Berkley Sensation Titles by Carolyn Jewel

SCANDAL
INDISCREET
NOT WICKED ENOUGH

Not Wicked Enough

≫≪

CAROLYN JEWEL

B

BERKLEY SENSATION, NEW YORK

THE BERKLEY PUBLISHING GROUP
Published by the Penguin Group
Penguin Group (USA) Inc.
375 Hudson Street, New York, New York 10014, USA

Penguin Group (Canada), 90 Eglinton Avenue East, Suite 700, Toronto, Ontario M4P 2Y3, Canada
(a division of Pearson Penguin Canada Inc.)
Penguin Books Ltd., 80 Strand, London WC2R 0RL, England
Penguin Books Ireland, 25 St. Stephen's Green, Dublin 2, Ireland (a division of Penguin Books Ltd.)
Penguin Group (Australia), 250 Camberwell Road, Camberwell, Victoria 3124, Australia
(a division of Pearson Australia Group Pty. Ltd.)
Penguin Books India Pvt. Ltd., 11 Community Centre, Panchsheel Park, New Delhi—110 017, India
Penguin Group (NZ), 67 Apollo Drive, Rosedale, Auckland 0632, New Zealand
(a division of Pearson New Zealand Ltd.)
Penguin Books (South Africa) (Pty.) Ltd., 24 Sturdee Avenue, Rosebank, Johannesburg 2196,
South Africa

Penguin Books Ltd., Registered Offices: 80 Strand, London WC2R 0RL, England

This is a work of fiction. Names, characters, places, and incidents either are the product of the author's imagination or are used fictitiously, and any resemblance to actual persons, living or dead, business establishments, events, or locales is entirely coincidental. The publisher does not have any control over and does not assume any responsibility for author or third-party websites or their content.

NOT WICKED ENOUGH

A Berkley Sensation Book / published by arrangement with the author

PRINTING HISTORY
Berkley Sensation mass-market edition / February 2012

ISBN: 978-0-425-24660-3

PRINTED IN THE UNITED STATES OF AMERICA

10 9 8 7 6 5 4 3 2 1

*To all the wonderful readers
who've let me know how much they enjoy my books.
Thank you.*

Acknowledgments

To my amazing agent, Kristin Nelson: thank you, thank you, thank you. Similar thanks to my editor, Kate Seaver, and the entire Berkley team.

I'd also like to thank Allen Joslyn of the Antique Doorknob Collectors of America, who pointed me in fruitful directions, which included two of their newsletter issues that were directly on point regarding specifics about doorknob construction in the early nineteenth century. Thanks to Terry Herbert over there in England who uncovered the Staffordshire Hoard. I shamelessly stole your discovery and moved it across time and space. I must also acknowledge the Birmingham Museum & Art Gallery for putting all those astonishing pictures online.

More thanks go out to Nyree Belleville and Jacqueline Yau for the friendship and dinners. I am so glad you guys moved to my part of California. Special thanks to Julie McDermott and Robin Harcher for all the ESC and hours spent talking about academia, romance, books, writing, and reading. You guys keep me sane. Much love to my sister, Marguerite, and my son, Nathaniel, whose skill in the kitchen includes Nutella sandwiches—you're the best! Love to my nephew, Dylan, and my nieces, Lexie and Hannah.

Chapter One

1:00 AM, Bitterward, seat of the Dukes of Mountjoy,
near High Tearing, Sheffieldshire, England, 1816.

LILY WELLSTONE WASN'T THE ONLY ONE TO HAVE
been caught in the downpour. She ignored the rain dripping
off her bonnet and gazed at the other occupant of the
entrance hall.

He was tall with dark hair and an ill-fitting and very wet
greatcoat about his broad shoulders. Raindrops darkened
his worn boots and glistened in his hair. His eyes were deep-
set and private. This was a man who did not share his
secrets, a man who could only be unraveled bit-by-tortuous-
bit. Not for a moment did she mistake him for a fellow caller,
though his clothes were hardly better than something a
country squire might wear.

This most fascinating man stood at the opposite side of
the room from the front door, near the magnificent arched
doorway to the second floor. To the right, if she was correct
about Bitterward's architectural integrity, that same archway
ended at the butler's pantry. Two sets of crossed swords hung
on the wall on either side of the doorway's pointed top.

As the shape of the doorway proved, Bitterward was

Gothic. Legitimately several centuries old and therefore not a reconstitution of the medieval as was the fashion of the recent past. Such follies as the modern Gothic only demonstrated, in her opinion, a failure of imagination.

Her as yet silent companion could have passed for the ghost of one of Bitterward's ancient lords. His present-century clothes spoiled the effect, but notwithstanding that anachronism, the ancient spirit gazing out of his eyes sent a shiver of anticipation through her.

Behind her, a servant pushed the heavy wooden door closed with an ominous *thunk*. The drum of rain diminished. On the table beside the door, a lantern threw her elongated shadow onto the marble floor. The floor was not the original surface, of course, but the marble, laid out in horizontal stripes of *V*s that alternated black and white, was worn enough to be quite old.

The gentleman's wet boot was planted in the shadow of her head. Sensible footwear, those boots. Not even five minutes in the rain, and her slippers were soaked through. The damp from her shoes and the rain dripping off her cloak already penetrated her bones. Neither her shoes nor her coat had proven sufficient protection against this night's weather.

The footman who'd met her carriage and held the umbrella over her head all the way up the front stairs—for all the good it did what with the wind blowing the rain sideways—disappeared through a side exit, umbrella in hand, leaving but one footman with her and the mysterious stranger.

"Welcome to Bitterward," the gentleman said. He did not smile that she could see. The gloom of the entryway made it difficult to tell. Smile or no, the sound of his voice was intimate and very much at odds with the roughness of his clothes. That voice was a thing of dreams, entwining with her emotions, already at a high pitch after too many hours traveling and then this downpour that had her chilled to her marrow.

She resisted the urge to take a step back and instead indulged a fancy that she would be unable to move until he removed his boot from her shadow. She removed her bonnet to stop the water from falling into her face and passed the back of a hand over her forehead. Her glove was too damp, as it turned out, to do much besides redistribute the wet. His gaze followed the motion of her hand. In the dimness, she was forced to guess his age. Thirty, she thought. The prime of life for a gentleman, be he real or ghost.

"Thank you, your grace." She peeled off her gloves. The gentleman did not deny he was entitled to the honorific. She removed her cloak, too, and gave it a shake. Water cascaded onto the floor. Her traveling gown had been spared the worst of the drenching, thank goodness.

The remaining footman stepped forward to take her cloak. She dropped her gloves into the well of her upturned bonnet and handed that over, too. "Thank you." To the duke, she said, "I hope you have ordered your sister and me better weather tomorrow."

He didn't react right away, and she had the impression he was deciding whether she had amused him or convinced him she was a fool. Perhaps a bit of both. Well. She was cold and wet. His boot yet pinned her shadow to the floor, so she remained where she was. Behind him, she caught a glimpse of a stone staircase that quickly narrowed and turned as it spiraled toward the first floor and disappeared into darkness.

Lily pointed to the painting on the wall beside the stairs, a gentleman dressed in the fashion of the Italians from two hundred years ago. "Is that a Gossart?"

"Yes," he said without a glance at the portrait she meant. "It is." He cocked his head. "I am informed my great-granduncle brought it here from the Continent." As everyone knew, the line of descent from the first duke to the fourth was not a straight one. The title had gone into abeyance for a time, and the Crown, she understood, had been poised to take back the lands. Mountjoy had not yet reached his majority when his existence was discovered and his lineage proven. Imagine that. An orphan, living with his younger brother and sister in the home of a maternal uncle. On a farm. On which he himself had labored.

"He had excellent taste." She declined to mention there was now a Gossart in her own house, but wasn't that the oddest coincidence?

His mouth quirked on one side. "Thank you, Miss Wellstone."

The duke might be rough around the edges in respect of his clothes, but there was nothing deficient in his intellect. She curtseyed and caught a glimpse of water stains on her hem. "You're welcome, your grace."

"George," he said to the footman who still held her cloak and bonnet. The silk flowers she had so painstakingly made and affixed to her bonnet might never recover from the damp and, now, from being crushed in the footman's hands. "Do you know which room my sister meant for Miss Wellstone to have?"

"The Lilac room, your grace."

"Lilac?" A wry smile appeared on his mouth. "I'd no idea we had a room with a name like that. I don't know how anyone keeps them straight."

George bowed. "Your grace."

"See to it her trunks are taken there forthwith." He spoke well, with no trace of an accent, a Sheffieldshire one or any other for that matter. "Tell Miss Wellstone's maid she may have a meal in the kitchen once she's seen to her mistress's comfort."

"Your grace." The footman bowed and departed to carry out his employer's instructions, which left Lily wholly alone in the entryway with her friend Ginny's wholly impressive eldest brother. For a man in such inferior clothes, his manners were faultless, but then he'd been some nine years in possession of the dukedom, and nine years was time enough to acquire some polish. Though, apparently, not quite enough.

"You must be exhausted after traveling for so long." He moved toward her, treading further on her shadow. Since she was a tall woman, she preferred men who did not make her feel she was a giant. The duke was quite a bit taller than she. Six feet at least. His mouth curved in the most devastating smile. "In such inclement weather as I had ordered up this evening."

"I forgive you the inconvenience."

His gaze flicked over her, reminding her, forcefully, that she was female to his male. "Will you?"

"Already done, your grace." Now that he'd stepped farther into the light cast by the lantern, she adjusted her opinion of his apparent age. He was younger than she'd thought. Not more than twenty-eight or nine, and with his looks, a good deal more dangerous to a woman's virtue, too. "I will correct you in one respect, your grace, and say that I am not the least tired. I never am at this hour."

"Duly noted."

Ginny was fair-haired and blue-eyed. She'd expected both her friend's brothers to have similar coloring. The duke's hair was dark brown, and his eyes were an extraordinary green with thick, sooty lashes she would have killed to have herself. To say that the duke was handsome, however, would do a disservice to men who actually were.

Lily stayed where she was, meeting his gaze without blinking or looking away. According to the terms she'd set herself, she could not move while he trod on her shadow. The thought made her smile.

The duke didn't look away, either. Nor did he smile in return. The effect was . . . bracing.

"I never fall asleep much before four or five in the morning," she said. "Often as late as six."

"Is that so?" His voice sent a shiver down her spine. He was doing that on purpose. "I would be happy to show you the library. In the event you would like to take something engaging back to your room."

She gazed at her slippers, as ruined as the flowers on her bonnet. When she looked up, she saw a condescending smile flitting about his mouth. But she had indeed understood his double entendre. She smiled as if she had not. "Thank you."

Mountjoy's eyes widened.

Well then. Excellent. She maintained her most innocent expression though, in fact, she was no longer innocent. A spinster she might be, but she was not decrepit yet, thank you. "I do hope you have something thrilling to show me."

Chapter Two

MOUNTJOY CONSIDERED THE PERMUTATIONS OF WHAT his sister's acquaintance had just said. Regardless of her actual age and experience of life, Miss Lily Wellstone possessed a disconcertingly guileless face. With her dainty, too-pretty features, she looked an innocent incapable of matching wits with anyone, let alone a man experienced with women of all sorts, proper and those not so proper.

Miss Wellstone was young enough to flirt and more than pretty enough to know she had an effect on a gentleman's passions. And she was unmarried. As was he, which she must surely know. Never mind that he was all but engaged to a suitable woman. Until he was actually married, he would be pestered by hopeful parents and girls with ambition.

I do hope you have something thrilling to show me.

She was flirting, he decided. He was alarmed to realize he did not feel entirely impervious to her charm. Which was considerable.

Without responding to her comment, he fetched the lantern from the table then held out his arm, and they proceeded up the stairs, with her shockingly bare hand on his sleeve. Her fingers were long, very pale, and slender. She wore two rings, a ruby on her first finger and a diamond on the one next to it. The gems were not gaudy, but they weren't small, either.

When the stairs became too narrow to navigate side by side, he dropped back, allowing her to take the van but holding the lantern high enough to light her way. Her hips swayed as she climbed the stairs. He appreciated the view.

"Aside from the abysmal weather," he said from behind her, "was your journey here a pleasant one?"

"It was, your grace. Until the very moment one of the horses threw a shoe. We were obliged to stop for several hours while we waited for the farrier to assist us." They passed narrow, slitted windows with deep ledges, and she glanced out of each one even though there was nothing to see at this hour. "Your family were Yorkists, I presume," she said as they made another dizzying turn of stairs. "During the War of the Roses."

"Why would you presume such a thing?"

"To my recollection, which I confess might be imperfect, there are no Hamptons listed on Edward IV's Act of Attainder."

At least she wasn't one of those women who pretended they were ignorant. "The Hamptons supported the House of York until after Edward was king. It's how my ancestors eventually became dukes. After that it's less clear. The situation was fluid."

She lifted her skirts higher. Since by happy accident he was looking down, he caught a glimpse of two slender ankles. "Not surprising, if your relative fought valiantly."

"We have been given to understand that he did, Miss Wellstone." He paused, just the merest hesitation before he committed to an inappropriate reply as a test of his theory that she was not as guileless as she appeared. "All we Hampton men have valiant swords."

"Thank goodness," she said without missing a beat and with such artlessness that he frowned. Then she glanced over her shoulder at him, eyes dancing with amusement. "Everyone has need of a valiant sword from time to time. Don't you agree?"

It was all he could do not to laugh out loud. She was an amusing thing, wasn't she? "Some more than others, I daresay."

Outside, the wind shifted and drove the rain against the windows. "The weather," she remarked, "is another reason I was so late getting into Sheffield and then to High Tearing."

"Left at the top."

"Thank you." She reached the landing and went right.

He arrived at the top of the stairs and found she'd not gone far. She was waiting a few feet away. He joined her, holding out his arm for her to take. The air here was cooler, and he saw the skin up and down her arms prickle from the cold. "Left, Miss Wellstone."

She sighed. "I never can tell the difference." She gave him another heart-stopping smile. "Given the nature of my one and only defect, you'd be astonished how rarely I become lost."

"I assure you, I am already astonished."

"At any rate," she went on as he got them headed in the correct direction, "I had thought to beat the rain, but I miscalculated. My coachman ought not to have listened to me. He ought to know better by now."

"Had he a choice?"

"One always has a choice, your grace." She spoke matter-of-factly, and he could feel her experience of life behind the words. "The difficulty comes when one or more of the choices is unpalatable. I'm sure my coachman considered whether his position was worth his silence. He's new to my employ. I'll warrant he does not know I would never dismiss any servant for politely voiced opposition."

"No?"

"Certainly not."

They passed portraits of family members he'd never met and whose names he did not know unless he read the plates on the frames. None of the subjects bore much resemblance to him, but there were two from the sixteenth century that could have been his brother, Nigel. He liked the still lifes better than the portraits. A draft swirled the air around them as they passed a marble statue set into a niche, not Greek, but an Egyptian deity with the head of a jackal. Miss Wellstone shivered.

Without comment, Mountjoy stopped to set down the lantern and remove his greatcoat. He placed it around her shoulders, pulling the garment close around her and holding both sides near the collar until she had a grip on it. Her eyes were the darkest brown he'd ever seen on a woman as blond as she. He stood there, holding his coat around her. He allowed his attention to slide from her eyes to her mouth.

A kissable mouth. He waited to find out whether he might be invited to discover if he was right. He oughtn't be thinking such things. There was Jane, after all, who was, whatever one thought about the weight of everyone's expectations about them, perfectly suited to be a duchess. Miss Wellstone was a guest in his home, a friend of his sister's. No gentleman would dream of seducing a lady under such circumstances.

She cocked her head then took a step back. "Thank you, your grace. That's very kind of you."

He nodded and picked up the lantern and continued walking. This time, because she was holding his greatcoat around her, she did not put her hand on his arm. He led her down a stone corridor beneath an arched and ribbed ceiling. She slowed until he had to stop or leave her behind. He faced her, curious about what had caught her fancy.

"Do you have ghosts here?" she asked.

Good Lord, he hoped she wasn't serious. With that innocent face of hers, he couldn't be sure. "Not to my knowledge," he said.

"You ought to consider it."

He was at sea. One moment he was convinced she was a helpless sort of female, none too bright, the next that she must be daft. Or intelligent beyond what her sex typically allowed a man to guess. There was more than a hint of the contrary about her, and besides, how many unintelligent persons knew about any Act of Attainder? "I beg your pardon?"

She stuck a hand through the opening of his greatcoat so she could wave. As before, her smile transformed her from pretty to ethereal. His breath caught.

"In my experience," she said with a smile still on her lips—so, not entirely serious?—"a ghost improves a residence immeasurably. I have two where I live. I've instructed the staff to relate the stories to visitors on the days when the house is open to the public. They tell their friends, relations, and acquaintances when they return to their homes, and invariably, they visit, too. You ought to do the same."

"Does that not lead to more strangers traipsing through your house?" He began walking again.

She caught up to him. His coat flapped against her legs and dragged on the floor in the back. "I adore visitors. Don't you?"

"No." He opened the door to the library, and, yes, it was in fact the library, one of the few rooms he could regularly find in the labyrinth that was Bitterward. He allowed her to precede him in. "Present company excepted."

"I'm hardly a stranger," she said on her way past him. "Ginny and I are practically sisters."

He stopped walking. "You are not practically a sister to me."

The moment the words were out of his mouth, he realized he ought to have said nothing. Best to think of her as a sister since there must be nothing between them but an acquaintance.

A few feet inside, she turned in a circle, scanning the room but pausing in the motion long enough to face him and say, "I've always wanted a brother."

"I am happy to be a brother to you."

"How lovely." She stopped with her back to him and breathed in. Mountjoy was sorry his coat hid her figure. He crossed to a table by the door, lit another lamp, and the darkness before them receded. He moved so that he could watch her face, studying her while she was not aware he was doing so. Her eyes were closed. She was a woman of delicate beauty with golden blond hair, pale skin, and a slender, elegant figure. He could not imagine why a woman like Miss Wellstone remained unmarried.

"There is nothing quite like the smell of books." She opened her eyes and examined the nearest shelves. "My father is not one to collect books or read much himself. He does not approve of novels." She approached a set of shelves. "When I moved to Syton House, I supplemented my aunt's library with all the books my father forbade me to take from the subscription library. And more."

"Did he not object to your library additions?"

"I'm sure he would have. If he'd known. Now, it's true, he thinks my library is a deliberate offense to him. In a way, I suppose he's right."

He watched her walk, but with his coat around her, he could no longer see the sway of her hips. "There is a famous home called Syton House in Exeter," he said. "Notable for its gardens, if I recall correctly." Eugenia had lived in Exeter with her husband. "Is your Syton House also located there?"

She looked at him over her shoulder, no sign of that breathtaking smile anywhere. "There is only one Syton House, sir, and it is mine."

That shocked him to silence. He didn't remember if Eugenia had mentioned the very interesting fact that her bosom friend Miss Lily Wellstone was bloody rich. "Indeed?"

"Yes." She held a hand toward the shelves. "I can feel the tingle of all those stories waiting to be known to me." She stayed there awhile with her hand outstretched. "Are you absolutely sure you don't have ghosts?"

"Yes."

"I just felt the most mysterious thrill. I would not be surprised to learn you are wrong."

"You are fond of reading?" he asked in a low voice. He

leaned a hip against the table. If she owned Syton House, she had very good connections, and the money to keep company with them. She wasn't much like the women he'd met who came from families with those sorts of connections. Ghosts, for pity's sake.

"Very fond," she said.

"Tell me what books you prefer to read. I could recommend something for you, if you like."

She turned to him, another smile on her lips. He could not imagine a woman more dissimilar to him. She was joy and wit, and, he was sure, the sort of woman who thrived among crowds and at parties. He did not.

"Adventure, your grace." She smiled, and his body reacted with a sexual jolt. "Passion." Though he was sure she exaggerated her emotions to amuse him, he suspected she meant every word. "To have my heart pound until I feel it might burst from my chest."

He continued to gaze at her. She did not break the silence, and in the quiet he felt the pull of attraction. Nothing was wrong with that. He was a man, after all. Men admired women all the time without any intention of seducing them. "You were Eugenia's neighbor. In Exeter."

She blinked. "Yes."

"You were a good friend to her, during her husband's final days."

"I hope I was, sir."

"She spoke highly of you, Miss Wellstone, after I brought her home."

The melancholy in her dark eyes receded. "She was kind to me, too, your grace."

He liked her for that. Very much, indeed. Eugenia deserved that sort of loyalty and regard.

She turned back to the shelves, and he moved the lantern to the other side of the table and placed it so she could see the titles better. She reached for one of the volumes and opened it. In a soft voice she said, "Your sister was always kind to me. Despite everything."

His voice stayed low, too. They were entirely alone here, and the household was asleep. "What would that be, Miss Wellstone? The everything to which you refer?"

She turned, book in hand, close enough to him that he could smell, very faintly, violets. It was a scent he happened to particularly like on a woman. Her expression turned more serious. "You aren't the sort of man one easily deceives."

"No."

With a nod, she clutched the book, and her smile reappeared. "Best not to omit what someone will inevitably discover, I always say." Her mood was oddly bright for a woman with news she seemed to think he would not like to hear. "The *everything* that makes you so curious is that I was once disowned by my father."

He frowned. Her connection to Syton House puzzled him even more. "Once? Do you expect him to disown you again?"

"I can't be sure. My father has always been convinced I am of a wild nature."

"Is he right?"

She replaced her book on the shelf and stood there, her back to him, hand still on the spine of the volume.

"Miss Wellstone?"

"Yes," she said, reaching for another book. "He is. But then you already suspect that of me."

"I am not used to any lady being so forthright."

"Oh, you may rely on that with me." She turned, and he had the impression she had been struggling to hide her emotion. She hadn't entirely succeeded. Her smile was brittle, and it made him want to take her in his arms and promise no one would ever again make her sad. Such was the effect of that angelic face of hers. She hugged a book to her chest. "My father went bankrupt, you see; that was nearly two years ago now. He hasn't a penny left. If he had not come to live with me at Syton House, he'd not have a roof over his head."

"I should think he'd be grateful."

"He resents his circumstances extremely. Indeed, it's why

I have so little time here. I had to promise the servants I would be home before May or I own they would have refused to look after him. I fear he's a difficult man to like. I don't like to have the staff abused, you understand." She opened her book, stared at the pages, then closed it with a sigh. "I can make an excuse, your grace, before Ginny knows I have arrived, if you would rather not have me in your home. I would appreciate, however, the recommendation of a nearby inn. It's far too late to think of driving all the way back to Sheffield."

He considered her offer. He liked an orderly household, and it was plain as anything that Miss Wellstone would disrupt his peaceful country existence. This was not a woman who would sweetly make herself invisible. There was also the fact that she was quite beautiful and an accomplished flirt. He was not impervious to any part of that.

"Your grace?"

"No," he said. He shoved his hands into his coat pockets. "I won't deny my sister the company of someone she recalls so fondly and likes so well as she likes you." This was true. Eugenia had been looking forward to Miss Wellstone's arrival since the day two months ago when the visit had been agreed to. His gaze traveled the length of her, from head to toe. He did like a tall woman. "Nor myself the pleasure of learning why she adores you so unreservedly." His mouth twitched. "Despite everything."

She pulled his greatcoat tighter around her. "My dear duke," she said in a voice of mock sorrow. "It is my sad duty to tell you that I am reformed."

Her smile was an invitation to sin, and he was feeling very much inclined to sin right now. Unthinkable, of course. But knowing all the reasons he should not act on his impulses didn't divert the direction of his thoughts. Not in the least. "That, Miss Wellstone," he said, "is a very great pity."

Chapter Three

LATE THE NEXT MORNING LILY STOOD IN THE ENTRY-
way of Bitterward and slid the rest of the way out of her
cloak. She was aware the duke himself had arrived at the
door moments after she had and that he now stood behind
her. Doyle, the duke's butler, stepped away from her with
her cloak in hand. Already, he was reaching to take Mountjoy's gloves, hat, and greatcoat.

She exchanged a glance with Mountjoy. He nodded at
her. Say what you would about his grace's undistinguished
manner of dress, his servants were efficient and meticulous
in their duties.

"Lily!"

Lily looked away from the duke and saw Ginny hurrying
down the stairs to the entryway. "Ginny."

"Lily, you're here. Doyle! You should have sent someone
to fetch me the instant she arrived." She came down the last
steps. "Oh, hullo, Mountjoy. When did you arrive?"

"Last night," the duke said.

"I meant Lily, not you."

"Never mind that," Lily said to her friend. "Let me see you." She raised her hands so that Ginny would stop, which she did. She was not pleased with what she saw. She had expected to see Ginny recovering from the loss of her husband. She wasn't. Sadness inhabited her eyes, and she was too thin in a gown black as night and drab beyond words. "You should be glad no one woke you when I arrived," she said to cover her shock. "It was well after midnight."

"Last night?" Ginny crossed the black-and-white tiles, hands extended. "Good heavens, Lily. So late. You must be exhausted."

"I," said the duke, "am not in the least tired. Thank you for asking after me, Eugenia."

"Couldn't be helped," Lily said. She took Ginny's hands while her friend made a face at her brother. "But I'm here, and I've just come back from a bracing walk and feel ready to face a bit of tea and something to eat. Will you join me? I'll tell you everything that's happened since you left me bereft at Syton House." She glanced at Mountjoy, standing by the door. "You, too, duke."

Ginny enveloped Lily in a hug. Lily breathed in her perfume of roses and citrus. A new scent for Ginny, but she liked it very much. "How wonderful," Ginny said, "that at last you've come to visit after so many months of my pleading with you."

"I ought to have come sooner." Indeed she ought to have. If she'd had any idea the case was so dire, she'd have come immediately. She kissed Ginny's cheek. "You know how I am. Never as organized as one ought to be." Lily tightened her arms around Ginny and softly said, "My darling, you are far too thin." She stepped back and released Ginny.

Mountjoy said, "Doyle, bring us tea, won't you?"

"In the Oldenburg salon," Ginny said.

"Yes. There." The duke gestured. "Something to eat as well."

Lily added, "A substantial something if it's not too much trouble."

"Your grace. Lady Eugenia." The butler bowed at the waist, but he was smiling, which seemed auspicious, though Lily wondered who had decided Ginny was not to be called Mrs. Bryant. "Miss Wellstone."

Ginny put her arm through Lily's and headed for the stairs, ignoring her brother. He followed them despite that. "You have the room next to mine, did you know that?"

"The Lilac room I was told. It's lovely." Heavens, but she was glad to be here. In Exeter, Ginny had become a very dear friend. "I am now determined to have a room with lilac accents when I'm back at Syton House."

"I knew you'd love the view of the garden." They continued walking arm in arm until the stairs were too narrow, and Lily took the lead. She was far too aware of the duke behind them. "They're not the gardens at Syton House," Ginny said. "That goes without saying, but we do very well here, all the same."

Lily walked backward up the stairs so she and Ginny could face each other. His grace continued up the stairs, a pleasantly bland expression on his face. "You were right that I would adore the view. I gazed for several minutes upon the prospect when I arose." After all this time, Ginny still wore black. There was no question Lily was needed here. Ginny must not be allowed to founder here as she had been. "How have you been, my dearest Eugenia?"

"Oh, very well, thank you. Do you still not sleep well at night?"

"Abysmally, I fear." *Oh, Ginny*, she thought, *you should not be so sad*. She touched her left hand to the stone wall and held her skirts out of her way with the other as she continued her backward walk up the stairs.

"We keep country hours here," Mountjoy said.

"I'm sure you do, your grace. Everyone but me keeps them at Syton House. I assure you I'll muddle along whilst I am here." She waved her left hand then returned to skimming the wall with her fingertips. "I always do, don't I, Ginny?"

"Yes, Lily."

She looked past Ginny to her brother. "Don't dream of changing your schedule on my account, your grace."

"I shan't. Right at the top," Mountjoy said.

"Right, is it?" She reached the top of the stairs well ahead of Ginny and her brother and turned. She took several steps before she realized the corridor looked familiar. That couldn't be correct.

"Right," said the duke from somewhere still on the stairs.

"Lily?" Ginny's voice came from behind her. "You've gone left. It's the other way." Lily returned to the stairs and found Ginny and her brother waiting for her. "I should have pointed," Ginny said.

"No harm," she said. "For here I am. Safe and sound."

They reached the Oldenburg salon without further incident. The salon proved to be a smallish room set in a tower at the west end of the house. While not strictly a castle, Bitterward was an old enough structure to have been built with two round towers at the east and west. The Oldenburg salon had the architectural advantage of having windows along the curved outer wall that overlooked the very garden that had attracted her admiration before. The early roses were in bloom, and she wanted to walk outside again just to breathe in the scent.

The salon was charming, with a fireplace mantel of carved mahogany polished to a sheen, as were the paneled walls and ceiling. Very pretty, though she would have preferred if the room had retained more of its Gothic decorations rather than a Tudor character. "This is a newer part of the structure, I presume?"

"Relatively," Ginny said. "I believe this wing was remodeled during the reign of Charles I. Mountjoy would know."

"Yes," the duke said. He tugged on the bottom of his waistcoat, but nothing was going to improve the lay of the fabric except for a pair of scissors and needle and thread. "This wing was extensively redone."

Ginny put her palms on Lily's shoulders and slid her

hands down until they were clasping hands. "She adores ruins, Mountjoy."

"Does she?"

"Yes," Lily said, looking at him from over Ginny's shoulder. "She does."

"After we've eaten," said Ginny, "perhaps you'd like a tour of the church? It's not far, and I've been told it's Anglo-Saxon."

Lily gave Ginny's hands a squeeze before she released her and strolled to a love seat upholstered in dark green velvet. The green would make a striking contrast with her primrose gown. She was never going to marry, for her heart was no longer available for such emotion. But that was no reason not to show herself to advantage when the opportunity arose. Life ought to be lived with due consideration for the beauty of one's surroundings, and that included the elegance of one's attire.

"I should adore that," Lily said.

Ginny sat on an upholstered chair that made her look even more drab and wan than she had in the hall. Lily made a mental note to speak with her brother the duke at her earliest opportunity regarding his lack of attention to his sister. Surely, he had not brought her home to her family only to abandon her to loneliness all these months? She feared he had.

The duke moved a chair nearer his sister and sat. He did not seem much at ease, and yet he was the most vital man she had met in her life. Full of repressed energy.

"I don't know how much we shall see of Mountjoy," Ginny said. "He's the parish magistrate, and the Sessions are on. He's forever doing this and that about the property. Always meeting with someone or attending to business that keeps him from home."

His eyebrows rose. "The responsibilities of an estate like Bitterward are not ones I care to delegate."

"Then I imagine we'll see very little of you, your grace."

He nodded. "To my great regret, of course."

Though she did not say so to Ginny, industrious and useful occupations seemed in keeping with the man. She suspected as well that a man as vital as him had a mistress or a lover or two somewhere not far away.

"He's going to marry the daughter of one of our neighbors. Miss Jane Kirk. You'll meet her by and by. You'll like her exceedingly. She's two younger sisters, both delightful. You won't meet Miss Caroline Kirk, though. She's away just now."

"Congratulations on your upcoming nuptials, your grace."

"Thank you, though your good wishes are premature."

"Come now, Mountjoy, of course you'll marry Jane."

"I will," he said.

Lily leaned against the sofa, stretching an arm along the top and extending one leg. She considered what Ginny had said and the manner of her delivery. "I take it this is one of those situations in which everyone agreed the match was a splendid idea even before you'd met."

"Yes," Mountjoy said. "That's it exactly."

"You love her madly, I hope."

Ginny leaned forward. "Everyone loves Jane."

"I adore a romantic tale. She loves him madly, too, am I right?"

"How can she not? He's Mountjoy, after all. He has a way of getting what he wants."

She looked to the duke. "Indeed, your grace?"

"Yes, Miss Wellstone"—he smiled—"I do."

A servant brought in the tea and refreshments, and while the tray was set on a table near the sofa, Lily used the silence to study her friend. "Ginny." She extended her hand, and after a moment, Ginny took it. Lily drew her to the sofa. "Have you been ill?"

"I enjoy very good health." At twenty-three, Ginny was two years younger than Lily, and though they were both blondes, Ginny's hair was much lighter than hers, and her eyes were blue, not brown.

"I can't say the evidence supports you."

"I don't know what you mean."

"You miss him," Lily said. "I know that." She handed Ginny her handkerchief. Ginny shook her head, but took the handkerchief anyway.

"I do." She pressed the embroidered silk to her eyes.

She understood loss, and Ginny knew that. She glanced at the duke again, meeting his gaze as she spoke. "You have your family to rely on, and that is something fine, Ginny."

"Yes, yes, I do." She balled up the handkerchief. "I do know how fortunate I am." Ginny knew about Lily's estrangement from her father, and that, until her father came to Syton House, she had lived on her own from quite a young age.

When the tea was ready, Ginny, being the excellent hostess that she was, poured while Lily prepared plates of food for herself and the others. Cucumber and watercress sandwiches, cold ham, bread, crackers, and cheese. The butter was stamped with Mountjoy's crest, a swan, wings spread and wearing a duke's coronet with a broken chain around its neck. She arranged and rearranged the food on the plates until she was satisfied with the placement and balance of colors and textures.

"I will engage to fill your mind with happier thoughts," she said when she'd handed out the food and sat with her plate. Though she was hungry, she didn't eat right away. She wanted time to admire the palette of her breakfast plate. "One does not easily recover from the loss of a deep and abiding love."

"No," Ginny said.

"I am proof one can go on and even be happy." She leaned to cup a hand to Ginny's cheek. "We must, you know, even when we've lost the person we love most in all the world."

"Have you suffered such a loss, Miss Wellstone?" The duke set his plate and his tea on a table near him.

"I have, your grace."

"My condolences."

"Thank you."

Ginny covered Lily's hand with hers and gave it a squeeze. "I've told everyone about you. Even Mountjoy, when he was here before."

"Don't change the subject." She cocked her head. Lord, Ginny must get out of black. "What have you said, Ginny?"

His grace sipped his tea then answered for his sister. "That you are wonderful and amusing, and the best friend she could ever have."

"I adore being flattered." She intended to discover why Ginny's brothers had neglected her until she'd become this pale, wan creature devoid of the spirit she so loved about her. Had neither of them seen how heartbroken and unhappy their sister was? Had they even tried to entertain her? To occupy her hours? Introduce her to suitable and compatible gentlemen and women who would befriend her?

"Now that you're here," Ginny said, "we're going to have such a lovely time."

"Oh, indeed we are. Depend upon it." Lily crossed her ankles to one side and ate what proved to be a devilishly good watercress sandwich. The rest of the food was just as superlative, better than what her own cook produced, and he was so French she barely understood a word he said. The crackers were crisp and flavorful, the bread fresh, and the Brie and Stilton first-rate. "Does your dairywoman make a Devonshire cream? If she does and it's as lovely as this, I warn you, I may never leave."

"She does, it is, and you are welcome to stay here for as long as you like."

"You'll regret saying that." Lily ate another sandwich. "If only it were possible."

Ginny picked at her food while Lily eyed another watercress sandwich and wondered if she ought to simply get another plate before she'd finished her first. "I shan't," Ginny said. She gave her brother a defiant look. "In fact, I wish you would live here."

"How sweet of you to say so." The duke ate one of the finger sandwiches. Such a quiet man, and extremely attractive in a visceral manner. Miss Jane Kirk was a lucky woman. "I am very glad to be here." She slathered Brie on a cracker. "You must eat, Ginny. I insist. I won't rest until you have."

Ginny smiled, and that encouraged her. "You needn't ever go home."

"Would you eat more if I agreed?" Lily ate her cracker, and the rich, buttery tang of the cheese spread over her tongue. She closed her eyes in bliss. "Oh, my. I shan't leave until I've spoken with whoever obtains this Brie." Likely the local smugglers supplied the duke's household. "I must know who you get it from."

"You have my leave to inquire of the cook."

"Thank you, your grace. This Brie is astonishingly good. Have some, my dear Ginny."

"I shall, Lily." Ginny made no move to do so.

Lily put down her food and stood, hands on her hips. Stern measures were called for. She was not at all in charity with the Duke of Mountjoy for neglecting his sister. "I see I was too conservative before. I'll fix you a proper plate while you pour more tea." So saying, she returned to the tea table and selected a slice of bread, butter, crackers, a bit of each of the cheeses, and a small portion of ham. No point overwhelming her with too much food. As she had with her own plate, she settled everything into a pleasing combination of shapes and colors. "I still like my tea sweet," she said while she perfected her arrangement of Ginny's plate. She sculpted a pyramid with the butter she put on the plate. "Do be generous with the sugar."

"I haven't forgotten."

Back at the sofa, she accepted her tea and handed Ginny the plate. "Try the Brie."

Ginny gazed at the plate. "You've created a work of art, Lily. This is too lovely to eat."

"Humph." She tapped her foot. Mountjoy snorted, but she ignored him.

"Yes, Mama." Ginny rolled her eyes.

"So long as you eat, I shan't take offense."

While she watched Ginny spread Brie on the corner of a cracker, a blindingly handsome gentleman strolled in. He had Ginny's coloring, with blue eyes and even blonder hair. Unlike his brother, he knew something about how to dress himself. His clothes fit impeccably and complimented his physique and coloring. He was tall, though not as tall as Mountjoy, and possessed a smile that made her like him before she had any right to have come to that decision. He made his way to Ginny and bent to kiss her cheek.

"Good afternoon, Eugenia," he said. "Mountjoy."

"Nigel." Ginny paused with her cracker halfway to her mouth. "Where have you been?"

"Went to see the Misses Kirk. I am commanded to tell you hullo and ask you to come to tea as soon as you can. So, hullo from all the Kirks, Eugenia."

"Tea?" Ginny asked her brother. "The Kirks love my brother. I can't imagine why."

"What?" Lord Nigel put a hand to his heart.

"Perhaps his excellent waistcoats?" Lily said. The garment was a delicious shade of cream silk that perfectly complimented his sober blue coat.

The vision of male beauty quirked his eyebrows in Lily's direction. "You must be Miss Wellstone," he said in the loveliest voice. No country accent, just the crisp syllables of an educated man who spent his time among the Ton.

"I am," she said. His coat fit precisely, and his cravat was neither too plain nor too lacy. She most definitely approved. And good heavens, he was lovely. She would have known him for Ginny's brother anywhere.

"Delightful to meet you at last, Miss Wellstone. Eugenia's praised you to the skies every day for the last month."

"Good heavens, Ginny." She raised her teacup but did not drink. "I fear I will only disappoint your brothers. Do eat that cracker. I can't have another drink of this lovely tea until you do."

The cracker hovered near Ginny's mouth. "I've not told anyone a thing that isn't absolutely true."

"I die of thirst," Lily said, inflecting her words with enough passion and suffering to break the hardest heart. "My throat . . . it is a veritable desert."

Ginny laughed and ate the cracker.

Lord Nigel Hampton smiled fondly at his sister. "According to Eugenia, Miss Wellstone, you are perfection itself."

"She is," Mountjoy said. "As you will soon discover for yourself."

Lily took a sip of her tea and found it acceptably sweet. How odd that she, who admired all things elegant, preferred the duke's looks and manner to his brother's. She said, "Lies, I'm afraid. Shame on you, Ginny."

"You traveled here from Exeter, am I right?"

"Yes, Lord Nigel, I did."

"That's a devilish long trip." He bowed. "But I forget my manners. Nigel Hampton, at your service." His blue eyes lingered on her face. "I'm Eugenia's favorite brother in case she didn't think to praise me."

Lily helped herself to more Brie. "She said something about a pest and bother, but I may be mistaken."

"Oh, Lily!" Ginny laughed, and it was gratifying to hear. "No, no. I said he was a perfect bother." She smiled insincerely at him. "Never a pest, Nigel, dearest."

Having grown up the only child born to her parents, the interactions of siblings had always fascinated her. She loved to imagine what it would have been like to have a brother or sister.

While Mountjoy snorted, Lord Nigel put his hand over his heart, partly turning toward Lily. "You wound me, sister. And you, Mountjoy, you don't defend me? Your only brother?"

"Delighted to meet you, Lord Nigel." Lily gave him her most engaging smile, and Lord Nigel stared. Men often did. She had been told more than once that her smile was beyond lovely, though she'd never quite seen it herself. According to Greer, he'd fallen in love with her smile first. "This Brie is excellent. Tell Ginny she ought to have more."

"Eugenia, do have more of the Brie." Lord Nigel remained

standing. He couldn't be much older than twenty-two. Despite his youth, he had a Town polish. Doubtless because when Mountjoy ascended to the title, Lord Nigel had been young enough to be sent to Eton and then to Oxford. Eugenia did fix herself another cracker and Brie.

"My brother," Mountjoy said dryly, "can be charming when he wishes to be."

Lily extended a hand, and Lord Nigel Hampton bent over it. "Delighted to meet you, Miss Wellstone," he said. He held her gaze longer than was proper. Dear Lord. He was a boy. Beautiful as he was, she had no interest in a boy. "Welcome to Bitterward."

"Thank you, Lord Nigel." She smiled faintly. For good or ill, she was much more interested in the Duke of Mountjoy.

Chapter Four

NEAR MIDNIGHT, MOUNTJOY LEFT THE STABLES AND headed for the rear entrance that led to his room. He hadn't intended to be gone for so long. He owed his sister an apology for his absence. Eugenia had particularly asked him if he could come home for supper this evening, and he had agreed he would. He ought to have been, given that in the week since their guest's arrival, he'd managed to dine at Bitterward exactly once.

The most direct way to the private entrance took him through the rose garden, a familiar walk now. There was a full moon, and that meant he did not need a lantern to light his way. Finely crushed gravel crunched under his boots as he walked. Once, Bitterward had been a foreign place to him, cold and demanding of his time and attention. Over the years, he'd come to see his legacy as a living thing. He had been required to learn its secrets and shepherd the lands, tenants, staff, and a thousand other dependencies. In return, the estate gave him shelter, food on his table, ready money in his pockets and his brother and sister an income. Properly managed, Bitterward would support his wife, children, and future generations of Hamptons who would one day gaze at his portrait in the gallery hall.

Halfway to the house, he stopped. A woman limned in silver moved with silent grace onto the path ahead of him. Her back was to him, and damned if he didn't wonder if the apparition was entirely of this world. Then she turned her head toward the roses along the path, and he recognized her.

"Miss Wellstone?"

She let out a soft gasp and whirled, a hand to her heart. Moonlight scattered soft prisms of light from the combs in her hair. "Your grace."

He walked to her and, God help him, he was on point, far too aware of her as a woman. He schooled himself against the reaction. "Were you perhaps expecting the gardener?"

Too late, he understood the insult he'd just leveled at her. They spoke at the same time, Miss Wellstone with more than a hint of frost in her tone.

"I was not expecting anyone, your grace."

"Forgive me, Miss Wellstone. That was thoughtless of me."

"It was." Her pale shawl had slipped into the crooks of her elbows, leaving her shoulders and bosom exposed and all the rest of her indefinably luscious in full evening dress.

"I only meant to remark your unexpected appearance out here." He, on the other hand, wore the same clothes he'd put on this morning. While he rarely gave a thought to his appearance, Miss Wellstone made him wonder if he ought to care more. He removed his hat and held it by the brim then thought what his hair must look like. He smoothed a hand over the top of his head. "I intended no insult."

"We hardly know each other, yet here I am giving you my forgiveness again."

Her eyes, Mountjoy thought, gave away the mind behind those innocent, delicate features. Again too late, he realized he was staring and that his silence could be construed as rude. He opened his mouth to speak, too late, of course.

"Twice in an acquaintance seems excessive, don't you think?"

"For a man who is little more than a country oaf? Hardly." Ahead of him the path led to the house. To his right, a narrower walkway lay half in shadow from the roses in full bloom. And in front of him, a vision that made him think of sex and the silk of a woman's form.

"Ridiculous, your grace," she said. Her smile was gentle and inviting and not at all as cold as he deserved from her. "You're no oaf."

"Am I to be forgiven?"

She plucked at her shawl until the two sides were even, then gave him a look from beneath her lashes. "I suppose."

"You are all that is generous, Miss Wellstone." She was a flirt, Miss Wellstone was. A charming, delightful flirt.

"In fact, I am." Moonlight turned her gown silvery gray. "Which you would know if you were ever at home."

"Another failing of mine." He bowed. "I attend to duty before pleasure."

"I expect that of you." She touched one of the roses, a bloom just beyond full. "It's a lovely evening."

He put a hand over his heart. Because he was a damn fool. Because she was beautiful and alluring. "Exactly as ordered."

"For which I sincerely thank you, your grace."

"Might I ask what brought you out here at such an hour?"

"This and that. Ginny and your brother have retired for the night." She tilted her head.

He completely lost his ability to see her as his sister's unmarried friend. Untouchable. Beyond a man's base desires. Before him stood a woman of flesh and blood, and he lusted after that woman.

"I couldn't sleep. I never can this early. I came out here because I wondered if I would still be able to smell the roses." She drew in a deep breath. "I can. I've been standing here these ten minutes or more breathing in the scent of your Gallicas."

Her features were exactly the sort of sweet and delicate form that made men feel a woman must be protected. No darkness or unhappiness should ever enter her life. Women like her were made to be spoiled and coddled and granted their every whim. He felt the urge himself, though he knew she was far from helpless.

"We missed you at supper tonight," she said. "Ginny seemed sure you would join us."

"I sent a note when I realized I would be detained."

"Yes. We received that." She had a narrow nose, perfectly balanced cheekbones, and a tenderly shaped mouth. Head-on or in profile, she was an angel. Her figure only added to his impression that here was a woman too fragile for her own good. His preference was for lovers who wouldn't collapse into a heap at the slightest exertion. He was willing to overlook that with her. "All the same, your grace, that does not mean we were not disappointed."

"I beg your forgiveness again."

"Three times I have been called on to forgive you." She shook her head and gave him a smile of mock ruefulness. "Now that *is* excessive."

Mountjoy moved closer to her. She was not unaware of her appeal, he knew that, but she had not been spoiled by it, as women sometimes were. A gold medallion hung from a long ribbon onto which were knotted several gold beads, spaced every three or four inches. In the dark, it was impossible to tell what color the ribbon was.

"It is." He wasn't awkward around women. He never had been. Even in the days when he'd been merely a farmer with just enough prospects to call him gentry, women liked him, something he'd realized early on. He felt awkward now because he was attracted to her and did not wish to be and suspected he was not going to resist. "I'm sure you would rather enjoy the garden in solitude."

"Actually, no." Her fingerless lace gloves matched the

moonlit silver of her gown. Had she worn those to supper? He found the informality profoundly arousing. "I dislike being alone." She gave him a sideways glance, and Lord, but her eyes were not innocent. She wasn't flirting with him, he understood that. She was a woman, not a girl, and quite plainly knew her own mind and desires. "Would you mind keeping me company? At least for a while."

God, no. Still holding his hat, he gave her a half bow. "I should be delighted to."

She laughed. "You poor gentlemen, obliged to accept trivial requests from we ladies even when you'd rather not." She waved him toward the house. "Go on, your grace. I only meant to walk to that hedge and then back. I can tolerate my own company for that long."

Mountjoy stayed where he was. She'd given him an easy way to escape his fate, and he stood there, unable, unwilling to take it. "It's a pleasant enough night."

They said nothing for two heartbeats, a long silence for a man and a woman alone. With no one near. Not even a servant. Mountjoy was far too aware of that fact. Was she? He rather thought she was.

"Ginny said you were at the Sessions," she said.

"I was. Until quite late."

She moved down the path, and Mountjoy followed. When he caught up, he took her arm as if they were relatives or it was broad daylight. As if there was no tension zinging in the air between them.

"Am I keeping you from your supper?" she asked. She did not sound as if she were in any way aware of the impropriety of them being alone here. "Or have you dined?"

Some of her nonchalance transferred to him. There was no reason to be anxious about being alone with her. She was a guest at Bitterward. They must naturally meet, and spend a moment or two in conversation, and without any of the speculation that attended a man's attentions to a woman at a formal social gathering. "With the mayor of High Tearing."

"Does he have pretty daughters?"

"No." The scent of roses carried on the breeze. They walked in silence for several steps while Mountjoy idly and improperly wondered what sort of lover she would be. Not passive, but warm, inviting. Adventurous. How could a woman like her be anything but adventurous in bed?

"Will you believe," Miss Wellstone said, "that until now I've never been farther from Syton House than I can walk in a day?" She let out a breath. "It seems I ought to be able to go home by mere thought alone. Or at least as quickly as a walk over the next hill, rather than a week's travel."

"You prefer the comforts of your home?" Mountjoy said. He'd have assumed a woman like her would be in constant search of entertainment. One party after another and an endless cadre of admiring men, not keeping at home with only herself and her cantankerous father for company.

"Very much, your grace." She shrugged, and the movement of her shoulders was achingly graceful. "I love Syton House. It's been my home since I was nineteen." She looked away from the roses and grinned at him. "All this time I thought I'd be terribly travel sick. I was before. I was so dreading the journey north. For naught, as it turns out."

"When was that?" he asked. "Your previous journey."

Her expression went blank for just a moment, but whatever thought had clouded her eyes vanished. "When I moved to Syton House. It was an unpleasant excursion. I confess, I found the carriage ride to Bitterward by turns dull and exhilarating. But this time, I was never once ill."

"A long journey always has its moments of tedium."

"If it weren't for my father, I'd travel more often." She faced him on the path, and though he was taller, she didn't have to lift her chin to look into his face. "I had an adventure on my way to Bitterward," she said.

His belly hollowed out. "Did you?"

"Shall I tell it to you?"

"Please." They stood close. Enough for him to see the lace that trimmed her gown. Enough to see the rise and fall of her bosom, the smoothness of her skin. She gestured. Her shawl slid down one of her arms, and he reached out to twitch the material into place over her shoulder.

"Thank you."

"Tell me your adventure." The side of his finger brushed her bare shoulder. Neither of them acknowledged the contact. Not yet.

"We'd stopped in Tewkesbury, as I particularly wished to see Tewkesbury Abbey. The nave, I'm told, retains some Norman features, and I hoped to inspect it. I don't know if Ginny told you of my fascination with architecture."

"She did."

Her shawl slipped off her shoulder again. Mountjoy stooped to pick up the trailing end, but instead of handing it to her, he fingered the material. Cashmere, and unutterably soft.

"It's one of the reasons, your grace, that I am so pleased to be here at Bitterward." She clasped her hands behind her back and rocked on her heels. "The house is an excellent example of the Gothic. I'm very much looking forward to exploring and taking some sketches. That's if you don't mind. I hope you don't."

"Draw the entire house if you like." The neckline of her gown was low enough to offer him a view of the curve of her breasts, and, yes, he looked.

"Thank you." She took a step away from him and plucked a leaf from one of the rosebushes. He reminded himself of how improper it would be to close the distance between them. She folded the leaf in half lengthwise then in half again. He had the impression Miss Wellstone was never still for long. Despite her physical delicacy, she was not a languid woman.

"Your adventure?"

She unfolded the leaf and then began again, folding in the opposite direction. "It began when I saved a Gypsy king's dog from certain death."

"A Gypsy?"

"He wore the most colorful clothes. They made me dizzy

with delight and astonishment." The leaf succumbed to the folding and tore. She dropped it at the side of the path. "You never saw a more handsome man in your life. He wasn't as tall as you, but he was well made, with dusky skin and the most languishing eyes."

"Did you fall in love with him?" he asked. He took a step toward her.

"Madly. Desperately. Head-over-heels." Her smile broadened, and Mountjoy thought he'd do anything to see her smile like that again. "If only for a moment. I do believe if he'd asked me, I'd have run away with him and his charming puppy to learn to dance, read fortunes, and live the Gypsy life."

Mountjoy began to understand why her father thought her wild. The idea of her running off with a Gypsy was more than a little arousing, and he suspected she knew that. They were alone. Completely. He did not think only he felt the tension between them. He touched her cheek and began his slide to Hell for what he intended.

"Don't you think that would be a most exciting life, your grace?" She didn't move away from his caress. He wasn't far gone enough not to know he hadn't merely touched her. "I wonder if I ought to have done so."

"Eugenia would have been devastated to miss your visit."

She lifted her chin. "I was only in love for a moment, but what a moment it was." Her laughter was a beguiling thing to hear. No titter or practiced trill, but a full-on burst of amusement. "I had already imagined our ten beautiful children, all of them Gypsy princes and princesses."

"Ten of them?"

"Yes." A breeze came up, and she shivered. She rubbed her palms up and down her arms.

"You're cold."

"Perhaps a little."

Mountjoy arranged her shawl around her shoulders so it didn't droop uselessly down her back. Then he curled his fingers in the cashmere and pulled her toward him. He shouldn't do this, but it seemed he was going to anyway. Because she was beautiful and intriguing, and not at all the innocent he'd imagined when they met. "Will you let me keep you warm?"

She smiled as if she knew a secret, and he wondered just who was seducing whom. He moved her closer to him.

"Better?" he said.

"Mm."

He brought both sides of her shawl closer around her. He could not do any of the things on his mind. He couldn't. But if he did? "Since you did not run away with the Gypsy king, there must be more to your adventure. Or was meeting him thrilling enough?"

Their eyes locked, acknowledging what their words did not. "He thanked me profusely and genuinely for rescuing his puppy, which he intended to give to one of his daughters."

Mountjoy kept her close. "If the Gypsy king had a daughter of his own, then he must have already been married, and you could not have run away with him to become his Gypsy queen."

"Well. I suppose you're right." She stood with her head tipped to one side, as if she'd never considered the possibility. Perfect, an absolutely perfect picture of innocent confusion. "It's fortunate I did not run away." Her eyes twinkled. "In any event, he was so grateful he gave me this medallion." She held up the ribbon around her neck, high enough to display a gold circle the size of a guinea that hung from the end of the ribbon. "You see?"

He leaned closer to examine it, taking the metal in his hand, angled so the moonlight illuminated it. One side was engraved with a bow and arrow. He turned it over to show a cherubic face on the obverse.

"The medallion is magic," she said. "He promised me that."

Mountjoy glanced up. They stood quite close. "Will it bring you riches and good health for all your life?"

She took the medallion from his hand and studied it. "He

told me that whoever possesses this charm will be united with the individual with whom she or he will be happiest in love. Ginny says I must sleep with it under my pillow."

Mountjoy said, "Isn't that how such charms work?" Her future husband would take her to bed. He'd cover her body with his and put himself inside her and make love to her. And she would enfold her husband in her arms, kiss him, caress him, and if the man were not a dolt, she would sigh and call out his name.

"Oh, the medallion can't work for me."

He held her gaze. "Why not?"

"I have already met the man I was destined to love."

"The Gypsy king?"

"No." She stood motionless with no sign of her previous animation.

"If you are in love, Miss Wellstone, why haven't you married the man?"

"I meant to. We intended to."

His heart clenched because he remembered too late that she had admitted she'd lost someone dear to her. Whoever he was, she truly had loved the man. He cupped the side of her face. He wanted to stop her from hurting, and he didn't know how. "What happened? What broke your heart?"

"He was a soldier."

"I'm sorry." Not for a moment did he think a man who'd won her love would jilt her. Impossible. "How long ago did he die?"

"Five years."

Briefly, he closed his eyes. "What a terrible loss, Miss Wellstone."

She gave a tiny nod, and he was pleased to see some of her sorrow ease. "So you see, your grace, the medallion can't work for me." She tipped her head into his palm. Only for a moment. He let his hand fall to her shoulder. "I am resigned to my single state. It suits me, for I can't love another like that. I wouldn't wish to ever again." She rubbed one side of the medallion. "It's a pretty thing," she said. "I like it exceedingly."

"Are you sure it won't work?"

"It can't possibly when my heart is incapable of being aroused."

"What if you're wrong?"

"I'm not."

"Can you be sure? Who have you encountered today, Miss Wellstone?" he asked. By some miracle he injected the perfect hint of humor in his voice. She bit back a laugh, but smiled. "Any mysterious gentlemen? Any premonitions or chills along your spine? Perhaps an irresistible urge to demand an introduction to some strapping young fellow?"

She shook her head solemnly, but he could see the laughter in her eyes. "None at all. Unless you count your butler. We nearly collided earlier." She let a beat go by. "Is there, by any chance, a Mrs. Doyle?"

"Yes," Mountjoy said. "There is."

"Ah. A shame."

Mountjoy was horrified by how badly he wanted to kiss her.

And, so, after they'd stood there staring at each other, neither of them moving, he did.

He curled his fingers into her shawl and used that to bring her closer. She came to him with a soft sigh and then lifted her arms to his shoulders. He'd broken, amicably, with his mistress when he was last in London, for no reason other than boredom. Therefore, it had been some weeks since he last held a woman in his arms. He was randy as hell. So he told himself.

Lily Wellstone did not kiss like a virgin.

Jesus, no.

He held back nothing. He was far too wound up for a circumspect kiss. From the moment he touched her without either of them pretending nothing would happen, the possibility of restraint flew from any list of his abilities. The world, it so happened, had just become limited to the two of them. He was lost to every selfish and sexual urge a man might have in respect of a woman and to the scent of her, the taste of her, the feel of her body against his.

She took his hat from him, and if she dropped it to the ground, he surely didn't give a damn because she buried her fingers in his hair and, oh, yes, indeed, she was kissing him back.

Her hips pressed into him, gently against his erection and then the moon disappeared behind some clouds and they stood there in the dark of the garden, still kissing, breathing in each other and the scent of roses.

By the time she drew back, and it was she who did, one of his hands cupped her bottom. The other was curved around the nape of her neck. He took a deep breath, but at the end, though she had put a few inches' distance between them, he leaned toward her and kissed her again. She allowed the kiss to linger, a light touch of their mouths, and then no more.

"Goodness," she said, looking at him from under her lashes. "That was lovely."

"I do know how to properly kiss a woman."

Her secret smile reappeared. "You do, your grace."

He kissed her again. She pressed her hand to his cheek as this kiss lingered, too, but she drew away too soon. Far too soon. She dropped her hand to his chest and kept it there.

"I don't mean for you to get the wrong idea," she said.

"What would the wrong idea be?"

"This." She shook her head. "The two of us."

"It doesn't feel wrong."

She leaned against him, her hand pressed to his chest. "I confess I find you extremely attractive."

"Thank you."

She pushed on his chest and stepped away. "This is not wise, your grace. We can't. Much as I like . . . all that— Well. You understand."

"What do you like?"

"Don't be obtuse. You know precisely what I like. Kissing you." She placed a finger across his lips. "Touching you. You're so very lovely, which I am sure you know, but it would be unwise to continue this when more is impossible between us."

He wrapped his fingers around her wrist. "Are you certain?"

"Your sister is my dear friend," she said. "And you are to be married."

"I am aware," he said. Lord, yes, he was aware now. He hadn't been when he was kissing her.

They stood there, in the darkened garden. Lily looked away, and he bent to retrieve his hat from the path, and there they stood again, mere inches apart. She looked like a woman who'd been kissed. Thoroughly.

She let out a short breath. "Despite what you must think of me, I'm not a woman of loose morals."

He nodded his agreement.

She met his gaze. "I wanted to kiss you." She brushed a hand over her face, then to her throat. "I suppose that makes me wicked. Wanting you to kiss me. Then allowing you to do so."

"It doesn't." He reached out and took her Gypsy medallion between his fingers. "I blame this," he said.

She laughed, and the sound lightened his heart. "Of course." She plucked another leaf. "That must be the cause. We had no power to resist the magic."

"You see? We are not at fault here."

"Better you than Doyle, I daresay."

He let go of the medallion and laughed outright. Quiet descended, and during the silence, she adjusted her shawl over her shoulders and closed the distance between them. Mountjoy slid an arm around her waist, and the tension was back, singing through him. But all she did was lean in to kiss his cheek.

"I'll tell you good night, your grace, and see myself inside." She touched his cheek. "Thank you for your company."

He didn't let her go. Not until she cleared her throat. "The pleasure was mine, I assure you."

She curtseyed to him and then left him. Alone.

He watched her walk away, and since the moon had come out from behind the clouds he had no trouble discerning the sway of her hips until, at last, the shadows hid even that.

She was right. They couldn't when nothing would come of it. He was going to marry Jane. He could not seduce his sister's friend. Affairs always ended. Eugenia would never forgive him when their inevitable break cost her Lily's friendship. His sister had few enough friends as it was.

He wanted to, though.

Chapter Five

JUST BEFORE LILY BLEW OUT THE CANDLE AT HER
bedside, she took off the Gypsy's medallion and slipped it
underneath her pillow. Not that she believed in the power
of the medallion; she just didn't want to lie to Ginny about
whether she had done so, and Ginny would ask. She marked
her place in her novel with an ivory bookmark and set it on
the table beside her. The candle was barely an inch tall. Her
inability to sleep at night meant she would have to ask the
housekeeper to see that there were extra candles in her room.

Dawn was just touching the windows as she pulled the
covers to her shoulders. The room was no longer dark, and
at last, sleep dragged her eyes closed. Her sheets smelled of
lavender, and while she breathed in the scent, she imagined
the coolness of the Gypsy's medallion lay not beneath her
pillow but beneath her fingers. She could still feel the duke's
mouth on hers, the solidness of his body. The taste of him.
The bewildering response of her body to him. He was not
Greer, and she could not help feeling she'd betrayed the man
she loved. And yet, to be held like that. Kissed like that. She

tried to summon Greer's beloved face and she couldn't, and her heart broke anew.

She fell asleep as the first light of morning filled her room, turning dark shadows to gray, and gray to palest lilac. She dreamed. Vividly. She was outside, a spade in her hand, looking into a hole in the ground. In her dream, she knew she was searching for treasure.

Footmen stood around her, wilting in the afternoon heat, soon dirty and sweaty from the work of digging the trench. They'd cast off their coats and rolled up their sleeves, though it was she who held the shovel. Ginny and the so very young and handsome Lord Nigel Hampton stood to her right. Across from her, on the other side of the trench, stood the Duke of Mountjoy, his eyes green as moss.

Their gazes connected, hers and the duke's, and her heart beat hard in her chest. He wasn't as lovely as his brother, but there was a look in his eyes, a certainty about him that appealed to her immensely. Surely, she thought, he would not ask more of her than she had in her to give.

She broke from his gaze and returned to her digging. After turning a few spadefuls of dirt, her shovel hit something that was not dirt. Carefully, she reached in to scrape away the dirt. Gold gleamed from the shadowed trench. She bent closer and the shadows resolved into an iron pot full of gold coins that, even in her dreaming state, she thought looked suspiciously like her medallion. Why, with these, the whole unmarried population of High Tearing would be able to find their truest and happiest loves.

The footmen applauded as she bent to touch the coins, and she grinned with triumph. She stood up, the pot in her arms, and no one, least of all herself, remarked that such a pot would be too heavy for her to lift, though she held it easily. She gave everyone present one of the discs. Except for the duke, who stood on the other side of the excavation, his arms crossed over his chest. Refusing to accept one.

She walked the perimeter of the trench until she reached Mountjoy. There, she handed him the pot of coins. "You see? We succeeded. Look at your sister." Ginny stood beside Lord Nigel, wearing a sky blue frock instead of a black one. "Do you see how happy she is? She ought to wear colors all the time."

"Yes," he said. "She ought to." Mountjoy turned away from the crowd, but she followed him, and they were soon in the library, quite alone. The coin-filled pot sat on the largest table. Each disc in the pot exactly resembled her medallion. She smoothed one of them between her fingers. They were heavy enough to be solid gold and therefore must be worth a fortune.

Mountjoy stood beside her, silent. Brooding.

"Are you angry, your grace?" she asked.

"No."

She gave him a disc and this time, he accepted it.

"Thank you, Lily."

In her dream, his voice sent a shiver down her spine. Yes, the man did have the loveliest voice, edged with smoke and silk. She touched his coat, poorly cut for a man whose shoulders were so broad. Mountjoy was an active man and his body reflected that. One heard things, if one paid even the least attention. On occasion, the duke worked alongside his tenants, and the plain truth was that with his advice, crop yields were up. He had a reputation as a horseman able to turn even the most bad-tempered mount into an obedient ride. He was not considered an approachable man, but his neighbors solicited his opinion about horses and farming. The Duke of Mountjoy was, if not well liked, then well respected.

"You ought to hire me on as your valet." She was perfectly serious, and Mountjoy took it as such.

His eyes stayed on her face. Such a pure and intense green, framed by dark, thick lashes and a tilt at the edges that made her think of his kisses. Her pulse raced out of control so that she could scarcely breathe. "I won't pay you more than twenty pounds per annum."

"So long as I have room and board, that is acceptable."

Since she would be working for the duke, she'd have to close Syton House, though the garden tours must continue. Syton House was famous for its gardens and that brought visitors who spent money at the local establishments. If enough of her staff agreed to stay on even though she no longer lived there, the public tours of the house could continue. The moment she had the chance, she'd write to her steward to put that into motion.

"Then the position is yours," the duke said just as if there was nothing unusual about hiring a woman as his valet. "You'll start immediately."

"Excellent, your grace, since you require an entirely new wardrobe."

He picked up one of the discs and spun it on its edge. "Do I?"

"Indeed, sir, you do. You won't regret it. I'll make you the envy of every man in England. Everyone will beg to know the name of your tailor."

"Make it so, Wellstone."

She laughed, tickled that he should have fallen immediately into calling her by her last name. Oh, yes, she would be the most excellent valet in the Empire and the Duke of Mountjoy would be her triumph.

"Wellstone." He caught the still spinning coin between his fingers.

"Yes?"

"There is one other duty you'll have."

"Yes?"

"This."

Then he kissed her, and she was not an inexperienced girl who could only guess at the passion possible between a man and a woman. He kissed her the way he had in the garden. Tenderly then passionately, holding nothing back, and beneath her fingers she felt the strength and warmth of his body, and she wanted more than anything to touch him when he was nude. To slide her fingers over his magnificent physique, over the muscles that formed his body, to touch and taste and tell him how astonishingly lovely he was.

Her body betrayed her memory of Greer, because she clung to Mountjoy as if no one else had ever mattered to her. In her wicked, wicked dream she kissed him back, and it was wonderful to feel a shiver of arousal when his arms slid around her, the soft touch of his mouth. He pulled back to look at her, his eyes a deep and unfathomable green, and the world dropped away.

She held his face between her hands, sweeping her thumbs underneath his eyes. His skin was warm and alive. She'd felt like this the first time Greer touched her. Shaky, full of anticipation, nervous, aroused, and completely without doubt that they were right to do this. To hold each other, to kiss, to enjoy the physical. Mountjoy's arms tightened around her as the chasm that was her grief opened up and threatened to swallow her whole.

"You work for me now," he told her in a gruff voice. "No one but me."

"Yes."

"I shan't ask you to forget him. Never that." His hands moved over her, caressing, sliding along her shoulders, over the curve of her breasts, her bottom, and everywhere else he could reach and in between he pressed kisses on her, and she melted a little at each one. "Eugenia is right. You can find happiness with another man."

In her dream, she wondered for the first time if that might actually be possible for her.

Chapter Six

MOUNTJOY CAME HOME TO A QUIET HOUSE EVEN though it was early afternoon. He thought nothing of it, supposing, erroneously as it turned out, that Nigel was visiting the Kirks again, and his sister and her friend were shopping or making calls. He admitted to a certain disappointment at the empty house because Lily Wellstone was a sensual pleasure to watch. She was his secret and guilty pleasure. Addicting, actually. She was in his thoughts too often and, lately, in his dreams, too.

They had succeeded, however, in putting aside that mad incident in the garden. He stayed away from home more than he might have otherwise, and if they happened to meet, they were cordial to each other and nothing more, whatever his private thoughts might be.

He nudged aside the guilty thought that he ought to take the opportunity to call on the Kirks himself. One day, Miss Jane Kirk would make him as suitable a wife as any woman of his acquaintance. Her father had made it clear an offer from him would be welcome, and most of High Tearing behaved as if their marriage was inevitable. He should get the thing done and propose to her. As soon as the time was right. When he had a moment to breathe amid his duties. When more of his affairs were settled. When he did marry, he wanted the thing to be done right, with all the sincerity and sobriety the marriage deserved.

In his room, he put on fresh clothes, breaking his valet's heart yet again by ignoring his suggestions as to alternate attire. The man took every opportunity to suggest, by deed or look or allusion—Mountjoy had forbidden overt remarks on the subject of his clothes—that his wardrobe was deficient. Why should he mind his clothes when he was in his own home and no one was here? He wasn't one of those noblemen born into money and position, and he saw no reason to behave as if he had been.

Dressed in his most comfortable clothes, he left Elliot to his incipient despair and went downstairs in search of a bite to eat. He passed one of the salons on his way and heard voices and laughter, the deeper tones of a man and then a woman's laugh. Two women, he thought.

The salon door was ajar, though not enough for him to see what was going on. His ability to keep the names and functions of the various rooms in the house straight wasn't improving, in part because he didn't care and in part because he'd grown to manhood in his aunt and uncle's home, a house with two floors and seven rooms, including the kitchen and servants' rooms.

Why did anyone need four salons? Or was it five? He could not recall if this salon had a particular use or name. The music room? He pushed open the door and looked in. He didn't think he'd been in it more than a dozen times since he came to Bitterward with his sister and brother in tow.

He did not see musical instruments.

What he did see was Nigel standing by a table, his back to the door, one hand on the top rail of a chair occupied by Miss Lily Wellstone. A paisley shawl draped down her back. Nigel was bent over her shoulder, intently watching something. Eugenia and Miss Jane Kirk were here, too, as intent as Nigel on the table. Jane sat enough to one side that if she were to look up, she'd see the door. And him. Her gloved hands were pressed together and her cheek rested on her uppermost hand. He was struck by what a pretty woman Jane was. He could not do better for his duchess. Like Nigel, Eugenia and Miss Kirk were absorbed in whatever Miss Wellstone was doing.

As best he could tell, Miss Wellstone appeared to be writing or perhaps drawing. Sketching the room as she liked to do? Her intention, she'd said, was to draw the entire house before she departed. Rather than continue in and interrupt them, he leaned against the door and drank in the sight of Lily. He remembered how she'd melted in his arms, the taste of her, the touch of her lips, the roar of passion through him.

She laughed in that heartfelt way of hers, and Eugenia leaned closer to look. His sister giggled. So did Jane, for that matter. Miss Wellstone reached forward with one hand, did something, then drew back. An action consistent with dipping a quill into ink. So. She was writing or drawing something.

"Have a care," Nigel said.

Miss Wellstone spared his brother a quick glance. "I am being very careful. Honestly, Lord Nigel. Has disaster struck yet?"

"No. But you're tipping it."

She did something with whatever they were looking at. "That's because you distracted me." She wrote or drew something. "Don't distract me, my dear young man, and all will be well."

Eugenia propped her chin on a fist this time and said, "What are you going to write next?"

Jane craned her neck to look. Her dark hair contrasted with the blond of the others. She would do well as his duchess. Very well indeed. He wondered if they had decided to write a play. There were enough young people in the environs of High Tearing to put on a creditable production. Lord, he hoped they did not intend to perform their creation at Bitterward. The house would be overrun, and he'd be forced to lock himself in his office to escape the agony.

"Something dramatic," Miss Wellstone said. "Something to pull at our hearts. Unless anyone wants to compose an extempore poem, a line from Shakespeare I think. *Out damn spot!*" She made a flourish in the air then returned to her paper and wrote something down. "Out, out, you dreadful lout."

Nigel guffawed. "Oh, poetess!"

On the other hand, Mountjoy was convinced Miss Wellstone would prove an adept actress. It would be amusing to watch her in a dramatic role. If they were writing a play, he would not object to having the performance here despite the disruption to his schedule. So long as they did not disturb him with their rehearsals.

"'Yet who would have thought the old man to have had so much blood in him?'" Miss Wellstone did a creditable Lady Macbeth, full of fearful lunacy.

Nigel said, "Write something else."

"Such as?"

"I don't know. 'The weather is fine today'?"

"No," Jane said. "Write, 'Mountjoy has not smiled these seven years.'"

Nigel gave her a quick look. Miss Wellstone continued writing, pausing frequently to dip her pen in what Mountjoy presumed was an inkpot. "Why would I write that?"

"Because it's true," Jane said. "Isn't it, Lord Nigel?"

"He has a great many duties, Miss Kirk, to occupy his thoughts. Though it's true, he does not smile often," Nigel said.

"Not unless he thinks he has to," Jane said.

"I don't think that's so," said Miss Wellstone. She kept writing.

Mountjoy pushed off the doorway and headed for the table. Best join them before they said something about him that would embarrass them all.

Jane looked up, and her eyes met Mountjoy's. Her cheeks flushed pink. She stood and squeaked out a set of nonsense syllables he presumed was meant to be his name. Good God. Did he actually frighten her?

Nigel and Eugenia continued unaware, and Miss Wellstone was too absorbed in writing out her sentence to notice Jane's reaction or the reason for it.

"I'm not going to write something that isn't true," Miss Wellstone was saying. She looked at Nigel instead of Eugenia or Jane. "How about 'The Duke of Mountjoy is in dire need of a new wardrobe'?"

Eugenia saw him, and she started. She cleared her throat and got out the words that had stuck there. "Mountjoy. Whatever are *you* doing here?"

Miss Wellstone froze.

Nigel looked over his shoulder, saw him, and turned the color of old porridge. "You."

"Good afternoon, Nigel," he said as if he'd overheard nothing. "Eugenia. Miss Kirk." He headed for the other side of Miss Wellstone's chair so as to have a view of the table. There was no reason on earth for Jane Kirk to be afraid of him or believe he never smiled. None. "What has you four so occupied?" he asked. He was near enough now to see a sheet of paper on the table. Unlikely as it seemed, the words glowed a sickly yellow. He made out the lines from Macbeth. She had not, it appeared, gotten around to writing down Nigel's little ditty about him nor her own suggestion. "What the devil?"

"Your grace," Miss Wellstone said with a brilliant smile that left him momentarily witless. "Good afternoon." She held a quill in her right hand and in her left a phial of water. There was a small pot on the table, capped. The tip of her quill appeared to be wet.

He was aware that Nigel, Eugenia, and Jane had gone quiet, but in that silence he forgot how to breathe. Because Lily Wellstone, when she smiled like that, was quite literally breathtaking.

"We are engaged in a scientific experiment." She gestured with the hand that held the quill. He did not think he was mistaken that the point of the quill was emitting the same eerie yellowish light as the words on her sheet of paper.

"An experiment?"

"Indeed, your grace." She lifted the paper. "Behold!"

He hadn't been wrong. The words were glowing.

"If the room were dark," she went on, "I'm sure the effect would be even more dramatic. I was about to ask Lord Nigel to draw the curtains. Do you mind if he does?"

"What is that?"

She used the quill to point to a book that had not yet been bound. The cover was still the ashy blue cardboard sheets. He could not read the label pasted on the spine. "A book I bought shortly before I left for Sheffieldshire. *The New Family Receipt Book*. It's filled with the most fascinating information and advice. Invaluable to household management. If you're interested, I'd be happy to provide your cook with a recipe for coffee made with acorns."

"Acorns." She kissed like an angel.

"Or potatoes."

"Coffee from potatoes?" He shot a glance at Jane. She sat with her hands clasped on her lap, and she did look terrified. He smiled at her before returning his attention to Lily. "Forgive me, Miss Wellstone, but that's vile."

Her lips pressed together and she managed, somehow, to look down her nose at him even though she was sitting and he was standing.

"You think it's not vile?"

"I think it's narrow-minded of you to judge without evidence. It is an ingenious receipt." She waved the quill again. "Think of the savings."

He rocked back on his heels and smiled again. "The household can yet bear the expense of actual coffee. There's no need for substitutes."

"Perhaps you'd like to give your cook a better method of stuffing a goose."

He gazed at her, torn between thoughts of kissing her senseless and informing her that his household ran perfectly well under his supervision and Doyle's.

"No?" she said. "Another means of making excellent ink? There are several, and I mean to try them in any event so it's no trouble at all." She smiled again. "I'm happy to report the results to you and recommend the best."

Nigel fidgeted and said, "Miss Wellstone?"

"What experiment are you performing?" Mountjoy asked. Some of his wits returned, and he realized everyone except Lily was wary.

"Ah. Yes." She stopped waving the quill and held it up between them. "A phosphorus pencil."

"Phosphorus?"

"Miss Wellstone!"

She turned on her chair. "How may I assist you, Lord Nigel?"

"The quill must be kept wet."

Mountjoy saw her blink and glance at the phial of water in her other hand. He frowned. "A phosphorus pencil? Are you mad?"

"Oh." She blinked again. "Lord Nigel, I do thank you for the reminder. Your grace, I'm quite sane, but thank you all the same for your concern."

"The water," Nigel said.

"Yes, yes. Phosphorus, as I am sure you know, your grace, ignites on contact with air. Hence the precaution of keeping the quill wet. The instructions were quite explicit on that point."

Mountjoy watched her hand. The hair on the back of his neck prickled. "I am well—"

Light flashed at the head of the quill. Nigel shouted and that made Miss Wellstone startle. Her reflexive jerk sent sparks showering over the sheet of paper. At the same time, she dropped the phial of water. The container struck the edge of the table and broke, scattering glass and the contents onto the rug. His Axminster rug, valued at several hundred pounds in the most recent inventory and originally installed by the second Duke of Mountjoy.

"Miss Wellstone!" Nigel leaned in, reaching for the burning quill. Ominous dark spots appeared on the paper.

Eugenia and Jane cried out.

"Good God." Mountjoy swept up the smoldering paper and threw it into a large Chinese vase fortuitously within his reach.

"The pencil!" Nigel said.

Mountjoy stopped Nigel from snatching away the quill. "You'll burn yourself, you fool." He whipped off his coat, prepared to wrap Miss Wellstone's arm and the now flaming quill in the garment.

"There is no need for panic." Miss Wellstone, holding the quill by the feathered tip, walked briskly to the vase. The paper he'd tossed into it had fully caught. A strong smell of smoke and burning phosphorus permeated the air. The light was intense as flames appeared above the rim of the vase and continued to burn all out of proportion to a single sheet of paper. Miss Wellstone tossed the burning quill before she quite reached the vase.

Not that he blamed her for doing so since she might otherwise have severely injured her hand. But Mountjoy, with visions of the quill missing the vase and setting fire to the carpet and thence to the room, roared, "No!"

The quill, half in flames, seemed to dance through the air. It made a graceful arc and landed.

In the vase. The flames and light intensified, and they all held their breath while they waited to see if the fire would stop or continue to a conflagration that required an evacuation of the house. The flames sputtered, then died down.

No one said anything. Except for Miss Wellstone, who had her back to him and could not see his black expression as could Nigel and the others. She dusted off her hands. "That's that, then."

Chapter Seven

"MISS WELLSTONE."

Lily turned. Without his coat, the Duke of Mountjoy was both physically magnificent—there was no disguising the perfection of his form—and a sartorial disappointment. His waistcoat bagged at the sides, and his cravat was a horror. One might as well not even bother having suits made. Did his tailor not know how to cut fabric for such a specimen as Mountjoy? Did not his valet understand how to properly starch and fold a neckcloth?

"Do you know, your grace, if *I* were your valet, I wouldn't permit you to step foot outside your dressing room with a cravat like that."

"I beg your pardon?"

Lord Nigel said, "I've told him so many a time, Miss Wellstone. Perhaps he'll listen to you."

"You do not appear to be happy, your grace. It's only a poorly tied cravat. Easily remedied."

"How observant of you, Miss Wellstone."

"Yes, well. Who could be happy wearing such inferior attire?"

"I am. Might I point out that you are not my valet, Wellstone?"

Her heart did a flip, but no one, including the duke, seemed to notice what he had called her. "More's the pity, I say."

He glowered at her, actually, and she hadn't done anything to merit such a glare. She gave him a quick smile. True, there had been a moment when the fire might have done more than singe the interior of the vase, but nothing worse had happened. He squeezed his coat, which he held in one hand. "Did you burn yourself?"

She shook her head, flattered that he was worried on her behalf, yet cautious on account of his dark expression. "There was never any danger of that."

"Your phosphorus pencil was on fire." Their relations since their encounter in the garden had been, if not warm, then at least distantly cordial. She understood the reason for his reserve. They had transgressed propriety that night. One could not help but expect a certain discomfort as a result. But that did not warrant his present behavior. His fingers tightened around the coat. If it were a living thing, the garment would be dead by now. With that happy thought, she was forced to look anywhere but at his hand lest she imagine him choking the life from some poor, innocent creature.

"Well, yes, sir, it was on fire. A little."

"A little."

"You distracted me, and the tip dried out. If you hadn't interrupted, we would still be writing out glowing words from the immortal bard. It was great fun. It's a pity we didn't finish."

" 'The weather is fine today'?" he said. At least his tone was milder. " 'Mountjoy has not smiled these seven years'?"

"No one wrote those words."

He arched his eyebrows and glanced at the vase. "The proof of that is nothing but ashes."

"I don't see that I need to prove anything." She licked her lower lip. He didn't seem to be any happier. "Would you like to try for yourself? There's plenty more phosphorus."

"Where?"

"Just here, your grace. We are fully outfitted for a lengthy experiment." She was aware the man was angry, but she wasn't about to let him get away with spoiling their afternoon. "This is excellent. Your participation in our adventure is most unexpected, I must say." She half turned. "Lord Nigel, have you another quill?"

Lord Nigel, pale as a sheet, gripped the back of the chair she'd been sitting on. His knuckles were white as bone. "No, Miss Wellstone, I haven't."

She knew perfectly well he did, but Ginny was as ashen as her younger brother and Miss Kirk was far too somber. She herself, having never had relations of any degree who acknowledged her existence, did not know what it was like to have a brother. For all she knew, everyone feared one's eldest brother. She doubted that, though.

"I'm sure," she said, turning back to the duke, "that we could send for another quill." She walked toward the bell-pull. She no longer permitted anyone to bully her, and that included noblemen of any rank. "Shall I do that?"

"No," the duke said in a pleasant voice that nevertheless frosted her ears. "You shall not. I meant, Wellstone, where is the phosphorus?"

"On the table." She pointed. His eyes darted that direction, and she knew instantly what he intended. She took a step back and to the side, placing herself in front of the table and between the duke and her phosphorus, arms outspread. "It's mine, sir. I purchased it at the apothecary earlier today. I'm afraid I cannot allow you to take my property."

"Mountjoy—" his brother said.

"And I"—the duke spoke with deceptive calmness—

"cannot permit anyone to continue in possession of a substance capable of burning down my home."

Lord Nigel spoke up again, loudly. "See here, Mountjoy. You've no call to address her like that."

The duke could glower all he liked. She would march to her doom willingly and alone. Brave to the very end.

"You and I will speak later," Mountjoy said to Lord Nigel.

Lily looked at Lord Nigel and then at Ginny and Miss Kirk. Lord Nigel was still pale, but his eyes were fiery. He'd taken a step toward Jane, and Lily silently applauded his instinct to protect the young woman and his sister. Ginny stood with her hands to her mouth and was blinking rapidly. Jane, very sensibly, sat quite still, but she was not holding up well either. There would be tears any moment, and Lily would not stand for that.

"If there is blame to apportion, it belongs to me alone," Lily said. "I proposed the experiment. I convinced the others. And I acquired all the necessary materials." She picked up the container of phosphorus. "Might we discuss this in private, your grace?"

"No."

She fixed him with a glower she hoped was every bit as intimidating as his. "But, your grace," she said. There wasn't enough sugar in the world to match her sweetness. "I require a word in private with you." She walked to him and put her arm through his free arm—he still had his coat in a choke hold in the other—and headed for the door. "Ginny, I'll meet you and Miss Kirk in the Oldenburg salon in a quarter of an hour. Twenty minutes, at the most." She glanced at the duke and amended her estimate. "Perhaps half an hour. And you, as well, Lord Nigel. I expect tea will be as lovely as always."

She tightened her fingers on Mountjoy's arm and said in a voice pitched low, "Do come along."

Mountjoy did. She wasn't surprised. She'd found over the

years that men responded to decisive action, perhaps especially from a woman. Nursemaids trained them to obedience from an early age.

Lily strolled out of the room with Mountjoy at her side. "Which way?"

"Left."

"Thank you." She marched down the hall only to have him refuse to follow.

He drawled, "The other left, Miss Wellstone."

"Never mind then." She opened the nearest door. "This room will do."

Mountjoy reached around her in time to hold the door for her. When she'd swept in, he followed, holding out a hand after they ended up facing each other. He continued strangling his coat with the other.

"The phosphorus, Wellstone."

"I told you, it's mine." She crossed her arms, but she was distracted by the breadth of his coatless shoulders. He wasn't a huge man, but there was substance to his frame and none of it to spare. "You'll think me bold and impertinent, your grace, and you will be right."

"I always am." His voice was steel and smoke, but there was something else there, too. Something hungry that sent a frisson of anticipation racing down her spine.

"Do please put on your coat," she said. "I don't think I can bear to look at your waistcoat another minute."

The duke drew in a long, slow breath. "Forgive me."

"Again?"

He put on his coat and rapidly buttoned it. "An improvement, I hope."

"No." She examined him from head to toe. "Your valet ought to be dismissed."

"So you've said, Wellstone."

"I don't think I have."

"You have in my dreams."

She braced herself against showing how his remark

startled her. "I swoon, your grace, to think I have been honored to appear in your dreams."

"Did I say dreams? I meant nightmares."

"Your coat, sir, is as atrocious as your waistcoat. But I did not ask for this interview to chastise you for your attire."

"No?" A note of something wild curled around the edges of his voice.

She sat on a sofa with a large harp set at an angle to one end and gestured for him to take the chair across from her. As he did, she slid a finger over the strings of the harp. The instrument was out of tune. "For a time, in my extreme youth, I had harp lessons. I did not enjoy them."

"I thought all young ladies enjoyed their music lessons."

"Did you enjoy yours?"

"Farmers do not have the luxury of a musical education."

"You're not a farmer."

"Did you mean to ask me if I could play you a song on the harp? I can't."

She set the phosphorus beside her. Mountjoy eyed the jar. "It's tightly sealed, your grace."

"It had better be."

"It is. I assure you. But please. It's your sister I wish to speak to you about. I knew her when her husband was alive, how happy and in love she was. I saw her in her grief when he died. When you came to take her home, I thought, thank goodness. She'll have someone to look after her. Family upon whom to rely."

"She has that," he said.

Lily sniffed then glanced down and winced. The man was in need of a decent bootmaker, too. "My God," she said in a low voice. "Those boots." No amount of polish or oil could save his footwear. She shook her head. "Now that I am here, your grace, it is my particular aim to see your sister amused." She folded her hands on her lap. "It's something you and Lord Nigel have failed to do. You ought both of you to be ashamed. I intend to continue to encourage her to leave the house, make calls, and engage in divers recreation that will refresh her heart."

"Wellstone, please believe that I do not for a moment doubt your devotion to my sister—"

"If writing sentences with a phosphorus pencil amuses your sister, and it did, sir, then how can you object to that?"

His eyes widened. "Because it is dangerous."

"Oh, pshaw. We'd been writing for some time before you interrupted us. In fact, Lord Nigel, Miss Kirk, and your sister had already had their turn."

"I object to my house burning down."

She lifted her hands, palms up, and looked from side to side. "Your house has not burned down."

He spread his thighs and propped his hands on his knees as he leaned forward. "Pure luck."

"Hardly."

"The quill burst into flames. You might have brought the house down."

She snorted. "Tell me, do you come home every day and say to yourself, 'Thank God, today I was not savaged by wolves'? Or 'killed by a runaway carriage'?"

He yanked on his cravat. There was at least no way to make it look any worse. He would be passionate in bed, she was certain. Capable of gentleness, but more than able to set tenderness aside if the moment called for more. "There are no wolves in England."

"Precisely my point."

"But there are runaway carriages, and when I am in the presence of one, yes, I am grateful to continue among the living." He leaned back on his chair and raked his fingers through his hair. Such beautiful, thick hair. She wanted to run her fingers through his hair again. "Phosphorus is a dangerous substance."

"So is gunpowder. Have you removed every trace of it from your estate?"

"Of course not. There are precautions, Miss Wellstone."

"Thank you for making my point."

He stared at her. Lily stared back, and the heat between them had nothing to do with phosphorus pencils. "I've never covered a quill in the stuff and thrust it into the flames."

"What an absurd thing to say, your grace. Did you see me do that?"

"Tell me, Wellstone." He leaned back, arms crossed over his chest, legs apart. "If you were to survive a fall from a twenty-foot cliff, would you then presume you would be unharmed when you jumped the second time?"

"Argument by analogy is hardly logically sound."

"Yes it is." His eyes flashed. "But allow me to speak without resort to analogy. What I mean for you to understand is that this is my home, and I consider phosphorus to be an element so dangerous that I do not wish to have it present. With or without precautions. I don't want Eugenia, Miss Kirk, or Nigel to be injured. Or you, Lily." He spread his arms. "Is that unreasonable?"

"No, sir. It's not." She tapped her chin. She was aware that she'd been outmaneuvered and could not help admiring him for it. "I cannot disagree it must have been alarming to you to enter upon such a scene."

"Indeed."

"Without knowing the various precautions we followed."

"They were not sufficient."

"I admit that phosphorus is volatile." She fingered her medallion, smoothing a finger over the surface as was becoming a habit with her. "We followed the instructions almost without deviation. Lord Nigel was there, and if there had been any danger, I am confident he would have acted quickly to prevent harm from befalling anyone." She gestured. "It was a lark, your grace. You must have seen your sister. Before our phosphorus pencil caught fire, that is."

He nodded.

"She was laughing. How often have you seen her laugh since she came home? The entire project amused her, and that can only be good."

The duke relaxed a little on his chair, and Lily began to

hope she'd brought him round to her point of view. He fell silent a moment. "I've not seen her laugh like that for far too long."

"You see?" She leaned over far enough to pat his knee, and it was no surprise that his attention followed her bosom. Or that she felt that shivery sense of anticipation. "We do agree on something. That's lovely, isn't it?"

"It seems we do." Mountjoy stared at his thigh. And then at her, turning the full force of his gaze on her. She'd kissed him, and she wanted to again even though he wasn't Greer. She hadn't in all this time thought of another man in that way. So intimately.

"Can we not be friends?" she asked.

He did not answer straightaway. "Would you be as loyal to me as you are to my sister?"

Her heart tripped because his voice had gone softer. Not sweet so much as silky. It was the voice she heard in her dreams. That shivery sensation climbed inside her again, and she was hard-pressed not to melt in her seat. "If I find you deserving, yes, absolutely."

"I will endeavor to deserve your devotion, Wellstone."

Lily looked at him sideways. His face was perfectly bland. "You should not call me that."

"I would prefer, Wellstone," he went on in a voice that was oh so slightly less silky, "that you give the phosphorus to me for safekeeping. I will return it to you when your visit has concluded."

"You were not present to see the care we took."

He kept his thighs spread. "You failed to keep the quill wet."

"Lord Nigel reminded me." She reached for the jar and held it out to him. He had a point. This was his home and surely a man expected to make the rules in his own home. "Consider it a gift, your grace."

His eyebrows lifted. "A gift?"

"You needn't return it. I can always buy more when I am back at Syton House."

"I pray there is a local firefighting association."

"As a matter of fact there is. I donated the very newest engine."

He took the jar from her and slipped it into his pocket. She rose and he, too, stood. He offered her his arm. "Now that we have settled matters between us, may I escort you to the Oldenburg salon?"

Lily tucked her hand under his upper arm so that her fingers rested lightly on his biceps. If she kissed him again, would it be as wonderful? "You'll just have time to change before tea."

"I've already changed."

She very nearly laughed, but she had the good fortune to look at his face in time to stop herself. He was serious. "Do you mean to tell me, sir, that these are your best clothes?"

They reached the door before he answered. "No. These are among my most comfortable clothes."

"You have the oddest notion that fashionable clothes are necessarily uncomfortable ones. You are wrong." The duke reached for the knob. "A properly fitted suit not only makes the most of a man's assets, and yours are considerable, but it is also comfortable. Because it fits."

"I am perfectly at ease in these clothes."

"You're serious."

"Why wouldn't I be?"

"You really ought to hire me as your valet."

"Perhaps I ought."

She gestured at him, and he took a step nearer her. Away from the door. "As bad as that?" he said in that silky voice.

"Worse," she said. She grabbed a handful of his cravat and pulled his head to hers. His lips caught at hers, slanted over her mouth, and he parted her lips or, perhaps, he didn't have to.

Not a kiss between friends. Not at all.

Mountjoy's arm snaked around her waist, and he pulled her close. She ended up with her back pressed against the door and his forearms on either side of her head while they kissed each other as madly as they had before. More.

He wasn't gentle this time, and she was swept along, and by the time they separated, they were both breathing hard and she was weak behind the knees. "We can't do this, Wellstone," he said, his mouth inches from hers.

"No. Positively not," she whispered.

"Go. Go have tea, and give my regrets to Eugenia and Miss Kirk." He didn't release her, but even if he had, she wouldn't have moved.

"I'd rather stay here."

"Impossible." He pressed a kiss to her ear.

"It's the medallion," she said, arching her throat to give him the access he wanted. His lips slid along her shoulder. "We have no power to resist."

He rested his forehead on hers but managed to reach behind her and pull the door open enough that they had no choice but to move. "Damned magic."

"At the moment, I find it rather thrilling."

Mountjoy gave a low laugh. "It is at that. Go or I won't answer for the consequences."

Chapter Eight

TWO DAYS LATER, LILY SAT WITH GINNY AT THE FAR side of the Kirks' salon, listening to Miss Caroline Kirk play the piano. Lily wore a gown of pale pink satin while Ginny wore a frock that was at least not quite black. One took small steps. There was no point in asking more of Ginny than she was yet prepared to give. Gray, even a very dark gray, was a triumph.

Jane Kirk sat beside her sister, turning pages. The middle of the Kirk sisters, Miss Caroline, had only yesterday returned from a visit to relatives in the north of England. This gathering was a welcome-home for her. Most of the High Tearing gentry were here on her behalf. Lord Nigel sat a few rows nearer the front while Mountjoy sat closer to the door, beside Mr. Kirk, who would one day be his father-in-law. All in all, Lily thought the connection would be a good one for both families. At the moment, Jane was rather outmatched by Mountjoy, but that would change.

Miss Caroline was a better than excellent musician, and Lily was glad that the room was comparatively quiet while she played. She'd chosen a difficult piece by Scarlatti, and such was her talent that Lily had some time ago stopped worrying about whether she would make a mistake and was simply enjoying the music.

The salon door opened to admit a late arrival, but the butler, wisely, did not announce him. Nevertheless, Lily and several other guests turned for a better look at the latecomer. From the whispers, she gathered he was someone important. He looked to be in his late twenties, quite handsome and distinguished, but with a decidedly cold air about him. He reminded her of someone, but she couldn't think who.

The new arrival elected to stand near the door, well within her view as it happened. He surveyed the room as if he were searching for someone. Whoever he was, she approved of his taste in clothes. Heartily. Mountjoy could learn a thing or two from this stranger's example.

Whoever he was, though he took no sartorial risks, his clothes fit him to perfection. Even from where she sat, she could tell the fabrics were first-rate. The very best grade of wool and silk, the finest lawn for his shirt. His cravat was subdued yet folded and knotted to perfection. His boots gleamed and though there were no tassels, she felt the lack suited him. If his attire was a trifle severe, he'd relieved the effect by wearing an embroidered fob of an overly cheerful yellow. An intriguing whimsy.

When Caroline had done playing and the applause had not yet died down, Lily leaned to Ginny and whispered, "Don't be obvious"—she held Ginny's forearm to prevent her from turning around—"but do you know who that is? The gentleman who's just come in."

Under cover of adjusting her gown, Ginny glanced across the room. "Who?"

"With the yellow fob."

"I don't see anyone with a yellow fob."

"There. By the door. I've the strangest feeling I've met him before, but I can't think where."

Ginny frowned. "What's *he* doing here?"

"You *do* know who he is."

Ginny straightened. "Yes." Her lips thinned. "Lord Fenris."

Lily's heart frosted over. "Fenris, you say."

"Yes. He's Camber's heir."

"The Duke of Camber?"

Ginny rolled her eyes and huffed. "I don't know how anyone stands him."

"Camber?" Lily put her fingers over her mouth, then immediately lowered both her hands so that Ginny would not see her trembling.

"No, Lily. Fenris." Ginny looked over her shoulder and frowned in the man's direction. "Though I hear Camber is no better."

"Does Lord Fenris know one of the Kirks, do you suppose?"

Ginny turned her back on the man. "Mr. Kirk wouldn't keep a connection like that quiet. He'd have told Jane to marry Fenris instead of Mountjoy. Better if your son-in-law is to be the ten thousandth duke than merely the fourth."

"Perhaps he met Caroline while she was away, and she invited him?"

Ginny sniffed. "Poor Caroline Kirk if that's the case."

Feeling she needed to proceed carefully, she said, "Miss Caroline Kirk is an attractive girl. He might be here on her account, don't you think?"

"Fenris?" Ginny made a face. "Marry a Kirk? A mere Miss? He'd never stoop so low."

"I take it you don't like the man." Lily didn't know whether to feel she'd been vindicated or not.

"No," she said. She adjusted her shawl. "I'm sorry, I don't. Don't let his looks fool you, Lily." Ginny lowered her voice. "He's handsome enough, I'll grant you that, but Lord Fenris is a judgmental bore."

Lily glanced in Fenris's direction. "I wasn't aware you knew him well enough to have any opinion at all."

"I do," Ginny said with more passion than Lily had seen

from her since she'd arrived. "You can't go falling in love with him. You can't." She paused and then lowered her voice again. "I don't care how perfect his clothes or how handsome you think he is."

"In love?"

"Don't admit to a fault around that man unless you want a lecture on the evils of imperfect comportment. He once told Miss Abigail Archer she ought to think more and laugh less, and Abigail Archer is an absolutely delightful young lady."

"I'm sorry to hear that." Lily clasped her hands on her lap.

"What does it matter if she's prone to laugh too often? It's charming, if you ask me." She sniffed. "I wonder what he's doing here?"

"If he's no prior acquaintance with any of the Kirks, I fear there is only one possible reason for his presence here."

"Oh?" Ginny said.

Lily nodded soberly. Her heart remained frozen solid. "I expect he's here on account of me."

"But you didn't even know who he was." Ginny started to say something more, but a footman walked by with a tray, and she held back her comment.

People were leaving their seats and heading for the back of the room where servants were setting out food. Lily watched a footman enter with a salver of strawberries, but her attention returned to Fenris. Now that she could study him, there could be no doubt he was searching for someone.

"I am very much afraid Lord Fenris and his father mean to wrest control of my fortune from me."

"I don't understand," Ginny said. "Why would they want to do that?"

Fenris continued scanning the room, and Lily's heart thumped when she realized he was now looking over the area where she and Ginny sat. He did look at them, and she did not think she was mistaken that his attention paused, but whether he was looking at her, whom he had never in his life met, or at Ginny, whom he did know, was impossible to say.

He headed across the salon, but the flow of guests to the food impeded his progress. He hadn't got far when Mrs. Kirk intercepted him. He took her hand and bowed over it, and the cadences of their exchange, if not the specific words, floated over the sound of conversation. His manners were impeccable, she had to grant him that. Fenris broke free of Mrs. Kirk, and this time she could not doubt that he was headed toward her and Ginny.

Lily jumped up, grabbed Ginny's hand, and pulled her along to the back of the room, hoping to blend in with the crowd.

"Lily," Ginny said. "What on earth?"

From the corner of her eye, Lily saw Fenris adjust course. She zigged through the crowd and when she peeked again, Fenris had done the same. "What if he knows who I am? What if someone described me to him?"

"Good heavens. You're afraid of him." Ginny pulled on Lily's hand and they stopped. "Honestly afraid. If you're worried about Lord Fenris's intentions toward you, we ought to tell my brother. He will help you. He will."

"Lord Fenris and his father are my concern. Not his. Or yours."

"Lily." Ginny pressed her hand. "Lily, you are not alone. If Lord Fenris has made himself odious to you, Mountjoy will intervene on your behalf."

"Your brother has more important matters to deal with."

"He's just there." She glanced in Mountjoy's direction. "Tell him, Lily. He won't leave you to that odious man's mercy. You'll see."

Her heart stayed cold as ice. "If only he could help."

"But he will. I know he will. Why wouldn't he?"

"Because Lord Fenris is my cousin. One of my few relations, actually."

Ginny's mouth opened and for a moment no sound came

out. "Fenris? Is your cousin?" She groped behind her for a chair, found one, and sat down. "But how?"

She stayed close to Ginny, keeping her voice low. "The previous Duke of Camber was my mother's father."

Her eyes widened. "Your grandfather?"

"The present duke is my uncle. And that, I fear, makes Lord Fenris my cousin."

Ginny put a hand to her heart, her hand pale against the gray of her gown. "Lord Fenris? Your cousin?"

"My aunt Lily, I've told you about her—"

"She left you Syton House."

"To me, instead of Camber." The subject of her relation to the Duke of Camber was painful. She had years ago stopped thinking they would ever meet under any circumstances but unpleasant ones. "Aunt Lily was a Talbot before she married." Talbot being the Duke of Camber's family name.

Ginny, no fool she, tilted her head. "Ah."

Yes, Ginny understood. "Precisely."

"You poor thing, to be related to such a man."

Lily remained on her feet. They were only partially hidden by the guests, but for the moment at least, Fenris seemed to have lost sight of them, for he was now looking in the opposite direction from where they were. Because, she realized, Ginny was sitting down. She looked down at her friend. Wasn't that interesting? Was it possible her cousin was following Ginny and not her?

"Ginny, my dear. How is it you know Lord Fenris?"

Ginny's mouth thinned. "He was Robert's friend. Before we married."

"But not after?"

She looked at Lily and passion flashed in her eyes. "He did his best to stop Robert marrying me. He did not approve of me, you see. My brother, after all, was nothing but a farmer who, in his opinion, didn't deserve his title. And me? Why, I was only an ignorant country girl with designs on his friend."

"Much worse than a judgmental bore," Lily said with a nod.

"Why didn't you tell me"—Ginny twisted on her chair and looked behind them—"that such a hateful man is your relation?"

She shrugged. "I've never met my mother's family. They've never wanted to meet me. Camber and Fenris disapprove of me, too, you see. Because my father had married so far above his station. My father, they believe, did not deserve my mother. Just as Fenris believed you did not deserve Robert."

"Judgmental bores the lot of those Talbot men," Ginny said fiercely. "Well, whatever he's planning, he's not going to succeed." She squeezed Lily's hand again. "Don't look, but he's coming this way."

Lily froze. The idea of meeting her cousin when she was so thoroughly unprepared and with no notion of his immediate intentions unsettled her. If there was to be an unpleasant confrontation, let it not be here, in front of Ginny's friends. "Fenris?"

"No, Lily." Ginny touched Lily's arm. "Mountjoy. Behind you."

"Eugenia." Mountjoy's voice wound around Lily's senses. "Miss Wellstone."

She turned and curtseyed to the duke. His coat was the wrong color of blue for his waistcoat. "Your grace."

Without warning, Ginny shot from her chair and threw an arm around Lily's shoulder, putting her mouth by Lily's ear. "Pretend you are about to faint."

"I've never swooned in my life."

"Didn't you say you once wanted to be an actress?" Ginny looked over her shoulder again. "Swoon, Lily, or you will meet Fenris now and there will be an awful scene. Do you want that here? In front of everyone?"

Lily believed in action with conviction. Half measures only made things worse. Therefore, she grabbed the back of a chair and went limp with the intention of landing, ever so delicately and safely, on the chair.

"Mountjoy," Ginny said. "Thank goodness you're here. Help."

Lily found herself not on the chair but enfolded by the duke's arms. There was nothing for it now but to see the thing through.

"Oh, dear!" Ginny spoke too loudly. "She needs fresh air, Mountjoy. Do help her outside."

Mountjoy, already supporting her, swung Lily into his arms. She willed herself boneless in his embrace. Her head lolled back, and one arm dangled toward the floor.

"Mrs. Kirk," Lily heard Ginny say as Mountjoy carried her out. "Yes, yes. I know. I don't know. Thank goodness my brother was here. The crowd, you understand. Stifling. So many people in the room. A little fresh air, I think . . ."

Ginny's voice faded. By the time Mountjoy had carried her out of the salon, however, Ginny had caught up with them. Lily cracked open one eye and caught a glimpse of Ginny's gray gown as the duke moved away from the gathering. She opened a door for her brother. In an excess of caution, in case they were followed, God forbid, by the hateful Lord Fenris, Lily remained limp against Mountjoy's broad chest until they were inside.

Mountjoy said, "Eugenia?"

Lily bestirred herself and, still in Mountjoy's arms, reached for Ginny's hand. "Thank you, Ginny. You are a good friend. The very best."

"As are you, Lily." Ginny patted her brother's shoulder. "Look after her, Mountjoy. Do not under any circumstances leave her alone. I'll be back as soon as possible." Ginny left, pulling the door closed behind her. Mountjoy looked down, and Lily blinked at him.

They were alone. The door was closed, and Lily was far too aware of the impropriety of that. The duke drew in a breath and put her down on a small and infernally maroon sofa. He took a step back. "Have you a vinaigrette?"

She looked around and shuddered. "I am wearing entirely the wrong colors to be in this room. My God, whoever thought maroon was anything but a hue with which to accent?"

"A mystery," Mountjoy said.

"Indeed, sir." She left the sofa for the window but stood sideways so she could see Mountjoy. He was so very handsome, and she could not stop thinking that they were alone. *Alone*.

"If you're not well, are you certain you should be on your feet?"

She pushed aside the curtains to get a better view of the garden. "You know perfectly well there's nothing wrong with me."

He crossed his arms over his chest. "You could have a career on the stage, Miss Wellstone. I was convinced you'd lost your senses."

She turned her head to glare at him, but his comment was so beautifully double-edged that she couldn't help but be impressed. And amused. "I would have been ashamed if you had not been. At my father's home when I was a girl, I mean, not Syton House. I was renowned for my Ophelia. I had her every line memorized before I was ten. I did Lady Macbeth, too. My father lived in fear of my running away whenever a traveling troupe came into town."

The curtains, the same unfortunate maroon as the sofa, were giving her a headache. The view, on the other hand, was spectacular. She thought of Ginny, facing Lord Fenris on her own. She was a Wellstone and not ashamed of her family or herself. Let him stare down his aristocratic nose at her and tell the world she was non compos mentis or whatever nefarious scheme he planned to carry out.

"If there's nothing wrong with you, dare I ask, Miss Wellstone, what your most impressive swoon was meant to achieve?"

"I wished to avoid Lord Fenris." She smoothed her skirts and gazed out the window. She would never be free of the hatred between the Talbots and the Wellstones if she ran at the first possibility of a confrontation.

"I meant to warn Eugenia he was here," he said, "but it seems that's unnecessary." Mountjoy joined her, standing behind her, too close if anyone should see them, and not close enough. "I know my sister has no reason to like the man, but has he done something to upset you as well?"

"You might say so."

"Will you?"

"Your grace." She put her back to the window and told him the history between her and Lord Fenris. She could see him making all sorts of mental leaps of logic. "Naturally my father objected to my correspondence with my mother's sister. He never forgets a slight done him. Speak a word to him in anger and twenty years later he will repeat to you the exact circumstances of the offense. He regularly reminds me of all of mine, and there were many." She looked up at the duke. "I am now more than a quarter of a century old, and he has held a grudge against my mother's relations since before I was born. I can only marvel, sir, at his tenacity. My maternal grandfather is no longer living, and my father cannot and, I assure you, will never forgive any relative of the man who disowned my mother for marrying him."

"Ah."

"I could not tell him my mother had maintained a secret correspondence with my great-aunt any more than I could confess I'd carried on as she did. If he had known, he would have forbidden it, and I would know nothing of my mother's life."

"And he would never forgive you."

"No. He would not. And does not." She crossed her arms and tapped one finger on her upper arm. "Even so, I was betrayed. After a fashion."

"How so?"

"She meant me no harm, you understand. Quite the opposite. But when Aunt Lily passed on, she left me Syton House. My father was furious. That I had been rewarded for my treachery only made it worse, you see."

His expression stayed thoughtful. "Her legacy to you cost you your father. The only family you had left."

The enormity of his understanding shook her. No one, not even Ginny, had understood what it had meant to lose her father, even though he'd never been the sort of loving family she knew Ginny had grown up with. All she could do was nod.

"Syton House." Mountjoy rubbed one cheek. "Quite a legacy, I'd say."

"The disaster was total. She left me everything and destroyed Camber's hopes of combining her fortune with his."

"Everything?"

She sighed. "Eighty-six thousand pounds and two estates besides Syton House. One in Scotland, a castle near Edinburgh, and another estate in Kent."

His eyebrows rose.

"They are leased with fifty more years remaining. I make a tidy sum on them both. I don't have any expectation that I will be forgiven for that from any quarter. I do believe my father would be a happier man if I were reduced to living under a tree."

"Why would you ever go home to him? Why not travel the world until he passes to his reward? Let him live in another of your houses."

She shrugged. "He is my father, and the only person I know who remembers my mother. Sometimes he'll even tell me about her. Things I never knew because I can hardly remember her. When he does, I begin to understand why she married him, for he loved her beyond life. There was room for only one love in his life; my mother. Just as Greer was the only love for me."

Mountjoy cocked his head and, after considering her a moment, said, "Shall I ask Lord Fenris to leave? Or would you prefer I take you home?" He put a hand on her shoulder, and Lily's senses focused on that contact between them. His fingers curved over her, touching her gown and bare skin, too. Her heart beat too fast. "To Bitterward, I mean." She faced him, and in so doing, his hand fell away from her. He meant nothing by that casual touch. They were close enough to touch again. But neither of them moved. "What are you thinking?" Mountjoy asked.

She could not remember a time when any man had made her so relentlessly aware that she was a woman. The man made the back of her knees positively weak. "Nothing."

He laughed, and her belly tightened. "Wellstone. The day you are thinking of nothing is the day the world ends."

"Very well." She shook her head, amused by him. "I am imagining myself calmly telling Lord Fenris that I am indeed his cousin and that if he chooses to withdraw from High Tearing on account of my being an unwanted connection, that is his choice to make. He will leave, mortified and secretly happy with his narrow escape, and that will be that."

"Begging your pardon, but that does not sound like you. Or Fenris."

"No?" She resisted the urge to touch him. "More likely, he'll accuse me of stealing his watch. Or his gloves. Or perhaps his horse. That's a hanging offense."

Mountjoy snorted. "I very much doubt he plans that."

"You know what he's like. What he did to Ginny. Or nearly did. Why else would he be here, if not to pursue his family's vendetta against mine?"

"Coincidence?"

"My attorney once warned me Camber might try to declare me mentally incompetent."

Mountjoy frowned.

"Camber wants Aunt Lily's legacy. He thinks it should have gone to him. Or to Fenris."

"My God, you're serious."

"You've no idea the rancor he holds toward me. I didn't think he'd ever give up." She glanced away. "I don't think he did. Not really. He's been biding his time." She laughed softly. "Thank goodness Camber never spoke to my father. If he had, he might have found grounds."

He frowned again. "Would your father allow such a thing to happen?"

"Perhaps not deliberately."

Mountjoy didn't answer right away, but he continued to frown. "I can take you home if you'd rather not meet Fenris today."

"Thank you, your grace." She touched his sleeve. "That's kind of you. But not necessary."

He cocked his head, a thoughtful expression on his face. "It might be wiser to meet him at Bitterward where you are surrounded by friends and people he cannot bully as easily as he must hope to bully you."

At first, she thought that by *friends* he meant Ginny, but then she realized he meant more than that. Just as Ginny had promised, he was extending an offer of his personal support. In all her life, she had never had anywhere to look for assistance but to herself and those whom she hired to act on her behalf. The idea that Mountjoy intended to help her was as disconcerting as it was astonishing. "You mean that."

He regarded her in silence. Lily held her breath, expecting any moment that he would withdraw his offer or chastise her for putting him to such an inconvenience.

"I do," he said. "You are my sister's friend. My friend as well, if I am permitted to be so bold. Even if you were not, I would not leave any woman to the mercy of Lord Fenris. Certainly not you." He smoothed the front of his coat. Not that it did any good. Nothing would improve the appearance of his coat. "Not while you are under my roof. Even if you weren't, I should hope you'd know you could appeal to me for assistance."

Lily swallowed the lump in her throat. She didn't care if he dressed as if he'd never set foot in a tailor's shop. His support touched her deeply. "Thank you, your grace." She swallowed the lump in her throat. "But I think I ought to meet him now, if only to give him a face to go with the devil's spawn he's been imagining all these years."

"I'll go with you. To make the introduction."

Tears jammed up in her throat and further words were impossible. All she could do was nod her agreement.

"We will present him a united front of persons of whom he can disapprove all he likes and to no avail."

She wanted to thank him, but if she spoke she'd sound as if she were crying, and she never cried. Instead, she nodded.

"Very well then." Mountjoy headed for the door, but Lily, having mastered herself, stopped him from opening it. To know that she was not alone made more difference to her than she would have believed.

"Best let me go first," she said.

He nodded, and she reached for the door. As she pulled it toward her, the metal knob came off in her hand. She didn't understand at first what had happened, only that the door remained closed. "How odd."

"What is it?" Mountjoy said from behind her.

She showed him the doorknob. "I've broken the door."

Chapter Nine

"BROKEN? HOW CAN THE DOOR BE BROKEN?" Mountjoy took the bit of metal she handed him in answer. While he examined it, Miss Wellstone tried again to open the door.

"I've never seen anything like it," he said. The metal had sheared clean off, leaving only the brass plate affixed to the door. He looked up when she let out a frustrated huff. "What?"

"I am unable to open the door."

His first inkling of disaster hit. He clutched the broken doorknob. "What do you mean?"

"I mean, my dear Duke," Miss Wellstone said a bit too evenly, "that when Ginny left, she closed the door, and with the knob no longer attached, there is no way to open it."

"Allow me." Mountjoy dropped the doorknob into his pocket and examined the faceplate. The metal was smooth except where the knob had been attached, and only the smallest bits of twisted metal remained behind. She was right. Without the broken-off knob, there would be no easy way to pull the door open.

"My hands are smaller than yours. Perhaps I can grasp a bit of the metal." She stripped off her gloves, and he took them from her while she bent to the door. Her tongue appeared at the corner of her mouth.

"Caution, Wellstone. It's sharp."

"Thank you for that reminder of the obvious." She arranged her fingers over the spot where the knob had been attached and pulled. The door moved forward an infinitesimal amount, then her fingers slipped. "Drat."

Mountjoy didn't think anything except that she had failed to open the door until she hissed and caught her left hand in her right. Blood welled between her fingers. "You've hurt yourself."

"It's nothing." She looked at him, eyes wide, features so impossibly delicate, now ashen because she had hurt herself and was trying to hide it. His chest tightened.

"It's not nothing." He reached for her hand. "How bad is it?"

"I don't know," she said.

"Let me see." He caught her injured hand in his. The moment she released her grip on her fingers, blood flowed even faster from a cut along the side and across the pad of her index finger, covering her skin in brilliant red. He pulled out his handkerchief and wrapped it around her fingers. Blood soaked through almost immediately. "I ought not have let you near the door."

"I am an experienced door opener, I'll have you know."

He glared at the door. There were other reasons to get them out of here as quickly as possible, but her injury was the most pressing at the moment. "Do you see the key anywhere? I might be able to use that as a lever to pull the door forward enough to open it."

"Brilliant idea."

The key, however, was nowhere by the door, and they both looked.

Mountjoy scowled. "If it fell from the lock, I'm dashed if I can see where it landed."

"Do you suppose it could be in a drawer somewhere?"

If they weren't able to open the door in the next five minutes, he was going to have to call for help with all the unpleasant ramifications that such a public action entailed. Jesus, the house was full of people. And that prig Fenris, who probably already thought the worst of Lily, would have his prejudices confirmed. Should they be discovered alone, in a room that had been closed against intruders, scandal would be the inevitable result. At least he liked her well enough. More than well enough. He got on well with Lily. If it came to that.

If.

"Why," he said with more tartness than was required, "would someone put the key anywhere but in the door?"

"Look around you, your grace, what do you see?"

He was helpless to act except in a way that would not please either of them, and he was not a man prone to help-lessness in anything. "Furniture. A window. An average room."

"Are you blind?" She winced and brought her hand closer to her body. "The room is maroon, sir."

"What's that to do with anything?" The handkerchief around her hand was more red than white now. He stripped off his gloves and tried to get some kind of leverage on the decorative metal plate, but his hands were too big and the bits left of the doorknob were far too small and razor sharp besides.

"I regret to say," she said in a thin voice, "that anyone who would decorate a room with such a singular lack of consideration to what is pleasing and restful to the eye is not likely to have been sensible about where the key ought to be kept. You'd best pray Miss Kirk has better taste than her mother."

He ignored the dig, but, Lord, the thought of anyone having a hand in making over Bitterward gave him the shivers. "I'll look again, then." He walked to a highboy and opened a drawer at about his waist height on the theory that the key wouldn't be kept inconveniently high or low. "How is your hand?"

"Better." From the corner of his eyes, he saw her study the room, gripping her handkerchief-wrapped fingers and tapping her toe. "It wouldn't have to be the key to the door would it?" she asked.

"Of course it would."

Lily walked to a secretaire. "Why? The door is not locked. All we need is leverage. Any key, any object capable of catching in the lock will do."

He shut another drawer of the highboy and acknowledged that with a tight nod. "Quite so."

With both hands, she pointed to the key sticking in the upper lock of the desk. "This one will do nicely I should think."

If he did have to marry her, he was unlikely to be bored anytime soon. Exasperated, yes. Amused, often. But bored? Never. "Quick thinking, Wellstone. Please"—he strode to her—"don't use your hand. I'll get it." He extracted the key from the secretaire. A tassel of reddish purple silk hung from the end. He didn't like the color much himself, but what did he know? As he wriggled the key into the lock, someone knocked on the door.

Lily understood the seriousness of the moment, for she stood beside him, quite still and silent. Not that it mattered who it was. At this point, his duty was to get her out of here to have her injury looked after and never mind explaining why he had been closeted away with an unmarried lady.

"Lily?"

That was Eugenia's voice. Thank God.

"Yes, Ginny, I'm here."

"Is everything all right?"

"Yes, yes. Tell me, Ginny, is anyone there with you? Or are you alone?"

"I am not alone."

He and Lily exchanged a look. "It can't be helped, Wellstone," he said in a low voice.

"Ah," Lily said for Eugenia's benefit. Her somber nod of understanding was for his benefit. "If you wouldn't mind opening the door, there's been a malfunction of some sort. We are not currently able to open it from this side."

"Oh, dear."

Mountjoy put an arm around Lily's waist and drew her away. "Be so good as to open the door, Eugenia."

The door rattled, then moved smoothly inward, and Eugenia walked in, one hand on the side of the door. Lord Fenris and Mr. Kirk came in behind her. Eugenia took one look at Lily's hand and blanched. "What happened?" She whirled to him. "Mountjoy, what happened?"

"Shall I fetch a doctor?" Fenris asked. He pulled out his handkerchief and, as Mountjoy had done, handed it to Lily.

"Thank you, my lord." Lily gave him a nod and wrapped Fenris's handkerchief around her hand.

"That's blood," Mr. Kirk said. "Blood all over your hand."

"Yes, sir, it is. I had the misfortune of doing myself an injury."

Mr. Kirk turned the color of chalk. His eyes rolled up in his head. He wasn't a tall man, but he made considerable noise when he hit the floor and landed at Lily's feet.

"Someone had best call a doctor," she said, staring down at the insensible Mr. Kirk.

"Dr. Longfield is here somewhere," Eugenia said. "Perhaps we ought to fetch him."

Lord Fenris crouched and patted Mr. Kirk's cheek. The man did not respond. "An excellent notion, Mrs. Bryant. I'll see to him until the doctor has looked after Miss Wellstone."

"Thank you," Lily said. "That's very kind of you." She walked briskly past Fenris and Kirk. "You can't imagine how badly it hurts, Ginny." Her voice trembled, though Mountjoy could not help the impression that she was, at last, exaggerating her injury and the pain she was in. Eugenia put an arm around her shoulders. Lily shuddered. "Imagine the horror if blood had gotten on my gown. And yes, let's do find Dr. Longfield. Quickly. I believe I'm feeling faint."

Mountjoy watched Lily and Eugenia walk down the hallway, their heads together. "Thank God the man passed out," Fenris said from his position at Kirk's side.

"Why is that?"

"I suspect he'll not recall that you were alone with Miss Wellstone." He stood. Slowly. "I, however, will not."

He gazed at the marquess. "Nothing happened, Fenris."

Fenris ran the bottom of his thumb over his fingernails. "That's never the point where scandal is concerned, is it? Your grace."

"I don't give a bloody damn what rumors you start, Fenris."

"Gossip can be quite vicious."

"I'll marry her if I must."

The marquess flinched. "Where I am concerned, you are, for now, both safe from that fate." Kirk moaned, and Fenris hauled him to his feet. "You might wish to make yourself scarce."

Mountjoy walked away and waited in another corridor where he counted to one hundred before he returned to the salon. On the way there, he stopped a servant and ordered his carriage to be brought around. He found Nigel and let him know they would be returning to Bitterward.

Not long after Mountjoy's unexceptional return to the salon, there was a commotion that proved to be Lily returning with Dr. Longfield. Her injured finger was done up in a plaster. Eugenia walked at her side, an arm around her waist. He met them halfway.

"She'll have an aching finger tonight, your grace," Dr. Longfield said. "A glass of your best sherry will go a long way to relieving her discomfort."

"Thank you."

Longfield continued to address Mountjoy. "I'll call in a day or two to confirm everything's going well with my most beautiful patient. Put a fresh plaster on it tomorrow and don't hesitate to send for me if anything seems amiss."

Mountjoy nodded. "I will."

The doctor left to attend to Mr. Kirk, and Mountjoy took that opportunity to tell them he'd ordered the carriage. Lily said nothing, but he thought both women looked relieved to have avoided another encounter with Fenris. Their good luck did not last, for just as they reached the stairs that would lead to the entrance hall, Fenris intercepted them.

"Your grace," he said, bowing to Mountjoy. For a man who had done nothing to make himself agreeable to Mountjoy or his siblings, he had some nerve accosting them. Fenris looked between Eugenia and Miss Wellstone, but his attention lingered on Eugenia. Mountjoy, well aware of the role Fenris had played in attempting to convince Robert Bryant not to marry Eugenia, silently counted to ten. The urge to plant his fist in the man's face did not fade. "Mrs. Bryant."

Eugenia, whom Mountjoy had never in his life seen cut anyone, turned her back on Fenris. Lily said nothing. Fenris blanched, but that was the only sign that he was affected by Eugenia's refusal to acknowledge him. Could he truly have expected anything else from her when his offense against her was so grave?

The marquess bowed to Lily. "Cousin."

Mountjoy kept his hand on Lily's elbow. He didn't like the man, and now that he knew of his relationship to Lily, he liked him even less. "We are on our way out, Fenris."

"I shan't detain you long," he replied.

A flash of irritation passed over Eugenia's face. "Mountjoy, we ought to go now. Lily is not well at all. She's had a shock."

Fenris took an abortive step forward. "Miss Wellstone," he said quickly. "Did you know you look very much like your grandmother? And mine."

"How would I know such a thing?" Lily said, her words clipped.

Fenris paled.

"Enough is enough, my lord." Mountjoy shifted so that he stood between Lily and her cousin. "Another time you might be welcome. But not now."

The marquess gave them both a curt nod and once again, his gaze slid from Lily to linger on Eugenia. Did the man still resent her for her marriage to Robert Bryant? Mountjoy found himself making a fist of his free hand. He would not allow anyone to cause Eugenia any more pain. Most especially not this man. Bloody officious prig.

Fenris bowed again. "Your leave, Mrs. Bryant. Mountjoy." He hesitated, as close as Mountjoy had ever seen to uncertainty. "Cousin Lily."

"Good day," Mountjoy said.

They left Fenris standing at the top of the stairs. Quite alone.

At the front door, Mountjoy took the doorknob out of his pocket and handed it to the Kirks' butler. "You'll want to have this repaired."

Lord Fenris, Mountjoy thought as he handed his sister and Lily into his carriage, had not behaved like a man who despised his estranged cousin. Quite the opposite.

Chapter Ten

HAVING FINISHED VOLUME ONE OF THE NOVEL SHE'D selected the night of her arrival, Lily made her way to the library in search of the second volume. She carried a lantern in one hand and the first volume of her novel in the other. She had not bothered yet to dress for bed and still wore the gown she'd worn at supper, a sumptuous white silk trimmed with lace she'd tatted herself last winter at Syton House. Amid the lace were gold gauze flowers no larger than her littlest fingernail that she'd spent most of one Easter week making. Similar flowers around the hem complimented the burgundy bodice. Her slippers were white satin embroidered with matching burgundy flowers picked with tiny gold accents.

Pearls were her jewelry of choice tonight: at her ears, her throat, and even a strand wound through her hair and one on the first finger of her left hand. Her injured hand was not yet healed enough for jewelry. She'd changed the ribbon of her Gypsy medallion to a white silk that matched her ensemble. Her shawl was white cashmere embroidered with gold silk and gold accents to match her slippers. Even at four-thirty in the morning, one ought to look one's best.

In the library, she set the lantern on the table nearest the bookcase where the novels were shelved. She kept her volume in hand while she admired the room. The ceiling, though not visible at its highest point, was the original Gothic structure, vaulted with structural ribs that supported the central dome. One of these days she would add a sketch of this library to her growing collection of architecturally interesting structures and rooms. There were no windows here, and what walls were not covered with shelves were carved stone. In one such corner stood a suit of armor, supported by a stand and polished to a sheen. Upon closer inspection, she found some wag had placed a book of poetry in its upraised steel hand.

She stood before the armor, rapt. Which ancestor of the duke's had last covered himself in all that metal and ridden to battle? A dent marred the chest plate, a small defect near where the man's ribs must have been. She imagined Mountjoy's ancestor standing beside his destrier, sword in his hand, defending himself—no—attacking his enemy.

Footsteps echoed in the corridor. She recognized that determined stride, having by now heard it on those occasions when the duke was home. She was therefore prepared when she faced the doorway. The shiver down her spine was familiar, too.

Mountjoy appeared in the doorway but stopped without stepping over the threshold.

"Good evening, your grace," she said.

He leaned against the side of the doorway, looking, for once, especially dashing in a luxurious midnight blue silk banyan. Gold embroidery of Arabian flair decorated the fabric. The banyan was nipped in close around his arms and chest, though he'd not closed the garment but left it open to show his waistcoat and shirt. The silk fell to the tops of his shoes, draping in a way that came only from superior workmanship. And the colors. Blue and gold were luscious on him. His waistcoat was a match for the banyan, with the same fabric and embroidery, by which she assumed banyan and waistcoat had been purchased as a set.

"Wellstone."

She wanted to drink him in, caress that gorgeous fabric, and tell him how very lovely he looked. Instead, she pointed to the corner. "Do you know, sir, when that suit of armor was last worn?"

His eyes followed the direction of her arm. "March the twenty-ninth, fourteen and sixty-one."

"The Battle of Towton?"

He nodded. "It was." He used his shoulder to push himself upright. "You know your history."

"I do, your grace." She didn't say so, but she appreciated that he was not bothered by her historical knowledge. It had been her unhappy experience that some men disliked the mere hint of erudition in a woman. As a child, there had been little for her to do but read what books were in her father's library. Books of history, for the most part. And a great many treatises on architecture. She had become expert in both subjects. Had it not been for the housekeeper taking pity on her she might never have learned more feminine occupations.

"An ancestor of mine fought at Towton. He took an arrow in the thigh."

"Was he badly hurt?"

"Not enough to keep him from continuing to fight. He was loyal to King Edward." He walked in. "Up late as usual I see."

His coming so near set off tingles in her chest and the backs of her knees. One of the inappropriate dreams she'd begun having, now for several nights running, had as its setting this very library.

"You don't sleep well," he said in his smoke-edged tenor. "Why is that?"

"Why does the sun rise in the morning and set at night? Because the world is made that way." She shrugged. "I am not made to sleep at night. Since I shall be up one or two more hours at least, I've come down to fetch the next volume of the novel I selected the night I arrived."

"You are enjoying the story?"

"Very much. It's quite exciting."

"Then you did take something thrilling from the library that night."

"I did, sir." She wasn't sure whether she ought to respond to the suggestion that lurked in his comment. "The heroine, Miss Quince, has been attacked by banditti whilst escaping from her uncle who wishes to force her to marry his odious son. She is in love, sir, with a poor young man who possesses a noble brow. I suspect the author's use of *noble* is no accident and that he is a prince in disguise. Or else unaware of his heritage."

"And vast fortune."

"Indeed." She smiled, pleased to have him join in. "I further suspect that the captain of the banditti is the brother she believes was lost at sea when she was a girl."

He kept walking toward her. She did enjoy watching him move. He was a graceful man. The most shocking notions came to mind while she did, and really, where those thoughts came from did not bear examination. Him nude, bending to kiss a woman, moments from sliding into her willing body. As he had slid into hers in her dreams. More than once.

Her experience with Greer had taught her just how much she adored the male physique. Even though she'd not been with anyone since, there were times she longed for intimacy, for the pleasure a man's body could give. There had been occasions when she'd thought even a man she did not love would do. The Duke of Mountjoy put just those sorts of thoughts into her head.

"What *are* you thinking, Wellstone?" His banyan shimmered in the light. This was the sort of fabric he ought to wear all the time, rich and flattering to his coloring and features.

"Nothing I will confess to you, sir."

He was now in front of the suit of armor and mere inches from her. Lily was nearly five feet and ten inches, and

Mountjoy was at least two inches taller than she. He gazed at her.

More wicked thoughts occurred to her, more images from her dream, more forbidden longings. Whatever might happen, she would be safe. The Duke of Mountjoy was a decent man who had no expectations of her outside of this room. Her fortune was of no consequence to him. To him, her family connections meant nothing. Before much longer she would go home to Syton House, and if she had lovely memories of Mountjoy to add to her visit, then she would be a lucky woman indeed.

"Dr. Longfield is right. Your eyes are very fine. Full of life and spirit."

"Good heavens," she managed, somehow, to reply in a cool voice. She did not feel about him the way she'd felt about Greer, and he had no deep feelings for her, either. They could flirt in this way that was not innocent and have no fear of unwanted entanglements. "Was that a compliment buried in there?"

"Yes."

"Thank you. To you and Dr. Longfield." Her belly tightened. She'd worked so hard to suppress her attraction to him and all that simply vanished. He filled the room with his presence. She wanted to touch him. Yearned to touch him. To taste his skin, his mouth, feel his hair beneath her fingers, his breath warm against her skin.

"When I was in town this afternoon I happened to see him. He asked after you."

"I hope you told him I'm well."

"I did. He then described your eyes to me at length, but he was certain they were black."

"Why on earth would he say anything at all about my eyes?" She walked away from him, heading for the shelves. "It was my finger he treated."

"I've no idea. But one wants to know such things precisely," he said. "When one is forced to listen to a man prattle on for the better part of half an hour about a woman's eyes. Could my memory be faulty, and your eyes are black? Or some other color entirely?"

She clutched her book. He had a way of making even a large room feel small. "Five minutes or twenty-five, I observe that he did not trouble himself to discover their actual color."

"I grant you that." He didn't quite smile, but there was a lightening of his countenance that suggested he might. She resisted taking a step back when the duke took a step forward. Under no circumstances would she retreat from this spot. She intended to stand here as if her slippers were glued to the floor. "What color are they? Let me see, Wellstone."

She lifted her chin and opened her eyes as wide as she could. "As you can see, a very common brown, your grace."

He took her book from her while she blinked to recover her vision. What he did with the book she had no notion whatever. "There's nothing common about you."

Since he was so close, she put her hands on his chest. She knew immediately she oughtn't have. Because everything changed. Her world was no longer safe. Mountjoy tensed, but he didn't move away. He stayed just where he was, his moss green eyes on her face. The silk beneath her palms was as rich as she'd imagined.

"This is lovely," she said, stroking the material. "You look a god in this."

"A god?" His low voice sent a thrill through her, a warmth that centered in her belly.

"Yes." She left her hand on his chest. "Arrayed in gold befitting your status as a deity."

"It was a gift from a friend who traveled to Anatolia."

What could he mean but a former lover? Of course he had had lovers in his life. A man of his great physicality must have lovers. "Was she very beautiful?"

The distance between them became smaller yet, and that made her pulse leap. A hint of citrus clung to his skin. "Why do you assume it was a woman?"

She curled her fingers around the lapels of his banyan, just beneath his chin, and that was the moment that sealed her fate, because he still did not move away. And she didn't want to. She didn't. Because she wanted to kiss Mountjoy. And more. The anticipation was delicious. "Wasn't it?"

"No." He smiled, and it killed her to see the curve of his mouth, the tender shape of his lower lip. He had kissed other women. Taken them in his arms and whispered endearments to them.

"I hate them all," she said. "Your previous lovers. All the women you've held and loved."

"You shouldn't."

She leaned forward, dizzy with the images in her head and the longing for him to do . . . something.

"The friend who gave me this was a man," he said. "I met him not long after I came into my title. He was in the army at the time and was soon after deployed near Constantinople. He's only recently retired to the English countryside where he lives a very dull existence, so he tells me."

"He has exquisite taste." She stroked the silk, traced one of the sumptuous patterns embroidered in the fabric of his waistcoat. "You need more clothes like this."

"My valet, Wellstone, says much the same thing." He didn't move. Neither did she. "He's in raptures whenever I wear this."

He was going to kiss her. She knew it and wanted it. Desired his mouth on hers beyond anything. Lily tightened her hands on his lapels. His head came nearer to hers, and she made sure to meet him. She closed her eyes in anticipation. But there was no brush of his lips against her, and she looked at him through her lashes.

One of his hands cupped the nape of her neck. So warm. His thumb slid toward her jaw. "Horrible man," she whispered.

His hand moved along her jaw, and then his thumb brushed the line of her lower lip. "Are you sure?"

"Yes. You're horrible." She rolled her eyes. "I shan't fall in love with you, your grace."

"I don't expect you will," the duke said in a soft voice.

She wouldn't. She couldn't. Her heart had died with Greer. "You won't fall in love with me, either."

"No." He laughed. "Given our mutual defects in respect of our hearts, tell me, what would you like to happen between us?"

"I've been thinking about that these ten minutes at least."

His arm tightened around her. "Something shocking?"

She leaned closer. "You don't strike me as a man easily shocked."

He laughed, low and throaty. "I swoon, Wellstone." He continued touching her face, but his other hand now rested on her waist, very near her hip. "But I shall endeavor to bear up."

"I want you to make love to me."

There. She'd put words to the feelings building in her.

His hand had moved up to cover the side of her face and then angled down until his first three fingers were underneath her chin. His eyes stayed locked with hers. "You relieve my mind."

"Indeed?"

"I'd begun to think I'd put on this banyan for nothing."

"You wore this for me?"

A grin pulled at his mouth. "You are welcome to see the matter in that light, yes."

"Oh, you are horrible." She tugged on his lapels. "I wish you weren't so tall," she said. "I thought I liked that about you, but I don't. Not in the least."

"Is this better?" He lowered his head to hers.

At last.

At last his mouth brushed hers.

Lily opened her mouth and kissed him, and he made a sound in the back of his throat and kissed her back. Before she was quite ready for the contact to end, she pushed him back. "Aren't you worried we'll end badly?"

"Yes." He pulled her closer. "But right now I don't give a farthing for that."

She didn't either.

Chapter Eleven

❧

As a lover—potential lover—Lily was unfamiliar to him and he was, quite honestly, overcome with sensation. The entire time he was sticking his tongue down her throat and sliding his hands over all the parts of a lady a gentleman never touched, he understood he was crossing a line that shouldn't be crossed. The knowledge aroused him even more.

Her skin was warm and her mouth hot beneath his, the shape of her body against his undeniably feminine. She tasted good and smelled even better, violets again, sweet and delicate.

No, at the moment, he didn't give a damn that he shouldn't be doing this. He wanted her, and he meant to have her.

She kissed him just as hungrily as he kissed her, and when both his hands cupped her arse, she tightened her arms around him and pressed harder against him, as if she couldn't get enough either.

He entertained thoughts of laying her on the table, throwing up her skirts, and getting himself between her legs.

Would she object? Would she let him take her right here? Now? With just this desperate kissing and touching before they got there?

Then she moved back a step, not far because she was still kissing him like the angel she resembled. Heavenly. She removed a hand from his shoulders, and he prepared himself for an end to whatever was going on between them. Only he didn't want to stop kissing her yet. Not yet.

Her hand slipped between them, inside his banyan that she so admired and then along the fall of his trousers. Her fingers, damn the woman, slid very deliberately over the top of his cock, tracing the shape, and it just couldn't be his good fortune that she was touching him there. Like that.

Miss Lily Wellstone couldn't possibly be a virgin.

Neither was he.

Wasn't that a happy coincidence?

Indeed, yes.

Her fingers curved around his cock, pressing gently, stroking up, then down, and he could feel his eyes crossing behind his closed lids. When a woman caressed a man's prick like that, surely she was at least thinking about fucking him. Please, God, let her want to fuck him here and now. He took her head between his hands and tilted her face toward his to get a better angle on her mouth. There wasn't anything refined about the way he was kissing her. Or she him.

She unfastened one of the buttons at the fall of his trousers and then another, and the whole time she did that, part of him was thinking he really shouldn't let his happen, not with his sister's friend, but more of him was thinking he'd come to the library for reasons that weren't pure and he was lucky, lucky, lucky for that. Then all such thoughts faded to nothing because now he thought if she stopped he'd go out of his mind.

Mountjoy sucked in a breath when her bare fingers touched his belly and then, God help him, curled around his member. He nipped at her mouth, but his concentration was on what was going on with his prick and her hand. Little else existed. At some point he became aware she was pushing him back, toward the table, and he went along with that, kissing her the entire time.

Out of control. Beyond wicked. Bloody arousing.

He ended up sitting on the reading table with her standing between his spread thighs. She drew her head back from his and looked at the disarray of his trousers. His eyes fixed on the tops of her breasts, and Lord, he wanted to see her body laid bare to his every desire. At the moment, he was perfectly willing to let her take the lead because, damnation, she was good with her hands.

Angelic, oh so innocent, delicate, and fragile Miss Lily Wellstone unfastened enough of his trouser buttons to expose his cock, and he did nothing to discourage her. In fact, he spread his thighs wider.

"My, your grace," she said in a gratifyingly breathless voice while she put her hand on him. Around him. He threw back his head and concentrated on what she was doing to him. "How beautiful you are."

Eyes on her face for now, he put a palm on the table and let that arm take his weight while he leaned back to give her better access. Though he had, of course, been complimented any number of times, he could not recall any past lover specifically calling his prick beautiful. If one had, then she hadn't sounded half as earnest as Miss Wellstone. No one could mistake the look on her face for anything but heartfelt sincerity.

"I adore a man's body," she said in that same breathless and admiring voice. Sultry, that was what she looked like and sounded like. Reverent, even, and it made him even harder, even more aroused. Her fingers swept down and caressed his balls before sliding back up his shaft. "But you, your grace, you are simply magnificent." Lord, but he loved the glitter in her eyes. "Do you find that too wicked of me?"

Once he realized she wasn't asking him a rhetorical question, he said, "Very wicked, Wellstone. Pray continue." And she did. God, yes, she did. The first shivers of incipient orgasm built, promising him bliss. He cupped his other hand around her elbow.

He tightened his fingers on her arm, and then around her hand so she'd know what he needed from her. She caught on, and he released her hand to grip the back of her neck. He wanted to kiss her, but he was incapable of anything but pushing his cock harder into her palm. "Jesus."

"There's no need to take the Lord's name in vain," she said. Her fingertips touched his sac. "*Lily* will suffice."

"Lily." His breath hitched in his chest, caught there as he began to peak. "Finish me."

She leaned in, her hand gripping him, sliding up and then down his shaft from the base of him to the crown. He rocked his hips into her hand, and when he was teetering at the edge of spending, with him not giving a damn about the mess or anything but getting to his release, she came in close enough to kiss his throat, just by his jaw.

His hand, still on her nape, gripped her hard, and as his eyes fluttered closed, she said, "I don't want to ruin that lovely waistcoat of yours, your grace. You're going to have to stand up."

He tried to focus on her, but his brain was incapable of thinking of much besides impending orgasm. Fortunately, she took him in hand. Because he was already there, in a manner of speaking. He stood, not really understanding what she wanted from him. "I don't give a damn about the waistcoat," he said.

"But I do." And then she went down on her knees and the next thing he knew her mouth was around him, and her tongue was licking the head of his cock, then his shaft and, hell, just hell, he was deep in her mouth, and he buried his fingers in her hair and held her head. He didn't need but a few strokes of her tongue along his length before his crisis was on him.

Too fast. He was going to come too fast and not have the time to savor her mouth. God. "Lily."

One of her hands spread over his belly. The other stayed around his cock. Jesus. Jesus, Jesus. Her fingers curled over the waistband of his breeches, just by the fastening of his braces, and he came. Lord, he came hard, his cock pulsed and he thrust forward and cried out, some incoherent sound, and he had never in his life had a mistress who made him believe without question that she loved having him in her mouth, but he believed it of Lily.

When he had the presence of mind to let go of her head, and he'd withdrawn from her, he slid his fingers beneath her chin and tilted her head so that he could look into her eyes. Her hand remained around him. And then, very daintily, she leaned forward and kissed his prick and proceeded to put his clothes to rights. He let her because he liked seeing her on her knees. Because apparently he was a base rogue without any tender feelings toward a woman, a lady, who was a guest in his house, whom he'd just debauched. And hoped to further debauch in as short a time as possible.

He did, however, extend a hand to help her up when she was done. Except just as she was putting her hand in his to rise, the sound of someone walking down the corridor, humming something out of tune, froze them both before she was on her feet.

Whoever it was came into the library.

"Oh," said a woman. The word itself was a squeak of alarm.

Mountjoy lifted a hand to Lily, signaling her to stay where she was. The table was between them and the door, and his banyan was open. Chances were good Lily would not be seen if she stayed where she was. His eyes met hers. So dark and beguiling. Hers were wide open, but she crouched down more, making sure her head was not in sight. He turned enough to see the door and the maid who had stopped several steps into the room. She clutched a bucket in one hand.

"You may tend to the fire here later," he said as easily as he could under the circumstances. The girl curtseyed. From the look on her face she was frightened half to death.

"Your grace," she said, hardly audible.

"Thank you. Stay there," he said to Lily in a soft voice when the servant had gone.

Mountjoy adjusted his trousers then walked to the library door and closed it. He did not think the maid had seen Lily. The girl hadn't looked scandalized, only shocked to have come across her employer. But what if she had? He didn't care to think of making a spectacle of himself in front of the servants, and even less about publically compromising Lily. Privately, of course, the deed was done.

When he faced the table, Lily was standing up, and she looked . . . stunningly pretty. Her hair was disheveled, but in a way that made him think about her mouth on him again. Or him covering her while he fucked them both out of their minds. He wasn't engaged yet, he told himself. He'd made no promises to anyone yet, not to Jane and not to her father.

Her eyebrows drew together. "That was . . . more excitement than even I had anticipated." She cleared her throat. "Perhaps I ought to retire, your grace."

He nodded, but didn't move when she walked toward the door. He caught her arm as she passed. He had no idea, none at all, what this meant to her. An interlude she'd sooner forget or one she wanted again?

"Yes?" she said coolly.

"Lily."

"*Lily*," she said with a frown.

"Am I not permitted to call you Lily?"

"You may, certainly. When we are private. But isn't it odd that I prefer when you call me Wellstone?"

"It's what I call you in my dreams."

"How odd." She tilted her head. "It's what you call me in mine."

He drew her close and kissed her again. Just once. But it was a kiss that curled his toes. And she did respond to him. He drew away, not much because she looped an arm around his neck and then her hand slid into his hair. "Thank you."

"Lovely, lovely man." She pulled away. "We must do that again."

"Yes," he said.

"Good night, your grace. Or, rather, good morning."

"Sweet dreams. Wellstone."

He watched her all the way out the door and wondered how his dreams would change now that he knew for certain what her mouth was like.

Chapter Twelve

MOUNTJOY HAD NEVER BEEN MORE VISCERALLY AWARE of a woman than he was of Lily Wellstone at this moment. This morning he'd awakened having dreamed even more scandalous things about her than he'd yet done so far. Shocking dreams that had him satisfying his lust on his own.

He hadn't explicitly intended to see her so soon. This morning, he *could* have left the house as he did most days. He hadn't. Even before Eugenia had asked him to drive her and Miss Wellstone into town, with Miss Wellstone standing quietly to one side watching him as if she expected to be disappointed, he'd known he would agree.

Of course he was going to agree. She wasn't going to be here much longer, after all, and it would be a shame if they did not explore more of what had happened between them in the library while they could.

Besides, Lily believed he neglected his sister, which he did not do any more than could be helped given the demands on his time; and in the time remaining for her stay, he intended to prove to her that he didn't. He also wanted Lily's company, and that meant that the words *I would be delighted, Eugenia* had actually passed his lips despite a long list of appointments and tasks he had before him.

Even though he wasn't delighted. At all. He'd said so anyway. He could ill afford the time away from the management of his estate. His state of anxious desire was nigh onto intolerable and all he wanted was to have Lily in his arms again. To be in her arms again.

"Eugenia," he said when the two women came downstairs. "I don't recognize you. I surely do not." He bowed. "I'd forgotten what you look like in colors."

Lily speared him with a meaningful gaze. "She's lovely, don't you agree, your grace?"

"Yes, Miss Wellstone. She is." It was true. His sister was transformed. "That shade of green looks very well on you, Eugenia."

"You see, Ginny? I told you so."

He helped the two into the carriage and frowned as it occurred to him, now that he was actually looking at Eugenia, that his sister was only a year or two older than Jane. How odd that he'd come to think of her as a matron of no particular interest to men, when she surely would be. Surely must be. It did not speak well of him that he'd allowed that conviction to creep into his mind and stay there.

Was there some truth to Lily's accusation that he overlooked or even neglected Eugenia?

When they reached High Tearing, Lily walked at his side, her hand on his arm, as cool and collected as if last night's encounter had never happened while he could scarcely think of anything but that. He told himself that one encounter between them could be blamed on the lateness of the night, or on his poor judgment, or his moral weakness. He could not, however, say he hadn't seduced her, because, in point of fact, he had. He'd done nothing to avoid their meeting or what happened afterward and a great deal to bring it about. All of it.

Her visit to Bitterward would soon be over, but as long as she was here and there was this heat between them, why not indulge? Why not? While they walked, his mind was occupied with all the ways he might get his sister's friend on her knees again. And then on her back with him driving into her. Lord, he hoped she wanted more of what had happened between them because it would be a crime against nature to leave that passion unexplored.

How soon? became a drumbeat in his head. How soon could he get her alone? Eugenia waved and the motion jostled him out of his thoughts. Thank God.

"Nigel!" She waved again. "Look, Mountjoy, it's Nigel and the Misses Kirk."

Indeed, Nigel was walking in the opposite direction on the opposite side of the street, with Jane and Caroline Kirk on either side of him. Mountjoy waited with Eugenia and Lily for Nigel to safely escort the Kirk sisters across the street.

Nigel greeted them with, "You'll never guess who I met. Completely by luck, of course. I met them coming from the stationer's."

Eugenia looked gravely around her and said, "By any chance was it the Misses Jane and Caroline Kirk?"

There were fond greetings between the women, compliments for Eugenia's appearance, and then, without Mountjoy knowing how it had happened, they were walking, all of them, to the milliner's.

For God's sake, the milliner's.

Inside the shop, which reminded him of a closet in which bits of a woman's wardrobe had exploded, the ladies carried on an animated discussion of the wares. Their conversation slid past him. He didn't retain a single word they said between them, not even when they spoke directly to him or Nigel. Nigel had no trouble offering his opinion, requested or not. He *had* neglected Eugenia, he thought. He had allowed his sister to fall into her grief and stay there. She'd lived here so quietly, managing all the things a woman managed for a household, and he had let her wthout a thought to the consequences for her isolation. Shouldn't he have remembered before now that Eugenia had once been more like Lily than him? Happy and quick to laugh. His sister had not always been content to keep to herself the way he was.

He had the presence of mind to step to the counter when Eugenia approached the clerk with the ribbons she'd selected. They were white, pink, and yellow, and for several seconds he wondered why that seemed odd. It was, he realized, because they weren't black.

"I hope, Eugenia," he said, "that this means we shall soon see you in matching gowns?"

"Perhaps you shall," Eugenia said. She smiled, and he was reminded of the way she used to smile before.

Lily leaned her forearms on the counter. Last night, only an untimely interruption had prevented him from taking her on the library table. "I daresay we might, your grace," she said. She picked up the pink ribbon. "This is an excellent color for you, Ginny. What do you think?"

"Have a gown made in that color," he said. "Yellow, too. And blue. I remember how well you look in blue." He paid for Eugenia's ribbons, aware that Lily was smiling in his direction as if nothing indecent had happened between them. "It's time," he said. "No more black, Eugenia."

Eugenia glanced at Jane. "What about you, Mountjoy?"

"No pink for his grace," Lily said. "It is not his color." Enough laughter followed that he was not obliged to respond to his sister's hint about the state of matters between him and Jane.

Nigel insisted on paying for the Kirk sisters' selections. Jane had chosen green and lavender, and Mountjoy duly admired them when she showed them to him afterward. He wasn't without sensibility. Admiring her ribbons was nothing more than any soon-to-be-engaged man would do. It was about time he behaved as if he were. In any event, if she was pleased with her ribbons, that was exactly what she ought to be. Caroline Kirk slipped her packet into her reticule.

Lily approached the counter with a batch of ribbons and gewgaws of the sort that ended up on ladies' hats and gowns, and Mountjoy hesitated to approach the counter again.

He'd bought ribbons for ladies before that damned attorney called on him and changed his life. But he had not done so since. He'd understood very early on after he came into the title that his attentions to a woman, particularly a young, unmarried woman, created expectations he was not ready or willing to fulfill.

Lily didn't have those sorts of expectations. No one would think anything of it if he paid for her ribbons. Everyone, including Lily, knew he was going to marry Jane.

Nigel reached again for his wallet and the paper money there. "Allow me, Miss Wellstone," his brother said before Mountjoy could act.

"How kind, Lord Nigel, but not necessary." She lifted a hand and dazzled the clerk with a smile.

After which commenced one of the most ruthless bargaining sessions he'd witnessed in some time. She never lost her smile and she did not denigrate the merchandise other than, perhaps, to frown as she fingered a bit of fabric. She relentlessly made it clear that without a discounted price, she could buy nothing. Why not add another length of ribbon since she was buying so much, and by the way, if anyone asked, she'd instantly tell them where she'd obtained the items that adorned her gowns. There was to be dancing at Bitterward, you know. A Spring Ball, everyone would be there.

She had her coins counted out and on the counter before he or Nigel could even attempt to pay for her purchases.

They left the shop, Jane on Nigel's left, Caroline beside her while Lily took Nigel's right. He took Eugenia's arm and they made their way to the confectioner's for chocolate and perhaps some candies and tortes, so the ladies declared. They were nearly there when Lily released Nigel's arm.

"Oh," she said. From her tone, one imagined that the world had just come to an end.

Everyone stopped to see what was the matter.

She stood motionless. "Disaster has struck."

"What is it?" Jane asked. "Are you unwell?"

"I knew I should have worn the half boots. You know the ones I mean, Ginny. With that darling fold by the ankle. But these slippers are such a perfect match for this gown that I thought the risk worth it."

"What's happened?" Caroline asked.

"My slipper has come unlaced." Her shoulders tipped as, Mountjoy surmised, she balanced on one foot. "Not just unlaced, I fear, but damaged." She made a shooing motion. "Pray don't wait for me. I will attempt to effect a repair and rejoin you as soon as possible." She waved them off. "Lord Nigel, take Ginny and the Misses Kirk to the confectioner's. If my slipper cannot be repaired, I'll send Mountjoy for the carriage. Oh, do please, go," she said, forestalling objection. "I'll feel just awful to have spoiled our outing."

"Ought we to return home?" Eugenia asked.

"By no means," Lily said. "I won't hear of it."

"I would be happy to fetch the carriage if required," Mountjoy said.

"Go on, Ginny." Lily waved them on. "See that you drink an entire chocolate for me."

Once the others had moved off, she hopped on one foot to the side of the shop where they'd stopped. Mountjoy was both resigned to his fate and on edge with anticipation.

"Give me your arm, your grace," she said. He did so, and she actually blushed as she stooped, one hand gripping his arm for balance. A moment later, she had her slipper in hand. "Dear. Much worse than I feared." One of the ribbons that tied around her ankle had shredded where it was affixed to the inside of the slipper. "You'll have to fetch the carriage," she said so mournfully his heart actually dropped. "I did so want a cup of chocolate."

He held out his hand, palm up. "Allow me?"

"It won't fit you, sir."

"I am crushed, Miss Wellstone. Crushed."

She put the slipper on his palm and continued to hold on to his arm. "I can't walk without it fastened, as you can well imagine. It will never stay on."

She was entirely correct about that. The slipper was hardly more than a leather sole with a bit of fabric attached.

"I'll wait here for you to return with the carriage."

Mountjoy pulled the sapphire stickpin from his cravat and held it up. "With your permission, I think I can make a temporary repair." He wanted to pull her into his arms and cover her with kisses. "In the alternative, I can carry you to the confectioner's where you can wait in comfort with the others while I take your slipper to the cobbler two streets over."

Her eyes widened. "Oh, you clever, clever man. Do you think you can? I should hate for your stickpin to be damaged."

He smiled and did his best not to think of her on her knees. "We can but make the attempt. Shall I?"

"Please."

"I'll need both hands. And the ribbon."

"Oh, yes. Naturally." She gave him the ribbon. "Do be careful, your grace. I shouldn't like for you to be injured."

Mountjoy met her gaze. "For you," he heard himself say, "I would slay dragons."

Her smile struck him dumb, and the truly astonishing thing was that she appeared genuinely touched. Why? A woman like her had to have heard such nonsense from dozens of other men ever before he uttered such an inanity.

"How gallant of you to offer. But I require only my slipper."

His idea was a complete success. Her slipper was made of a material more than fine enough to pierce through with the added thickness of a folded section of the ribbon. The pin itself was long enough and sturdy enough that he fully expected it would hold until they returned to Bitterward.

"Voilà." He held up her slipper, pinned side toward her. "You are rescued."

Her smile threatened to stop his heart. They stayed where they were, gazes locked. She lifted a hand to his face but stopped short of touching him, while he wished she hadn't. She whispered, "What a lovely beast you are."

"Lovely, I can't agree. But a beast?" He leaned closer. "There are all manner of beastly things I wish to do with you."

He knelt at her feet. She pulled up her skirts and obligingly extended her stockinged foot. Her ankle was slim and her arch delicate, and he wrapped his hand around the back of her ankle, sliding a finger over the lace clocking along the outward side of her silk stocking. She slid her foot forward. They were in public, he reminded himself. Not someplace where he could lock the door and to hell with what was right and proper. He slid his smallest finger upward, to her calf. Lily remained still. He didn't dare more.

Neither of them spoke while he retied her slipper. When he was done he stood and stared at her mouth, and in his head was the image of her on her knees before him. She gazed back. Quiet. Serene.

"Shall we, then?" he said. There were a dozen possible meanings, and he meant every bloody one. Was there a man alive who could look at that angelic face and not think of what it would be like to have her beneath him? He wanted to touch her, caress her, and he had to fist his hands to prevent himself from doing just that. It was bad enough to have compromised her in private. To do so in public would be reprehensible.

"Yes," she said with a decidedly wicked grin. "I think we should."

He held her gaze while he extended his arm and walked, metaphorically speaking, through the gates of Hell. "Excellent, Wellstone."

"Oh. I'm Wellstone now?"

"You know very well you are. Come along." The confectioner's was yet twenty yards distant, at once too far and not far enough away. She was tall enough to keep pace with his longer stride, but he maintained a slow walk out of concern for the repair to her slipper.

"What sort of beastly things were you thinking?" she asked.

"Do not provoke me, Wellstone." He glanced at her and found her watching him. He had a mad desire to drag her into some dark corner of High Tearing and kiss her, to lift her skirts and take her up against a wall or find a private room anywhere he could and get her on her back. She knew what he was thinking, too. He watched her front teeth press into her lower lip.

"Will you think me terribly wicked if I ask you a favor now?" she said.

He forced himself to look away from her mouth. He shouldn't rise to that delectable bait, but he did. "I should like it if you did," he said. "Your favors are quite rousing as I recall."

"Not that." Her cheeks pinked up. "I would like your assistance with a project that I think will engage your sister's spirits."

"That's all?"

She nodded.

"Does it by chance involve flaming pencils?"

"No, your grace." She laughed, and he felt unduly proud to have amused her. He was not known as a man who amused people. "But I daresay you won't like my idea."

"What?" He wanted to put her on her back right now, having stripped her naked and then himself.

"You heard me mention a ball at Bitterward when we were buying ribbons."

"Did I?"

"You know you did." Her fingers tightened on his arm, a gentle reproof. "I was perfectly serious about a ball. I was astonished to learn you've never had dancing in all the time you've lived at Bitterward."

"For most of that time, I did not have a hostess." Not that his single state was an excuse. "When Eugenia came home, she was in mourning."

"You ought to have had a ball before now." They continued walking. Slowly. They were neither of them in a hurry. "If only for the ladies of the parish. All those beautiful Kirk sisters, and you've never given a ball. For shame, sir, when Bitterward has a splendid ballroom."

"Are you asking for permission now?" he asked. "I'll

wager you've already invited most of High Tearing." They weren't walking very fast, but they were nearly to the confectioner's.

"Yes, I am." She gave him a narrow look, full of suspicion. "Do you mean to refuse? Could you be that heartless?"

"I surely am, Wellstone." True. "I am heartless as you well know. But I am also selfish. Any favor that puts you in my debt is one I mean to grant."

"Is 'thank you' the correct reply?"

"It is. Have whatever parties you like. I'll tell the staff you are to be accommodated in your every requirement in that regard."

She stopped walking. "Do you mean it?"

"Why wouldn't I? So long as you inform me of expenses over fifty pounds before they are incurred. Or if your expenses exceed two hundred pounds in total."

"Tyrant." They started walking again. Even more slowly than before.

"A solvent one, Wellstone."

"I trust you will engage to attend." They'd reached the confectioner's and now stood only a few steps from the door.

He sighed. Through the low shop window, he saw Eugenia and both the Misses Kirk at a table, each with cups of something to drink. The fabled chocolate no doubt. Nigel had his back to the door but appeared to be dancing attendance on the ladies. Another gentleman in the shop sat with his back to the windows. "So long as you tell me when and where I am to be."

"I will slip a note amongst the bills."

"Be certain you inform my secretary. He keeps my appointment calendar."

"I will do so, your grace. Now, I have another project in mind."

"Two favors will cost you dearly."

"Wretch." She grinned at him and they stood there, not daring to stand closer. He did want her. Quite badly. "No phosphorus is required."

"You relieve my mind." He laughed and didn't care who

saw. He was doing his duty to his family, and he was damned if he'd feel guilty for enjoying himself. "What is the project you really want me to approve?"

"Too clever by half, your grace."

"I am the eldest brother. I am required to be clever simply to survive two devious siblings such as I have. What is your project?"

"Treasure."

He stood in front of the window. Nigel, facing the window but with his attention entirely on the ladies, put a hand on the back of Jane's chair and bent to whisper something in her ear that made her laugh. He wondered if Jane had refused other suitors because everyone, including him, expected he would marry her. Had other men declined to court her as a result? "I beg your pardon?"

"You and Jane suit you know."

He nodded and looked away from the window. He did not want to think about Jane just now. "What is your favor?"

"I've been having the most astonishing dreams. About finding treasure at Bitterward. And I thought, why not?"

"Why not what?"

"Why, why not search for treasure? My project, your grace, my brilliant notion to amuse your sister and recover her spirits, is to find buried treasure somewhere on Bitterward lands."

"Treasure." He frowned. "Am I expected to conjure up this treasure you've dreamed about?"

"I misspoke, your grace." She clasped her hands behind her back. "Not treasure. A treasure hunt."

"You seem convinced you'll find it."

"I have the very highest hopes for success. It happens all the time, some farmer . . ." She hesitated, he knew, because she was remembering that he had once been a farmer. "An earnest farmer toiling among his parsnips uncovers an ancient artifact. A cache of Roman coins, part of an ancient road, pots, a sword or poleax, or jewelry, all having been buried for hundreds of years. We shall search for treasure, Ginny and I. After all, the Romans were here in the north. We'll survey the property, make maps of suspicious mounds or likely caves. Why, you might be engaged for weeks with the project, long after I've gone home."

"Does not a search for treasure require that someone dig holes in the ground?" The idea gave him a chill since he vividly recalled dreams in which he stood with her at the edge of a wide trench, surrounded by servants who'd been digging in the ground. Three of his footmen, staring at him from across a hole. And Lily. Beautiful, alluring Lily Wellstone.

"Unavoidable, I should think." They remained partially in view of the shop window. Nigel had not noticed them, but Jane had. She was pretending she hadn't, but her eyes flickered to the window too often, sliding away when otherwise she might have looked directly at Mountjoy. "My plan is to have two or three burly footmen do the digging."

"Three?"

"That seems a proper number to me. Perhaps several energetic boys if you can't spare us assistance from your staff, or I can hire men from High Tearing."

"Have you reason to think there might be treasure of any kind on the property?"

"None at all." She grinned. "But why shouldn't there be? Sheffieldshire is rich in history, as you well know."

"Someone will break a leg in one of those holes you dig."

She rolled her eyes. "We'll have them filled in. You'll never know anyone put a spade to the earth. I promise you."

He ought to refuse, but aside from his disinclination to allow anyone to dig holes in the ground, he could think of no objection she wouldn't quickly dismantle. "So long as you fill in the holes after you have dug them, you are free to search for treasure anywhere on Bitterward lands."

"Excellent." She smiled again, that private, personal, incandescent transformation that made his heart thump against his chest. "Have you a survey map of the estate? I should like to copy it."

"I will make a copy available to you."

"Thank you." She leaned in to kiss his cheek, then checked herself. He knew why. Because her instinct wasn't innocent. Like lovers determined to hide an affair, they didn't dare touch in public.

She was precisely the kind of tonnish woman he preferred to avoid, except she wasn't. She wasn't like the women he met in London, no matter her exquisite clothes and her managing ways. "Have you considered the effect of your eventual disappointment when you fail to uncover treasure?"

Lily waved a hand. "We'll never finish before I go home, so who's to say we failed?" She reached past him, opened the door herself, and swept inside. "Ginny," she said in response to the greetings. "Jane. Caroline. Two hearty huzzahs for the duke. My slipper is repaired."

As he followed her inside, the gentleman with his back to the window rose. Mountjoy passed him on his way to the table where Lily now stood. Nigel held a chair for her. The two Kirk girls smiled, but Eugenia kept a stony silence, one hand curled around her cup of chocolate.

The man who'd stood turned to Mountjoy and bowed to him. "Your grace."

No wonder Eugenia had gone so quiet. And Lily. "Lord Fenris."

The marquess nodded to each of the Kirk sisters, studying them with a cold eye. "Ladies. Miss Wellstone. Mrs. Bryant."

Eugenia stared into her cup.

Lily gave him a cool look. "Good afternoon, my lord."

Lord Fenris let a hand drift to their table. Just his fingertips touched the surface. "I hope I have found you in good health, Miss Wellstone."

Lily inched closer to Eugenia and put a hand on her shoulder. "I'd offer my wishes for your health, but I don't think they'd be well received."

"On the contrary," he replied.

The edge of Lily's mouth twitched. "Then do accept my wishes for your continued health."

He bowed. "Thank you."

"Good day, sir."

There was a moment's awkward silence until Fenris removed his hand from the table. "Ladies." He bowed again, his gaze sliding to Eugenia. "Mrs. Bryant."

Eugenia took a sip of her chocolate and stared in the direction of Nigel's shoulder. On his way out, Fenris placed a coin on his table and, after one more bow, left.

Into another awkward silence, Nigel said, "May I fetch you a chocolate, Miss Wellstone?"

"Chocolate would be delightful, Lord Nigel. And some sugared walnuts, if it's not too much trouble. I adore them. Don't you, Miss Kirk?"

"Yes, thank you, I do." Jane smiled and Mountjoy had not the slightest reaction, even though Jane was pretty when she smiled. "Very much, Miss Wellstone."

"The ones here are particularly good," Lily said. "It is my goal to convince the proprietor to give me the recipe."

"Sit down, Nigel. I'll order for myself and Miss Wellstone." Mountjoy headed for the counter.

While Nigel did so, Lily put her hands on the table. "About our ball," she said.

He stood at the counter, staring at the table where Fenris had been sitting, wondering why a man whose family wanted nothing to do with their relative had come all the way to Sheffieldshire. And stayed.

"I am considering a Venetian theme," he heard Lily say. "What do you think, ladies?" From where he stood, Mountjoy saw her prop her elbows on the table. "Shall we flood the ballroom and do our dancing via gondola?"

Mountjoy said nothing. He was preoccupied with the realization that Lord Fenris had not come here to exact some sort of petty revenge on Lily. He was here to mend fences with her.

Chapter Thirteen

LILY PACED BEFORE THE FIREPLACE IN HER ROOM. IT was three o'clock in the morning, hours before she would be able to sleep. There was no moon out or she might have thrown on her cloak and gone for a walk. What she wanted to do was wander the house until she met with Mountjoy. Handsome, magnificent Mountjoy.

She hated feeling she was confined to her room when she wanted to be moving. To be doing something. Anything. Anything to take her mind off Ginny's brother. She did so hate to be alone with nothing to divert her from her thoughts.

She plucked her shawl off the chair where she'd left it after she'd retired to read and discovered she could not concentrate. Her situation was desperate indeed if she found no solace or distraction in a book. She knew the reason for that. There was no point denying she was infatuated with Mountjoy or that her attraction to him was the cause of her current unrest.

Even now, so many hours after their return from High Tearing, she felt the warmth of his fingers on her ankle, sliding, caressing, that quick slip of his fingers along her calf. If she closed her eyes she could see again the flash of heat in his eyes.

Thoughts like hers were not appropriate for a lady. Her father had once told her she'd been born wicked, and she suspected he was right. What proper lady, never married, took a lover, regretted nothing, and dreamed of taking another? Even as a girl, she'd dreamed of men who fell in love with her and to whom, in those dreams, she yielded all. Until Greer, naturally, her imaginings had been vague on the details of her surrender to passion.

Now that she'd kissed Mountjoy, touched him, tasted him, heard him groan in the passion she'd brought him to, she wanted more. Solitary enjoyments no longer sufficed. She wanted to caress him, to stroke his body and see his face when he reached his pleasure. Even more, she wanted the duke to touch her and kiss her and, yes, do some of those beastly things he'd alluded to when he'd fixed her slipper.

Mountjoy was nothing like Greer. He hadn't Greer's easy manner or his passion for history or his flights of fancy. Not his way with words either. The duke did not and would never love her the way Greer had, and she would never feel about Mountjoy the way she'd felt about Greer. She would always have that place in her heart where Greer still lived, and all the joy and happiness and the black despair of his loss remained locked away there. Safely guarded.

The only sounds in the house were the typical ones heard in a large and very old building. Syton House had inured her to such creaks and groans, the distant sound of the wind. She faced the door to the corridor, and tried to breathe, but the stale and thin air was suffocating in here.

She walked away from the door to unlatch and open the window. Night air whooshed over her, damp with the promise of rain. The hooting of owls stopped then started up again. She breathed in deep draughts of air and still felt she could not pull enough into her lungs and that she would never be able to catch her breath.

The sky was utterly dark. No moon, no stars, and no

promise of dawn, and that wet heaviness of impending rain. She leaned out the window and let the breeze riffle through her hair. Her skin rippled from the chill. It was spring, for God's sake. Not winter.

She stayed at the window until she could bear the cold no longer. Or the solitude. She could not stay here with the walls closing in on her and the air going away and her wicked, wicked mind whispering that she could find Mountjoy's room and settle entirely the question of what it would be like to make love to someone other than Greer. If she remained with nothing here capable of distracting her, she would reach a point where staying became intolerable, and she then really might search out Mountjoy's room.

Self-denial, she'd found, was the unfailing precursor to overindulgence in the very thing one sought to avoid. Her father excelled at denying himself and those around him, and she had always rebelled against his strictures.

She closed the window and pressed a palm to one of the panes of glass until the cold seeped into the bones of her hand. Hers was not an aesthete's character. That was, frankly, a truth to which she had long ago been reconciled. Her nature was, quite simply, not a proper one for a woman.

Lily picked up her sketchbook, pencil, and an oil lamp. She would wander the house looking for architectural details to sketch for her collection of oddities and grotesqueries and if, by chance or purpose, she and Mountjoy met? Well.

The moment she stepped into the corridor, the tightness in her chest released. Thank God. She walked to the Armory Hall, so called because the walls were hung with medieval weapons and there were at least ten separate suits of armor, including one for a horse. The door she'd entered through was at one of the short ends of the rectangular room. Three double-branched candelabra decorated a long oak table in the middle of the hall, gleaming silver in the lamplight. There were twenty-two chairs around the table and overhead a crystal chandelier, though with just the light of her lamp, there were no prisms of color to be seen.

A sideboard sat in the middle of the wall opposite the windows, but all along the rest of this long side were the suits of armor, in various attitudes of martial valor as was possible through the clever use of wire. Some held weapons: a sword, a dirk, or a pike. Another had a mace at its feet, yet another an axe.

According to Ginny, the Armory Hall was sometimes called into use as an informal dining room. The knights faced the windowed wall, and she fancied they had each come to know their separate views quite well. Every few feet opposite the knights were tall, multipaned windows inset in a bowed area topped by a small dome. Each dome contained a different carved ivory medallion: a face, a medieval beast, an open book with an inscription in Latin. One of the medallions was a swan with a broken chain around its neck, the very beast from Mountjoy's coat of arms.

To a careless glance, the last wall appeared to be nothing more than a wall that ended without a passage into yet another room. But Ginny had shown her the concealed doorway there that opened if one knew just where to press.

She set her light on the table and considered sketching each of the windows. There were seven. Enough for one a night for a week. Or, perhaps she'd sketch one of the suits of armor. There were eleven of them. As she was deciding that she would begin with a sketch of the swan, the hair on the back of her neck prickled.

She turned in time to see the concealed door swing open.

Lily's breath caught in her throat. Mountjoy had denied there were ghosts here, but if ever a house ought to have a ghost or two, it was Bitterward. But it wasn't a ghost that entered the hall. It was far, far worse than any spectral apparition.

The duke halted when he saw her, and they stood there, she fancied, in mutual disbelief that they should meet. Again. At this hour. When they had agreed they must avoid each other at such times as this.

"You," he said.

She curtseyed. "Your grace."

He wasn't wearing that lovely banyan of his. Alas, tonight he was dressed in his usual inelegantly fitted clothes. He put down his candle and pointed at the frescoed ceiling that, at the moment, was not possible to see. "Doyle tells me that in fourteen hundred something, my ancestor hired an Italian master to paint the ceiling."

She looked up as if she could see that far in the darkened room. She did recall from her previous tour that the paintings were sublime. Her heart thudded in her ears.

Why encounter him now when she was not feeling at all virtuous? On a night when she'd been entertaining salacious thoughts about the man across from her? She was already weak where he was concerned. "Do you know who he engaged?"

"Family legend is that it was Fra Angelico, but I've seen nothing to prove that. The claim seems suspect at best."

Lily stood close enough to the table to put her hand on it. The wooden surface had been polished until she could see her reflection. In her room, she had imagined herself taking actions that she was now barely able to contemplate. Not with the duke here in the flesh, with his guarded eyes and somber expression.

It seemed another time and place entirely that she had unfastened his trousers and his fingers had been buried in her hair.

But then, disaster.

Mountjoy left his candle where it was and crossed the room to her. He ended standing mere inches from her.

Oddly enough, her nerves settled. "Your grace."

"I have decided," he said in the manner of a man who was used to deciding a great many things, "concluded, that we cannot be lovers." He drew a fingertip along the line of her shoulder. "I'm sorry," he said softly. "I'm sorry, but it just can't be. You and I."

She leaned in to him, and his eyes swept downward to fix on her bosom, which she found a gratifying reaction.

"I'm sorry, too." She curled an arm around his neck, which required that her upper torso press against his chest. His arm snaked around her waist, and she gave a little tug of her arm and just like that, his mouth was in reach. She kissed the side of his jaw.

Mountjoy laughed, a low, velvet sound of ironic mirth, and he dipped his head toward hers. In return, she brushed her lips across his. So soft, his lips were. Again, nearly a kiss this time.

And then a kiss.

That was all the two of them needed. She'd known the moment he'd come in that she hadn't the strength to continue in a ladylike manner. He was here, and she wanted him to stay.

His lips parted, and he nipped at her mouth, soft kisses that turned into heated kisses, and Lily melted against him. She adored the way he kissed. The Duke of Mountjoy knew what he was about. His other arm went around her waist, too, pulling her tight against him. His tongue dipped into her mouth, caressed, beguiled, turned her bones to jelly.

He lifted her up, and she did not know what he intended until she was sitting on the table, close enough to the edge that had he not stood between her legs she would have worried about falling off. He planted his hands on either side of her thighs and returned to kissing her mindless. Which he did very, very well.

Lily returned his passion, accepted everything he did, and tightened her arms around his neck. She pushed her fingers into his hair. She gave a moan of protest when he lifted her up a second time, but as she learned, it was only to lift her skirts and set her down with her bare bottom on the table. Cool against her skin. Thrilling. One of his hands ended up on her knee. Just above her garter.

"Lily," he said, shaking his head. "You and that damned medallion. You're constantly in my thoughts. My dreams. I can't keep my damned hands off you."

His fingers curved around her leg as potent proof of that.

Her belly tensed and a quiver of arousal spread upward from her breasts to her throat, and lower, too, between her legs. She felt her need for him there especially.

She gasped when his fingers slid higher. Oh, heavens, higher yet, until he was touching her exactly there. She was wet and slick, and he knew where and how to stroke her, and she angled herself into his hand. They weren't kissing anymore; she hadn't the breath for it now. For a time, he watched her face while his fingers were busy.

Mountjoy leaned in to kiss her once. Just once before he slid his mouth downward, along her jaw and then back to her mouth. He drew away, then kissed her ear and said, very low, in nearly a growl, "We can't be lovers, but it wouldn't be gentlemanly of me if I did not repay the favor you recently did me."

"That's so," she managed to say. He knew what to do with his hands. He'd found that place that made her weak with need. Not weak, she thought, strong. Stronger because of her need and her determination to satisfy it, and stronger because he was so very close to fetching her. Stronger because she trusted her body and its reactions and welcomed the pleasure. Stronger because her feelings and reactions were true. She pulled him toward her, tightened her arms around his shoulders.

"You *are* wild," he whispered. "Wild and lovely beyond words. I worship you for that. I thank God for that." He slid a finger inside her, and this, this was the moment to allow her control to slip away. "You're hot around me, Lily," he whispered. He beguiled. Seduced, except she'd been seduced from the very moment she'd set eyes on him. A second finger joined the first, and while he stroked his fingers in her, he managed to keep contact with that spot that made her grateful for her wildness. "Every time I looked at you today I thought of your mouth fetching me."

She could barely speak, but she managed to say, "I, too."

He lay her back and, though she wanted to touch him and could not, except to touch his head and thread her fingers through his hair, he used his mouth instead of his fingers. He kissed her sex, and that was not something Greer had ever done for her.

She would go mad. No woman would survive what his mouth demanded of her. One of his hands stroked her thigh, and she felt the coolness of the air on her skin, the warmth of his hands, the pounding of her heart when his fingers and palm followed the curve of her leg. She did not last long. His tongue flicked over her, and she was done. Climax washed over her, swept her away.

His name fell from her lips, but only his title, *Mountjoy*. Because that's all she knew as she clutched his head and gave herself over to sensation. Pleasure rolled through her, wrung her out, and then, when she thought there was nothing more, when he'd slowed and then stopped, and she was breathing again, he blew on her, and it electrified her. He licked and waited, then kissed her there again, and she wasn't finished after all. She came again, and she was his in that moment, his utterly, for as long as her heart continued to beat.

When she could think again, she opened her eyes and saw Mountjoy standing over her, one hand on her belly and the other resting on the outside of her thigh, and his green, so green eyes watching her. "What a shame," she said, and she actually did mean every word, "that we cannot be lovers."

Chapter Fourteen

MOUNTJOY USUALLY TOOK THE SAME ROUTE WHEN he returned to the house after riding out, but today he changed his mind. His horse, Fervent, fancied a gallop, so rather than take the road from High Tearing to Bitterward upon reaching the edges of the estate lands, he took Fervent over the stone fence into the field and let him have his head.

He was delaying the inevitable return home, he understood that, but it was also true that Fervent wanted a run. Since it was their mutual decision that they should not pursue an affair, he preferred to avoid Lily when possible. Fervent therefore got his way.

For a quarter mile, he and Fervent flew, taking a line that followed the river Tear and curved past the woods, and he hardly thought at all about her skin, the taste of her, the way she kissed, or the sound of her calling his name when she came. He and Fervent were both breathing hard when he slowed down. He put his horse into a trot and headed more or less in the direction of Bitterward.

Lately, whenever he stayed at Bitterward he missed London

less and less, and he'd never missed Town all that much. He wasn't a proper duke; he never had been and probably never would be. He'd much rather be in the country than sitting in the Lords or whatever Mayfair gentlemen's club would have him for a member. If there weren't duties in Town that required his presence there, he'd be content to stay here the rest of his days. Every time his presence in London was required, he missed Bitterward more and more. He belonged in the country with his sleeves rolled up and his hands full of dirt.

He took the climb to the last substantial field before the more manicured lawns at a walk. At the crest of the slope he had a view of Bitterward to his right, and to his left, the Saxon church that was still in near pristine condition. The view, as always, took his breath. Everything within his sight belonged to him. Unless he married and begot himself a son or two, one day Bitterward and all the rest of his inheritance would belong to Nigel or Nigel's sons. The dukedom was his by right of birth. He worked and managed the estates with his own sweat and blood, and he wanted to raise a son of his own to step into the role of Mountjoy.

He had no business chasing after a woman who did not want what he did from life. Tomorrow, he thought. He would offer for Jane tomorrow, and he would then be obligated to put Lily out of his thoughts. He would settle down to the business of ensuring his line endured.

As he neared the church, he saw there was a veritable crowd outside the doors. This was so even though, according to Doyle, the last services held there had occurred when the centuries were still in three digits. He rode closer and saw a woman marching away from the stone building in a deliberate, measured stride. Was she counting off steps? And why?

Nigel stood near Eugenia, whom he did not immediately recognize because she was wearing colors again. Jane was a few feet away, watching Lily pacing away from the church. Lily stopped her marching and faced Nigel and the others.

He continued riding toward them, and his heart sped up

even though there could be nothing more between him and Lily. This was, however, an opportunity for him to begin a formal courtship of Jane. He came close enough to see that Lily wore a blue riding habit that flattered her figure extremely. A round hat perched jauntily on her head. For her, it seemed, every day was an adventure for which she must be exquisitely attired. She had a leather case under one arm, and as he approached, she opened the case, took out a sheet of paper that rattled in the breeze, and made a notation with a pencil.

By now, all three of them had heard his approach and turned. Lily, farther away from him than the others, stayed where she was, a hand lifted to shade her eyes. He remained on his horse, aware, as he had rather not be, that Nigel was as beautifully clothed as Lily and his sister.

"Eugenia." He nodded to her, and it was as if he hadn't seen his sister in months. His heart turned over. She was too thin. Far too thin, and he ought to be hanged for not having noticed before. "You look lovely again."

"Thank you, Mountjoy."

"It's good to see you in colors, Eugenia." He was very much aware of Lily several feet distant from them. And of Jane, of course. His future duchess. He dismounted and handed the reins to the footman who held the other horses. The ground was soft from the recent rains. Lily remained standing several yards from the church, still engaged in writing something down on her paper, using her leather case as a makeshift table. "Miss Kirk," he said. "Good afternoon."

Her cheeks turned pink, a reaction she attempted to hide by ducking her head while she curtseyed to him. "Your grace."

"I hope you're well today."

Jane's eyes went wide. "Yes, sir."

Good Lord, he terrified the girl. That must be remedied as soon as possible. He smiled at her, but it didn't seem to help.

Lily, meanwhile, had finished with her writing. She tucked her pencil away and strode toward them without the deliberation that had so marked her walk away from the church.

"Your grace," Lily said when she reached them. She extended a gloved hand as if she were a queen and he a mere flunky. Her gaze traveled him from head to toe, and he did not think, alas, that she had in mind her remarks about him being a splendid animal. In fact, that was a shudder when her attention reached his neckcloth, which he had yanked loose during his gallop. His clothes, so comfortable, felt even more inadequate. His damned grooms looked better than he did. He wondered what Jane thought of his appearance and realized he had no idea what she thought about anything.

"Lovely to see you, sir," Lily said.

"A pleasure to see you, too, Miss Wellstone." Mountjoy bowed over her hand and stepped back. He hadn't ridden out expecting to escort their guest on a tour of the property. And yet, ridiculously, he wished he'd not worn his oldest riding clothes or his battered greatcoat that, this morning, had seemed just the thing.

"We've been examining your church." Her eyes sparkled. "Did you know the baptismal font is still in place?"

"Is it?"

"I've made a detailed sketch, but really, there's simply no way to capture the sense of all those ancient hands that must have touched that stone." She put a hand on her head to keep the breeze from whipping off her hat. "How lucky you are to have such a splendidly preserved example of Anglo-Saxon architecture on your property. Lord Nigel didn't know when the church was last used, but I'd say it must be centuries, and yet so wonderfully intact. Down to the sundial!"

"Your enthusiasm inspires, Miss Wellstone." He knew what she tasted like. He knew what she looked like when she came. He knew her skin was soft and her limbs sleek. He wanted to know the rest.

"I've made a note of all the likely spots hereabouts." She held up her leather case as if that explained all.

"Likely spots?"

She walked the rest of the way to where he stood with Eugenia, Jane, and Nigel, her leather case under one arm. He watched the sway of her hips as she walked. Mud dotted the hem of her riding habit and clung to her boots, but this was England in spring, and they had been subjected to frequent storms, some of them with the chill of the past winter at the edges. Her cheeks were rosy from her brisk walk. "For finding treasure, of course."

"Treasure."

"You did agree to our searching." She gave him another of those head-to-toe looks, and this time he knew she wasn't thinking about the fit of his coat. "Don't tell me you've forgotten."

"Not at all." Last night—this morning, rather, he'd held her bottom in his hands, and he was, say what you would about him not being a proper duke, thinking it would be better than pleasant to do so again. Never mind what was proper. If she was willing, if she had no more expectations of him than he had of her, why not?

"Who knows what we might find? At home, my neighbor, Mr. Bardiwill, was hunting in a corner of his property when he came across an entire cache of Roman coins partially dug up by one of his spaniels. They'd been stored in an amphora, but alas, his servants broke the vessel whilst they were digging it out. It would have been wonderful to see the amphora intact."

"You expect to find Roman coins?" In London, on those occasions when he was looking to spend a few hours in a woman's arms, he appeared in those places frequented by women looking for lovers and the thing was done. He never pursued married women. He'd only once become involved with a widow, and she had not been a woman of the Ton. His past lovers were never women like Lily. She was unique among females. He took a step nearer Jane but found his brother had already offered Jane his arm. "What else, dare I ask?"

"Who knows?" She grinned, losing herself in her enthusiasm. "The foundation of an ancient Roman garrison. A Viking ship."

"This far from the shore?" Eugenia said.

"A hoard of gold, then." She gestured with her free hand, then put it back on her head to prevent her hat from blowing away. "Goodness, the wind. At any rate, your grace, one never knows. We might find anything at all."

"I suppose that's true."

"In the meantime, I, for one, am famished. Aren't you, Ginny? Miss Kirk? Shall we return to Bitterward for tea?" She headed for her horse, a very fine mare, Mountjoy noted, that she must have brought with her as it was not an animal from his stables. "Were you on your way home, your grace?" Her eyes pierced him and killed the denial on his lips. "Or had you business elsewhere when you saw us?"

He could tell her yes, that he had business away from Bitterward. But he didn't. He frowned to see Nigel whispering something to Jane. "On my way home. Miss Kirk," he said. "May I assist you to your horse?"

Jane turned pink as a sunrise. "Yes, your grace."

While he did so, with Nigel stepping aside, one of the grooms bent to offer Lily a hand up. She looked over her shoulder at him. "If you're on your way home, your grace, we should adore your company."

"Thank you."

He looked into Lily's eyes, and he could have sworn he lost a little part of himself to the joy he saw there.

"Will you hold this for me, please?" She handed her leather case to Mountjoy, and he, being closer to her than anyone else, accepted it with a nod. She set her booted foot on the footman's cupped hands and mounted gracefully. She sat her mare with complete confidence. He wondered if her father had given her lessons when she was young or if her skill was more recently acquired.

"Thank you, your grace." She leaned down to collect her case, and he handed it to her.

"You're welcome, Miss Wellstone." There. What could be more proper than that?

With a glance at Eugenia and Jane, both of whom were now mounted, Lily gave him a smile that bedazzled. She gave absolutely no sign that he'd brought her to climax only a few hours ago. "Talk with Miss Kirk, won't you, your grace? She'll be pleased if you do."

He nodded again, afraid that if he spoke or stayed where he was even a moment longer he would give himself, and Lily, away.

"Lord Nigel," she called. "Come tell me everything you know about the church. And is it true there are caves on the property?"

She'd managed them all. Nigel. Eugenia. Jane. Him, too, and not even for the first time. In the normal course of things he did not care for women who wanted to manage him. With Lily, he wasn't at all sure he minded. He remounted and, as instructed, dropped back to accompany Jane. Nigel, Eugenia, and Miss Wellstone rode ahead.

Mountjoy discovered his impression that Jane was terrified of him was an accurate one. He kept to safe topics such as the weather, her family, and, in a moment of daring, phosphorus pencils, and she said hardly a word. They spent the entire return to Bitterward in this utterly boring and safe manner. Once there, Jane declined tea, claiming a prior engagement. He suspected she was afraid of being trapped in conversation with him again.

He would have insisted on escorting her home, but Doyle came down the front stairs, a letter in his hand. "Your grace, the messenger has been instructed to wait for your immediate reply."

The letter was from Mr. Thomas Plummer, the vice-chancellor. Indeed, his immediate attention was warranted. "Nigel," he said. "Would you be so kind as to see Miss Kirk home?"

"Of course."

When Mountjoy came downstairs sometime later, he was late for tea but his response to the vice-chancellor was on its way back to London. He'd refused to give in to his desire to dress with more than his usual attention to his appearance. For whose benefit would he do such a thing? This was his home, and if there was anywhere a man ought to be comfortable, it was in his own home.

The moment he walked into the Oldenburg salon, he regretted his stubborn refusal to give in to his valet's hints that perhaps *this* time he might attempt something new in his dress.

Eugenia presided over the tea while Lily sat at a table, a pencil in one hand and a rectangle of paper before her. Nigel had one hand on the table and was bending over Lily's shoulder. A familiar scene. But there was no phosphorus, thank the Lord, and the pencil was a normal pencil of the sort anyone could use to write with no danger of flames engulfing the house.

"Your grace," Lily said with a smile when he came in. She rose to curtsey, but he lifted a hand.

"No formality between us."

"That's very kind of you." She sat again. She'd changed from her riding habit—of course—and now wore white muslin trimmed with pale blue. Some sort of cap perched atop her hair, plain enough not to interfere with anything. The colors suited her. She wore a chain of silver beads that reached to the middle of her stomach, and her medallion on a velvet ribbon of the palest blue.

She looked, as she always did, very well. Devilishly pretty with her golden hair and chocolate eyes. He'd known a few women who were more beautiful, but he'd begun to believe he'd never known any woman more alluring than her.

"Eugenia," he said. "You're well, I trust."

"Yes, Mountjoy." She looked at him with a smile. "I'm so glad you could join us." Once again, he was taken aback at seeing her in colors. How had he forgotten what she'd been like before her husband's death? Happy, he recalled. Smiling. Intelligent, that was a Hampton trait. "We thought you might not."

"I'm famished," he said. "And in dire need of tea."

"Lily's brought some Lapsang Souchong for us to try. Will you have some of that?"

"Yes, thank you." He went to the table where there were laid out several cheeses, some biscuits, bread, butter, a yellow cake, various jellies and preserves, and Devonshire cream. There were apples and grapes, too, as well as some early strawberries. "May I bring you anything, Eugenia?"

"No thank you, Mountjoy."

He gathered a plate for himself. "Miss Wellstone?"

"Are there more grapes?" She did not look up from her paper. "I should love more grapes."

Nigel said, "I'll get them for you."

"Lord Nigel," Lily said sternly. She barely looked at Nigel. "Your brother is half an inch from the food. He can trouble himself to bring both of us grapes and perhaps a slice of that cake." She glanced in his direction, but her attention was directed more at the food than at him. "And a bit of that delectable Devonshire cream."

"I should be delighted, Miss Wellstone." He only just stopped himself from rolling his eyes in self-disgust. Was that now his favorite phrase? *I should be delighted.* Lily Wellstone had his life turned upside down.

He brought her and Nigel plates with the requested items, then accepted his tea from Eugenia, which he took with him to study the paper Lily had spread over the desk. No one could think anything of his doing so since Nigel was doing the same.

"What do you think?" Lily asked him. She smelled good. Just enough of violets to be pleasant and to remind him of the scent rising from her skin, the taste of her flesh, and the sound of her sexual release.

"I can't make heads or tails of what that is." He nodded at her paper.

Nigel laughed at him. "She meant the tea, Mountjoy. What do you think of the tea?"

"Did she?" He took another sip, slowly because it was hot and Lily was watching him. "I still can't make heads or tails of that." There was a smokiness to the tea that he liked. The flavor hovered on the edge of too much. "It's quite strong."

"It is a bold tea," Lily said. "And therefore not for everyone." She put her elbow on the table and her chin on her hand. "I suspected you might like it."

"Why?"

"You are like this tea. Bold. Opinionated." Her lips quirked in a smile. "And something of an acquired taste."

Nigel gave a yelp of laughter.

"Few people have acquired that particular taste," Mountjoy said.

Lily met his gaze. "Perhaps they've not given you a sufficient chance."

"Where do you get this?" No one could blame him for staring at her. Her smile could resurrect a dead man. "I should like to have a supply laid by."

She reached across the table for another sheet of paper and wrote on it. "The name of the tea, and the tea merchant my steward swears by. If you write to him and tell him that I particularly recommended you to him, I'm sure he'll sell you some."

Mountjoy had been duke long enough to know he was unlikely to need any introduction or recommendation. His name would be more than enough. "It's quite good."

"But not a tea everyone cares for." Lily sat at the table like a queen, in command of them all. "I recognize that and for that reason bring my own personal supply. Ginny, for example, did not care for the taste, and your brother, I fear, only pretends that he does."

Nigel hastened to say, "There's no pretense, Miss Wellstone." He took another sip of his tea but it was obvious to all he was restraining a grimace. "Perhaps a bit," he said with a shake of his head. "I have hopes it will grow on me. Like Mountjoy eventually did."

"So very amusing, Nigel," Mountjoy said.

"Don't quarrel," Lily said. She looked between him and Nigel, touchingly anxious. "Not on my account."

"If I didn't mercilessly tease him over something like that," Nigel said, "he'd wonder what was wrong with me."

"My dear brother, I have no need to wonder." Mountjoy sipped his tea again. "I've known for years what's wrong with you."

"Gratifying to hear." She gave the paper to Mountjoy. "I'll write to my steward and have him send more. That way you will have some of your own after I'm gone and while we hope that Mr. Philby agrees to take you on as a client."

"Whyever should he not?" Nigel asked. His eyebrows soared upward. "I can't think of many merchants who would refuse my brother's custom."

"Mr. Philby is exceedingly particular. My great-aunt transacted all her tea-related affairs through him, and I suspect he only deals with me because he feels a sense of obligation to her memory. It's rather sweet of him, actually."

Mountjoy drank more of his tea. He did like the taste. If Lily had met Mr. Philby in person he knew exactly why she was his customer. One look at her, and only the most hard-hearted man could refuse her. "I hope your good word will persuade him to my side."

She looked at him, and when their eyes met, she did not look away. Nor did he. The sexual thrill was familiar. Compelling. Addicting. She looked at the papers before her, and he felt in some absurd way that he'd won. "One hopes, your grace. One hopes."

"May I ask what you are doing with these papers here?"

"An excellent question, sir. Marking down the likeliest spots for us to find ancient treasure. Your sister and I have done a preliminary survey of the property and determined where we believe some ancient tribe or Roman Legion might have had occasion to travel or live."

"It's all very scientific," Nigel said. Mountjoy remembered the way Nigel had been leaning over Lily when he came in. Was it possible Nigel was developing tender feelings toward Lily?

"I am sure it is," he replied.

Lily ate a grape, eyes closed, savoring the flavor as if she'd never tasted anything sweeter in her life. "They are ever so faintly chilled. Your cook keeps these on ice, I presume." Slowly, she opened her eyes. Mountjoy was aware of his brother's stare at Lily, and of his own. His gaze met hers, and he thought of sex. Hot, passionate, blood-burning sex. "Do you know," she said, "that once I ate some grapes that had been frozen through? They were wonderful. Ginny, my darling"—she turned on her chair—"have you ever eaten frozen grapes?"

"I don't believe so."

She plucked another grape from the bunch Mountjoy had set on her plate. "I think I'll write to Mr. Stevens and tell him I am quite settled that this year we shall have a new icehouse built. Our ice never lasts the summer. Late August becomes intolerable with nothing cold to drink."

"And Mr. Stevens is?" Nigel asked too quickly.

She ate another grape, languidly and with as much single-minded attention as before. Mountjoy had the wicked image of her stretched out naked on a bed—his bed—enjoying grapes while he stripped to his skin and joined her.

"My steward," she said, unaware of his wayward thoughts. "He's absolutely devoted to me."

And who, Mountjoy wondered, was not eventually absolutely devoted to her?

Chapter Fifteen

LILY STOPPED WALKING WHEN SHE HEARD THE ECHO
of footsteps on the stone floor. Her pulse jumped with
anticipation. She waited and, as she knew would happen,
moments later the duke appeared from around the far corner.
He held a shielded candle, and when he saw her he, too,
stopped.

Of course the duke.

From habit, her fingers closed around her medallion.
Who but the duke would she meet at this dark-of-night hour?

"Your grace." She curtseyed to him, and he nodded and
crossed the remaining distance between them. They were
in a gallery hall of sorts, though it contained no paintings,
with original-to-the-structure Gothic arched windows along
one wall and a bare stone wall opposite. The ceiling was
ribbed and domed in the Gothic fashion. Light from the
duke's candle and hers flickered off the walls and the window glass. Had it been daylight she would have been able
to enjoy sunlight rippling through the thick panes of glass
instead of reflected candlelight.

"Wellstone." He gave her a half grin that sent her heart pounding. "Imagine us meeting like this."

"I'm not sure it's entirely safe," she said.

He gave her an inscrutable look then held up his candle to illuminate the windows. "Have you sketched this part of the house yet?"

"Several pages of my notebook are dedicated to this passageway." Half a notebook, actually. "The masonry and stonework are exemplary. And quite beautiful."

"What will you do with all your drawings?" Mountjoy stayed where he was. As did she. And yet, the connection between them tugged at her. She was more flustered by him than she cared to admit.

She shrugged. "Assemble them into a book I should think. I'll call it *A Study of England's Ancient Homes, Volume the First*, and publish under a man's name. Professor L. Carter Farnsworth. What do you think of that for a scholar's name?"

Mountjoy smiled. She did love the shape of his mouth. "That Professor Farnsworth cannot fail to find a publisher for such a work. There must be upward of half a dozen people in the whole of His Majesty's Empire who would put such a book in pride of place in their library."

"Would you?" She cocked her head. "Acquire me for your library?"

"My dear Wellstone, I would love to have you in my library."

"Between the royal quarto sheets, your grace?"

He didn't answer right away because he was trying not to laugh. "But of course."

Lily was close enough to the wall to stroke one of the stone ribs that lined the windows. "I think this corridor is my favorite in the whole of Bitterward."

The edge of his mouth twitched with a suppressed smile. "Yes. Just now this corridor is my favorite, too."

"I can feel the past here. Can't you?"

"No." He reached out and tapped one of the windowpanes. "But I can feel someone calculating my window tax."

She gave him a sideways look. "If ever there was a place to encounter a ghost, this precise spot is it." In the quiet, she gestured toward the windows. "Sometimes when I find myself in a place like this, I feel as if the world is weary of we humans."

"I as well."

"Whenever I walk here, I imagine knights and their ladies, feudal lords walking past these windows on their way to the Great Hall for a meal where the food is flavored with salt and saffron and pepper that costs half a year's income. I see Jesuits with prayer books in hand on their way to Matins."

"I don't believe Bitterward ever housed Jesuits."

"That does not signify, your grace. That is what I imagine. I hear them speaking in Latin as they walk."

"What an eccentric mind you have."

"It's an odd fascination of mine, I admit," she said. His coat was atrocious, yet she itched to put a hand on his chest.

"Born in your father's library."

"Yes. And come of age after I moved to Syton House." Her father's housekeeper, the woman who had, in effect, raised her after her mother died, had not accepted Lily's invitation to come with her. She had a husband and children who kept her there. "I found myself solely alone and in want of occupation in my free hours." She smoothed a wrinkle from her skirt. She was glad she still wore her evening gown. One did so want to look one's best at a time like this. "Out of sheer boredom, I inspected the house from top to bottom. I discovered the foundation was built on a Roman villa, or if not a villa, some such structure at any rate. There is a Roman bath belowstairs."

"I should like to see that."

Lily hesitated, on the brink of telling him that he must come to visit. She couldn't say such a thing. That presumed too much. Far too much for them both, for it assumed the sort of friendship from which one could not simply walk away.

"Given your interests, Miss Wellstone, there is a room here I think might well send you into raptures."

"Indeed?" She kept her hands buried in her skirts or she really would touch him. "Other than the east tower, I thought I'd been in every room in Bitterward." A portion of that part of the house was inaccessible. When she had asked Doyle about the locked door that blocked her access, he had politely informed her that he did not have a key, which she had taken, sensibly enough, to mean that Mountjoy did not wish anyone to enter that part of the tower.

"Yes." He held her gaze.

"Your grace. If you have a room in which to give me raptures, I should very much like to see it."

"Lily," he said, laughing at last. "Lily, you'll drive me mad."

"I don't see why."

"May I show you?"

She nodded, fully aware that she was agreeing to more than a tour of a usually inaccessible part of the house. "I should like that."

"Come along then."

She followed the duke out of the stone gallery hall. They turned a corner, then another, and at the end of that passage was a plain wooden door with a threshold worn to a curve in the middle from all the feet that had passed over it. Decorative ironwork covered the door from the hinges to the latch. Beside the door was an empty niche the height of her two hands with a scallop design carved into the stone above it. She took his candle while he fit a key to the lock and opened the door.

Mountjoy stepped across the threshold, his back to the door, keeping it open for her. Narrow stone stairs spiraled upward. As she went in, he pulled the door closed, and she said, "Do keep the key safe, your grace."

"I will." He took the lead in climbing to the very top of the tower. The passageway narrowed as they ascended. At the top was a door with no landing, just a stone threshold curved in the center simply from centuries of feet stopping there. Mountjoy opened that door, too. The latch operated by a simple rope one pulled to lift the bar on the interior of the door. He took his candle from her and they went in.

"I came across this room shortly after we moved here," he said. Lily set her candle on a stone table by the door while the duke set his candle next to hers. The air inside was cool. She could not see much beyond a few feet, though she could tell the room was round and that there were windows in the opposite wall.

With a flint he took from the stone table just by the door, he lit a lantern. "Nigel was at Rugby by then," he continued. "I don't recall where Eugenia was. Visiting our aunt and uncle in Haltwhistle, I think." He snuffed out their candles and lifted the lantern. "Mind your step," he said. He walked farther in.

Lily, too, walked into the center of the tower room. "Oh." The walls were bare stone, and it seemed that every inch was carved with fanciful figures, grotesqueries, and scrollwork.

"What do you think?" he asked.

She put a hand to her heart and found she could barely speak. "Magnificent." She spared him a glance before she craned her neck to see the ceiling. "Thank you. Thank you for bringing me here."

"You're welcome." Mountjoy crossed the circular room, which was not large, and lit a second lamp. Here, the windows were deep wells that narrowed to panes of glass. An archer could have stood in the well, before the glass had been installed, aiming at advancing hordes. But it was the carved stone in between the windows that caused her stunned admiration.

Mountjoy cleared his throat. "My apologies if you are offended."

"I'm not offended." She stifled the urge to giggle. "What a marvelous sense of humor the stonemasons must have had."

"They're lewd, Wellstone, not comic."

"A fine line, sir. Very fine." She took a step closer. "Marvelously fine."

"In that case, I'll give you a key so that you may take sketches at your leisure." She could hear the smile in his voice. "For Professor Farnsworth, you understand."

"Yes, thank you." She looked at him from over her shoulder and returned his grin. "I think you'll find him very grateful."

His gaze traveled slowly from her head to her toes. "I hope so, Wellstone."

She went to stand beside him at one of the windows. "The view from here must be breathtaking during the day."

"It is."

She examined the room, aware that Mountjoy was watching her. The ceiling, too, was covered with stone figures and yes, some of the figures were engaged in sexual acts. "This is astonishing," she said. She turned in a circle, slowly, taking in as much detail as she could.

"I hoped you might appreciate it."

Absurdly touched that he'd thought to bring her here, to a room that was so plainly a private retreat, she could barely speak. There were Turkish carpets on the floor and blankets piled on a chest against the wall because with no fireplace the air here would certainly never be very warm. There was one chair that looked quite comfortable to sit on, and beside that a table with several books and near that a chaise that couldn't be more than a few years old. On the table beside the door were a decanter, a humidor, a flint, glasses, and several bottles.

"Thank you," she whispered.

"I don't allow anyone in here but a few trusted servants."

Lily put a hand on his arm. "I'm honored you've shown me. It needn't go in the professor's book, you know. It's enough that I've seen this."

He gave her a sheepish grin. "I was quite a young man when I came to Bitterward. You can suppose the effect this room had on someone of my tender years. I kept it secret from Nigel and Eugenia. They were far too young to see . . ." He gestured at a vaguely bearlike creature in congress with a centaur.

"I understand completely."

"Before I knew it, this room was the only place where I could escape my fate."

"Sanctuary." She tilted her head, her hand still touching his arm. "I have a similar retreat at Syton House. Without the stonework, alas. I am green with envy that you have monsters and gargoyles."

"By all means study them."

"I will." She turned to the wall and drank in the cavorting beasts and monsters.

From behind her, Mountjoy said, "I remember the day the attorney came to Haltwhistle, that's where Eugenia, Nigel, and I were living at the time, with our mother's sister. He sat at the best table in the only parlor we had and showed me the family lines that led to me. I made him go over and over it, and each time, he ended up at our branch of the Hamptons. With me." He let out a breath. "He'd been researching five years, he said, on behalf of the dukedom. Following the branches. They'd somehow lost track of my father's branch for a while. I suppose in those earlier days they thought us too remote. The attorney, it happens, had set out to prove the line was extinguished. Instead, he found me. Each time we went over what he claimed was incontrovertible proof, I thought sure he'd find he'd made a mistake, that if anyone was to be the next Mountjoy, it would not be me."

She turned just enough to see him. "Yet, here you are."

The duke shrugged. "There was no time to air out the country smell or knock the dirt from my boots." Lily went still when he came to stand behind her. She found it difficult to concentrate on anything but him. Why, oh why, had he been so kind as to show her a room like this? He would break her heart. He truly would. "I went from Haltwhistle to the house in London, then Bitterward and a seat in the Lords with hardly a breath in between."

"Who doesn't dream of one day discovering one is secretly royalty?" To her left stone animals cavorted above and between the windows; a stag, a bear, a boar, and even a swan. She could make out the broken chain that identified the creature as representing the Hampton family sigil that had found its way into the Mountjoy coat of arms, with the later addition of the ducal coronet.

He leaned a shoulder against the wall where there was a smooth space between the window-well and the carved stone forest. His mouth twitched. She did so like the way he looked when he was trying not to smile. "I never did. Never once."

"Well, I can assure you I grew up convinced I was a princess."

"You would."

Lily's stomach did a flip. They stood so close. So close. "Hidden away for safety while my father bravely and in secret fought against our country's enemies. I was to have married a prince and taken my place on the throne of my beloved subjects."

"Where you would prove yourself a fair and benevolent ruler."

"Precisely. Alas, no one ever came to the house with papers to prove my true identity. My father is my true father. Not that I'd want any other. I love him. Despite everything."

"I've not met the man, but I'll own I do not care for what I've heard." He frowned. "He neglected you when you were a girl. He abuses your generosity now that you are a woman. Was there no one besides you and your father in the house? A governess to see to your education?"

She tipped her head to one side. "Our housekeeper taught me to read and do figures. To sew and knit, too, and how to cut fabric. She was a genius with scissors and a needle."

"And she taught you to run a household."

Her urge to touch him rose up again, threatening to overwhelm her. "Skills that have stood me in good stead all these many years, I must say."

"Could your father not spare twenty pounds to educate you?"

"Why would he, when I was so wicked that my education would surely have been a waste?"

He backed up a step to allow her to advance along the wall and continue her study. "Because he was your father. Did he never sing to you or read you stories?"

"Others are not as lucky in their families as you were."

"I'm no prince, but I was indeed fortunate in my parents."

"There's still hope that someone will inform me that I am a princess and much beloved by my subjects who long to have me back in my rightful place as a gentle and benevolent ruler."

He grinned. "You'll tell me the moment that happens, won't you?"

"Oh, certainly."

Mountjoy put a hand on a smooth bit of the wall by the window. "I was fortunate in my aunt and uncle, too, that they took in a family of orphans. We might have been split up, you know, Eugenia, Nigel, and I." He smiled, but his eyes stayed serious. She did not speak into the silence. The quiet went on too long. With his other hand, he touched a rabbit carved at his eye level. "My good fortune persists, Lily, for you came here. To Bitterward."

"You flatter me, your grace."

"Flattery?" He drew a finger along the stone back of a gargoyle having sexual relations with a nymph, and she, God help her, watched the slow movement of his finger. "Have you any notion, Lily, of the effect you have on men?"

"Some. I'm not a fool about that."

"You walk into a room, and no one can think of anyone but you. Where before there was tedium, now there is life. We all want that warmth and joy for ourselves."

"We?"

"Dr. Longfield. My brother. Every man to cross your path."

"You?" she asked.

His eyes pierced her through. "Beautiful. Elegant. Never wearing anything that isn't the height of fashion and exquisitely made."

"I spent too many years deprived of elegant attire, forbidden anything pretty." She licked her lower lip. "Now that I am free of that, I refuse to live my life without fashion or beauty. When I'm old and wrinkled and breathing my last, I won't be sorry for having lived a life with beauty in it."

"Your damned father. You shouldn't go back to him."

"I must. You know that. Besides, if I were to stay here, you'd soon reach a point where you wished me gone. Best to leave while your hosts still like you, that's what I've always felt." She breached the space between them to touch his cravat. "You could do with a little of my conceit. Don't deny you aren't aware of *your* appeal."

"Tonight," he said, "I deny nothing." He stepped forward and put his hands on her shoulders. His thumbs brushed along her collarbones. "Not you. And not me."

The world vanished from beneath her feet.

Chapter Sixteen

IN THE BACK OF HIS MIND, MOUNTJOY KNEW HE STILL had a chance to stop this from happening. He could step away from her and turn the conversation to her plans for treasure hunting or to bloody architecture. Lily, being the intelligent creature that she was, would know he'd lost his nerve.

To be honest, though, whatever guilt he might feel over involving himself with a woman besides the one he was supposed to marry, he could tuck away very far from this particular moment. He stayed where he was, his hands on her shoulders and his thumbs sweeping over her soft skin. Her eyes stayed on his face, and he could see she was deciding what she would allow to happen.

There was no telling what she would decide about the two of them.

Without letting go of her he said, "I dreamed about you last night."

"I'm not responsible for your dreams."

"No, but that damned medallion of yours might be." He

reached out and touched the metal. "What if that Gypsy's magic works and that's why I can't get you out of my head or my dreams?"

She burst out laughing. "Oh, it doesn't, and well you know it."

"Are you certain?" He dropped the medallion and moved closer. She retreated, but that put the wall at her back.

"Very," she said. "There's no such thing as magic."

Their eyes locked, and he smiled because of the challenge there. Beyond anything, he wanted her in his arms. "Last night," he said, "my dreams were filled with you."

"Proper dreams, I hope."

"Not very."

"How odd, your grace. For I dreamed of you last night."

"Was yours a proper dream?"

She lifted her chin. "You kissed me."

"On the cheek, I presume?" He held her gaze. He wanted to be sure he would leave this room having stripped them both naked and left no passion unexplored between them. The uncertainty of gaining what he wanted aroused him. She was so maddeningly forthright and in control of herself. She might well tell him no.

"No, your grace. That was not where you kissed me."

"Perhaps it was your forehead I kissed. I might have done that."

She put her hands behind her back and shook her head. "Not there either."

He arched his eyebrows. "Your hand?"

"No."

"I confess myself baffled." He moved close enough to draw a finger along the top of her shoulder. "Such warm skin, Lily. Soft beneath my touch." He continued stroking her. Caressing her. He trailed the backs of his fingers along her collarbone. "Yours is skin a farmer or a duke would enjoy beneath his own."

She pushed away from the wall and walked past him to the table. She turned with a motion that sent the fabric of her skirts snapping. Her eyes swept over him from head to toe. "I do believe you are being deliberately wicked, your grace."

"Do you object?" He walked to her, and he took her in his arms and turned so they ended with him backed up to the table and her with a hand on his chest.

"Wickedness does not become you."

"I think it does," he said. "But in any event, I cannot help my dreams." He resisted the urge to pull her into his arms. Lord, but she was astonishingly pretty. "Or what you do in them. And you have done things in my dreams, Wellstone. Such things."

"Infamous, your grace, that you lay the fault at my feet."

He gripped the edge of the table on either side of his legs. He was mad. Mad to be pursuing this. He could not imagine doing anything but this. "In your dream, where did I kiss you?"

A grin flashed over her face. "Where else but in the library?"

He'd brought her here, where they would not be interrupted, and if it was not a bedroom, that hardly mattered. They were alone. He leaned forward, still holding on to the edge of the table. He was very much aware that he was responsible for what was happening between them. He wanted to fuck her, and she knew it and had come here with him. "That's not where I kissed you in *my* dream. Shall I show you?"

She touched a finger to his chin. "Let me guess."

Once, he thought. Once with her would be enough, though if this alluring, fascinating woman wasn't averse to an affair, well, then. His life would become much more interesting for as long as they lasted. "Try."

"Only if it would please you, your grace."

"I'll tell you if you don't."

She took a step closer and went up on her toes. His stomach bottomed out. He saw her lips part just as his eyes closed. She put her hand to his cheek and slid the cool tips of her fingers across his skin. She kissed his chin and drew back.

He stayed just where he was, leaning slightly forward. He opened his eyes. "How disappointing."

"In what way?"

"That's not where you kissed me."

Her eyes glinted with humor. "I'm sure it's where I meant to kiss you."

They weren't far apart. He leaned forward another inch or two and brushed his mouth over hers. She went still. Only for a moment, but enough that his heart gave a lurch. Then her palm cupped the side of his face, and she kissed him, and he let her. He invited her to kiss him, and she closed the distance between them until she stood between his spread thighs, and her torso pressed against his.

He leaned into the kiss and opened his mouth over hers, and she did reciprocate. Her hands moved to the back of his neck and her fingers pulled his head to hers. Lily Wellstone kissed the way she lived. Boldly. According to her taste. With conviction. Never married, and she kissed like this? Like a courtesan.

For all that she was bold and taking exactly what she wanted, she wasn't a courtesan or his mistress. He knew better than this and didn't give a damn.

His hands disengaged from the table, and he was holding her tight against him. Bringing her closer, closer. Jesus, not close enough. The hell with holding anything back. No man in his right mind would hold back with her.

She made a small sound in the back of her throat, and his tongue was in her mouth, and hers met his, touched, swept away, and her hands cupped his face as if he were precious to her, when, how could he be?

She did not break the kiss but gentled it. So tender, and he was content with that, too. Part of his mind was engaged with imagining her naked and accepting the pleasure her body afforded. They'd burn to ashes, the two of them, if things progressed to that.

At last, she drew away. Her hands stayed around his shoulders. He left his arms around her waist. "*Mmm*," she said, low and throaty. Gratified. She ran her fingertips underneath his eyes, along the line of his cheek, his nose and jaw. And his mouth. "I suppose your other lovers tell you how much they adore kissing you."

Other lovers. He wanted that to mean she now considered herself a member of that cadre. "Not in so many words."

She smiled. "Well, you're a lovely, lovely man, and I adore kissing you."

"But not enough to make you lose your head?"

"Or you yours," she said.

"It was a near thing, I promise." He lowered his head to hers, his lips hovering above hers. "Perhaps we ought to try again. See if we can discover where we went wrong."

"Perhaps we should." She drew away, but he closed his thighs, trapping her gently between his legs. She could move away if she wished. "I wanted to kiss you tonight, and now I have."

"And?"

Her eyes lost their glitter of humor, but he didn't dare ask her what made that vanish. Not yet. "And," she said, "I quite enjoyed it. Did you?"

"You know the answer to that." He brought her close. The smile that curved her mouth made him mad to know what she was thinking, what she intended. Had she decided what would happen here? Between the two of them?

"I don't think I do."

They ended up looking at each other, and Mountjoy didn't know what to do or say in response. So he kissed her again, and she melted against him and damn him to Hell if he wasn't even more aroused. He took the lead this time and, yes, her kisses drove him mad. Wonderfully mad.

When they broke apart again, his brain must have been addled because he heard himself say, "Have you been to bed with a man before?"

That pert smile of hers danced on her mouth. "Have you been to bed with a woman?"

He stared at her lips and then looked into her eyes. She

was a passionate woman, but unmarried, and whatever else had happened between them, she might not be as experienced as he'd assumed. "Several times. Have you? Been to bed with a man?"

"Of course."

"Your soldier."

"Does that bother you?"

He brought her closer. "That you've been with a man before? Not at all." A half-truth. He was jealous of her previous lover, of the way he'd captured her heart. "But if this was to be your first time, I'd be more careful. That's the only reason I asked."

"How thoughtful." She leaned closer. "If this were your first time, I promise I would have been gentle with you."

She never failed to amuse him at the most unexpected times. "Thank God I'm no virgin."

"I should say so."

He touched the medallion around her neck. "In my dream," he said, "you wore this." He smoothed a finger over the scrollwork etched in the metal. "Strange that I recall that detail so vividly."

"You have a labyrinth of a brain, sir."

"I parted ways with my mistress before I came here from London."

"Why?"

He shrugged. "No reason other than she no longer interested me, and I had a friend who was enamored of her. As well let her move on to a lover inclined to be more generous than I was."

"Are you stingy with your lovers?" Her smile knew too much, but then Lily was unique among the ladies he knew. "That surprises me."

He traced the line of her lower lip with his finger. "I am generous. But not as generous as a new lover is apt to be."

"Did you enjoy making love to her?" Her voice was languid, warm silk, inviting, appreciative, and underneath a taste of need that resonated in her words, her half-shuttered gaze, the curve of her body against his. He brought his hands to the side of her throat and slid them down, fingers spread over her skin, along the curve of her bosom. She tipped her head back, and he wanted to bask in his reaction to her. He understood the mystery that was Lily, knew the contradiction between the sweetness of her face and the sharp wit behind it.

"I did. But then as you know, I am a man of country appetites." He dropped a kiss at the corner of her mouth. He kissed her again, and she melted against him. She responded with a soft moan and a step forward that brought her torso even closer against his. His hands wandered down her corseted back to the softness of that dip of her spine just before the swell of her bottom. The contact turned raw and needy, and he was halfway to climax already. The tingle of arousal centered in his nether parts, and he wanted that climax, the sweetness of completion in a woman's body.

Lord, but this was the kind of kiss that led to naked bodies. He drew back, but kept his arms around her and only enough to say, "How far. How far are you willing to let this go? More than just a kiss? More than your mouth on me or mine on you?"

Her eyes fluttered down, lashes dark against the pale skin of her cheek. "Two kisses, I think." She looked at him through her lashes. "Someplace convenient."

"Two kisses seems a paltry number on which to decide." He tightened his arms around her. "There ought to be a third, don't you agree?"

"There ought to be a sufficient sample."

"Four?"

"Four seems excessive to me."

"Wellstone." He trailed his thumbs along the inner curve of her breasts then pushed his fingers into her hair. A few pins came loose and he picked them out and kept going until her hair fell around her shoulders in golden waves, and it was wicked, seeing her with her hair down. Forbidden. As if she'd stepped from her boudoir. And not one word of protest passed her lips. "I'll take whatever you offer me."

He waited while she drew in a breath and slowly let it out. He stood straight, moving them away from the table but still holding her head between his hands.

"Tell me what you want, your grace. Is it only a few kisses? Or is there more?"

"I want to see you in your bare skin. Lily. Will you do that for me? Every inch of you nude for my eyes to devour?"

Chapter Seventeen

>≈<

WOULD SHE? LILY COULD SCARCELY THINK, SO DRUGGED was she from his kisses and the wicked promise of his voice. Lord, what wouldn't she do for him? His request was outrageous. Brazen. If she were a proper sort of woman, she'd swoon with outrage. If she were a proper sort of woman, she wouldn't be here with him. Alone.

She couldn't imagine telling him no, even though she ought to.

There was no pretense between them in respect of physical desires, and that was at once frightening and exhilarating. She had been on her own, directing her own life for long enough to have gotten used to that. Tonight, he would be the perfect lover, if things went that far, this man who made her heart race for the first time since she'd lost Greer.

"Lily?" His thumbs brushed over her cheeks. His hands stayed in her hair, holding her in place, and all Lily could think was that this beautiful and fierce man wanted her. He wasn't after her fortune, which other men certainly had been. He didn't *want* her in any way but the carnal sense, and that meant he wanted her. Only her. Only for what she was right now. He wanted nothing of her besides greedy pleasure. Best yet, he was indulging her love of words and play, a patient man. Thoughtful.

Lily leaned toward him. The sight of him, the scent of him, the warmth of his hands on her made her imagine the moment when he would push inside her body, and just that made her shiver with longing. He must know how much she wanted him.

"You are the most unusual creature I've ever met," he said. "What the devil *are* you thinking?"

She could let this happen and if afterward the situation became uncomfortable or went badly, she could retreat to her solitude at Syton House, and she would be safe. No one would know she'd been wicked because Mountjoy would never tell a soul.

"I am thinking," she said slowly, "how improper it would be for me to remove my clothes."

"Very." His mouth twitched.

"A gentleman would not ask it of me."

He took her medallion between the fingers of one hand and rubbed the surface. "I am aware."

She put a finger to his lips to still his smile then put that same finger across hers. She studied him. "If I agree, your grace, I have a requirement."

"Oh?"

"Just one."

"I'm a generous man." His smile was an invitation to sin, but she could see caution flickering around the edges of his mouth. He was a duke, after all, and women must surely have schemed with demands of him before. "Within reason."

She managed to hold off a smile. She wanted him to suffer. He deserved it before she ceded the very last bit of power she had over him. "That's a pity because I think you'll find my request unreasonable."

"Then why make it?" That was frank curiosity on his part.

"Because it is the one requirement I have before I give up everything." She took a step back, and he released her.

"Put me out of my misery, Lily, and tell me what you want from me so that we either proceed or go our separate ways."

"It's a simple thing."

"You say."

"It is. I promise." He arched his eyebrows at her. "Allow me to take your wardrobe in hand."

He gaped at her, and she reached with her free hand and tapped the underside of his chin. A laugh burst from him, and he let go of her hand to rake his fingers through his hair. "My wardrobe?"

"Give me an hour with your tailor, two if he is a stupid man, and I can manage your clothes no matter where I am. From Syton House if need be." She drew off a glove, slowly. He watched. She dangled it from one hand. "I make your wardrobe a condition because I don't know how much longer I can stand to see you dressed as if you don't care a fig what you look like."

"I don't."

She sighed. "Such a disappointment, your grace." She looked at her glove. "Should I put this back on?"

"Witch," he said. "Temptress."

"Lord, I hope so." She crossed her arms beneath her bosom and tapped her toe on the carpet. "One's appearance matters. One ought to take pride in looking well. You are a duke. You ought to dress as if you believe it of yourself." She fingered the bottom hem of his coat. "Look at this. It's only a decent fit. And your shirts ought to be made of a finer material." She took another step back and worked her fingers free of her other glove. "I'm not suggesting anything but that you ought to care how you look. It affects Ginny and your brother, you know."

Mountjoy snorted. "They're more affected by the fact that I can afford to pay their debts and expenses and put a better than decent roof over all our heads."

"No one disputes that. Not for a moment. But, your grace, you are such a lovely man. I'm not suggesting you set fashion, though I think with my assistance you would. I am suggesting that you wear colors that flatter you and clothes that fit your magnificent body. Clothes that make others think, here is a man worth knowing." She touched his cheek. "Because it's true. Not to mention, you might have more success with Miss Jane Kirk if you dressed the part of a duke."

For some time he regarded her with a solemn expression, and she really had no idea what he was thinking. She thought of all the colors she could put him in that would accentuate his green eyes and take advantage of the drama of all that thick, dark hair.

"If I accede to this requirement of yours, I want you to take off every stitch you have on right now." Lily looked him up and down, and Mountjoy waited while she did that.

"Everything, you say?"

"Yes." Mountjoy walked over to the side table and filled a glass with two fingers from one of the decanters there. "I have a decent Madeira. Port, as well, if you'd like something to drink."

"No, thank you." Stubborn, stubborn man.

He walked back to her but stopped halfway to tug on his coat and take a sip from his glass. "What's wrong with my coat?"

"The pattern is unimaginative, it doesn't suit a man of your size and form, and the cloth is inferior wool." She waved a hand at him. "The color, my God, what am I to call that color? Mud? Ditchwater? You're fortunate you're handsome."

"You are aggravating in the extreme." He took a drink. "Has anyone told you that before?"

"Many times."

He walked toward her until he stood an arm's length away, this time with the cut-glass tumbler in one hand. His eyes scoured her. "My wardrobe?" he said in a low, silky voice. "Is that really all you ask?"

"You told me what you wanted," she said. "I told you what would convince me to agree to such an outrageous and improper request as yours."

"Every stitch, Lily?"

"I think you made yourself plain."

His expression turned so subtly wicked she could have sworn the room got warmer just from the effect. "That's not all I want."

"It's no concern of mine if you failed to clearly convey your request."

"I want to touch you. And, forgive me if I use a country term, *cover you.*"

She adored his willingness to draw out their wordplay. "I believe *fornicate* is the more accurate term."

"I suppose it is." He took another drink, but not in time to hide the twitch of his mouth. "So?"

"You know my terms." She shook her hair behind her shoulders.

His gaze lingered on her mouth before dropping to her bosom. "Done. I put myself into your hands."

Her stomach dropped. Too late now to back out. She'd made her pact with the devil.

He set his drink on the table. "Lily," he said very softly. So softly she could barely hear him.

"Yes?"

His gaze raked her up and down. "I've agreed to everything you asked of me."

"So you have, your grace."

She turned her back to him. She could not see out any of the narrow windows, just bits of faint reflections in the glass. Mountjoy came close enough to work the fastenings down the back of her bodice. His fingers brushed her skin from time to time. Or lingered there, on her back. She managed the tapes herself when the time came. Her petticoat rustled to the floor. She caught her gown when it was loose enough for her to step free of it, though she didn't. She turned and found Mountjoy's attention on her, gaze traveling over her.

One must do the outrageous with style. With élan. With complete conviction.

Lily dropped her gown. It caught on her hips, and she reached down to push the fabric free. She turned her back to him again. "Unlace my corset?"

"Of course." His fingers nimbly worked the lace, and when it was loose enough, he drew it over her head. He stepped away. She wore just her chemise now, and her slippers and stockings. "Turn around, Lily."

She did, and watched him watch her. He stood with his eyes half closed, one loosely fisted hand held to his lips. He lowered his hand enough for her to see his mouth.

She unfastened her garters, one then the other, and shed her stockings and now she stood before him in her chemise.

"Go on," he said.

Lily threw herself over the brink. She drew off the chemise, and when the linen came over her head, the room fell utterly silent. She kept her eyes open because she was no coward. Not that it mattered. Mountjoy wasn't looking at her face.

Lily stood in the froth of her gown and petticoats around her calves, holding her chemise in one hand. Cool air washed over her skin. She was aroused and abashed at the same time, and yet there was also a shiver of anticipation. She was exactly as she was meant to be.

The duke reached behind him for his tumbler and drank half the contents. Glass in hand, he walked toward her. "Stay just as you are," he said. He paced a circle around her. Slowly. When she could see him again, he returned his drink to the table behind him. "Simply ravishing."

"Thank you." She knew, of course, that she was not unattractive and that her figure was one men admired, but she knew nothing of how her body compared with any other woman's when a man experienced in sin was thinking of indulging in more.

He held out his hand, and after a moment's hesitation she put her bare palm on his. With his assistance, she stepped over her clothes and found that without her shoes she had to tilt her chin to look at him. He made no move to touch her beyond the contact of their hands; he just continued to inspect her. "So very lovely," he whispered. "I could look at you all night."

"Is that all?"

With his other hand, he cupped the back of her head, fingers spread out on her skull, tipping her head to his. "I told you what else I wanted." She adored the gruffness of his voice. "Tell me what will convince you to agree to that. Diamonds for your fingers? Sapphires around the column of your throat? Ropes of pearls? I assure you, my taste in jewelry is exemplary."

"I don't need any of that."

"What do you need?"

She met his gaze. "To know you want me."

"Do you doubt it?" His voice roughened, and she found herself pulled against him, her bare skin against his torso. "Christ, how can you doubt it?"

"Easily enough, as here I stand without any finery to hide my flaws. You want sex, but do you want me?"

"What flaws? It's you I want. Lily Wellstone. No one else will do for me and therefore, if there are flaws, I want those, too." The fingers of one hand glided down her shoulders, along her spine, and to the small of her back and lower. "Your skin is unconscionably soft, and that, my dear Wellstone, is no flaw."

"Thank you."

"Are we too near the windows? I don't want you to be cold."

"I'm not."

"Good. That's very good." Both his hands slicked up her body. He picked her up and carried her to the chaise longue, and the very first thing he did after he'd laid her down was say, "Shall we see how convincing I can be?"

Chapter Eighteen

HE WAS MAD TO BE DOING THIS. UTTERLY MAD. JUST now, he'd not trade madness for sanity, not for the world. She was nude, and he had never in his life wanted a woman as much as he wanted Lily right now.

So here he was, sitting beside her on the chaise, and she was in her bare skin. The little witch had seduced him with that pert smile of hers and her quick wit and by shocking him out of his usual dour habits and left him with nothing but need. She'd beguiled him and aroused him, and now at this moment, if she were to ask him for carte blanche in return for allowing him to touch her, he might actually agree, he was that far gone with lust.

Because, good God, Lily Wellstone had the face of an angel, the body of a goddess, and the spirit of the devil glinting from her eyes. She was a woman worth losing his soul for. Mountjoy thought he'd never in his life seen a more erotic sight than her stretched out naked the way she was. The chaise longue was dark blue, and her skin was smooth and alabaster white against the fabric. Her Gypsy medallion glittered gold against the upper part of her stomach, not far below her breasts, and her hair spread out in golden waves.

"What a lovely body you have," he said. She was not familiar to him like this, her lush curves bared to his examination, her eyes soft on him, her will, at the moment, in abeyance. Patient. Waiting for him. No matter her boldness and passion, she was not, he thought, as experienced as lovers he'd taken in the past, though he did not doubt for a moment that she knew what she wanted. "I've wondered what you would look like. Dreamed about that."

He took his time studying her, his Venus. Her smile widened while he did, but there was a reserve to her expression that puzzled him. He lifted a hand along the line of her leg, but did not touch her. Not yet. Anticipation was almost enough. The thought of having even a moment of mastery over her, fleeting though any such moment might be, was unbearably luscious.

"You've seen me almost every day since I came here." She shifted a little, stretching, not in the least shy. And yet, there was a center of quiet in her that made him think she was not as sanguine as she appeared.

"True," he said. "I have. But not like are you now." Lily was a frustrating delight to be around. She challenged everything he believed about himself, and more than once through her reactions to him or through his reactions to her, there was reflected back to him a man he barely recognized as Mountjoy. A stranger whom he thought he might actually like. "I do like a woman with long legs," he said. "Most of your height is in your legs."

"Then I am fortunate, your grace," she said.

He cocked his head, tracing with his eyes the curve of her breasts, the slope of her waist. "I've always preferred brunettes. And women who do not look as if I'd break them. And here you are, with your golden hair." He touched one of her curls. "And your slender figure and a face that makes me think you must be protected from the world, let alone from me, and I cannot imagine any woman I want more than you."

"Good fortune rains upon me."

"You're no delicate flower to be cosseted and pampered."

She tipped her head. "Not even a little?"

He touched her hip, curved his fingers around the outside of her there, and the room got smaller. The world held just the two of them, with hardly room for his desire. "You'd be bored in a week if I did, Lily."

"All the same, a little pampering would not go amiss."

He was aware that there was more to the pitch of his arousal than *what* she was, which right now was stark-naked and gazing at him from half-lidded eyes. This was Lily, a confident, curiously independent woman who fascinated him, challenged him, and wasn't ashamed to admit her passions. There was also, quite undeniably, the lure of the forbidden. He really shouldn't. They shouldn't. But he was far beyond denying himself anything Lily would consent to do with him.

She adjusted herself on the chaise longue, on her back, with one knee raised, an arm underneath her head, and all her beautiful curls spilling onto the fabric beneath her. Mountjoy wondered for a moment if he would last long enough to get inside her, if she agreed to that. She might not, though he was determined to convince her.

He knelt on the floor beside her and put one hand on the far side of the chaise, near her rib cage. He lowered his head to her belly but kept his eyes on her face. A man didn't need a title to be a good lover. Even before he was Mountjoy, he'd learned how not to be a fumbling boor when he took a woman to bed. "What would you say if I asked permission to kiss you here?"

"I would ask you why you'd want to do such a thing."

"To see if your skin is as soft as it looks." He bent closer. "Why else would I want to do such a thing to a beautiful woman?"

"I admit I'm curious to know the answer."

"Allow me to discover for us both." He kissed her right below the spot where her medallion lay. The scent of violets was sweet near her skin, and he kissed his way upward until he reached her breasts. She'd denied she was cold, but her skin rippled with a chill and was cool to touch.

"Liar," he whispered.

Her hand fluttered onto his shoulder. "Your grace, I protest." Her dark eyes were mischievous. "I almost never lie."

"But you are cold." He dipped his head to her stomach, and in a moment of pure whimsy, kissed her Gypsy medallion, too. She arched toward him, and he worked his way to her navel, dipping his tongue in and out of the indentation.

"I'm feeling much warmer now."

"Your skin is indeed very soft." He moved back up and hovered over her breasts. "But what about here? Are you sensitive here? If I kissed you here, would that give you pleasure?"

"I confess I wonder that myself."

"Allow me, then, to help us discover the answer."

"In a spirit of inquiry, I think you ought."

Her breast fit his cupped hand, and, oh, so pretty. As lovely as the rest of her. He flicked his tongue over her nipple, and she made a soft noise of appreciation. He closed his mouth over her while he cupped the outer curve of her breast. Lord, but she was soft, and the way she filled the curve of his palm was going to drive him mad. Her nipple tightened in his mouth, and that aroused him even more.

He did the same to her other breast, then kissed his way down again, and though he'd thought about pressing kisses along her legs, what he did was part her thighs and set himself to the task of finding out what would fetch her. What touch did she prefer? Did she like to have her breasts stroked, held, or gently pinched? What other parts of her body intensified her physical reactions?

He gave no quarter because after what she'd done to him she didn't deserve any. At one point, he replaced his mouth with his fingers and watched her face, and that was that for him. Her lips were parted, her eyes looking inward, the middle of her back arched off the chaise, and then he found the rhythm she needed, and he stopped long enough to earn him a fiery look.

"Rogue," she said. "Horrible man."

"I've been called worse." But he did himself and her the courtesy of finishing her with his mouth. Her hands clutched his head, and after just a moment longer, there, she shuddered and cried out.

She held nothing back. His name broke from her as she broke, and the sight, her reaction and his, was everything he'd imagined and more. While she came down from her orgasm he kissed the inside of her thighs, one then the other, and drew his fingers along the length of her outside leg.

Her eyes fluttered open. "Oh, my," she said in a low voice. "You are a very talented man."

Next to her, Mountjoy turned onto his side, half sitting to unfasten his breeches and free his stone-hard cock from his clothes, and she held out her arms to him and like that, in a smooth transition he was over her body, sliding himself inside her.

Oh God. Inside her. Warm and soft, and it was like he'd never been with a woman before, as if this were his first time and had no idea what to expect. He lost his ability to speak from the very first thrust into her, and she moaned long and deep and wrapped her legs around his hips and her arms around his shoulders.

He could barely open his eyes or focus when he did; all he could do was try to keep up with the sensation. God help him, this was Lily at last, warm and soft beneath him, hot and slick around him, her breath on his skin. Her arms holding him close, her body moving with his, meeting him. Matching him. Her fingers pressed into him, urging him deeper.

After they'd let the wonder settle between them, she worked the buttons of his coat, and he paused long enough to shrug it off, because if that's what she wanted, he wasn't going to deny her, and then he went back to fucking her. Her hands stayed busy removing his cravat then opening his waistcoat, and he had to stop again to remove that hindrance to her pleasure, and then pull out of her long enough to shrug off his braces and pull his shirt over his head. Where the hell that landed he didn't know and didn't care.

"I want to see you," she said. She sat up and ran her palms over his chest, along his shoulders, and down his spine to the curve of his behind.

"Later."

"Now." She grabbed his head with both hands. "You beautiful man, I want to see you. And feel your skin against mine."

Maybe the delay to remove the rest of his clothes wasn't so bad, because he'd been very close to climax, and not nearly ready to be done. He pulled off his boots and stockings and when he stood to shuck his breeches and small-clothes, she leaned on one elbow and gave him a look that melted him. He put his hands on his hips and gazed at her.

"Come here, your grace," she said after she'd thoroughly examined him. She held out a hand. "I'll catch my death otherwise."

"We can't have that." He rejoined her on the chaise, and she was right. They were skin to skin now, and her body was warm against his, her breasts soft against his chest, and he kissed her until she pushed him back, palms on his chest, until he was on his back.

She stroked him, trailed her fingers down his chest and to his belly, and he couldn't take his eyes off her. "I knew you would be lovely to look at." She drew in a breath. "But I didn't know I'd want to lick you from head to toe."

"Deny yourself nothing." He pushed his fingers into her hair.

She laughed and bent to kiss his chest, and when her tongue flicked over his nipple he groaned. The entire time she was doing this, pressing kisses on his body, her hand wandered toward his belly, along his thigh, and, Christ, yes, to his cock. He held his breath, hoping for her mouth, though her hand around him, then on his sac was enough to make him hiss with pleasure.

She looked up at him, and said, "Am I too wicked, your grace?"

"My love, if I may be honest—"

"Please."

"You're not wicked enough."

Her eyes widened, and slowly, she smiled. "Tell me what would be wicked enough. Better yet, show me."

His fingers tightened in her hair and he gently pushed her in the direction of his sex. "Use your mouth on my prick. The way you did before."

And she did. He about went out of his mind. Her tongue traced the length of him, then followed the head of his cock, moved down to his bollocks, and she'd have kept going until he came in her mouth if he hadn't stopped her.

"Why?" she asked.

"I don't want to come yet."

Her fingers remained lightly wrapped around him. "I adore your cock. He's lovely and awe-inspiring."

Mountjoy laughed. "Do go on."

"He tastes delicious, and I love the sound you make when I kiss him."

He took her upper arms and pulled her up until she lay on him. "Sit," he said. She ended up straddling his belly. "Like so. I want to look at you some more."

"I'd rather kiss your cock, your grace."

"Madam," he said. Lord, she was an unmarried woman, not a widow or a courtesan. But she was no innocent, either. "Another time you'll take me to completion that way again, but not tonight."

She gave him another melting look. "Do you promise?"

"I do." He covered her breasts and levered himself up enough to kiss the tips and run his hands along her stomach, all that soft, smooth skin under his fingertips. He put her under him again and while he entered her, slowly this time, as every moment passed he wondered why he didn't feel that he was at all mastering her. The more he tried to think about fucking, the more images of her flashed through his head. The way she smiled, her in the breakfast room making Eugenia laugh. In the library, facing him with that insouciant smile of hers.

Eventually, he pushed up on his hands and watched her, watched their bodies. Her face, the depths of her eyes. The sound of their breathing, the slide of him inside her. Her legs wrapped around him, her hips moving against his, and this was heaven for him for quite some time.

He withdrew again and, with no words between them, he turned her over and, a firm grip on her hips, came into her from behind. He had the idea that he had surprised her, but she adjusted. Her round bottom pressed against his groin and for a time he was content to take in the curve of her hips to her waist, and glide the flat of his hand along her spine. Then he started to move in her again, and the quiver of his sexual completion stayed just enough out of reach that he was confident of lasting awhile longer, and yet close enough, intense enough, that he wanted to find out sooner than later just how high that peak would be.

They ended up on the floor, her torso and arms on the chaise, him still behind her until his orgasm was too close. She understood the urgency, and he had her on her back again with her gorgeous legs around his waist, and he drove hard, and she met him, thrust for thrust.

His body raced toward a pleasure that seemed just out of reach, but he couldn't be so selfish as to not bring her again when he knew she was close, too. He reached between them and stroked her, once, again, and she shattered again. Her arms tightened around him and she said in a low, fierce voice, "Harder."

He obliged her. Of course he did. He could deny her nothing. It seemed a miracle to him that he was able to withdraw in time, and even so, even not finishing inside her, his climax roared through him, and she wasn't squeamish about the result, but rather took him in hand and in that moment, he ceased to exist.

When he had his wits and his breath back, he said, "Next time, I will procure a *baudruche*."

To which she replied, "What is that?"

"A sheath. To cover me. So that when next we do this, I can finish inside you." And then he remembered that he'd just fucked his sister's best friend within an inch of both their lives. And promised to do so again soon.

He didn't feel at all guilty.

Chapter Nineteen

LILY THOUGHT IT A MIRACLE THAT SHE WAS OUT OF
bed and outdoors two monstrous hours before noon. Had
someone told her she'd ever be out of bed before one in the
afternoon, she'd have laughed herself silly.

Yet here she was at not even half past ten, standing mid-
way between the back of the house and the stables. She wore
a cotton muslin walking dress two shades darker than her
eyes, the better to hide the dirt that would inevitably stain
her hem whilst she tromped about in the fields. Her dark
gold spencer was trimmed with gold braid and epaulettes,
and there was a gold silk bow tied beneath her bosom.

After some internal debate, she'd elected not to wear the
turban that went with the gown, but, rather, a toffee-colored
top hat with an egret plume. The turban would have been
more adventurous but she hadn't the heart to forgo the match
of the top hat that, with its gold trim, was a twin to the braid
on her spencer. Her walking coat she left open because it
was warm. Who would have guessed a spring morning would
be anything but cool? Not that it mattered. It would have

been a pity to hide her frock when everything coordinated so wonderfully. Her sole reservation was that she had on her second-best boots, but since that was her only concession to the reality of mud, all in all, she had achieved the perfect ensemble for a morning to be spent searching for Roman treasure.

They were taking two dogcarts to the location Lily and Ginny had ranked first on their map of likely locations for uncovering treasure. The site had clear signs of ancient habitation. It was her intention to excavate the foundations of what she hoped would prove to be the remains of a Roman garrison. A few well-placed questions around High Tearing had uncovered tales of coins, glassware, and bits of pottery having been found by people who hiked along the river Tear until they decided to take the shortcut into the village, which shortcut ran, not coincidentally, through Mountjoy's field and past their excavation spot.

Would not a Roman Legion have made the same trek? Perhaps even on their way to and from their barracks.

Lily supervised the loading of the cart that would transport the shovels, spades, and three footmen enlisted to dig, ticking off items on her list as they were placed on the carts. No point driving all that way only to learn something crucial had been omitted from the supplies. One needed the planning skills of a general and a quartermaster's talents of organization for such an endeavor as this.

While she counted shovels, picks, rakes, and sorting baskets, another cart, loaded with an awning, folding chairs, tables, and hampers containing refreshments, started on its way, carrying as well two serving maids, one of the undercooks, two more footmen, and grooms to manage the horses.

The morning was a fine one without a single cloud in the sky. A breeze kept the heat from becoming unbearable, but for anyone who stood in the sun, she imagined one would soon be uncomfortably warm. Lily stopped a footman on his way back to the house. "See that there's plenty for all of you to drink, won't you?"

He bowed. "Yes, miss. I'll speak with Mr. Doyle right away."

"Thank you." She intended to do some digging herself, of course, but it was the footmen with their brawn who would do the brunt of the work. They were all of them in for a day of what would likely be the tedious labor of uncovering the foundation of the structure she hoped was there.

Before long, the second cart went on its way, too, fully laden with all the implements required for her excavation. Lily brushed off her skirt. Excitement for the day's adventure curled in her stomach. Bronze oil-paper parasol in one hand and her map in the other so that she could finalize her approach to the area she'd chosen to start their digging, Lily headed for the front of the house. There, she found Ginny and Lord Nigel waiting underneath the portico for the carriage that would transport them to the site.

"A most thrilling morning, don't you agree, Ginny?" she said as she joined them. Ginny was very pretty in pale rose muslin and sarcenet and a delightful cap pinned slantways on her head. The ensemble was one of the gowns Lily had offered in the hope of tempting Ginny into remaking it for herself. Though impractical for an outing, did it matter when she looked so lovely? She put her arm through Ginny's. "It's unlikely we'll find anything the first day out, but we might. We just might."

"What do you think, Nigel?" Ginny asked. "Will we have good luck and find treasure straightaway?"

Lord Nigel took off his hat and bowed. "The first day?" He smiled a bit too heartily. Lily narrowed her eyes at him. "I don't see why we won't find something."

"We mustn't forget Lily's Gypsy magic," Ginny said. "That's bound to help us."

Lily pressed Ginny's arm. "Magic or no, we shall stand firm and not give up even if we are disappointed today. I'm sure we'll have work for the better part of a month before we've excavated whatever building is there."

"Of course." Ginny patted Lily's arm just as a groom brought the carriage around. "We stand firm."

Thank goodness there would be plenty of food and drink to sustain them through the afternoon. She had no worries about Ginny's fortitude, but she did not expect Lord Nigel to have her enthusiasm nor to withstand the inevitable tedium of an endeavor such as this.

"You ought to make a good luck wish on your medallion before we go," Ginny said.

"Excellent notion, my dear." Standing beside the carriage, she held her medallion, closed her eyes and counted to three, throwing in a hasty wish for good fortune and lots of treasure—no harm in that—and then opened her eyes. How odd that the metal was warm against her fingers. Had she been in the sun long enough to heat the gold? "There. All done. Shall we go?"

She accepted Lord Nigel's hand up into the carriage. "Come, Ginny." She patted the seat. When Ginny was seated, Lily held up her medallion. "You ought to wish for good fortune as well."

"Do you think it will work?"

How wonderful to see Ginny smile. "It can't hurt."

"Is there a best form?"

She rubbed the medallion between her fingers. "I think it's sufficient if you close your eyes and wish wholeheartedly, but whatever you feel is efficacious would be much appreciated."

Lord Nigel, now perched in the driver's box, snorted. Ginny stuck out her tongue at her brother's back. Then she closed her eyes, medallion in her hands. "There," she said. "I've wished for us to find a treasure trove."

From the driver's box, Lord Nigel snorted again.

"You ought to wish for good fortune as well, Lord Nigel."

"I do," he said. "I do."

"Well. That's that then." She leaned back. Lord Nigel snapped the reins and they were off. He was perfectly put together. It was a pity, really, that she did not like blond men and that he was, in any event, far too young for her. She did admire the cut of his driving coat. If only Mountjoy had a coat that fit his marvelous form as perfectly as Lord Nigel's coat fit him. Of course, very shortly, he would.

When the day came that Mountjoy dressed in clothes worthy of his physique, no woman would be able to resist him. To be fair, she doubted many women resisted him now. There were times when his eyes positively smoldered. What woman could deny a man who gazed at her with such open passion?

As they drove, Lily kept her map spread over her lap, studying her sketch. She didn't believe for a moment they would find any artifacts, not the first day, but she saw no reason not to apply her intellect to the matter of exposing a building, whether it once housed Roman Legionnaires, medieval serfs, or a family of Angles or Jutes.

She set aside her study of the map when Ginny said, "I've been thinking, Lily, about what we should serve for our spring fete."

"Have you?"

"Yes. I've been wondering about a menu."

Lily took out her notebook and pencil and found a blank page. "What do you think?"

"We ought to have pheasant."

"Yes, I think we should."

"I'll ask the cook if any is laid by."

As best she could given they were driving the carriage over a road rutted from the season's late rain, Lily made a note about the pheasant. "Duck, too, don't you agree?"

"Jane says to ask her father if we haven't any. He hunts every season, and she says there's always an abundance."

She noted that, too. She wondered when Mountjoy would offer for Miss Kirk. Not until after she left Bitterward, she hoped. She and Mountjoy had no future beyond her stay here, yet the thought of his eventual marriage felt bittersweet to her. Her preference would be to read of the engagement in a letter from Eugenia, not witness it personally. "Duck Mr. Kirk."

"Cakes, too," Ginny said. "And other sweets from the confectioner's in High Tearing."

"Oh, certainly. We ought to meet with the cook tomorrow. To plan a menu." She made a note of that, too.

Ginny sat sideways on the seat, a smile on her face, and Lily was strongly reminded of the woman who had become her friend in Exeter, before the heartbreaking loss of her husband. "We should have music and dancing for the young people, don't you agree?"

"Heavens, yes. We must have dancing for everyone who wishes to. Including you, my dear."

"If you will, I will. If anyone asks, that is."

"You may be assured of that."

"I haven't danced for ages and ages, Lily. I'm not sure I remember how."

"Everything will come back to you as soon as you hear the music." Lily waited for the carriage to pass over another rut before she made that note. "Is there a local orchestra you can recommend or should we send to Sheffield?"

"We've a very good one here." Ginny leaned in and pointed at Lily's notebook. "Put down that I'll hire them."

And so it went until Lord Nigel slowed the horses and looked over his shoulder at them. "We're here. The awning isn't up yet so now's the time to say something if this isn't the spot you meant, Miss Wellstone."

She looked around. They were on the northeast corner of the property at the rock-strewn meadow she and Ginny had felt was the most promising. The field was no more than a thirty-minute walk from the ruins of the Norman church and within sight of the river Tear. A likely place, as she'd thought from the very first, for a fortress.

"Yes," she said. "This is the place."

Lord Nigel put on the brake and secured the reins before getting down to assist his sister and then her. Interesting, she thought, that the degree of Lord Nigel's attentions to her could be predicted by whether his brother was present. In the former case, she could count on Lord Nigel flirting a little too much. But without Mountjoy? He was merely a very polite young man.

By the time they'd crossed the meadow, the servants had put up the awning and were arranging table and chairs underneath. Farther away, the rest of the men were unloading the shovels and other excavation implements.

Lily put up her parasol and walked smartly to the spot she thought was the place to begin. Lord Nigel and Ginny came along. The ground was strewn with rocks, most smaller than her fist, though a few were larger. She strongly suspected and hoped to confirm that the rocks were all that was left of a Roman garrison. Larger stones that would have once formed the walls had likely been long ago scavenged for fences or homes elsewhere. Like Lily, Ginny held a parasol over her head to ward off the sun. The day was really quite warm. Lord Nigel's hat did not provide him sufficient shade. He'd be brown as toast before long.

"See there?" She pointed for Lord Nigel's benefit as he had not been present when she and Ginny first examined the site. "Those impressions in the ground along there and there? They are too straight to be natural and surely mark the location of an ancient structure. Ginny and I noticed that the first time we came here."

"You think it might be Roman?" Lord Nigel said, a bit too jovially.

She gave him a sideways look. "Perhaps."

"Or Viking," Ginny said. "Or Norman. Or whoever was here before that."

Lord Nigel suppressed a grin. "Or after."

"Given the Roman artifacts so often found around here," Lily said, "I have high hopes this was the site of a garrison." She squinted to narrow her field of focus to the outline of the foundation. On which side should they begin?

"Cromwell might have done that," Lord Nigel said. "Leveled a building. He was mucking about here with his cannons. Or it might have been our great-great-granduncle—or was he a cousin several times removed?—the first duke. Any one of the ancestors who preceded Mountjoy, actually."

Lily, who didn't want to dampen anyone's spirits, continued her study of the foundation lines. She pointed at another series of furrows barely visible in the grass. "Could there have been two buildings here?"

The footmen with their shovels, picks, and spades had reached them and were now awaiting instructions. "Do you mean for us to dig here, miss?" the eldest of them asked. He wasn't more than twenty-five and looked a strapping man. He nodded at Lord Nigel. "Perhaps we ought to dig by the river. That's a likelier spot than this one, I say."

Lord Nigel, it seemed to her, made a particular point of looking away from the fellow. And now she rather thought Lord Nigel and the footman were both trying to hide a smirk.

"Is it?" she said. The ground by the river hadn't even the faintest sign of human habitation. Flooding over the years would have washed away any structure built so foolishly near the water.

"Yes, Miss Wellstone. It is."

She didn't like the way the eldest servant looked at Lord Nigel, nor Lord Nigel's overly hearty tone of voice.

Something was afoot, and she meant to discover what it was.

Chapter Twenty

LILY THOROUGHLY STUDIED THE THREE FOOTMEN Mountjoy had been kind enough to allow on this adventure. The eldest was Walter, she learned. A smile continued to twitch at the corners of Walter's mouth. Lord Nigel had interfered in some way. She was sure the two of them were partners in some plot.

"You recommend we start near the river?" she asked the young man. She smiled at him quite deliberately. He goggled, but only for a moment because another of the footmen poked him in the back.

"Aye."

"May I ask why?"

"Heard tales about it when I was a lad." Walter nodded as if that were of vital importance. As if, perhaps, he'd rehearsed the words. "Romansford, it was called. Isn't that so, boys?"

Romansford. Oh, for pity's sake. The two hadn't even bothered to come up with a believable name. "Is that so?" Lily asked dryly.

"It was?" Ginny asked. "How odd. I don't think I ever—"

"Eugenia." Lord Nigel, standing a bit behind his sister, grabbed her by the shoulders and leaned on her in a hearty manner. "Romansford. Everybody calls it that. How could you fail to remember that? Mountjoy and I were out here the Easter after we moved to Bitterward, and we found an entire cache of coins along the banks. I remember it as if it were yesterday."

Ginny shook her head, craning her neck to look at him. "I don't recall that."

"Aye, milady." Walter nodded with enthusiasm. "I found a wee coin there once." He nudged one of his companions. "Didn't I?"

"You did, Walter," the young man said.

"Mountjoy still has them, Eugenia. Ask him if you don't believe me."

"I don't think you found any coins at all," Ginny said, one hand on her hip.

"Did too."

"In fact, I'll wager anything you like that you can't produce a single one of them," Ginny said.

Lily slowly turned her parasol in a circle over her head. She was highly tempted to close it and give Lord Nigel a sharp rap over his head. "Can you, Lord Nigel?"

"I don't know precisely where they are. Somewhere in the house."

"Nigel." Ginny shook her head.

Lord Nigel put his hands in his coat pockets and looked sheepish. He cleared his throat. "Just because I don't know where they are now doesn't mean we didn't find them."

Ginny rolled her eyes.

"Do you remember the winter I built a model trebuchet? The year before you were married." He held his hands about two feet apart. "About that big."

"Yes," Ginny said, looking at him with her arms crossed over her chest.

"I tested it."

"Mountjoy told you not to. He said you'd break a window if you did."

Lord Nigel drew himself up. "That's why I used the coins instead of pebbles. I shot most of them off the west tower roof."

"What about the rest?"

"Into the lake."

"Does Mountjoy know?"

"Good God, no, Eugenia. He'd have skinned me alive if he'd found out."

"Allow me to understand," Ginny said. "By your own admission, my dear little brother, the coins you claim you found, if ever they existed, are stuck in the gutters at Bitterward or sunk to the bottom of the lake."

"Yes."

"Do you really expect us to believe any of that?"

"Yes."

"Rubbish, Nigel."

"It's not."

Ginny snorted. "If you've interfered with our adventure, Nigel, Lily and I are going to be peeved with you. Very peeved."

He lifted his hands in protest. "This is the thanks I get for trying to help?"

"Thank you, Lord Nigel," Lily said in a firm voice. "That is indeed helpful information. Very kind of you to share, and so important to the cause." She rested the handle of her parasol on her shoulder and braced it underneath her forearm so as to have both hands free to hold her map and consult the sketches and notes she'd made. "That clump of rocks is intriguing, don't you think?" She pointed away from the river. "Perhaps the threshold of the garrison building."

"The riverside, miss," Walter said. Again, too heartily. "You'll want the river. It's the best spot."

"Shall we toss a coin?" Lord Nigel reached into a pocket and came out with a coin, which he flipped into the air and caught on the back of his hand. "Heads it's the river, tails, your meadow of rocks there."

Ginny scanned the meadow as Lily had done. "I think Lily's medallion ought to determine where we start."

"Brilliant idea," Lily said. One never did want to accuse one's host of cheating, but she was convinced, among other things, that Lord Nigel Hampton had rigged his toss of the coin. Or else so thoroughly seeded the area with "treasure" that her project was hopelessly compromised. "You are clever beyond words, my dear Ginny."

Lord Nigel lifted his hand, but tilted it so she couldn't see the coin. "Heads." He glanced at her. "Right then. The river it is."

While Lord Nigel was still looking at her, she clapped a hand to her chest and stared to her right. "Good Lord!" She added a hint of alarm to her words. "What on earth is that?"

Lord Nigel looked.

She snatched the coin off his hand, placing a finger over the side that had been facing up. "Just as I thought." She sniffed and handed back the coin. "Tails, sir. Not heads."

Lord Nigel had the grace to look abashed, but in the end, he shrugged. "Does it matter?" He pointed. "The ground is softer by the river. Why make these poor fellows dig among the rocks when the day promises to be so warm?"

"Do you find it warm?" she asked. "I do not. It's rather cool out in my opinion."

"Romansford it is," Walter said. He pushed off on his shovel, ready to go. The other two propped their shovels and picks on their shoulders and prepared to follow him to the river.

"I do not care for luck that is no luck at all," Lily said with a meaningful look at Lord Nigel. "Ginny's idea appeals to me." She smiled. "Let's have my medallion choose."

"Give it a spin," Ginny said, "and whichever part of the face is nearest the two locations, the river or the foundation, why, we'll start there."

Lily met Lord Nigel's eye. There was not the slightest hint of flirtation in his gaze. There never was unless Mountjoy was around. Which she found interesting. "Gypsy magic is useful for any endeavor involving a search for treasure." She patted Ginny's shoulder. "I ought to have thought of it myself."

Lord Nigel snorted. "Toss a coin, spin your medallion, what difference does it make? It's only chance."

"I agree with the principle, but only when others are not actively attempting to influence the outcome. Or when magic is involved."

"Magic?" Lord Nigel said, hands on his hips.

"Magic," she said. She pulled the ribbon over her head. "I can think of no better cause in which to call upon Gypsy magic than this. Can you?"

"Several, but go on." Lord Nigel gestured for her to continue.

She spun the medallion and they watched the ribbon twist, reach a point at which it could turn no more, and then spin again in the opposite direction, untwisting the ribbon. She waved a hand around the spinning disc. "I call on your magic to help me find that which I most desire."

Ginny giggled.

She cocked an eyebrow at her friend. "Do not mock the mysterious forces at work here. It's unbecoming of you and disruptive to the power of the medallion."

"Oh, I should never mock." But Ginny couldn't stop grinning. Lord Nigel was doing the same.

The medallion slowed.

Lord Nigel looked past them. "Blast."

Lily sniffed. "You won't fool me with that trick. Honestly. Do you take me for a fool?"

"No. But I mean it. Blast."

"Oh, dear," Ginny said in a way that reminded her of how Mountjoy had surprised them all during their experiment with the phosphorus pencil. The man was stealthy when he wanted to be.

Lily gazed at the slowly turning medallion, willing it to stop before it made her too dizzy to stand. "Is there an apparition?" Wouldn't that be rousing, to think the medallion had called up a specter to point them in the direction of treasure? "The ghost of a Legionnaire, perhaps?"

"No," Lord Nigel said. "Something much more terrifying than that."

"What could be more terrifying than the ghost of an ancient warrior?" Her stomach was feeling a bit tender, what with watching the spinning medallion.

"Mountjoy."

Lily's stomach somersaulted, but this time the sensation had nothing to do with the spinning medallion. She turned in the direction Lord Nigel meant, clutching the ribbon of the medallion in one hand and her parasol in the other. It was indeed Mountjoy. Her heart thumped.

He rode his chestnut gelding and, truly, was there ever a man to sit a horse the way he did? She didn't move because the sight of the Duke of Mountjoy had frozen her in place. An invisible line connected them and pulled on her heart. *Yanked* might be a more apt description of the sensation. She forgot, utterly, the business with the medallion.

When he reached them, he pushed back the brim of his hat. "Nigel." He nodded at his brother. "Eugenia." There was nothing untoward about his greeting. He sounded bored, as he so often did. "Miss Wellstone."

Ginny curtseyed. "Mountjoy."

Lily did the same. She was never nervous around others, but she was now. How did one behave with a man with whom one had been illicitly intimate? Her time with Greer had been so short and private. Those final days and hours had been spent alone, exactly as if they'd been husband and wife just married, and then he'd gone off to war and she'd never seen him again.

From atop his horse, Mountjoy gazed at them, careful, so careful, not to look at her any longer than was polite. Possibly his gaze lasted less than was polite. His coat was indifferently cut, and his cravat had not survived whatever journey he'd been on. The folds were now uneven though, knowing him, he'd probably started his day with his cravat tied like that. "You are about to dig up my field, aren't you?" he said.

"Yes." Lily smiled because anything else might give away the state of her nerves. Their encounters so far did not mean they were engaged in an affair. They weren't lovers yet. They might never be. How could they when she would not be at Bitterward much longer? Her heart was not involved. Nor was his. So why, then, was her pulse racing so?

"Where will you start?" he asked.

"We'll dig here." She pointed at Mountjoy. "If you wouldn't mind moving aside, your grace? We have a Roman garrison to uncover."

Lord Nigel said, "Isn't this the site of the old stables? I remember hearing somewhere that the second duke tore down the original house and rebuilt where Bitterward now stands."

"Not another word from you, Lord Nigel."

"What about at Romansford?" Ginny said, all sweetness and innocence.

"Romansford?"

"You remember, Mountjoy. Where you and Nigel found the coins?" Ginny spoke without the slightest indication she believed the story was a false one. "Over there, by those rocks. You remember, don't you, Mountjoy? The Easter after we came here from Haltwhistle."

Mountjoy frowned. "Was it there?" He gave a more convincing performance than his brother. "No, it was closer to the river than that, wasn't it, Nigel?"

"Infamous, your grace," Lily said.

His eyebrows rose in that infuriating way he had. "I beg your pardon?"

"You're in on the plot with your devious brother."

He dismounted and dropped the reins to the ground. His mount flicked its tail and nudged a clump of grass under its nose. Its back hoof dislodged a small rock. Lily stared at the rock and the too square bottom surface. That was no naturally occurring shape. He turned, one hand resting on his saddle. "Nigel, take Eugenia to the awning to await the excavation of the Romansford Garrison. I need a word in private with Miss Wellstone." After his brother and sister left them in relative privacy, he looked her up and down with a gaze that would have broken a woman of weaker will than her. "What plot would that be, Wellstone?"

She did not bother hiding her annoyance. "You and your brother have colluded to be sure we dig by the river and not here."

Mountjoy returned his attention to her, and her stomach took flight again. "Why would we do that?"

"So we find the artifacts you buried for us to discover."

The duke scanned the area before he replied. "The ground would be softer by the river, and it is where Nigel and I once found some Roman coins."

"You, sir, are incorrigible."

He returned his attention to her. He crossed his arms over his chest, and it did not matter to her one bit that his waistcoat had no style whatever or that his coat and buckskin breeches both should have long ago been handed over to his valet for disposal. He met her gaze, and her stomach went spinning away. They had been intimate. He'd been inside her. She knew what he looked and sounded like when he climaxed.

"I don't think you can produce a single Roman coin, your grace. In fact, if you can produce even one of the coins you claim you found, why, why . . ."

"Yes?"

"Why, I'll wait on you hand and foot for an entire day, that's what."

"And if I cannot?"

"You will do the same for me." She held out her hand and met his gaze straight on. "Be forewarned, your grace. I am without mercy."

His mouth curled into a smile that made her too giddy to

think straight. She wanted her hands on him again. Her mouth. Her tongue. She wanted to feel the weight of his body over hers. More than anything she wanted to look into his eyes when he slid inside her. "Bloodthirsty girl, aren't you?"

"You've no idea."

With that devastating smile still hovering around his mouth, Mountjoy tapped his riding whip against his open palm. "I never make a wager I am not confident of winning."

"Nor do I, your grace." Was it possible he wanted her with the same intensity? Heavens, she hoped so. "Do you accept?"

"Done." Mountjoy clasped her hand.

"Prepare to grovel, your grace, for when *I* win our wager, I'll have you on your knees to me."

"Delightful as that sounds, Wellstone," Mountjoy said far more evenly than she liked to hear from him, "I never grovel."

"I am adding, Mountjoy, to my very long list of tasks I will demand you perform. I hope you enjoy dancing."

"I abhor dancing," he said.

Lily took her notebook and her pencil from her pocket and prepared to write. "Item the first," she said to herself. "Dan . . . cing . . . duke." She made a flourish underneath the words. "There."

"When I win," he said in a low voice, "I'll have *you* on your hands and knees. Again. Tonight, I hope."

She licked her lower lip. "Best go, your grace, and join your brother and sister. I've serious work to do."

Mountjoy bowed, and while he walked away, she returned the notebook and pencil to her pocket. Coolly as she could, she walked to where Walter and the other footmen waited. "If you would," she said, closing her parasol and using it to indicate the area she meant, "dig a trench from here to about there. At least two feet deep, I should think. More, if possible. Do not, under any circumstances, disturb the foundation when you've reached it. The goal is to uncover what remains and leave it in place. We are not here to salvage the stones."

Walter bobbed his head. "Miss."

She would stay here, valiantly supervising the work. She opened her parasol again, shading herself from the sun and, incidentally, hiding her face from Mountjoy, who was by now back at the awning. She stayed near the footmen as they worked and soaked in the scent of fresh earth, the *shick* of a spade biting into the dirt, the soft comments from time to time between the men. She kept her parasol over her head, but the sun beat down unmercifully, as hot as Lord Nigel had predicted.

Half an hour later, Ginny called to her from the awning. "Lily, darling. Do come have something to drink."

"No, thank you." She waved. A trickle of sweat ran down her spine. "Would you be so good as to have someone bring the men something to drink?"

Refreshment was duly brought to the men, who leaned on their shovels while they drank from the clay jars brought to them. In the meantime, Lily fidgeted. She never wanted to sit or stay still when she was outside. She wanted to walk, to explore. To see the world around her and breathe it all in. She wanted to be alone with Mountjoy.

She walked to the edge of the hole and looked in. As yet, there was no sign of a foundation.

"What do you see?" Ginny called from the edge of the awning.

"A great amount of dirt." She turned. Underneath the awning, a maid handed Mountjoy a glass of lemonade. Ginny cooled herself with an ivory fan. She held a glass in the other.

The footmen dug steadily, leaning over more and more as the trench became deeper and longer. There was nothing but dirt down there, and it was unrelentingly dark and damp-ish from the spring storms. Perhaps her idea of digging for treasure had a flaw. Days and days of uncovering nothing but dirt wasn't so very adventurous. Oh, perhaps they'd uncover the occasional root or rock, but the predominant finding was going to be dirt.

She ignored the entreaties from the others to come out of the sun or to have a cool, refreshing glass of lemonade. There was a minor bit of excitement when one of the men uncovered a bit of metal, but examination proved the object to be a horseshoe nail.

The sun climbed higher in the sky. More sweat rolled down her back and beaded at her temples. She blinked because for a moment, she was sure she saw something that wasn't the color of dirt. After all this time, even a rock would be a thrill. The merest hint of the foundation would be lovely. Even if it was all that remained of a stable.

One of the servants brought up a clump of something on his shovel, but after another bit of excitement, the object turned out to be a piece of broken slate and yet another horseshoe nail. Ginny called her again, and Lily turned just enough to see her.

"Strawberries," Ginny said, holding up a plate. "They are excellent. Will you come have one?"

She waved a refusal. "How good of you to ask, but no, thank you." She ought to sit under the awning with the others, drinking lemonade and eating strawberries. In the shade. She could admire Mountjoy's shoulders and imagine him naked. Bother with her commitment to the tedium of treasure hunting.

In the trench, Walter emptied his shovel of dirt and went back for another. The shovel made an odd sound, and he stopped before the bottom of his stroke down. Another of the footmen stopped digging, too, arrested by the sound.

"What is it?" Lily asked. Had they reached the foundation at last? Or had they found a horseshoe to go with their collection of nails?

"A root, miss," Walter said.

A root. She could practically hear him thinking how much he'd rather be digging by the river.

"Have you found something?" Lord Nigel called.

Lily waved a dismissive hand. "Carry on," she said to the footmen. They did, all three in a line and all of them more miserably hot than she was.

"Walter," said the man at the far end of the trench. "Give me the smaller shovel?"

The implement was duly handed over and Walter tossed the larger one onto the lip of the trench. Lily considered walking to the awning. The shade would feel delicious.

"Oi!" Walter waved one arm over his head. "Oi there, miss!"

She arrived at that end of the trench in time to see the other footman drop to his knees and reach into the hole. "Have you reached the foundation?"

When his hand came out, by some trick of the sun, his fingers glittered with gold.

Chapter Twenty-one

MOUNTJOY ACCOMPANIED EUGENIA AND NIGEL TO see what was causing the fuss, but hung back when they reached the edge of the trench. The scene was eerily familiar. All three of the footmen had taken off their coats and hats and rolled up their sleeves. As in his dream, one stood at the rim of the trench, leaning on his shovel and staring down into the trench they'd dug. The other two stood in the excavated area. Lily, on the other side of the excavation, stared at something in the trench. Her parasol was closed and on the ground at her feet, exactly as he'd dreamed.

He'd known for days about the treasure hunting project and that it would involve digging. Therefore, his dreams about this weren't so unusual. Women commonly had parasols outside. The details of Lily and her treasure hunting were hardly earth-shattering, and yet, the hair on his arms prickled.

The servant nearest to Lily held out a bit of twisted, dirt-encrusted metal. The piece wasn't much larger than his palm but he'd scraped off enough dirt to expose the unmistakable gleam of gold. There appeared to be flashes of red, too. The man grinned as if he'd just been handed a fortune of his own.

Mindful of Lily's accusation that the field had been seeded with treasure, Mountjoy looked at Nigel, but his brother looked as shocked as everyone else. If this was whatever Nigel had buried here himself, which he suspected his brother had done, Nigel was a better actor than Mountjoy thought.

He walked to the lip of the trench and peered down. A jumble of objects, all of them covered and encrusted with dirt to the point where he could not form the shapes into anything recognizable, lay at the bottom. Most appeared to be quite small. He didn't see anything that looked like pots or glassware or the sorts of jars that turned up in areas where the Romans had established forts or cities. Another of the footmen crouched in the trench, bringing out what looked at first glance like more dirt-covered rubbish.

Every so often, gold glittered from beneath the dirt, and some of the bits of metal that could be glimpsed were obviously of exquisite workmanship. If whatever these things were had once been contained in something, that material had long ago rotted away. He looked at his brother again. Was Nigel responsible for the find? If so, he'd gone to a great deal of trouble by burying them so bloody deep and making the items look as if they genuinely had been underground for seven or eight hundred years. He frowned because he didn't see how or why or where anyone could have acquired unidentifiable items in order to perpetrate a fraud. It made no sense. Yet.

On the opposite side of the trench, Lily knelt and tucked her outer coat underneath her knees. It was too warm a day for a coat, he thought. She moved her parasol out of her way and used one hand to brace herself so she could reach down with the other. They'd dug down three feet in some places. The man nearest her in the trench extended a hand to steady her before he placed a dirty lump on her palm.

"Gold, miss," he said in awed tones.

Lily clutched the object and speared Nigel with her gaze. "Are you responsible for this?"

"No, Miss Wellstone." He raised his hands, palms out. "I assure you I am not."

She glanced at the eldest of the three footmen. "Walter, fetch the baskets, please."

"Right, miss." Without bothering to put on his coat—it was too warm for a man who'd been laboring in the sun these past hours—the young man jumped out of the trench and hurried toward the dogcarts.

The servant who'd steadied Lily bent down and handed her a second lump of dirt. "Another one, miss."

Lily leaned back and gently scraped debris off the object. It was button shaped, domed on top, but too large to actually be a button. Like the other piece, it shone gold and red where she'd dislodged enough of the dirt.

"Whatever is it?" Eugenia asked. She held her parasol over her head.

Lily scrubbed at the object then held up the bit of metal. An elongated, U-shaped stem made the button look vaguely mushroomlike. She brushed away more dirt. "My dear Ginny," she said in reverent tones, "I do believe it's the top bit from the pommel of a sword. A decorative button."

"Where's the sword, then?" Eugenia asked. She peered in the trench, and Mountjoy did, too. Everyone did. He saw nothing that looked like a sword.

Lily sat back on her heels, the button in her gloved hand. She'd removed more of the dirt and just then the sun hit a bit of the red material. It shimmered. "Oh," she said. "It's lovely." She wiped her forehead with the back of her gloved hand before she held up the object. "Do you see?" Sunlight reflected off the now cleaner edges of the metal she held. "How beautiful this will be when it's been washed."

Walter returned with the baskets and Lily supervised the transfer of objects from the trench to the baskets. There were hundreds of them, few of them of any decent size.

This was scavenged metal, Mountjoy thought. Bits of

metal torn from fallen warriors, the remnants of bridles, armor, anything that could be quickly carried from a battle-field. Now that he understood what he was looking at, he could see there were buckles and brooches, broken finials, tabs and buttons, twisted shards of gold torn from whatever they had been attached to. There were gems, too, cabochons that had fallen out of their metal settings. One of the last items pulled from the dirt, though, was a set of daggers, then the decaying metal bits of a scabbard, and a sword.

After nearly an hour with the sun continuing to climb in the sky, Lily agreed they would find no more buried objects without considerably expanding the trench. Mountjoy, who by now happened to be standing nearest her, helped Lily to her feet. He steadied her when she wavered on her feet. With a laugh that sounded too feeble for someone like her, she bent to brush the dirt and grass off her skirt.

Her cheeks were pink, and Mountjoy wondered if she'd gotten too much sun or if that was just the flush of excite-ment. "Eugenia," he said, "kindly bring Miss Wellstone some lemonade."

Eugenia took a step forward. "Lily?" Her voice rattled with worry. "Lily?" Lily swayed, and if he hadn't grabbed her arm she might have fallen. "Oh, Mountjoy, help! She's going to faint."

"Nonsense," Lily said in a shaky voice. "I never faint."

Mountjoy caught her around the waist because Eugenia was right, and he did so not a moment too soon. Lily's legs crumpled beneath her. With Nigel at his side, he carried her to the awning and set her down on a chair. "Eugenia," he said. "Fetch that lemonade now."

She did. Moments later she pressed a glass into Lily's hands.

"Thank you, Ginny, dear," Lily said. She drank deeply and then pressed the cup to her face. Her cheeks remained flushed while the rest of her skin was chalky white. She closed her eyes and swayed on the chair.

"Take off that blasted coat," Mountjoy said. He helped

her out of the garment and scowled to find her skin clammy to touch. "Whatever possessed you to wear such a thing on a day like this?"

"It goes with my gown." She looked at him without her usual penetrating gaze. "How was I to know the day would be so dreadfully warm?"

If he hadn't had a hand on her upper arm, he might not have noticed she was trembling. He didn't like her flushed cheeks and too bright eyes. "Have you a fan, Miss Wellstone?"

She shook her head. "I tell you, this is why I prefer to sleep through mornings." Her voice faltered, as if she couldn't spare the breath for words.

"Have you one, Eugenia?" Mountjoy said. He put out a hand when his sister nodded. Eugenia pulled a fan from her reticule and moved close enough to fan Lily's face. "Wellstone, drink more of that lemonade." He made sure she did, then made eye contact with one of the serving girls. "Another lemonade for Miss Wellstone, if you please. And fetch a damp cloth, as cold as you can get it."

Nigel hovered nearby, silent. The servants had gone quiet, too.

"Thank you, Eugenia." He was grateful for his sister's quick action. "Better, Miss Wellstone?"

She closed her eyes and touched her hand to the side of her head. "I've the most awful megrim coming on."

"Nigel," Mountjoy said. "See that the carriage is ready to go. She needs to get home. Inside. Where it's cool."

Lily opened her eyes. "Don't make a fuss." Her voice remained indistinct. "I promise not to be a bother. I need a moment is all."

He grabbed her hand and yanked off her glove. Her palms were damp with perspiration. He removed her other glove, too, and let it drop to the ground. "You're too warm."

"Give me back my gloves. Those are the very finest kid."

"I've seen this happen before," Mountjoy said. "To a man in the heat too long."

"What happened?" Eugenia continued to fan Lily.

A maid handed him a damp cloth, and he took it. Mountjoy gave his sister a look and shook his head. The man had died. He'd been much worse off than Lily was right now, but then Lily was a delicate woman, not a man inured to labor, and there was no knowing how badly she'd react. He wiped her face and pressed the cloth to the back of her neck. She wasn't reviving as she ought to. Instead of protesting, she bowed her head and groaned.

"More lemonade," he said, pressing another glass into her hand.

Nigel returned. "Carriage is ready," he said. "How is she?"

Mountjoy looked past Nigel. "Put the top up." While Nigel did so, a maid brought a second dampened cloth. He wiped her wrists and face again.

"Perfectly fine," Lily said.

"You're not."

She opened her eyes and gazed at him. Her eyes were unfocused. She stood, but swayed once on her feet. "I won't be a bother."

"You of all people ought to know I am always correct," he said. He pushed her back onto the chair. "I'm going to carry you to the carriage. I wouldn't object if I were you. Things will go badly for you if you do." She opened her mouth to protest, but he forestalled her by gathering her into his arms. Wonder of wonders, she sighed and rested her head against his shoulder.

"Adorable man," she whispered.

Mountjoy stood, seeing the concern on the faces of the gathered servants. Eugenia gave no sign she'd overheard Lily's endearment, thank God. Then again, he could not see her face while she bent for Lily's parasol and gloves. When he could, though, and Eugenia had the parasol shading Lily from the sun, he saw nothing but concern from her. From any of them. She hurried beside him, keeping the parasol over them while Mountjoy strode to the carriage with Lily inert in his arms.

Chapter Twenty-two

MOUNTJOY CLIMBED INTO THE CARRIAGE WITH LILY while Nigel helped Eugenia up before leaping into the driver's box. He settled Lily on the seat between them. She went limp, as boneless as her garments permitted. He and Eugenia exchanged a look. Lily turned her head toward him and set a bare hand on his cheek. Her skin was warm and clammy. "Such a lovely man, Mountjoy. Have I told you that?"

"Thank you, Miss Wellstone." He didn't look at his sister to see what she thought of Lily's boldness. Best pretend there was nothing untoward about it or that he believed she was not entirely in her right mind. "She's still got on too damn many clothes," he told Eugenia. "Help me get this off, will you?"

"Yes, of course." Eugenia assisted in the removal of Lily's spencer, a process that required some contortions from them all. That done, Eugenia began fanning Lily again, briskly enough to lift strands of his hair.

"Ah." Lily sighed. "That does feel good. Thank you, my dear Ginny."

"How are you?" Eugenia smoothed Lily's hair. "Feeling any better?"

"You're such a dear, Ginny, to look after me."

"Is your megrim improved?"

"Some." Lily rested her head against the back of the seat, eyes closed. Every so often Mountjoy wiped her still-flushed face with the damp cloth he'd kept for the purpose. The carriage bounced over a rut, and Eugenia braced herself on the seat.

A few minutes later, Lily tried to sit up and adjust her gown. "None of that," he said. He put a hand on her shoulder and gently pushed her back. "You'll rest until the doctor's examined you and agreed you're well."

"My gown will be wrinkled."

"Oh, Lily—" Eugenia said.

"Damn the gown," Mountjoy said. Lily tried to sit up again, and this time he leaned over her, put a hand on her shoulder, and growled. "Pray do not exert yourself. I insist."

"Beastly man."

He said, "If your frock cannot be restored to its original splendor, Lily, I will buy you a new one."

Eugenia coughed softly, and he realized what he'd said. What could he do but pretend he'd not called her by her Christian name?

"My God, Ginny, he's threatening me." Lily grasped Eugenia's free hand and pretended to swoon. "In my weakened condition, no less. It's a wonder I don't have a relapse." She gave him a look that went a way toward relieving his mind about her condition. "Besides, look at your brother's coat. I wouldn't trust him to buy me an apron, let alone a frock."

"I know how to buy a woman an extravagant gift." At least she was feeling better. His attention flicked downward, and Lily noticed. Probably Eugenia noticed, too, but he was beyond caring anymore. Lily leaned against the seat, gazing at him from under her lashes.

"Buying a gift is simple," she said, with a lift of her chin. "It's choosing one that's fraught with danger."

"Don't lecture *me* about buying a woman gifts. I assure you I've done it often."

"Mountjoy," Eugenia said, more a whisper than anything else. "Really."

"I've bought you many a gift, Eugenia, and never heard you complain."

"Well, no, but, then I am your sister."

"Were you dissatisfied?"

"No, Mountjoy. But that's hardly the same as telling Lily you'll buy her a gown. That's not . . . proper."

"Then you buy it for her, so long as the woman stops thinking a deuced frock is more important than her health."

"Better Ginny than you," Lily said. Eugenia laughed at the rejoinder and, well, if the laugh was at his expense, at least Eugenia had been distracted from his inappropriate remarks.

In the ensuing silence, he traced lazy circles on Lily's palm. He *did* know how to choose an extravagant gift. Several minutes passed before he realized that all this time he'd been holding Lily's hand. He ought to let go, but that would only draw attention to the fact that he'd been doing so all this time. Eugenia didn't appear to have noticed.

By the time they reached the turn to Bitterward, Lily had improved to the point of taking the fan away from Eugenia and declaring she had half a mind to break it lest she turn into a block of ice.

Another carriage waited at the head of the driveway. A groom—not one of Mountjoy's servants—held the bridle of the lead pair. A Bitterward footman had a hand on the carriage door, ready to open it as Nigel brought the coach to a halt as near to the door as he could manage.

Mountjoy got out, and, while he reached to take Lily in his arms, from the corner of his eye he saw the occupant of the other carriage emerge. Fenris. The bloody Duke of Camber's heir. Nigel stayed in the coachman's seat and called down, "I'll fetch Longfield."

He spared his brother a glance. "Thank you."

Fenris approached, eyes wide and fixed on Lily. "My God, Mountjoy, what's happened?" He succeeded by look and words in implying that Mountjoy had injured Lily himself. "Is she badly hurt? Is there anything I can do?"

"Fenris—"

Fenris pulled up short. "Where is your sister, Mountjoy? Has something happened to her?"

He hardly had time to register the sharpness of that last question before Fenris glanced away and saw Eugenia ready to step from the coach. He moved smoothly to the carriage door and held out his hand, cutting off the groom ready to assist Eugenia. "I'll see to Mrs. Bryant," Fenris said. "Mountjoy, take my cousin inside. And do try not to do her further injury."

"Lily," he said in a low voice as he climbed the front stairs with her in his arms. "You would be easier to carry if you didn't behave as if you'd rather leap to your death than touch me."

"What if someone should see us?"

"They will assume I am carrying you to your room so that you may be properly looked after." She turned her head away from him, but she did slip an arm around his shoulder. "Thank you," he said. Doyle opened the door and Mountjoy strode inside.

She rested her head against his upper shoulder, and, well. Her bodice gaped and the shift in her position provided ample evidence of the curves he wanted so much to caress again. "I'm sorry to be a bother," she said.

"You are not a bother. Which way is your room?"

At the top of the stairs, Lily pointed right and said, "Left here."

He went left and moments later he'd found Lily's room. The Lilac room. The predominant color was indeed lilac, from the canopy over the bed to the pattern in the wallpaper. He laid her down on the bed and stepped back. "You see? I did not drop you."

They gazed at each other, and Lord, he thought he might

go up in flames. This was her room. The bed in which she slept. What would happen if he locked the door, with him still inside?

Her lips parted, and she licked her lower lip. "I didn't think you would."

"Nor ravish you," he said in a low voice. He could hear someone, a servant or perhaps Eugenia, moving down the corridor. Close. Too close to risk anything.

"Were you at least tempted?" She lifted one knee, only a few inches, but that movement was enough to expose a slender ankle.

As Eugenia came in, Mountjoy held her gaze, not hiding a thing from her, and said, "Yes." To his sister he said, "Is Fenris still here?"

"I gave him leave to depart." Eugenia went to the wash-stand. A moment later, she came to the bed with a basin and a cloth. She gave him a peculiar look and said, "Go on, Mountjoy. You're not wanted here anymore."

He cleared his throat and bowed to her and then to Lily. "I leave you in my sister's capable hands, Miss Wellstone. Please accept my hopes that you recover enough to join us for supper."

"A cool bath will be just the thing," Eugenia said. "Very refreshing."

His gaze slid from Lily's ankle to her face. While he'd been engaged with thoughts of her legs and regions north, she'd slipped a hand underneath her head. His eyes locked with hers again. That she understood the carnal nature of his perusal of her was no fault of hers. Or, no more than it was his. He didn't look away when he ought to have. Neither did she, and he felt a burn of desire start up in his belly.

Christ. He wanted her still. Again. More. Much, much more. More than any woman he could recall, he wanted Lily Wellstone, fascinating, desirable, infuriating creature, in his bed as often as he could convince her to join him there.

"Shoo, Mountjoy," Eugenia said. She put a hand on his shoulder and pushed him toward the door. Was that amusement in her voice? "She needs a bath and to rest and you aren't helping by standing there like you've turned to stone."

"Ginny? Are you saying I am Medusa?"

"No, Lily. Of course not." Eugenia threw him a last glance. "Go, Mountjoy. I'll have a word with you later."

"As you wish."

In the hallway after Eugenia closed the door behind him, he wondered what the hell had happened to his formerly regulated life. He had only himself to blame. Lily wasn't chasing after him. He knew what it was like to be chased after. He was the one pushing matters between them. He'd done that. Him. Because he wanted to take her to bed, and now that he had, he wanted to do so again. If he wasn't careful, he was going to care more for her than was safe. This was a first for him with a woman—the worry that he might want more than she did.

He left the hallway and ensconced himself in his office and did a pisspoor job of responding to the correspondence his secretary had left for him to go through. Hours and hours went by, except when he looked at his watch, it had been exactly fifty-seven minutes since he'd sat down. Just over an hour since he'd carried Lily to her room. A little more since he'd come home to find that damned Fenris waiting. He returned to his letters and another eternity.

Someone tapped on the door.

Mountjoy muttered, "Thank God," and threw the letter he was reading onto the top of the pile of correspondence he would have to read again.

It was Doyle, with Dr. Longfield, whom Nigel had brought to the house to look after Lily. Mountjoy stayed at his desk and waved the doctor to a seat, privately glad of the interruption. Doyle retreated. Mountjoy was very good at appearing to be busy and engaged in important matters. Matters of State, even. "How is Miss Wellstone?"

The doctor perched on the edge of the chair across from his desk. "Quite a remarkable woman, as I'm sure you know."

"Do you think so?"

"Delightful smile and—*ahem*—extremely beautiful woman. Very well formed, I must say. Brilliant mind, too, if one can say that of a female."

He quirked one eyebrow.

"Very spirited and amusing, which I'm sure your grace has noticed."

Mountjoy tapped a finger on the table. He recognized in the doctor all the symptoms of infatuation with Lily Wellstone. "Since you found her spirited, am I permitted to assume that her health is no longer a matter of concern?"

"Her finger is well healed, I was pleased to note."

"Excellent." He forced a smile, but it wasn't her bloody finger that worried him.

Dr. Longfield grabbed the top of one knee and rocked on his chair. "How is it she's unmarried? A puzzling thing that at her age no man should have snapped her up."

Mountjoy moved a pile of correspondence from one side of his desk to the other. He didn't trust himself to look the doctor in the eye, torn as he was between wanting to laugh out loud or tell the man if he so much as breathed Lily's name he'd find himself outside of the house looking in. "Ought we to be more concerned with her present health than with her marital status, doctor?"

"Provided she does not overexert herself, she's as well as can be expected, which is well enough, your grace. And so I told her."

Mountjoy stood abruptly. Ten more seconds of this prattle and he'd go stark raving mad. "You see no need for concern?"

"Very little."

"Then thank you for coming here on such short notice."

"I've warned her she's far too delicate to stand in the sun as she did."

Mountjoy came around from behind his desk to put a hand on the doctor's shoulder and guide him to the door.

"She mustn't be permitted to engage in such excess again.

A delicate thing like her. You may tell her, your grace, that I forbid it."

"I will do exactly as you advise, thank you, doctor." Mountjoy opened the door. "You may rely on it."

He tugged at his coat. "Excellent."

"You know the way out?"

"Indeed, sir." The doctor crossed into the hallway then turned and bowed. "Give Miss Wellstone my regards, won't you?"

"I shall."

"Good day, your grace."

"Good day, doctor."

Mountjoy returned to his desk and stared at the patterns in the grain of the wood. He wanted to see Lily. Alone. He wanted to throw away all this damned correspondence and lock himself away where he and Lily would not be disturbed. He picked up the next letter in the batch he was supposed to read through. The words ran together like ants drunk on blue fire.

Half a lifetime passed and he got through precisely none of the letters. Someone knocked on the door, and he practically shouted in relief. "Enter."

His sister came in. She was a different woman since Lily had come. So young and pretty, if one could think such a thing about one's sister. "Mountjoy."

He rose and gestured to the chair Dr. Longfield had vacated. "Eugenia."

Instead of sitting she stood behind the chair, her hands resting on the top rail. "You'll think me presumptuous for this. Oh, do sit down, Mountjoy."

He did, leaning against his chair and picking up his pen. The ink had dried on the nib. "Yes?"

She bit her lower lip. "I've come about Lily."

He picked up his penknife and set himself to sharpening the point of his quill. "Dr. Longfield assures me she's in excellent health, though he warned me she's to stay out of the sun."

"He said the same thing to me. But Mountjoy, that's not why I've come."

"Oh?"

"I'm worried you'll be hurt."

"I beg your pardon?"

"Lily is my dear, dear friend. I love her better than anyone. She's amusing and intelligent and very, very beautiful."

"Yes," he said carefully. "She is all that. But I fail to see what that has to do with me."

Eugenia licked her lips. "You won't be surprised to know that other men have loved her." She gripped the top of the chair. "But Mountjoy, she never cared for a one of them, and . . . I don't think she ever will. She never led them on, she's not that sort of woman. She's like me after Robert."

"Eugenia . . ."

"Please don't interrupt, or I'll lose my nerve."

He gestured.

"I'll never love any man but Robert. And Lily, she's met the only man she will ever love." His sister's eyes were too bright.

"There is no need for tears," he said. He dropped the penknife on the blotter and offered her his handkerchief.

She waved it off. "I'm not crying."

"As you say." He continued to hold out his handkerchief.

"I'm not." Eugenia took it from him and dabbed at her eyes.

"I won't disagree with you that Miss Wellstone is a beautiful and vivacious woman."

"She is."

"I enjoy her company. Most of the time. So does your brother. I'm glad she's here, for she's done you a world of good."

Eugenia gave him a tremulous smile. "That's true."

"She's made me see that I have neglected you. I have not done my duty by you, and for that I apologize."

"Oh, no, Mountjoy. Never."

"She took me to task for my treatment of you, and she

was right to do so, but you mustn't think I'm angry with her for that."

"Angry?"

He steeled himself and said, "Is that not why you came here?"

"No." She sat on the chair, one hand over her heart. "You can't imagine how relieved I am to hear you say that." She shook her head. "You'll think me such a goose. I was worried she might have engaged your affections without your knowing, that's all."

"Engaged my affections?"

"I apologize, Mountjoy. Of course that's not happened. We all know you love Miss Kirk. It's just I've seen it happen to other men where Lily is concerned."

Mountjoy schooled his expression. "Eugenia." He laughed, and he even sounded convincing. "I am not in love with Miss Wellstone."

"Thank goodness. I am sorry, Mountjoy for jumping to conclusions about your feelings for Lily."

"You've no need to apologize." He smiled and picked up his pen. "Please close the door when you go."

Another century passed with him having given up any pretense of working. Then Doyle tapped on his office door and informed him it was time to change for supper.

He absolutely was not in love with Lily.

Chapter Twenty-three

LILY CAME DOWNSTAIRS FOR SUPPER PRECISELY AT SIX o'clock that evening, much recovered from the morning's treasure hunting experience and firm in her conviction that morning activities were to be avoided at all costs. She wore her very best evening gown, a crimson silk worked with gold embroidery and a gold underskirt that peeked from the scalloped hem. She had spent several afternoons before her departure for Bitterward fashioning the trim on the bodice and hem.

One curl of her hair was loose and trailed along the side of her neck. A matching arrangement of gold lace and crimson roses was affixed below a gold-filigree hair comb in the curls pinned at the back of her head. She'd even changed the ribbon for her medallion to a red one.

From the doorway, she had a view of Mountjoy and his brother before either man saw her. Every atom of her attention was for Mountjoy. He was seated on a chair, reading a paperbound journal while Lord Nigel stood staring into the fireplace, one foot on the grate. Mountjoy was as badly dressed as ever, yet the sight of him made her happy.

She straightened her skirts, adjusted the gold lace at her neckline, and tugged on her bodice before she walked in. Mountjoy saw her first, but all he did was set his journal on his lap. Lord Nigel turned his back to the fire and gave her an elaborate bow of the sort he only gave her when his brother was around to see it. Mountjoy stood, setting his volume on the table beside him.

She curtseyed. "Good evening, your grace. Lord Nigel."

"Miss Wellstone." Lord Nigel came forward to take her hand. "I hope you're feeling better."

"I am, thank you."

"You look lovely."

As a matter of fact, she was quite sure she did look lovely. She glanced at Mountjoy, but he stayed where he was, hands behind his back. If he admired her appearance tonight more, or even less, than any other time, she could not tell.

"I hope you haven't been waiting long," she said. He was supposed to have changed for supper, but could one even be sure? His cravat, which was not sufficiently starched, was loosened, and his coat was unbuttoned. Not unforgivable, that unbuttoned coat, but his waistcoat, that was unforgivable. The garment was muddy brown silk with small red lozenges that did not hide the knobs in the weave. Silk, yes, but poor quality. The design was not bad, but the colors and tailoring were unfortunate and inferior. She made a mental note to visit the man's tailor as soon as possible.

Mountjoy approached her at last, and with a flicker of his attention to her bosom, he bent over her hand. "Good evening, Miss Wellstone."

"Your grace."

He took something from his pocket. The corners of his mouth twitched. "I have something you ought to see."

"What could it be?" She was no longer shocked at the hard thump of her pulse when their eyes briefly locked.

There was nothing astonishing about her finding another man attractive, after all. She'd reacted that way to Greer even before she'd fallen in love with him and long before Greer had let her know he felt the same.

He opened his hand and held it out. "This."

She came close enough to see an irregularly shaped circle no larger than her smallest fingernail and so dark a copper that the object, at first glance, appeared black. Her heart sank after she plucked it from his hand. "Where did you get this, sir? From a shop in High Tearing by chance?"

The twitch of his mouth broadened into a smile. A very smug smile. "I kept several of them back from among the coins Nigel and I found near the river that day. They've been in my quarters ever since. Safe from the inquisitive fingers of boys who build trebuchets."

Lily stared at the coin in her hand. She hated to lose. Abhorred it.

"I believe, Miss Wellstone," he said in a low voice, "that I have won our wager."

She would have answered, but Ginny's arrival gave her an excuse to silently return the coin. He pocketed it, still with his smug grin.

"What wager is that?" Ginny crossed the room to envelop Lily in a quick embrace. "Lovely to see you. I was worried you wouldn't feel well enough to come downstairs."

"I'm quite well now, Ginny."

She held Lily at arm's length. "Don't you look lovely?" She glanced at her brothers. "Doesn't she look lovely?"

Lord Nigel made another elaborate bow and said, "As ever."

Mountjoy said nothing, but Lily felt the heat of his gaze.

Lord Nigel coughed into his hand. "Eugenia, I have business that will take me to London tomorrow. Is there anything I can bring back for you?"

"You're going to London?" Mountjoy asked.

Ginny turned to her younger brother. "You'll be back in time for our ball, won't you?"

"Wouldn't miss it for the world." He bowed to the duke. "Yes. I've business there. I won't be long. A few days."

"You'd better not," Ginny said. "We're counting on you to dance with all the young ladies too terrified to dance with Mountjoy."

"Of course, Eugenia. Your errands?"

"Would you mind stopping at Hookam's for me? There are several books I'd like. I'll write down the titles for you." Ginny headed to the writing desk to do just that, sweeping her skirts out of the way as she sat. She wore white, and Lily thought she looked just splendid.

"Miss Wellstone?" Lord Nigel asked. "Anything for you? Books? Ribbons? Candied almonds? I know you're fond of them. When I go to London I always bring back nougat for Eugenia."

"Thank you, Lord Nigel, that would be lovely."

"Mountjoy, what should Nigel bring back for Jane?" Ginny said from the desk where she was writing her list. She looked over her shoulder. "My dear brother," she said. "Do not tell me you haven't any idea."

Lily shot a glance at Mountjoy, who stood impassive.

"Then I must remain silent."

Ginny sighed. "Nigel, bring her back some lace. I'll write down the name of the shop. Brussels lace if you can get it."

"I promise you," Lord Nigel said quickly, "I'll bring back everything she requires."

"Something for all the Misses Kirk," Ginny said, still writing.

"Certainly." Lord Nigel turned to his brother. "What have you done with the treasure, Mountjoy? It's not still in the wagons, is it?"

"No," the duke answered smoothly. "I took the liberty of moving the artifacts to the old stillroom. If you are not familiar with the location, Miss Wellstone, Eugenia can show you where it is."

"Thank you." Their eyes met again. Head-on, and she lost all sense of anyone or anything but him, and she did not often lose her self-possession. He did not look away. Or smile. Goodness, but his eyes were an astonishing green, and his hair, though worn a shade too long, suited his careless manner.

"Here." Ginny stretched backward over the desk chair, extending the notepaper to Lord Nigel, who took the sheet from her and slipped it into an inside pocket of his coat. "Thank you, Nigel."

Lily tore her gaze from Mountjoy. "We'll need a detailed inventory of what we found, Ginny. Perhaps you and I could begin tomorrow?"

"If you like. But I've just had the most wonderful idea," Ginny said.

"Oh?"

She shifted to face her younger brother. "Nigel, what if Lily and I went to London with you?" She turned again, this time to address Mountjoy. "May we stay at the town house?"

"That would not be convenient," Lord Nigel said.

"Whyever not?" She gripped the top of the chair and leaned over it. "No one stays there when Mountjoy's at Bitterward. As well open the house for one person as three. We won't bother you, Nigel, I promise."

"I'm very sorry, Eugenia," Lord Nigel said. He wiped his hands down the front of his coat. "But I'm leaving before dawn, and I'm not taking the carriage."

"A trip to London is a lovely idea, but, Ginny, I cannot go," Lily said, partly because it was true, but also because Lord Nigel obviously did not want their company. "Not tomorrow, at any rate."

"Why not?"

She sent a quick glance in Mountjoy's direction. She had so little time before she had to return to Syton House, and she did not want to spend any of it away from Mountjoy. "Your brother has produced a coin that was the subject of a wager we made earlier this afternoon."

Ginny leaned her forearm over the back of her chair. She looked from Mountjoy to Lily. "A wager?"

"Yes."

"Oh dear. You lost, didn't you, Lily?"

"Yes."

"If only you'd told me. I would have warned you. Nigel and I learned as children never to wager with him." She shook her head. "How much did you lose?"

"Alas, Ginny, I am now obliged to wait hand and foot on your brother for a period of twenty-four hours."

Ginny tried to stop a laugh and failed. "Say it's not so, Lily."

"I'm afraid it is. We'll go to London another time, I promise you. On this occasion, sadly, Lord Nigel will have to make do without our company."

"However will I manage?" Lord Nigel said.

"Fortitude, sir. A great deal of fortitude. As I must now have. Your grace," Lily said to Mountjoy, "would you not like to sit down?" She walked to a chair and, standing behind it, put her hands on either side of the back.

"I do believe," Mountjoy said, pointing to a chair on the opposite side of the room, "that I would like to sit in that chair."

"But of course. Would you care for a blanket, perhaps?" she asked as she walked across the room. He went along and sat, with great ceremony, on the chair. "Or a pillow upon which to rest your weary noble feet?"

"That stool there," he said with a wave at a round ottoman on yet another side of the room. She fetched it for him and placed it at his feet. "*Hmm*," he said in a doubtful tone as he shifted around. Lord Nigel snickered while Ginny gawped at her elder brother. "I'm not sure this one is as comfortable as I'd hoped."

Lily gave him a curtsey worthy of a meeting with the Prince Regent. "Allow me to search the house for another, your grace, for I can think of nothing but your pleasure and happiness."

The arrival of Doyle to announce dinner prevented her carrying out that plan. Mountjoy rose and held out his arm. "Miss Wellstone."

He escorted her to the dinner table, seeing her to her seat at his right. She took care to over-attend to his needs. She even unfolded his napkin and draped it over his lap for him.

"Thank you, Wellstone."

No one seemed to notice his slip, thank goodness. The food, as always, was excellent, the conversation as good as ever. They discussed the treasure they'd uncovered, what it might be, how they might clean it and whether it was Roman or something much older. Or younger. It was Mountjoy who mentioned an acquaintance at Oxford who they might call in to have a look, which Lily thought an excellent idea.

As they talked, servants brought each dish to the duke first, but to much amusement Lily made a point of examining the dishes and selecting the most delectable slice of beef, the lightest, flakiest fish. She tasted his wine for him, and when she found it acceptable, which she did because the cellars at Bitterward were first-rate, she filled his glass rather than allowing one of the footmen to do so.

"Mountjoy," Ginny said. "Since Nigel will be gone tomorrow, would you be so kind as to drive Lily and me into High Tearing?"

Mountjoy drank some of his wine and casually held out his glass for Lily to refill. She did, with the wonderful French Beaujolais that had been opened. "I am free in the afternoon, if that's convenient for you."

"Two o'clock?"

He nodded. "I should be delighted."

As the meal came to a close, the staff brought out plates of fruit and cheese, which were, naturally, arranged so they were before Mountjoy since he presided over the table. Lily took his knife and cut and cored an apple and then a pear. She arranged the fruit and added slices of cheese until the contents were balanced and pleasing to the eye. Ginny and Lord Nigel snickered while she did.

When it came time for them to leave the men to the table, she and Ginny walked arm in arm to the salon. There, Ginny leaned against the wall beside the door and laughed. "Oh,

Lily, you were astounding. Priceless. The way you waited on Mountjoy— Oh, I will adore you forever for this night."

She, too, thought Mountjoy had been magnificent. He'd played along wonderfully and made the evening much more amusing that she'd ever have expected. She took a seat near the fire and retrieved her embroidery. She was working on new trim for one of the gowns she was having remade for Ginny. Ginny brought over the lamp and placed it so she had the best light for the work.

"Thank you, dear. So thoughtful of you." She was going to miss the companionship when she was back at Syton House.

"It's the least I can do." She sat on the chair beside Lily. "What else will you do for him?" she asked. "Please torture him. It's so wonderful to see him suffer. He cannot bear being made a fuss of."

She set her needlework on her lap, smiling. "You're so very right, Ginny. I really must make him suffer. Until he begs me to stop."

"Oh, do, please do. This is much better than going to London."

"He won't last another hour."

The door opened and Lord Nigel came in, followed by Mountjoy. The duke's eyes flicked to her, and Lily's breath caught in her chest.

"What shall we do to entertain ourselves tonight?" Lord Nigel made for a seat near the fire. When Mountjoy sat, she hurried to spread a blanket over his lap. Lord Nigel snorted when Mountjoy pushed away her hands. "You look a proper old man now, Mountjoy. Miss Wellstone, I think he needs a blanket for his shoulders, too."

"No, I do not."

"I've grown accustomed to our nightly discussions of strategies and plans for finding treasure." Lord Nigel grinned at them. "Now that we've found it, what's left for us?"

"I am compelled to point out we may not have found Roman artifacts," Lily said. She retook her seat and put away her embroidery. "Nor did we uncover a foundation. No, there is yet a great deal of work remaining, despite our initial successes." She addressed Mountjoy next. "Your grace?"

He threw the blanket off his lap. "Miss Wellstone?"

"May we continue our excavation, or have you given up on that?" She pulled a skein of green yarn from her basket and held it up, squinting at Mountjoy as she did.

"Dig as many holes as you like, so long as they are filled in when you are done with them. May I ask why you are waving that yarn in my face, Miss Wellstone?"

"Ginny, what do you think of this color for your brother?"

"It matches his eyes."

"Old men need mufflers," Lord Nigel said. "Wards off the chill in their creaky bones."

"I intend to knit you a scarf, your grace."

"I don't need a scarf."

"In respect of your wardrobe, sir, you have no authority."

"And you do?" The man knew very well that she did.

"I have decided you must have something to remember me by once I've gone home. And as your brother so wisely points out, a scarf will ward you from chills. Very useful, I should think. I am contemplating whether I should work your coat of arms into this. What do you think, Ginny? Is that not an excellent idea?"

"Oh, yes."

She found the loose end of yarn and proceeded to make a neat ball. Mountjoy, however, brought his chair closer to hers and dutifully held up his hands to act as a guide for her winding the yarn into a less tangled form.

"My father used to do this for my mother," he said. He watched Lily over the tops of his fingers.

"Yes," Ginny said. "I remember Papa would read to us or recite a poem. Or sing. Do you remember that, Nigel?"

"I do."

Instead of feeling left out of these reminiscences, Lily felt as if she belonged. As if the memories, though not hers, were hers to share. She could almost believe that she, too, had grown up in a warm and loving family. They spent the next hour taking turns reciting poetry or singing or telling tales. Lord Nigel and Ginny both sang very well, Lily had a tolerable voice, and even Mountjoy wasn't as bad as he'd claimed he was.

Lord Nigel knew long passages from Milton's *Paradise Lost*, and he recited them beautifully. After that, Mountjoy fetched a copy of *A Midsummer Night's Dream* and she wanted to hug him close for remembering her childhood dream of running away to tread the boards. She did love to act out a scene. They read scenes from the play, at one point swapping the roles so that the ladies read the parts of the men, and Lord Nigel and Mountjoy the parts of the ladies, and it was great fun.

For the first time since Greer's death, Lily felt there were people on whom she could rely. People who welcomed her for who and what she was. Flaws and all. The feeling that she was wanted here, a friend even, made the evening magical. Like her time here at Bitterward, the feeling that she belonged would end too soon.

Lord Nigel was the first to retire, as he had an early day tomorrow. Mountjoy remained to talk for a while longer, and the subjects were never anything deep, just stories about how the Hampton children had grown up, a bit of politics, though not much, and then Ginny yawned and Mountjoy stood.

"Come ladies, I'll walk you to your rooms and say good night to you both. I want to see Nigel off in the morning."

Ginny's room was closest and they stopped before her door and said good night. As Ginny went inside, Mountjoy made it seem he would walk away once her door closed. But he didn't.

Lily and Mountjoy were alone with fifteen paces yet to travel before they reached her door. "Wellstone."

She looked up at him. "Your grace?"

He came close and studied her so intently she wasn't sure what to think. "Thank you for a lovely evening tonight."

"Thank you." She touched his hand. "When I was a girl, I had to read all the parts myself. It was great fun reading with you."

"I'm pleased you enjoyed yourself."

"I did. This isn't a night I'll soon forget."

"You're sure you're well after all you endured today?"

"Perfectly." She took a step back, but somehow the distance between them did not change. She took another step back and found her shoulders pressed against the wall. The distance between them still had not changed.

"I'm glad you are here with us at Bitterward," the duke said. "I can't recall the last time I saw Eugenia smile as much as she did tonight. Or when I've had my every comfort so thoroughly looked after."

"You are ingratiating yourself with me, aren't you?"

"I am," he said.

She put a hand on his chest. "You do it beautifully."

"Thank you."

"Diabolically clever of you, sir." His mouth was inches from hers, and he was stealing all the air.

"There are one or two more things I'd like from you tonight, Wellstone."

"What could that be?"

"Come with me, and we'll discuss it."

They returned to the east tower room, but, as it turned out, there was very little to discuss, and in any event, Lily was kept busy seeing to Mountjoy's every whim. He had a great many.

Eventually, she lay in his arms, exhausted and happier than she'd been in longer than she could recall. Her last thoughts before she gave in to sleep were that she'd come out the winner in their wager and that she would be very sorry to leave here.

Chapter Twenty-four

❧❧

MOUNTJOY LOOKED AT HIS REFLECTION IN THE CHE-val glass and tugged on his waistcoat. A man's clothes didn't prove much besides how much money he wasted on his tailor. Except now that he was studying himself, he wondered if Lily wasn't right. She'd been to see his tailor and there were, he was told, great events in the works. "Elliot. Are you sure this fits as it should?"

His valet hovered behind him, squinting, hands clasped in front of his heart. His graying eyebrows made a straight line across his forehead, then smoothed out. "Your grace?"

The note of resignation in his valet's response pricked his conscience. True, he'd made it clear he didn't want Elliot fussing and interfering with his wardrobe. He wanted to get dressed and go about his business. "The truth," he said. His favorite coat hung over the chair behind him. "It doesn't fit properly, does it?"

Elliot blanched. "I don't presume, your grace, to have an opinion about what suits you."

He turned around, irritated beyond belief to have his

words of so long ago parroted back at him. "It's your bloody job, man."

"Sir." He backed up a step then bowed. "Your grace."

"Elliot. I beg your pardon. That was not fair of me." Elliot bowed but his expression remained cautious. Mountjoy sighed. "The waistcoat does not fit, though I'm damned if I can tell why."

"Perhaps if you had allowed your tailor to do the additional fittings . . ."

"Does it matter when my coat will hide it?" He remembered the days after he'd ascended to his title and how Fenris and others had sneered about farmers dressing up as dukes. Mountjoy's response had been hardly more than irritation. He simply hadn't cared much for anyone's opinion of his clothes when so many other things mattered more. For some absurd reason, it mattered to him that Lily found his wardrobe inferior.

Elliot shifted his weight between his feet, and his eyebrows met again. He coughed once. "Your grace is concerned with fashion?"

"No." But for his promise to Lily, he would barely have glanced at himself in the mirror this morning. He wouldn't have given a moment's thought to the fit of his waistcoat. "Perhaps a change is in order."

"A change, sir?" He licked his lips, slowly, plainly considering what words he would use. "Do you intend something more substantial than new buttons? If I might inquire. So as to be prepared."

He tugged on the bottom of his waistcoat again. The moment he let go, the sides sagged. She was right about his clothes. "Is there another tailor you'd recommend?"

Elliot sucked in a breath. "In High Tearing or Sheffield?"

"I was thinking of London."

There was a moment of heavy silence. Elliot coughed softly. "London, your grace?"

"Yes, London."

"Oh," Elliot said. "Oh. Do you, by any chance, mean a

Bond Street tailor?" He whispered the words *Bond Street* as if the mere mention would bring God himself down to earth.

He could hear himself telling Elliot, not so long ago and quite possibly in a curt tone, that he was forbidden to mention the words *Bond Street* and *tailor* in the same sentence. He'd also said he didn't give a damn what he looked like, and that he didn't need any tailor but the one he'd patronized since he was expected to buy his own suits.

"We shall see." He turned back to the mirror. He'd let his prick do his thinking for him, and now he was fending off a rapturous valet. He didn't regret it as much as he ought to.

In fact, both he and his prick wanted Lily again.

If letting Lily dress him up meant he would have her again, she could put him in tassels and purple silk, and he wouldn't care. Except she wouldn't, because Lily had exquisite taste. "What about the color?" he asked.

"The color, your grace?"

His coat was green. So was his waistcoat. Why wouldn't green go with a coat that was nearly the same color? He thought of Lily's reaction to his banyan, the way she'd smoothed her hands over the fabric. She loved beautiful things. Beautiful to look at, to touch, and to taste. "Does this waistcoat go with that coat?"

Elliot, face as gray as his hair, shook his head. "In my opinion, no, your grace. Begging your pardon, sir."

Damn. The coat he had insisted he would wear today was comfortable, and he'd last worn it five days ago. Why oughtn't he to wear it again? Mountjoy walked away from the mirror and sat down, looking sideways at Elliott. The poor man was frozen in place. Elliot had once valeted the younger son of an earl. A bit of a rogue from what one heard. Elliot had elected to stay in England when his previous employer was shipped off to India to avoid unsavory rumors and inconvenient debts. Quite a come down for the man to valet a duke with no taste.

Mountjoy sighed. "You've tried to tell me."

Elliot swallowed hard and picked up the lint brush. He held it like a shield over his heart. "Your grace."

"What coat does go with this waistcoat?" He waved a hand. "Never mind. It's the one you tried to get me to wear."

"Sir."

He stood. "I suppose none of my coats fit."

Elliot clutched the lint brush to his chest and shook his head again. He looked sadder than ever, yet Mountjoy did not think he was wrong there was a glint of joy in the man's eyes. Once he had new clothes, Lily would look at him with a glint in her eyes, too.

He plucked the other coat off the top of the chair. His most comfortable coat, his favorite coat. An old friend. He threw it on the seat of the chair where one sleeve drooped to the floor, looking to him like a fair match to the olive green of his waistcoat. He was stubborn. He knew that. He'd kept to his old habits of dress out of sheer muleheadedness. Daring people to think the Duke of Mountjoy mattered less because of his clothes and not more because he'd saved the title from extinction and then done his bloody duty every day of his life since.

Mountjoy sighed. "Bring me a coat that goes with this waistcoat, then."

His valet broke into a smile. "Yes, your grace."

While Elliot brought out the better coat, Mountjoy returned to the cheval glass. He looked like himself. More to the point, he looked much the same as he'd looked when he was not in possession of a title, an estate, or the income that went with it. But he wasn't that boy. God knows he'd changed in just about every way since then. In truth, he was a bigger man, two inches taller and still as broad through the shoulders as the farmer he'd once been. Older by a dozen years. A man, now, not a boy. Not a farmer, whether by his choice or not, but a duke.

As far as he was concerned, the new coat looked very much like the old one. Except not as comfortable. His valet went at him with the lint brush, and he gritted his teeth, resisting the urge to snatch the brush away and throw the damned thing out the window. "Thank you, Elliot."

"Your grace."

He headed for the door but halted halfway there. He turned. "I will be ordering a new wardrobe presently. If there are London tailors you think are suitable, please write me a list of names."

His valet smiled. "Your grace."

"In future, Elliot, I will endeavor to listen to your advice."

The servant beamed at him as if he'd handed over the damned Crown Jewels and told him they were a gift from the Prince Regent himself. "Sir."

He headed downstairs. Eugenia had made a particular point of asking him to attend her tea this afternoon, and he had agreed. Duty and all that. Nigel wasn't due home from London for another two or three days at least, leaving him the only Hampton male to attend. Besides, Lily would be there.

The function Eugenia had begged him to attend, since Nigel's business in London kept him away, was in the Oldenburg salon, and he arrived to find at least twenty people crowding the room. There seemed to be a great deal of food either on trays or being carried about the room by footmen in livery. Everywhere he looked were dainty sandwiches, petit fours, cheese, bread, biscuits. Jellies, and cold ham and pastries he did not recognize. Three other footmen strolled through the room, one collecting abandoned or unneeded dishes, another with a tray of meringues, and the last with a salver of assorted sweetmeats. This was the sort of gathering a duke ought to have, he thought.

He recognized the vicar, holding a plate of half-eaten cake, deep in conversation with Dr. Longfield. He saw several of his neighbors. Fine men, all of them, some of whom would have traveled upwards of two hours to reach Bitterward. At least half of the people in his house were young ladies of the sort mothers and fathers liked to have introduced to men like his brother Nigel. And him. He stayed in the doorway and scanned the room for Lily without admitting that he was.

He'd been living at Bitterward for more than ten years, but he had not had a formal gathering since Eugenia was married. No dinners or fetes. He didn't hunt much, and he had never attended any of the dances in town. Other than irregular appearances at church and somewhat more regular evenings at the homes of neighbors he liked, he'd kept to himself. He knew the gentlemen but not their wives and children.

Lily stood by the window, fingering her medallion, counting up and down the gold beads worked into the ribbon. Several men were gathered around her, some more boy than man, but they all had the same besotted expression. Eugenia stood next to Lily, wearing a lavender gown. She was laughing at something, and, Lord, his sister was still young and pretty.

Good God.

Jane Kirk was here, too, sitting for now with her mother and sisters. The woman everyone thought was his future wife. He was aware he was an object of her interest and even trepidation. He stayed where he was and watched Lily while she was unaware of his presence. She'd been naked in his arms, and he'd looked into her face while he thrust into her. She'd had her mouth around his cock, and he'd had his hands on her, everywhere he could reach, and she was smiling as if none of that had happened. Lovers for a few days and nothing more? Would she return to Syton House and her dratted father and never think of him again?

"Your grace." The vicar walked across the room to him, sketching out a bow while holding his plate of cake. Dr. Longfield had joined the crowd around Eugenia and Lily. "Delighted to see you, sir."

"Vicar."

"You really must try this cake." He picked up his fork and pointed at the remains of a slice of yellow cake on his plate. "I had no idea your cook was capable of such transporting delights."

"You ought to come to tea more often," he said.

"I shall, oh, I shall. Now that you ask. And you, your grace, I hope will one day accept my invitation to tea at the vicarage."

"I will, sir." He imagined sitting there with Lily beside him.

"Lovely tea," the vicar said.

"Thank you." Mountjoy, with the vicar in tow, joined his sister.

"Mountjoy," Eugenia said. Her smile transformed her into the sister he remembered from years ago. She went to him and kissed his cheek. "Thank you so much for coming."

Lily was right. His public support of his sister mattered a great deal, but he'd rather be tromping through the fields than standing here in a room full of people he barely knew.

He glanced at Lily. Nothing could be more natural. A gentleman ought to greet his houseguest. Their eyes met, all innocence between them. Mountjoy acknowledged her with a nod.

"Your grace," she said. She was regally calm.

By God, there would be another time for them.

Lily said, "Shall I fetch you a plate of food, your grace? There is the most astounding Edam, and some delightful strawberry preserves. Cakes, too, if you'd like some."

The vicar lifted his plate. "His grace must have a slice of cake."

At Lily's confirming look, Mountjoy said, "Yes, thank you." Anyone who looked at him must surely know he'd had carnal knowledge of her. "Miss Wellstone."

Lily went to the sideboard. He contented himself with counting the number of men who stared at her. Damn near every man in the room. Including him.

"Tea, Mountjoy," Eugenia said.

He waved her off. "Not hungry."

"Dear brother. You drink tea, not eat it." Eugenia's eyes sparkled, and he tore his gaze from Lily. "I made some for you with Lily's Lapsang, but if you'd rather have the gunpowder, I'd be happy to make that for you instead."

"The Lapsang is perfect. Thank you." With a smile, he took the cup and saucer from his sister. They were using the best china today. The Mountjoy crest was painted on every piece. He took a sip of his tea. Someone had taken the vicar aside and left him standing more or less alone with his sister.

"Mountjoy?" Eugenia said.

"Yes?"

"May I ask a favor of you?"

He sipped his tea and liked the flavor even better than before. "You may."

"I'd like you to speak to Lord Fenris."

He set his cup on its saucer too hard. What he remembered was the way Fenris had asked after his sister, how quickly the man had gone to Eugenia's assistance. If he'd made himself unpleasant to her, he'd see that Fenris was sorry he'd ever stepped foot near Bitterward. "Why?"

"He's not to be trusted. I know from personal experience that's true. He means Lily no good." She put a hand on his arm. "Protect her, Mountjoy. She deserves better than whatever Fenris has in store for her. Will you promise me?"

Chapter Twenty-five

MOUNTJOY WATCHED LILY CHARM EVERYONE. SHE wore a frock with a pink bodice and a white skirt with narrow pink stripes. Her slippers were pink.

He was aware that he might be ignoring her too assiduously. He'd left the knot of men he'd been speaking with and had made a point of moving from one group to another, the epitome of a good host. One of the young ladies from High Tearing was sitting at the piano in the corner of the salon playing Bach and doing a creditable job, too. He spoke with his neighbors, made the acquaintance of wives, sons, and daughters, and observed that his clothes were, in the main, flavorless compared to anyone else's.

At one point, he found himself in a crowd that included Jane Kirk. He should get his proposal done with. Invite her to stroll with him, and tell her he hoped she would consent to be his duchess. "Miss Kirk." He bent over Jane's hand. She smiled coolly. There was just nothing between him and Jane. No spark. He could not deny she was a pretty woman. He liked her. She was pleasant and intelligent and there was simply nothing between them. Had there been, he might have done something about the two of them when the sly innuendos about a match first began.

"Delightful to see you at Bitterward," he said to her. "My brother will be devastated to know he missed you today."

"Your grace." She flushed and didn't meet his gaze.

They stood there with nothing more to say to each other. He opened his mouth to ask her if she would like to see the roses and what came out was, "I beg your pardon, Miss Kirk. There's someone I must speak to."

He escaped the room and, taking in great breaths of air, leaned against the wall just beside the door. The sounds of the gathering carried on the air. Laughter. The clinking of cups. Mountjoy rested his head against the wall. He was no good at parties. No good at all. He would speak to Jane another time, when his house was not full of people he barely knew. He would get to know her.

"Your grace?"

He opened his eyes and saw Lily standing before him. "Lily."

She curtseyed. "Are you well?"

"I am now."

"Mr. Kirk was asking after you."

"I will find him presently."

She put her hands behind her back and rocked on her heels in that way she had. "Is aught well?"

"When do you intend to take command of my wardrobe?" he asked in a low voice. The question reminded him of the luscious curves of her body, and the sound she made when he entered her. He did not want to think of the inevitable time when she would be gone, but it killed him to know she would be. At his side, he clenched his fists then released them.

"Your tailor will need additional measurements. I trust you will oblige him." She leaned back and swept her eyes over him. "I'll be sending fabric samples and strict instructions for how the cloth is to be cut."

The electricity between them made him feel alive. He pulled at his cravat.

"Stop," she said. "You're making things worse."

"The bloody thing is strangling me. Come with me, Lily, and fix it."

She glanced at the door and then at him. "Is that all?"

"No." He took a step toward her. "You know that's not all."

"Your sister has guests, Mountjoy. I can't abandon her. Or them." She put a hand on his sleeve. "Come back inside."

"I've had enough, Wellstone." A servant came out of the salon with a tray.

"Poor man."

"You like all that. The people. The talk and noise."

"I do."

"I don't." He speared her with a look. "All I want is to be alone with you."

She smiled, and he thought his heart would break at the sight. "Later, Mountjoy. I promise you."

"Now," he said.

"You know I can't."

"I won't go back in there."

She shrugged. "Then go, your grace. You're no good to anyone scowling like that anyway."

"I've done my duty to Eugenia."

"You have."

He checked the hall again and, seeing no one, risked a touch to her cheek. "Do what you must, then. Enjoy yourself." They were so different, the two of them. "So long as you know I want you with me."

She didn't return his smile. "Your grace."

He walked away, thinking he ought to have gone back inside, but equally aware that the crowd would have quickly worn away his civility. Some minutes later he ended up in his office, which, it happened, overlooked the same back lawns as the Oldenburg salon. The guests had moved outside, Lily among them. He gazed out the window, unable to work, though there was a mountain of correspondence and ledgers awaiting his attention. He ignored it all.

She would leave him. Every minute that passed brought them closer to that moment. That had been the understanding from the beginning. If he were honest, that impermanence had, at the start, been a relief. It would eventually happen that they would go their separate ways. But not yet. Not just yet. Even from a distance one could tell Lily was the leader, the others followers, she the sun, everyone else planets in orbit around her. She was the light of any room. In a crowd, one noticed her. Exuberant and full of spirits. Passionate beyond belief. Beautiful in his arms.

He rested a hand on the sill and his forehead on the casement. He was endangering his good name and his family's trust by thinking for even half a second that he could safely conduct an affair with Lily for the rest of the time she was here. Not with his blinding need for her. How long did they have? Two weeks. Three? Could he convince her to stay for a month? What about a year?

The rest of his life?

Today the sun shone bright, and the guests outside were laughing and gesturing and dashing about. Someone's dog was barking, and the sound carried through the window. Two servants came out, each carrying a basket filled with what looked like apples.

Lily was now arm in arm with Eugenia and Jane, and Caroline Kirk, too. They looked well together, the four of them. Several of the gentlemen held tennis racquets. He grabbed the windowsill and stood there, staring at Lily in that pink frock that fit her like a dream. No other woman out there looked half as fine as she did.

Miss Caroline threw a stick for the dog, a spaniel of some sort. It dashed after its prize. The footmen set the baskets on an invisible line, with the guests gathered behind them. Lily began an animated explanation that involved gestures and pacing. Dr. Longfield stepped forward, a tennis racquet in hand. At a signal from Lily, he took an apple from one of the baskets.

The doctor threw the apple into the air, a wizened thing it was, and hit it a smashing serve. The fruit came off the racquet like an overstuffed Christmas goose. Bits split off and plummeted to the ground.

The demonstration appeared to have been successful, for the doctor bowed once, turned his racquet over to the next gentleman in line, and the rest of the guests lined up. Two at a time, they took turns throwing an apple or other unappetizing fruit into the air and hitting it with the racquets. From time to time one of the gentlemen would lob the fruit into the air for one of the ladies.

There were a great many misses and an indecent amount of mirth. Not everyone hit their target the first time. Whenever someone hit one of the apples particularly well, cheers and applause rose up. There was, he could see from his vantage, spirited betting going on among certain of the spectators.

His guests—Eugenia and Lily's guests—were having a splendid time. The footmen retrieved any apples that hadn't disintegrated upon being hit and that appeared as if they could be abused again. Lily stepped up to the line and accepted an apple from Jane Kirk. She tossed her missile into the air and *whack*! The fruit spiraled through the air, shedding bits until the entire thing came apart.

Mountjoy left the window. At his desk, he dashed off a quick line on a half sheet of paper and put the folded page into his coat pocket. By the time he reached the lawn, Lily had another apple and a racquet in hand. Everyone was laughing and smiling, even people who had failed to hit anything while he'd been watching.

Lily put her toe to the line again. As before, she threw her apple into the air. He could see that most of one side of the fruit was a discolored brown.

Thwack!

The apple shot into the air, split into several pieces, and whirled three different directions. Cheers went up.

"Good shot, Miss Wellstone!"

"Applesauce!"

Footmen ran out to retrieve what pieces of fruit they could.

He crossed the lawn, aware of a sudden silence. From the corner of his eye, he saw Jane Kirk, ashen, a hand over her mouth. Did they really think him as awful as that? "Miss Wellstone—" He held out his hand to Lily. What little conversation was still ongoing ceased.

He heard Eugenia whisper, "No, Mountjoy."

"Give me the racquet, if you please."

Lily handed it to him with only a slight tilt of her head. During the exchange, he shoved his note into the top of her glove. Racquet in hand, he turned to his left.

"We're saving the pieces, Mountjoy," Eugenia said. She held her hands to her mouth, then lowered them. "They're to be fed to the chickens and the stoats."

He stooped for an apple. It was discolored and soft. "Even this one?"

"Yes," Ginny said. Behind her, Jane Kirk shook her head. Caroline looked at him as if she expected him to bite off someone's head.

"It's hardly fit for a pig."

No one said anything.

Mountjoy tossed the apple into the air and hit it with all his strength. It shot through the air like a thing possessed, whirling and spinning and then disintegrating. Bits of apple rained down, yards and yards distant, he saw with some satisfaction, from where anyone else's had landed.

Caroline Kirk leaned over to Eugenia and said, not too softly, "Applesauce."

Jane shushed her.

Lily kept a straight face. "Well hit, your grace."

He handed the racquet to Lily. "That's how it's done."

"Indeed, your grace."

"See that the scraps are fed to the livestock." And then he stalked away like an ogre retreating to its lair.

Chapter Twenty-six

MOUNTJOY PACED WHILE HE WAITED. HIS REGULATED life was falling to bits. Nothing was as it should be. He no longer knew how to behave toward Lily in public and it seemed whatever he did only made Jane's opinion of him worse. People were noticing a difference in him, too. Since Lily's arrival, the men he regularly met with had all remarked, in small ways and large, that he was a changed man. Eventually, he was going to say the wrong thing to Lily in front of someone, if he hadn't already, or pay too much attention to her and not enough to Jane. He'd be caught staring at Lily, not Jane, and the rumors would start.

When the door to the tower room opened, Mountjoy stopped pacing and wondered at the way his heart beat so hard. He said nothing. His life came to a halt. She had a key. He'd given Lily the key to the tower room he considered his sanctuary.

Lily closed the door and leaned against it, hands behind her. She was . . . serene. "Are you angry?"

"Not angry," he managed. He must break with her. Send

her home to Syton House now. He must say the words he had ready.

"Eugenia and Jane had nothing to do with it."

He nodded.

"It was all in good fun. I didn't think I needed your permission for a game. The new apples are already put by. We only hit the ones that no one would ever eat."

"Close the door." Heart sinking to his toes, he knew he wouldn't say what he should. He was still enthralled. The boredom would come, and then he'd break with her. But not yet. Not while she was at Bitterward. Surely, he could manage until she left. Then his life would go back to the way it was.

She did, then faced him again. Patient. Lovely beyond his understanding. "I daresay the hens will thank me for saving them from eating all the really rotten bits."

"It was your idea." He sounded a bloody fool. Hadn't she already told him so?

Her chin lifted. "Every part of it."

"I'm not angry."

"I am glad to know it." Cool as ice, she brought her hands from behind her and drew his note from the sleeve of her glove. "You'll want to burn this."

"Come here."

"I am here, your grace." God, that inscrutable expression of hers, as if nothing he could do or say could ever touch her. "At your pleasure."

"You should be here." He glanced at his feet, well aware there was a crude interpretation to his words and action.

Her mouth curved, and the last of her wariness slid from her eyes. "Maybe you should be here."

"Come here. To me."

She leaned her head against the door. "I think I will be safer here."

"Yes," he said. "You would be. Much safer. Is that what you want? To be safe?"

She pushed off and walked toward him. He watched her approach. "Are you sure you're not angry?"

"Quite."

"Well then. If you're not angry, why the imperial summons?" She waved his note.

"I thought I would go mad watching you. They admire you, all of them. Too much. Especially that damned Dr. Longfield."

"Don't be jealous," she said when she reached him. He took back his note, the dratted thing. "It's unbecoming a duke."

He drew her into his arms and brushed his mouth over hers. They fell into a kiss so carnal his initial thought of indulging just in this, just the kissing, flew off with his good sense. He pulled away. "I have a sheath," he said. "From Venice. I'm told they make the finest."

At first she didn't understand, and he felt a pang of guilt that she was innocent enough not to know what he meant. But then her expression cleared. "Oh. I see." Her cheeks turned pink. "Have you?"

"Yes."

"What of it, Mountjoy?" Her arms stayed around his shoulders. One of her hands played in his hair.

"I have it with me." He patted his chest in the location of an interior pocket of his coat.

"Convenient."

"I want to fuck you here." The words sounded crude, not what he meant at all. "Right now. With you wearing that pretty frock."

She drew in a sharp breath. "Wicked man."

He released her and walked to the sideboard to pull the salver from beneath the bottles there. He put an edge of his peremptory note to the flame of the lantern until it caught. When the fire licked down nearly to his fingers, he dropped what was left on the salver and waited until nothing remained but ashes. He also found some still water, thank God, and dropped his sheath into a glass of it so it would soften.

"Best stir the ashes," Lily said. "To be sure no one can reconstruct the note."

"It's gone up in smoke." He looked over his shoulder at her. She remained standing in the middle of the room. "No one will be reading it, I promise you."

"I can see most of the shape of the paper."

"And?"

"I once read a novel in which a spy was uncovered in just such a manner. The clever heroine was able to read the words etched into the ashes of the page."

"Balderdash."

"Upon such convictions are nations brought down." In a softer voice, she added, "And reputations destroyed."

She was right. And it would be her reputation that was shredded. There was no reason for the risk, far-fetched as it might be. He sighed and stirred the embers with his finger until all that was left was curling bits of blackened motes. He splashed some brandy on his fingers and wiped off the ashy residue with his handkerchief. Turning, he said, "Do you think we're safe now?"

"Not at all," she said.

Carrying the glass with his sheath, he returned to her and set it on the floor by the chaise. He put his hands on her shoulders and brushed his thumbs over her exposed skin. "You're right, Lily. Neither one of us is safe now."

She smiled. "Not in the least."

Taking her hand in his, he sat on the chaise where he drew her between his open thighs. He reached for the buttons along the side of her glove. One tiny pearl after another, he unfastened her glove enough for him to pull it off. He did the same with the other and draped them both over the top of the chaise.

"Thank you," she said. "The better to touch you."

He slid his hands underneath her skirts. His hands glided up her legs until he was touching the bare skin of her thighs. "The better to touch you. Like this."

She gazed down at him. "It's not wise."

"We've established that." He cupped the back of her thighs and pulled her forward. She was careful to lift her skirt, and he took care not to crush her frock more than necessary. She straddled him, knees on either side of him, and gasped softly when his fingers pressed between her legs. Soft skin, the folds of her already slick with want. Of him. He unbuttoned one side of his breeches and opened the fall to free himself.

Lily dropped her hands to his shoulders and watched him retrieve the sheath. Her skirts hid his hands sliding the lambskin over his cock and fastening the ribbon, but she knew what he was doing.

"Ready?" he whispered.

Her dark eyes stayed on his face while he adjusted them both. He brought her down on him, hands cupping her hips while he pushed up. Her body surrounded him, and as he closed his eyes and gave in to the exquisite sensation of being inside her and surrounded by the soft slickness of her, she whispered, "You feel good. So good."

When he was seated in her, pressing her down on him, he opened his eyes and said, "Say my name."

"Your grace."

He brought his hips toward hers and angled himself so the side of his cock, the sensitive head of him, rubbed harder against her passage. He pulled her forward sharply and thrust hard into her. "That isn't my name."

"Mountjoy." Her lips parted, and he disengaged his hands from her skirts and wrapped one hand around the nape of her neck. He kissed her. Hard and deep, tongue sweeping into her mouth. He moved his other hand to her belly, as far as he could reach before the bottom of her corset barred the way. He angled his fingers so he could stroke her. He knew where to touch a woman to bring her to pleasure, and he did so for her.

Lily's fingers dug into his shoulders, and he drew back from their kiss to watch her while he brought her closer to the edge. Closer. Until she shattered, and then he lay back, angled on the chaise, drinking in the heat in her eyes, the sensual curve of her mouth.

"Like that," he said. "God, yes. More."

She moved on him, rode him, sent him out of his mind with delight, and the same happened to her. When she came, she did so without reservation, and he adored the way she gave herself over to her pleasure. Her reaction made him feel potent, a lover worth keeping.

"Beautiful," he whispered as she used his body.

Her eyes opened slowly, a satisfied smile curving her mouth. "And you?" she asked.

"I'm close. Very close."

"What do you need?"

He sat up and rearranged them so that her back was to his front, her gown safely tucked up, with his arms under her shoulders, her legs spread over his thighs, and he pushed into her again. Thrust. Pulled back, thrust again, and she understood the motion he needed. His felt his reaction spiraling tight, out of reach yet closer with every thrust, with every clench of her body around his cock.

"I'm going to spend inside you," he said.

When he came, his peak hit hard, spun him out of his mind, out of his control. The only thought on his mind was more. More of this. Let him be thrown out of his mind. Inside his chest emotion quivered. He damn near let go of her because he was completely lost to his reaction to her. Releasing inside her.

Once he had his breath back, when he was back inside his body, and they'd separated, he said, "Don't leave, Lily."

Saying her name cracked his heart in half.

She did not answer.

"Don't leave me," he whispered. "Not so soon. Not yet."

"I have to go back outside before much longer."

"That isn't what I meant."

She pushed up on one elbow and peered into his face. "What do you mean?"

"Stay here." He curled a strand of her hair around his finger. "At Bitterward. At least a little longer."

She looked away.

"Why not?" he asked.

"My father needs me. I can't gallivant around the country for weeks and weeks. He gets lonely, you know, and he hasn't any friends. When he came to live with me, he gave up all that. No one should be lonely when they're old and frail. What sort of daughter would I be if I left him alone like that?"

"If he'd raised you with half the thought you give him now, you'd have had a happy childhood. He'd be the sort of man who could make new friends."

"I'll be here another fortnight. That's a long time yet for me to impose on your good graces."

"You're no imposition."

She leaned down and kissed the tip of his nose. "And when I do leave you'll think just the same. That I was a delightful guest. You'll have fond memories of me."

"More. You know that."

"Yes," she said without smiling this time. "Yes."

What would he do if, after he'd tried everything he knew, she left him anyway?

Chapter Twenty-seven

><==

AT BITTERWARD'S FIRST BALL, MOUNTJOY WORE ONE of the new suits that had arrived at the house just the day before. He felt foolish even though he knew he looked, in some indefinable way, more like a duke than he ever had before. Everyone was staring. In the last two hours, he'd had more compliments about his appearance than he'd had in the last ten years. He accepted each surprised remark with a nod but could not help thinking he remained the same man he'd been every day before this.

The fit was as comfortable as both Elliot and Lily had promised, but his cravat had a deal more starch than he was used to. His shirt was of so fine a linen that even he, with his dislike of any change and his aversion to even a tacit admission that he had been a stubborn ass, had to admit he liked the way his coat slid on and left him with no urge to pull or tug at the parts that bunched up. Now and again, he caught sight of himself in a mirror or a fortuitously reflective surface, and he scarcely recognized himself. He looked a dandy, but without the fussiness he associated with those overdressed fools.

This was a night in which he learned he'd been wrong-headed about more than his clothes. Obviously, Mountjoy had completely underestimated the importance of social entertaining. In London he rarely went to events that weren't political or for some purpose of business, his or the government's. He had not been to a ball these five years at least and had yet to as much as hint that a voucher for Almack's would be put to use. He did not care to be turned down by the Almack's patronesses—he wouldn't be the first duke to suffer that humiliation—any more than he would actually care to attend such an affair.

He ought to have begun formal entertainments here years ago. He really should have.

Here he was. A duke from the skin out, in a house full to the rafters with what looked to him to be the entirety of High Tearing and half of Sheffield. There was a steady procession of people through the room where samples from the treasure Lily had uncovered were on display. The pieces, though they appeared to be metal parts and fittings torn or removed from centuries-vanished armor and other equipage, were nevertheless beautifully worked. With the dirt removed and what repairs the local goldsmith felt competent to make, the displayed collection took one's breath.

An hour of talking to his neighbors had cemented better relations with them than all his years of appearing at the Sessions or at any of the official or ad hoc governance meetings that had taken place over the years. A good many of the men were genuinely interested in his opinions of the management of an estate, its tenants, lands, livestock and crops, and other holdings. The men's wives knew a great deal of their husbands' interests. More than one extended a verbal invitation for a social meeting that even he, at last, understood was at least as much a business opportunity as it was luncheon or supper or tea.

Presently, he was standing at the edge of the ballroom watching the dancers in the last set before the orchestra took an intermission and his guests could sit down for an informal meal. Nigel was not yet back from London, which had caused much consternation and upset with Eugenia. The Kirk girls were here, but for Jane, which was odd. Somewhere, though not within immediate sight, was Lord Fenris, who had not been invited but who had come nevertheless.

Eugenia was dancing with the mayor of High Tearing. She was lovely in pale blue silk, happy and smiling as she had not been for far too long. Miss Caroline Kirk was dancing with Dr. Longfield. He did not see Lily anywhere. He scanned the room, expecting to find her easily and feel that rush of his pulse that happened whenever he laid eyes on her.

Her ball gown was the color of the champagne coming from his wine cellar in such copious amounts, and he did not see that so distinctive hue anywhere in the room. He stayed until the set ended, watching his guests enjoying themselves while he looked for Lily. She'd danced several times tonight, but he hadn't asked her yet. He wanted to waltz with her.

People applauded the orchestra when the members put down their instruments, and soon after couples and groups formed for the meal that would be served during the intermission. They were enjoying themselves, he thought. Young and old alike, and he had Lily and Eugenia to thank for that.

He headed for the terrace by way of his office where he kept his cigars. His office was at the end of this corridor and ought to be closed, as that was not a room intended to be open to his guests. The door was ajar, however, though there was no light inside other than the moonlight through the windows. Mountjoy walked in, reaching as he did, for the flint by the door. He did not light the lamp because the room was occupied.

"Is that you, Wellstone?"

"Your grace," she said. She was on the sofa by the fireplace. Her soft greeting was forlorn. So very unlike her on a night that was her triumph. Success in everything, the ball, the house, Eugenia smiling and in colors, and him looking like a man born to his title.

He pushed the office door closed and crossed to her. "Are you all right?"

"No," she said. "I don't believe I am."

"Tell me what's the matter." Anything. He'd do anything to keep her from being unhappy.

She didn't answer. Instead, she turned her head away from him.

"Are you crying?" He sat beside her and took her hand in his. With her other hand, she swiped at her face.

"Certainly not. I never cry." When she faced him, her features were composed. She rested a hand on his upper chest, but her voice quavered when she spoke. "Have I told you, Mountjoy, how absolutely splendid you look tonight?"

He could not bear the thought of her in tears, not for any reason. She was too subdued for him to believe all was well. It wasn't, and that tugged at his heart. "Thanks entirely to you."

"Your valet put you together very well. The success is his, I assure you."

"He was in raptures when the first of the suits arrived."

Lily opened her mouth to speak but didn't. He watched, helpless, as she simply dissolved. He put an arm around her shoulder, and she collapsed against him, tears flowing. He'd seen women cry before, some of those tears heartfelt, but the fact of Lily, confident, happy Lily, sobbing against his chest broke something in him.

"Lily. Darling, what is it? What's happened?"

She shook her head.

Mountjoy held her until some of the tension went out of her shoulders. "Can you tell me?"

She kept her hand on his chest. "Lord Fenris is here, and it's upset Ginny. She does not like the man. Not at all."

He thought of his sister, dancing with the mayor. "He seems to have upset you as well. Has he insulted you? Shall

I find him and send him away? I will if having him here pains you."

"I've never had any family." Her fingers curled around the lapel of his coat. "No one but my father, that is. And now, after all this time thinking Lord Fenris meant me no good, I wish there were a way for us to mend things between us."

Mountjoy fished out his spare handkerchief and handed it to her. He wanted very much to vilify the man, but he didn't. Though he didn't make an endorsement of him either.

"Thank you." She took his handkerchief and pressed it to her eyes. She sucked in a breath and let it out. "I've been his relation all along. Why take notice of me now? It's just that . . ." She looked at him, her eyes glittering with tears. "I should like to have family of my own. Is that so terrible?"

"Lily," Mountjoy said. He took his handkerchief from her and dabbed at her cheek. "My dear Lily."

"Ginny dislikes him. With reason, I know that. He treated her infamously, and I wouldn't for the world force her to tolerate anyone she holds in such abhorrence. I can't."

He cupped her face with one hand and could not for his life parse out what he was feeling. "You are a loyal friend to my sister."

"I told you that the day I arrived."

"So you did." He kept his hand on her cheek. "I'll talk to him for you. Find out once and for all why he's here."

She leaned her head against his chest, and Mountjoy put an arm around her shoulder, keeping her close. She held up her medallion. "If only the magic would make my relations pleasant people. Now *that* would be useful."

Mountjoy laughed. "Lily, darling," he said without thinking, "this is exactly why I love you."

She sat up, though he kept his arm around her. Neither of them spoke for the space of half a breath. The quiet was fraught. He'd never said those words before, not to anyone, not on purpose. Nor on accident. Not even when he was a green boy.

Until now.

Mountjoy kissed her to stop the quiet or her potential question, he wasn't sure which. He hadn't meant that he *loved* her, not precisely. As was always the case with him and Lily, the kiss was immediately carnal. Wonderfully, wholly uninhibited. He didn't want to ruin her ball gown nor the arrangement of her hair, not when there was still more dancing to be done, so he fetched her with his fingers and his mouth, and when he'd had the pleasure of hearing, seeing, and tasting her pleasure, he found he couldn't think why she shouldn't use her hands on him, which she did, and then she finished him with her mouth, and he clamped his hands on the sofa while she did, so that he wouldn't reach for her head and leave her hair a tangled mess.

While he came, he thought he'd be damned if he let Fenris hurt her. Damned. Not for any reason.

Chapter Twenty-eight

LILY LAY CURLED UP IN HER BED, IN A STATE THAT WAS not quite awake yet not asleep either. Her maid tapped on the door between her dressing room and the bedchamber. She ignored the sound, including the creak of the connecting door as it opened. Her dream was vivid in her mind, and she did not want to give it up. In between lovely, slow kisses, Mountjoy was declaring himself head over heels in love with her.

"Miss?"

He'd said those words. *I love you, Lily.*

He hadn't meant them, but the effect on her had been nearly the same as if he had. She pulled the covers over her head and tried to fall back into her already fading dream. Something delicious about Mountjoy.

"Miss," her maid said. "Doyle said I ought to tell you, or I'd not bother you at this hour. Not for anything."

"What?" she said from beneath the sheets. The linens smelled of lavender and they were warm around her body. Perfect for hours more dreaming.

"You have a caller, miss."

Who on earth would be calling on her here? She stayed with her legs drawn up and the covers warm around her. "What time is it?"

"Half past eleven, miss."

"Eleven?" She groaned. She was going to have to see whoever it was. But that did not make her any fonder of mornings. Even if her maid went away this very second, her cozy half-dreaming state was over, and she would never get back to Mountjoy and his wonderful dream kisses and declarations of love. "In a moment," she said.

"It's the Marquess of Fenris himself, and Doyle said you ought to be told he's waiting."

She turned over and lowered the sheet enough to see her maid's expression was serious. Her heart thudded as the name registered. "Lord Fenris?"

"Yes, miss."

"Does Lady Eugenia know he's here?"

"She went into High Tearing this morning. With the duke."

Now that was a stroke of luck for Fenris, wasn't it? To have arrived when both Ginny and Mountjoy were out. Coincidence? Or something else? She pushed herself onto her elbows. "Did Lord Fenris happen to mention the purpose of his call?"

"Why, I suppose, to speak with you."

"Is there anyone with him?" A lawyer, perhaps, with papers to serve on her. "Another gentlemen. Probably carrying a leather case?"

"No, miss. At least Doyle didn't say. Shall I tell him you're not at home?"

She wished she weren't. "No. I'll see him."

"You ought to wear your rose frock, I think," her maid said.

Lily sighed. "Oh, very well." She was going to have to face Fenris sooner or later, if only to tell him he must leave her in peace. She might as well do so now. "Tell him I'll be down shortly."

"Yes, miss."

She folded the covers to below her chin and spoke to her maid's retreating back. "I suppose someone should offer him tea and something to eat."

"Miss."

"When you return, would you bring some chocolate and perhaps a roll and butter? Porridge if there is any."

"Yes, miss."

She groaned and stretched out on the mattress. By the time the maid returned with the food—her roll was still warm, there was honey and butter in the porridge, and the chocolate was steaming hot—she was standing in front of her wardrobe working out what frock one ought to wear while meeting a long estranged relative whose fondest wish might be to have her locked away for a madwoman, never to be seen again.

"What parlor is he waiting in?" Lily asked when she approved of the results of her hair. "The Oldenburg?"

"No, miss. He's in the Prussian salon."

"Ah." The predominant color of the Prussian salon was blue. There was, in fact, a sofa in a gorgeous shade of the blue after that name. "You're right about the rose frock. I'll wear that."

"Yes, miss."

The ash pink bodice would look delectable when she sat on that Prussian blue sofa. The hours she'd spent affixing ribbon of the exact right color to the gown, no more the exquisite Brussels lace, had been more than worth the time. The dress was brought out, and while her maid took it off to press, Lily ate her breakfast.

Forty minutes later she was outside the Prussian salon, as nervous as she'd ever been in her life. She took a deep breath to compose herself before she opened the door.

Her cousin stood with his back to her, staring out the window opposite the door. His hair was cut close to his head, so short that she wondered if he'd recently been ill. He was tall and well made with a wiry build. Not at all sickly. His clothes were once again severe yet perfectly cut.

"My lord?" She walked in. Whatever he wanted, she would soon know. Reconciliation, as she hoped? Or something far more dire? "My apologies for keeping you waiting."

Fenris turned. His eyes flicked down to her slippers and back to her face. He smiled, but without warmth. "It's hardly been a moment, Miss Wellstone."

She approached him and curtseyed while he bent over her hand. Fenris was more handsome than she remembered, with brown eyes, though not as dark as hers. She studied him and did not know if she found similarities between them because she so badly wanted there to be, or whether there really was a likeness between them. "Shall I send for tea?"

"No, thank you." He seemed to be studying her as acutely as she did him.

"My lord." She walked to the Prussian blue sofa and perched on the edge, back straight, feet planted squarely on the floor. She gestured to a chair. "Will you sit?"

"Thank you, but I prefer to stand." He was holding a packet in one hand. Her heart sank, for she was beyond certain those were legal documents.

"As you wish."

"How is your hand? Has your injury healed? I trust it was not serious."

She wriggled her fingers. "A nuisance, really. It's nearly healed now. Thank you for asking."

"And your . . . illness? The day Mountjoy carried you into the house?"

Fenris, she thought, seemed garrulous for a man who intended to destroy her life. "Perfectly recovered."

Silence fell, and she left it to Fenris to make his purpose known. If he wished to serve her with papers, why hadn't he sent an attorney to do that for him?

He cleared his throat. "I don't know how much you know about me. . . ."

She met his gaze forthrightly. "You are the heir to my uncle, the Duke of Camber. The previous duke was your grandfather and mine. My mother was your aunt, and therefore, Lord Fenris, you have the misfortune of being my cousin."

"Hardly a misfortune."

"I confess, sir, after all this time, I wonder what business you think you might have with me."

"I find myself in a difficult situation." He paced, the packet of documents still clutched in one hand.

Oh, no doubt he did. She clasped her hands on her lap. Honestly, did he expect her to sympathize with his effort to destroy her life?

"For days, I've walked from one end of High Tearing to the other, turning matters over in my mind. Wondering what I ought to do."

"A very bracing walk. I'm sure it's improved your constitution."

He stopped his pacing and stood with his hands behind him. "My grandfather, our grandfather, never spoke of your mother. Nor did my father. I was at Eton at the time she married. They told me," he said, "that she'd passed away."

She quirked her eyebrows in response.

"I had no reason to believe my father lied to me, Miss Wellstone. I was a boy at the time, still at school when he wrote with the news."

"I cannot, and do not, blame you for what happened when you were a boy."

He blanched. "Would that my own family had been as tolerant. As you might imagine, there was an uproar when we learned Great-Aunt Lily had left everything to you. That, Miss Wellstone, was when I learned of your existence."

"Indeed?"

"Quite."

She remained silent.

"I was shocked to discover my aunt—your mother—hadn't died as they told me she had, but had instead married and even had a child." He drew in a long breath. "I was equally shocked to learn I had a cousin I knew nothing about." He drew another breath, but Lily said nothing. "Everything in secret." He paced again. "I was . . . appalled by the lies, Miss Wellstone. My own father, perpetuating such a deception." He stopped walking. "Upon learning of your inheritance, my father immediately met with his attorneys."

"I am aware."

He looked sheepish. "Yes, you must be. At any rate, as you also know, the properties and the monies were Aunt Lily's to dispose of as she wished, and eventually the family lawyers had no choice but to advise my father he would be unlikely to prevail if he continued to pursue the matter."

Lily pressed her lips together. Was he about to tell her he'd secured a more favorable legal opinion? In such a case, would she not be hearing from an attorney, and not Fenris himself? Ah, but then there was that mysterious packet he carried. The one that contained legal documents. "I see."

"I persuaded him there was nothing to be gained by going forward as he wished. Other than the enrichment of our lawyers. And yours."

If he was already in possession of papers that declared her incompetent, he would he have brought the bailiff to secure her. Or was he confident she would simply go along with a heinous plan to lock her away? "Sir. I have yet to understand why you are here. Nothing you've said is anything my own solicitor has not already told me. Perhaps not the particulars, but the result is what matters, I daresay."

"True."

"Nevertheless," she said, "I thank you for your intervention with your father. You saved us both a great deal of aggravation and money."

He nodded. He was quite a handsome man. Not like Mountjoy, but appealing nonetheless. "A few weeks ago I came across letters that my aunt—not your mother, I mean, but our great-aunt and your namesake—left behind at my father's house. She kept a study there, and after she passed, my father never went through the room." He stood very straight, as a military man might.

Lily's stomach dropped. "You found another will."

"A will?" His eyebrows drew together. "No. Not at all. I found letters. From you." He held out his packet. "I thought I ought to return them to you."

Lily rose with all the dignity at her command. "There is only so much ill will I'll tolerate from anyone, even a future duke. You traveled all this way, spent all these days here in order to make the grand gesture of returning Aunt Lily's letters to me? Because, naturally, you would not wish the letters of such a woman as I am to remain in your house." She held out her hand. "Please give me the letters so that you may be on your way home."

He blanched. "You misunderstand."

"It was made very clear to me that your family—"

"We Talbots are your family as well."

"Much to my regret. Besides Aunt Lily no Talbot has ever wanted anything to do with a Wellstone." His last words penetrated and she gave a brittle laugh. "You say Talbots are my family, too? What family returns a child's letters but one that wants no association with her? For I assure you, I was a child when I first wrote to our grandfather. And to your father, too. They returned my letters unread. Now you do me the favor of returning my letters to Aunt Lily. My collection is now complete. Thank you, Lord Fenris, for it's better that I have the letters than that they stay in the hands of anyone with the name Talbot."

"My father admitted to me that he refused your letters." He briefly closed his eyes. "I hope you'll accept my apologies for that."

"Aunt Lily was the only one of you who wanted anything to do with me. She loved me, and I loved her. Not a day goes by that I don't wish she were still alive."

"Miss Wellstone. Please."

She held out her hand again, shaking with anger that he felt he'd needed to see her personally to cut off relations they'd never had in the first place. "I am happy to accept the letters and see you on your way. Thank you, my lord, and good day."

"Cousin."

"I have no cousin." She heard in her words and the manner of her saying the echo of her father. So determined to punish any slight. If anyone deserved that, was it not the Talbots?

He stared at the letters without handing them over. So did Lily. She remembered the paper, the smell of the ink as she wrote the letters, and how deeply she'd longed to meet the woman she'd been named after. Fenris spoke softly. "You weren't more than fourteen or fifteen when you wrote these letters."

"You read them?"

"Of course I read them." He lifted his chin, and the look in his eye reminded her of Ginny's opinion of him. A judgmental man, and from what she could see, the very worst sort who probably believed he was justified in his lectures and moral superiority. "They were among my Aunt Lily's effects. I found them in the house where I live."

She lifted her hands. "Keep them, then, if you feel you must assert ownership. Or would you feel better if I gnashed my teeth and wept bitter tears?"

"No."

"For I tell you, I won't give you the satisfaction."

"I wished only to tell you that it's plain from these pages that you loved her, and that Aunt Lily had a great deal of affection for you and your mother." He checked himself. "I suppose that's obvious seeing as how she made you her sole heir. Heiress. Miss Wellstone. Cousin Lily. I read your letters to her and wanted to meet you and tell you I am sorry, very sorry, that my grandfather refused to acknowledge you and that my father did the same."

She sat on the sofa and opened her mouth to speak and found she had no words. The desire to send him away still burned hot. Why should she reconcile with any Talbot after what his family had done? She stared at her lap and struggled to compose herself. This unreasoning sense of betrayal was her father's way, and she would not follow his example. She looked up. "That's decent of you."

"I wish I'd met your mother. I wish I'd known you were corresponding with Aunt Lily before it was too late. Miss Wellstone." He took a half step forward and stopped himself. "I am here because I do not wish the estrangement between our families to continue."

"You don't?"

"You *are* my relation, Miss Wellstone. Not a Talbot by name, but my cousin nevertheless. Cannot you and I make our peace?"

"What does your father think of your visit here?"

His mouth twisted. "That does not signify."

"He doesn't know you've come."

"I'm a grown man." He laughed. "I make my own life, and my father, I do assure you, is well aware of that. I respect his advice and opinion, but my life is my own."

"Ah."

Fenris tapped the letters on his palm. "I have given our situation a great deal of consideration. Yours and mine."

"My inheritance or our estrangement?"

He colored but soon recovered. "Both, I suppose. I can see, Miss Wellstone, that you are a woman of spirit, though that has no bearing on my presence here. There's no way I could have known before I left to find you that I would encounter such a striking, vibrant woman as you."

"What is your point?"

"Naturally, your letters suggest the spirit I see in you now. I never did expect to find an ordinary woman, not after reading these."

"I'm not certain you mean that as a compliment, but I'll take it as one."

"You should. It is not and never was my intention to slight you in any way. I did not come here merely to return the letters as some sort of insult to you." His chagrin was honest, she felt. Miraculous, even. "I thought you might want them as a memento of the woman you loved."

She held out her hand. "I would like that very much. Thank you."

"Perhaps it won't be necessary for me to return them."

"Why not?"

"Because you are my cousin." He went still, composing himself much as she had needed to do. "You would be welcome to read these letters as often as you like."

The tension in her melted away. His wish for a reconciliation was genuine, and that meant she had a cousin. "I should be glad, very glad, to know you."

"It is my hope, Miss Wellstone, that we will have more than an acquaintance."

"Oh?" She leaned against the sofa back. "How so, if your father and mine have not changed their minds? Do you propose we carry on a clandestine correspondence such as Aunt Lily and I did?" The idea amused her enough that she smiled at him, and he tipped his head. "We wrote to each other in care of a particular stationer's. Her letters to me were always franked, but I wouldn't expect you to do the same. That expense is now one I can bear. But to keep our secret, my lord, I could write my letters to you in lemon juice, as a precaution against them being intercepted. Your father would think someone is sending you blank papers. Imagine his confusion. You might tell him it's a new stationer you're thinking of patronizing and the paper is a sample."

Fenris blinked once then again. "There's no need for a secret correspondence or letters written in code or lemon juice."

"How disappointing."

"Miss Wellstone." He smiled. Barely. A Tablot smile, she thought. "Have you not foreseen the reason for my visit?"

"No. Since you haven't brought the baliff, I rather think I have not."

"I am here to make you an offer."

She frowned. "Of what? The letters?"

"We can right the wrongs of the past, you and I."

"I'm not sure I follow."

He went down on one knee. "Lily Wellstone, marry me. Become my future duchess."

At that point, the door opened, and Mountjoy walked in. He took one look at Fenris kneeling and his eyebrows shot to his forehead. "What the devil is this?"

Lily didn't answer because, for once in her life, she had no idea what to say when it must be perfectly clear what was going on.

Chapter Twenty-nine

❧❧

On Mountjoy's return to Bitterward, Doyle informed him that Lord Fenris was here and that Lily was presently entertaining him in the Prussian salon. Mountjoy went directly there. Almost directly. He opened two wrong doors first.

When he found the right room, he stopped at the threshold of the doorway, his heart hammering as if he'd returned to find his house had been robbed and he was only now understanding the scope of his losses. Lily sat on the sofa, luminously beautiful in a gown in a shade of pink that flattered her complexion. As if she would ever wear a color that did not.

What the devil was going on, indeed.

Mountjoy raked his fingers through his hair in what was probably a futile attempt to make himself presentable. He wore his riding clothes, for pity's sake, which had not yet been altered for him or sent to him new. Mud and, no doubt, unspeakable matter spattered his boots. In all likelihood there was dirt on his face. He looked disreputable and unkempt and there was nothing he could do about it.

It was bloody obvious what was going on.

That damned prude Fenris was on one knee. In front of Lily. Holding her hand and staring into her face with the sort of stunned awe he'd seen before from other men.

The fool was proposing to her.

To Lily.

She did not look angry or horrified or even mortified. She did not look like a woman who had just refused an offer of marriage from someone she had every reason to dislike.

Mountjoy didn't question the panic that washed over him. Not that he hadn't taken into account the possibility that Fenris would do this. What he hadn't accounted for was Lily's reaction. He'd assumed Fenris would be a pompous prick and that Lily would refuse him because she had better sense than to entertain thoughts of marriage to a man like Fenris. That assumption was a serious miscalculation on his part. If she married Fenris, whether she was in love with the man or not, she would have the family she'd always longed for. She would belong, and for her, that would be a powerful incentive to accept.

Fenris rose and gave him a look that took in and dismissed his well-ridden-in clothes. "Your grace."

Lily looked between him and Fenris, and he realized he had no idea if she'd just accepted a proposal of marriage from the man or whether he'd interrupted the question or the answer or both. His heart lurched.

He did not own Lily, he told himself. They had no understanding except that she was leaving before long. What had he offered her besides physical passion? Nothing. Fenris, on the other hand, had just offered her the family connections she'd always longed for. Camber himself would come to terms with a daughter-in-law who brought with her a fortune he'd had to give up for lost. For that sort of fortune, even the Duke of Camber might see his way clear to recognizing her father.

"Might Miss Wellstone and I have a few moments longer?" Lord Fenris said. One corner of his mouth twitched. "I've matters to . . . discuss with my cousin." When Mountjoy didn't move, Fenris said, "They are of a personal nature, your grace. I'm sure you understand."

If he knew anything about Lily it was that she knew her own mind, and this self-righteous prick was going to treat her as if she did not. As if her desires, whatever they might be, were of no consequence compared to his. He fought his urge to throw the man out on his ear. "Wellstone?"

Lily rose slowly. She did not, as another might have done, pretend the moment wasn't awkward. "Lord Fenris, thank you very much. You do me a very great honor. I'm deeply flattered." She held out her hand for him to take. "And taken by surprise, as you must imagine. Though I thank you for calling on me."

Fenris turned his back on Mountjoy. "Have you an answer for me, cousin? Or do you need time to consider your reply?"

Her cheeks pinked up. "No. No answer yet, my lord."

Not yet.

"Is there a time when I might know my fate?"

"Tomorrow," Lily said. "If that's agreeable to you."

"If I must wait, I shall. Thank you." He took her hand and bowed over it. When he straightened, he put a packet into her hands. "In the meantime, keep these. Please. To remind you of my sincerity."

The emotion that flooded her face brought a lump to Mountjoy's throat. "Thank you." She took Fenris's hand in hers and pressed it. "Thank you very much."

"Until tomorrow."

"At two o'clock, if you don't mind."

"Certainly." He brought Lily's hand to his mouth and kissed her knuckles. As he walked past Mountjoy, they traded looks. Mountjoy waited until Fenris was past him before he said, "Perhaps you and I ought to have a word. My lord."

Mountjoy turned to find Fenris had done the same. They now faced each other. "You're not her father, Mountjoy."

"No, but she is an unmarried woman staying in my house. I am responsible for her while she is here."

Lily cleared her throat, but they both ignored her.

"Your concern for my cousin does you credit. Thank you." Fenris looked past him to Lily. "Tomorrow at two, Miss Wellstone."

"Not a moment sooner."

With that, Mountjoy was alone with Lily. "Would you rather I leave?" he asked. He closed his eyes. Of all people, Fenris was in a position to know just how wealthy Lily was. It made sense to bring that money back into the control of his family. Fenris would know that a man in his position married for reasons of dynasty and that he would please his father beyond words if he were to bring back Lily's fortune. Marrying Lily was a far cheaper solution than laywers.

Would she agree?

She shook her head and sat on the sofa. She placed the packet Fenris had given her on the table beside the sofa. "I confess, Mountjoy, I am at a loss just now. And I am rarely at a loss."

He stayed where he was, just past the door. She had not given Fenris an answer yet. Not yet. But tomorrow?

She looked at him, and for once she did not seem impossibly confident of herself. She clasped her hands on her lap. "I thought he'd come here to tell me they'd found another will and that I must leave Syton House and give back everything." She gazed at him. "All this time I've been imagining the awful things he must be plotting against me. His offer was completely unexpected."

He checked the hall to be sure Fenris had really gone. "He will be a duke one day. His title is an old one."

"Oh that. Yes, I suppose so. But he is my cousin, Mountjoy. I've never had a cousin before." She twined her fingers on her lap. "And he wishes to know me. After all this time, he wants a connection between us."

It killed him, but he said, "Commendable of him."

She fixed wide eyes on him. "My father would never forgive me."

"Does it matter if you add one more item to his list of your unforgiven sins?"

"Oh, Mountjoy, you do make me laugh." She smiled. "When you put it like that, perhaps it doesn't."

"Don't let your father ruin this for you, Wellstone. You mustn't."

"But what of your sister?" Her amusement slowly faded. "Ginny will never forgive me."

"She will," he said.

"I wouldn't. I wouldn't forgive a thing like that. My dearest friend marrying the man who tried to prevent my marriage?"

He took a breath. "Eugenia will understand."

"If she doesn't? I couldn't bear to lose her friendship. I couldn't."

Her despair broke his heart. "Come." He held out his hand. "We'll walk in the garden and talk. Or say nothing, if you prefer. Or speak of everything that is inconsequential."

She walked to him and put her hand in his. She squeezed his hand. "Thank you, Mountjoy."

Not ten minutes later, they were walking side by side in the rear garden. She'd fetched a cloak and had that around her shoulders. In silent accord, they headed past the formal grounds. He held the gate for her, and they walked a path that led to the lake, the bottom of which he now knew contained a good number of Roman coins. There was a bridge at the narrowest part of the water, and they followed the gravel path that wended that direction.

"I don't know what to do, Mountjoy," she said when they'd exhausted subjects such as the weather and whether they preferred lemon tarts to sweet puddings. "I've half a mind to sneak home in the dark of night."

"Impossible. You are engaged to be here another eight days."

"Stop making me laugh when I feel so miserable."

He tucked her arm under his. "Listen to me, Wellstone, because I ask this in all seriousness. Is marrying Fenris the condition of this connection he is so suddenly pursuing?"

They walked several feet before she answered. "No. I don't think so." She looked away. "I don't know. He might have meant that." She stopped walking. "I am aware that I am in possession of some very valuable properties and a fortune the present Duke of Camber believes should have gone to anyone but me. So don't imagine I do not understand my cousin's financial incentives. He wouldn't be the first to have them."

"Believe me, I do not dismiss your understanding of anything."

She shot him a look. "It was not my impression that Fenris agrees with his father about me. At least not now."

"He's a bloody good little son, to come haring halfway across the country to propose to the woman his aunt made her sole heir."

They walked a few yards before she replied. "I wonder what he would have done if I had turned out to be an aged and wrinkled old hag?"

He drew her closer. "How large did you say your fortune is?"

"About eighty thousand. More now. Rents are up and my investments have done quite well."

"Then he'd have gone down on his knee to you whether you proved a hag or a shrew. Or both."

"There's an excellent basis for marriage." She released his arm to straighten her cloak. "Mutual ignorance of each other's character."

"Marriages have been contracted on far less than that."

"They have been."

"I thought you had determined you would never marry."

They strolled a ways before she answered. "Not for love."

Mountjoy stopped walking. "For what reason would you marry?"

Her fingers tightened on his arm. "I don't know. When he can't possibly expect me to love him. When it makes such sense."

"You think it makes sense to marry Lord Fenris?"

"Objectively, it does."

He crossed his arms over his chest. "Suppose," he said, "that I told you I could never love you and that I understood you would never do something so inconvenient as to love me in return. In such a case, would you agree to marry me?"

Her gaze burned into his. "Are you asking me under those conditions?"

"That is not the point. Our discussion is a purely academic one."

"To answer your question, no. I would not."

"Why not? If your only criterion is that there be no love between you and your husband, it seems to me that any unmarried man will do. Therefore, why not me instead of Fenris?"

"You're twisting my words."

"No, Wellstone. I am attempting to unravel that nonsense."

"All right then. For reasons of dynasty. I'd marry him for that."

"I am in need of an heir. For reasons of dynasty." He took her arm again and continued down the path. He scowled the entire time they walked. "Why would you marry Fenris but not me?"

"Because."

"Because?"

"Because marrying you would be a betrayal of Greer."

"Why?" he said softly.

"Because you're going to marry Jane."

"Jane has nothing to do with Greer. But suppose that was not the case, that I was free to marry anyone I wished."

She pressed her lips together before she answered him. "No, I would not marry you."

"Why not?"

She glared at him. "Because you are my friend."

"Your friend."

"Yes."

"As your friend, I say you ought not marry a man whose character you do not know. You needn't tell Fenris yes or no tomorrow merely because you said you would. If you need more time to decide, for God's sake take it." He took her arm again when they reached a rough portion of the path.

"But I promised, Mountjoy."

"You told him he would have a reply."

"Exactly."

"Tomorrow reply to him that if he wishes to win your hand, you must at least know him well enough to give your approval of his character. If he's serious, he'll wait for you to make your decision."

"Shall I languish in the tower of yon castle, while I ponder on the subject?" She pressed the back of her hand to her forehead. "I cannot marry any man but one who proves himself worthy. By slaying a dragon. Or fetching me a golden fleece."

Mountjoy chuckled. "I don't advise that you languish, though you may if you like. If you mean *that* tower"—he tipped his head in the direction of Bitterward—"I'd find a way to keep you occupied while your cousin performs his mighty works."

She gave a sigh and leaned her head against his shoulder while they walked. "If he turns his back on me when I tell him I cannot answer him? What then?"

He stopped walking and faced her, hands on her shoulders. "Wellstone. You are an extraordinary woman. A woman worth knowing." He wanted to be selfish and tell her to stay the hell away from Fenris, but he couldn't. It wouldn't be right. "Fenris is a damned fool if he didn't know that from the moment he laid eyes on you. Don't let anyone, especially him, make you think that's not so. If you marry anyone, at least make sure the man deserves you."

Her mouth quirked. "No one deserves me."

He chose to ignore the double meaning. "God knows Fenris doesn't. He's done nothing to deserve your love." His fingers tightened on her. "Don't settle for marriage without at least respect between you. You can't live like that. Not you, Lily. I know you loved Greer, and I believe you'll never love another man the way you loved him. But does it follow that you can never love? Does a parent love only one child? A child only one parent? May we love only one friend? You, Lily, you of all people must have love in her life. Genuine love from a man who understands the wonderful eccentricities of your mind. Accept nothing less. If Fenris proves himself that man, then marry him but not until then. That's my advice to you."

"Ginny's right about you." She touched his cheek. "You give excellent advice."

"Will you take it?"

"I should think you'd be cackling in glee at the thought of him ending up married to me."

He took a step back. "Do you find me as petty as that? I wouldn't wish that on you. I want your happiness."

"No, Mountjoy. No I don't think that of you."

"If you're going to do something as harebrained as marry in cold blood, then marry a man who understands your worth."

She pushed away from him and spread her arms wide. "Imagine the clothes I could have if I were a nobleman's wife."

"You have those clothes now."

"Yes." Her eyes sparkled. "But I wouldn't be spending my money on them. There are economies I would not feel compelled to make. I could have a dress entirely of silver cloth without feeling a moment's guilt. I should look perfectly stunning in a gown of silver cloth."

He grinned because he couldn't help it. "You wouldn't feel guilty if you had one now."

"True." They remained standing quite close. "But I feel I ought to. If I were Lady Fenris, I would feel it my duty to wear only the most fashionable and tasteful gowns and slippers. And jewels. I don't see how I could get by without quite a lot of jewels. Ruinously expensive jewels." She touched her head. "I've always wanted a tiara."

"Is that your sole criteria for marriage? Clothes and jewels? Then by all means tell him yes. When you've confirmed he's the money to keep you in the style to which you wish to be accustomed."

"If I did say yes, would I have your blessing?"

"No." The word burst from him, hard as a diamond.

She stepped back, but he followed. "Why not?"

"Because you would not be happy."

"A casket or two of fabulous jewels would make me quite happy."

"Buy your own jewels." He clenched his hands. "You have the money."

"They're so much prettier when someone else buys them." She drew her cloak around her and headed for the bridge. He followed. Of course he followed. When he caught up, she said, "I don't get many gifts, you know. And that's an argument in favor of marriage I hadn't considered. My husband would be obliged to buy me a gift from time to time. Don't you think?" She touched the medallion around her neck. "Do you know, Mountjoy, that this is the first gift I've had these dozen or more years at least?"

"A dozen years?"

"That was when my father stopped speaking to me."

"What?"

"Well, he did now and then, that couldn't be helped. It would have been awkward to refuse to speak to one's daughter in front of the vicar or one's neighbor. But I recall he once went five months without saying a word to me. Thank goodness for our housekeeper or I might have been as silent as him." She waved a hand, as if to say it no longer mattered. They were at the bridge and neither of them spoke until they reached the other side. He didn't know what to say to her. What could he say to her that would not reveal his outrage on her behalf? Her bedamned father had much to answer for.

Back on the path, she faced him while he stood at the end of the stone bridge. "It has occurred to me, Mountjoy, that perhaps the medallion is working as the Gypsy king said it would."

"It is?"

"Consider the matter." She crossed her arms beneath her bosom. "Fenris showed up here, didn't he? Completely unexpected. And he has proposed to me knowing his father will never approve. Why, it must be the medallion. No other explanation makes sense."

"You can't be serious."

She tilted her chin. "Why can't I be?"

"Because it's absurd to think magic has anything to do with Fenris pursuing you."

"Perhaps we're fated lovers, Fenris and I. Why else would he come all this way to make an offer of marriage to a woman he does not know and of whom his father disapproves?"

He'd never felt as powerless as he did right now. The world was slipping away from him and he did not know how to stop it.

"A dozen reasons."

"Name three."

"The estate is bankrupt."

"It isn't."

"You asked for three likely reasons. I'm suggesting the obvious ones. You're rich. He needs money. He means to anger his father; he sincerely wishes to mend the break between your family and his. He finds you beautiful."

"That's five."

"I can give you five more if you like."

"That would only be ten, not a dozen."

"My point, my dear Wellstone, is that any of those are more likely than a bit of metal having the power to draw your lover to you."

"You, sir, do not possess a poet's soul."

"A poet's soul?" He swept his arms wide, to indicate that

she should examine his attire. "You've been here all this time, Lily. Why the devil would you think I have anything like a soul, poetic or otherwise?"

"If I have to explain it to you there's no hope for either of us." She turned around and walked away.

"That's absurd," he called to her back. Were they having their first argument? He watched the sway of her backside and then followed. "Wellstone."

"Stop calling me that." She kept walking.

He caught up and put a hand on her shoulder. Lily turned. "What?" she said.

"This."

He kissed her. He kissed her with all his heart and soul.

Chapter Thirty

WHEN THEIR MOUTHS PARTED, LILY STUDIED HIM IN a way that made the world smaller than it was. He hadn't meant to kiss her, not like that, but he had and he wasn't sorry.

His belly tightened. "Lily," he said softly. "Whatever are you thinking?"

"I could not possibly tell you," she said, without a trace of a blush.

"Would you if you had sufficient inducement?"

"Doubtful."

Mountjoy tightened his arms around her, and she did not push away from the closer embrace. "Perhaps if I guessed?"

Her smile turned liquid. "How amusing that might be if you did. Do try."

"You are a beautiful woman," he said. "You know that's so."

She shook her head. "Not what I was thinking. But thank you."

He was off-kilter where she was concerned. He'd only met her a short time ago, and they had embarked on an affair with the understanding that their relations would end when she departed Bitterward. No emotions were to be involved. Part of him knew that this was different, that his feelings for Lily were considerably more complicated than lust. But that did not warrant declarations from him. Hell, he wasn't certain what he would declare to her and was even less sure she would welcome a declaration of any sort from him.

Tomorrow, she might agree to marry someone else.

"I would risk a great deal for you. You know that." He didn't know where those words came from, but he'd said them and neither could nor would take them back. The words were true, and yet he felt he was deceiving himself, that there was more to this for him.

She gave him a pert smile. "Also not what I was thinking."

He ran a finger underneath her lower lip and tried again. And failed, he knew as the words came out. "We're lovers, you and I. Lovers such as more poetic souls than I can express."

Her smile faded, and now she looked as uncertain as he felt. "Are we?"

"We can at least admit that to each other."

"I admit absolutely nothing."

"Why should we give that up when it suits us so well?" Again, true words, and yet they also deceived. He was at a private impasse, unable to find words that would convey his true sentiments. How could he when he wasn't sure himself what he felt? "What reason is there for you to marry your prig of a cousin without love and at the risk of your independence?"

She lifted her chin, and he repeated the touch of his finger along her mouth. "We'd grow to love one another. That's a reason."

"No. It's not, and well you know it." Lord, she was quick to see beneath his words. Quicker than anyone he knew. "He was a soldier, your Greer was, going off to war. And you loved him." He touched her cheek, a caress, a plea for her to stay close. "I know you loved him; Lily, my love, I wish you had not lost him. But there's me now, to touch you like this and show you that you are adored and desired, and to wish for so much more between us." He stared into her eyes, thinking he might never sound the depths there. He slid his finger along the line of her cheek. "Will Fenris understand that about you?"

She did not move her head, but placed her palm lightly over his hand. "I knew," she whispered. "I knew Greer would not return. But I would not change a thing."

"Passion, once awakened, is not forgotten. Nor love. We never forget that we have loved."

"No."

"Lily," he said. He cajoled. He entreated. "Lily, come to bed with me again. And again. Whenever we so desire it. Don't leave here until you are well and tired of me."

She shook her head, but she was not telling him no. "You should not have kissed me like that." She bit her lower lip. "That wasn't fair of you at all."

"I will take you under my protection." The words came in a rush of desperation. "I am generous, you know I would be. If it's jewels you want, you may have them. All the gowns you could possibly wear. Ten of silver lace and another ten in gold. I promise you discretion. I promise you your privacy. In bed, you shall have all the passion you desire. No entanglements, no need to give up your independence." He touched his forehead to hers. "Hell, take me under your protection, if you like."

She kissed his chin. "And what gifts should I shower upon you in that case?"

"All the waistcoats, coats, and pantaloons you'd like." He kept his head near hers. His desperation stayed, took up residence in his chest. In his heart. "A set of enameled dueling pistols, if you're set on indulging my whims. A horse to ride when I am in Town. A carriage. Well sprung."

She laughed.

Mountjoy continued caressing her. "Are you insulted I've asked?"

"I ought to be, but I'm not." She frowned, but stayed in

his arms. "I suppose that is due to my nature. You're right. I don't wish to give up my independence, and Fenris would expect that of me."

"You have the means to assure your future whoever you take as a lover. For as long as you like."

"I can't leave my father on his own."

"I'll come to Exeter."

She lifted her eyes, very quickly, to his. "Would you?"

"I've just told you so. I can manage my properties from there."

"And if there are consequences, Mountjoy? If we remain lovers, what if there are consequences?"

A gentleman took care of his bastards, that went without saying, but Lily wasn't one of the demimonde, nor a woman used to such arrangements. "We'll do what we can to prevent that, of course, but if that should come to pass, I won't abandon you." His heart raced in his chest, his pulse drummed in his ears. He wanted Lily with him on whatever terms she would accept. "It happens sometimes, you must know that. Even when a man is careful. Even when the woman is careful."

She chewed on her lower lip.

"I'll find a home near Syton House and buy you a town house in London. You can come to Town when the Sessions are on. Or we'll chose someplace halfway between Syton House and Bitterward and see each other there. Say yes, Lily. Say yes."

"You've given me a great deal to think about."

"So long as your answer is not no out of hand."

"It's not." She put her hand on his arm and they returned to the house. They didn't speak again until they were in the corridor that led to her room. She faced him and said, "May I ask you a question?"

"You know you may."

She frowned. "I know why Ginny dislikes Fenris, but why do you?"

"When I was new to the title, hardly a man and rough

about the edges, he was of the opinion, freely shared, that I still stank of dirt and manure. I confess that did not endear him to me."

"I don't imagine it would."

"I was offended, as anyone might be when they discover they are disliked for themselves."

She patted his hand. "I'm sure he'd say different now."

"If I were wearing my new clothes, yes."

"So you admit I was right."

He laughed softly. "Blast you, yes."

"New clothes or not, you are completely splendid, Mountjoy." She stroked his waistcoat, one of his old ones.

He leaned closer. "Don't refuse him because I don't care for him." He hated himself for playing devil's advocate with her. "He will provide you much that you deserve." But not love. Not the adoration she deserved. "He may be a prig, but he's an honorable prig. He would take care of you." He couldn't stop himself from brushing his fingertips along the side of her face, and then along her lips.

"Now there's a recommendation. An honorable prig."

"Wellstone." Mountjoy put his hand under her chin and tipped her face toward his. She closed her eyes, and he leaned in and kissed her eyelids, one then the other, and he didn't give a fig about the possibility that a servant might come upon them. Or even Eugenia. He drew back, and she opened her eyes, and he kissed her lips this time and hers were soft beneath his. Familiar now and every bit as devastating as the first time he'd kissed her.

No chaste or tentative kiss between them. Not from the very first.

He didn't have enough sense to stop, or pull back, or keep his damned tongue out of her mouth. Or his hands from wandering. Nor his brain from shutting down any and all objections his good sense might assert.

She closed the distance between them and slid her arms around his shoulders. She kissed him back. It was a lover's kiss, he did not delude himself about that. The kiss was carnal. Wicked. A prelude to sex. She kissed with the unreserved passion she had for everything she did. Her kiss was full of life and spirit, and he didn't want to give that up.

Her lips softened under his, accepted his ardor and returned it. He'd been waiting for this for too long. Her arms slid around his shoulders and drew him down to her, accepting his greedy need. One of her hands snaked through his hair and covered the back of his head. His body went taut with anticipation, ripe with lust.

He pulled back. "I want to make love to you in a bed, where there's room for us both and more."

"My room?"

He stood. "No. Mine."

"No, Mountjoy. We're safer in the tower room. That's ours together."

He took her hand in his and wondered why her answer pained him so.

Chapter Thirty-one

"THE BUTLER TOLD ME I MIGHT FIND YOU HERE."

Lily looked up from the garden bench and rested the letter she was rereading on her lap. "Good afternoon, Lord Fenris."

Mountjoy was right. He was a relation of her mother's, and he had reached out to her. He was family. And she owed it to them both to see what sort of ties they might form. One did not choose one's family, after all.

He stopped in front of her, hands clasped behind his back. His coat was a deep claret with a wider lapel than was usual and silver buttons embossed with the coat of arms of her mother's family. He carried off the boldness quite smartly. "Am I disturbing your letter reading?"

"I'm rereading it. Do sit." She made room on the bench. If she'd had a brother, he might have been a great deal like Fenris. "It's from a dear friend from the days when I still lived in my father's home. She's married now, the mother of two beloved children and soon a third to kiss and hug and lavish with affection."

The corner of Fenris's mouth slid up. "You sound as if you long for children of your own."

"Long for them?" She straightened on the bench. Where on earth did the man get an idea like that? "No, I don't think I long for them."

"Don't all women?"

"I've no notion what other women do. I'm not always certain what I want. Do all men long for the same thing?"

"No," he said. "But it's natural for men and women both to long for children. Don't you agree?"

She liked the easy way he asked the question. "We don't all have the life we would wish. Not everyone marries, my lord, just as not every married couple has children."

"Some things are in God's hands, Miss Wellstone."

"Do you long for children?" She wondered how they'd ended up on the subject of children. Well, she'd asked him, hadn't she?

"I do."

"Out of duty?"

He nodded solemnly. "Yes, but for more than that. I want children because I think I would love them very much. A son like me. A daughter with my eyes." He gave her a considering look. "But not you," he said, slowly.

"You must think me unnatural."

"No," he said. "I think you stopped thinking of children whenever it was you decided marriage was not in your future."

"Am I so obvious?"

He took her hand in his, and she allowed him to hold it. "What if you were to marry? Is it not possible that you would then change your mind about children?"

"Did you come here to turn me inside out?"

"I make you no reply to that," he said, and with a smile that made her notice how handsome a man he was.

She looked away and stared at the horizon. Her heart deeply misgave her. "When I was a girl I used to imagine the children I would have. I thought there was no question

I would one day have them. But then, I dreamed as well of exploring the world and discovering a comet." She returned her attention to him. She would have wanted Greer's children. If he had not died, she would have married him. "But that is not what befell me. I haven't explored the world or found a comet in the sky."

"You might yet have your friend's life. A husband and beloved children." He turned on the bench to face her. How cold of him, she thought, to offer marriage to a woman he did not know. To decide that a stranger ought to bear his children. "A proper home, with a husband to manage what is not your domain."

"I've become settled in my ways."

He nodded. "As I am settled in mine. I admit that to you. Can we not embark on the adventure of a new life together?" He gave her a quick grin. "I will buy you a telescope so you may search the heavens every night."

"Lest you think my friend nothing but what a woman ought to be, she is also a poetess of no small talent."

"Is she?" His eyebrows rose. "Many times blessed, then."

"Yes."

He said, "Even a mother's life can be more than the demands of home and hearth."

"Her powers of observation are acute, sir, and I do enjoy reading and rereading the verses she copies into her correspondence to me. Little rhymes, she calls them, but they are far more than that. One day I intend to publish them for her."

"A lady publisher for a lady's verses." He crossed one leg over the other. "You might sell a copy or two, I suppose."

She folded the letter and slipped it into her pocket. "I daresay you are not here to listen to me rattle on about friends you've never met and publishing ventures of which you disapprove and children I shall never have."

"I don't disapprove, Lily. May I call you that?" She nodded, and he turned a little on the bench. "It's unusual, I grant you that, but from the moment I saw you, I could see you are not the usual sort of woman." He lifted her hand between them.

She met his gaze over her hand. His eyes were a lighter brown than hers. "I cannot change my essential nature, sir. More to the point, I will not."

Fenris nodded in answer. "Nor I. I would be a poor man if I expected you to transform yourself into another creature entirely, just to please me."

She pulled her hand free of his and clasped her hands on her lap. In her head she heard the laughter of children. A family. A husband. Children she would love and cherish. "Don't think I'm not flattered. I am, sir. But I don't wish for such an alteration in my circumstances. I have arranged my life exactly to my tastes. I would miss all the things to which I've become accustomed."

"Such as?"

"I go where I like, when I like. If I wish to travel, I can. I came here, for example." Her stomach contracted to the size of a pinhead.

"Do you travel often?" He smiled, and she had the unsettling idea that he knew she rarely left home.

"That is beside the point. The point, sir, is that if I wished to leave England and visit China, I could."

"Without a husband?"

He was right about that. A visit to China on her own would be fraught with difficulties. "I don't want to visit China. That was merely an example. Be that as it may, I could certainly visit Bath or York or even Edinburgh if the fancy took me. I could sail to America if I wished and I could do so without consulting anyone or asking anyone but my banker for the funds to do so."

"If you had a husband, you could visit China." He rocked back on his heels. "With very little notice. You might even find that all the details had been taken care of for you and that more of the mystery of that country would be open to you simply because you have a husband with connections."

She looked him in the eye. "Well, I haven't got a husband."

"Miss Wellstone. Lily. You know why I am here."

For a bit, they said nothing.

"What are we to do, my lord?"

He leaned against the bench and extended his far arm along the top, away from her. "Marry. We ought to marry."

"Without any hope of love?"

He glanced at her and there was a world there that he was not admitting to her or, she thought, to himself. Lord Fenris, she realized, was in love with someone else. He had, for whatever reason, given up hope of winning the woman's heart or he would not be here with his offer.

"Does your father know what you're about? Asking me to marry you?"

"No."

She frowned. "You intend to bring home a bride you know he dislikes and a wife you do not love."

He turned more on the bench, until he was nearly facing her. "No, Cousin Lily. I will bring home a bride who is beautiful, charming, and unique. A bride who is an heiress and whose antecedents are, in fact, as impeccable as my own."

"And whose fortune once belonged to your family."

"It's your family, too." He took her hand in his again but this time he lifted it to his lips. His eyes locked with hers over the top of her hand. "Come now. It's a sensible solution. Marry me, Miss Wellstone, and you will make me a very happy man."

Her life stuttered.

"Everything come right at last. Our family whole at last."

"My lord." She jumped to her feet, dislodging her hand from Fenris's. He, too, stood, though more slowly. "You do not know me."

His expression darkened and again, she had the sense there was a great deal he wasn't telling her. "And you do not know me. That will change."

"What if I told you I'd had a lover?"

He clasped his hands behind his back and frowned. Not at her but at some internal thought of his. Then his attention fixed on her. "Have you?"

"All men want a virgin on their wedding nights. Well, you would not have one in me, sir. If you married me, you would not have the sort of wife you imagine." There. That flash of disapproval on his face reminded her of why Ginny disliked him, though in this case, could she blame him? The women men like him married were supposed to be pure, and she was not.

"Thank you for your honesty." He tipped his head to one side. "Are you with child?" he asked softly.

She let out a sharp breath. "No."

Fenris said nothing.

She stood her ground. She had long experience with men who disapproved of her. "I'm sorry you came all this way only to learn how horribly unsuitable I am."

"My offer stands. In any event, you and I needn't hurry to the altar. We can wait several months. A year."

She shook her head. He meant, of course, that he would marry her after the birth of any child she might have conceived. "Chivalry ill becomes you. It will only turn to resentment."

"And yet, my mind is unchanged."

"Why?"

"Lily." He took her hand again but just held it. "I don't mean to force you to accept me." He frowned. "But we will suit. You'll see."

She cocked her head, and everything Mountjoy had told her rushed into her head until she was dizzy with it. "My lord, if I were to marry, it would be to a man who makes my heart race. I want my stomach to drop to my toes, my limbs to quiver with passion."

Fenris studied her in his quiet way. "Are you convinced we would not have that?"

"I haven't the faintest notion." Her words came out too quickly, her breath too short.

"Sometimes affection between a man and a woman grows slowly, upon deeper acquaintance." He flushed, and that made her wonder if he was thinking about the woman he loved. The one who'd broken his heart. "Love is not always a fire that roars through you. It can be a flame that is small yet steadfast over the years."

"I want my husband to love me and admire me and believe he cannot live without me." She took a step away and threw her arms wide. "I wish myself to be madly in love in return, Fenris. Can you promise me mad love? Can you imagine yourself so desperately in love with anyone that you would rather lose your soul than lose her?"

He stood straighter, but she recognized the bleakness in his eyes. "Yes."

"Not with me," she said. "Can you really imagine yourself in love with me? Be truthful or there's no hope for us. None at all."

He eyed her. "I imagine there are very few men who cannot envision themselves madly in love with you."

"Can you? Could you?"

"I am not a man of public passions." He held her gaze and then smiled. "That does not therefore mean I have no passions, I assure you of that. Marry me," he said in a low voice, "and that will change. I promise you. My family will be doubly your relations. They will recognize you and accept you."

"Marry you and I'll have everything I've ever wished for?" She frowned. "Is that a threat, my lord?" She lowered her voice to a basso note. "Marry me or you will never meet your uncle the duke."

He had the audacity to laugh at her. "I wouldn't call that a threat. Quite the opposite."

"What would you call it?"

"Persuasion."

She stopped smiling. "Tell me true, if I say no, will I lose any hope of reconciliation? If I'm not your wife, is there any circumstance under which Camber will accept me?"

"No matter what my father says or does, you are my cousin. And Camber's niece. I won't turn my back on you merely because you refuse my offer of marriage. I am a man of quieter passions than you," he went on, "but not shallower ones." And then he gave her a penetrating look. "One hears that Mountjoy will soon be married to one Jane Kirk."

"What does Mountjoy have to do with this?"

"Everything."

"Why?"

"Because you are in love with him."

Chapter Thirty-two

IN MOUNTJOY'S ROOM, LILY PRESSED HER BACK AGAINST the wall beside the door, not wanting to look away from him. Not yet. Her heart beat faster when he closed and locked the door. His room. She drank in everything about his private quarters. Every detail revealed him to her and made her heart ache. He'd brought her here where, without meaning to, he would break her heart. She knew it. He hadn't asked her about Fenris. If he did, what would she say? What could she possibly tell him that would not ruin everything else?

The curtains were open, but the sun was at the other side of the house and his rooms were cool and shadowed. The decor was reassuringly spare, as suited the man, but not austere. She stopped examining their surroundings and watched Mountjoy. He stood by the door, a hand on the latch. Silent.

Here she was. Alone in a room with a man to whom she was not married. With a man who had just admitted for them both that they were lovers now and who had asked her to be his mistress. He'd not used the word, but he'd meant that.

Still with his hand on the door, Mountjoy cocked his head and gazed at her, the faintest of smiles curving his mouth.

She said, "I'm nervous to be here with you. I don't know why. I oughtn't be."

"Tell me what I can do to make you feel better." He stayed where he was, just at the door, but with his body angled toward her. Shadows darkened the edges of his face.

"Kiss me?" She meant it in jest, but it wasn't. Not really. She wanted the comfort and steadiness of his arms around her.

He leaned over to kiss her lightly on the mouth. She raised her chin, and his mouth lingered on hers. Her stomach flew away. Mountjoy continued kissing her, softly, tenderly, but not at all politely. How strange it was to pretend during the day that she never once thought about throwing herself into his arms. The truth was she did. She was happy around him. Giddy.

Hunger rose up in her as they continued to kiss, and she found herself leaning into him. She coiled an arm around his neck.

After a bit, he drew back, one hand lifted to brush her cheek. His head stayed by hers. "A moment."

He pushed away from the door and lit a lamp which he set on a table on the other side of the door from where she stood. Across the room he locked an interior door. So that his valet or some other servant, she supposed, would not accidentally come upon them. He left the other interior door open. She presumed that one led to his bedchamber.

The lamp made it possible for her to see there were the usual things one found in a room meant for a gentleman's privacy and relaxation. In the middle was a gleaming cherry-wood table and chairs, against another wall, a cherry writing desk with gold fittings. Books, a newspaper, and several volumes of a gentleman's magazine were on the desk. One of the torques from the treasure hoard sat atop the desk. A claw-footed sofa faced the fireplace. On one wall was a landscape from somewhere in Yorkshire.

The room and its decor suited him. It was easy to imagine him sitting in here, tending to his private affairs. Writing letters. Reading. Having a drink before he retired for the night. She committed the sight to memory so that she would have the image with her always.

She left the door to sit sideways on the nearest of the mahogany chairs, one hand gripping the top rail. This was Mountjoy's private domain. His room. He lit the tapers in a branched candelabra and the room grew brighter. He seemed so matter-of-fact, going about mundane tasks while she could scarcely breathe. Next, with a glance at her, he walked to a side table. "I know it's afternoon, but would you care for a cognac?"

"I've never had cognac."

"It's time you tried, then." He picked up a decanter and removed the top. With his free hand, he turned over two tumblers and poured cognac into both glasses. He walked to her, holding out one of the glasses. The other he left on the table. "A sample, to see if it's to your taste."

She accepted the glass and took a sip. It burned going down, but mellowed quickly enough that she was able to suppress a cough. Warmth spread through her chest. She looked up at him, still gripping the top of her chair. "My."

Neither of them said anything for a while. She didn't know what to say and knew even less what might be going through his mind just now. Had she really agreed to continue seeing him? Being here with him was a deliberate enough choice that she was forced to admit that yes, they were lovers. If he came to Exeter, she would gladly continue as his lover.

He broke the silence. "Are you having second thoughts, Wellstone?"

She shook her head because words of denial stuck in her throat. They had done this before, been alone together in a room locked against intrusion. They had been to bed before. Conducted their illicit affair out of sight of family and staff. But the intimacy of being here was too real.

"If you'd rather not, I understand."

She clutched her glass. She did not want him to send her away, and yet, if he did, she would spare herself the tension squeezing her heart. "How sanguine, Mountjoy," she said. "Are you so indifferent to my presence?"

He smiled. "I would be disappointed if you left, don't misunderstand. At the same time, if you are not certain you want this, then don't feel you must be here or that you must stay simply because earlier you agreed." He gave a quick look at the ceiling. "Damn me for saying such a thing. I'm not usually so noble."

"Yes you are. You are the noblest man I know."

His eyes landed on her again. "I want you to stay. Please. Stay. Make me forget again that the world consists of anything but you and me."

"It seems different now." A part of her mind shouted that she should leave immediately, that if she did this with him here, her life would change irrevocably. Her heart would never be the same. "Why is that?"

"Have you changed your mind?"

She held his gaze. Somehow, Mountjoy had become her friend, and she did not want to give him up. "No. Have you?"

He held out his hand and waited for her to take it. "Not in the least."

She put her hand on his palm, and he tugged the merest bit until she must either resist or stand. She stood.

He took the cognac from her and placed the tumbler on the table. His fingers tightened around hers, and he pulled her close to him. Closer than was proper, but then when they were behind locked doors they were never very proper, were they?

He dipped his head to hers, not to her mouth, but to the side of her throat. "I am unbearably aroused by you. And I ask you, why is that?" His breath warmed her skin. He trailed his fingers up her arm to her shoulder. His lips touched her skin just above her collarbone, and his mouth parted. She shivered at the touch of his tongue, the kisses he dropped. "I want to see you reclining on my bed," he said. "With your hair down and your legs spread, looking at me with that imperious gaze of yours."

"Imperious? I'm sure I don't know what you mean."

"I adore that about you. The way your eyes snap with intelligence."

"I should think you ought to at least be overcome by the perfection of my figure."

He laughed. "I am. I am and hope to be so very soon."

She leaned toward him, and his arms tightened around her. "I should like to see you unclothed as well, Mountjoy."

He lifted his head. His arms remained around her. "Ah yes, you and your fondness for splendid animals in their natural state."

"Extremely splendid, Mountjoy." She kissed his lower lip. "And very, very natural."

"Your every wish is my desire. After all, you've done the same for me, haven't you?" He took a step back and shrugged off his coat. He dropped the garment on a chair, all the while looking at her. He unfastened his watch chain and tucked the watch into a pocket of his waistcoat before he undid the buttons.

"Do you require assistance?"

He kept unbuttoning his waistcoat. "Kind of you to ask, but no. But make a note, Wellstone, that you'll need to order me new riding clothes. These won't do for me at all. Not anymore." He tipped his chin in the direction of the chair she'd been sitting on. "You may sit down again, if you like."

"I'll just stay here." She leaned against the table.

He dropped his waistcoat on the chair with his coat. "Mind your cognac."

She moved the tumbler to the middle of the table.

Mountjoy undid his cravat next, exposing the placket of his shirt. He sat down to remove his riding boots. And then his buckskins. The rest of his clothes followed. He didn't hurry, but he was naked soon enough.

Lily gazed at him in silence.

He waited, arms at his sides, his weight on one leg. She

made a motion with one finger and, with a grin, he obliged her by turning in a circle. Muscle shaped his long legs, his torso, too, front and back. He had, as she knew, little hair on his body. His body, so magnificent, demonstrated the effects of the hours he spent in the saddle or working with his tenants and neighbors. He walked to her and, taking her cognac from the table behind her, drained the tumbler. Her heart sped up.

He set down the glass and took a step back. "What will you do with me, Wellstone, now that I'm at your mercy?"

"I'll worship your body."

He grinned. "Is that all?"

"Isn't that enough?"

"No."

"Greedy man."

"Lovely, devilish, clever Lily." He clasped his hands behind his head and stretched. His member was not yet erect. "Should I confess that I dream about you every night? About you being here with me. In this very room. It's unwise, I think, but now I've gone and said it."

"Do you?" She reached for her medallion, out of habit fingering the cool surface. "Tell me what happens in your dreams." She went to him and rested one hand on his shoulder and curled the other around his nape. His body warmed hers. This was what she wanted, to have someone close, to be connected with another person in the way only lovers could be. "Is it my laughing eyes and dulcet tones you dream of? Or is it my intelligence?"

"In my dreams, I call you Wellstone."

"Mine, too. What else?"

"Your soft and naked skin." He put a hand on her waist. "Your mouth doing unspeakable things to me."

"Unspeakable?" She leaned against him and slid her hands up and down his back, over the curves and valleys of his muscles. "Mountjoy, my heart races trying to imagine what you mean. Do tell me. Or, since you cannot speak of it, show me."

"We have all day," he said. "What's left of it. I've locked the door. There'll be no servants interrupting. My bed is just there." He tipped his head in the direction of the open door. "Waiting for my most wicked dreams to become reality."

"Wicked of you, I agree, but hardly unspeakable."

He took a step closer. "I'd like for you to fetch me with your mouth."

She twined her fingers through his hair. "I'd like that, too. You know I would."

"Here?" he said. "On your knees?"

She trailed her fingers down his chest. "That is very wicked, your grace." She pressed her palm to his hip, and Mountjoy cupped the back of her head, fingers tense. She wanted to caress his cock, his beautiful manhood, and so she did. He was warm, and firm, erect now, to be sure, and his skin was soft. Without saying a word, he wrapped his hand around hers.

"On your knees," he said in a low voice. Not quite a question. Yet, not a command, either.

She knew his body by now, enough to know she adored the shape and taste and scent of him. The thought of bringing him to completion in that way aroused her. She longed for the pleasure it brought him. With a glance at him, she adjusted her gown and sank to her knees, sliding one of her hands from the middle of his chest to his groin as she did. "Like so?"

"Yes," Mountjoy said. With the lamp and the candles burning she could see the green of his eyes. His body was lean and well muscled, and she could spend hours worshiping his form with her hands, her eyes, and even her mouth.

She kissed the top of his penis, and that part of him flinched. He set his fingers lightly on her head, and a thrill shot through her at the contact. She wrapped her hand around his shaft.

"You needn't be gentle," he whispered. "You know what I like. Yes," he said again when she took him in her mouth.

With word and deed, Mountjoy showed her what he

wanted from her, and she loved his reaction to her, the tension in him, his groan when she used her hands, her mouth, and her tongue. Before long, his body tensed, and his directions to her turned insistent. His moan deepened her arousal.

His fingers tightened around her head again, and he pressed forward. "Like that. Christ . . . Like that."

She used her tongue on him, cupped his sac, and touched, so lightly, the base of him because she remembered once that he'd told her he liked that, and he shouted, and pushed into her mouth and came. His hands lost contact with her head, then returned. She kept her mouth on him until there was no question he was done. In such moment, he was hers.

Only then did she sit on her haunches, the back of her hand pressed to her lips.

His eyes held hers. "Are you disgusted with me?"

"No." She stood, with the aid of his hand. "Are you disgusted that I enjoyed that and would gladly do so again?"

"No. God, no. Never."

She put her hands on his chest. "Perhaps your bed would be more convenient?"

His eyelids lowered halfway so that she could barely see the green of his irises. "Yes, I think it would." He picked up the candelabra and walked to the door he hadn't locked. She followed, watching his naked backside.

He put the candles on a table opposite the bed and she looked around. His bed very much suited a duke. Four posters and a canopy of burgundy silk with yellow silk tassels holding back the hangings. The duvet was embroidered with his coat of arms, red and blue and with the swan picked out in silver thread. He pushed it away then stretched out on the mattress and extended a hand to her. "Come."

Lily kicked off her slippers before she joined him on the bed. She lay beside him, on one flank, and touched his chest. He raised a knee and tucked a hand underneath his head. "Do with me what you will," he said.

Lily stroked him, watched his face and body for reactions. His nipples were sensitive, she knew. To her fingers and her kisses.

"I think it's time you were naked, too," he said after not a very long time.

"That seems only fair."

He snaked an arm around her and brought her in for a kiss. "And convenient to our purpose."

She turned her back to him, and he unhooked her bodice. Between them, sometimes clumsily, they removed her garments. She left the bed, wearing little but her chemise and stockings, and carefully draped her clothes over a chair. She rejoined him and knelt on the mattress between his spread legs when the last of her clothes came off.

"You've converted me," he said. "From liking brunettes to worshiping blondes. Loosen your hair, Lily. So I can see it down around your shoulders."

She pulled the combs that held her hair back, and he took them from her to place on a table near the bed. She shook out her hair and arranged it so most of it fell over her shoulder.

Mountjoy held out his hands and she straddled him. "Lovely," he murmured. "So very lovely." He cupped her breasts and the flush of heat through her body astonished her.

He lay her back, and kissed his way from her shoulders to her toes and back up to her thighs. He buried his face there, kissing her and finding clever things to do with his tongue and fingers until she could hold back no longer. He stroked her body while she came, whispering her name, whispering, *Lily darling, I adore you*.

When she came back to herself, Mountjoy had himself recovered. He opened a drawer in the bedtable and took out one of his sheaths, made of the finest lambskin, he'd told her. He left the bed long enough to wet it with water from a basin as the fit was more comfortable for them both if the sheath was damp. She helped him put it on and even tied the ribbon around the base of his cock.

She lay back, and he came over her, and slid inside, and

though they'd not in the past been silent lovers, they were strangely silent now. Her heart had become too big for her chest. Mountjoy's expression was intense, and his strokes in her at first were slow and luxurious. Until he pushed harder once, then again, and she felt that stroke all the way to her heart.

He pushed up on his hands and worked her harder, and she met him stroke for stroke and still they did not speak. She couldn't. Though she'd already come, and not so long ago, pleasure rushed back, the quiver built and she hovered there at the edge, holding back because she did not want to come again so quickly when he'd hardly begun.

"Let go," he said. His words were gruff. "Give yourself to me entirely."

She raised her knees, and he thrust harder and she had to reach up toward the headboard to brace herself. "More," she said.

"I oblige you, madam."

Close, she was so close to a magnificent release, and she knew Mountjoy was close himself. She put a hand around his waist and then his hips, lifting to meet him. Once again, they had no words but the words of their bodies until he shifted the angle of his cock and she spiraled tight, so close, so close.

"Mountjoy." She arched beneath him and there were words building in her too big to hold in and far too big to speak. He held her around her waist and rocked hard into her. Her breath hitched, and she forgot anything but her need to climax, her frustration that she had not reached that point yet. He must have been close himself because his thrusts came faster and faster.

And then she crested, and lost herself completely and utterly to his body, and at the last, she felt something inside her that wasn't usual, but all that mattered was that he didn't stop, that he was coming, too, and he was calling her name and she held him tight.

"Oh, Jesus, Lily."

She opened her eyes. He wasn't looking at her fondly but with eyes wide open, staring. "What's wrong?"

He pushed back and slowly withdrew from her, looking at his member as if his cock had betrayed him, which it certainly had not, as far as she was concerned. He closed his eyes tight, then opened them again. "Lily."

She put her weight on one elbow. "What?"

He did something with his sex, and when she looked, she saw the ribbon of his condom was still tied around the base of him, but she could see only part of the sheath. The rest of his member was bare. "I'm sorry," he said. "The sheath broke."

Lily licked her lips and remembered that moment when something had not felt right. "Just now?"

"No." The rest of the sheath was in his hand. "I'm sorry. I didn't know. Didn't realize." He shut his eyes then opened them. "No, not just now. I came inside you, Lily."

Chapter Thirty-three

❧❧

MOUNTJOY FOCUSED ON THE LETTER BEFORE HIM. HE blinked. Was this the one about the declining output of one of the Mountjoy coal mines? Or was that the one before, and this one reported a threefold increase in sales of Mountjoy wool? There were other letters, too, all of them running about in his head without his knowing anything but that he'd read the subject matter at some point. There was a need to better fund the parish orphanage. The sheriff was concerned that the local smugglers were bold and getting bolder, and someone else had requested that he bring a pressing matter to the attention of the House of Lords during the next parliamentary session.

His concentration was broken by a disturbance somewhere in the house. The commotion appeared to be coming nearer. Footsteps thudded down the corridor—more than one man—and he heard Doyle saying very sternly, "Sir, I assure you his grace is not at home."

"Get out of my way," a man shouted. "I'll have the bloody farmer's head, see if I don't."

"Sir," Doyle said, his voice nearer and nearer. "That is—"

"Mountjoy!" His name became a roar of agony.

He started for the door, but he didn't get far before the door slammed open and Mr. Kirk burst in, his coat still on, his hat missing, and a riding whip clutched in one hand. Doyle dashed in after the man, two footmen behind him.

"Your grace," Doyle said, wringing his hands. The two footmen stopped in the doorway when Mountjoy signaled them to leave.

Mr. Kirk's eyes were wide and staring, his cheeks flushed red, but every hair on his graying head was perfectly in place. He pointed at Mountjoy with a shaking arm. "You."

"Sir." He took a step toward the man. Lord, what could this be but that Mr. Kirk had found out about him and Lily?

"You—" Kirk said. That he'd been crying at some point was patently obvious.

"Doyle," said Mountjoy. "Please bring Mr. Kirk a brandy."

His butler bowed. "Your grace."

"I don't want a bloody brandy," the man said.

"That will be all, Doyle. Thank you. I'll call you if you're needed."

When they were alone, without servants in sight, Kirk took a step forward, whip hand raised. "I want what's right."

Mountjoy was thirty years younger and a good deal larger than Kirk. He had no difficulty taking the riding whip away. He kept a grip on the older man's wrist and leaned over him to speak deliberately. "You will sit down. And you will tell me in a civilized manner what has brought you here to my house in such a state."

"She's my girl," Mr. Kirk said. He stared past Mountjoy. "My firstborn. The best of the lot of them if you ask me. She's ruined. Ruined!"

"Has something happened to Jane?" He lifted a hand palm out. "Choose your words carefully, sir."

Kirk took a deep breath. "As if you don't know, when she's pregnant with your bastard."

He blinked twice. "I beg your pardon?"

"Don't deny what you've done. All these years you've kept her from meeting a man who will marry her. Leading her into sin. Seducing her." Kirk scrubbed his hands over his face and when he looked up, he seemed to have collected himself. "Do you think we don't know your reputation when you are in London? Opera girls and ballet dancers. Do you think a father can't see his daughter's weakness? Jane loves you. She loves you enough to do whatever you ask of her because you're the bloody duke."

Mountjoy pressed his lips together. "Has she actually accused me?"

Kirk set his jaw. "Who else would seduce her? To whom else would she give herself except to the man she believed would marry her?"

"Someone besides me," Mountjoy said.

"You'll marry her," Kirk said. "You'll marry her as quickly as you can. It's only right when you've ruined her for anyone else. I'll sue you for breach of promise if you don't."

"What promise would that be? I never asked permission of you to marry any one of your daughters."

"You didn't need to. Everyone knew you'd marry Jane. Ask anyone, and they'll tell you."

"If you stand before a judge and swear that I promised any such thing, you'll consign yourself to Hell." Anger slipped into his voice because until now he'd considered Mr. Kirk a friend, and the man was here, sitting in his house, attempting to force him into a marriage he did not want. "Nor did I ever speak to Jane or any of her sisters about marriage. I won't marry your daughter, Kirk." He leaned over the man. "Drag this farmer's name through the mud if you feel your reputation and your soul are worth the lies."

Kirk blanched. "Agree to acknowledge her bastard as yours, then. The bastard son of a duke might do very well in life."

"No." He felt for Kirk's pain, for the scandal and disgrace if it was true Jane was with child. Sadly he must consider the possibility that Kirk was lying in an attempt to force a marriage. "If it's true, I am very sorry. But I am not the father. I will not marry a woman pregnant by another man any more than I would support another man's bastard simply because a distraught father accuses me."

"We are at an impasse." Kirk lifted his head, eyes bleak. "It must be you. It can only be you."

"There's no impasse, sir. I am not the man responsible for your daughter's misfortune."

"Then she's ruined and some rogue will not do right by her."

"So long as we agree that the rogue is not me." Mountjoy walked to the bellpull and called for Doyle. When he turned, Kirk was slumped on his chair, head down, hands clasped between his open knees. "Doyle will show you out."

Still with his head in his hands, Kirk said, "What am I to do?"

He held out Kirk's riding whip. "Go home to your family. Surely you or your wife can convince her to tell you who is responsible."

The man shook his head. "If it were someone who was free to marry her, she would have told my wife."

Doyle appeared, and Kirk, after a shaky sigh and a curt bow, left the room. Mountjoy returned to his desk, but he could not concentrate on the tasks at hand. He wished Doyle had brought a brandy.

Someone tapped on his door. "Come," he said.

The door opened. Slowly. Too slowly for the efficient Doyle.

He knew it was Lily before he saw or heard her. "Mountjoy?"

This should not be happening to him, that a woman's presence should make his heart pound and his body shiver with anticipation, with doubt, and with outright lust. Shouldn't, but was. He stood, though he stayed behind his desk, fingertips resting on top. "Yes?"

Lily was so beautiful it hurt his heart to look at her, yet

what he wanted to see from her wasn't that angelic perfection but the impish smile that meant she had the measure of him and intended to make him pay. Mountjoy, still on his feet, carefully, very deliberately, capped the ink and placed his quill in the stand.

"May I come in?" She gripped the side of the door. "I understand you're busy, but I'll only bother you for a moment." She put her other hand over her heart. "I promise."

He made the same gesture to the near chair as he'd done for Mr. Kirk. "Please."

She came in and sat on the chair, back straight, hands resting lightly on her lap. She wore a pale gray muslin with narrow vertical stripes of a darker gray. A fiery orange ribbon was threaded through her hair. The effect was, as ever, flattering to her, without there being any obvious reason why. "Sit down, your grace."

The door was open. If he could have closed it with a look he would have. If he could have changed whatever thought or concern had made Lily choose to leave it open, he would have done that, too.

"You heard all that I suppose."

"Yes."

He didn't sit down. "It isn't true," he said. "About Jane and me."

She leaned forward. "It was impossible not to overhear. He was quite angry." She met his eyes, and all he could think was how she'd looked in his arms last night, the sound of his name on her lips, the way she'd felt around him. "Is aught well with you?"

"I am not the father of her child."

"I know you're not."

He came around from behind the desk and stood before her. "There will be gossip."

"I fear Mr. Kirk intended that result."

He gave a dark laugh and gestured at his desk. "My responsibilities must be met. Every day. Every minute. I do meet them and have done so since the day I became Mountjoy. Duty to my family, my title, my tenants, the people who live in this parish, and those where I am an absentee property owner they know only by name. To those in my employ and to my king and country. But I do not owe Jane Kirk a father for her child."

"No, I suppose you don't." She let out a breath. "What if you married her after the child comes?"

The world stopped. His heart no longer beat. "You can't marry Fenris. Not now. No more than I can marry Jane. You know that. You know why."

"Mountjoy, don't."

"Don't what? Am I to do nothing while you marry a man you don't love? Should I marry a woman I don't love? For God's sake, you can't mean that."

She stood, too, and he closed the distance between them and the hell with the open door, he thought. He kissed her, mouth open from the start, and twined an arm around her waist to bring her close. She moved with the forward impetus of his arm, melted against him and now, for this moment, he felt right. Whole. Her arms went around his shoulders, both of them so that she was pressed against him. She slid her fingers into his hair and brought his head down to hers and kissed him senseless.

They parted, eventually, each of them breathless. They'd ended up with her backed up to a tall and thankfully sturdy cabinet that stored various documents and supplies. Paper. Ink. Letters, deeds, the last will and testament of the third duke.

"I'm not going to marry Fenris," she said.

"I'm not going to marry Jane."

"Very well, then."

"Have you made up your mind what you'll do about me?" he said. When he made up his mind that he wanted thus and such a woman, he'd never had any difficulty getting her into his arms. He'd watched other men flirt and seduce and cajole, and he had never had to do that. Until now. Until Lily. He touched her shoulders, her low back, the sides of her throat.

She leaned against the cabinet. "I can't think when you kiss me like that."

"You do want me." He wasn't a man of sweet words. To his knowledge he had no particular way with women the way other men did, just good sense about them. "You couldn't kiss me like that if you didn't."

Her impish smile flashed. "Perhaps you're right."

"I'm always right." He kept her close. "Have you changed your mind about us?"

"No. Have you?"

"No," he said. Relief blew through him, but it was followed by the unsettling conviction that he'd just made a serious mistake. Though, how could that be when Lily wasn't leaving him?

Chapter Thirty-four

MOUNTJOY OPENED THE DOOR TO LILY'S ROOM AND slipped in as quickly and unobtrusively as he could. Lily was in bed, a single candle providing the light by which she'd been reading. She had a book in her hand, but it was facedown on her chest, and her eyes were closed.

She sat up, though, blinking when he turned from the door he'd just locked. "Mountjoy?"

He put a finger across his lips and whispered, "Don't send me away."

"I shan't." If she hadn't been asleep, then she'd been near to it. Her hair was down, but braided so that it would not tangle while she slept. Half past six in the morning and she was only now falling asleep. "What is it?"

"Lord, where to start." She was the first and only person he wanted to talk to, and he had taken a risk, coming here with the servants already up and about.

"In the middle, if you please." The curtains were drawn, but her candle and a soft morning light kept the room from darkness.

"Nigel came home late last night." He walked to her dressing room door and closed that, too. And locked it.

She set aside her book and sat with her legs curled underneath her. If he were a painter, he'd take her likeness posed like this. As if she were fresh from her lover's embrace, even though she wasn't. A frown creased her brow. "And?"

"He arrived home in possession of a special license. In order to marry Jane Kirk. Which he has done, I should add, without my prior knowledge or consent. In the middle of the night."

"Don't tell me you object."

"It wouldn't matter if I did. They are married and are even now sitting downstairs having come here to inform me I have a sister-in-law. I have just listened to my brother confess that he has been in love with Jane Kirk for months and that he is responsible for her inconvenient situation."

"What does Mr. Kirk say? Does he know?"

"Not yet." He scrubbed his hand through his hair. "Directly he obtained the special license, Nigel went to Jane. Not here. He did not come home to consult the head of his family. He went to the Kirks', got a ladder, put it up against Jane's window, and carried her away."

"He did?"

Mountjoy looked down and saw her eyes wide and, God help him, filling with tears. "For pity's sake, don't cry. There's nothing to be done now. He did not consult a soul, the fool."

She blinked, and two fat tears rolled down her cheeks. "I always cry when there's a happy ending. I can't help myself. A ladder, you say? It's so romantic."

"Romantic?" He pulled his handkerchief from his pocket and handed it to her.

"Thank you, your grace. That's simply the loveliest story. He adores her. Did he throw pebbles at her window, or was she waiting up for him?"

"I haven't the faintest idea." He resisted the impulse to

kiss her. For now. "Wouldn't it make more sense for him to climb the ladder and tap on the window?"

"I think he must have thrown pebbles." She put her book on the bedside table. "It's what all the heroes do when they carry away their ladyloves."

The tension in his chest eased because he'd just seen his future. He was looking at it now. He knew exactly what he had failed to recognize before. "You don't think it's a scandal? Eloping with the woman everyone thought was to marry his brother?"

"Of course it's a scandal. A delicious, wonderful scandal of true love, Mountjoy." She extended a hand, and without thinking, he took it. "You'll have to have a wedding party for them."

He groaned. "More people in my house."

"I'll help you plan it."

"That's your advice for me? Have a party?"

"We'll invite everyone."

"I'm not writing a single invitation."

"Ginny and I will manage everything. Don't worry. You won't have to do a thing except pay the bills." She patted the mattress, and he sat beside her.

"What am I to do about this, Wellstone?"

"Which?"

"Any of this. You." He stretched himself over her, laying her back on the mattress, then drew back with a sigh. "I haven't got a sheath with me."

"Another time, Mountjoy."

"I want you now." He kissed her and kissed her some more and only just recalled himself. "If we were married, Wellstone, we could dispense with sheaths and withdrawal. I could come inside you again right now."

"That seems rather shortsighted of you, don't you think?" Her arms were around him, and she spoke in a low voice. "Is that worth a night or two of pleasure?"

"It's morning."

"A day then. A day of pleasure."

"Do you think as badly of me as that? Why not you for my duchess? We get along. You amuse and delight me. I never know what you'll do next. And you would be a splendid mother to our children. They'd be exceptional. How could they not be with us to raise them and lavish them with love?"

"A point, sir."

He pulled her close enough that she could not fail to know he was aroused. "You see?" he said. "I want you. I always do. I have from the day we met. I won't behave anymore as if I don't adore you more than Nigel adores Jane. I want the right to touch you, kiss you, to make my life with you in public and in private."

"You're overwrought, Mountjoy. Swept away by your brother's grand gesture." She gave him a look. "Or is it lack of sleep that's made you like this?"

Mountjoy bent to kiss her forehead, then let her go and slid off her bed where he stood staring at her with his heart racing. "Will you wait here?"

"Where would I go? I should like a few hours' sleep." She covered a yawn.

"Don't sleep."

"Why not?"

"Promise me?"

She reached for his hand and squeezed it. "I don't believe it's wise for me to indulge your whims like this, but if you insist."

"I do."

Twenty minutes later, Mountjoy was outside her window wrestling a ladder into position. It scraped against the wall and listed dangerously far to the right. Several of his groundskeeping staff watched him. He saw one of them scratch his head. One of the gardeners who'd been pruning the roses came to lend a hand. "Ground's too soft here, your grace. Begging your pardon, but that ladder will fall over, and you'll break your neck."

Mountjoy pointed. "I need it there. At that window."

"Your grace." Between the two of them and another of

the staff who came over to assist, they got the ladder into place. The top rails banged against the windowsill. He stooped for a handful of pebbles, but that proved unnecessary since the noise had brought Lily out of her bed to see what was happening.

Mountjoy climbed the ladder but before he got to the top, Lily had already opened the window. He gripped the top rung with one hand and threw his handful of pebbles at the glass. Most of them showered to the ground below, but a few ended up on the sill and one or two inside her room.

"Mountjoy?" She brushed away the pebbles that had landed on the sill. "What are you doing?"

"There's no easy way to say this so I'll just say it." He took her face between his hands. "Lily. Lily, you are mine." He knew from her frown that he'd not spoken well. "I want you to belong to me. Mine," he said. Which he knew was exactly the wrong thing to say to her, but the word fell from his lips as if it had been waiting there to send him to perdition and now the moment had come.

"Am I?" she whispered. The ladder wobbled and he had to let go of her to steady himself.

"Mountjoy?" someone called out from below.

Lily waved from the window. "Felicitations to you Lord and Lady Nigel." She closed her eyes. "And our audience is now complete, Mountjoy. Here is your sister."

"Mountjoy?" said Eugenia. He didn't bother looking. "Good heavens."

"Good morning all," Lily said. "Your brother was concerned for my safety when he saw a crack in my window. He's saved my life, I daresay."

Mountjoy looked down and saw his brother and Jane on the lawn with the groundskeeping staff. The couple held hands. Eugenia was there, too, in her night-robe. He returned his attention to Lily. "Never mind them. Come away with me, Wellstone."

"And do what? Scandalize your family and all of High Tearing?"

"Marry me," he said, and where the demand had been hiding from him all this time, he did not know. He ought to have said it days ago. He ought to have made her understand days and days ago. "We shall deal with your father."

She pressed a finger to his mouth. "It's far too soon for that. Nothing is certain, Mountjoy. Not yet. You needn't."

He reached for her again and brought her head to his and kissed her, and as always, they were immediately in lust. In high passion. She pulled back. Below, he heard a whistle and applause.

"Come inside, you foolish man, before you fall and break your neck."

"Don't be absurd. What would everyone down there say if they saw me climb into your room? No, there's nothing for it but for you to come down the ladder with me." He reached in and got an arm around her waist. "Or," he whispered in her ear, "I can go down alone and tell them it's not the window that's broken."

"Mountjoy," she said. "Oh, Mountjoy, what am I to do?"

"If you'll take my advice, fetch your prettiest night-robe and come down the ladder with me."

"I have a jade green one, with the most cunning darker stripes running through it."

"You are spectacular in green. Fetch that one." Ten minutes later, he managed to get them safely down to the lawn. "You see? You will always be safe and sound with me." He used the sides of his thumbs to brush away her tears. "What's this? More tears?"

"Impossible," she whispered. "I'd never cry over something like this."

"Marry me, Lily." He pulled her into his arms. "I want to spend my life learning about you. Being with you. Trying to make you as happy as I will be with you as my wife."

She gazed at him and blinked twice. "Good God, Mountjoy."

"Marry me, my love."

"Have you considered the negatives? You'd have me for

your duchess when I am sure to invent a ghost or two for Bitterward. What will people say?"

"That I'm a damned luckier man than anyone deserves. They'll say I climbed a ladder to propose to the woman I love, that's what they'll say. Besides, after Eugenia tells you how sorry she is you're going to have such a one as me for a husband she'll be over the moon at having you as a sister."

Behind them, someone coughed.

"Ignore them." He gripped Lily's shoulders. "Say yes, Wellstone. I'll make you happy, I promise you that with my last breath."

"It's not your duty to make me happy."

"It would be my joy. I want to. I want you to be happy." He stared into her face and understood he had not been honest yet. Not with himself and not with her. "The bald truth. I love you." He cupped her face between his hands. "You are the most remarkable woman I've ever met. I adore you. I want to be with you. I don't care how short a time it's been since we met, my life is no longer what it was, and I am unutterably grateful to you for that."

She turned her head to one side and kissed his wrist. "That is because at last you understand the value of a decent waistcoat."

"I love you, Lily. Marry me. Please make me the happiest of men." He drew a strand of her hair away from her face, and she looked at him again, her gaze serious, unreadable except that she was not smiling and had not told him yes. Or no. Or that he needed to prove himself to her. "Love me," he said. "Love me in whatever way a woman like you can love a man like me."

More tears slid down her cheeks. "Oh, Mountjoy. Don't say such things."

"If you don't love me, for God's sake, refuse me, but if you do or if you think you could, then marry me. Be my wife, and my lover, and my friend. Be the mother of our children. Let me spend the rest of my life with you, and I will be the luckiest, happiest man on this earth. I love you,

Lily. I think I fell in love with you the moment I saw you, and all this time I've been too stubborn to admit it."

She did smile, and he was grateful for that. "You are a very stubborn man, I'll grant you that."

"That I am."

She held his face. "Do you mean this?"

"Lily," he said. "I am prepared to make an enemy of your father."

She leaned her head against his chest. "Oh, Mountjoy."

"So tell me, is there room for me in your heart?"

She looked up, her eyes bright with tears. "My dear, dear man. I think I should very much like being a duchess."

"Does that mean yes?" He kissed her once. On the mouth. "You'll marry me?"

"Yes. Yes, I'll marry you."

Behind them, the servants hooted and cheered and applauded, and amid all that joy he heard Nigel and Eugenia cheering as well.

"I feel," she said, "I ought to tell you that you have Fenris to thank."

"Say it isn't so."

"But it is. Fenris was the one who told me I am in love with you." She kissed his hand. "He was right."

"About?"

"That I love you, Mountjoy."

"I've always wanted a cousin," he said.

She twined her arms around him and for quite a while they were lost to each other, and Mountjoy felt at last he'd done exactly the right thing.

Epilogue

Three weeks later. The Anglo-Saxon church at Bitterward.

EUGENIA TRIED NOT TO SNIFFLE AS HER BROTHER, THE Duke of Mountjoy, slid a ring onto Lily's finger. Then the final benediction was over, and her brother and her best friend were married. Eugenia just couldn't be happier. It was obvious to anyone that Mountjoy was head over heels for Lily and that Lily felt the same about Mountjoy.

The wedding was beautiful, and her brother looked so handsome in his new suit of clothes. He was smiling, her brother was. Smiling. The way he'd started smiling shortly after Lily arrived, only bigger and broader and at last without him trying to pretend he wasn't. Beside him, Nigel elbowed him and whispered something Eugenia couldn't hear but that made Mountjoy grin.

She heard a sniffle and glanced across the chapel where Miss Caroline Kirk had a handkerchief pressed to her eyes. The wedding was an intimate one, with only friends and family in attendance, a fortunate thing since the invited guests fit very snugly in the church.

The location had been Mountjoy's idea and there had

been three weeks of frantic work so that the church could be used. The walls had a fresh coat of whitewash, pillows had been laid on the stone pews, and the break in the altar had been repaired. Banners with the Mountjoy coat of arms hung from the walls and another flew outside. The path had fresh gravel laid down.

Lily's cousin, that awful man, the Marquess of Fenris, heir to the Duke of Camber, was in attendance as the lone representative of her family. He'd sat quietly during the ceremony, very proper and unapproachable. If he had tender feelings for the bride as she pronounced her vows, they were not in evidence. She resented Fenris for all that he had done, but she could not, after all, begrudge him a place at his cousin's wedding. Their aunt and uncle were here as well, all the way from Haltwhistle, as proud of their nephew as any parent could be of a son. Two of Mountjoy's close friends had come up from London and Cornwall respectively. A small gathering, but Mountjoy never wanted a fuss.

Eugenia dabbed a handkerchief to her eyes as Mountjoy bent to kiss his wife. Her aunt, who was sitting beside Eugenia, pressed her hand, but she sniffled, too. Silently, Eugenia wished Lily and her brother all the happiness in the world.

Afterward, everyone walked outside into the bright afternoon sun. A few yards distant, several carriages waited to carry the guests and the Duke and Duchess of Mountjoy back to Bitterward for a reception.

She walked out with her aunt, but they'd only got partway down the path when she heard Lily call out, "Ginny!"

With a word to her aunt, Eugenia returned to her brother and her sister-in-law. She smiled and curtseyed. As any who knew Lily would expect, she was exquisitely dressed. She wore ivory silk overlaid with silver lace with tiny silver blue flowers knitted into it. "Yes, your grace?"

"Here." Lily removed her Gypsy medallion and, before Eugenia could say a word, hung it around her neck. "For you, my dear Ginny."

"But this is yours!"

Lily pulled Mountjoy closer to her. "I've all the good luck I need, Ginny. The medallion has done its work for me." She pressed Ginny's hand and they locked gazes. "It's someone else's turn now."

"I thought you didn't believe any of that," Mountjoy said.

"Why wouldn't I?" Lily asked. "The magic worked exactly as the Gypsy king said it would." She patted his cheek with her free hand. "After all, the medallion brought me you. There's no better magic than that, Mountjoy."

"True," he said, dropping a kiss on his wife's cheek.

"Thank you, Lily," Eugenia said. She touched the medallion, tracing a finger over the bow and arrow engraved on it. The metal was warm.

Lily leaned in to give her a kiss. "I'll take good care of your brother, Ginny. I promise you."

"I know you shall."

"Be sure you sleep with the medallion under your pillow."

She laughed. "I will."

"Promise?"

"I promise."

A few minutes later, Mountjoy had escorted his bride to their carriage and they were on their way to Bitterward where they were to say good-bye to their guests before leaving for Syton House and parts south.

Eugenia sniffled again as her brother's carriage rolled away from the church. At the same time she was turning to rejoin her aunt, the Marquess of Fenris was heading for his carriage. Eugenia's vision was blurred with the remnants of her tears and did not realize how close he was to her. Fenris was inattentive as well, for he collided with Eugenia on the path. If he'd not caught her, she might actually have been injured in a fall.

She found herself clasped in the arms of the man who had told Robert he was making the biggest mistake of his life, marrying her. The man who'd done everything in his power to prevent her marriage. When she had her feet underneath her, she pushed him away.

"I beg your pardon," Fenris said.

Eugenia stepped away from him. "It's nothing. I beg *your* pardon." He was her new sister's cousin, and therefore she felt she could not cut him dead. That did not mean she had to be anything but cool toward him. She didn't like him and never would. She dropped him a curtsey and returned to her aunt.

"He seems a polite young man," her aunt said when they were once again arm in arm. "And very handsome."

"The man who nearly knocked me over?"

"I didn't mean the vicar, dear."

"I suppose." Eugenia didn't bother looking at Lord Fenris or she would have seen that he was watching her. She did at least lower her voice. "But I dislike him exceedingly."

Look for the next Romancing the Rake novel
by Carolyn Jewel

Not Proper Enough

Coming in September 2012
from Berkley Sensation!

THE LION

"Timely and terrific...one of the greatest storytellers of our or any time." —*Providence Sunday Journal*

"Let the pulse pounding begin." —*New York Post*

"You won't be able to put this one down, and you learn about the roots of terrorism to boot."
—Lisa Scottoline, on the *Today* show

"DeMille's combination of character and action are fun to read...The conflict between Khalil and Corey is an extraordinarily well-matched one." —*Denver Post*

"If you like CIA, FBI, and terrorist plots, you'll love DeMille's tale. It's a chilling reminder of how vulnerable we still are despite all our homeland security measures." —*Chattanooga Free Press*

"Nelson DeMille has not lost a step...Mr. DeMille puts on a clinic demonstrating how to move a story along with memorable characters and a plot that is all too plausible in the aftermath of September 11."
—*Washington Times*

"Very creative and exciting...a well-constructed and satisfying sequel, full of exciting visual imagery."
—*Booklist*

The Panther

NOVELS BY NELSON DEMILLE
Available from Grand Central Publishing

By the Rivers of Babylon
Cathedral
The Talbot Odyssey
Word of Honor
The Charm School
The Gold Coast
The General's Daughter
Spencerville
Plum Island
The Lion's Game
Up Country
Night Fall
Wild Fire
The Gate House
The Lion
The Quest

WITH THOMAS BLOCK

Mayday

Nelson DeMille

The Panther

VISION

NEW YORK   BOSTON

Copyright © 2012 by Nelson DeMille

Vision
Hachette Book Group
237 Park Avenue
New York, NY 10017
www.HachetteBookGroup.com

Vision is an imprint of Grand Central Publishing.
The Vision name and logo is a trademark of Hachette Book Group, Inc.

The Hachette Speakers Bureau provides a wide range of authors for speaking events. To find out more, go to www.hachettespeakersbureau.com or call (866) 376-6591.

The publisher is not responsible for websites (or their content) that are not owned by the publisher.

Printed in the United States of America

Originally published in hardcover by Hachette Book Group
First international mass market edition: April 2013
First oversize mass market edition: April 2014

10 9 8 7 6 5 4 3 2 1
OPM

Author's Note

Regarding the spelling of Arabic words in this novel, I've used a variety of sources in transliterating. There is no standard transliteration of Arabic script into American English, and in some cases I simply used phonetic spelling to make it easy for the reader. I mention this up front with the hope that I can persuade the reader not to send me an e-mail saying I spelled an Arabic word wrong. However, if you see an English word misspelled, let me know.

The Panther

— PART I —

Marib,
Yemen

CHAPTER ONE

A man wearing the white robes of a Bedouin, Bulus ibn al-Darwish by name, known also by his Al Qaeda nom de guerre as al-Numair—The Panther—stood to the side of the Belgian tour group.

The Belgians had arrived in a minibus from Sana'a, four men and five women, with their Yemeni driver, and their Yemeni tour guide, a man named Wasim al-Rahib. The driver had stayed in the air-conditioned minibus, out of the hot August sun.

The tour guide, Wasim, spoke no French, but his English was good, and one of the Belgians, Annette, a girl of about sixteen, also spoke English and was able to translate into French for her compatriots.

Wasim said to his group, "This is the famous Bar'an Temple, also known as Arsh Bilqis—the throne of the Queen of Sheba."

Annette translated, and the tour group nodded and began taking pictures.

Al-Numair, The Panther, scanned the ruins of the temple complex—over an acre of brown sandstone walls, towering square columns, and open courtyards, baking in the desert sun. American and European archaeologists had spent many years and much money uncovering and restoring these pagan ruins—and then they had left because of tribal suspicion, and more recently Al Qaeda activity. Such a waste of time and money, thought The Panther. He looked forward to the day when the Western tourists stopped coming and this temple and the surrounding pagan ruins returned to the shifting desert sands.

The Panther looked beyond the temple complex at the sparse vegetation and the occasional date palm. In ancient times, he knew, it was much greener here, and more populous. Now the desert had arrived from the East—from the Hadhramawt, meaning the Place Where Death Comes.

Wasim al-Rahib glanced at the tall, bearded Bedouin and wondered why he had joined the Belgian tour group. Wasim had made his arrangements with the local tribal sheik, Musa, paying the man one hundred American dollars for the privilege of visiting this national historic site. Also, of course, the money bought peace; the promise that no Bedouin tribesmen would annoy, hinder, or in any way molest the tour group. So, Wasim wondered, why was this Bedouin here?

The Panther noticed that the tour guide was looking at him and he returned the stare until the guide turned back to his group.

There were no other tourists at the temple today; only one or two groups each week ventured out from the capital of Sana'a, two hundred kilometers to the west. The Panther remembered when these famous ruins attracted more Westerners, but unfortunately because of the recent reports of Al Qaeda activity in this province of Marib, many tourists stayed away. He smiled.

Also because of this situation, the Belgians had arrived with an armed escort of twenty men from the National Security Bureau, a para-military police force, whose job it was to protect tourists on the roads and at historic sites. The tourists paid for this service, which was money well spent, thought The Panther. But unfortunately for these Westerners, the policemen had also been paid to leave, which they were about to do.

Wasim continued his talk. "This temple is also known as the Moon Temple, and it was dedicated to the national god of the Sabaean state, who was called Almaqah."

As the Belgian girl translated, Wasim glanced again at the bearded man in Bedouin robes who was standing too close to his tour group. He wanted to say something to the man, but he was uneasy about him, and instead he said to his group, "This was one thousand and five hundred years before the Prophet Mohammed enlightened the world and vanquished the pagans."

The Panther, who also spoke English, nodded in approval at the guide's last statement.

He studied the Belgian tourists. There were two couples in their later years who seemed to know one another, and who looked uncomfortable in the burning sun. There was also a man and a woman, perhaps in their early twenties, and The Panther saw they wore no wedding rings, though they were obviously together, sometimes holding hands. The remaining man and woman were also together as a couple, and the girl who was translating appeared to be their daughter or a relative. He noted, too, that the women had covered their hair with hijabs, a sign of respect for Islamic custom, but none of them had covered their faces as required. The guide should have insisted, but he was a servant of the non-believers.

They were all adventurous travelers, thought The Panther. Curious people, perhaps prosperous, enjoying their excursion from Sana'a, where, as he knew, they were guests of the Sheraton Hotel. Perhaps, though, this excursion was more difficult and adventurous than they had been told by the tour company. So now, he imagined, they might be thinking about their hotel comforts, and the hotel bar and dining room. He wondered, too, if a few of them were also thinking about security matters. That would be an appropriate thought.

Again Wasim stole a glance at the Bedouin, who had intruded even closer to his small tour group. The man, he thought, was not yet forty years of age, though the beard and the sun-browned skin made him appear older. Wasim also noticed now that the man was wearing the ceremonial jambiyah—the curved dagger of Yemen, worn by all males in the north of the country. The man's shiwal, his head covering, was not elaborate nor was it embroidered with costly gold thread, so this was not an important man, not a tribal sheik or the chief of a clan. Perhaps, then, the Bedouin was there to ask for alms from the Westerners. Even though Wasim had paid Sheik Musa to keep the tribesmen at a distance, if this Bedouin asked for alms, Wasim would give him a few hundred rials and tell him to go in peace.

Wasim again addressed his group. "This temple is believed by some who practice the American Mormon faith to be the place to which the Mormon prophet called Lehi fled from Jerusalem in the sixth century before the Common Era. It was here, according to Mormon scholars, where Lehi buried the prophet Ishmael. And when this was done, Lehi built a great ship for himself and his family and sailed to America."

Annette translated, and one of the male tourists asked a question, which the young girl translated into English for Wasim, who smiled and answered, "Yes, as you can see, there is no ocean here. But in ancient times, it is believed there was much water here—rivers, perhaps—from the Great Flood of Noah."

The young woman translated, and the Belgians all nodded in understanding.

Wasim said, "Follow me, please." He ascended fourteen stone steps and stood before six square columns, five of which rose twenty meters in height, while the sixth was broken in half. He waited for his group to join him, then said, "If you look there to the west, you will see the mountains where the local tribes believe the Ark of Noah came to rest."

The tourists took pictures of the distant mountains and didn't notice the bearded man climbing the steps toward them.

Wasim, however, did notice, and he said to the Bedouin in Arabic, "Please, sir, this is a private tour group."

Al-Numair, The Panther, replied in Arabic, "But I wish to learn also."

Wasim, keeping a respectful tone in his voice, replied to the Bedouin, "You speak no English or French, sir. What can you learn?"

The Panther replied in English, "I am a poor man, sir, who comes to entertain the tourists in my finest tribal robes."

Wasim was taken aback by the man's perfect English, then replied in Arabic, "Thank you, but Sheik Musa has assured me—"

"Please, sir," said the Bedouin in English, "allow me to pose for photographs with your Western friends. One hundred rials for each photograph."

Annette heard this and translated into French for her compatriots, who had seemed anxious about the exchange between the two Arabs. Hearing now what this was about, they all smiled and agreed that this would be a very good thing—an excellent souvenir photograph to take home.

Wasim acquiesced to his clients' wishes and motioned to the Bedouin to proceed.

The Belgians began posing alongside the tall, bearded Bedouin, individually at first, then in small groups. The Bedouin smiled for each photograph, and he was very accommodating to the tourists as they asked him to move around the temple to set up various shots with the ruins in the background.

One of the older men asked him to draw his dagger, but the Bedouin explained almost apologetically that if the jambiyah is drawn, then it must be used. On hearing the translation of this from Annette, the older Belgian said to his compatriots, "Then we will not ask him to draw his dagger," and they all laughed. But Wasim did not laugh.

Wasim glanced at his watch. Though they had left Sana'a at eight in the morning, the bus had not arrived at the nearby town of Marib until after noon. The tourists had lunched, too slowly he thought, at the Bilqis Hotel tourist restaurant, and there Wasim had to wait too long for Sheik Musa, who demanded two hundred

American dollars, saying to Wasim, "The other tribes are making problems, and so I must pay them to allow you safe passage on your return to Sana'a."

Wasim had heard this before, but he explained to the sheik, as he always did, "The tourists have already paid a fixed price to the travel company in Sana'a, and a price for the police escort. I can ask no more of them. And there is no profit for me if I give you more money." But, as always, Wasim promised, "Next time."

The sheik and the tour guide from Sana'a had agreed on the one hundred dollars, but Wasim had decided there would be no next time. The road from Sana'a to Marib was becoming unsafe, and it was not only the tribes who were restless, but also this new group, Al Qaeda, who had entered the area in the last year. They were mostly foreigners—Saudis, Kuwaitis, people from neighboring Oman, and also Iraqis who had fled the Americans in their homeland. These people, Wasim thought, would bring death and unhappiness to Yemen.

In fact, Sheik Musa had said to Wasim, "These Al Qaeda people are becoming a problem. They are attracted by the American oil wells and the American pipelines, and they gather like wolves waiting for a chance to strike." The sheik had also told Wasim, "You cannot buy those people, my friend, and the police cannot protect you from them, but I can. Three hundred dollars."

Again, Wasim had declined to make the extra payment, and Sheik Musa had shrugged and said, "Perhaps next time."

"Yes, next time." But Wasim was now sure there would be no next time.

Wasim al-Rahib, a university graduate with a degree in ancient history, could not find a job teaching, or a job anywhere, except with this tour company. It paid well enough, and the Western tourists were generous with their gratuities, but it was becoming dangerous work. And also dangerous for the tourists, though the tour company would not say that. All the guidebooks— written years ago—said, "You cannot leave Yemen without seeing the ruins of Marib." Well, Wasim thought, they would have to see them without him.

Wasim watched the tourists, talking now to the Bedouin through the English translation of the young girl. The Bedouin seemed pleasant enough, but there was something unusual about him. He did not seem like a Bedouin. He was too at ease with these foreigners, and he spoke English. Very unusual, unless perhaps he worked for the Americans at the oil installation.

In any case, it was now past three in the afternoon, and they had not yet visited the Temple of the Sun. If they stayed here much longer, they would be traveling the last hour to Sana'a in darkness. And it was not good to be on the road after dark, even with the police escort, who themselves did not want to be on the road after dark.

Wasim spoke in English to the young woman, and to the Bedouin, "We must now leave. Thank you, sir, for your hospitality."

But the Belgians wanted a photograph of the entire group together with the Bedouin, taken by Wasim. So Wasim, thinking about his gratuity, agreed, and took the photographs with four different cameras.

Wasim then said to the Belgian girl, "I think if you give this gentleman a thousand rials, he will be very happy." He made sure she understood. "That will be about five euros. A very good day's pay for this kind man."

Annette collected the money and handed it to the Bedouin, then said to him, "Thank you, sir."

The Bedouin took the money and replied, "You are very welcome." He also said to the girl, "Please tell your compatriots that Bulus ibn al-Darwish wishes them a happy and safe visit to Yemen."

Wasim was looking to the north where the minibus had parked on the road behind the army truck that carried the security police. The bus was still there, but the truck was not. In fact, Wasim could not see any of the National Security police in their distinctive blue camouflage uniforms.

Wasim made a call on his cell phone to the police commander, but there was no answer. Then he called the bus driver, Isa, who was also his wife's cousin. But Isa did not answer his cell phone.

Wasim then looked at the Bedouin, who was looking at him, and Wasim understood what was happening. He took a deep breath to steady his voice and said to the Bedouin in Arabic, "Please, sir . . ." Wasim shook his head and said, "This is a very bad thing."

The tall Bedouin replied, "You, Wasim al-Rahib, are a bad thing. You are a servant of the infidels, but you should be a servant of Allah."

"I am truly his servant—"

"Quiet." The Bedouin raised his right arm in a signal, then lowered it and looked at Wasim and at the Belgians, but said nothing.

The four men and five women were looking at their guide, waiting for him to explain what was happening. Clearly, something was wrong, though a few minutes earlier everyone had been smiling and posing for pictures.

Wasim avoided the worried stares of his group.

Annette said to Wasim in English, "What is wrong? Did we not give him enough?"

Wasim did not reply, so Annette said to the Bedouin in English, "Is there something wrong?"

Al-Numair, The Panther, replied to her, "You are what is wrong."

The Belgians began asking Annette what had been said, but she didn't reply.

Then one of the men in the group shouted, "Regardez!" and pointed.

In the temple courtyard below, where they had been standing, a group of about twelve men suddenly appeared from the dark recesses of the ruins, wearing Bedouin robes and carrying Kalashnikov rifles.

At first, all the tourists were silent, but then as the Bedouin began running up the stone steps, a woman screamed.

Then everything happened very quickly. Two of the Bedouin pointed their rifles at the Belgians while the others bound their hands behind their backs with tape.

Annette shouted to Wasim, "What is happening? Why are they doing this?"

Wasim, whose wrists were also bound, was at first afraid to speak, but then he found his voice and said, "It is a kidnapping. Do not be frightened. They kidnap for money. They will not harm us."

And as Wasim said this, he hoped it was so. A tribal kidnapping of Westerners. It was a common thing— what was called a guest kidnapping—and they would spend a week, perhaps two, with a tribe until money was delivered. And then they would be released. These things usually ended well, he knew, and Westerners were rarely harmed, and never killed unless the army intervened and attempted to free those who were taken by the tribes.

Annette, though she was terrified, said to her compatriots, "It is a kidnapping. For ransom. Wasim says not to be—"

"Shut up," said the tall Bedouin in English. He then said to Wasim in Arabic, "This is not a kidnapping."

Wasim closed his eyes and began praying aloud.

Bulus ibn al-Darwish, The Panther, drew his curved dagger and moved behind Wasim. With one hand he pulled Wasim's head back by his hair, and with his other hand he drew his curved dagger across Wasim's throat, then shoved the man forward.

Wasim fell face first onto the stone floor of the Temple of the Moon and lay still as his blood flowed quickly and spread across the hot stones.

The Belgians stared in horror, then some of them began screaming and some began crying.

The armed men now forced all the Belgians to their knees, and The Panther moved first to Annette, coming around behind her, and said to her, "So you don't have to watch the others die," and with a quick motion he pulled her head back by her long hair and sliced open her throat with his curved dagger, then moved on to the others.

Some cried or begged for mercy, and some struggled, though it was futile, because the jihadists held them in a tight grip as The Panther cut their throats. A few accepted their fate quietly. Only one prayed, an elderly woman whom The Panther saved for last so she could finish her prayers. It was interesting, he thought, to see how people died.

In less than two minutes, it was over. All nine infidels and Wasim their servant lay on the floor of the temple, their life blood flowing freely onto the ancient stone.

Bulus ibn al-Darwish, al-Numair, The Panther, watched the infidels as, one by one, they went into a final death throe, then lay still.

One, however, the man who was the father of the young woman, suddenly stood, his wrists still bound behind his back, and began running down the stone steps. He quickly stumbled and fell face first onto the stone, then tumbled down the steep steps and came to rest at the bottom.

The Panther said to his jihadists, "I hope he was not injured."

The men laughed.

The Panther stared at his jambiyah, red with blood, then slid it into its sheath.

He retrieved one of the tourists' cameras and looked at the digital images on the small screen, which made him smile.

He called to one of his men, "Nabeel," and handed him the camera to take pictures of the slaughter.

The Panther looked at the dead Europeans and said, "So, you came to Yemen for adventure and for knowledge. And you have found both. A great final adventure, and a great knowledge of this land. You have learned that in Yemen death comes."

— PART II —

New York City

CHAPTER TWO

If the earth had an anus, it would be located in Yemen. And speaking of assholes, my boss, FBI Special Agent in Charge Tom Walsh, wanted to see me, John Corey, at 5:15 P.M., and Detective Corey was now five minutes late. But not to worry—my wife, Kate Mayfield, who also works for Walsh, was on time for the meeting and had undoubtedly made excuses for me, like, "John is in a passive-aggressive mood today. He'll be here when he feels he's made his statement."

Right. Another five minutes. I logged off my computer and looked around the empty cube farm. I work on the 26th floor of 26 Federal Plaza, which is located in Lower Manhattan in the shadows of the Twin Towers. Well... not anymore. The Towers, I mean. But I'm still here.

It was Friday—what we call Federal Friday—meaning that by 4:30, my colleagues in the war on terrorism, mostly FBI agents and NYPD detectives, had left to beat the bridge and tunnel traffic, or they'd gone off on special assignments to the surrounding bars and restaurants. With any luck, I'd be joining them shortly.

But first I had to see Tom Walsh, who is in charge of the New York Anti-Terrorist Task Force. And what did Mr. Walsh want to see me about?

His e-mail had said: *John, Kate, my office, 5:15. Private. Subject Yemen.*

Yemen? Typo, maybe. Yemex? A new kind of explosive? Maybe he meant "Yes-men." Too many yes-men in the organization.

Walsh doesn't usually state the subject of a private meeting—he likes to surprise you. But when he does state a subject, he wants you to think about it—he wants it to eat at your guts.

If I thought this out, I could conclude that Tom Walsh wanted to assign Kate and me to the Yemen desk. Do we have a Yemen desk here? Maybe he just wanted us to help him find Yemen on the map.

Another possibility...no, he was *not* going to ask us to *go* to Yemen. No, no. I'd been there for a month to investigate the USS *Cole* bombing. That's how I found out it was an anal cavity.

I stood, put on my jacket, straightened my tie, and brushed the chips off my shoulders—a well-balanced detective has a chip on *both* shoulders—then made my way toward Walsh's office.

A brief history of this elite organization. The Anti-Terrorist Task Force was founded in 1980, when the word "terrorist" was not synonymous with Islamic terrorist. The ATTF in those days had its hands full with Irish Republican Army guys, Black Panthers, Puerto Rican separatist groups, and other bad actors who, to paraphrase William Shakespeare, thought that all New York was a stage, and every bad actor wanted to play Broadway.

So the first Federally funded Anti-Terrorist Task Force was formed here in New York, made up of ten FBI agents and ten NYPD detectives. Now we have a lot more people than that. Also, we've added a few CIA officers, plus people from other Federal and State law enforcement and intelligence agencies. The actual number is classified, and if someone asks me how many people work here, I say, "About half."

The New York Task Force experiment worked well, and prior to September 11, 2001, there were about thirty-five other anti-terrorist task forces across the country. Now, post-9/11, there are over a hundred nationwide. A sign of the times.

The theory behind these task forces is that if you mix people from various law enforcement and intelligence agencies into a single organization, you will get different skills and mind-sets coming together to form synergy, and that will lead to better results. It sort of works. I mean, my wife is FBI and I'm NYPD and we get along and communicate pretty well. In fact, everyone here would get along better if they slept with one another.

The other reason for including the local police in the Federal Task Force is that most FBI agents—my wife included—are from non-urban areas, meaning the 'burbs or the boondocks. So in a big city like New York, it's the local cops who know the territory. I've instructed new FBI agents on how to read a subway map and I've pinpointed for them the location of every Irish pub on Second and Third Avenues.

In any case, I'm actually a contract agent here, meaning I'm a civilian. Until five years ago I was NYPD, but I'm retired on medical disability as a result of being shot three times in the line of duty, all on the same day. I'm fine physically (mentally maybe not so fine), but there were other reasons to take the offer to retire. Now, like a lot of ex-cops, I've found a new career with the Feds, who have zillions of anti-terrorist dollars to spend. Do I like this job? I was about to find out.

CHAPTER THREE

My boss and my wife were sitting at a round table near a big window that faced south with a good view of Lower Manhattan and the Statue of Liberty in the harbor; a view now unobstructed by the Towers, though on the window was a black decal of the missing buildings with the words "Never Forget."

No one, myself included, commented on my lateness, and I took a seat at the table.

I am not overly fond of Mr. Walsh, but I respect the job he does, and I appreciate the stress he's under. I'd like to think I make his job easier, but . . . well, I don't. I have, however, covered his butt on occasion and made him look good. He does the same for me now and then. It's a trade-off for Tom. So why did he want to send me to Yemen?

Tom informed me, "Kate and I haven't discussed the subject of my memo."

"Good." Bullshit.

Kate is career FBI, which is maybe why she likes the boss. Or maybe she just likes him, which is maybe why I don't.

A quick word about Special Agent in Charge Tom Walsh. He's young for the job—mid-forties—good-looking if you like store mannequins, never married, but in a long-term relationship with a woman who is as self-absorbed and narcissistic as he is. Did that come out right?

As for his management style, he's somewhat aloof with his own FBI agents, and he's borderline conde-scending to the NYPD detectives under his com-mand. He demands total loyalty, but he's forgotten that the essence of loyalty is reciprocity. Tom *is* loyal to his superiors in Washington; everyone else is expend-able. I never forget that when I deal directly with him. Like now.

But human beings are very complex, and I've seen a better side of Tom Walsh. As a for-instance, in our last major case, involving the Libyan terrorist Asad Khalil, a.k.a. The Lion, Walsh exhibited a degree of physical bravery that matched anything I've seen in my twenty years with the NYPD and my four years with the Task Force. If it wasn't for that one act of incredible courage, when he put his life on the line to save thousands of innocent lives, I'd now be thinking about another job when my contract expires next month.

Tom got right to the point and said, "Let me get right to the point." He glanced at an e-mail in front of him and informed us, "Two overseas postings have come down from Washington."

I inquired, "Paris and Rome?"

"No," he replied, "two jobs in Sana'a." He reminded me, "That's the capital of Yemen."

"Not happening," I assured him.

"Hear me out."

Kate said to Tom, "If my husband is not interested, then I'm not interested."

Actually, she didn't say that. She said to me, "Let's hear this."

Thanks, partner. Kate is always putting career and country ahead of her husband. Well, not always. But often. I have notes on this.

Also, my detective instincts told me that Tom and Kate had, in fact, started without me. FBI people stick together.

Walsh continued, "One posting is for a legat, and the other is for an ERT person." He added, "Both in Sana'a, but with some duties in Aden." He informed us, "The Sana'a embassy currently has no Legal Affairs Office, so this is a new position, beginning next month."

He then went into an official job description, reading from a piece of paper. I tuned out.

A legat, FYI, is a legal attaché, attached to the U.S. Embassy in a foreign capital, or to a U.S. consulate office in a major city. In this case, it would be Sana'a and maybe Aden, the only two cities in Yemen as far as I knew.

Kate, like many FBI Special Agents, is a lawyer, so I, as a detective, concluded that the legal job was hers. The ERT is the Evidence Response Team—the Fed equivalent of forensic or crime scene investigator—so I concluded that that was to be my job.

The crime in question, I was certain, was the bombing of the USS *Cole*, a warship that had been refueling in Aden Harbor. This took place on October 12, 2000, which was why I had been in Yemen in August 2001. The investigation of this terrorist act is ongoing and will continue until everyone involved is brought to justice.

As for Sana'a, the capital of Yemen, the word in Arabic means A'nus. And by the way, the port city of Aden is no treat either. Trust me on this.

Mr. Walsh continued, "As John knows from his last visit, the Yemeni government will issue only forty-five-day visas to our ERT personnel who are investigating the Cole bombing. But with some pressure, we can usually get this extended for up to a year."

A year? Are you kidding?

Walsh editorialized, "The Yemenis are being cooperative, but not *fully* cooperative." He explained, "They're walking a fine line between pressure from Washington and pressure from sources inside and outside of Yemen who want the Americans out of their country." He further explained, "The government in Sana'a is currently going through an anti-American phase."

I informed him, "I don't think it's a phase, Tom." I suggested, "Maybe we should stay home and nuke them."

Tom ignored my suggestion and continued, "Kate's job with the embassy comes under diplomatic rules, so she can be there for any reasonable length of time."

How about five minutes? Does that work?

Tom further briefed us, "Bottom line, you can both figure on a year." He added, "Together." He smiled and said, "That's not so bad."

"It's wonderful," I agreed. I reminded him, however, "We're not going."

"Let me finish."

This is where the boss tells you what's going

to happen if you say no, and Tom said, "Kate's time here in New York is approaching a natural conclusion in regard to her career trajectory. In fact, Task Force headquarters in Washington would like her to transfer there. It would be a good career move."

Kate, who is from someplace called Minnesota, did not originally like New York, but she's grown fond of being here with me. So why wasn't she saying that?

Tom continued, "If Kate accepts this overseas hardship assignment, the Office of Preference will move her to the top of the OP list." He explained, unnecessarily, "Meaning, after Yemen, she can return to New York—or any place she chooses."

Kate nodded.

Tom said to me, "If you accept this assignment, your contract, which I understand is about to terminate, will obviously be renewed for the time you're in Yemen, and we'll add two years afterwards."

I guess that was the carrot. I think I liked the stick better—don't renew my contract.

Tom had obviously thought about that, too, and said to me, "Or, after your return from Yemen, you can have a Federally funded job with the NYPD Intelligence Unit." He assured me, "We'll take care of that."

I glanced out the window. A crappy February day. It was sunny in Yemen. I looked at the nearby brick tower of One Police Plaza. It would be nice to be back on the force, even as a Federal employee, though I'd be working in intelligence rather than homicide. Still, I'd be out of 26 Federal Plaza, which would make me and Tom equally happy. Kate and I could fly paper airplanes to each other from our office windows.

Tom seemed to be done with the carrot and the stick, so I asked the obvious question. "Why us?"

He had a ready answer and replied, "You're the best qualified." He reminded me, "You've already been there, and the team in Yemen would appreciate someone with experience."

I didn't reply.

He went on, "You two work well as a team, and the thinking is that a husband and wife might fit in better."

"I'm losing you, Tom."

"Well . . . as you know, women are not fully accepted in some Islamic countries. And professional women and unmarried women run into many obstacles. But Kate, as a married woman traveling with her husband, can move about more freely." He added, "And more safely."

Neither Kate nor I responded to that, but I was getting the feeling that he wasn't talking about Kate's work as a legal attaché at the embassy.

In fact, Kate asked, "What's this about, Tom?"

He didn't reply directly, but said, "You both may be asked to go beyond your official job descriptions."

I inquired, "Do we have to kill somebody?"

He didn't laugh and say, "Of course not, you silly man." In fact, he didn't say anything, which said a lot.

Tom stood and went to the sideboard. He returned with three glasses and a bottle of medicinal brandy. He poured, we clinked, said "Cheers," and drank.

He turned and stared out the window awhile, then said, as if to himself, "There were seventeen American sailors killed—murdered—when a boat pulled up beside the *Cole* in Aden Harbor and the suicide bombers on board detonated a large explosive device that blew a hole in the side of our warship. Thirty-nine sailors were injured, some very badly." He added, "A multi-million-dollar warship was put out of service for nearly two years."

Right. That was almost three and a half years ago, and the ongoing investigation has had mixed results.

The Evidence Response Team in Yemen, by the way, has long ago discovered any existing forensic evidence, and the crime scene—Aden Harbor—has been dredged, and the USS *Cole* is repaired and returned to duty. So this is an Evidence Response Team in name only—a designation that our reluctant Yemeni allies can live with. In fact, the ERT team in Yemen interrogates suspects, witnesses, and informants, and is actively involved in hunting down the perpetrators. That's what I did when I was there. So maybe that's what Tom meant about us going beyond our job descriptions. Or...he meant something else.

Walsh sat, then confided to us, "We have identified one of the masterminds of the attack, and we have good intelligence that this individual is now back in Yemen." He added, "The focus of our team in Yemen is to find and apprehend this man." He looked at Kate and me and said, "You would be part of that effort."

Neither of us replied, so Walsh continued, "This assignment could take you out of Sana'a and out of Aden and into the tribal lands."

I thought about that. The tribal lands, otherwise known to the Americans there as the Badlands, or Indian Territory, were basically lawless. Also known as dangerous.

Walsh said to us, "As John knows, this could be risky."

Right. Now I knew the answer to "Why us?" Walsh wanted me dead. But he liked Kate. So...maybe I would be the only one riding a camel into the Badlands, looking for this guy.

I pointed out to Walsh, "You're not making this job sound very attractive."

He replied, "I'm not going to sugarcoat it."

"Right. I appreciate that, Tom. But I just don't see what's in this for us."

"Why is it always about you?"

Well, that made me feel bad. Tom knows how to do that. So I said, "Look, Tom, I'm a patriot, a soldier in the war on terrorism, and I've never backed away from my duty or from danger—"

"I know that. Both of you are brave, dedicated—"

"Right. But I sort of like my danger in an urban setting. Like here." I reminded him, "I've been there. We slept with our boots on and our guns in our hands." I assured him, "I'm not thinking of my own safety. I'm thinking of Kate."

Kate, of course, said, "I can take care of myself, John."

"Right." *You* go.

Walsh told us, "You would need to report to the American Embassy in Sana'a no later than next weekend. So I'll need your answer Monday at nine." He added, "If you say yes, then I can give you the classified details of your assignment. Once you have those classified details, you are committed to the assignment."

"In other words, we don't know what we're saying yes to until after we say yes."

"Correct." He assured us, "If you say no, there will be no record of this meeting and no adverse entry in your file." He reminded us, "Your careers will take a normal course."

Right. I'd be unemployed in New York, and Kate would be in Washington.

Walsh continued, "This assignment—if you choose to accept it—will ensure your futures—"

"Shorten our futures?"

He ignored me and continued, "Even if this mission is not successful. If successful, you and the other members of the team who are already in Yemen will be appropriately honored by a grateful government. That's all I can say about that."

Honored where? Arlington National Cemetery?

He had some good news. "Your assignment in Yemen would actually be over as soon as you apprehend this man."

Good incentive to wrap it up in a week. The other side of that deal is that our assignment could be over if this guy found us first.

Tom looked at me and said, "This assignment will give you ample opportunity to demonstrate your sometimes unorthodox methods, which are not always appreciated here, but will be invaluable over there."

How should I take that? Loose cannon makes good in Sandland?

Kate said, "We'll think about it." Then she asked Tom, "Can only one of us say yes?"

He nodded.

Well, I was seeing the old handwriting on the wall here. What did I do with my desert duds from my last trip to Sandy Arabia?

Tom stood and we also stood. He said, "I'll see you both here in my office, Monday, nine A.M. Have a good weekend."

We shook, and Kate and I left.

On the way back to our cube farm, I suggested, "Let's get a drink."

She didn't reply immediately, then said to me, "John, we have to do this."

"Absolutely, and we'll have dinner, too. Where would you like to go?"

"We have to go to Yemen."

"Why not Ecco's?"

"I'm going."

"Good. Should I call ahead for a table?"

"And I'd like you to go with me."

"I wouldn't let you drink alone."

"Are you listening to me?"

"No."

We grabbed our coats, rode down in the elevator, and exited the lobby of 26 Federal Plaza onto lower Broadway.

It was windy and cold on the street, but I like the cold. Good drinking weather. Yemen was hot and alcohol was illegal.

On the plus side, I could, as Tom said, and as I had discovered myself in Yemen, be free of the bureaucratic bullshit here, and free of the political correctness that permeated 26 Federal Plaza. I could be me. Nuts.

Also . . . I had the feeling that someone in Sandland needed to be whacked. That could be interesting. I mean, I never had or wanted a license to kill—but I could conceive of a situation where this might be necessary and right. Especially since 9/11.

This was a lot to think about, and I think better at the bar.

We got to Ecco's on Chambers Street, and as we made our way to the crowded bar, Kate said to me, "We're getting into a rut here. I'm ready for a change. An adventure."

"Let's go to a different bar."

"We'll appreciate our lives and jobs more when we come back."

"Right." But not everyone who went to Yemen came back.

CHAPTER FOUR

Ecco's is an Italian restaurant, but the bar is sort of old New York, though the prices are new New York.

The place was hopping on this cold Friday night after work, and most of the clientele were lawyers, judges, police officials, and politicians whose wallets hadn't seen the light of day in years.

Kate and I found a place at the bar, said hello to a few people we knew, and ordered the usual—Dewar's and soda for me, a Pinot Grigio for the lady.

Kate asked me, "Are there any places in Sana'a or Aden where you can get a drink?"

"Is that all you think about?"

My ex, Robin by name, is a high-priced criminal defense attorney, and she introduced me to this place years ago, and she still comes here. I don't care, and I don't dislike her, but I don't like her life's work, which is defending the scumbags I spent twenty years trying to put in jail. That caused some strain on the short marriage. Now I'm married to another lawyer. As I often say, I like to screw lawyers.

Kate and I clinked and said grace. "Thank God it's Friday." There was a piano in the corner, and the player was just getting started. I said to Kate, "Ask him to play 'Midnight at the Oasis.'"

She rolled her big baby blues.

A word about Kate Mayfield, a.k.a. Kate Corey. We met on the job when we were both working on the first Asad Khalil case. FBI and NYPD are different species, but we fell in love, married—about four years ago— and it's still heaven.

Kate is a little younger than me—actually, about fourteen years—and the age difference is not an issue; she's mature beyond her years, and I can't seem to grow up.

She's originally from Minnesota, as I said, and her father is retired FBI and her mother is a loon. They both hate me, of course, but being from Minnesota they're really nice about it.

Also on the plus side, Kate and I have been shot at together, which is good for any relationship, and she's cool under fire. If she has any faults, aside from her divided loyalty, it's that she doesn't fully appreciate my NYPD work habits or methods. Also, the Feds are almost humorless, while cops are funny. I'm trying to get more serious, and Kate is trying to see the funny side of terrorists.

Away from the job, we get along well. I wondered, though, how we'd do in Yemen, where we'd be on the job together 24/7. Maybe she'd appreciate my cowboy style better in a place where the only law is a man with a gun. Better yet, maybe we'd never find out.

I asked for a table and was happy to learn it would be a thirty-minute wait. "Another round," I said to the bartender. Can't walk on one leg.

Kate said to me, "If we don't take this assignment, your contract may not be renewed, and I may wind up in Washington."

"He's bluffing."

"He's not."

"I don't respond well to threats," I assured her.

"It's not a threat. It's a transfer."

"Whatever."

"Would you live in Washington?"

"I'd rather live in Yemen."

"Good. We'll be together. In a year, we'll be back in New York."

"Right. It's that year in Yemen that might be a career killer."

She didn't reply.

Regarding my last visit to Yemen in August 2001, the same month I was there, Kate was in Dar es Salaam, Tanzania, as a legat investigating the 1998 U.S. Embassy bombing, which was an Al Qaeda attack, planned by Osama bin Laden, whose name was then unknown to most of the American public. A short time after Kate and I returned from our respective overseas assignments, Osama bin Laden and Al Qaeda both became famous for murdering three thousand people.

Our separate assignments overseas, by the way, were a sort of punishment—or a warning—resulting from my and Kate's unauthorized snooping into the mysterious midair explosion of TWA Flight 800. So off we went. Kate to Dar es Salaam, which was not such a bad place to be, and me to Yemen, which is like the Siberia of the Task Force, though I did feel like I was doing something useful. We returned to New York a

few days apart, as I said, just in time for September 11.
Tom Walsh was not the boss then, so I can't say he was
now making another effort at adjusting my attitude. So
what was he up to? Kate was taking this at face value.
I was not. Tom doesn't do things *for* people; he does
things *to* people. Also, this came from higher up. John
Corey has to go to Yemen. But why?

Anyway, all this was running through my mind as I
stood at the bar in Ecco's, observing Western civilization at its best or worst, thinking about my career, my
marriage, my country, my life, and my future.

I normally don't reflect on any of this, and I pride
myself on a low level of introspection and zero self-
awareness. But I'd just been unexpectedly presented
with a life-changing choice, and I needed to think
about my response.

Kate asked me, "What are you thinking about?"

"There's a new Monet exhibit at the Met."

She looked doubtful, then said, "John...if you
don't want to go, I will understand."

I said to her, "You should take my word that this is
not a place you want to be for a year."

She reminded me, "A lot of our people are or were
there. And we have troops in places like Iraq and
Afghanistan who are making great sacrifices every
day." She informed me, "You can't pick where you want
to fight a war. You have to go where the enemy is."

"They're *here*, Kate," I reminded her. "We're manning the ramparts of Fortress America."

She thought about that, then said, "We've done a
good job here. But now we need to go into the belly of
the beast."

"The asshole," I corrected.

Our table was ready, and as we made our way through the restaurant, who should I see but my ex, sitting with yet another beau. I mean, this lady has had more mounts than a Pony Express rider.

She saw me and waved, so I went to her table and said hello and got introduced to Mr. Right Now, who looked like he was about halfway through a sex change operation.

Kate, who is cool about this, said hello to Robin and her date, and Robin asked us, "How's the war on terrorism going?"

I informed her, "The alert level is still yellow."

Robin didn't respond to that, but said, "God, sometimes I think they're going to blow this place up."

Kate had a nice comeback and said, "Why would anyone want to kill lawyers, judges, and politicians?"

Robin wasn't sure how to take that and asked me, "Are you still in the apartment?"

The apartment in question is the former marital residence, a very expensive place on East 72nd Street that Robin had lived in when I met her. She'd signed over the long-term lease to me on her way out, a very nice gesture that took care of most of my monthly income. I said, "Still there."

"Good. I wanted to send you both an invitation for a fund-raiser I'm running. It's for the Downtown Association for the Arts." She explained, "To raise money to commission artists to create murals and sculpture in Lower Manhattan."

More shit.

"It's at the downtown Ritz-Carlton. Black tie. March twenty-sixth. You'll be my guests."

I found myself saying, "Thanks, but we'll be out of the country."

"Where are you going?"

"Classified."

"Oh...well...good luck."

"Thanks."

We followed the hostess to our table, and Kate asked me, "Does that mean you'd rather go to Yemen with me than a black-tie fund-raiser with your ex-wife?"

"You know I'd follow you to hell."

"Good. We leave next week."

CHAPTER FIVE

It was Saturday, and Kate and I agreed not to discuss Yemen until Sunday evening.

Kate went to the office Saturday morning to clean up some paperwork and to identify cases that she would need to hand off if, in fact, she was going to Yemen.

I had an appointment with a guy named Nabeel, who coincidentally was from Yemen. I didn't know Nabeel, but he'd called the ATTF office, using only his first name, asking for me by my full name, and saying to me that we had a mutual friend. I doubt that, but that's how I get half of my contacts in the Muslim community; my business card is all over town. Well, Muslim neighborhoods. It pays to advertise.

My brief phone conversation with Nabeel revealed that his legal status in the country was a little shaky, and he wanted some help with that in exchange for some information he had. Nabeel worked in a delicatessen in Brooklyn, so I wasn't sure what kind of information he had for me. Phoney baloney? Exploding beans?

A little-known factoid is that many Yemeni immigrants work in delis in Brooklyn and Queens. Why?

Who knows? Why do the Turks own so many gas stations? Why do Indians own all the 7-Elevens? Who
cares as long as the Irish still run the pubs?

Anyway, I told Nabeel to meet me in Ben's Kosher
Deli on West 38th Street, a place unlikely to be frequented by others of the Islamic faith—though, ironically, kosher food is halal, meaning okay for Muslims,
so this works.

And here I was now in Ben's, sitting in a booth
across from Nabeel. He had to get back to his deli in
Bay Ridge, Brooklyn, so this was going to be a happily
short meeting.

Nabeel looked to be about mid-thirties, but he was
probably younger, with a scruffy beard, dark skin, and
teeth stained green by khat—a narcotic leaf that keeps
ninety percent of the male population of Yemen per-
petually stoned and happy. I wished I had some now.

Nabeel ordered tea and a bagel with hummus, and
I had coffee.

I asked Nabeel, "Where did you get my name?"

"I tell you on phone. From friend." He also
reminded me, "Cannot tell you friend."

"Was it Abdul?"

"Who Abdul?"

"Which Abdul. Who's on first?"

"Sir?"

"Talk."

Nabeel talked. "There is big plot from peoples of Al
Qaeda. Saudi peoples. No Yemen. All Saudi. Plot is to
make bomb exploding in New York."

"Can you be a little more specific?" And maybe
grammatical?

"Yes? What more?"

"Bomb where? When? Who?"

"I have all information. I give you. I need work visa."

Maybe I could give him my visa to Yemen. I asked him, "You have ID on you? Passport?"

"No."

They never do. I really didn't want to speak to this guy unless I could see his passport, so I said to him, "I need you to come to my office." I took a card from my pocket and asked him, "What's your last name?"

He gave me a scrap of paper on which his name was written in badly formed Latin letters—Nabeel al-Samad—saying to me, "I copy this from passport." He said proudly, "I can sign name."

"Wonderful." I wrote on the back of my business card, *Nabeel al-Samad to see Det. Corey.* I signed it, dated it, and handed it to him, saying, "I'll have an Arabic translator and I'll have someone from Immigration for you to talk to. Capisce?"

"Yes? You arrest me in office?"

"No. I can arrest you here." And fuck up my day. Not to mention yours.

"Talk here first."

"Okay. Talk."

Nabeel confided that he was in contact with people who knew more about this bomb plot, but he needed more time—like a six-month visa—to get the details. Sounded like bullshit. But you never know.

Finally, he agreed to come into the office on Monday if he could get the morning off. These guys work twelve-hour days, six or seven days a week, and they send what amounts to a fortune home to their wife and ten kids. A deli in Brooklyn is like a gold mine in Yemen.

I asked him, "Where you from in Yemen?"

He named some place that sounded like "Ali Baba."

"You like it there?"

"Yes. Beautiful country. Good people."

"Then why do you want to stay here?"

"No work in Yemen. I go home, two months. Three months. See family. Come again here. Go again Yemen."

A Yemeni jet-setter. I tore a sheet out of my notebook, gave it to him with a pen, and said, "Write your info."

Unfortunately, he couldn't write English beyond his name, so I said, "In Arabic." No luck. Illiterate in two languages. "Spanish?"

"Sir?"

Three languages. I asked him the name of his deli in Brooklyn, his place of residence, and his cell phone number.

He spoke—slowly, please—and I wrote in my notebook, saying to him, "I want to see you Monday morning at 26 Federal Plaza or I'll send a police car to pick you up. Have your passport with you. And your visa—expired or not. They'll have your name at security. Bring my card. Understand?"

He nodded.

I dialed the cell number he'd given me and it rang in his pocket. Trust, but verify. I threw a twenty on the table and left.

I was supposed to meet Kate at the Met to see the stupid Monet exhibit. I should learn to keep my mouth shut.

I had some time, so I began walking the forty blocks. Good exercise.

I thought about Nabeel. Most informants have or can get you some information, or they wouldn't come to you. All of them want something in return. I've never seen a Mideastern informant who just wanted to do their civic duty to their adopted country. In Nabeel's case, as with most of them, he wanted permanent citizenship or a green card in return for ratting out someone. Sometimes they just wanted money. Money for informants was easy—green cards not so easy. Meanwhile, I still can't figure out why they want to live here. Could it be that their beautiful countries suck?

I have a theory about immigration. Wherever you were born, stay there.

Kate and I made cell phone contact and met at the Met. We had lunch in the museum restaurant, then went to the Monet exhibit. Was this guy going blind? Or do I need glasses?

Saturday night we joined two other couples at Michael Jordan's Steak House. This is a cool place. Cholesterol and testosterone.

The restaurant is located on the balcony above the Grand Central Station Concourse, with an overhead view of the famous clock under which lovers and others meet. I watched the mass of humanity arriving and departing by train—a scene that hasn't changed much in a hundred years, except now there were soldiers and police watching everything. No one seemed to notice them anymore; they were part of life now. That sucks.

Cops tend to hang with cops, but I've expanded my social circle since joining the Task Force, and tonight we were with Feds. Fortunately, the two guys, Ed Burke and Tony Savino, were ex-cops like me, working for the Feds like everyone else these days. One of the wives, Ann Burke, was an MOS—Member of the

Service—and still on the job, working in the 103rd Precinct. The other lady, Marie Savino, was a stay-at-home mom with two crumb snatchers under five and one in the oven.

Which gave me an idea. If Kate were to get pregnant—like about four hours from now—then the Yemen thing was off. I reached under the table and ran my hand over her thigh. She smiled.

Anyway, we tend not to talk business when we're out, but tonight I said, "Kate and I have been asked to apply for a posting to Yemen."

Ed Burke, a former NYPD detective with the Intelligence Unit, advised, "Just say no."

Tony Savino said, "I know two guys who were there."

I inquired, "What do they say about it?"

"I don't know. No one has ever heard from them again."

This got a big laugh. Cops have a sick sense of humor.

I informed everyone, "I was actually there for a month in August 2001. The beaches are topless. You get your head blown off."

Good laughs.

"John."

"In Yemen, the men are men and the camels are nervous."

"Enough, please," said Kate.

So I dropped the subject.

But Tony said, "Seriously, the two guys I knew who were there said there's no place safe outside the American Embassy." He added, "They know who you are when you get off the plane, and you have a target on your back every time you move."

I already knew that. And now Kate had heard it from someone else—but she did not waver. In fact, she's stubborn. She said, "If we don't go, someone else will have to go."

Hard to argue with that. But the problem, as I saw it when I was there, was that we had a very small American presence in a very hostile environment. A recipe for disaster. Ask General Custer about that.

We dropped the subject completely, or so I thought until Ed Burke said to the waiter, "I'll have the camel dick on a stick."

Everyone's a comedian.

Sunday morning we got up late and I offered to make breakfast. I asked Kate, "Do you feel like pickles and ice cream?"

"What?"

"You should make sure you're not pregnant before we see Walsh tomorrow."

"John, I'm on the pill."

"Right. How about scrambled eggs?"

We had breakfast, read the *New York Times*, and watched a few morning news shows. The BBC is really the best source of world news that Americans don't give a shit about, and we tuned in just in time to discover that there was yet another civil war going on in Yemen.

Apparently some tribal leader in the north named Hussein al-Houthi was trying to topple the government in Sana'a and restore the Imam to power and create an Islamic fundamentalist state. Hussein, according to the reporter with the British accent, wanted to kick out all the foreigners and infidels in the country and return Yemen to Sharia law. Not a bad idea. Kicking foreigners out, I mean. Me first. Hussein also wanted to cut off the head of Yemen's longtime dictator president, a guy named Ali Abdullah Saleh. Hussein sounded like a guy who took the fun out of fundamentalist.

Kate hit the mute button and said to me, "I didn't realize there was a war going on there."

"There's always a war going on there." I inquired, "Did you know that Yemen has the highest ratio of guns to people in the whole world?" I explained, "They have to do *something* with those guns."

She didn't reply, but I could sense she was rethinking her year abroad.

We belong to a health club on East 39th Street, and we spent a few hours there, burning off the beef fat from Michael Jordan's and sweating out the red wine.

Kate and I stay in pretty good shape, and we also spend time at the pistol range. If we were FBI accountants, we probably wouldn't bother with any of this.

I needed a drink after the health club, so we walked up to Dresner's, a neighborhood pub where they know my name too well.

We took a table near the window and ordered two beers to rehydrate.

Kate asked, "Do you want to talk about Yemen now?"

I replied, "I thought that was a done deal."

"Well...I'm still leaning toward it, but I want you to go with me."

What she actually wanted was for me to talk her out of it. My role—if I choose to accept it—is that of bad guy. But I didn't want to play that role or that game. I said, "If you're going, I'm going."

"I don't want you to do something you don't want to do."

"I want to do whatever you want to do, darling."

"Well...maybe we should weigh the pros and cons."

I couldn't think of a single pro, but in the spirit of weighing all the issues, I said, "Maybe your parents could come for a long visit."

She seemed a little annoyed and said to me, "If you're going to be flippant about this, then I say we should just go."

"Okay with me."

End of discussion. Right? Well, no. It doesn't work that way. She said, "I don't think you mean that."

Obviously Ms. Mayfield was wavering, and I was elected to give her the push one way or the other. I could have killed this thing right then and there, but I was taking some perverse pleasure in this. I mean, she was gung-ho for Yemen on Friday, but now some reality had set in.

Oddly enough, I was starting to think of some reasons why we *should* go. Not good reasons, but reasons—the biggest being that like most husbands, I sometimes let my wife do something I've advised against, which gives me the pleasure of saying, "I *told* you so!" I was actually looking forward to that moment. I pictured us in the desert with an overheated vehicle—maybe with bullet holes in the radiator and all the tires shot out—surrounded by Bedouin tribesmen with AK-47s. As I was slamming a magazine into my Glock, I'd look at her and say, "I *told* you so!"

"What are you smiling at?"

"Oh...I was just thinking about...how beautiful the desert is at night. Lots of stars."

The waitress came by and I ordered a bacon cheese-burger with fries and another beer. Kate did the same. Hey, life is short. I informed Kate, "Not much beer or pork in Yemen."

"If we go, I don't want to hear you complaining for a year."

"I'm not a complainer."

"That's a joke—right?"

"Complaining is a New York thing. It's an art."

"It's annoying."

"Okay. I won't complain in Yemen. No one there gives a shit anyway." I added, "Or they just kill you. End of complaint."

She suppressed a smile.

I said, "There's actually an off-Broadway theater in Sana'a, and they've got a long-running musical called 'Guys and Goats.'" I broke into a show tune: "I got the goat right here, the name is al-Amir—"

She reminded me, "You're an idiot."

Back in our expensive apartment, we had coffee and watched some TV. The History Channel had yet another documentary about the end of the world, this one about the End of Days, as predicted by the Mayan calendar. December 21, 2012, to be exact. But they weren't saying what *time* this was going to happen. I mean, you wouldn't want to be sleeping and miss it.

Anyway, I felt like a cigar, so I went out to the balcony, lit up, and looked out over the city. It was a clear, cold night and I had great views to the south, and from here on the 34th floor I could see where I worked. We used to be able to see the Twin Towers, and after they were gone we could see the smoke rising for weeks, and then a few weeks later twin light beams rose high into the sky to symbolize the Towers. And now there was nothing.

Kate came out wearing a coat and carrying one for me. "Put this on."

Real men don't wear coats while they're smoking a cigar on their balcony—but I put it on.

We didn't speak for a while, and we watched the moon rising over the magical lights of Manhattan Island.

Finally, Kate said, "I'm actually going to miss New York."

"You'll appreciate it even more when you get back."

She said, "This is obviously not a routine foreign assignment. This is something important. And Tom is showing confidence in us by asking us to take the job."

"It's very flattering," I agreed.

"Which is why it's hard to say no."

"I thought we were saying yes. But if you want to say no, that's easy." I reminded her, "I signed on for domestic anti-terrorist work. So I have no legal or moral obligation to go to Yemen or anywhere else outside the U.S. You're in a different position. So if you feel you need to go, I'll go with you."

She thought about that, then replied, "Thank you." She said, "This may be a chance for us to make a difference. To actually apprehend the mastermind of the *Cole* attack."

"Right."

I looked toward the skyline where the Towers once stood. We'd both lost some good friends that day. And tens of thousands of other people lost friends, family, and neighbors. We were all heartbroken. Now we're pissed.

Kate stayed quiet awhile, then said, "I really wouldn't have gone without you."

"You would have. But you're not."

We went inside and I settled into my soft leather La-Z-Boy recliner. I was really going to miss this chair.

Kate was curled up on the couch with her laptop, and she said to me, "You were right—Yemen has the highest ratio of guns to people in the world."

"It's a typical baby shower gift."

She also informed me, "It's the most impoverished, backward, and isolated country in the Mideast."

"And that's from the Ministry of Tourism. Wait until you read what the critics say."

"Over a hundred Westerners—tourists, scholars, and businesspeople—have been kidnapped in the last ten years and held for ransom. Some were killed."

I didn't respond.

She continued, "Did you know that Yemen is the ancestral homeland of Osama bin Laden?"

"I did. It's also the homeland of Nabeel al-Samad."

"Who?"

"My breakfast date."

"He was Yemeni? Did you talk to him about Yemen?"

"Yeah. He said don't drink the water."

She went back to her computer and informed me, "Yemen is known as the Land That Time Forgot."

"Sounds romantic."

"In ancient times, it was the Kingdom of Sheba—where the Queen of Sheba came from."

"Where's she living now?"

"She's biblical. King Solomon's lover."

"Right. As long as you're up, can you get me a beer?"

"I'm not up." She read her screen silently for a minute or two, then said, "This place is a shithole."

"What was your first clue?"

"You never said much about it when you got back."

"I don't like to complain."

I launched myself out of my chair and got two beers from the refrigerator. I handed one to Kate and said, "You understand that if we tell Tom we're going, and he tells us more about this, then there's no turning back."

"Tom thinks this is right for us and I trust him."

"I don't. Tom only knows part of this. We get the real deal after we land." I added, "It's like quicksand."

"I'm still in. As long as you promise that after we get there, you won't say, 'I told you so.'"

"That's the only reason I'm going."

"No, we're going there to apprehend the man who masterminded the murder of seventeen American servicemen."

"Correct." We clinked bottles and drank.

CHAPTER SIX

Monday morning.

Kate and I got to 26 Federal Plaza at 8 A.M.

The lobby elevators are surrounded by thick Plexiglas walls and a Plexiglas door with a security pad. I punched us in and greeted the three armed and uniformed security guards, who are actually FBI Police. I gave the senior guy, Larry, my card, on the back of which I'd written Nabeel's info, and told him, "Arab gent to see me. He's supposed to show in the A.M. If he's late or he doesn't have his passport, beat the shit out of him until I get down."

Larry thought that was funny. Kate, Ms. FBI poster girl, pretended she didn't hear that. But on the way up in the elevator, she said to me, "Tom's right. You'll do better overseas."

"I do just fine here."

"Every Islamic civil rights group in the city has a wanted poster of you hanging in their office."

I assured her, "I just joke around."

"Like when you punched that Iranian U.N. diplomat in the groin?"

"He slammed his nuts into my fist."

Anyway, we got to our office on the 26th floor and separated. Kate is in the FBI cube farm, I'm on the NYPD side. The FBI gets more sunlight, but the cops are closer to the elevators.

I gave ICE a call. Immigration and Customs Enforcement is in the same building and they work closely with us. I explained to a woman I know there, Betty Alvarez, that I had a possible informant and he had a work visa problem. I gave her the info from my notebook, and she said she'd try to check him out in her data bank. She asked, "Do you have his passport info?"

"No. But if he shows, I will."

"Okay. Call me later."

"Right." I asked her, "Are you here legally?"

"John, fuck off."

"Okay. Thanks."

I was feeling a little nuts this morning, a result no doubt of the liberating effect of my pending departure to Siberia.

I used my landline phone to call Alim Rasul. Alim is NYPD, working for the Task Force. He was born in Iraq, but now lives in Brooklyn and calls himself Al.

He answered, and I said, "Are you around this morning?"

There was a second of silence, then he asked, "Is this Corey?"

"Yeah. Are you around?"

"John, I'm sitting right next to you."

"Good. Do you speak Arabic?"

"Why are you calling me on the phone?"

"This is a secure landline."

"You're a fucking idiot."

"*Me?* You're the one still talking on the phone."

He hung up and came around to my cube. "What can I do for you?"

I explained about Nabeel and said, "I need you to be in the interview room."

"To translate?"

"No, Al. I just need you to hold him while I head-butt him."

Al smiled politely.

I said, "I have to see Walsh at nine. If Nabeel shows while I'm with El Cid, maybe you can go down and get him."

"Sure."

I also informed him, "I may be out of town for a while. Maybe you want to handle this guy."

"Okay." He asked, "Where you going?"

"Sandland."

"That's a derogatory term."

"Sorry. I'm going to the shithole of Yemen."

"You screw up?"

"Not recently." I let him know, "This is a promotion."

He thought that was funny. He asked me, "Kate?"

"She's coming."

"Good. It's b.y.o.b. in Yemen."

"Yeah? I thought the babes were hot."

"No, it's the guys who will make you lose your head."

So, with all the cultural jokes and slurs out of the way, I thanked Al for sitting in on the interview— formerly known as the interrogation—and I promised to bring him back a crucifix from Yemen.

I spent the next half hour on my computer, reviewing and updating my cases for whoever was going to get them.

Kate came over to my desk and said it was time to go see Tom.

On the way up the elevator to Tom's office, she asked me, "Are we still okay with this?"

"I've always wanted to go to Sweden."

"It's Yemen, John."

"Oh ... well, that's different."

We got off at the 28th floor—housewares, supervisors, aggro, and bullshit—and walked to Tom's door.

I was about to knock and enter, but Kate said, "Last chance."

I knocked on the door and said to her, "You make the decision. Surprise me." I added, "Remember the *Cole*."

I opened the door and we entered.

CHAPTER SEVEN

Tom stood and greeted us at his desk. He asked, "How was your weekend?"

I informed him, "We saw the Monet exhibit at the Met." And I got laid Saturday night. How about you?

All the pleasantries aside, he asked us, "So have you reached a decision?"

Kate, without even a glance at me, said to Tom, "We'll take the assignment."

He smiled. "Good. Have a seat."

There's a grouping of armchairs and a couch around a coffee table that Tom uses for important people, or people he needs to screw nicely, and Kate and I took the chairs facing the window. Tom sat on the couch and began, "First, I want to say that I appreciate your willingness to accept this overseas assignment."

And so on. We got a short speech that he probably gives to everyone who's going off to some craphole or another.

I interrupted Tom's good-bye, good-luck speech and asked, "Are you going to tell us what this is about?"

He feigned surprise at the question and replied,

"It's pretty much what I said Friday." He elaborated, "One of the three masterminds who were behind the *Cole* attack is in Yemen. He has been indicted in absentia. You will be part of a team that is looking for him."

I asked, "What do we do with him when we find him?"

"You arrest him."

"And?"

"And, we will extradite him to the U.S. Or maybe to Guantanamo."

"Right. But as I was told when I was there, and as you probably know, Tom, the Yemeni constitution specifically forbids extradition of any Yemeni citizen for any reason—including terrorism and murder."

"Yes…that's true. But they make exceptions. And that's what Kate will be working on as our legal attaché."

"They haven't made an exception yet, but okay." I asked him, just to set the record straight, "Are you sure we're not supposed to terminate this guy?"

He informed me, "We don't assassinate people."

"We don't assassinate people," I agreed. "But we have used Predator drones with Hellfire missiles in Yemen and elsewhere to…let's say…vaporize about fifty or a hundred people."

"That's different."

"I'm sure the vaporized guys understood that."

Tom seemed a little impatient with me and said, "I'll give you both a piece of information that you will get in Yemen. This suspect holds an American passport. He claims dual citizenship—Yemen and U.S. So yes, we have a good case with the Yemeni government for extradition." He also reminded us, "We don't kill U.S. citizens."

"Actually we do if they're enemy combatants. Also, as you know, if we do apprehend him and turn him over to the Yemenis, we may never see him again." I reminded him, "Some of the *Cole* plotters were captured, put in Yemeni jails, and miraculously escaped."

Tom nodded, then said, "Let's not get too far ahead of ourselves. First things first. First, we need to apprehend this man."

"Right. So to recap, we find this Yemeni with U.S. citizenship, turn him over to the Yemeni government, and hope they give him back to us."

"Correct."

"Can we at least torture him? Just a little?"

Tom asked, "Any other questions?"

Kate asked, "What is this man's name?"

"You'll be given his name when you get there. But he goes by the nom de guerre of al-Numair. Means The Panther."

It seems to be my fate to get mixed up with Arabs who name themselves after big cats. The last guy was Asad—The Lion. Now I've got a panther to deal with. Hopefully, the next one will call himself Kitty.

Anyway, it seemed to me that Tom wanted to say as little as possible at this end. Or he didn't know much.

In fact, he said to us, "To be honest with you, I don't have a need-to-know, and what I know is what you now know. You'll be fully briefed when you get there."

Since Kate and I were about to depart on a dangerous mission into a hostile country, I felt I could be a little disrespectful of Tom with no consequences, so I reminded him, "You indicated Friday that what you were going to tell us was classified, and that once we heard it, we were committed to the assignment. Correct?"

He nodded.

I continued, "What we've heard is nothing. We could get up, go back to work, and forget about Yemen."

"I suppose you could. But that wouldn't make me happy. Or you happy."

"Okay, let's try a different approach. On a scale of one to ten, how dangerous is this mission?"

He thought about a reply, then said, "Capturing a top-ranking Al Qaeda leader is dangerous."

"One to ten."

"Ten."

"Because?"

"Should be obvious." He explained the obvious, "He'll be guarded, he'll be in hostile territory, he's aware that he's a target, and our resources and assets in Yemen are scarce."

"Right. And we're not going to vaporize him with a Hellfire missile because . . . ?"

"I suppose because we want him alive. To interrogate him."

"So we're not really turning him over to the Yemeni government. Our job is to kill his bodyguards, take him alive, and sneak him out of the country for interrogation."

"You'll be briefed over there." He added, "As I said, you'll be part of a team."

Kate asked, "Who is on this team?"

"I have no idea."

Kate had an important question. "If we're detained by the Yemeni government, who comes to our aid?"

"The embassy. You'll both have diplomatic immunity, of course."

Love that diplomatic immunity. It works about half the time when you get caught breaking the local laws. The other half of the time, the embassy can't seem to remember your name.

I thought I understood one reason why Kate and I were chosen to participate in what amounted to a Black Ops mission. It had to do with my cover and Kate's cover. Officially, the U.S. was there only to aid the Yemeni security forces in investigating the *Cole* bombing, and our FBI personnel, people like me, rotated into and out of the country on a regular basis. As long as we kept the numbers small and didn't stay too long, the Yemeni government was okay with Americans operating on their soil.

Most of the Americans doing anti-terrorist work were attached to the embassy for cover—as Kate would be—so that the Yemeni government could take the public position that their country hadn't become an American ally or outpost. In fact, if the USS *Cole* hadn't been bombed in Aden Harbor, we wouldn't have anyone in Yemen except a small embassy staff. But now we had our foot in the door—or in this case, the Yemenis had let the camel get his nose under the tent. But they didn't want the whole camel sleeping inside.

And for all those reasons, the CIA was not welcome, but a few CIA officers were tolerated.

I asked Tom, "Is the CIA involved in this operation?"

"I'm sure you'll find out when you get there."

"I'm sure we will." I reminded him, "You said this guy was Al Qaeda."

"Did I?" Tom fessed up, "He's actually the head of the Yemen branch of a newly formed group called Al Qaeda in the Arabian Peninsula—AQAP."

"Thanks for sharing."

He reminded me, "You have no need to know this now, and you didn't hear it from me. When you get there, you'll know more than I know. But I will tell you that this guy is wanted for other crimes aside from the *Cole* bombing."

"Such as?"

"The usual. Murder, kidnapping, conspiracy, and so forth." Tom added, "He's killed a lot of people— Yemenis, Europeans, and Saudis—before and after the *Cole*." He let us know, "Most terrorist activities in Yemen can be traced to The Panther."

"Bad dude," I observed.

"One of the worst," Tom agreed. He added, "And a traitor to his country."

"He's an asshole." I asked, "Is there a bounty on this guy's head?"

"The Justice Department is offering five million."

"Not bad. Dead or alive?"

"Either."

"How much do we get to keep?"

"None of it." He reminded us, "You get a paycheck every two weeks."

"Will the Justice Department use the reward money to spring us if we wind up kidnapped or in a Yemeni jail?"

He replied, "I'll make sure of that for Kate." He smiled. "You're on your own."

I smiled in return. Tom *can* be funny. Especially when the joke is on me. I asked him, "Are you going to miss me?"

"No."

He stood, and we stood. He said to us, "Make sure you go to the Medical Office today, and call the Travel Office. I've asked Legal Affairs to assist you with whatever you need. Also, I'll set up a meeting for you with the Office of International Affairs—for a cultural awareness briefing."

Oh, God. Not that. Before my last trip to Yemen, I'd managed to avoid this four-hour State Department lecture, but I'd heard about it from other guys who'd had to sit through it. I said, "That's cruel, Tom."

"It's mandatory for Kate," he informed me, "but I know you'll both benefit from it." He concluded, "You have until Thursday to put your personal affairs in order. I'll see you here Friday, ten A.M., for a final briefing and contact info in Sana'a. You leave Friday night. Any questions?"

Neither Kate nor I had any further questions, so we all shook hands and we left.

On the way to the elevator, Kate said, "I can't believe we're going to Yemen to capture one of the masterminds of the *Cole* bombing—the head of Al Qaeda in Yemen."

She sounded excited, but maybe a little apprehensive. Indeed, this was a big deal with a big upside for us professionally, and a big victory for the home team if we got our man. The downside was also big—like, we could get killed or captured. I've come to terms a long time ago with getting killed. But getting captured by terrorists in a foreign country was, as they say, a fate worse than death.

"John? Are you still good with this?"

I didn't recall ever being good with this. But I do

like a challenge. And I was still pissed about how I and the other FBI agents in Yemen had been jerked around by the Yemeni police and their political security force when I was there. They were playing both sides in the *Cole* investigation, not letting us do our job and also tipping off the bad guys. Great allies. Actually, assholes. So this was a chance for me to shove it up their butts.

"John?"

"There is an old Arabic saying—'It is easier to kick a camel in the balls than it is to capture a black panther who's eating your ass.'"

"Do you have more of those?"

"I'm afraid so."

"Can you keep them to yourself?"

"Maybe they sound better in Arabic."

"This is going to be a long year."

"Be optimistic. We'll be dead before then."

CHAPTER EIGHT

I got back to my desk, and Al Rasul informed me that he'd called downstairs, but Nabeel hadn't shown up yet.

It was still early, so there was no reason to send a cop car to get him. I did call Nabeel's cell phone, and it went to voice mail—Arabic and English. I left a message in English, then gave the phone to Al, who left the same message in Arabic—except Al's tone was very sharp. He explained to me, "That's how the police talk to citizens in Sandland."

"Right." Anyway, Nabeel al-Samad was the least of my priorities today, but you have to follow up on everything because sure as hell the thing you didn't follow up on is what comes back to bite you in the ass. The people who dropped the ball on the pre-9/11 clues can verify that.

I gave Al a pencil and said, "Transliterate the Arabic word for 'panther' into real letters."

"'Panther'?"

"Yeah. Big black cat."

He took a scrap of paper from my desk and said,

"There are a few ways to transliterate..." He wrote, *Nimr—Nimar—Numair*, and said, "The last is maybe the most standard transliteration." He pronounced the word for me.

"You need a tissue?"

He asked me, "What's with panther?"

"If I tell you, I have to kill you."

"Anything else I can do for you today?"

"Yeah, if Nabeel shows up." I added, "Thanks."

Al's a good guy and he takes a lot of crap well. But he also knows how to dish it out. If you're an Arab and you work here, you have to have a sense of humor—and very thick skin. I wondered why Al Rasul wasn't asked to go to Yemen. Right?

I checked my e-mail and found a note from Tom to me and Kate telling us that we were expected at Legal Affairs and the Medical Office before noon. I've never seen government workers move this fast. Tom really wanted us out of here, which compelled me into some paranoid thought processes, and the word "expendable" kept popping into my mind.

I had an e-mail from Betty Alvarez informing me that she had no info on a Yemeni male named Nabeel al-Samad. She asked for his passport info and visa, if any. I replied: *Still waiting for subject to show.*

I used my ATTF password to access the internal files on ACS—the Automated Case System. I didn't have a case name, but I typed in "USS *Cole*," which got me hundreds of hits, though probably nothing I didn't already know. I typed in "Panther," which got me nothing, then "Numair"—thank you, Al—which got me a file that said "Restricted," followed by rows of Xs. Usually you get something, even on the restricted files, like when the file was opened, what the classification level was, and who to see about getting access to the file. But apparently all this was above my pay grade, and all I saw was "Numair" and Xs. Well, at least Walsh didn't make that up.

I e-mailed Walsh and asked him about getting access to the Numair file, based on my recent need-to-know.

A few minutes later, he replied: *Your need-to-know begins when you're in Yemen. P.S. Stop snooping.* He didn't actually write that, but that was the message.

Kate came over to my desk and asked, "Where to first? Legal or Medical?"

"Medical. We need our heads examined."

"That could take all day. Legal first."

The FBI Legal Affairs Office here normally deals with cases, warrants, wiretaps, documents, and so forth, and not with employees' problems or work assignments. But this was a special case, and it needed to be done on an expedited basis.

We had a few papers to sign, including a new confidentiality statement, and also a statement having to do with "interrogation under duress." As I signed it, I said, "As a married man, I am an expert on interrogation under duress."

No laughs.

Our wills were on file and we checked them over, then we were given powers of attorney to fill out and sign. Jennifer, a young lawyer I'd seen before my first trip to Yemen, explained, "This is in case you're abducted or go missing."

I asked, "So we just show this to our kidnappers?"

"No. You—"

Kate interrupted and explained to me, "If we're

dead, the executors of our wills handle our affairs. But if we're missing or unlawfully imprisoned, then someone has to act on our behalf—someone to write checks, pay our bills, and so forth. It doesn't have to be an actual attorney." She inquired, "Didn't you do this last time?"

"Right. I named you as my attorney-in-fact."

"Good. We'll name each other. But...if we share the same fate, we'll need an alternate."

This was getting a little heavy.

Kate said, "It should be a family member." She suggested, "How about my father?"

Am I related to him? I mean, what if we both wound up kidnapped or missing, then got free and found out that her father had spent all our money on his collection of J. Edgar Hoover memorabilia?

"John?"

"Yeah. Fine." They'll never take me alive anyway.

We filled out the forms, signed them, and Jennifer notarized them.

Finally, Jennifer produced our black diplomatic passports, which had been kept in a safe since our last make-believe diplomatic assignments to Tanzania and Yemen.

Jennifer also informed us that the State Department had called the Yemeni consulate office and our visas should be ready after 1 P.M. for us to pick up.

There aren't many Americans who go to Yemen, so by now our Yemeni allies were aware that John Corey and Kate Mayfield would be arriving soon. Maybe they'd have someone at the airport to greet us.

Another thought popped into my head—a thought about the speed of all this paperwork—and I asked

Jennifer, "When did State call the Yemeni consulate about our visas?"

She replied, "Thursday."

Kate and I glanced at each other. *Thursday?*

Anyway, we finished up with Jennifer, who said, "You get to do exciting things. I wish I was going."

I wish you were, too, Jennifer.

As we walked down the hallway, Kate said, "*Thursday?*"

"The Friday meeting was just a formality. Yemen is our fate. It is written in the sands of time."

No reply. Clearly she was not happy with her friend Tom. Good.

I said to Kate, "By the way, I went into ACS and there's a file called Numair, which is Arabic for 'panther,' and it's restricted."

"Who do we see about getting access?"

"Didn't say."

"Odd." She suggested, "We'll ask Tom."

"Did that. He said go to Yemen."

We took the elevator down to the nurse's office, where a young lady named Annie was expecting us.

Because Kate and I were scheduled for departure within five days, we couldn't get the shots spaced over the recommended seven days, and sweet Annie stuck us like we were voodoo dolls.

We got eight shots—diphtheria, dysentery, typhoid, anthrax, scarlet fever, and three diseases I've never heard of. I especially enjoyed the two shots in the butt. Annie gave us each a starter vial of malaria pills and said, "Start taking these now." She added, "Come back Friday morning for the rest of the shots."

"How many more diseases could there be?"

"Leprosy, for one."

Jeez.

She advised us, "You have a lot of vaccines in you, so you may not feel well later."

"Can I have alcohol?"

"Sure. Just be close to a toilet."

We went to Kate's desk, and she called the FBI Travel Office at Headquarters in D.C.

Kate put it on speaker phone, and a woman answered, "Travel Office. Mrs. Barrett speaking. How may I help you?"

Kate said we were calling from the New York office, and she gave our names and our travel authorization numbers.

Mrs. Barrett replied, "Hold on...yes, here you are. Sana'a."

"Santa Ana," I corrected. "California."

"No...Sana'a. Yemen."

Kate picked up the phone and disengaged the speaker, saying, "Ready to copy."

She listened to Mrs. Barrett, made some notes, then said, "Thank you," and hung up. She said to me, "American Airlines to London, British Airways to Cairo, Egyptair to Sana'a. First class."

"Hard to believe there are no direct flights to Sana'a."

"There are. From Cairo."

"How do the deli guys get back and forth from Brooklyn?"

"I'm sure I don't know." She informed me, "If you really want to go direct, there is a military flight twice a week from Dover Air Force Base in Delaware. One to Sana'a, one to Aden."

That was interesting. Sounded like we were getting our noses a little farther under the tent.

Kate said, "If we want to go that way, Mrs. Barrett will check it out. Departure times and days vary."

"Yeah. Let's check it out. Might be interesting to see who and what is going to Yemen." Also, this was probably the way we'd sneak The Panther out of Yemen. Direct U.S. Air Force flight from Yemen to Guantanamo. The shithole to hellhole express.

I went back to my desk, and Al informed me that Nabeel had not shown. It was 12:15.

Al called Nabeel's cell phone, but got his voice mail again and left a loud message. I phoned the deli, a place named George's in Bay Ridge, and spoke to some guy with an accent who wasn't helpful. Al took the phone and spoke sharply in Arabic, then discovered that the guy was Mexican. Funny. What a great country.

Al volunteered to drive us to George's Deli, but I had lots to do and Brooklyn was not on that list. I suggested, "Find one of our guys in the area and ask him to check out the deli and Nabeel's home address."

"No, I'll go. I could use a break here. What's this guy look like?"

"Green teeth." I described Nabeel's other features and related a little of my short conversation with him in Ben's Deli. I suggested, "See if this deli is under the eye for any reason. Maybe we have surveillance photos."

"I did that. Nothing."

"Okay. Thanks, Al. I owe you one."

My next task was to go to a separate stand-alone computer where I could access the Internet. We can't do that from our desk computers, or we'd be playing video games all day. I did a Google search on Al Qaeda in Yemen, and got a few hits on al-Numair, The Panther, and I actually got his real name from Wikipedia—Bulus ibn al-Darwish. No wonder he changed it.

Apparently some of this info was not as classified as Tom thought. In fact, there is little that is not available online if you know what you're looking for.

I checked out the Wikipedia entry. Bulus ibn al-Darwish, a.k.a. The Panther, was born in Perth Amboy, New Jersey, on May 8, 1965, making him thirty-nine years old in May, if he lived that long. So he was not a naturalized citizen—he was actually born here. Interesting.

His parents were both Yemenis who'd immigrated to America, but there was no further info on them. Dead? Alive? Living where?

Little Bulus attended public schools in New Jersey, then graduated from Columbia University in 1987 with a degree in economics—making him an Ivy League terrorist. He should have gone to Wall Street—same work, better pay.

At some point, according to the entry, Mr. al-Darwish became radicalized and went to Yemen in the early 1990s.

The remainder of the entry was a mix of facts and speculation about his activities in Yemen, Saudi Arabia, and perhaps Iraq. He was identified as one of the planners of the attack on the USS *Cole* and also the 2002 attack on the French oil tanker *Limburg* in the Gulf of Aden.

Additionally, the subject asshole had been implicated in two or three armed attacks on Westerners in Sana'a, Aden, and the surrounding areas, resulting in a number of deaths and kidnappings. Plus, while he was at it, he'd planned two rocket attacks—one on the American Embassy in Sana'a, one on the Sheraton Hotel in Aden. Both attacks had been thwarted. The planned attack on the Sheraton interested me, because that's where I stayed with the other American personnel in Aden. We called the place Fort Apache.

And last but not least, Mr. al-Darwish and some friends had been involved in a shoot-out at the Saudi Arabian border last year, resulting in the deaths of six Saudi soldiers.

Bottom line, this was a bad guy. Maybe fearless, maybe nuts, and definitely angry about something. Maybe he got teased in school.

Also, I'd never heard of this guy. And I knew the names of lots of terrorists. So this guy was being kept under wraps. Why? Probably because this was strictly a CIA case, and they were not sharing the info with the FBI. Until now. The Agency only talks to you when they need you.

I clicked next onto the website of the U.S. Embassy in Sana'a and checked out Citizen Services and what's called Warden Messages. The Department of State, I saw, was concerned about Al Qaeda in the Arabian Peninsula and had issued a Travel Warning for Yemen regarding "possible attacks by extremist individuals or groups against U.S. citizens, facilities, businesses, and perceived interests."

I guess that included the embassy itself, not to mention everyone working or visiting there.

The embassy website further informed me that "travel on roads between cities throughout Yemen can be dangerous." Really? "Travel outside Sana'a is restricted." Right. That's where those roads are.

"Travel in tribal areas north and east of Sana'a is particularly dangerous, and kidnappings are common." Best to avoid the whole country.

There was also a mention of the ongoing civil war that Kate and I had seen reported on the BBC. This rebel leader, al-Houthi, was taking control of bigger parts of North Yemen. And that led me to wonder why anyone wanted to rule this fucked-up place.

So to recap, Yemen was ruled by a corrupt dictator, and the country was half overrun by a rebel leader, and the rest of the place was run by tribal warlords, except the areas that were infiltrated by Al Qaeda. Plus, the Red Sea and the Gulf of Aden were infested with pirates. The good news was that everyone was stoned on khat and didn't give a shit.

I read a last entry on the embassy website, which advised, "From time to time, the U.S. Embassy in Sana'a may temporarily close or suspend public services as necessary to review its security posture and its adequacy."

With luck, they'd shut down before I got there.

Anyway, I could have spent a week surfing the Internet, getting background on Yemen and Al Qaeda in the Arabian Peninsula and The Panther, but why bother? By Saturday or Sunday I'd be in the belly of the beast.

I logged off the computer and went back to my desk.

CHAPTER NINE

Kate and I decided to have lunch at Fraunces Tavern, the place where Washington gave his farewell address to his officers, and where I would now give my farewell address to Washington.

We exited 26 Federal Plaza onto Duane Street, which since 9/11 has been blocked to vehicles between Broadway and Lafayette on the theory that someone might want to detonate a car bomb under my window.

In fact, all of Lower Manhattan has become a security zone since that day, and though it's not too intrusive, it's annoying. More to the point, it's a constant reminder that these bastards have made America the front lines. So maybe taking the war to them is good quid pro quo.

We got to Fraunces Tavern, in business since about 1762, which is a lot of grog.

A hostess showed us to a table in the crowded main dining room. The clientele was mostly out-of-towners who wanted to tell the folks back in Peoria that they had lunch at the very table where George Washington dug his wooden choppers into a mutton chop.

Mindful of Nurse Annie's warning about mixing alcohol and vaccine, I ordered club soda with a shot of scotch on the side. Does that work? Kate had a Coke, and we looked at the menus. Mostly traditional American fare. I said, "I think I'll have the Yankee noodles."

"Dandy."

We ordered—sliced steak for me, a sissy salad for Kate.

There's another piece of history here that you won't find in most tour guides, but you will find on the Automated Case System—back in January 1975, a group of Puerto Rican separatists exploded a bomb here during lunch hour, killing four people and injuring more than fifty. I'm not sure what kind of statement they were trying to make, but the attack shocked the city and the nation, which was not then used to terrorism on American soil.

It was this attack, along with some other Puerto Rican separatist activities and the activities of the Irish Republican Army and the Black Panthers, that led to the formation of the Anti-Terrorist Task Force in New York in 1980.

Now the focus has shifted, and The Panther I was looking for was an Arab. But he wasn't here—he was in Yemen, by way of New Jersey and Columbia University. Hard to figure that out. I mean, I can figure out the foreign-born terrorists, but I can't figure out the increasing number of American-born Muslims who have defected to Islamic countries that they've never even seen, and who have taken up arms against America. What was *that* all about?

Kate asked me, "What are you thinking about?"

"About when this place was bombed by the FALN.

And I was also thinking about The Panther. Did you know he was born and educated in the U.S.?"

"I did. I went on the Internet after you did."

"So why would a man who grew up in relative comfort, in a free society, and who went to one of the best universities in the country, choose to go to the backward and dangerous country that his parents had left, to engage in terrorist activities against the country of his birth?"

"When you find out, let me know."

"But we need to find out why the melting pot is not working. There's something wrong in our thinking— or their thinking."

"Maybe both." She added, "It's about jihad, but that doesn't fully explain it." She observed, "Even scarier is that John Corey is thinking about all this. What happened to the guy who used to say, 'Nuke 'em all'?"

"Well…I guess because we're going to Yemen to find this American-born Islamic terrorist, I'd like to get into his head a little." I added, "It might help us."

"It would, if we could do that."

I thought a moment and said, "When I worked Homicide, we did a lot of psychological profiling on murder cases, especially serial killers, and it was helpful. But this is different. The common criminal is usually stupid, though they're smart enough not to want to be killed or captured. These people don't care if they die. They blow themselves up. They fly airplanes into buildings. Then they go to Paradise. That's where the wine and virgins are. For us, it's the opposite. We get our wine and women here, then we go to hell and get more."

"Theology may not be your strong point."

Our food came as my cell phone rang, and it was Al, who said, "Our guy Nabeel is not working today, and the twenty Yemenis living at his address haven't seen him since Saturday, and he's not answering his cell phone. I'm checking out the local hookah bars, the storefront mosques, other delis, and so forth."

"Check the jiggle joints."

"Is that an order?" Al went on, "Nabeel worked in that deli for only a week and no one knows anything about him, or his family, or friends." He speculated, "Maybe he just got here, he got spooked by his conversation with you, and he bolted."

I replied, "He said he was a regular guest worker."

"Well, maybe he worked someplace else. No one at George's knows him."

"Maybe people are lying to you, Al."

"They don't lie to *me*, John. They lie, they die."

"Right." We need more guys like Al Rasul. I'm too easy on the usually uncooperative Mideastern community. Well...maybe "easy" is not the right word.

Al said, "I've asked for a surveillance team on his apartment and his place of business, and a trace on his cell phone. Meanwhile, I'll keep checking out the neighborhood."

"Okay."

"There's something not right about this."

"Could be," I agreed.

"See you back at the fort."

I hung up and Kate asked, "What's happening?"

"My Yemeni disappeared."

"Not to worry. I know where to find lots of them."

After lunch, we took a taxi to the Yemeni consulate on East 51st near the U.N.

The offices of the Yemeni Mission to the United Nations wouldn't win any design awards, though the walls of the consulate section were decorated with very nice tourist posters showing spectacular scenery and happy people, not a single one of whom was carrying an AK-47.

We seemed to be the only customers today, though I'm sure this place is usually mobbed with people who want to travel to Yemen.

The receptionist was a middle-aged man, reminding me that women in Yemen didn't get out of the house much. I stated our business, and the man took our passports and disappeared for a few minutes—long enough to photostat them—then returned with another middle-aged man who introduced himself as Habib, who asked me, "When and by what means do you plan to arrive in Yemen?"

This was none of his business, and he knew he shouldn't be asking that of Americans with diplomatic passports.

I replied, "We're awaiting our travel orders."

"Yes? But you requested your visas for not later than Wednesday."

I informed him, "We're here to pick up our visas—not answer questions."

He didn't like that, but he ignored it and flipped through our passports, checking our photos against our faces. He said to me, "I see you have been to Yemen."

I didn't reply.

He glanced at Kate, but did not speak to her. Then he asked me, "Do you plan to arrive in Sana'a or Aden?"

"I plan to leave here with our visas in two minutes."

He didn't respond, but said something to the receptionist, who put two completed visa forms on the desk. I looked them over. My visa was for forty-five days, and Kate's was for an indefinite stay. Both listed us as American Embassy staff with diplomatic status. The purpose of our visit was government business. No mention of Panther hunting.

I did notice that, as per security procedures, the State Department had falsified our home address by giving it as 26 Federal Plaza. Also, our U.S. contact information was the State Department Foreign Office in Washington. Fine, except that falsifying the required info on the visa app could get your diplomatic immunity nullified, or at least compromised if you got into some trouble in the host country. Well, I'd worry about that if and when there was a problem in Yemen. Or I'd let our friends at the State Department worry about it. I was on a diplomatic mission. Right?

Everything else looked in order, and Kate and I signed the visas along with two copies. The receptionist stamped the forms, then stamped our passports, and Habib said to me, "There is no charge. A diplomatic courtesy."

They should pay *me* to go to Yemen.

We left the consulate, hailed a cab, and went back to 26 Fed, my home away from home.

By five we'd posted updates on our computers for all our cases and sent e-mails to friends and colleagues announcing our imminent departure to Yemen.

Most return messages wished us luck; some suggested we were crazy.

Al returned and reported that he'd had no luck

locating Nabeel al-Samad, and that Nabeel's cell phone was not sending a signal according to CAU—the Communications Analysis Unit. Al said he'd make a report and see what the bosses wanted to do, and I said I'd do the same.

Bottom line here, Nabeel al-Samad was not high on anyone's list of people to find. Informants, Mideast or otherwise, are notoriously fickle and usually liars. And sometimes these guys are playing a double game, so I had the interesting thought that Mr. al-Samad had another job outside the deli, and he just wanted to get a look at me. Maybe he took a picture.

As Annie predicted, Kate and I were not feeling well, so Typhoid Kate and Anthrax John went home.

Back in the apartment, Kate got into her pjs and went on the Internet. I channel surfed. The History Channel had a special on Adolf Hitler's dog.

Kate informed me, "According to the website of the Yemen Tourism Promotion Board, Yemen is, quote, 'Arabia's undiscovered gem, and so little is known about the real Yemen, that when visitors travel across the country, it is almost always a beautiful voyage of discovery.'"

"Watch that 'almost.'"

She continued reading: "'Camel racing is one of the old favorite sports of Arabs and of course Yemen, as Yemen is the origin of Arabs.'"

"I thought they came from Brooklyn."

"'Paragliding,'" she went on, "'like in the legend of Suleiman and his bird, who cross the Yemen to see the Queen of Sheba, have fun and discover our country by flying above mountains and seas.'"

"Like Predator drones."

"I don't see anything about that."

"Al Qaeda ambushes?"

"That might be under trekking and hiking."

"Right. What's for dinner?"

"A malaria pill."

We took our malaria pills and watched a rerun of *I Love Lucy*. Could the world have been that simple?

CHAPTER TEN

Tom Walsh, as promised, arranged an appointment for Kate and me with the State Department Office of International Affairs for our cultural awareness course. The OIA is right here at 26 Fed, which is convenient, but still sucks.

On Tuesday morning at 8 A.M., we met Mr. Buckminster Harris—where do WASPs get these names?—in a small, windowless conference room. Mr. Harris asked us to call him Buck, and he invited us to sit.

Buckminster Harris was a well-dressed gent of about sixty, and I guessed he'd seen some of the world during his long and I'm sure distinguished career with the State Department. This was probably his last posting before he retired to some genteel WASP enclave in the Northeast where he'd write his memoirs for Yale University Press. Meanwhile, he was stuck with me for the morning, and I with him.

There were apparently only two people going to Yemen this week—Kate and me—so the class was small and intimate. Kate had a notepad, of course, so I didn't need the one I forgot.

There was a colored map of Yemen on the wall, and on the table were State Department handouts, which I'd be sure not to forget.

Mr. Harris took a seat at the head of the table and began, "So you're going to Yemen?"

Why else would I be here?

He informed us, "I was there during the civil wars."

I inquired, "How many were there?"

"A few."

"Right. Who won?"

"The north," he said.

"Good. Right?"

"The south was Marxist."

"Karl or Groucho?"

He chuckled and continued, "The north is tribal, backward, and fundamentalist."

"Glad the good guys won."

I thought Buck was going to take me out in the hallway for a scolding, but he smiled and said, "They told me about you."

Really?

"I understand you've been to Yemen."

"Correct. Short assignment. Back in '01."

"Well, nothing there ever changes, except for the worse."

"Looking forward to seeing that progress."

He smiled again, then said, "It's a country you can love and hate at the same time."

Actually, it's a country you love to hate. But this was Buck's class and I wasn't going to be like those dopey students who spent a month someplace and tried to impress their teachers with their half-assed observations.

Buck continued in his very prep school accent, "The capital of Yemen is Sana'a. South Yemen, also known as Adan, with an A, had its capital in the city of Aden, with an E."

Also known as the Shithole, with a capital S.

He also let us know, "The country was unified in 1990 after another war that the north won, but there is still a separatist movement in the south, and also a movement to restore the Imam as ruler in Sana'a."

Kate stopped taking notes and said, "Led by the warlord Hussein al-Houthi."

Buck was happy to have at least one bright student in the class and smiled. "Yes, very good. I see you've done some homework."

I mean, who gives a rat's ass? I wasn't going to Yemen to make friends or discuss politics. I was going there to probably whack some asshole who needed whacking. Sorry—to capture a prime suspect in the *Cole* bombing and return him to American justice. Maybe, though, I could learn something here that might help me. But probably not.

Buck said a few words about the al-Houthi rebels and the tribal warlords. I sort of listened. Warlords are interesting. I'd like to be a warlord.

Buck said, "There are dozens of Bedouin tribes that hold power in their respective regions. And now, to add to the political and social divisions, we have Al Qaeda, who have gained influence in some of the towns and villages." He concluded, "Yemen is a failed state."

Right. Not even worth nuking.

Buck recapped the history of Yemen, which was mostly a history of civil wars, revolutions, and invasions. Also, there was a period of British colonial rule in

Adan until the 1960s when the British left after another war. Buck said, "You'll see some vestiges of British rule in the south. Like a statue of Queen Victoria in Aden, which the Yemenis have left standing for some reason." He added, "She is often veiled by fundamentalists."

I actually saw that when I was there. I thought it was a statue of Elton John in drag.

Buck continued, "When the British left, South Yemen became Marxist—the only Communist Arab country in the world." He added, "You'll also see some vestiges of the Soviet presence in Aden during this period, such as ugly architecture, black-market vodka, and a Russian nightclub that features Russian strippers and prostitutes."

Address?

Buck continued, "During this period, there were a series of wars between the north and south, alternating with reunification talks. With the collapse of the Soviet Union, the Russians left and unification was achieved, but then the south changed its mind and waged a new war of secession, which failed and led to the present reunification."

Who's on first?

Buck further informed us, "I was in Sana'a and Aden during this period. It was a very bloody time and the scars remain." He added, "Yemenis have become used to war, which has led to a sort of national psychosis, and which is why Yemen is an armed camp."

I glanced at Kate, who seemed to be getting that Yemen wasn't the Switzerland of the Mideast.

Buck continued, "During the first Gulf War, Yemen sided with Saddam Hussein, which annoyed their large and powerful neighbor of Saudi Arabia. The Saudis retaliated by expelling a few hundred thousand Yemeni guest workers."

Who are now in Brooklyn.

Buck continued, "The Saudis and Yemenis are currently engaged in a border dispute." He explained, "They share a long border including the area of Ar Rub al Khali, what is called the Empty Quarter, an uninhabited expanse of scorching desert and shifting sands." He added, "This area includes the border province of the Hadhramawt, which means 'the Place Where Death Comes.'"

The Yemen tourist board should really think about renaming that. I mean, the Empty Quarter is bad enough, but Death Comes is not a winner.

I asked Buck, "And the loser of the border dispute has to keep this place?"

"There is oil there," Buck answered, then continued. "It is a porous, ill-defined border and a suspected crossing point of AQAP—Al Qaeda in the Arabian Peninsula."

Right. Maybe that's where The Panther had a shoot-out with Saudi soldiers. I'm glad I didn't have to go there. Right?

Buck concluded, "This brief history brings us to the *Cole* bombing in October 2000. Since then, as you well know, the U.S. has gained a foothold in Yemen, but it is a very tenuous foothold and our mission there could end suddenly if the Yemenis have a change of heart or a change of government."

That would be nice.

Buck took an ornate curved dagger out of his briefcase, which he unsheathed as he said, "I can cut your throat with this."

Not if I get to my gun first, Buck.

He smiled and said, "But only if you fall asleep." He informed us, "This is called a jambiyah, and it's worn by most men in Yemen. You can buy a jambiyah at a souvenir stand for about three dollars, but the ones made by artisans can cost thousands of dollars. This one is an antique with semi-precious stones and a rhinoceros-horn handle, and is worth about five thousand dollars. According to the last owner, it has been used to kill at least six people."

Buck advised us, "Never ask to see a man's jambiyah." He explained, "A man only unsheathes his jambiyah if he is going to use it."

He continued, "There is an old Arab war song"—he didn't sing, but recited—" 'Terrible he rode alone, with his Yemen sword for aid; ornament it carried none, but the notches on the blade.' "

Right. I'd actually heard those words before, from a guy named Gabe Haytham, an Arab-American on the Task Force, when I was working the case of Asad, The Lion.

Buck was going on now about religion—ninety-eight percent of the country was Muslim, the rest were Christians, Jews, and Hindus. He said, "Before the creation of Israel in 1948, the Sana'a government tolerated its Jews, who are part of their heritage from the days of King Solomon and the Queen of Sheba. In fact, many Yemenis were Jewish until the arrival of Islam."

Maybe that explains the Yemeni delis in Brooklyn.

He informed us, "Most of the Jews fled to Israel after 1948." He continued, "The Yemeni constitution supposedly provides for religious freedom for minorities, but there are no churches or synagogues remaining where you can attend services." He added, "As in most Islamic countries, the conversion of a Muslim to another religion is prohibited, and punishable, usually by death." He warned us, "Do not proselytize. It's a capital offense. Though you may quote from the Old and New Testaments, which Muslims consider sacred texts. But try to learn a few passages from the Koran as well."

"Which Korean?"

"The *Koran*, Mr. Corey."

"Right."

Buck continued, "Yemenis speak Arabic, including ancient dialects. Yemeni Arabic is considered the most pure form of the language—unchanged for thousands of years because of the isolation of the country. Many Arabic-language scholars, including Westerners, go to Yemen to study the language. Think of Yemeni Arabic as Shakespearean English, though it is much older."

I asked Buck, "Do you speak Arabic?"

He replied in Arabic, and I said, "That's easy for *you* to say."

Kate accidentally kicked me under the table.

Buck said, "Sex."

I sat up.

"Sex," he repeated. "We all know or think we know about the Muslims' attitude toward sex, so I won't repeat all that you've heard, but I'll recap. Sex outside of marriage is forbidden, and adultery is punishable by death."

"Right. Screw the divorce lawyers. Get that jambi-yah sharpened."

Buck smiled and said, "That shouldn't be a concern for a happily married couple."

Correct, but I had to ask, "Do guys get the death penalty for screwing around?"

"Not usually, but—"

Kate interrupted, "They do with me."

"Just asking."

Buck also informed us, "Homosexuality is often punished by death, but rape is usually settled with a cash payment to the victim's family. But if the rapist claims the sex was consensual, which they always do, then the victim, if she can't produce four witnesses to the contrary, is sometimes killed by her family. What they call honor killings."

Okay, we knew all of this, but it was jarring to hear it.

Buck next discussed marriage and family. "Polygamy is legal under Islamic law, and a man may have up to four wives, but polygamy is not common in Yemen."

"Why not?" Kate asked.

Because what guy wants four women telling him to take out the garbage?

"Because," said Buck, "most men can't afford more than one wife."

Most men, Buck, can't afford *one* wife.

Buck continued, "Most marriages are arranged."

I asked, "Do they have Match.com?"

"Yes, but the women in the photos are all veiled and they have no hobbies, interests, jobs, or education."

Funny. I liked Buck. Even Kate laughed.

Buck informed us, "Custom regards the ideal marriage as a marriage between cousins."

Like in Kentucky.

"Women are viewed as subordinate and must serve their fathers, husbands, brothers, and even their male children."

This might be a good year.

Buck said, "The Yemeni constitution states that women are equal to men, but then incorporates many aspects of Sharia law, which negates that equality. For instance, in a court of law, the testimony of one man equals that of two women."

My lawyer wife asked, "How can they call that equal?"

I volunteered, "Buck just told you. One equals two. Do the math."

I got another kick. Restless leg syndrome?

Buck also told us that the Yemenis had the highest birthrate of any Arab country—six to ten children were not uncommon—so something was happening when those veils came off.

Buck also said, "There's a population explosion in progress, and there are now more than twenty million Yemenis, mostly young, in a small, impoverished country with few natural resources. This is a demographic time bomb waiting to go off, and most analysts predict social upheaval within ten years." He added, "We're seeing it already."

Recalling Nabeel, I suggested, "More Yemeni delis in Brooklyn."

He replied, "In fact, there is a high emigration rate to America, Western Europe, and the oil-rich countries of the Arabian Peninsula, which serves as a safety valve for Yemen and is a source of outside money. But millions of unemployed youths remain in the country."

Right. I remembered hordes of young men hanging around the streets and souks in Aden with nothing to do. A surefire recipe for trouble, and a fertile ground for Al Qaeda recruiters.

Buck finished up with love and marriage; divorce is easy for men—just say, "I divorce thee" three times— but nearly impossible for women. Pre-nups—marriage contracts—exist and are enforceable, unless you get an asshole judge like I did.

Buck switched to the subject of clothing. "Ninety percent of the population wears traditional Arab dress that probably hasn't changed much since biblical times." He advised us, "Buy a set of traditional clothing for yourselves."

"Why?" I asked.

He replied, "Just for fun. Or you might wear it when wandering around the streets and souks." Buck confessed, "I often dressed as a native when I left the embassy."

I inquired, "Do you have a picture you can show us?"

He smiled, then described to us the native Yemeni attire. The men wore headgear called a thob or shiwal, usually white, and in the north they dressed in a white fouteh, a robe, and in the south the men wore a white sarong. Underwear optional.

Sometimes, I recalled, they also wore a ratty Western-style sports jacket over their robe, the pockets stuffed with khat and magazines of the metal variety. They all wore sandals, and the whole country needed a pedicure.

Two things a man never left home without were his dagger and his rifle. The right to bear arms in Yemen seemed to be an obligation, and ninety percent of the males over the age of about fourteen toted an assault rifle, usually an AK-47, capable of taking out all his friends and neighbors in a few seconds of automatic

fire. Oddly, though, there was little random gun violence or crime. I mean, everyone was packing, so you
thought twice before you walked into a store and said,
"This is a stickup." Everyone in the place would blow
you away. Right?

Non-random gunplay was another matter. Most people who got whacked got whacked for a reason. Usually
something to do with politics, or honor, or a business
dispute that couldn't be settled over a khat chew. Also,
Westerners were rarely robbed at gunpoint. If you got
a gun stuck in your back, you were not likely to hear,
"Your money or your life." Instead, you'd hear, "Come
with me." The purpose of kidnapping Westerners was
not only money, but also a way for the Bedouin tribes to
embarrass the central government and/or extort favors
or services from them, which was a common pastime of
the tribes. These abductions were called "guest kidnappings," and kidnap victims often reported that nothing
was taken from them, except maybe an admired watch
or piece of jewelry that should be offered as a gift while
you were waiting for the ransom money to arrive. Your
food and upkeep isn't free, you know. And you were
getting an authentic experience.

When I first got to Yemen, I was, I admit, a little
taken aback by the sight of almost every male carrying an assault rifle. But after about a week I didn't even
notice it—in fact, what caught my attention were men
without rifles. Who were these wimps?

Anyway, Buck was done with menswear and we
moved on to ladies' wear. Almost all the women wore
the balto, like a burqua, an all-encompassing cloak
that, like the first Model T Ford, came in any color you
wanted as long as you wanted black.

Buck then moved on to the subject of veils. He said, "Very few women show their faces in public, and those who do are often harassed by fundamentalists."

"Because they're ugly?"

"No, Mr. Corey, because it's *immodest*."

"Right." I wondered if I was going to get a cultural awareness certificate in my personnel file.

He continued, "As for Western women"—he looked at Kate, who is from Minnesota—"you are not required to wear a veil, but you may feel more comfortable on the street if you cover your face with a hijab, a head scarf that can also be wrapped around your face."

Kate stated, "I have no intention of covering my face."

Buck nodded in solidarity with his compatriot, but advised her, "It's best to wear a pantsuit with long sleeves, but it has to be loose-fitting." He informed us, "There have been reports of Western women traveling in the rural villages who have been jeered at and even had stones thrown at them for their seemingly immodest attire."

I mean, what do you say about that? Nothing.

Buck looked at his watch and said, "Fifteen-minute break."

CHAPTER ELEVEN

Out in the hallway, Kate said to me, "I am very impressed with your probing questions and your astute observations. I can tell, too, that Mr. Harris is in awe of your insights and your instinctive grasp of the material."

"Thank you."

"Can you do me a favor when we go back in there and shut the fuck up?"

"I'm trying to make it fun."

"This is serious. Pay attention."

"I divorce thee."

"Speak to my lawyer." She looked at her watch and said, "I need to freshen up." She turned and headed toward the ladies' room.

I think Kate was annoyed with me. I mean, I'm not good in classroom situations, but I usually listen. Maybe it was the subject—Yemen, Islam, and cultural awareness, which meant cultural sensitivity. How many people from the Mideast take a cultural sensitivity class before they come to America? Why is it always us who have to be sensitive to other cultures? Works both ways.

But maybe I could learn something useful. Like where to pull a guy's shiwal to spin him around like a top.

I went back into the classroom where Buck was sitting, looking over some notes. I said to him, "Sorry if I was a little...inattentive."

He looked up, smiled politely, and said, "I'm enjoying your participation."

See? *He* didn't think I was annoying. I was brightening his morning.

Kate returned and sat, and Buck picked up where he left off and said, "The only absolute requirement of dress in Yemen is modesty. For men, therefore, shorts and short-sleeved shirts are not acceptable. For women, all that may show is their eyes, their hands, and their feet. The rest," said Buck with a smile, "is left to the imagination." He glanced at me as though expecting a good joke, but I just gave him a studious nod.

Buck had some good news about bare skin and said, "As Mr. Corey will remember, there are a few resort hotels around Aden where parts of the beach are set aside for Westerners to wear modest bathing attire." And bad news. "But these beaches are sometimes visited by fundamentalists who cause a scene."

Right. I recalled playing volleyball with the Marines on the beach behind the Sheraton in Aden where we were quartered, and we wore shorts and T-shirts, but there were no women on the beach except a few female FBI colleagues who wore similar outfits. This didn't seem to be a problem, but that's because we also had a few fully clothed and armed Marines at both ends of the beach. I recalled, too, that I felt naked and exposed without my gun on my hip, though our weapons were always nearby. Also, we weren't supposed to swim, because that would make us sitting ducks. I mean, between the terrorists and the fundamentalists, I wasn't having much fun at the beach.

Buck moved on from bare skin to balls. He said, "As a warrior people, Yemenis hold courage in the highest esteem—higher than other virtues such as hospitality or honesty."

In fact, in my experience there, honesty was very low on the list of virtues, and lying was elevated to an art, if not a virtue. The Yemenis were, however, brave, and I could relate to that and respect it. In fact, this was something to keep in mind when I met The Panther.

Buck continued, "Conversely, cowardice is viewed with extreme contempt. If, for instance, the sight of armed strangers on a street corner makes you uncomfortable, you cannot show fear. If you appear fearful, then this invites an aggressive reaction from the men."

"In other words," I said, "they don't like pussies."

"Correct. Look a man in the eye and say, 'As-salaam alaikum!' Peace be upon you. He will reply, 'Wa alaikum as-salaam'—and upon you be peace."

"Okay. How do you say, 'Make my day, punk'?"

Buck continued, "Women may appear fearful without inviting contempt. Also, women should never look a man in the eye and say anything. Women lower their heads and pass by a man quickly."

I asked Kate, "Got that?"

She had no reply. Clearly, Ms. Mayfield was having a little trouble processing this. But she'd be fine when she got there. She adapts easily.

"Hospitality," said Buck, "is very important to the Yemenis, and it must be accepted when offered. Even if you knock on a man's door to ask directions, he must offer you something to drink or eat, and you are obligated to accept it. Be aware not to give offense to a man who offers you something."

Right. Especially if he's carrying an AK-47 and offers to blow your head off.

Buck informed us, "Women are mostly exempt from the rules of hospitality." He advised us, "Read the handouts on these subjects."

Buck continued, "The Yemenis tend to be creative with the truth, which is a diplomat's way of saying they lie."

Right. I remembered having to deal with the authorities in the central jail where the *Cole* suspects were imprisoned. I didn't mind the prisoners lying to me, but when the cops, jailers, and translators all lied to me, I had to wonder if the whole country wasn't pathological liars. I recalled, too, getting into screaming matches with the above assholes, and a few times I thought we were headed for a shoot-out.

Buck said, "They lie to each other, so don't feel you're being singled out because you're a Westerner." He added, "The truth is hard to come by for someone trying to do a job there, and basically you should trust no one. Having said that, you *will* get the truth if the truth will serve the person you're speaking to. As an example, if someone wants to betray someone else, he'll tell you where you can find that person. The problem is, you have no way of knowing if you're being given good information, or if you're being set up for a kidnapping—or worse."

This was true, and didn't even need to be said, but it's good to be reminded. Also, Buck apparently knew we had other duties in Yemen beyond evidence recovery and legal attaché.

Buck continued, "Yemen is a land of distrust, which in a way removes any ambiguity. Trust no one and you won't be betrayed or misled. If a government official is assigned to assist you, he is not there to assist you. All informants lie, even the ones you pay. If an ordinary man begs you to get him a work visa to the States in exchange for information, he is working for the government or for Al Qaeda, and he just wants to get close to you and obtain your trust. Why? You'll find out the hard way. Any questions?"

I thought of Nabeel and said to Buck, "Same with the Mideastern guys I talk to here."

"Then you understand." Buck continued, "The tribes. They make up the majority of the population, and they live mostly in the highlands in the north, though there are also tribes in the south. Some tribes are nomadic Bedouin, but most live in small settlements. Some tribesmen have emigrated to the towns and cities, but the individual retains his loyalty to his tribe."

Sounds like Kate's family.

Buck continued, "The tribes are led by sheiks or chieftains who are usually elected, but sometimes inherit the title." He added, "We sometimes call these sheiks or chieftains warlords, though they may consider that a derogatory term." He advised us, "If you should happen to meet one, address him as sheik."

I had the feeling that Buck was giving us a mission briefing and that a sheik was in my future.

Buck went on, "The tribes distrust the central government, and they distrust one another, though they will form alliances of convenience, even with the government, but these are shifting alliances and it's hard to keep score on who is allied with whom on any given day."

Sounds like 26 Federal Plaza.

"The tribes have a primitive, pre-Islamic code of honor, and in many ways they are chivalrous. If you are their guest, whether by invitation, chance, or kidnapping, they will show you extreme hospitality. They have no particular animosity toward the West, but they're not presently happy with the American officials in Yemen, who they see as propping up their government, which they hate." He reminded us, "The friend of my enemy is my enemy. That said, if you should somehow wind up as guests of a tribe, you aren't automatically dead. But don't try to pass as innocent tourists. Be up-front about who you are. But be sure to criticize the government in Sana'a."

"That's easy."

"And it may save your life."

"That's good." I reminded him, however, "We'll be working in Sana'a and Aden. No tribal lands on the agenda."

He didn't reply to that and said, "You'll be briefed more fully on these subjects when you arrive."

Kate asked, "What is the tribal attitude toward Al Qaeda?"

"Mostly negative," replied Buck. "Al Qaeda doesn't fit into the social or political matrix of tribal society. Neither did Marxism, obviously. The tribes are distrustful of all foreign ideologies, urban dwellers, intellectuals, politicians, and even Muslims who are not Yemeni. They like things the way they were two thousand years ago."

"But they were all Jews then," I reminded him.

He smiled and replied, "Don't remind them." He added, "Another thing to remember about the tribes is that they tend to be monarchists. They actually owe allegiance to and take orders from the exiled princes, sheiks, and sultans who live mostly in Saudi Arabia and who command the loyalty of different tribes. We, meaning the Foreign Office, are in contact with many of these Saudi princes and sultans and through them we can gain the assistance of certain tribal chieftains. In fact, if you do go into the tribal lands, you may be provided with letters from these exiled princes, sultans, and sheiks asking the tribal chieftain to give you safe passage or assistance."

We seemed to have returned to this subject of us going into Indian Territory.

Kate asked, "Do these letters actually work?"

"Sometimes."

And sometimes not. Like, hey, chief, I got a letter here from Sultan Salami asking you to help me out. Oh...that's the next tribe? You don't like Sultan Salami? He did *what* to your brother? Sorry. Which way to the next tribe?

This was moot anyway, because we weren't going into the tribal regions. Or did Tom mention that we might do that?

Buck said, "The social and political situation in Yemen is complex beyond understanding—part feudal, part Islamic, and part modern dictatorship—and the Yemenis themselves are confused by shifting alliances and a central government that sends mixed signals to friends and foes alike. Their president, Ali Abdullah Saleh, has said, 'Governing Yemen is like dancing with snakes,' and I couldn't have said it better. So you have some challenges ahead of you."

"We love challenges," I assured Buck.

"Good," he said. "You're going to the right place."

I thought maybe the class was over, but Buck continued. "Khat. It's cheap and plentiful. About ninety percent of the males chew khat. And almost eighty percent of the arable land is used for growing it, which has caused food shortages, water shortages, and widespread malnourishment—not to mention a population that is under the influence from about noon to bedtime." Buck also said, "Part of the malnourishment is a result of khat being an appetite suppressant, which works well in a country with food shortages."

Right. Not like pot, which gives you the munchies.

Buck continued, "Khat is an amphetamine-like stimulant that causes excitement and euphoria. Individuals become very talkative and may appear to be emotionally unstable."

My last girlfriend must have been a khat chewer. Also, I hope that the ninety percent of the men who chew khat are not the same ninety percent who carry assault rifles. On the plus side, they probably couldn't shoot straight. Right?

Buck said, "Khat can also induce manic behavior and hyperactivity."

Maybe Tom Walsh chews khat. But I was thinking about khat as an appetite suppressant. I saw an opportunity here to make a fortune in lard-ass America. Amber waves of khat.

Kate asked, "Do women chew khat?"

Buck replied, "About half the women do. The other half get the work done."

I was really getting excited about this. Lose thirty pounds in thirty days. Also good for alcoholics. Dry out, stay blitzed.

Buck continued, "Some people say khat is a mild aphrodisiac, or at least it makes people uninhibited, which may account for the high birthrate."

Triple wow. Lose weight, get high, get laid. Does it get any better than this?

"Mr. Corey? I seem to have lost you." He brandished his dagger playfully.

"Oh...sorry. I was just thinking about...any downside to khat?"

"I just told you. Loss of appetite, erratic behavior, plus it turns your teeth green."

"How green?"

"Long-term use can cause male impotence."

"Viagra."

"And the withdrawal symptoms are very unpleasant."

Why stop? Anyway, every drug has a few side effects, and that never stopped Big Pharma. Let's focus on appetite suppressant. Thirty days, thirty pounds. America can be thin again.

Buck broke into my reverie and said to me, "I don't know if you tried khat when you were there, but I warn both of you, khat has been the downfall of many a Westerner in Yemen."

I observed, "But if you're thinner, you make less of a target."

He smiled, then got serious and said, "Khat will get you through a bad day in Yemen, but it will not get you through the year."

"Day at a time."

I had the thought that Buck must have been a good American diplomat—Arabic speaker, cross-dresser, khat chewer, culturally sensitive. I asked him, "What was your job with the embassy?"

He replied, "Cultural Affairs."

Right. And I'm going there to gather evidence on the *Cole* bombing, and Kate is there to issue visas. We all lie like Yemenis.

The khat chat was finished, and Buck moved on to climate—sucks. Geography and topography—empty beaches, lethal deserts, dangerous tribal highlands. Health concerns—every disease known to man, plus some. Medical facilities—get evacuated to someplace else. Relations with neighboring Oman and Saudi Arabia—pretty bad. Boating on the Gulf of Aden or the Red Sea—pirates. Food—tastes good, but you might get sick. Local water—tastes bad and you will get sick. Security concerns—not much petty crime; just kidnapping and getting whacked. Tourist attractions— lots of good ones, but that's where you'll get kidnapped or whacked. Agriculture—eighty percent khat, twenty percent wasted on food. Manufacturing—incense, per- fume, and AK-47 knockoffs. Entertainment—khat and kidnapping. Sports—soccer and shooting. Tourism— down slightly from none. Leisure activities—khat. Arts and crafts—daggers. Government—dysfunctional and oppressive, except where non-existent.

There were a few other areas that Buck covered, and basically I was getting the impression of a country that had lots of problems and no solutions.

Buck, in fact, had painted a picture of the land and the people that didn't look like the tourism website. And yet I had the impression that Yemen historically had once been part of the world, an important center of trade and commerce between East and West, a center of learning, and a happier land than it was in the twen- tieth and twenty-first centuries. It had, unfortunately, devolved into a hell on earth. Shit happens, but in Yemen it happened hard.

Buck was finished with the required tutorial, and he said to us, "I'm aware that your mission to Yemen is not entirely diplomatic, and I hope you learned something this morning that could be useful to you—though you may not recognize it at this time."

Neither Kate nor I replied to that leading statement, and Buck concluded with what was probably his standard wrap-up. "Yemen is an ancient land where time has stood still, and where you can see glimpses of an almost biblical civilization. It is where the Arabs are thought to have originated, where the people practice customs and rituals that are rooted in a forgotten, pre-Islamic past. Whatever you know or think you know about the Mideast is not necessarily true in Yemen. So keep an open mind, and think of your time there as a unique and incomparable experience. And good luck."

Eleven A.M. Not bad.

We stood and shook hands with Buck, who gave Kate his card and said to her, "If you think of any questions, don't hesitate to call or e-mail me, even after you've arrived in country."

To me, he said, "I would strongly advise you, Detective, not to underestimate these people. They may be backward, but they're not stupid, and they will use your Western arrogance and disdain to play you like a lute."

"I've figured that out."

"Good. You're intelligent." He said to both of us, but really to Kate, "And don't go the other way, as some Western people do, and patronize them, or try to find excuses for their sometimes unacceptable customs and practices." He advised us, "Remember who you are, why you're there, and what you believe in, and they will respect that."

"Good advice," Kate agreed.

He concluded, "You will have no natural allies there, but neither will you have natural enemies—except Al Qaeda. With everyone else, it's very situational. Learn to read the situation. And above all, learn how to make a good deal. It's all about the deal. But don't promise what you can't deliver. And keep in mind, the Yemenis can't always be bought with money. As with the Italian Mafia, it's often about favors. If you can help a group or an individual in a vendetta against another group or individual, they will help you in your mission." He looked at us and said, "For instance, the Sana'a government helps us locate Al Qaeda targets for our Predator drones and Hellfire missiles. In exchange, the government tells us which tribal chieftain or political opposition leader they'd like to see dealt with in a similar manner." He added, "It's all about quid pro quo."

Neither Kate nor I responded to that, and Buck told us, "You didn't hear that from me."

The post-class chat seemed to be finished, so we thanked him, said our good-byes, and Kate remembered to take the handouts.

CHAPTER TWELVE

O ut in the hallway, Kate remarked, "An interesting man."

"Especially at the end."

"CIA?"

"No. He was too nice. Maybe State Department Intelligence."

She nodded. "That would fit."

"Right. Hey, do we get a certificate for this course?"

"Just a note in our file so we don't have to take it again when we do another tour in Yemen."

Not funny. We got on the elevator and rode up to the 26th floor. I said, "I think we just got a mission briefing—a glimpse of how we're going to find and eliminate The Panther."

She nodded.

And did I have a problem with that? "That" being a promise to the corrupt and nasty Yemeni government to vaporize some poor tribal leader or political opponent if the government gave us the location of Al Qaeda targets, including, hopefully, The Panther.

And how did Kate and I fit into this? Maybe we were on the team that would coordinate this with the Yemeni government, and/or we would be on the waste collection team, i.e., going out to the hills or desert where a Hellfire missile just turned some guys into hamburger, then collecting fingers for a print match or a DNA analysis to make sure we got The Panther.

Well, no use speculating. We'd know when we got there.

We got off on the 26th floor and Kate said to me, "I'm feeling a little more prepared for the country, but still not sure about the job."

"Cultural awareness is ninety percent of the job."

We returned to our desks and got some work done. I love reading memos and electronically checking that I've seen them. Plus, some e-mails needed a response. It occurred to me that none of this had anything to do with me anymore. I was going to the front. I was free.

Before I knew it, it was noon, and the sacred lunch hour had begun. Short of a national emergency, you cleared the building at noon. To have lunch at your desk was unpatriotic or suspicious, and you might be questioned by the Office of Professional Responsibility.

I grabbed my topcoat and met Kate at her desk, and we left the building with no plan other than to get some air and clear our heads.

Before we'd left on our last overseas assignments, Kate and I had gone for cocktails to the Windows on the World in the North Tower of the World Trade

Center. That was no longer possible, so we walked to the observation deck at the WTC site.

It was a cold day, but there were dozens of people on the deck, mostly tourists, but also some office workers, construction guys, and a group of elementary school kids.

We don't come here often—we don't need to—but today seemed like a good day to reconnect with this place, to remember, as Buck said, who we are, why we're here, and what we believe in.

We walked down to Battery Park, got a coffee and hot dog at a food cart, and sat on a bench, looking out at the harbor.

There was a time when everyone coming to New York from overseas—tourists, immigrants, and Americans returning home—had to sail past the Statue of Liberty. Now, ninety percent of overseas travelers came in through the airports, and they were definitely missing something. Almost everyone arriving here—immigrants, tourists, people on work or student visas, and businesspeople—was here for legitimate reasons. The ones who weren't, like the bastards who took down the Towers, became my problem.

But now I was going to one of the breeding grounds of this sickness—to find one diseased sonofabitch. A guy who helped kill seventeen American sailors as well as other innocent people. Tom Walsh keeps telling me it's not about revenge; it's about justice. I keep telling him to get real.

Kate asked me, "Any other thoughts on what Buck said?"

"No, not about what he said. But about what he didn't say."

"Meaning?"

"Why us?"

"I'm sure he has no knowledge of that. And you can keep asking that all week and you'll never get the answer. The answer is in Yemen."

"Right." But I think I already knew the answer.

CHAPTER THIRTEEN

On Tuesday night, some of our civilian friends gave us a going-away dinner in what used to be the basement speakeasy of the 21 Club. We celebrated the end of Prohibition in America, and drank enough to get us through a year of Prohibition in Yemen.

I invited everyone to come to Yemen and promised an exciting visit, including a civil war reenactment, except, I confessed, they weren't acting.

We used Wednesday and Thursday to settle our personal affairs, including the usual of having our mail forwarded—in this case to a State Department address in Washington where it would be sent on to the U.S. Embassy in Sana'a in a diplomatic pouch. Can't wait to get those Victoria's Secret catalogues.

Our travel orders instructed us to take only a week or two's worth of clothes and necessities, and to arrange with the State Department Travel and Relocation Office for a hundred pounds each of additional personal items to be shipped at government expense to an address in Yemen, which was not yet known. I wondered if I could sneak my La-Z-Boy recliner into the shipping container.

We arranged with Alfred, our excellent doorman, to let the shippers in and to have someone look after our apartment. I gave Alfred a nice tip and promised him a jambiyah when we got home.

We also saw our lawyer and gave him power of attorney for certain legal matters, including the shipment of our mortal remains—but only if we were dead. He asked for the name of a local funeral director, so I said, "Walsh Funeral Home," and gave him Tom's home address.

Kate wanted to shop for modest clothing that would be appropriate for wear both in the embassy and on the streets of Sana'a or Aden. I suggested, "A black balto is good for day or night wear, as well as the beach, and you can accessorize with different-colored veils."

Kate had managed to get us a direct military flight from Dover Air Force Base to Sana'a, but later we got an e-mail from DOD—Department of Defense— informing us that the flight was full. I suppose a big C-17 could be full, but the question was, what was it full of? Military equipment? Troops? Hellfire missiles? Or maybe people we weren't supposed to see or talk to. The e-mail further advised us that we were authorized to use a commercial air carrier, which we knew.

On Thursday night, a number of our Task Force colleagues—NYPD and FBI—gathered at Walker's, a neighborhood pub on North Moore, a few blocks from the office. The supervisors, including our pal Tom Walsh, made an early appearance before the gathering got out of hand and before the owner had to call the police—most of whom were already there.

The FBI and NYPD don't usually socialize, but this was a going-away party for two extremely popular colleagues, one of whom was FBI, and the other NYPD.

There were a few NYPD guys there who'd been to Yemen with the Evidence Response Team, and one female FBI agent who'd spent half a year there. They all had some useful advice, like sleep with your gun, never travel alone, and don't chew the khat. The FBI lady, however, said to Kate, "Without alcohol, the only way your marriage is going to survive with this guy is to chew khat."

Al Rasul was there, of course, and he got behind the bar and did a funny impersonation of a Yemeni bartender telling his customers it was ladies' night and the women could drink for half price, but no women were allowed, and neither was alcohol. Al also accused the Christians of turning his water into wine.

Later, Al told me, "Still nothing on Nabeel."

On Friday at 10 a.m., after getting our final shots in the nurse's office, we were sitting in Mr. Walsh's office.

Tom asked us how the rest of the evening went and apologized for not staying longer.

I assured him, "The party died when you left."

We were again sitting in the preferred seating section, and Tom had thoughtfully ordered coffee, which I needed.

Tom Walsh is not really a bad guy—well, he is, but he's not much different than any NYPD boss I've ever dealt with. It comes with the job—or it comes with ambition.

Tom, however, had been a little deceitful in the past, lying mostly by omission, then telling me after I'd found out the truth that I had no need to know what he hadn't told me. When I was a cop, the bosses told you all they knew because you had a need to know everything about a criminal case. But this was a different game. Lots of classified information, compartmentalization, firewalls, and outright lies. Some of this was necessary; most of it was not. It's gotten better since we lost three thousand people on 9/11, but old habits die hard.

With all this in mind, I listened to Tom Walsh's final briefing. Basically, he had nothing new to add, but he did say, "You will be part of a five-person team. Two are already in place, and one will join you later."

He put a manila envelope on the coffee table and said, "These are your travel documents, including your airline tickets. Also included is your contact info for when you arrive at Sana'a Airport." He continued, "The Travel Office did the best they could, but you'll be arriving in Sana'a at about two-thirty A.M. on Sunday morning. You'll be met, of course, but in the event you're not, you have instructions that will tell you what to do."

I asked, hopefully, "Take the next flight home?"

"No."

Kate inquired, "Why would we not be met?"

Walsh replied, "Things can go wrong."

"So," I inquired, "if four guys in white robes ask us to get into a black van, we should say no?"

"You should definitely say no." He added encouragingly, "We've never lost anyone at the airport."

I inquired, "Anyone ever *delayed* at the airport?"

"Now and then." He reminded us, "But you're traveling on diplomatic passports, so you're not required to answer any questions, except for your destination, which is the American Embassy." He added, "Demand a phone call to the embassy. The night duty officer is alerted to your arrival."

"If he doesn't answer, can I call you?"

"No." Tom continued, "You will be met before you go through passport control. You will not have to go through customs, but if someone demands that you open your bags, then open them. And make sure there is nothing in your luggage that is offensive, compromising, or contraband."

"Like soap?"

"Like weapons, alcohol, or certain magazines. Or anything made in Israel."

"So no Uzi submachine guns?"

He informed us, "There's a list in the envelope." He continued, "Assuming all goes right at the airport, there will be a three-car convoy to take you to the embassy."

I asked, "Do our guns travel in the dip pouch?"

"No. You will leave your handguns here. When you get in your vehicle in Sana'a, you'll be issued handguns which you are authorized to carry at all times."

Kate asked, "Who's our contact person at the airport?"

Tom replied, "His name is Paul Brenner. There's a photo of him in your envelope. I understand he's former Army CID—Criminal Investigation Division. He's now working for the Diplomatic Security Service."

Kate asked, "Does he know why we're in Yemen?"

"I don't know." Tom stood and said, "I want to thank you again for taking on this assignment. And I want to wish you both the best of luck." He looked at me and said, "I know you have some reservations about this, John, but I also know that you will become more enthused about this assignment when you learn how important it is to the country."

"I can feel it already, Tom."

"Good." He said to Kate, "You'll have a more difficult time as a woman—and as the member of the team who has to keep John in line."

They both got a chuckle out of that. Really funny.

Tom and I did a good, firm handshake, and Kate got a hug, which in a Federal building is sexual assault.

We promised to stay in touch by e-mail and send cards on the holidays.

Out in the hallway, Kate said, "I can't believe we're getting on a plane tonight to go to Yemen for a year."

"Did you unplug the toaster?"

"Well... maybe it won't be a full year."

"Probably not."

She asked me, "Are you excited?"

"I keep pinching myself to make sure I'm not dreaming."

She stayed silent as we walked to the elevators, then said to me, "I feel better that we're together and we can look out for each other."

"Right." I remembered an old Arab saying. "When walking through a minefield, make one of your wives walk fifty paces in front of you and your camel." I didn't say that, of course. I said, "If I had three more wives, we'd have a whole five-person team looking out for each other." Actually, I didn't say that either. I said, "We always look out for each other."

She kissed me as we waited for the elevator, and we held hands on the way down.

CHAPTER FOURTEEN

A l Rasul said he wanted to see me before I left, so I went to his desk and he suggested a cup of coffee in the break room.

We sat at a table with our coffees, and I said to Al, "Tom has agreed to send you to Yemen with us."

He smiled, then said, "You know, I've never actually been to a Muslim country."

"Except Brooklyn."

He smiled again and said, "I don't think I'd like it. I know my wife wouldn't."

"She Muslim?"

"Yeah. But born here. She sees the new immigrant women with the scarves and veils and it makes her crazy."

Which reminded me of the question that had been bugging me, and I asked him, "Maybe you can tell me why some American-born Muslims have gone to Sandland to fight for the bad guys?"

Al Rasul replied, "The short answer is jihad. The long answer is God, history, Sharia law, and lots of hate. And here's a secret—they hate the West only slightly more than they hate their own corrupt governments, and a little more than they hate themselves."

I thought about that, and I guess I understood what he was saying. But it didn't really answer the question of how all this had translated into a growing jihad.

Al had part of an answer and said, "Islam began with military conquest, forced conversions, religious fundamentalism, and an intolerant theocratic state. And then there was a period of enlightenment. But what you're seeing now is a return to the good old days. The Dark Ages."

"Right. But don't forget those seventy-two virgins in Paradise."

He smiled, then got serious and said, "The fundamentalists take that literally. If you kill innocent non-believers, you don't go to hell where you belong—you go to Paradise." He added, "Their goal on earth is Sharia law and world domination. Their spiritual goal is to ascend into Paradise." He advised me, "Don't try to make sense of it. And don't think that what these homegrown radicals need is a good dose of Western civilization and a few beers. They've had that—here and in Europe—and they reject it."

"*You* don't reject it."

"I'm a bad Muslim. At least by their standards. I'm also a marked man."

"Right. Don't sit so close to me."

I looked at the Department of Justice wanted posters on the wall. Mostly bearded guys with dark, dead eyes. Almost all the captions said *Wanted for Murder*, some said *Suspected Murder*, and some said *Conspiracy to Commit Murder*. Murder used to be my game, but this wasn't murder. It was something else, and it wasn't war; it was sick and it was evil.

Happily, a lot of the posters had big red Xs on them, and notations: *Killed*, *Captured*, *Convicted*.

There was no wanted poster for Bulus ibn al-Darwish, a.k.a. The Panther, and I wondered why not. I guess for the same reason that al-Numair came up empty on the automated case system; The Panther had gone from wanted by the Department of Justice to the CIA kill list.

Anyway, assuming that Al Rasul wasn't Al Qaeda, I confided in him, "I'm going to Yemen to look for an Al Qaeda guy who was born here."

"I know that. The Panther. Al-Numair."

"How do you know that?"

"If I tell you, I have to kill you."

"Right. Any advice?"

"Yeah. Watch your ass."

"That's it? That's the total wisdom of the East?"

"That's the total wisdom of East Flatbush, where I grew up, and the Lower East Side, where you grew up. But here's another tip—this guy is not some rural desert hick like your last big cat, The Lion. You may or may not be able to get into The Panther's head, but he's multicultural so he's already in *your* head."

"Right. I know that."

"Good. So don't try to guess what he's going to do as an Arab. Try to guess what his conflicts are. His strength as a Westernized Arab is also his weakness. His head is on Channel One some days, and Channel Two other days, and sometimes both channels, and that's when he gets static. He would tell you that he has no sympathy and no admiration for the West, and that the West is not in his heart or soul. But it *is* in his head, and if he were honest with himself, he'd understand that his hate was, in fact, a form of respect. You don't bother to hate what you think is contemptible."

"Right." And Al Rasul knew all of this because...? I asked him, "How do I actually find this guy?"

"You know very well that he will find you."

I was afraid he was going to say that.

"Make sure you let *everyone* know you're looking for him. The word will reach him—if it hasn't already." He reminded me, "You understand that you have somewhat of a reputation after The Lion. Asad Khalil was not Al Qaeda, but as you well know, he worked with Al Qaeda on his last mission here. And he was a respected jihadist, and because you sent Khalil to Paradise, you are not unknown to Al Qaeda." And then the kicker. "In fact, Al Qaeda would like to see you in Yemen to even the score."

Actually, that thought had occurred to me. In fact, it kept occurring to me, but I'd put it into my denial file. Now good old Al had pulled it out for me. Also, I think Tom Walsh forgot to mention that I was actually going to Yemen to be red meat for The Panther. See what I mean about Tom?

I asked Al, "Did someone tell you to brief me?"

He hesitated, then replied, "Not officially. And not Tom Walsh." He confided to me, "I'm working this end of the case. Mommy Panther and Daddy Panther in New Jersey." He let me know, "They're clean. Good citizens. Very upset. But they're not giving up their son...Still, we might get some leads through them."

"Let me know."

"Will do." He also let me know, "Bulus ibn al-Darwish is on the CIA's kill or capture list, and Mom and Dad have actually brought suit in Federal court to get their son removed from the kill list. Their reasoning is that their son is an American citizen and therefore can't be assassinated by the American government."

"Okay. But did anyone explain to them that their son has killed American citizens? Like seventeen U.S. sailors."

"In fact, that's why they may get their son removed from the CIA kill list." He explained, "His parents have also made the legal argument that what their son did, did not constitute an act of terrorism, but was an act of war." He further explained, "This legal theory is backed by some past decisions in American courts and the International Court. So if attacking an American military target—as opposed to attacking civilians—is ruled an act of war, then The Panther has committed no crime and he will not be brought to trial. He will be detained as a prisoner of war, and under the Geneva Convention he is not obligated to give any information other than his name, rank, and service number."

That sucked. I mean, not only couldn't I kill him, I couldn't even torture him. I said to Al, "Sounds to me like Mom and Dad are playing it both ways. First, their son is an American citizen with Constitutional rights. Next, he's a soldier in a foreign army and he has protections under the Geneva Convention."

"Right. Whatever works."

I said, "What he actually is, is a traitor to his country, and that's a hanging offense."

Al agreed, but reminded me, "We don't assassinate traitors. We put them on trial. Bottom line, Mom and Dad may get Junior removed from the CIA terrorist kill list."

I didn't reply, but I wondered now what the goal

of the mission was. It's a lot easier to whack someone than it is to capture them and return them to U.S. soil. Therefore, someone—like the CIA—had perhaps decided that Bulus ibn al-Darwish needed to be killed quickly, before some Federal judge got him removed from the kill list. After The Panther was dead, the lawsuit became moot. Strange war. I mean, judges, lawsuits, and all that.

Al advised me, "You didn't hear any of this from me." He stood, we shook, and he said, "Good luck."

"Thanks. See you next year."

"Maybe sooner."

I found Kate strolling around, saying a few good-byes to colleagues, but I hate long and repetitious good-byes, and I got us out of there in five minutes.

We began the six-mile walk back to our apartment— her idea, not mine—and we took in the sights and sounds of New York City, my hometown. Could be the last time, but with luck, we'd be back.

I thought about telling Kate of my conversation with Al Rasul, and how I'd just discovered the real reason I was being sent to Yemen. *Bait*. But...well, did she have a need to know that? Actually, yes. But she wanted to think that her pal Tom chose us for this mission because we were the best of the best. And we were. So Tom only half lied to us.

Also, Tom knew I wouldn't go alone, so he told the bosses in Washington that they had to include Kate, who he knew would want to go. Plus, Kate had worked the Asad Khalil case with me, so for all I or Washington knew, Kate was also on The Panther's menu.

A sane man would have pulled the plug on this. But...did it make any real difference? If Tom had told us we were bait, would we have said no? And if I confronted Tom with this, he'd say, as he always did, "I didn't know that. Nobody told me that. Where did you hear that?"

In any case, I now understood what had happened behind the scenes. Actually, I always understood.

We spent our last afternoon in our apartment, taking care of some final details and calling our parents. Hers were in Minnesota, as I said, and mine were retired in Florida. Thank God none of them would visit us in Yemen. The place sucked enough.

I'd already convinced my parents that Yemen was the Switzerland of the Mideast, so they weren't too concerned, though my mother warned me about getting too much sun. "You know how you burn, John."

Kate's parents were a little more hip to the situation, and they expressed a mixture of pride and concern for their little girl. And some advice for me. "Take care of our daughter."

How about me? Maybe they were in on this with Tom.

Funny, though, that when all is said and done, the last thing you do is call Mom and Dad. I wondered if The Panther ever called home.

At 5 P.M., we phoned Alfred, our doorman, and told him we needed a porter with a luggage cart and a taxi to JFK.

As the porter was loading our luggage into the taxi, Alfred, who knew what we did for a living, and knew we were going to someplace in Sandland, said to us, "Thank you for your service to our country."

Kate and I shook hands with Alfred, then got into the taxi. Kate, I saw, was wiping a tear from her eye.

I took her hand and squeezed it.

At least, I thought, I was going into the jaws of the beast armed, finally, with the truth, as revealed by Al Rasul. The truth is good, except when it's bad.

And there was another truth that had occurred to me—another reason we were being asked to go to Yemen, and it also had to do with the past—but not The Lion—something else that happened years ago, that involved Kate and the CIA.

I put that thought in the back of my mind, but not too far back. The answers to Why me, why Kate, and why Yemen, were in Yemen.

PART III

Marib,
Yemen

CHAPTER FIFTEEN

Bulus ibn al-Darwish, al-Numair, The Panther, wearing the white robes and shiwal of a Bedouin, stood before a gathering of his fighters; forty-two jihadists, armed with AK-47 assault rifles and shoulder-fired rocket launchers.

It was past the midnight hour, but he could see his men sitting cross-legged in the bright light of a waxing half moon, and he could see, too, the flat, desolate landscape of rock and powdery soil, stretching to the star-filled horizon.

The Panther said to his men in a loud, clear voice, "This night, you will achieve a great victory for Islam!"

The men cheered and raised their rifles in the air.

"You will kill the infidel and cleanse the sacred soil of Islam with their blood!"

Another cheer.

The Panther looked out at his soldiers. They were mostly new recruits, hastily trained in the mountain camp. But among them were four hardened jihadists from Afghanistan, and two officers of the defeated Army of Iraq.

These two former officers had met the Americans in battle and had fled their homeland after the defeat, and they were now here in Yemen to avenge that humiliation. What they lacked in the spirit of holy war, they more than compensated for in hate.

One of the officers, Behaddin Zuhair, a former captain of the elite Iraqi Guard, would lead the attack on the American-owned Hunt Oil installation. The other Iraqi, Sayid al-Rashid, would be his second in command.

The Panther had great faith in these combat-proven soldiers, and he knew they would give courage to the young recruits. With these two Iraqi officers, and with the four battle-hardened jihadists from Afghanistan within the ranks, The Panther saw no reason to lead this attack against the American oil facility himself.

The Panther reminded his men, "The security forces of this foreign compound are all paid mercenaries— men who have no loyalty to the Americans, only to the American dollar. They will surrender and beg for mercy, or they will run—or they will die at your hands!"

The men cheered more loudly.

The Panther knew, as did his officers and men, that the Americans had also hired a hundred men of the Yemeni National Security Bureau to provide additional protection for the oil installation—the housing units, the offices, the trucks, the machinery, and the pipelines and pumping equipment. These one hundred para-military policemen were well paid by the Americans but poorly trained by the government in Sana'a, poorly equipped, and poorly motivated. And, as The Panther recalled from his dealings with these men at the Bilqis ruins, they were easily intimidated and more easily bought.

He reminded his fighters, "The police camp is outside the perimeter of the oil company, on the north side, and you will attack from the south." He also assured his men, "The police will not engage you. And you will not provoke them." He smiled and said, "They will be sleeping like lambs and will hear nothing."

The men laughed, but Bulus ibn al-Darwish could sense that it was forced, nervous laughter.

Men on the edge of battle, he knew, were fearful. This was understandable. But faith overcame fear. Leadership overcame inexperience. And that was his job—to foster faith and show leadership.

He said to his fighters, "You have been shown the plans of the defenses of this American colony on the soil of Islam. You know that this place is weak, and you know the secrets of these defenses. And you know that the mercenaries who guard this place for the Americans are infidels without heart or soul. And the Yemeni laborers who are with them have sold themselves to the Americans and are unworthy of God. They are all sheep to be slaughtered this night!"

The men stood and cheered wildly.

Captain Behaddin Zuhair stood to the side and watched his men, then looked at his chief, Bulus ibn al-Darwish, who called himself The Panther, though some called him al-Amriki—the American, which al-Darwish did not like.

Behaddin Zuhair thought that al-Darwish had great presence and spoke well. The Panther had become a legend since he planned the successful attack on the American warship in Aden Harbor, so the men listened to him, trusted him, and revered him. Al-Darwish, thought Zuhair, was a great inspirer of men, a smart planner, and perhaps a great thinker. But he was not a great military strategist. In fact, he knew nothing about war. If the truth be known, this attack on a fortified compound, executed with poorly trained troops, had all the ingredients of disaster. But no one would tell that to Bulus ibn al-Darwish.

The men were still cheering, and The Panther motioned them to sit.

He let the silence fall over the desert, and he looked out at the star-filled night. A soft, hot wind came from the north, from Ar Rub al Khali, the Empty Quarter, the desert of the blazing sun and the massive, shifting dunes of scorching sand where even scorpions died.

It was here where God put the oil, and here where the Americans came to drain it from the soil of Islam. And The Panther was moved to say, "It is here where the Americans and their paid servants will die. And the dunes will march south and cover their bones and cover every trace of them, and all evidence that they were here and have polluted the sacred soil of Yemen and Islam."

The men raised their voices in agreement.

The Panther shouted, "You will be victorious!"

The men stood again and shouted, "Victory!"

"You will show no mercy!"

"No mercy!"

"You will kill the infidels and their servants! No one escapes alive!"

The men cheered and continued cheering.

Captain Zuhair, too, cheered, as did his lieutenant, Sayid al-Rashid. But they exchanged glances with each other. These officers, who had seen battle against the Americans, against the Kurds and the Iranians, and against the Iraqi rebels who fought against the great leader Saddam Hussein—these two men knew victory and defeat, and they knew fear, cowardice, bravery, and death. The Panther knew none of this.

Zuhair looked at his men. Too young—not in their years, but in their hearts and their heads. Too many idealists and religious scholars who came from comfort. Too many Saudis who had seen battle only on television.

Well, thought Zuhair, what they lacked in hardness, perhaps they made up for in faith and zeal.

Zuhair looked again at Bulus ibn al-Darwish. The Amriki, too, must have had these thoughts and doubts. Which perhaps was why al-Darwish was not leading the attack tonight.

The Panther called out to his men, "You have gathered here from many nations of Islam to engage in jihad. Tonight will be the first victory, followed by many more, until the Americans are driven from Yemen. And then we will turn to Sana'a and annihilate the corrupt government men who have invited the Americans into holy Yemen." The Panther raised his voice and said, "We will hang the ministers and the generals from the lampposts of Sana'a and celebrate our victory in the palace of the puppet president, Ali Abdullah Saleh!"

The men stood again and shouted, "Death to Saleh!"

The Panther smiled and raised his arms, but his thoughts were elsewhere. He himself would not be leading this attack, though some among his jihadists might question why he was not joining them. In fact, Captain Zuhair had raised this issue.

Bulus ibn al-Darwish did not fear death, but he did fear capture, especially at the hands of the Americans, his former compatriots. He feared prison, he feared torture, he feared the humiliation of having his family in America—his father, his mother, his sister—seeing him kept like an animal in an American prison.

Death was far better, and to die during jihad would assure his immediate ascension into Paradise. But there was no guarantee of death in battle.

If he were taken prisoner, the entire jihadist movement in Yemen would suffer or collapse. So for that reason, and because God willed him to stay alive and free to fight the Crusaders, he could not join the attack.

But he did intend to be there to join in the victory, and to oversee the execution of the survivors.

He motioned for his men to be silent, and he said to them, "I will be with you at the moment of victory." He drew his jambiyah from its sheath—still stained with the blood of the Belgians—and raised it high. "I will join you in cutting the throats of all who fall into our hands. No mercy! No prisoners!"

The men cheered wildly.

Captain Zuhair tilted his head toward Lieutenant al-Rashid and whispered, "He *does* know how to cut throats."

Al-Rashid nodded.

Bulus ibn al-Darwish turned and faced toward the Kaaba in Mecca, raised his arms, and called out, "God is great!"

"God is great!"

"Let us now pray."

It was not the time of the dawn salat, though the dua—the prayers for supplication in times of crisis or danger—could be said at any time, so Bulus ibn al-Darwish sat cross-legged facing Mecca, as did his men, and he recited from the Koran, " 'When the heavens are stripped away, the stars are strewn, the seas boil over, the tombs burst open, then shall each soul know what it has given and what it has held back.' "

The Panther then said, "Let each man now pray silently to God for strength, for courage, and for victory in battle."

Again the desert went silent, except for the wind from the Empty Quarter.

Bulus ibn al-Darwish prayed silently, beseeching God to give his men courage. He prayed, too, for himself and said, "Let me cut many American throats this night."

But as often happened when he prayed for American deaths—such as before the *Cole* attack—other thoughts intruded into his prayers and his mind; thoughts of his childhood and school years in America. Thoughts of his family, and his former home.

These were troubling thoughts, confused memories, and they weighed heavily on his soul.

He had not been happy in America, but he was happy now in the land of his ancestors. Yemen was ancient and once pure, and he would make it pure again.

He looked up at the wondrous desert sky, a sky that had not changed since the days of his forefathers—since the day of Creation. He vowed, "The land of Yemen shall be as clean and pure as the sky above it."

And God spoke to him: "You, Bulus ibn al-Darwish, will be the savior of Yemen and Islam."

He felt a light touch on his shoulder and looked up to see Captain Zuhair, who said softly, "If you have a moment, sir, before I move the men to battle."

The Panther stood and followed Captain Zuhair into a mud hut.

Inside the small hut, lit by a single candle, was Lieutenant al-Rashid.

Captain Zuhair began, "I am confident, sir, in total victory tonight." He paused, then said, "But I must report to you, sir, that I have just received, by cell phone, some information from our friend who is inside the American compound." Zuhair continued, "This man reports that the Americans and their security forces, who number perhaps thirty, are arming themselves and their laborers, including our friend, and they are preparing themselves for an attack."

The Panther stood quietly in the dark and did not reply. Could this be true? Or could it be that Captain Zuhair was losing his courage?

Captain Zuhair suggested, "Perhaps, sir, we should delay this attack until another night. Perhaps a week. The men can train further. Also, sir, we should consider adding more fighters to the force."

Again The Panther stayed silent, but then he said, "We attack tonight. And we cannot add any men to this force." He reminded Captain Zuhair, "Forty men are as of this moment making their way to Aden to attack the Sheraton Hotel, and to kill the American soldiers and spies who live there. Another forty will soon be on their way to Sana'a to attack the American Embassy. And that, Captain, is all the fighters we have in the camp."

"This is true, sir. But perhaps we should not divide

our forces. Perhaps we should concentrate our forces on the American oil installation to ensure a complete and rapid victory."

The Panther had already discussed this with Captain Zuhair, and now the man was speaking of it again—on the eve of battle.

The Panther said with some annoyance and authority, "I have made the decision to attack on three fronts. This will cause the government to react with fear and confusion. They will not know when or where to expect another attack, and they will become paralyzed with indecision, and they will begin arguing with the Americans, who always want action and decision."

Captain Zuhair had no reply.

The Panther reminded Captain Zuhair, "I have told you this before." Then he reminded the captain, "The Americans are arrogant and the government is cowardly. You will see both when these attacks are successful."

"Yes, sir."

"If you had been here after the attack on the *Cole*, you would understand what I am saying and doing."

Like all bad generals, Zuhair thought, this one is reliving his victories and forgetting his defeats. But Zuhair said, "Yes, sir."

The Panther turned to Lieutenant al-Rashid and commanded, "Speak. What do you say?"

Sayid al-Rashid said nothing, but then drew a deep breath and said, "I can certainly see the concerns of Captain Zuhair, but..." He glanced at Zuhair, then said to The Panther, "But I can also see that what you say, sir, is true."

The Panther nodded.

Al-Rashid continued cautiously, "We...Captain Zuhair and I are simple soldiers, sir, and we think of tactics. But you, sir, know of strategy. And it is an excellent strategy. To throw fear into the government and cause strife within the government—"

"And between the government and the Americans."

"Yes, sir. And of course, our victory tonight will be all the greater because of your leadership and planning."

The Panther nodded curtly, then said, "If there is nothing further, I suggest you speak to each man now to be certain they understand the plan of attack." He also said, "You will say nothing of what you have just said to me."

"Yes, sir."

He reminded them, "It is six kilometers to the oil installation, and if you start now, you will be there in less than two hours." He ordered, "The attack must be completed at least two hours before dawn so that we may withdraw into the hill camp under the cover of night."

Both men replied, "Yes, sir," then Captain Zuhair said, "Nabeel would like a word with you."

"Now?"

"He says it is important."

"All right. Tell him to come in." He also ordered, "You stay."

Lieutenant al-Rashid ducked out of the hut and returned seconds later with Nabeel al-Samad, a junior aide to The Panther.

The Panther looked at his aide in the dim light of the candle. Nabeel, like himself, had lived in America, though Nabeel was an occasional visitor who went there only for business—Al Qaeda business. And also to deliver a verbal message now and then to the family of Bulus ibn al-Darwish, and to bring a message in return from his father, mother, and sister. Nabeel had already done this three days before, so what now did he want?

The Panther asked his aide, "What is it, Nabeel?"

Nabeel al-Samad made proper greetings, then said, "Sir, I have just heard from our friend at El Rahaba."

"Yes? And what do you hear from our friend at the airport?"

Nabeel reported, "There is an Egyptair flight arriving in Sana'a at two forty-five this morning. The manifest for this flight lists two Americans from New York City who are traveling on diplomatic passports." Nabeel also said, "We knew of these people perhaps two weeks ago when the American State Department applied for visas in their names."

"Yes? And?"

"One of these Americans is a man named John Corey, and the other is a woman called Katherine Mayfield, who is his wife."

"And they are diplomats?"

"No, sir, they are both agents of the Federal Bureau of Investigation."

The Panther nodded and said, "Continue."

Nabeel further reported, "Our friend in the New York consulate office informed me when I was in New York that these agents had arrived to pick up their visas, and our friend gave me copies of the visas and their passports. Both of these agents had listed their home address as the government building in which they work. Further inquiries revealed to me that they both are employed in the office of what is called the Anti-Terrorist Task Force."

Again, The Panther nodded and motioned Nabeel to continue.

"This, as you may know, sir, is an internal American security agency, but the agents are sometimes sent to various places in the world—"

"Yes, I know that. They are *here*."

"Yes, sir." Nabeel continued, "The man, Corey, was in fact in Aden approximately three years ago. Now he is back."

The Panther stayed silent awhile, then asked, "And how is this man and this woman different from the other American agents who come here?"

Nabeel informed The Panther, "These two agents have been specifically placed by name on the assassination list of the Supreme Council."

"Yes? And why?"

"This man, sir, is the American agent who killed Asad Khalil, The Lion, in New York."

The Panther nodded. He certainly remembered that. Was it a year ago? Perhaps less.

Nabeel reminded The Panther, "Asad Khalil had traveled to New York to kill this man, Corey, and his wife, Mayfield."

"Yes, I recall." But it had not gone well. Khalil was a Libyan, and he had gone to America on an earlier mission to avenge the bombing of his homeland by the Americans. He had exacted a degree of revenge, but not all that he wished. So he returned. And this time, they killed him.

Khalil was not within Al Qaeda, but he worked *with* Al Qaeda. And thus the Supreme Council had sought to avenge his death by calling for the assassination of this man Corey, who had killed the great jihadist, Asad Khalil, The Lion.

The Panther inquired, "Why do you think this man has come to Yemen again?"

Nabeel replied, "Perhaps, sir, to kill *you*."

That came as no surprise to Bulus ibn al-Darwish. The Americans had a special hatred of Muslims who had been born or achieved citizenship in America and then joined the jihad.

The Americans, he understood from his more than twenty years in that country, were so arrogant as to believe that anyone who lived among them would come to love them and love their corrupt and licentious country. And when you did not love them, they hated you for your lack of appreciation of them and their wonderful nation. True arrogance and true vanity. *Pride goeth before destruction*, as it is written in the Hebrew Book of Proverbs.

And of course, the Americans in Yemen were here to avenge the killing of seventeen seamen on the American warship. And Bulus ibn al-Darwish knew from his parents and other sources that his name had been placed on what was called the CIA kill list. And this list, according to custom, or perhaps law, had to be approved by the President of the United States. That was interesting. Interesting, too, that this man Corey, who was perhaps here to kill him, was himself—along with his wife—on a similar assassination list that was approved by the Supreme Council of Al Qaeda. So the hunter and the hunted were listed for death. The question was, Who is the hunter, and who is the hunted? The answer for now is, Both are both.

Also, he knew, his mother and father had engaged an American attorney to have his name removed from the CIA list. Corey's name would be removed from the list of the Supreme Council when he, Bulus ibn al-Darwish, killed him.

The Panther thought about all this. To him, it was an honor to have his name placed on that American list. But his mother and father—and probably his sister, who was an American—would rather see him rotting his life away in an American prison. They did not understand him because they had been too long in America. They did not understand martyrdom, and perhaps they had even ceased to believe that martyrdom in jihad earned a man his rapid ascension into Paradise. His parents, he thought, would someday go to hell.

"Sir?"

The Panther returned to the present problem and said, "So if this man and this woman are in Yemen to kill me, then they have made it convenient for me to kill them."

Nabeel nodded, but said nothing.

It was possible, thought The Panther, that these two Americans were not here specifically to kill him, but in any case the man Corey had killed The Lion, and for that reason the Supreme Council had ordered a death sentence for him. So if he, Bulus ibn al-Darwish, could kill this American agent, he would gain great honor with the Supreme Council.

He said to Nabeel, "Kill them both."

Nabeel nodded, then asked, "When? Where?"

"Whenever you can, wherever you can." He added, "In Sana'a. Or in Aden if they should go there." He thought a moment, then said, "Or in Marib, if they should come here seeking me. Take as many men as you need and kill them at the first opportunity."

"I will see to it, sir."

The Panther was about to dismiss Nabeel, but then Nabeel said, "I have actually met this man."

"Yes? Where? How?"

"In New York, sir. Just last week." Nabeel had been waiting for this moment to impress his chief with his knowledge of the enemy, and to show his usefulness in America. Nabeel enjoyed his visits to New York, and he wanted those visits to continue. He explained, "After I received this man's name and office address from our consulate in New York, I telephoned the number on his visa application and asked to speak to John Corey with the claim that I had important information for him about terrorist activity."

The Panther smiled and said, "Well, that is a true claim."

Nabeel and the two Iraqis, seeing that The Panther was smiling, laughed.

Nabeel continued, "Corey came to the telephone and I explained that I had gotten his name from a man who did not wish to be identified. We spoke briefly and arranged to meet."

The Panther asked, "At the government office?"

"No, sir. That is not the procedure for the first meeting." Nabeel thought this could be amusing, so he had rehearsed his English and replied in that language, "The agent Corey and I arranged to meet at a Jewish delicatessen."

The Panther smiled again, but the Iraqis spoke no English and they did not understand.

Nabeel, emboldened by his chief's smile, continued

in English, "Ben's Jewish deli—on West three-eight."
He asked, "Do you know it, sir?"

The Panther said in English, "West Thirty-eighth
Street." He seemed no longer amused and said abruptly,
in Arabic, "Tell me of this man."

Nabeel did not want to say that the meeting was
brief, or that his poor English inhibited the talk, but he
did say, "The man was arrogant."

"They are all arrogant."

"This man more so." Nabeel thought back to his
brief meeting with the American agent and said, "He
was abrupt, and his manner was that of a man who had
little respect for me or those of our faith who live in
America." Nabeel wasn't certain if that was completely
true or accurate, but this is what his chief wanted to hear.

The Panther nodded and said, "Arrogant."

Nabeel continued, "He seemed anxious to leave—
it was Saturday last, and the agents do not want to
work on Saturday or Sunday. So I arranged with him
for me to come to this government building for a new
meeting—on Monday, in the morning." Nabeel did
not mention the need for an Arabic translator.

The Panther asked, "And did you go to this
meeting?"

"No, sir. That would be dangerous."

The Panther smiled and joked, "So perhaps it is *you*,
Nabeel, who this man is looking for in Yemen, and you
who he wishes to kill."

"No, sir, it is you. But I will kill him first."

"You will. And his wife." He asked, "Is that all?"

Nabeel replied, "That is all, sir. But I wish you to
have this—" He reached into his fouteh, and the Iraqi
officers became alert.

Nabeel produced a small white card and handed it respectfully to The Panther, saying, "This is the business card of the agent, John Corey. He gave it to me to present at the government building when I called on him."

The Panther took the card and held it near the flame of the candle. He read:

John Corey, Detective
N.Y.P.D./FBI
Anti-Terrorist Task Force
26 Federal Plaza
New York, N.Y. 10278

There was the office telephone number for contact, but not the man's cell phone.

Also on the card were two seals—one of the Federal Bureau of Investigation and one of the New York Police Department.

Bulus ibn al-Darwish stared at the card for longer than it took to read it, then he turned it over and read, *Nabeel al-Samad to see Det. Corey.*

Nabeel was aware that some men who worked for and with Al Qaeda in America at times exaggerated their deeds and accomplishments, so this card was good proof to have of his work—and his truthfulness.

The Panther handed the card back to Nabeel, who said, "It is yours, sir. I have no use for it."

"Neither do I. And neither will Corey after you kill him, so keep it, Nabeel, to remind yourself of your task."

Nabeel took the card and said, "Yes, sir."

Nabeel made to leave, but The Panther said, "Wait."

He thought a moment, then said, "There will be a good reward for you, Nabeel, if you are able to capture this man instead of killing him. Capture him and bring him to me. And also his wife."

"Yes, sir."

"But do not allow this reward to blind you to the task of killing them if that is the only way."

Nabeel vowed, "This man and his wife will be captured and brought to you, or they will be killed." He further vowed, "They will not return to America."

"And neither will you if they escape."

"Yes, sir."

Nabeel again made to leave, but The Panther again said, "Wait." He said to Captain Zuhair and Lieutenant al-Rashid, "Begin the preparations for the march."

Both officers saluted and left the hut quickly.

Bulus ibn al-Darwish, alone now with Nabeel al-Samad, recently arrived from America, inquired of his aide, "So they looked well to you?"

Nabeel knew who "they" were and replied, "As I said, sir, they looked well, and they send you their greetings and their blessings." He added, because his chief wanted more, "Your father is prospering in his business and your mother has become closer to her faith."

The Panther nodded and asked, "And Hana?"

"She, too, has become more devout, and as I have said, she is very content in her work at the office of your father."

None of this was true, of course—at least about the sister and the mother. The father *was* prospering, but he had aged badly in the three years since Nabeel had begun visiting them after the *Cole* attack. The mother, too, looked drawn and sad. Hana, however, was more angry than sad, and she had told Nabeel, "I have no brother," but Nabeel would never tell that to his chief.

The parents of al-Darwish had given Nabeel photographs and letters for their son, but he could never allow these things to remain on his person, and he had burned everything at the first opportunity after he left these meetings, which were always arranged for a public place in Manhattan or Brooklyn—a park or a museum, or sometimes a department store. The authorities, he was certain, did not know of him, though of course they knew of the al-Darwish family. The authorities sometimes watched their house, and their mosque, and the father's place of business. But the family was not under constant surveillance, and they traveled often to the city for shopping and entertainment. Also, Nabeel knew, they had a sense, after all these years, of knowing if they were being watched.

Still, it was a danger to meet them, and Nabeel was glad that he had to do this only once or twice in a year. But it was also a good thing for him to do this, because it raised his status with his chief.

Bulus ibn al-Darwish said, "You did not say if my sister was still betrothed."

"She is, sir."

"And is there a date set for the wedding?"

"Not yet, sir." He added, "But soon." Or perhaps not. In truth, Nabeel had not asked the family about any of this, and Hana had said nothing to him on this subject.

Nabeel always found himself in a difficult situation on these occasions—in New York, and in Yemen. He needed to be careful. A lie was not good, but sometimes necessary. And the truth was not always good.

The Panther stayed silent with his thoughts. He did not want to ask a question that Nabeel had answered three days before, and he did not want to seem overly concerned about any of this. So he said nothing.

He knew that one day he would again see his mother, his father, and his sister, and it would be here in Yemen. And that day would be soon after his total victory. He would see them in Sana'a—in the palace of the president. On the day he became Supreme Leader of Yemen. On that day, his family would be with him to share in his triumph. And they would never again return to America.

The Panther looked at Nabeel and said, "That will be all."

Nabeel bowed and left the hut.

The Panther remained standing in the light of the flickering candle, then blew it out and went into the night.

Zuhair and al-Rashid were preparing the soldiers for their movement, and The Panther motioned them to him.

He said to his two commanders, "Well, you have heard Nabeel. The Americans are sending more agents here, and soon they will be sending soldiers unless we kill the small numbers who are already here." He added, "More reason to attack the embassy and the Sheraton Hotel in Aden."

Captain Zuhair thought that the opposite might be true; every attack on the Americans in Yemen increased the number of Americans in Yemen. The jihadists, he thought, should be attacking the Yemeni Army and security forces, but Bulus ibn al-Darwish, the Amriki, had a hard hate in his heart for his former countrymen. Nevertheless, Captain Zuhair said, "Yes, sir."

The Panther said to his two officers, "Let us go now and begin the march."

The three men moved closer to the soldiers, and Captain Zuhair called out to them, "It is time!"

The men cheered.

The Panther, too, called out a last time to his jihadists, "We will meet again, amid the inferno of the oil camp, and among the corpses of the Americans—or we will meet in Paradise!"

The men let out a long, loud shout: "Victory!"

Captain Zuhair and Lieutenant al-Rashid paid their final respects to their leader, who blessed them and blessed the jihadists. Then the officers took charge of their men and began the march toward the American oil compound.

The Panther watched them disappear into the dark, then he turned and walked toward five waiting vehicles, filled with his personal bodyguards. He would remove himself from this place and await the outcome of the attack in a nearby Bedouin camp. It was necessary, he knew, to keep moving, to not stay in one place too long, and to take shelter under a roof or in a cave away from the probing eyes of the American Predator drones. And it was for this reason that he wore the robes and long beard of a Bedouin.

He glanced up at the desert sky. It *looked* the same as it did since the beginning of time—but there was something new up there, something that had already killed too many of his fellow jihadists. And they were looking for him. And now, perhaps, the Americans had sent a man—and maybe a woman—to look for him also. Well, he thought, the Predators would not find him, and the man Corey would not find him. He could not kill the Predators, but he could kill the man. And kill the man's wife. And kill any American who came to the sacred soil of Yemen to find him.

The Americans may rule the air, but he, Bulus ibn al-Darwish, The Panther, ruled the land.

— PART IV —

Sana'a,
Yemen

CHAPTER SIXTEEN

It was 2:35 in the morning and the Egyptair flight from Cairo was approaching Sana'a International Airport. The airport had a name—El Rahaba—which according to my Arabic dictionary means, "I'd like the fruit salad." No. That can't be right.

Anyway, it had been almost three hours since we'd left Cairo, and this leg of the flight was unexpectedly full; mostly young men, probably all Yemeni guest workers bringing home a few bucks so their families could eat. It was a sad country.

Kate and I were sitting in first class and the other gentlemen in first class were dressed Western, but looked Mideastern; maybe Yemeni and Egyptian businessmen or government officials. A few of them had their wives with them, and the women were dressed in traditional clothing. Most of the ladies had been unveiled in flight, but now that the aircraft was landing, they all had scarves and veils in the full upright position.

Kate, FYI, was wearing loose blue pants and a matching high-collared blouse with long sleeves. Buck would have approved, except that Kate had no head covering and her medium-length blonde hair was completely exposed for every man to see, as was her pretty face. Also, FYI, she'd gone light on the makeup.

As for me, I had on my usual tan slacks, navy sports jacket, and a blue shirt, which was a Christian Dior. Christian—get it?

The big Airbus continued its descent, and I leaned over and peered through the window. It was a clear night and I could see hills in the distance, and below was an expanse of arid landscape washed in blue moonlight. In the near distance I saw a few scattered lights that must be Sana'a.

As we crossed over the airport boundary, I could see the military end of the airport: two jet fighters with Yemeni markings, a few helicopters whose markings I couldn't make out, and a huge United States Air Force C-17 cargo plane. The outpost of Empire.

We touched down and the aircraft rolled to a halt, then taxied to a hardstand a hundred yards from the terminal. The engines shut down and Kate said, "He's not taxiing to the gate."

"We walk."

"I'm assuming that's a joke and it's not funny."

Clearly Kate was a bit anxious, not to mention tired and cranky after a nearly thirty-hour journey. I said to her, "This whole country is a joke. Learn to laugh or you'll go crazy."

No reply.

Everyone was standing, and I stood and moved to the exit door and looked through the porthole at the terminal, which I remembered from last time; a low building not much longer than a strip mall, badly lit by three stanchion lights. I could see the headlights of the mobile staircase, followed by a bus, heading toward the first-class exit door, which reassured me that the peasants in the rear wouldn't be on my bus.

I returned to my seat, and Kate and I collected our things and moved into the aisle.

The staircase pulled up without smashing the aircraft, the door opened, and I could smell the fresh, cool morning air rushing into the cabin. Yemen.

So down the stairs and across the tarmac to the waiting bus. Our fellow passengers from first class were all seated, but Kate and I stood in the rear. Kate was the only unveiled woman on board, and the men, who had not taken much notice of her on the aircraft, now looked at her, as did the women. It was as if we'd all been on a nude beach, then got dressed and boarded a bus, except that one of the women was still naked.

There are two gates in Sana'a Airport, and we stopped at the one called two. We let everyone get off first, then followed. So far, so good.

Inside the terminal, our cabin mates moved toward the passport control booths. Only two booths were manned at this hour, and the booth marked for VIPs, diplomats, and crew was closed. Also, there was no one around who looked like us, and Kate said, "Maybe we have to go through passport control."

"We're supposed to be met here."

So we waited. The buses that were filled with coach peasants started arriving and the passport lines got longer. Two Yemeni soldiers carrying AK-47s were giving us the eye.

Kate said, "Let's call the embassy number."

"The pay phones are on the other side of passport control, and I'm not standing in line with the peasants."

"We can't stand here."

"Okay, let's cut the line."

I went to the head of the line at one of the booths and Kate followed. No one objected and I recalled that the Yemenis, for all their faults, were exceedingly polite and tolerant of Westerners, whom they expected to be arrogant assholes.

Kate and I went to the passport guy and presented our diplomatic passports. The guy checked our visas, then our faces against the passport photos, and he stared at Kate. I mean, every woman in line was veiled, so this guy must be good at eyes. Right?

He stamped our visas, then motioned us to pass through. For some reason—instinct—I glanced back and saw he was on the phone.

Before we got to the double doors marked EXIT, a tall guy with a two-day beard, wearing a crumpled suit but no tie, approached and without identifying himself said, "Come this way," and motioned us to follow him to a side corridor. I said to him, "We're meeting someone here from the American Embassy."

He seemed to understand and said impatiently, "Yes, yes. Embassy man is this way. We must discuss your visa."

Sounded like bullshit to me, and I didn't want to leave the public area—not that it mattered a whole lot where you were when you got arrested. But if we stayed here, we might see our embassy guy. I said, "We are traveling on American diplomatic passports, as you know, and we have been instructed to wait here, and we're not moving from here." I suggested, "Go get the embassy man."

He seemed very annoyed, and at this point he should have IDed himself and asked for our passports, but instead he said, "Wait," and walked toward the corridor.

The two soldiers with the AK-47s moved closer to keep us company. Meanwhile, the Yemenis from the flight were giving us furtive looks as they hurried toward customs.

I said to Kate, "See what happens when you cut the line?"

"John, what's going on?"

"I don't know." And I wasn't waiting around to find out. I eyed the double exit doors that led to baggage and customs, and thinking our contact guy might be there, or in the terminal, I said to Kate, "Let's go."

"He said wait—"

I took her arm and we moved toward the exit doors. "Walk like an Egyptian."

We got within ten feet of the doors before I heard a shout, and the two soldiers suddenly rushed ahead of us and we found ourselves looking into the muzzles of two AK-47s.

Our Yemeni friend reappeared and shouted, "I say to you wait here!"

"Yeah, you also said the embassy man was with you."

"Yes. Now he is here."

"Mr. and Mrs. Corey, I presume."

I turned, and walking toward us was a guy wearing jeans and a windbreaker. He was, in fact, the guy in our photograph. Paul Brenner.

He said to Kate and me, "Sorry I couldn't meet you. I was speaking to this gentleman about your visas."

I told him, "The Yemeni consulate in New York assured me there was no charge."

He smiled, put out his hand to Kate, and said, "Paul Brenner. Nice to meet you, Mrs. Corey. Welcome to Paradise. I hope you had a good flight."

"Yes...thank you."

He extended his hand to me and said, "Your reputation precedes you."

"Apparently it does." I asked, "Who is this joker?"

Brenner introduced the joker as Colonel Hakim of the Political Security Organization—the Yemeni secret police. Colonel Hakim didn't shake hands, but said to Brenner, "I will now wish to speak to your colleagues in private."

Brenner replied, "I told you—not happening, Colonel."

"Do you say no to me?"

"I say you must either arrest all of us or let us leave."

Colonel Hakim seemed to be considering his two choices, then said to Brenner, "You may join us."

"That's not one of your choices."

It was my turn to be alpha and I said to Colonel Hakim, "Tell these guys"—I pointed to the soldiers—"to lower their rifles."

He hesitated, then barked something in Arabic and the soldiers lowered their rifles. Hakim said to me, "There is a problem with your visa, and that of your wife. A discrepancy of address. So I may ask you both to leave Yemen."

Who said there's no God?

Brenner said to Hakim, "That's not a decision for you to make, Colonel."

Sure it is. Shut up.

Colonel Hakim had no reply.

Brenner said to him, "The embassy will lodge a formal protest with your foreign minister tomorrow. Good evening, Colonel."

Colonel Hakim again had no reply, but then Brenner unexpectedly stuck his hand out and Hakim hesitated, then took it. Brenner said to Hakim, "We must remain allies in the war against Al Qaeda. So cut this crap out." He added, "As-salaam alaikum."

Colonel Hakim, given the chance to save face in front of the soldiers, replied, "Wa alaikum as-salaam."

I said to Colonel Hakim, "Let me know if you're ever in New York."

And off we went into the second ring of hell, the baggage and customs area.

As we walked, I asked Brenner, "What was that all about?"

He replied, "Just the Yemeni government trying to assert its authority." He added, "They think they run the place."

Kate inquired, "Don't they?"

Brenner replied, "No one runs this place. That's why we're here."

Right. Nature abhors a vacuum. Or, to be more positive, we're here to help.

I said to Brenner, "Actually, our visas list our home address as 26 Federal Plaza."

"These clowns don't need your home address."

"Right. We practically live in the office anyway."

Brenner muscled his way through the maze of carts and people, saying something in Arabic, like maybe, "Excuse me, we're Americans and we need to get out of this shithole. Thank you."

Brenner said something to a porter, who nodded.

The carousel showed no signs of life, and Brenner said to us, "This could take a while." He added, "Sometimes the carousel doesn't work. Then they carry the bags in, and pandemonium breaks loose. It's fun to watch."

I asked Mr. Brenner, "How long have you been here?"

"Too long."

"Me, too."

He smiled.

Mr. Paul Brenner looked to be in his early fifties, tall—but an inch shorter than me—not bad-looking, well built, full head of black hair, and very tanned. Under his blue windbreaker he wore a gray T-shirt that I now saw said "Federal Prisoner." Funny. Not so funny was the collar of a Kevlar vest that I could see above his T-shirt. Also under his windbreaker was a bulge on his right hip.

He informed us, "We have a three-car convoy that will take us to the embassy."

"Guns?" I asked.

"Guns? You want guns, too?"

Paul Brenner seemed to have a sense of humor. I know someone with a similar sarcastic wit. This was not going to make us buds; there's room for only one top banana in the show. I didn't think Mr. Brenner was part of our team, but to find out I asked him, "Will we be working together?"

He replied, "I'm with DSS—Diplomatic Security Service. I work for the State Department to provide security to American Embassy personnel and official visitors."

That didn't answer the question, but I left it alone, and said, "Sounds interesting."

He let us know, "I was Army CID. A homicide investigator. Like you were, Mr. Corey. I was a chief warrant officer. You were a detective second grade, NYPD. Now we are both civilians, pursuing second careers."

"Right. Except I'm not exactly pursuing my second career."

"I hear you."

Kate commented, "This is the only career I've got."

Brenner smiled, then looked at her and said, "You've got a lot of guts to come here."

She didn't reply, but to set the record straight, I told Brenner, "It was her idea."

He let us know, "It's a tough assignment, but you'll get through it, and you'll be able to write your own ticket when you get back."

I replied, "We're hoping for Afghanistan next."

He laughed, then said to me, "So you were here in August '01?"

"Yeah. Forty days altogether. Mostly in Aden."

"Right. Well, things have heated up a bit since then." He explained, "Al Qaeda is here."

I informed him, "They were here when I was here. They blew up the *Cole*."

"Right. Well, now they're all over." He went on, "If possible, this place has become more dangerous."

Typical war-hardened vet trying to scare the newbies. I said, "In my day, when we walked down the street in Aden, we had to throw grenades just to go get a newspaper."

He laughed again and said, "Well, in Sana'a we fire

so many rounds from the embassy that we wade knee-deep through the shell casings."

Kate said, "Please."

It's a guy thing, sweetheart.

Anyway, we chatted awhile as we waited for our luggage, and Brenner said to Kate, "Take what I'm about to say as a professional observation—you're very good-looking, and you have a face that, once seen, is not forgotten. That may be a liability."

Kate smiled nicely and replied, "That's never been a liability before."

"Let me make a suggestion," said Mr. Brenner. "You should always wear a long head scarf that you can wrap or hold over your face. The Western ladies here find this is a good compromise to the veil."

"Thank you," replied Kate a bit coolly.

The carousel jerked to a start and the baggage began dropping out of a hole in the wall.

I've never actually seen so much stuff on a baggage carousel—boxes, crates, weird shapes wrapped in plastic, and some of the worst luggage I've seen since my aunt Agnes visited from Buffalo. I said, "I hope our chickens made it."

The Yemenis picked the carousel bare like piranha stripping a carcass.

Our first-class bags were among the last, and Brenner asked, "Is that all you've got?"

I informed him, "There is a large cargo ship sailing out of New York with the rest of my wife's luggage."

Kate smiled. She loves sexist jokes.

The porter had our suitcases and overnight bags on his cart and we moved toward the customs counters, but Brenner led us directly toward the doors. A customs guy in uniform hurried toward Brenner, and Brenner held out his passport from which protruded an official document called a thousand-rial bank note— about five bucks—that the guy snatched as he waved us through.

Brenner commented, "This is one of the worst airports in the world in terms of security and screening. There's no watch list, so Al Qaeda guys and other bad actors can come and go. Also, you could ship a bomb out of here addressed to someplace in America."

I said to Kate, "We should have given them Tom Walsh's home address."

We went out into the badly lit and nearly deserted concourse, which was as run-down as I remembered it. The few shops were closed, as was the only car rental and the Yemenia airline counter. I saw a big sign that said, in English and Arabic, NO KHAT CHEWING. I'm not making that up. But smoking was okay, because a soldier had a butt in his mouth.

We went through the exit doors, and at the curb were three black Toyota Land Cruisers with dark-tinted windows. Standing close to each SUV were two guys toting M4 carbines, who were obviously also DSS, and they were eyeing everything around—especially the six Yemeni soldiers with AK-47s. How come everyone else gets a gun?

Brenner said, "We're in the middle."

As Kate and I moved to the middle vehicle, two DSS guys opened the rear doors and we slid in. Brenner got in the passenger seat, and the other DSS guys grabbed our luggage and jumped in the front and rear vehicles. Brenner said to the driver, who was Yemeni, "Yalla nimshee," which I remembered means, "Let's go," and off we went.

Brenner informed us, "These are FAVs—fully armored vehicles—and the glass is bullet-resistant." He added, "Resistant as in duck. There are two flak jackets in the rear. I suggest you put them on."

I turned and retrieved the two heavy military-issue flak jackets, which could stop anything from a bullet to antiaircraft fire. I helped Kate into one and put on the other.

This all seemed a little like overkill, but I recalled being met this way the last time, and it was considered standard operating procedure; also known as the embassy covering its ass if something went wrong.

We cleared Sana'a International Airport in less time than it takes to say "Sana'a International Airport," and we were on the surprisingly decent four-lane road toward Sana'a. This was the way I'd come to Yemen last time, and it was a bit of déjà vu—except for being met by Colonel Hakim. More to the point, this was a good introduction to Yemen for Kate, who by now must be thinking, "I should listen to my husband."

Brenner broke into my thoughts and said, "Half the fun is getting there."

No, half the fun is *me* making wisecracks—not you.

Anyway, a rival wiseass was the least of my problems. I asked Brenner, "How long you got left here?"

He replied, "As long as you've got left. We're all leaving together."

Well, maybe that answered part of the question of who else was on the Panther team.

I suggested, "Let's wrap it up in thirty days."

He replied, "Now that you're both here, that's very possible."

I hadn't yet given Kate the good news that we were

here to be Panther bait, and she was missing some of the nuances, so she said, "That's very flattering, Mr. Brenner."

He said, "Please call me Paul."

And call me red meat.

CHAPTER SEVENTEEN

There wasn't much traffic at this hour—it was now 3:55 A.M.—and we clipped along at 120 KPH. The Yemeni driver yawned loudly. The khat must have worn off.

Brenner said to Kate and me, "This is Mohammed. We pay him a dollar an hour to drive for us. Two dollars to stay awake."

Mohammed laughed, so he understood English, or he'd heard the joke so many times he knew he was supposed to laugh.

I asked, "Why the Yemeni driver?"

Brenner explained, "The Yemeni government now insists that we have at least one Yemeni driver in a convoy at night for our enhanced security." He further explained, "Partly it's so we have an Arabic speaker who can talk to the idiots at the checkpoints, or call for police or army backup if we get into a situation."

I said, "That sounds almost plausible."

"Right. But it's bull." Brenner let us know, "We actually don't know who Mohammed works for, do we, Mohammed?"

He replied, "I am just a simple driver, sir."

"Right. And I'm the cultural affairs attaché."

"You are, sir."

That out of the way, Brenner turned and said to us, "The only incident we've ever had happened at this hour."

Kate said, "Thanks for sharing."

I asked, "Guns?"

"Oh, right. You want guns." He passed us a black canvas bag and said, "You'll carry the M1911 Colt .45 automatic, A1 model."

I opened the bag and saw the two military-issue automatics, a dozen magazines, two boxes of ammo, two hip holsters, and a cleaning kit.

Brenner asked, "You familiar with these?"

Kate replied, "I'm qualified on this."

Right. Very qualified. In fact, she killed someone once with a Colt .45 automatic. I assured Mr. Brenner, "I've been shot at with this gun."

"Good. Kate can give you a quick lesson on how to shoot back."

Wise guy.

I made sure both guns had a loaded magazine in place, and checked that there was a round in each chamber and the safety was on. I left the guns in the bag, but kept it open between us.

I asked Brenner, "Do we get automatic rifles?"

"If you should need to leave Sana'a or Aden."

"Right." I asked, "How's the civil war going here?"

"I don't know." He asked Mohammed, "How's the civil war going?"

"Oh, I do not know, sir. I only know what I read in the newspaper."

Brenner informed us, "The government is down-playing it, and it seems to be contained to the north of here, but for all I know we could wake up one morning and find rebel troops outside the embassy."

"They could be there now," I suggested.

"I think someone in the embassy would have called me."

Mindful of Mohammed, we didn't speak much on the drive into the city, but Brenner spent some time texting on his cell phone. He let us know, "I'm making a report."

"Spell my name right."

He looked at a text message and said to us, "We'll stop at the embassy before going to your apartment."

I didn't ask him for any details. In fact, there wasn't too much we could talk about with Mohammed listening, and anything Brenner said was probably disinformation for Mohammed's consumption.

I'd noticed about five military checkpoints so far, though no one had stopped us, but I wouldn't be surprised if they reported our position.

The lead vehicle and the trail vehicle were keeping fifty-foot intervals, and now and then Brenner would speak to the American drivers on his hand-held radio.

Mohammed said he had to make a cell phone call—"a security requirement," he assured Brenner. I didn't know how much Arabic Brenner understood, but apparently not enough to let Mohammed call his buds and say something like, "Hey, Abdul, where's that ambush supposed to be? Did I miss it?"

Brenner said to Mohammed, "La," which means no.

Mohammed shrugged.

The good road had ended and we were in an

unpleasant slum now. There weren't many vehicles or people on the dark and unmarked streets, some of which were dirt, making them excellent places to bury an explosive device.

Brenner, feeling an urge to be a good host and guide, said, "We're close to the center of Sana'a, the old walled city, which is a World Heritage Site with buildings over a thousand years old and still standing." He informed us, "The city, however, has spread out and the population has grown to nearly two million people, most of whom live in squalid shantytowns like this one, without indoor plumbing or sewers."

In fact, I noticed an aroma strong enough to penetrate the bulletproof SUV, which I guess wasn't gasproof. The good news was that we could all fart freely and no one would notice.

Brenner said, "I'll show you around old Sana'a tomorrow if we have time."

Kate said, "That would be nice."

I had missed seeing old Sana'a last time I was here, and I wouldn't mind missing it again, so I didn't second that. But I'm sure Mohammed made a mental note of it, which was maybe why Brenner said it. Bait has to advertise.

We made a few turns that I could tell were solely for the purpose of varying the route to the embassy. In fact, Brenner said, "We never go the same way twice." Brenner also let us know, "If we get hit, my first shot goes through Mohammed's head. Right, Mohammed?"

Mohammed did not reply.

I glanced at Kate and saw she was handling this well. So maybe this wasn't the right time to say, "I told you so." I'd know the right moment when it arrived.

We were now in the hilly eastern suburbs, a better part of the city, and Brenner said, "Five minutes to the embassy unless we run into an ambush. Then you have to add ten minutes."

Mohammed thought that was funny. It occurred to me that everyone here was crazy. Maybe I was in the right place after all.

We approached the illuminated walls of the American Embassy compound, and I could see Yemeni soldiers sitting on the concrete barricades or lounging in white plastic chairs.

Brenner commented, "These guys are members of an elite unit called Sleepy Company, part of the Slacker Brigade."

I inquired, "Is this their day off?"

"Every day."

The lead vehicle stopped, and one of the soldiers stood and ambled over to the driver.

The embassy walls were about fifteen feet high, except around the gates where an ornate section rose about thirty feet. Embedded in the wall over the gates was the Great Seal of the United States. A welcome sight.

Brenner informed us, "If this place got hit, I'm confident these fine Yemeni soldiers would give their lives to protect the American Embassy."

"They look half dead already."

He laughed.

The electric gates slid open, and two United States Marines with M-16 rifles, wearing body armor and battle dress uniforms, stepped outside as the lead vehicle entered the embassy compound into what's called a sally port—a walled-in pen with another steel gate that opened as the first gate closed.

It was our turn, and as we passed through the gates, two more Marines stood at attention and saluted. Kate, I thought, looked a little more relaxed. In fact, we both removed our flak jackets and threw them in the rear.

We passed through the second checkpoint, and I could see the main embassy building—the chancery—about fifty yards ahead at the end of a wide driveway.

The chancery building was of recent construction, and in the spirit of cultural sensitivity, it looked like a theme park sultan's palace, with big arches, a white stone façade, and lots of fretwork.

The embassy compound, I recalled, was about five or six acres, surrounded by high walls. On the grounds were several ancillary buildings, including the ambassador's residence, Marine guard quarters, housing for embassy staff who lived inside the walled compound, and other structures that housed everything you'd need if you were suddenly cut off from the world, including an electric generator and a water tank. For fun, there was a small movie theater, a swimming pool, and two tennis courts that doubled as a helipad. Also, alcohol was served.

The first time I saw this place, I recalled thinking, "Not bad if you had to live and work here." I also recalled, however, that there had been a few terrorist plots to launch rockets into the embassy, which I recently learned were planned by The Panther himself. No Mideast assignment is perfect. In fact, none of them are. I remarked to Brenner, "I don't see any shell casings."

"The incoming rockets blow them into little pieces."

Kate giggled. I think she found this guy funny. But if *I* had said that, she'd roll her eyes. What's with wives?

We stopped at the big front doors of the palace-like chancery building, and Brenner opened his door and said, "You can leave your luggage in the car."

I opened my door and said to Kate, "Take the guns, leave the cannolis."

Kate got out with the gun bag, which she gave to me to carry, and we followed Brenner up the steps of an arched portico. The three SUVs pulled away, and I saw that our luggage had been deposited at the curb.

Brenner informed us, "You're actually staying here tonight. Just in case Colonel Hakim is on the prowl. Later today, you go to the Sheraton Hotel."

Kate asked, "Why not our apartment?"

Brenner informed us, "There is no apartment." He let us know, "You may not be here long."

Kate asked, "Why not?"

"We need to discuss a few things later."

Right. Like, do we want to be Panther bait? Or do we want to go home?

Kate and I followed Brenner past a Marine guard who saluted. Former Chief Warrant Officer Brenner returned the salute.

The big atrium lobby looked as impressive as it did two and a half years ago, assuring me again that our tax money was well spent.

There was a huge American flag on the wall, and also some photos of the chain of command, starting with the president down to the current ambassador, Edmund James Hull, who had a big smile on his face like he just got the word he was leaving this hellhole. In fact, according to the embassy website, his posting had come to an end. Lucky Eddie. I should be so lucky.

As we passed through the empty lobby, Brenner said

to us, "FYI, Mohammed probably works for Colonel Hakim's Political Security Organization. Or maybe an outfit called the National Security Bureau, which was formed in 2002, after John was here, to patrol the main roads, protect tourists at historical sites, and protect oil fields and foreign oil workers in Yemen." He added, "Sounds good, but they're just a branch of the PSO."

I speculated, "So maybe Mohammed wasn't his real name."

Mr. Brenner further informed us, "The PSO and the NSB have been infiltrated by Al Qaeda from other Arab countries. The Yemeni government knows this and doesn't seem to care." He concluded, "With allies like this, we don't need enemies."

Nuke 'em all.

Brenner stopped and said, "I know you're tired, but before I show you to your room, I thought we'd have a nightcap and meet someone."

"Nightcap is good," I agreed. Meeting someone maybe not so good.

Brenner got on his cell phone and texted. He explained to us, "I can use my regular cell phone in Sana'a, because we have a secure cell station and tower on the embassy roof. But away from here, we have to use satellite phones, which I'll give you later."

I replied, "Same as last time."

"Right. I keep forgetting you were here."

"I don't."

While we waited in the lobby to meet someone, Kate asked Brenner, "Is my office here in the chancery building?"

Brenner replied, "Yes. Most working offices are on the second and third floors. The legal attaché office in

Yemen has just been authorized by a strategic framework agreement, but will not officially open for a week or two."

I said to Kate, "You won't be the first government employee with nothing to do."

Brenner said to Kate, "Your boss will be a man named Howard Fensterman, who arrived a few days ago. He is the chief legal attaché, and you are his assistant." He added, "Mr. Fensterman, like you, is FBI."

Right. Everyone here has two hats, but they keep one in the closet.

Brenner went on, "As you may have heard or read, the ambassador, Edmund James Hull, has just left Yemen and will not be returning."

"Right." And the official reason for his departure was given as personal, which could mean anything from diarrhea to his wife packing up and leaving this shithole.

When you're assigned to a small diplomatic mission in a small, backwater country, you actually get to meet the higher-ups, who are happy to speak to anyone from the States. Even me. So when I was here last time, I got to meet the former ambassador, Her Excellency Barbara Bodine, who had been in Yemen when the *Cole* was bombed. I'd spoken to her here in the embassy on two occasions, and once down in Aden when she'd visited the *Cole* investigators in the Sheraton Hotel and played volleyball with us on the beach—wearing knee-length shorts and a T-shirt. She was an attractive woman, and not a bad person, but I came to share the opinion of the FBI and others here that she had . . . let's say, not handled the *Cole* crisis well. She, too, must have come to that conclusion, and she left in August

2001, about the same time I did. This place can make you or break you.

Brenner said, "I don't know when we can expect the new ambassador, and to be honest, things run better—for us—when the ambassador is on home leave, or quits." He confided, "We have different agendas."

Right. The dips are here to make nice; we are not.

Also, I was getting the impression that Paul Brenner's job went beyond meeting people at the airport. He may actually be DSS, but as I said, everyone here has a second job. Brenner's second job, which I'm sure he volunteered for, was panther hunting. Hey, anything to get out of the embassy. The real issue was, could I work with this guy? Did I have a choice?

Brenner got a text and said to us, "This way."

We followed him to a set of glass doors that I remembered led out to a small covered terrace overlooking a patch of greenery.

Brenner opened one of the doors and said, "We can sit out here. It's a nice evening."

It was actually about five in the morning, and there was nothing nice about it so far, but for a drink I'd sit anywhere.

There was wicker furniture on the terrace, and a man was sitting with his back to us. As we approached, he stood, turned, and said, "Welcome."

It was dark, but I recognized that preppy voice. It was, in fact, Mr. Buckminster Harris.

CHAPTER EIGHTEEN

Bucky!" Kate and I did a group hug with Buck and we all spoke excitedly.

Actually I said, "What the hell are *you* doing here?"

He walked over to us, and I could see him smiling as he said, "I thought I'd continue my class here."

I replied, "I thought we were done."

"You're never done learning, Mr. Corey."

He took Kate's hand and said, "Welcome. I hope you had a pleasant journey."

Kate replied, "We did until we met Colonel Hakim."

"Ah, yes," said Buck. "Colonel Hakim is like goat droppings—he's everywhere."

Kind of funny. Anyway, Buck was wearing one of those white linen jackets that you see in 1930s British colonial movies, and for some reason I had an urge for Kentucky Fried Chicken. I asked him, "Did you take the C-17 direct to Sana'a?"

"I did. Awful flight. Uncomfortable, and the meals come out of a box. And no alcohol." He asked, rhetorically, "Have we become Muslims?" He assured us, "You did better taking the slow route."

"Well," I said, "we're taking the fast route out of here when the time comes."

"You will."

And then I had a mental image of a human remains box in the back of a C-17. Be careful what you wish for.

Buck returned to the subject of Colonel Hakim and said to Kate and me, "Paul texted me about your delay at the airport, and it's nothing to worry about." He added, "We will file a formal complaint."

"Good," I replied, not giving a damn. I said, "Thank you, a scotch and soda would be fine." I thought you'd never ask.

Buck invited us to sit, and he played host and moved to a rolling bar, asking, "And what would Mrs. Corey like?"

"Just water, please."

Brenner, too, wanted water. Wimp.

Buck seemed to be drinking what looked like a gin and tonic with lime, but no little paper umbrella.

So we sat around a cocktail table, lit with a few bug candles, and Buck raised his glass and said, "To a successful mission." We all clinked.

Buck informed us, "I'll be joining you on this assignment, as will Paul."

Mr. Buckminster Harris didn't look like the killer type, but I've been surprised before. And as I suspected, Mr. Brenner was on the team.

Buck reminded us, "I speak fluent Arabic and you'll need that." He informed us, "Paul speaks a little, but it's not conversational. It's giving orders, such as, 'Get out of my way, you son of a goat.'"

Brenner and Harris both got a chuckle out of that, as though they'd shared this joke before. So obviously they knew each other, and obviously Buck worked here, or maybe he shuttled back and forth to D.C. and/or New York. He had me fooled back at 26 Fed, and I was sure it wasn't the last time I'd be fooled here, but it was the last time I'd take it so well.

Buck continued, "There is a fifth person on our team, but he's not here tonight."

Kate asked, "Where is he, who is he, and when can we expect him?"

Buck looked at her and replied, "I can't answer that now."

I said to Buck, "Maybe you can tell us now who the boss is."

"I am," said Buck.

"And may I ask who you work for?"

"The United States government, Mr. Corey, the same as you do."

There's always a CIA guy when it's an overseas whack or snatch job, but as I'd concluded in New York, Buck didn't look or act like any CIA guy I ever had the pleasure of knowing or working with, including the late Mr. Ted Nash. More on Mr. Nash later. Nevertheless, for the record, I asked Buck, "Company man?"

"No."

I looked at Brenner, who shook his head. Well, I wasn't CIA, and I didn't think Kate was, so if everyone was telling the truth then the fifth person was the guy.

I like to know who I'm trusting my life with, so I asked Buck, "SDI?"

He nodded. State Department Intelligence was sort of a gentlemen's game, so that fit.

I looked at Brenner, who said, "DSS, as I said."

He added, "But this job sounded interesting, so I volunteered."

Buck leaned forward and said in a soft voice, "I'm enjoying the cool morning, but we'll need to go inside to speak more freely."

Right. The embassy walls could have electronic ears, though that was unlikely here in Yemen. I mean, this wasn't the Cold War, the Arabs weren't the Russians, and the PSO weren't the KGB. Still, you had to follow security procedures, and not make the common mistake of underestimating these people.

Buck said to us, but really for anyone listening, "We have a number of very good leads on the location of six of the Cole plotters." He winked and continued, "We have good sources inside the Political Security Organization." Then for fun he said, "This Colonel Hakim that you met at the airport is actually on our payroll."

We all got a smile out of that. And if the PSO *was* listening, then poor Colonel Hakim would have electrodes clipped to his nuts in about an hour. Payback's a bitch, Colonel.

Buck, on a roll now, continued, "We've also been able to plant listening devices inside PSO Headquarters."

Okay, Buck, don't push your credibility.

Clearly he was enjoying this game, and you'd never expect Buck Harris to be so delightfully devious, or such a con artist. I had the thought, based on Buck's age and my instincts, that Mr. Ivy League of State Department Intelligence had been an old Cold Warrior, and maybe this new war on terrorism was just a way to occupy his time and his mind at the end of his career. Or, like me, Brenner, and thousands of other men and women since 9/11, he was retired and called back as a contract employee to fill the ranks in the new war.

He asked me, "What are you thinking about, Mr. Corey?"

"You." I inquired, "Do you also speak Russian?"

He replied in Russian.

I didn't know what he said, but I told him, "I'm impressed."

"And well you should be." He informed me, "When the Russians were the foreign power in South Yemen, I spent many years there keeping an eye on them."

"Then you must have spent a lot of time drinking vodka in that Russian brothel."

"Nightclub," he corrected. He smiled at me and said, "You're not as simpleminded or unsophisticated as you pretend to be. In fact, you're very bright and perceptive."

"That's very perceptive of you."

"But stupid people think you're like them, and they lower their guard and say things they shouldn't say."

I replied, "There are probably a hundred people still in jail who made that mistake." I added for Mr. Brenner's benefit, "And a few dead people."

"I'm sure." Buck let me know, "When the idea of asking you to go to Yemen came up, there was some thought that you might not be right for the job. My job, then, was to make an evaluation of your fitness for this assignment, and thus our time together in New York had a dual purpose."

I admitted, "I didn't know I was on a job interview."

Buck smiled again and continued, "I assured the people in Washington who are running this mission that you were not only qualified for this assignment, but that I was certain you would be an invaluable addition to the team, and that I looked forward to working with you."

"Thank you, sir. I will be forever grateful for this opportunity."

I think Buck was tired of smiling at my wit, and he said, "Prove me right." He added, "Our lives now depend on each other."

"Indeed they do." And by the way, when are you going to tell me why I'm *really* here? That my strongest qualification for this job is that The Panther would like to eat my ass?

He turned to Kate and said to her, "You are career FBI and you would be here if ordered, but it's my understanding that you wanted this assignment, and there's no substitute for enthusiasm and spirit."

That's true if you're a cheerleader, but this was a little more complex and dangerous than yelling, "Go, team!"

Buck, understanding that, continued, "Your record speaks for itself, including your excellent work on the embassy bombing in Dar es Salaam, and I also know that you've exhibited a high degree of courage and composure under fire and against great odds."

Kate, to her credit, said nothing, not even mentioning the guy she whacked with the Colt .45. But I was certain Buck already knew about that.

Buck turned his attention back to me and said, "You're a very lucky man."

Then why am I here?

He got his smile on again and said to me, "By the way, you had me thinking about some possible medicinal uses for khat." He added conspiratorially, "Perhaps when we're done with this business, we can explore that further."

Brenner laughed, so I guessed that Buck had shared some of my classroom wit with him.

Buck said to me, "You enlivened my class, Mr. Corey."

I replied, "Your class, Buck, was like waterboarding without the water."

Everyone got a good laugh out of that.

Buck looked at Kate and said, "You've chosen your clothing well, but you need a head scarf." And he had one for her. He presented Kate with a paper-wrapped package that she opened, revealing a long black scarf.

Kate said, "Oh, this is beautiful. Thank you."

Buck said, "It's called a hijab. It's made from a very fine mohair, and it comes from a shop here in Sana'a called Hope in Their Hands." He explained, "It's a non-profit co-op that sells handcrafts made by women throughout the country, and all the proceeds go directly to these women to help them improve their lives and the lives of their children."

"That's very nice," Kate said.

Buck further informed us, "Most of the embassies, expats, and tourists shop there as often as possible." He added, "Good quality, good prices, and a good deed."

Indeed. I asked him, "What did you get for me?"

"Nothing. But I'll give you the name of the best jambiyah shop in Sana'a."

"Thanks. I left mine home."

Kate draped the scarf over her head, and Buck leaned toward her and showed her how to wrap it with a long tail, saying, "Use your left hand to hold it over your face."

"Is that custom?" she asked.

"No, it frees your right hand to draw your gun."

Joke? No.

He assured us, "Sana'a is actually quite safe compared to most of the country. There is very little crime in the city and very few political or religious attacks directed against Westerners. However, it does happen, and there have been a number of plots against the American and British embassies, so you need to be vigilant while you're here."

I asked, "How long will we be in Sana'a?"

"I'm not sure."

Brenner said, "I know you're exhausted, but we'd like to finish this conversation inside."

It was still my turn to carry the gun bag, and we went back into the lobby and up the elevator to where I knew that the SCIF—the Sensitive Compartmented Information Facility—was located.

It was in that room, I was sure, where Buck would mention the small and apparently forgotten fact that Kate and I were here not to find The Panther, but for The Panther to find us.

CHAPTER NINETEEN

The SCIF was on the third and top floor, a window-less and soundproof room, lined with lead and kryptonite or something, impervious to directional listening devices and other types of electronic buggery.

Half of the big, dimly lit room was filled with commo and crypto, and the other half, partitioned with thick glass, was taken up with work stations and a round conference table.

A young woman was attending to the electronics, and when we entered she stood and greeted Brenner and Buck, said hello to Kate and me, then closed the glass door between us.

We'd had a similarly purposed room in the Sheraton Hotel in Aden, but that had been an emptied bedroom in which a lead-lined tent was pitched. The world of spying has come a long way since the days when gentlemen did not read each other's mail, or when it was bad manners to listen at the keyhole or stand outside a building and literally eavesdrop. Today, even pissant countries like Yemen had access to off-the-shelf electronic listening devices and decoding equipment, and the world of secure communication had become a game. The Americans had the best equipment, but you never knew who just developed something better.

Buck Harris broke into my thoughts and assured us, "We can speak freely here."

Right. Except, of course, every word was being recorded.

Brenner got on the intercom and made contact with the Yemenis in the kitchen, and ordered in Arabic.

Buck got down to business and said to me and Kate, "There is something else about this mission that you may not have been told."

I didn't reply.

"Or maybe you *were* told."

Again I didn't reply. He was fishing to see what we knew, and I was waiting to see if he'd actually tell us why we were in Yemen.

Buck glanced at Brenner, then said to Kate and me, "Well, then, I'll fill you in." He hesitated a second, then said, "One of the reasons you were both picked for this assignment is because the CIA has knowledge or belief that Bulus ibn al-Darwish, The Panther, would likely make you a target if he knew you were in Yemen."

"Actually," I replied, "it is the *only* reason we were picked." I said to Kate, "The Panther is looking for payback for The Lion." To be sure she understood, I added, "We are Panther bait."

Kate looked at me, then Buck, then Brenner, and said, "I see."

"Good," I said, "and that makes us the best-qualified people for this job. Just as Tom told us."

She thought about that, then instead of saying, "That bastard," she asked, "Do you think Tom knew that?"

Jeez. Sweetheart, your buddy is a deceitful prick. I said, "Uh...let me think—"

Buck interrupted my sarcasm and said, "None of us knows if he did or not, and it's really a moot point."

Not for me, so I said to Buck and to Brenner, "It would have been nice if Tom Walsh or anybody had given us that information in New York so we could have made an informed decision about whether or not we'd like to be bait for a homicidal terrorist." I asked, "Agreed?"

"Agreed," agreed Buck. "But you're here, you've heard *why* you're here, and now all you have to decide is if you want to stay here or get on that Air Force plane and go home."

Brenner, to help us decide, pointed out, "Does it really matter who is the hunter and who is the hunted? It doesn't change the tactical approach that much."

Actually, it does if you happen to be the hunted. But I understood his point and said, "Right. But we're talking about truth in job advertising here. We're off on the wrong foot."

Brenner replied, "I never lied to you. And I never will."

We looked at each other and my instincts said to believe him.

I looked at Kate, who I knew was annoyed that she was the last to know. As for me, I've gotten used to being lied to by the Feds, but Kate was still capable of being upset by all the bullshit and need-to-know crap.

She said to me, "Apparently you knew about all this, and yet you didn't tell me."

I knew that was coming and I replied, "I wanted you to hear it here. And not from me."

She nodded, but said nothing.

Buck suggested, "We can leave you alone to discuss this."

I reminded him, "Every word is being recorded. You may as well hear it live and not have to play the tape."

Brenner said impatiently, "Just give us your decision, please. You already know in your guts what you want to do. So let us know."

Well, this shouldn't be that tough of a decision. Do we stay in this dangerous shithole and dangle ourselves from a meathook to attract The Panther? Or do we go home and have dinner in a nice restaurant?

There *were* career considerations, but that wasn't too important to me, though it was for Kate.

The bottom line was really about the *Cole* victims, the war on terrorism, this asshole called The Panther, and maybe a little payback for 9/11. When it's only about you, you do what's best for you. But when it's about something bigger than you, you do what's right, not what's best.

I knew why I was here, so I said, "I'm in."

Kate said, without hesitation, "Me, too."

"Good," said Buck. "You won't regret...Well, you might, but with luck and good teamwork, it will be The Panther who regrets your decision, as well as his own bad decisions."

Brenner added, "As I said, now that you're here, we have a good chance of wrapping this up quickly and successfully." He smiled. "And I can get the hell out of here."

Buck seconded that, then looked at us and said, "I was Yale, Class of '65, and in those days, before

Vietnam got ugly, and before we lost confidence in ourselves and lost our innocence, we believed in the school motto—'For God, for Country, for Yale.'" He smiled and said, "Well, Yale doesn't give a damn, and I'm not sure about God, but we do this for our country. Not for the government, but for the people, and for the innocent victims of terrorism. There's no other reason to be here."

Can't argue with that. I mean, the pay is okay, but not good enough to put your life on the line. The ego needs feeding once in a while, but my ego was already stuffed. Adventure and danger are interesting, but I did that every day. So what was left to motivate people like me? Maybe Buck had the simple but rarely spoken answer: patriotism. But also something else that is usually not said in polite American society, and I said to Buck, "Don't forget revenge."

He nodded and said, "With the Soviets, I never thought of revenge. But now I think about it often."

Brenner agreed, "Revenge is good."

Kate said, "I'll stick to God and country."

There was a buzz on the intercom, and Brenner said, "Breakfast. Then we can go over the plan."

It was good to hear that there was a plan. I was sure I wasn't going to like the plan, but the bait never does.

CHAPTER TWENTY

The SCIF was off-limits to Yemenis, so Brenner left to meet the kitchen guy in the hallway.

I took the opportunity to ask Buck, "What are *his* qualifications for this job?"

Buck replied, "Paul is a Vietnam vet—two tours, one as a combat infantryman, one as a military police-man. He's been decorated for bravery, and he has a B.S. in criminal justice. He's also been to post-war Vietnam on a clandestine mission." He added, "Forget that."

"And how does all that qualify him for *this* mission?"

Buck seemed a little impatient with me and replied, "He understands police work, as you do, and what we're doing here is basically looking for a fugitive from justice." He added, "Also, Paul has been shot at, so if that happens here, he knows how to shoot back."

"All right." Basically, Paul Brenner was no more qualified for a Black Ops job than I was—but they weren't bad qualifications. And I had one up on him—I had a target on my back. Who the hell put this together?

Kate said, "I think we have a good team so far."

Buck replied to her, "I know we do. And when we apprehend this suspect, then you, as an FBI agent with arrest powers, and as a legal attaché, will make the formal arrest in the name of the people and the government of the United States."

Kate said, "I'm looking forward to that."

Me, too. Then I'll put a bullet in his head and save everyone a lot of trouble.

Brenner returned pushing a cart on which was tea, coffee, and fresh-baked muffins.

We helped ourselves, and Buck informed us, "Yemen is where mocha coffee originated." He asked me, "How is that?"

"It was probably good last week."

We were sitting again and Buck said, "I'll outline some of what we're thinking, but our fifth team member has a more detailed plan."

Well, if this was a CIA plan—which it was—then it was probably over-planned, over-thought, and over-complicated. But I'd keep an open mind. My concern was that this plan might rely too much on Mr. and Mrs. Corey's roles as red meat.

Buck began, "First, we're positive that Bulus ibn al-Darwish is somewhere in Yemen. That's why we're here. What we don't know is if he knows that John Corey and Kate Mayfield of Lion fame are also here. And third, we can't be certain that The Panther would make an attempt on your lives if he knew that." He added, "But we'll make those assumptions, based on CIA information."

Brenner said, "As for The Panther knowing you're in Yemen, the names of all Americans coming through a port of entry are considered a saleable commodity—especially Americans traveling on a diplomatic passport. Those names go to the government, of course, and to the local police and the PSO. And as I told you, the PSO is infiltrated with Al Qaeda members and sympathizers, so Al Qaeda knowing you're here is not a problem."

Sounded like a problem to me. But I guess that was the whole idea.

Buck picked up the ball and continued, "We're hoping and assuming that AQAP—Al Qaeda in the Arabian Peninsula—is competent enough to identify the arriving John Corey and Katherine Mayfield Corey as people whom they'd like to kill."

"God, I hope so."

Even Kate laughed. I mean, as I said, you have to laugh.

Kate had a good question and asked, "Don't you think Al Qaeda will suspect that this is a setup to lure The Panther into a trap?"

Buck reminded us, "You both have good cover and plausible reasons to be here. John has returned to continue with the *Cole* investigation. Kate has been assigned to our new Legal Affairs Office." He added, "It's not unusual to assign a husband and wife together when possible. Hopefully, Al Qaeda will not think much beyond that."

Kate wasn't sure and said, "It seems too pat."

Buck got philosophical, or maybe metaphorical, and asked, "Does the panther or the lion know that the meat is a trap?" He answered his own rhetorical question and said, "I think he does on some instinctive level. Have you seen those wildlife documentaries where the big cat approaches the live bait—the tethered goat or lamb? He doesn't charge at the animal. He stalks it and approaches with caution. But the important thing is that he goes for it. Every time. Why? Because he's hungry and because he's at the top of the food chain and he's strong and confident." Buck paused then said, "And then he's trapped. Or dead."

I asked, "What happened to the goat?"

Buck replied, "Who cares? Goats are expendable. But people are not." He assured us, "You'll always be covered. More importantly, you can both think for yourselves and defend yourselves. Goats and lambs can't."

I looked at my watch and asked, "Can we still make that flight?"

Buck took this as a joke, smiled, and didn't reply.

Brenner said to Kate and me, "You're both free to modify any final plan if you think it's too risky."

Goes without saying. Also, I had the thought that the CIA would in fact be okay with The Panther eating the goat if it meant getting The Panther. Paranoid? Maybe. But we'd already been lied to, and lies are like cockroaches—if you see one, there are more.

Buck continued, "Al Qaeda in Yemen, like us in Yemen, are small in numbers. They have perhaps four or five hundred hard-core members. But they also have thousands of sympathizers and active supporters, including, as I said, inside the PSO, and also inside the army, the police, and probably the government."

I inquired, "How many sympathizers and supporters do we have in Yemen?"

"Two," replied Buck. "The lady who runs the craft shop and the man who cuts my hair—and I'm not sure about him."

Good one, Buck.

He continued, "But as I told you in New York, among the general population there is not an attitudinal animosity here against the West or Americans. But neither can we expect any help from the average citizen, except maybe from a Jew or Christian. Also, some tribes can be rented on a short-term lease with an unknown expiration date."

Brenner said to us, "The sheiks who are tribal chieftains are mostly clients of the Saudi government, and our arrangements and payments to the tribes go through the Saudi royal family. The Saudis are our allies and they've been helpful—except when they're not."

Buck reminded us, "As I said in New York in answer to Kate's question, the tribes do not like Al Qaeda, and the feeling is mutual. However, a few tribes have now and then accepted Al Qaeda money—or Al Qaeda favors—so we can't always trust them."

I observed, "It sounds like the tribes are part of the plan."

Buck replied, "They have to be. They control most of the countryside."

Kate asked, "Does that mean we're going into the tribal lands?"

Brenner replied, "That's the plan." He explained, "The cities and towns are where the government security forces are strongest, and we don't want any interference from them, and we don't want to get into a shooting match with Al Qaeda in a complicated urban setting." He further explained, "In the hinterlands we have the advantage of tribal help, or at least tribal neutrality. Also we have the big advantage of Predator drones armed with Hellfire missiles."

Right. I always knew this would play out in Indian Territory, but I asked, "How do we know The Panther will meet us on that turf?"

"We don't," Brenner replied, "but if he wants you, he'll go where you are."

"We're in Sana'a," I reminded him.

Brenner replied, "As I indicated, we're not staying here." He further informed us, "In a day or so, we're traveling by road to Aden, and with luck we'll run into trouble on the way."

It seemed to me that Paul Brenner's idea of good luck and my idea of good luck were not the same.

Buck let us know, "I'm not certain that The Panther himself would lead a frontal attack on our convoy, but it's possible he would, and also possible that we can capture someone who knows where he is."

Right. You bring the water, I'll bring the board.

Buck continued, "Also, we don't know if The Panther would like to kill you or capture you." He said, unnecessarily, "Killing is easier, but capturing both of you would be a real coup for Al Qaeda and The Panther. A major humiliation for the U.S."

"Not to mention a major inconvenience for me and Kate." I observed, "I see you've thought this out, but I'm not hearing an operational plan that's based on concrete information."

Buck replied, "As I said, our fifth team member will provide that."

"Okay."

Buck also said, "It's my understanding, Mr. Corey, that you're not plan-oriented. That you shoot from the hip and make it up as you go. So you shouldn't be too concerned about a detailed plan." He added, "In fact, that's one of the reasons you were invited to be here."

"Right." The other reason was the same reason that the turkey is invited to Thanksgiving dinner. I said, "I'm flexible."

Kate, in a rare instance of agreeing with her husband, said, "John is very good at reading a situation and changing tactics on a dime." She added, "But sometimes he bends the rules."

That's my girl.

Brenner and Buck made a mental note of that, and then Brenner continued, "We don't want to run this operation from the embassy, which can cause problems. So Aden will be our operational base. From there, we'll go where we think we have to go. Also, Aden is where Al Qaeda has many eyes and ears." He looked at me and said, "You remember that, and it hasn't changed much. Point is, if we're at the Sheraton in Aden, The Panther will know it. Also, Aden is where you're supposed to be for the *Cole* investigation."

"Got it."

So we spent the next ten minutes talking this out, and I was alert despite the lack of sleep. Maybe it was the mocha coffee. Maybe the subject matter. War and talk of war focuses your mind and body like nothing else can, except maybe sex.

It occurred to me that Buck and Brenner, via the CIA, knew something I didn't know—like hard information from a radio or satellite phone intercept, or a paid informant, or a vigorously interrogated detainee— that indeed Al Qaeda already knew Kate and I were here, and that The Panther would strike.

It also occurred to me that the State Department's

application for our visa—before we even knew we were coming to Yemen—was the trigger that set Al Qaeda in motion, long before we landed at Sana'a Airport. In any case, whatever information the CIA had was not necessarily going to be shared with Mr. and Mrs. Corey at this time. And whatever information The Panther had would be shared with us at a time and place of his choosing.

Buck and Brenner wrapped it up and Buck said, "You must be exhausted. So I thank you for your attention." He smiled and said, "I hope this was more interesting than my class in New York."

I assured him it was, except for the info on khat.

Before we retired to our rooms, I said, "One thing that's bugging me—Bulus ibn al-Darwish. We haven't focused on him, and I'm trying to figure out why an American-born Muslim would defect *from* America. I mean, most defectors defect *to* America. Right? What's motivating this guy? What's his problem?"

Brenner replied, "I don't know, and I'm not sure I care. But when we get him into an interrogation room, you can ask him."

I replied, "At that point I don't care either. But if we knew *now* why he turned against his country, and if we could get into his head a little, it might help us predict what he'll do and what his strengths and weaknesses are."

Buck informed us, "In fact, the CIA has a psychological profile on him that we'll see shortly, and that might be helpful."

"Good." It takes crazy to know crazy. Not that I meant the CIA was crazy. Or did I?

Buck asked me, "Are you aware that the suspect's

parents are bringing suit in Federal court to have their
son removed from the CIA kill list?"

"I am."

Mr. Brenner said, "That's one reason why we need
to make every effort to take him alive."

Actually, it was a good reason to whack him quickly,
before some Federal judge intervened.

I looked at Brenner, who motioned toward the ceiling to remind me that we were being recorded. Then
Paul Brenner made a cutting motion across his throat.

Great minds think alike. I was starting to like
this guy.

CHAPTER TWENTY-ONE

Brenner said the guest house in the embassy was full, but we could get a few hours' sleep in the chancery building before going to the Sheraton, and he showed us to a bedroom on the second floor where our luggage had been delivered.

He informed us, "We had to convert a few offices here in the chancery into sleeping quarters." He explained, "If the threat level goes up, embassy personnel who live outside the compound are required to move into the compound, so it gets crowded inside the fort until it blows over."

I asked him, "Is that why the guest house is full?"

"It is."

Well, I was glad we were getting out of Sana'a. Unfortunately, we were going to Aden.

Anyway, the room looked comfortable enough for an embassy staffer on the lam from psychotic jihadists. Two stars.

Brenner informed us, "The bathroom is down the hall."

One star.

Brenner told us, "You'll check in at the Sana'a Sheraton this afternoon." He assured us, "It's heavily guarded, and more comfortable than here."

"Also," I added, "you'd like us out there to see if we come to the attention of the person we're looking for."

"That is correct." He also told us, "I'll have satellite phones for you later, but meanwhile feel free to use the room phone, though as I remind everyone, we record everything for security purposes, and the PSO records for their own purposes. And in answer to your next question, there are no electronic bugs in your room— only real bugs." He smiled.

I believed him, because if Kate and I found a listening device in our bedroom, we all knew that would be the end of our Yemen visit.

Kate asked him, "Do you live in the embassy?"

"No. I have an apartment not far from here."

"And are you staying there even though the alert level is elevated?"

He smiled. "I'd rather take my chances with terrorists than living with State Department people."

Me, too.

Kate also asked him, "Are you alone here?"

He looked at her and replied, "I am."

"Sorry...I didn't mean to ask a personal question."

He assured her, "Over the next few weeks or months we'll learn a lot about each other." He let us know, "There's someone back in the States."

He changed the subject and said, "I'd like us to meet in the lobby at, let's say, eleven A.M. Is that good?"

Kate and I said it was.

He informed us, "There is a non-denominational

church service at eleven in the parlor if you'd like to attend."

Kate thought that would be nice, and I was trying to think of a reason why it wasn't.

Brenner said, "You can decide when you come down." He advised us, "Bring your luggage down and we'll go over to the Sheraton, then if you'd like we'll take a walk around town." He smiled. "Hopefully someone will try to kill or kidnap us."

Especially if Mohammed dropped a dime on us. Maybe we should go to church instead.

He reminded us, "Sana'a is relatively safe. But bring your guns."

Goes without saying.

He also advised us, "If you hear a siren, move immediately to the basement."

"Wine tasting?" I asked.

He thought that was funny. I think I was one up on him.

He said, "There is a safe room down there. Blast-proof. Use the stairs, not the elevator, and come as you are." He reminded us, "Take your guns with you."

He gave us instructions on how to find the safe room—follow everyone else—and he wished us a good sleep and left.

Kate said, "I didn't know what to expect here, but I wasn't expecting this."

"Meaning?"

"I don't know...I guess I didn't understand the security situation."

"Sure you did."

"I guess...also, I thought we'd have an apartment, then I'd spend some time in my office..."

I reminded her, "You're not really the legal attaché."

She nodded and said, "I was surprised to see Buck here and surprised to discover that we were bait for The Panther."

"Were you?"

"Maybe not." She asked me, "How did you know about that?"

I was almost certain the room wasn't bugged, but I didn't want to say "Al Rasul," so I said, "I figured it out," which was partly true. I told her, "So did you."

She nodded again, then asked me, "What do you think of Paul?"

"I feel the beginning of a beautiful friendship."

She said, "I like him and I trust him."

"Let's see how he and Buck handle the CIA guy. That could be the game changer."

She advised me, "Don't let your past experiences with the Agency prejudice you."

"Of course not. My mind is open to a miracle."

I took both Colt .45s out of the bag and asked Kate, "Which one would you like?"

"They're the same, John."

"The serial numbers are different."

She didn't reply so I threw both guns on the bed.

Kate looked around the room, then out the window. The sky was getting light, and she said, "I can see the city from here. We're on a hill."

"Right." And in the surrounding hills were guys with mortars and rocket launchers who could target this big compound with their eyes closed.

As though reading my mind, Kate asked me, "If I hear the siren, would you like me to wake you, or let you sleep?"

Do we need a third wiseass? I said, "The explosions will wake me."

I went to the phone on the nightstand and picked up the receiver.

Kate asked, "Who are you calling?"

"Tom."

"It's"—she looked at her watch—"past eleven P.M. there."

"The FBI never sleeps." I dialed zero and got the embassy operator. I gave him Walsh's cell phone number and he said to me, "This is not a secure—"

"Right."

He put the call through, and I got Tom Walsh's voice mail. I said, "Tom, John here. I thought you'd be waiting up for my call. Well, as you may have already heard, we're here. And guess what we just found out? I can't say because it's not a secure phone, but you know what I'm talking about. Cat food, Tom. This is exciting and I wanted to thank you for this opportunity." To mess with his head, I added, "We may take the next flight out and thank you in person. Don't give away our desks." I hung up.

Kate asked rhetorically, "Was that necessary?"

"Tom wanted to hear from us."

She reminded me, "We have no business with Tom anymore and vice versa."

"That was a personal call."

She had no further thoughts on that subject, and she began to undress, so I did, too. There didn't seem to be a closet in the room, so we threw our clothes on a chair, and I put a gun on each nightstand.

Kate collapsed on the bed, naked, and said, "We need to burn those clothes. And I need a shower."

"Down the hall." I reminded her, "If we hear the siren, it's come as you are to the safe room."

She smiled and said, "That could be fun."

I asked, "Is the bed hard?"

"No."

"Well, I am."

"Oh...my goodness. How can you think about sex now?"

"That's a silly question from a naked lady."

She smiled again, then motioned me to hop aboard.

CHAPTER TWENTY-TWO

Kate and I came down to the atrium lobby with our luggage, dressed in our Sunday best—Kate in a tan pantsuit, and me in fresh khaki trousers, black blazer, and another Dior shirt. Onward Christian Dior.

For footwear, we both had black running shoes; the mark of the urban guerrilla. To accessorize, we carried our Colt .45s—Kate's under her loose top, and mine discreetly strapped to my pants belt. Kate was also wearing her new scarf draped over her shoulders, and my outfit would be complete when I bought a jambiyah.

Paul Brenner, wearing his blue windbreaker, black pants, and a sports shirt, was waiting for us in the lobby, and he had another man with him—a guy in his early forties, sporting a mustache and wearing a dark suit, who I thought might be our CIA guy. But Brenner said, "This is Howard Fensterman, the new legal attaché."

Kate and I shook hands with Mr. Fensterman, who said to Kate, "I'm looking forward to working with you."

Kate replied, "I'm excited about opening the new office."

So maybe Kate really was the assistant legat, and I was going down to Aden to join the *Cole* investigation. Great. Better than Panther bait.

But Mr. Fensterman cleared that up by saying, "I'll be providing any legal assistance you might need for your mission in Yemen. Feel free to call me when you leave Sana'a if you have any questions or need any clarifications regarding procedures."

"Thank you," said Kate.

I mean, did George Patton have a lawyer on his staff? Hey, Counselor, can the Third Army cross the Rhine yet? Are we still waiting for a legal opinion?

Mr. Fensterman asked us to call him Howard and continued, "I'm working closely with State and Justice regarding extradition procedures, and I'm being kept up-to-date by Justice regarding the Federal lawsuit brought by the suspect's parents."

I said, "I hope you're also working on covering our asses if by chance the suspect should meet an untimely end during his apprehension."

Howard replied, "I'll address that if and when it occurs." He added, "It's all a little complicated because, as you know, the suspect is an American citizen." He reminded us, "He has Constitutional rights."

"Of course." And I had the answer to all those pesky rights on my hip.

Howard informed us, "I'm about to attend the church service in the parlor. Would you like to join me?"

"No," I replied. "We're carrying guns, and we're pagans."

"That's all right," Howard assured us. "I'm Jewish."

Huh?

Howard told us, "Friday night I went to one of the mosques that allows non-believers to enter. Saturday, I went to services in the home of a Yemeni Jew. So today I'm going to the Christian service here in the embassy."

I asked him, "Are you very spiritual?" Or confused? Or maybe covering all your bases?

He replied, "The three religions have much in common." He also said, "I'm bored."

Try khat.

Howard really wanted company, and he also wanted to show Kate her office after the service. Kate didn't want to disappoint her new boss, and Brenner was in no hurry to get to the hotel, so Kate, I, and Brenner accompanied Howard to the parlor.

The big, sunlit room was filled with about fifty people—embassy staffers and spouses and about ten uniformed Marines. Everyone was sitting on the upholstered furniture or in folding chairs, and they were all dressed nicely. The American taxpayers, who were there in spirit, had provided vases of cut flowers.

The preacher, or whoever he was, was standing at a lectern wearing a celestial blue suit, and he greeted us and introduced himself as Ed Peters, adding, "It's always good to see new faces, and I'm happy to see Mr. Brenner."

As we searched for empty seats, I saw Buck sitting comfortably in an armchair, still wearing his white jacket. I found a folding chair in the rear on which was a photocopied program of only four pages. Thank God.

Mr. Peters began, "Welcome to all who slept late and missed the service in the British Embassy."

A few chuckles.

It occurred to me that maybe half of these people never went to church back home, but when you're in weird-land you get religion, or maybe you just want to accentuate the difference between you and the people on the other side of the embassy walls. How's that for insightful analysis?

Mr. Peters asked us to rise to sing "Rock of Ages," the words to which were in the program. There was a baby grand in the parlor, and a nice lady in a floral dress tickled the ivories.

I could see Kate standing near the window and she seemed angelic singing in the sunlight with a post-coital glow.

Buck was singing without looking at his program, and Howard was belting out the hymn like he was auditioning for the church choir. Brenner was two seats away from me and he was moving his lips like he was reading an eye chart. As for me, I hummed along.

Anyway, we got through that, sat, and Mr. Peters read from the Old Testament, the First Book of Kings: *When the Queen of Sheba heard of the fame of Solomon . . . she came to test him with hard questions.* And my favorite: *King Solomon loved many strange women.* And from the New Testament, Matthew: *Ye shall hear of wars and rumors of wars.*

We sang two more hymns and recited two prayers, then Mr. Peters gave a talk or homily about the sacrifices we were all making here in the service of the American people, and about the difficult times we lived in.

He also urged us to see this time as a growing and learning experience, and he predicted that when we looked back on our service in Yemen, we would all come to appreciate our days in this shithole. But he used another word.

Mr. Peters went on a bit about reaching out to the Yemeni people, about being guests here, and about tolerance of the host country even though it was fucked up beyond all understanding. Or words to that effect.

According to my program there was no Holy Communion, so we were basically finished as soon as this guy wrapped it up. Is that a siren I hear?

But then Mr. Peters asked for a minute of silent prayer for our military and civilian personnel who were serving in Iraq, Afghanistan, and all over the world, including this hellhole. Amen to that.

After the minute of silence, Mr. Peters invited us all to join him in the lobby for refreshments and fellowship. He concluded, "Go in peace."

That's not why I was here, but I needed a cup of coffee, so Kate and I, along with Brenner and Howard Fensterman, went to the lobby and mingled.

There was an employee cafeteria off the lobby that provided what looked like good approximations of American cookies and cakes. They even had bagels, which made me homesick.

The congregants of the First and Only Church of Jesus Christ in Sana'a seemed like nice people. Among them were not only embassy staffers and a few spouses, but also expats and others who were seeking company, God, or a small piece of America. Probably all three.

I noticed there were no children—a sure sign that this was a dangerous place.

Life in the Foreign Service was unlike any other overseas experience, except maybe the military or being a missionary. How do people do this? But then I started thinking about Paul Brenner and the Diplomatic Security Service. Maybe that's the job I should ask for if we got our man. A few years in Paris, London, or Rome. Kate would be a legat. Something to think about.

I chatted with a few of the Marines and they were all very professional and called me "sir," and they seemed gung-ho and mission-oriented. They assured me that if the embassy were attacked, the twenty Marines and ten DSS guys could hold the fort until the Yemeni Army arrived. One guy explained, "Then we'd have new targets—the Yemeni Army." Everyone laughed. Everyone here was nuts.

I moved over to Buck, who was in his element here, mingling with his Foreign Service brothers and sisters, most of whom I'm sure shared his background and some of whom also had funny first names, like Livingston, Kelvin, and Winthrop—a.k.a. Livie, Kel, and Winnie. You can't make this up.

Buck said to me, sotto voce, "There was an Al Qaeda attack near Marib early this morning."

I wasn't sure where Marib was, but I hoped it wasn't too close to the embassy lobby.

Buck continued, "The target was an oil installation partly owned by Hunt—an American company." He let me know, "Security forces killed six of the attackers and took one wounded prisoner who said he was Al Qaeda." He added, "The Company is questioning the prisoner about our man."

The oil company? No, the CIA. I asked, "Where is Marib?"

"About two hundred kilometers east of here." Buck speculated, "This could be a sign that Al Qaeda is beginning attacks against American and Western interests in Yemen." He added, "Al Qaeda attacks are rarely isolated."

"Right."

He also informed me, "The al-Houthi rebels have ambushed a military convoy north of here."

"Any good news this morning?"

"Yes. I flew in with a fresh shipment of Boodles and dry vermouth. Martinis tonight."

Make mine a double, hold the vermouth.

Anyway, I finally got my coffee and a bagel with cream cheese, and as I was munching, Mr. Peters came up to me and said, "Welcome to Sana'a."

"Thanks. Good service, Padre." Short.

He informed me, "I'm a lay preacher. Non-denominational."

"Me, too."

He thought that was funny and continued, "My weekday job is chief of DSS here."

"Yeah? How do I get a DSS job?"

"Apply. We're short-staffed all over the Mideast. No one wants the job. Everyone wants Paris, London, and Rome."

"Wimps."

He informed me, "Paul is my second in command. He's a good man."

"Right."

"Hate to lose him."

"Where's he going?"

"With you. Then home."

I didn't know how much Peters knew, so I didn't respond.

Mr. Peters said he wanted me to meet someone, and

he led me over to a big guy who looked like a weight-lifter wearing his First Holy Communion suit.

Peters said to me, "This is John Zamoiski, DSS. You might remember him from the airport."

"Right." One of the guys in the lead car.

We shook and the guy gripped my hand like it was the last cold beer in hell.

John Zamoiski said, "Call me Zamo."

"Okay. Call me John." Later we'll switch.

Mr. Peters said to me, "Zamo will be with you when you drive to Aden."

"Good."

"He'll also be with you if you go into the Badlands."

"The more the merrier."

Mr. Peters continued, "Zamo was an Army sniper in Afghanistan."

I looked at Zamo. He still had a military haircut— you don't want hair blocking your crosshairs—and a face that didn't move much. He wasn't more than thirty, and I noticed that his dark eyes never blinked. He seemed to be a man of few words, but he had Mr. Peters to speak for him, and Peters said, "Zamo is also a martial arts expert."

"You draw soldiers?" I asked.

His mouth turned up in a smile. He liked me. Good boy, Zamo. *Sit!*

Brenner joined us and suggested that we get moving. He said to Zamo, "You'll accompany us to the Sheraton."

Zamo finished eating his coffee cup and nodded.

I guess Zamo was the team sniper. It's good to have a trained killer on the team. And a churchgoer at that.

Thinking back on our time since we landed, I had

the same feeling that I'd had the last time I was here; I'd stepped through the looking glass and everyone on this side was crazy, and they'd been crazy for so long that they made sense to one another, but not to anyone who just arrived from Earth.

Anyway, Brenner and I found Kate, who was with a group that included Howard, and I said to her, "Time to go."

Howard reminded us, "I wanted to show Kate her office."

Brenner suggested, "Tomorrow would be good."

I wasn't sure of the pecking order here, but in places like this, security guys had some weight, so Howard said, "Fine. See you at nine." He added, "I need to give you a copy of the arrest warrant for the suspect."

I asked Howard, "Can I have a copy of the CIA kill order?"

Howard didn't reply.

Anyway, Kate and I collected our luggage, and we met Brenner out front where a single Land Cruiser was waiting for us. It was a bright, sunny day, but already getting hot.

Kate said, "What a beautiful day." She asked me, "Isn't this better than New York in February?"

"No."

Zamo loaded our luggage in the rear, then slid behind the wheel. Brenner got in the front and Kate and I sat in the back.

I asked, "Where's Mohammed?"

Brenner replied, "Getting fitted for a suicide belt."

Funny. I was really getting into this place.

So off we went, and I commented that there was no lead or trail vehicle. Brenner said, "It's only about six hundred yards to the Sheraton and we don't want to attract undue attention on the street or at the hotel."

Right. So only one armored Land Cruiser, two armed security men, and two armed passengers. No one will notice.

We got to the outer gates, which slid open, and we were on the street. The Yemeni soldiers were still sitting around, at the top of their game.

Brenner and Zamo had their guns in their laps, so Kate and I did the same.

Across the way from the embassy I saw another walled and guarded compound that I remembered from last time, called Tourist City for some reason, though it was actually a complex of apartment houses and shops for resident and transient Westerners, some of whom were staff from the various embassies. Also living in Tourist City were aid workers and a few poor bastards who were transferred here for business, mostly the oil. This was probably where Kate and I would have lived if we were staying in Sana'a.

Yemenis, I recalled, were not allowed in Tourist City, except as trusted servants, though it was rumored that a few of these servants were Al Qaeda, which you'd expect. In my opinion, it was the least safe place in Sana'a; a terrorist attack waiting to happen.

The best thing about Tourist City was the Russia Club, owned and operated by two entrepreneurial gentlemen from Moscow whose personal mission it was to bring alcohol, drugs, and hookers to Yemen, thereby spreading the benefits of European civilization to this benighted nation. The Russia Club had a second location in Aden, as Buck mentioned in his class, and I'd been invited to both clubs on my last trip to Yemen, but I'd declined. Honest.

We turned right onto a narrow, tree-shaded road, and I asked, "If I roll down my window, will someone lob a grenade in?"

"Probably," replied Brenner. "Just throw it back."

We all got a laugh at that.

This was going to be a fun assignment.

CHAPTER TWENTY-THREE

Brenner passed us a nylon bag, saying, "Two satellite phones with chargers, and two hand-held radios. The sat-phones are programmed with the speed dial numbers you'll need. The radios have a selection dial for twenty frequencies, but we are using only two—zone one and zone two. There's also a list of radio call signs in the bag." He informed us, "The radios have a short distance—basically point to point—because we don't have antennas or repeaters here."

I asked him, "Is our absent team member programmed?"

"Not yet." He instructed us, "If death or capture seems imminent, destroy the phones and radios." He suggested, "A bullet will do it."

If I have a bullet left, I'm not shooting my phone.

Brenner also informed us, "Our radio call sign is Clean Sweep." He added, "This has some significance regarding the USS *Cole*." He explained, "Warships returning to port after an engagement often tied a broom to their mast which signaled 'Clean Sweep.' In other words, 'We got the bastards.'" Brenner further informed us, "The name of this operation is also Clean Sweep."

Every operation needs a code name, something that doesn't give the enemy any info. Clean Sweep was good. Avenge the *Cole*.

Paul Brenner, man of many bags, passed us another bag, a big blue one, and said, "Two Kevlar vests. Size should be okay."

I asked, "Is that it for the bags?"

"I was going to give you a bag of cookies, but now I'm not."

Kate laughed.

As we continued on, Brenner informed us, "This neighborhood is where the U.S. and U.K. embassy people live who don't live in the embassy compound, or in Tourist City."

Kate inquired, "Is this where you live?"

"No, I live near the khat souk. Not too far from here."

Kate processed that for a second and said, "Khat souk...?"

"Biggest open-air drug market in the world." He assured us, "They sell other things—chickens, cows, firewood, and guns."

"So," I speculated, "you can get high, buy a cow, shoot it, and cook it, all right there."

"That's what I do most Saturday nights."

We pulled into a circular drive and headed toward the portico of the Sheraton, which had a mock Mideastern façade, sort of like the embassy.

I'd spent two nights in this Sheraton on my last visit to Sana'a, which I had thought was my last visit to Sana'a.

Zamo stayed with the vehicle, and Brenner, Kate, and I got out and moved toward the front doors where two men in blue camouflage fatigues and blue berets stood with AK-47s. Brenner said, "They're NSB guys—National Security Bureau." He added, "Tonight they could be Al Qaeda."

"Should we tip them?"

We entered the air-conditioned lobby, and Kate and I went to the front desk, while Brenner stood near the doors. The check-in clerk said, "Welcome, sir and lady."

"Thank you, man."

We gave him our passports, and he looked us up on the computer, then assured us, "You have beautiful mountain view room. See sunrise."

"Great." And at night we can see the mortar flashes before the incoming rounds hit the building.

He also said, "You stay with us four nights."

News to me.

The hotel charges were pre-paid, though the clerk didn't know by whom. And neither did I. There's an old saying in this business—"It's not important to know who fired the bullet; it's important to know who paid for it."

If I had to guess, I'd say it was the Agency, a.k.a. the Company, not the embassy or the FBI who was paying for all this. Which brought me to the Golden Rule— whoever has the gold makes the rules.

As the clerk photocopied our passports and visas, he told us about the hotel's amenities—fitness center, safe deposit boxes for our guns, medical services if we got wounded, pool, tennis courts, cocktail lounge, and so forth.

"Can I chew khat by the pool?"

"Yes. But please not to spit."

Sounded reasonable.

Brenner came over to us and said, "You can stay here, or as I mentioned last night, we can take a walk in the Old City."

"Thanks, but—"

Kate piped in, "I'd love to see the Old City."

"Good. I'll meet you here in the lobby. How about half an hour?"

How about never? Does that work for you?

Kate said, "See you then."

Brenner suggested, "Guns and Kevlar." He also said to Kate, "And your scarf, and a camera if you have one."

We followed the bellhop to the elevators, where an NSB guy with an AK-47 sat in a white plastic chair contemplating his navel. We rode up to the fifth floor of the six-story building, which put a floor between us and incoming.

Our room was nice, and it did indeed have a mountain view and a minibar, and even a bathroom. Three stars. Four if the window was bulletproof.

I tipped the bellhop two bucks, and as Kate and I unpacked, I said to her, "We could get into a contact situation with Al Qaeda, but not with The Panther." I added, "This is not like The Lion, who personally wanted to kill us."

She said, "I'm assuming, as Buck and Paul mentioned, that the CIA knows something we don't know."

"They always do," I agreed.

Well, now that I was here, I was looking forward to the job. But something was bothering me, something I'd thought about back in New York, and it had to do with the CIA. They were devious, not team players, and they had their own agenda. And those were their good points.

More importantly, they had long memories, and they were into payback. Their official company motto was, "And ye shall know the truth and the truth shall set you free." And their unofficial mission statement, also biblical, was, "An eye for an eye, a tooth for a tooth." I'm all for that, except if it's my eye or tooth that they want.

And why, you ask, would the CIA want to get even with me or with Kate? Well, once upon a time, Kate and I had inadvertently screwed up a major CIA plan—Operation Wild Fire—that, if it had been successful, would have turned Sana'a and other Islamic cities into nuclear ash. The plan was clever, diabolical, illegal, and very dangerous to human life on earth. Other than that, it was a good plan. Actually, it wasn't.

But it didn't matter what I thought—as I said, Kate and I got caught in the middle of it, and without going into details, Kate and I found ourselves looking down the barrel of a Glock held by the previously mentioned Mr. Ted Nash, CIA officer, and I think Kate's one-time lover, which may or may not be relevant to what happened next. Bottom line, Kate was a half second quicker than Ted, and Ted was dead. Self-defense. Except for the next seven shots. But the police and FBI cleared her of excessive target practice. The CIA, however, did not, and they were not happy.

I didn't worry too much about Kate or me being on a CIA kill list—I mean, I *thought* about it, but it had been a year and a half since the incident, and officially it was over, and the CIA had been advised that they should forget it. But there's only one way to get off a CIA kill list.

Back in the States, it would be unlikely that Kate or I would meet with an unfortunate accident. But overseas, especially in a place like this where the CIA is its own law, it was quite possible that John Corey and Kate Mayfield could have that unfortunate accident. That is, if The Panther didn't get us first. A win-win for the Agency would be dead Panther, dead John, and dead Kate—and all these deaths obscured by the fog of war.

Crazy, I know. I shouldn't even be *thinking* like this. I mean, yeah, this was a CIA operation, and yes, the Agency wanted me and Kate in Yemen—but not to settle an old score. No, they wanted us in Yemen to lure The Panther into a trap; not us into a trap. Right?

Anyway, I didn't think I should share these thoughts with Kate at this time. Maybe I'd wait until we met our CIA guy and see if I picked up on anything that didn't smell right.

Kate asked me, "What are you thinking about?"

"The CIA wants to kill us." No, I didn't say that. I said, "The CIA has been taken to task for failing to predict, suspect, or warn of the attack on the USS *Cole*. It was a total intelligence failure."

Kate replied, "There's enough blame to go around. Naval Intelligence, Defense Intelligence, and the Navy itself for not instituting better security procedures when entering a hostile port."

"Right. But the CIA always catches the flak. So I think they're motivated and anxious to even the score." I added, "They never forget a failure, especially if their failure leads to American deaths." How's that for planting a thought in her head?

Kate didn't reply for a second, then said, "The FBI

is no different." She asked me, "What point are you trying to make?"

"I'm not sure. Just thinking."

We put on our vests, put a few things in the room safe, then spent the next fifteen minutes getting familiar with our satellite phones and hand-held radios.

The problem with satellite phones was that you needed a clear view of the sky, and the antenna needed to be clear of obstructions, so the sat-phone didn't work well in the woods or work at all indoors. That, plus the line-of-sight limitations on the hand-held radios could make for some interesting situations if the feces hit the fan.

As Brenner said, the satellite phones had about a dozen speed dial numbers, all identified by initials in case the phones fell into the wrong hands. I scrolled through the directory: B.H.—Buck Harris; J.C.—Jesus Christ or John Corey; K.C.—Kate Corey; P.B.—Paul Brenner; and M.D., which could be the closest McDonald's or a doctor. Last time I was here, we usually had a medical doctor with us when we traveled. Not a bad idea.

The embassy number was also on speed dial, plus about six other initials, including H.F., who was probably Howard Fensterman. It's always good to have your lawyer on speed dial when you're out and about trying to whack someone.

I pretended to call and said, "Hello, Howard? Look, these guys are firing submachine guns at us. Can we return fire? What? You'll call Washington and get back to us? Okay. I'll hold."

Kate laughed, then said, "Be nice to Howard."

Anyway, I didn't recognize the other initials, but I

guessed they were our DSS drivers and shotgun riders. None of them, according to Brenner, were our
CIA guy, who wished to remain anonymous until he
revealed himself. The Agency loves secrecy and drama.

I next looked at our list of radio call signs. On Frequency One were most of the same people as on our
satellite phone speed dial. Buck was Clean Sweep One,
Brenner Clean Sweep Two, I was Three, Kate was Four,
and so forth.

The second radio frequency was to be used by and
for Command and Control—the U.S. Embassy in
Sana'a, and the Sheraton Hotel in Aden, i.e., the bosses.
But as Brenner said, the transmitting and receiving distances were short, so as soon as we were out of Sana'a,
we were out of radio contact with the embassy, and
same for the Sheraton in Aden. This could be good in
regards to upper-echelon meddling. But it could be bad
if we needed help.

Next, Kate showed me how to field-strip the Colt
.45, then gave me a few tips on aiming and firing.

I'm sure this gun brought back bad memories of
when she capped Ted. In fact, as we rode down the elevator, she said to me, "We haven't worked with the CIA
since that last time."

"Right. How did that work out?"

She didn't reply, then said, "I just had a troubling
thought."

"Keep that thought."

She nodded.

CHAPTER TWENTY-FOUR

We met Brenner in the lobby and went out to the Land Cruiser where Zamo was still behind the wheel. I said I wanted to ride shotgun, so Kate and Brenner got in the rear, and off we went.

Brenner said to us, "We won't be in Sana'a long, but it's good if you have a general sense of the city in case something comes up and we're told to stay here awhile."

"Also," I reminded him, "we want to see if anyone tries to kill us."

"Right. That too." He reminded me, "We want to advertise your presence in Sana'a."

"How about a billboard?"

Zamo laughed.

"Also, that's why you mentioned in front of Mohammed about us seeing the Old City today."

"Correct."

So, tell me how sharp I am. But he didn't, so I moved on and said, "We're checked into the hotel for four days."

Brenner informed me, "That usually means one or

two days." He explained, "We don't give out information to Yemenis."

"Right." And not much to me either.

As we drove downhill toward the Old City, Brenner announced, "Sana'a was founded by Shem, the son of Noah, after the Flood subsided."

Maybe it was waterfront property then.

Brenner continued, "Sana'a claims to be the oldest inhabited city in the world."

Kate, sitting next to our guide, said, "That's amazing."

I inquired, "How about lunch?"

Brenner replied, "We'll have lunch in the Old City."

He pointed to another walled compound on the left and informed us, "That's the new British Embassy." He let us know, "If you're in a tight situation and can't make it to the American Embassy, or if our embassy is under attack, the Brits will let you in."

"What if they're also under attack?"

"Go to Plan B."

"Right." Plan B was bend over and kiss your ass good-bye.

Brenner continued, "Coming up on the right is the Mövenpick Hotel, where you also have a reservation." He explained, "Confuses the enemy."

Not as much as it confuses me.

Brenner also let us know, "The hills to the east of here, that you can see from your room, are good places to launch rocket and mortar attacks toward the U.S. and U.K. embassies, as well as Tourist City and the hotels."

"That was mentioned in the hotel brochure."

Zamo laughed again. I liked Zamo.

Brenner continued, "About six Al Qaeda plots have been foiled in the last year, including one plot to ambush the British ambassador when his convoy left the embassy, and another plot to drive a truck bomb through the U.S. Embassy gates."

"I thought you said this was a safe neighborhood."

"I think I said heavily guarded."

"Got it." I had a realtor like him once.

Mr. Brenner informed us, "The farther east you go, toward Marib, the more you're in tribal territory and Al Qaeda territory." He pointed to a road sign and informed us, "That road to Marib city has become very dangerous, and Marib province seems to be the center of Al Qaeda activity in Yemen."

I asked Brenner, "Did you hear about the Al Qaeda attack in Marib on the Hunt Oil installation?"

"I did."

I said to Kate, "Early this morning. Buck mentioned it."

Brenner had nothing to say on that subject, and we continued in silence. I wondered if we'd be going to Marib. In fact, we probably were.

Brenner continued his country orientation and said, "As you travel south toward Aden, which we'll do in a few days, you're in the tribal lands for a while. Then as you get toward the Gulf of Aden, you're in Al Qaeda territory again, and you're also in the territory of the South Yemen separatist groups who are still trying to secede from North Yemen." He completed his briefing by saying, "To the west, as you get to the Red Sea coast, there are also Al Qaeda operatives who are in cahoots with the Somali pirates."

So, to recap, al-Houthi rebels to the north, Al

Qaeda to the south and east, Al Qaeda and pirates to the west, separatist rebels to the south, and tribal warlords in between. Not much room left for camping, hiking, and boating.

Kate asked, "What does the government control?"

Brenner replied, "Mostly main roads and towns. But that changes and you have to check with the military, who lie."

"Then why bother to check?" she asked.

"Protocol."

Zamo pulled over at a wide bend in the road, and Brenner suggested we get out and look down into the city.

So we got out and stood on an overlook, though Zamo stayed close to the SUV.

We used the opportunity to do a commo check with our sat-phones and hand-held radios. You need to check government-issued equipment.

The old walled city of Sana'a was about half a mile to the west, and the newer parts of the city spread across the high plateau, as far as the surrounding hills and mountains.

Brenner said, "Old Sana'a is famous for the tower houses which you can see rising up to ten stories above the walls. There are thousands of them, some going back to the eleventh century, and they are said to be the world's first skyscrapers."

Kate took a few photos from the overlook, then insisted that Brenner and I pose, which we did without putting our arms around each other's shoulders. Then Kate gave me the camera, and I took a shot of her and Brenner, who did put their arms around each other.

The photo ops were finished, and Brenner returned to his narrative, saying, "Up until the early 1960s, the old walled city was the entire city of Sana'a, with a population of only about sixty thousand. Now there are about two million." He added, "The water table is dropping quickly, and food is becoming a problem." He informed us, "Sana'a has become politically and socially unstable, and the city is full of troops and security forces to keep the population in line."

"More khat."

"Khat," replied Mr. Brenner, "is not the solution. It's part of the problem."

It's actually both, but I didn't want to argue with my tour guide. I asked, "Does Al Qaeda do khat?"

"Good question. The answer is no. Most Al Qaeda members in Yemen are not Yemenis, and those who are, are prohibited from using khat. So Al Qaeda is sober all day, and everyone else here is spaced out after lunch." He added, "That's one reason why I think Al Qaeda is going to win here. Unless we can stop them."

Right. Like in Vietnam, Paul. How did that work out for you?

Mr. Brenner put on his tour guide hat again and said, "If you look to the west, beyond the tower houses, you'll see what used to be the Jewish and Turkish quarters of the city." He informed us, "The Turks are long gone, the Jews mostly gone, and the few remaining Christians live up here now where it's safer."

"I think you said heavily guarded."

"Right." Brenner continued, "In 1948, during some civil war, tribes from the north laid siege to the walled city and broke in. They looted, pillaged, and burned for days, and a lot of the Old City still remains damaged." He added, "That's when the new state of Israel organized what they called Operation Magic

Carpet and airlifted about fifty thousand Yemeni Jews to Israel."

Kate said, "That's fascinating."

Lunch?

Brenner continued, "Sana'a has a long history of being conquered and looted by foreigners, but the main threats have always come from the tribes, who see the city as a piggy bank, a place full of gold, spices, art, and other things they don't have." He added, "The population of Sana'a still fears the tribes, who most recently besieged the city in 1968. And now there are the al-Houthi tribesmen, who have come as close as sixty kilometers to the city."

Kate commented, "Sounds almost medieval."

Actually, it sounded like fun. I want to be a warlord.

Brenner switched topics and said, "Down there, you can see ath-Thawra Hospital—Revolution Hospital—and on the other side of the city is the Kuwait Hospital. If you can't get to the embassy, it's good to know where the hospitals are if you're sick, injured, or nursing a gunshot wound."

I asked, "Do they take Blue Cross?"

"No, but they'll take your watch."

Good one.

Brenner further informed us, "There are also a number of traditional healers and folk remedies available." He smiled and said, "If, for instance, you get malaria, you can sell your disease to the ants."

"Excuse me?"

"You lie down on an ant mound and proclaim your intent to sell them your malaria."

I wasn't sure I'd heard him correctly, but I asked, "Why would the ants want to buy your malaria?"

"I'm not sure," Brenner confessed, "but there have been a number of cures reported." He speculated, "Maybe it has something to do with the ant venom."

I asked, "Who do I sell my hemorrhoids to?"

"Another asshole." He didn't say that, but I know he was *thinking* it.

Anyway, Brenner pointed out a few other sights and landmarks, including the khat souk, near where he lived, and a place called Ghumdan Fortress, which was built into the eastern wall of the city. He informed us, "This is the site of the famed Ghumdan Palace, built almost two thousand years ago. The palace was said to be twenty stories high, and the roof was made of alabaster that was so thin and transparent you could see birds flying overhead."

Kate asked, "How did they clean the bird shit off the alabaster?"

Actually, I asked that. Kate said, "John, please."

She always says that. Meanwhile, we've been standing here too long, twenty feet from the armored vehicle, and at least a dozen vehicles had passed by and slowed down. Zamo was standing with the Land Cruiser between him and the road with his M4 carbine at his side.

Brenner, oblivious to my concern, continued, "Ghumdan Palace was destroyed in the seventh century by the Islamic armies that were sweeping across the Arabian Peninsula. The stones were used to build the Great Mosque, which you can see over there." He added, "The Qalis Cathedral was also destroyed, as were the synagogues." He paused, then said, "Islam had arrived."

Right. And as Al Rasul said, what we were seeing now was a return to a dark and bloody past.

Brenner continued, "Ghumdan Fortress was built on the palace site by the Turks during the Ottoman Empire, and it now houses Yemeni military barracks and a political prison." He let us know, "Later, we have an appointment to speak to a prisoner."

I asked, "You mean the Al Qaeda guy captured in the Hunt Oil attack?"

"Correct."

"Good." I like interrogating starving prisoners after I've had a big lunch.

We got back in the SUV and continued down toward the city along a winding road.

Kate, sitting next to Brenner, said to him, "Thank you for an interesting history lesson."

Brenner replied, "This is a fascinating place. It grows on you."

Not on me, Paul.

Today being Sunday, and thinking about Noah, Shem, Sana'a, and all that, I asked, "After God sent the Flood to cleanse the earth of the sinful and the wicked, do you think he was pissed off that the people who repopulated the earth got it so wrong again?"

No one replied to my profound question, and no one bothered to defend the earth's inhabitants. Amen.

CHAPTER TWENTY-FIVE

We came down onto the plateau and into a drab neighborhood of modern concrete buildings that sat between the hills and the east wall of the Old City.

Brenner pointed across the road and said, "That's where I live," indicating a three-story concrete slab structure that looked like it had seen better days. He informed us, "Built in the late sixties when the city first started spreading outside the walls. It has hot water and a manageable vermin population." He added, "Ten bucks a month for Yemenis, forty for me."

I asked, "Does that include parking?"

"It does. I keep my motorcycle in the foyer."

So Mr. Cool has a motorcycle. Figures.

He informed us, "That's the best way to get around this city, and I can go where assassins in cars can't go." He added, "I can be in the embassy in five minutes if I push it."

I had the thought that Mr. Brenner was showing off a little for Mrs. Corey. Guys are assholes.

Anyway, Zamo pulled over beside a concrete wall, and Brenner said, "We'll walk through the khat souk, then into the Old City." He told Zamo, "I'll call you every half hour, or call me."

So we left Zamo in the nice air-conditioned armored Land Cruiser and walked toward a gate in the concrete wall where a guy sat cradling his AK-47.

Brenner said, "This is a fairly new souk, built I think in the seventies outside the Old City wall, but the mentality was still walls, so this souk is walled, as you can see."

Right. Walls are good. Moats, too. Keeps the riffraff out. Especially riffraff with guns.

Brenner suggested to Kate, "You might want to wrap that scarf over your face."

Kate did that and I asked her, "Would you like a cigarette?"

She mumbled something through the scarf that sounded like, "Fook-yo." Arabic?

Anyway, we passed through a gate into the khat souk, which was sort of like a farmers market, filled with jerry-built stalls in the open plaza and surrounded by permanent buildings along the perimeter walls.

The place was bustling and crowded with white-robed men wearing jambiyahs, who shared the space with donkeys, cows, and camels. Some of the cows had been disassembled and their parts were hanging from crossbeams, covered with flies. And did I mention that the ground was covered with shit?

Brenner said, "It's relatively safe here, but let's stick close."

We were the only Western people I saw, except for some young guys in jeans and T-shirts who were snapping pictures of piles of green leaves that I assumed were not spinach. I mean, this was junkie heaven. I had a sudden urge to make a bust.

I didn't see any women in the souk, except for Kate, and oddly no one seemed to be paying much attention to us. But now and then, when I looked back over my shoulder, I caught people watching us.

Brenner stopped at a khat stall and said something in Arabic to the proprietor, who looked very happy with his career choice. Brenner said to us, "There are dozens of varieties of khat. This gentleman claims he has the best khat in all of Yemen, grown in Wadi Dhahri, and picked fresh daily." He also informed us, "This man claims he is the purveyor to the president."

"George Bush chews khat?"

That got a laugh.

Anyway, we did a walk around the souk, avoiding the cow pies and donkey bombs. Brenner took Kate's camera to shoot pictures for her, and he paid a kid about ten cents to take a great shot of the three of us standing in front of a shoulder-high pile of wacky weed. I couldn't wait to send the picture to Kate's parents with a nickel bag of khat and a note: *Chewing khat with Kate. Love, John.*

After admiring the cow pens and the piles of firewood, we stopped in the sporting goods department, where there were tables of fully automatic assault rifles sitting along a wall.

Brenner said, "Most of these AK-47s are cheap knockoffs, some are better-made Chicoms—Chinese Communist—but a few are the real deal, made in Mother Russia. Those go for about five hundred bucks—a year's pay for a working man."

But a good investment for the future.

Brenner informed us, "I have one in my apartment." He added, "It's a good gun." He picked up an AK-47 and stared at it a long time, then said, as if to himself, "A very good gun."

Right. And obviously it brought back some memories for Paul Brenner of another hellhole.

He put the gun back on the table, and the proprietor said in English, "Five hundred for you. And I give a hundred rounds for free."

I said to him, "Throw in a cow and you got a deal."

We left sporting goods and headed through a gate that led toward the high wall of the Old City.

Brenner speed-dialed his satellite phone and said, "Leaving the khat souk, entering the Old City." He listened, then said, "Okay. Four-thirty at the al-Mahdi Mosque." He hung up and said to us, "Our appointment at Ghumdan prison is for five P.M. We'll meet Zamo at the mosque on the other side of the Old City, then drive to Ghumdan." He also informed us, "Kate has to stay in the vehicle."

Girls miss all the fun around here.

We passed through an opening in the city wall, and it was literally like stepping back in time. Huge tower houses with ornate façades blocked the sun from the narrow, alley-like streets, and the sound level went from loud internal combustion engines to the hushed murmur of people and animal-drawn carts.

Brenner said to us, "This is the largest and most pristine walled city in the Mideast, covering an area of over one square kilometer. The old Jewish and Turkish quarters on the west side of the city cover another square kilometer." He further informed us, "The east and west halves of the city are divided by Wadi as Sa'ila. When the wadi is dry, as it is now, it's used for vehicle traffic."

"And when it's wet, how do they paint the white line?"

He smiled politely, then continued, "The Mahdi Mosque is near the wadi. If we get separated, our rendezvous point is there."

"Okay. Mahdi at the wadi." My appetite had recovered from the shit souk, and I asked, "Where is lunch?"

"Up ahead in a tower house converted into a guest house."

So we continued on through a maze of alleys and narrow, twisting streets, some of which led into souks that were crowded with people, animals, and motor scooters.

We noticed the buildings that had been damaged or destroyed by the 1968 storming of the Old City by the tribes, and Brenner said, "The tribes could come again. Or maybe Al Qaeda this time. And that could be soon."

Right. But first, lunch.

Anyway, I was sure we didn't have a tail, and the place seemed safe enough, but I was happy to be packing heat and wearing a vest.

Brenner motioned to the tower houses and said, "The first few floors as you can see are made of stone, and the upper floors are mud brick. The ground floor is used for animals and to collect human excrement from the upper floors."

"Sounds like 26 Federal Plaza."

Brenner continued, "Each tower house has a shaft for excrement, and another shaft that's used to haul up well water." He informed us, "This presents a sanitation problem."

"You think?" I asked Brenner, "Is this restaurant on the ground floor with the animals and excrement?"

"No. Two floors up." He explained, "That's called the diwan, where guests are received."

And no one would know if you farted.

He continued, "Above the diwan are the floors where the extended family lives, sharing a single kitchen." He concluded, "The top floor is called the mafraj, literally, a room with a view—sort of the penthouse, and this is where honored male guests gather to chew khat and watch the sunset."

I need a room like that. Hey, guys, let's go up to the mafraj and stare into the sun and get wasted. Then we can bungee jump down the excrement shaft.

Anyway, Kate seemed overwhelmed by the experience, and she took lots of photos and asked Brenner lots of questions, and he was happy to share his knowledge with her, or make up answers. If he was a peacock, his tail feathers would be fully fanned out by now.

We continued our walk without seeing much evidence of the twenty-first century. There were a few other Westerners wandering around on some of the streets, so we didn't stop traffic. But these annoying kids kept following us asking for "baksheesh, baksheesh," which I remembered from Aden meant either alms or get-the-fuck-out-of-here money. Brenner said to ignore them, but Kate wanted to engage them in playful conversation, or take their pictures, which cost five cents.

Brenner also said, "If the kids suddenly disappear, we may be having a problem."

Gotcha. "Hey, Abdul, you want a piggyback ride?"

Anyway, as a detective, I noticed what was missing. Women. I'd seen fewer women on the streets than I'd seen dead rats.

I asked Brenner about that and he replied, "The women do their errands in the morning, usually with male escorts, then they stay indoors to cook, clean, and take care of the kids."

"Sounds grim," said FBI Special Agent Kate Mayfield.

Brenner had a joke and said, "But Thursday is wet burqua night at the wadi." He added, "Bring your laundry."

Funny. But Kate didn't laugh, so I didn't either. You gotta be careful, even here.

Sunday wasn't the Sabbath around here so everyone who had a job was at work. But what I noticed, as I'd noticed last time in Aden, were hundreds, really thousands, of young men on the streets and in the souks, obviously unemployed and killing time. Their futures would probably take one of three paths: petty crime, emigration, or Al Qaeda. Or maybe someday they'd just revolt against the government, hoping that anything that came after would be better than this. Indeed, they were a demographic time bomb waiting to explode.

Brenner said, "Here's the restaurant."

Kate said, "That was fascinating."

Brenner offered, "If we don't go to Aden tomorrow, I can show you the rest of the city."

I thought we'd already pushed our luck. But this was the guy who did a second tour in Vietnam. But hey, you gotta die somewhere.

CHAPTER TWENTY-SIX

The restaurant was called, appropriately, "Old Sana'a," and so was the tower guest house in which it was located.

I assumed Brenner had been here and he hadn't died of *E. coli* or a gunshot wound, so we followed him through an open arch into a large, high-ceilinged space, lit only by sunlight coming through narrow windows in the stone walls. I was relieved to see that the space had been cleared of livestock and excrement, though a hint of all that remained in the air.

We climbed a spiral staircase to the diwan level, where a white-robed man sat behind a table, on which was a stack of assault rifles. I guess you had to check your guns here. The man smiled, decided we were probably English speakers, and said, "Welcome. For lunch or room?"

Brenner replied, "Restaurant, please."

The desk clerk/maître d'armaments stood, grabbed three menus, and we followed him through one of those *Casablanca*-type archways with hanging beads into a large, sunlit dining room that took up the whole floor of the tower house. He escorted us to a low round table with beanbag chairs near an open window and said, "Good looking."

I wasn't sure if he meant the view, or if he meant me or Brenner. Kate was scarfed, so he didn't mean her. I replied politely, "Thank you. This is a Christian Dior shirt."

"Yes?"

So we sat cross-legged on these horrid stuffed cushions, and I looked around. It was a pleasant enough place, with ceiling fans, oil lamps on the tables, and carpets on the floor—sort of a cross between Rick's Place and the den of Ali Baba and the Forty Thieves.

I asked Brenner, "Come here often?"

"Now and then." He explained, "It's not a good idea for a Westerner to be a regular anywhere in Sana'a."

"Right." Except maybe the Russia Club.

I looked out the window into the backyards of several tower houses. The yards were crowded with vegetable gardens, goats, and chickens. There were no play swings or slides, but a few barefoot kids were having fun chasing the poultry. A woman in a full black balto and veil was scrubbing clothes in a copper tub. In some weird way, this scene reminded me of the tenement I grew up in—sans goats. It was such an ordinary, peaceful scene that it was hard to believe the rest of the country was descending into violence and chaos.

Brenner said, "That's our emergency exit if we need one."

"Right." About a twenty-foot drop into a pile of manure. How would I phrase that in my incident report?

There was a weird, smoky smell in the air, which

I commented on, and Brenner informed me, "That's frankincense."

"Where's he sitting?"

"It's an Arabic gum resin. Used in perfume or incense."

"Yeah? How about frankin-khat chewing gum? Yes?"

Kate interjected, "Stop."

Brenner further informed us, "The Yemenis believe it was a Yemeni wise man who brought the gift of frankincense to the baby Jesus."

Better than fruitcake. Right?

Anyway, the place was about half full on this Sunday afternoon, mostly young Westerners, male and female, but also some weird-looking dudes wearing daggers and white robes, with dark beards and black eyes, who were glancing at us. There were no Yemeni ladies lunching.

Kate still had her scarf over her face, which limited her choices on the menu, but Brenner said to her, "You can uncover your face here, but I'd advise you to keep your hair covered."

Kate did that, and I said to her, "I forgot how beautiful you were."

Brenner also said to Kate, "It might be best if John or I gave your order to the waiter." He explained, unnecessarily, "Men don't take orders from women."

"Incredible," Kate said.

Brenner was right—this place could grow on you. But to show my sensitivity to women's issues, I said, "Unbelievable."

Brenner agreed and said, "The male guest workers who return from Europe and America have seen the twenty-first century, and they've been subtly influenced by what they've seen in the West."

I thought about Nabeel, and also The Panther, and I wondered if this was true. Or, if they *had* been influenced by the West, it wasn't in a positive way. Bottom line, the winds of change that were sweeping Islam were blowing backwards. They were happily miserable and rigid, and we should leave them alone—except for knocking off a few of them who fucked with us. Like Osama bin Laden. And The Panther.

A waiter dressed in theme costume came over, and Brenner suggested the local fruit drink or the shai, a spiced tea. Kate said to Brenner, "Shai," and Brenner repeated it to the guy and ordered one for himself. The menu was written in Arabic and bad English, and I saw that they had non-alcoholic beer, which possibly had fermented in the bottle, so I said to Kate, "Tell Paul to tell the waiter I want a beer." Did I get that right?

Anyway, we made small talk, and Kate asked Brenner, "Where are you from?"

"South Boston."

"Do you miss it?"

"I don't get there much. I live in Virginia now. Falls Church." He added, "That's where CID Headquarters is, and it was my last duty station before I left the Army."

Kate seemed to want to know more about Paul Brenner, and with some prodding, he gave her his history—drafted into the Army at eighteen, infantryman in Vietnam, decided to make the Army a career, went to military police school, second tour in Vietnam as an MP, then transferred to the U.S. Army Criminal Investigation Division, and served in various Army posts around the world. He had apparently been in a special CID unit that handled high-profile and/or sensitive cases, and his last case involved the murder of a female U.S. Army captain who was also the daughter of an Army general who had been highly decorated in the first Gulf War.

I thought I remembered this case, because it had made the news at the time, a year or so after the Gulf War, and I had the impression that this case had somehow led to the early retirement of Chief Warrant Officer Paul Brenner.

Brenner didn't mention his clandestine mission to post-war Vietnam, either out of modesty or because he still wasn't allowed to talk about it. This mission, though, must have redeemed his reputation or something, and maybe the Army's equivalent of Tom Walsh asked him to name a job, and Brenner picked the Diplomatic Security Service. Fun and travel. In fact, Brenner told us that he'd served with the DSS in London, then Athens. I wonder what he did wrong to get sent here.

Brenner concluded his edited history, and I noticed it was all professional, lacking any personal details, with no mention of marriage or divorce, kids, or the current lady back in the States.

Kate didn't prod him on that subject, and I certainly didn't. All I wanted to know about Mr. Paul Brenner was if I could trust him, and whether or not he had a set of balls. He seemed okay in both categories. He also seemed bright, which was good, but I couldn't determine if he had good or bad professional judgment, which was crucial. I myself display impressively bad judgment on occasion, but I always temper that with acts of irrational risk taking. Ask my wife. Brenner, I suspected, was a little like me in those respects, which is the sign of the alpha male. Most of us are dead by now, of course, or incarcerated, or permanently disabled, but some of us are lucky. I'm lucky. And smart.

Anyway, I thought I could work with this guy, and I didn't think he was going to get me killed—I could do that on my own, thank you.

Kate, too, seemed impressed with Paul Brenner, though I doubt she'd analyzed why. Women's intuition.

Our cocktails arrived, and the waiter asked if we had made a choice for lunch. We hadn't, but a quick scan of the menu showed me that my choices were limited to animals that I could see from the window.

Kate said to Brenner, "Why don't you order for us?"

Brenner had to order for Kate anyway, so I agreed but warned him, "No organs."

Brenner ordered in Arabic, then asked us, "Do you want utensils? Or do you want to use your fingers?"

We didn't know one another that well, so we agreed on utensils, and when the waiter left I took the opportunity to speak to Brenner without Buck present. I asked, "Why do we need a CIA guy on the team?"

"It's their show. Also, they have all the information we need."

"Let's get the information and leave the CIA guy in Aden."

Brenner asked me, "Why wouldn't you want a CIA officer on the team?"

Because the CIA wants to kill me and my wife. But that would sound silly if I said it out loud, so I replied, "They tend to complicate things. And they're not team players."

"Neither are you from what I hear."

"If I'm on the team, I play with the team."

Kate said, "That's true." She remembered to add, "But John sometimes makes up his own rules."

You see why I love my wife.

Brenner stayed quiet a moment, then said, "To further answer your question, it's my understanding that Predator drones with video surveillance cameras are an important part of this operation. And as you may know, in Yemen only the CIA has operational control of the Predators. So that's why we need a CIA officer with us when we go into the Badlands—to control the Predator drones on aerial reconnaissance missions." He explained, "We can have real-time video surveillance transmitted directly to a video monitor on the ground."

"And then the Predator launches a Hellfire missile against the target."

He didn't reply for a second, then said, "I suppose that's an option." He added, "That has been very effective here and in Afghanistan. We've killed dozens of important Al Qaeda leaders that way."

"Right." They leave their cave or mud hut to go take a leak, and next thing they know, they're holding their dick in Paradise.

I asked Brenner, "What about taking this suspect alive?"

Brenner shrugged and replied, "I don't know. I'm not sure what the actual goal is."

"That makes three of us."

He continued, "The way I see it, Washington would like to take this guy alive, but it's easier to kill him. So maybe if the opportunity to capture him presents itself, then that's what we'll try to do. But if that seems impossible—or too dangerous—then we fix his location and call in the drones and Hellfires."

I nodded, and added, "Then we Ziploc some pieces for ID."

"Right. We have the suspect's prints on file—and also DNA from his family."

Kate commented, "Maybe I don't need my arrest warrant."

Brenner assured her, "We need you and your arrest warrant in case we have the opportunity to apprehend the suspect."

Kate nodded tentatively. Actually, Kate and her arrest warrant were cover for what was most likely the assassination of an American citizen. I had no problem with that, and I was happy to have the cover in case this thing came back to bite us in the ass vis-à-vis Mr. and Mrs. al-Darwish's lawsuit, or some other silly legality. Fucked-up war.

Kate also asked, "If we do apprehend the suspect, do we turn him over to the Yemeni authorities, then ask for extradition, or do we attempt to get the suspect out of the country?" She added, "In other words, extradition or rendition?"

Brenner shrugged again and replied, "This is all beyond my pay grade."

"Why," I asked, "is State Department Intelligence involved?"

Brenner replied, "First, keep in mind that Buck Harris is officially a diplomat, attached to the economic assistance mission, which is why he travels around the country. Forget SDI. Second, we want a diplomatic component to our operation." He stressed, "We want to involve the State Department."

"Right." Meaning that if things went wrong—or even if things went right—the State Department could do what they do best: apologize to the host government for violating their sovereignty and offer them a few million bucks to forget it. That's what diplomats are for.

Brenner reminded me, "Buck is an invaluable asset. He knows the country, the people, and the language."

"Right. We love Buck. But he knows more than he's sharing."

Brenner said, "Let's take it a step at a time and see how it plays out." He also suggested, "We'll get some clarification from our Agency guy."

Paul Brenner had apparently not worked with the CIA before.

Our food came and it was served family style in big bowls, and everyone around us was eating directly out of the bowls with their fingers. We, however, had plates, serving spoons, and utensils. The food actually tasted good, whatever it was. Did I take my Cipro this morning?

I said to Brenner, "Tell me about this wounded Al Qaeda guy that we're seeing in the slammer."

Brenner told us, "We got this appointment because we told the PSO that we think this attack could have been planned by one of the *Cole* plotters. Therefore, Mr. John Corey of the FBI Evidence Response Team would like to speak to the prisoner." He added, "We have an understanding with the Yemeni government, based on cash and other good and valuable considerations, that they will cooperate in anything having to do with the *Cole*." He concluded, "I have no idea if this prisoner knows anything about the *Cole* or The Panther, but we'll certainly ask."

"Can we torture him?"

"I'm sure that's been done." He added, "But the PSO was probably focusing more on the oil installation attack than on The Panther."

"Right. But when we ask this guy about The Panther, the PSO guys who are present will know what our focus is."

Brenner replied, "That's okay." He explained, "Assuming someone in the prison is reporting to Al Qaeda, then this is one way of getting the message to The Panther that John Corey is in town looking for him." He reminded me, "That's the point."

"Right. Why do I keep forgetting I'm bait?"

"Not bait," Brenner corrected. "That's such a negative word. I like to think of you as a lure."

Funny? Maybe not.

Kate asked, "Will Colonel Hakim be at the prison?"

Brenner replied, "Probably." He explained, "He seems to be the PSO guy who is assigned to keep an eye on the American Embassy."

I asked, "Whose side is he on?"

Brenner replied, "The CIA thinks he's loyal to the Yemeni government—but what does that mean? It doesn't mean he's pro-American, or anti–Al Qaeda. Like most people here, his first loyalty is to himself, then to his faith—or vice versa. His next loyalty is to his ancestral tribe, his clan, and his family, followed by a loose loyalty to the concept of being a Yemeni. His last loyalty, if it exists at all, is to the government."

I could see why this country wasn't working. I said to Brenner, "The question is, Does Colonel Hakim have ties to Al Qaeda?"

Brenner replied, "He may have contacts. Most

high-ranking people do. But in this country, that doesn't make him a traitor. It makes him smart." He added, "People with money or power are covering all their bets until they see who looks like the winner here." He further explained, "The Americans are putting their money on a bad government, but it's the only play we have."

I suggested, "Let's whack who we have to whack to avenge the *Cole*, and get the hell out of here before we get in deeper."

Brenner thought a minute and said, "It sort of reminds me of Vietnam...a corrupt, double-dealing government, backed by the U.S. out of necessity, fighting a tough, single-minded enemy who terrorized a population that didn't care who won as long as they could live in peace...Even the hill tribes here remind me of the hill tribes in Vietnam who hated and fought both the government and the Viet Cong. And we were right in the middle of it. The quagmire. And we keep doing the same thing, expecting different results."

No argument there.

Kate said, "It's the same situation in Iraq and Afghanistan."

Brenner seemed to have returned from the jungles of Southeast Asia to the sands of the Middle East, and he said to me, "I understand you've had some experience with interrogating *Cole* suspects in Aden."

"Right. But not too successfully." I explained, "Everyone had fun lying to the Americans—the police, the PSO guys, the prisoners, and even the translators. And after we left the prison, they probably all had a khat chew together and yucked it up." I added, "Assholes."

Brenner assured me, "The Yemeni government

is a little more worried now, and they've been more cooperative."

"You mean like Colonel Hakim at the airport?"

Brenner didn't reply, and asked me, "When you were interrogating the *Cole* suspects in Aden, did the name Bulus ibn al-Darwish or al-Numair—The Panther—ever come up?"

"No. I don't think the FBI or CIA knew about him at that time." I thought a moment, then added, "But I remember now there was some suspicion, or a rumor, that an American-born Muslim may have been involved."

Brenner nodded, then said, "It was apparently The Panther's idea to attack an American warship that was on a regularly scheduled refueling stop in Aden Harbor." He informed us, "This was different from most Al Qaeda attacks in Europe or the Mideast, which are directed against soft targets. This was a rare attack against the American military." He added, "Very bold, with a high risk of failure. And yet they succeeded in crippling a high-tech American warship and killing seventeen American sailors."

Right. But in a way, The Panther miscalculated. This attack got the Americans into Yemen, and now Al Qaeda in the Arabian Peninsula was under pressure. I said, "As with 9/11, Al Qaeda got more than they bargained for."

"Agreed. And that's what we have to show them. There is a price to pay."

Kate said, "They know that. But it hasn't stopped them from escalating the attacks. In fact, they're stronger in Yemen than they were at the time of the *Cole* attack."

Brenner replied, "That's partly due to a dysfunctional government."

I asked, "Ours or theirs?"

Anyway, we called for the check, which was written on a scrap of paper—eight million rials or something, which came to about three bucks, drinks included, and Brenner treated. I could live like a sultan in Yemen.

I would have asked for a doggie bag, but the waiter might misunderstand and I'd wind up eating Fido later.

I asked, "Does anyone have to use the excrement shaft?"

On the way out, I said to the guy at the front desk, "Everything was terrific. We'll be back tomorrow for lunch. One P.M. John Corey." Tell The Panther.

"Good. Tomorrow."

"Is one of these guns mine?"

"No, you don't bring gun."

"Okay. I think I left it on my donkey—"

"John."

"Ciao."

Kate wrapped her scarf over her face, and Brenner checked in with Zamo, then we went down to the street into the bright sunlight where it had gotten hotter.

Without any discussion, we checked out the crowded street, then crossed to the other side and watched the door to the restaurant.

You always need to go through the drill, even when things look and feel safe. In fact, that's when you most need to keep your head out of your ass. And you needed to keep reminding yourself that the hunter is also the hunted.

CHAPTER TWENTY-SEVEN

B renner knew his way around the narrow, twisting streets of the Old City, and he said we had time to stop at Hope in Their Hands before we met Zamo.

I'm usually good at spotting a tail, but half the men here looked alike, with the same white robes, headgear, and beards. And we three had the opposite problem; there weren't many Westerners in Sana'a, and we stuck out like pigs in a mosque.

We reached Hope in Their Hands and entered. The clientele were all Western—male and female backpackers, a European tour group, and some ladies who could have been aid workers or Western embassy people.

Brenner said to Kate, "You can remove your scarf here."

I suggested, "Wrap it around your eyes while you shop."

"Maybe I'll wrap it around your neck."

I saw that coming.

Kate unwrapped, revealing herself as the best-looking woman in the shop, except maybe for a twenty-something backpacker with an Australian accent and long red hair. But I digress.

As Kate looked around the shop, and Brenner looked at the door, I got into a conversation with a young guy, an American named Matt Longo from New York. Young Mr. Longo was living in Sana'a in a tower guest house, though not the one where we had lunch. He was a Yale grad with a degree in Mideast studies, spoke passable Arabic, and he was here to learn the more pure and ancient Arabic in the Land That Time Forgot. He'd been in Yemen a month, and he had another month to go.

I asked him, "Has anyone tried to kidnap you yet?"

He thought that was funny and replied, "No. These are really nice people."

"Right. But the State Department keeps issuing travelers' warnings about the not-so-nice people here."

He shrugged and said, "They overreact. I've been all over the Middle East. Never had a problem."

"Good. But watch yourself."

He confessed to me, "I'm half Jewish, so I get it."

"Keep that to yourself."

"Yeah." He asked me, "Have you seen the Jewish Quarter yet?"

"It's on my list."

"It's worth seeing. Still mostly deserted. Like, houses with Stars of David on them that haven't been lived in for fifty, sixty years. It's weird. Like, why don't the Yemenis tear them down? Or move in? It's like they're waiting for the Jews to come back."

"That might be a long wait."

"Yeah. But you never know."

"Maybe after the next flood."

He told me, "Next week, I'm going to Marib with a few people." He explained, "The pre-Islamic ruins. Temples to the sun and moon gods. Queen of Sheba's palace. You should check it out."

"You should check out the security situation first."

"Yeah. I know." He informed me, "There's like a police force here—the National Security Bureau. They protect tourists. For a price. They're giving us, like, twenty armed guys for the trip for two hundred bucks. Includes transportation."

I reminded him, "You get what you pay for." I gave him some recent intel. "There was an attack in that area last night. American oil installation. Looks like Al Qaeda."

Mr. Longo, who was twenty-something and immortal, did not seem concerned.

He asked me, "Why are you here?"

"I thought the travel agent said Sweden."

He laughed, then assured me, "You'll get more out of this."

"I plan to." I asked, "You alone?"

"My girlfriend's coming in a few days."

I advised him, "Register your names and local address with the consulate at the embassy."

"Okay."

"You know where the American Embassy is?"

"No."

"Find out."

"Okay."

"Do I sound like your parents?"

"Sorta."

I told him where I was staying, and I said, "If I'm still in town when your girlfriend gets here, come on over to the hotel and my wife and I will buy you dinner and a real drink."

"Thanks." He said, "If you want to go on that Marib trip, we have room." He added, "About twenty bucks a head."

That's about what Al Qaeda pays for a head.

I took his satellite phone number, wished him good luck, and joined Kate in the veil and balto department.

It occurred to me that Sana'a was a deceptively serene city; not dangerous enough to keep you off the streets, but not safe enough for a Westerner to be wandering around alone. I think it all depended on who you were and what the situation was at the moment. For us—American Embassy people—Sana'a was always an adventure. For Matt Longo, it was one stop on a long journey.

Anyway, the Yemeni ladies who ran the shop were nice, spoke English, and seemed to be of the educated class. One of them, Anisa, insisted on taking us upstairs where Yemeni women—mostly widows and divorced ladies, Anisa said—were cutting fabrics and sewing garments by hand or on old treadle sewing machines.

It's rare for women in this country to work outside of the home, but this shop and factory seemed to be tolerated because of its charitable purpose. Brenner informed us, "The Koran exhorts Muslims to be charitable and help the poor."

"What Korean?"

"*Koran.*"

"Oh, right." How many more times could I use that one?

Anyway, Kate helped the poor to the tune of three shopping bags full of clothes, reminding me that her clothes were still in New York awaiting a Yemen mailing address. She also bought a black balto, which, as Buck suggested, is not a bad garment to own if you should need to blend in. They didn't sell men's dresses, or whatever they call those things, so I was off the hook on that. Kate's stuff came to about twenty bucks, so I couldn't complain, and I was moved to donate another twenty to the charity, partly in gratitude for the third-world factory outlet prices.

We left the shop, and Kate wrapped her pretty face in the scarf. We crossed the street to the jambiyah souk, a small square that looked like it had been there since the Year of the Flood. Literally.

Brenner steered me toward a tiny shop that Buck had recommended, and where the proprietor, Mr. Hassan, seemed to remember Mr. Brenner. I wouldn't be surprised if Brenner and Buck got a kickback. Or if Mr. Hassan made a call to someone after we left.

Brenner seemed happy to share with me his knowledge of curved daggers, and within fifteen minutes I found myself the about-to-be proud owner of a mean-looking jambiyah with a sheep-horn handle. A hundred bucks, marked down from three hundred because we were Americans. Or marked up from twenty bucks because we were Americans. Arguing price with an Arab in a souk is not one of my many strengths, so I gave Mr. Hassan the hundred bucks, and he threw in a hand-tooled leather belt and a silver-tipped sheath.

I asked Mr. Hassan, a wizened old man with a long white beard, "Anyone ever killed with this?"

He understood enough English to smile, and he was honest enough to reply, "No. For you to make first kill."

I had this sudden fantasy image of me in Tom Walsh's office, saying to him, "I have something for you from Yemen. Close your eyes."

The transaction completed, we left the knife shop with me wearing my belt and sheathed dagger, which, if you're interested, is worn not at your side, but in front, with the curved tip pointing to the right. Left if you're gay. I made that up.

Kate said to me, "That knife cost five times more than all the clothes I bought."

"Boys' toys are expensive," I reminded her.

We didn't have time to visit the nearby donkey market, which was a disappointment, but something to look forward to another day. We headed west until we came to the wide wadi that separates the Old City into east side and west side, sort of like Fifth Avenue does in Manhattan. And there the comparison ends. The wadi was dry, as Brenner had said, and the streambed was partially paved and heavy with traffic. We crossed at what looked like the only bridge and headed south toward the al-Mahdi Mosque.

If Al Qaeda was following, this was their last chance to make a move before we got in the armored vehicle—and I would have welcomed an early opportunity to use my new gun. The only thing I really worried about was someone with a car filled with explosives or someone wearing a suicide belt who wanted to be in Paradise before dinner. Everything else, I and my companions could handle.

Brenner called Zamo on the radio, and we stayed in contact until we spotted one another.

Zamo pulled up as we were walking, and we jumped into the Land Cruiser and continued south along the wadi, with me riding shotgun again.

Brenner asked Zamo, "Anything interesting?"

"Nope. Just some guy giving me a crate of mangos." He added, "It's in the back."

Brenner said, "The mangos are ticking."

They laughed.

Obviously these two had developed a gift for frontline humor. I guess this kept them sane. Or they were past that point.

CHAPTER TWENTY-EIGHT

As we headed toward Ghumdan Fortress, I pulled out my jambiyah and showed it to Zamo, who glanced at it and said politely, "Nice." He advised me, "No one should ever get close enough that you have to use a knife."

"Agreed." I remembered my last meeting with The Lion and said, "But it happens."

"Yeah. But it should only happen if you want it to happen."

"Right." I changed the subject and asked him, "So, how many kills you got?"

He replied matter-of-factly, "Eleven confirmed, two possible, one miss." He added, "The asshole bent over for some reason." He laughed and said, "Maybe he saw a nickel on the ground."

"His lucky day." I again changed the subject and asked, "What do you do here for fun?"

"I'm doing it."

Within five minutes, we were approaching the walls and watchtowers of Ghumdan Fortress, a forbidding-looking place of dark brick that dominated the landscape.

Brenner said to us, "The Turks built this place in the nineteenth century, on the site of the ancient Ghumdan Palace as I mentioned." He added, "The Turkish occupation was brutal, and it was said that no Yemeni who entered Ghumdan Fortress ever came out."

Right. Most old cities have a place like this, an iconic fortress-prison with a bad history whose very name strikes fear into the city's inhabitants—especially the kids. Like, "Clean your room, Amir, or you're going to Ghumdan." Most of these places in the civilized world are now museums and tourist attractions, like the Tower of London. But here, it was still in the same old business, under new management.

As we pulled up to the gates of the fortress, I advised, "Veils for those who need them."

Brenner lowered his window and said something in Arabic to the soldier, and I heard the names Corey and Brenner. That's us. The soldier stared at Kate, then said, "Wait," and went back into the guardhouse.

I asked Brenner, "Been here before?"

"Once." He explained, "Some idiot from D.C. on an official visit to the embassy was speaking to a Yemeni woman on the street. She was upscale, unveiled, and smiling too much." He added, "They both got busted."

I pointed out, "It was all her fault. If she was wearing her veil, none of that would have happened—not the chatting up, and not the smiling."

Brenner had no comment on that and said, "Anyway, I sprung him and got him on a plane home."

Kate asked from behind her scarf, "What happened to her?"

Brenner replied, "Don't know. Probably got slapped around and got a warning."

Definitely hard to get laid here.

An officer came over to our vehicle, and he was quite pleasant, saying, "Please to park car near flagpole and await a person." He added, "Lady not go from car."

Brenner said something in Arabic, including "As-salaam alaikum," and off we went.

The center of the fortress was a large, open field of dirt and gravel, probably once a parade ground and muster area, now used mostly for military equipment. A few soldiers sat around in white plastic chairs, chewing something. What could it be?

Brenner pointed out some old Soviet tanks and self-propelled howitzers, plus newer American Humvees and trucks. He said, "We're supplying them with as much equipment as we can spare from Iraq and Afghanistan. But we don't want to give them too much because this place could become Al Qaeda nation in a year or two." He further explained, "Also, half this stuff sits here needing parts or repairs, and they don't have trained mechanics or a parts inventory system, which they don't really need anyway because most of the parts get stolen. And the equipment that works is used to fight the tribes instead of Al Qaeda."

Who cares? Not me. I just need to whack one guy and get the hell out of here. Brenner has been here too long.

He also told us, "The Yemeni government doesn't want American military advisors who could straighten out their logistical and training problems, but they want American money and equipment, neither of which they can handle responsibly."

Same at 26 Fed.

"It's like Vietnam," said Brenner, who understandably

saw a lot of the world through that prism. "Incompetent and weak-willed allies fighting an enemy who are motivated by something higher than saving their own worthless asses." He added, "But we could turn it around with a few Special Forces units, maybe a Ranger battalion, and a Military Advisory Team."

I pointed out, "I think that's what the Pentagon said about Vietnam."

"Right...but..." He said to Zamo, "Park here."

Zamo pulled into a space near the flagpole between two American-made trucks.

Brenner said, "Okay, Kate and Zamo will stay in the vehicle, and John and I will get out and await a person." He added, "If we're not back by Wednesday, call the embassy."

That got a chuckle, and Zamo added, "It's easy to get in here, but not so easy to get out."

Not so funny.

Brenner said to Zamo, "Call in a sit-rep."

I asked Kate, "You okay with this?"

"I'm fine. I have Zamo and a Colt .45."

Brenner advised her, "Keep the scarf on."

In the spirit of cultural outreach, I kept my jambiyah on, and Brenner and I got out and walked away from the parked vehicles where we could be seen by the person, whoever he was. Actually, I was pretty sure I knew who was meeting us.

I looked at the surrounding stone and brick buildings. Some old forts are romantic; some are sinister and depressing. This place would get the Midnight Express award for Creepiest Turkish-Built Prison.

Brenner reminded me, "You are here as the interrogator for the FBI Evidence Response Team investigating the *Cole* attack. But if you don't mind, I'd like to take a shot at the prisoner."

"Sure. You go first. Then I'll show you how it's done."

He took that well, but also reminded me, "I was a criminal investigator."

"Right. But if this is like the Central Prison in Aden, don't expect too much."

A Humvee came across the dusty field and stopped a few feet from us. The rear door opened and out came Colonel Hakim of the Political Security Organization. He was dressed in a uniform this time, but that didn't make him any more attractive than the last time I saw him.

He glanced at my jambiyah and smiled—or was that a sneer?—and motioned us to the vehicle. I got in the front with the driver, who had spent the day with livestock, and Brenner kept Colonel Hakim company in the rear.

Colonel Hakim said something to the driver and off we went.

Brenner, sticking to protocol, said to Hakim, "Thank you, Colonel, for meeting us."

Colonel Hakim replied, "I am not for this arrangement, but I follow my orders."

What a gracious man. Hey, shithead, you're riding in a Humvee that I helped pay for.

Brenner reminded the colonel, "We have the same enemy, and the U.S. is here to offer assistance."

No reply.

To confirm what Buck said about the CIA, I asked Mr. Happy, "Have any other Americans come to speak to the prisoner?"

He didn't reply at first, then asked, "Do you not know?"

"I just got here."

"Yes? So you ask your friends."

Asshole.

We stopped at a particularly grim-looking four-story building, and even without the bars on the windows, I would have known this was the prison.

I've seen too many prisons in my life. And too many prisoners. And each visit to a prison took something out of me, and left something with me.

Colonel Hakim said, "You have half hour. No more."

But I'm sure Colonel Hakim was hoping that the next time he brought us here, it would be for more than half an hour. Like maybe twenty years. Meanwhile, we were just visiting.

CHAPTER TWENTY-NINE

We entered the prison through a rusty iron door into a dark stone vestibule where a guard stood and snapped to attention.

We followed Colonel Hakim down a quiet corridor whose walls were covered with rotting stucco. This building may have a mold problem.

My mind went back to the Central Prison in Aden, which had been built by the Brits when they ran South Yemen. That, too, was a grim and creepy place, but this place made the Aden prison look like a health spa.

Colonel Hakim led us into another quiet corridor of closed wooden doors. I guess it was past quitting time, but when we passed a narrow staircase that led to the second level, I heard a man scream, followed by a man shouting, then another scream. Glad to hear someone was still at work.

Colonel Hakim opened a door, and we followed him into a room where two men sat in plastic chairs at a small table. Along one wall were file cabinets, and on the far wall was a barred window without glass that let in sunlight and whatever else wanted to fly in. A floor fan moved the bad air around.

On one wall was a large picture of Yemen's President for Life, Ali Abdullah Saleh, a mustachioed Saddam Hussein look-alike, who was desperately trying to avoid the same fate as his Iraqi idol.

On another wall were signs and posters in Arabic that I guessed were not the prisoners' bill of rights, though one of them may have said EMPLOYEES MUST WASH HANDS AFTER BEATING PRISONERS.

Anyway, the two men were standing now and neither of them looked like a prisoner. In fact, Hakim introduced one as the interpreter, and the other as a doctor. Hakim explained, "Prisoner speaks no English and prisoner is sick." Makes sense.

The interpreter, a young guy in Western clothing, asked us to call him Sammy, and the doctor, an older gent in a ratty suit without a tie, introduced himself as Dr. Fahd. Brenner introduced himself using his former military rank, so I introduced myself as Commander Corey. Why not?

The interpreter invited us to sit, which we did, though Hakim remained standing, and Dr. Fahd sat with a newspaper and lit a cigarette. Sammy had a dossier in front of him and he flipped through it, then said to Brenner and me, "The prisoner's name is Rahim ibn Hayyam—"

Brenner interrupted and said, "Can we have a copy of that?"

Hakim, standing near the window, asked Brenner, "Do you read Arabic, Mr. Brenner?"

Brenner replied, too politely I thought, "No, but I can have it translated."

Hakim informed him, "That is a classified dossier and may not leave this room."

I took out my pen and my detective's notebook, which I never leave home without, and said to Sammy, "Can you spell that name?"

Hakim said, "No. No notes. I tell you to listen."

Brenner said to me, "We'll put in a request through channels."

Sammy continued, "The prisoner says he is twenty-two years of age, and that he is a Saudi citizen by birth. His passport was taken from him by Al Qaeda, so all this is his word. He tells us he is from a good family of the upper middle class who live in Medina. He has two years of university in Riyadh. He further states that he is a good Muslim, he answers the daily calls to prayer, and he has made the Hajj."

That's good. I guess. Sammy went on a bit about the prisoner's religious background—he was a Sunni Muslim—and his devotion to the teaching of the Koran and so forth.

I mean, did I need to know this? But I guess around here this was important stuff. Why? I have no idea. Maybe a good Muslim got better food or one less kick in the balls. Meanwhile, the clock was ticking, and I give Brenner credit for saying, "Can we move on to other information?"

Sammy glanced at Hakim, who knew he had wasted as much time as he was going to get away with, and Hakim nodded.

Sammy flipped a page of the dossier and continued, "The prisoner says he was recruited by Al Qaeda in Medina four months ago. He does not know the family names of his recruiters, only their given names, and that they, too, were Saudis. Shortly thereafter, he was flown on Yemenia airlines to Sana'a on his own passport with a tourist visa. He was met at the airport by two unnamed men, then taken to a house in an outlying district, the location of which he does not know. He stayed in the house for five days, with two other recruits from Saudi Arabia, and they passed their time fasting and praying."

Some guys have all the fun. No wonder they wanted to join Al Qaeda. Travel, adventure, meet new people, fast, pray, get shot, and go to jail where you get tortured. Sign me up. I mean, what the hell are these people thinking? That is the question.

Sammy continued, "On the fifth day, at dawn, the prisoner and the two others were put into a Toyota Hilux with a driver and traveled east on the Marib road. They were stopped at three military checkpoints, but upon showing their Saudi passports and saying they were tourists and students on their way to the Marib ruins, they were allowed to pass. The driver, a Yemeni, told the soldiers he was a paid guide." Sammy commented, "This is a place of ancient temples from the times of Sheba, and the place where the Ark of Noah is said to have come to rest, so it is interesting to Jews, Christians, and Muslims."

Right. And American oil companies and Al Qaeda. Lots going on around Marib. Maybe Matt Longo was right—this was someplace I should see.

Sammy continued, "This was a five-hour journey on the Marib road, and then another half hour into the mountains. The prisoner claims that he cannot tell us or show us where he was traveling in the mountains or where he ended because the three men were asked to bind cloths over their eyes."

I hope the driver wasn't blindfolded. But seeing how these people drove, it wouldn't matter much.

Sammy said, "The prisoner, with his two compatriots, arrived in a mountain camp, which he describes as primitive. Mud houses and caves, and also some Bedouin tents. Perhaps it was once a Bedouin camp. This, he says, was the Al Qaeda training camp, populated by perhaps a hundred recruits from various countries, including Oman, Iraq, Egypt, and Kuwait. And also ten or twelve others who were officers, military trainers, and spiritual guides."

Spiritual guides? Maybe that's what I needed instead of a supervisor. There was no spiritual element to the Anti-Terrorist Task Force. How could we be Crusaders without spiritual guides? Anyway, it seemed to me that Islamic jihadists, including Al Qaeda, had medieval heads and twenty-first-century weapons. And that, I thought, made this war very different. I missed the godless Communists.

Sammy flipped a page and said, "The training in the camp lasted for three months—training with rifles, explosives, maps, and communication equipment. The prisoner described the training as very tiring and very hard, and the food was of poor quality."

This was sounding like more fun every minute. But, I mean, you gotta give these bastards credit. My teenage nephew won't clean his room, but Al Qaeda gets these mostly middle-class kids to leave their air-conditioning, televisions, and indoor plumbing and go out to the boondocks to live in mud huts and eat goats and learn how to be fighters. Sort of like the Peace Corps, except for the guns. And then there was The Panther from Perth Amboy, New Jersey. What's going on here?

Sammy continued, "The prisoner says there was

a medical person in the camp, but this person lacked skills and supplies. He says one recruit died of a fever, and one of injuries received in a fall from a mountain path. He says there was much sickness in the camp."

Right. They didn't have a nurse sticking needles in their ass before they got to Yemen. Bottom line, Al Qaeda in Yemen was in stage one or two of development; they had arrived, they were setting up camps, they had recruits and a training cadre, but they weren't strong enough yet to make a major move toward toppling the government. Meanwhile, Al Qaeda was gaining confidence and respect by mounting attacks against foreign interests and individuals—tourists, embassies, and businesses—and not taking on the Yemeni military, which would make even a lazy and incompetent army retaliate. And then there was the USS *Cole*, the first and so far most spectacular and successful Al Qaeda attack in Yemen. That got them noticed.

Sammy continued, "When this training was complete, the prisoner and forty others traveled by vehicle to the region north of Marib town. There they lived in the huts of sheep herders who were not present. And there they planned and prepared for the attack on the American oil facility, which is nearby."

Sammy looked up from the transcript and said to us, "That is as far as the interrogators got before the prisoner became ill and had to be taken to the prison hospital."

Right. It's always a delicate balance between vigorous interrogation and putting the prisoner in the hospital. Or the morgue.

Sammy assured us, however, "The prisoner is somewhat better now and you may speak to him." He also editorialized, "This is a misguided young man who is frightened, and he cries for his parents and his good life in Saudi Arabia."

No shit. This kid was looking at ten or twenty years in a Yemeni slammer, which was a death sentence. Unless, of course, Al Qaeda sprung him. Or if Al Qaeda took over here. Then he'd be a hero. Meanwhile, he needed to survive, and the best way to do that was to talk, which he sounded happy to do if these idiots didn't kill him first.

Brenner asked Sammy, "Did the prisoner say who his leaders were?"

Sammy replied, "As I have said, he has stated that he knows his companions only by their given names."

Okay, but how about a description of the leaders? Their nationality? Like did one of them have a New Jersey accent and a Jersey shore T-shirt? I mean, if I had this prisoner alone for two hours, I'd wring him dry. But these interrogators, as I saw in Aden, were inept sadists. All they wanted, ultimately, were more names and a full confession. I wanted to know what the prisoner had for breakfast and what his favorite TV show was, and we took it from there.

Brenner asked Sammy, "What did the prisoner say about the relationship between his camp and the local tribes?"

Sammy replied, "He says nothing about that."

Brenner then asked, "Why wasn't he asked? How could this camp exist without the permission of the tribal chieftains?"

Sammy shrugged, then speculated, "Perhaps they had an arrangement. Or this camp was too strong for the local tribe. Or—"

Hakim interrupted, "Do not interrogate the translator, Mr. Brenner. He is here only to say what the prisoner has said."

True. But as long as Sammy seemed chatty and helpful to the Americans, I asked him, "Was the prisoner cooperative with the other Americans who were here this morning?"

Sammy replied, "Yes, but the prisoner was sick, in the hospital, so it was a short talk."

I asked Colonel Hakim, "Were you here this morning when the CIA was here?"

"You should ask them, not me." Colonel Hakim had become impatient with us and said, "Let us see now the prisoner."

Dr. Fahd grabbed his medical bag, and we all stood and followed Hakim out of the room and down the corridor.

I wasn't sure if all this was bringing us any closer to The Panther, but it was at least interesting. A small insight into Al Qaeda's modus operandi, though not their heads. Probably I'd never get into their heads—we weren't even on the same planet. But I thought I understood a little about Rahim ibn Hayyam, though I hadn't yet met him. He was a scared kid, and he was happy to talk. He might not think he knew much about the bigger picture, but he probably knew more than he thought he did.

With any luck, Rahim had met The Panther, and with any more luck, The Panther was still in the Marib hills. And if he stayed there, he'd have John Corey up his ass.

CHAPTER THIRTY

We came to an iron door where a guard was taking a khat-nap in a white plastic chair. Hakim kicked the man's leg, and the guard stood quickly and opened the door.

Hakim entered first, followed by Sammy, Dr. Fahd, Brenner, and me.

The cell, probably an interrogation room, was about ten feet square, lit only by a high, barred window and a single hanging lightbulb. The walls were whitewashed brick with some interesting reddish stains around the perimeter, including a few red handprints.

A filthy mattress lay on the stone floor, and on the mattress was a young man with a wispy beard, wearing dirty white prison pajamas that were bloody around his left leg where his wound had bled through the bandages. I noticed, too, that his right eye was swollen shut. Also, his lower lip was split, and his hooked nose was crooked. I also saw that his arms and legs were shackled, and the leg chain was bolted to the floor.

Hakim explained to his American guests, "He is chained to prevent him harming himself."

Right. He has lots of people to do that for him.

Hakim snapped at the prisoner, who sat up slowly and moved his back against the wall.

Hakim also explained, "As you can see, this man has been injured when he resisted capture by the security forces at the American oil company."

I recalled the same bullshit in the Aden prison. Interesting that the Yemenis thought they had to lie to the Americans about beating prisoners. My jokes to the contrary, I'm not a big fan of torture. It's messy, risky, not productive, and not right. What you want from a prisoner is in his head, so you have to beat up his brain, not his body. Takes longer, but you get better results.

Dr. Fahd moved a chair beside the prisoner to check out his vitals.

There were four other white plastic chairs in the room, and Colonel Hakim invited me, Brenner, and Sammy to sit facing the prisoner. Hakim moved a chair against a wall between us and the prisoner and sat.

As my eyes adjusted to the dim light, I saw an empty plastic water bottle near the prisoner, and a full basin of what looked and smelled like urine. There were old cigarette butts on the floor, and what appeared to be well-masticated khat leaves. The whole room reeked of a hundred years of misery.

Dr. Fahd looked in the prisoner's eyes with a light, took his temperature, listened to his heart and lungs, then took his blood pressure.

The good doctor stood and said, "The prisoner is well."

Actually, the prisoner looked like he'd just gone ten rounds with Mike Tyson. But maybe his vitals were good.

Dr. Fahd sat in a corner and lit a cigarette. I guess it's all right for doctors to smoke here.

Colonel Hakim spoke to the prisoner, obviously introducing his visitors, and I heard the word "Amrika."

The prisoner closed his good eye and nodded.

Hakim said to us, "You may begin."

I nodded to Brenner, who looked at Rahim ibn Hayyam and asked, "How are you feeling?"

Sammy translated, Rahim replied, and Sammy, who apparently forgot or wasn't told that Brenner understood some Arabic, said to us, "He is feeling well."

Brenner corrected, "*Not* well. And he says he needs food and water."

Sammy glanced at Colonel Hakim, and Hakim said to Brenner, "If your Arabic is so good, I will send the translator away."

Brenner replied, "My Arabic is good enough to know when I hear a false translation."

Hakim ignored him and looked at me. "And you, Mr. Corey? How is your Arabic?"

"Better than your English."

Hakim didn't like that, but he said something to the guard, who left. Hakim said to Brenner, "Continue."

So having established that we couldn't be totally conned, Brenner, with the clock ticking, got right to the point and asked, "What is the name of your commander?"

Sammy asked, Rahim replied, and Sammy said to us, "As he has stated, he knows only given names."

"Okay. What was the given name of his commander?"

Sammy asked and Rahim replied, "Sayid." Rahim

said something else, and Sammy told us, "This was one of the men who died in the attack."

Well, I guess that's a dead end.

Brenner asked, "What was Sayid's nationality?"

The answer was Iraqi.

The guard returned with a bottle of water that he threw on the mattress, and Rahim opened it and finished it in one long gulp.

Brenner asked a few more questions about Rahim's comrades in arms. Bottom line, this platoon-sized unit of fighters really didn't know each other's full names, which was good security in the event one of them, such as Rahim, was captured. They did, however, know nationalities and some hometowns, and Brenner established that about half of them were Saudis—our good allies—and some were from Kuwait, the country that we liberated from Iraq in the first Gulf War. There were also a few recruits from neighboring Oman, a few from Egypt, and only five Yemenis—probably recovering khat chewers. Interestingly, most of the spiritual guides were from Saudi Arabia, and most of the military trainers and commanders were Iraqis, former members of the now-defunct Iraqi Army, who were currently employed by the group called Al Qaeda in Mesopotamia. Hey, you got a kill skill, you gotta sell it somewhere.

Anyway, Brenner, ex-soldier, then asked Military Intelligence–type questions about command structure, equipment, morale, and so forth, and he got some interesting information to pass on to the embassy military attaché. But we weren't any closer to The Panther.

In fact, this interrogation, as we both knew, had some problems. Not only was time short, but Colonel

Hakim of the Political Security Organization was listening to every word, so he'd know what we were looking for, and he could figure out what we already knew or didn't know.

If these people were real allies, it wouldn't matter much. But they weren't. In fact, for all I knew, Colonel Hakim, and maybe the interpreter and the doctor, had a brother-in-law in Al Qaeda. I remember having the same problems with interrogations in Aden.

Considering all that, Brenner and I had to do a balancing act. This was probably our only shot at the prisoner, and we had to maximize the opportunity without giving away too much to our allies. Or our enemies. On the other hand, we did want Al Qaeda to know one thing—John Corey was looking for The Panther from Perth Amboy.

Brenner now put on his cop hat and said to Sammy, "Tell Rahim that if he continues to answer truthfully, the Americans will assist in returning him to his home."

Sammy glanced at Hakim, who nodded, and Sammy passed on Brenner's kind bullshit. I mean, Rahim was an Al Qaeda jihadist who just attacked an American-owned oil facility, so he had a better chance of being repatriated by the Yemenis than by Americans—and if Rahim ever wound up on American soil, the place would be called Guantanamo. But the offer must have sounded sincere to the desperate Rahim, and he nodded vigorously.

Brenner then asked, "Did any of your companions or commanders ever live in America?"

Sammy asked the question, and Rahim seemed to hesitate, then replied. Sammy said to us, "He says one of his companions, Anwar, the Egyptian, lived for a time in America. He also says he had heard that a high commander once lived in America."

Brenner was smart enough not to ask a quick follow-up question and changed the subject. He asked, "Did you receive any assistance or information from any of the tribes in the Marib area?"

Rahim listened to the translation, then said something that Sammy translated as, "He says a sheik of the Yafi tribe—a local chieftain of that tribe—took money from Al Qaeda for safe passage and for the use of this Bedouin camp."

It was interesting that Al Qaeda was able to make a deal with the local chief. All differences aside, money talks. Or, as Buck said in New York, favors were exchanged.

Brenner followed up with, "What else did this sheik provide?"

Sammy asked Rahim, then said to us, "He says the sheik provided food, guides, and information concerning the security of the American oil installation. He also says he and his comrades were told by their commanders that with this information, their attack would be successful."

Rahim volunteered something else, which is always a good sign, and Sammy told us, "He says the American oil company security forces appeared to be expecting them, and he now believes that someone betrayed them to the Americans or to the Yemeni security forces."

Hey, welcome to Yemen, Rahim. Only here we don't call it betrayal, we call it business as usual. And it was probably the local sheik who was playing both ends of that business.

Brenner asked, "What is the name of this sheik?"

Sammy asked, but Rahim said he didn't know.

Brenner said to me, "The Yafi are a large tribe around Marib, but like all tribes, they're broken into many clans that sometimes take their name from their ancestral sheiks. So if we had this sheik's name, we could identify the local tribe and maybe get a fix on this Al Qaeda camp." Brenner then said to Colonel Hakim, "You should look into this."

Hakim replied curtly, "Do not tell me what I should do."

Ally or asshole?

Brenner thought asshole and explained to me, "The PSO doesn't like to leave the safety of the cities."

I thought Hakim was going to blow a gasket, but he controlled himself and said to us, "Five minutes." He added, for the record, "The prisoner is sick and must rest."

I pointed out, "The doctor said he was doing great."

"Five minutes."

Brenner said to me, "Your turn."

Okay. As I said, I like to soften up the prisoner with personal questions and sports talk, but we had a big cultural divide here, and I had about four minutes, so I went right for the big enchilada and asked a typical leading question. "When was the last time you saw Bulus ibn al-Darwish—al-Numair?"

Rahim's puffy eyes opened wide even before the translation.

Sammy translated, and I could see that Rahim was struggling with his response. Finally, he replied.

Colonel Hakim sat stone-faced as he listened to Rahim, and Brenner was nodding as though he understood every word—or at least every third word.

Finally Sammy translated, "He says...al-Numair—The Panther—was present on the evening of the attack. Last night. Al-Numair spoke to the fighters and assured them they would be victorious. They prayed together...then al-Numair entered a vehicle and drove away."

I exchanged glances with Brenner, then I asked a standard police question. "What kind of vehicle? What color?"

Sammy asked, then told us, "He says it appeared to be a Toyota Hilux. White."

Brenner informed me, "A very common SUV in Yemen. And ninety percent of the vehicles in this country are white."

"I noticed." So The Panther was tooling around in a commonly used vehicle, which was no surprise. But what was surprising was that he seemed to have safe passage in this tribal area.

I asked, "How many vehicles were with him?"

The answer was five, and Sammy said they were all white SUVs, though Rahim couldn't be certain of their makes or models.

I asked another standard police question. "What was al-Numair wearing?"

The answer was traditional North Yemen clothing—a white fouteh, and a shiwal on his head. No Jersey shore T-shirt. The Panther, it seemed, was returning to his roots.

I tapped my dagger and asked, "Jambiyah?"

Sammy didn't have to translate, and Rahim nodded and said, "Jambiyah."

"Facial hair?"

Yes. A long black beard.

"What was his general appearance? Sick? Healthy? Heavy, thin?"

Sammy asked and said to me, "Rahim believes this man looked healthy. But very thin."

I asked, "Does Rahim know that Bulus ibn al-Darwish is an American citizen?"

Sammy seemed surprised at that, though Rahim did not. Sammy said to me, "He has heard this. But did not know if it was true."

In a normal interrogation, I'd now mention the big reward and ask, "Where is he hiding?" But I was sure that Rahim didn't know. Not even for five million bucks. And if he did know, and if he told us, it wouldn't be the Americans who got there first. In fact, it would probably be someone telling The Panther to beat feet. Or if the Yemeni Army gave it a try, they wouldn't necessarily ask us to help, and left to their own proven incompetence, The Panther would get away.

So instead of "Where is he hiding?" I asked, "Where and when is the next attack?"

Sammy translated and Rahim replied. Sammy said to me, "There was talk in the camp of attacks on the oil pipeline between Marib and As-Salif, attacks on oil engineers, aid workers, and Western tourists." He added, "And talk of an attack on the American Embassy."

This was hardly hot news, and I doubted if a low-level jihadist had any specific times or places for these attacks. I thought of young Mr. Longo and his planned excursion to see the temples of Marib. Maybe he should just visit the website of the Yemeni Tourist Board, click onto Marib, and call it a day.

Remembering that The Panther got his big start in

Yemen with the *Cole* attack in Aden Harbor, and knowing that criminals sometimes return to the scene of
their crimes, I asked another leading question. "What
is al-Numair's target in Aden?"

Rahim seemed to understand the question before it
was translated and replied in Arabic to Sammy.

I heard the word "Sheraton," which was not the
word I wanted to hear.

Sammy said to me, "The Sheraton Hotel. He says he
was told there are many American soldiers and police
in the hotel...infidels on sacred Islamic soil...He says
his companions who did not participate in the attack
on the American oil installation are now traveling to
Aden. But he has no further knowledge of this."

I said to Brenner, "That might be interesting information to anyone planning to stay at the Sheraton in
Aden."

Brenner did not respond.

Colonel Hakim said, "Your time is finished."

I ignored him and said directly to Rahim, "Thank
you for your cooperation. If you continue to cooperate
with the Americans, we will do everything possible to
help you return to your home."

Sammy didn't translate, and Hakim stood and said,
"It is finished."

As I suspected, Rahim, like most educated Saudis, actually understood a little English, and he probably enjoyed contraband American DVDs—maybe
The Sopranos or *Sex and the City*, and he said to me,
"Please, sir. Help me. I help you."

I looked at Rahim sitting against the wall, his eyes
on me. If he got sprung, I wondered if he'd go home
and get his life together, or if he'd rejoin the fight.

About twenty-five percent of the jihadists released from Guantanamo had turned up again on the battlefields of Afghanistan. And others had been rearrested for terrorist activities in Saudi Arabia, Iraq, and Europe. I wasn't sure about Rahim, but from experience I know that all prisoners are sorry for what they've done. Once freed, however, they're only sorry they got caught.

Maybe Rahim was different. But even if he was, he didn't join Al Qaeda to promote world peace. And he didn't go to the American oil installation looking for a job; he went there knowing he was going to kill people. And if his jihadists had overrun the facility, they'd have killed everyone in it—American and European civilians, security people, Yemeni workers, and anyone else who lived or worked there. It didn't turn out that way, but it could have. And now Rahim was sorry.

"Please to help me. I help you."

I turned and left.

CHAPTER THIRTY-ONE

In the better air outside the prison, Brenner said to Colonel Hakim, "Thank you for your time and assistance."

Hakim didn't reply to Brenner, but he did say to me, "Your visa, and that of your wife, remains a problem."

"Sorry. Hey, maybe I need a tourist visa like all the Al Qaeda guys have who come through Sana'a Airport."

Colonel Hakim didn't have much to say about that, but he did advise both of us, "Be very careful here."

If Ghumdan had a soundtrack, this is when I'd hear an ominous organ chord.

Brenner said to Hakim, "We can find our way back to our vehicle." Then Brenner did a nice thing and saluted, and Colonel Hakim returned the salute. Military guys do that, even when they hate each other. Good bonding.

As Brenner and I walked back to the Land Cruiser, he said to me, "You shouldn't piss him off."

"Me? How about you?"

"He's got some power, and we may need him at some point."

"He and his government actually need us more than we need them."

"True. But they don't get that yet."

"They will."

It was good to be out of that prison. The place was rotting, and everyone in it was rotting. In fact, this whole country was rotting.

Brenner asked me, "What did you think of all that?"

"Let me speak to my spiritual advisor and I'll get back to you. Meanwhile, I did get some insight into Al Qaeda in the Arabian Peninsula."

"Right. The Yemenis don't know what they're in for, or that they have a small window to snuff out Al Qaeda before these guys get their game on."

"Well," I pointed out, "if the Yemenis don't know what's coming, it's no one's fault but their own."

"Correct. But the Yemeni Army and government are obsessed with their tribal problems, and their ongoing fight with South Yemen." He added, "They think Al Qaeda is an American obsession."

"Well, it is. But with good reason."

"Correct." Brenner said to me, "Good question about Aden."

Actually, all my questions were good, but I replied, "I'm surprised the Sheraton in Aden hasn't been attacked yet." I pointed out, "Aside from the embassy, that's where to find the most Americans in one place. And it's not that secure."

He nodded. "I've been there."

"Me, too, and we're going there again."

We made our way through a cluster of decrepit buildings that looked like barracks. I could smell food cooking somewhere, and at the end of the barracks I saw the minarets of a small mosque. Soldiers lounged around, smoking and chewing whatever, and giving us the eye. Garrison life is no treat, but I'm sure the Yemeni Army liked it better than mounting field operations against a tough and motivated enemy. Same with the National Security police, who apparently sat out the attack on the Hunt Oil installation.

Brenner asked me, "Do you think The Panther is still in the Marib area?"

"I think he's found a tribal sheik who's giving him a secure base—a sanctuary."

"Sounds that way." He added, "But Marib may get hot for him after that attack."

I motioned toward the crack troops sitting around and asked, "Will it?"

"Well, maybe not."

On another subject, Brenner said to me, "The PSO always knew we were looking for The Panther. Now they know that a guy named John Corey has arrived to join the search." He reminded me, "Assuming this information gets to Al Qaeda, then we have to hope that the name John Corey has some meaning to The Panther."

Right. Like, "Hey, isn't John Corey the guy who killed Asad Khalil? Let's kill John Corey." I said, as I'd already said, "God, I hope so."

We were now crossing the dusty parade ground and I could see the Land Cruiser where we'd left it. I thought I saw Kate's head in the rear seat. I really didn't think there'd be a problem, but anything was possible in Yemen.

I asked Brenner, "So what's with this tribal sheik who helped Al Qaeda?"

"Don't know. But it happens. Either for money, or because a sheik wants to poke the government in the eye." He assured me, "Next week, this sheik could be helping us."

"Maybe he already did."

"Right—Rahim thinks someone betrayed them. But that was Rahim's first introduction to the battle-field, and what looked to him like a setup could just have been Hunt's hired mercenaries doing what they get paid for." He also informed me, "Our military atta-ché and the CIA are doing an analysis and report of the attack."

"Can't wait to read it." I reminded him, "The CIA was here before us."

"Correct. They're looking at the bigger picture. We're looking for The Panther."

"That *is* the bigger picture."

"Good point."

I returned to the subject of this tribal sheik and said, "If we go out to the Badlands, are we supposed to trust the sheiks of Araby?"

Brenner assured me, "They're good for their word—until someone makes them a better offer."

"You can't buy that kind of loyalty."

Brenner said, "At least the Montagnards—the hill tribes—stayed loyal to the Americans right until the end."

"That'll teach them."

"Well, we projected great power. No one bets on a loser. Right now in Yemen, no one can say who has the power, and who the winner is going to be. But if Al Qaeda starts to look like a winner, they'll be able to recruit young Yemenis in great numbers. Then we have a problem, and we either have to cut and run, or get involved in a third land war."

"Nuke 'em. It's cheaper."

He ignored my suggestion and said to me, "We can buy some time if we kill or capture Bulus ibn al-Darwish. He's the driving force behind recruiting, training, and motivating this small but growing movement. Also, he apparently has some access to big money and he's a hero to the jihadists because of the *Cole* attack. So if we get him, that will be a strategic and psychological blow to Al Qaeda here and around the world."

"Right. And don't forget that The Panther is an American. So maybe he thinks more clearly and logically than most of these whacked-out jihadists."

"Maybe."

We were closer to the Land Cruiser now, and I could definitely see Kate in the rear. Sometimes I forget how much I love my wife, and maybe I don't always say it or show it, but then when a situation becomes dangerous, I realize I could lose her. I try to picture a life without her, living alone in New York in a big apartment on the fashionable Upper East Side, surrounded by trendy bars and restaurants bursting with single women... Is this coming out right?

I asked Brenner, "Any chance of us getting Rahim alone, with an embassy interpreter?"

"Not a chance."

"Right." Same as when I was questioning the *Cole* suspects in Aden. The PSO was the five-hundred-pound gorilla in the room. "Any chance of another chaperoned interview?"

"We'll put in a request. But to be honest, the Agency

has first dibs on Rahim." He added, "You got your FBI Evidence Response Team shot."

"Right." I also asked him, "Are we going to Marib?"

"Maybe. But we're going to Aden first to set up a command post in the Sheraton."

"When?"

"Could be tomorrow."

We got to the Land Cruiser, and I wanted to sit with Kate, so Brenner sat up front. Zamo started the SUV and off we went.

Kate unwrapped her scarf and asked, "How did it go?"

I replied, "Not bad, but not great. Hakim was in the room, and we had only half an hour, and the prisoner wasn't feeling his very best."

Brenner said, "We'll bring you up to speed when we see Buck."

Zamo was heading toward the watchtowers, and we sailed through the open gates into the city.

Brenner said, "I'll drop you off at the Sheraton, and Zamo will pick you up at seven." He informed us, "Martini night at the embassy."

Kate, of course, asked, "What is the dress?"

Brenner replied, "People dress a bit."

I suggested, "Wear your new balto."

She suggested, "Why don't you wear it?"

That got a laugh. We were really having a good time.

Brenner reminded us, "Guns will be worn. Vests optional."

We pulled up to the Sheraton, and Zamo got Kate's shopping bags out of the rear. I didn't see the exploding mangos.

Brenner also reminded us, "We may be leaving for Aden tomorrow, so think about packing."

He and Zamo pulled away, and we walked past the National Security Bureau guards and into the lobby.

I stopped at the front desk to see if there were any messages for us, and the desk clerk handed me an envelope, which I opened on the way to the elevator.

It was a fax from Tom Walsh, sent not from the ATTF office, of course, but from a Kinko's near 26 Federal Plaza. I read the fax aloud. "Dear John and Kate, Thanks for your call. Hope you're enjoying the sights and the good weather. Snow here today. You're lucky to be in Yemen. Have a wonderful trip. See you soon."

I commented, "Asshole."

Kate reminded me, "You started it."

There was a P.S., and I read, "You knew what this was about before you got on the plane."

Double asshole. But he was right. And yet here I was. What was I thinking? Not much.

The NSB guy at the elevator didn't ask to see our key or anything, and we took the elevator up.

We ran a bit long in the shower, and by the time we got dressed it was a little after seven.

I had a tie and jacket on, and Kate was wearing a nice black dress. She had her gun in her purse, and I had mine in my holster. She talked me out of wearing my jambiyah, and neither of us had our Kevlar vests, but Kate had her scarf on to walk through the lobby.

Down in the lobby, I noticed a lot of Mideastern-looking men in sunglasses, dressed in Western clothing, heading for the bar. Guilty pleasures aren't the same for everyone, everywhere. Here, narcotic leaves were guilt-free, a martini was not.

Kate commented, "They go out without their wives."

"What's the fun in that?"

Anyway, Zamo was waiting in the Land Cruiser, and we hopped in, me riding up front.

He said to us, "Looks like we're heading to Aden tomorrow."

I asked him, "Have they improved the road?"

"No. But we've improved our armor and firepower." He laughed.

I love being the straight man for a comedian doing sicko humor.

As we headed up the road toward the embassy, I said to him, "The prisoner we spoke to today said Al Qaeda was planning an attack on the Sheraton in Aden." I added, before he could, "But no problem. We'll probably never make it to Aden."

He laughed, then confided to me, "I like you."

Kate said, "I need a drink."

CHAPTER THIRTY-TWO

Cocktails were in the embassy's atrium lobby, and this was for staff only, not an embassy reception, which would be held in the more formal parlor.

The unstated reason for this free alcohol was that the new ambassador had not yet arrived, and this was everyone's last chance to get snockered before he showed up.

And if we needed another reason for the taxpayers to buy us a drink, this was a welcome party for the two new legal attachés, FBI Special Agent Howard Fensterman and FBI Special Agent Kate Mayfield, a.k.a. Mrs. Corey. And, I guess, it was a hello party for me, too, though I wasn't on staff here, and I'd be saying good-bye shortly.

I suspected that there were not many social demands on the American Embassy staff in Sana'a, nor were there more interesting things for them to do in Yemen on a weekend, so I was sure most of them were here tonight.

The size of an embassy staff is classified, but I'll say we had three bartenders, and six Yemeni men passing hors d'oeuvres. Hopefully, the Marines or the Diplomatic Security Service had checked them all out for suicide belts.

None of the Marines were in attendance, except for the two officers, a captain, and a young lieutenant who told me he'd served in Afghanistan. I asked him, "Would you rather be here or Afghanistan?"

He replied without hesitation, "Afghanistan," explaining, "There you know you're in a combat zone, and so does everyone around you. Here, everyone around you—the civilians—pretend there's no war, and that's dangerous."

"Right." Which was probably not much different than the mind-set in the presidential palace and the government ministries. Except now and then, reality intruded into the deep bunkers of denial.

I looked around at the embassy people, who were nicely dressed, sipping cocktails and chatting. This could have been anywhere in the civilized world, including New York. But outside the guarded walls was another world that had absolutely nothing in common with this world. Except, to be optimistic, a shared humanity, a love of children and family, a hope for peace, prosperity, health, and happiness, and a belief in a higher being who was loving and kind—except when he got pissed off and sent plagues and floods to get rid of everyone.

Kate was making the rounds, getting to know her new colleagues, who actually would never see her again. I chatted with people who came up to me and welcomed me to Yemen. Everyone seemed to know I was going to Aden with the FBI Evidence Response Team, and that my stay in Sana'a would be short.

Interestingly, no one wanted to know anything about the *Cole* investigation. I think the dips put a distance between themselves and those men and women who used the cover of the embassy for other kinds of work.

Among those who did that kind of work was the military attaché, a.k.a. the Military Intelligence officer, who introduced himself to me as Colonel Drew Kent, U.S. Army, a tall, middle-aged man in mufti. His job here, he informed me, was challenging, but fulfilling. A few minutes later he modified that a bit and said, "The Yemeni Army is a friggin' joke. The unwilling led by the incompetent. Ill-paid, ill-equipped, ill-trained, and unmotivated."

"But are they good?"

He thought that was funny and advised me, "If you need to depend on them to provide security for your work—whatever it is—make sure you watch your back and sleep with your boots on and your gun handy. Better yet, stay awake."

I asked him, "How about the National Security Bureau?"

"You mean the blue clowns? Half police force, half tourist protection service, and all corrupt. They don't have a clear mission or a clear chain of command. They're used and abused by the politicians to further their own agendas. If you need to rely on them for security, make sure you pay them well—half up front, half if you get back alive."

I hoped Matt Longo knew all that. I inquired, "How much is well?"

"About two dollars per man, per day. Extra if they have to fire their rifles."

"Sounds reasonable."

He informed me, "The blue clowns did a disappearing act on a bunch of Belgian tourists last August. At the Marib ruins."

"Really? What happened to the tourists?"

"They disappeared, too. Maybe kidnapped, but no one has heard from them."

"I hope they're all right."

"Don't bet on it. Their Yemeni guide and their bus driver were found with their throats slit."

Ouch. I didn't remember hearing about this, but bad news out of Yemen wasn't big news in the States unless it had to do with Americans. I mean, I'd been surprised to discover there were over a hundred Westerners kidnapped in the last ten years, mostly Europeans. Now and then you'd hear about tourists being killed, sometimes in a crossfire between Yemeni security forces and tribal kidnappers. But what Colonel Kent was describing didn't sound like a tribal kidnapping.

I asked him, "Could that have been an Al Qaeda attack?"

"That seems to be the consensus. But the Yemeni government plays down these incidents." He let me know, "They like the tourism. In fact, tours still go to the Marib ruins."

"How many come back?"

On the subject of Marib as an exciting place, Colonel Kent said, "There was an Al Qaeda attack last night on the Hunt Oil installation north of Marib."

"I heard."

"Did you?" He continued, "Hunt hires its own security force—mostly American and European mercenary types. Unfortunately, the NSB insists on being in on the arrangement—for money, of course. But as I said, you can't trust them, so when the excrement starts to fly, you don't know if the NSB has your back, or if they ran away, or if they joined the other team." He concluded, "Tactically, it's a damned nightmare."

"Right. But the Al Qaeda guys were routed."

"Luck. Or maybe the Hunt guys knew they were coming. Information is cheaper than a barrel of oil around here." He added, "Maybe the Al Qaeda force was inept."

I thought of Rahim and partly agreed. But I was also sure that the Al Qaeda guys were going to get better.

Colonel Kent said to me, "They got an Al Qaeda prisoner from the attack."

I didn't respond, so he asked me, "You know about that?"

"You know I do and that's all I can say."

He accepted that and advised me, "The Agency always knows more than they're saying. If you're FBI, which I guess you are, you'll get more help from my office—Military Intelligence—than you'll get from our Comrades In Arms."

"Right."

"And be aware that State Department Intelligence cozies up to the CIA more than they should." He opined, "SDI should be working more with MI."

Who's on first? Anyway, Colonel Kent seemed to be a man of opinions, so I asked him, "What's your opinion of the Political Security Organization?"

He replied, "Like any internal political security force, they can be nasty. In most countries in the Mideast, they're called the Mukhabarat, which they were once called here. But that name has a lot of negatives attached to it—like the old KGB or the Gestapo—so they changed the name here. But it's the same bunch of thugs. And as in every other dictatorship, people are frightened of them and people think they're everywhere. Truth is, they're not, but they promote fear and distrust." He advised me, "Steer clear of them if you can. They answer to no one except the president and his inner circle."

I wondered if they were hiring—or did I really want to be a warlord? Anyway, I asked Colonel Kent, "Do you know this PSO guy, Colonel Hakim?"

"Sure. Nasty thug. But not stupid."

"Whose side is he on?"

"He's on his side. He wants to keep his job and his high status no matter who wins. He'll shoot an Al Qaeda captive one day, then let another one escape another day. He does the same with the tribal rebels. But someday he's going to get a bullet in the head from one side or the other."

I wouldn't mind doing that myself. I asked him, "Who's going to win here? The government, the al-Houthi rebels, the South Yemen separatists, or Al Qaeda?"

"Well... in the end, the tribes always win—if they can agree on a leader. This al-Houthi guy may be the one. There's another one—a Bedouin sheik—in Marib who could unite the tribes. If not, I'd put my money on Al Qaeda."

"Why?"

"Because they're organized, disciplined, and they believe they are the future."

"They're the past."

"That is the future."

"Right."

Then he said to me, sotto voce, "If you're here to find The Panther, I wish you luck. But I'll also tell you that it might be best in the long run if Al Qaeda won in Yemen."

"Why?"

He explained, "This regime is broken. They're the walking dead. If Al Qaeda wins, they control Sana'a, and the Saudis will find that intolerable, and the Saudis, with American military help, will unite the tribes and get rid of Al Qaeda in Yemen." He informed me, "The Saudis have united the tribes before when they didn't like the government in Sana'a, and also when the Communists took over in Aden. But first, Al Qaeda needs to be out in the open—in the presidential palace. In other words, the quickest way to win this war is to lose it. Follow?"

Maybe I needed another martini to follow this. But I think I got Colonel Machiavelli's line of reasoning. I suggested, "So we get to fight a real land war with Al Qaeda as soon as they win here."

"That's it. Same as with the Taliban in Afghanistan." He let me know, "Al Qaeda should be careful what they wish for."

So should we.

Colonel Kent asked me, "What's your clearance?"

"About six foot two inches."

He smiled politely at the old joke and said, "I'll tell you an open secret. Our goal here is to force the Yemeni government to sign a treaty giving us a ninety-nine-year lease on a big chunk of waterfront property near Aden. We need to do this before the government collapses. We need to build a land, sea, and air base for operations and refueling. An American Gibraltar. From there, we can control the Red Sea and the Gulf of Aden, and we'll do it with a friendly government that we help install later, like the British did two hundred years ago when they grabbed Aden. We can mount operations against Al Qaeda in the Arabian Peninsula and the Horn of Africa. And we can also wipe out the Somali pirates who are in league with Al Qaeda. Plus, we'd have a place other than Guantanamo and closer to the battlefields to warehouse and interrogate enemy combatants." He got a dreamy look in his eyes and said, "Sweet."

"Beautiful," I agreed. Grand strategies and geo-politics always give me a little headache, but to be polite I said, "I like multi-purpose land use." Maybe I could put my khat spa there.

Colonel Kent continued, "And while we're at it, we can tell the Saudis to go fuck themselves, and we can shut down our bases in Saudi Arabia before they tell us to get out." He asked me, "Understand?"

"Sounds like a plan."

"And here's the kicker. The biggest construction company in this part of the world is bin Laden Con-struction. Owned by that asshole's family. So we con-tract them to do some of the work." He asked me, "See the irony?"

"I do. But watch the cost overruns."

"Right." He looked at me and said, "You didn't hear any of that from me."

"Correct." I needed another drink, so I excused myself and headed for the bar.

On the way, I was intercepted by Brenner's boss, the

sometimes reverend Ed Peters, who asked me how my day went, and I told him I was disappointed about not seeing the donkey market.

He assured me it wasn't that interesting, then asked me, "What did Colonel Kent have to say?"

Well, Colonel Kent reminded me a little of the general in Dr. Strangelove, but I didn't want to share this thought with Ed Peters. I mean, I had no idea what the interpersonal relationships were here, or who thought who was a loon, or who was jockeying for position. As I said, everyone here seemed a little nuts to me, and my short-term goal was to get out of this embassy, find The Panther, whack him, and go home. In fact, Tom Walsh was looking very good to me right now.

I said to Ed Peters, "The colonel gave me a briefing about the Yemeni Army."

"That's always good for a laugh."

"Right. We need more serious allies."

"You won't find any in this part of the world." He shifted into diplomatic mode and said, "The irony is that the Yemenis are good people, and they could be good allies if they—or we—got rid of their government."

"Let's hope the people choose a better government in the next election."

"This country is three thousand years old. There hasn't been an election yet." He changed the subject and said, "We're using a five-vehicle convoy tomorrow. That should be all right."

"I'm sure we can get away with three."

"Five is better."

How about twenty? I asked him, "Why don't we fly?"

"We don't trust Yemenia air. And we don't have any of our own air assets here. I wish we did, but these idiots won't let us bring in helicopters."

"How about Spook Air?" Meaning the CIA air assets.

He replied, "I don't know if anyone asked."

"How about the C-17?"

"We like to have one sitting at Sana'a Airport in case we have to move the whole embassy out of here."

"Good thinking."

He explained, "When one C-17 comes in, the other leaves for the States, and the one that came in waits for another to arrive."

"Got it." I asked him, "Why don't we charter an aircraft to take us to Aden?"

"We do that sometimes. But not this time."

"Why not?"

"I don't know."

Well, I did. We were driving to Aden because someone wanted to see if Al Qaeda snapped at the bait. Which reminded me, if I needed reminding, that Al Qaeda fighters were on the way to Aden, and I asked Peters, "How would you evacuate the American personnel at the Sheraton in Aden?"

"By ship."

"Whose ship? And how do we get to it?"

"I'd try the backstroke."

Why do I think he's used this joke before? But it *was* funny, so I gave him a chuckle. But seriously.

He said, seriously, "My DSS counterpart in Aden, Doug Reynolds, will brief you." He asked me, "What was your evacuation plan when you were in Aden last time?"

"I think it was the breaststroke."

While I was wondering if I should mention that I'd just discovered that the Sheraton in Aden was in imminent danger of attack, Howard Fensterman came over to me, and Ed Peters excused himself. There seemed to be an unwritten rule here that conversations needed to be compartmentalized, so it was like a Shakespeare play where the actors entered, delivered their lines, then exited, making way for new actors who didn't know what the last ones said, which usually led to some misunderstanding or troublemaking, which in turn led to someone getting whacked. That's what happens when people don't communicate. Right?

Anyway, Howard said to me, "You and Kate went into Sana'a today with Paul."

"We did."

"I would have joined you."

"We thought you were attending the Catholic Mass at the Italian Embassy."

He smiled, but he wasn't amused. He said to me, "I have your satellite phone numbers and we'll stay in touch when you're on the road."

"Why don't you come to Aden with us?"

"I would, but I have a lot to do here to get this office up and running." He informed me, "There was an attack last night on an American oil installation in a place called Marib."

"I heard."

"One suspect was captured. I'm trying to get permission from the Ministry of Justice to interview him."

So do I tell him—been there, done that? He was the FBI legat, Kate's supposed boss, but no one had told him that we'd been to Ghumdan. Who the hell was in charge here? And what was going on behind the scenes? For some reason I pictured Buck as the guy with all the strings in his hands, manipulating the whole puppet show.

I said to Howard, "You need to speak to Buck Harris about that."

"I do? Why him?"

"Why not?"

Howard asked me, "What is his actual job here?"

"I don't know. Protocol officer?"

Howard changed the subject and said to me, "I told Kate she needed to see me first thing tomorrow. I have the arrest warrant, a copy of the indictment, and instructions on how to effect a lawful arrest on a suspect in a foreign country who claims dual citizenship." He also let me know, "You need to read him his Miranda rights, but you first need to establish that he understands English."

"When can I kick him in the balls?"

He ignored me and said, "I also have all this in Arabic—the warrant, the indictment, and his Miranda warning for him to read and sign."

"Howard, is this a joke?"

"No, it is not. This arrest will be made lawfully and properly, and it will stand up in an American court of law."

Well, if I had any second thoughts about whacking The Panther, Howard just put them all to rest.

I said to him, "Brief Kate on all this."

"I will. But I want you, as one of the likely arresting agents, to understand this."

"Okay."

He assured me, "I'm just trying to keep you from

making a mistake that could jeopardize a Federal prosecution, and get you or us in trouble."

"Thank you."

"That's what I'm here for."

"Right." I actually liked Howard, and I could see that he was bright enough to learn how the world really worked. After a few months in this place, he'd lose his idealism and his fine legal scruples and he'd be helping the PSO torture suspects in Ghumdan Prison. Well, maybe not. But like all of us who've been on the front lines too long, and all of us who lived through 9/11, Howard Fensterman would become a little more like the people we were fighting. Of that, I was sure.

Buck came over to us, and instead of Howard asking him about the captured terrorist—sorry, the suspect—Howard asked him, "What time are you leaving tomorrow?"

Buck replied, "Before eight A.M." He explained to Howard and to me, "It's about four hundred kilometers to Aden, and it can take anywhere from four to six hours. So we want to get there in time for the convoy to turn around and get back to Sana'a not too long after dark." He further explained to us, "We'd rather the DSS agents not stay overnight in Aden, because we need those resources here."

I thought we might need them more at the Sheraton.

I again suggested to Howard, "Come along for the ride. If we get ambushed, you can tell us when we can legally return fire."

Even Howard laughed at that.

Buck said to Howard, "We have room, and we can always use another gun. We gather in the chancery parking lot at seven."

Howard acknowledged that and exited stage left.

Buck asked me, "Were you giving him a hard time?"

"Not me."

"He's doing his job," Buck assured me. "Unfortunately his job makes our job more difficult."

"Not for me."

Buck changed the subject and said, "Paul told me you learned a few things at Ghumdan."

"We did. Our allies are assholes."

"Did you learn anything you didn't already know?"

"Maybe." I informed Buck, "Howard didn't know we were at Ghumdan."

"Is that so? Did you tell him?"

"No. I told him to see you."

"I'll speak to him." He added, "We're not sure how the legat fits into this."

"Let me know when you know."

"I will." He asked me, "What did you speak to Colonel Kent about?"

"The Yemeni Army."

He let that go and asked, "What did you learn at Ghumdan?"

I never liked it when an NYPD boss wanted to debrief me without my partner present. There could be a misunderstanding. So I replied, "I think Paul wanted the four of us to discuss that."

"Of course." He asked me, "So how did you like Ghumdan?"

"It has a way to go to become a model penal institution."

"I thought so, too."

I asked him, "Were you there this morning?"

"No, but I've been there many times in the past."

"When will we see the CIA report on their interrogation of the prisoner?"

"After it's been seen by the station chief."

I had not yet been introduced to the CIA station chief in Yemen, so I asked, "And who is that?"

"You don't need to know." Buck added, "And he doesn't need to know you."

I asked, "How many games are in town?"

"Several. But ours is the main game at the moment." He added, "You ask good questions."

That's not what he meant, but I said, "Thank you."

"Paul said Colonel Hakim was his charming self."

"He was obstructing American justice."

"That's his job."

I told him, "The fact is, if we had two or three hours alone with the prisoner, with an embassy interpreter, we'd know a lot more about Al Qaeda in Yemen than we do now."

Buck replied, "If the situation were reversed—if it was *your* prisoner in New York, Detective Corey—would you allow a foreign policeman or intelligence officer to question him alone?"

Spoken like a true diplomat. But not a rhetorical question, so I replied, "You're assuming some sort of equality, and there is none. We're here to save the ass of a weak and corrupt government. The least they can do is get out of our way."

Buck nodded, then informed me, "Sometimes they do. But as we say in the world of diplomacy, it's about quid pro quo. We give them something, then they give us something." He informed me, "I think it's our turn to give them something. Aside from money."

"Like what?"

"Well, as I told you in New York, they want our help to...neutralize some particularly aggressive and dangerous tribal leaders."

"And?"

"And we're reluctant to do that."

"Why?"

"We want to keep the goodwill of the tribes."

"I didn't know we had their goodwill."

"We do, but not directly. As I also explained to you, the tribes are culturally and historically closer to the monarchy in Saudi Arabia than they are to the republican government in Sana'a. And the Saudis are our allies, and our link to the tribes."

"So we don't want to vaporize tribal chieftains with our Hellfire missiles and piss off the Saudis."

"Correct. But we might...neutralize a few sheiks and chieftains in exchange for the Sana'a government giving us more help in locating and eliminating Al Qaeda leaders."

"Right. But they should do that anyway. It's good for them, too."

"That's what we're trying to explain to them, and believe me they know it, but they're using our fixation with Al Qaeda to force us to use our Predator drones and Hellfire missiles against these tribal chieftains as well as the South Yemen separatists."

"Got it. And round and round it goes."

"Indeed it does." He further explained to me, "It's a delicate balancing act, and it all comes back to quid pro quo."

"Got it."

He returned to my complaint and said, "Regarding our interrogation of their prisoners, the PSO really doesn't want us getting free information. They want to sell it to us. So if they give us some good information on The Panther, for instance, then they want us to give them a bucket of guts that used to be an annoying tribal sheik."

The graphic imagery sort of surprised me, but it made me remember that Buck Harris was only ten percent diplomat, and ninety percent intelligence officer. In fact, in the good old Cold War days, Buck and his pals would have a cocktail and talk about the nuclear obliteration of hundreds of millions of people. Now the potential body count could be measured in terms of a bucket of guts. That's progress.

On a more immediate subject, I said to him, "I assume Paul told you that the prisoner told us there are about forty jihadists on their way to Aden to attack the Sheraton."

"Yes, Paul did mention that, and we've alerted our people there."

"Good. Especially since we are going to be some of those people." I suggested, "Maybe the Yemeni Army can intercept them."

He informed me, "The Yemeni Army seems to have little luck in intercepting Al Qaeda fighters when they come out of the mountains." He added, "We believe that Al Qaeda travels in small groups or individually, in civilian clothing, and they may even take public transportation. Buses, planes, hired vehicles." He reminded me, "Men in Yemen with AK-47 rifles aren't stopped and questioned because of the rifles. That would be like stopping men with umbrellas in London."

Buck was getting three-martini clever, and I smiled.

He glanced at his watch and said to me, "We're actually meeting Paul at eight upstairs. It's that time."

"I'll get Kate."

"I think she's already there."

"All right." So we ditched our drinks, went to the elevator, rode up to the third floor, and made our way to the secure communications room.

Interesting cocktail party.

CHAPTER THIRTY-THREE

Mrs. Corey and Mr. Brenner were sitting at the table chatting, and two commo people were manning the electronics on the other side of the glass wall. I was sure there was a lot of traffic today between here and Washington.

We sat, and Brenner told us, "The recording devices are off."

Now I'd never know what Paul and Kate were talking about. Actually, I'd never know anyway.

Buck asked us, "So did you all have a good day in Sana'a?"

I replied, "How could anyone have a bad day in Sana'a?"

Buck smiled, then urged us to tell him about our day.

So we did, and Buck listened without comment, except to ask us how the food was at Old Sana'a, and to ask Brenner if he was sure he'd gotten me the best jambiyah for the best price. He also asked Kate if she'd been successful at Hope in Their Hands.

This was Buck's schtick, of course, putting life-and-death topics on the back burner and asking us about lunch and shopping. This is a good interrogation technique, but an annoying debriefing technique.

Buck moved on, asking us, "And you're sure you weren't followed?"

I'd already said we weren't, so I got a little pissy and said, "Buck, I'm a cop. I know if I'm being followed."

Buck pointed out, "This is not New York."

"Assholes are the same everywhere."

Buck smiled, then said, "Well, I'm sure that someone, somewhere today saw you and made a phone call, which is actually what we want." He added, "It's good, though, that no one acted on that information while you were in an exposed situation." He said to Brenner, "Maybe you should have had DSS backup."

Brenner replied, a bit testily, "I felt it was safe enough to go out without backup."

Well, it wasn't. But safety wasn't the point. Backup is easily spotted and scares off the bad guys, and that's not what Paul Brenner or John Corey wanted to do.

Buck said, "All right. All's well that ends well. So... oh, by the way, Mr. Corey, that was good of you to give the lady in the shop an extra twenty dollars. We like to support them."

Had I mentioned that? No, I had not. So probably one of those Westerners in the shop was his snitch, or more likely he'd just called the shop and chatted in Arabic with the manager. In any case, in the world of spooks and spies, it's all illusion, and nothing is as it seems. Old Buck had been at this game a lot longer than anyone in this room, and he wanted everyone to know it.

Point made, Buck said to me and Brenner, "Tell me and Kate what happened at Ghumdan."

So we did. And as former cops, we got right into sync and gave Buck and Kate a clear, concise, and accurate report of our Ghumdan experience.

Buck listened intently, as did Kate, and neither of them interrupted.

When we were finished, Buck stayed silent awhile, then said, "You seem to have gotten more information than we usually do at these interrogations." He said to me, "I suppose your past experience in Aden was helpful."

I replied, "To the extent that I knew what to expect." I informed him, "The prisoner was more cooperative than our ally, Colonel Hakim."

Buck said to us, "I'll ask Howard to put in a formal request with the Ministry of Justice to get the transcript of this prisoner's interrogation by the PSO." He let us know, "They won't honor that request, but then we have something new to complain about."

I asked Buck, "Is the PSO more cooperative with the CIA?"

He looked at me and said, "Good question. The short answer is yes." He smiled. "Birds of a feather." Then he added quickly, "I'm not suggesting the PSO and the CIA have anything in common."

I thought he just said birds of a feather.

Buck informed us, "They have their own understanding between themselves. Very much quid pro quo."

That was a little scary.

Kate, who I was certain was the only person here who had once slept with and shot a CIA officer, said, "I'm assuming our fifth team member can fill in some of our information gaps."

Buck replied, "That is our expectation."

Right. The CIA is happy to fill you in. Unfortunately, they lie.

Mr. Brenner had no comment on this topic, and he returned to the subject by reminding us, "The Panther could know from his fighters that one of them was taken prisoner—but he might also think Rahim was killed. So we don't know if The Panther is worried about a prisoner talking about his location." He added, "I hope this prisoner wasn't mentioned in the government press release."

Buck assured us, "The Sana'a government is not that stupid. They are, in fact, crafty, which is why they're not all hanging from a noose. So they will report the attack, but claim four killed. Or twenty. Or whatever number they like. There will be no mention of a prisoner."

True. But I reminded everyone, "Someone at Ghumdan could tell Al Qaeda that there's a talking prisoner who said he saw The Panther at Marib."

Buck replied, "That's very possible, but let's hope it doesn't send The Panther running." He reminded us again, "If there is a leak from Ghumdan to Al Qaeda, they will also mention the name of John Corey."

Right. That's why I was at Ghumdan.

Buck asked Kate, "Any questions for John or Paul?"

Kate asked me, "Is it possible that this prisoner was rehearsed? That what you heard was not the whole truth?"

I really don't like being interrogated by my wife, but it was a good question and I replied, "It's possible. But the prisoner had the appearance of truthfulness." I looked at Brenner, who seconded that and added, "This guy was scared, hurting, and desperate."

Kate asked Brenner, "What was Colonel Hakim's demeanor during the interrogation?"

Brenner replied, "Not a happy guy. He really wanted us out of there, which is why I think this wasn't rehearsed and wasn't disinformation."

Kate and Buck both nodded. So we kicked this around awhile, and after about ten minutes Buck said, "All right. It appears we've been handed an opportunity. So in the absence of any new or contradictory information, I think our first excursion into the countryside from Aden will be to Marib."

Obviously.

He continued, "If The Panther is not there, we can at least see those magnificent pre-Islamic ruins."

Who gives a shit? You wanna see ruins? Go to Newark. I pointed out, "We really won't know if The Panther is still there, but if we stay there looking for him, I'm sure he *will* know that. Also we now know that The Panther has assets around Marib, including a tribal sheik, so even if he moved because of this attack, he'll return to meet us on his turf."

"Precisely," agreed Buck. "And we can see the ruins while we're waiting for him."

"There you go."

Brenner commented, "Now we know where to set and bait the trap."

Bait? What happened to lure?

Buck said, "Assuming Colonel Hakim is thinking along the same lines, don't be surprised if we see him there."

Right. Could get crowded at Marib. And we could scare off The Panther. But I was betting that John Corey on The Panther's turf would be irresistible to him.

Buck next brought up the subject of the possible Al Qaeda attack on the Sheraton in Aden and assured us,

"The FBI SWAT Team, the DSS men, and the Marines at the Sheraton are on full alert, as are all American personnel in the hotel. Also, we are officially notifying the Yemeni government at the highest level about this possible attack, so they have no choice but to increase their security around the hotel."

I, of course, remarked, "That will make us sleep better."

Brenner assured us, "You'll never sleep as well as the Yemeni Army."

Funny. But not.

"The last time the Sheraton in Aden was attacked," Buck said, "was before the Americans were there. During one of the civil wars in the eighties. A rebel group lobbed a few mortar rounds into the hotel." He added, "The Communists ran South Yemen in those days, and they allowed alcohol—which is the best thing I can say about them. In any case, this rebel group was fundamentalist, and the cocktail lounge offended them."

I reminisced, "When I was at the Sheraton, we made up fun names for the cocktails." All right, I'll tell you. "High Explosive Mojito. Martini Mortars. My favorite was the Incoming Cosmo."

No one thought that was funny. I guess you had to be there.

Anyway, Kate asked Buck, "Is there any other place for us to stay in Aden?"

"No. The Yemeni government has given us two floors of the Sheraton, and that's our operational base in Aden." He assured us, "I wouldn't worry about this too much." He added, "Unless you start to see Arab guests checking out."

Funny? Maybe.

Kate also asked, "Do we have an evacuation plan?"

Yes, the breaststroke.

Buck replied, "We'll ask Doug Reynolds, who is Ed Peters's DSS counterpart in Aden."

Buck then said to us, "Final subject. The road trip to Aden. We haven't notified the Yemeni authorities of our movement, so, theoretically, Al Qaeda will not be tipped off that we are taking a convoy to Aden tomorrow morning. In that respect, we aren't advertising this trip in advance with the hope of making contact with Al Qaeda—but as soon as we leave the compound, cell phones will be ringing all over Sana'a and along our route, so our movement will then be known."

Brenner continued Buck's thought and said, "The longer we're on the road, the more chance that Al Qaeda will try to set up an ambush or roadside bomb along our route." He added, "It will be obvious that we're headed to Aden. But if we maintain good speed, and maybe vary the route, we should be able to stay ahead of anything they try to plan."

Buck reiterated, "It's not as though we're *trying* to get into a fight with them, but it may happen, and we are prepared—and we may be able to kill or capture a key Al Qaeda leader."

That sounded a bit optimistic, but since we were driving to Aden anyway, I guess we might as well kill some bad guys on the way. Right?

Buck had some good news and said, "We may be crazy, but we're not stupid. So we've arranged to have two Predator surveillance drones on station along our route." He informed me and Kate, "They have infrared video cameras that can see through cloud cover if necessary, and the high-resolution cameras can operate from as high as twenty thousand feet and still see a man with a rifle." He concluded, "We should know about an ambush long before we reach it."

Well, that *was* good news. The bad news, of course, was that the surveillance drones might still miss fifty jihadists sitting in a mud hut waiting for us to come by. Or miss a roadside bomb. I asked, "And what do we do if we get this aerial surveillance information?"

Brenner, ex–combat vet, replied, "I will make the decision about how we react to an ambush warning."

"Give me a call," I suggested.

Kate asked a good question. "How about Hellfire missiles?"

Buck replied, "We are not authorized to use Hellfire missiles without the explicit permission of the Yemeni government."

Kate, the lawyer, asked, "Not even as a purely defensive means to save lives?"

Buck informed us, "Unfortunately not." He also let us know, "It takes a very long time to get this permission from the Yemeni authorities, so we can't count on Hellfire missiles in a rapidly developing situation."

I thought about that and said, "I assume that the Predator surveillance drones *will* be armed with Hellfire missiles, and that we will in fact use them if we're ducking AK-47 rounds."

Buck didn't reply directly, but said, "To ask permission is to invite rejection. We do what we have to do, then apologize."

"Right. And give the Yemenis another million."

"Maybe two." He smiled and said, "In Yemen, we pay to play."

Right. Even wars have rules, but the rules here in Yemen did not favor the Americans. The good news was that we broke the rules. The better news was that the punishment was a small fine. Two million. Hell, give the Yemenis ten million and carpet bomb the whole country. Better yet, nuke 'em. Check's in the mail for that.

Bottom line on this trip to Aden was that it was more than a method of getting from Point A to Point B; it was also trolling for sharks—fishing for Al Qaeda.

Buck announced, "That's all I have. And if no one has anything further, this meeting is adjourned."

Wonderful.

But Buck said, "Let me buy you all dinner at the Mövenpick. They have a new French chef."

I said, "I'd love to, but—"

Kate interrupted, "That would be very nice."

"Good," said Buck. "Afterwards, if you're game for it, we can go to the Russia Club."

I reminded everyone, "We need to get up early."

Buck told us, "We can sleep on the way to Aden." He smiled and assured us, "The roadside bombs will wake us up for the ambush."

I felt like a guy who thought he'd joined an ace fighter squadron and found out it was a kamikaze group. I mean, bravery is one thing; war psychosis is something else. I said to Buck, "You've been here too long."

"I know. But we're all going home." He added, "One way or the other."

CHAPTER THIRTY-FOUR

So we left the embassy and squeezed into the armored Land Cruiser with Zamo driving and Buck up front for the short drive to the Mövenpick Hotel.

It was a nice hotel, and I was glad I was checked in there, though I was staying elsewhere.

I'm not a big fan of Continental cuisine, except French fries, preferring instead pigs-in-a-blanket, but the restaurant was good, and if you let your mind wander, you could be anywhere but here. I'm sure the new French chef felt the same way.

We had a nice, wine-fueled, getting-to-know-you dinner, and talked a bit about ourselves.

Buck Harris, it turned out, was married, with a wife in Silver Spring, Maryland, outside of D.C. I got the impression he had some family money, and he didn't rely on his State Department salary to buy five-thousand-dollar jambiyahs. So for Buck, maybe the Cold War had been a gentleman's hobby, something to keep him busy. What, then, was the war on terrorism? Probably the same thing, but with the added incentive of revenge, as he said. I could imagine him being buddies with his former Soviet enemies, but I couldn't imagine a day when he, or any of us, would be having drinks with former jihadists. For one thing, they didn't drink. More to the point, this was a war without end, and there would be no forgiving or forgetting.

Buck had a grown son and daughter who he said did not share his ideology or his enthusiasm for fucking America's enemies. Buck told us, "They believe we should try to understand Islam." He speculated, "If they'd been old enough during the Cold War, they would have told me I should try to understand Communism." He assured us, "I understand both."

Right. Hey, it sucks when your own kids think you're part of the problem.

But Buck said philosophically, "The important thing is that I know I've spent my life doing what I thought was right—not just for me, but for my country, and for civilization—and also for my children and their children."

Kate assured him, "You don't need to justify your life or your work to anyone."

Buck agreed, but said, "In this business, however, you are sometimes forced to compromise your own beliefs in the interest of the greater good—national security, global strategy, and so forth." He confided to us, "During the Cold War, there were a few occasions when I had to betray or abandon an ally as part of a complex plan."

No one commented on that, but I did wonder if he was hinting that the past was prologue to the future. Hopefully not.

Kate, too, spoke a bit about her background,

including her wonderful FBI father, now retired, and her loony mother who was a gun nut, though Kate mentioned that only in the context of growing up around guns and learning at a young age how to hunt and shoot.

This was a great opening for her to tell everyone about how she whacked Ted Nash, but she didn't go there. Maybe she was saving this interesting story for when we met our CIA teammate, thinking that the retelling of it would be even more interesting to a CIA officer. But I'm sure everyone in the CIA already knew this story.

I used our bonding occasion to tell some funny cop stories, which made everyone laugh. But to show it wasn't all fun and games on the NYPD, I mentioned getting shot on the job, and my medical retirement, and my rocky transition from NYPD to the Federal Anti-Terrorist Task Force, and of course, my first case, where I met Kate Mayfield, the love of my life.

Paul Brenner seemed to have had an interesting and adventurous life in the military, but like most combat veterans, he downplayed his war experiences, and again he didn't mention his clandestine mission to post-war Vietnam. But he did say he'd had a brief wartime marriage, though he didn't say anything about his current lady in the States, and I didn't expect he would; he seemed to be a private person. Also—how do I put this?—he was smitten with Kate Mayfield. Hey, no big deal. I think Tom Walsh has the same problem. And it wasn't my problem.

Anyway, four-fifths of the A-team got to know one another a little better, which might or might not make us work better together. And with luck, we'd all get home and have a few stories to tell. Or, in this business, not tell.

I suggested a reunion. "We'll meet at seven under the clock at Grand Central Station, just like in the movies, and we'll go to Michael Jordan's Steak House."

Everyone liked that happy ending and we agreed to be there, date to be determined by fate. I wondered who, if anyone, would make it.

Buck paid for dinner as promised—sixty bucks, including tip, wine, and drinks. That's a month's pay for a Yemeni, and about four drinks in a New York bar. Maybe I should buy a retirement house here.

Anyway, showing the poor judgment of the intoxicated, we thought it was a great idea to go to the Russia Club.

Zamo drove us the few hundred meters up the road to Tourist City. The half dozen guards at the gate appeared to be Eastern European, and they looked tough and menacing with their flak jackets and AK-47s. But they recognized the American Embassy Land Cruiser, and probably recognized Zamo, and waved us through.

I said to Brenner, "They seemed to know you."

No response.

Tourist City was a collection of five- and six-story concrete slab buildings, not unlike an urban housing project for the poor. But here, in Sana'a, it was the height of luxury, and more importantly, it was guarded. Not safe. Guarded.

I could see why Paul Brenner might choose not to live here; it was sort of depressing, but also an admission that you felt unsafe on the outside. And macho men would never admit that. They'd rather die. And often did.

There were a few low-rise buildings on the grounds, including a few shops, and in one of the buildings was the Russia Club.

Zamo pulled up and we piled out.

There were two more armed guys in front of the place, and they definitely recognized Mr. Buckminster Harris. In fact, they greeted him in Russian, and Buck replied in Russian with what must have been a joke, because the two guys laughed.

Ironic, I thought, that Buck Harris, who'd spent most of his professional life trying to screw the Russians, was now yucking it up with them in Yemen, where he'd spent part of the Cold War spying on the now-defunct Evil Empire. If you live long enough, you see things you could never have imagined.

We entered the Russia Club, and the maitre d' saw me and shouted, "Ivan! It is you! Excellent. Tatiana is here tonight. She will be delirious with joy!"

Just kidding.

But the maitre d', Sergei by name, did know Buck, though not Paul Brenner, which disappointed me. I would have liked to discover that Mr. Cool dropped his paycheck here every month, boozing and whoring. Kate, too, would find that interesting.

Anyway, the place looked a bit sleazy, which it was. There was a long bar to the right, a raised stage, and a ceramic-tile dance floor surrounded by tables, half of which were empty. A DJ was playing some god-awful seventies hard rock, and a few couples were on the dance floor, looking like they were having seizures.

The bar was crowded with casually dressed men

and barely dressed women. I mean, I haven't seen so much deep cleavage since I drove through the Grand Canyon. The men looked Western—Europeans and Americans—and most of the ladies appeared to be from Eastern Europe and Russia, though there were a few black ladies who, I'd once been told, were from Djibouti, Ethiopia, Somalia, and Eritrea, which is not far from here if you cross the pirate-infested Red Sea. Also at the tables were a few Western-looking women accompanied by their gentlemen friends or husbands. I recognized two men and women from the embassy, but they didn't wave.

If there were any Yemeni customers or service staff in the Russia Club, I didn't see them. In fact, I'm sure one selling point of this place was the promise that you didn't have to see a single Yemeni, unless you stayed until closing time and watched them mop the floor under the eye of armed Russians.

Kate broke into my thoughts and asked me, "Been here before?"

"They've named a cocktail after me."

Anyway, Sergei escorted us to a table, though I'd have preferred the bar.

Buck ordered a bottle of Stolichnaya on ice, a plate of citrus fruit, and zakuskie—snacks.

My last case, involving The Lion, had taken me to a Russian nightclub in Brighton Beach, Brooklyn, which is home to many Russian-Americans. The club, Svetlana by name, was a lot more opulent than this place, and the clientele were mostly immigrants from the motherland on a nostalgia trip. This place, named simply the Russia Club, was the Village of the Damned in the Country of the Lost.

Anyway, the vodka came quickly and we toasted, "Na Zdorov'e."

Kate seemed comfortable enough in the proximity of horny guys and hookers, and her only complaint was the volume of the bad music.

Mr. Brenner asked her to dance, of course, and she accepted and walked unsteadily onto the slippery dance floor with Brenner holding her arm.

Buck said to me, "She's a delightful woman."

"She is," I agreed. More so when she's had a few. However, if it was me who'd suggested coming here, she might not be such delightful company.

Kate slipped on the tile floor, but Brenner caught her, and Kate kicked off her shoes and they danced to some horrid disco tune.

An attractive, scantily clad lady came over to the table carrying a tray suspended from a strap around her neck, and in the tray were two huge hooters and a selection of cigars and cigarettes. Take your pick.

Buck found three Cubans hiding under the lady's left humidor, and gave her a twenty-dollar bill, which included tax, tip, and a light.

The lady said to Buck, in a heavy Russian accent, "I don't see you for many weeks."

Buck replied in Russian, and the lady laughed and tousled his thinning hair. Buck was apparently still fucking the Russians.

The lady checked me out and asked, "You are new in Sana'a?"

"I feel I've been here all my life."

"Yes?" She further inquired, "Is that your wife or girlfriend? Or his?"

"My wife, his girlfriend."

She thought that was really funny, then said to me, "Maybe I see you again."

"Tomorrow night."

So Buck and I sat there, smoking Cuban cigars, drinking Russian vodka, listening to American disco, and watching the human comedy.

I was sure that if you stayed in Yemen long enough—like more than a month—you'd develop a deep fatalism, which led to strange and risky behavior. I'm not being judgmental—just expressing an awareness that the people I needed to work with and trust had gone a little around the bend.

Anyway, the DJ switched to American big band, and an instrumental of "I'm in the Mood for Love" filled the room while a Russian chanteuse on the stage did her best to sing along.

"Ahminda moot fa loov, zimply becus yerneermee..."

Brenner and Kate were getting to know each other.

On the subject of fatalism, I imagined that every dangerous mission from the dawn of time through World War Two and the Cold War to the war on terrorism began with an alcohol binge. Or should begin that way. Hey, eat, drink, and be merry. Nothing puts things into perspective like the thought that you might die tomorrow.

I said to Buck, "This was a good idea."

"It's the thing to do on the eve of battle." He added, "War is a good excuse for any type of behavior."

Indeed.

The DJ was now playing "Moonlight Serenade" and Kate, observing the one slow dance rule, came over to the table, took Buck's hand, and led him to the dance floor, leaving Mr. Brenner and me to dance if we chose to.

Before I could ask, Brenner sat and said, "Oh, good. Cigars." He busied himself with pouring a vodka while getting the attention of the cigarette lady, who came over and clipped his Cuban, then lit it for him.

We didn't have much to say to each other, but he did say, "Good cigar."

Mr. Brenner, I thought, was becoming less funny and less interesting as he became more distracted by Ms. Mayfield. I'll write this off to too much alcohol and too much time in the land of limited dating opportunities. Not that you had to be drunk or horny to find Kate Mayfield attractive.

Anyway, I watched Buck and Kate sharing the dance floor with Western European and American men, and Eastern European and African hookers. It was great that so many diverse cultures could get along so well. It would have been even greater if we could get the Arabs out there in their robes and veils, all liquored up, doing the Bristol Stomp.

A few ladies came by to ask if they could sit or have a dance, and Mr. Brenner and I politely declined.

To make conversation, I said to Brenner, "Someday a rocket is going to come through this roof."

He informed me, "They have steel planking and sandbags on the roof."

"It should say that on the menu."

"Moonlight Serenade" ended, and it was my turn to dance with my wife.

The DJ was still spinning big band and the smoky air filled with trombones and saxophones playing Tommy Dorsey's "I'll Never Smile Again."

Kate and I danced, and I didn't spin her much because I could tell the room was already spinning in her head.

She didn't have much to say, and I walked her back to our table.

It was past midnight now and the Russia Club was in full swing. Buck suggested cognac, which was not a good suggestion.

Kate said, "I'm ready to go home."

Me, too. Let's go to the airport.

Brenner picked up the tab—about forty bucks, which he paid in American dollars.

Sergei showed us to the door and said to us, "Tomorrow is belly dancing show. You come."

Buck said we'd be back. We left, and Zamo pulled up to the door. I put Kate in the front seat and the boys squeezed in the rear.

As we passed through the gates of Tourist City, Zamo suggested we have our guns handy, which was a good idea considering we were so drunk it would take five minutes to find them.

Zamo also suggested that he drop Kate and me off first at the Sheraton, then double back to the embassy. His final suggestion was that Brenner should stay in the embassy tonight since Zamo had no intention of driving him to his apartment after midnight.

So just another night out in wild and crazy Sana'a.

Kate and I got dropped off at the Sheraton, and Zamo said he'd pick us up at 6:45. Buck told us not to check out, and Brenner said to wear the Kevlar. I said, "Good night and good luck."

I stuck my gun in my belt and steered Kate into the

lobby, which was empty and quiet, though I could hear music from the cocktail lounge.

We went to the elevators, where there should have been a security person, but the chair was empty. We drew our guns and rode up to our floor, where I told Kate to keep an eye on the corridor while I cleared the room.

There were no terrorists under the bed or in the closet so I motioned Kate in, and I closed and bolted the door. The drapes were open and I drew them shut.

Kate, not feeling her very best, collapsed on the bed.

I looked around the room to see if anything struck me as wrong—like a stuffed black panther on my pillow. Everything looked kosher—or I should say halal—and I lowered myself into the stuffed chair.

All in all, this was not a bad day in the Land That Time Forgot. I mean, we learned a lot, and we could make good use of what we learned, and by now, maybe The Panther knew that John Corey, who'd killed The Lion, was now here to kill him. There ain't room in this country for both of us, asshole.

My teammates seemed more than competent, and I trusted Brenner. Professionally, I mean. Not so much with Kate. Buck seemed trustworthy, though he had a self-admitted history of throwing friends under the bus—but only for patriotic reasons.

Our CIA person was as yet unknown, but not for long. That could change the team balance.

Kate was still gung-ho, and she was a fast learner. I was honestly glad she was with me and I looked forward to that moment when I could say, "I told you we should have stayed home."

So, tomorrow the road to Aden, which I'd traveled

round-trip last time. This time, there would be no round trip. It would be one-way to Aden, then to Marib. And that, too, could be one-way. But to be optimistic, let's say Marib was the last stop before home. And the last stop for The Panther.

— PART V —

Death Highway,
Yemen

CHAPTER THIRTY-FIVE

At 7 A.M., everyone who was going to Aden had assembled with weapons and baggage in the small parking lot at the side of the chancery building.

It was a nice morning, dry and cool, with a clear sky for the Predator drones.

Standing around the five black Land Cruisers were about fifteen people, all men, except for Kate and a woman in tan cargo pants and a white T-shirt. She was, according to Buck, our doctor, and her name was Clare Nolan. She looked very young, and I asked Buck, "Is she old enough to use alcohol swabs?"

"She's very competent," Buck assured me. "She worked in an inner-city hospital trauma unit for six months. Gunshot wounds and all that."

"Can she treat a hangover?"

"You look fine, my boy." His satellite phone rang and he excused himself and went off to speak to someone in private.

I was actually feeling not too bad, considering I'd had a few glasses of wine with dinner, after the martinis and before the bottle of vodka.

Kate also looked good, but that may have been the makeup. I hoped she remembered that she'd saved the last dance for me.

On that subject, Mrs. Corey and Mr. Brenner seemed to have little to say to each other this morning. Ah, yes. Been there myself.

Anyway, Kate and I had chosen desert boots and jeans for Death Highway and she wore a black pullover, under which was her Kevlar vest. Over my vest I wore a khaki shirt that I'd worn last time I was in Yemen—my good-luck shirt. And since we were going through Indian Territory, we had our .45s unconcealed, strapped on our hips.

The uniform of the day for the DSS guys was cargo pants and sleeveless bush jackets over black T-shirts, and that's what Mr. Brenner was wearing along with his heart on his sleeve.

Howard Fensterman had decided to show up, and he looked ready for adventure in his bush shirt with his Glock slung low at his side. All FBI Special Agents are trained and qualified on a variety of weapons, but some are more qualified than others. Still, I'd been surprised before by who was a good gunslinger. It's all in the head.

Howard also carried the most lethal of lawyers' weapons: his briefcase. In the briefcase, he informed Kate and me, was all the paperwork we needed to make a lawful arrest of one Bulus ibn al-Darwish, a.k.a. al-Numair, a.k.a. The Panther.

Mr. Fensterman also informed us, "I have copies of everything for both of you and for Buck."

I was tired of giving Howard a hard time so I said, "Thank you."

"I also have copies of the suspect's fingerprints, and

three color snapshots of him taken in the U.S. about twelve years ago, plus his last driver's license and U.S. passport photo."

"Good." If you look like your passport photo, you're already dead.

Anyway, I thought we'd get all this in Aden, but it was good to have it now in case we ran into the suspect on the road.

Mr. Fensterman continued, "He's clean-shaven in these photos, but we know from various sources that he's grown a beard."

That's what Rahim said at Ghumdan.

Howard further informed us, "He's also wanted by a number of foreign governments for attacks against their citizens."

"Right. The Saudis want him for killing some of their border guards."

"Correct. And the Belgians for a possible kidnapping and suspected murder."

I'd just heard about this from Colonel Kent, but I hadn't mentioned it to Kate, who asked, "What was that about?"

Howard replied, "Back last August, nine Belgian tourists disappeared at the ruins near Marib."

Kate said, "I remember reading something about that in the Times."

She may have read it in the *Post*, but she always cites the *Times*. I do the opposite.

Howard continued, "It looked like a tribal kidnapping, but there was no ransom demand, and there was blood found at the ruins." He added, "The Yemeni tour guide and bus driver were found...dead." He added, "Throats slit."

Didn't sound good for those tourists. I asked, "Why does the Belgian government think it was The Panther?"

Howard replied, "The Belgians arrested an Al Qaeda suspect in Brussels on an unrelated charge, and apparently this information came out during the interrogation."

Right. That's how we get half our information; bad guys know lots of bad things.

Howard said to us, "So, aside from the Yemenis, other governments, including the Saudis, will want to be notified if we make an arrest, and they may ask for extradition. So we need to make a strong case for our *Cole*-related charge."

"Right." The Saudis could be a problem if we did snatch The Panther and had to beat feet with him across the Saudi border. Therefore, we were probably not taking The Panther to Saudi Arabia, and certainly not handing him over to the Yemenis. It occurred to me that there was more going on here than I knew. I'm shocked.

Bottom line here: A bullet in the brain settles all extradition requests, jurisdictional disputes, and silly lawsuits.

Howard also informed us, "I'm going to stay on with you in Aden."

Shit. But I said, "Great." I felt obligated, however, to advise him, "We have intel that the Sheraton in Aden might be the subject of an Al Qaeda attack."

"Really?"

"With luck, this will happen before we get there and the cocktail lounge won't be damaged."

Kate suggested to Howard, "You might want to return to Sana'a today."

Howard thought about that—Death Highway back to Sana'a this afternoon, or Ground Zero in Aden tonight? Personally, I'd head inside for a muffin. But Howard said, "No, I'll stay in Aden until a convoy heads north again." He added, "I want to be close to this."

"Your call."

Zamo came over and asked us to join him at his Land Cruiser for a quick course on the M4 carbine.

He handed each of us a weapon and said, "This is the Model A1, a shorter and lighter version of the standard military M-16 assault rifle, which I'm sure you're all familiar with."

I hefted the carbine in my hands. It felt good. It felt *bad*.

Zamo, warming to his favorite subject, said, "It has a telescoping stock, and this model fires fully automatic." He continued, "It takes the standard 5.56mm cartridge, and has a thirty-round magazine. The cyclic rate of fire is seven hundred to nine hundred and fifty rounds a minute."

Kate asked, "Effective range?"

"You'll get good accuracy at three hundred yards." He further explained, "The short barrel reduces the effective range, but we have day and night scopes that I'll give you."

I inquired, "Do you have your sniper rifle with you?"

"Does the Pope leave home without his cross?" Zamo continued, "This gun is built for close-in defense and medium-range offensive use. So if we get into a situation where the bad guys are firing from a distance with AK-47s, then you have to compensate by laying down full automatic suppressing fire to keep their heads down." He assured us, "What the M4 lacks in long-range capability, it more than makes up for in its high cyclic rate of fire."

Howard asked a good question. "Any jamming problems when it gets hot?"

Zamo replied, "Theoretically yes, but no one has reported a combat jam."

Maybe because they were dead.

Zamo continued, "The small size makes it easy to transport and conceal. Easy to carry it in and out of tight and confined spaces like vehicles or caves."

Caves?

Zamo looked at Kate and said to her, "Its size, weight, and low recoil makes it popular with the ladies."

I asked Zamo, "Will it chip her nails?"

Zamo laughed and Kate said, "Fuck you." Which made Zamo laugh even more. This was fun.

So Zamo went on a bit about the M4, using more words than I'd heard him use all day yesterday.

All in all, the M4 seemed like an excellent weapon. I hoped I never had to use it, but if I did, I knew I'd have a blast.

On that subject, Zamo said, "I'm sorry we never got a chance to test fire, but we'll go out in the Badlands tomorrow and give it a rip." He added, "We might even find live targets."

I reminded him, "We might find those on the road this morning."

"Right." Zamo asked, "Any questions?"

Howard asked, "Which thing is the trigger?"

Funny.

Okay, so deadly force course completed, Kate and I and Howard slung our M4s over our shoulders, and

Zamo gave us each a black satchel stuffed with loaded magazines and telescopic sights. He said to us, "Good luck and good hunting."

Mr. Brenner, the caravan master, had gathered the DSS drivers, and he was now speaking to them, reading from a sheet of paper that outlined the route and the order of march. I wondered if by chance Mr. Brenner and Mrs. Corey were riding in the same vehicle. Would he do something so stupidly obvious? Why not? I would.

Ed Peters had come out of the chancery building, though I didn't think he was going to Aden with us. Maybe he was here to bless the caravan.

Kate and I were standing with Buck now, and Peters came over to us and said to Buck, "I've got only two fully armored vehicles left, and I have to pick up the new ambassador next week, so don't get ambushed."

Buck assured him, "You can get five new vehicles on a C-17."

Peters replied, "That can take over a week." He said to me, "I hate these trips to Aden."

"You're not going," I reminded him.

"My vehicles are."

"Sorry. Is there a bus I can take?"

Clearly Mr. Peters was worried about his vehicles. And, of course, his DSS agents. As for his passengers, they were the cause of his worries. A larger issue was the lack of American helicopters in this dangerous and inaccessible country. Without them, we had to drive through Indian Territory, and basically we were no more mobile than Al Qaeda in their Toyotas.

On the plus side, we had Predator drone surveillance—and maybe Hellfire missiles—but I didn't know if Peters knew that, or if he knew we were taking his men and vehicles on the road to see if we could get into a fight with Al Qaeda.

Mr. Peters thought he might be causing the newbies some anxiety, so he said to me and Kate, "We've never gotten hit on the Sana'a–Aden road."

Buck, too, assured us, "The most dangerous thing about the trip is the Yemeni truck drivers."

Kate asked Buck and Peters, "Aren't the National Security police supposed to provide road security?"

Peters replied, "Sometimes the police themselves are the problem."

Right. In Yemen, even the good guys are bad. This place sucked. Did I already say that?

Bottom line here was three possible outcomes of this trip: a nice drive in the country, a successful encounter with the enemy, or headlines in tomorrow's newspapers. *American Convoy Wiped Out in Yemen; Thirteen Dead.*

Public reaction would be total bewilderment—Where's Yemen?

Good question.

CHAPTER THIRTY-SIX

Buck got another sat-phone call, and he moved off to speak. Maybe it was his wife in Maryland questioning him about all the Russia Club bills on his Amex.

Anyway, Buck returned and we chatted awhile, though he didn't mention the phone call.

Brenner came over to us and said, "We're ready to roll in five minutes." Mr. Brenner glanced at Mrs. Corey, but asked me, "You all squared away on the M4?"

"We are."

Brenner summoned everyone to draw near and said, "Listen up, please."

As everyone gathered around, Brenner began, "First, let me introduce you to Dr. Nolan, who some of you may already know."

The young doctor raised her hand and waved. She wasn't bad-looking if you like the looks of, say, Scarlett Johansson. But I digress. What was I saying? She looked competent. Right.

Brenner informed everyone, "Dr. Nolan is fully

equipped to treat carsickness, and gunshot wounds smaller than nine millimeters."

That got a good laugh. Even Howard laughed on his way back inside the embassy. Just kidding.

Dr. Nolan said, "I make house calls."

Brenner then introduced "our very important passengers, Mr. John Corey of the FBI Evidence Response Team, and Ms. Kate Mayfield, our new legal affairs attaché."

I held up my hand and said, "I'm John. That's Kate."

That got a few laughs. I mean, we were the reason for this risky trip to Aden, so I thought I should show everyone we were just nice, silly people.

Brenner also introduced Howard Fensterman, then said to everyone, "Okay, the order of march." He read from his paper, naming the five DSS drivers and their assigned vehicles, and informed everyone, "I will be in the lead vehicle."

Or as they say in the military, on point— theoretically the most dangerous position in a convoy, so if Mr. Point Man thought Kate was riding with him, I'd have to correct that.

Brenner, however, moved on, saying, "Mr. Harris will be riding shotgun in Vehicle Two."

Buck raised his hand and informed everyone, "I am second in command if Mr. Brenner is not able to perform his duties."

Right. Like dead.

Moving right along, Brenner announced, "Mr. Corey will be riding in Vehicle Three."

The middle vehicle was usually the safest one in a convoy, sometimes reserved for the commander. But Mr. Brenner had assigned me the place of honor. Why?

Because he liked me? No, because I was actually the goat that needed to be delivered as safely as possible to the trap.

Brenner then announced, "Also in the middle vehicle will be Dr. Nolan."

Well, how about *that*? Actually, it was standard procedure to put the medical person in the middle, so that's how that happened. Nothing to do with my prayers. But where was Kate riding?

Brenner answered my question. "Ms. Mayfield will be riding in Vehicle Four."

I was really disappointed that Kate wasn't riding with me and Clare.

Brenner continued, "Also in V-4 will be our other new legal affairs attaché, Mr. Fensterman."

Poor Kate. Just kidding. I really liked Howard. But if I had to spend five or six hours with him in a car, only one of us would walk out alive.

Howard, perhaps reading my and everyone's mind, said, "Kate and I are available by sat-phone if anyone has any legal questions about returning fire."

That got a big laugh of recognition from everyone who had to deal with this nuttiness. Even Howard laughed at himself, bringing him another step closer to reality.

Brenner went on, "The trail vehicle is our enhanced security unit." He named the two DSS agents, one of whom was Zamo, who'd be riding with the DSS driver. He added for the newbies, "This vehicle has specialized armaments and security devices." He quipped, "This is our Bondmobile." He also told us, "The Bondmobile may change positions and may drop back or move out front to scout."

This all sounded like standard convoy security procedure with maybe some variations based on past experience. Bottom line here, Paul Brenner was responsible for five expensive vehicles, lots of pricey commo and weapons, some sensitive paperwork, and thirteen American lives.

This was not the kind of job you trained for; it was the kind of job you were born or not born to do.

I wasn't sure if Paul Brenner was enjoying this, but it was obvious to me that he was at home here. Back in the States, he'd be looking for another job, and in London, Paris, or Rome he'd be just another cog in the big embassy wheel; here, he was one of the wheels. I had a feeling he was staying in Yemen, though he himself didn't know that.

Brenner said, "Commo. The hand-held radios should work well when we stay in line of sight, but remember there are some mountain curves and dips in the road. If necessary, we can relay radio messages. Also, please keep the radio chatter to a minimum for security and tactical reasons. I will initiate most calls." He continued, "Each vehicle is equipped with a sat-phone antenna jack. If attempting a call, please don't forget to plug in your phone."

This got a few laughs, and it was obvious that some lunkhead had forgotten to do that once. These guys had a history together, and Kate and I were just a new chapter. And hopefully not the final chapter. It was also obvious that the DSS agents liked the boss, and that told me a lot about Paul Brenner. Actually, I liked him, too. He had good taste in women.

He continued, "As for other calls, specifically calls of nature, we may not be able to stop, so there are male and female bottles in each vehicle." He advised, "If you don't know which to use, call me."

Good laughs, though they'd heard this one before.

He also informed everyone, "We have brown-bag lunches in each vehicle, compliments of the cafeteria." He added, "Dr. Nolan can treat food poisoning."

There was really a lot of good material in Yemen. A joke a minute. I couldn't wait to get to Ecco's and try out some of this stuff. "So, this camel walks into a bar in Sana'a, and the bartender says, 'Hey, why the long face?'"

Brenner continued, "Because these Land Cruisers are FAVs—fully armored vehicles—they are heavy, and we will have to make a refueling stop."

He glanced at the paper in his hand, then said, "The route. We are taking the main road to Yarim. There we will decide if we'll take the Ta'iz road, or the new road to Aden, depending on the security situation."

He concluded, "I'll be in sat-phone contact with the embassy and also with the Sheraton in Aden to see if they have any info for us en route." He then announced, "We have been promised Predator drone surveillance, but I can't promise that it will be extensive or effective."

I noticed that Brenner didn't mention that those surveillance Predators might be armed with Hellfire missiles, or if they were, that the Hellfires would be used. Bottom line for any commander is don't promise more than you know you can deliver. The men know the risks, and they appreciate honesty. Bullshit is not part of the pre-mission briefing.

Brenner also informed everyone, "The Yemeni authorities have not been advised of our movement, but as always, we'll encounter National Security Bureau police on the road as well as local police and military checkpoints. If we're asked to stop, Mr. Harris will deal diplomatically with the situation."

Buck said something in Arabic, then translated, "Get out of my way, you stupid sons of diseased camels."

Big laugh from the boys. It was obvious that no one here had a very high regard for the host country or its citizens. I could certainly see why this was so—but American arrogance led to over-confidence, and that led to mistakes.

Brenner also reminded everyone, "Flak jackets will be worn even though you're wearing Kevlar vests. We will maintain the top speed possible, and I will set the speed. Vehicle intervals are determined by speed or terrain."

He then got down to the tough stuff and said, "As per our training, we will not deploy or return fire if fired on—we will trust our armor, and we will drive through the ambush, even if our so-called puncture-proof tires are flat. If a vehicle is disabled by an explosive device, we will encircle the disabled vehicle, take up defensive positions, and return fire if fired upon. If we are engaged by a moving vehicle while we are moving, you may at that time lower your windows and blow him the fuck off the road."

That got a big cheer. Even Howard let out a whoop. I'm starting to worry about him.

I watched Mr. Paul Brenner, combat veteran, and I could see, as I said, that he was very much in his element here, getting the troops psyched up, showing a mixture of professional confidence and personal aggressiveness. This was a competent leader, and a man everyone could trust—except maybe if you happened to have your wife with you. But, hey, no one is perfect. I just hoped he was focusing more on the mission than on his lonely dick.

I glanced at Kate while Brenner was speaking, and I could see she was somewhat taken with Mr. Macho. She had that admiring look in her eye that she usually reserves for me and Bon Jovi.

Anyway, Brenner wrapped it up with, "We have no reason to expect any problems on the road, but if we do have an encounter, we're more than equipped and ready to handle anything. I wish us all a safe journey and a nice ride in the country."

Everyone applauded. Bravo. Encore. Well, maybe it was time to go.

Ed Peters, part-time preacher, called out, "Godspeed, and safe home."

And bring those Land Cruisers back in one piece.

Brenner shouted, "Mount up! Let's roll!"

Everyone gathered their gear and made their way to their assigned vehicles, but I, of course, walked Kate to Vehicle Four. Howard was already sitting in the passenger seat with his M4, talking to the driver, and I loaded Kate's luggage in the rear compartment beside Howard's.

I closed the hatch and said to Kate, "Sounds like a milk run."

She didn't respond to that, but advised me, "Behave yourself."

I put on that confused look that I do so well and asked, "What are you talking about?"

"You sit up front."

"Of course. Shotgun."

"Give me a kiss."

We did a hug and kiss, and she said, "See you at the refueling stop."

Or sooner.

So I threw my bags in the rear of the middle vehicle, where Dr. Nolan's CPR unit and oxygen were stowed. I got in the front seat and said hello to the driver, whose name was Mike Cassidy.

Dr. Nolan was already in the rear seat with a big medical bag, wearing her flak jacket, and I turned to her and said, "Hello, Doctor."

"Call me Clare," said Scarlett.

The big engines of the five Land Cruisers all fired up, we buckled up, and off we went.

Both gates of the sally port were open, and the convoy passed quickly out of the American Embassy compound and into Yemen.

CHAPTER THIRTY-SEVEN

Across the road was Tourist City, the scene of last night's Russian adventure. Thinking back, I was certain that Buck knew of Mr. Brenner's interest in Mrs. Corey, and I wondered what the wise old diplomat would advise his friend. I'm sure Buck would tell Brenner to cool it. Mission first.

"John?"

I turned in my seat. "Yes, Clare?"

"Have you driven to Aden?"

"Actually, I have. About two and a half years ago." I asked, "How about you?"

"First time." She told me, "I just got here three weeks ago." She asked me, "How long will you and your wife be here?"

Who? Oh, my wife. I replied, "Hopefully not long. How about you?"

"I signed on for a year." She told me, "The State Department is helping me repay my student loan."

"Right. Me, too."

She laughed.

I asked, "How do you like Yemen?"

"Sucks."

"Give it time."

Mike Cassidy, our DSS driver, assured her, "It doesn't get better."

We continued south, past the British Embassy and the Mövenpick Hotel, then turned onto the Marib road, which was not well traveled, making it easier to see if anyone was following. Then we doubled back to intersect with the main road heading south again.

The Bondmobile reported on the radio, "We're alone."

There was some truck, bus, and SUV traffic going both ways, as well as motorcycles and scooters. The more traffic the better. Not that we were blending in—I mean, five big black Land Cruisers caravanning in the land of little white vehicles were attracting some attention, and it was obvious to even the densest Yemeni that this wasn't a tour group. Probably, I thought, everyone in Sana'a knew these SUVs, and it wouldn't be long before Abdul called his cousin Abdullah who was a fink for Al Qaeda. Cell phones. Everybody had one. Even here.

We passed through the ramshackle outskirts of Sana'a, and the traffic started to thin out.

Mike Cassidy announced to his passengers, "I have three weeks to go here."

I asked him, "Where you heading?"

"Home. Daytona Beach, Florida. Then I got a great gig in Madrid."

"You deserve it," I assured him. I asked, "Ex-military?"

"Yeah. Six years in the Army. One deployment in Afghanistan with the Tenth Mountain Division, one in Iraq with the First Cav."

Clare said, "Thank you for your service."

"Still serving," Mike said. "But the pay is better."

I thought about Mike Cassidy, John Zamoiski, a.k.a. Zamo, and the other DSS agents, and even Paul Brenner. We'd built this extensive and expensive intelligence and security apparatus, of which I was a part, to fight what amounted to a pissant war. But this war could turn very deadly in a heartbeat, as we saw on 9/11, and on other occasions such as the *Cole* bombing. And when you put nukes into the equation, or biological and chemical weapons, you were talking nightmare time. Day to day, however, no one in the States gave much of a rat's ass about any of this since 9/11, but 9/11 would come again, and this time we couldn't say we were surprised or unprepared. Meanwhile, we followed leads, guarded embassies, chased shadows, and now and then whacked a major asshole, which made the homeland just a little safer. That's why I was here.

Mike asked me, "How long are you signed on for?"

"I have a forty-five-day visa with the ERT, subject to extensions."

"You should think about those extensions."

"Right. But my wife is here with the embassy for at least a year."

"That can be tough."

"Right." Especially if I *did* get sent home after my visa expired, and Kate stayed on in the embassy with Paul Brenner. Definitely gotta get that Panther.

Mike asked me, "We got any new leads on the *Cole* bombing?"

"I'll find out in Aden."

Clare asked, "Are you investigating the *Cole* bombing?"

"I am."

"That was awful."

"Right." It was murder.

So the three of us got to know each other a little. Dr. Clare Nolan was from someplace called Iowa and this was her first trip outside of America—except for the week she spent in Washington, D.C., before coming here.

Mike said to me, "The guys in Aden are very good. You'll enjoy working with them."

I wasn't going to be working with them, but I said, "Looking forward to it."

He did a quick rundown of his fellow DSS agents in Aden, who numbered only six. Like last time, there was also an FBI SWAT Team in the Sheraton, numbering ten, and also, like last time, an FBI doctor. My FBI Evidence Response Team, Mike said, numbered five at the moment, but that varied. There was also a Marine FAST Team of twenty men out of Dubai, for hotel security. So, give or take, there were about forty Americans in the Sheraton—pretty much the same as last time I was here. Enough people to do the job, but maybe not enough to defend Fort Apache if the Indians attacked—which seemed to be a real possibility.

Also in the Sheraton, but not officially counted as warm bodies, were CIA officers and Military Intelligence officers. When I was there, I counted three of each, but they kept to themselves. They didn't even play beach volleyball with us.

Clare said, "Someone told me the Sheraton was okay. Pool, gym, beach."

"And a bar," I assured her. I asked, "Are you staying?"

"I am."

Ah. "I didn't know that."

She informed me, "If you need to go into the Badlands, I may go with you."

"You sure you want to do that?"

"No. But if you need me, I'll go."

I couldn't think of why we would need a doctor in Indian Territory. Well...maybe if I thought really hard, I could imagine a situation where people were firing automatic weapons at us.

Clare also said, "I wouldn't mind seeing some of the country."

Mike suggested, "You're seeing all you need to see now."

Clare didn't respond.

I opened the manila envelope that Howard had given me and slid out the photos of Bulus ibn al-Darwish.

The first photo, in black and white, was of a young man in a cap and gown. The caption read: *Bulus ibn al-Darwish, Columbia University graduation, 1987.*

Young Bulus was not bad-looking in an exotic sort of way, with a hooked nose, dark eyes, and high cheekbones. His long hair was swept back, and I was surprised to see that his thin lips were smiling. He was happy to be graduating. He had the whole world in front of him.

The next two photos were color blow-ups of what were captioned *Driver's License photo, 1982*, and *Passport photo, 1990*. In the passport photo, he was still clean-shaven, but his demeanor had changed. He looked serious, or maybe he was thinking about returning to his ancestral home. By this time, he'd gotten his head full of radical thoughts, probably from radical clerics' audio tapes, and maybe from some local spiritual guides who had a different view of Islam than most Muslims had, and who preyed on young men such as Bulus ibn al-Darwish.

The last three photos were color snapshots, and one of them showed a big Victorian house in the background, and it was captioned *Perth Amboy, home, May 1991. Last known photo.*

Bulus, twenty-six years old in this picture, looked older, and without reading too much into the snapshot— but with the knowledge that he'd gone to Yemen a year or so after this photo—I had the impression of a young man who was about to sever his ties to home and family; a man who had seen his future and was anxious to make his mark in the world.

Who, I wondered, took the photo? Probably Mom. Taken in May, so maybe a birthday photo. And did Mom and Dad know that their boy was about to leave the nest and fly east? Probably.

I wondered, too, if Bulus had a girlfriend. Was he getting laid? Did he have only Muslim friends? Or did he also pal around with Christians and Jews? Did he watch American sitcoms on TV? Maybe he did all that in college and afterwards. But somewhere along the line, young Bulus started slipping away into an alternate universe. And now he was here, killing people— American sailors, Europeans, Saudi co-religionists, and his own countrymen.

What happened? Maybe I'd never know. Maybe he himself didn't know what happened, or how it happened. But at some point he'd come to a fork in the road, and he'd taken the wrong one. And I was on a collision course with this guy. If I had a moment with him, I'd ask him about all this. But more likely, there would be no moment of discovery; there would be a quick death. Mine or his.

Mike asked, "Is that the subject asshole?"

"It is."

Mike glanced at the birthday photo and said, "Looks normal."

Right. Some monsters look normal.

Clare leaned forward and asked, "Who is that?"

"That," I replied, "is Bulus ibn al-Darwish. He is a mass murderer."

She didn't reply for a few seconds, then asked, "Are you here to find him?"

"I am."

"Good luck."

I took a last look at the subject, then put the photos in the envelope.

If he knew I was here, maybe he had a photo of me.

CHAPTER THIRTY-EIGHT

Brenner was maintaining a good speed, and we were passing slow-moving vehicles, which is always interesting on a two-lane road with large trucks coming at you.

After a particularly close encounter, Mike remarked, "These armored SUVs don't respond well to the gas pedal."

"You're doing great," I assured him. I asked Clare, "You carrying anything aside from that medical bag?"

"You mean...like a gun?"

"Yeah. Like that."

"No. Well...yes." She informed us, "It's in my medical bag."

"What is it?"

"A gun."

"Right. Can I see it?"

She opened her medical bag and produced an unholstered 9mm Glock.

I unfastened my seat belt, leaned between the seats, and took the gun from her. I checked it out—full magazine, no round in the chamber. I gave her a one-minute lesson on how to chamber a round, how to change magazines, and reminded her that the Glock had no safety.

She said, "Paul Brenner showed me all this."

"Good. Did he also tell you how to aim and fire?"

"He said to hold it with both hands, arms outstretched, look down the barrel, and squeeze the trigger."

"That's about it." I reminded her, "Aim for the center mass of the target. Heart is on the right."

"Left."

"His left, your right, Doctor."

She nodded.

I turned and refastened my seat belt.

The traffic had gotten lighter, and we were picking up speed. Winter is the dry season here, and the high rolling plateau was brown. I saw fields of what looked like newly planted grain, and scattered fruit trees. But mostly I saw what I knew was the cash crop—khat shrubs with dark green leaves and pretty white flowers. The goats seemed to like the khat. Happy goats.

I mentioned the khat cultivation to my driving companions, and Dr. Nolan gave us a medical analysis of *Catha edulis*, a.k.a. khat. She made no moral judgment, but her medical opinion was that you shouldn't operate machinery under the influence. Probably you shouldn't fire a submachine gun, either.

Our radios crackled to life now and then, mostly negative sit-reps from our leader, and from our trail vehicle. Indeed, this looked like a milk run, but it could turn on a dime.

I noticed that when there was no oncoming traffic, Brenner moved the convoy into the left lane. He was either practicing for an assignment in the U.K., or he was keeping away from possible roadside bombs whenever he could. Good thinking.

About fifty miles south of Sana'a, Mike pointed out an oil pipeline that he said came from Marib and went to the Red Sea port city of As-Salif. He informed us, "The hill tribes to the east of here blow up the pipeline about once a month."

"For fun?"

"Fun and profit. They make the government and the American oil company pay them protection money."

"Protection money is supposed to stop them from blowing up the pipeline," I pointed out.

"Yeah, but this is Yemen."

Right. Case closed.

The radio said, "Ma'bar, two K."

Mike and the other drivers acknowledged, and we started to slow down. Mike said to us, "Small town."

I was remembering this road a little, and I recalled that there weren't many towns along the way, and Ma'bar, about sixty miles from Sana'a, was the first.

What I also remembered about my trip between Sana'a and Aden was that the road wasn't considered too dangerous two and a half years ago. I mean, it wasn't totally safe, but it wasn't ambush alley either. Things, however, had changed, and not for the better, as Buck mentioned in New York, and the embassy website said.

The convoy slowed down, and Mike said, "Expect a checkpoint."

We entered the small town of Ma'bar, which I sort of remembered, a collection of two-story mud brick buildings, goats, children, and chickens.

There was indeed an army checkpoint in the center

of town, and we stopped. I saw Buck get out of the second vehicle and walk up to the soldiers. He shook hands with the honcho, said something that made the soldiers laugh, then got face-to-face with the boss, Arab style, and had a serious conversation with him. And while he was at it, he slipped the guy some baksheesh, which made everyone happy.

Buck got back in the Land Cruiser. Piece of cake.

As we passed the checkpoint, the Yemeni soldiers looked into the dark-tinted windows, and though they couldn't see inside, Mike flipped them the bird anyway, saying, "They should be paying *us*."

Brenner's voice on the radio said, "Dhamar, thirty K. Expect another stop."

Within twenty minutes we were in the larger town of Dhamar. I recalled that an earthquake had pretty much leveled this place back in the eighties, and it was still half in ruins. This country can't catch a break.

Clare asked, "What happened here?"

"It wasn't a battle," I assured her. "Every two years the residents smash up the town with sledgehammers. It's called the Festival of Al-Smash."

Silence from the rear. But Mike laughed.

Clare said, "This is going to be a long day."

My wife says that. Every day.

Anyway, we were stopped again in the center of town, and Buck again got out, but this time Brenner accompanied him and they had a conversation with the soldiers.

Mike said to us, "They're talking about road security."

"And why do we trust these clowns to give us good information?"

"We don't, but if you talk to all of them, like Brenner is doing, you can get a feel for the situation. Like, if they're bullshitting."

"Right." The other thing to consider, of course, was what the surveillance drones had seen—or not seen—and what to make of those video images that were being transmitted to some ground control station somewhere. I mean, in a country where everyone carries an AK-47, how does an analyst determine who's up to no good? Right?

I looked out the rear, and I could see that Zamo and another DSS agent had lowered the windows of the Bondmobile and were covering our rear with their M4s.

Buck and Brenner were now heading toward their SUVs. The radio crackled, and Brenner's voice said, "Continue on the main road to Yarim."

And off we went, through the ruined town of Dhamar.

The road from Dhamar to Yarim was mostly uphill and I saw that the plateau was rising. There was a map in the glove compartment and I looked at it.

Mike said, "When we get to Yarim, we can pick up the new road that goes to Aden, or we can stay on this road—the old caravan road—to Ta'iz, then to Aden."

I wasn't sure I wanted to share the road with camels, so I asked, "What's the difference?"

Mike replied, "The new road is good, and more traveled, but there are more mountains, and better places for ambushes and IEDs."

"Okay. And the camel road?"

He replied, "Less traveled, so it's easier to avoid suicide trucks. Also, it's mostly low hills, except for about sixty miles of mountain."

Clare asked, "Which is the *safest* road?"

The answer, of course, was neither, but Mike said, "Depends."

Anyway, we got to the small decrepit town of Yarim, which Mike informed us was a hot springs resort town with old Turkish bathhouses—sort of like Saratoga Springs, except this place sucked. I mean, I wouldn't wash my socks here.

Anyway, we stopped again at a military checkpoint, and Buck and Brenner got out to talk to the soldiers.

Mike said, "Whichever road we take will be radioed in by the military to some headquarters, and that info can get to the wrong people." He added, "In either case, we're passing through territory where Al Qaeda has a presence." He further informed us, "That territory starts here in Yarim."

I suggested, "They should have a road sign: Al Qaeda, Next 100 Kilometers." But seriously, this sucks.

I watched Brenner and Buck talking to the soldiers, and I imagined the conversation. "So, guys, which road should we take to avoid ambushes and roadside bombs?"

And the soldiers laughed and replied, "You should take the Long Island Expressway."

Anyway, Buck and Brenner got back in their SUVs. The radios came alive and Brenner said, "We will head toward the new highway, but then double back around this checkpoint and take the old road to Ta'iz."

Everyone acknowledged and we moved past the checkpoint.

Buck came on the radio with some good news. "Predator reports no suspicious activity on the Ta'iz road."

That's because the bad guys didn't know yet what road we were taking.

In fact, Mike had the same thought and said, "There are a thousand eyes and five hundred cell phones along either route. So it really doesn't matter what road we take."

"Right."

He further added, "We just need to be fast and try to keep ahead of anything that Al Qaeda tries to put together for us."

Clare said, "This is scary."

What was your first clue?

Anyway, we did the old, "I'm going this way, fellas," then the switcheroo and the double-back, and within ten minutes we were south of Yarim on the old caravan road to Ta'iz.

Mike said, "I think this is a smart move."

That depended on whether or not we actually wanted to make contact with Al Qaeda.

Clare asked, "Is this really Al Qaeda territory?"

Mike replied, "According to what's called the CIA Areas of Influence map." He added, "But you can't always go by the map." He assured her, "The CIA likes to overstate the danger. Keeps them in business."

Overstating the danger is also called covering your ass, as in, "Hey, we *said* the roads were dangerous. Sorry about what happened to that convoy."

CHAPTER THIRTY-NINE

The old caravan road wasn't bad, and it was lightly traveled so we were making good time, about 120 K per hour, and within half an hour I could see the mountains on the horizon.

As we came over a hill, I saw the brake lights of the two lead vehicles, and on the road ahead I saw a convoy of five military trucks. I took the binoculars from the console and focused on them. There were about twenty men in each open truck, wearing the berets and blue camouflage fatigues of the National Security police.

The radio crackled, and Brenner said, "We'll pass one at a time."

The drivers acknowledged, and Brenner's lead vehicle pulled out into the oncoming lane and accelerated. But suddenly, the last police truck swerved in front of him, and the Land Cruiser had to brake hard, drop back, and get back into the right lane.

Mike said, "Assholes."

Clare asked, "What's happening?"

Mike replied, "Probably a shakedown." He informed

us, "The military has some discipline, but the police are banditos in uniform."

The police convoy slowed, then one of the trucks moved into the oncoming lane, and all the trucks came to a stop. Roadblock.

The five Land Cruisers also came to a halt, but we kept thirty-foot intervals between us. This was a lonely stretch of road, and the only vehicles around were us and them.

Brenner said on the radio, "Everyone stay in their vehicles, but be prepared to make a show of force."

Brenner and Buck were out of their vehicles, and unarmed; they stood where we could see them and waited. Brenner was carrying his hand-held radio, and Buck was talking on his satellite phone, probably in contact with the embassy. Or maybe the Predator drone ground station. Good. Or at least it looked good.

Mike said, "These clowns want Brenner to walk to them. Not going to happen."

Clare asked, "Should I be frightened?"

Mike replied, "I think pissed off is better."

This seemed to be a standoff, and it could go on for a while. I wasn't sure of the protocol here, but male egos I understood.

The tailgates of the trucks started dropping and the police began jumping out, carrying their AK-47s. Their blue cammies were covered with dust, and I saw that most of them had dust bandanas covering their mouths and noses, making them look, indeed, like banditos. They didn't make any moves toward the Land Cruisers; they just milled around, and some of them used the opportunity to take a leak.

I saw Brenner raise his radio, and he said, "Everyone just sit tight."

I saw that Buck was now conversing with a few of the National Security police guys, probably telling them to go get the boss, but it didn't seem to be working.

Patience is not one of my many virtues, and it was about time I made Buck and Brenner understand I wasn't just along for the ride, so I opened my door and got out with my M4 slung over my shoulder.

Mike said, "Brenner is going to be pissed."

Clare said, "Be careful."

I walked past the two Land Cruisers in front of us, and Brenner saw me and said, "Get back in your vehicle."

I didn't respond. I took Buck's arm and said, "Let's go find the boss."

Buck resisted for a moment, then came along with me, and we walked up the road through the mob of police. Brenner stayed behind so he could be in sight of us and keep point-to-point radio contact with the convoy.

I said to Buck, "Find out what these idiots want, and let's get moving."

Buck replied, "All they want is to show us who's the boss here, and a few hundred dollars."

"They're not going to get either."

Before we got to the lead vehicle, a tall guy with important-looking insignia on his uniform walked up to us and said something in Arabic.

Buck replied in Arabic, and the guy didn't seem surprised that Buck spoke the language—I guess he'd been briefed by radio—and he and Buck started jabbering.

I interrupted, "What is this clown saying?"

Buck said to me, "This is Captain Dammaj of the

National Security Bureau, and he wants to know who we are and where we're going."

"He knows damn well who we are and where we're going. Tell him to go fuck himself."

Buck said something to the guy, but probably not what I suggested.

The guy replied, and Buck said to me, "He says this road is closed for security reasons, and we must go back to Yarim and take the new road."

"Yeah, well, here's your chance to say, 'Get out of my way, you stupid son of a diseased camel.'"

Buck said something to the guy, but I didn't hear the Arabic word "gamal," which I knew.

Buck listened to the guy, then said to me, "He says he will provide security for us through these mountains to Ta'iz." Buck added, "Five hundred dollars."

"Tell him we'll provide security for him. Six hundred dollars."

"John—"

The guy said something, and Buck said to me, "He senses you are angry, and he believes you are insulting him."

"Me?" I smiled at Captain Dammaj and said in a pleasant tone, "I'll give you two minutes to get the hell out of our way."

Buck, ever the diplomat, also smiled and said something to Captain Dammaj.

They chatted, maybe negotiating the deal.

Anyway, I'd really gotten myself worked up, maybe for no reason, and maybe I was being overly aggressive and making an annoying situation into a bad situation. But thinking back to what Buck had said in New York, the Yemenis didn't like pussies. No girly men here. So

I was just following Buck's advice, though Buck didn't seem happy with me.

Anyway, I could hear someone on my hand-held and I put it to my ear, and Buck did the same.

It was Brenner, who said, "What is going on there? John, I want you back here."

Buck replied, "The officer in charge says this road is closed for security reasons. We're trying to work out a deal. Over."

Brenner said to me, "John, let Buck handle this."

I replied, "Negative. Out."

I could see that Kate had gotten out of her SUV and she was in a serious discussion with her friend Paul about something, maybe saying, "I told you John wasn't a team player." Or maybe she thought I was just trying to show her I was much cooler than Paul Brenner. That was totally not true. Well...maybe a little true.

Buck and Captain Dickhead exchanged a few more words, then Buck said to me, "He'll take four hundred dollars—"

"Highway robbery. I know they get two bucks a man."

Buck was looking a bit unsettled now, and he said to me sharply, "John, please calm down." He told me, "The money is in the budget. It's not your money, and you're making this more difficult than it needs to be."

"It's not about the money, Buck. It's about balls." I reminded him, "You told me to be aggressive with these people."

"No. I told you that if you look fearful, it invites aggression on their part."

"Oh...did I get that wrong? Sorry about that." I let

Buck know, "We're playing good cop, bad cop. I'm the bad cop. So you talk nice to this asshole and tell him I'm the boss and I'm being a prick, but I'll agree to a hundred bucks."

Buck seemed a bit frustrated with me, but he forced a smile and said something to Captain What's-his-name.

As he spoke, I prompted him by saying, "Tell this clown the Yemeni government should be kissing our asses for being here."

Buck interrupted his conversation with the captain and said to me, "John, shut up."

"Okay." I don't think I'd make a good diplomat.

Finally, Buck turned to me and said, "Two hundred. That's as low as he'll go." He reminded me, "In Yemen, it's all about the deal. This man needs to save face now. And we're not exactly bargaining from strength, and we don't want to go back to Yarim, so I'm giving him two hundred dollars and we'll be on our way."

"Until the next shakedown."

Buck said something to Captain Dammaj, who replied, and Buck said to me, "He'll give us...let's call it a laissez-passer, in diplomatic language. A written pass to Aden."

Sounded like bullshit to me, but Buck was getting stressed, and the police were finished urinating in public, and they were getting restless, plus Brenner was totally pissed off, and Kate looked worried. Or pissed at me. Also, she was unveiled, and these clowns were giving her the eye. So...I said to Buck, "All right."

Buck said something to Captain Dammaj, who nodded and smiled at me.

I asked Buck, "Do I hug him?"

"Just shake hands."

So I extended my hand to Captain Dammaj, we shook, and I smiled and said to him, "You're a thief."

He smiled in return and said something that Buck translated as, "You are a brave man and a hard negotiator."

I don't know if Dammaj really said that—maybe he said, "You're a total asshole and you eat goat shit"—but Buck was intent on smoothing things over.

Buck got on his radio and said, "We'll be on our way in a few minutes."

Captain Dammaj walked to one of the trucks, I guess to write a pass or something.

Buck said to me, "I could have handled this without your help."

"I made it fun."

Captain Dammaj returned with a piece of paper, and he and Buck exchanged the pass and the money. As Buck was reading the pass, I asked him, "Did he sign it Ali Baba and the Forty Thieves?"

Captain Dammaj smiled and said to me, in English, "You are not so funny."

Whoops.

Buck almost dropped his laissez-passer.

Captain Dammaj said to both of us, "Be very careful on the road. And have a pleasant stay at the Sheraton."

"And you have a nice day," I said.

Before he turned to walk off, he said to me, "Go fuck yourself."

Buck looked at me, but he seemed at a loss for words.

On the walk back to the Land Cruisers, I asked Buck, "Do you think there really is a security problem ahead?"

Buck replied, "We'll find out soon enough."

We got to the lead Land Cruiser where Brenner and Kate were standing. Brenner, showing a lot of restraint, said to me, "I appreciate your initiative, but it's Buck's job to handle these situations."

I didn't respond to that and kept walking.

Kate caught up to me and asked, "What is wrong with you?"

Sounded like a rhetorical question, so I didn't answer, but I said, "You were told to stay in the vehicle. Follow orders."

"Me? How about you?"

"I don't take orders from Paul Brenner."

She didn't reply to that, but said, "I'll see you later," and kept walking.

I got in my Land Cruiser, and Mike asked, "How much?"

"Two hundred."

"That's about right."

Clare asked, "Is everything okay?"

"We're good to go."

The police truck that was blocking the left lane moved over, and Brenner's lead vehicle pulled out and led the way for the Land Cruisers to pass the stopped trucks.

I looked in my sideview mirror and saw that the police trucks were doing a U-turn. We were on our own.

Within a few minutes we were clipping along and the police convoy was out of sight.

About twenty minutes later, we were on a steep upgrade, and the road narrowed and turned through a mountain pass.

Brenner got on the radio and said, "Niner-niner"

—meaning all personnel—"it gets interesting here. Spread out, but keep the vehicle in front of you in sight." He added, "Stay alert."

Goes without saying, Paul. But I wasn't worried. We had a pass from Captain Dammaj.

There was no oncoming traffic on the mountain road, and Mike informed me, "That's not a good sign."

"Right."

Mike asked me, "Did the police say anything about the security situation?"

"I think the chief did say something about the road being closed for security reasons."

"Yeah? And?"

"Just a sales pitch. He wanted five hundred bucks to escort us."

Mike didn't say anything for a while, then suggested, "He may have been telling the truth."

"We'll see."

"Yeah . . . anyway, you can't trust the police to provide protection—even if you pay for it."

"Right." I thought about those Belgian tourists at Marib. They didn't get much for their money.

Clare said, "Maybe we should turn around."

Mike replied, "That's for the boss to decide, and he's already decided."

Right. Paul Brenner wasn't turning around. In fact, we'd gotten ourselves into a dicey situation. But I think that was the goal.

Mike said, "Well, we got the road all to ourselves."

"I hope so."

The road skirted a town high up on a hill, and Mike said, "That's Ibb. Last town we'll see in these hills." He added, "Almost no government presence here."

"Good. We're almost out of shakedown money, so that works."

He continued, "The tribes rule here, but they won't take on this convoy." He reminded me, however, "Al Qaeda is the new boy on the block here."

Right. And they don't want your money. They want your head.

CHAPTER FORTY

The mountains were parched, and there were herds of goats nibbling at the brown vegetation. I could see mud huts on the slopes and in the alpine meadows. People lived here, but I hadn't seen anyone for a while. Khat time?

White clouds had developed around the peaks, but the Predator infrared cameras should be able to see through them.

The narrow road was paved, but clouds of dust partly obscured the two Land Cruisers ahead of us. We were driving mostly on the left to lessen the damage from a roadside bomb planted on the right. But a bomb could also be planted on the left.

We were maintaining a speed of about a hundred KPH—about sixty miles an hour—which was pushing the limit here.

The radios were quiet, and so were my companions.

Finally, Mike said, "In about thirty minutes we'll be coming down onto the plateau."

I could tell by Mike's tone of voice that he seemed to have a mountain phobia, and probably with good reason.

Every now and then I scanned the terrain with the binoculars, but I didn't see anything suspicious. Not that I'd know what suspicious looked like around here. But I'm sure if I saw it, I'd know it.

I asked Clare, "How you doing?"

No reply.

I turned and saw she was sleeping. I guess that's the best way to get through a terrifying ride through enemy territory. I said to Mike, "You should try to catch some sleep, too."

I thought that was funny, but he didn't laugh. I hoped he wasn't flashing back to Afghanistan.

The radio crackled, and Brenner's voice, cool and calm, said, "Predator reports ambush ahead."

That got my attention.

Mike said, "Shit!"

Clare, awake now, asked, "What did he say?"

I said to her, "Get down below the windows. Now. Quick."

She unfastened her seat belt and got flat on the seat.

Brenner said, "Maintain max speed."

I focused my binoculars on the road ahead, and about three hundred yards in front of Brenner's lead vehicle I saw three things: a mud hut close to the right side of the road, then fifty yards farther a white Toyota SUV on the narrow shoulder with its hood up, and finally at a bend in the road a donkey cart and driver coming toward us.

Mike said, "There's the ambush—maybe IEDs..." He said to me, "Get below the windows."

I kept looking through the binoculars.

Brenner's lead vehicle was literally seconds from the mud hut, and I saw his brake lights come on, and he swerved to the far left on a collision course with the donkey cart. Then all of a sudden I saw a streak of smoke coming out of the sky, and a second later the mud hut exploded, then erupted again in a secondary explosion whose shockwave rocked the SUV.

Clare screamed.

Holy shit.

Two more streaks of smoke came out of the sky, and in quick succession the Toyota and the donkey cart erupted in deafening explosions.

Debris was falling out of the sky, the brown grass was burning, and black smoke billowed from what remained of the Toyota.

Brenner's vehicle hit a chunk of donkey as it shot through the devastated area, followed by Buck's vehicle, then ours. Something hit the windshield and left a thick red smear on the glass.

Mamma mia.

I looked in the sideview mirror and saw Kate's vehicle coming through the smoke and the debris field, followed by the Bondmobile.

Then something else hit our SUV, and it took me a second to realize we were taking rounds.

Mike hit the gas and we two-wheeled it around the S-curve as we got hit again. A loud noise filled the SUV and I turned to see a big dimple in the back windshield where it had taken a bullet. I could also see green tracer rounds coming from the hills around us, streaking toward the speeding convoy.

I really wanted to lower my window and return fire, but Brenner had said not to do that, and maybe it wasn't a good idea with bullets coming at us. But when I looked again through the back windshield, I saw that someone in the Bondmobile, wearing a flak jacket and

Kevlar helmet—maybe Zamo—was leaning out of the rear driver's side window gangster-style, firing back at the streaks of tracer rounds. The other DSS guy riding shotgun was doing the same, and the Bondmobile was drawing most of the fire now.

The Land Cruiser took another hit, and Clare shouted, "Stop!"

Mike yelled, "Look!"

I turned, and on the road coming toward us was another Toyota SUV traveling at top speed, quickly closing the distance between him and Brenner's lead vehicle. Bad guy? I'd never know, because a white smoke trail angled down out of the blue and the Toyota erupted in a ball of flames, followed by a loud explosion.

Brenner's and Buck's SUVs swerved and shot past the burning wreckage, and by the time we reached it, pieces of burning junk started falling on us, and something bounced off the hood. Mike was temporarily blinded by the black, billowing smoke, and we were going off the pavement, but he jerked the wheel back in time to avoid an off-road trip into a ravine.

I unfastened my seat belt and looked out the back windshield. Kate's SUV was right behind us, and the Bondmobile was coming up fast. We seemed to be out of the killing zone and I didn't see any tracers following us. I took a deep breath and looked down at Clare, who was now on the floor, her face and chest covered by the big medical bag. I said to her, "It's okay. It's over."

She didn't respond and I reached down and lifted the medical bag. She stared up at me, but said nothing. I asked, "You okay?"

She nodded.

I turned back toward the front and Mike said, "Three fucking weeks."

"Right." In fact, time is relative. The ambush seemed to last forever, but it was probably less than two minutes since the first Hellfire hit.

Mike had the windshield washers on now, and the wiper blades were smearing a red goo across the glass.

The hand-helds crackled and Brenner's voice, still calm and cool, came over the radios. "Sit-rep. Vehicle One okay."

Buck said, "Two is...fine." He sounded surprised.

Mike had a death grip on the steering wheel, so I transmitted, "Three okay."

I waited for V-4 to transmit, and I was getting concerned, but then Kate's voice, almost upbeat, said, "Four okay."

The Bondmobile reported, "Trail okay...but Z has a graze wound."

I said to Clare, "One customer for you."

The mountains were receding off to the left and right now, and the terrain started to flatten on both sides of the road. Brenner increased the speed and we were flying down the middle of the crumbling blacktop. The color had returned to Mike's face, but his knuckles were still white.

Brenner transmitted, "Predators see nothing ahead."

Everyone acknowledged the good news.

Mike found his voice and said, "Predators usually operate in pairs...two Hellfires each...so we're out of missiles."

"Right. But the bad guys don't know that."

"Yeah...and they don't want to find out."

I hope.

Clare was sitting low in the rear seat, and she had her radio in her hand. She transmitted, "V-5, M.D. here. How's Z?"

Z himself replied, "Don't need you."

Then the other DSS agent transmitted, "Bullet passed through his brain. No damage."

Everyone was on an adrenaline high now, happy to be alive and very happy to joke about death.

Someone else transmitted, "I feel bad about the donkey."

Another guy said, "Legat, legat. Permission to return fire."

Howard replied, "I'm checking."

Brenner said, "Can the chatter."

So we continued on in radio silence.

Clare confessed, "I've never been so frightened in my life."

Mike replied, "Welcome to the club."

I focused my binoculars on Buck's SUV, then Brenner's. I could see some raw metal where they'd taken hits. Also, Brenner's back windshield had been hit. I wondered what the new ambassador would say when he was picked up at Sana'a Airport with these vehicles.

The road was straightening out, and we were definitely on the downslope. I began seeing more mud and stone huts, livestock, and people, plus a few motor scooters raising dust on the mountain trails.

We increased our speed, and as we crested a hill I could see flatlands in the distance.

Mike's knuckles were pink again.

Mike had his sat-phone plugged into the antenna jack, and I speed-dialed the DSS driver in Vehicle Four. The driver answered, "Steve."

"Is Ms. Mayfield awake?"

"Yeah...hold on."

Kate's voice came on the line. "Who is this?"

"Just called to see how you're doing."

"I'm doing fine. How about you?"

"Good." I asked, "How's Howard?"

"Fine...a little concerned that there may have been ICs back there."

"Only the donkey was an IC." I added, "And by the way, I *told* you this place was dangerous." *Finally*, I got to say it.

Kate replied, "You may be right for a change."

"See you later."

I hung up and Mike said to me, "As we used to say in Iraq and Afghanistan, we can't tell the ICs from the jihadists, so kill them all and let Saint Peter sort them out."

"They're Muslims," I pointed out.

"Right. So the innocent Muslims get the seventy-two virgins, and the jihadists get to jerk off for eternity."

Interesting theology. More importantly, Mike Cassidy, who seemed like a regular guy from Daytona Beach, had apparently become a little callous, maybe numbed by years of this stuff. Well...maybe it was happening to all of us, by small degrees, and we didn't see it.

We were onto the plateau now, and there were farms, people, and vehicles around. I'd say we were back in civilization, but that would be stretching the definition of civilization.

The radio crackled and Brenner said, "Fuel status."

Mike looked at the computer display: 96 kilometers left to empty.

Everyone reported about the same, and Brenner said, "Refuel in Ta'iz. Details to follow."

Mike let us know, "Ta'iz is a big town—maybe three hundred thousand people, and a dozen gas stations. But sometimes they're out of gas."

I thought they produced oil here. The only thing this place was never out of was ammunition.

The radios crackled and Brenner said, "We're not out of the woods yet, so stay alert." He added, "Everyone did a good job back there."

Thanks, Paul. The drivers actually did a great job, and so did Zamo and the other DSS guy who literally stuck their necks out to return fire. The rest of us didn't do much except keep our sphincters tight and our bladders full.

The best job was done by the Predator ground pilots, and if I ever met them, I'd give them a big hug. But I'd never meet them. I didn't even know what continent they were on.

I said to Mike, "Good driving."

"Thanks."

Clare seconded that and added, "I thought we were dead."

Mike admitted, "It was a little close."

Clare offered brown-bag lunches, but all anyone wanted was water.

We continued toward Ta'iz, then Aden, then maybe Marib. The Panther, apparently, had found us. And now we had to find *him*. And kill him, before he killed us. This was simple. I like simple.

CHAPTER FORTY-ONE

We didn't want to go into Ta'iz with shot-up vehicles, and Mike also explained that Ta'iz was a hotbed of Al Qaeda and anti-government activity, and that the Commies were still strong there.

Sounded like the San Francisco of Yemen.

The good news was that the Predators had spotted an open gas station outside of town. The Predators are better than GPS—they shoot missiles.

Anyway, we followed Brenner's vehicle and up ahead we saw the gas station.

Brenner got on the radio and said, "Vehicles One and Five, fill up. Everyone else take up positions."

Mike parked on the side of the road with the engine running, as did Buck's and Kate's SUVs, while the lead and trail vehicles pulled up to the two pumps.

Brenner, carrying his M4, got out of the SUV and went to the trail vehicle to check on Zamo.

Buck, also armed, got out, and Clare said, "I need to make a house call," and exited with her medical bag.

I got out, too, carrying my M4, and checked out my surroundings as I walked. The gas pumps were modern, but the parking area was dirt, and the building was a small concrete-block hut, from which emerged six Yemenis in ratty white robes, all carrying their Yemeni walking sticks, a.k.a. AK-47s. I haven't seen this much firepower at a gas station since my road trip through Alabama.

Two of the Yemenis were the gas attendants—no self-service here—and the other four were nosy. They checked out the shot-up Land Cruisers, and Buck was conversing with them. I had no idea what he was saying, but he should tell them we were just shooting at each other for laughs. They'd totally believe it.

Clare had gotten into Zamo's SUV, and Brenner had his head stuck in the window. He made room for me and I poked my head in. Zamo was sitting in the rear seat, and Clare was unwrapping a bloody first-aid pressure bandage from his left forearm.

I asked him, "How you doing?"

"I'd be doing better if people stopped asking me."

Clare got the bandage off and said, "This is not bad."

"I know that," said Zamo.

"I'll clean and dress it, and maybe suture it when we get to the hotel." She handed Zamo a vial of antibiotics and asked him, "You want a painkiller?"

"No."

Brenner asked the doctor, "Is he okay for duty?"

Zamo himself answered, "Good to go."

Everything seemed under control here, so I walked into the station hut looking for the restroom, and thinking maybe I could buy a few Slim Jims and a Dr Pepper. But there was nothing in the hut except some white plastic chairs and a prayer rug. Which way is Mecca?

Buck joined me and said, "The restrooms are out back."

We went through an open doorway where there was a slit trench, and we held our noses and dicks and did our business, joined by a few of the DSS guys, in shifts, then Brenner, then Kate, who asked, "Who left the toilet seat up?"

We stood watch with our backs to Kate as she used the unisex trench. This was a great bonding experience, and I was sure there'd be more of them in the Badlands.

Anyway, the A-team was all assembled, so we used the opportunity for a quick meeting before we got back on the road.

Buck informed us, "I've reported the incident to the embassy by sat-phone, and they have relayed my report to Washington." He added, "The State Department will notify the Yemeni government. But we are not admitting to any unauthorized use of Hellfire missiles."

I pointed out, "I don't think rifle fire can cause that kind of damage, Buck."

It was Mr. Brenner who replied. "Small-arms fire can detonate roadside bombs and fuel tanks." He added, "The Yemenis don't have the sophisticated forensics to determine otherwise."

Right. Whatever.

Kate then said, "Howard may want to report this as it happened."

Buck said to Kate, "Tell him I'd like a word with him."

Kate nodded and left.

Buck explained to me and Brenner, "It's important that there are no conflicting accounts of what happened."

"Right," I agreed. "Especially true accounts."

Buck further explained, "We were the victims of an apparent Al Qaeda attack. We don't want to be seen as aggressors or provocateurs." Buck also informed us, "There are certain groups in the States who are not in favor of our Hellfire assassination program." He added, "This incident, if it became public, could be misinterpreted as offensive rather than defensive."

Right. We don't want to upset human rights groups in the States with our HAPPY program—Hellfire Assassination Program to Pacify Yemen. I made that up.

Buck also said, "It is important that we four are not declared persona non grata and asked to leave Yemen."

I agreed, but pointed out, "If it wasn't for the Hellfires, we'd all be declared persona non breathing."

Buck ignored that and continued, "This attack, along with the Hunt Oil attack, will cause Washington to re-evaluate our military mission in Yemen." He added, "Just as the Cole did."

Right. So, bottom line here, you sometimes need an attack to get things going your way. The Alamo, the *Maine*, Pearl Harbor, the Gulf of Tonkin, the USS *Cole*, and so forth. Sometimes the attack is an unprovoked surprise, and sometimes it isn't.

Howard appeared from the hut, spotted the trench, and used it. He then said to me, "I don't know how I can ever repay you for inviting me along."

"I'll think of something."

Buck had already thought of something and said to Howard, "This is a national security matter, Howard, and a sensitive diplomatic matter at the highest level." He added, "Please do not say anything to anyone that would jeopardize this mission."

Or we'll kill you.

Howard, practicing not saying anything to anyone, just nodded, then left.

We all assembled in front of the station. The Land Cruisers were topped off, the windshields were cleaned of mortal remains, and we got in our vehicles. Gentlemen, start your engines. And off we went, southeast toward Aden.

Brenner transmitted, "Predators still on station until we reach our destination." He added, "Two new Predators with Hellfires on the way."

Great. So, what did we learn from our drive in the country? Well, we learned that Al Qaeda knew of our trip to Aden—but that was almost a given. We learned, too, that Al Qaeda was willing and able to attack an armored American convoy. They were getting their act together. What Al Qaeda didn't know, however, or didn't expect, was Hellfire missiles—and that was because the Yemeni government idiots usually said no to Hellfires. But we solved that problem by not asking. This was a new game.

What *we* didn't know was if Al Qaeda knew that Mr. John Corey was in the convoy. But we could assume they did. In fact, Al Qaeda knew that John Corey and Kate Mayfield would be in Yemen before we knew we were going. What we didn't know was if The Panther was now in Paradise, or in Marib, or someplace else. Wherever he was, he was pissed.

Good. I was pissed, too.

CHAPTER FORTY-TWO

The convoy continued on toward Aden.

Mike informed Clare and me, "The farther south we go, the less Al Qaeda is present."

"Good."

"But Al Qaeda is strong again around Aden."

"Bad."

"Also, when we cross into what used to be South Yemen, you have secessionist rebels."

Clare asked Mike, "Is there any part of this country that's...like, safe?"

"Not one square inch."

You're safe with me, sweetheart.

She said, "At least we can feel safe in the hotel."

Uh...about that hotel, Clare...

We were on the downslope from the central highlands and making good time toward the coastal plains despite the traffic on the well-traveled Ta'iz–Aden road.

Mike said, "About a hundred K to Aden."

Brenner's voice came over the radio. "New Predators with Hellfires on station. No suspicious roadside activity ahead. But stay alert for suicide vehicles."

The fun never stops.

Mike informed us, "The Predators can keep flying for up to twenty-four hours without refueling."

Correct. And the pilot was on the ground, and he could hand off the controls every few hours. The Predator drone with Hellfire missiles was an awesome weapon system. This was probably how we'd bag The Panther, if we hadn't already vaporized him back in the hills. American military technology is a beautiful thing—unless you're on the receiving end.

I asked Mike, "Where are the Predators stationed? And where are the ground control units?"

He replied, "No one knows. But I'd guess Oman, or Saudi Arabia. Or maybe Djibouti across the strait."

"So not here?"

"Not in this screwed-up country."

"Right."

It was almost 1 P.M., and we'd made okay time considering we took the old caravan route, though I hadn't seen a single camel. The ambush hadn't actually delayed us—in fact, it sort of moved things along. Nothing like getting shot at to get your ass moving.

We intersected the new highway that came from Sana'a and headed due south toward Aden. It was a good road, and if we'd taken it, I wonder if we'd have had the same exciting experience we had on the caravan route. I was fairly sure that it was the Predator controller who advised us to take that route. In the end, the CIA—who had operational control of the Predators—got what they wanted: a show of American force, dead bad guys, and an incident.

I asked Mike, "Will you guys be able to get back to Sana'a before dark?"

"Maybe... We'll see what Brenner wants us to do."

I used that opening to fish. "He seems like a good guy."

Mike replied, "He's good." Silence. "But he pushes his luck sometimes."

Which meant pushing everyone else's luck. Maybe he had nothing to live for. But maybe he'd just found a new interest in life. I said to Mike, "He told me he had a lady in the States."

"Yeah. She was here once." He let me know, "A real knockout."

"So no embassy romance?"

Mike realized he was saying too much about his boss and replied, "Not that I know of." He added, "Slim pickings here."

Clare piped in, "I beg your pardon."

That got a laugh.

Clare also offered, "I think he's cute." She added, "But a little old for me."

What? He couldn't be five years older than me. I'm crushed. I wish I had died in the Al Qaeda ambush.

We were on the coastal plain now, and up ahead I spotted a road sign, one of the few I'd seen in the last four hundred kilometers, and I focused the binoculars on it. It said something in Arabic, but beneath that it said ADAN—with an A—GOVERNATE.

Mike said, "We are crossing into the former South Yemen, also once known as Adan." He added, "It's almost like another country in some ways."

Actually, it was once. But I said, "Looks like the same crap hole to me."

"Different attitudes here. A little more modern, maybe because of the British influence, then the

Soviets, and all the ships coming into Aden Harbor from around the world."

"Right. Like the Cole."

Mike replied, "Al Qaeda is new in Aden." He added, "South Yemen is regressing."

Actually, the whole Middle East was regressing.

A half hour later, we were in the outskirts of Aden. I looked to the southeast, where I knew the Sheraton was located, and I didn't see any smoke rising into the air, so that was a good sign.

The Sheraton Hotel is located away from the city, on a peninsula that juts into the Gulf of Aden. The landscape was formed by a hopefully extinct volcano, and there are high hills and bluffs overlooking the beaches, which is very scenic, but not good for security.

There was a construction project up ahead, and a big sign in English said: BIN LADEN CONSTRUCTION COMPANY, which reminded me of what Colonel Kent said in Sana'a. I'm sure most of the Yemeni-based bin Laden family were good citizens, but it was sort of jarring to see that—like if I saw in Germany ADOLF HITLER VOLKSWAGEN DEALER. Right? They might want to change that company name.

We passed the airport and began an uphill climb into the high ground above the beaches.

I could now see the Sheraton below, a white six-story contemporary-style building, sitting peacefully in the sunlight. Behind the hotel was a stretch of white sand and palm trees, and the calm blue waters of the Gulf of Aden. Paradise. Not.

Clare said, "Looks nice."

Looks like a target.

Mike asked me, "Bring back memories?"

"Lots."

We came down a narrow road on the downside of the high bluffs, and right in front of us was the Sheraton Hotel. Brenner radioed, "Niner, niner. We have arrived. Good job, everyone."

Mike and the other drivers blasted their horns as we pulled into the hotel driveway.

I have returned.

— PART VI —

Marib,
Yemen

CHAPTER FORTY-THREE

Bulus ibn al-Darwish, al-Numair, The Panther, wearing the white robes and shiwal of a Bedouin, sat on the dirt floor of a goat herder's hut situated in a narrow gorge in the highlands south and west of Marib town. The sun was low over the mountains and the hut was in shadow, though a shaft of sunlight came through the doorway.

Sitting around the walls of the stone hut were ten men—his inner council of advisors, and also his most senior aide, Altair, an older man, from the province of Ta'iz where the al-Darwish family originated. In fact, Altair was a distant kinsman, and the old man had known the father of Bulus's father, and had also known Bulus's own father as a young man, before he emigrated to America.

Nearby was the camp of The Panther's jihadists, but he could not go there for this meeting because of the American Predator drones. The drones may have seen the camp—though from the air it appeared to be a Bedouin village of tents and also stone and mud huts. And in fact it once was a Bedouin village, but not any longer, thanks to Sheik Musa, who had given—for a price—this village to the jihadists of Al Qaeda. The Panther did not know if the Americans had become suspicious of the camp, but in any case he had called for a gathering here, in the narrow gorge, which was also not far from The Panther's maghara, his cave, where he lived alone—except for a woman—and which was known to only a few of his most trusted aides, including Altair.

The Panther addressed his council of advisors, saying, "God is testing us."

The men nodded.

The Panther had just recently received the news that the ambush on the American convoy had failed—because of the Predator drones firing Hellfire missiles—and many jihadists had been killed and wounded.

He said to his council, "The Americans are operating freely on the sacred soil of Yemen. And they are doing this with the blessing of the government in Sana'a—the corrupt lackeys of the Americans who sell their souls for the American dollar."

Some of the men made sounds of agreement. But not all.

The Panther continued, "We will avenge these deaths."

Again, there were only a few signs of agreement among his ten advisors.

Bulus ibn al-Darwish knew that some of these men had been against the attack on the Hunt Oil installation. And for that reason, he had not consulted with them about mounting an ambush on the American Embassy convoy. This was the first they were hearing of it, and they were not pleased.

He had suffered two defeats at the hands of the

Americans within days, and he needed someone to blame for these defeats. He also needed a victory.

He reminded his advisors, "Forty of our jihadists are as of this moment on their way to Aden. They will attack the Sheraton Hotel and kill all the Americans there—the spies and the soldiers who are using the hotel as a base on the holy soil of Yemen—and also the Americans from the embassy who have arrived from Sana'a. All of them will die within the next few days."

A few in his council of advisors nodded, but The Panther was aware that some of them were beginning to doubt him—to doubt that he was blessed by God.

He continued, "And forty jihadists have journeyed to Sana'a and will mount an attack on the American Embassy compound."

A senior advisor, Jawad, reminded his chief, "This council must approve of the embassy attack and it must also be approved by the Supreme Council."

The Panther did not reply.

Jawad also reminded his chief, "If the embassy attack is successful, and if our jihadists enter the embassy compound and kill all the Americans— perhaps a hundred who live and work there—this act will have consequences which go beyond these borders." Jawad also told his chief and the others, "I fear an invasion of American soldiers in our country if these attacks on the embassy and on the hotel in Aden are successful—or even if they are not." He also reminded his chief, "You recall what happened after the successful attack on the American warship."

The Panther replied, "Yes, Jawad, I recall." He told Jawad and everyone, "Men and money flowed to us in abundance."

"And so did the Americans flow into Yemen in abundance."

The Panther again did not respond.

Another man on the council said, "We are not ready yet to attack. We must build our forces. We need another year, perhaps."

The Panther replied, "The more we attack, the more men and money will come to us."

Altair, sitting at the right hand of The Panther, looked at the advisors in the dim light and he could see their doubt. His young friend, Bulus, he thought, was still glowing in the victory of his bold and successful attack on the American warship, the *Cole*. But that was over three years ago, and since then Bulus ibn al-Darwish had only small victories against the Sana'a government and no victories against the Americans. The council was willing to wait, but The Panther was not.

Altair knew also that the killing of the nine Belgians and the two Yemenis at the Bilqis ruins had not been celebrated by all jihadists, or by all sympathizers to the cause. True, the Supreme Council of Al Qaeda had approved the attack, but the population of Marib province, including the Bedouin tribes, were not happy that the foreigners had been killed, and many saw it as an act of cowardice, and many in the province had suffered financial loss because the tourists had ceased to come to the ruins.

Altair knew also that if the attacks on the Sheraton Hotel in Aden and on the American Embassy in Sana'a did not result in victory, then his young friend's leadership would be in jeopardy. Also, perhaps, his life.

The Panther was still addressing his council of advisors, and Altair thought he was saying too much. What

more was there to say? What had already happened—
the two defeats—spoke for themselves. If his jihadists
were successful with their attacks in Aden and Sana'a,
that, too, would speak for itself.

In any case, Altair did not believe in The Panther's strategy of attacking the Americans. The jihadists should be attacking the government forces. If
al-Darwish wished to someday live in the presidential
palace, as he said, then he needed to defeat the hated
government—not the Americans, who were here in
small numbers.

He knew also that if the government was not
defeated, the corrupt men in Sana'a would give in to
American pressure to let the Americans build a military
base in Aden, as the British and then the Russians had
done. And if that happened, then the Yemeni people
would have the Americans with them for a very long
time. But al-Darwish could not see that far into the
future. He was blinded by the sight of a small number
of Americans, and did not see the ones waiting for an
excuse to do what they had done in Iraq and Afghanistan. That would be a disaster for Yemen.

Altair leaned toward al-Darwish and whispered,
"We have much to do."

The Panther paused in his address to his council,
then said to them, "We will meet again in perhaps one
week—after our victories in Aden and Sana'a."

The Panther stood and his advisors stood also. The
advisors left the hut silently, and only a few took their
leave with proper expressions of respect.

The Panther and Altair stood alone, and Altair said,
"Perhaps you should reconsider these attacks."

The Panther replied with a question. "How can you

live as a Muslim and as a Yemeni while the Americans are on the sacred soil of Yemen?"

Altair replied, "They are here because the government invited them. And they are here because you attack them here." He advised, "Destroy the government and the Americans will leave."

"They will not leave unless we kill them here."

Altair had already had this discussion with al-Darwish, and he had concluded that his young friend was more interested in killing his former countrymen than in a wise strategy to free their country from the corrupt men in Sana'a.

Altair did not want to argue with this man—and if the attacks in Aden and Sana'a failed, he would not need to argue with him. But he advised, "Hate blinds us to the truth."

The Panther had no reply.

The Panther's junior aide Nabeel al-Samad was standing a respectable distance from the open door, and Altair motioned him to enter. Nabeel entered quickly and made proper greetings, kissing the hands of both men.

The Panther remained standing and said to Nabeel, "Tell me and tell Altair what happened with this ambush, and also about your mission in Sana'a to kill the American agents."

"Yes, sir."

Nabeel did not wish to make this report, but if he was truthful and direct, it would go better. As he began to describe the ambush, The Panther interrupted and said, "Tell us first about your failed mission in Sana'a."

Nabeel licked his dry lips, then said, "Yes, sir . . ." He related his journey by vehicle to Sana'a after The

Panther had given him the mission to kill the two Americans who had landed at the airport.

Altair interrupted, "I did not know that. Who are these Americans?"

It was The Panther who explained to Altair about John Corey and his wife, and that these two American agents were on the assassination list of the Supreme Council of Al Qaeda. The Panther explained also that the Americans were marked for death because the man Corey had killed Asad Khalil, The Lion.

Altair nodded and said to Nabeel, "Continue."

Nabeel was surprised that The Panther had not consulted his most senior and trusted aide on this matter, but he knew why that was so; Altair did not want to provoke the Americans, thinking correctly, perhaps, that the Americans were seeking an excuse to send more forces into Yemen—as happened after the *Cole* attack. The Panther, however, wanted to kill more Americans.

Nabeel continued, "Friends at the airport informed me that Corey and his wife had left that location in a convoy of three armored vehicles which took them to the American Embassy, where they spent the remainder of the evening."

Nabeel continued his report, saying that embassy watchers as well as friends in the Sheraton Hotel confirmed that the two Americans had been transported to the hotel in the late morning by a single armored vehicle, and that they had registered there and gone to their rooms.

Nabeel also said, "I arranged for our watchers in Sana'a to keep them under observation, and I also called together four jihadists with myself to assassinate the Americans at the first opportunity."

The Panther commented, "That opportunity apparently did not present itself."

Nabeel took a long breath and replied, "It is difficult in Sana'a—"

"Continue."

"Yes, sir." Nabeel related what he had heard from the watchers. "The two Americans were later met at the Sheraton Hotel by two American security men from the embassy, with an armored Land Cruiser, and they drove into the city."

Nabeel then told The Panther and Altair of the movements of these four Americans in Sana'a—the khat souk, the Old City, lunch at Old Sana'a, the shop called Hope in Their Hands, the jambiyah shop, then the drive to Ghumdan Fortress.

The Panther already knew from his sources in the Ghumdan prison that Corey and the security man called Brenner had come to the prison and had spoken to Rahim ibn Hayyam, his jihadist, who had been taken prisoner at the Hunt Oil installation. This was troubling, because if Rahim ibn Hayyam had given information to the Americans, or to the Political Security Organization, then perhaps Rahim ibn Hayyam had revealed that The Panther was in Marib province on the night of the attack. If that were the case, then he, The Panther, could expect more Predator drones and perhaps more government activity, or even the presence of Americans who might come here to find him.

Altair also understood this and said to al-Darwish, "Perhaps you should leave Marib province before the government forces—or the Americans with their drones—come here to find you."

The Panther did not think Altair should have said

that with Nabeel present. In any case, he replied, "It is acceptable for men in our situation to hide, but it is not acceptable to run." He vowed, "I will remain here."

Altair responded, "As you wish." He thought Bulus ibn al-Darwish would be wise to remove himself from this province, but al-Darwish was not wise; he had acquired in his youth the arrogance of the Americans whom he so hated.

Altair also understood that if the prisoner, Rahim ibn Hayyam, had revealed the location of The Panther, he may also have revealed the plans to attack the Sheraton Hotel in Aden—if he knew of these plans. And Hayyam *might* know from talk in the camp. And Bulus knew this, and yet he had said nothing to the council, and he had not halted the plan to attack the hotel. Truly this attack could end in disaster if the Americans were alerted.

Altair took al-Darwish aside and asked him about this.

The Panther replied, "Even if Hayyam is speaking under torture, he would not know of this plan to attack the Americans in Aden."

Altair disagreed. "Soldiers in camp talk, my friend."

The Panther told Altair, "We have many watchers at the Aden hotel, and they report no increase in the security there. No army troops have been dispatched to the hotel."

Altair thought about this, then said, "The Americans may have chosen not to ask for additional soldiers." He explained to al-Darwish, "They may be waiting for the attack, and they may welcome it. Just as they did at the Hunt Oil installation—and as they may have also done with the ambush."

The Panther did not reply.

Altair said to him, "Do you not see? This is how they conduct war. You think you are surprising them, but they are surprising *you*, Bulus."

The Panther replied, "That is not true. You will see."

Altair looked at Bulus ibn al-Darwish. Clearly this man did not have the wisdom or patience of his forefathers. In Yemen, war is a slow thing, a never-ending struggle against the invaders and also against whoever sits in the palace in Sana'a. But al-Darwish, al-Amriki, did not understand how war was done in Yemen. And Altair was not going to tell him again how it was done. He would discover that for himself—and become either a great leader, or a dead man.

Also, Altair knew, this man was dangerous. He killed those who disagreed with him and those who proved him wrong. Altair did not fear The Panther, but perhaps he should.

Altair returned to Nabeel and asked him questions about what he had related, and Nabeel stressed that his watchers had been thorough, and that they kept in contact by cell phone with friends who watched outside the embassy, and friends in the Sheraton Hotel. Even the proprietor at the Old Sana'a restaurant had called an assigned telephone number to report the presence of the Americans.

The Panther nodded in approval. He had gone to great lengths to build a telephone network of friends in each town and city in Yemen. These friends, who asked only a few rials for their trouble, numbered in the hundreds, and most of them, he thought, did not know or care whom they were reporting to when they called the telephone number assigned to them. Some of them would be surprised to learn it was Al Qaeda who wanted this information about the movements of the Americans and British, and also other Westerners—but most understood who was paying them. There were so few Westerners in this small country that they could be tracked by only a few hundred friends. The Panther believed that his network of informants was even larger than that of the PSO, who in any case were more interested in Yemeni political opponents than in Westerners.

Also, The Panther knew, the number of Westerners who came to Yemen for tourism, business, and aid work was smaller each year as the security situation became worse for them. And this was the purpose of his attack on the Belgians. Soon, he thought, the number of Westerners in Yemen would be reduced to the embassy staffs—and also the American spies and military men in Aden.

Nabeel was now speaking of the embassy party on the Sunday night. Two of the Yemenis working in the embassy kitchen were friends. Nabeel continued, "Four Americans then left the embassy with a security man who drove the armored vehicle to the Mövenpick Hotel, where the Americans had dinner." Nabeel informed his chief and Altair, "Two of our watchers entered the hotel and confirmed to me that two of the Americans were Corey and his wife, and one was the security man, Brenner, and one was a diplomat called Harris."

The Panther nodded again. This would have been a good place for Nabeel and the jihadists to visit and kill all four Americans at dinner as they drank alcohol. The Mövenpick employed National Security police and private guards on the premises, but these were of no consequence. What *was* of consequence was the money paid by the Mövenpick and other Western hotels to Al Qaeda in return for peace. But if The Panther had known of the four Americans in the hotel—if Nabeel had telephoned him—he would have ordered the assassination in this case.

Nabeel continued, "The Americans then drove in their vehicle to the Russia Club." He reminded his chief, "The security in this compound is very strong, and we have no friends in this place."

The Panther responded, "Soon, when our jihadists enter Sana'a, there will be no one alive in that filthy place."

"Yes, sir." Nabeel completed his report, which on balance, he thought, showed that he had done a very fine job of knowing where the Americans were throughout the day and evening.

The Panther, however, said, "So, it was good that you knew every movement of the Americans. But I believe you were supposed to kill them."

Nabeel explained, "As you know, sir, these are trained men and they take precautions." Nabeel reminded The Panther of the armored vehicles, the weapons, the bulletproof vests, and the possibility that other American security men were watching their compatriots. Nabeel also said, "And, of course, sir, the PSO also watches the Americans."

The Panther stared at Nabeel for a long moment, then asked him, "Were you frightened, Nabeel?"

Nabeel replied quickly, "No, sir. We were waiting for the moment when we could be certain the Americans could not escape our bullets—when they could be shot in the head, to ensure—"

"But that moment never arrived."

"Not on that day, sir. But for the next day, we set forth a plan to—"

"Or were you waiting for the opportunity to kill only the security men, then kidnap Corey and his wife and claim your reward?"

Nabeel hesitated, then replied, "No, sir. A kidnapping was not possible in Sana'a with the police, the PSO—"

"Enough!" The Panther said to Nabeel sharply, "So on the following day, your two fortunate Americans again escaped death. Correct?"

Nabeel took another breath and replied, "They were taken from the Sheraton Hotel in an armored vehicle in the early morning and delivered to the American Embassy. Sometime later, the embassy watchers observed a convoy of five vehicles leaving the embassy." Nabeel reminded his chief, "The armored vehicles have black glass, so neither the watchers nor a soldier who is a friend could say for certain if Corey or his wife were in any of the vehicles, but—"

"But you made the assumption that they were."

"Yes, sir." He explained, "Corey and his wife had arrived at the embassy at an early hour, then perhaps half an hour later the convoy passed through the gates, so—"

"I understand, Nabeel. So it was at this time that you decided to ambush the convoy."

Nabeel had made no such decision. He had, in fact, called The Panther, who agreed that Corey and his wife were most probably in the convoy, and that an ambush should be set for the convoy. But this was not what The Panther wished him to say with Altair present.

Altair asked Nabeel, "Are you saying that you took it upon yourself to authorize an attack on the American Embassy convoy?"

Nabeel lowered his head and replied to Altair, "I did attempt, sir, three times to call al-Numair on the cell phone and satellite phone."

The Panther said to Nabeel, "You should have attempted calls to others around me."

"Yes, sir." Nabeel knew that if the ambush had been successful, then this conversation would not be taking place in this way. He remembered something from the Hebrew Book of Leviticus: *Let him go for a scapegoat into the wilderness.*

The Panther said to Nabeel, "Now tell us what you know of this ambush."

"Yes, sir." Nabeel could take no blame for the failure of the ambush—that blame went to Faris, the local Al Qaeda leader who had organized the ambush—but by taking the blame for ordering it, Nabeel knew he had perhaps condemned himself to death.

"Nabeel? Speak."

"Yes, sir." He stood straight and addressed The Panther and Altair. "When I received word of the American convoy leaving the embassy, I immediately contacted our provincial leaders along the expected route."

It was actually The Panther who had told him to do this, and it seemed a good strategy. Nabeel continued, "The route, as usual, was south, toward Aden, which is where the Americans go by convoy."

The Panther said, "That was a good thought, Nabeel. I would have approved—if you had contacted me."

"Yes, sir." He continued, "Many friends along

the route reported on the location of the convoy, and within hours, Faris had assembled fighters for an ambush in the hills south of Ibb."

"Excellent," said The Panther. "So is the convoy destroyed? Are all the Americans dead?"

Nabeel had been witness to his chief's unusual manner of speaking to men who displeased him. He wondered if Bulus ibn al-Darwish had learned that way of speaking in America.

"Nabeel? Am I not speaking loudly enough for you?"

Nabeel drew a deep breath and replied, "I apologize, sir, for my slowness in responding—"

Altair interrupted, "Continue, Nabeel. What happened with this ambush?"

Nabeel continued, "Faris has told me that the ambush was well planned, with twenty jihadists, a car bomb, a roadside bomb, and a bomb in a donkey cart, whose driver was prepared to become a martyr, but—"

"Enough." The Panther had already been told that the American Predator drones had seen the ambush and launched Hellfire missiles at the jihadists, so he said to Nabeel, "I have heard enough from you."

"Yes, sir."

He said to Nabeel, "I wish to see Faris. He is to travel to Marib town and await further instructions."

"Yes, sir."

"Or perhaps I should have someone else call him. Perhaps you will not be able to contact him with your troublesome cell phone."

Nabeel did not reply.

The Panther commented, "You seem frightened, Nabeel. What is frightening you?"

Nabeel again lowered his head and replied, "My

own inadequacy frightens me, sir." He looked directly at The Panther and said, "I have failed you, and I have failed our great cause."

"I agree with you, Nabeel. I agree that you failed to kill the two Americans as I ordered, and I agree that you ordered an ambush that ended in disaster. And what do you think your punishment should be?"

"Whatever you wish, sir."

"Even death?"

"If it pleases you, sir."

The Panther drew his jambiyah from its sheath and held the razor-sharp blade against Nabeel's throat.

Nabeel felt his body and legs begin to tremble, and felt himself losing control of his bladder.

Altair said, "That is not necessary, Bulus."

Perhaps, hoped Nabeel, the old man suspected that The Panther was lying and that it was The Panther who had ordered the ambush. Altair knew Bulus ibn al-Darwish well—perhaps too well. Nabeel prayed that Altair would save his life.

The Panther pressed the blade harder against Nabeel's jugular vein, but did not draw the dagger across his throat. "Look at me. Look into my eyes."

Nabeel looked into the eyes of The Panther and saw hate, but not of him, he thought. The hate was always there when the talk was of the Americans.

The Panther said to Nabeel, "So the Americans are now at the Sheraton in Aden, Nabeel. They are perhaps swimming in the pool. Or on the beach. Or perhaps they are having alcoholic drinks in the bar room. And how many jihadists lie dead in the hills and on the road because of your stupid decision to attack this convoy? How many, Nabeel?"

Nabeel swallowed and felt the blade press deeper into his flesh. "Ten, sir . . ."

"I think more."

Altair said, "Bulus, we have been here too long." He reminded him, "If the drones and the missiles trouble you, then we need to leave before they visit us."

"Yes, but first I need to cut a throat."

"Yes, but not this man's throat. Another throat awaits you."

The Panther did not reply to Altair, but he said to Nabeel, "Perhaps your throat can wait for another time."

Nabeel felt a flood of relief passing through him and he closed his eyes, which filled with tears, and he nodded.

Still holding his curved dagger to Nabeel's throat, The Panther said to his aide, "You are to travel to Sana'a with all speed, and board an aircraft to Aden. You are to take a room in the Sheraton Hotel and complete the task I have given you."

Though he knew this was a suicide mission, Nabeel managed to say, "I will, sir."

"And if you do not, or if you should leave Yemen out of fear, I assure you I will find you. And if I do not find you, I will find your family." He asked, "Do you understand?"

"Yes, sir. I will kill—"

The Panther drew his blade across the left side of Nabeel's neck and cut into his flesh.

Nabeel let out a sharp sound of surprise and pain, staggered backwards, and grasped his neck with his right hand. Blood ran between his fingers as he probed the wound and satisfied himself that it was not fatal.

The Panther slipped his bloody jambiyah back into its sheath and said to Nabeel, "Come outside. I want you to see that I do know how to cut a throat."

The Panther and Altair left the hut, and Nabeel hesitated, then, pressing his hand against his wound, he followed.

Outside, sitting on the rocks of the narrow gorge, were the survivors of the failed Hunt Oil attack. Kneeling on the ground facing the men was their commander, Captain Behaddin Zuhair. His wrists were bound behind his back and his head was bowed so he did not have to look at his men, who had passed the time in conversation while waiting for The Panther.

The men grew silent as their chief and the old man, Altair, stepped out of the hut.

The Panther walked directly to Captain Zuhair, but he did not address him. Instead, he addressed his jihadists and his council of advisors and his aides, and called out, "This man, Behaddin Zuhair, showed cowardice and stupidity as he led his brave jihadists against the American oil facility. He ignored the advice of our council and of his own lieutenant, Sayid al-Rashid, who died a hero's death while his captain cowered behind a rock." The Panther continued, "When Zuhair should have pressed the attack to total victory, he hid, then fled like a woman as the Americans and their mercenaries fired their weapons."

The jihadists and the council of advisors sat silently.

The Panther continued, "I share in the blame for this defeat, because it was I who failed to see that Zuhair was not a true leader of men."

The Panther's council of advisors remained silent, but one of his personal aides called out, "No! No! It is Zuhair who is to blame!" Another aide shouted, "Zuhair spoke bravely, but hid his cowardice!"

The Panther motioned for silence. He noticed, as did Altair, that no man in the council of advisors had spoken for their leader as they were expected to do when the leader publicly confessed to a lapse of judgment or a wrong decision.

But he also noticed that the jihadists who were with Zuhair in the attack did not say anything in defense of Zuhair. They sat quietly, avoiding the eyes of their captain, and of The Panther.

The Panther knew he had to end this quickly, so he moved closer to Zuhair's side and shouted at him, "Confess your cowardice and your incompetence and I promise you a quick and merciful death."

Zuhair turned his head toward The Panther and spoke in a loud, clear voice, "I have nothing to confess. I have done my duty on the field of battle—"

"Quiet! I have asked you for a confession. Not excuses."

"I make no excuses." Captain Zuhair faced his men and, still kneeling with his wrists bound, he exhorted them to come to his defense. "Tell what you know! Tell what you saw! Speak truthfully of my actions—"

"Quiet!"

Zuhair suddenly stood and shouted, "Have I not led you well? Have I not done my duty...?" He looked out at the men who had trusted him with their lives—his men who themselves had faltered under the intense fire from the American compound. Did they not remember that he had rallied them and shouted words of encouragement and comfort as they lay on the ground, paralyzed with fear?

But no one spoke for him.

He called to them, "I do not fear death in battle, but I do not deserve this death. I do not deserve to have my reputation and honor—"

A shot rang out, and Zuhair fell forward on his face.

Everyone looked at the old man, at Altair, who had fired the shot from a pistol.

They then looked at Captain Zuhair, who was still alive, and those who were closest saw that Zuhair had been shot in the left buttock, where blood was spreading across his white fouteh.

The Panther looked at Altair, who was now standing close to him, and Altair said softly, "You let him speak too long, Bulus. Now finish it your way."

The Panther nodded, then ordered two fighters to lift Zuhair into a kneeling position.

The Panther drew his jambiyah and came up behind Zuhair as the two men held him up. The Panther said to Zuhair, "You have chosen this death."

Zuhair summoned all his energy to shout, "You will burn in hell!"

The Panther had heard too much already from this man, so instead of cutting his jugular and his arteries, he sliced deep into Zuhair's throat where his larynx sat, and said, "Satan will be pleased not to hear you speak."

The two men held Zuhair in the kneeling position as the man began choking and spitting up blood.

The minutes passed as Zuhair continued to drown in his own blood.

The Panther took this opportunity to mock Zuhair, saying to him, "You were too cowardly even to confess your cowardice. A man of honor, a soldier, would have said he had lost his courage and begged for a quick death. But instead, you dishonored yourself further by lying. You—"

Another shot rang out and the front of Zuhair's head exploded with bone, brain, and blood.

Altair holstered his pistol and said to the jihadists, "Bury him quickly and deep so the animals do not find him."

To Bulus ibn al-Darwish he said quietly, "You may show no mercy, Bulus, but you may not show such disrespect." He reminded The Panther, "We are civilized."

PART VII

Aden,
Yemen

CHAPTER FORTY-FOUR

The Land Cruiser's outside temperature gauge read 102 degrees Fahrenheit, so I wasn't too shocked when I opened my door and got hit by a blast furnace.

Clare and I left our flak jackets in the SUV and I told Clare to go ahead inside.

I took the binoculars and looked up at the hills that rose above the hotel. Last time I was here, there was no Yemeni Army security up there, and I didn't see any now.

The perimeter security seemed to consist of the dozen Yemeni soldiers I saw along the entrance road, sitting on their asses in their white plastic chairs under sun umbrellas, chatting on their cell phones. Ice coolers completed the picture of intense vigilance. Did anyone tell these guys that Al Qaeda was heading this way?

Also, as I recalled, there was a white tent pitched on a ridge that ran down to the beach on the south side of the hotel, which the Yemenis said was an army observation post. But our commo people said it was a PSO listening post to intercept our radio and sat-phone communications—which was one reason we had the lead-lined tent on the fourth floor. The other reason was Al Qaeda, who also had some commo intercept capabilities.

I focused the binoculars on Elephant Rock on the north side of the hotel. There was still a Yemeni Army pickup truck on the rock, and on the flatbed of the truck was a .50 caliber machine gun manned by four Yemeni Army assholes who liked to keep the gun pointed at the hotel instead of at the surrounding hills. They probably thought this was funny; we did not.

The National Security Bureau, whose job it was to guard hotels, didn't exist when I was here last time, and I was happy not to see their blue cammies here this time, even though I'd developed a special relationship with Captain Dammaj.

As for our own security, we had the Marines and FBI SWAT Team, and I recalled that there were always four Marine snipers on the roof, and four or five Marines with M-16s on the beach. At night, that figure doubled.

I shifted my attention to the convoy. Everyone was out of the Land Cruisers—all thirteen of us—and one of the DSS agents was overseeing the transfer of luggage and equipment into the hotel lobby, while the others were keeping an eye on things out here.

A few Arab guests, who looked like rich Saudis, in full robes and headgear, exited the lobby doors and spoke to the doorman about the shot-up vehicles.

It's not often that you have armed military and paramilitary groups staying in a hotel where civilian guests are also staying. But this was Yemen, and the guests didn't seem to mind our presence as much as we minded theirs. In a way, though, we provided protection for each other—Al Qaeda probably wouldn't shoot up a hotel full of their co-religionists. Right? I recalled Buck saying not to worry unless the Arabs started checking out.

I also recalled that this Sheraton franchise was owned by a Saudi prince, but I wasn't sure if that was a good thing or a bad thing in regard to the hotel getting blown up by Al Qaeda. Probably depended on who the prince was paying off or pissing off.

Anyway, all the luggage was inside, so I slung my M4 and moved into the cool lobby.

A few DSS agents, including Mike and Zamo, were keeping an eye on the luggage cart, and Brenner was at the front desk checking us in without showing passports or giving names, which was none of the hotel's business. The Americans owned floors three and four, forever, and the Saudi prince had a great cash cow going here, compliments of the American taxpayers.

The lobby had just been remodeled when I was last here, and it wasn't bad—lots of mahogany woodwork and wicker furniture; sort of British tropical colonial, like hotels I'd been to in the Caribbean. And there the similarities ended.

I noticed the ubiquitous photo of Ali Abdullah Saleh, President for Life—until someone killed him— hanging on a wall. Big Ali is watching you.

I also noticed a few Western guests, probably clueless Europeans who got a good deal on a winter getaway. American tourists had the big advantage of never having heard of Yemen or Aden, and neither had their travel agents, and if they had, they didn't want to go anyplace where Americans were not welcome— which was just about everywhere these days. Europeans thought they were welcome all over, which was another kind of ignorance or arrogance.

Also in the lobby were two Yemeni soldiers with AK-47s, and two U.S. Marines with M-16s. What must those European tourists be thinking by now? Great beach, cheap rates—but what's with all these people carrying assault rifles? They must be shooting a movie.

I saw that a welcome committee of our colleagues had arrived, and Buck was speaking to three men and one woman in the sitting area of the lobby. Buck seemed to know them, and none of them looked like they could be our CIA guy, who I was sure would reveal himself in a more dramatic way—like maybe paragliding onto the beach. Or a more clandestine way, like if that potted palm over there started whispering to me. "Psst. Corey. Over here. The palm tree. Don't look at me. Just listen."

My wife, who'd gone off to freshen up, came up to me and said, "This isn't a bad place." She asked, "Did you have a good time here?"

That question was more loaded than a sailor on shore leave, and I replied, "Without you, darling, there are no good times."

She seemed to doubt my sincerity, then moved on to, "How did Dr. Nolan handle the problem back there?"

That wasn't the real question, but I replied, "Shook her up a bit."

"Were you able to calm her down?"

"I was too busy fighting her for her tranquilizers."

Kate suppressed a smile, then informed me, for the record, "I'm still annoyed at you for that police stop."

"Well, try to get over it." I reminded her, "Life is short."

She softened and said, "You're a brave man, John, but reckless and arrogant."

"Thank you. Hey, the bar here is not bad. Can I buy you a drink?"

"Paul says drinking alcohol is on hold until further notice."

"Yeah? Then how about a beer?"

Howard, who had also gone off to freshen up, came up to us and said, "Not a bad place. But is it safe?"

"No," I assured him. I suggested, "You may want to return to Sana'a."

"I think I've had enough car travel for one day."

"I'd hate to see you miss the return-trip ambush."

He actually laughed. Howard was now a combat vet who laughed at death.

He informed us, "I live on Long Island. I love the beach and I'm a competitive swimmer."

"Good. The sharks love competitive swimmers."

Clare, too, joined us and said to Kate, "Your husband is a very brave man."

Kate replied, "He's my hero." Actually, she said... well, nothing.

Clare continued, "I've never been so frightened in my life. But John—and Mike—were totally cool and calm, and John made sure I stayed below the windows."

"And," I added, "I covered her with my body." No, I didn't say that. I'm not *that* brave.

Kate had no comment.

Brenner was finished at the front desk, and he came up to us and handed out key cards in envelopes with our room numbers on them. Brenner had remembered to put me in the same room as my wife, so I think he was over Kate.

Brenner suggested, "Let's meet our Aden colleagues."

I asked him, "Where is our Company man?"

"I don't know."

Okay. But if I had to guess, I'd say our missing teammate was in the commo room speaking by radio to his station chief in Sana'a, asking if there was any intel about the Hellfires vaporizing The Panther. Wouldn't that be nice? Or did I really want to whack this guy myself? It's been a while since anyone from the New York Task Force personally whacked a bad guy, and I think I had the last kill. The Lion. Which was why I was here for an encore performance. Also, maybe Kate whacking a CIA guy was the other reason we were here.

In any case, I was on a roll with killing big cats, and I hoped to continue my winning streak.

CHAPTER FORTY-FIVE

We moved to where Buck was chatting with the welcome committee, and Buck did the honors and said to the four people, "You all know Paul Brenner. And this is FBI Special Agent Kate Mayfield, our new assistant legal attaché in Sana'a, just arrived from the ATTF in New York. And this is Kate's husband, also known as Detective John Corey of the FBI Evidence Response Team, also from the New York ATTF." Buck added, "John, as I told you, has been here before and he was homesick for Aden."

That got a laugh, but not from me.

Buck also introduced Dr. Clare Nolan, and FBI Agent Howard Fensterman, the new legat, adding, "Howard volunteered to come along for the ride."

Did I hear someone say, "Schmuck"?

We shook hands all around, and each person introduced himself and herself.

The lady was Betsy Collins, Supervisory Special Agent and Team Leader of the five-person FBI Evidence Response Team. She seemed pleasant and welcoming, and assuming my reputation had preceded me, she was probably thrilled to have learned from Buck that she didn't actually have to work with me.

Brenner's Aden counterpart in the Diplomatic Security Service was Doug Reynolds, whose title was Regional Security Officer, and who looked like ex-military.

I took the opportunity to tell him, "The DSS did a hell of a job getting us here."

He nodded and said, of course, "That's what they get paid for."

The second guy was Lyle Manning, Supervisory Special Agent of the ten-man FBI SWAT Team. He was a young guy, obviously in great physical shape, and like most FBI Special Agents, he wasn't sure if an ex-cop was his peer. He was okay with Kate and Howard, though, who were in the club. FBI, by the way, means Fabulously Boring Individual. Just kidding.

The third guy was easy to identify—he wore desert cammies, a Marine cap with globe-and-anchor insignia, captain bars on his collar, and a nametag that said "McAndrews," though he said, "Call me Mac."

We all pulled up wicker chairs, and we stacked our rifles neatly against the cocktail table. A hovering waiter put menus on the table and said, "Welcome, new sirs and new ladies, and already honored guests to the Sheraton Aden. I am Masud. Please to inform me of your wishes."

"Water for me and a scotch for my rifle."

Anyway, we all ordered soft drinks, and Masud floated off to the lobby lounge.

Captain McAndrews said to the Sana'a contingent, "So you had a little excitement on the road."

Brenner replied, "Five hours of boredom, two

minutes of pure terror." He added, "Predators did a great job." He further added, "Road security is going downhill fast."

Doug Reynolds, the DSS guy, said to Brenner, "I spoke to Ed Peters and he's okay with your men staying here overnight—not happy, but okay. Meanwhile, I've put in a request through channels for a Yemeni Army escort back to Sana'a."

Brenner replied, "Normally I wouldn't want that, but I'll take it if we can get it." He added, "If we get offered a National Security police escort—for hire or for free—the answer is no."

I interjected, "Especially if it's Captain Dammaj."

Buck and Brenner both laughed. See? *They* weren't pissed at me.

Doug asked, "Who's Captain Dammaj?"

Buck replied, "An NSB officer we met on the road. I sat-phoned that in." He further explained, "John told him to go fuck himself." Buck apologized to the three ladies for my language and added, "Unfortunately, we didn't know that Captain Dammaj spoke English."

Everyone got a good laugh at that.

Buck told our colleagues, in case they didn't know, "This country is close to dysfunctional."

Betsy Collins said, "Dysfunctional would be an improvement."

As I said, and as I saw the last time I was here, our relations with our Yemeni allies were not good. The Americans saw the Yemenis as corrupt, devious, and inept, and the Yemenis knew what we thought of them. I had no idea what they thought of us, but it was easy to guess.

And to make matters worse, we were stretched so

thin here that we were barely able to accomplish our mission, and barely able to protect ourselves from our enemies, not to mention our Yemeni allies.

The soft drinks came, and Doug proposed a toast. "Welcome to our guests, and here's to much success on your mission." He added, "Whatever it is."

That got a few conspiratorial chuckles. Plausible deniability is important with Black Ops jobs.

I didn't think we'd have much to do with these Aden people once we left here to find The Panther, and as with most Black Ops missions, we'd be mostly on our own. Also, though we might never see them again, they might see us if they were assigned to a body identification and recovery detail. But think happy thoughts.

Doug asked Clare, "How's your patient?"

Clare replied, "He'll be fine. But I'll have to see if he needs sutures, and he needs to keep it clean."

Captain Mac offered, "Infections are rampant here." He added, "This whole place is a petri dish."

Shithole.

Lyle Manning, the FBI SWAT Team Leader, changed the subject and said, "We're a little concerned about this reported threat of an Al Qaeda attack on this installation."

Actually, it wasn't an installation; it was a hotel with plate glass windows. I reported, "Paul and I heard this firsthand from an Al Qaeda prisoner at Ghumdan, and the prisoner seemed credible."

My buddy Paul agreed and added, "Al Qaeda has lost the element of surprise, so I'm sure we can deal with anything Al Qaeda tries here."

Captain Mac added, "If, as reported, it's only forty

or so enemy combatants, it won't be a problem. In fact, it's an opportunity."

Why was I not seeing these Al Qaeda attacks as opportunities? What is wrong with me?

I glanced at Clare, who looked like she wasn't hearing this correctly. *This hotel is an Al Qaeda target? Did I miss that memo?*

More importantly, Howard, as an attorney and an employee of the Department of Justice and an honest man, did not need to be hearing things he didn't need to hear. We hadn't gone there yet, but we would, so I suggested, "If it's all the same to Mr. Fensterman and Dr. Nolan, and the rest of us, I think Howard and Clare might want to recon the hotel and the beach." I said that nice. Right?

Howard and Clare got it, stood, and excused themselves.

Brenner inquired of one and all, "What are the Yemenis providing or promising in the way of extra security?"

Lyle Manning replied, "To be honest, we haven't requested anything."

Say again?

Lyle looked at Buck, who informed us, "It was I who suggested that we not ask the Yemeni government for a large show of force."

What were you thinking, Buck? I reminded him, "You said back at the embassy that you were going to notify the Yemeni government at the highest levels that we needed extra security here."

"Yes, I did say that." He explained, however, "If I asked the Yemenis for extra security, that would alert Al Qaeda that we knew this hotel is a target." Buck continued his reasoning. "If Al Qaeda thought we had information about an attack on the Sheraton, they would also think that we had information from the same source—the prisoner in Ghumdan—about the last known location of The Panther."

No one had anything to say about that, and I had the feeling that the Aden contingent agreed with the old Cold Warrior's crafty thinking—though they were sitting in the bull's-eye.

More interesting, Buck seemed to have the power of life-and-death decisions. Buck was a big man.

Captain Mac also reminded us, "The fewer Yemeni Army people we have around here, the better I like it." He smiled and confided to us, "The first targets we take out are the Yemeni Army's .50 caliber along with the Yemeni commo tent."

Don't forget the guys under the sun umbrellas.

On the subject of tipping off Al Qaeda, no one was suggesting that we evacuate the European or Arab guests. I guess the attitude was "Fuck them." There's a reason for cheap high-season rates. If you don't know the reason, that's your problem. Indeed, we had become a bit callous. Except when it came to American lives. Everyone else was expendable. Well, maybe our European and Arab allies needed a deeper appreciation of what the Americans were up against. They could stand on the sidelines if they wanted, but they could get killed there, too.

Lyle Manning let us know, "The entire SWAT Team will be pulling all-nighters until further notice."

Doug Reynolds added, "We also now have the DSS men from Sana'a."

Brenner reminded him, "Only for tonight, Doug."

He let us know, "There's a new and credible threat to the embassy, and they need to get back."

The safest place in Yemen might be swimming in the gulf with the sharks.

My other thought was that any attack on Americans would trigger the *Cole* response. Within two weeks of the *Cole* attack, there were close to two hundred American military, intelligence, and anti-terrorist people in this hotel and on ships out in the harbor. The Yemenis had made us scale down since then, but there were people in Washington who wanted to ratchet it up. All we needed was an excuse. And a few more dead Americans.

Kate, who hadn't said anything so far, now said, "I understand the decision not to increase security here. But I also don't want to risk any of our team being... becoming casualties here." She added, "We need to depart this location as soon as possible and go to where we think we will make contact with the suspect."

Buck replied to Kate, "We understand that." He let our colleagues know, "We hope to be out of here—and out of your hair—as soon as we get the intel we need."

This brought us to the subject of our missing team member, but I wasn't sure any of the Aden people had any info on that, so I didn't bring it up. That was up to Buck, and he wasn't saying anything about the CIA.

But I did want to know about the evacuation plan, though I think I already knew the answer to that. Nevertheless, I said to Doug Reynolds, "Ed Peters said you'd brief us on an evacuation plan."

Doug smiled, which was not what I wanted to see. He said, "Ed tells everyone coming here to ask me about that." He confided to us, "It's called the Alamo plan." He asked me, "Any questions?"

I guess not.

Betsy Collins did say, however, "If we have advance warning from our sources, and if we could get to the airport, we have air resources in the area that could evacuate us." She added, "Or, if we could get to the harbor, we can rendezvous with or commandeer a ship."

I pointed out, "I think we actually have advance warning of an impending attack." Remember?

Captain Mac ignored my sarcasm and cautioned, "The worst thing we could do would be to destroy all our equipment here, then evacuate and find out there was no imminent attack." He added, "That would make us look bad."

Looking bad is not as bad as looking dead, but to be a team player, I responded, "Sounds good."

Betsy Collins asked me, "What was the evacuation plan when you were here, John?"

"The backstroke."

Good laughs. I was being accepted by the inmates.

I did ask, however, "What about the civilian guests here? And the hotel staff?"

After a long silence, Captain Mac replied, "You should ask Al Qaeda that question."

Right.

Buck did have some good news and informed us, "We now have two Predators on station twenty-four-seven, reconning the area."

I asked, "With Hellfires?"

Buck nodded.

Good. I had recently become a big fan of Hellfire missiles.

We also spoke about the ongoing *Cole*

investigation—slow progress—then we discussed recent developments in Aden and the surrounding area. The big concern was that Al Qaeda was becoming politically stronger around Aden, though not yet a military threat—notwithstanding the forty jihadists on their way from Marib. The CIA and Defense Intelligence were closely monitoring the situation and keeping everyone here informed. Glad to hear that.

We seemed to have covered all topics and Buck said, "We'll let you all get back to your jobs, and we can meet again tonight in the cocktail lounge if you don't have other plans."

Betsy Collins said, "We do have a full social calendar here, but if we're not in a firefight with Al Qaeda, we'll be in the bar."

Funny.

We all stood, shook hands, and set the time for cocktails at 7 P.M. At least something important had been decided here.

CHAPTER FORTY-SIX

Buck, Brenner, Kate, and I walked back to our luggage, which was still under the watchful eyes of Mike and Zamo.

Brenner informed Mike, "You're all staying here tonight on full alert. Secure the vehicles, then get some sleep." To Zamo he said, "You can return to Sana'a with the convoy tomorrow. We'll ask for a SWAT sniper for the team."

Zamo, of course, replied, "I'm staying."

"Okay. But see Dr. Nolan ASAP."

Bellhops were not permitted on the American floors, so we gathered our bags and walked toward the elevators.

Buck said to us, "Everyone is free until seven. I'm going to the pool in an hour."

I'm going to get laid in ten minutes. Getting shot at makes me horny.

But Kate said to Buck, "We'll see you there."

Sitting at a desk near the elevators was a Marine with an M-16 rifle and a hand-held radio. He stood and we made the acquaintance of Lance Corporal Brad

Schiller, who asked to see our passports and creds. Schiller checked our names against his list, then handed each of us a red-and-white plastic ID card on a chain that said, "American Embassy—Sana'a Yemen." On the other side of the card was a bull's-eye. Just kidding.

Corporal Schiller said, "I'll call upstairs." He added, "Welcome to Paradise."

Everyone's a comedian.

We rode up to the third floor, which I recalled was reserved for the FBI Evidence Response Team, the FBI SWAT Team, the Diplomatic Security Service, the FBI doctor, and transient guests, mostly from the embassy, and rarely from Washington. There was also a common room on the floor where we used to sit, drink, play cards, and complain.

On the fourth floor were the twenty Marines, two to a room, plus our offices and our equipment and supply rooms. At the end of the fourth-floor corridor were rooms for our CIA colleagues and Defense Intelligence Agency officers, who mostly kept to themselves, which made everyone happy. Also on the fourth floor was the CIA's lead-lined SCIF in a cleared bedroom.

These two floors constituted the American outpost in Aden. The camel's nose under the tent. But if people like Colonel Kent had their way, we'd soon be building an Arabian Guantanamo down the coast. Call bin Laden Construction.

We stopped at the third floor, and Buck said, "I'm on four. See you at the pool."

Kate, Brenner, and I got off, and there was a Marine in the hallway standing behind his desk, on which was his M-16 rifle and radio.

We introduced ourselves to Lance Corporal Wayne

Peeples. He directed us to the right, and as we walked I checked my room number again to be sure Kate and Paul weren't sharing a room.

Actually, Brenner's room was next to ours, and we all said, "See you later," and entered our rooms.

We had a room overlooking the Gulf of Aden, as I'd had last time. Same room? Are those my socks on the floor?

Kate said, "This is nice."

"Nothing is too good for Christian Crusaders."

We threw our luggage and weapons on one of the two king-size beds, and I suggested we throw ourselves on the other.

Kate thought that was a swell idea.

Afterwards, we stood on the balcony and looked out at the turquoise water. This was the view I'd had for forty days of living in this hotel, and it brought back some memories.

The bay, called Gold Mohur Bay, was formed by two ridges of bare volcanic rock that ran down into the water.

Kate spotted the lonely white tent on the south ridge and asked, "What's that?"

"That's the tent that Captain Mac was referring to." I explained, "It's either a Yemeni Army observation post, or a PSO eavesdropping facility. In either case, the men inside the tent are not there to help us."

Kate nodded, then looked to the right at Elephant Rock, which indeed looked almost exactly like the head of an elephant, complete with a long trunk which formed a stone arch that ended on the rocks below.

At the risk of stating the obvious, I said, "That's Elephant Rock."

"I wonder why they call it that."

Kate noticed the pickup truck farther down the elephant's back with the .50 caliber machine gun pointed our way. "What's that?"

"That's our Yemeni Army security."

"Why is the gun pointed at the hotel?"

"They're sending us a subtle message."

She had no comment on that, and she looked down at the stone terrace below, where we used to have barbecues at night and pretend we were in Hawaii waiting for the hula dancers.

Beyond the terrace was the pool where about a dozen tourists were sitting or swimming, and beyond the pool was a white-sand beach where the volleyball net was still strung, but there was no game at the moment.

There was also no one sunning on the beach or swimming in the bay, but I did see four Marines in full gear at either end of the beach.

The hotel had planted small palm trees all over, but the climate here was so hot that even the palms had trouble staying alive.

Kate said, "Now I can picture where you were."

"Right." I hadn't taken many photos, and the ones I'd taken were designed to show the port city of Aden as the shithole it was—mostly dilapidated buildings, barefoot urchins, women in black baltos, and men with guns. I mean, I didn't want anyone thinking I was having a good time here.

Kate said to me, "My forty days in Dar es Salaam were no treat, but it wasn't Yemen."

"There is only one Yemen," I assured her.

I pointed toward Elephant Rock and said, "On the other side of that peninsula is Aden Harbor, where the *Cole* was anchored on October 12, 2000."

Kate nodded.

Seventeen American dead and thirty-nine wounded, some disabled for life. And that suicide boat should never have gotten anywhere near an American warship.

So, what have we learned from the *Cole* and from 9/11 and from all the terrorist attacks before and since? Two things that we'd forgotten over the years: Kill them before they kill you, and if they kill you, hunt them down and deliver lethal justice. That's why I was here.

CHAPTER FORTY-SEVEN

Kate wanted to go down to the pool, so, good husband that I am, I said I'd keep her company. Also, Clare was in the pool, but that had nothing to do with my decision.

Our rooms here are considered secure, so we were able to leave our rifles in the room, but we locked our papers in the safe, as per regulations. We did need to take our sat-phones, radios, and handguns, which we stuffed in the pockets of our bathrobes, and we took the elevator to the lobby and went out to the pool.

Buck and Brenner were also there, as was Howard, and they got out of the pool, along with Clare.

I should mention here that pool attire for gentlemen was long bathing trunks or shorts, and a T-shirt. For women it was long shorts and a long, loose T-shirt. And that's about as risqué as it got at any of the hotels or beaches in Yemen. So if I was looking forward to seeing Clare in a bikini—and why would I be?—I would be disappointed.

Clare, however, still looked good in a wet T-shirt. In fact . . .

"John."

"Yes, dear?"

"We're sitting over there."

"Right."

We all sat around a table under an umbrella and ordered a pitcher of iced tea. There was no sea breeze from the gulf, and it was *hot*.

A few Western tourists swam in the pool or lay on chaises, but there weren't any Mideastern guests at the pool, and there never would be. Not that I was dying to see Abdul or Afiya in shorts and T-shirts, but it might do them some good to get a little sun on their skin— vitamin D—and learn how to swim. Or am I being culturally insensitive again?

Anyway, we all chatted awhile and drank iced tea, which is as bad a drink as anyone ever invented.

Buck, holding court, said, "Local legend says that the graves of Cain and Abel are located here in the Ma'alla quarter of the city."

I had an old homicide sergeant who claimed he worked that case.

Buck further informed us, "The Yemenis also believe that this is where Noah's Ark sailed from."

Lucky for life on earth that suicide bombers didn't blow a hole in its side.

Buck concluded, "The Yemenis like to appropriate history from the Old and New Testaments and move it here." He added, "The American Mormons have also speculated that some of their history began here."

Yeah? Why *here*? Maybe because the great truth about Yemen was that it was the land of lies and half-truths. As I was discovering.

"I never thought I'd say this," Buck confided to us,

"but this place was better under the Yemeni Communists." He explained, "They were secular, and they kept the fundamentalist Muslims in line—with Russian help." He added, "Now that South Yemen is dominated by the north, it is slipping back into fundamentalism."

On a more important topic, Clare had put on her bathrobe. Which has nothing to do with anything. Why did I even mention that?

Buck informed us, "I was here in January 1986, when the thirty-day civil war devastated Aden. Thousands were killed, and I was almost one of them."

He got a faraway look in his eyes, then continued, "The war of 1994 was particularly devastating. This city was under siege for two months and the water pumping facilities were destroyed and people were dying of thirst."

Kate asked him, "Did you stay in the city?"

"I did, and I sent radio reports to the State Department..." He let us know, however, "I had several months' supply of Seera beer put away for such a situation." He informed us, "The Seera brewery was built by the British, and it supplied the whole country with beer. But when the North Yemenis took the city, they blew up the brewery." He added, "Bastards."

That got a chuckle. But it was also a hint of what went on here not too long ago. And also a hint of what Buck Harris had experienced here over the years. I had no doubt that this man was a dedicated professional. What troubled me, though, was his profession. I have a thing about intelligence officers, no matter what alphabet agency they work for. I mean, they do a necessary job, and I respect what they do, but if you're not one of them, you can wind up on their expendable list, as Buck himself had confessed in vino veritas.

On that subject, I was still waiting for our CIA guy to show himself, and my instincts said it would be soon.

We were all baking in the heat, so we unrobed and dove into the pool, which was warm as bathwater.

Everyone, I assumed, had a gun and extra magazines in their bathrobes, and the staff knew that and stayed away from our table. Also, as per my last visit here, there was a Marine sniper on the roof keeping an eye on the pool and beach. Every resort hotel should have a sniper on the roof. Helps you relax.

Anyway, after about a half hour of pool frolics, I suggested a beach volleyball game, admitting, "I got very good at this when I was here."

We carried our bathrobes down to the beach and hung them on the net pole, then chose up sides: Buck, Clare, and me against Brenner, Kate, and Howard.

We played best out of five, and I seemed to be the only one who knew how to play the game. My team swept the first three, with me as the high scorer, of course. Hey, I played this stupid game for forty days. That's why I suggested it.

Brenner, I noticed, was a competitive player, and not a very good loser. Neither am I, which is why I play games I can win.

Buck suggested a walk on the beach, so we asked one of the Marines to watch our backs and watch our robes and guns, and we all went down to the water. As I said, naked on the beach in Yemen means you don't have your gun.

Howard announced, "I want to take a swim. Who's coming in with me?"

How could I resist saying, "Do you know why sharks don't eat lawyers? Professional courtesy."

Okay, old joke, but it got a laugh because of the immediate proximity of the lawyer and the sharks.

Brenner, of course, took the challenge, and I did, too, but Kate said, "John, I don't want you—any of you—to go in."

Buck informed us, "It's very dangerous."

Well, that settled it. Howard, Brenner, and I ran into the surf and dove in. The gulf was calm, the salt water was buoyant, and the tide was running out, so it was an easy swim, even with the weight of our heavy shorts and T-shirts.

We got about a hundred yards out when I spotted two gray dorsal fins about twenty feet away. Holy shit.

Howard said hopefully, "Could be dolphins."

I suggested, "Tell them the lawyer joke and when they laugh we can see if they have sharp teeth."

Anyway, we headed for shore and made it back to the shallow water, where Buck, Kate, and Clare stood waist-deep in the surf watching us set a swim speed record.

Buck asked, "Sharks?"

I replied, "I didn't ask."

We all waded ashore, and Kate said to me sharply, "We didn't come all the way here and survive an ambush so you could get eaten by a shark."

"Yes, dear."

Brenner was probably rethinking his infatuation with Kate Mayfield. My rule is, if you're thinking of having an affair with a married woman, first see how she treats her husband.

Anyway, we all decided that the pool was safer, but before we began our walk up the beach, I saw Buck looking at a guy who was standing about thirty feet

away at the water's edge, smoking a cigarette and staring out at the sea.

I had the impression that Buck knew this guy and
knew he would be there.

Buck said to Clare and Howard, "You go ahead.
We'll join you later."

So we were about to meet our last teammate.

CHAPTER FORTY-EIGHT

The guy flicked his cigarette into the surf, then began walking toward us.

He looked to be in his mid-thirties, medium height and very lean, though I had the impression he'd once carried more weight. He was barefoot, wearing white cotton pants and a green flowered tropical shirt, which was unbuttoned.

His hair was long and straight, and it was bleached almost white by the same Saudi sun that had burned his skin almost black. His eyebrows, too, were sun-bleached, and as he got closer I saw that his eyes were a weird, almost unnatural blue.

At first glance, you'd say beach bum or surfer dude. But if you looked closer, you'd see a man who'd been here too long; a Westerner who had not gone native, but had gone somewhere else.

Buck met him halfway and they shook hands. I heard the guy say, "Good to see you again." His voice was flat as was his whole affect, but he did force a smile.

Brenner, Kate, and I joined Buck, who introduced us to Chet Morgan. He knew who we were, of course, and now we knew our CIA guy, though Buck hadn't mentioned Mr. Morgan's affiliation.

He shook hands with Kate first, saying, "Glad you could come," then with Brenner, saying, "Good job on the road."

Brenner responded, "Thanks for the Hellfires."

He didn't acknowledge that, and as I shook his hand, he said, "Thank you for coming here."

Weird. And for the record, his handshake was more of a jerk than a shake, and his skin was cold. Maybe he was dead.

Chet, as he wanted to be called, suggested a walk on the beach, so we walked toward Elephant Rock.

Chet hadn't said walk and talk, so we walked in silence, like we were old buds just enjoying the moment together.

I glanced at Buck, who seemed subdued, which is not like Buck.

Chet lit another cigarette.

I didn't give a shit if this guy never said another word, but Brenner broke the silence and asked Chet the standard question, "How long have you been here?"

Chet replied, "Since the *Cole*."

So that was about three and a half years. No wonder the guy was buggy. But Buck had been in Yemen on and off for a lot longer, and he was okay. Maybe if I stayed here another six months I'd think Chet was okay, too.

As a cop, I can spot someone who is indulging in a controlled substance, and I had the thought that Chet was on something, maybe khat. So maybe the A-team had a junkie on board. Terrific. Takes the pressure off me.

Brenner, a man of few words himself, was apparently uncomfortable with a man of no words, and he asked Chet, "Any chance our target was KIA in the ambush?"

Chet drew on his cigarette and replied, "I don't think so." He added, "Chatter puts him in Marib."

Well, I guess we were going to Marib to end the chatter.

Buck asked Chet, "Do you or your people think that this attack on our convoy in any way compromises our mission?"

Chet replied, "I'm not hearing anything. But it's a good question." He added, "I think we need to move fast before somebody in Washington starts asking the same question."

Right. As always, it came down to the age-old clash between the hawks and the doves—the ballsy and the ball-less—just like during the Cold War. The Pentagon, the State Department, the intelligence establishment, and the White House all had different agendas. The only people who had a clear agenda were the terrorists.

Kate asked, "Why would anyone in Washington not want to go ahead with apprehending The Panther?"

"There are legal issues," Chet replied, "and diplomatic issues."

Right. The Yemenis had this silly idea that their soil was sovereign. Plus there was Mommy and Daddy's lawsuit. Also, there was a chance we'd be kicked out of Yemen for using the Hellfires today. I asked Chet, "How fast do we need to move?"

"Maybe tonight." He added, "It may not be safe here."

When was it safe here?

We continued our walk along the beach, past a Marine patrol, and reached Elephant Rock, which jutted into the gulf.

There were about a dozen fishing boats moored or anchored in the shallows, and Chet waded into the water toward one of them, so I guess we were supposed to follow.

He pulled himself into an open twenty-foot wooden boat with an outboard engine, and Buck followed. Kate and I and Brenner glanced at one another, then climbed aboard.

Chet unfastened the mooring line, put a key in the ignition, set the throttle, and pulled on the starter cord. The engine caught, and off we went. But where were we going?

The only seat in the open boat was in the stern near the engine, and that's where Chet sat and steered. The rest of us sat on overturned white plastic buckets. The boat smelled fishy, and our bare feet were submerged in about four inches of nasty bilgewater.

Also, not to complain, but the sun was starting to burn my exposed skin, and I could see that Buck, Kate, and Brenner were getting a little lobsterish as well. A more immediate concern was that our guns and commo were back on the beach.

Chet Morgan, I concluded, was crazy. And we were following him. That didn't make us crazy; it made us stupid.

There were a few rocks sticking out of the water, and on one of the rocks stood a large black-and-white bird. As we got within fifty feet of the rock, Chet reached under his shirt into the small of his back, pulled a .40

caliber Glock, took aim, and popped off a round at the big bird. Kate, who hadn't seen Chet pull his gun, was startled; the rest of us were astonished, and Chet was annoyed because he missed. The bird flew away.

To make him feel better, I said, "To be sure of hitting the target, shoot first and call whatever you hit the target."

Chet ignored that and informed us, "That was a masked booby." He assured us, "Not endangered."

I remarked, "And never will be with shooting like that."

I thought Chet was going to shoot me, but he laughed—a real laugh, which almost made me think he wasn't nuts. He said, "I'd never shoot a white-eyed gull. They're endangered. And they bring good luck."

Whatever you say, Chet. Now put the gun away.

But he put it on the seat beside him. Well, at least one of us had a gun. Unfortunately, it was the crazy guy.

Chet glanced up at Elephant Rock, and I followed his gaze. The Yemeni Army guys in the pickup truck had swung their heavy machine gun toward us, and one of the soldiers was looking at us with binoculars.

Chet commented, "They get jumpy when they hear gunfire."

Me, too.

He said to us, "If we have time, I'll take you shark fishing. I have good luck nearly every time I go out." He smiled and said to me and Brenner, "The sharks almost got lucky when you went out." He laughed.

So, here we were on a small boat with an armed psychopath. How do I get myself in these situations? I need to check my contract.

I glanced at Brenner, who I knew was thinking

what I was thinking. Kate, too, seemed a bit unsure about Mr. Morgan, but she has a history of giving CIA nut jobs the benefit of the doubt. Up to a point. Then she shoots them. Well...only one so far.

Buck had a dopey smile on his face, and I knew he had a lot of tolerance for screwy behavior as long as the screwball was a colleague and a peer. I mean, I had the feeling, based partly on their preppy accents, that Buck and Chet had gone to the same schools or similar schools and came from the same social stratum. Chet was the bad-boy frat brother who was always on double-secret probation, and everyone loved him as long as he didn't actually get anyone killed. Later in life, however, what had been funny and zany behavior progressed into something less entertaining.

Also, with these CIA guys, they all cultivated eccentric behavior, which became part of their self-created legend. They wanted their peers to tell stories about them and to spread the word of their unique flamboyance.

Kate's aforementioned pal, Ted Nash, was a good example of all this. Plus Ted was an arrogant prick. But now he was dead, and you shouldn't speak ill of the dead. Even if they were assholes. Which brought me to another thought: Did Chet Morgan know Ted Nash? Probably. But this wasn't the time to ask.

Anyway, Chet Morgan had set the stage for his entry into the show, and as they say in the theater world, if you show a gun in the first act, you need to use it in the final act.

We rounded the peninsula and Chet set a course for the middle of Aden Harbor. I knew where we were going.

We sailed into the setting sun for about ten minutes, then Chet killed the engine but didn't drop anchor, and the boat drifted out with the tide.

Chet said, "This is where the *Cole* was moored."

I informed him, "I've been here."

He nodded.

In fact, nearly everyone who worked this case had been taken out to this spot where seventeen American sailors had been murdered.

Chet lit another cigarette and stared into the blue water. He said, "The USS *Cole*, a Navy destroyer, under the command of Commander Kirk Lippold, sailed into Aden Harbor for a routine refueling. The mooring was completed at nine-thirty A.M., and refueling started at ten-thirty."

Everyone knew this, but this is the way you begin— at the beginning.

Chet continued, "At around eleven-twenty, a small craft, like this one, with two men aboard—two suicide bombers—approached the port side of the destroyer. A minute or two later, the small craft exploded, putting a forty-by-forty-foot hole in the side of the armored hull." He added, "It's estimated that four to seven hundred pounds of TNT and RDX were used." He asked rhetorically, "Where the hell did they get that much high-grade explosive?"

The answer was, just about anywhere these days. The real question had to do with the two Al Qaeda guys who woke up that morning knowing they were going to die. They worked hard to load the boat with the explosives that were going to kill them, then sailed the boat into the sunny harbor. I sort of pictured them watching the gulls flying overhead, and I wondered what they said to each other or what they were thinking in the last few minutes of their lives.

"Asymmetric warfare," Chet said. "A small boat like this one, worth maybe a few hundred dollars, two guys who probably had no military training, and they crippled a billion-dollar, sixty-eight-hundred-ton state-of-the-art warship, built to take on any enemy warship in the world. Except the boat that attacked them." He flipped his cigarette over the side and said, "Fucking amazing. Fucking ridiculous."

Fucking right.

"And how were they able to do this?" asked Chet, and answered his own question. "Because the Navy's Rules of Engagement were rewritten by some committee of politically correct, ball-less wonders in the bowels of the Pentagon."

Right. Worse yet, the *Cole*'s crew and commander actually followed the new Rules of Engagement. I wouldn't have. But I'm not military.

Chet informed us, "For hundreds of years, naval rules called for challenging an approaching ship by voice or signal to identify itself. If the ship keeps coming, you sound the alarm for battle stations and fire a shot across its bow. And if it still keeps coming, you blow it the hell out of the water." He reminded us, "The *Cole* did none of that, even though this is known as a potentially hostile port. They let an unidentified ship come alongside, right here, and blow them up." He added, "Because internationally recognized rules of the sea had been changed, for no reason except political correctness."

The only good news is that the Navy has re-evaluated its new, sensitive Rules of Engagement after seventeen sailors died on the *Cole*, and we've all re-evaluated the rules of war after 9/11. As for poor Commander Lippold, he was officially exonerated of any fault—he was just following stupid rules—but unofficially his career was finished and he was passed over for promotion and retired. I'll bet he wished he had that ten minutes to live over again.

Chet continued, "To make this attack even more incomprehensible, Al Qaeda had tried the very same thing nine months earlier in January of 2000 as part of the millennium attack plots." He reminded us, "The USS *The Sullivans*, right here in Aden Harbor. A refueling stop, just like the *Cole*. A boat approached *The Sullivans*, but it was so overloaded with explosives that it sank before it reached the ship."

Right. In my former business, that's a clue that somebody wants to kill you, and you know they'll try again. Same with the February 1993 truck bombing at the World Trade Center. A cop on the street can see the pattern, but the geniuses in Washington were whistling in the dark through the graveyard with their heads up their asses. Well, we all woke up after we lost three thousand people on 9/11. But that wasn't going to bring back the dead.

Chet continued, "The enemy are not the brightest bulbs in the room, but they only have to get it right once. We have to get it right every time."

Chet lit another cigarette and looked toward Aden. "See that brown apartment building on the hill? Five Al Qaeda operatives were in there on the morning of the attack and they were supposed to get over to the Al-Tawahi clock tower and videotape the explosion."

I looked at the clock tower, a tall Victorian structure

built by the British over a hundred years ago. I'd been in the top of the tower, and from there you had a good view of the harbor. But the videotape guys never saw that view.

Chet continued, "Unfortunately, the idiots were asleep in the apartment and missed the whole show." He commented, "Total fuckups. But even fuckups get lucky once in a while."

I'd also been in that apartment, which had been sealed off as a crime scene when I was here and maybe it still was. Hard to believe that five jihadists had slept through the big moment. I mean, total assholes. They were probably sleeping off a big khat chew. But as Chet said, even fuckups get lucky, and the two guys in the boat got very lucky that day—if lucky is the right word for blowing yourself up—helped a bit by the Pentagon.

We were drifting with the outgoing tide and a small land breeze had come up and was pushing us farther out into the open gulf. Around us were a few dozen fishing boats, and like most men in Yemen, including fishermen, the guys on board were probably packing AK-47s. I mean, I wasn't concerned per se, but I don't like to get myself in exposed situations for no good reason. Chet, however, seemed unconcerned or unaware, so maybe he had some backup out here on the water. Or he was, as I suspected, crazy. Maybe arrogant, too.

Chet said to us, "The place on the hull where the jihadists detonated the explosives was the ship's galley where crew members were lining up for lunch, which is why there were seventeen dead and thirty-nine injured." He thought a moment and continued, "So it would seem that Al Qaeda knew the location of the galley and knew it was the first lunch shift."

I thought about that. A hundred or more crew members clustered in the galley for lunch. And right on the other side of the armored hull was a boat filled with maybe seven hundred pounds of explosives. The question was, Did Al Qaeda know—or did The Panther know—where and when to detonate those explosives? Or, like most of their successes, was it just dumb luck?

Chet concluded his briefing, "The crew fought the flooding and had the damage under control by nightfall. Divers on board inspected the hull and reported that the keel was not damaged, so the billion-dollar ship was salvageable." He continued, "Because we have no military base in this part of the world, the *Cole* was on its own for a while. But there was a Royal Navy frigate in the area, the HMS *Marlborough*, that proceeded at top speed and provided medical and other assistance. Eleven of the most injured sailors were flown by medevac to the French military hospital in Djibouti for surgery before being flown to the U.S. military hospital in Landstuhl, Germany. The rest of the injured—and the dead—were flown to Landstuhl." He added, "Fortunately, none of the thirty-nine injured died, but many are disabled for life."

No one had anything to say, but then Chet surprised us by suggesting, "Let's say a silent prayer for the dead and injured." He bowed his head, so we all did the same and said a silent prayer.

I'm not good at this, but I did pray that the two suicide bombers were burning in hell with their dicks blown off and not getting any wine or sex in Paradise. Amen.

"Amen," said Chet, then he started the engine and we headed back.

I looked at Chet Morgan, who was staring off into space with those glassy blue eyes. This guy was either very good at what he did, or very nuts. Maybe both. In any case, he needed close watching.

CHAPTER FORTY-NINE

Chet opened the throttle, and we were making good time around the peninsula and back toward Elephant Rock.

There were a lot of big dorsal fins gliding around close to the boat, and if Kate and I had been alone now with Chet and his Glock, I might have been a little concerned. But then I remembered that we were here to be Panther bait, not shark bait.

Chet said to his captive audience, "If you recall, we weren't certain that Al Qaeda was responsible for the Cole attack. This was pre-9/11 and Al Qaeda was only one of many terrorist groups that were causing us problems."

Right. And Al Qaeda never claimed responsibility for the attack. But on the Arab street, the word was out that Al Qaeda was behind the *Cole* attack, and Al Qaeda recruitment went way up, just as it did after 9/11.

Chet continued, "By August 2001, right before 9/11—about the time Mr. Corey was here—we identified Bulus ibn al-Darwish, al-Numair, The Panther, as one of the three main plotters. That's when a lot of this started to make sense." He asked rhetorically, "Who else could have thought of this, organized it, and executed it so perfectly? It had to be an American." He reminded us, "Most of these so-called jihadists are too stupid to even *think* of something like this, and too inept to pull it off."

I partly agreed, but I said to him, "Some of the top guys are very smart and very sophisticated."

"True," replied Chet, "but I see a Western-educated head behind this attack. Not someone like bin Laden who's really a country bumpkin and a clueless fundamentalist and two-bit philosopher who has his head in the clouds when it's not up his ass."

Interesting, and maybe true. At least the CIA thought so.

Chet continued, "No, it was someone who understood us. Someone who had knowledge about our idiotic Rules of Engagement, and someone who may have had some knowledge of the *Cole*'s layout and the time and date that the *Cole* would put into Aden Harbor, and the time of the refueling and the first lunch shift. Also someone who understood the psychological impact of an attack on an American warship that caused the death of so many American sailors." He added, "This bastard, Bulus ibn al-Darwish, has a big hate toward America and this attack was a manifestation of that hate—a humiliating kick in our balls."

No argument there, and I'd add that Chet Morgan had a big hate, too. I guess we all did, but Chet seemed to be taking it more personally than most of us. I mean, we're not supposed to get into the hate game, which can screw up your judgment and your performance. You need to be cool, and most people in this business are cool to the point of cold-blooded. Hot is not cool.

But Chet had been here a long time, and he was probably frustrated and under pressure to get results. Plus he had more info than we did about The Panther, including the asshole's psychological profile. As sometimes happens in a long investigation, the case officer starts to obsess on the fugitive and begins to see him as the cause of all his problems. It's kind of complex, but I've been there. The other thing that struck me was that Chet, who had initially come across as a bit burned out, was now very animated, like a switch had been turned on. Or maybe the khat had kicked in. Or the hate.

Chet continued, "This attack has not been fully avenged. But it will be. These bastards, including Mr. al-Darwish, have to learn that there is a price to pay."

"They know that," Kate assured him, "and they are ready to pay it."

"And we're ready to make them keep paying."

Chet was into revenge, which was good regarding terrorists, but maybe not so good regarding Ms. Mayfield whacking Chet's colleague. But that was another subject, and probably not on today's agenda.

I wasn't sure I had a good take on this guy, but I was certain that Buck knew about him, though Buck doesn't always share.

Chet had said he'd been here since the *Cole* was bombed, but I didn't remember him. On the other hand, the spooks were in and out, flying off to Sana'a, Djibouti, Oman, Qatar, Bahrain, and Saudi Arabia. And even when they were in the Sheraton in Aden, they were nearly invisible. Part of their mystique.

It must be a lonely job, and I often compared CIA officers to vampires who only hung out with other vampires and had no human friends. That's not nice. Maybe I have CIA envy.

Chet continued his history of the *Cole* incident and said, "The first FBI agents sent to Yemen in response to the *Cole* attack worked in a very hostile environment. They were met at Aden Airport by Yemeni soldiers pointing AK-47s at them when they got off the plane." He confided to us, "I was with the FBI that day, and I can tell you, we thought we were going to get into a firefight right there on the tarmac." He added, "Assholes."

So, another ugly American who didn't like the Yemenis. How are we going to win this war on terrorism if we don't win the hearts, minds, and confidence of our Islamic allies? Right? I mean, true, they were assholes. But they were *our* assholes.

Also, I was sure that Chet had been very frightened that day when he was threatened by Yemeni Army guys with lots of firepower. And when you let something or someone frighten you, you get very angry later. And you want to redeem your manhood—by killing someone. Same as on the mean streets of New York. Maybe that's what some of this was about.

Chet continued, "Speakers in the Yemeni Parliament were calling for jihad against America, like it was *us* who did something wrong, and this was broadcast live on radio and TV every day." He added, "Most of the Americans here—tourists, oil workers, and businesspeople—left the country quickly."

Buck informed us, "The embassy was in lockdown and we sent all nonessential staff to Oman or Riyadh."

Chet nodded, then went on, "The Yemeni government was sending us mixed signals. They said it was okay to bring our people in, but when we got here, we were threatened."

Buck explained, "There was a lot of confusion and panic within the government."

Ours or theirs?

Chet then related another scary story, one I'd heard when I was here. "The American response team was given the two floors of the Sheraton, but one night the hotel was surrounded by a few hundred men wearing traditional dress, though they had military jeeps and were armed with military weapons, so we knew they were Yemeni soldiers and maybe PSO men in disguise." He stayed silent a moment, undoubtedly recalling that night, then said, "We organized defensive positions on the roof and on the ground floor, and we wouldn't let any of the Arab guests leave the hotel." He added, "There were still a few Western tourists in the hotel, and they were afraid to leave, so we gave them handguns for self-defense." He let us know, "We all thought we were going to die that night... The officer in charge of the Marine unit issued a single order—'Take a few of them with you.'"

Right. No surrender. No American hostages. And when I was here in the Sheraton, that order still stood. *Take a few of them with you.*

No one spoke for a while and the boat continued on toward the Sheraton beach. I looked at Kate, who appeared to have acquired a new appreciation of the situation here, and maybe a new appreciation of her husband who'd spent a month in this dangerous place. It wasn't all beach volleyball, sweetheart.

To Buck and Brenner, Chet's stories were nothing new, but it probably reinforced their resolve to get the job done and get the hell out of here. There comes a

time in every hazardous tour of duty when you realize you've used up your quota of luck. Buck, Brenner,
and Chet were past that time, but the goal was finally
in sight; just a few hundred kilometers from here, in
Marib.

Chet continued, "By dawn, all these assholes surrounding the hotel had disappeared. But we were
ordered to get out of the hotel, and we were ferried by
boat to U.S. naval vessels in the harbor. Two days later,
the Yemeni government said it was safe to return to the
Sheraton, so we took Navy helicopters back to the beach.
But on the way in, the helicopters got radar lock-ons
from SA-7 ground-to-air missiles, the pilots had to drop
down to sea level, and we came in over the water ready
for a shoot-out." He looked out at the water and the
approaching beach as though this scene brought back
that memory, and continued, "But there weren't any
hostile forces on the beach—I think the Yemeni military
probably thought we'd turn around when the choppers
got the missile lock-ons, and when we kept coming they
beat it out of there. So we retook our two shitty floors in
the Sheraton and we've been there ever since."

Right. And Mr. Chet Morgan, a privileged child of
a superpower country, had had a lot of time since then
to reflect on the poor reception he'd received in Yemen.
He came here to help—well, not really, but officially—
and the Yemenis treated him like a piece of crap, and
threatened to kill him, and he wasn't leaving here until
he evened the score. Of course by now he was nuts, so
even M-16 therapy wasn't going to make him a happy
man—but it would help.

Chet wrapped up his background briefing. "The
weeks after the *Cole* was bombed had a surreal quality

to them…maybe more like slapstick comedy with the Yemeni government and military running off in different directions like the clowns they are, saying, 'Welcome Americans,' then 'Yankee go home.'" He concluded, "Totally dysfunctional country."

Dysfunctional, as Betsy Collins said, would be an improvement.

We were about a hundred meters from the beach now, and Chet backed off on the throttle as he steered around some sandbars toward the shallows near Elephant Rock.

There were a lot of gulls on the rocks, but Chet left them alone, and instead he flipped the bird at the Yemeni Army guys manning the machine gun. Chet needs some anger management classes.

As he maneuvered the boat, he said, "In the old days of gunboat diplomacy, if some pisspot country attacked Westerners, a naval fleet would assemble and bombard the port city until it burned to the ground. Now…well, the primitive little assholes of the world get away with too much. But there will be a day of reckoning." Chet thought a moment, then said, "In fact, every day since 9/11 has been a day of reckoning." He nodded to himself and added, "And for Mr. Bulus ibn al-Darwish, a traitor to his country and a mass murderer, his day is close at hand."

I hoped so. What I knew for sure was that there would, indeed, be a day of reckoning here in Yemen, but I wasn't sure who would be reckoned with.

CHAPTER FIFTY

The cocktail hour had arrived, and Kate and I joined our colleagues in the hotel bar. Chet Morgan did not make an appearance, but he had asked us to meet him in the SCIF at 10 P.M. to discuss the operational plan.

Chet had stayed with his boat after dropping us off in four feet of water, and we had returned to the hotel pool where Howard and Clare were watching our things and apparently getting to know each other better.

Howard and Clare knew not to ask us about our new friend on the beach, but Clare did say she was worried when we were gone so long. Clare really cares about me.

Kate and I had gone back to our room to shower and dress for dinner and/or a trip to Marib later that night, as per Chet. Once things start to roll, they roll fast, and you have to keep one step ahead of the terrorists and two steps ahead of Washington.

Kate and I discussed Mr. Chet Morgan of the Central Intelligence Agency, and I confided to her my suspicion that Chet was a chewer. She thought about that, but wasn't sure, so I dropped it.

I didn't share with Kate my other thoughts about Chet in regard to his nuttiness or what was driving him, but I did say, "He seems a bit intense. When he's not spacey."

Kate replied, "You have a built-in prejudice against the Agency."

Me?

Anyway, Kate was reserving judgment on Chet. Unfortunately, we needed to make a quick decision about going up to Marib with this loon to find The Panther.

I also broached the delicate subject of her complicated relationship with Ted Nash and said, "I think we should ask Chet if he knew Ted, and how he's feeling about your last encounter with the deceased." How's that for subtle?

Kate didn't reply for a few seconds, then said, "I'll take care of that."

Actually I would take care of that, but I said, "Okay."

Well, we were now down at the bar for drinks with our colleagues, including our DSS guys from Sana'a and most of the Aden team, except for the twenty Marines, who were on guard duty.

Unfortunately, because of the high alert, and our possible trip into Indian Territory tonight, alcohol was still off the menu. The bartender was whipping up fruit drinks in the blender, and I had a mango slushie. It sucked.

But the conversation was good, and we talked about home, family, and everything but the war on terrorism, and no one mentioned the forty Al Qaeda guys heading our way. I noticed, though, that everyone was wearing Kevlar vests and sidearms and had automatic rifles with them, which is not SOP in the bar. The bartender, waiters, and the civilian clientele noticed, too, and they were looking a bit concerned. I wondered which one of them had a suicide belt. Maybe the fat Saudi guy in robes sitting by himself drinking scotch. This was a lot more exciting than Ecco's.

At 8 P.M., Captain Mac, thinking maybe we'd pushed our luck a bit, and that we needed to get serious about security, asked all American personnel to leave the bar and return to their rooms or their posts.

A few of us, however, had a dinner meeting scheduled, and we went out to the back patio where the grill was blazing.

We sat at a round table—me, Kate, Buck, Brenner, Betsy Collins, Doug Reynolds, Lyle Manning, and Captain Mac.

It was still hot, but the sky was clear and the stars were out, and a half moon was rising in the east. Out on the water I could see the lights of big cargo ships and oil tankers. A few Western tourists were cavorting in the pool, and the really dumb ones were strolling on the beach, probably wearing T-shirts that said, "Kidnap Me." This place was a headline waiting to happen.

The barbecue was good, as I recalled from last time, though I passed on the goat kebobs. We all drank non-alcoholic beer and chatted about how wonderful it was to be living the dream and working for the government—foreign travel, great pay, appreciative bosses in Washington, and a chance to make a difference by killing some assholes who wanted to die anyway.

We got around to security concerns, and Doug Reynolds told us he'd sent a message to Washington requesting a standby ship in the harbor for possible evacuation, and an unmarked charter aircraft—meaning CIA—at Aden Airport. So far, he said, no response. It occurred to me that Washington might be looking for an excuse to land a thousand Marines on the beach.

Captain Mac, who preferred a fight instead of a flight, said, "I can't kill them if I'm not here."

Right. You stay here. Good balls, though.

Buck announced, "We may be leaving tonight."

No one, of course, asked where we were going, but everyone wished us good luck.

I said, "And good luck here." And don't pay for the rooms if you have to check out under fire.

Captain Mac assured me, "We don't need luck. We've got twenty Marines."

No one asked us how we were getting to wherever it was we were going, but Betsy Collins did say, "Travel at night is risky."

Buck informed her, "We're flying."

Really? How did he know that?

It was understood that this was probably a CIA operation, so no one had any further comments or advice. But I sensed that the Aden team might open up if asked a direct question, so I asked directly, "What do you think of Chet Morgan?"

Silence.

Okay, so that answered that question. I said, "For the record, I think he's been in the sun too long."

Buck interjected, "John, we don't need to—"

I continued, "We could be going up to Marib with him tonight—I guess by plane—and I'm concerned that Mr. Morgan may be suffering from in-country stress and fatigue."

No one argued with that, but they'd have to report my statement in the event some of us didn't return from Marib alive.

The dinner and the conversation seemed to be finished, and Buck said, "If you'll excuse us, we have a meeting in the SCIF."

Buck stood and we all stood and did handshakes, good-byes, and good luck.

Lyle Manning, who didn't seem to like me, surprised me by saying, "You've made a good evaluation of the situation."

This was one time I wouldn't have minded being wrong.

So we went into the hotel, and Kate, Brenner, Buck, and I rode the elevator up to the fourth floor. On the way up, Buck said to me, "You have permission to leave anytime, but you do not have permission to discuss this operation with anyone at any time."

"The subject, Buck, was Chet Morgan."

Buck assured me, "I've known Chet for three years. He's a good man."

"Right. I could tell by what everyone said about him."

Kate interjected, "John, let's discuss this after our meeting with him."

Brenner said, "I'm more interested in the plan than in Chet Morgan."

Well, you're wrong. The reason the best-laid plans of mice and men often go astray is not the plan; it's the mice and men. And Chet was about ten rials short of a Happy Meal. But to be a team player, I said, "Fair enough."

We got off the elevator, greeted the Marine guard,

and walked down the corridor to the Sensitive Compartmented Information Facility.

Bottom line here, The Panther was only one of my problems. My teammates were another. But hopefully the plan wasn't as crazy as Chet.

CHAPTER FIFTY-ONE

Buck had a key for the locked door and we entered.
A black tent filled most of the emptied guest room, and we ducked inside through a flap. The dim interior of the SCIF tent was about fifteen feet by twenty, crammed with electronic equipment, desks, and file cabinets, lit only by a few desk lamps and the glow from the computer screens.

Sitting at the shortwave radio was a young man in a T-shirt and shorts, wearing headphones. He noticed us and said, "Chet's on the balcony."

Good. I hope he jumped. But probably he was smoking; a slower form of suicide.

We left the tent and went around to the balcony, where, sure enough, Chet stood at the rail with a butt in his mouth, contemplating the moonlit sea. He was still wearing his white ducks and silly Hawaiian shirt, and he was still barefoot. Time for home leave, Chet.

Without turning around, he said to us, "Yemen was known to the Romans as Arabia Felix—Happy Arabia." He added, "No one has called it that since then."

Right. Now it's called Shithole.

Chet continued, "If Afghanistan is the graveyard of empires, then Yemen is the slaughterhouse of imperial ambitions."

God save me from a nutcase with an Ivy League education. Right?

Chet informed us, "Alexander the Great sent a colony of Greeks to Socotra, an island off the coast here, but it didn't last long, and the Romans invaded from the north and got as far as Marib before their army was decimated by battle, hardship, and disease."

Marib? Isn't that where we're going? Don't forget the Cipro.

Chet continued, "Yemen has seen a succession of conquerors and would-be conquerors—Egyptians, Persians, Romans, Ethiopians, Turks, the British, and the recently departed Russians. But no one has ever controlled all of Yemen. Not even the Yemenis." Chet concluded, "I wouldn't want to see us in a land war here, which is why these surgical operations need to succeed."

I suggested, "Nuke 'em."

Chet assured me, "I have no problem with that."

Maybe he really wasn't crazy after all. I mean, he agreed with me. And I'm not crazy. Right?

Anyway, Chet dropped his cigarette into a pail of water that had been put there for that purpose—and maybe as a khat spittoon—and he turned toward us.

The light was bad, so it was hard for me to tell if he had been chewing, or where he was in the rising and falling arc of a khat trip. But if I had to guess, I'd say he was on the upgrade of the roller coaster, about twenty feet from the top. Coming down is a bitch.

Chet said, "I'm sorry I couldn't join you tonight,

but I heard you had an interesting conversation at dinner." He looked at me.

Well, first off, you weren't invited, and second, I guess someone told him I'd commented on his mental health. But I didn't think that Betsy, Doug, Lyle, or Captain Mac would give Chet Morgan a call about that. And Buck didn't have the opportunity to speak to Chet. Probably Chet just assumed, from past experience, that someone called him a nut job, and he further assumed it was me. Good deduction, Chet. Or...he had a directional listening device and he heard us down on the patio. That's really not nice. But I guess that's why they're called spies.

Anyway, Chet led the way into the tent.

There was a small map table in the corner, and Chet invited us to sit.

As my eyes adjusted to the dim light, I saw taped to a wall the official photo of President Ali Abdullah Saleh, but this one was captioned *Asshole of Arabia.* Funny.

I also noticed a few steel-cut axes, burn boxes, and paper shredders, all necessary office equipment in a sensitive facility that was located in hostile territory. I pictured Chet high on khat, swinging an ax at the computers, and someone shouting to him, "I said there were *tourists* in the hallway—not terrorists." Whoops.

Anyway, the young man at the radio couldn't hear us with his headphones on, and Chet said, "There are no recording devices activated for this discussion." He added, "Operation Clean Sweep is top secret, of course, and you will never divulge or reveal what was said here, or what happens here."

Right. Just like a bachelor party in Vegas. What

annoys me is that the CIA thinks they have to re-pledge you to secrecy. Like no one but them gets the concept of keeping your mouth shut.

Bottom line, the CIA doesn't like joint operations, and they see them as babysitting jobs. On the plus side, if something went wrong, they had someone else to blame.

To get something straight, I asked Chet, "Who is running this operation?"

Chet replied, "Buck is the team leader."

"I mean, who in Washington is running this? Who do *you* report to?"

"You don't want to know."

Then why did I ask? But obviously this was a CIA operation, directed from the highest level. If it was FBI, they'd make everyone wear blue windbreakers with big white letters that said "FBI." They like to advertise. The CIA does not.

I asked Chet, "What is your job on this team?"

He reminded us, "I have operational control of the Predators."

"Right. So we're going to vaporize this guy?"

He also reminded us, "Predators are used primarily for aerial observation."

Then why are they called Predators? Why not Doves with good eyesight?

Chet added, "I'll get to the goal of this mission later."

You usually start with the goal, then outline the plan. But Black Ops jobs were a little different, mostly because the goal—like whacking someone—was not always legal and therefore not spelled out; it was understood.

Chet began, "First, our intelligence sources—human and electronic—put The Panther in the vicinity of Marib."

Brenner informed him, "This is what John and I heard from the prisoner in Ghumdan."

"Right."

I added, "And your colleagues in Sana'a also questioned the prisoner—or you did."

No reply.

I asked, "Do you have a transcript of that interrogation?"

"Not yet." He added, "Translation problems." He inquired, "May I move on?"

"Sure."

He continued, "Second, I have to tell you that we'll be leaving here about midnight and flying to Marib, and we may not be coming back."

Brenner asked, "Can you phrase that a bit differently?"

Chet actually smiled, then clarified, "If the mission is a success, we will not return here." He advised us, "Pack only what you absolutely need, and leave everything else in your rooms, to be forwarded on."

To *where?* Next of kin?

Brenner inquired, "And if the mission is not a success?"

"Then we may return here to continue the operation." He added, "Unless we're dead."

Got it.

I informed Chet, "Just to let you know, Kate and I need to hear and approve of the operational plan before we go anywhere. That was the deal."

Chet didn't seem to know there was a deal and said,

"I think you've passed the point of no return on that, Mr. Corey."

Buck interjected, "John and Kate have volunteered to be bait, so they can suggest some changes to the plan as it relates to their roles." He then said to Kate and me, "But I must tell you, this may be our only chance to apprehend The Panther before he disappears again."

Kate replied, "We understand that."

Chet continued, "We are flying out of Aden Airport on a DHC-6 Twin Otter." He explained, "This is a two-engine short takeoff and landing plane, with reinforced fixed landing gear, capable of putting down on a road, which we will do."

Say again?

He also informed us, "The Otter is registered in Kuwait as a regional charter craft, but it will be flown by two American pilots."

Thank God. The Otter, of course, was actually owned by a CIA front company, and the pilots were CIA employees, though both those facts would be difficult for anyone to prove. The Company has excellent air resources all over the world, known in the trade as Spook Air. If anyone was ever able to count all the aircraft owned by the CIA, Spook Air would probably be bigger than American Airlines.

"Flight time," said Chet, "will be under three hours."

On that subject, Spook Air could have gotten us safely from Sana'a to Aden in under three hours without an ambush. But some idiot had decided to see what Al Qaeda knew, and what they could do. And also to see what the Hellfire missiles could do to Al Qaeda. I don't remember volunteering for that, but if we'd blown up The Panther, I'd be patting Chet on the back now and getting ready to fly to New York instead of Marib.

Brenner asked, "Will there be a pathfinder on the ground?" Meaning a guy with a flashlight or at least a cigarette lighter.

Chet replied, "Yes, a trusted local."

Brenner informed him, "No such thing." He flashed back to some jungle clearing in Southeast Asia and said, "It has to be an American."

"That's not possible here." Chet assured Brenner and the rest of us, "We've used this man before. He is well paid." Chet added, "And he has family in the States whom he'd like to see again."

Me, too. Well...not my in-laws.

Chet continued, "This man, who is code-named Tariq—which means 'night visitor'—has a hand-held radio that will work on the frequency that the Twin Otter will monitor." He said, "To mark the runway portion of the road, Tariq has a backpack full of small, self-contained electronic transponders that he'll place as instructed along the road, and also at the beginning and end of the runway portion of the road to mark the thresholds." He further explained, "The pilots will be able to see the signals from these transponders on the GPS flight panel display in the cockpit." Chet assured us, "Tariq has done this dozens of times and so have the pilots."

"And you?"

"Many times." Chet continued, "All the transponders will be turned on when Tariq sets them on the road, but just before our arrival, Tariq will consider wind conditions and other factors, then turn off the threshold transponders at one end of the runway—the end he doesn't want us to approach from. The pilots will now know the direction of their landing, but more importantly, if all the transponders are still on at both ends of the road—or if none of them are on—that would mean that Tariq, for some reason, is out of action."

"Or sleeping like those schmucks who were supposed to videotape the *Cole* explosion."

Chet forced a polite smile and continued, "That will be our first indication that we need to pull up and keep going." He went on, "If the transponders are all set properly, then the pilot will ask Tariq by radio a single question—'Any dust?' Tariq will say 'Yes' if there are unfriendlies in the area, or if he has a gun pressed to his head. If Tariq says, 'No dust tonight,' then it's all clear. And he will double verify that he is not under duress by also saying 'Safe landing' as we approach the runway." Chet added, unnecessarily, "If he doesn't say those words, or if the threshold transponders are not properly set, then we fly directly back to Aden."

I saw this in a World War II movie once, but the pathfinder got captured by the Nazis, who tortured him and made him give them the sign and countersign for all clear. Everyone on the incoming aircraft was captured or killed. War is hell.

Buck told us, "I've made a few night landings around the country under similar circumstances, and it's always gone well."

Obviously, or you wouldn't be here to say that.

Chet added, "Al Qaeda is too stupid to have identified Tariq as working for us, but even if they did, they're too stupid to follow him, and too stupid to turn him around. They'd just kill him." He added, "They're not Germans."

He must have seen that movie. But Al Qaeda was not *that* stupid.

Chet also assured us, "Predators will be watching our approach and landing."

Kate said, "I'm okay with this. Let's move on."

Chet continued, "After we land, we will be met by a local sheik. Sheik Musa." He explained, "No operation in the tribal lands can succeed without the cooperation and armed security of at least one local sheik. Musa's tribesmen will take us by car to a remote safe house and his men will provide security for us."

Really? What are you chewing, Chet? I mean, letting Tariq in on this was risky enough—but letting a whole tribe of crazy Bedouin in on it was suicidal.

No one had anything positive to say about the travel arrangements, and I sensed that Chet was losing the confidence of the team. Chet understood that, too, and continued matter-of-factly, "Sheik Musa has provided us with assistance in the past, and he is well compensated for his help."

Silence.

So Chet further informed us, "Musa's tribal lands encompass the ancient ruins of Marib, and he provides security and protection to tour groups, scholars, archaeologists, and others who visit the ruins. This is a very lucrative arrangement for him," he assured us, "and on that basis alone he can be trusted to do what he's paid to do and what's best for him, which is to keep the peace."

I guess. Money talks. But didn't I just hear that nine Belgian tourists disappeared at the Marib ruins? And weren't their guide and driver found with their throats cut? Maybe that was another Marib.

I waited for Chet to mention this, but he went on, "Sheik Musa is not happy with Al Qaeda, most of whom are not Yemenis and not royalists as he is—"

"Excuse me," I interrupted. "I seem to remember that nine Belgian tourists went missing at the Marib ruins last summer."

Chet looked at me and I could see his icy blue eyes narrowing in the dim light. Finally, he said, "I was about to get to that."

"Sorry. I thought you forgot about that."

He informed us, "No one knows who was involved in that incident, but it certainly wasn't Sheik Musa."

"Right. But Sheik Musa, protector of Western tourists and scholars, fell down on the job. No?"

I could see that Chet was annoyed, Kate was concerned, and Brenner, who had to know about this incident, was quiet.

Buck, who'd forgotten to mention this to me and Kate, explained, "Sheik Musa took full responsibility for his failure to protect these tourists, and he's provided Yemeni and Western authorities with some leads." He added, "The sheik was embarrassed and angry, and he has vowed to avenge this insult to his honor and his reputation." Reminding me and Kate of his classroom lecture, Buck said, "When a Yemeni extends his hospitality, and someone else violates that hospitality, that violator becomes the subject of a blood feud."

Chet added, "And for that reason, Sheik Musa can be trusted."

Right. Lots of reasons to trust Sheik Musa. And for all I know, he's looking for a visa to open a deli in

Brooklyn. Still, I had some doubts. Also, it seemed to me that Buck, who had denied detailed knowledge of the operational plan, knew more than he'd let on. But I already knew that.

Chet said, "Al Qaeda are the primary suspects in this incident, but it could also have been a tribal kidnapping that went badly." He added, "Not Musa's tribe, obviously."

I informed Chet, "The Belgian authorities were told by a captured Al Qaeda operative in Brussels that it *was* Al Qaeda, and that the Belgians are probably dead."

Chet wanted to ask me where I got my information, but he didn't. He said, "Point is, Sheik Musa works for us. Not Al Qaeda, and not the Yemeni government."

Buck also informed us, "The sheik owes his loyalty to the Saudi royal family, who have him on retainer." He further advised us, "A Saudi prince has had a letter delivered to Sheik Musa, a copy of which I have, asking him to provide us with hospitality, safe passage, and any assistance we may need." Buck let us know, "That letter to the sheik from the Saudi prince is worth more than all the gold, money, or weapons we could give him."

I inquired, "Is there anyone you forgot to tell that we're going to Marib?"

Buck did not reply, but Chet said, "We have no choice but to reach out to people who are . . . situational allies."

I asked, "Do our Yemeni government allies know we are going to Marib?"

Chet replied, "Not from me."

"Can they guess?"

"Maybe."

I thought of Colonel Hakim, but I didn't ask.

Chet inquired, "Can we move on?"

Everyone nodded and Chet continued, "Sheik Musa will have two SUVs at the safe house for us to use. We will stay in the safe house overnight, then at about one or two P.M. we'll drive to Marib town, as though we've just arrived from Sana'a, and we'll check into the Bilqis Hotel where we have reservations under our own names. Then we drive to the ruins, to see and be seen. We're trying to pass as tourists, but virtually no one will believe that. The word will be out that we're on an Al Qaeda hunt—a Panther hunt." He continued, "Sheik Musa will provide protection for this trip, though it's only about ten kilometers between the safe house, the town, and the ruins. At the ruins, there may also be National Security police for protection."

Brenner said, "I hope we're not there on the day they're working for Al Qaeda."

Funny. Unless you were going there.

Brenner inquired, "Can we carry our M4s at the ruins?"

"No," replied Chet. "As I said, we're going as tourists."

I thought tourists carried automatic rifles in Yemen. If they didn't, they should. There'd be fewer dead tourists and more dead terrorists.

Chet assured us, however, "We will wear Kevlar and carry our handguns, concealed."

Brenner asked, "How about Zamo?"

"He will stay with our vehicles close to the ruins with his sniper rifle. Also, our M4s will be in the vehicles."

Brenner didn't seem keen on this, but he said nothing.

I really wanted to ask if Dr. Clare was going with us, but Kate might misconstrue my question. Maybe I should cough, then ask.

As if reading my mind, Kate asked, "Is Dr. Nolan coming with us?"

"No," replied Chet.

Why not?

Chet told us, "It's too dangerous."

That's why we need a doctor, Chet.

Well, no one had anything to say about that, but Chet's statement certainly put things into perspective.

I said, "I hope we're taking Howard along to advise us if we're doing anything illegal."

Chet replied, "If this was an FBI operation, we'd need six lawyers."

Touché.

Chet continued, "On our way back from the ruins to the Bilqis Hotel, about dusk, our two vehicles will be stopped by tribesmen in vehicles, and we will offer no resistance as we're kidnapped."

Huh?

Chet continued, "We will be taken back to the safe house to await developments."

Developments? Like what? Having our throats cut?

But Buck assured us, "It's all a sham, of course. The kidnappers are Sheik Musa's men. We'll have our weapons, and we'll be under the watchful eye of Predator drones armed with Hellfire missiles."

Great. And who controls the Predators? Chet. And he's been kidnapped.

Chet clarified that and said, "At the safe house is a van, which is a mobile Predator ground monitoring station, so I won't actually be with you when you check into the

Bilqis Hotel, or at the Marib ruins, or when you're kidnapped. I'll be at the safe house, watching the live camera feeds from the drone that is watching you, and the other drone that is watching the safe house." He added assuringly, "If something happened to me, or to the ground monitoring station at the safe house, then the Predators will pass under the control of the distant ground control station where the pilots maintain satellite radio control of the drones." He added, "They will, if necessary, use the Hellfires." He asked us, "Understand? Any questions?"

Lots of questions, but Chet was on a roll so we shook our heads.

Chet continued, "Once we're all assembled back at the safe house, ostensibly as the kidnapped guests of Sheik Musa, the sheik will get the word to the Al Qaeda operatives in the area that the sheik has a present for them—a team of American intelligence operatives, including Mr. John Corey and Ms. Kate Mayfield, both of whom work for the Anti-Terrorist Task Force, and who are both on Al Qaeda's kill list." He added, "Buckminster Harris is also known to Al Qaeda, and they would like to question him. Mr. Brenner, I'm sorry to say, is not that important to them, though they'd like to question and kill him as well. And your sniper, Zamo, would make a nice trophy, and they'd like to have his sniper rifle." He paused, smiled, then said, "As for me, Al Qaeda has never killed a CIA officer, so cutting my head off will make them look good."

And it might make the rest of us feel good. Sorry. That was not nice. Actually, I was developing some real respect for Chet Morgan. He had balls. He was also crazy, and probably a liar. But very cool, very smart, and apparently fearless.

Chet added, however, "Since I won't be with you when you all check into the Bilqis Hotel, or go to the ruins and get kidnapped, then I'm not known to be in Marib, and I won't be offered to Al Qaeda." He further explained, "Al Qaeda in Yemen equates CIA officers with Predators and Hellfire missiles, and we don't want to put that into their heads."

Right. That's why they're called spooks. They're there, but no one can see them. But I was okay with this, and Kate and Brenner seemed to be, too. Buck, of course, already knew this plan.

Regarding the plan, I had a few problems with it, and I asked, "Why would The Panther or Al Qaeda think that Sheik Musa would kidnap Americans if he's paid to protect Westerners and if he wants Marib to remain a must-see tourist destination?"

"Good question," replied Chet. He explained, "The sheik has promised Al Qaeda that his tribal lands will be neutral. Tourists and scholars are welcome, but American intelligence operatives are not. They—we—are fair game."

"Okay. Sounds plausible. But why would Sheik Musa go to Al Qaeda with the six—sorry, five—kidnapped Americans if the sheik is not on good terms with Al Qaeda?"

Chet nodded as though he expected the question and replied, "Money." He expanded on that. "Al Qaeda believes they have established an accommodation with Sheik Musa, based on money." He informed us, "Al Qaeda and the sheik negotiated a deal for Al Qaeda to set up their training camp in one of the sheik's Bedouin camps, so while Al Qaeda doesn't trust Sheik Musa, they think he can be bought."

I pointed out, "Sounds like he *was* bought."

Chet shook his head and explained to me patiently, "That was our idea, Mr. Corey. Now we know where the training camp is."

Right. Clever. If true. I asked, "Why don't we take out the camp?"

"It's better to watch it." Chet also let us know, "It appears from Predator observation and from local sources that The Panther never goes to the camp, but if he did, and if we could establish that, we'd have put a Hellfire up his ass a long time ago."

"Got it."

"As part of Musa's neutrality deal with Al Qaeda," Chet continued, "Al Qaeda is not allowed to carry out any armed operations within Sheik Musa's tribal territory. But when Al Qaeda kidnapped—and murdered— the Belgians, and made it look like a tribal kidnapping, Musa told Al Qaeda he was pissed off. Al Qaeda denied any involvement in the disappearance of the Belgians, but they gave Musa some money and weapons and smoothed it over. But Musa didn't believe them, so when he got word of the planned Al Qaeda attack on the Hunt Oil installation, he tipped us off—for ten thousand dollars—and we sent observation drones into the area and relayed the info to the Hunt security forces, who, as you know, were ready for the attack. But Al Qaeda can never be sure who, if anyone, ratted them out—though Sheik Musa told Al Qaeda he was looking into it."

It was hard to follow the lies and the liars without a scorecard. In the world I lived in, a lie was a deal-breaker—or got you some jail time. In this world, getting caught in a lie meant you needed a bigger and better lie, or at least a nice gift for the guy who caught you in a lie.

Chet said to me, "So to answer your question, Al Qaeda believes that Sheik Musa will make a deal with them, when it is in the sheik's best interest to do so." He also added, "The sheik has not canceled the lease on the Al Qaeda training camp—at our request—and Al Qaeda sees that as a positive sign that the sheik is in business to make money." On that subject, he informed us, "For five kidnapped American intelligence operatives, Al Qaeda will pay the sheik...maybe a hundred thousand dollars."

"Each?" I inquired.

"No. Together." He smiled. "Don't overestimate your worth."

Right. Life here is cheap.

Chet also told us, "The National Security police were paid about four hundred dollars to do a disappearing act on the Belgians."

Very cheap.

So, to recap, Sheik Musa was a double-dealing, double-crossing rat fink who was collecting bribes, rent, and retainers all over the place. He'd make a good New York City landlord. And was I supposed to believe that the Al Qaeda attack on the Belgian tourists was a complete surprise to him? Chet believed that. Or said he did. Buck, too. Sheik Musa's stated goal to make his tribal lands the Switzerland of Yemen—or Arabia Felix—seemed to have some inconsistencies and problems of the sheik's own making. But this was the Mideast, where nothing made any sense.

Chet, who could guess what I and everyone was thinking, said, "In the end, Sheik Musa knows that he's staying alive only as long as we don't let the Hellfires loose on him. He can play a lucrative double game now and then, but we control the endgame." He looked at us and said, "Hellfire missiles. The deus ex machina of this war. God shooting thunderbolts out of the sky. If you fuck with God, you're dead."

Okay. A little Latin is very convincing. But Chet wouldn't be the first Westerner who was hustled by the East.

I spent twenty years as a cop dealing with snitches, rat finks, stoolpigeons, and scam artists. And I always made sure they understood that if they double-crossed me, they'd be dead. Or wish they were. When you're dealing with people who have no moral center, no loyalty to anyone but themselves, you don't always get the logical results you expect, or the truth that you paid for.

And on that subject, I wondered about Chet's moral center and his devotion to the truth. Yemen was indeed the land of lies, a place where bullshit was a commodity and deception was the norm. In that respect, Yemeni culture and the CIA culture were not too far apart, despite the CIA's motto that the truth will set you free. And Chet, I suspected, had himself been corrupted by this culture of lying, and he thought he was better at it than the Yemenis, who he thought were stupid. I don't know if they're stupid, but I know they're cunning. That's how they've survived for three thousand years. And they'll be here long after we're gone, which could be soon.

"Mr. Corey?"

I looked at Chet.

"Don't overthink this."

I didn't reply.

Chet continued, "Musa will invite three or four Al Qaeda representatives to come to the safe house, under guard and, of course, blindfolded, to view the kidnapped Americans and to verify who they are." He reminded us, "Bring your passports. Then Musa will insist, as a matter of honor, respect, and trust, that The Panther himself negotiate the deal to buy the five Americans. Both sides will be allowed a fixed number of armed men, which the sheik will suggest should be ten or twelve, and that meeting will take place outside a goat herder's hut a few kilometers from the safe house. The sheik assures us that he knows what The Panther looks like, and to be doubly sure, we've shown him photos of Bulus ibn al-Darwish, with and without a beard."

Buck, who as I said knew a thing or two about this plan and this place, informed us, "This type of meeting between equal warlords is traditional in this culture, and a certain amount of good faith is expected on both sides. Nevertheless, both sides are armed, to ensure good behavior, but also to ensure that a third party does not take advantage of the meeting of the important leaders." He added, "It's a very medieval protocol, but in this case, the third party, the Americans, are not waiting in ambush behind rocks. We're watching from five thousand feet, and we can put a missile into The Panther's teacup."

Chet said, "If this meeting is to take place, I will call in two more Predators to be on station." Chet also assured us, "You will not actually be inside the goat herder's hut, of course. That's too close to what's going to happen. You'll still be in the safe house where I'll be in the Predator control van, talking to the four

Predator pilots and watching what's going on at the
hut, and what's going on around the safe house." Chet
continued, "Back at the goat herder's hut, when Sheik
Musa recognizes The Panther, he will greet him cor-
dially and give him the traditional embrace and hand
kiss."

Also known as the Kiss of Death.

But to be doubly sure I understood this, I said, "So
we're not going to make an attempt to apprehend the
suspect."

Chet replied, "No, we're going to kill the terrorist
with a Hellfire missile."

"So I don't have to read him his rights?"

"He has no rights."

That's what I've been saying. But it sounded a little
harsh coming from Chet. On the other hand...it was a
breath of fresh air.

Also, I was a little disappointed that I wasn't going
to whack The Panther myself—or at least be there when
a Hellfire turned him into protoplasm. I love the smell
of high explosives and burning flesh. But modern war
is impersonal. At least I could watch the action on the
video monitor from the Predator van at the safe house.
Would it be in color?

Chet went on, "After everyone greets everyone,
Sheik Musa, as host, will invite The Panther and a few
of his lieutenants to sit on a carpet for tea. But before
the negotiations begin for the Americans, Musa and his
close lieutenants will excuse themselves for a moment
and go into the stone goat herder's hut—maybe on the
pretense of retrieving the Americans. When I see this
on the monitor at the safe house, I will direct the Predator pilots to fire their Hellfires—two at al-Darwish

and his nearby retinue on the carpet, and two at the other Al Qaeda men and their vehicles." He assured us, "The surviving Al Qaeda guys will be totally stunned, and Musa's tribesmen will finish them off." He also let us know, "About the time this is happening, American Air Force fighter-bombers, operating out of a base in Saudi Arabia, will level the Al Qaeda training camp."

There was a silence in the tent while we all formed a mental picture of what Chet had just outlined. It sounded good...but there were some potential problems with the scenario. Like, people don't always do what you want them to do, or sit or stand where you want them to sit or stand. Right?

I asked, "What if it's raining on the outdoor tea party?"

Chet assured me, "It hasn't rained in Marib in two hundred years."

That might be an exaggeration, but it sounded like zero percent chance of precipitation.

Chet also informed us, "The second pair of Predators is our security at the safe house, and they will cover us as we drive to the scene to collect some bits and pieces of Mr. al-Darwish and the men around him for DNA and fingerprint ID." He added, "Some photos, too, though I don't think there will be any recognizable faces."

Chet was enjoying this. Hey, you earned it, Chet. Now you can go home and get your head tuned up.

Brenner had a thought and asked, "Won't this assassination and massacre put a little strain on Sheik Musa's relationship with Al Qaeda?"

Chet replied, "Sheik Musa, of course, will say he had no clue that the Americans were watching him, and he'll claim casualties of his own." He added, "There won't be any Al Qaeda witnesses alive to contradict his version of the attack. Also, after this, Al Qaeda won't be much of a problem in Marib province."

I asked Chet, "Does Musa get the five-million-dollar reward?"

"I think he earned it."

Right. Better than a hundred thousand from Al Qaeda. I inquired, "How much do we get?"

"The satisfaction of a job well done and the thanks of a grateful government."

"Same as last time."

Kate had a good question: "How do we get out of there?"

Chet replied, "As I said, we'll be covered by two Predators on our way to the scene. The Twin Otter will land on a nearby road and take us across the border into Saudi Arabia to a secret forward base in the Arabian Desert. We turn over the goo bags, the cameras, and our weapons, then the Otter will fly us to Riyadh Airport, where we will hop commercial airliners and fly home, wherever that is."

No one spoke as we all sat there in the dim, quiet tent, thinking about the plan, or about flying home first class or flying home in a box.

Well, I thought, this plan was based on a lot of past history, some of it true, some of it made up, and some of it not fully evaluated. The plan also depended on a lot of assumptions. The CIA, as usual, had come up with an operational plan that seemed clever, but was actually too clever by half. Keep it simple, stupid. But it might work.

Chet let the silence drag on, then asked, "Questions?"

Kate asked, "Don't you think The Panther will smell a trap?"

Chet replied, "The Panther, as a devout Muslim, would not believe that the sheik, also a devout Muslim, would betray him to the Americans, who are, of course, infidels."

I commented, "That's a good assumption, making me wonder why Musa *would* set up a fellow Muslim to be whacked by the infidels."

Chet replied, "The short answer is the five million bucks. But also Musa and al-Darwish don't have much else in common beyond their religion. Musa is a royalist and Al Qaeda is anti-royalist. Musa is a Bedouin, and the non-Bedouin Arabs, like al-Darwish, look down on the tribesmen. Plus, most of the tribes in Yemen want Al Qaeda out of their tribal lands." Chet added, "Also, I think Sheik Musa may not consider Mr. al-Darwish a true Yemeni. In fact, he probably thinks of him as an American intruder."

Everyone in this room is an American intruder.

Brenner observed, "You're making a good case for why Musa would betray The Panther, but not a good case for why The Panther would trust Musa and come to this meeting."

Chet nodded, then said, "The Panther needs a win after the Hunt Oil fiasco, and the recent failed ambush of our convoy, so the opportunity to get five Americans—not tourists, but intelligence operatives, including Mr. and Mrs. Corey, who are on Al Qaeda's kill list—will be so tempting that he'll talk himself into taking the risk." Chet added, "The Panther may not trust Musa, but he won't want to appear fearful and not go to the meeting." He also told us, "We have a psychological profile on al-Darwish that I'll show you on the way to Marib. Bottom line on Bulus ibn al-Darwish is that he's a megalomaniac." He looked at us and said, "Delusions of grandeur. Extreme egotism and narcissism."

Like everyone else in this room. Well...the guys. Kate was mostly normal.

Chet continued, "We can discuss this analysis on the plane. But to answer Mr. Brenner's question and Ms. Mayfield's concern, the worst-case scenario would be that The Panther just refuses to show up at the meeting to negotiate, buy, pay for, and take custody of the Americans."

Actually, I could think of a few even worse scenarios, but I saw Chet's point. If The Panther didn't show, then we'd just fly back to Aden and try another approach.

Brenner said to Chet, "The plan sounds okay in theory, and I see it's been well thought out and that you've done a lot of groundwork with Sheik Musa. But I don't trust the Yemenis, and this plan depends entirely on the assumption that everyone from Tariq to Musa is on our side." He added, "Our lives and this mission are in their hands, and not in our own hands." Brenner continued, "The only operations that really work are those that are completely run and executed by Americans—or by trusted Western allies. Not paid allies."

Spoken like a true soldier. And he was right.

Chet replied, "I agree, but that's not possible in Yemen." He added, "Ironically, this plan should work precisely because it depends on including some Yemenis in the operation. We've never done that before, so The Panther will not think we're now trusting a Yemeni to help us kill him."

Chet seemed to have an answer for everything. And they were good answers. And to give Chet some credit, he was putting his own ass out there on the front line. So I guess he believed in this plan.

Buck spoke up. "The plan is not foolproof, but it's not as dangerous as it sounds."

"Sure it is," I assured him.

Buck explained, "The downside for Sheik Musa if he betrays us is so severe—Hellfires and the wrath of the Saudi royal family—that I'm very confident of his loyalty." He added, "The sheik may switch loyalties next week or next year, but for now the deal is made and he will live up to his end of the bargain."

Chet agreed and added, "If Musa has changed his mind, he will just tell Tariq to wave us off, and we return to Aden."

I observed, "Musa may be trustworthy, but all it would take to get us killed is for one of his tribesmen to be working for Al Qaeda."

Neither Chet nor Buck responded to that, and Chet seemed a bit impatient and got down to the question of our participation in this plan. He looked at me, then at Kate and asked, "Are you all right with this?"

I glanced at Kate, who nodded. I said to Chet, "If you like it, Chet, then we love it."

"I love it," Chet assured us. "In fact, I conceived of it."

Wonderful. It takes an egotist to catch an egotist.

Chet looked at Brenner.

Brenner had probably been betrayed by the natives here and in Southeast Asia one time too many. Nevertheless, he was going to give it another shot and he said, "I'm in."

"Good," said Chet. "The A-team is ready to kill The Panther." He added, "And about a dozen of his jihadists."

As I said, the bait never likes the plan, but at least Kate and I weren't the only ones with skin in the game.

Chet, to further incentivize us, said, "I believe, based on what we know of the structure of Al Qaeda in Yemen, that if we kill The Panther and his top lieutenants, and destroy their training camp, then the Al Qaeda attack on the Sheraton won't happen."

Buck seconded that and said, "If the Marib operation is successful, Al Qaeda in Yemen will be in disarray and they won't risk an attack on the Sheraton, which could end in another failure." He added, "And that is also true for the suspected attack on the embassy."

Okay. I got it. Captain Mac would be disappointed if he couldn't kill jihadists attacking the hotel. Same for the Marines in the embassy. But for everyone else in the embassy and the hotel, they would be happy if the attacks didn't happen—or were at least postponed.

Chet said to us, "We'll meet in the lobby at midnight. Two DSS vehicles will take us to the airport, where the Otter will be waiting to fly us to Marib."

This is where the coach gives the team the pep talk, and Buck, our leader and life coach, said to us, "I believe we have assembled an excellent team for this mission, and I thank you for volunteering. There may not be any public glory in this, but somewhere your names will be recorded and known to future generations. You are risking your lives for a cause greater than yourselves, knowing that the success of this mission will make America safer and bring us closer to victory over those who wish us harm."

Sounds good. Buck had lived long enough to see the end of the Cold War—but none of us would live long enough to see the end of this war.

Chet Morgan got down to specifics and said, "Bulus ibn al-Darwish, al-Numair, The Panther, head of Al Qaeda in Yemen, is a traitor to his country of birth, a mass murderer of innocent civilians and seventeen American seamen, and a sworn enemy of America." He assured us, "We should have no moral qualms about ending his life and the lives of his jihadists on the field of battle."

That's much better than me trying to read him his rights in Arabic.

Chet concluded, "I know someone is watching over us to ensure our success and our safe return home."

Correct. The Predator drones.

We all stood, shook hands, and left the SCIF tent. Chet went to the balcony to fuel up on whatever, and the rest of us went into the bright light of the hallway.

Buck, obviously not wanting to engage in a post-coital chat, said, "See you later in the lobby," and walked toward his room.

Kate, Brenner, and I went to the elevator and rode down to our rooms on the third floor.

As I was taught, and as I'd learned over the years, if the goal is simple—like whacking someone—the plan should be simple. When the plan is complex, then something else is going on.

CHAPTER FIFTY-TWO

Zamo called our room at 11:30 and said he'd be around to pick up our bags and rifles, explaining, "The CIA guy doesn't want people in the lobby to see that you're going on a trip."

Okay. That's the problem with conducting anti-terrorist operations from a hotel in Sandland; there could be Al Qaeda snitches watching what you do. Chet had good tradecraft. Also, he probably watches too many spy movies.

Zamo also said, "Mr. Harris wants Ms. Mayfield to pack her balto."

"Wonderful." I hung up and said to Kate, "Great news. You have an occasion to wear your balto."

A little after midnight, Kate and I, wearing cargo pants, desert boots, black T-shirts, sleeveless bush jackets, Kevlar, and concealed Colt .45 automatics, walked into the hotel lobby.

The lobby was nearly deserted, and I didn't see any of our teammates. I said to Kate, "I'll look outside."

"No. Chet said to meet in the lobby."

Kate, who is usually cool before departing on a

dangerous assignment, seemed a bit subdued, maybe uneasy. And who could blame her? I mean, just getting to the airport at this hour had some risks.

Anyway, we took a seat in the lobby and waited for our teammates.

After our meeting with Chet, Brenner had called our room and asked to come by to talk. Not a bad idea.

I was ninety-nine percent sure there were no listening devices in our room, but recalling Chet's possible eavesdropping, and because of the PSO tent on the nearby ridge, I turned on the TV. Some guy in a beard and robe was literally screaming about something, and I kept hearing the words, "Amrika," "jihad," and "mawt," which means "death."

I asked Brenner, "Is he a stand-up comic?"

"He's a mullah," Brenner replied.

Actually, he was an asshole.

Anyway, we moved three chairs together and leaned close. Brenner got to the point and told us, "I'm not sure about the plan."

Kate agreed and added, "If I was The Panther, I'd see a setup and smell a trap."

Thinking about panthers, lions, and other predators, and remembering what Buck said back in Sana'a, I reminded them, "The Panther is always going to be cautious and on his guard. But he wants to eat." And recalling what Chet said, I added, "If he does smell a trap, he'll just not show up." I concluded, "He's either in the trap or he's a no-show. I don't see the danger to us."

Of course I certainly *did* see the danger to us. But I wanted to see if Kate or Brenner saw it.

In fact, Brenner said, "The immediate danger isn't from The Panther. It's from this guy Sheik Musa. Musa is holding all the cards. Not us, not the CIA, and not even The Panther."

Kate agreed with Mr. Brenner and said, "We have no idea what the politics are here, or who owes who what, or who is ready to betray whom."

I agreed with that, but to continue to play devil's advocate, I said, "Chet and Buck made a good case for why Sheik Musa could be trusted, and I don't see any holes in that logic. I mean, what's in it for Musa to betray us to Al Qaeda? Hellfire missiles. There's much more in it for him to take our five million bucks to get rid of Al Qaeda and The Panther." I explained, "That would not only make the Americans happy, but also make the Saudi royal family happy as well as the idiots in Sana'a. It's a win-win-win for Sheik Musa."

Kate and Brenner thought about that, and they both nodded, though reluctantly.

Of course there were other parts and pieces to this plan and to the bigger picture. For one thing, Brenner might or might not know that his new friend Kate had whacked a CIA officer. But was that relevant to what was going to happen in Marib? Possibly.

And then there was the Political Security Organization. Yemen's CIA. Birds of a feather, as Buck said in an unguarded moment. Why did Chet not address the question of his Yemeni counterparts?

Kate, thinking along the same lines, said, "Chet never mentioned the PSO, the National Security Bureau, or the Yemeni Army. That's like totally discounting the fact that even this place has a security apparatus." She added, "Colonel Hakim knows from the prisoner where The Panther was last seen, and he can guess that we're going there."

Brenner agreed. "This is true. We could wind up in a confrontation with the army, the NSB, or the PSO."

The devil's advocate replied, "The tribes and Al Qaeda rule in Marib province, and the security forces are scarce there. So maybe that's why Chet didn't address that." I added, "Or Operation Clean Sweep has been cleared with the Yemeni government at the highest levels, but neither Chet nor Buck is authorized to share political information."

Again, Kate and Brenner nodded reluctantly.

I'm smart enough not to believe my own bullshit, and I certainly didn't believe Chet's bullshit or Buck's bullshit. In fact, there *was* something else going on here, and I was beginning to get a picture of what it was. But not so clear that I could put it into words and share it with Kate or Brenner, or confront Chet or Buck with my suspicions.

Brenner was worried about Sheik Musa, and Kate was worried that The Panther would smell a trap, and they were both worried about the Yemeni authorities. My worry was the CIA. I mean, it was *their* plan. And there seemed to be something wrong with the plan. And the CIA, for all its faults, is not stupid. So if the plan seemed flawed, it really wasn't. The fact was, there was actually another plan.

But to calm the troops, I said, "Bottom line, Chet and Buck are putting their asses on the line with us." I said to Brenner, "In the Army, you would never send your men on a mission that you yourself wouldn't go on or didn't believe in. Correct?"

He nodded.

So we kicked this around for a few minutes while the mullah was working himself into a frenzy about

Amrika or whatever. I mean, the whole Mideast was fucked up long before we got here, and it would be fucked up long after we left. And with all the Jews gone, who are they going to blame for all their problems? Amrika. Truth is, as Al Rasul told me, they really hated themselves. Nevertheless, we were about to give them another reason to hate *us*—a whack job perpetrated by the infidels on the sacred soil of Islam.

Brenner said, "Well, we have to make a decision."

I informed him, "The decision has already been made. Unless you two can come up with a fatal flaw in this plan—something other than it sounds dangerous—then we're getting on that plane tonight and flying to Marib." I reminded everyone, "We all volunteered for this. And what did we think we were volunteering for?"

Brenner looked at me and said, "I've volunteered for missions in Vietnam and other places that were more dangerous than this. But I always had guys I could trust to watch my back. We don't have that here."

"Sure we do," I replied. "Buck and Chet. And Zamo. And don't forget the Predators."

Kate, who knows me too well, said, "John, you feel the same as we do about this mission."

"Maybe. But forewarned is forearmed. We'll keep an eye out for one another, keep an eye on Chet and Buck, keep Zamo close, and be ready to take charge if things start to smell bad. Agreed?"

Kate and Brenner nodded, and Brenner asked me, "What's motivating you? Aside from the *Cole*?"

"That's enough motivation. But aside from that, all of us are in this business, and this is not a safe business. Never was, never will be. Look at Buck. He's put his balls on the line for over thirty years. And even Chet, living in this shithole for three years to avenge the *Cole*. And you, Paul, you've been in harm's way for a good part of your life. And so has Kate. This is not a career, it's a calling. It's not a paycheck, it's a life." I concluded, "We're making the homeland just a little safer." Plus, I have a big ego, but I didn't mention that.

Brenner nodded and said, "I'm still in. I just wanted to see if you two understood the problems with this plan and this mission."

Kate said, "We all understand. And I'm glad we spoke about it." She added, "We'll keep alert for problems." She looked at me, then at Brenner, and said to him, "John actually likes bad plans from higher-ups. He can't wait to change the plan, rescue the mission from disaster, and show everyone how smart he is."

Totally not true. That's just the way it happens. Anyway, I said, "First things first. First we have to get to the airport without getting kidnapped."

We all stood, and I said, "See you downstairs," and Brenner left.

The guy on the TV was still going nuts and I thought he was going to pass out like that TV newscaster in *Network*. I wondered if the Evening News with the Mad Mullah had a big market share.

"John?"

I shut off the TV. "Yes, dear."

"I know you know what you're doing."

"Absolutely." Not a clue.

"And I'll trust you on this."

"Smart move."

She let me know, "I think Paul still has some valid misgivings, but not enough to pull out."

"We actually don't need him even if he does." To be provocative and snotty, I added, "And I know you won't think any less of him if he hightails it back to the safety of the embassy."

"You're an asshole."

"I am an alpha male on the A-team. We will kill The Panther, then go to Washington and get a handshake. Maybe we'll take a week and go to a nude beach in St. Maarten. No Muslims on a nude beach to worry about. And if there were, where would they hide a gun or a suicide belt?"

She didn't reply to that, but she did give me a kiss.

So we stuffed some things in our overnight bags, and Zamo called to say he'd come for our bags and rifles, and now here we were in the lobby, waiting for the rest of the A-team.

CHAPTER FIFTY-THREE

My cell phone, which worked near the hotel SCIF, chimed and I looked at the text message: *Parking lot*.

Kate and I went outside and walked to the unlit parking area in front of the hotel, where I saw one of the Marines with a bomb-sniffing dog. As the Marine approached our five Land Cruisers, he commanded, "Cummins, search!" Good doggie. A journey of a thousand miles can end quickly if your car blows up when you turn the key.

Cummins seemed happy with all the Land Cruisers, but he growled at Chet, sensing a CIA man. Or maybe Cummins smelled the khat. Also, FYI, Chet had changed into dark clothing and he'd found his shoes. This was getting serious.

Two of our DSS drivers from Sana'a, including Mike Cassidy, loaded the bags in the back of the two vehicles and handed us our rifles.

Brenner said to everyone, "Top speed, we stop for nothing, keep your rifles at the ready."

Right. Just in case we run into the forty Al Qaeda guys heading for the hotel.

Brenner, Buck, and Chet got in one vehicle with the driver, and Kate and I got in the rear of the other with Zamo up front and Mike behind the wheel.

Mike said, "I thought I was done for the day."

"Me, too."

Brenner's Land Cruiser pulled out of the parking area, and we followed, past the Yemeni Army lawn chair brigade.

I asked Zamo, "Did you see Dr. Clare?"

"Yeah..."

Bullshit. Some guys look for the million-dollar wound that will keep them out of action, and some guys who get the wound, like Zamo, are afraid it will keep them out of the action. I wondered what motivated Zamo. Probably he liked to kill jihadists with his sniper rifle. That simple.

We accelerated uphill on the narrow, winding road that cut through the hills and bluffs above the beach. There were no other vehicles on the road, and we stayed in the middle of the blacktop, hitting 120 KPH. As we crested the bluff and got into the flatlands, Brenner's driver gunned it, and Mike followed.

This was the road we'd come in on, and it skirted around the city, then ran along the Gulf of Aden. In less than five minutes, I could see the lights of the airport, but I didn't see any aircraft flying at this hour.

We followed the lead vehicle into the airport and shot past a manned guard booth without stopping, then veered off the road that led to the terminal and headed across a dusty field toward the runway.

At the end of the runway, I saw a high-winged twin-engine prop aircraft that must be the Otter. The paint job was a monotone gray, the official color of Spook

Air, and the small tail markings were almost unreadable, another indication that this was a Company aircraft. Also, the cockpit and cabin windows were dark, and as we got closer I saw that the cabin shades were pulled and the boarding door was closed.

As we approached the aircraft, the cockpit lights went on, both engines fired up, and the props began spinning.

The two SUVs stopped near the rear boarding door, and everyone piled out. Mike said, "Good luck. Look me up in Daytona or Madrid."

"Will do."

We quickly retrieved our bags from the rear, including Zamo's sniper rifle case, some backpacks, and a heavy duffel bag that I hoped held junk food and extra ammo. As we got to the left rear boarding door, it opened and one of the pilots dropped a short ladder down, and up we went. At the top of the ladder I glanced back and saw that our two DSS drivers were covering the situation with automatic rifles.

The copilot was making his way up the aisle back to the cockpit, and I saw that the dimly lit cabin had rows of double seats on the right and single seats on the left that would hold about fifteen people. Here near the tail were two facing bench seats along the wall, I guess for napping. Chet pointed out an open baggage area to the right of the door where we threw our bags and weapons as Chet pulled up the ladder, closed the boarding door, and then directed everyone to take seats toward the front. Chet went up to the cockpit and spoke to the pilots for a few seconds, then returned to the cabin and took a single seat across from Buck in the row ahead of Kate and me. Brenner and Zamo had slid into single seats across the aisle, so the aircraft seemed balanced for takeoff.

The dim cabin light went out, then the PA speaker crackled and one of the pilots made a boarding announcement, "Welcome aboard," and a safety announcement, "Get ready for takeoff."

And thank you for flying Spook Air. I noticed, too, that neither pilot introduced himself by name. Not even a first name. Company policy.

The engines revved and we buckled in as the aircraft began rolling fast down the runway. In less than ten seconds, the Otter abruptly pitched up and we were airborne. The aircraft seemed to strain as it continued to climb at a very steep angle.

I reached across Kate and opened the window shade and looked down at the lights of Aden and the harbor where all this began. I mean, had Commander Kirk Lippold challenged the approaching boat and fired a shot across its bow, I wouldn't have been here two and a half years ago, and I wouldn't be here now. But for sure, I'd be someplace else. There was no end to this.

The ground was falling away at a fast rate as we continued our steep, full-throttle climb, and I turned my attention to my seat mate. "How you doing?"

"Can we go back and get my stomach?"

I knew she'd start to see the funny side of antiterrorist operations in dangerous, fucked-up places.

I said, "This is nothing. Wait until you see the landing."

"Not funny."

"Just trying to lighten the moment."

"Try jumping out."

Anyway, a few minutes after our thrilling short-takeoff maneuver, the pilot, still climbing at a steep angle, banked hard right, which caused the aircraft to shudder and caused Kate to grip her armrests. A voice on the PA said, "Sorry, folks. There was some traffic ahead."

I hate it when planes collide in midair.

The pilot or copilot also announced, "We're flying dark—no exterior lights, and please keep all the shades down if you turn on your overhead light."

I lowered my shade.

A few minutes later, we came out of our gravity-defying climb and leveled off. I turned on my overhead light and scanned the aisle for the beverage cart.

The pilot came back on the PA and said, "Marib is almost due north of here, but unfortunately I forgot to file a flight plan with the authorities." He chuckled. A little CIA pilot humor. He also told us, "To confuse anyone watching us on radar, we'll take a northwesterly heading towards Sana'a, then as we approach Sana'a we'll drop below radar coverage and head east into Marib." He informed us, "Marib has an airstrip, so if someone thinks we're going there, they'll think we're heading for the airstrip."

Right. Because no one would think we were stupid enough to land on a road in the dark.

The pilot also assured us, "Weather is good en route, and we have some moonlight to fly by and we have night vision goggles for the landing."

Do we have parachutes?

"Flight time is about two and a half hours."

Well, we had reached the point of no return regarding Operation Clean Sweep.

Actually, Kate and I had reached that point when we walked into Tom Walsh's office to talk about Yemen.

And here I was.

And here we all were, all six of us, with not much in

common except one goal—to kill someone. I'd be lying if I said I didn't have some misgivings about this, but I'd be lying more if I said I wasn't looking forward to the kill. That's the reason I came here. Well, one of the reasons.

— PART VIII —

Marib,
Yemen

CHAPTER FIFTY-FOUR

The pilot announced that we'd reached our cruising altitude of thirteen thousand feet, and we were free to help ourselves to refreshments from an ice chest in the rear.

So we all got up and fished soft drinks and bottled water out of the chest, and Chet invited us to sit on the facing bench seats. Zamo had no need or desire to know what Chet was going to say, so he returned to his seat with a Dr Pepper. Was it my imagination, or did his left arm seem not to be moving normally? I mean, if you take a hit like that, with soft tissue trauma, it's going to stiffen up, and maybe it was also infected. Great. A sniper with a bum arm.

Anyway, Kate, Brenner, and I sat together, and Buck and Chet sat facing us. Chet turned on an overhead light and I saw that he had a file folder in his hand—what the CIA calls a dossier, just to be très cooler than the FBI.

Chet spoke over the steady din of the twin engines. "This is our psychological profile and background analysis of Bulus ibn al-Darwish. It was put together by a team of FBI and CIA psychologists and investigators over the last three years since we identified Mr. al-Darwish as a prime suspect in the Cole bombing." Chet also informed us, "This report is based on interviews with the suspect's parents, a younger sister, childhood and college classmates, teachers, school counselors, Muslim clerics, and others who knew the bastard in the States."

I asked, "Any girlfriends?"

"Only one that we know of."

"There's the problem. He wasn't getting laid enough."

"John, please."

Who said that?

Chet agreed, "Young men without women are a problem in this culture, and that often leads to male aggressiveness and other abnormal behavior."

"Right." When I get horny, I get mean.

Chet continued, "It may not seem necessary to know all of this, considering that we're going to terminate the subject. But I thought you'd find this interesting, maybe for future assignments. And maybe you'd also just like to know what's inside the head we're going to blow off."

I would. And I'd also like to know what's going on in Chet's head.

Chet continued, "Also, if you know how al-Darwish got to where he is, and who he is, you'll see why I think he's going to walk into that meeting with Sheik Musa and get himself killed."

Chet, as I said, was a small breath of fresh air after my four years with the FBI, which, as part of the Department of Justice, needed to at least *sound* legalistic. Ergo

Howard. And Kate, too. But I was working on Kate. The CIA, on the other hand, made few public statements, and therefore they had not developed a politically correct vocabulary for public consumption. Maybe I should consider asking Chet for a job. I was sure I could explain about my wife killing one of his colleagues.

Chet informed us, "The subject, as he is called in this report, was born in New Jersey to Yemeni-born parents. As I said, he has a younger sister, Hana. His father, Jurji, was and is a successful importer and wholesaler of Mideastern goods, and he commutes to his office in Newark. He uses the name George, which is Jurji in Arabic. The mother, Sabria, is a stay-at-home housewife. They live in a large Victorian house in the waterfront section of Perth Amboy, which is more affluent than most of the working-class city."

Right. The house I'd seen in that photo.

Chet said, "FYI, Bulus means Paul, but the subject never used Paul to identify himself to non–Arabic speakers." He added, "We shouldn't make too much of that, but it's interesting that his father calls himself George, and mother's and sister's names are nondescriptive—Western-sounding."

Right. A shrink would have a field day with that. More importantly, in a few days Bulus would be known as Mayit—Dead.

Chet also told us, "The al-Darwish family and the wife's family in Yemen are city dwellers—Ta'iz—and they remain there. We have asked the PSO to keep these families under surveillance, but nothing has come of that." He added, "I'm sure the suspect doesn't go to Ta'iz for family visits. The senior Mr. al-Darwish, George, sends money to his and his wife's relatives, and he used to visit now and then on business, but since the Cole, George hasn't set foot in Yemen."

Right. War separates families and divides loyalties, and for the emigrant, the fatherland can become a dangerous place. As for jihadists like Bulus, who do come home, they discover they can't pop in on Uncle Abdul for a cup of tea. They are alone. Except for their new friends with AK-47s.

Chet continued, "The family in Perth Amboy kept a halal home, read the Koran, and attended a storefront mosque in the downtown section of the city. The mosque has not come to the attention of the authorities and neither has the al-Darwish family." He added, "Mr. and Mrs. al-Darwish have been known to have a cocktail or two with Christian friends."

I hoped they reciprocated with a khat chew.

Chet flipped a page and continued, "The subject terrorist attended the public schools and had few friends in grade school or high school, possibly because he lived in a non-Muslim community. The people we interviewed claim, however, that the subject's social isolation was his choice and not a result of any prejudices in the community. As possible proof of this, most of those interviewed confirmed that the subject's parents and sister had friends and social contacts in the non-Muslim community." Chet speculated, "If we believe that, then maybe the subject wrongly perceived prejudice and animosity, and reacted accordingly, and that reinforced his social isolation."

Right. Little Bulus was an angry, unhappy, and weird kid, and this made him a prime target for other kids. And that's why he wanted to be a terrorist when he grew up.

Chet continued, "The subject seems to have ignored the fact that his parents and sister were integrating well into the community, and the analysts believe that this shows the subject's tendency to exclude any realities that don't fit his preconceived beliefs."

Kate suggested, "That describes half the world's population."

Chet nodded, but said, "The subject takes it to an extreme." He also said, "But to be objective, we need to concede that the subject, being a Muslim, may have experienced some degree of prejudice."

Right. But it's how you handle it that determines if you're going to move on and live the American dream or if you're going to become the American nightmare.

Chet went on, "Bottom line on this is that the subject could never see himself as anything but an outsider in American society, and he had no attitudinal loyalty to the country of his birth. His alienation and anger were, of course, reinforced by the daily news, which gives extensive coverage to foreign and domestic acts of terrorism, the wars in Iraq and Afghanistan, our strained relations with Islamic countries, and so forth."

Unless you listen to NPR.

Chet reminded us, "Young people are impressionable and sensitive and there is a whole generation of American-born Muslims who are growing up in what some of them perceive as a hostile environment, especially after 9/11." He added, "Ironically, their foreign-born parents are better adjusted because they have voluntarily made the decision to become Americans. Most of them are happy with that decision, and if they're not, they can move back to wherever they came from. Children don't have that option, and the children of Muslim immigrants sometimes feel trapped and blame their parents for bringing them to America or for having been born in America. In contrast to earlier immigrants, these children sometimes romanticize their ancestral land and think they would have been happier if they'd never left there." Chet concluded, "We think this is what happened to Bulus ibn al-Darwish, based on statements he's made, letters and e-mails he's written, and long, rambling audiotapes that he's recorded and distributed."

"So," I said, "this is all Daddy and Mommy's fault."

"For starters." Chet added, "He became completely alienated from his parents in college, which is very unusual in this family-oriented culture."

Brenner commented, "But al-Darwish must know that his parents are trying to save his butt."

Chet replied, "Doesn't matter. He doesn't thank them for the opportunity of a better life in America—he blames them for coming to Christendom and living among the infidels." Chet also informed us, "The parents actually did screw him up, but not in the way he thinks." He told us, "As their only son—a rarity in traditional Muslim homes—they spoiled and indulged the little bastard the way most Western parents do with their children. Possibly the parents felt guilty about their decision to live in America, and they overcompensated by not pushing the kid to go play baseball or something."

Kate commented, "We see a lot of that in our work—young Muslims who are caught between two worlds." She added, "American culture does not fit them as well as it fits other immigrants, and their response is alienation, which eventually leads to radical websites and then radical friends."

Right. Plus, America is *the* superpower, and America makes war on Islam, so Muslim Americans think of themselves as the neighborhood face of the enemy. And sometimes they're right.

The aircraft droned on as Chet flipped through the dossier and also droned on a bit about little Bulus's boyhood and adolescence. Chet concluded, "The subject was treated like a prince at home, an outsider in school, and a target on the streets of Perth Amboy. He was headed for trouble, but not the kind of trouble we usually associate with an angry, alienated male." He added, "You can take this analysis for what it's worth. If the subject was ever brought to trial, you'd hear the same crap in the courtroom, and the media would dutifully report it. Therefore, no one will ever hear how and why the defendant got his head messed up by a cruel, uncaring, and prejudiced society."

I agreed that it was probably better to terminate the subject rather than apprehend and prosecute him—for sure it was the easier thing to do. But I asked, for the record, "Doesn't he have info we can use?"

Chet replied, "Lots. But his legal status as a U.S. citizen puts him and us in an awkward situation." He explained, "We would probably have to inform him of his right to remain silent, and that's exactly what he'd do. Plus, of course, his parents are all lawyered up. So…"

Right. Mr. al-Darwish as an American citizen with the right not to be taken to a secret location and waterboarded was a problem. Therefore, as I'd guessed from the beginning, Bulus ibn al-Darwish had to be terminated. End of problem.

Chet moved on to the subject's college years and

said, "Despite the bastard's problems in public school, he did well academically and got accepted to Columbia University, which as you know is one of the best schools in the country."

I asked Chet, "Where did you go to school?"

"Yale."

I pointed out, "So you and the subject terrorist have something in common. You both went to Ivy League schools."

Chet ignored that and informed us, "He actually has a genius I.Q.—top two percent of the population—and he could have joined Mensa, but he didn't join anything in college except a campus Muslim group and a mosque."

I wondered if the subject asshole was smarter than me. I don't think I've ever met or killed anyone smarter than me. This could be interesting.

Chet continued, "Being a genius doesn't make you smart, happy, or successful. In fact, sometimes the opposite. Studies have shown that people with genius-level I.Q.s are often unhappy, alienated from the society around them, impatient with people of lesser intelligence, angry at how stupid and ignorant the world is, and generally self-absorbed and untrusting. In fact, they only trust themselves and they rarely take the advice of others."

Why is everyone looking at me?

Chet went on, "As this relates to what may or may not happen in the next few days, we believe that Bulus ibn al-Darwish will ignore any advice or warnings he gets from his aides or advisors about the meeting with Sheik Musa. He is driven first by hate and what he sees as revenge against America for our attacks on Islam, and by the American military presence on the sacred soil of his country and other Islamic countries. And somewhere deep in his subconscious he's remembering all the shit he got from his schoolmates in Perth Amboy, and this is payback time." Chet added, "The *Cole* was payback, too, but that was impersonal. He wasn't even there to see the Americans die—and as you know, he didn't even get to see a videotape." Chet let us know, "But this time...Well, this is his chance to get his hands on five live Americans—his former compatriots—people who remind him of all those years of misery and loneliness." He let us know, "If you—we—ever did fall into his hands, don't expect a quick death."

I already knew that. In fact, what we could expect was months or years of brutal captivity, until The Panther got tired of playing with his captured mice, then he'd saw our heads off. I glanced at Kate, Buck, Brenner, and Chet, and thought about spending years with them as a prisoner. I mean, The Panther wouldn't even have to torture me; a few weeks with Chet and Buck would be torture enough.

Chet continued, "The subject's college years were unremarkable, but this is the period when he seems to have become radicalized." Chet informed us, "As you may know, Columbia has a large Jewish student body, and it's generally understood that these Jewish students, and in fact most of the students at Columbia are, let's say, overly tolerant and empathetic toward the relatively small Muslim student body." He speculated, "You'd think that this would have opened al-Darwish's eyes and mind to the idea that not everyone was against him or against Muslims. He could have fit in very well in college, and gotten happier and made non-Muslim friends. Instead, he ignored the generally open and liberal atmosphere on campus and withdrew into a narrow world of like-minded Muslim friends on and off campus." Chet also informed us, "Interestingly, to appease his father, he majored in economics, but he minored in Middle Eastern studies."

Ironic that he learned about his culture at an American university.

"He also took Arabic-language classes to improve his proficiency in the language," Chet went on, "and he lived off campus in an apartment with other Muslim students, American and foreign-born, who were observant of the calls to prayer, the dietary laws, and other strictures of the religion." Chet added, "He studied the Koran...I guess you'd say religiously...and did well in class."

Young Bulus wasn't exactly Joe College. I mean, every American knows that you go to college to get drunk, get laid, and give your parents heartburn. But this idiot actually studied. I'm surprised he didn't come to the attention of the FBI as a possible subversive. But maybe he did. I asked, "Any problems with the law?"

"Just once. The girlfriend." Chet explained, "He was dating a European Muslim lady from Bosnia, who had become Americanized. She was secular, liked a drink now and then, dressed Western, and apparently had sex outside of marriage. This was interesting, because in every other way Mr. al-Darwish was a strictly observant Muslim. But he became involved with this lady who was not exactly the ideal Islamic woman by Mr. al-Darwish's standards."

I was happy to learn that even fundamentalist

Muslim men think with their dicks. A ray of hope in the war on terrorism.

Chet informed us, "We interviewed this lady where she lives in Manhattan, but she wouldn't say much except that her college boyfriend, Bulus, was not a barrel of laughs." He added, "They dated for two semesters, then she broke it off and began dating a non-Muslim. A Christian. Well, Mr. al-Darwish became violent and he physically assaulted her in her apartment, someone called the police, and they came and arrested him." Chet let us know, "She refused to press charges and the case was dropped."

Right. Before I was a homicide detective, I responded to dozens of domestic violence cases. Most of the guys involved would turn up again in one way or another, usually another violent crime. Mr. al-Darwish, too, had turned up again—big-time.

Chet went on a little about the subject's college years, and truly there was nothing remarkable about his four years at Columbia. One instructor described him as "brooding," another as "quiet." One Muslim student, however, described him as "seething." Most of his classmates couldn't remember him at all. Not exactly big man on campus, and not a campus trouble-maker. Interestingly, no one recalled him ever making anti-American remarks, or anti-Semitic statements. In fact, the impression I got was of a young man who was quiet in public, but filled inside with bad stuff. Like a ticking time bomb.

Chet also told us, "This brush with the law—arrest, the booking procedure, which probably included a strip search, the night in jail—seemed to have a pro-found effect on him. A few college classmates said he became even more withdrawn and went into a deep depression."

Right. For the average middle-class kid, this was a traumatic experience. The upside was that most of them got scared straight and kept their noses clean. But as I said, when you're frightened you later get angry, and you look for payback. If I fell into this guy's hands, I should probably not mention that I'm former NYPD. But I'm sure he already knew that.

Chet continued, "Interestingly, although al-Darwish apparently visited a number of radical websites, he did not seem to be under the influence of any specific fundamentalist or radical religious mentor as many of these radicalized young people are. Our profilers and behavioral science people believe he saw himself as his own inspiration, and quite possibly he believed then, and believes now, that he's being guided from above."

Right. Like, I hear voices. I've had a couple of those. Scary people.

Chet added, "But we don't know if he's that kind of nut job. And we'll never know."

"Well," I pointed out, "if he walks into the trap we'll know that no one from above warned him."

Chet conceded, "Good point." He continued, "If you study the lives of men who've gone on to become powerful dictators and mass murderers, you'll discover that many of them were like this bastard—angry, driven, obsessed, and sociopathic—but they were also quiet as boys and young men, as though they were biding their time until they could break away from the restraints of society and the law." Chet continued, "It was almost inevitable, in retrospect, that al-Darwish would go to Yemen, a country that shares many of his beliefs, and also a country that's dysfunctional enough for him to gain some power. In other words, he was a zero in America, but here in Yemen he filled the void in the power vacuum and blossomed into a feared and respected leader." Chet added, "Ironically, being an American—or as the Arabs say, al-Amriki—gave him some cachet and credibility. And some respect."

Right. Everyone else here was born in this shithole and lived and died here. Bulus ibn al-Darwish came from Amrika to save and serve his people, and they thought that was pretty cool. It *was* ironic. Plus, the bastard knew America—Islam's number one enemy—firsthand. I recalled what Al Rasul told me about The Panther being multicultural and the conflicts in his head. I wondered what language he dreamt in. Maybe it depended on the dream. Sex dreams in English, killing Americans in Arabic.

Chet let us know, "There are a growing number of American-born or American-raised Muslims who have followed this path back to their ancestral countries and become leaders in the jihadist movement." He added, "To be fair, however, many Muslim Americans have returned to these countries to do good."

I observed, "That's what al-Darwish thinks he's doing."

"Maybe. But he's not. He's a sick puppy."

I agreed, "He sucks."

Chet continued, "Under the category of megalomania and delusions of grandeur, Bulus ibn al-Darwish is not content to have become the leader of Al Qaeda in the Arabian Peninsula. According to an Al Qaeda defector who knew him, al-Darwish has bigger ambitions. He sees himself as the supreme leader of Yemen.

The prodigal son returns and takes over. He wants to unify and purify Yemen, to kill or kick out all foreigners. And while he's at it, he wants to wipe out all political opposition, including the Westernized intelligentsia in the cities, and then he'll move on to the armed opposition, including the al-Houthi rebels, the tribal sheiks and warlords, and the South Yemen secessionists."

Sounds like a lot of work. But maybe he'd enjoy it.

Chet continued, "Al-Darwish wants to restore Sharia law in Yemen and make the country into a medieval theocracy."

I asked, "How can we help him?"

Chet nodded in understanding and maybe agreement. I think everyone in this business was a little tired of trying to save these people from themselves. It was a thankless task and usually counterproductive. If left to their own devices, they'd find a century they were comfortable with—maybe the tenth century—and go live in it.

The problem was assholes like bin Laden and al-Darwish who engaged in attacks on the West. If they were smart, they would cut this shit out and the West would ignore them—as long as the oil kept flowing.

On that subject, Chet told us, "Yemeni oil is not important to us now, but geologists believe there are vast oil deposits in Ar Rub al Khali, the Empty Quarter, which straddles the undefined border with Saudi Arabia." Chet said, unnecessarily, "We want to control that oil with the Saudis."

Of course we do.

Chet continued, "Aside from that consideration, if al-Darwish actually did gain power in Yemen, our political analysts are certain that Yemen would become a big Al Qaeda training camp, as Afghanistan was, and that Bulus ibn al-Darwish, the American, would surely export violence—not oil—to America." Chet let us know, "Aside from avenging the Cole, *that* is what is at stake here."

Right. It always comes back to oil and to protecting the homeland against terrorism. The terrorist thing I get. The oil...well, produce more corn alcohol. You can drink it, too.

Anyway, Chet changed the subject and continued, "The Panther is also known within Al Qaeda as al-Amriki—the American. Oddly, this is not used in a pejorative sense. There are a number of men in Al Qaeda and other Islamic groups who are known as al-Amriki. But it is our understanding that Mr. al-Darwish does not like this nickname. Possibly this reminds him that he is an outsider here—just as he was an outsider in America."

His whole life might have been different if he'd just called himself Paul, or even Al.

Chet went on, "Our sources tell us that al-Darwish often misses the nuances of Yemeni culture, society, and even the language, which is understandable for someone who spent their first twenty-five years or so in another culture. Al-Darwish tries to compensate for this by acting more Yemeni than the Yemenis, and more Islamic than the mullahs. But in the end, he has no tribal affiliation, he wasn't born in a mud hut, he never raised goats, he doesn't chew khat, and most importantly he was not imbued by his father and male relatives with the warrior ethos that is common here. And yet he's come a long way, mostly because he's been a successful jihadist, and because Al Qaeda has suffered from the loss of so many leaders, in battle and in assassinations—Israeli bombs, American Hellfires, and unfortunate accidents." Chet smiled, gave himself a CIA pat on the back, and added, "Also, maybe al-Darwish does sometimes think logically like an American, and therefore he's made some good career choices, plus he's had some luck in murdering people."

Brenner said, "I think it was more than luck. The *Cole* was an intelligence failure on our part."

Chet, a member of the intelligence establishment, didn't like that and he stayed silent. Well, Chet was not here just to avenge the *Cole*, but also to redeem the reputation of his Company. Everyone is driven by something.

Chet picked up his train of thought and said, "Think of an Italian-American from, say, New Jersey, who goes to his ancestral Sicily to join the Mafia. His accent and mannerisms are wrong, but his head and heart are in the right place. People such as this may be accepted and even trusted, but at the end of the day... well, they are different."

Right. You can take the boy out of New Jersey, but you can't take New Jersey out of the boy.

Chet added, "Al-Darwish's American background might impress most Yemenis, but it does not impress the Bedouin, who would be distrustful of anyone born and raised outside of Islam." He said, "Sheik Musa is not impressed, and this is another reason why Musa would betray al-Darwish, al-Amriki."

I guess. But the A-team are *real* Americans. Like, Christians and all that. Chet, I thought, was overanalyzing this. But that's what the CIA does.

Chet further informed us, "Regarding the warrior

thing, al-Darwish has gone out of his way to be a hands-on warlord. We're sure he was present when the Belgian tourists were killed, and he's led his jihadists in attacks against Saudi soldiers on the border. But for some reason he didn't lead his men in the failed attack on the Hunt Oil installation—maybe God told him to sit it out—and I'm sure that didn't look good to his close lieutenants or his jihadists. Plus, The Panther has just had another setback with the failed ambush on our convoy. So when Sheik Musa requests The Panther's presence at this meeting to negotiate the sale of the Americans, Bulus ibn al-Darwish, the weirdo from Perth Amboy, has little choice but to be there—to be The Panther, and to meet with the great tribal sheik on equal terms, man to man, Yemeni to Yemeni, warlord to warlord." Chet concluded, "That is my analysis."

Either Chet had been here too long or I'd been here too long, because some of this made sense to me.

So we all sat there for a minute as the Otter continued toward Marib, sipping our drinks, thinking about Bulus ibn al-Darwish. Killing this guy would be good for everyone, including maybe Mr. al-Darwish himself, who didn't seem to enjoy life. But when you kill these guys, they become martyrs, and they go on beyond death.

And yet maybe when all was said and done, that's where he belonged. Dead. Remember the *Cole*.

Chet asked, "Any questions? Any comments?"

No one had either and we all returned to our seats.

Kate said to me, "Chet is overconfident. This thing could easily go the other way."

"We all know that."

So, did I now have my question answered? Like,

how could someone born in America, in a free and open society, raised in material comfort and educated in a liberal atmosphere, become a fucking terrorist? A murderer.

Maybe. But not completely. The answer wasn't in the externals of life. The answer was deep in Bulus ibn al-Darwish's head. The mind excludes external reality, or processes it differently, and justifies nearly anything.

No matter what kind of society we created, the terrorists, the murderers, the bullies and the wife-beaters and the sexual predators and all the rest would always be with us and among us.

So, no, I still didn't know how Bulus ibn al-Darwish got to where he is, and what happened on that long, strange journey from Perth Amboy to Marib. Only he knew that.

And in the end, it didn't matter. It only mattered that he died very soon.

The big, lumbering Otter flew on through the night, toward our rendezvous with Bulus ibn al-Darwish, who I imagined was sleeping now, unaware that his fate had been discussed and sealed. Or someone—maybe the voice in his head—had tipped him off and it was *our* fate that had been sealed. We would know soon enough.

The pilot said, "Landing in about an hour."

CHAPTER FIFTY-FIVE

The cabin was pitch dark, and I couldn't even see Kate sitting next to me, but we were holding hands. I wondered if Chet and Buck were holding hands in the dark.

I could feel our speed and altitude decreasing, and I reached across Kate and opened the shade. There were no lights on the ground, but the moon illuminated a silvery expanse of jagged hills. I estimated we were at about three thousand feet, traveling at less than 200 MPH. It was 2:45 A.M., so we must be close.

Kate glanced out the window, but didn't have anything to say. In fact, no one had much to say since Chet's briefing, and the cabin was quiet except for the drone of the prop engines.

The PA crackled and the pilot said, "About ten minutes."

It's times like this when you wonder what the hell you were thinking that got you in situations like this. I remembered what my father used to say to me when I got in trouble with my friends: "An idiot will try anything. That's how you know he's an idiot."

The pilot informed us, "Transponders are set correctly. Our designated road runs east–west, and we'll come around and land from the east." He added, "Light winds, good visibility."

The Otter began a tight left turn, then leveled out and continued at the same speed and altitude. We were now lined up with the electronic transponders that marked the road.

The pilot left the PA on so we could hear him transmitting on his radio. "Night Visitor One, this is Night Visitor Two. Read?"

A few seconds of silence passed, then we could hear the faint response coming through the PA speaker. "Night Visitor Two, this is Night Visitor One. Over."

The voice had a distinct Arabic accent—nit veeseetor tow—and I thought of Brenner's objection to the Arab pathfinder. I could see his point.

The pilot transmitted, "Any dust?"

Again, a long silence, then a response that I couldn't make out over the PA speaker.

Kate asked, "What did he say?"

I hoped he said, "Get the hell out of here," but the pilot said to us, "He reports no dust tonight."

Chet got out of his seat and opened the cockpit door so we could have visual contact with the pilots in case things started to go downhill.

Chet then said, "Shades down. Lights on so we can get our weapons."

I pulled down my shade, and we all turned our overhead lights on and made our way to the rear.

Buck said to Kate, "Please put your balto on over your clothes." He explained, "Sheik Musa and his men would be offended to see a woman dressed in men's clothing."

I added helpfully, "No cross-dressing here. This is not New York."

Kate said something unladylike, but pulled her balto from her bag and slipped it on over her mannish attire.

We all retrieved our weapons and returned to our seats and buckled up.

I assured Kate, "Sheik Musa won't give you a second glance."

"Lights off," said Chet. "Shades up. Give a holler if you see anything that doesn't look right."

Kate put her shade up and we both looked out at the terrain, coming up fast. It was much flatter here than it had been a few minutes ago when we passed over the hills. I thought I saw a light here and there, but mostly it was a dark landscape, though the moon was bright enough to reveal some isolated areas of cultivation.

The Otter was in its final approach and it was getting a little bumpier as we came in lower.

The pilot came on the PA and said, "Night Visitor has wished us a safe landing."

Well, that was the final okay, and we had truly reached the point of no return.

I had this mental image of Tariq with a gun to his head, surrounded by smiling jihadists while The Panther and Sheik Musa were having a good laugh as they sharpened their daggers. Or maybe Tariq was in on it, too, and he was high-fiving Musa. Right?

The aircraft suddenly decelerated, and the pilot said, "Two minutes."

Chet said, "As soon as the aircraft comes to a halt, we jump out and take up defensive positions in the drainage ditch on the left side of the road."

Is that an FAA-approved procedure?

But there was some good news, and the copilot called out, "Predators report no negative indications."

Great. But how can they tell? Good-guy and bad-guy white robes and AK-47s all look alike. Right?

The high-mounted wings gave us an unobstructed view below, and we were all focused on the terrain outside the windows.

I didn't see anyone or anything in the dim moon-lit landscape below. No people, no vehicles, no build-ings. Just rocks, dry flatlands, some scrub brush, and a few stunted trees. The roadside drainage ditches, how-ever, had some vegetation, and this would give us good concealment—and also good concealment to anyone waiting for us.

Chet informed us, "We're going to put down in the middle of our designated landing strip, then roll out past the end of the transponders."

Right. Just in case the bad guys were waiting at the end of our expected rollout. But the bad guys knew this trick, too, and they'd be farther down the road.

The pilot said, "About thirty seconds."

Kate said to me softly, "Well, we're not drawing fire."

"That's good." In fact, if there *were* bad guys down there, they wouldn't shoot the Otter out of the sky; they'd let us land and get out, then shoot up the Otter, then try to take us prisoner. Well, that wasn't going to happen.

Chet called out, "Order of exit—me, Paul, Buck, John, Kate, and Zamo last."

At about fifty feet above the narrow dirt road the Otter's engines suddenly got quieter and we dropped quickly. The reinforced fixed landing gear hit hard, and we began a jarring series of bounces over the rough road, throwing up a cloud of dust. The aircraft fishtailed, but the pilot kept it on the road.

The pilot was pressing hard on the brakes and the Otter was decelerating rapidly.

Chet said, "Unbuckle, get ready to move." He stood, slung his rifle, and moved quickly toward the rear door as the Otter was still rolling out. Before the aircraft stopped, Chet opened the door, letting in a cloud of dust.

Everyone stood, slung their rifles, and lined up in the aisle. I asked Buck, standing in front of me, "How do you say in Arabic, 'Don't shoot. I'm an American with diplomatic immunity.'"

Buck replied, "I'll do the talking, you do the shooting."

Buck's okay for an upper-class, Ivy League, State Department bullshitting twit.

Chet grabbed a few bags from the luggage bin as the aircraft lurched to a sudden halt. He called out, "Let's go!" then threw the bags out and jumped after them. Brenner and Buck did the same, and as I got to the door, the copilot came up behind me to shut the exit door and said, "Good luck. See you on the return."

Is this a round trip? I threw my overnight bag out, said "Geronimo," and jumped the three or four feet to the ground.

Kate was right behind me, then Zamo, and we all scrambled into the drainage ditch with our baggage.

The Otter's door closed, and a second later the engines roared and the aircraft began accelerating rapidly down the road.

If this was an ambush, this was when the Otter would begin taking fire. I divided my attention between my surroundings and the big, lumbering aircraft, which was quickly disappearing in the dark. Within ten seconds, I saw the Otter pitch up and go airborne at a very steep angle. No tracer rounds followed it, and I knew we were okay—for the moment. In fact, we were alone in the middle of Al Qaeda territory.

CHAPTER FIFTY-SIX

Chet said to keep low and keep still.

But Brenner, ex-infantryman, said, "You don't stay where you were seen taking cover. Follow me. Leave the equipment."

So we ignored the CIA guy and followed the combat vet through the drainage ditch in a running crouch.

After about fifty yards, we stopped and Brenner and Zamo crawled out of the ditch and scanned the dark road and countryside through their rifle-mounted nightscopes.

Brenner, looking east toward the direction we'd flown in from, said, "I see a vehicle on the road, moving this way, no lights."

Chet was on his sat-phone and he said, "Tariq. This is Mr. Brown."

I thought his name was Morgan.

Chet listened, then asked, "Is that you in the vehicle near the touchdown spot?" Then, "Okay, keep coming."

We could hear the vehicle now and we all poked our heads above the brush and peered through our nightscopes at a small pickup truck that was approaching slowly.

As it got closer, I could see a man behind the wheel, but no one was in the passenger seat—and hopefully there were no jihadists crouched in the rear. The truck stopped where we'd jumped out of the Otter.

Chet said into the phone, "Keep coming."

The pickup truck continued on.

Chet said to us, "Stay down, cover me," then he stood and raised his hand toward the truck, which came to a stop next to him.

Tariq stayed in the vehicle and he and Chet shook hands through the window and exchanged a few words. Chet said to us, "Pile in the rear."

So we all stood and jumped in the rear of the small pickup. Chet hopped in beside Tariq, who did a U-turn and took us back to our baggage, which we quickly collected, and off we went, up the bumpy dirt road we'd landed on.

Following Brenner's lead, we were kneeling on one knee, scanning the terrain through our rifle scopes. All I could see through my scope were long stone fences that penned in a few sheep and goats. Zamo was standing, steadying his sniper rifle on the roof of the cab as he peered ahead through his nightscope. It seemed to me that his left arm was definitely hurting.

Aside from that, so far, so good. We were on the ground, six cowboys in the middle of Indian Territory. But where was the cavalry?

I reminded everyone, "I thought Sheik Musa's guys were going to provide an armed escort."

Buck replied, "We can't see them, but Musa's tribesmen are all around us."

If you say so. Did that goat just wave to me?

Buck also told us, "Musa himself will meet us up the road."

What else does he have to do at 3 A.M. in Marib province? I mean, for five million bucks, I'd even go to Brooklyn to meet Musa in his new deli.

Kate was looking a bit tense, so I patted her cheek and said, "Don't forget your veil when you meet the sheik."

Anyway, after about a half mile, Tariq turned off the road onto a goat path or something, and up ahead I could see six white SUVs parked around a stone hut. Tariq stopped, and Chet got out and said to us, "Okay, let's go meet the sheik."

So we threw our bags out, opened the tailgate, and jumped down.

Tariq did a U-turn and off he went, back to the road to collect the transponders for the next idiots who wanted to land on a road at night. Hopefully that would be the Otter coming back to pick us up.

The stone hut was another fifty meters up the goat trail, so Chet said to leave our stuff there, and he and Buck led the way toward the hut. Kate remembered to wrap her hijab over her hair and around her face, and Buck suggested we sling our rifles as a show of trust and respect. Hey, why don't we just drop our rifles and walk with our heads tilted back to make it easier for them to slit our throats? Is that culturally sensitive enough?

Anyway, we were long, long past the point of no return on this one, so we strode confidently and cheerfully toward the hut, humming, "We're off to see the wizard."

No one was coming to greet us, so we marched

right up to the hut. I would have knocked, but there was no door.

Buck entered first and called out, "As-salaam alaikum!"

No one shot him, and I heard several voices returning the greeting, "Wa alaikum as-salaam!" Did someone say, "It's jambiyah time"?

Buck invited us to enter, and we all squeezed through the short, narrow doorway into the small hut.

The hut was lit with two kerosene lamps that hung from the ceiling beams, and around the stone walls, sitting on nice carpets, were six bearded gentlemen in white robes, wearing jambiyahs. All of them had AK-47s leaning against the walls, and in front of them were little piles of green leaves, the breakfast of champions.

One guy was resplendent in his snow white robes and jeweled jambiyah, and his head was crowned with a shiwal that looked like it was embroidered in gold. Must be the sheik.

Buck said to us, "It is customary that we all greet each man, individually, using your first name, beginning with the most senior. Follow my lead." He informed us, "They will not stand, but that is not a sign of disrespect." He further advised, "Kate, you just stand by the entrance. Eyes on the floor, please."

I need a picture of this.

Anyway, Buck began by greeting Sheik Musa, the guy with the golden hat, and Sheik Musa made the intro to the guy next to him, whom Buck greeted in Arabic, as Chet greeted Sheik Musa in English, and Musa replied in Arabic, and Mr. Brenner was now calling himself Bulus, and round we went, Bedouin by Bedouin. The Arabs don't generally shake hands, but we all nodded our heads in respect. Hi, I'm John. What's your name again? Another Abdul. At some point in the round-robin I got confused and greeted Zamo.

Anyway, that over, the American men were invited to sit, and Buck advised Kate to keep standing near the door. So we five gentlemen squeezed in between the six Bedouin, whose deodorant had quit a few weeks ago.

Sheik Musa said something and Buck said to us, "The sheik offers us khat, but we will decline. It's all right to say no."

I protested, "Let's have some khat, Buck."

Buck said something to the sheik and he nodded, then ordered one of his guys to pass around bottled water from a crate. Brenner, who was closest to Kate, passed a bottle to her. Then someone passed a pizza-sized piece of flatbread, and everyone broke off a piece. Pass the Cipro, please. Kate took a piece of bread from Brenner, though I didn't see how she could eat or drink without dropping her scarf and causing a ruckus. Not my problem. I was a man amongst men. Fuck Manhattan. Fuck 26 Federal Plaza. Hello Bedouin. Where's my camera?

So with cocktails and hors d'oeuvres served, Buck addressed Sheik Musa in Arabic, and the sheik was listening intently, or he was wasted on khat, and he nodded a few times. Some of the other Bedouin were speaking to Buck and to one another.

Chet knew a few words of Arabic, too, and he used them, but Bulus Brenner kept his Arabic to himself.

Recalling Captain Dammaj who hid his English from us, I asked Buck, "What are these nice people saying?"

Buck replied, "They are confirming our under-standing."

"Right. Five million bucks."

"And they confirm that they've received the letter from Prince Imad of the Saudi royal family."

"Wonderful." I smiled at Sheik Musa and said, "Prince Imad is tops." I gave the prince a thumbs-up.

Buck suggested, "Please be quiet."

Right. I do the shooting.

On that subject, I looked at Zamo on the other side of the room. He'd been sitting very still the whole time, but his eyes were moving around from Bedouin to Bedouin, who undoubtedly reminded him of Afghan tribesmen. I had the impression he was com-mitting these faces to memory in case he saw them again through his telescopic sight. Good boy, Zamo.

Anyway, Buck and the Bedouin jabbered away for a minute or so and Buck announced, "The sheik con-firms that the van with the Predator ground monitor-ing equipment is here and is now at the safe house, guarded by his men."

Great. And speaking of Predators, the sheik had to know they were circling overhead and that he had to be nice to us or he'd be toast.

Buck, Musa, and the other Bedouin exchanged a few more words and I heard, "al-Numair" and "Al Qaeda" a few times. Also, the word "Sana'a" came up, as did the word "Mukhabarat," the PSO. It's good to get briefed by the locals, except when the locals have their own agenda.

I looked at Sheik Musa in the dim, flickering light. The guy looked imposing, almost regal, and he had a terrific beak—one of those ice cutters like on the bow of a ship. His eyes were alert despite the hour and the green chew, and his skin looked like my leather La-Z-Boy, which, by the way, I missed. I don't like sitting cross-legged.

The sheik said something that caused his five guys to nod and make approving sounds.

Buck said to us, "The sheik says we are brave men."

Hey, Kate's got balls, too. And we're all idiots.

Buck continued, "He says that we have a common enemy. Al Qaeda. And of course, he says, the enemy of my enemy is my friend."

Right. Until that changes. Not to mention that the sheik was doing business with our common enemy.

The sheik stood and we all stood. He said something, and Buck translated, "He says we all must be tired from our long journey, so he will have us driven to our house and he wishes us a pleasant sleep, and a safe stay in Marib."

He probably said the same thing to the Belgian tourists. But they didn't have five million bucks and Predator drones, so maybe this time he meant it.

Buck thanked the sheik and his trusted lieutenants for their hospitality and their assistance. The sheik decided to shake and he offered his hand to Buck, who took it and shook it. Then we all sheiked. Except for Kate, who kept admiring the carpet.

There were a dozen armed guys outside now, all dressed in robes, and they indicated three of the big Toyota Land Cruisers, which already had our bags in the back. So Kate and I got into one of the SUVs with two Bedouin up front, Buck and Chet got in another, and Brenner and Zamo got in the third. And off we went, down the goat path and onto the road, heading west, toward the rugged hills in the distance.

I announced to Kate, who was still wearing her scarf over her face, "I want to be a warlord."

No reply.

"But I want to ride a white Arabian stallion. Not a Toyota."

"The only leather that's ever come in contact with your ass is your La-Z-Boy."

Wives bring you down to earth. Every day.

Anyway, it seemed to me that Sheik Musa could be trusted. If he was going to turn us over to The Panther, he'd have already done that.

On the other hand, this was the Middle East. The land of the mirage, the shimmering pond in the sand that drew you farther into the deadly desert, and when you arrived at the lifesaving water, it disappeared, and you discovered the bones of those who'd been there before you. You discovered death.

CHAPTER FIFTY-SEVEN

The three-vehicle convoy continued on the road that had been our landing strip, toward the hills we'd flown over. Buck and Chet were in the lead vehicle, Kate and I in the middle, and Brenner and Zamo were bringing up the rear.

The SUVs had their lights off, but there was still enough moonlight to see the straight road, which was also defined by the drainage ditch. I doubted if the Bedouin had valid driver's licenses, but they seemed to know how to drive in the dark. I mean, camels don't have headlights. Right?

Question: If the tribes rule here, why don't these guys have their headlights on? Answer: There are other tribes. One is called Al Qaeda.

The night was cool and dry, and the starry sky was crystal clear. The half moon was sinking into the western hills and it would soon be dark, except for the starlight. The desert at night has a stark beauty, an otherworldly feeling that somehow changes your mood and your perception of reality. Maybe this was what drew The Panther to Yemen.

All Arabs were once nomadic, and they originated here, in Yemen, so maybe the desert was in The Panther's genes, and in his blood. So it would be good for him to die here. Better than dying in New Jersey, which is redundant.

Our driver and shotgun guy were jabbering away to each other while also speaking on their cell phones. Maybe they were calling their wives. Hi sweetheart, yeah, gotta work late again. Don't wait up. I'll grab some roadkill.

Actually, neither of these guys spoke English, which limited our ability to gain some knowledge of their culture and their lives. That was the good news. On the downside, I had no idea what they were saying. Hopefully it was all good.

Within half an hour we were at the base of the jagged hills, which, as I saw from the air, were more like a series of eroded plateaus or mesas.

The road suddenly got narrow and twisty as we climbed up a ravine on the face of the plateau. The moonlight was almost gone, but the drivers continued on without their headlights. As we continued up the plateau, the road became a stone-strewn goat path. Then a chipmunk path.

Finally, we came to the top of the plateau, which was not flat like a real plateau, but was studded with huge rock formations. I mean, if the flatlands below were the middle of nowhere, then this place was the top of nowhere. Good place for a safe house, though.

There was still some moonlight up here, and as we drove a few hundred meters across the rocky plateau, I could see the outline of a large structure up ahead, silhouetted by the sinking moon.

The vehicles all stopped near the structure, and I saw Buck and Chet getting out of the SUV. This must be the place.

Kate and I got out and so did Brenner and Zamo, and we all stared at our new safe house away from home.

Rising in front of me was a square tower, like the tower houses in Sana'a. This one was about six stories high with randomly spaced windows beginning about twenty feet from the ground. The top floor of the tower was formed by open arches, and attached to the tower was what looked like a walled-in courtyard, probably the camel parking lot. The entire structure was built out of the only building material around here: rocks. And more rocks. Also, I noticed, the tower sat at the edge of what looked like an eroding cliff.

Buck was speaking to two Bedouin who'd come out of the courtyard to greet us, and we all walked over to them.

Buck said to us, "This is called a nawba, a watch-tower or fortress, and it's named Husin al-Ghurab— the Crow Fortress."

Right. You'd have to be a crow to get here.

Buck, sounding like a realtor trying to dump a white elephant on clueless yuppies, said, "It was the property of Sultan Ismail Izzuddin ibn al-Athir."

I wouldn't want to have to sign autographs with that name.

Buck told us, "The sultan was expelled with all the Yemeni sultans after the 1967 revolution and he lives in exile in Saudi Arabia. Sheik Musa, who is his nephew, keeps an eye on the fortress for his uncle until he returns someday." Buck informed us, "A floor of the tower has been cleaned for us, and bedding provided."

I wasn't going to think about that bedding, but I did ask, "Water? Electricity?"

"Neither," Buck assured us. He continued, "The top of the tower, the mafraj, is good for observation and sat-phone communication."

Right. The room with a view. Pass the khat, and call home. Hello, Tom? You're not gonna believe where I am. Asshole.

I inquired, "Is there an excrement shaft in the tower?"

"I'm sure there is."

Great. Maybe I can get Chet to stand under it.

Anyway, Buck exchanged a few words with one of the Bedouin, who led us toward the small fortress. I didn't see a door in the tower, but there was a gated opening in the courtyard wall, and we passed through into the large walled-in area where two small SUVs were parked. Also parked in the courtyard was a thirty-foot box van. The van was white and on the side was something written in Arabic and a picture of a red fish. On top of the van's roof was what appeared to be a refrigeration unit, though I knew this was the sealed dome of a satellite dish.

One of the Bedouin spoke to Buck, who said to us, "The two Hiluxes are for our use. The truck, as you know, is our communication system and Predator monitoring station." He also let us know, "This truck came into Sana'a Airport with me on the C-17."

Which was another reason why Kate and I couldn't get a ride on the C-17. I wondered what else or who else was on board.

Buck and Chet went over to the two rear doors and satisfied themselves that the doors were padlocked. Buck had a penlight and he confirmed, "This is the same padlock from the aircraft, and the wax seal is intact."

Good. Recalling the Trojan horse, I wouldn't want to discover that the van was now filled with jihadists. Or explosives.

Buck also informed us, "I have the padlock key." He added, "We'll open it in the morning."

It *is* morning, Buck.

Chet confirmed that he had the backup key, then he unlocked the cab and checked that the ignition key was in the ignition lock, and Buck and Chet confirmed that they both had backup keys. Also, one of the Bedouin turned over a set of keys to Buck.

So obviously a lot of this had been pre-planned back in the States, including getting Mr. and Mrs. Corey to come along. And now it was all coming together here, in Marib province, where apparently the planners knew The Panther would be. And they knew this before the attack on the Hunt Oil installation. It occurred to me, not for the first time, that what I was seeing was the tip of the iceberg. That in itself was not unusual—you only need to know what you need to know in this business. But I had the feeling that there were things I *did* need to know that I didn't know.

Brenner asked Buck, "How did the truck get here?"

Buck replied, "We turned it over to two of Sheik Musa's men at the airport, and they drove it directly here, without incident, accompanied by a discreet armed escort of SUVs, also provided by Sheik Musa."

The sheik was earning his five million Yankee

dollars. He was incentivized. Money talks. Loyalty is just a word.

Kate, who was still recalling the thrilling ride up to this plateau, asked, through her scarf, "But how did they get this truck up *here*?"

Buck informed all of us, "My driver, Amid, told me there is a better road coming up here from the north." He also let us know, "Amid says the sheik has that approach guarded."

Great. So we were protected by men and terrain. Unfortunately, protected also means boxed in. But to be positive, like Buck, I had to admit that Sheik Musa seemed to be living up to his end of the deal. And yes, we couldn't have done any of this without the help and cooperation of a local sheik. In this case, Sheik Musa.

The three Toyota Land Cruisers that we'd arrived in pulled into the courtyard and the Bedouin began unloading our bags.

Two of the Bedouin led us across the courtyard to a narrow opening in the base of the stone tower, and as we entered the dark space, I immediately recognized it as the livestock level, complete with dirt floor and pungent smell. I looked up at the high ceiling for the opening of the excrement shaft, but I couldn't see much in the dark.

The two Bedouin had flashlights and they pointed the beams at a stone staircase, then led the way up.

The second floor of the six-story walk-up was the diwan level, the prime space in the tower, and the Bedouin stopped there and said something to Buck, who said to us, "This is where we stay."

Our hosts began lighting kerosene lamps, illuminating the large open space that was the entire floor of the tower, supported by stone pillars. A few window openings let in some moonlight, air, and birds. The floor was rough-hewn planks covered with bird shit, and the walls were unplastered stone. This whole place was basically a pile of rock, like a medieval castle, hardly fit for a sultan, let alone six finicky Americans. Well…maybe not all of us were finicky. In any case, this was where we'd be returned to after our staged kidnapping to await the Al Qaeda guys who'd be taken here by Musa's men to see us. Hopefully that wouldn't be a long wait.

As my eyes adjusted to the light of about ten lanterns, I spotted our bedroom—six ratty blankets spread over a bed of straw. I also noticed a small wooden shed in the far corner, and if I had to guess I'd say that was the master bathroom, a.k.a. the excrement shaft. Other than a washbasin on a stand, there wasn't a single stick of furniture in the place, leaving lots of room for a La-Z-Boy recliner. Also, it goes without saying that the only items in the room from the twenty-first century were us.

Buck said, "All the comforts of home."

Right. If home was Dracula's castle.

Buck also said, "Someday, when this country is at peace and tourism returns, this will be a quaint country inn." And he named it for us: "The Sultan's Crow Fortress. Fifty dollars a night."

"Great view," I agreed. But don't put the reception desk under the excrement shaft.

A few of the other Bedouin began arriving, carrying our bags, which they deposited near the straw and blankets. Nice chaps. I would have tipped them, but if things went right, they'd be sharing in Musa's five million bucks. Warlords and tribesmen can do okay if they get tight with the Americans and the Saudi princes. I need to look into a career change.

Buck exchanged a few more words with our Bedouin bellboys, who, said Buck, wished us good sleep. But why were they grinning and fingering their jambiyahs? Or was it just the light?

With all the Bedouin gone, Kate pulled off her scarf and balto and threw them on a blanket.

Brenner quipped, "Hussy."

That got a laugh—the first laugh in a long time. I think we were all relieved to have gotten this far.

We were one step closer to The Panther, and soon he'd know we were here, if he didn't already know. Let the hunt begin.

CHAPTER FIFTY-EIGHT

We spent a few minutes exploring our accommodations, discovering a crate of bottled water and a sack of flatbread.

Chet excused himself to go up to the mafraj to make a sat-phone call, probably to his station chief in Sana'a, or maybe mission control in Washington. Also, he'd want to speak to the Predator ground control station, which could be anywhere in the world. And while he was doing all that, he might as well have a little chew.

Zamo was in his sniper mode, going from window to window, sighting his rifle and nightscope at the surrounding terrain. He let us know, "Great perch. But too many rocks down there for cover and concealment. But no concealment between the rocks."

Zamo saw life through a telescopic sight. Someone else would see a nice view. Position determines perspective.

Kate and I looked out a window into the courtyard below. The six Bedouin who'd driven us here were apparently staying with the two Bedouin who'd been here watching the van, and I could see them all in the fading moonlight sitting in a circle on a carpet that they'd rolled out. They seemed to be brewing tea on a camp stove and chatting away.

Chet returned and informed us, "Predators report no unusual or suspicious activity in the area."

I guess Chet told them that the eight Bedouin they saw in the courtyard were on our side. The problem with aerial reconnaissance, no matter how sophisticated, was that it couldn't read minds or hearts and couldn't predict intentions. That's where human intelligence—HUMINT—came in. The problem with human intelligence, however, was that not all *Homo sapiens* were sapient.

Brenner, who was our security guy, said, "It's only a few hours to first light. So I suggest we stay awake, and at first light we'll post two lookouts, and sleep in shifts."

Everyone, I was sure, was sleep-deprived, but you gotta do what you gotta do to avoid the Big Sleep.

There was a carpet laid out near our sleeping area, which I guess was the living room, and Buck suggested we sit.

Kate and Brenner brought over some bottled water and the sack of bread.

So we sat cross-legged, drank water, and passed around the flatbread, which Buck said was called tawwa, which must mean "fresh last week."

Chet didn't seem particularly hungry or tired and I guessed he had a chew in the mafraj. Maybe there was something to this stuff. Chet asked if we minded if he smoked, reminding us half-jokingly, "We could all be dead tomorrow anyway." Well, if you put it like that, Chet . . .

Zamo chose to pull guard duty and he extinguished all the lanterns except one near the carpet, then he began walking from window to window with his night-scope, while also keeping an eye on the stairwell.

When Zamo was on the far side of the room, I said to Brenner, "I think his arm is hurting."

Brenner replied, "He's taking Cipro."

It's times like this when you realize you need a good-looking female doctor.

We chatted a minute about Sheik Musa and the Bedouin tribesmen, and Buck, the old Arabist, told us, "The Yemeni Bedouin are the most romanticized of any people in the Mideast, and they are also the most feared and the least understood."

Now you tell us.

Buck continued, "In semi-desert regions like Marib province, the distinction between the traditional nomadic Bedouin, who herd goats and ride camels, and the Bedouin who are settled farmers is becoming blurred." He explained, "Decades of drought and centuries of war and climate change have caused the settled Bedouin to return to a nomadic way of life." He further informed us, "Marib is the cradle of Yemeni civilization, and in ancient times it was more green and more populated. Now that the desert has arrived, the population is regressing to a pre-agricultural nomadic survival mode."

Chet, not a big fan of Arabs in general, said, "On all levels of society, these people are clinging more to their Korans, their guns, and to Sharia law."

Buck agreed, and said, "South Yemen in the seventies was becoming an open and enlightened society.

The British and the Russians had left their mark on the educated Yemenis, but that's all gone."

Along with the brewery.

"There is oil here," Buck also informed us, "but the Bedouin see virtually no money from this oil, and they resent that. Tourism could bring in revenue, but some tribes are hostile to foreigners, and the security situation has been made worse by Al Qaeda." He added, "Marib is economically depressed, politically unstable, socially unraveling, and it's becoming an ecological disaster as the desert encroaches."

I suggested, "This would be a good time for you to buy this fort cheap."

Buck smiled, then admitted, "Those of us who dream of a better Yemen—and a better Mideast—are fooling ourselves."

Chet said, "The only thing keeping the Mideast alive is oil. When that runs out, it's back to the Middle Ages here. Forever."

Buck advised, "Be careful what you wish for. When the oil runs out here, it runs out at your local gas station. But in any case, you see what the situation is here in Marib, and we are trying to...let's say manage this instability to further American interests." He confessed, "It's about the oil—and Al Qaeda is not good for oil exploration, oil recovery, and oil pipelines. The tribes would be more helpful with eliminating Al Qaeda if the Sana'a government was fair to them, but this idiot Ali Abdullah Saleh is stealing the oil from the tribal lands and keeping the money. Al Qaeda promises to share the wealth, which is why they're tolerated by the tribes. So we need to do a delicate balancing act between the government, the tribes, and the Saudis, who are in conflict with the Yemeni government over the oil and most other matters."

Chet said, "But first we have to wipe out Al Qaeda, who is a new player. And a new problem."

Buck agreed, then informed us, "Sheik Musa is a particular enemy of President Saleh and the government."

"And why is that?" I asked.

"Because," Buck replied, "Musa is strongly allied with the Saudi royal family, Musa has blown up a few pipelines to the coast, Musa demands millions in oil revenue, and Musa has defied the central government on every issue and at all levels. Also, Musa is a rallying figure for the other sheiks who are looking for a strong leader to unite them against the central government."

In other words, Sheik Musa was on President Saleh's hit list. And one of those thoughts in the back of my mind now became clear—Bulus ibn al-Darwish might not be the only chief who was going to die in that Hellfire attack. This was what Buck was talking about in New York.

Everyone else seemed to be thinking this too, but no one had any comment.

Chet, who also had to know about this—he had operational control of the Predator drones—said, "Some things that we do may not seem right, but we do what is best for our country." He added, "There is a bigger picture."

There always is in this game.

Buck expanded on that and said, "We need the cooperation of the Yemeni government in our war against Al Qaeda, and President Saleh needs a favor."

Got it. This was a two-fer. We get rid of Musa for the Yemeni government, and the Yemeni government lets the Americans mount an operation in Marib using Hellfire missiles to get rid of The Panther. The Panther deserved whatever he got from us, but Sheik Musa, even if he was a double-dealer, did not necessarily deserve to die in an American Hellfire attack.

I suggested, "This might not be a nice way to repay Sheik Musa for his assistance and his hospitality."

Buck shrugged, then said, "Accidents happen—which we will explain to the Saudis." He assured us, "If we kill The Panther, the sheik's family and tribesmen will get the five million dollars."

"The late sheik would have been happy to know that."

Kate, who was processing all this, said to Buck and Chet, "You owed us this information before we got here."

Buck replied, "You had the information in New York. You should have come to the conclusion."

Brenner, the former soldier who'd probably killed more bad guys than all of us put together—except for Zamo—said, "I've killed soldiers in ambushes who were just walking along and were not an immediate threat to me, but I've never killed anyone who was helping me."

Chet replied, a bit sharply, "*You* are not killing anyone." He added, however, "This was not part of my plan, but it is now part of my orders." Chet further reminded us, "I don't need your cooperation or your approval. I just need your silence."

Buck said nicely, "We've given you this information as a courtesy. You, John, Kate, and Paul, are professionals and you're intelligent enough to see that we are playing the long game. The goal here is to wipe out Al Qaeda in Yemen, and to avenge the Cole, and also to avenge 9/11 and all the other Al Qaeda attacks on Americans and American interests—and other Western interests—and to keep Yemen from becoming a staging area for Al Qaeda attacks against our country."

Don't forget the oil.

Buck continued, "We may not like President Saleh, but he's all we've got between us and Al Qaeda in Yemen."

Right. So what's one dead Bedouin sheik? I don't even know the guy. Still, it sucked.

Also, this new information explained why Chet was not concerned about a possible run-in with Colonel Hakim and his PSO. The fix was in, and the government in Sana'a was giving us a free hand to deal with The Panther if we would also deal with Sheik Musa while we were at it.

So every time I got a new piece of information, something that didn't make sense made sense. It was like peeling layers off an onion; you keep seeing more onion, and the onion gets smaller. And at the center is something you probably don't want to see. But I don't think I've gotten there yet.

I said to Chet, and to Buck, "I'm assuming the sheik is not going to get vaporized at the same time as The Panther. Correct?"

Chet replied, "Correct. But soon after we're safely out of here."

Right. We can't be here in the van watching Sheik Musa getting blown up by a Hellfire while the sheik's

Bedouin tribesmen are here watching us, and maybe speaking on their cell phones to their Bedouin buddies, who are with Musa at the scene of the attack. Like, "Hello, Abdul, an American Hellfire just landed on our sheik."

Also, the Bedouin at the scene of the attack needed to finish off the Al Qaeda guys. And we needed to drive from here to the scene of the carnage and collect bits and pieces of The Panther and his lieutenants before we jumped on the Otter.

I asked, "How do you explain this terrible accident to the Saudis?"

Chet gave me a straightforward CIA answer. "You have no need to know that."

Buck assured us, "I'm personally unhappy about having to…sacrifice Sheik Musa, but Chet and I wanted you to understand why there will be no interference from the Yemeni security forces."

Chet said, "We're also telling you about this because you may be asked about this someday. John, you, Kate, and Paul don't know anything about what happened after you left Marib."

I didn't reply. But it occurred to me that Chet, by telling us not to say anything after we got out of here, was also saying that if we didn't promise to keep our mouths shut, we might not get out of here. Or was I getting paranoid again?

Something didn't smell right here, and I needed to talk this over with Kate and Brenner as we'd agreed back in Aden. Meanwhile, I said to Chet, "Okay. I understand." I looked at Kate and she understood, too, and said, "I'm all right with this."

Brenner got the drift and said, "Sorry, I wasn't paying attention."

Chet nodded, then stood and went to his duffel bag and retrieved a bottle of Hennessy cognac. Good move, Chet.

He passed the bottle around and we all took a swig, then passed it again.

The sky outside the east-facing windows was starting to get light, and I could hear birds singing. A black crow perched on a windowsill, then flew in and walked cautiously toward us.

Chet broke off a piece of bread and threw it toward the bird, who went right for it. Don't shoot the bird, Chet.

More crows arrived and more bread was tossed, and the cognac kept making the rounds.

The dawn came, which was one of the few things you could rely on in Yemen, along with death.

Kate and I volunteered for the first guard shift and we relieved Zamo, who literally hit the hay and was quickly asleep with his boots on and his rifle across his chest.

Buck, Chet, and Brenner also lay down with their guns and boots on, and Buck said to everyone, "We leave here for the Bilqis Hotel about one P.M. Then we go to the ruins." He assured us, "You'll enjoy the ruins."

I'm sure the Belgians enjoyed them, too, except for that problem.

I went to an east-facing window and watched the flat, distant horizon growing lighter.

Somewhere out there was Bulus ibn al-Darwish. It was hard to believe that this weirdo loser from Perth

Amboy had come all the way here to metamorphose into The Panther.

And harder to believe I'd come all the way here to find and kill him.

In a day or two we'd see whose life journey had come to an end.

CHAPTER FIFTY-NINE

The straw bed was predictably uncomfortable, and the wool blankets smelled like camels or something.

And now a few words about the excrement shaft; it was basically a six-story indoor outhouse, with a hole in each floor. A squatter. So you had to look up, and if you saw someone's ass above you...well, too much information. More importantly, the shit shaft could be a means of escape. Always look for an escape.

Buck was kind enough to share a roll of TP he'd thought to steal from the Sheraton. A man who thinks of TP is a man who thinks of everything.

We heard noises in the courtyard and I looked out the window. The eight Bedouin were kneeling and prostrating themselves on their rug, facing Mecca, which around here is northwest.

Buck informed us, "They are performing the noonday salat—the call to prayer."

I looked at my watch. Right on time.

Buck also informed us that we were invited for

lunch with our Bedouin hosts, but unfortunately the invite did not extend to Ms. Mayfield, who though she dressed like a man was still a woman. Kate took that well—she didn't give a shit and she didn't want to wear her balto anyway—and she took some bread and water up to the mafraj to keep an eye on our surroundings. Good thinking.

So the men of the A-team went down to the courtyard, and the Bedouin, who pride themselves on their hospitality to travelers, had hot tea for us and bowls of hot oats or groats, or some weird glutinous cereal product.

They also gave us plastic spoons, and Buck commented, "They eat almost everything with their fingers, but they've discovered spoons for certain foods."

There's progress. Next, napkins.

So we sat cross-legged on the rug with our eight new Bedouin buddies and we ate this glop, which was at least hot. The tea was herbal and did nothing for my cognac headache.

It was a little cooler here in the highlands than it was in Aden at this time of year, and on that subject my calendar watch showed that we'd rolled into March. You lose track of time when you travel back a few centuries.

The stone wall around the courtyard was about ten feet high, and the wooden gate was closed, so no one could see us, but neither could we see anyone approaching. There were, however, a few stone platforms around the walls for observation and shooting. I glanced up at the mafraj and saw Kate standing in one of the open arches with her M4 slung across her chest, enjoying the view through a pair of binoculars.

The Bedouin seemed very interested in our M4s, and Buck, against all regulations and common sense, allowed them to examine his weapon, which they passed around, fully loaded. They seemed amused by the compact size, small caliber, and light weight of the automatic carbine, and they passed around one of their AK-47s to show us what a real rifle felt and looked like. Yours may be bigger than mine, Abdul, but I can paint you red in a heartbeat with my little rapid-fire plastic toy.

The Bedouin also seemed interested in Zamo's sniper rifle, but Zamo wouldn't let them touch it and they seemed to respect him for that. But they did want to know about it, and Brenner said it was okay to let them know what this rifle could do.

So Zamo, through Buck, explained that he was carrying an M24 Sniper Weapon System, and it fired a 7.62mm NATO cartridge, which he said could blow their heads off at a thousand meters, though I don't think Buck translated all of that.

Zamo also said that the U.S. supplied this rifle to the IDF—the Israel Defense Forces—and again I was sure Buck did not translate that provocative fact to these Muslim gentlemen.

They were fascinated by the telescopic sight, and Zamo explained that the magnification was adjustable from three-power to nine-power, meaning that at its highest power, an object that is nine hundred meters away looks like it's only a hundred meters away.

The Bedouin seemed impressed, and since I can't keep my mouth shut, I said to Buck, "Tell them that Zamo has killed fifty men with this rifle."

Buck hesitated, then translated, and the Bedouin all looked at Zamo like he was a rock star. That's worth another bowl of glop.

Anyway, I wasn't sure this was a good strategy. I mean, on the one hand, it was good for Musa's men to know that Zamo could put a bullet through someone's head from a kilometer away. On the other hand, why advertise what you can do? People should find out the hard way.

Bottom line, though, there was a warrior thing going on here, and the Bedouin wanted to make sure they weren't being overly nice to a bunch of girly men. You know, like guys who dragged a woman along to do a man's job.

I mean, we weren't even on the same planet with these people, but in some strange way I was getting to like them. I thought about bringing two or three of them back to 26 Federal Plaza to show some of the suits what real men looked like.

Maybe I was getting a little carried away with the moment.

Brenner, though, said to the team, "They remind me of the Montagnard tribesmen in 'Nam—basic, no bullshit, brass balls, and ready to kill without hesitation."

Zamo, who also fit that description, and who'd fought men like this in the mountains of Afghanistan, said, "Guys like these are hard to the core. They live, eat, and breathe war."

Right. This must be what the world looked like a thousand years ago. But the tribesmen did have modern weapons and vehicles and also cell phones. Things to make killing easier and more efficient. Nice to see, though, that they still carried their jambiyahs and dressed weird. Good for tourism.

Regarding the warrior thing, I'd worn my jambiyah for the occasion and the Bedouin thought that was funny. Unfortunately, by custom, none of us could draw our daggers to pass around—only to cut someone's throat—but the Bedouin next to me, a guy named Yasir, examined my sheathed jambiyah, and Buck told me, "He says it seems of excellent quality," making me feel better about the hundred bucks it cost me.

Our hosts insisted we have more tea and they pushed some khat on us that Buck took "for later." Chet, of course, had his own stash, but he said, "Shuqran." Thanks.

So I liked the Bedouin. Too bad we were going to whack their sheik. Hey, Abdul, it's nothing personal. Just business.

Or for all I knew, Chet intended to whack these guys, too, on our way out of here. It would be nice if Chet told us what the hell was going on. But he probably figured that unpleasant information should be rationed out, like shit in a spoon.

Anyway, the picnic lunch was finished and it was time to examine the van.

Buck thanked our hosts for the meal and conversation, and Brenner told Zamo to keep Kate company. I asked Zamo how his arm was and he said it was fine, but it wasn't. I also asked him to bring Kate some tea and gruel in case she was tired of tawwa bread. I am a great husband.

Chet, Buck, Brenner, and I moved across the courtyard to the twenty-first century.

The thirty-foot windowless box van sat on the

chassis of a Mitsubishi truck, and the van didn't open into the driver's compartment.

I asked Buck, "What does this say?"

Buck read the Arabic on the van. "'Musa'—which means Moses—'purveyor of fine fish.'" He also translated, "'Fresh to market from the Red Sea.'" Buck smiled and said, "Someone in Washington had fun with this."

Right. A real knee-slapper. Musa—Moses—Red Sea. Get it?

Anyway, Chet did the honors and unlocked the padlock, opened one of the rear doors, and jumped inside. We all followed.

The interior of the van was high enough for us to stand, and the walls, floor, and ceiling were lined with Kevlar and, I assumed, lead. Unsurprisingly, there were no fish inside. Instead there was a large electronic console in the front of the van, similar to a pilot's cockpit array. In front of the console and the twin monitors were two swivel chairs.

Chet took a seat in the left chair and he invited Buck, the oldest gentleman, to take the other seat. Brenner, ever vigilant, stood against a wall where he could divide his attention between the courtyard and the van.

There were a few more electronic devices mounted on the long walls of the van, and on the floor were metal boxes marked with the names of the replacement parts that they contained. More importantly, there were three cardboard boxes of canned food on the floor and I read the American brand labels—mixed fruit, mixed vegetables, and, maybe as a joke, canned tuna. Who's supposed to eat this shit? Where's the chili? Is this the best those bastards in Washington could do?

Chet said, "The electronics are low-powered so that everything can be run from our onboard generator." He hit a switch on the console, and a few seconds later I could feel the vibration and hear the steady hum of the generator from somewhere under the floor. Chet also informed us, "There are electrical outlets in here so we can recharge our sat-phones, cell phones, and hand-held radios."

Chet glanced up at a gauge on the panel. "Voltage is steady," he announced as he hit another switch and the dark console suddenly lit up. "We're in business."

Chet played with a few dials, then switched on the two monitors and we immediately saw moving images on the screens—aerial shots in full color of two differ-ent landscapes gliding by.

Chet read some electronic info on his screen and said, "The right-hand monitor is the view from a Predator drone that is, at this moment, running autonomously—meaning without an active ground pilot. The drone is executing a reconnaissance flight over this area using a pre-programmed computer plan."

The screen showed the rugged and unpopulated terrain west of here that we'd flown over last night. It was easy to see how guerrilla forces could disappear in those hills. And easy to imagine The Panther making those hills his home. It might not be so easy to draw him out of there. But with the right bait—Mr. and Mrs. Corey and company—The Panther might come out to eat his former American compatriots.

Chet said to us, "The images from both these

Predators are transmitted by Ku-Band satellite link to this van and also to a ground control station where one or two pilots and aerial image specialists are sitting at a console similar to this one—in a van or in a room."

I asked, "Where is the ground control station?"

Chet gave me a CIA reply. "It doesn't matter. Could be in Saudi Arabia, could be an Air Force base in the States, and it could even be at Langley." He also had a Zen reply. "With satellites and advanced electronics, real time is more important than real place. The only real place that matters is the target."

Whatever. Thanks. I also asked, "Where are the Predator drones based?"

Chet replied, "I really don't know or care to know." He added, "And neither do you."

Actually, I do, asshole. But I let it go.

Chet continued, "The pilots have a flight control stick like this one, but my stick is deactivated."

Have you tried Viagra? Maybe less khat.

Chet confessed, "I'm not a pilot. But I can speak directly to the pilots and instruct and guide them regarding what I want or need." He reminded us, "I am the one who has operational control of the Predator drones and the Hellfire missiles during the execution stage of the mission." To make sure we understood, he also said, "I, along with the aerial image specialists, identify who or what is the target and I give the order to the pilots to launch the Hellfires."

Right. That's why it's called the execution stage.

Chet, on a little power high, also said, "This is what we call SAA—stealthy aerial assassination." He concluded, "Awesome."

Indeed. But not as awesome as me blowing The Panther's head off with my Colt .45.

And then there was our sometime friend Sheik Musa, who was a full-time enemy of our sometime friend President Saleh. Some genius in Washington had figured out how to make this plan work for everyone. The idiots in Sana'a feared the tribes more than they feared Al Qaeda, but the Americans were obsessed with wiping out Al Qaeda. So if we put those two obsessions together, then Washington and Sana'a, the so-called allies, could solve their different problems in the same way—a thunderbolt out of the blue. It actually *was* a smart idea, and even Sheik Musa, who knew a few things about double-dealing, would appreciate it. Probably The Panther would, too. They could both talk about it in Paradise.

Chet directed us to the screen in front of him and said, "That's us."

And sure enough, there was a nice overhead image of the Crow Fortress on the screen. The slow-flying Predator drone was flying a tight circle over the plateau and we could see a few hundred meters in all directions, including the road we'd taken here, and also the better road that came from Marib in the north.

Chet punched in a command on the keypad and the Predator's camera enlarged the view of the fortress. I could see the Bedouin in the courtyard, sitting around, chatting and chewing.

Chet said, "The Predator is about ten thousand feet, but with the fifteen-hundred-millimeter computer-enhanced zoom lens, the view looks like it's from about fifty feet."

In fact, one of the Bedouin was taking a leak against

the stone wall and I could see he wasn't circumcised. Okay, maybe I assumed that.

Chet put his headphones on and made radio satellite contact with the ground control station. "Clean Sweep zero-zero, this is Clean Sweep six-six. Commo check."

A few seconds later, a voice with a nice Down South accent came over the speaker. "Sweep six-six, loud and clear."

Six-six said to zero-zero, "I called in a sat-phone sitrep at five hundred hours, and I repeat, all okay."

"Roger, six-six." Zero-zero inquired, "Whacha'all have for lunch down there? Looked like grits." Zero-zero laughed.

Hey, were we having fun or what?

Chet, a.k.a. six-six, and zero-zero, whoever and wherever he was, exchanged some technical information, then Chet said to zero-zero, "I'll give you a heads-up when Clean Sweep is mobile—two small white SUV Hiluxes that you see here, plus the three white larger SUV Land Cruisers containing local escorts. Destination, Bilqis Hotel, Marib. Details to follow."

"Roger. Predator Two will follow. Predator One remains on station above you." He added, "Both heavy." Meaning armed.

Chet also told him, "I'll be away from this station until the team goes mobile, so if you see anything in the area that we should know about, call my sat-phone. If I'm not able to receive, you have the five other sat-phone numbers."

"Roger." Zero-zero asked, "Anything further?"

"Negative."

Zero-zero said, "Good luck."

Chet signed off and said to us, "I wanted you to see and hear that everything is in place, and that we are covered by the Predators."

Wonderful, Chet. But can the Predators predict if our Bedouin buddies are going to smell a double cross and whack us? Or worse, turn us over to The Panther? No. We have to figure that out ourselves.

Chet explained a few other features of the Predator monitoring equipment and informed us, "As I said in Aden, during the execution stage of the operation we'll have four Predators. Two over the target, and two over this location for security, each armed with two Hellfires." He further explained, "I can split these two screens and watch all four images."

I asked Chet, "How do we get this million-dollar van out of here?"

"We don't. We can't."

"So the Predators take care of it?"

"Correct."

That's why my taxes are so high. I said jokingly, "I assume we will be out of the van when the Hellfire hits it."

"That would be a good idea."

The show-and-tell seemed to be finished, so Chet, Brenner, and I each took a case of canned food and we exited Moses' fish van and Buck locked it up.

Buck said we should share our bounty with our hosts, to reciprocate for their hospitality—thanks for the glop, here's a can of tuna—so we did that and made our way back to the second floor of the tower.

Chet seemed upbeat, and I imagined he saw the end

in sight—the end of all his work and his frustration, and the end of his time here in Yemen.

All we had to do now was go check into the hotel, go see the stupid ruins, then get kidnapped.

And then wait for The Panther.

CHAPTER SIXTY

At 1:15 P.M., the A-team, minus Chet Morgan, piled into our two Toyota Hiluxes, compliments of Sheik Musa. We left most of our personal items in the Crow Fortress because we'd be coming back later today as kidnapped Americans, also compliments of Sheik Musa. But we did take our overnight bags with us for when we checked into the Bilqis Hotel for a few days of sightseeing fun, cut short, unfortunately, by the above-mentioned kidnapping.

The purpose here, according to Chet's complex plan, was to make it appear that we were tourists driving in from Sana'a. And at the same time, we were obviously not tourists, so therefore we were Americans on a mission. Hopefully our arrival would come to the attention of The Panther, who would conclude, correctly, that his former compatriots were here to kill or capture him. The Panther, in turn, would make plans of his own to kill or capture *us*. But before he could do that, a third player—Sheik Musa—would upset The Panther's plan by doing what the Bedouin do best: kidnapping foreigners for ransom. And the first person who was offered the chance to buy the Americans would be The Panther. The Panther, theoretically, would not smell a setup or a trap because it would appear that Sheik Musa just happened to get wind of the American presence and was taking advantage of an opportunity.

And that's the way the CIA thinks. It's not the way I think—I'm a bit more direct and a lot less into the smoke and mirrors that the CIA loves. But, hey, it's their show and Yemen is the stage, so maybe they've got this one right. We will see.

Anyway, in my overnight bag, if you're interested, I'd packed some bottled water, a can of tuna, and yesterday's boxer shorts. Also, Chet had provided each of us with a toilet kit to complete the appearance of overnight visitors from Sana'a.

We were carrying our concealed sidearms, we wore our Kevlar, and our M4s were across our laps. Kate also wore her black scarf so she could cover her hair and face when appropriate, like when she was kidnapped by Muslim gentlemen who would be offended to see her face.

The three Bedouin Land Cruisers that had taken us to the Crow Fortress would now provide a discreet escort for us to the town of Marib, to prevent a real kidnapping—or assassination—by someone else. Two of the Land Cruisers had gone ahead to check out the road, and the third would trail behind. And if anyone noticed the Bedouin's SUVs, they would or should appear to be stalking us, not protecting us.

The two Bedouin who'd been here watching the Predator fish van when we arrived were staying here to hold down the fort, literally, and to provide security for

Chet. I hoped they didn't cut his throat. We needed Chet to talk to the Predator pilots.

As for CCC—Command, Control, and Communication—the Bedouin had provided Chet, Buck, and Brenner with local cell phones so the convoy could stay in touch if a security situation arose. Also, we had our hand-held radios for point-to-point contact with one another, and our sat-phones, though they'd work only if we had clear sky, meaning not in the vehicles, unless we had our heads out the window.

The order of march was: Hilux One, Buck driving and Zamo riding shotgun; Hilux Two, Brenner driving, me riding shotgun, and Kate in the rear.

We gave the two lead Bedouin Land Cruisers a five-minute head start, then Chet wished us a safe drive to Marib, a nice day at the ruins, and a pleasant kidnapping. Chet thought that was funny. He waved good-bye, then stepped into the van, where he could watch us getting abducted as he ate a can of tuna.

Buck and Zamo pulled out of the courtyard, and Brenner, Kate, and I followed.

Buck didn't head back to the steep ravine we'd come up, but headed north and west across the plateau, following the tire tracks of the two Land Cruisers ahead of us, whose raised dust we could see in the distance. Follow that Bedouin.

The gray, rocky plateau looked like the video images from the first moon walk. This place could use another forty days and forty nights of rain.

Brenner said to Kate and me, "I've been thinking about this thing with Sheik Musa."

I asked, "You mean about us killing Sheik Musa?"

"Yes." He admitted, "I see the reason for it. But I don't like it."

"Neither will Sheik Musa," I assured him. But the sheik *would* know the reason for it.

"Aside from the ethical issues, there are practical issues," said Mr. Brenner.

"You mean like, how do we explain to the Saudis that we whacked their Bedouin ally?"

"Yes, not to mention that the Bedouin here in Marib and elsewhere may not want to do business with us in Yemen ever again." He let us know, "They have long memories and they hold grudges for about a thousand years."

I said, "Maybe Washington has figured out a way to make Sheik Musa's death look like an accident or that someone else did it."

Brenner replied, "Assuming we use a Hellfire missile on Musa, that reduces the possible murder suspects to one. Us."

"Right. But it's not murder. It's termination with extreme prejudice, in CIA lingo." I added, "Sounds better."

Kate, who's been hanging around me too long, said wisely, "When you see a double cross, look for a triple cross."

Brenner agreed with Ms. Mayfield and added, "As we said in Aden, let's keep an eye on this and talk to each other."

Paul Brenner was a good guy, a former cop, and a straight shooter. True, he seemed to have Restless Dick Syndrome, but, hey, we all have a little of that. I wondered what Clare was doing now. Probably floating in the pool with Howard. How did I get from Paul Brenner to Clare Nolan? Could I have RDS?

Anyway, it was interesting that the three of us didn't completely trust the two intelligence officers. Comes with the territory, I guess, though we were all on the same team. Whatever lies we were told and whatever information Chet and Buck withheld was based on the strong principle of need-to-know. If we needed to know, we'd be told when the time came, and if we never needed to know, we'd never know. And what we didn't know couldn't be gotten out of us if we were captured—or worse, interrogated by a congressional committee. And what we don't know can't hurt us. Wait. Let's back up on that one.

Anyway, Kate, Brenner, and I were now on the same page, and we had our antennae up, to mix metaphors.

Brenner's Bedouin-issued cell phone rang and he answered and listened. Are you allowed to drive while talking on your phone in Yemen? I guess if you're allowed to fire assault rifles out your window, you can talk on your phone.

Brenner hung up and said, "That was Buck seeing if these cell phones actually worked."

"Good thinking," I agreed. Not that we didn't trust Sheik Musa; it was the Yemen Telephone Company that could be the problem. Especially here. Lots of dead zones. Also, I wondered how the Bedouin paid their phone bills.

Brenner informed us, "Buck said he got a cell phone call from Chet saying Predators report no suspicious activity ahead."

Didn't they say that on the road to Aden?

The north side of the plateau, as I saw on the

Predator monitor, was a gradual slope, and Buck followed the rutted track as it descended into the flatlands. I could see a road in the distance, a few vehicles, houses, and cultivated areas.

Halfway down the slope, I spotted a white SUV parked behind a big rock formation, and as we got closer I saw four men with AK-47s sitting on the rocks. Obviously they were Sheik Musa's men, guarding this approach to the fortress as promised. Our two lead escort vehicles had apparently sailed right past these guys, so everyone was in the same tribe. Right? On the other hand, this was Yemen and nothing was as it appeared.

Buck slowed down, and so did we. It's times like this when you fully appreciate fully armored vehicles. Beats the hell out of a Kevlar vest.

I took my M4 off safety and told Kate to do the same. Brenner drew his Colt .45.

Buck stopped about fifty meters from the men and they waved their arms to continue on. Like, "Come on, people. Haven't you ever seen four guys in robes with assault rifles?"

The cell phone wasn't ringing, so I guess Chet and the Predator pilot were okay with these guys—or the pilot was about to put a Hellfire on them.

Our trail vehicle caught up to us, then our handheld radios all crackled and Buck's voice said, "They're Musa's tribesmen."

Buck continued on and we followed. I reminded Kate, "Scarf. Don't make eye contact unless you're firing at them."

Brenner thought that was funny.

As Buck drew abreast of the Bedouin, he lowered

his window and did his peace greeting—As-salaam alaikum—which they returned. So I lowered my window and called out, "Shalom aleichem!"

Kate said, "That's Hebrew, John."

"Sounds the same."

We continued on, and our trail escort dropped back.

We came down into the flatlands and followed the rutted track north through a sparsely populated area of small irrigated fields and brown pastureland where skinny goats wandered around looking for something they might have missed. Life here is tough. And short.

Brenner, Kate, and I made small talk, because to keep talking about the mission sounds like you're a little jumpy. And that was not cool.

Brenner informed us, "I once flew to the Marib airstrip from Sana'a—about a year ago, before things started to go downhill here." He explained, "Some VIPs from Capitol Hill wanted to see the ruins, and I led an advance team from the embassy to check out the security situation."

"And?"

"And I strongly suggested they not come here." He added, "It was okay for tourists...until the Belgians disappeared last summer. But I couldn't guarantee the safety of congressmen and their staffs."

I said to him sternly, "Are you telling me that you missed an opportunity to get rid of some congressmen?"

That got a laugh. I'm way funnier than Paul Brenner.

Anyway, we intersected a paved road, and Brenner followed Buck, who turned right—east toward Marib.

Brenner said, "This is probably the Sana'a-Marib road. The one we saw the sign for in Sana'a."

Right. And I thought Sana'a wasn't safe. Sana'a was looking like Geneva about now.

Bottom line about third-world travel is this—there's always someplace more dangerous and fucked up than where you are. In this case, however, we had reached the very pinnacle of Places You Don't Want to Visit.

We continued east, toward Marib. I was looking forward to a cold beer and a hot shower in the hotel before I got kidnapped.

CHAPTER SIXTY-ONE

As we approached Marib, Brenner suggested to Kate that she rewrap, and I assured her that the black scarf made her look more mysterious—and thinner.

We entered Marib, which was a ramshackle but bustling town—the provincial capital, according to Brenner, and the only market town for many miles.

The main street was a collection of open-front shops and stalls, government offices, and a few gas stations, but not a single saloon. But to make the town lively, nearly every male was carrying an automatic rifle. I also noticed there was nothing ancient about the place, and Brenner explained, "This is New Marib. Old Marib is a few kilometers from here and it's mostly abandoned."

"Why?"

"The Egyptian Air Force bombed it in 1967."

"Why?"

"Marib was royalist during the civil wars, and the Egyptians were allied with the republican government in Sana'a."

These people went to war the way kids choose up sides for a football game. And we're getting involved in

Yemen, why? They don't need us to help them kill each other.

The town smelled of diesel exhaust and dung, but I also caught the aroma of the outdoor grills in front of the food shops and my stomach growled. Maybe I should eat that tuna.

I asked Brenner, "Where exactly is the Hunt Oil installation?"

He replied, "About sixty miles north and east of here. At the edge of Ar Rub al Khali—the Empty Quarter." He told us, "It's a hundred twenty degrees Fahrenheit in the summer."

"How come oil is always located in shitty places?"

"I don't know. But I do know that geologists think the oil fields are huge and extend into Saudi Arabia. We thought we could control this oil because Yemen is weak. But then Al Qaeda showed up." He also told us, "This installation is heavily fortified, but the oil wells can't be expanded until the threat from Al Qaeda is eliminated."

"Right." I asked, "Who the hell would want to work there?"

"There are only about a dozen Americans there. The rest are foreign workers and Yemenis. And mercenaries for security."

"How much do the mercenaries get?"

"I hear about two thousand a week."

I said to Kate, "Honey, I just found us a better job."

"Send me a postcard," said Mrs. Corey through her scarf.

Anyway, we continued to move slowly along the dusty, vehicle-choked main drag, and I asked Brenner, "Where is this hotel?"

"The Bilqis is just outside of town."

"Did you stay there?"

"No. I was just here for the day. But I checked it out for the VIPs. It's not bad."

"Is there a bar?"

"No. Strictly forbidden in Marib province."

The cold beer in my head evaporated like a mirage. I hate this place.

Buck made a right turn and we followed.

Brenner informed us, "The other guests at the Bilqis are foreign aid workers, oil company visitors, the occasional American intelligence officer, and other shady characters." He thought that was funny, and added, "The passports of arriving guests are faxed to the National Security Bureau and the Political Security Organization, and photocopies are also sold to Al Qaeda. Or maybe they get them for free."

"Probably free."

The town thinned out after a few hundred yards, and up ahead on the right I could see a long white wall with two open gates, which Brenner said was the Bilqis Hotel.

Buck pulled over before we got to the gates and so did Brenner.

We had to get our rifles out of sight, which was why we had Chet's duffel bag.

I noticed that the two Bedouin Land Cruisers in front of us had continued on, and the trail SUV now passed us and kept going.

Buck and Zamo were out of the Hilux and we got out, leaving our M4s in the vehicle.

Zamo was carrying the duffel bag, which was long enough to hold his rifle and big enough to hold our four compact M4s.

Zamo threw the duffel in the backseat, then got in the Hilux and gathered up our weapons and magazines, putting them in the bag and wrapping them in what looked like Chet's underwear.

Buck asked us, "Did you enjoy the ride?"

Why does he always say things like that?

No one replied, which was his answer. Buck briefed us, "We check in, go to our rooms, and meet in the lobby in, say, thirty minutes." He assured us, "That's enough time to enjoy a quick shower."

Buck had new passports for us—same names, same photos, but different passport numbers, and these passports had standard blue covers, i.e., not diplomatic. Now we were tourists.

I asked Buck, "Where did our escort go?"

"I don't know, but I know we'll see them again later."

"Will they be kidnapping us?"

"Correct."

"Good." I wouldn't want to be kidnapped by strangers.

Zamo had finished wrapping our hardware in Chet's underwear, and we all got back in our vehicles.

Buck drove up to the big double gates and we turned in.

At the end of a long drive was an unexpectedly large hotel of white stucco, consisting of two three-story wings that flanked a single-story entrance structure. The hotel grounds were landscaped and irrigated and it was almost jarring to see green.

Buck stopped in front of the lobby doors and we pulled up behind him.

We all got out and a bellboy appeared who put our

overnight bags on a cart, then took the duffel, which was, of course, heavy. Buck, pretending he had only a few words of Arabic, said something to the bellboy, then to us he said, "I told him to be careful. We have expensive cameras and photographic equipment in there."

Right. I guess telescopic sights could be photographic equipment.

Anyway, we moved into the large, oval-shaped lobby, which was nearly empty.

Buck informed us, "This hotel was constructed in the late seventies for tourism and archaeologists, and this entrance lobby is supposed to be built in the oval shape of the Mahram Bilqis Temple."

Who gives a shit?

He further informed us, "There was a lot of hope for Yemen after the civil wars and revolutions of the sixties and seventies." He let us know, in case we didn't, "It hasn't worked out."

The desk clerk was all smiley, like we were the first guests he'd seen this year. We produced our new but worn passports, which he handed to another guy to photostat for the PSO, the National Security Bureau, and the hotel, with a fourth copy for Al Qaeda. Another guy looked up our reservations on the computer. On the check-in card, we gave our Yemen address as the Sana'a Sheraton, where I assumed we were all registered. The CIA has good tradecraft and lots of money to make it work.

Because no one had been shot or kidnapped in Marib since last August, the rooms were fifty bucks a night. I noticed we were booked for four nights.

The desk clerk, Mr. Karim, asked in English, "How was your drive from Sana'a?"

Well, we first drove to Aden and got ambushed by Al Qaeda, then we flew in on a spy plane and landed on a dirt road at night, and some Bedouin gave us a lift to Dracula's Castle, and here we are. I replied, "We took the scenic route."

He nodded, but advised us, "It is good if you stay on the main roads."

"Are there main roads here?"

Buck, in the role of tourist, asked Mr. Karim, "Are any of the ruins closed to visitors?"

The clerk replied sadly, "Unfortunately the Mahram Bilqis remains closed." But he brightened and said, "I think, however, I can arrange a private visit for you."

Of course you can.

Buck asked a few more tourist questions while Brenner and Zamo kept an eye on our bags, and Kate stayed modestly quiet, admiring the floor.

So did we look like American tourists, or did we look like Americans who were trying to look like tourists? One of the guys behind the desk was definitely checking us out, especially Zamo. I mean, innocent faces aside, we were all wearing Kevlar and sidearms, which though covered by our bush vests could still be spotted by someone who knew what they were looking for. I had the impression that one of these guys behind the desk would be on his cell phone in two minutes talking to someone about us. PSO? Al Qaeda? Probably both. The good news was that the PSO was giving us a free hand—or said they were. The other good news was that Al Qaeda would soon know we were in town. Does it get much better than that?

Mr. Karim returned our passports and gave us four key cards.

He then asked if we'd like a dinner reservation, as though there could be a problem getting seated. Buck asked the clerk to book us for 8 P.M. Buck told us quietly, "This is where the Belgians had lunch before they went on to the ruins."

Thanks for that.

We followed the bellboy to the south wing, third floor, where our adjoining rooms awaited us. The bellboy showed Kate and me to our room, which was sparsely furnished, but not bad. Nice green lizard on the wall.

I went out to the big balcony and Kate followed. Below was a swimming pool in the shape of two attached ovals, so I guess ovals were the theme here. There was absolutely no one out on the terrace or in the pool.

Kate said, "This place is empty."

Maybe it had something to do with tourists getting kidnapped and murdered. I mean, even Europeans on a budget might find that unacceptable.

Kate said, "This all seems unreal."

"It's real."

"Do you hate me for getting you into this?"

"Ask me later."

She stayed quiet as we stared out at the empty pool, then asked me, "Is this going to be okay?"

"Why shouldn't it?"

She didn't reply.

So with Buck's time clock ticking, we went back in the room, undressed, and showered and shaved together to save time and water.

We got dressed and left our overnight bags and toilet articles in the room. What happens to the luggage of kidnapped tourists? We took the stairs down to the lobby. Never trust the elevator in a third-world country.

Buck and Brenner were looking at some tourist brochures, and Zamo had the duffel with our photographic equipment.

The desk clerk, Mr. Karim, came over to us and said, "It is not advisable for you to visit the ruins without an escort." He assured us, "I can obtain the services of three or four Bedouin within fifteen minutes."

Buck replied, "We're meeting some Bedouin at the ruins."

Who are going to kidnap us.

The clerk shrugged and further advised us, "Be careful."

Better yet, we're armed.

Our Hiluxes arrived and I said to Mr. Karim, "If we're late, hold our table."

We walked outside, and Buck said, "We'll go first to Old Marib, then to the Bar'an Temple—the throne of the Queen of Sheba."

"Will she be home?"

Buck smiled. "She was kidnapped." He said to Brenner, "I know the way. Stay close."

Goes without saying, Buck.

We got into the Hiluxes and off we went.

I said to Kate and to Brenner, "Just to remind everyone, the difference between a staged kidnapping and a real kidnapping is not always so clear."

Brenner replied, "That's what I've been saying."

I hear you.

CHAPTER SIXTY-TWO

We headed south on a paved but disintegrating road, and within ten minutes we turned off on a worse road, where up ahead, on a hill, I could see the dark tower houses of Old Marib.

We stopped near a crumbling wall at the edge of the city, and we all got out and looked around. We had clear views down the hill, and there was no one in sight.

Buck said to us, "Paul will stay here with Zamo. John, Kate, and I will go into the city for about half an hour of sightseeing."

I told Buck, "I've seen the South Bronx. I'll stay."

Kate said to me, "I want to see this and I want you with me."

I asked Buck, "If we're not getting kidnapped here, why are we here?"

"We need to be seen."

"There's no one around, Buck."

He informed me, "There are people around, and they notice everything and everyone in a place like this. Especially Westerners. And they all have cell phones and phone numbers to call."

Sounds like Kate's hick town in Minnesota.

Buck further explained, "We need to give any potential kidnappers enough time to discover we are here and call men together to kidnap us." He added, "Our kidnapping needs to appear to be real."

I see a CIA brainstorming session at work; clever people thinking of stupid things. Or Buck just wants to see Old Marib.

Regarding our kidnapping having the appearance of being real, I asked Buck, "Isn't it unusual for us not to have hired some Bedouin to be with us? Or National Security police?"

Buck replied, "There was a time when you could come here on your own. But it's not advisable now, though adventurous travelers—or unknowing travelers—still come here without armed escorts."

"Okay." I asked, "Are the Predators watching?"

"Of course."

I pictured Chet in his van watching us right now. Should I flip him?

Buck also said, "Our Bedouin escort is close by and we can call them if a situation arises."

Or when we're ready for them to kidnap us.

Zamo put the duffel bag with the serious guns on the hood of his Hilux and he and Brenner stayed behind to cover our backs.

Buck led the way and Kate and I followed him into the city, carrying only our concealed sidearms and a camera.

The dirt streets of Old Marib appeared deserted, but I noticed fresh goat droppings and recent foot-prints in the dust.

The mud brick tower houses rose as high as eight

stories, except the ones that had collapsed from age or were blown up by the Egyptian Air Force in Civil War Twenty-nine, or whatever. More than half the city was gone, but you could see the surviving foundations filled with drifting sand and rubble.

Buck said to us, "Several thousand people once lived here. Now maybe a dozen families remain."

"Well, parking's not a problem."

The place was creepy, and the dark mud brick buildings looked like high-rise haunted houses. It was deathly still, except for a weird wind that whistled through the streets and through the shells of the buildings, and small dust devils that appeared and disappeared in the roads and rubble. The words "post-apocalyptic" crossed my mind.

I mean, the place *smelled* dead—like old ashes and rotting...something.

I glanced at Kate, who seemed fascinated, but also anxious.

Buck said to me, "Be honest. Isn't this interesting?"

"No."

Buck chuckled. He was having a grand time, and he spotted a huge foundation stone in one of the tower houses, which he examined, saying, "This is from a Sabaean temple. See the Sabaean writing carved in the stone?"

Kate dutifully got closer and examined the whatever. I kept an eye on the street.

Buck also found a square stone column that had been incorporated into the doorway of the building, and he informed us, "This, too, is Sabaean. It's probably three thousand years old."

I asked, "What does the writing say?"

"It says 'Yankee go home.'"

Funny. But not a bad idea.

Buck also let us know, "This hill is actually the result of layer upon layer of civilization here. Someday, archaeologists will excavate this right down to the first human settlement on this spot."

And find the world's first delicatessen.

Anyway, it was time for a sit-rep, and I used my sat-phone to call Brenner.

He answered and I asked, "Anything happening there?"

"Negative." He asked, "Am I missing something good?"

"I see dead people."

"Get a picture."

"Roger."

So we continued to wander around, and Buck was all over the place, looking for bits and pieces of broken stone with this weird writing carved in it, which to me looked Martian. He took lots of pictures, and I was starting to believe we *were* tourists.

Buck asked us, "Do you want to go into one of the houses?"

"No."

"We can climb up to the mafraj and get a wonderful view."

"Buck," I said sternly, "these towers are on the verge of collapse. I don't even want to be in the *street* next to them."

"Well...all right. But if we see real kidnappers—or Al Qaeda—we'll have to duck into a tower house."

"I'd rather shoot it out on the street."

We continued on, and Buck, ever the instructor,

informed us, "Islam has an ambivalent attitude toward pre-Islamic culture and artifacts. Some Muslims see these ancient pagan cultures as visible evidence that the early Arabs were civilized and very advanced. But the fundamentalists reject anything that is pre-Islamic and pagan, and they often destroy these artifacts—the same as the early Christians destroyed and defaced the statues and temples of pagan Rome."

"Right. They knocked the dicks off the statues."

"Correct. The fundamentalists here do the same."

Can we leave now?

But he continued, "The Bedouin feel some affinity for these ruins. The Sabaeans are their direct ancestors. But people like Bulus ibn al-Darwish want to erase all evidence that a civilization existed anywhere in the Middle East before Islam." He added, "And that is why the Western archaeologists have been threatened here, and why so many attacks on Westerners have occurred in and around pagan archaeological sites here and elsewhere in the Middle East."

I thought that Westerners were attacked at archaeological sites because that's where Westerners went. And also because these places were isolated. That's what happened to the Belgians. They should have stayed in Sana'a. Actually, they should have gone to Paris.

But I got Buck's point. Westerners coming here were like people going to an African game preserve; the visitors want to see the wild animals, and the wild animals see the visitors as a lunch that walked into their dining room.

In any case, we were in the right place. Or the wrong place.

Buck reminded us, "The Romans besieged this

city, and Marib has been besieged dozens of times and survived until the Egyptian Air Force destroyed it in 1967."

Jet fighters with two-thousand-pound bombs are a bitch.

Buck looked around and said sadly, "War is senseless."

I think the old Cold Warrior was going soft. I mean, this was nothing compared to thermonuclear Armageddon.

We came into an open area that Buck said was once a souk. There were goats wandering around the square and also a few kids—meaning young children, not baby goats. Anyway, the kids—the children—spotted us and stared at us like they'd seen ghosts. I guess they don't get many tourists here.

Finally, they got their courage up and about ten of them ran toward us, yelling, "Baksheesh! Baksheesh!"

I said to Buck, "Tell them to walk with us and we'll pay them."

Buck nodded and said something in Arabic, and the children left their kids behind and surrounded us as we doubled back to our vehicles.

I mean, I hate to use children as shields, but they were getting paid.

About half an hour after we'd entered Old Marib, we came back to where we'd started.

Buck asked us, "Did you enjoy that?"

Kate said, "It was fascinating. Incredible."

Sucked.

We walked out of the ruins and I was happy to see Zamo and Brenner, who had not been kidnapped or murdered.

We paid off the urchins, and I advised them, "When you grow up, relocate." But stay away from Perth Amboy.

Brenner wanted to ride with Zamo awhile, so we switched and Buck got behind the wheel with me still riding shotgun and Kate in the back. Buck took the lead again and we drove down the hill, toward the next dead ruin, the throne of the Queen of Sheba.

I pictured the headline in the *New York Post*: *Five Yanks Yanked Seeing Sheba*. Or, *Bedouin Bad Boys Snatch Our Boys*.

Hey, it's all make-believe. Part of a clever CIA plan.

So how about this? *Panther Pulverized by Predator in Perfectly Planned Ploy.*

I like that.

But first, a friendly kidnapping.

CHAPTER SIXTY-THREE

We headed south from Old Marib and crossed a narrow bridge over a flowing stream, the first running water I'd seen in Yemen that didn't come out of a tap.

In fact, Kate said, "Nice to see a river."

Buck informed her, "There are no rivers in Yemen. That is a seasonal wadi, usually dry at this time of year, but the gates of the new Marib dam must be open upstream."

Right. Gotta water that spring khat.

Buck also informed us, "The old Marib dam was built about two thousand years ago, which made the Sabaean civilization possible. The dam collapsed in 570 A.D., the year Mohammed was born, which Muslims take as an omen." He explained, "The end of paganism, and the beginning of a new world."

That's how I felt after the collapse of my first marriage.

Buck also told us, "The new dam was built in the 1980s—fourteen hundred years after the old dam collapsed."

"Union problems?"

Buck also let us know, "A bridge limits your ability to go off-road."

Right. That's where I'd set up a kidnapping.

Anyway, within ten minutes we were approaching the archaeological site of Bar'an. I saw a white minibus parked on the dirt road, and a blue military truck, probably belonging to the National Security police.

Buck parked behind the truck, and Brenner and Zamo parked behind us.

We all got out and looked around. There were patches of scrawny trees here and there and date palms and also a few irrigated fields, but mostly it was brown dirt and dust.

Buck, too, was looking at the arid landscape and said, "The desert, when it decides to come, is relentless. The dam and the irrigation pumps are fighting a losing battle."

So are we. And ironically, so are the jihadists. There will be no winners here. Except the desert.

We weren't out of the vehicles two minutes before we were attacked by kids yelling for baksheesh, then souvenir vendors, then two young men who said they were guides for hire. And finally, an NSB officer butted in and offered protection for twenty dollars. He must be related to Captain Dammaj.

I hope there's an ATM around here.

But Buck was our ATM, and he gave the NSB officer some rials, then paid off the kids to beat it. He also gave the two guides a nice tip for doing nothing, and he spoke pleasantly to all of them in Arabic. Buck is a good American diplomat; he gives money to anyone and everyone.

The police officer was looking at us as though his instincts told him we weren't the clueless tourists we appeared to be. I wondered if he could tell we were wearing Kevlar, and if so, did he conclude we were carrying? Or did he think we were stupid enough to be here unarmed?

He said something to Buck, who translated for us. "He says the police are leaving, and we should not stay here too long."

As though these clowns could be of any help. But thanks for the tip. I said to everyone, "I wonder if these are the same NSB guys who took a hike on the Belgians."

No one replied.

Anyway, the Keystone cop left, but the souvenir guys, six of them, hadn't been paid off yet, and they were waving their wares at us—cheap jambiyahs, probably made in China; shiwals, one size fits all; sandals, ditto; and postcards.

Buck gave the souvenir vendors a few hundred rials, took a few postcards, and we were now free to approach the entrance to the ruin.

Zamo stayed behind to provide security, as per the plan, and the four of us walked to a stone arch that looked new, where four Bedouin sat, chewing, and they hit us up for an admission fee of about three bucks each. At the end of the day, it is the Bedouin who control all movement and all access here.

The ruin was elevated above the surrounding land, and we climbed up some stone steps and looked out across a few acres of excavations and broken walls surrounding a paved courtyard. Across the courtyard, at the top of a flight of steps, were tall square columns where a group of tourists stood listening to their guide. Nice ruins. Better than Marib, which was creepy. Time to go.

But Buck, our unpaid guide, said to us, "This is the Bar'an Temple, also known as the Temple of the Moon, and also known as Arsh Bilqis, which means the throne of Bilqis, which is the Sabaean name for Sheba." Buck continued, "Not far from here is the Temple of the Sun."

Makes sense.

"This temple was dedicated to the Sabaean god called Almaqah."

Please, someone kidnap me.

Buck went on awhile, as he does, and Kate, of course, asked questions. She's always trying to improve her mind, and as long as she doesn't try to improve mine, I'm okay with that.

Meanwhile, the real tourists were assembling in the courtyard with their guide, and I counted fifteen of them. I looked for my Sana'a pal, Matt Longo, but these were mostly middle-aged people, probably Europeans by their pale winter skin and atrocious footwear.

The guide led his clients toward the exit, and as they approached, Buck said something to the guide in Arabic, and they chatted a minute, then the tour guide moved on toward the minibus.

Buck said to us, "Half the tour group are German, the other half are Danes."

Totaling one bunch of adventurous idiots. Clueless in Bilqis.

Buck told us, "They're returning to Sana'a." He added, "No one stays here overnight anymore."

I inquired, "Why does anyone even *come* here?"

Buck replied with impatience, "To learn, Mr. Corey. To see history. To experience another culture."

Okay. I guess the Belgians experienced another culture.

Buck reminded me, "If you stay home, the terrorists win."

That's what everyone in New York said after 9/11, so we all went out and filled the bars and restaurants. Fuck Al Qaeda. Make that a double, bartender. God bless America!

But this was different. This was the belly of the beast. And for all I knew, the tour guide, the NSB officer, and everyone else here was on their cell phone right now telling someone there were American turkeys here to pluck.

Buck glanced at his watch and said to us, "This area will be deserted within half an hour. We'll wait until then, then we'll head back to the Bilqis Hotel."

Kidnapped at the oasis. Waylaid at the wadi.

Buck, with time on his hands, informed us, "The Western archaeologists won't return here, and the local authorities won't remove the drifting sand." He concluded, "In ten, maybe fifteen years, all this will be covered again, except for those columns."

Kate said, "That's sad."

Maybe they can put an oil well here.

Buck turned, looked toward the west, and said, "Those hills on the horizon are the ones we flew over, and where the Crow Fortress is." He told us, "The Yemenis believe that Noah's Ark came to rest in those hills after the Flood." He also told us, "About forty kilometers farther west of the Crow Fortress is where the Al Qaeda training camp is. Also somewhere in those hills is where we believe The Panther's personal hideout is located."

Maybe he's hiding out in Noah's Ark. I suggested, "The Predators should look for the Ark while they're looking for The Panther's hideout."

Buck reminded me, "The Panther is coming to us."

"Right." We had as much chance of finding The Panther as we had of finding the Ark. The Panther, however, would find us.

The sun was starting to sink in the western sky and I shielded my eyes as I stared at the distant hills. So the Crow Fortress was not too far from the Al Qaeda training camp, which would soon be pulverized by American fighter-bombers if all went well. And also up there in those desolate hills was Bulus ibn al-Darwish, a long way from New Jersey. And maybe Noah's Ark was sitting up there, too. A profound thought was taking shape in my mind, a unifying thread, perhaps, that would link all this together, and I said, "This place sucks."

Buck turned impatiently and led us down into the sunken courtyard. I noticed we were hidden from the road, and there wasn't a soul in sight. I drew my .45 and slipped it in the pocket of my bush vest. Brenner did the same.

Buck, addressing Kate and Brenner but not me, said, "This is the temple that some Mormon scholars believe is the place where their prophet Lehi came after he fled from Jerusalem in the sixth century B.C." He added, "It was here where Lehi is said to have buried the prophet Ishmael."

I hope Ishmael was dead.

I was really looking forward to my kidnapping.

Buck also told us, "The Mormons also believe that it was here that Lehi built a ship for himself and his family and sailed to America."

Hold on. Did that ship have wheels?

But Buck clarified, "There is strong evidence that there was a river here at that time which flowed to the sea."

Got it.

Buck led us across the courtyard and up fourteen—count 'em—wide and steep stone steps. At the top were five square columns, rising about sixty feet high. There was a sixth column that was broken, and Buck related a story about the symbolism of the broken column—something to do with the five undisputed pillars of Islam, and the one disputed pillar of the faith. I think he makes this stuff up. In fact, he makes up a lot of things.

Buck finished the story, then stayed uncharacteristically silent for a few seconds before saying, "This is where the Belgians were presumably killed."

No one responded to that. But in fact that thought had crossed my mind. And Buck wanted to save this moment for now.

Buck looked down at the paving stones at the base of the columns and said, "The Yemeni Army personnel who were first called to the scene said these stones were covered with blood."

In fact, they were still stained, but if you didn't know what happened here, you wouldn't know it was blood.

Buck continued, "There were two older couples, retirees from Brussels, and a young unmarried couple from Bruges who were touring the Middle East, as well as a married couple, also from Brussels, with their daughter, age sixteen."

Again, no one responded.

Buck continued, "They were all staying at the Sheraton in Sana'a as part of a larger tour group. Those nine people decided to sign up for this day excursion to Marib."

Bad idea. *Very* bad idea.

Buck again stayed silent and I noticed that the ruins were completely deserted now, and the bus and police truck had left. There was no sound from the road or from the ruins around us. We were alone.

Buck said softly, "These people weren't here to hurt anyone, and the only thing they did wrong in Yemen was to be Westerners. Europeans. Christians. And for that, they paid with their lives."

Indeed.

Buck continued, "The bodies of the Belgians were never found, but their tour guide and the bus driver, young men from Sana'a, were found in a drainage ditch a kilometer from here with their throats cut...so they were able to receive a proper Muslim funeral." He added, "Their crime was associating with infidels, and the penalty was death."

Kate said quietly, "How awful...senseless."

Brenner said, "This is not war."

Buck agreed, "It was a merciless, cold-blooded act of butchery."

I asked, "And we think The Panther was here when it happened?"

Buck nodded and replied, "That is the information we received from the Al Qaeda prisoner in Brussels."

Well, if anyone had any qualms about killing those

bastards with Hellfire missiles, those thoughts were now gone. In fact, high-explosive oblivion was too good for Bulus ibn al-Darwish.

Buck's sat-phone rang and he answered. He listened, then said, "All right," and hung up. He said to us, "That was Chet." He informed us, "It's time to leave here and return to the Bilqis Hotel."

Which was another way of saying, "It's kidnap time."

CHAPTER SIXTY-FOUR

The kidnapping itself was sort of anticlimactic.

I was with Buck in the lead vehicle, sitting in the rear of the small Hilux, and Kate was up front so she didn't have to sit with the kidnapper. I am a gentleman.

Brenner and Zamo were about twenty meters behind us.

We had pulled over after we left the ruins and everyone had retrieved their M4s, which we now had on our laps, and Zamo had his sniper rifle. Most importantly, Kate was wearing her scarf for her kidnapping. All was right with the world—if your world was Yemen.

As we approached the narrow bridge over the wadi, a white Toyota Land Cruiser pulled onto the road from the shoulder and slowed down on the bridge. A second white SUV pulled onto the road behind us and in front of Brenner. A third SUV fell in behind Brenner. So we were boxed and sandwiched. This might be a staged kidnapping, but these guys had done this before, for real.

The SUV in front of us came to an angled stop at

the far end of the bridge and Buck stopped about ten meters from him.

I turned to see the SUV behind us stopping close to our rear. Brenner, too, came to a halt, then the last SUV stopped behind Brenner and bottled up the bridge. Nice job everyone.

Kate, who probably thinks all Bedouin look alike, asked, "How do we know these are our...people?"

I assured her, "Our Bedouin were bearded and wearing white robes, and these guys in the SUVs are bearded and wearing white robes."

Buck was a bit more reassuring and said, "Those are Musa's three vehicles, and I'm sure those are the men who escorted us last night and today."

I added, "We had lunch with them." And Musa is still working for us. Right?

My Colt automatic was still in the pocket of my bush jacket, and I took it off safety.

I noticed a number of women on the banks of the wadi washing clothes, and some boys were wading in the water, and some men were fishing. A few of these people glanced up at the five SUVs stopped on the bridge: two Hiluxes and three Land Cruisers. They must have figured out it was a guest kidnapping—happens all the time—so they looked away.

Up ahead, a big truck stopped at the approach to the bridge, but he wasn't blasting his horn the way they would in New York. Just be patient, Abdul. The Bedouin are kidnapping a few tourists. Takes a few minutes.

The rear door of the Land Cruiser in front of us opened and a Bedouin got out, carrying an AK-47. I looked behind me and saw another Bedouin approaching Brenner's Hilux.

I recognized the Bedouin coming toward us—it was Yasir, the guy who had fondled my jambiyah—and he was waving the business end of his AK-47 at us as he opened the rear door next to me. He slid in quickly, slammed the door, and rested his rifle across his chest with the muzzle a foot from my head.

He didn't have much to say, but there wasn't much that needed to be said.

The Land Cruiser in front of us began moving, and Yasir said to Buck, "Yalla nimshi." Let's go.

We drove past the stopped truck and I looked at the driver, who was literally covering his face with his hands. I mean, he didn't see *nuthin'*!

Anyway, the kidnap convoy continued north, toward Marib, but before we got to the Bilqis Hotel, the lead vehicle turned left on a dirt trail, west toward the hills, and we all followed.

Our passenger seemed to relax a bit and he said something to Buck, who replied.

Buck said to us, "This gentleman, Yasir, says it is good to see us again."

I asked Yasir, "Have you done this before?"

Anyway, everything seemed cool so far, and I didn't pick up on anything wrong or suspicious. Bottom line, I had my Colt automatic in my pocket, my M4 on my lap, my Kevlar in place, and my antenna way up.

Regarding that, everyone's hand-held radio crackled and Zamo's voice said, "Clean Sweep Five here. Read?"

I replied, "Sweep Three, loud and clear."

"Everything good?"

"So far."

"Same." He added, "This sucks."

Could be worse. Could be real. Or it could turn real.

There weren't many vehicles on this dirt trail, and not too many people in the scattered fields, but there were a number of goat herders sitting around on stone fences, and they seemed interested in the five-vehicle convoy kicking up dust.

Buck made small talk with Yasir, who still seemed a little jumpy. Probably, I thought, despite the fact that this was Bedouin territory, Yasir didn't want to run into an army patrol, or even the National Security police, though the NSB was bought and paid for. I doubted if Yasir and his friends were worried too much about the Mukhabarat, a.k.a. the PSO, a.k.a. the secret police, who operated mostly in the towns. In any case, the fix was in with the government, though Yasir didn't know that, and neither did he know why the fix was in—because the Americans were going to whack his sheik as a favor to President Saleh.

The other thing on Yasir's mind would be Al Qaeda. They were on my mind, too. It was possible that Al Qaeda had been tipped off by now about the Americans at the Bilqis Hotel and at the ruins, and maybe they had put together a snatch job of their own.

Bottom line, though, if Al Qaeda was around, they'd have to defer to the Bedouin, who'd been here for two thousand years. Right?

Anyway, I saw that we were going southwest, and I could see the hills ahead, meaning we were on our way back to the Crow Fortress, which was the plan. If, however, we were going someplace else—like the Al Qaeda training camp—I was ready to cut this trip short.

I said to Buck, "No detours, no bullshit from Yasir."

Buck replied, "Relax, please."

"I'll relax when I'm on that Otter."

Kate said, "I'm going to call Chet."

"Good idea."

She opened her window and leaned out to get clear sky and dialed Chet on her sat-phone, but he didn't answer.

Yasir didn't seem to care if we used our hand-held radios or sat-phones or that our automatic rifles were on our laps, so maybe I shouldn't be paranoid. We were on our way to the safe house, the Crow Fortress. However, if we found Chet there with his throat cut, that would not be a good sign. Or was I ambivalent about that?

I reminded Kate, "The Predators are watching us."

Kate reminded *me*, "You have a Bedouin sitting next to you with an AK-47."

"Right. I'm on top of that."

Buck said, "This is all going as planned."

And it was. So I said to Yasir, "Where did you go to college?"

Buck translated, and Yasir replied, and Buck said to me, "He thanks you for your compliment."

"What compliment?"

"I told him you said you admired his shiwal." Buck added, "He might give it to you. Then you have to wear it."

"Thanks, Buck."

"And if you keep making me translate silly remarks, you'll be wearing his underwear."

Kate thought that was funny, and I was happy she was starting to relax.

Anyway, I gave up on trying to make conversation with Yasir, and I paid attention to where we were going.

Within ten minutes we intersected the wide dirt road that I recognized as our landing strip, and we turned right toward the plateau where the Crow Fortress stood.

Kate said to me, "Try Chet."

So I opened my window, leaned out, and dialed Chet.

He answered and I said, "We've been kidnapped."

He replied, "I saw that."

I reminded him, "In case you forgot, we're in the two small Hiluxes. Tell the Predator pilots."

"Thank you. Anything further?"

"Any dust?"

There was a short pause, then he replied, "No dust tonight." Chet let me know, "You should be here in fifteen minutes."

"Keep the beer cold."

"Further?"

"Negative."

So I sat back and relaxed.

Chet thought I was funny, but annoying. Maybe even a bit silly. And it was good that he should think that. There are a lot of felons in jail who thought that.

Brenner, however, ex-cop, recognized the act. Zamo, too, may have seen beyond the jokes, and Buck had also been perceptive enough to figure out my M.O.

Kate, of course, had seen me play dumb and funny with suspects, as well as supervisors. Playing dumb is smart. People let their guard down. And make mistakes.

Buck and Chet were my colleagues, my compatriots, and my teammates. But they were not my trusted friends. In fact, they were up to something.

We got to the ravine at the base of the plateau, and up we went. This was actually scarier in the daylight.

We made it to the top and headed toward the Crow Fortress.

I had no idea how long we were going to be here waiting for the Al Qaeda delegation to come check us out and confirm who we were. But if I had to spend more than a week with Chet and Buck, I'd surrender to the first jihadist who came through the door.

Meanwhile, I had to keep an eye on Chet and Buck. Especially Chet. I could wait to see if Chet was here to settle an old CIA score with Kate and me, or I could confront him with it. If I waited, it might be too late to tell him, "I knew you were up to something." So maybe I needed to make a pre-emptive strike. Before he did the same.

CHAPTER SIXTY-FIVE

The five-vehicle kidnap convoy drove through the open gates into the walled courtyard of the Crow Fortress and we all got out of the SUVs.

The two Bedouin hadn't cut Chet's throat, and he greeted us and said, "It looked picture perfect on the video monitor." He added, "I hope enough locals saw it happening, and that by now the word has gotten back to Al Qaeda."

I asked Chet, "What if the locals or Al Qaeda know or suspect that we're in the Crow Fortress?"

Chet replied, "That's possible. But Al Qaeda is not going to interfere with a Bedouin kidnapping or mount an operation against a fortress occupied by Sheik Musa."

Probably not. But I wouldn't want to leave here again until The Panther and his jihadists were ready for the goo bags.

We thanked our Bedouin hosts for a pleasant kidnapping experience and climbed up to the second floor of the tower, where we would await further developments, as per Chet's briefing in Aden.

Chet had retrieved a sat-phone antenna from the van that he'd rigged up in one of the windows, and he plugged his phone into one of the antenna cable jacks, saying, "Now we don't need clear sky to be in direct sat-phone contact with the Predator ground control station."

That's good.

"Or with the embassy, Langley, 26 Fed, or Washington, or anyone who needs to call us."

That sucks.

He advised us, however, "Sat-phone reception is sometimes spotty and also the PSO could be listening. Maybe even Al Qaeda if they have the capability. So we'll keep our sat-phone calls to a bare minimum." He assured us, however, "The satellite radio signal from the van is very strong, and it's scrambled and encrypted, so that's secure."

Bottom line, this was a well-thought-out mission, but the ability to operate in this environment was severely limited. Chet, though, wanted this to work, to show that the CIA could mount surgical strikes in hostile territory as they did so well at the beginning of the Afghan war. The U.S. military and others, however, would like to see boots on the ground. Lots of them. I found myself rooting for the CIA on this one.

So now that we saw the new sat-phone antenna, what else do we do for fun? Maybe we could play Chutes and Ladders with the excrement shaft.

Before I could suggest that, Buck said, "I brought along some magazines, paperback novels, and crossword puzzles to kill the time."

I asked Chet, "Any more cognac?"

"One bottle for a celebration."

Let's celebrate.

Anyway, we all sat cross-legged on the carpet, except for Zamo, who went from window to window with his rifle and binoculars.

Kate asked Buck and Chet, "How long do you think it will take for Sheik Musa to contact Al Qaeda?"

Chet replied, "Could be a day or two." He explained, "Musa will make it appear that he's biding his time, maybe exploring his options, or maybe waiting to see if Al Qaeda contacts him to inquire if he knows anything about some kidnapped Amriki." He added, "It has to play itself out and we don't want to micromanage Musa."

No, but we want Musa to get his ass in gear.

Chet also reminded us, "The Panther could have felt the heat here after the Hunt Oil attack, and maybe he left the area. If so, when Musa offers him five kidnapped Americans, The Panther will have to make the decision about coming back here or not, because Musa is not going to leave his tribal lands and go to The Panther with the five Americans." Chet concluded, "So it could be a long wait. But I'm confident that one way or the other, Bulus ibn al-Darwish will show up in the crosshairs of a Predator drone video camera."

Maybe. But the problem was the long wait, and I asked Chet, "How long do we wait?"

"As long as it takes."

Holy shit. I asked, "What happens when the tuna runs out?" I prompted him, "Come on, Chet. What's the max time we sit here doing crossword puzzles?"

Chet thought about that, then replied, "I say we give it two weeks. After that we may have a security problem."

Not to mention a mental health problem. I mean, *two weeks* in this dungeon? We could get a disease. Call Clare.

Chet also informed us, "The decision is not wholly ours to make. I need to consult with Langley on a day-to-day basis." He added, "We'll play it by ear."

I suggested, "We should also stay in touch with Sheik Musa. He's the guy who's in touch with Al Qaeda."

Chet replied, "We don't call Musa. Musa calls us."

Buck also informed us, "The Arabs in general, and the Bedouin in particular, have a different sense of time than we do in the West." He let us know, "They can negotiate for months over even a simple matter. They're in no rush."

But Chet was more reassuring and said, "The Panther, having a half-American head, will probably come to a quick decision." He added, "He's impatient. And hungry."

"Me, too."

So we had a long wait. Or a short wait. In the end, the best-laid trap still depends on the guy you're trying to trap.

Kate had a good question. "Will our disappearance— or kidnapping—be reported to the media?"

Buck replied to that. "There is a news blackout at the embassy PIO office." He smiled and said, "Which is redundant since the PIO doesn't put out many news releases from Yemen anyway." He added, "As for snooping Western journalists, there are virtually no resident American news organizations in Yemen. Only the BBC has an office in Sana'a, and the lone reporter there is on extended home leave. As for Yemeni journalists, or government sources, they either know nothing or they've been told to know nothing."

Right. This was truly the Land That Time Forgot, and the black hole of the Mideast, and you could be missing here for months before anyone outside of Yemen noticed.

Kate asked, "What if our friends or family don't hear from us, or are trying to contact us?"

I said to Kate, "If you mean your parents, consider this a vacation." No, I didn't say that. I kept my mouth shut.

Buck replied, however, "Each of us will write a note that will be delivered by our respective offices in the States to anyone on your list." He advised us, "Keep it general, and don't mention that you've been kidnapped." He smiled.

Buck also advised us, "Any inquiries to our offices coming from friends or families will be handled by the embassy in Sana'a." He added, "We should have no problem staying incommunicado for a week or two."

Chet informed us, "I stay out of touch with friends and family for weeks at a time." He added, "Comes with the job."

Also, no one gives a shit if they don't hear from you. In fact, they welcome it. That's not nice. Someone somewhere loved Chet.

On that subject, we knew virtually nothing about Chet's personal life, and he never volunteered a word. But Kate took the opportunity to ask him, "Are you married?"

Chet hesitated a second, then replied, "I am estranged from my wife."

Maybe that has to do with Chet being strange.

Kate said, as women do, "I'm sorry."

The wife is probably not.

Chet volunteered, "This assignment and the separation has put a strain on the marriage."

I'll say. And I did feel a little sorry for him. On the bright side, he could have four wives here...or maybe only three. He's already got one. Right?

Buck, who had seemed to make his marriage work despite decades of foreign assignments—or maybe *because* of that—said, "This business is difficult for family life. We sacrifice a great deal for our country and sometimes I'm not sure it's appreciated by the country."

How about never? And why do we care? We do what we do for other reasons. Appreciation is not part of the plan.

Buck said, regarding the long or short wait here, "Let's be optimistic and assume that we'll be on a plane heading home before anyone even knows we are missing."

Okay. Let's be optimistic.

I opened one of the crossword books and said, "An Arab who ran out of ammunition? Eight letters."

Brenner, who knew the joke, replied, "A moderate."

CHAPTER SIXTY-SIX

It was dinnertime and we feasted on canned tuna, cold mixed vegetables, and tawwa bread, all washed down with warm bottled water. Chet had a smoke.

The light was fading and we lit a few kerosene lanterns. Out in the courtyard it was prayer time again and the Bedouin were praying loudly, making me homesick for Brooklyn.

After the call to prayer, Chet announced that he had to do a sit-rep and he was going to use the secure radio in the van. I said I'd keep him company, and we both went down to the courtyard where he unlocked the van and we entered.

Chet checked his voice mail and text messages, then made his sit-rep—all okay—then signed off and swiveled his chair toward me. He asked, "You wanted to talk to me?"

"I do." I remained standing and said to him, "About Ted Nash."

He nodded.

"You knew him."

He nodded again, then said, "But not well."

"Whatever. Here's the deal, Chet. My wife, before we were married, was involved with Nash." I looked at his face in the dim light of the console. "You know that?"

"I heard."

"So what happened was maybe more personal than business."

He didn't respond.

I continued, "On the other hand, Nash, a few seconds before his death, had a gun pointed at us—at me and Kate—and that was business. Did you know that?"

"I don't know the details."

"I'm giving you the details. Here's another detail. Nash was involved in a rogue operation that would have caused a nuclear attack by the U.S. on the world of Islam." I asked, "Did you know *that*?"

"If I did, I wouldn't tell you that I did." He added, however, "I did not."

"Now you know." I further informed him, "That might sound like a good idea to you—nuke 'em, as I said, and you agreed. But wiping out tens of millions of innocent people and leaving the Mideast a nuclear wasteland is not really a good idea."

He smiled and replied, "That's your opinion."

"Yeah. And my opinion was the one that counted." I also informed Chet, "Kate and I were prisoners of a nut job who was going to kill us. And Nash knew this. In fact, after Kate and I whacked the nut job, Nash showed up and was going to finish the job for the psycho. Follow?"

"I guess."

"So we're talking about self-defense, with maybe a little personal history between the parties."

"Okay. But what does this have to do with me? Or this mission?"

"You tell me."

"Okay. Nothing."

"Try again."

Chet stayed silent a moment, then said, "I think I see how your paranoid mind is working. And to be honest, I can understand how you might reach some wild and erroneous conclusions. But—"

"No buts, Chet. Do you think I'm stupid enough to believe that Kate and I were asked to come here because we're perfect for this job?"

"You *are* perfect for this job, John. And so is Kate."

"Right. Perfect in every way."

He asked me a question that I'd asked myself. "If you really believe what you're suggesting, why in the world did you come here?"

"Because, Chet, this is the belly of the beast. And you are the beast. And I am here to talk to the beast, and if I have to, to kill the beast."

He had no reply to that.

I advised him, "When I walk out of here, you will cable or speak to Langley, and you will let them know that you spoke to me, and that this problem better be finished."

Again he stayed silent, then said, "I'll pass on our conversation." He added, "But as far as I know, you and your wife being asked to come here has nothing to do with what happened to Ted Nash. It has to do with you and Kate being good Panther bait— because you killed The Lion. Nothing more, nothing less." He further informed me, "I don't like being threatened."

"I'm not threatening you. I'm telling you that if I smell a rat, or if something happens to Kate, you're dead."

He was getting a little pissed off and snapped, "If something happened to Kate, you can be sure the same thing would happen to you."

"Not if I blow your fucking head off first."

He backed off a bit and said in a controlled voice, "I understand how you might come to the conclusion you came to...And you know what? You could be right. But I don't think you are. But if you are, it has nothing to do with me. I'm not here to settle a score with your wife, or with you. I'm here to kill Bulus ibn al-Darwish." He assured me, "I don't assassinate American citizens...well, except for al-Darwish."

"I'm happy to hear that, Chet. And if you leave here alive, it's because I didn't kill you. So that evens the score. Tell the boys back in Langley."

He nodded, then said to me, "I need to send some cables. Are we finished?"

I turned and left the van.

Well, that was out of the way. Now Chet knew that I knew, and he could think about it and report it to whoever had the bright idea of sending me and Kate here to become unfortunate casualties of war.

I mean, I always thought that there was a CIA contract out on us since Kate whacked Ted, and this seemed like a good time and place for the Agency to act on that. And nothing that Chet said made me believe I was wrong. So, to further answer Chet's question of why I was here if I thought that, the answer was, "You can't run from the beast forever." You have to meet the beast. And you meet him on his turf. And you kill him.

Or, because we're civilized, and because the beast has friends, you might make a deal with him.

I hope Chet understood the deal. If not, the Otter wouldn't be carrying as many passengers on the return trip.

CHAPTER SIXTY-SEVEN

Without electricity—except in the van—there wasn't too much to do after the sun went down. Also, I'll never again take hot running water for granted. Or a chair to sit in, or a cold beer.

I mean, I'm not a softie or a sissy; I'm an urban fighter. Urban is good. Comes from the Latin for city. As in electri-city. Right?

Well, maybe this rustic experience will do me some good. I'll get in touch with my inner Bedouin. But maybe I should rethink the warlord thing.

Also, it could be worse; this could be a real kidnapping. I could be waiting to have my head sawed off.

Anyway, we were all sleep-deprived, so it was no problem hitting the hay early. We posted a two-person guard for three-hour shifts—Brenner and Zamo first, me and Kate second, Buck and Chet last. That should take us to dawn. And Paul Brenner, I should point out, was fulfilling his desire to sleep with Kate—though probably not the way he envisioned it.

Chet and I had not revisited our conversation at any point during the evening, which in any case was not really possible in a communal setting. But Chet did say to me, in a rare moment of privacy, at the door of the excrement shed, "I sent a cable relating your concerns." He added, "No reply."

Bullshit.

During my and Kate's guard shift, as we looked out a window at the black night, I said to her, "I spoke to Chet about Ted Nash."

She didn't reply for a few seconds, then reminded me, "I was going to do that."

"I handled it differently than you might have handled it."

"Meaning?"

"Meaning I shared with him my suspicion that you and I were asked to come to Yemen so that the CIA could even the score. Meaning you whacking Ted Nash."

She stayed silent for a while, then said, "I don't necessarily agree with your suspicion." She added, "It's too . . . crazy."

"You think? Look, it's not only about you terminating Ted, and you being cleared of any wrongdoing. It's also about you and me screwing up the CIA's plan to nuke Islam. That was a biggie. And we *know* about it."

"We've stayed silent—as per the deal."

"Right. But that's not good enough for worried people in Langley. Dead is better."

She didn't reply.

"So that's why we're here."

Again, she didn't respond, but asked me, "What else did you say to Chet?"

"Well, I told him if anything happened to you, or if

I even *thought* you or I were being set up, I was going to blow his head off."

"You shouldn't have said that."

"All right. I'll tell him it's okay for him to kill us."

"What I mean, John, is that you may be *wrong* about this."

"If I'm wrong, I'm wrong, and there's no harm done."

"You don't threaten someone's life without some harm done. Especially if that person has done nothing wrong—or knows nothing."

"Okay. But Chet took it well. He was even pleasant to me after he returned from the van. Did you notice?"

"You may be as crazy as he is."

"Crazier, I assure you." I reminded her, "*You* said to look for the triple cross."

She didn't reply.

I continued, "What's in a name? Why is this called Operation Clean Sweep? Why are you and I here?"

"All right. I get it. But . . . what did he say?"

"He neither confirmed nor denied my suspicions. Actually, he said he could understand how I might come to such an erroneous and paranoid conclusion, and that I might actually be right, but he has nothing to do with whatever it was that I was wrongly suggesting." I asked, "Follow?"

"No."

"I guess you had to be there. Bottom line here, I let the cat out of the bag, and Chet cabled his people in Langley. Or maybe he actually spoke to them. So I think we now have less than a fifty-fifty chance of becoming victims of friendly fire—or winding up whacked by Musa or Al Qaeda."

Kate nodded, then said, "In this business, the past comes back to haunt you."

I'm not haunted by anything. My problem is when the past comes back to *kill* you. Like The Lion. Like Ted Nash. This business is a cycle of vendetta, an ever-widening circle without end. Someday, maybe when I'm old, sitting in a rocker, someone from the past will get me. But not today. Not this week.

To make Kate feel better, I said, "It was self-defense. You saved our lives. Don't replay it."

She nodded.

So we finished our three hours of guard duty and woke Chet and Buck. Chet was actually already awake. Maybe he had a bad dream about someone cutting his throat while he slept.

The five gentlemen of the A-team had breakfast with the eight gentlemen of the desert down in the courtyard, while Kate used the opportunity of privacy to wash up with bottled water.

Breakfast was the same glop, except the Bedouin had added tuna.

After breakfast, Chet, Buck, Brenner, and I went into the van and watched TV. Both screens had reruns of yesterday's show—beautiful Yemen from the air. I felt like I was soaring.

Chet did a commo check and a sit-rep, and ground control reported no unusual activity in the area. Just another routine day in the tribal lands, and a quiet day in Al Qaeda territory. But that could change quickly.

We walked around the courtyard for exercise, the way convicts walk around the prison yard. I counted fourteen lizards.

Later I suggested to Buck, "Ask our Bedouin hosts if they can get us a soccer ball. Also some real food from Marib. I'll buy."

Buck informed me, "They've told me they're not allowed to leave here. And no one can come here unless the food and water runs out." He explained, "We're all in lockdown until further notice."

"When do we start killing and eating the camels?"

"There are no camels. But there are goats outside the walls and our hosts seem to be killing one a day."

"How many are left?"

"Enough for a long siege."

On that subject, Kate, Brenner, and I bugged Buck and Chet about getting some info about how Sheik Musa was doing in his talks with Al Qaeda.

But Buck and Chet both agreed that it was premature to send a message to the sheik.

Buck said, "It would be impolite to ask him now. Maybe in a few days."

Chet agreed. "Let it play out." He added, "We need to appear trusting, unworried, and cool."

Who makes this shit up?

Anyway, we had lunch on the diwan level where we lived. Tuna again. Buck explained away the poor provisions from Washington by saying, "We don't want to accentuate the differences between us and our Bedouin allies."

"That's idiotic, Buck. We should *celebrate* our differences. Like with pork chops."

Buck continued, "Also, we don't want to look too good for the Al Qaeda men who come to see us. We're supposed to be subsisting on goats and oats." He smiled and added, "We can't be getting fat in captivity."

I pictured another CIA committee discussing this. They really are into smoke and mirrors, and as I just discovered, they are believers in method acting. The A-team had to starve a little to look the part of kidnap victims. Not to mention we all needed a shower and shave.

Anyway, there wasn't a lot to talk about anymore, without saying stupid things, so we all sort of retreated into ourselves, and read, and did crossword puzzles. Kate exercised a lot, and Mr. Brenner joined her a few times, twisting and bending. I should call the Bedouin in to see this.

We had a first-aid kit, and Brenner helped Zamo change his dressing, and later Brenner assured us that Zamo was okay. Maybe he was. But maybe we had to get him out of here.

We also wrote out in longhand our required notes of assurance to friends, family, bookies, and whom-ever. These notes would be e-mailed to the parties we indicated.

Buck had some suggested wording for the last paragraph, and it went something like this: *I'll be out of communication in a remote area for a week or two, but if you need to contact me, this is the U.S. Embassy e-mail address set up for this purpose. I may not be able to respond for a week or more, but be assured I will see your e-mail and I will contact you shortly.*

I said to Kate, "Tell your parents I miss them."

Chet and Buck gathered up the handwritten notes from Kate, me, Brenner, and Zamo, then took them down to the van for encrypted transmission to the embassy, or to Washington—they weren't clear about that.

I said to Kate, Brenner, and Zamo, "This is like the stupid postcards you had to send to your parents from camp." Except there was something creepy about this.

The day passed, the Bedouin answered all their calls to prayer, and all their cell phone calls. We walked around the courtyard, and we explored each floor of the six-story tower, which was all the same except for the open-arched mafraj level. Good view. Also, to break up the monotony, I took a leak from the mafraj down the excrement shaft—six stories to the ground floor, which was piled high with shit. Longest piss I ever took. TMI. The other highlight of my day was recharging my commo equipment in the van. It's fascinating to watch the charge levels rise.

The Bedouin, by the way, never seemed bored. They had an infinite capacity to sit around and bullshit. And when they weren't talking to one another, they were talking on their cell phones. They made tea all day, prayed, and slept when they felt like it. They had some kind of washing ritual associated with the call to prayer, but it seemed more symbolic than rub-a-dub-dub.

Now and then one of them would climb one of the stone platforms and peer out over the wall, but they didn't seem to take guard duty too seriously. Probably because they didn't take the Yemeni Army too seriously. And they didn't yet understand the new boys on the block—Al Qaeda.

Also, I don't think the Bedouin really understood about the Predator drones watching us, or that we could see, on our monitors in the fish van, what the Predators saw from five or ten thousand feet.

I asked Chet about this, and he said, "If I showed them the monitors, they'd understand the capabilities without understanding the technology. Just like with their cell phones." He added, "They know it's not magic, but the less they know, the better."

Right. But I'm sure Sheik Musa knew a little more about Predator drones carrying Hellfire missiles; he knew he didn't want to appear on the video monitor with an X between his eyes.

Anyway, I suppose I could wax poetic about the Bedouin, and maybe romanticize them the way most Westerners did—but basically they were just simple, uncomplicated, and understimulated people who took small pleasures in a cup of tea. And these eight guys in the courtyard were happy to be sitting around here and not busting their butts herding camels or goats, or scratching out an existence in the dead fields.

As Chet said, they had their Korans to read—if they could read—their guns, and their faith. Also a little khat to help pass the time and elevate their mood.

Speaking of which, Chet took about three trips a day to the mafraj and always came down with a smile. I had this mental image of him stumbling into the excrement hole and dropping six stories into a pile of shit. That could happen.

On a completely different subject, getting laid is no big deal, but *not* getting laid is a *very* big deal. Capisce? Enough said.

Evening came, and we dined al fresco with the Bedouin to do something different. Oats, groats, goats, tawwa, tea, and tuna. Canned fruit for dessert. The Bedouin liked the syrupy canned fruit and ate up most of our stock.

Kate was allowed to join us if she wore her balto and hijab and sat by herself off to the side. Sounded reasonable to me, but Kate balked. Buck, however, urged her to have dinner with us at a distance. He explained, "This is a big break with custom and we should take advantage of the opportunity to bridge the cultural divide."

I agreed and suggested, "About forty feet should do it."

Kate agreed reluctantly, and it was good to have her at dinner.

Anyway, early to bed, three guard shifts, restless sleep, and dawn. I never before appreciated the dawn. I can see why ancient people worshipped the sun. The sun was life. The night was death.

On the third or maybe fourth day, as I was re-reading the mixed vegetables label, Kate asked me, "How are you holding up?"

"Fine. I've named all the crows." I asked, "How are *you* doing?"

"Okay." She added, "Physically, fine. But I'm developing Stockholm Syndrome." She smiled. "I'm beginning to identify with the Bedouin."

"They're great guys," I agreed. "Even though they've never seen your face, they knew you'd make an attractive dinner companion."

She smiled again and said to me, "It's very reassuring that you're still an asshole."

"Thank you." In fact, I knew that Kate would appreciate me more here in this manly country.

Another thing I noticed is that I didn't miss the news. Or the sports scores. When you're cut off from the civilized world, you go through a few days of withdrawal, and then one day you realize it's all bullshit.

What difference does it make what's going on in Washington, London, Moscow, New York, or Cairo? They don't care what *I'm* doing. I would, however, like to know how the Yankees were doing in spring training. But someone could fill me in if I ever got back. And if I didn't, it was sort of moot.

On the subject of getting back alive, neither Chet nor I mentioned our conversation in the van. There was nothing more to say, and he wasn't going to tell me what his bosses in Langley said to him.

Look, I could be way off base on this, in which case there was nothing more to say or do. But if I was right, Chet and his people were now trying to figure out if Operation Clean Sweep should include John and Kate.

It would have occurred to them, too, that if John Corey knew or suspected a whack job way back in New York, then I would have left one of those "To Be Opened Only in the Event of My Death" notes with someone.

Maybe I should have, but I didn't. Maybe because I didn't intend to get whacked here by the CIA. Or maybe because if Kate and I got killed by Al Qaeda or The Panther, I wouldn't want the CIA to be suspected of a crime they didn't commit. No matter how I felt about the Agency, in the end they are our first line of defense, and I am a dedicated and responsible professional.

Early the next afternoon, after salat and after the last can of tuna had been eaten, Chet's sat-phone rang. He went to the window where it was plugged into the antenna, and answered.

He listened, then said, "Okay, thanks," and informed

us, "Predator reports three white Land Cruisers approaching from the north and heading toward this plateau."

Kate asked, "Who do you think they are?"

Chet replied, "Could be re-supply...or it could be the men we've been waiting for."

Brenner asked, "Why didn't Musa give us a heads-up?"

Buck replied, "He would give his men a heads-up—not us."

And sure enough, we heard a commotion in the courtyard.

We all went to the window, and I saw that our eight Bedouin were on their feet, AK-47s in hand, and one of them was on his cell phone. Then four armed Bedouin ran toward the tower and we could hear them coming up the stone stairs.

Everyone grabbed their M4s and we spread ourselves strategically around the stairwell. Buck stood at the top of the stairs with his M4 slung.

The four Bedouin were on the staircase now, shouting loudly and excitedly as they ran up the stairs.

Buck said to us, "Al Qaeda is coming to see the kidnapped Americans."

Great. I mean, you know you're bored when you look forward to a visit from Al Qaeda.

CHAPTER SIXTY-EIGHT

Chet, looking very happy, said to us, "The Panther has bitten."

Right. But The Panther wasn't biting Chet, who, being a spook, was not really here. So Chet excused himself, saying, "I'll stay in contact with the Predators." And off he went down the stairs and into the van.

So now we had to look like prisoners of the Bedouin, who fortunately treated their kidnapped guests well.

Kate wrapped her hair and face in her black scarf as the four Bedouin came up the stairs and quickly gathered up most of our things, including our sat-phone antenna from the window. It might be hard to explain to the Al Qaeda guys if we got a phone call, so we also shut off our hand-held radios, sat-phones, and cell phones.

The four Bedouin carried our baggage up one level, as well as our boxes of canned food and our reading material, leaving only our bread and water on the floor. Our friend Yasir and another Bedouin rolled up our carpet and also carried it up the stairs.

The Bedouin wanted our M4 carbines and Zamo's rifle, but Brenner flat-out refused, and we stowed them under our straw bedding. We also kept our Colt .45s concealed in our holsters, which we moved to the small of our backs, though we had to take off our Kevlar vests in case the Al Qaeda guys were sharp enough to notice. Kate took care of that, modestly, in the indoor outhouse.

We also gave the Bedouin our watches and the non-diplomatic passports that we'd used to check in at the Bilqis Hotel, but we kept our diplomatic passports in case we needed to make a dash for the Saudi border.

We'd thought this out over the last few days, and it seemed that we'd thought of everything. But then Kate said, "Chet's blanket."

Right.

Buck picked up the blanket and tossed it out the window. I would have tossed it down the shit shaft.

So, did we look like prisoners who'd been cooped up here for four days? We certainly *smelled* the part.

Last thing. We scuffed up the floor where our carpet had been and Buck impressed us with his tradecraft by saying, "Perhaps we should put some bird droppings here."

I told him, "That's your job, Buck." But he let it go.

We heard something in the courtyard and we all went to the window. The gates were open now, and a white Land Cruiser drove into the courtyard. Then another, and another.

Al Qaeda was here.

We continued to watch as the four Bedouin in the courtyard opened the rear doors of the Land Cruisers and assisted the black-hooded occupants from the vehicles. There were five of them, dressed in white foutehs and sandals. Also, they had their AK-47s slung over their shoulders. I mean, even blindfolded negotiators carried guns here.

Brenner remarked, "They've got to know they were driven up to the Crow Fortress."

Buck assured us, "There are a number of places like this in the hills."

That's good. I hope the Bedouin drivers were smart enough to drive these assholes in circles for a few hours.

Anyway, we watched as the five hooded Al Qaeda guys were walked across the courtyard toward the tower. Don't bump into that Predator van.

So now it was time for us to look like five prized Amriki worth a hundred thousand bucks.

We all sat on the bare wooden floor. From left to right it was Brenner, Zamo, Buck, me, and Kate on the far right. The four Bedouin produced three chained ankle shackles and keys. We refused their kind offer to shackle us and did it ourselves—Brenner and Zamo shared a set of shackles, as did Buck and I. Kate, being a woman, had her own set of shackles. We kept the keys. Last thing, we pulled off our shoes and socks, and the Bedouin put them under the straw.

Buck reminded us, "Scuff the soles of your feet on the floor."

Right. Never underestimate the intelligence or the perceptive powers of the enemy. They're not as dumb as they look. In fact, these guys probably knew what prisoners were supposed to look like.

This could be a setup, of course, and we could be real prisoners in about five minutes, or real dead. But Musa and his Bedouin had other opportunities to double-cross us. And bottom line, our hands were free and our guns were ready to be drawn.

Someone called out in Arabic from the stairwell and our buddy, Yasir, called back.

I asked Kate, "You okay?"

"I'm fine."

Buck reminded her, "Keep your head and eyes down."

A few seconds later, the five hooded Al Qaeda guys with three Bedouin guiding them came up the stone stairs and into the tower room.

The Bedouin placed the five Al Qaeda guys in a line, shoulder to shoulder, about five feet in front of us, then one by one they pulled off the black hoods. And we were face-to-face with the enemy.

CHAPTER SIXTY-NINE

The Al Qaeda delegation looked like a firing squad, lined up with their rifles slung on their shoulders.

Also, five men were more than they needed to ID the Americans, so this was a power play or a show of force, and the Bedouin shouldn't have allowed it. But they did, so I expected the Al Qaeda guys to throw their weight around.

Four Bedouin remained in the diwan, including Yasir, who seemed to be hosting this occasion.

The Amriki were supposed to look frightened, nervous, tired, and dejected, which meant mostly just looking down and keeping our mouths shut, unless spoken to. On the other hand, Al Qaeda knew we were not tourists, so we could show a little defiance now and then.

I looked at the five Al Qaeda fighters standing in front of us. They were on the young side—maybe early to mid-twenties, though their faces appeared weather-beaten and old beyond their years. They were beardless, but not exactly clean-shaven, and they looked pretty grim, though they should have been enjoying this.

The guy on the far right, however, was smiling and looking at me, which seemed strange. And then I recognized him.

Nabeel al-Samad said to me, "Hello. You remember me?"

My teammates all turned their heads toward me, and the four Bedouin, who spoke no English, seemed confused that the Al Qaeda guy was smiling and speaking to the American captive. Hey, we had bagels together.

I was supposed to just nod, but I said, so my teammates understood who this guy was, "Nabeel and I had a breakfast meeting in New York." I added, "He had some important information for me."

Nabeel thought that was funny and he translated for his compatriots, who also thought that was funny.

What wasn't so funny was Nabeel saying to me, "Jewish deli for me not funny. You not funny. You not go home ever."

Nabeel needed help with his verbs, but I got that I was supposed to appreciate the moment and the message, which in better English was, "So, Detective Corey, we meet again, and this time the situation is reversed, is it not, Detective Corey?" Hee-hee-hee. Fuck you.

Anyway, I played the game and looked down at the floor.

Bottom line here, soon after the State Department applied for my and Kate's visas, that information had gotten to Al Qaeda in Yemen. Happens all the time and it's not usually a problem for American tourists, businesspeople, or diplomats heading to Sana'a—unless their names happen to be on the Al Qaeda kill list.

Anyway, the fun part was over and it was time for business.

Nabeel said something to Yasir, who handed Nabeel our five non-diplomatic passports.

Nabeel had sheets of paper in his hand, which I was certain were the photostats of these passports gotten from the Bilqis Hotel. Nabeel passed the five passports and photostats around to his four buddies, who studied the passport photos and looked at us.

Nabeel, who had seemed to me like a pleasant putz in New York, had another side to him, and he said to the Amriki sharply, "Look up! Look to me!"

We all looked at Nabeel as the other A.Q. assholes glanced between us, the photostats, and the passports.

Nabeel, of course, made a positive ID on Detective John Corey, and the other Al Qaeda geniuses seemed to agree that Buck, Brenner, and Zamo were the Amriki in the passport pictures. The problem was Kate, wrapped in her scarf, and Nabeel said to her, "Take off hijab."

So Kate pulled her scarf away from her face, and the five Al Qaeda assholes stared at her a long time. I mean, how many women's faces had they seen in their lives?

They all seemed to agree that Kate's photo matched her face, and Yasir collected the passports.

Nabeel said to Kate, "Put on hijab!"

Nabeel then produced two more sheets of paper, which he showed to Yasir. Yasir nodded, then said something to Buck in Arabic. Buck replied in Arabic, and said to us, "They also have copies of John and Kate's diplomatic passports—probably from the Yemeni consulate in New York. And they want to know where—"

"Shut up!" shouted Nabeel. Then to all of us he asked, "Where diplomatic passports?"

Buck replied in English, "At the embassy."

"You lie."

But Yasir jumped in and said something, maybe assuring Nabeel that the Bedouin had searched us and not found any diplomatic passports in the possession of the Americans.

So Yasir, Nabeel, and the other four Al Qaeda assholes got into an argument, and Buck, sotto voce, was translating snippets, saying, "They want to search us . . . and search the bedding . . . and search the diwan."

Right. These things never go the way you want or expect. I asked Buck, "Who the hell is in charge here?"

Buck said to us, "Yasir seems to be losing control."

Great.

Nabeel interrupted his argument long enough to tell me and Buck to shut up.

But Buck, understanding these people, said something to Yasir in Arabic, and his voice was firm. I heard the word "Musa."

Yasir seemed to find his balls and backbone, and he shouted at Nabeel and at the other Al Qaeda shitheads, who shut up.

I mean, what's the pecking order here? You tell 'em, Yasir. Meanwhile, I glanced at my compatriots, and I could see they were a bit uneasy. While Nabeel and Yasir were talking, I said in a low voice to Brenner, Zamo, and Kate, "If I say pull, on the count of three, you know what to do."

They nodded.

As Kate likes to point out, I sometimes change the plan. But only when Plan A is not going well. I mean, bottom line here, The Panther's prize was right in front of his jihadists, and I wouldn't put it past them to get the drop on the Bedouin and re-kidnap us. Or just blow us away.

So if we had to, we would draw on these five bastards and waste them all before they even got their AK-47s unslung. And that would be the end of the negotiations and the end of Operation Clean Sweep, and unfortunately the end of any chance we had of vaporizing The Panther with a Hellfire. But sometimes you gotta think of yourself first, and you have to take what you can get—like five jihadists who were getting a little too aggressive.

Nabeel and Yasir seemed to have settled down a bit, and they were still jabbering away.

Meanwhile, I noticed that the other four Al Qaeda guys were eyeballing us as if trying to determine if we looked like real guests instead of kidnapped guests.

The Al Qaeda delegation was also eyeballing the big tower room, and they all glanced out the windows to try to figure out where they were. Crow Fortress? Or some other tower in the hills?

The tip-off would have been the window behind them that overlooked the courtyard, and more importantly overlooked the fish van. Hey, Abdul, what's that doing here?

The other three Bedouin were standing directly behind the Al Qaeda guys, to keep them literally in line, head and eyes straight ahead. But then one of the Al Qaeda assholes tried to sneak a look over his shoulder, and I was surprised and pleased to see one of the Bedouin smack his head with the barrel of his AK-47. Like, "I said no peeking, asshole. Try that again and your brains will be on the floor." Good. It's your show, boys, and your fort.

More importantly, I could see there was no love lost between these two groups. The Bedouin ruled and have ruled for two thousand years; Al Qaeda was tolerated, as long as they understood whose land this was. Nabeel, however, had spent a little time in Amrika and he'd forgotten his manners. Interestingly, it was Buck who had to remind Yasir that Al Qaeda was not top dog here. Not yet.

But back to business.

Nabeel shouted at me, "What you do here? Why you here?"

It was Buck who replied—Buck does the talking, I do the shooting—"We are embassy personnel on a visit to see the ruins."

Nabeel, of course, said, "You lie! Why you go to Aden?"

"Embassy business."

"You lie! How you come to Marib?"

"By car."

"You say to hotel you come from Sana'a."

"You know we came from Aden."

Nabeel, perhaps realizing his English was too limited to get at the essential truth, took advantage of Buck's Arabic and continued his questions in that language. I heard the words al-Numair, Al Qaeda, Amrika, Sana'a, Aden, and Marib, and even the word Ghumdan.

Obviously Nabeel strongly suspected that we were here to find al-Numair. And the answer was, Why else would we be here, stupid? But Buck wasn't going to give them anything. I couldn't understand what Buck was saying, of course, but I trusted the old Cold Warrior to just stick to the story, no matter how implausible it sounded.

Also, I was certain that Nabeel and his compatriots, as well as their boss, al-Numair, were very pissed off about the Hellfire attack that killed their buddies. Not to mention getting their asses kicked at the Hunt Oil installation. So obviously the Al Qaeda guys were not in a good mood. In fact, they'd like to kill us. But first they had to buy us.

Nabeel, on the instructions of his boss, I'm sure, was trying to determine if the Amriki knew or suspected that The Panther was in Marib—and maybe Nabeel was trying to figure out if this was a trap set by the Amriki with the help of Sheik Musa. And *that* was the real issue. But Nabeel was not going to get that information from the Amriki, unless we were prisoners of Al Qaeda, which we were not—yet.

It's not easy questioning someone else's prisoners, as I discovered last time I was here, and more recently at the Ghumdan prison, and Nabeel seemed frustrated with Buck's replies, so he ended the conversation, then said something to Yasir.

Buck said to us, "Nabeel now wants to see whatever weapons we were carrying when we were kidnapped."

That was my cue to say, "One, two, three—pull!" and show them the weapons. But maybe I should see how Yasir handled it.

Yasir and Nabeel seemed to be getting heated again, and Buck took advantage of the shouting to say to us, "Yasir refuses to show these gentlemen anything—except us." He added, "John's New York acquaintance may be smelling a rat."

Right. Al Qaeda is not stupid. I wish Chet was here to see and hear all of this. He might learn something—like how unpredictable people are.

Yasir, too, was getting the impression that Nabeel was smelling a rat, so he did a smart thing and shouted at Buck, probably telling him to shut up. Then Yasir did a smarter thing and kicked Buck in the chest, knocking him on his back. It was all an act—I think. Buck didn't seem to be hurt by Yasir's half-hearted sandal kick to his chest, and he sat up again. I would have kicked Buck in the balls—just to make it look real, of course.

Nabeel, taking his cue from Yasir, took a step toward Buck as though he intended to kick or hit him, but Yasir went ballistic and shoved Nabeel back and shouted at him.

The other four Al Qaeda guys looked like they were ready to get into a fight, but the three Bedouin behind them stepped back and leveled their rifles. One of them shouted, probably saying, "Make my day, suckers."

Anyway, Yasir seemed to be tired of his visitors, and he shouted, "Imshee!" Go away.

The Bedouin began slipping the black hoods over the Al Qaeda dickheads, but before Nabeel was hooded, he looked at me and said, "In Yemen, you die." Then to my compatriots, he also promised, "You die. But maybe not die. Maybe wish to die."

Well, Nabeel, *you're* not getting an American work visa.

Anyway, I wasn't sure now if we were going to lure The Panther into a meeting with Sheik Musa, so why shouldn't I yell "Pull!" and bag these bastards? Right?

I glanced at Brenner, who was looking at me, and I could tell he was thinking the same thing. Zamo actually had his right hand behind his back, ready for the count.

But Buck, the voice of reason, who could sense that the A-team was on the verge of some messy business, said softly, "Let it go."

Did he say, "Pull"?

The Al Qaeda delegation was all hooded now, and whacking them would be easy, but not fun or sporting. And maybe not a good idea. I mean, I didn't think the Bedouin would like that, and I suppose there was still a chance that The Panther would schedule the meeting with Musa—if Chet was right about Bulus ibn al-Darwish taking chances. But for now, it was Kate who'd been right about Al Qaeda smelling a rat. As for Brenner not trusting the Bedouin, he seemed to be wrong about that so far. But this deal hadn't played itself out yet.

The four Bedouin marched the five hooded Al Qaeda guys down the stairs, and we were alone.

Kate was the first to unlock her shackles, which she threw across the room, saying, "Damn it!"

Then, showing her feminine side, she asked Buck, "Are you all right?"

Buck assured us all that he was fine, saying, "Yasir pulled his kick."

Yasir has more self-control than I do.

Anyway, we all freed ourselves from our shackles and stood.

Okay, this had all been a sham, but the five Al Qaeda fighters standing in front of us were real, and their AK-47s were real, and I think all of us were a little tense for a while there. I'm sure there's a better way to earn a living.

Anyway, we all went to the window.

The Al Qaeda delegation was being walked across the courtyard, and within a minute they were inside the three Land Cruisers, which headed toward the gate. Arrivederci, assholes.

Buck said, "It could have gone better."

You think?

Zamo said, "We shoulda fuckin' wasted them."

And possibly that would have been the right thing to do.

But Kate, who'd grown up hunting game with her nutty parents, said, "Sometimes you let the does go and wait for the buck."

Agreed. Let's shoot Buck. Sorry.

Kate said, "I assume that was the informant you were looking for in New York."

"Yeah. Sorry I bought him a bagel."

Buck said, "Al Qaeda's organization in America is sometimes more extensive than we realize."

Right. But with a few million Muslims in America, we shouldn't be too surprised. Still, it was creepy that Nabeel had set me up for a look-see. Next time I see him, I'll kill him.

Anyway, Chet was not getting out of his van, so he was probably watching his video monitors.

Brenner asked Buck the sixty-four-thousand-dollar question. "Do you think they suspected a setup?"

"I don't know," replied the wise man. "But we will know soon enough."

Brenner suggested, "If they did suspect a setup, and if The Panther still wants to meet with Sheik Musa, then it's possible that The Panther is going to kill Musa—and us."

That was not a happy thought, but it was a possible outcome of what just happened. Another possibility was that The Panther and Sheik Musa would work out another deal between themselves. In Yemen, any deal is possible.

Anyway, if Chet Morgan was not coming to us, then we had to go to Chet Morgan. I suggested, "Let's get some air."

So we put on our shoes and Kevlar vests, and we took our M4s, which we always carried when we went down to the courtyard. But this time we took extra magazines. The situation had changed, and I don't think we fully understood how it had changed, or what the Bedouin were thinking now. Zamo stayed in the tower and covered the courtyard with his rifle.

So Buck would speak to Yasir, and we'd all speak to Chet, the mastermind of Operation Clean Sweep, and we'd decide on our next move. But I already knew what Chet was going to say: We wait. The next move belongs to The Panther.

CHAPTER SEVENTY

Buck, Kate, Brenner, and I stepped into the van.

Chet was sitting at his console, watching the three Land Cruisers on his monitors, and he glanced over his shoulder and asked, "How did it go?"

Buck replied, "Not very well."

Chet pulled himself away from his screens, swiveled his chair, and asked, "Why not?"

Buck explained, "I think they're suspicious."

Chet replied, "Of course they are. They're not stupid."

I reminded him, "You said they were stupid."

"Yes. But they're also cunning and paranoid." Chet reassured us, "If The Panther wasn't interested in getting his hands on you, he wouldn't have even sent that delegation." He explained, "You don't make an appointment to see a car you're not interested in buying."

True, but sometimes you go look at the car because you want to steal it.

Anyway, Buck gave Chet a quick briefing of what happened and Chet listened carefully, then again assured us, "Al Qaeda is just doing due diligence. They need to protect The Panther, and they always proceed on the assumption that a double cross is possible." He reminded us, "This is the Middle East."

Right. Not the Midwest. Definitely not Kansas.

Chet said to me, "So you knew this guy, Nabeel?"

I replied, "He knew me before I knew him." I explained about the leak in the Yemeni consulate in New York, and I suggested, "The State Department should declare the whole consulate staff persona non grata."

Buck, Mr. State Department Intelligence, said, "The leak could be in the Foreign Ministry office in Sana'a." He informed me, "We like the Yemeni consulate staff in New York. They also sell information to us."

Right. It's a game. Double-Dealing for Dollars.

On a more important topic than me being pissed off about buying Nabeel a bagel in New York and him making me look silly, I said, "I think these Al Qaeda guys knew where they were taken."

Again, Chet didn't seem to care, and he asked rhetorically, "What are they going to do about it?"

But the question wasn't rhetorical and I said, "They're going to send a hundred jihadists to the Crow Fortress one night and kill everyone here."

Chet replied, "That would be war with Sheik Musa, and they do not want war with Sheik Musa."

Buck agreed and added, "It's not these walls or our weapons that protect us. It's the wrath of all the Bedouin tribes that protects us."

Chet added, "And the Predators."

"Okay." But I suggested, "We could use another ten or twenty Bedouin here."

Chet informed me and all of us, "The last thing

we want here are more armed Bedouin. If things go wrong, or turn around," he explained, "we can handle these eight guys. We can't handle any more."

I reminded Chet, "Sheik Musa is our trusted ally."

"He is," agreed Chet. "But alliances shift." He reassured us, however, "All that I said in Aden about Sheik Musa remains true. Unfortunately, with the Bedouin, they change their minds a lot."

Was that in the Aden briefing?

Buck, Mr. Arabian guy, said, "There are no constants in the lives of the nomadic Bedouin. Even the desert that they travel changes with the shifting dunes. Their only constant is the tribe, and they will always do what is best for the survival of the tribe." He added, "Fortunately, what's best for Sheik Musa's tribe at the moment is to ally themselves with the Americans. And it's important that he keeps believing that."

Right up until the time we put a Hellfire up his golden shiwal.

Chet said, "The critical time is now, when Musa's tribal council speaks to The Panther's council to determine if The Panther wants to buy the Americans, and if he will do the deal in person." Chet added, "That discussion could produce a variety of possibilities, not all of them favorable to us."

"Did I miss that memo?"

Chet said to me, Kate, and Brenner, "I'm being honest with you."

Kate responded, "Honesty that comes late is not honest or useful."

Chet advised us, "Keep an eye on the Bedouin here. They're simple people, and if you see a change in their attitude or demeanor, let me or Buck know."

Actually, I was more interested in a change in Chet's demeanor.

Chet changed the subject and turned back toward the monitors, saying, "You can see the three Land Cruisers heading north, toward Marib. See them? What's going to happen is that the Bedouin drivers will drop off the five Al Qaeda men in Marib—where the Bedouin picked them up, and where, unfortunately, they will disappear in the crowds or the buildings. Then at some point they will leave Marib, individually, by truck, bus, or SUV, driven by an Al Qaeda operative or a sympathizer, or just somebody looking to make a few rials. They will be let off near the highlands here, and make their way on foot to the Al Qaeda camp— which is actually one of Musa's Bedouin camps, located about forty kilometers from here." He explained, "That is an effective way to escape Predator surveillance, because the Predators will have lost them in Marib, and five men traveling individually will not look like a target of interest to the Predators because every male here carries a weapon." He continued, "Unfortunately for Al Qaeda, we know where their camp is, so they waste a lot of time and energy trying to elude aerial surveillance." He looked at us and smiled.

Chet, I think, was in love with his Predator drones. That's what broke up his marriage.

Chet turned in his seat and punched in a command on his console, saying, "I'm directing Predator One to go on station above the Al Qaeda camp."

We watched the monitor as the terrain slid by, showing the dry, rocky plateau west of here. Then the Predator began a counterclockwise turn, and on the monitor we could see tents, huts, and vehicles spread out across a flat expanse of the plateau that was surrounded by large rock formations.

Chet said, "That's the Al Qaeda camp."

We all moved closer to the monitor and I could now see people moving on the ground. There were also map grid coordinates on the screen, which I made a mental note of. Why? Because you never know what information you might need.

Chet twisted a dial and the image grew larger. He said, "It was—and still looks like—a Bedouin camp. But there are clues that it's not." He explained, "First, most of the men in the camp are not dressed in traditional Bedouin robes. Second, they're *all* men. No women, as you'd find in a Bedouin camp, and no children. Third, the men don't sit around and chew khat or herd goats as the Bedouin do. In fact, they train with rifles. Also, we spotted a mortar and rocket launchers, which are not typical Bedouin armaments."

Chet concluded with a smile, "But the big clue is that Sheik Musa told us the location of this camp that he rented to Al Qaeda."

Right. Aerial reconnaissance analysis is impressive, but nothing beats someone on the ground telling you what you're really seeing from the air.

Brenner asked, "Why does Al Qaeda think we wouldn't figure this out?"

Chet shrugged, then said, "I don't think they fully understand what we can see from the air, and that we can accurately analyze what we're seeing. Also, they don't know that we've dramatically increased the number of Predators in Yemen."

I watched the image on the screen and saw a few men in white foutehs walking around. So this is where

Rahim ibn Hayyam lived for a few months before he was sent to attack the Hunt Oil facility. Even from the air, the place looked like a shithole. He's better off in jail.

Chet further informed us, "The camp once held about a hundred fifty men, but now we're counting about fifty. About a hundred jihadists have left the camp—half on their way to the embassy and half on their way to the Sheraton in Aden."

Right. And maybe the other fifty were headed for the Crow Fortress. But Chet or the Predator pilots who were watching twenty-four hours a day would notice if more men started leaving the camp.

Chet said, "It's not a large camp, and it will be much smaller after the fighter-bombers level it." He added, "There are about five more camps like this in Yemen, and this is when we need to start eliminating them—because if we don't, there will be fifty, then a hundred, and then we have a real problem."

Right. Kill the beast in the cradle.

Chet reminded us, "We still don't know where The Panther's personal hideout is, and as with bin Laden in Afghanistan—or maybe Pakistan—it's almost impossible to locate a few individuals who are most likely living and hiding in caves. So we have to get The Panther out of his cave and kill him in the open." He added, "They all come out in the open eventually, for one reason or another." He looked at us and said, "And you, who have just been eyeball to eyeball with Al Qaeda, are a very good reason for Bulus ibn al-Darwish to come out of his cave."

No one had anything to add to that, but I confessed, "We came close to wasting those assholes."

"Not a smart move," said Chet.

Brenner said, "A bird in the hand."

"Tempting, maybe. But we have a bigger animal to kill."

I asked Chet, "What's the plan now?"

"We wait."

"We're out of tuna."

Chet didn't even smile, and he said, "I can almost assure you that Bulus ibn al-Darwish will have an answer for Sheik Musa within two or three days."

Buck needed to speak to Yasir, Arab to Arab, so he left the van. Kate and Brenner volunteered to put our cozy quarters back together, so they, too, left. I said I'd be along shortly.

Alone now in the van with Chet, we looked at each other for a few seconds, then he said to me, apropos our last private discussion, "There's no problem. Never was."

Wonderful news. I really felt awful about being paranoid and threatening Chet's life and all that.

I said to him, however, "There *was* a problem. And if there's *still* a problem, then I am still *your* problem."

He didn't reply.

I left Chet to watch his monitors and think about his problem.

CHAPTER SEVENTY-ONE

The A-team of Operation Clean Sweep, including Chet, gathered in the mafraj, whose high, open arches gave us an unobstructed view of the terrain for miles around. These watchtowers were the Predators of the last millennium. Hey, Abdul, there's a bad guy— drop a rock on him.

We all had our M4s and Kevlar, and Zamo did his march around the perimeter of the mafraj. The rest of us stood on the carpet of bird crap.

Buck began, "Yasir had little to offer regarding whether or not the Al Qaeda delegation seemed suspicious about this kidnapping. Yasir did say, however, that he didn't like these men, and especially didn't like Nabeel, al-Amriki."

Well, if Nabeel al-Samad was an American, then I'm a Bedouin. But from the Bedouin's perspective, Nabeel could have come from Mars.

Buck also told us, "Yasir says he thinks that only Nabeel was a Yemeni. The rest, he believes, are from someplace else." Buck added, "The Bedouin do not trust these people."

And the feeling is mutual. Recalling Chet's new-found concerns regarding Sheik Musa, I asked, "So do you think we can still trust Musa and his men?"

Buck replied, "The Bedouin practice a primitive democracy. Which means that even if their sheik wants to switch sides and make common cause with Al Qaeda, the tribesmen won't necessarily go along with it."

We could use some primitive democracy in the ATTF.

Anyway, it occurred to me that the Bedouin tribesmen might not actually know that The Panther and his retinue were going to be vaporized by Hellfire missiles, so I asked Buck and Chet about that.

Buck replied, "Musa and his men who will be with him obviously know what's going to happen at this meeting. And if one Bedouin knows something, they all know it. Also, the Bedouin know this was a sham kidnapping, so they all understand that the Americans aren't really being offered to Al Qaeda."

Brenner said, as he did back in Aden, "That is a massive security breach. All it would take is one Bedouin to tip off Al Qaeda."

Chet replied, "We're trusting that whatever the Bedouin know stays with the Bedouin." He reminded us, "They are very clannish."

Let's hope so. Otherwise we have a problem.

Buck also told us, "From what I can gather from my conversations with them, the Bedouin think that one of the purposes of this meeting is to discuss important matters which need to be resolved between the tribes and Al Qaeda." He added, "Sheik Musa is wise to take that approach, and it's a compelling reason for The Panther to show up in person. The two warlords need to talk. And even if they can't agree about the Americans, they have other pressing issues to discuss, man to man, chief to chief."

Right. Like the rent on the Al Qaeda camp. Musa is smart. Five million bucks makes you think.

On another subject, Buck said, "As we also know, neither the Sheraton Hotel in Aden nor the embassy in Sana'a have been attacked, and I believe, as do my colleagues in the embassy, and Chet's colleagues as well, that The Panther has put those attacks on hold until he makes his decision."

Good news for everyone in Aden and Sana'a, except people like Captain Mac who were looking for a fight.

Chet added, "Those attacks could end in disaster for Al Qaeda, and they are signs of The Panther's desperation or recklessness. The Panther, however, now sees an easier way to score a win."

Buck continued, "And The Panther knows he can still order those attacks after the deal is done with Musa." He reminded us, "But of course he'll be dead if he shows up at the meeting, and those attacks, we believe, will probably not be ordered by his successor."

Well, not right away. But someday.

I thought the mafraj meeting was over, but then Buck, who saves the best for last as he did at the Bilqis ruins, said, "Yasir gave me a sealed envelope that was given to him by Nabeel." He pulled a long white envelope from his pocket, and I saw that the logo on it was from the Bilqis Hotel. Our bill?

Buck told us, "Nabeel told Yasir it was for Detective Corey, but I took the liberty of opening it." He explained, "In case it contained anthrax, or a letter bomb."

Do I thank him for risking his life to open my mail?

Buck slid a stack of photographs from the envelope and handed them to Chet, saying, "I warn you, some of these are not easy to look at."

Chet looked at the first photo, then passed it to me. It was a group shot, taken in front of the columns at the Bilqis ruins. It showed what I assumed were the Belgian tourists—two older couples, two younger couples, and a pretty young woman, maybe sixteen or seventeen years old, all smiling into the camera. In the center of the group was a tall, bearded Bedouin in robes wearing a shiwal, and also wearing a jambiyah. He, too, was smiling. And what was making this murderer smile?

I passed the photo to Kate as Chet passed a second photo to me. This one was of the young woman standing close to the Bedouin—Bulus ibn al-Darwish, The Panther—and they were both smiling, though neither had their arm around the other. I passed the photo to Kate, who said, "That bastard."

The next few photos showed other posed shots with the couples and the man they thought was a Bedouin.

I knew what was coming, of course, but even so, the next photograph was difficult to process immediately, but then I recognized a close-up of one of the older women lying on the brown paving stone, her throat cut from ear to ear, and a pool of red blood around her head and face.

I stared at it. The woman's eyes were open, and there was a look of terror on her face. She could have been alive.

Kate, who was looking at me, asked, "What is it?"

I passed the photo to her, and she stared at it, then said softly, "Oh my God...oh..."

Brenner took the photo from her, looked at it and said, "Sick."

Buck asked, "Do you want to see the rest of them?"

Chet took the photos from Buck's hand, flipped through them quickly, then handed them to me.

I, too, went through them quickly, noting that some of the long shots showed all nine Belgians dead with their wrists bound behind their backs, and around them were men dressed as Bedouin who were actually Al Qaeda jihadists.

In one photograph I could see a man at the bottom of the steps who had been pushed or had tried to run. One close-up photograph was of a young man who looked Arabic—the guide, I assumed—who had probably taken the group photo of the Belgians with the tall Bedouin who turned out not to be a Bedouin.

The last photograph was a close-up of the young woman. Her eyes were wide open, and her parted lips looked very dark against her white, bloodless skin.

I passed the photos to Kate, who passed them to Brenner without looking at them.

Zamo had come over to see what was going on, and Brenner gave him the stack of photographs.

Zamo slung his rifle, shuffled through the photos, and handed them back to Brenner without comment, then he walked to one of the arches and stared out into space.

Buck said, "Obviously, we can identify the man in the posed shots dressed as a Bedouin." He added, "There was no note with these photographs, but there was this..."

He handed me a business card, and I saw it was my card, the one I'd given to Nabeel in Ben's Kosher Deli a million years ago. On the back I saw where I'd written, *Nabeel al-Samad to see Det. Corey.* And someone, obviously Mr. al-Samad, had drawn a smiley face. Good cultural awareness, Nabeel. Asshole.

I gave the card to Kate, who looked at it, then she asked of no one in particular, "Why did they give us these photographs?"

It was Buck who replied, in Latin, no less, "Res ipsa loquitur." He translated, "The thing speaks for itself."

Indeed it does. And I got the message.

I said, "I think this answers our question about what The Panther is going to do. He is not showing us what he's capable of doing, or what he's done—he's showing us what he is *going* to do. To us." I concluded, "He's made his decision. He will meet with Sheik Musa."

Everyone agreed, but I still wondered if The Panther would want to avoid that meeting and try the direct approach by storming this fortress.

Either way, Bulus ibn al-Darwish had a lot of murders to answer for. And he would not answer for them in an American court of law. He would answer for them here, in Yemen, in an appropriate act of violence. He may not have been born here, but he *was* going to die here.

CHAPTER SEVENTY-TWO

The eight Bedouin again invited us to dine with them, which was a good sign that we were still their honored guests, because Bedouin hospitality demands that you don't kill your guests. I mean, from their perspective this was all a big pain in the ass. Not only did the Bedouin have to share their daily goat with us, but they'd also had to deal with the five Al Qaeda assholes who, in some existential way, were a threat to their ancient way of life.

We dressed for dinner—Kevlar and guns for the gentlemen; balto, hijab, Kevlar, and guns for the lady.

Buck said he'd be along shortly, after he made a sat-phone call. I, too, excused myself, saying I needed to visit the excrement shaft, so Kate, Brenner, and Chet went down to the courtyard. Zamo ordered goat take-out and went up to the mafraj.

Before Buck made his call and before I hit the shaft, I asked him, out of curiosity, "How many tribesmen live around here?"

Buck replied, "There hasn't been a census since the Queen of Sheba, but I'd guess there are about thirty thousand Bedouin in and around Marib province, and they make up about ninety percent of the population." He added, "Musa's tribe—men, women, and children—number maybe ten thousand."

I did the math and said, "Five million dollars is about five hundred bucks for every man, woman, and child." I added, "That's about a year's pay."

Buck informed me, "Musa will actually take the lion's share, and he will also share some of that with the other tribal sheiks as a traditional courtesy."

Actually, Musa will be dead, but I asked, "How about bribes to government officials?"

"A few." Buck asked me, "Why does this interest you, John?"

"Because five million is a lot of money and it's a good motivator, but big bounties attract other people."

"Who did you have in mind?"

"Well, Colonel Hakim comes to mind."

Buck said, "I doubt if the U.S. government would pay Colonel Hakim if he killed The Panther."

"If they'll pay Musa for The Panther's head, they'll pay anyone for that head." Except us. We get a paycheck. I asked Buck, "Is the Yemeni government offering a reward for the death or capture of The Panther?"

"Yes, but it's our money they're offering." He reminded me, "Al Qaeda is *our* problem."

"How about a Yemeni government reward for the death or capture of Sheik Musa?"

"Definitely not."

"Why not?"

"Because if the Yemeni government put a price on the head of *any* tribal sheik, no matter how much they wanted him dead, that would cause a tribal uprising all over the country."

"So that's why the Americans are whacking Sheik Musa, as a favor to the Yemeni government. Musa is President Saleh's problem, but our job."

"Correct." He looked at me and asked, "What is it that you don't understand about this?"

"I don't understand how we can help a corrupt, brutal, and treacherous dictator and his government kill a tribal sheik who has done nothing to us, and who is helping us in a very important matter."

"We've been through this, John." He informed me, "I've done worse during the Cold War." He let me know, "The ends justify the means."

I didn't reply, but on a related subject of people getting whacked, I inquired, "Did you know that Kate killed a CIA officer?"

He nodded.

I asked him, "Do you think that's one of the reasons that Kate and I are here?"

"I'm not following you."

"Of course you are."

He didn't reply directly but said, "I believe you and Chet have discussed that."

"Correct. And he assured me there was no problem."

"Then there is no problem."

"I'm relieved."

"Good." He asked, "Anything else on your mind?"

"Yes..." I confessed to him, "I want to be a warlord."

He forced a smile and informed me, "The Panther is a type of warlord, but he can never be a sheik, and neither can you."

"Warlord is okay."

"Good. I have a class on that."

I smiled. Buck was easy to like. But not easy to trust.

The smell of dinner wafted through the window and I said, "Smells like Italian sausage at the Feast of San Gennaro in Little Italy."

"Goat."

"Again?"

I didn't really have to answer a call of nature, but Buck really did have to make a call in private, so I went down to the courtyard where a fresh, whole goat was roasting on a spit. Good. I hate leftover goat.

Buck joined us a bit later, and Kate said she'd dine in the van and monitor the electronics. I think she felt awkward at a stag dinner. Also, the van was running and the generator was powering the small air-conditioning unit, so Kate shut the doors, saying, "It's hot in this balto. Enjoy the fresh air, gentlemen."

Right. A dozen gamey guys and a roasting goat. Does life get any better?

Anyway, after a simple and simply awful dinner, we joined Kate in the van and watched a little TV—Channel One was showing a rerun of the infrared night view of the Crow Fortress, and Channel Two was showing our immediate area of concern, meaning a wider view of the plateaus and the surrounding flatlands. Nothing seemed to be moving out there, except a diminishing herd of goats.

Chet announced that he was going to sleep in the van—which could be locked from the inside—so he could be near the screens, and in case he got a radio or sat-phone call from the Predator pilots, who remained vigilant through the night. Sounded like a good idea. Sleep light, Chet.

The rest of us went up to the diwan and posted our guard—Kate and I took the first shift, Buck and Brenner the second, and Zamo pulled the last shift alone.

During our guard duty, Kate said to me, "I have to be honest with you, John, those Al Qaeda men and those photos shook me up."

"That's what they wanted. But you should also be angry."

"I am . . . but . . . I want to get this over with."

I told her, "You can actually leave. If you think about it, we're not needed here anymore. Al Qaeda saw the bait, and they won't see us again. The next thing they and The Panther will see is Sheik Musa, followed by Hellfire missiles."

She thought about that and nodded, but said, "I'm not going anywhere without you, and I know you're staying, so I'm staying." She looked at me. "We need to see this through to the end."

We actually didn't, but we did. I said, "If you change your mind, I'm sure we can get you to the Marib airstrip, then to Sana'a Airport, or back to the embassy."

"This subject is closed."

"Okay." We separated and looked out different windows—north and west for me, south and east for Kate.

Right. We could actually leave now. So could Buck, Brenner, and Zamo for that matter. Only Chet had to stay behind to direct the Predators and the Hellfire missiles, and then, if all went well, he could go alone to collect pieces of the garbage. And even that wasn't completely necessary for a successful mission.

But I, and the rest of us, couldn't leave Chet here by

himself. I mean, our differences and egos aside, we'd sort of bonded as a team. Right? We'd come a long way and all of us wanted to be here to see this through together. Also, I wanted to see what Chet was up to.

And to be honest, we all wanted to see the blasted corpses of The Panther and his jihadists—to smell the burnt flesh and bone—to see what we had done by remote control that we would have liked to have done up close and personal. And, like warriors since the beginning of time, we wanted to take mortal evidence of our victory back to our camp—in this case, a forensic lab. Warfare has changed, but the heart of the warrior remains the same; it remains primitive.

CHAPTER SEVENTY-THREE

The following day brought no word from Sheik Musa about Al Qaeda, and I was beginning to think we weren't worth a hundred thousand dollars, which was a big hit on my ego.

The real problem, of course, was the provision in the deal that it had to be negotiated by the principals. No underlings.

I had the thought that many chiefs from the beginning of time had also found themselves in this quandary. I mean, do you show up and take a chance that the other chief has a surprise for you? Or do you strap on your brass balls and take the meeting?

I guess that decision depends on how brave you are. Or how stupid you are. Or how paranoid you are. Or, in the end, how hungry you are for what was being offered.

By the second day, the A-team was beginning to doubt my conclusion—and their hope—that The Panther would say yes to the meeting. But I kept thinking about those photographs—the message *was* clear: I hate the West, I hate America, and I will do anything I have to do to cut your throats.

At about half past three of the second day, we had our answer.

Chet got a radio message from a Predator pilot reporting that a single Toyota Land Cruiser was climbing the north slope of the plateau, on its way toward the Crow Fortress—code-named Point A, in case anyone was listening.

The A-team went up to the mafraj and watched the Land Cruiser coming from the direction of the rock pile where Musa's men guarded the northern approach to the plateau and the fortress.

The Bedouin in the courtyard, who'd been called by the Bedouin guarding the approach, opened the gates and the white Land Cruiser entered.

We watched from the mafraj as five armed Bedouin piled out of the SUV and began talking to the eight men in the courtyard.

Chet said to us, "They're not delivering food or water, so I think they're delivering a message."

Good CIA thinking. But I would have welcomed a few chickens.

Chet and Buck volunteered to go down to the courtyard to see what was going on, and Chet also said, "I need to see what's happening in the van. Cover us."

Well, I'll cover Buck. You're on your own, Chet.

Buck and Chet, armed and armored, moved quickly down the stairs to the courtyard.

Brenner said to Zamo, "Cover, but don't aim at anyone." To us he said, "Same. But be ready. Don't misinterpret. Only I give the order to fire."

I thought Brenner was overreacting to what seemed like a non-threatening situation. But something *was* happening—a transitional moment in the routine and rhythm of life in the Crow Fortress.

Buck and Chet appeared in the courtyard, and Buck walked directly toward the Bedouin, who now totaled thirteen. That's a lot of AK-47s. Chet unlocked the van and disappeared inside. No one stopped him, and that was a good sign.

Buck was now speaking to one of the newcomers who seemed to be the boss. Yasir was in on the conversation and the other Bedouin stood around listening. With the Bedouin, when the bosses speak, the rank and file stand around and listen. Just like at 26 Fed. Not.

Anyway, it appeared that Buck and the Bedouin were having a normal, though slightly excited, conversation.

Finally, Buck did his Go in Peace thing and entered the van to report to Chet. The Bedouin continued their conversation.

Brenner told Zamo to stay in the mafraj, and we went down to the diwan where we could be closer to the situation, whatever it was.

Finally, Buck appeared from the van and moved quickly toward the tower.

He came up the stairs, slightly out of breath, and announced, "The Bedouin say that The Panther has sent a verbal message directly to Sheik Musa." He smiled and told us, "They will meet in about two hours"—he looked at his watch—"at six P.M. to discuss various matters of mutual interest, and also to discuss the sheik's offer of the five Americans." Buck added, "The Panther just tacked that on as though it was of peripheral importance." He further informed us, "Typical Arab bargaining technique."

And not a bad technique. Like, "Hey Abdul, let's talk about camel grazing rights. And by the way, how much do you want for your wife?"

Anyway, this was good news indeed, and we all did high-fives—even Buck, who didn't know what a high-five was.

Buck also told us, "The meeting will take place at the same goat herder's hut where we met Sheik Musa."

That must be the sheik's Camp David. More importantly, it was near the road where the Otter had put us down, and would now pick us up after we filled the goo bags.

I glanced out the window and saw that the five Bedouin who'd arrived were still there, and I asked, "Are they staying?"

Buck replied, "Yes. For extra security and also to escort us to the scene of the attack."

I reminded Buck, "I thought we didn't want more Bedouin in the courtyard."

"It's their property," he reminded us. "They are on our side."

"Right," I agreed, "but maybe they could be on our side someplace else."

Buck assured us, "The Bedouin won't be here long, and neither will we. In fact, we are two hours away from a successful mission, and maybe another hour away from jumping on that Otter."

Right, and we should take Sheik Musa with us. He has some big bucks coming to him, and I know a deli in Brooklyn he can buy, and the Yemeni government would be just as happy to see him gone as see him dead. But happy endings are not always so neat and tidy in real life.

It also occurred to me that what was driving The Panther—hate, revenge, and too many frustrating defeats—was the same thing that was driving Chet. And that's when your judgment gets clouded.

But to be more positive—like Buck and Chet—and maybe to be less cynical than usual, it could be that what we were seeing was what we were getting: one dead Panther who put his instincts aside and went for the meat.

Buck, who doesn't like it when he sees me thinking, asked, "What's on your mind, John?"

"Not much." I asked him, "What's Chet doing in the van?"

Buck replied, "Coordinating all aspects of a stealthy assassination attack." He let us know, "Two more Predators are coming on station over the goat herder's hut. They'll be ready for the meeting." He also told us, "Two Predators remain on station here, over and around the Crow Fortress. They will cover us when we drive with Musa's men to the scene of the attack, and they will cover the landing and takeoff of the Otter."

"Right." I asked, "Who has the goo bags and latex gloves?"

"Chet."

"If The Panther's head is in one piece, can I take that home?"

Buck didn't reply at first, but then said, "We're primarily interested in the fingers for the prints and DNA."

"Right." I like being a little nuts now and then, and I said, "I hope that little shit Nabeel is there. I want his balls in a Ziploc."

Kate finally said, "John, that's enough."

"Sorry. I'm excited."

Brenner, who'd seen war firsthand, and who may have taken a head or an ear himself, said nothing. War is hell, ladies and gentlemen, and all the euphemisms are not going to change the nature of the act. Kill them before they kill you, then celebrate.

Brenner said to Buck, "I'll leave Zamo in the mafraj for cover and we'll join Chet in the van."

But Buck informed us, "Chet needs an hour or so by himself." He explained, "What's happening now is top secret. He's actually speaking to people in Washington by radio, getting the necessary clearances and go-aheads."

Kate asked the obvious question. "What is he saying that we can't hear?"

Buck replied, "Just about everything." He explained, "This is all verbal so there is no written record of anything, and there can be no witnesses to what Chet says and what is said to him." He further explained, "Chet is speaking through the secure telephone unit, so names of personnel in Washington are en clair, and we don't need to hear those names—or hear anything."

I could almost hear Chet now. "Hey Dick, hi Ralph, Chet here. So, we're ready to vaporize some asshole jihadists and burn The Panther's traitorous ass with a few top-secret Hellfire missiles. You guys still okay with that? Any problems at that end? Just nod . . . Oh, sorry, I mean just say yea or nay."

Sounded reasonable. But who knew why Chet wanted to be alone or what he was saying and hearing? Not us.

So we had some time to kill before we were allowed to go into the van and watch the drama taking shape— the arrival of Sheik Musa and his merry Bedouin at the goat herder's hut, the arrival of The Panther and his retinue, the kiss of death, the tea party on the carpet, and finally the sheik ducking inside the hut on some pretext. And where, I wondered, would the sheik's men be? Hopefully not too close to The Panther and his men who were going to be hit by four laser-guided Hellfire missiles, each warhead packing twenty pounds of high explosives. Maybe all of the Bedouin would need to go off to take a piss at the same time.

There is an old saying among detectives: Never overlook the obvious.

And what was obvious to me was that Sheik Musa and his men, along with The Panther and his men, were actually going to share the same fate at that meeting. So obviously the A-team was not driving to the scene of the carnage, where some of these men—Bedouin and Al Qaeda—might still be alive and very pissed off.

If the obvious were true, then how do we, the Americans, get out of the Crow Fortress with thirteen Bedouin around us who would know soon enough from the survivors what happened to their sheik and their buddies? Right?

Well, we will see how it actually plays out. I could be wrong. Or I could be half right.

Buck said he was going down to speak to the Bedouin again and see if he could get a better sense of what they knew about the sheik-Panther meeting, and also what their instructions were.

It's good to have an Arabic speaker on the team. We couldn't have even attempted this mission without Buck. Next time I volunteer to go into Al Qaeda territory, I want Buck with me. Or maybe another Arabic speaker who wasn't so full of bullshit. Or better yet, maybe I'd take a pass on the next offer.

Buck left, and I brought up my concern of Hellfire missiles causing collateral damage to friendlies, meaning Sheik Musa and his men, and thereby putting us in a dangerous situation here at the Crow Fortress.

Brenner, who has seen a lot of high-explosive warheads ripping people apart, said, "I was thinking about that myself." He added, "As accurate as these missiles are, they throw out a lot of shrapnel. You don't want to be anywhere near a hit."

Kate said, "Why didn't you—we—bring this up at the meeting in Aden?"

Brenner replied, "I was thinking that Chet knew what he was talking about."

Well, he does, but sometimes he forgets the details.

Brenner continued, "I'm thinking that when Sheik Musa excuses himself to go into the stone hut, that's obviously the signal for Chet to order the Predators to fire the four Hellfires—but it's also the signal for the Bedouin to haul ass and dive for cover." He added, "They have about four, maybe five seconds to do that before eighty pounds of high explosives and shrapnel turn the area into a slaughterhouse."

One, two, three, four... I could be in the next province if I knew a Hellfire was on its way.

Brenner also surmised, "It would take The Panther and his men a few seconds to realize what's happening, but before they could react, they'll be in Paradise."

Probably true. Nevertheless, I did say, "There could still be friendly casualties."

Kate and Brenner thought about that, and Kate

said, "God, I hope not." She asked, "How would we get out of here?"

"Very quickly."

On that note, we climbed up the stairs to the mafraj to talk to Zamo and give him a heads-up on some of this. Brenner also said he wanted to show us something up there. Maybe a new species of bird shit, and that wouldn't smell half as bad as the bullshit we were getting down here from Buck and Chet.

CHAPTER SEVENTY-FOUR

We told Zamo the good news about the Panther-sheik powwow, and Brenner also told him, "We're going home today."

Zamo, man of few words, just nodded.

Brenner then drew our attention to the excrement shaft and pointed out a square hole in the ceiling directly above the shaft, whose wooden walls rose about eight feet, only half the way to the high ceiling of the mafraj. Brenner said, "That's a vent hole."

Right. Shit flows downhill, but the smell rises.

Brenner said to me, "Give me a boost."

So we walked over to the half wall of the shaft and I boosted him up so that he was standing precariously on the top of the wall with his fingers barely touching the edge of the vent hole for balance.

The squatter hole on each floor below was large enough for a person to squeeze through and drop to the next floor, which I'd noted as a means of escape. But you wouldn't drop straight through each hole into the pile of excrement without some squeezing and twisting. Nevertheless, I warned Mr. Brenner, "Careful. It's about sixty feet down. But the pile of shit will soften your fall."

"Thank you." He stood on his toes and grabbed the edge of the vent hole with both hands, then pulled himself up through the opening onto the roof.

Good upper-body strength. Now what?

He knelt at the hole and said, "We can do this."

I saw his legs and body drop through the hole, and he dangled by his fingers at the edge of the rough-hewn roof plank, then he swung himself clear of the wall of the excrement shaft and landed on the floor, announcing, "The roof has a four-foot-high parapet around it, which is good cover if we're in a firefight." Brenner, whose last war, Vietnam, was all about heli-copters, also informed us, "The rooftop will easily hold a helicopter."

That was really good news if we were trapped on the roof and taking fire, but I reminded him, "We have no helicopters in Yemen."

"Correct. But we're about one hundred seventy-five miles from Najran airfield, right across the Saudi border—about an hour flight time." He further informed us, "That's where the Predators come from, and probably also where the Otter is now."

"Okay. And?"

"And, if we have to, we can get a U.S. Army or Air Force chopper here to take us off this roof."

"Why," Kate asked, "would we have to do that?"

"Because," he replied, "if the Al Qaeda delegation figured out where they were taken, they may try to save a hundred thousand dollars and also show Sheik Musa who's the boss, not to mention avoiding that meeting."

"I hear you," I said.

Brenner continued, "I'm also not sure about our Bedouin allies, so we need to have a plan of escape."

And I thought *I* was paranoid. But this wasn't paranoia; this was Plan B from Point A.

Kate said, "It seems to me that a helicopter from Najran would be a better way of getting out of here and across the Saudi border than an Otter landing on a road."

"It would be," Brenner agreed, "but the Otter is Company run and this is a Company operation. Also, the helicopter—with or without U.S. Army or Air Force markings—can be easily identified as American, and that's not what the plan calls for. But if it's an emergency situation—here, or at the scene of the attack—then a chopper is what we'll need."

"Right," I agreed. "But an hour is a long time to wait for the cavalry to arrive."

Brenner agreed. "It is, but it's better than waiting for nothing to arrive."

Kate asked the obvious question. "Can we contact whoever it is we need to contact to get this helicopter?"

Brenner replied, "I made a sat-phone call to Ed Peters in the embassy, and he's trying to locate a contact number for the American installation at this Saudi airfield." He told us, "Officially, the U.S. is assigned there as a training group to the Royal Saudi Air Force, but everyone knows we also have some CIA and NSA resources at Najran to keep an eye and ear on the Yemeni situation. That's where the F-15s will come from to pulverize the Al Qaeda base camp."

Interesting. I asked, "Are we sharing this information with Chet and Buck?"

Brenner replied, "I would bet money that Chet

and Buck already have a direct sat-phone number and radio frequency for the American chief of operations at Najran airfield. And if they don't, they can radio the CIA at Najran." He also pointed out, "They haven't said a word to us about Najran or about helicopters."

Right. I mean, there was some crap going on here, but maybe not as much or as deep as my paranoid mind had imagined. There could be rational and logical national security explanations for everything that wasn't adding up. But if it keeps quacking like a duck, and keeps telling you it's an American eagle, you gotta be a little suspicious.

I asked Zamo, "Can you pull yourself up there?"

"Why not?"

"Because your arm is fucked up."

Brenner said, "I'll go first, you second, and we can easily pull up Zamo and Kate."

Did we forget old Buck? How about Chet?

Kate let us know, "I'm sure I can pull myself up."

I looked at the wall of the excrement shaft, which as I said was about eight feet high, and I pointed out, "The last person won't have anyone to boost them up."

Brenner replied, "That washstand in the diwan will hold Zamo's weight, and he's the heaviest person here."

I guess they already tried that. You can always count on military guys to show initiative and good skills in solving field problems.

I let Brenner and Zamo know, "Good thinking and good job. But let's hope we never have to get to the roof." On a related subject, I said, "You may have noticed that the squatter hole on each floor is big enough for any of us—even Zamo—to squeeze through."

Brenner, the expert on tower houses, said, "They're made big so it's easier to dump kitchen garbage and chamber pots down the hole to the excrement level." He also informed us, "The excrement shaft is a primitive fire escape in the tower houses."

You learn something new every day. Anyway, I pointed out, "If we need to go down the shaft instead of up, we can also manage that."

We all agreed that the excrement shaft had multiple uses, but before we adjourned the meeting, I brought up a perhaps moot subject and said to Brenner and Zamo, as I had said to Kate, "After the Al Qaeda guys came here and saw the bait, all of us, except for Chet, could have gotten out of here."

Brenner nodded and said, "I thought about that back in Aden."

And that would have been an excellent time to bring it up, Paul.

Brenner continued, "But"—he looked at me, Kate, and Zamo—"I don't think any of us ever intended to leave."

"No," I agreed, "we never did, but for the record, and for later, no matter what happens in the next few hours, we should acknowledge that we stayed beyond the time we were needed. We stayed to see how it ended."

No one had anything to add to that, except maybe the words, "Brave but dumb."

So the mafraj meeting was adjourned for probably the last time, and Kate, Brenner, and I went down to the diwan, leaving Zamo to contemplate the abstract thought that excrement shafts go up and down and either way could get you out of deep shit.

This was all coming to a head, and we had lots to think about, but the bottom line was the mission: Kill The Panther. Then worry about how to get out of here alive.

CHAPTER SEVENTY-FIVE

It was time to join Chet and Buck in Moses' Red Sea Fish van so Kate, Brenner, and I went down into the courtyard.

The sinking sun cast a shadow along the west wall, and the thirteen Bedouin sat or squatted in the shade, drinking herbal tea and chatting. Little piles of green leaves sat on the ground between them. It was the happy hour.

Kate, Brenner, and I went into the van where Chet was sitting in the left-hand chair, staring intently at the video monitor. Buck was in the right-hand chair doing the same.

Chet's screen showed the aerial view of the sheik's goat herder's hut, with a very close resolution of maybe a few hundred feet.

Buck's screen had a higher and wider image of the area around the hut, showing a two- or three-kilometer radius. I saw five white Land Cruisers heading for the hut from the east. The Bedouin? Or Al Qaeda? Probably the sheik and his men, who as hosts needed to get there early to make tea.

As we all knew, each of the two Predator drones over the hut had, in addition to video cameras, two laser-guided Hellfire missiles, each with a high-explosive warhead, ready to launch, then seek and destroy whatever was in the crosshairs of the monitors. Awesome.

Chet came out of his electronic trance and said to us, "Look. The sheik is arriving."

We looked closely at his screen and saw the five Land Cruisers pulling up about thirty yards from the hut, which was farther away than they had been when we'd arrived from the Otter to meet the sheik. In fact, the vehicles were far enough away from the kill zone to avoid winding up in an auto body shop.

As we all watched, the Bedouin began piling out of the five Land Cruisers, and I counted a total of fifteen, all carrying AK-47s, except one—the sheik.

Sheik Musa was distinguishable in his clean white robes and his regal shiwal. I couldn't see his face, but from this computer-enhanced height of a few hundred feet, I could actually see his awesome proboscis. I mean, that thing cast a two-foot shadow, and probably had its own zip code.

The Bedouin were unloading the SUVs—three carpets, and what were probably crates of bottled water, plus burlap bags of what was maybe bread and tea. They were carrying other things that could have been camp stoves and pots to boil water—but no khat for their Al Qaeda guests. Other than that, they had everything they needed for a Yemeni picnic, even ants in case someone had malaria. And, of course, they had their AK-47s, because later, in a gross breach of Bedouin hospitality, they'd kill any of their guests who hadn't been killed by the American Hellfires.

Sheik Musa ducked into the hut with a few of his men, and the rest of the Bedouin began setting up for the powwow.

Chet said to us, "The Panther and his men will arrive in about an hour or more. It's okay to be late, but never early."

If they had a woman with them, they wouldn't have to worry about being early. Sorry. That just slipped out.

Chet hit a button on his console and said, "The video is on record. So we can play the final few seconds of Mr. al-Darwish's life over and over again."

There was still the question of friendly fire casualties, and Brenner asked Chet about that.

Chet had a ready answer and replied, "The two sides don't mix. Al Qaeda is on their carpet or around their own vehicles, and the Bedouin do the same. Only the sheik and The Panther sit together on their own carpet and speak privately, and when the sheik excuses himself to go into the stone hut with a few of his men to drag out the Americans, that's the signal for the Bedouin to take cover." He added, "I then give the order to fire, and about four seconds later, it's all over for Mr. al-Darwish and maybe half his men. The Bedouin will finish off the survivors." He reminded us, "We discussed this in Aden."

We did, but maybe Chet was still full of shit and everyone down there was going to die. Or at least lose a body part. And then we had to get out of here. Quickly.

Chet split his screen and the left half now showed a wide view of the Crow Fortress taken from one of the second pair of Predators on station over the plateau. Chet said, "There's no one out there."

Right. No Al Qaeda army ready to storm the Crow

Fortress. So that was one indication that things were going as planned and that The Panther was going to show up at the goat herder's hut.

Chet said to us, almost matter-of-factly, "There's been a change of plans."

A little buzzer went off in my head.

He swiveled his seat toward us, looked at me, Kate, and Brenner, and said, "But a good change."

The buzzer got louder. Also, I noticed, Buck had been uncharacteristically quiet since we'd entered the van. Was he thinking about something? Or worried about something?

Chet continued, "It has been decided at the highest level that you three will leave here. Now."

Neither I nor Kate nor Brenner asked why. That was coming.

Chet said to us, "Your role in this mission is finished, and in fact it's been finished since the Al Qaeda delegation saw you."

We all knew that, but this was the first time Chet had mentioned it.

He answered the unasked question. "The thinking in Washington was that you would stay around for a few days after these Al Qaeda guys saw you, in case they figured out where they were taken, and in case Al Qaeda was watching the Crow Fortress to attack it or to see if anyone left." He went on, "But now that everything is in place and moving toward a conclusion, the mission planners want to split the team to ensure that we don't have all our eggs in one basket."

Again, the three eggs who were going to be put into another basket didn't raise any questions. Best to let Chet talk.

And he did, saying, "Buck and I will stay here until the Hellfires do their job. We'll keep Zamo here for security. And we will also have a Predator overhead for observation and security—the other Predator follows you." He looked at us again and said, "You will take one of these Land Cruisers and drive it down the north slope, pick up the Sana'a–Marib road, and drive to the Marib airstrip, where you will meet a chartered aircraft—a Company plane—that will take you to a location in Saudi Arabia, and then to Riyadh International Airport and home." He informed us, "If you push it, you can be at the airstrip in less than an hour."

Thirty minutes, if *I* was driving. Wow. This sounded too good to be true.

Chet asked, "Any questions? Any problems?"

It was Kate who said, "We intend to stay here until it's over. We are going to the scene of the attack with you and we are flying out of there together on the Otter."

Chet informed her, "That's not going to happen, Kate." He reminded us, "These are orders from the top." He added, nicely, "But I appreciate your dedication."

Brenner asked, "What's the purpose of us leaving now? I'm not understanding *why* we're splitting up."

Chet explained, "Something could go wrong as we drive between here and the scene of the attack, or at the scene, or something could go wrong with our rendezvous with the Otter." He further explained in a paternalistic tone of voice, "There is no reason for all of us to take that risk, and there is every reason to split up so as to ensure that . . . well, some of us get out of here."

Right. But who?

Chet added, "We don't want a situation where the mission is successful but the whole team is lost."

Like, the operation was a success, but the patient died. Got it.

Kate asked Chet, "Do you think it's safe for a single vehicle to drive from here to the Marib airstrip?"

Chet assured her and us, "The roads are safe enough in the daylight, and you don't have to worry about a Bedouin guest kidnapping in Sheik Musa's territory, and you don't even have to worry about Al Qaeda, who rarely leave these highlands in the daylight." He reminded us, "If you move fast, you'll be at the airstrip before anyone even knows you're on the road, or even knows who you are. These Land Cruisers are generally recognized as Bedouin vehicles, and as you know, the windows are tinted, but Kate should wear her balto and sit in the rear." He again assured us, "You'll have a Predator covering you just in case, and we have sat-phone contact with each other. The drive to the airstrip should be a piece of cake." He inquired, "Any worries?"

I, like Buck, had remained uncharacteristically silent, but I now asked, "Any reason we won't have a Bedouin escort?"

Chet replied, "You don't need that, and quite frankly, if something goes wrong at the scene of the attack, the last thing you want is a carload of Bedouin near you talking to other Bedouin on their cell phones."

Chet, it seemed, was concerned about our safety and our survival. And he and Buck would do the dangerous job of driving to the scene of the carnage, then they'd do the dirty work of collecting, bagging, and labeling the mortal remains of The Panther and his men, and maybe they'd also take some photos of the dead—as The Panther had done at the ruins. As for Sheik Musa, I was sure he and his Bedouin would be long gone from the scene, either in their Land Cruisers—or on their way to Paradise. So either way, Chet and Buck didn't have to deal with them. Check's in the mail, sheik.

And did Brenner, Kate, or I need to be here for any of that? Not really, but I was going to miss the blood and guts, and the smoking bones and flesh. That's not fair.

Chet asked us, "Any other worries?"

"Worries" was a word designed to make us look and feel like nervous troops who needed to man up and follow orders. Chet, like most crazy people, thought he was the smartest man in the room—or in the fish van. Well, he wasn't. That would be me.

Anyway, I looked at Kate, then at Brenner, and we exchanged glances of, I guess, acceptance of the situation.

I said to Chet, "Okay. No worries."

Kate said, "I'm not okay with this, but I understand."

Brenner said, "I also understand the reasoning. But Zamo will make his own decision about coming with us or staying here."

Chet said, "His orders are to stay here and provide security."

Brenner replied, "I don't care what his orders are. He's not under your control. He's under the control of the DSS and me."

Chet didn't reply, and Buck didn't explain to Chet about embassy procedures and protocols.

Finally, Chet conceded, "All right. It's his decision."

But we—Kate, Brenner, and I—had no decision to make. We had been ordered to get out. Not by Chet, but by someone at the top. To be honest, I was more than a little ambivalent about this. Getting a head start on the trip home was good, and the road trip to Marib airstrip was a much smaller danger than sticking around here for the fireworks. Still, this was a big disappointment, and I'm sure Kate and Brenner felt the same. But Chet and the mission planners were right—if we split up, there was a better chance of someone getting back to make a full report, and Washington needed a few people alive to congratulate.

Chet said to us, "Take only what you need and be on the road in ten minutes. When you land in Saudi Arabia, you'll turn in your weapons, Kevlar, and commo, and you'll be flying up to Riyadh Airport within fifteen minutes." He further instructed us, "Burn the passports that Buck gave you and take your dip passports for the international flight to the U.S."

Chet kept mentioning that flight home as though us hearing it would make us believe it was going to happen. And maybe it was. And maybe it wasn't.

Chet also reminded us, "Stick your head in here before you leave."

I promised him, "We wouldn't leave without saying good-bye, Chet."

He smiled.

I said to Buck, "See you later."

He nodded, sort of smiled, and said to us, "See you later."

The now-unemployed members of the A-team left the fish van, mission completed.

CHAPTER SEVENTY-SIX

We returned to the tower, and Brenner called Zamo down from the mafraj and told him what was happening.

Brenner said, "It's your decision if you want to stay here and cover Buck and Chet or come with us to Marib."

Zamo didn't agonize much over his decision and replied, "I work for you." He also reminded Brenner, "I don't get paid to make decisions."

Brenner did get paid to make decisions, and he said to Zamo, "You'll come with us."

I suggested, "Let's get moving."

We gathered up what we needed, which all fit into our overnight bags, and we left everything else for the Bedouin, including my socks and underwear.

Kate slipped her balto over her clothes, and we went down to the livestock and excrement level and built a small bonfire of passports and crumpled magazine pages, which Zamo lit with a match from his field survival kit. We made sure everything burned, then we went out into the fading sunlight of the courtyard.

The Bedouin were still sitting and squatting along the wall, probably thinking about their approaching sundown prayers, and a new recipe for goat.

Kate covered her face with her hijab, and Brenner, in his limited Arabic, seemed to be thanking our hosts for their hospitality. The Bedouin remained sitting as they all said, "As-salaam alaikum."

Brenner responded with, "Wa alaikum as-salaam."

And arrivederci.

Brenner said something to Yasir, who stood and waved his arm toward the parked SUVs, and Brenner told us, "He says take any one we want."

"Which one has the bag of khat?"

Brenner didn't ask, but Yasir did give us three shiwals, one off his own head and two from his buddies, and Brenner said to us, "This is a gift to remember them by."

And they have my underwear to remember me.

Brenner told them that everything we'd left behind, which was mostly luggage, clothing, and one can of mixed vegetables, was theirs to keep. And, no, they couldn't have Zamo's sniper rifle.

I said to Yasir, "See you in New York. Ben's Deli." I also said, "Shuqran," which means "thanks."

We threw our overnight bags into the rear of one of the Land Cruisers, and carrying our weapons, we all walked to the fish van.

Chet and Buck were still watching the screens, and Chet was on the radio speaking to someone. As we entered, he said into the mic, "I'll call you back. Out."

He and Buck stood, and Chet said, "So, you're taking Zamo."

Brenner replied, without explanation, "We are."

It was Buck who said, "The Bedouin in the courtyard are all the security we need, and some of them will accompany us to the scene."

So we said our good-byes without getting too teary-eyed, and we all agreed that the A-team had performed admirably.

Chet said to us, "Thank you for your very professional performance." He admitted, "It hasn't always been easy to work together, but we've put our differences aside in the service of our country." He looked at me and said, smiling, "You have been a challenge, Mr. Corey, but I'd rather work with a man like you than someone who never questions authority."

"Thank you." I think. Why do I always get singled out? This started in grade school.

Anyway, Buck added, "You can all be proud of your work here. Thank you for volunteering and for putting your lives at risk." He reminded us, "The homeland will be a little safer after Bulus ibn al-Darwish is dead."

I reminded Buck, "We have a rendezvous under the clock at Grand Central Station."

"I'll be there," Buck promised. "We'll stay in touch."

Chet said, "I'll try to be there, too."

You weren't invited, Chet. But, hey, anyone who's alive at the end of today is invited.

Buck, and even Chet, hugged Kate, we all shook hands, and we wished each other good luck and Godspeed.

Buck said, "As-salaam alaikum."

To relive our first meeting a million years ago, I smiled and said, "That's easy for you to say."

He smiled.

We left the van and piled into the Land Cruiser. Brenner was behind the wheel, Zamo was riding shotgun, and Kate and I were in the rear. The gentlemen had their shiwals with them, but no one saw any need to wear them at this time.

Yasir got off his butt and ran across the courtyard to open the gate as we approached it. We all waved to Yasir, who seemed delighted to see us go. But not as delighted as we were.

Brenner drove around the courtyard walls of the Crow Fortress, our home away from home, and we headed across the rocky plateau, toward the rock pile where the Bedouin guarded the northern approach to the fortress.

Brenner was following the dusty tracks of the other vehicles that had been to the Crow Fortress, and I asked him, "Do you know where you're going?"

He hesitated, then replied, "Down the north slope...to pick up the Marib road." He assured us, "I've been to the airstrip and I can find it."

"Good." We continued on toward the north edge of the plateau.

Kate said, "I can't believe this is happening."

Brenner assured her, "It is, and within an hour we'll be on board a Company aircraft lifting off and heading for Saudi Arabia." He added, "Probably Najran airfield."

Kate asked, "Does anyone feel...sorry or disappointed that we didn't stay until the end?"

Brenner and I, who are really in touch with our feelings, agreed that we would have liked to be there for the grand finale. Zamo, probably not into his feelings, said, "Tactically, this makes sense." He added, "But it sucks."

We continued on, and up ahead I could see the big rock formations and the SUV at the edge of the plateau where Musa's men sat in the shadows of the rocks.

I said to Brenner, "Slow down."

He reduced his speed and asked me, "What's up?"

I replied, "Here's what's up, Paul. Not too long ago, Kate killed a CIA officer—in self-defense." I asked him, "Did you know that?"

He hesitated, then replied, "I heard."

"Good." And you still have the hots for her? Brave man. I sleep with one eye open. Just kidding. I continued, "I think the Company is looking for some rough justice on that."

Kate said, "John, we are not supposed to discuss this—"

"This is really important, Kate. Do not interrupt." I continued, "As if Kate killing this guy wasn't bad enough, we had also inadvertently messed up a CIA plan to turn most of the Mideast into a nuclear wasteland."

It was quiet in the Land Cruiser, and I continued, "So, Kate and I know this big secret, and we're sworn to silence forever—in exchange for the Company giving Kate a pass on the firearm incident. But the CIA doesn't really work that way."

Brenner, happily, agreed with me and said, "No, they don't."

"Right. They might let the gun incident go, but they are not comfortable with two witnesses walking around with that knowledge about the nuclear Armageddon that they'd planned for Sandland."

Brenner was driving even slower now, and he seemed to be thinking. Finally, he realized I'd said my piece, and asked, "So what...what are you saying?"

"I'm saying that Kate and I, and anyone who happens to be with us, are not getting out of Yemen alive."

No one had a response to that, and I explained, "That's why Kate and I are here—this is the perfect killing zone. No one answers to anyone for anything here. It's a black hole." I added, "And this is Operation Clean Sweep."

Brenner stopped the Land Cruiser. He glanced in his rearview mirror and said, "Kate? Do you believe this?"

My soul mate replied, "No, I do not."

Zamo, who usually has no opinion, said, "I do."

There you go. It's settled.

Brenner asked the obvious question. "How do you think this...this is going to happen?"

"I'll get to that later, but I can say it will happen between right here and the Marib airstrip."

No one had any response to that.

I asked, "Why do you think we're in this SUV, out of the Crow Fortress and away from Chet and Buck?"

Brenner replied, "What Chet said makes perfect tactical and operational sense."

"Indeed, it does, which is why my paranoia wasn't supposed to kick in. And you know what? I'm only, let's say, seventy-three percent sure I'm right about Chet wanting to get me and Kate whacked."

Kate said, "If we sit here all day, we *could* get killed. We need to get to the airstrip."

Brenner asked me the next logical question. "What does this—if it's true—have to do with me, or with Zamo?"

I replied, "You are just in the wrong place at the wrong time. It's logical that you would be ordered to leave with Kate and me, and if you weren't, that would look suspicious. As for Zamo, he was never going to stay behind. That was all bullshit to make this look like a tactically sound plan." I informed Mr. Brenner, "Buck knew exactly what you were going to say about Zamo staying here, and one way or the other, Zamo was not going to stay with Buck and Chet." I added, "And if he did, Chet would kill him with an AK-47, take his sniper rifle, and make it look like the Bedouin did it."

Both men remained silent, then Brenner said, "I'm just not buying that Zamo and I are going to get wasted by our own people just because we happen to be with you."

"You should believe it, but here's another reason you're not in a good place—for all Chet knows, I or Kate have confided in you about my suspicions, and you are therefore a person like us who knows too much." I reminded him and everyone, "And in this business, when you know what you're not supposed to know, you become a worry to the Company." I added, "The Company chose well when they chose Chet Morgan for this job." I explained, in case no one noticed, "He's crazy."

Brenner, Kate, and Zamo thought about all that, and I could imagine them concluding that John didn't need a Kevlar vest as much as he needed a strait-jacket.

But Brenner, either avoiding the topic of my paranoia, or maybe testing it, asked, "So do you think Buck is in on this?"

That was a tough call. The answer was that Buckminster Harris had been in the deception business so long, he really didn't know what was real and what he was making up. Right and wrong was a little blurry, too. Plus, he just enjoyed the game. I was sure he liked me, Kate, and all of us, but if Chet presented him with a national security problem and a solution, then Buck would work with Chet on both. Nothing personal.

Finally, I replied, "Buck has to be in on it."

Well, by now, Paul Brenner was waiting for me to announce that I'd been abducted by space aliens. But he was smart enough to be concerned, and he was still enough of a cop to want all the info. He said to me, "Even if you're right . . . I mean, you're giving Chet a lot of credit for being some kind of genius . . ."

"He's out of his fucking mind," I assured everyone. "But he's smart. I, however, am smarter." I asked my seatmate, "Right?"

She didn't reply. Clearly Kate was upset, and she was obviously worried that I'd slipped over the edge.

Brenner, in fact, said, "Look, we've all been under a lot of stress—"

"All right," I said, "drive on." I promised everyone, "We'll see what happens."

But Brenner didn't drive. He asked me, "What do you *think* is going to happen?"

I replied, "I think that a Predator drone, under the command of the Central Intelligence Agency, and under the operational control of Chet Morgan in his fish van, is going to launch a Hellfire missile at this vehicle and kill everyone inside it." I added, "The Predator pilot, wherever he is, will be clueless, or at least unsure, but he'll do what the operational control guy on the scene—Chet—tells him to do."

It was Zamo who spoke first. "Yeah. That could happen."

It sure could. I also said, "The Company has picked this method of a friendly fire accident to send a clear message that it wasn't friendly and it wasn't an accident."

Brenner stayed quiet awhile, then said to me, "Okay . . . what are *we* supposed to do?"

"What we're not going to do is drive down that slope and head cross-country toward the Marib road, because if we do, we're not going to get to the Marib road."

Brenner asked, "Then why are we even in this Land Cruiser? Why didn't you tell us this back in the Crow Fortress?"

"If I had, what would we have done?"

"Tell Chet and Buck what you just told us."

I replied, "At least they would believe me. But here's the deal—the mission comes first. Chet is poised to kill The Panther. And we will let him do that. But we will not let him have a friendly fire accident on our way to Marib."

Brenner sort of nodded.

I said to him, "Let's go."

As we moved toward the rock pile and the Bedouin guarding the approach to the plateau, I said, "Chet has not directed a Predator to watch us because the Predator pilot and other ground controllers would see that it was us who got into this Land Cruiser, and they would not fire on it." I explained, "Chet will get a Predator on station when he thinks we're traveling cross-country toward the Marib road. He will tell the pilot to keep us in his sight, then at some point he will inform the pilot that the Land Cruiser is a confirmed target. And then Chet will execute the assassination stage of the flight and order the pilot to take out the target." I added, "Kate's balto and our shiwals will be mentioned in the incident report as one reason for the misidentification of the people in the Land Cruiser as a target." I added, "Souvenirs can be dangerous."

No one had anything to say about that, so I asked, "Would anyone have a problem with asking one of those Bedouin to drive this vehicle down the slope and toward the Marib road?"

Zamo replied in a heartbeat, "Not me."

Brenner said, "I would have a problem with that... but..."

Kate didn't reply, and I said to her, "If nothing happens, then you're right and I'm crazy."

She hesitated, then replied, "I...would not want to see an innocent person killed..."

I pointed out, "You said I was wrong."

"I'm not making that decision."

"Okay. I'll make it."

The Bedouin around the rocks were watching us, and Brenner pulled close to them.

I said to him, "I need your Arabic."

Brenner and I got out of our Land Cruiser and everyone did their peace thing.

There were five Bedouin with AK-47s and they had one white Land Cruiser with them.

I said to Brenner, "Tell them we will give them mucho rials if one of them will take our vehicle to the airstrip and pick up an Amriki who is waiting there for us."

Brenner glanced at me, hesitated, then began speaking in halting Arabic.

The five Bedouin nodded in understanding, and Brenner said to me, "This gentleman"—he pointed to a bearded guy in his thirties or forties—"will go for us."

I nodded and smiled at the guy.

"He says he'll take his own vehicle."

"No." I took Brenner's arm and we stepped onto a small flat rock. I said, "See that?"

Brenner stared at the roof of our Land Cruiser, whose dusty white paint was smeared with what looked like blood, probably goat blood. He kept staring at the smear, then said, "Jesus..." He looked at me.

I stepped down off the rock and asked him, "So what do you think, Paul?"

He seemed at a loss for words, but then reminded me, "Yasir told us to take *any* vehicle."

"Right. Pick a card. Any card." At the risk of stating the obvious, I said, "They're all marked."

He nodded.

I said to him, "We can wipe the red target off, or since all the Bedouin vehicles are communal, we can swap cars with these gentlemen, and we can proceed to the Marib airstrip, and hopefully not get vaporized on the way. But I don't think there's anything or anyone waiting for us at the airstrip. So I suggest we go back to the Crow Fortress and deal with this." I checked my watch. "We should be there about the time The Panther is in Chet's sights."

Brenner, who has seen lots of death, has probably not seen lots of treachery and double crosses, and he still looked a little out of it. Hello, Paul?

Kate and Zamo were out of the Land Cruiser, and Kate glanced at Brenner, then asked me, "What's happening?"

I said to Brenner, "*You* tell her." She never believes me.

The Bedouin were watching us, curious about what

the crazy Amriki were talking about, so we didn't want to go look at the roof again and put ideas into their heads. But Brenner said to Kate and Zamo, "There is a red marking—looks like blood—on the roof of the Land Cruiser."

Zamo, who'd painted lots of people red with a red laser beam before he sent them to Paradise, got it in a heartbeat, and said, "Holy shit."

Well said.

Kate is quick, but stubborn, and she reminded us, "But Yasir said—"

"They're *all* marked," I informed her. "They weren't marked when we were up in the diwan or I'd have seen that, because I was looking for it. But when we went down to burn our civilian passports on the ground level, the Bedouin, at the prior request of Chet, marked all the roofs with goat blood, probably thinking that they were putting some kind of holy protection mark on the SUVs. You know, like the Passover thing with the lamb's blood." I added helpfully, "Exodus."

Well, maybe that was a stretch, but close enough. Or Yasir and his buddies had no idea why Chet gave them a few rials to do something weird. But they did know to keep their mouths shut about it. I further informed my teammates, "Chet also asked Yasir to give us the shiwals, which will be mentioned in the incident report."

Kate looked at me, and I thought maybe she'd say, "Sorry I doubted you," but she didn't. She asked me, and all of us, "What do we do now?"

I explained to Kate and Zamo that a road trip to Marib airstrip might not be productive, and I suggested, "We can let this kind gentleman here take the vehicle marked for death, and absolutely confirm that

Chet was planning to whack us." I asked, "Anyone need to see that?"

No one apparently did.

I suggested, "Let's go back to the Crow Fortress and talk to Chet and Buck."

Brenner agreed, but said, "They will deny everything."

Kate agreed, and so did Zamo.

Indeed, Chet and Buck would deny everything, and we had no proof that I wasn't totally crazy. And if we disobeyed orders and went back to the Crow Fortress and I accused Chet and Buck of plotting to kill us, that could get very weird, and I'd be the one answering charges back in the States. Not to mention that the Company would definitely see to it that Kate and I met with a fatal accident. So we couldn't go back to the Crow Fortress without proof, we didn't want to drive to Marib, and we couldn't stay here.

Zamo said, "Let the guy drive."

No one responded to that.

The guy in question, whose name was Emad, said something to Brenner, who didn't reply.

Okay, someone has to make life-or-death decisions, and like Brenner, I too get paid for that. And yet . . .

Finally, I said, "Let Emad drive to Marib airstrip."

Neither Kate nor Brenner seconded that, but neither did they object. Zamo, however, said, "Otherwise, you'll never know for sure."

Brenner hesitated, then said something to Emad, who smiled and got into our Land Cruiser. Emad didn't ask for his money up front, but Brenner pressed a handful of rials on him and said something to him in Arabic.

In truth, we were becoming more callous and more like the bad guys, but at least we had a conscience.

Emad waved and took off down the slope.

Well, part of me hoped I was wrong, but the blood on the roof said I was right. In fact, everything said I was right.

One of the Bedouin said something to Brenner, and Brenner said to me, "He wants to know if we need a ride back to the Crow Fortress."

I looked at my watch and said, "Ask him if we can borrow his vehicle."

Brenner asked, and it was no problem, and I tipped them with the last of my rials.

I drove this time, and Zamo rode shotgun. Kate and Brenner sat silently in the rear.

After a few minutes we could see the Crow Fortress ahead, and I spotted a pile of rocks on the left. I pulled over and said, "We can watch from here."

We got out of the Land Cruiser and climbed onto the rocks, which gave us a clear view of the flatlands below.

Zamo put his sniper rifle to his shoulder, adjusted his scope to full power, and said, "I got him."

Brenner, Kate, and I did the same with the weaker-powered scopes on our M4s.

I could see the white Land Cruiser driven by Emad kicking up dust about a mile away, heading north toward the Marib road.

There wasn't much vehicle traffic on the dirt roads that cut through the dry fields, and it was easy to follow the lone dust trail even as the Land Cruiser grew smaller.

The more time that went by without the SUV

erupting into a ball of flames, the more I began to think that maybe I was missing my flight out of here.

No one spoke, but I could imagine what Kate and Brenner were thinking: Poor John has gone gaga. Zamo, however, was looking through his scope like he was tracking a Taliban general. He was as still as a statue and his breathing was so controlled that I thought he'd gone into a trance.

I was half hoping that I hadn't sent an innocent man to his death, but as the seconds ticked by, I also hoped that a Predator pilot had the Land Cruiser in its crosshairs and was waiting for Chet to say, "Engage the target."

After three or four minutes I lost sight of the SUV in my scope, and so did Kate and Brenner, and they put their rifles down. But Zamo still had him and kept looking through his scope.

I said, "Maybe this will happen later."

No one replied.

Zamo said, "Lost him," and put his rifle down.

Brenner asked me, "What do you want to do now?"

I replied, "Sit here and wait for the streak of white smoke."

Again, no one replied, but Zamo was staring out at the distant horizon without his scope, so we did the same.

Kate said to everyone, "Let's ask one of the Bedouin back there to drive us to the Marib airstrip."

Brenner suggested, "Or let's walk back to the Crow Fortress and say our car broke down and we need another one."

Did I detect a note of sarcasm in his voice?

I said, "We can see the smoke trail for over twenty miles from up here."

Brenner informed me, "I'm not waiting half an hour for that." He said to Kate, "Please talk to your husband. We need to make a decision."

"John."

"Quiet."

So we sat on the rocks and stared out at the blue sky. The crazy guy was in charge. Or he needed to be humored until he came to his senses—or until they could get the drop on me.

So we continued to wait, but only Zamo and I were giving the sky our undivided attention. Kate and Brenner were exchanging glances.

Please, God, let me be right about the CIA wanting to kill me and my wife. That's not too much to ask.

Less than two minutes after we'd lost sight of the dust cloud, a white trail of thin white smoke cut across the blue sky. An instant later, there was a flash of orange light on the horizon, but no sound.

Zamo said, "Target killed." He added, "Holy shit."

Brenner stood, but said nothing.

Kate, too, stood, and stared as a column of black smoke began rising above the horizon. She said, "Oh my God..." I didn't know if she was addressing me, but she looked at me and said, "I can't believe this..."

Birds in the fields below suddenly took flight, then a muffled sound like distant thunder reached us and died away, leaving a stillness in the air.

Brenner was still staring at the rising smoke, and he said, "Those bastards."

Zamo said, "I guess John was right."

I guess so.

Kate said softly, "That poor man...he's dead."

No one responded to that.

Brenner said, "Okay, let's go back and talk to Buck and Chet."

I said, "They'll think they're seeing ghosts."

We got into the Land Cruiser and headed back to the Crow Fortress.

CHAPTER SEVENTY-SEVEN

I drove fast, but not so fast as to attract the attention of the Predator pilot whose job it was to watch the immediate vicinity of the Crow Fortress. But even if he saw us as we approached the fortress, all he'd see was the Bedouin Land Cruiser from the rock pile, so no reason to call Chet.

As for Chet and Buck, both their monitors would now be tuned in to the two Predators flying above the goat herder's hut. One of their screens would have been split to direct another Predator to follow the suspected target in the Land Cruiser—us—and Chet had just given the order to destroy the target. I wonder if Chet had a lump in his throat when he saw his teammates getting blown up.

We were now a few hundred meters from the Crow Fortress, and as I'd noticed since we'd been here, the Bedouin rarely posted a lookout on the walls of the courtyard—guard duty was the job of the Amriki in the tower—and I didn't see anyone as I looked at the wall in front of us.

When I got within fifty meters of the fortress, I

retraced my route to come around to the gate on the east side.

Brenner asked, "Do we have a plan?"

I replied, "There is no plan possible for this situation. Sometimes you just have to shoot from the hip." Literally.

Zamo suggested, "They need to die for what they did."

Good plan.

Brenner reminded Zamo and all of us, "I give the order to fire—but you can fire if fired upon."

Or if I feel like emptying a full magazine into those two bastards. But first we had to make sure that Chet had completed his mission and killed The Panther.

I pulled up near the gate, which was closed, and I turned the vehicle around, pointing it toward the edge of the plateau that we'd driven up on the night we landed in this shithole. I kept the engine running, and we all got out quickly, leaving the doors open.

Kate pulled off her balto for better mobility and access to her spare magazines, and Brenner said, "Rock and roll," meaning move your selector switches to full automatic.

I insisted on going in first and alone, and I lifted the latch handle, swung the gate in, and slipped into the courtyard.

The Bedouin were still where we'd left them, sitting along the shade of the west wall, chatting and chewing. I noticed also that all the vehicles were still there, so Chet and Buck had not yet left here to drive to the scene of the attack, meaning it hadn't happened yet. I checked my watch: 6:15 P.M., so apparently The Panther was late—or he wasn't showing up at all.

The Bedouin noticed me, but none of them looked surprised, though a few of them seemed to be discussing my return.

The doors of the van with the Predator monitors were closed, and the engine wasn't running, but I could hear the hum of the gasoline-powered generator.

I motioned to Kate, Brenner, and Zamo to come in, and I said, "Act normal," which meant walking casually across the courtyard to the van. The Bedouin were looking at us, and maybe they were unhappy that Kate was dressed like a man.

We stopped at the closed doors of Moses' Red Sea fish van and I saw that the padlock was not there, meaning someone was inside, which I expected. Hopefully it was both of them.

Well, I didn't want to interrupt Chet while he was in his stealthy assassination mode, but we couldn't stand here smiling at the Bedouin.

Brenner nodded toward the door and whispered, "Let's go."

Right. Chet and Buck would be unhappily surprised to see us, but they had a job to do and they'd do it, and then we could discuss other matters.

I leveled my M4 as Brenner and Zamo swung both doors open, and I jumped into the van.

Unfortunately, no one was there.

Brenner and Kate came into the van, and Zamo stayed outside to keep an eye on the Bedouin.

Kate asked, "Where are they?"

Definitely not here. But the consoles were fully lit and the monitors were both on, as though they'd just stepped out for a minute.

We moved to the front of the van and looked at the

screens. The left-hand screen—Chet's screen—showed the close view of the goat herder's hut, and the right screen had a split view, a higher and wider shot of the area around the hut, and another high shot showing a white SUV traveling on a dirt road.

As we watched, an electronic crosshair came onto the split screen over the SUV, and a few seconds later the white SUV was gone, replaced by a bright orange flash, followed by swirling black smoke and debris. A message came on the screen that said, "Target engaged."

Then I saw another, smaller message in the left-hand corner of the screen that said, "Replay." Then the original image appeared again and our SUV with the blood mark on the roof and Emad driving was vaporized again by the Hellfire missile. Ouch.

Brenner said, "Those *bastards*."

Kate said, "Look."

We focused on Chet's screen, which was also on replay, and watched silently as Sheik Musa, surrounded by about half of his fifteen men, walked from left to right toward another group of men who were moving from right to left.

Both groups stopped in the middle of the carpet, and after a hesitation, Sheik Musa took the hand of The Panther and kissed it. The Panther then did the same to Sheik Musa.

I don't know if they embraced or not, because the crosshair on the screen brightened, then an electronic message flashed "Fire," and the screen brightened again in an orange glow, followed by black swirling debris, then smoke and fire. The words "Target engaged" flashed on the screen.

Everyone, I was sure, including Sheik Musa and all the men around him, were dead or mortally wounded. Same for Mr. Bulus ibn al-Darwish—The Panther was dead.

I said, "Mission accomplished."

Brenner said, "Chet killed the sheik, too."

Kate pointed to the electronic clock counter and said, "At six-ten...seven minutes ago."

Right. And these images had been broadcast to people in Washington—to the mission planners in Langley, and maybe even to the White House. And everyone was celebrating. The Panther was dead. Congratulations, Chet and Buck. And then Chet and Buck left the van. But where did they go? Maybe to gather some things in the diwan, then they'd jump in an SUV and get out of here.

I looked at Buck's screen and I saw the replay again, but from a higher and wider perspective, which showed all the vehicles that had arrived—Bedouin and Al Qaeda—parked away from the hut. Two more Hellfires hit almost simultaneously, blowing up the two groups of men and vehicles. The secondary explosions of the fuel tanks sent fiery wreckage and burning gasoline into the air. A third Hellfire hit the roof of the goat herder's hut, just in case anyone was inside, and the stone walls of the hut collapsed.

Kate asked again, "Where are Chet and Buck?"

I didn't know, but I knew that they got out of here quickly, in case there were any Bedouin survivors at the scene of the attack who would call the Bedouin here saying that the Americans had killed their sheik. But where did our teammates go? I pointed out, "All the vehicles are here."

Kate concluded, "So they have to be in the tower."

"Maybe . . . but we need to get out of here in case the Bedouin here get those calls . . ." And then I remembered how Chet was going to get rid of this million-dollar van and I said, "The Predator over the Crow Fortress is about to vaporize this van."

We quickly exited the target, but we didn't want to spook the Bedouin so we didn't run. Brenner turned toward the gate, but I grabbed his arm and said, "We need to see if Chet and Buck are in the tower."

He hesitated for half a second, then nodded, and we began walking quickly toward the tower. Indeed, hate and revenge cloud your judgment. We should have been in the Land Cruiser now, tear-assing down the ravine to get away from here. But first we needed to settle up with our two teammates.

CHAPTER SEVENTY-EIGHT

As we got within thirty feet of the door of the tower, I noticed that two of the Bedouin were on their cell phones, and I knew what those calls were about; some of the Bedouin had indeed survived the Hellfire attack and were now telling their buddies in the Crow Fortress that the Amriki missiles had fried their sheik and everyone around him.

A few of the Bedouin started looking at us, then they all began standing. There was absolutely no reason now to act normal, so we began running toward the tower.

We let Kate in first through the narrow doorway, followed by Zamo, then Brenner. I took a quick look over my shoulder and saw the Bedouin running toward us, and a few of them were shouting and pointing their AK-47s at me.

Just as I slipped into the doorway, a deafening explosion filled the air, followed by the secondary explosion of the fish van's fuel tank, and the shockwave knocked me down. I could feel the earth shake under me as I got to my feet, and without anyone saying anything, we all ran for the staircase.

I don't remember hitting any of the stone steps, but within a few seconds we passed through the windowless storage level and we were all in the diwan, weapons at the ready.

Zamo ran to the indoor outhouse and kicked the door in, but no one was there. What was also not in the diwan was the washstand, and I pointed this out to everyone, who drew the same conclusion: Our missing teammates had headed for the roof.

Kate, Brenner, and I looked out the window into the courtyard. The van was a burning heap of twisted metal, and clouds of black smoke billowed from the wreckage. The courtyard was strewn with burning debris, and it appeared that three of the Bedouin had been killed or injured. The other ten seemed stunned as they wandered around the courtyard or stood dazed and silent.

Then one of them looked up and noticed us in the window, and he pointed and shouted.

Someone fired a full burst of rounds, which hit the stone above us, and without waiting for Brenner to give the order, Kate and I fired back with our M4s on full automatic, then Brenner pushed Kate away from the window and emptied a full magazine at the Bedouin down in the courtyard.

We didn't wait around for an accurate body count, but it looked to me as though we'd taken out about five of the remaining ten guys, including Yasir, who I'd seen fall. I said to myself, "Sorry."

The other Bedouin, unfortunately, had made it into the tower, and they were now right below us. Time to go, and there was only one way to go.

We raced up the stone steps and I could hear the shouts of the Bedouin behind us.

Brenner got to the next level first, and he called down, "Clear."

Kate and Zamo, with me bringing up the rear, charged up the stairs just as a burst of AK-47 fire came up the stairwell. Another burst ripped through the thick floorboards, close to where we were standing.

I fired a burst of rounds back through the floorboards as Kate fired down the stone stairwell. That seemed to quiet down the Bedouin, and we charged up the next flight of steps, then the next, which put us on the level below the mafraj.

So far, no sign of Chet and Buck, but they had to be in the mafraj or on the roof. Or they were up to their old tricks, so I fired a full burst of rounds into the wood outhouse, then kicked in the door and looked down the shaft through the holes, but I didn't see anyone.

I then looked up and I could see through the squatter hole in the floor of the mafraj, up to the vent hole in the ceiling. I thought I saw a shadow pass through the sunlight and I fired a short burst up through the vent, but I didn't draw any return fire.

I exited the outhouse and said, "I think they're on the roof."

As I said that, we heard a huge, thunderous explosion off in the distance, and we all turned toward the west-facing window. There was another explosion, then another, and in the far distance we could see black smoke rising into the blue sky.

Brenner said, "That's the airstrike on the Al Qaeda base camp—probably a flight of F-15s from Najran, dropping two-thousand-pound bombs."

Wonderful. Can they drop a smaller one on Chet and Buck?

The sound of the explosions kept rolling through the windows, and I counted twelve before it got quiet.

So that was the end of the Al Qaeda base camp—but there were more of them, and there'd be more coming. The Panther, however, was dead, and badasses like that were not as easy to replace as a camp full of jihadist recruits.

I said to everyone, "We need to get up to the mafraj."

Before we could make a move toward the stairs, Kate shouted, "Look!" and pointed to the window on the north side of the tower.

We looked out at the sky and in the far distance we could see a helicopter coming toward the Crow Fortress.

Brenner was covering the stairwell, firing single rounds down the stone staircase, but not drawing any return fire from the Bedouin, who were probably watching the helicopter approaching.

The helicopter was getting closer, and Zamo took a look at it through his sniper scope. He said in a quiet voice, "It's a Black Hawk...no markings, but it's got to be U.S....I see two door gunners..."

Great. The cavalry had arrived. Unfortunately, it had not arrived to save us; it had arrived, as per schedule—or a few minutes late from Najran—to save Buck and Chet's treacherous asses. This was the part of the plan that Chet and Buck forgot to mention, though Brenner had thought about it—but a little late.

Well, when the Black Hawk got to the roof, what they'd find was two dead guys.

"Let's go!" I said, and we all ran for the staircase as a long burst of AK-47 fire came through the floorboards around us, followed by another burst that came up the stairwell.

I led the way up to the mafraj and we fanned out along the four walls with our backs to the stone columns that supported the large arches. I saw the washstand sitting against the wood wall of the excrement shaft, confirming what we already knew.

I pointed my M4 at the ceiling, and everyone did the same. No one seemed to have any qualms about doing to our teammates what they had tried to do to us. Also, we had five or six Bedouin trying to kill us, and we might not make it back alive to see that justice was done—so we had to do it here.

As we were about to fire into the ceiling, a voice shouted in Arabic, and it took me a second to realize it came through the vent hole.

I didn't know what Buck said, but Brenner apparently did, and he shouted back, "It's not the Bedouin, Buck! It's us!" He added, "Alive and well. Surprised?"

Silence.

Well, maybe it was a good thing to let Buck and Chet know that we were still alive and well, but not very happy with our teammates. Then we'd kill them.

I shouted through the vent hole, "Come on down. We need to talk."

It was Chet, who replied, "Come on up." He let us know, in case we didn't, "There's a chopper inbound to get us out of here."

Us? Bullshit, right to the end.

Meanwhile, another burst of automatic fire came through the floorboards, splintering the old wood and lodging into the ceiling above us. But we were hugging the perimeter of the mafraj, standing on the floor where the boards rested on thick beams and masonry below, so we were relatively safe—for the moment.

Brenner shouted up, "Drop your weapons through the hole—pistols and rifles—then kneel at the hole with your hands on your heads."

Brenner, ex-cop, was trying to make an arrest. Corey, ex-cop, was trying to make two corpses.

Buck shouted down, "Paul, I don't know what you're thinking, or what—"

"Shut up, Buck!" suggested Paul. "Shut your fucking mouth and get your ass down here. You, too, Chet!"

Buck replied, "There are Bedouin down there. Are you all crazy? Get up here. We'll give you a hand."

Buck was stalling for time as the Black Hawk approached, and Brenner was intent on making a bust, then getting on that helicopter with his prisoners.

I'd had enough of this and I shouted to Buck and Chet, "You have three seconds to drop your weapons, or we ventilate that roof and you go on that chopper dead."

No response.

"One, two—" Everyone raised their weapons at the ceiling, and Brenner said, "At my command." Then to Buck and Chet he said, "Last chance!"

But before Brenner said, "Fire," someone else fired. In fact, it was the Black Hawk helicopter, which we could see through the big north-facing arch. It had gotten much closer, and the two door gunners were firing long bursts of machine-gun fire at the tower. We all hit the floor as red tracer rounds sailed through the arches. The rounds began hitting the columns and bullets started ricocheting around the mafraj. A spent round hit my arm, then a not-so-spent round hit the side of my Kevlar vest, knocking the wind out of me.

Chet was obviously in radio contact with the Black Hawk, and he'd told them there were bad guys below him and asked for protective fire. Psychos are smart.

I glanced up through the arch and saw the Black Hawk about a hundred yards away and coming fast. Another burst of machine-gun tracer rounds came through the mafraj and we all got into a fetal position as the bullets sailed above us or hit the stone columns and ricocheted around the stone walls.

I rolled on my back and emptied my magazine into the roof, hoping I'd see blood dripping down through the holes. But Buck and Chet were probably standing tight against the parapet now, and if they were smart, they'd also be standing on their Kevlar vests. Nevertheless, I slammed a fresh magazine into my M4 and fired again, and so did Brenner and Kate, but then another burst of machine-gun fire from the Black Hawk made us tuck in tightly against the floor and walls. Zamo, meanwhile, was lying flat at the top of the stairs, popping off rounds down the stairwell with his sniper rifle, just to let the Bedouin know we hadn't lost interest in them.

I couldn't see the Black Hawk any longer, and I knew the chopper was now flaring out above the tower and about to put down on the roof. The good news was that he couldn't fire through the arches at that angle, and he wouldn't fire through the roof with Buck and Chet there. The bad news was that we couldn't fire through the ceiling at Buck and Chet and take a chance of hitting the chopper. I mean, the four-man crew of the Black Hawk had no idea what the situation was except what Chet had told them, and Chet lies.

I could hear the rotor blades beating as the Black Hawk hovered above the roof. In about a minute, Chet and Buck would be airborne and on their way to Najran airbase, and we'd be left here to deal with the pissed-off Bedouin, whose sheik Chet and Buck had killed. Shit.

The chopper's rotor blades were getting louder, then I heard the thump of the wheels hitting the roof.

Chet and Buck would have some explaining to do at Najran and at every stop on their way to Washington—but they'd killed The Panther and that would make people happy, and happy people don't ask too many questions.

Unfortunately for Chet and Buck, the rest of the A-team was still alive, and we had a different story to tell. Now all we had to do was stay alive to tell it.

Brenner called out to everyone, "When the chopper lifts off, he'll open fire again to cover himself."

Correct. So let's get the hell out of here. The staircase was not an option, so without anyone saying the obvious, we ran in a crouch toward the excrement shaft.

As we got to the door of the shaft, we heard the Black Hawk's engine revving, and the pitch of the rotor blades changed as the big chopper began lifting off the roof. Almost immediately, two streams of red tracer rounds penetrated the roof and tore into the center of the floor.

We could now hear return fire from below—the Bedouin firing at the chopper through the windows. Then long bursts of machine-gun fire from the Black Hawk answered the Bedouin fire from below, taking the pressure off us for the moment.

We all quickly squeezed into the tight outhouse,

and Brenner said he'd go first and establish a beachhead on the next level, where the Bedouin were hopefully not using the squatter. He squeezed himself into the hole, dangled by his fingers, and dropped as quietly as possible to the next level, then got down on one knee and covered the door with his M4.

We could hear more bursts of AK-47 fire as the Bedouin continued to fire at the chopper, which must have been almost out of their range by now. There wasn't much good news at the moment except that the Bedouin undoubtedly thought that all the Americans were on that helicopter. No such luck.

It took a few minutes for each of us to drop, level by level, squatter hole by squatter hole, to the last level below the diwan, right above the excrement level, which was pungent.

We were all jammed into the indoor outhouse now and Brenner put his ear to the door, saying softly, "I don't hear anything."

The surviving Bedouin were either still on one of the higher levels, or they'd taken the stairs down and were in the courtyard, which would not be good.

Our choice now was either to get out of the outhouse and go down the stairs, or drop through the last hole and land in the pile of shit, which didn't seem so bad at this point. Both ways would get us to the ground floor, but not get us to our Land Cruiser and out of here. To do that, we might have to knock off the rest of the Bedouin, and to be honest I didn't want to kill any more of them. But neither did I want them to kill us. Actually, since we'd wasted a bunch of them, and since our Hellfires had vaporized their sheik and their buddies, we'd be lucky if they only killed us.

Kate whispered, "We can't stay here. The Bedouin from the rock pile could be on the way."

Good point. We didn't want to deal with more pissed-off Bedouin.

As we were contemplating our next move—stairs or free fall into the shit pile—we heard footsteps above us in the diwan, and voices in Arabic. If I had to guess, I'd say the Bedouin thought we were gone and they were rummaging through the stuff we'd left behind.

Well, before they took the stairs down, this was our chance to get out of here, and we all knew that.

The staircase was quicker and cleaner than the excrement route, so I threw open the door and we moved rapidly across the dark, windowless tower room, which was used to store hay, straw, and whatever. Zamo paused long enough to light a pile of hay.

I hit the stairs first and bounded down three and four at a time, then shoulder-rolled across the earth floor and got on one knee and covered the narrow doorway with my M4.

Kate came down next, followed quickly by Brenner and Zamo.

I stood, moved quickly to the door, and peered out into the devastated and body-strewn courtyard. Some of the wreckage was still smoldering, and the only people out there were dead.

I signaled all clear, pointed in the direction of the gate, and charged into the courtyard, with Kate, Brenner, and Zamo right behind me.

I got to the gate, stopped short, and spun around in a crouch to cover the courtyard and tower. I could see smoke seeping through the stone walls of the tower.

Just as Kate was getting to the open gate, a figure

appeared in the diwan window and fired. Kate went down and lay sprawled on the ground. I got between her and the tower and fired long, rapid-fire bursts at the window, glancing back at Kate, who was getting to her feet. No blood, so she'd taken a round in her Kevlar, and I yelled to her, "Move! Move!"

Kate and Zamo ran through the gate, but Brenner spun around and emptied his magazine at the window. The smoke was pouring out of the tower now, and I could see flames in the windows of the diwan.

I slammed a fresh magazine into my M4 and emptied it at the five vehicles in the courtyard, blowing out the tires and shattering the windows. Brenner did the same and one of the Hiluxes burst into flames. Time to go.

We ran through the gate and I saw that Zamo was already behind the wheel and Kate was in the rear, leaning out the window covering us. I jumped in beside her and pulled the door closed as Brenner jumped in the front. Before his door was even closed, Zamo was pushing pedal to the metal and we were shooting across the flat terrain toward the ravine.

Brenner and I lowered our windows, leaned out, and turned back toward the gate.

Two Bedouin came charging through the gate and all three of us opened fire, hitting one of them and making the other dive back behind the stone wall.

Within a few minutes we were at the edge of the plateau, and Zamo was slowing up, looking for the ravine. He spotted some tire marks and cut the wheel sharply to the right, then hit the brakes as the Land Cruiser's front wheels slipped over the edge of the plateau and into the ravine.

Zamo navigated down the steep, twisting terrain, going faster than was safe. But back there wasn't too safe either.

The sun was low on the horizon behind us, and the ravine, which was on the east side of the plateau, was in shadow, making it hard to see up ahead.

After a few minutes of escape-and-evasion driving, Brenner said to Zamo, "We shot up the SUVs, so anyone behind us is on foot."

Zamo let up on the gas and said, "Now you tell me."

We didn't exactly relax, but we were all breathing again.

I looked at Kate, who actually seemed fine, all things considered. She's cool under fire, and only loses her cool with me. I asked, "You okay?"

"Knocked the wind out of me...I'm okay..." She looked at me and said, "You can say it now."

A bigger man would have said, "I love you," but I'm not that big so I said, "I fucking told you so." And I meant it.

Kate said, "I love you."

Brenner, who had more important things on his mind, asked, "Anybody have any ideas?"

I asked him, "Can we get to the Marib airstrip?"

He replied, "Maybe. Maybe not. The airstrip has only a few charter aircraft going in and out, and there's usually no one there."

Kate asked, "Would the Bilqis Hotel be safe?"

Brenner replied, "Only if you want to run into someone like Colonel Hakim, or maybe Hakim himself if he came to Marib."

We didn't want to do that, and Kate asked, "How far is it to Sana'a?"

Brenner replied, "About four hours, but it might as well be on Mars. There are checkpoints all along the route, and we'll never make it without getting stopped by somebody who we don't want to meet."

Forget Plan C. Or was that D?

Zamo continued down the ravine, which was getting wider and less steep.

It went without saying that we were in the middle of nowhere, and the closest safe place might be the Saudi border, which, based on where Najran airbase was, would be about 175 miles north of here, as the crow flies, and we weren't flying—Chet and Buck were flying.

I asked Brenner about the border and he said, "Good thinking, but we'd never get past the Yemeni soldiers who patrol the border."

"We have our diplomatic passports," I reminded him.

He ignored my attempt to lighten the moment and said, "The best thing we can do right now is find a place to hide out and think about how to get out of here at dawn."

Kate had a better idea and said, "Let's use our cell phones to make contact with the embassy."

Eureka.

I pulled out my cell phone and lowered my window to stick my head out, but Brenner informed me, "Sorry to tell you, but Buck and Chet have by now notified the NSA that our sat-phones are probably in enemy hands, and the NSA will have called the carrier to discontinue service immediately."

Holy shit. I turned my sat-phone on and it lit up, but I couldn't get a tone.

To be sure, we all tried to get service, but all the phones were dead.

Plan D—or E—was a bust, so I suggested, "How about the Hunt Oil installation?"

Brenner didn't reply for a moment, then said, "That may be our only play. It's about two hours northeast of Marib town, and it's the only place in this province where we'll find other Americans—Americans with guns." He added, "But travel at night here is unsafe, and the Hunt people will shoot at night if we tried to approach. So we need to wait until dawn."

That sounded promising, but it barely lifted the dark mood in the Land Cruiser. I mean, we'd just exited hell with our shirttails on fire, and we were happy to be alive. But we'd only managed to pass from the center of hell to the next circle. This totally sucked. We'd gotten this far by our wits and our balls, without any help from anyone, and we deserved a break. Something good had to happen.

But this is not the land of good; this is the land of *not* good. We came down out of the ravine, and ahead of us, on the dirt road that we'd landed on—the road to the goat herder's hut—was what looked like a convoy of military vehicles.

Zamo said, "Shit."

The beginning of the road looked like the end of the road.

CHAPTER SEVENTY-NINE

When there's a military convoy coming at you, and the road you're on is the only road around, you don't have too many ways to avoid an encounter, except off-road, but that could end in a hail of bullets.

I could see three American-made Humvees in the front of the convoy, followed by four troop carriers that could hold up to a hundred soldiers.

Obviously, they'd responded to the Hellfire attack, and now they were headed toward the Crow Fortress. But why? And who, exactly, were they?

Brenner, Kate, Zamo, and I decided we had to meet them head-on, so to speak, then play it by ear. I reminded everyone, "We're supposed to have a deal with the Yemeni government, and we're supposed to have a free hand here in Marib."

Brenner pointed out, "That information came from Chet and Buck."

"Good point." Maybe the deal expired when Chet and Buck got on that helicopter.

Zamo moved to the right, and the convoy continued toward us hogging the middle of the road. When we got within a hundred yards of the lead Humvee, Brenner told Zamo to stop.

Brenner said, "Hopefully someone will speak English, but if not, I'll do the best I can."

The convoy also came to a halt, and we could see now that the vehicles were not painted with the brown and tan of the Yemeni Army; they were the camouflage blue of the National Security Bureau, a.k.a. the Blue Meanies.

Brenner said to me, "You and I will get out to meet them. Kate and Zamo will stay in the vehicle and cover us."

Kate said to me and Brenner, "Clip your sat-phones to your vests."

Good idea. They didn't work, but only we knew that.

Without Buck along to be diplomatic, we decided to carry our M4s, which we slung across our chests, ready to rock and roll. Take a few of them with you.

Brenner and I got out of the Land Cruiser and began the walk toward the lead Humvee, paid for with my tax dollars.

I noticed now in the far distance black smoke rising into the sky. That would be the scene of the Hellfire attack—men and vehicles still burning, and, of course, this convoy had already been there to see the carnage. I said to Brenner, who was also looking at the smoke, "Think about how to tell these assholes in Arabic that we have a dozen Predators with Hellfires watching us and the pilots have twitchy fingers."

He nodded.

Someone got out of the second Humvee and began walking toward us. Even from this distance I could see that it was Colonel Hakim of the dreaded secret police.

He was wearing cammies and carrying an AK-47, all ready for action. I love armed confrontations. They don't usually last too long.

We got within a few feet of Colonel Hakim and stopped. Brenner gave Colonel Hakim a half-assed salute, and Colonel Hakim returned the salute in a similar half-assed manner. He also eyeballed the sat-phones clipped to our vests, probably thinking about the American Embassy, or better yet about Predator pilots watching their monitors with itchy trigger fingers.

Brenner and Hakim exchanged peace greetings in Arabic, without much sincerity, and I said, "Buenos días," using my only second language.

Hakim ignored me and asked Brenner, "What are you doing here?"

Brenner replied, "You know what we're doing here, Colonel."

"Yes? Why would I know?"

I said to Brenner, "Just cut to the chase." I mean, these fucking people could beat around the bush until the bush died of annoyance.

Brenner asked Hakim, "What are *you* doing here?"

Colonel Hakim took offense at the question and snapped, "It is *my* country, Mr. Brenner. Not yours. And I will ask the questions of you."

Brenner, following my suggestion, got to the point and replied, "We are on a Yemeni-government-sanctioned mission to find and apprehend the Al Qaeda leader Bulus ibn al-Darwish, known as The Panther." He asked Hakim, "Don't you know that?"

Hakim replied, of course, "It is my business what I know."

Total asshole. But he'd come to meet us alone, and he

was talking and not shooting, so that meant he thought he might be on shaky ground. Also, it might mean he wanted something from the Americans. Hey, everybody does. And it's not advice or love that they want; it's money.

So I got right to that subject and said, "I assume you were at the scene of the attack"—I nodded toward the black smoke rising behind him and continued—"and if you escort us there, and assist us in identifying the Al Qaeda bodies, we will see to it that you share in the five-million-dollar reward for the death of The Panther."

That seemed to be what he wanted to hear, and his shitty demeanor softened ever so slightly.

He asked me, not Brenner, "And are you in that position to make such an offer?"

No, but you've got a hundred guns with you so I'll lie all day.

Brenner said, "We will do everything in our power to see that you are compensated for your assistance."

What kind of lie is that? Come on, Paul. Tell him the check's in the fucking mail. I mean, this is *not* the time for truth, justice, and the American way.

Colonel Hakim seemed to like me more than Brenner now, and he asked me, "How much?"

How about a mango up your ass? No? Then how about... "Two and a half million."

He'd have to work until he was about two thousand years old to make that kind of money, but he was a greedy shit and countered, "Three million."

"No," I replied, "we have to pay the Bedouin. Half for them, half to you."

He asked me, "And you?"

"Not a penny." I explained to him, "We get a paycheck every two weeks."

He didn't seem to believe that, but it was the sad truth.

Colonel Hakim thought about my offer, then said, "I will take you where you wish to go."

I want to go to New York, and maybe Hakim could help me get there. I informed him, "We are under surveillance by Predator drones. Capisce?"

He did, and he said, "Let us now go."

Colonel Hakim told us to follow his Humvee, and Brenner and I got back in the Land Cruiser.

Kate asked, "What's happening?"

I replied, "Colonel Hakim is taking us to the scene of the attack."

I explained to Kate and Zamo about the great deal we made and Kate reminded me, "You're not authorized to promise money, amnesty, immunity from prosecution—"

"I just don't feel like getting arrested and shot today."

Brenner said, "Hakim is our ticket out of here, or he's our worst nightmare. Either way, let's keep him happy and interested in our well-being."

Kate pointed out, "He's not going to let us out of here now until he gets his money."

I asked her, "Do you have a blank check on you? Or do you have a better idea?"

Zamo thought that was funny. Just like old times.

Brenner assured Kate, "We'll work something out with the embassy."

I also informed Kate, "Hakim thinks we're all on Predator TV."

"Good," said Ms. Mayfield. "And maybe we are."

Maybe. But hopefully Chet was no longer directing the show.

Anyway, Hakim's Humvee turned around, followed by another Humvee, and we all squeezed past the troop carriers and headed east on the straight dirt road, toward the smoke in the distance.

The third Humvee and the four troop carriers were moving now, and they continued on, west toward the plateau. I asked Brenner, "Why do you think they're headed toward the Crow Fortress?"

"They must be acting on information."

"What information?"

Brenner replied, "We'll ask Colonel Hakim."

Who was as honest and forthcoming as Chet and Buck. Everyone here carried a large sack of bullshit.

Bottom line, this was not the plan that Chet had laid out for us in Aden, but as I said then, and as we discovered, there was more to Chet's plan than he was sharing with us. And as Chet discovered, I had a few plans of my own. And as we all discovered, man plans, God laughs.

But part of Chet's plan had worked out. The Panther was dead, and Chet and Buck were heroes—and better yet, I was going to see what was left of Bulus ibn al-Darwish. I came a long way for this.

CHAPTER EIGHTY

On the way to the goat herder's hut, I said to Brenner, "We can take some evidence at the scene." We'll stop at a 7-Eleven for Ziploc bags.

Brenner replied, "We'll let the PSO and NSB do that and also take photos for us, and that will make Colonel Hakim think he's earning his two and a half million."

"Right." Just like Sheik Musa thought he was earning his five million. I mean, even I wasn't trusting the Americans anymore.

It took us less than twenty minutes to get to the scene of the attack, but I could see it and smell it before we got there.

Hakim's two Humvees pulled onto the path to the goat herder's hut and stopped.

We all got out of our vehicles and walked up the path to what remained of the stone hut. As we got closer, the smell of burnt tires and gasoline got stronger, and so did the smell of charred bodies. Kate wrapped her hijab over her face.

Despite my enthusiasm for seeing this, it was a bit

jarring. Most of the bodies were intact, though they'd been ripped up by shrapnel—Bedouin bodies in their blood-drenched robes, and Al Qaeda bodies in their foutehs. The ground was strewn with AK-47s, sandals, shiwals, and even cell phones.

Where the direct hits from the Hellfires had landed, the ground was blasted away, and the human remains were scattered in all directions, making me remember what an old Vietnam vet had told me about getting an accurate body count after an air or artillery strike. "Count the arms and legs and divide by four."

Brenner, who'd seen things like this, didn't seem fazed, and neither did Zamo. Kate, however, was a bit shaken, and the NSB guys were eyeing her, so Zamo walked her back to the Land Cruiser.

Colonel Hakim spoke first and said, "You see what has happened here. I have secured the area and I will cooperate with the American authorities in any way they wish."

Brenner said to Hakim, "We would like photographs of everything, and we will need your men to collect tissue samples of all the dead Al Qaeda who are identifiable by their clothing."

Hakim didn't seem to understand and he asked, "Why do you need that?"

Brenner explained, "We have DNA of Bulus ibn al-Darwish." He informed Colonel Hakim, "His family lives in America."

Colonel Hakim did not reply, and Brenner further explained, "We can identify al-Darwish by this means, and also by his fingerprints if you would be kind enough to include as many fingers as possible."

Again, Colonel Hakim had no reply, so I took a shot

at it and said, "We need a positive, scientific identification. Proof that al-Darwish died in this attack."

Colonel Hakim nodded this time and said, "Everyone has died. None escaped."

Well, not true. At least one Bedouin had survived and called his Bedouin buddies at the Crow Fortress. So it was possible that other Bedouin and maybe Al Qaeda guys survived. But probably not The Panther, who was in the crosshairs of the first Hellfire missile.

Hakim said, "The Panther is dead."

Brenner and I exchanged glances. Something was not right here.

I asked Hakim, "Were you able to identify al-Darwish?"

Colonel Hakim waved his arm around at the bits and pieces of men, as though saying, "Are you kidding?" He did say, however, "I have found the shiwal of Sheik Musa. That is all the proof I need of his death."

Musa's nose would clinch it for me, but, okay, the sheik was dead—score a hit for President Saleh. But we're talking about *The Panther*, Colonel. The bad guy.

I moved slowly through the blast area, and there were lots of heads intact, on and off their bodies, but about half of them were bearded, and most of the faces were disfigured by shrapnel or burns. The Panther's own mother wouldn't recognize him. Also, I was looking for Nabeel, who had a scruffy beard the last time I saw him, but people look different when they're dead.

One head was lying facedown on a shred of carpet, and I gave it a kick to turn it over. Most of the face was missing.

Brenner came over to me, away from Hakim, and

said softly, "Either he doesn't get what I'm saying, or we have a problem with positive ID."

I nodded, then I remembered the video replay—Sheik Musa had hesitated for a second before taking The Panther's hand and kissing it. Was Musa unsure of his guest's identity? I mean, to me, most fully bearded men looked alike, and forget bearded Arabs. They may as well be wearing veils. Musa, too, apparently had a moment of doubt.

Colonel Hakim came over to us and said, "You can congratulate yourselves on a successful attack."

Okay. Congratulations to us.

Brenner said to him, "I suggest you collect what we need and get it to the airport in Sana'a as quickly as possible. You will be met there."

I also suggested, "Get some ice from Marib. Maybe the Bilqis Hotel." They don't need the ice for cocktails.

Colonel Hakim informed us, "It is a sacrilege to do what you are asking." He told us, "All these remains must be buried as quickly as possible, according to our religion."

I figured that was coming, and I didn't want to argue religion with this guy, so I said, "Tell you what, Colonel, let's make this clean and easy for everyone. You get a hunk of hair from each head or beard here, number it, and deliver it to the embassy. We'll do a DNA match, and you get your money. How's that sound?"

Colonel Hakim couldn't think of any objection to that, so he said, "I think you are trying to change our arrangement."

"Not at all," I assured him. "We pay top dollar for dead Al Qaeda chiefs. But you can't tell me which of these heads belongs to al-Darwish. Right?"

"You know he was here. And you know that everyone here is dead."

Ergo, and so forth. I pointed out, "We don't know he was here. And neither do you." And I was starting to think he wasn't. Holy shit.

So we stood there, trying to figure out how to get this resolved. The stench of open body cavities and burnt flesh was overwhelming, and that smell, mixed with the acrid smell of smoldering vehicles and fuel, made my stomach heave. Anyone who thinks war is exciting should see and smell something like this.

I reminded Colonel Hakim, "We just need some hair. Like, no disrespect to the dead. Okay?"

"That is not possible."

Hokum, Hakim. I said to Brenner, "We have a problem."

Brenner nodded, then asked Colonel Hakim the question that had come up in the Land Cruiser. "Where were you going with your convoy?"

"That is my business, Mr. Brenner."

He reminded Hakim, "We are in business together."

Colonel Hakim did not reply, and he was probably thinking that his two and a half million bucks was slipping away. He might also be thinking that if he was going to lose the money, he might as well get rid of us. Or maybe kidnap us for ransom and make it look like a tribal kidnapping. In Yemen, anything was possible.

Finally Colonel Hakim said, "I was going to the Crow Fortress."

Brenner nodded and asked, "Why?"

He confessed, "There was a survivor of the attack. An Al Qaeda man. He has told me that a Bedouin in the Crow Fortress, a man called Yasir, who you may know from your stay there, has told Al Qaeda by cell phone that the Americans were not kidnapped, and that they were in fact guests of Sheik Musa at the Crow Fortress."

Brenner and I looked at each other, and Brenner said to me, "Like I said, all it takes is one rat, and there's always one rat."

Right. And usually the guy you least suspect. So what was in it for Yasir to rat us out? Probably the hundred thousand bucks that The Panther was going to pay to Sheik Musa to buy the Americans. And that would be a lot more money for Yasir than his share of his sheik's five million. Well, greedy Yasir was dead, and I was feeling not sorry about whacking him.

I said to Brenner, "Chet's ingenious plan actually sucked." I added, "He didn't factor in the human element." And how could he? He wasn't human.

Brenner agreed and added, "Even his plan to kill us didn't work."

That was almost funny.

Bottom line here, if The Panther knew we were actually guests of Sheik Musa, he also knew that the Americans would not be in this goat herder's hut at the meeting between him and Sheik Musa, and The Panther further knew this meeting was a sham and a trap.

I said to Brenner, "The Panther is not here and not dead."

Brenner nodded and looked at Colonel Hakim, saying to our new partner, "I'm not understanding why you were going to the Crow Fortress."

Colonel Hakim, probably trying to salvage a smaller reward, replied, "The Al Qaeda survivor has also told me that the jihadists from the Al Qaeda camp in the hills were preparing to attack the Crow Fortress and take the Americans."

I said to Brenner, "I think we always knew that."

Brenner nodded and said to Hakim, "And what were you going to do at the Crow Fortress?"

He replied, "It was my intention to come to your rescue."

What a nice man. Doing his duty. Actually, if Colonel Hakim was in business to make money, that was a good way to do it. But I doubted if he wanted a fight with Al Qaeda. More likely he was trying to get to the Crow Fortress before Al Qaeda got there, then he could arrest or attack his traditional enemy—the Bedouin—and say he rescued the Americans from the Bedouin. And that was worth some American dollars.

That didn't work out for him, but Colonel Hakim was still trying to figure out how to make a buck here. The dead Panther thing wasn't working out either, and rescuing the Americans from the Bedouin was a bust, so what was left?

Brenner said to him, "We appreciate your intentions, but as you can see, we don't need to be rescued."

Colonel Hakim said to us, "I am told by the Al Qaeda man who survived this attack that the Bedouin, Yasir, told him there were six Americans at the Crow Fortress."

Brenner informed him, "Two have left."

Hakim thought about that, then said, "I believe I saw smoke coming from the top of the plateau."

Well, that's a long story, but I shortened it and said, "We had a problem with the Bedouin."

He nodded and informed us, "They are treacherous."

They're amateurs, Colonel, compared to you.

Colonel Hakim also informed us, "According to this Al Qaeda survivor, the jihadist attack on the Crow Fortress was to begin after the meeting with Sheik Musa— but only if the Americans were not at the meeting."

"Right. Sorry we missed the meeting." Sorry, too, The Panther missed it. Bottom line here, The Panther was willing to sacrifice his men to see if the meeting was a trap—which it was—and The Panther was elsewhere. I asked Hakim, "Is The Panther supposed to lead this attack on the Crow Fortress?"

Hakim replied, "I asked that very question of the Al Qaeda survivor, but he did not know."

Right. The Panther kept things to himself. Which was why he was still alive.

Hakim said to me and Brenner, "I have no radio message from my men that they are encountering any Al Qaeda forces on the way to the Crow Fortress."

That's because the Al Qaeda forces in the camp have been turned into hamburger by the U.S. Air Force, but that was none of Hakim's business.

Recalling that the Bedouin in the courtyard of the Crow Fortress had taken a sudden dislike toward us, I said to Hakim, "We know that there was also a Bedouin survivor of this attack who called his friends at the Crow Fortress to report what happened here." I asked, "Where is this man?"

Hakim informed us, "Unfortunately, he died of his wounds."

I asked, "Hellfire wounds or a bullet wound in his head?"

To set the record straight, and set me straight, Colonel Hakim replied, "It makes no difference."

This guy was a cold, hard sonofabitch.

Colonel Hakim continued, "We have made this arrangement—the Americans and my government—and it has been a successful arrangement."

I replied, "You have your dead sheik, but I don't think we have our dead Panther."

Hakim replied, "I think you do, but if you do not, that is no fault of mine and no fault of my government."

Right. It's Chet's fault. In fact, Chet got hustled by the Yemeni government. They knew they'd get their dead sheik, and they didn't care if the Americans got their dead Panther. Now we were on the Bedouin shit list forever, and The Panther was still out there.

I said to Hakim, "Is this Al Qaeda survivor still alive or did he die of a bullet wound?"

Hakim replied, "I believe he is still alive."

Hakim was still trying to work the deal, but he didn't have much left to offer. Nevertheless, I said, "If the Al Qaeda man is still alive, and if we can speak to him, then our arrangement has not changed." You're still not getting shit.

Colonel Hakim nodded and led us toward one of the blue trucks.

We climbed into the open truck and on the floor was an older man with a white beard who didn't look as lucky as he was. Also, he didn't look like a jihadist. He looked more like a Bedouin, but he was naked, so it was hard to tell by the clothing.

Someone had bandaged him up, and his wounds didn't look too bad, and he had no burn marks on him, so he hadn't been too close to the blasts. He seemed to be shivering, and I thought a blanket would be a good idea, but the NSB and the PSO weren't famous for taking care of wounded prisoners, as I saw at Ghumdan.

There were bench seats in the truck, and Colonel Hakim invited us to sit, which we did, and he sat opposite us.

The wounded man was semi-conscious, but Hakim got his attention by kicking him.

The man opened his eyes, and Hakim said something to him in Arabic, and the man answered.

The man apparently wanted water, and Hakim called out to an NSB guy, who came in with a canteen and poured water on the old guy's face, then Hakim took the canteen.

Hakim said to us, "This man calls himself Altair, which means soaring eagle."

The guy looked more like a dying duck, but whatever.

Hakim told us, "That is his Al Qaeda name, and he will not give his true name unless he believes he is going to die. Then he asks that we tell his family of his fate."

Altair was looking at me and Brenner now, and I had the impression he didn't like us. Probably something to do with the Hellfire missiles.

I said to Hakim, "He doesn't look like a jihadist."

Hakim informed us, "Altair, who I know by name, is a senior advisor to al-Darwish." He added, "A friend of the al-Darwish family. And perhaps not truly Al Qaeda."

Interesting. And what did he advise The Panther about taking this meeting?

Brenner had the same thought and said to Hakim, "Ask him why he came here if he thought the Americans were not here and that this meeting could be a trap."

Hakim informed us, "I have already asked that of him, and he tells me that he did not believe that information from the Bedouin called Yasir."

I guess not, or he wouldn't be lying here all fucked up.

I asked Hakim, "Did Altair get that call directly from Yasir?"

Hakim again said, "I have asked him and he says no, he received that message from one of his jihadists who received the call from Yasir."

Right. And where would Yasir get the cell phone number of an Al Qaeda jihadist? Let me think. Well, maybe from the same person who gave Yasir those photographs. I asked, "Did Yasir make this call to a man named Nabeel al-Samad?"

Hakim replied, "In fact, it was that man." He added, "How do you know this?"

"I'm a detective." I asked Hakim, "Was this message, this warning, passed on to al-Darwish?"

Hakim replied, "Of course. Altair told me he delivered it personally."

"And were the jihadists told of this warning?"

Hakim looked down at Altair, then said to me, "He has told me that the jihadists were told, but I am not sure of Altair's truthfulness."

Right. The Panther kept this to himself, and the only one who acted on this warning was The Panther. In fact, he sent a double in his place, and he used his men to see what would happen at the meeting. If it wasn't a trap, and if the Americans were at the meeting to be bought, then all was well. If, however, it was a trap, then all it cost The Panther to discover that was about a dozen of his men. No big deal for The Panther, who wasted his men's lives for the cause—the cause being Bulus ibn al-Darwish's greater glory.

But The Panther had sent at least one senior advisor—Altair, a friend of the family. Why would al-Darwish do that? Maybe he was willing to risk the senior guy for appearances at the meeting. And Altair, apparently, was willing to take the risk for his boss. And if the meeting was legit, then Altair would advise The Panther's double on how to do the deal with Sheik Musa.

Brenner, too, concluded, "Altair was willing to take a big risk for his boss, and his boss was willing to send Altair and his men into what was sounding like a trap."

Right. The Panther really wanted the Americans, and he didn't care who he had to put at risk to get them—as long as it wasn't himself.

Recalling what Rahim ibn Hayyam told us at Ghumdan Fortress, about his boss's leadership style, I said to Hakim, "Tell this guy that his chief is a coward. That he sends his men into danger, but he hides in a cave, like he did when his jihadists attacked the Hunt Oil installation. Tell Altair he owes no loyalty to al-Darwish."

Hakim nodded and translated that, and Altair replied by spitting at me. And then he had the nerve to ask for more water. So Colonel Hakim, the soul of compassion, poured the rest of the canteen on Altair's face. Good practice for waterboarding.

I said to Hakim, "I assume you've asked this guy where The Panther is right now."

"Of course, and he tells me he does not know."

"You believe that?"

Hakim shrugged and said, "Only a very few people would know the hiding place of The Panther."

Right. And a guy like Altair might be one of those people. I changed the subject and said to Hakim, "Ask him if Nabeel al-Samad was here."

Altair understood the name and so understood the question, and replied to Hakim, who told us, "Nabeel al-Samad was not here."

Bummer. I wanted Nabeel's balls in a Ziploc bag. But I'd find him someday. Maybe back in New York.

Brenner, combat vet, wanted to know, "Where was Altair when the Hellfires hit?"

Hakim asked and Altair replied. Hakim smiled and said, "The old man had the need to urinate and so he went off behind the stone fence to do this. He says he was spared by God."

Or a bad prostate gland. Or he had a last-minute thought that standing on the carpet near The Panther look-alike and near Sheik Musa might not be the safest place around. Time for a piss.

Brenner asked Colonel Hakim, "What will you do with this man?"

Hakim replied matter-of-factly, "Probably I will shoot him."

I suggested, "You may want to bring him to Ghumdan, get him patched up, and continue the interrogation."

Hakim assured us, "He has nothing more to say."

Brenner informed me, "The Yemeni government doesn't like to have Al Qaeda prisoners." He explained, "The Al Qaeda guys have a way of breaking out of jail and embarrassing the government, or they radicalize the other inmates." He concluded, "So most of them are shot when captured, or die under interrogation."

Sounds a bit harsh, but I had a better idea and said

to Hakim, "If, as you say, you know Altair is a senior advisor to The Panther, then I'm certain he knows where his boss is hiding."

Hakim replied, "This could be true, but he will not tell us this, even under torture." He added, "Or even if you tell him unkind things about his chief."

"Try another approach," I suggested. "Offer him his freedom and, let's say, a hundred thousand dollars. The Americans will guarantee his freedom and the money."

Hakim thought about that, and maybe he saw a chance to get that money for himself, then shoot Altair anyway. He made the offer to Altair, who didn't respond, but neither did he spit.

I said to Hakim, "Remind him again that al-Darwish sent him and his men like sheep to the slaughter."

Hakim shrugged and spoke to Altair, who did not respond. When they don't respond, you're making progress.

I also suggested, "Maybe The Panther thinks such an old man is expendable. Maybe he doesn't like Altair." I said to Hakim, "Tell him that."

Hakim did and Altair closed his eyes, indicating he had no more to say.

Well, what now? I guess if you're partners with a PSO colonel, your options open up. And I had an idea.

I announced, "I have to take a pee," and jumped out of the truck. Brenner followed and I asked him, "What do you want to do?"

He replied, "We need to contact the embassy as soon as possible to report our status and to report what happened here."

"That's the right thing to do," I agreed.

"Then we need to get to the embassy first thing tomorrow."

"Right. But I'm thinking that Chet and Buck are bad-mouthing us wherever they are, and we may have some problems at the embassy." Like being locked in the basement bomb shelter waiting for the CIA station chief.

Brenner replied, "I don't think that's true—about having a problem...but in any case, Zamo and I need to report in person to the embassy." He thought a moment and said, "You and Kate, however, could probably go directly to Sana'a Airport and take the first flight out that's heading anywhere except Sandland."

"Good thinking. But here's another idea. Ready?"

He nodded tentatively.

"We throw Altair into the Land Cruiser and take him into the hills. He shows us where the Al Qaeda camp is, and we show him what two-thousand-pound bombs can do. We tell him that if The Panther was in the camp, he's probably dead, but if not, he should be because he's an asshole, a coward, and an incompetent fuck-up. And then we ask Altair nicely to show us where The Panther's hideout is. And if he does that, we'll save him from Colonel Hakim, give him a nice reward, and send him to the Bahamas." I asked Brenner, "What do you think?"

"I think you're crazy."

"Good. Look, Paul, Altair is our one and only link to The Panther, and I'm sure that old bastard knows where that asshole is hiding. We gotta give this a shot."

Brenner thought a moment, then said, "It's actually not a terrible idea, but we are definitely not authorized to make up our own missions."

"Why not? Someone authorized Chet to bump us off, so we can do whatever the hell we want."

Brenner took a deep breath and said, "We have no backup, no logistical support, no commo, and we're low on ammo."

"But we have a new partner. He's got what we need and we'll take him along." I added, "Hakim is authorized to do whatever he wants to do."

"Actually, Hakim should do this on his own."

"Hakim," I pointed out, "is incompetent, probably lazy, and he doesn't give a rat's ass about Al Qaeda or Bulus ibn al-Darwish."

"But he cares about the reward."

"Right. So he'll come with us. We need an interpreter anyway."

Brenner went into thinking mode, weighing the pros and cons of getting out of this shithole or getting deeper into it. He pointed out, "Altair may not be able to make the trip."

"He looks fine. He's a tough old goat. Or eagle. And if he dies, he dies. Better than Hakim's bullet in his head."

Brenner said to me, "I think you've been here too long."

"I've been crazy for years." I suggested to him, "When you get home, you'll realize how crazy *you* were here."

He forced a smile, ruminated, then said, "All right . . . if Hakim says okay to this, and if he comes with us, we'll go."

"Good. We're going to complete this mission."

Mr. Brenner asked, "How about Kate?"

"She wouldn't miss this for the world."

Brenner was about to say something about that, but Colonel Hakim, who wanted to see what his new partners were up to, hopped out of the truck and asked us, "So what do you do now?"

"Glad you asked." I explained my plan to him and he listened, nodding a few times. I assured him, "If we can kill or capture The Panther, I'll see to it that you get the three million you asked for." I pointed out, "The Bedouin were helpful to us, but one of them betrayed us, and we don't have a dead Panther." So fuck them.

Colonel Hakim nodded, but said, "The old man is perhaps not well enough to make this journey."

"Have your medic give him something to perk him up." But not Viagra. We've been fucked enough today.

Hakim nodded again, but said, "He may not be as cooperative as you wish. He will protect his chief."

"We won't know what he's going to do until we get up there."

Colonel Hakim asked us, "Do you know where this Al Qaeda camp is?"

"Altair knows," I assured him.

"He will not tell us."

"I'm sure you can make him tell us."

"Perhaps." He let us know, "I have some idea where it is."

"Good. And I happen to have map coordinates." I asked Hakim, "Do you have a map of the area?"

"Of course."

"Well, then, between you, me, and Altair, we're practically there."

Colonel Hakim excused himself, and Brenner and I walked toward our Land Cruiser. I asked Brenner, "How about Zamo?"

"He likes looking for jihadists in the mountains."

"Right. Doesn't everyone?" So Operation Clean Sweep, sans Chet, Buck, and Washington, continues. No complicated plans, no high tech, and no John and Kate for bait; just a bunch of guys in the hills trying to kill each other the old-fashioned way.

CHAPTER EIGHTY-ONE

Brenner and I explained the plan to Zamo and Kate, who signed on without a lot of questions. I mean, the more you think about bold ideas, the more problems you find. And if you keep going down that path, you'll come to an unpleasant truth: This is fucking dangerous. So why think about it? Just do it.

We had to do some fast talking to convince Colonel Hakim to take only one Humvee and not a hundred men with him, explaining that this was a stealth mission and not an invasion.

Hakim was in his Humvee with his driver now, along with two PSO thugs, plus Altair, who didn't want to take a ride with us, but one of Hakim's PSO goons hit him with a taser, then threw him in the rear compartment. On the plus side for Altair, he was now clothed, fed, watered, and alive.

Hakim had provided us with hand-held radios, and we left the scene of the Hellfire attack and headed into the sinking sun, back toward the highlands.

Hakim was in the lead, and we followed in the Land

Cruiser. Zamo drove, I rode shotgun, and Kate and Brenner sat in the rear.

The basic plan was to first find the Al Qaeda base camp, because we all agreed that The Panther's cave couldn't be too far from his camp, so that was a good starting point, and a good place to encourage Altair to point the way to his boss's hideout.

Colonel Hakim had also provided us with a military terrain map, and Brenner, who knew how to read these contour maps, was looking at it with Kate. I'd given them the coordinates of the Al Qaeda base camp that I'd taken from the Predator monitor, and we'd put a mark on the map. Brenner said, "Very inaccessible terrain...no roads, but maybe some mountain trails that aren't shown here."

I reminded Brenner, "We saw a few vehicles on the Predator video monitor, so there's some kind of vehicle access."

Brenner agreed, but said, "The airstrike may have caused rockslides."

"So we'll walk. Meanwhile, we don't have a lot of daylight left. Call our partner and tell him to step on it."

Brenner called Hakim on the hand-held radio and suggested, "We need to move faster, Colonel."

Hakim replied, "This is a good speed."

Brenner insisted, "A little faster." He signed off and said to me, "That's the story of the Yemeni Army, police, and government—too slow, too cautious, and too late."

"I don't think Hakim has much enthusiasm for this," I said.

"I can't imagine why not."

"He's a government worker."

"So are we," Brenner reminded me. He also reminded us, "He wants the money. But he doesn't want to get killed earning it."

"Same here."

So we continued on the long, straight road toward the plateau where the Crow Fortress sat, and where the highlands began. Smoke still rose into the air from the burning tower and I asked Zamo, "Why did you set the hay on fire?"

"Because it burns."

"Right." Well, so much for Buck's Sultan Crow Fortress Bed & Breakfast. And so much for American-Bedouin relations.

As we continued on, I thought about what was going on in our absence, and I had no doubt that Chet had concocted a good story about the friendly fire mishap to the Land Cruiser, though that would be a hard sell. The only people he could level with were the people in his Company who'd sent him on Operation Clean Sweep. And they'd cover his ass because Chet was a hero in Langley, and Buck was a hero at Foggy Bottom. The news release of this incident was already written, and the American public would be pleased to learn that Bulus ibn al-Darwish, the American traitor and a mastermind of the *Cole* attack, was taken out with a Hellfire missile. Unfortunately, in a separate but related incident, four unnamed Americans are missing in Yemen.

But if these Americans got back alive, they'd have, as I said, a different tale to tell, ending hopefully with me throwing The Panther's head on the table.

We were approaching the base of the plateau, and

after a quick radio conference with Hakim, we decided not to go into the highlands via the Crow Fortress approach. Instead, we'd go cross-country and skirt around the plateaus from the north, then we'd head into the highlands forty kilometers west of here, closer to where the Al Qaeda camp was hidden in the bad terrain.

We went off-road and the ride got a little rougher, and Hakim's Humvee slowed up. I said to Zamo, "Give him the horn."

Brenner chose his radio instead and urged Hakim and his driver to push it.

We continued on, across the arid fields and pastures, and whenever we came to a stone fence, Hakim in the lead found the gate and smashed through it, liberating hundreds of goats.

It took us an hour to travel forty kilometers along the base of the highlands, and we could see up ahead that the plateaus were now extending farther north, blocking us.

Brenner consulted his map and said, "The highlands get higher up ahead, and the only way through them is the Sana'a–Marib road, which takes us off course. So we need to head into the highlands around here . . . but I don't see any trails or paths on this map . . ."

I reminded him, "Rahim ibn Hayyam said he got to the camp by vehicle."

Brenner replied, "If you knew the uncharted trails, you could do it . . . but I do see some ravines that a four-wheel drive might be able to navigate."

"Great." I saw this in a TV commercial for a Jeep. "Let's do it."

Brenner radioed Hakim, who stopped, and we all got out for a map conference.

Zamo, too, was a good map reader, and even Kate had taken a map-reading course. I can read a subway map, and I can easily find my ass with both hands, but I had no clue about scoping out a terrain map. My contribution was reminding the A-team that we'd seen vehicles in the camp, and they weren't made there.

As the map committee was deciding on a route, I went to the Humvee to check on Altair, who was lying in the back compartment, covered with a blanket, holding a bottle of water. He didn't look great, but his color wasn't pre-croak, and his breathing seemed okay. "Hang in there, old man. God saved you to help us find Bulus ibn al-Darwish."

At that name, Altair shook his head.

Everyone got back in their vehicles and we took the lead now. Brenner sat up front with Zamo still driving, and he directed Zamo toward a shallow depression in the ground, saying to us, "The map shows a wadi here, and there it is." He further explained, "This is a stream which comes out of the highlands during the rainy season, and I'm thinking that this has to be flat from erosion all the way up into the hills."

Kate, who was born and raised in the great outdoors, said, "The streambed should be a layer of small stones, which will give us good traction."

I offered, "Just like the wadi highway that cuts through the middle of Sana'a."

"Correct," said Mr. Brenner.

Maybe I *have* been here too long.

So we drove into the wadi, and Zamo headed into the hills. It was easy to follow the dry streambed, and within fifteen minutes we were in a sort of gorge or valley between two towering plateaus. The streambed got very steep as we climbed farther into the highlands.

I kept checking to see if Colonel Hakim's Humvee was still behind us. I mean, I wouldn't put it past that bastard to throw it in reverse and go backwards all the way to Sana'a. But he kept right behind us, driven forward by duty, honor, country, and money.

The sun was definitely sinking, and the eastern sky was darkening, but there was daylight left to the west. After about an hour, we were driving in near darkness, but the half moon started to cast some light on these dead, dry hills, which almost shone in the moonlight.

No one had too much to say, and now and then Brenner and Hakim would exchange a few words on the radio. It occurred to me—a few times—that if there were any jihadists left in these hills, we were sitting ducks down in this wadi with high terrain all around us.

I asked Kate, "How you doing?"

"Still fine."

I was sure her ribs were very sore where that AK-47 round punched her Kevlar vest. Sometimes you get a broken rib, and always a big, ugly bruise. But, as we say, better red than dead.

The status of Zamo's arm was not his favorite subject so I didn't ask, but I could see by how he handled the wheel that his arm was stiff. Hopefully, we didn't need him to blow al-Darwish's head off from a kilometer away. Or take out some asshole firing at us.

The wadi was getting very narrow now, and the terrain was getting steeper and rougher. Brenner said, "We're coming to the end of where the rainwater drains into the wadi."

And?

"And the terrain ahead is unpredictable. It could rise up like a wall and that's as far as we go."

"Then we walk," said Kate.

"Right," I agreed. As my mother used to tell me, "God made feet before He made cars." There's no actual proof of that, but if it's true, then that's the reason for the gas pedal. On another subject, what the hell was I thinking?

We continued on, and we were in luck because there was no wall of rock as we crested the top of the rising terrain.

And there it was.

We stopped, and everyone got out of the vehicles and stood at the edge of a slope. Below us in the distance was a flat basin, maybe the size of four or five football fields, nestled among the rising hills around it. Just like we saw on the Predator monitor.

But the camp looked different now. The whole expanse of flat ground was smoldering, like the earth was cooking, and I counted twelve huge bomb craters, about thirty or forty feet across, and deep enough that I couldn't see the bottoms.

Brenner said, "Good bomb pattern."

I was just thinking that myself. *What?*

He continued, "See how they're evenly spaced? No overlap. The crew pretty much covered the target with twelve two-thousand-pounds." He also said, "Beautiful. Haven't seen that in a while."

"Looks great," I agreed. I asked him, "Anyone alive down there?"

"No." He explained, "The blast sucks the oxygen out of the air, and the shockwaves burst your lungs, and sometimes turn your brain into jelly."

Wow.

He continued, in a faraway voice, "Sometimes you do find people alive, but they're zombies...blood coming out of their ears, nose, and mouth."

"Yeah...well...good bomb pattern."

Zamo added, "We don't want to go down there." He explained, "There'll be, like, unexploded ordnance, like mortar rounds, or grenades, and they get sensitized by the shock, and if you step on something, they could blow and you're toast."

"Good to know that."

Meanwhile, Colonel Hakim and his three PSO goons were standing off by themselves, looking down at what the Americans had wrought. I had no idea what was going through their minds, but I thought that they had to be impressed, but also troubled, like they'd seen the future.

An acrid odor drifted up from the destruction, like burnt fuel and melted metal, and it took me a few seconds to recognize that smell. The Towers.

Kate, who hadn't said a word so far, now said, "Payback."

So we stood there and looked at the smoldering fires and the black gaping holes in the earth, lit by a bright rising moon; a little bit of heaven, and a lot of hell.

Now we find The Panther's lair, and if he's home, we kill him.

CHAPTER EIGHTY-TWO

The PSO goons dragged Altair out of the Humvee and they sat him on the ground facing his Al Qaeda camp in the basin below.

No one said anything to him, and we let him look. He showed no outward emotion, but instead he stared quietly at the moonlit landscape of bomb craters and smoldering rubble. Finally, he lowered his head.

Brenner said to Colonel Hakim, "Tell him this is what the Americans will do to all Al Qaeda camps in Yemen."

Hakim, who probably had a foot in those camps, hesitated, then translated.

Altair had no response.

Brenner continued, "Everyone down there is dead. Everyone who went with Altair to meet Sheik Musa is dead. Many jihadists who attacked the Hunt Oil installation are dead."

Hakim again translated, and again Altair did not respond, but kept staring at the ground.

Brenner then said, "But The Panther who caused all this death is still alive."

Hakim translated, but this time Altair responded, and Hakim told us, "He says The Panther was in this camp, so he is also dead."

I said, "Bullshit. Tell this sonofabitch that the next time he lies to us, he gets tasered."

Hakim nodded and passed on the good news.

Altair did not respond.

I also said, "If The Panther is dead, then Altair can tell us where his hideout is."

Hakim nodded, and translated, but Altair again had no response.

Okay, the taser was the stick, and here's the carrot. "Tell him if he shows us where al-Darwish's hideout is, the Americans will pay him one hundred thousand dollars, and send him anywhere he wants to go."

Hakim translated that and the other three PSO thugs looked interested themselves. I mean, if *they* knew where The Panther was hiding, they'd give him up in a heartbeat for a hundred large and a ticket out of here.

Altair, however, was not interested, and Hakim told us, "He says first that al-Darwish is dead in this camp, and that he does not want your American money, and that he will die in Yemen."

"That can be arranged." Well, so much for the carrot. Back to the stick.

Hakim had the same thought and he nodded to one of his goons, who hit the old man in the neck with a jolt of juice.

Altair screamed and toppled to the ground, thrashing around, then he lay still.

Kate turned away and walked back to the Land Cruiser.

Brenner said to Hakim, "Keep asking him the same question and if you get the same answer, repeat the process. Eventually he will tell us where al-Darwish's hideout is." Brenner cautioned, "Don't kill him."

Hakim, who didn't need much advice or encouragement on the subject of torture, asked Altair the question again, but Altair did not respond, and Hakim's goon shoved the taser prod into Altair's nuts.

Hakim went through the routine two more times until Altair passed out. Hakim said to us, "It is possible that he has no knowledge of where this hideout is located."

Well, that *was* possible, but we hadn't gotten there yet.

Brenner looked at Altair lying unconscious on the ground, then bent over and took his pulse, announcing, "He's...okay."

Maybe a little gray.

Well, if Altair didn't die here, Hakim would kill him anyway. We were trying to save the old guy's life, but he was making that difficult.

I moved away from Hakim and his goons, and Brenner followed.

Zamo, who'd told us about six times in the SUV that he didn't trust Hakim or his men, stood off near the vehicles with his rifle at the ready. I didn't trust Hakim either, but we were all here to do business.

I said to Brenner, "Altair knows where al-Darwish's hideout is and he'd tell us if he really thought al-Darwish was dead."

"Correct."

I continued, "He's not responding well to the carrot or the stick, so..." I thought about this and said, "So we need to try another approach."

"Maybe more carrots and a bigger stick."

"No. We're thinking the way we think, but Altair thinks differently."

Kate saw that the taser session had ended and she came over to us. "Any progress?"

"No. He's hanging tough."

"That's enough taser."

I agreed and said, "This guy doesn't want to rat out his chief and go to hell. Right? He wants to take the express elevator to Paradise."

Brenner nodded and said, "It's not a choice between living and dying. It's a choice of what kind of death he's looking for."

"Correct. So we have to help him become a martyr."

Kate asked, "How?"

"I don't know. But Hakim does."

The gentleman in question came over to us and asked, "What do you want to do?"

I said to Hakim, "It seems to me, Colonel, that Altair does not want to die a traitor and a coward. Right?"

Hakim, who was probably both, had to think about that, but then he nodded and said, "This may be true."

"So? How do we make a deal with Altair that lets him tell us what we want to know, but also lets him into Paradise?"

Again, Hakim had to think about that, and he replied, "That is difficult." He informed us, "You are the reason for his stubbornness." He explained, unnecessarily, "You are...infidels. He cannot betray his chief to you, or he will go to hell."

"Right. We get that." In fact, Altair should have mentioned that himself between tasers to his nuts. He would have saved himself a lot of pain, and saved us a lot of time. Not to mention saving all of us some discomfort. Well, the PSO guys didn't care—they did this stuff on their coffee breaks. Maybe, though, the pain was part of the process on the road to salvation.

Hakim interrupted my thoughts and said to me and Brenner, "There is also an issue of the money. Altair rejects it, but he will want this for his family." He explained, "It is a thing which worries the martyrs for Islam. Their families. So, Altair will give me his family name and I will promise that his family receives the money—in exchange, of course, for the information you need."

Hakim thought a lot about money, but he might be on to something.

"Okay," I said, "so how do we make all this work?"

Colonel Hakim replied thoughtfully, "First, we must offer Altair two kinds of death. The one will be a bullet in the head, right here, and he will die a defeated man, a prisoner, and not a martyr who has died in jihad and who would ascend directly to Paradise. And also there is no promise of money to his family."

Got it.

Hakim continued, "The other death, to die in jihad, a martyr to his faith, that is more difficult to arrange."

Maybe I should challenge Altair to a knife fight, but the old guy could get lucky and I'd be the one heading for Paradise.

Zamo, who was standing near the vehicles and who had spent some time in Islam, said, "Let the old guy go into the camp."

Yeah?

Hakim thought that might be a good idea and said,

"Yes, he can be with the dead martyrs, his jihadists. He will pray among them, and find peace."

Great. But first he has to do the open sesame thing with the cave.

Hakim continued, "When I spoke to him earlier, he believed two things—that God spared him for a purpose, but also that he had not achieved martyrdom as his jihadists had."

Right. A little survivor's guilt. We can help him with that.

Brenner said to Hakim, "Speak to him. But don't forget what we need from him."

Hakim said he certainly understood, and he reminded us, "Do not forget what I need from you."

How could we forget?

So Brenner, Kate, and I joined Zamo near the Land Cruiser to get out of Altair's sight.

Hakim's goons sat the old man up, gave him some water, and Hakim began talking to him.

About ten minutes later, Hakim came over to us and said, "Altair has told me that he believes Bulus ibn al-Darwish was in this camp, and that he died here."

That was not what I wanted to hear.

Hakim continued, "But he has also told me that because he believes his chief is dead, he can now reveal the place where al-Darwish once lived."

That's more like it. I think we all understood that Altair was bullshitting himself, but sometimes you gotta do that to save your soul, like me eating hamburgers on Good Friday and calling them veggie burgers. I mean, you can't bullshit God, but you can bullshit yourself.

We walked back to the edge of the basin and there

was Altair, stumbling down the slope toward the Al Qaeda camp, going home.

Colonel Hakim told us, "He will die here. And that is good."

Very good.

"Or, perhaps, God will again spare him, and we may hear from him someday."

"I hope not." But a deal is a deal, and on that subject, I asked Colonel Hakim, "Where is The Panther's hideout?"

Hakim looked off at the distant hills beyond the basin and pointed. "There."

"Can you be a bit more specific?"

He got specific and asked, "Do you see that peak? The one that resembles the sail of a ship?"

Were we getting directions to Noah's Ark?

It was hard to see much in the moonlight, but I thought I saw what Hakim was pointing to. Zamo, however, had his nightscope on it and he said, "I see it. It's about three klicks, across some rough terrain."

Kate and Brenner were also looking at it through the lower-powered daylight scopes on their rifles, and they said they could see it clearly in the moonlight. Great.

Colonel Hakim informed us, "Altair says there is a trail which begins on the far side of the camp. If you can locate that trail, it will take you to the other side of that mountain where the trail will ascend to the cave of Bulus ibn al-Darwish."

Piece of cake. Or a sack of bullshit. I asked Hakim, "Are you sure Altair was telling you the truth?"

"One can never be sure. However, he swore this to me, and I believe he was truthful." Hakim nodded to himself and said, "Altair understood that the thing I was giving to him needed to be repaid."

This place is starting to make sense.

Brenner said to Hakim, "I assume you are not coming with us."

The colonel replied, "I see no reason for that, and I have duties elsewhere."

Right. Like a swim in the pool at the Bilqis Hotel. I didn't want Hakim and his goons with us anyway, and neither did anyone else. We could handle this ourselves unless The Panther had a platoon of jihadists with him. I asked Hakim, "Would you guess that al-Darwish is alone?"

Hakim replied, "Al-Darwish is dead, according to Altair. But if he is not, then he is in that cave, and he is alone, or perhaps he has one or two trusted jihadists with him. But no more." He motioned toward the camp, indicating that there weren't many jihadists left for The Panther to invite to his hole.

Well, the only thing left to talk about was money, and I said to Hakim, "Whether or not we find The Panther if we find his cave, you will be rewarded as we discussed."

"Three million dollars."

And a small mango up your ass. "Correct."

Brenner confirmed that, and said to Colonel Hakim, "We will arrange to meet in Sana'a, perhaps at the American Embassy, or in your office. The appropriate people will be there from my government to arrange for your reward."

I lifted my foot, because the bullshit was up to my ankles.

But maybe Brenner would try to get *something* for

Hakim, and I guess that was okay. As with Altair, you do a little bullshit and a little chocolate ice cream. Point is, we weren't out of here yet, and Hakim could be the problem or the solution.

Hakim said to Brenner, "If you should capture al-Darwish—or find him dead—and you find yourself without means to transport him to Sana'a, I am at the Bilqis Hotel."

Of course you are. And the hotel is not charging a PSO colonel a rial for the room. Life is good if you're a policeman in a police state. It occurred to me that I had the right job, but in the wrong country.

Brenner said, "Thank you, Colonel. I'll let you know."

Actually, if we found The Panther, the only thing we'd have to transport was his pinky finger, and the rest of him could rot in these hills.

I hate long good-byes, so I said, "Good-bye."

But Kate, a compassionate lady, asked Colonel Hakim, "Did you tell Altair that his family would be taken care of?"

"Ah, yes, I did that. So we will need to discuss that as well."

I didn't think Uncle Sam was going to pay a terrorist's family a hundred grand, but they might pay Hakim something and Hakim could take care of that. Good-bye.

But Hakim had more to tell us, and he said, "The family name of Altair—it is al-Darwish."

I hardly knew what to say, so I said, "See you later."

Colonel Hakim and Mr. Brenner exchanged salutes, and the PSO guys got back in the Humvee I bought for them.

So, here we were. Alone at last.

They say the journey is the destination, but it is not. The journey is the journey; the destination is the end. And we were near the end of this journey—and so was Bulus ibn al-Darwish.

CHAPTER EIGHTY-THREE

We took what we needed from the Land Cruiser and began hoofing it.

The direct route to the head of the trail, if the trail existed, was through the Al Qaeda camp, but the camp was a hellish landscape of bomb craters, smoking earth, and dead bodies, not to mention unexploded munitions. So we began our way around the rim of the flat basin with the sloping hills to our right and the smoking camp to our left.

Every hundred yards or so, Zamo would look through his nightscope, checking out the terrain around us. He also looked down into the camp and told us, "I see the old man. He's wandering around."

Just as Zamo said that, there was a loud explosion and we all hit the ground.

Zamo said, "The old guy set something off."

Well, I hope he's on his way to a better place than this.

We continued on and the terrain was a challenge, with ridges of loose shale-like rock that gave way under our feet.

It took us half an hour to circumvent the Al Qaeda camp, and we were now approaching the far side of the camp where the trail was supposed to begin, according to Altair, who could not be re-questioned about that.

We stopped and took a break. Zamo passed his rifle around so we could look through the night-scope and do what he called "terrain appreciation and orientation."

I looked through the scope, which lit up the night with a weird green glow, like I was wearing tinted glasses. I'd trained on a similar nightscope, so my eye and brain adjusted to the monochromatic image, and I was able to fully appreciate that this whole place was a wasteland, deader than the moon. Not even a goat. Also no sign of Noah's Ark.

I looked across the smoking basin at the place where we'd started, and I could see our white Land Cruiser still there, which was a good sign that our deal with the devil was intact.

I passed the rifle to Kate, who focused on the sail-shaped peak and said, "Maybe another two kilometers."

We moved on, looking for the trail that we would have to intersect as we continued around the rim of the basin, but the ground was so rock-strewn that a foot trail wouldn't be noticeable. Also, the thought occurred to me, and probably to everyone, that Altair had pulled a fast one on Colonel Hakim, or Hakim himself had pulled one on us so he could get out of here and go someplace nicer and safer. Did I promise him the money for services already rendered? Or for results?

The A-team separated and doubled back, looking

for the trail, but we kept one another in sight as we closely examined the rocky ground in the dim moonlight.

I realized that this trail, if it existed, would not be well trodden. I mean, I doubted if The Panther invited a hundred jihadists up to his cave every night to play bridge and have a cigar, and I doubted, too, if The Panther made the trip down to the camp very often. So we weren't looking for an actual trail but more of a starting point into the hills.

It was Kate, with her obsessive attention to untidy floors, who spotted something, and she said in a quiet, enemy-territory voice, "Look here."

We went over to where she was standing and she pointed the muzzle of her M4 at something that would not be noticeable or remarkable in most places, but which here, on the moon, showed evidence of human presence; it was, in fact, a plastic bottle cap.

Kate picked it up and passed it around like a found diamond, and we all agreed that it was fairly new, and that the litterbug, whoever he was, had left us a trail marker.

So with our backs to the Al Qaeda camp, we had our starting point for the route that would take us where we needed to go.

We moved away from the basin and toward the hills to our front.

Kate, who'd kept the bottle cap as a souvenir, was looking for more, like Hansel and Gretel looking for shiny pebbles in the moonlight.

We also looked for the plastic water bottle that had been attached to the cap, but that seemed to be it for litter.

We had no second point to connect to the bottle cap, but as we moved on, the route became more clear because the terrain started to narrow between two ridgelines, like the narrow end of a funnel.

The ground rose more steeply and the loose rock was making noise as it slid beneath our feet, and noise was not what we wanted, so we slowed up.

As we came around a bend in the rising trail, it suddenly ended, and in front of us was a huge pile of rock, blocking the way.

We approached the rock pile and it was obvious that this was a recent slide, caused either by God telling us to go back, or by twenty-four thousand pounds of high explosives shaking the earth like an erupting volcano.

Zamo volunteered his rock-climbing skills, and Brenner held his rifle as Zamo picked his way up the broken rock with his Colt .45 automatic in his hand.

There was no doubt that The Panther, if he was in his cave when those bombs hit, had heard and felt the airstrike, and I imagined that he knew he'd lost a base camp and everyone in it. His unanswered sat-phone call to the camp would confirm that.

I had no idea what this psycho was thinking or feeling when his cave started shaking around him, but I hoped he realized that his world had gotten much smaller. That, and the lack of news from the goat herder's hut, told him he was alone, with a problem. Maybe Perth Amboy wasn't so bad after all.

Zamo called down in a loud whisper, "Clear."

Brenner slung Zamo's rifle across his back and we all picked our way up the rockslide.

At the top we could see the continuation of the trail and the sail-shaped peak off to our right.

Zamo took his rifle and scanned the terrain, saying, "Nothing moving...no scope looking back at me... There's like a deep gorge ahead that cuts through the trail...about six hundred meters...I see a stone hut..." He focused in and said, "Nothing moving around the hut..."

Brenner took the rifle and looked through the scope, saying to us, "It could be a sentry hut—between the base camp and the cave..."

"Could be," which meant we were on the right track.

Brenner said, "We can go around it."

I suggested, "Let's see if anyone is home."

We scrambled down the rock pile as quietly as possible and continued along the route.

There was nothing moving in this dead zone except us, and the night was silent, except for the crunch of brittle rock beneath our feet. The high terrain around us made me start to imagine that there were people looking down on us, and I was expecting the silence to be shattered any second by blasts of submachine-gun fire. Whose idea was this?

We were spread apart as we walked, but I moved closer to Kate and gave her an encouraging pat on the back, then continued on.

Zamo was on point now and he raised his arm, indicating halt. We stopped and everyone got down on one knee, rifles at the ready.

Brenner moved up to Zamo and they took turns looking through the nightscope.

Brenner motioned me and Kate forward, and we moved in a crouch to where he and Zamo were kneeling.

About fifty meters in front of us was the gorge we'd seen, and sitting in the gorge was the stone hut.

Brenner whispered, "I'll check it out."

Well, if you insist, go ahead. But I remembered whose idea this was so I grabbed Brenner's arm and made it clear that I was going. Kate wanted to come along, but that wasn't happening. I whispered, "Cover me."

I moved forward quickly in a crouch and got to the edge of the gorge, keeping my eyes on the stone hut. I flattened out on the ground and looked through my four-power scope to the right where the gorge descended between two hills. The moon was higher in the southern sky, and it cast good light on this south-facing slope. Nothing seemed to be moving uphill, and to my left was the hut at the bottom of the gorge.

I focused my scope on the hut. Like most of these huts it had no windows, only a narrow, doorless entrance. There was a crude ladder going up to the flat roof, and from here I could see that there was no one on the roof, so if this was a sentry post, the sentry was inside, which didn't make much sense in terms of vigilance.

I made my way on my butt down into the gorge, dividing my attention between the hut and everything else.

At the bottom, I crouched between two rocks and looked at the hut. There is the cautious approach, favored by most, and the let's-do-this-fast approach, favored by me. I sprang out of my crouch and charged across the rocky ground directly for the door of the hut.

I really didn't expect to find anyone inside, so when I tripped over a body lying on the dirt floor, I was as surprised as the guy I tripped over.

It was pitch dark inside the hut, except for a little light coming through the door, and I saw the guy getting to his feet at the same time I did. He'd just been rudely awakened, so he wasn't at the top of his game, but he instinctively kicked out and caught me in the gut. I grabbed his bare foot, twisted it, and he fell to the floor, then scrambled toward the door, grabbing what looked like his rifle on the way.

I dove on top of him, and he collapsed to the ground, but then he tried to lizard-crawl out the door. I gave him a roundhouse punch in the face, then another that broke his nose, and he was down for the count.

I stood, yanked his AK-47 away from him, and smacked the butt against his head to see if he noticed.

I heard something outside the hut, and I flattened my back to the left side of the door and held my M4 by the pistol grip.

It got quiet outside, and I waited, knowing that my team was covering me from the top of the gorge.

"John?"

"I'm here. Abdul is on the ground."

My teammates came into the hut, stepping over the other guy.

There wasn't much to say except that the guy on the ground was probably Al Qaeda and not an innocent civilian, and that he had been sleeping on the job.

We pulled the guy away from the doorway and sat him up in a corner.

Zamo frisked him while Brenner held a red-filtered flashlight on him. The guy had a 9mm Browning automatic and a sat-phone on him. He also had a cracked nose and a split lip, and his face was bloody. Before Brenner shut off the light, Kate took it and shined it closer to the guy's face. She's really good with faces, even when they've had a nose and lip job, and she said, "Nabeel."

Indeed it was. That called for a drink. Zamo opened a bottle of water and splashed it in Nabeel's face, then poured some between his lips as he slapped him around.

Nabeel coughed up some water, then half opened his eyes.

We didn't have a lot of time to get to the point, so I drew my jambiyah and put the blade to his throat, noticing the bandage on the left side of his neck, like he'd cut himself shaving, or maybe someone else had tried to get his attention with a knife. I said to him, "You owe me for that bagel."

He focused on me and there was real terror in his eyes, which made me feel bad, like *I* was the terrorist.

I said to him, "Here's the deal, Nabeel. You have your choice of living or dying, and by dying I mean I'm going to open up your throat like a ripe melon. Understand?"

He nodded his head without moving his neck.

I asked him, "Where is al-Darwish?"

He knew that was coming, and he said, "Please not to kill me and I say where is he."

"No, asshole, *I* say where is he. *You* say where he is. Where is he?"

"He . . . he is in . . . maghara . . ."

Brenner said, "Cave."

"Where is this cave?"

"Here. Close."

"Can you be more specific?"

"I tell you . . . not far. You go . . . go to where sun go—"

"West?"

"Yes. West. You see where to go. Up."

Brenner took over in Arabic, then said to us, "He says there are two people with al-Darwish. A sentry who he says sits on a rock, and a person inside the cave with al-Darwish."

Hopefully the sentry didn't have a nightscope, though he probably did, but maybe he, too, was asleep on the job. If not, we had to put him to sleep.

I said to Brenner, "Do you believe him about only two guys?"

Brenner replied, "We're about to find out."

Brenner asked Nabeel a few more questions in Arabic and English, and Nabeel claimed he'd never actually been to the cave, but he did confirm that the entrance to the cave was on the hill with the distinctive ship's sail peak. So that jibed with what Altair had said, making it a little less likely to be bullshit.

I was surprised that Altair and Nabeel gave up the boss, and I was getting the feeling that those who knew Bulus ibn al-Darwish did not love him. Just like back in the States.

Zamo asked, "Is this guy supposed to make a sit-rep?"

Brenner asked in Arabic, then told us, "He says yes, and he's happy to make that call now to al-Numair."

We all agreed that it was better if The Panther didn't hear from Nabeel that all was well, because there was a chance that Nabeel would give the code word for "I have a gun to my head." No news from the sentry sometimes just means the sentry is asleep.

Nabeel, trying to firm up his life-or-death deal, also offered to help us find the way to his boss's hideout, but it's never a good idea to take the enemy with you on a stealth mission.

Anyway, if we had time, we could have happily tormented Nabeel with the news about his buddies getting vaporized at the Sheik Musa meeting. Not to mention his camp being turned into a toxic waste dump. I would also have liked to take those photos of the Belgians, which I had with me, and shove them, one by one, down Nabeel's throat. But bottom line on Nabeel al-Samad was that he'd come to the end of his usefulness.

Well, the moment that we would have liked to avoid had come, and it was time to say good-bye to Nabeel.

Zamo said, "I'll tie and gag him."

We all nodded and left the hut. A second later, I heard the cough of the muzzle silencer, and Zamo stepped out of the hut, bolting another round in the chamber.

No one said anything as Zamo slung Nabeel's AK-47 over his shoulder and we moved on.

Kate noticed that the gorge was littered with plastic water bottles and similar evidence that a lot of people had been there, and we concluded that this was a meeting place, like an amphitheater, maybe where The Panther rallied his troops. If so, his cave couldn't be far off.

We climbed out of the gorge and continued on. I had point now, but Zamo was close behind me, scanning the terrain to our front, sides, and rear.

We were about a hundred yards from the base of the high hill where the cave was supposed to be, and I felt Zamo's hand press down on my shoulder. I dropped to one knee and glanced back to see him focusing on something up the slope of the hill.

He passed his sniper rifle to me and pointed, like a bird dog. I followed his outstretched arm and scanned the hill. About halfway up, sitting on a rock, was a man in dark cammies with what looked like a rifle across his knees. As I focused in, the man raised the rifle and began scanning the ground below him. I caught a brief flash of his nightscope lens as it swept past us, and Zamo and I hit the ground and rolled behind a flat rock.

As I passed the rifle back to Zamo, Kate and Brenner inched forward, and I said, "Sniper."

They both nodded and kept completely still.

Zamo was now refocused on the sniper, and Brenner inched closer to him.

Zamo said, "We can't move without that guy seeing us."

Meaning, permission to fire.

We all understand that if Zamo took that guy out, there'd be another dead sentry who was not reporting in. On the other hand, there seemed to be no way around that.

Brenner thought a moment, then said to Zamo, "Take him out."

Zamo seemed pleased with the assignment.

Zamo knew, and we all knew, that he had literally one shot at this. The sound of his shot would be muffled by the silencer, but the bullet, if it missed the target, would hit rock and even the most clueless sniper would know that he'd been shot at and missed. And by the time Zamo chambered another round and re-aimed, the enemy sniper would be behind a rock and raising the alarm. Then he'd start shooting back.

It looked to me like the sniper was maybe five or six

hundred meters up the side of the hill, still within the nine-hundred-meter effective range of Zamo's scope and rifle. But it wasn't an easy shot because it was a night shot, and because rising or falling terrain distorts your perception of the target's distance.

We all sat as still as the rocks around us while Zamo steadied his aim from a kneeling position. There wasn't a rock around that was high enough for him to use to steady his rifle, so he was aiming freehand, and I could see he was having a problem with his injured left arm, which couldn't hold its position long. In fact, Zamo lowered the rifle, then sighted again, then lowered it again.

Jeez. Come on, guy. You can do it. And do it fast before that bastard starts scanning the terrain again.

Zamo took a deep breath, then actually stood, took another breath, held it, then fired.

He dropped to one knee and chambered another round.

Brenner was the one to ask, "Hit?"

Zamo glanced back at him as though he couldn't understand the question. Finally, he said, "Yeah. Hit." Like, why bother to fire if you're going to miss?

Well, Zamo was feeling good about himself, and I was feeling that we were very lucky and that The Panther was not.

I suggested, "We really need to move it before The Panther hears all this silence."

Everyone agreed and we dispensed with stealth and caution and double-timed it up the trail that curved around the base of the high hill with the sail on top. We kept an eye out for what could be a climbing path up the hill, and after about a hundred yards Zamo spotted a small pile of loose rock on the trail.

We all dropped to one knee and hugged the side of the hill as Zamo scanned straight up and confirmed, "This is the way." He also said, "I don't see an entrance to a cave ... but I see, like, overhanging flat rocks ..."

I peered through my scope at the high hill and I could see rock strata jutting out, casting moon shadows across the face of the hill. The entrance to the cave would be under one of those overhangs.

So what's the plan? If Chet and Buck were with us, we'd sit here for a week with charts and diagrams, then call Howard and ask him to call Washington for clearance. But I had a better plan—go up the hill, find the cave, kill The Panther, go down the hill.

Brenner, however, had a few add-ons—Zamo was to stay here and cover our backs, then he, Kate, and I would go up and look for the entrance to the cave, but only one of us would go in. And who would that be? Well, whoever thought of this.

Brenner whispered, "Watch for tripwires—flares or booby-traps."

Thanks for that.

I went first, Brenner was behind me, and Kate brought up the rear as we began our ascent. The climbing path was mostly rock ledges, like a steep staircase cleared of loose stone. But now and then a piece of stone would fall and make a very loud noise, which I knew wasn't as loud as I heard it in my head.

I was happy with the small M4, which, as advertised, was light and compact, and I was sure it would be excellent in caves. The moonlight was bright enough to see the way, but not bright enough to see a tripwire, so I felt my way carefully, brushing my fingers around the stone ledges to feel for a wire.

This was slow going, but the idea was to surprise
The Panther, without being surprised ourselves by tripping a wire and getting blown to pieces. Or at the very
least, tripping an illumination flare that would light us
up like deer in the headlights, followed by a long burst
of AK-47 fire.

We had no way of knowing for sure if there were any
such devices on the approach to the cave, but if I was
living in a cave, I'd damn sure put something on the
path to alert me to visitors.

And there it was. I felt it with my hand—a taut
metal wire about six inches above the wide ledge I was
about to crawl onto.

I turned and motioned to Brenner, who was about
ten feet behind me, using the hand signal for tripwire,
which if you're interested is like pantomiming stretching a rubber band.

Brenner nodded, and I turned back and did a crab
walk carefully over the wire. You can't cut it because it
could also be set to trip if the tension is released. So you
leave it, mark it, and move on. I draped the wire with
my white handkerchief and kept climbing.

Brenner got over the wire, followed by Kate, and we
continued on.

We were about halfway up the hill, which was
maybe fifteen hundred feet high, and the slope was
becoming less steep, and this had the effect of making
it more difficult to see ahead to what was over the next
strata of rock.

Then something caught my eye to the right and I
froze. It was a man about fifty feet away sitting on the
same rock ledge that I was on. It took me a few seconds
to realize that this was the sniper's perch, and that the

man, who was leaning back against the rock, was not moving because he was dead.

I signaled to Brenner, who passed the signal along to Kate. They climbed to the ledge below me where they could see the dead man.

I moved sideways to my right and got to the sitting man, whose head was tilted back as though he was moon gazing. I could see that Zamo had hit his target full in the chest, slightly right of the heart, but fatal nonetheless.

The man's rifle, lying to his side, had the distinctive shape of the Soviet-made Dragunov sniper rifle, which it probably was. More importantly, the rifle had a nightscope whose lens was still illuminated, and I reached out to take it.

All of a sudden the silence was broken by a loud, piercing noise, like an alarm, which made me jump. Ringing phones always make me jump, and the phone rang again, then again. Well, it wasn't my sat-phone, which was dead, so it was the guy's phone and he was dead. If my Arabic was better, I'd have answered it and reported all was dead quiet here.

The phone finally stopped ringing, and I looked at Brenner and Kate below me. Obviously the sniper had missed his situation report, as had Nabeel, and whoever was calling—maybe The Panther himself—was getting a little worried. And with good reason. We, however, also had a problem now. But there was nothing we could do about it except continue on and get rid of the problem.

Brenner was signaling insistently that he would take the lead, and Kate was nodding in agreement and motioning me to come toward her. But I had come too far to drop back this close to the finish line, and I continued up the slope with my new sniper rifle. I got to the next ledge and used the nightscope to scan up the hill.

Less than thirty feet in front of me was a huge overhang, a long slab of rock that formed the roof of a deep, dark shelter—a cave. I focused the nightscope and saw something move in the darkness.

A figure suddenly emerged from under the overhang, carrying an AK-47, and I took aim with the sniper rifle. As I pulled the trigger, I realized the figure was wearing a balto. My shot hit her where I'd aimed, right through the heart, and her arms flew up, sending her rifle into the air as she fell backwards and hit the ground.

The bastard who was still inside the cave had fixed my position, and before I could take cover I saw the muzzle flash a half second before I heard the hollow popping sound of an AK-47 on full automatic. A tracer round clipped my hip and another round hit my Kevlar and knocked me backward off the ledge to the ledge below, and I lost the sniper rifle. It took me a few seconds to catch my breath, and when I looked up I could see green tracer rounds streaking down the slope right above where I was lying.

Kate and Brenner were returning fire, but they were probably low on ammunition from the shootout at the Crow Fortress and they weren't on full blast. The firing from the cave stopped, and Kate and Brenner ceased fire. It suddenly became quiet.

I was lying flat on my back on the rock, and I couldn't see Brenner or Kate, but I'd be able to see anyone who appeared on the ledge above me, and I had my

M4 on full automatic across my chest, ready to fire at anything that moved.

Only one AK had been firing and I assumed that was The Panther. The other person that Nabeel had mentioned must have been the woman. I don't know who she was—girlfriend or wife—but like all women around here, she was expendable, and al-Darwish had used her to draw my fire. Nice guy. And now The Panther was wondering if I was dead or alive. The name of this game is patience, deception, and surprise, and I was good at two out of three.

The minutes ticked by, and I was concerned that al-Asshole was flanking around to our sides, or worse, he could be hightailing it up the hill, heading for someplace far away. But if Zamo was in a good spot, he should be able to see that kind of movement and take care of it. Still, The Panther had the immediate advantage of the higher ground.

When you get hit, you don't always feel it at first, and I didn't, but now I could feel the pain where the bullet grazed my left hip, and the throbbing in my chest where the Kevlar had absorbed the second hit. I also felt some warm blood, but it wasn't gushing. Still, the hip would start to stiffen up when the initial shock wore off and the body said, "You got hit, stupid."

Another minute passed, and I was starting to think that maybe Brenner or Kate had been hit, but I couldn't think about that now. And I couldn't lie here all night waiting for The Panther to make a move—or a full retreat. So I took a deep breath, sat up quickly, and fired a long, sweeping spray of rounds up the slope. Bullets ricocheted from the rock as I dropped down, slapped another magazine into the M4, rolled down the slope, got up, and repeated the recon by fire.

But no one returned the fire and it got quiet again. I reached for another magazine in my bush vest and discovered that I was out of ammunition. Shit.

I drew my Colt .45 automatic and lay very still. I couldn't figure out what this asshole was up to, but he'd gone from panic-fire to very cagey silence. Or he was in the next province by now.

I yelled out, "Bulus! Asshole! Shithead!"

He didn't respond to his name, so I moved as far as I could along the ledge, still on my back, which was the only way to see what was above me without raising my head. I yelled out again, "Asshole! I'm talkin' to you, Bulus. You speak English?"

No response.

Okay, time to do it. I yelled, "Cover fire!" and I charged up the slope as Kate and Brenner, off to my right, opened up with their M4s. I zigzagged across the flat ledges toward the mouth of the wide cave in front of me, popping off a few rounds from the Colt. Brenner and Kate were firing full, long bursts of suppressing fire into and around the cave, and the bullets were ricocheting around me, but I wasn't drawing any return fire, so the bastard was either gone, ducking, or dead.

I got to the overhanging ledge, jumped over the dead woman, then shoulder-rolled into the mouth of the cave. I lay still on my side and peered into the darkness.

I realized I was lying on a very funky blanket. Some moonlight was penetrating the space under the ledge, and as my eyes adjusted to the darkness, I could see that the carpeted floor was strewn with what

I guessed was camping equipment. So this stinking
shithole was the lair of The Panther, the mastermind
of the *Cole* bombing, the head of Al Qaeda in Yemen,
and the target of the greatest power on earth. I mean, I
expected something like this, but now that I was here,
it was hard to believe that this crap hole was where
Bulus ibn al-Darwish, al-Numair, The Panther, lived
and plotted and ruled from.

Mr. al-Darwish pressed the muzzle of his AK-47
against the back of my head and said, in perfect English, "Throw your gun on the ground. Now!"

I threw the Colt .45 a few feet away.

He had backed off so I couldn't grab the barrel of
his rifle, and he said, "Hands on your head."

I put my hands on my head. Where were Kate and
Brenner?

"Who are you?" he asked.

"Your worst nightmare."

"No, I am *your* worst nightmare."

"I'm taking you back home, Bulus." I reminded
him, "Your momma's waiting for you."

He gave me a kick in the back of the head and asked,
"How many people are with you?"

"More than are with you. Everyone you know is
dead."

He had nothing to say about that, and there was a
long silence. Then he asked me, "How did you find this
place?"

"A soaring eagle told me." I translated for him,
"Altair." He didn't respond to that, so I went into my
police mode and said, "You're trapped, Bulus, and
you're going to die unless you surrender."

"Do not use my given name."

Shithead? I said, to make it official, "You're under arrest."

He thought that was funny and asked, "What is my arresting officer's name? That's my right as an American citizen to know your name."

Asshole. I told him, "John Corey, Anti-Terrorist Task Force."

"So you finally found me. Or have I found *you*?" He asked, "Where is your wife, Mr. Corey?"

"Where's yours? Dead?"

I thought that would send him over the edge and he'd try another kick, which would not go as well for him as the last one, but he didn't react. Maybe he had more wives.

He asked me, "Do you think this cave has only one entrance? Do you think I'm stupid?"

Yes, I do think you're stupid, and yes I thought this cave had only one way in and out. But I guess it had two. Shit.

He let me know, "I will be on the other side of this hill in ten minutes, you'll be dead, and anyone who follows me through the cave will step on a pressure mine and be blown up."

Holy shit.

"So I will say good-bye to Mr. Corey, and to Mrs. Corey in absentia."

I was certain he wouldn't fire, because he knew there were other people out there who would come charging in, firing—so he was going for his jambiyah to do it quietly.

I spun around on my buttocks and as I did I saw that he had his knife in his right hand, his rifle was slung, and his left hand was reaching for my hair. My legs caught him below the knees and he lost his balance and fell sideways.

I pulled my jambiyah, which he didn't see as he scrambled away from me and unslung his rifle.

Before he could level it, I was on top of him and I pressed my full weight down on him. He thrashed around, trying to get his rifle into a firing position, but I wasn't going to let that happen. He'd dropped his jambiyah, but now his right hand reached out for it, and he got hold of the handle and brought the tip around and buried it into my back. He realized it wasn't penetrating, and he brought it up again to stick it into my neck or head.

I gave him the old knee in the balls, which refocused his attention, then I put the curved blade of my jambiyah under his full beard and on his throat and said, "Remember the *Cole*, asshole."

Our eyes met for a second, then I pressed hard and drew the blade across his throat, which opened his jugular vein and both carotid arteries, causing his warm blood to spurt over my hand. I told him, "You have the right to remain silent."

I kept at it, sawing through his flesh, windpipe, muscles, and tendons until I got to his spine, which I separated with the blade, then I kept going until the blade hit the dirt floor.

I sat up, drew a long breath, then grabbed his hair and held up his head. I said to The Panther, "Payback, you fucking bastard. Payback for the men on the *Cole*, payback for the men, women, and children you murdered, you piece of shit. Payback—"

Kate said, "John...John...it's okay...it's okay... stop..."

Brenner grabbed the severed head by its hair, pulled it out of my hand, and threw it across the floor of the cave. He said, "Time to go."

Kate took my arm and I stood.

Time to go home. That's the plan.

PART IX

New York City

CHAPTER EIGHTY-FOUR

The big, four-faced stanchion clock read 6:50. Most of the commuters had departed for the suburbs, but arriving trains brought fresh blood—theatergoers, partiers, and others from near and far who poured into Manhattan every night through Grand Central Station.

Maybe, I thought, it was a little hokey to meet under the clock that had been used in so many movies as a rendezvous for lovers. But the clock had also served as a meeting place for tens of thousands of soldiers, sailors, and airmen coming home to their families, so this was okay.

Buck could not join us, but he was a gentleman of the old school, and he had sent his regrets, demonstrating not only good manners, but also tremendous chutzpah.

In other news from the front, Kate and I had been notified, officially, that Mr. Chet Morgan of the Central Intelligence Agency had been struck by a Bedouin bullet as he tried to rescue us in the Black Hawk helicopter. That's not quite how I remembered it, but in any case Mr. Morgan had died of his wound before the helicopter reached Najran airbase.

This was the second CIA officer whose death had been announced to me, the first being the aforementioned Ted Nash, who actually died twice, officially, before Kate whacked him for real. And I had the feeling that Chet Morgan, too, would experience a resurrection, and that I'd hear from him again. If not, he would hear from me.

Zamo, too, couldn't join us because he was on extended medical leave, recuperating from his injury, in Las Vegas. I hope his luck holds out.

We'd also invited Howard Fensterman and Clare Nolan, who had grown closer in the three weeks since we'd seen them, and they would have loved to be in New York with us, but their new duties in Sana'a prevented them from taking home leave at this time. They did promise, however, to be in New York for the holidays, all of which Howard probably celebrates.

Reunions sound good in theory, like my high school reunions, but in reality you don't always want to see the people who you bonded with at certain times and places in your life journey. The memories are good and they should be preserved and acknowledged with a holiday card or a quick e-mail and not be spoiled by actually having to see those people again. Clare, however, might be an exception.

Also, I was looking forward to seeing Paul Brenner. Mr. Brenner was home on leave, in Virginia, but as I predicted he was returning to Yemen. Some people can't get enough fun. I mean, this is the guy who did a second tour in Vietnam. One day, some tour in some shithole would kill him, but for now he was happy to feel alive by daring death. I suppose I could say the same about myself, and maybe even Kate, but...Well, no buts. We're back at 26 Federal Plaza, me with a new three-year contract, and Kate with a guarantee of three more years in the city she's grown to love with the man she loves, and tolerates. That's me.

But if we get bored or restless or tired of Tom Walsh's act, there are a dozen other hellholes where the Anti-Terrorist Task Force operates, and we may volunteer for one of them. Hopefully we won't have to take another State Department course in cultural awareness. The last one didn't work too well.

Kate and I watched Paul Brenner and his lady walking across the marble floor of the Main Concourse. They spotted the tall clock, then spotted us, and Brenner and his lady made their way through the crowd.

Kate said, "She's very attractive."

I wouldn't have expected less from a man who has good taste in women.

We waved, they waved, we all met and shook hands or hugged, and Brenner introduced us to his lady, who said to Kate and me, "I've heard a lot about you."

I couldn't say the same, but she seemed like a nice woman and we went up to Michael Jordan's Steak House on the mezzanine, where I got silly and asked the waiter for a Pink Panther, on the rocks.

When the ladies went to freshen up, Brenner said to me, "Buck."

I didn't reply.

Brenner asked, "Are we supposed to let that go?"

"We're supposed to believe that Buck was an unwitting accomplice."

"He wasn't unwitting."

Right. But Buckminster Harris had served his

country well and honorably since I was a milk drinker, so I said, "I don't want to see him disgraced in public."

Brenner nodded, then inquired, "How about dead in private?"

"Whatever you decide, I'm with you."

Brenner said, "I'm not buying that Chet is dead."

"Seems a little suspicious," I agreed. "When we see Buck, we'll get the truth."

Brenner leaned toward me and said softly, "I want both of them dead."

I nodded.

The ladies returned and we ordered another round. I could see that Kate liked Brenner's lady, whose name was Cynthia, and we learned that Paul and Cynthia had met on the job, just as Kate and I had. Cynthia Sunhill was Army, Criminal Investigation Division, and she'd requested a posting in Yemen. Good luck.

When the waiter came around, I, of course, inquired about any goat specials. Kate rolled her eyes. Brenner laughed.

It was a good evening and we parted, promising to stay in touch, which was inevitable because of the scheduled CIA post-op meeting in Washington. That should be interesting.

As for the thanks of a grateful nation, that hadn't yet been scheduled.

Hey, we were lucky we had jobs. Right?

Acknowledgments

First, my sincere thanks to Jamie Raab, Executive Vice President and Publisher of Grand Central Publishing, for taking on an additional job as editor of this novel. Jamie has been tireless, patient, and precise during the entire process, and this is a better book because of her keen editorial judgment and sage advice. We don't always agree on what I've written, but we always agree that the end product is a smooth combination of Jamie's yin and my yang.

Thanks, also, to Harvey-Jane Kowal, a.k.a. HJ, who came out of retirement from Hachette Book Group to work on another DeMille book. HJ is a master of grammar, punctuation, spelling, and fact-checking, and she saves me from looking uneducated. Our tradition for the last eleven books has been to celebrate the editing of the last page with a few Bloody Marys. Here's to you, HJ.

A book needs many editorial eyes and minds, and I thank Roland Ottewell, who has worked with care and precision on my last several manuscripts. And because my manuscripts are always late and due at the printer yesterday, Roland also works long hours to make the manuscript printer-ready. Thanks, Roland, for another job well done.

On the corporate level, I'd like to thank David Young, Chairman and CEO of Hachette Book Group. David takes the time from his busy schedule to read my manuscripts, though that isn't in his job description. David either enjoys my writing or he wants to see what he's paying for. I thank David, too, for his friendship and for his good taste in Scotch whisky.

As in all my novels, I've called on friends and acquaintances to assist me with technical details, professional jargon, and all the other bits and pieces of information that a novelist needs but can't get from books or the Internet.

First in this category is Detective Kenny Hieb (NYPD, retired), formerly with the Joint Terrorism Task Force and currently doing something similar, though I can't be specific. Kenny has been to Yemen in real life with the JTTF, and his experience there and his memories, notes, and photos of Yemen have all been invaluable to me as I constructed the world of this book. Thanks, Kenny, for your help, but more important, thank you for your work in keeping America safe.

I should say here that any errors of fact or procedures regarding police work, Anti-Terrorist operations, and related matters are a result of either my misunderstanding of the information given to me, or a result of my decision to take dramatic liberties and literary license.

Another eyewitness to Yemen was Matt Longo, who was in that country for more peaceful reasons than John Corey was. Matt, a college roommate of my son

Alex, is well traveled in many Arabic countries and he has been of great help to me in regard to the Arabic culture and the religion of Islam. I have included Matt as a character in this book with the thought that Matt represents a younger generation who may help define our future relations with the world of Islam, and bridge the cultural gap that exists between the two worlds. Thanks, Matt, for your help and your insights.

Many of my novels have benefited from the assistance of my childhood friend Thomas Block, U.S. Airways Captain (retired), columnist and contributing editor to aviation magazines, and co-author with me of *Mayday*, as well as the author of seven other novels. Although Tom has retired as an international captain, he has not retired from writing, which does not require good eyesight or quick reflexes, and Tom has recently published his seventh novel, *Captain*, available on his website: www.thomasblocknovels.com.

Many thanks, too, to Tom's lovely wife, Sharon Block, former flight attendant for Braniff International and U.S. Airways, for her timely and careful reading of the manuscript and her excellent suggestions, as well as her keen eye for typos and bad punctuation. Sharon's reading skills have been invaluable to both me and Tom, as our minds tended to wander in high school English class. What we were thinking about is another story, but we both knew we'd someday have a lady in our lives who knew how to proofread.

Thanks, too, to John Kennedy, Deputy Police Commissioner, Nassau County (NY) Police Department (retired), labor arbitrator, and member of the New York State Bar. John has read and assisted with all my John Corey novels, and he comes to this task with a unique combination of skills and knowledge as a police officer and an attorney. John is my reality check, and if he says something is not legally or procedurally correct, then I rewrite it—or I invoke the novelist's right to make up stuff.

This book would not have existed without the dedication and hard work of my two assistants, Dianne Francis and Patricia Chichester. I write my novels longhand, but for years no one could read my handwriting and it seemed that I had to learn to type or never be published again. But then along came Dianne, then Patricia, who could understand my illegible scrawl and put it into type form so I, too, could read what I wrote. Dianne and Patricia also read the manuscript, page by page, and their comments, fact-checking, and proofreading are nothing short of amazing. Thank you for that and for keeping my life and schedule organized.

As with dessert, the best is last, and that's my wife, Sandy Dillingham DeMille, who has shared with me all the agonies and ecstasies of book writing. Sandy's support and encouragement have pulled me through some tough writing periods, and her editorial suggestions and marginal notes are literally the last word on my manuscript before it gets sent to the publisher.

Sandy and I are celebrating our tenth year together, and it's all been one well-plotted and beautifully written romance novel.

The following people have made generous contributions to charities in return for having their name used as a character in this novel:

Howard Fensterman, who contributed to the

Crohn's & Colitis Foundation of America; and **John "Zamo" Zamoiski**, who contributed to the Irvington Education Foundation.

I hope they enjoy their fictitious alter egos and that they continue their good work for worthy causes.

VISIT US ONLINE AT

WWW.HACHETTEBOOKGROUP.COM

FEATURES:

OPENBOOK BROWSE AND
SEARCH EXCERPTS
•
AUDIOBOOK EXCERPTS AND PODCASTS
•
AUTHOR ARTICLES AND INTERVIEWS
•
BESTSELLER AND PUBLISHING
GROUP NEWS
•
SIGN UP FOR E-NEWSLETTERS
•
AUTHOR APPEARANCES AND TOUR
INFORMATION
•
SOCIAL MEDIA FEEDS AND WIDGETS
•
DOWNLOAD FREE APPS

BOOKMARK HACHETTE BOOK GROUP
@ WWW.HACHETTEBOOKGROUP.COM

"Well?" L_____ squawking as the ship went on alert.

Exedore turned to her. "These are not Tiresian ships, Admiral, I can assure you."

"Enhancement coming in now, Lisa," Rick said. The computer drew several clamlike shapes on the screen.

Breetai straightened up and grunted. "Invid troop carriers!"

"Could they have formed an alliance with the Masters?" Lisa asked.

"That is very unlikely, Admiral," Exedore answered her.

"Sir!" a tech shouted. "It's showing multiple paint through the field!" The clam-ships had opened, yawned, spilling forth an enormous number of small strike mecha.

"I want the Skull scrambled."

"General Edwards's Ghost Squadron is already out, sir," Blake reported from his duty station.

"What?!"

The threat board showed two clusters of blips closing on one another. Rick slapped his hand down on the com stud, demanding to know who ordered the Alpha Veritechs out.

"General Edwards," came the reply.

"Edwards!" Rick seethed.

Blake tapped in a rapid sequence of requests. "Sir. Ghost Squadron reports they're moving in to engage."

THE SENTINELS ™ #1
THE DEVIL'S HAND

Jack McKinney

A Del Rey Book

BALLANTINE BOOKS • NEW YORK

A Del Rey Book
Published by Ballantine Books

Library of Congress Catalog Card Number: 87-91376

ISBN 0-345-35300-5

Manufactured in the United States of America

First Edition: April 1988

FOR NICHOLAS, JEREMY AND MATTHEW
WHOSE ENTHUSIASM HAS BEEN A
CONTINUING SOURCE OF INSPIRATION.

ROBOTECH CHRONOLOGY

1999   Alien spacecraft known as SDF-1 crashlands on Earth through an opening in hyperspace, effectively ending almost a decade of Global Civil War.

In another part of the Galaxy, Zor is killed during a Flower of Life seeding attempt.

2002   Destruction of Mars Base Sara.

2009   On the SDF-1's launch day, the Zentraedi (after a ten-year search for the fortress) appear and lay waste to Macross Island. The SDF-1 makes an accidental jump to Pluto.

2009–11   The SDF-1 battles its way back to Earth.

2011–12   The SDF-1 spends almost half a year on Earth, is ordered to leave, and defeats Dolza's armada, which has laid waste to much of the planet.

2012–14   A two-year period of reconstruction begins.

2012   The Robotech Masters lose confidence in the ability of their giant warriors to recapture the SDF-1, and begin a mass pilgrimage through interstellar space to Earth.

2013   Dana Sterling is born.

2014   Destruction of the SDFs 1 and 2 and Khyron's battlecruiser.

2014–20   The SDF-3 is built and launched. Rick Hunter turns 29 in 2020; Dana turns 7.

Subsequent events covering the Tiresian campaign are recounted in the Sentinels series. A complete Robochronology will appear in the fifth and final volume.

CHAPTER
ONE

I leave it up to the historians and the moralists to judge whether our decision (the Expeditionary mission) is right or wrong. I know only that it is prudent and necessary—necessary for our very survival both as a planet and as a life-form. If the Protoculture has taught me anything, it is that one must simply act! When all is said and done the inevitabilities and reshapings will have their way, but to remain either complacent or inert in the face of those fatalities is to invite catastrophe of a higher order than any of us dare imagine.

From the personal journal of Dr. Emil Lang

IN THE MIDDLE OF THE NIGHT ON AN ALIEN WORLD, AN army of insentient warriors dropped from the sky. Tirol, as this small moon was known, represented a prize of sorts— the end of a long campaign that had taken the invaders through a dozen local star systems and across the varied faces of twice that number of worlds—the remote realms of the once great empire of the Robotech Masters, forged and secured by their giant soldier clones, the Zentraedi. But Tirol itself was all but deserted, abandoned almost a generation earlier by those same Masters. So in effect this conquest was something of a disappointment for the horde who had raised savagery to new heights, something of a nonevent.

1

But just as a rock tossed into a pond will make its presence known to distant shores, the Invid's arrival on Tirol would send powerful waves through the continuum; and nowhere would the effects of their invasion be more greatly felt than on the world already inundated by previous tides from this same quarter—a blue-white gem of a planet that had seen better days, but was struggling still to regain control of its own fragile destiny...

Earth had captured its second satellite in the year 2013, when a joint Terran and XT force had wrested it from the control of the Zentraedi commander, Reno, faithful to the Imperative even after Dolza's fiery demise. The factory satellite was an enormous monstrosity, well in keeping with the grotesque design of the Zentraedi fleet, that had been folded instantaneously through space-time by Protoculture-fueled Reflex drives. It was radish-shaped and rose-colored in starlight, with fissures and convolutions suggestive of cerebral matter. Attached along its median section by rigid stalklike transport tubes were half a dozen secondary sacs and appendages, smaller by far, but equally vegetal in aspect, veined and incomprehensible.

There were some 15,000 Humans and Zentraedi living onboard, a sizable portion of Earth's post-apocalyptic population. The majority of these men and women had labored for six years inside the factory's weightless belly to construct a starship, a dimensional fortress soon to be Tirol-bound—there to confront the Robotech Masters, and with luck curtail any threat of continued warfare.

Among those onboard were Vice Admiral Rick Hunter and his close friend and trusted commander, Max Sterling. From a viewport in the admiral's quarters, the two men were watching null-gee construction crews put the finishing touches on the massive ship's deliberately misleading superstructure.

"I just don't know whether we're ready for this," Rick was saying. He had turned from the viewport and was three strides toward the center of the room. "There are so many *variables*, so many things that could go wrong now."

Max followed him, a grin beneath the sympathetic look he had adopted. "Come on, what could go wrong?"

Rick whirled on him. "Maybe I'm just not *ready*, Max!"

Rick's voice cracked on the word and Max couldn't suppress a short laugh. "Ready? It's been six years, Rick. How much more ready can you expect to be?"

"Guess I'm not as good up against the unknowns anymore." Rick shrugged, lowering his gaze. "I mean, we've got something good going already. So why jeopardize it, why tamper with it?"

Max took his friend by the shoulders and gave him an affectionate shake. "Look, you and Lisa love each other, so quit worrying. Everything's going to turn out fine. Besides, everybody's excited about the wedding. And what are you going to do, walk out on ten thousand guests?"

Rick felt the wisdom of it sink in, and smiled, self-mockingly.

They had both aged well, the rigors of life on- and off-world notwithstanding; both had turned twenty-nine in March and had at least a few good years left in them. Rick stood taller and straighter now than he had during the war, and that combined with some added weight gave him a stronger, more capable look. This was enhanced by the cut of the Expeditionary Force's high-collared uniform and torso harness, a crisscross, tailed, and flare-shouldered affair of black leather worn over tight-fitting trousers. He still wore his black hair stylishly long, though—a fashion the Veritech flyboys of the Robotech Defense Force had been largely responsible for. Max, too, had left behind the innocent look that had been something of a trademark. While Rick, Dr. Lang, and Lisa Hayes had devoted themselves to the SDF-3 project, Max had been busy distinguishing himself in the Southlands, especially during the Malcontent Uprisings of 2015–18. He still favored the blue hair tint he had affected during the war, likewise oversize aviator glasses to contacts or corrective microsurgery. Less than perfect vision had never handicapped his flying skills, in any case.

Rick was glancing back at the SDF-3 now. "And everybody gets to ride in the limo." He smirked.

Fabricated from the hull and power drives of Breetai's dreadnought and the salvaged remains from the SDFs 1 and 2, the ship was itself a wedding of sorts. Pursuant to Lang and Exedore's requests, it was more Zentraedi than Terran in design: a nontransformable deepspace leviathan, bristling with antennae and blistered across its crimson surface with scanner ports and laser-array gun turrets.

"We'll make sure you two get the backseat," Max said. "For at least a couple of hours, anyway."

Rick laughed from across the room; Max joined him at the external viewport, Earth's incomparable beauty filling the view. Sunlight glinted off the alloyed hulls and fins of dozens of in-transit shuttles. Rick was staring down at the planet wistfully.

"When's Lisa due back?" Max asked him.

"Tomorrow. But I'm thinking of shuttling down to meet her."

Max made an approving sound. "I'll ride with you."

"When haven't you," Rick said, after a moment.

With the destruction of the SDFs 1 and 2 on that fateful winter night in 2014, Macross's sister city, Monument, had risen to the fore as Earth's unofficial capital. The irradiated remains of Macross had been bulldozed flat and pushed into what hadn't been boiled away from Lake Gloval. Three enormous manmade buttes marked the resting place of the superdimensional fortresses, along with that of the Zentraedi cruiser that had destroyed them. But those mounds had not been completed before volunteer teams of valiant Robotechnicians had braved slow death to salvage what they could from the devastation.

Thrice-born Macross, however, was not resurrected, as much by choice as anything else; but the name lived on in a kind of mythic way, and Monument City, to the southwest over a rugged ridge, was doing its best to carry the tradition forward. This would change after the SDF-3 departed, but in 2020 things were much as they were in the Macross of 2014. That is not to say that there weren't sinister currents in the air for one and all to perceive; but the Expeditionary mission to Tirol was foremost on the minds of those who could have prevented the subsequent slide.

Monument was the seat of the United Earth Government, but the most important building in that burgeoning city was the headquarters of the newly-formed Army of the Southern Cross, a politico-military party that had its origins in the Southlands during the Malcontent Uprisings, and had all but superseded the authority formerly enjoyed by RDF, most of which was slated for the Expeditionary mission. The headquarters was a soaring megacomplex whose central tower cluster had been built to suggest the white gonfalons, or ensigns, of a holy crusade hanging from high crosspieces. The high-tech needles were crowned with crenels and merlons, like some medieval battlement, announcing to all the world the ideals and *esprit* of the Army of the Southern Cross.

Just now the building was host to a final press conference held jointly by members of the Expeditionary Mission Plenipotentiary Council, the RDF, and the Southern Cross. Dr. Emil Lang and the Zentraedi Ambassador, Exedore, spoke on behalf of the twelve-person council, while the military factions were represented respectively by Brigadier General Gunther Reinhardt and Field Marshal Anatole Leonard. The press was there in force, crowding the hall, jostling one another for position, snapping off shot after stroboscopic shot, and grilling the four-member panel with an overwhelming array of questions from special-interest groups and insulated power bases as distant as Cavern City and Brasilia in the Southlands.

Lang was doing his best to respond to one of these; for the third time, someone in the press corps had returned to the issue of Earth's potential vulnerability in the wake of the SDF-3's departure. As the high priest of Robotechnology, Lang had little interest in such mundane concerns, but he was doing his best to restate the importance of the mission and repeat launch details that had already been covered in the press releases.

"Final selections for the crew are proceeding and we should have no trouble meeting our launch schedule. If we are to avoid a second Robotech War, we must make peaceful contact with the Robotech Masters and establish a relationship of mutual cooperation. That is the mission of the SDF-3."

Murmurs of discontent spread through the crowd, and several reporters hurled insults of one sort or another. But then, could anyone expect anything in the way of a concrete response from someone like Lang? When the man chose to be profound, there were perhaps only a handful of scientists on Earth who could follow him. The rest of the time he came across as alien as any Zentraedi. Rumors and speculations about Lang went as far back as the early days on Macross Island, when he and Gloval, Fokker, Edwards, and a few others had first reconned the SDF-1, known then as "the Visitor." He had taken a Zentraedi mind-boost, some claimed, a megadose of Protoculture that had somehow integrated his internal circuitry with that of the ship itself. Certainly his marblelike eyes lent credence to the tale. Although he had been more visible, more accessible these past few years, he was still the same ethereal man who had been the driving force behind Robotechnology since the turn of the century.

"I want to take this opportunity to reemphasize that the Robotech Expeditionary Force is intended as a diplomatic mission," Exedore added without being asked. "The SDF-3 will be traveling to the homeworld of the Robotech Masters, the third moon of the planet Fantoma, known as Tirol." The Zentraedi motioned to the huge projection screen behind the speakers' platform, which showed a color schematic of the ringed giant's extensive system.

"The Masters themselves have not engaged in actual combat for nearly six generations. However, it is impossible to predict with certainty how they will react to our mission. For that reason the SDF-3 has been outfitted with a considerable arsenal of Robotech weaponry. In the event that we are met with force, we shall be ready and able to defend ourselves. But I must press the point that the departure of the fortress will not leave the Earth undefended. Commander Leonard and his staff have all the capabilities for defense necessary to repel any invasion force. And as the planet is not presently threatened by any enemy, we feel confident that the Earth is in no jeopard—"

"If I may interrupt for a moment," Leonard said angrily, getting to his feet. He had been biting back his words for half the press conference, but had reached his breaking point when Exedore—the *alien*!—began to imply that the

SDF-3 would be facing greater potential danger than abandoned Earth. Reporters throughout the hall—certainly those who had been planted there by the Southern Cross command to steer the conference toward this very confrontation—took advantage of the moment to get shots of the bearish, shaved-skulled field marshal confronting and towering over the XT ambassador. Leonard's hatred of the Zentraedi was no secret among the general staff. He had never met Exedore full-size, as it were, but perhaps detested him even more in his Micronized state, especially since Terran cosmologists had gone to work on him, styling his hair with a widow's peak, and concealing the clone's dwarfish anatomy beneath specially-tailored uniforms. Leonard often wished that Exedore had been among the Zentraedi Malcontents he had hunted down in the Southlands. . . .

"I'm not as optimistic as the *ambassador* about the lack of an enemy threat," Leonard continued, his face red with rage. "Mark my words, the departure of the SDF-3 and its weapons systems will leave the Earth hopelessly vulnerable to attack! Even that factory satellite's going to be nothing but a useless shell when the Expeditionary Force leaves. They've stripped it clean—and you've stripped us clean!"

"Gentlemen, please," Lang tried to interject, stretching his arms out between the two of them. Reinhardt, with his bald pate, beard, and fringe of premature gray hair, leaned back in his chair, overshadowed by Leonard's bulk.

"It's all very easy for him to say we'll be safe," the field marshal ranted. "When the attack comes, *he'll* be on the other side of the galaxy!"

"Frankly, I think you're a bit paranoid, Commander," Exedore announced evenly, almost clinically. "What attack do you mean—by whom, from where?"

Leonard's great jowls quivered; his eyes flashed a

hatred even Exedore couldn't help but feel. "For all we know, there could be a fleet of your fellow Zentraedi out there just waiting for us to drop our guard!"

"That will be enough, Commander Leonard," Reinhardt said at last. "Alarmist talk is of no use to anyone at this point."

Leonard swallowed the rebuke as flashes strobed without pause. He was aware that his position with the general staff was still somewhat tenuous; and besides, he had made his point.

"Gentlemen, you're cutting our defenses to almost nothing," he concluded, as shouts filled the hall. "Once the SDF leaves orbit I won't be able to defend the Earth against a flock of pigeons."

The press conference was being carried live around the world, and to Luna Base, Space Station Liberty, and the factory satellite. But where many were finding cause for concern in Leonard's contentions, there was one viewer aboard the satellite who merely laughed it off. He had a drink in hand, his feet crossed on the top of the monitor in his spacious quarters.

Leonard was overplaying the role, Major General T. R. Edwards told himself as he set the drink aside. But his performance would have the desired effect nonetheless.

Edwards knew even then that the Southern Cross would eventually gain the upper hand. If necessary, Professor Lazlo Zand would see to that. And Senator Moran, whom they had spent years grooming for high office, would ascend to the seat reserved for him.

Edwards fingered the ugly raised scars that coursed across the right side of his forehead and face—diagonally, from his hairline to the bridge of his nose, and from there in a reverse angle to the heel of his jawbone. The eye at the apex of this triangular disfiguration was dead, sewn shut to a dark slash. He would not be around to reap the immediate rewards of these complex conspiracies and manipulations, but all that could wait until his return from Tirol. First, there were scores to settle with older adversaries, scores that went back more than twenty years.

Not far from the Southern Cross headquarters in one of Monument City's more upscale shopping districts, Admiral Lisa Hayes was being fitted for her wedding gown. She had chosen one her late father would have approved of; it had a traditional, almost antebellum look, lots of satin, lace, and tulle, with a full, two-petticoat tiered skirt, long sleeves, and a simple round neck. The veil was rather short in contrast, with baby's breath and two silk roses affixed to the headband. Lisa gave an appreciative nod as the two fitters fell back smiling, allowing her center place in the shop's mirrored wall. She ran her fingers under the flip of her shoulder-length auburn hair—still unaccustomed to the cut—and said, "Perfect."

In the front room, Dr. Jean Grant and Captain Miriya Sterling wondered aloud what was taking Lisa so long, not out of concern but anticipation. The day was something of a shopping spree for Jean and Miriya as well; in less than a week they would be on their way to Tirol, and on this trip out the SDF wouldn't be traveling with a full city in its belly. *And who knows what to expect in the way of shops on Tirol*, Max had quipped when the two women left the factory satellite. They had brought the kids along, Dana and Bowie, both nearing eight years old, presently bored and antagonistic.

Bowie had Jean's petiteness and dark honey complexion; his health had never been robust, but that didn't prevent blond and lanky Dana from teasing him whenever she could. He was standing sullen-faced in the shop's doorway when she snuck up behind him to yank his SDF cap down over his face.

"Hey, cut it out!" Bowie yelled. "Why'd you do that, Dana?"

She returned a wide-eyed look of innocence, elaborate concern in her voice. "I didn't do anything. I think your brain must be getting smaller."

"Ahhh, *whose* brain's getting smaller?" Bowie said, working the visored cap up to where it belonged.

"Okay, I admit it, I'm guilty," Dana answered him, sincere all of a sudden. "I guess I can't pull the wool over *your* eyes."

Jean and Miriya had both turned at the sound of Bowie's initial howl, but they had long ago decided on a policy of nonintervention when it came to the kids. Though children were included in the Expeditionary mission, Bowie and Dana would not be among them. In Bowie's case it was a matter of health—a fact that had since steered Jean into research medicine. But Dana was exempt for reasons less clear-cut; as the only child of a Human-Zentraedi union, she had been studied, tested, and evaluated since birth, and was judged too precious a commodity to risk on such an enterprise. This, in any case, was the thinking of Professor Zand, who had headed up the medical teams, and Max and Miriya had reluctantly accepted the logic of it. The decision was unalterable now, no matter what, and it was guaranteed that Bowie and Dana would grow up as near siblings under the care of the Sterlings' close friends, Rolf and Laura Emerson.

Miriya was thinking these things through while she watched the children's bickering escalate, then dissolve into playful banter. "Look at them, Jean," she said the way only a mother can. "Do you think we're doing the right thing?"

Jean gave one of the clothes racks a casual spin. "Of course we are, sweetie. You know that."

The two women showed strained smiles to one another. How often they had talked about the irony of their friendship; how often they had remembered Jean's sister-in-law, Claudia Grant, who died in Khyron's suicide run against the SDF-1. And perhaps the conversation would have taken a turn in this direction even then, had not Lisa chosen just that moment to present herself as bride-to-be.

"Well, what do you think?" she asked them, turning around for their inspection.

Miriya, who had worn her hair emerald green for years, was too surprised by the gown's conservative cut to say much; but Jean said, "I think you picked a beauty, Admiral. That gown is shipshape from stem to stern."

"Yeah, but how will it travel in hyperspace?" Miriya thought to ask.

"You two . . ." Lisa laughed, while her friends began to finger the gown here and there. None of them were aware that a newcomer had entered the ship until a female voice said, "Excuse me."

Lisa looked up and uttered a surprised gasp. Lynn-Minmei was standing in the doorway. Lisa had been thinking of her not five minutes before, standing in front of the mirror seeing new age lines in her thirty-five-year-old face and comparing herself to the seemingly ageless star of song and screen.

"I—I hope I'm not interrupting, Lisa, but I heard you were in town, and well, I just wanted to congratulate you before the wedding. I mean, it's going to be such a madhouse up there." They had hardly been strangers these past six years, but hadn't seen each other since the wedding date had been officially announced some five months ago. "I'd love to help out any way I can—that is, if you'd allow me to, Lisa."

"Minmei," Lisa said with a note of disbelief. "This is so unexpected. But don't be silly, of course you can help," she added, laughing. "Come here."

They embraced, and held hands as they stepped back to regard one another. Lisa couldn't help but marvel at Minmei's youth and radiance. She really was the one constant in everyone's lives.

"Oh, Lisa, I want so much to let bygones be bygones. That dress is lovely—I always knew you'd make a beautiful bride."

"Ms. Minmei's right, Admiral," enthused the shop owner, who had appeared out of nowhere. It was obvious that the man was thrilled to have a celebrity of Minmei's stature in his boutique; he risked a glance at the street, hoping some passersby had noticed her enter.

"I still think she should get married in her EVA suit," Bowie said from across the room, only to have Dana pull the cap down on his forehead again.

"Children!" Jean scolded as the bickering recommenced.

Minmei asked to see the engagement ring, and Lisa held out her hand.

"I can't tell you what it means to see you again, Minmei," Lisa said softly.

"That devious little Zentraedi's got the whole Supreme Council eating out of his hand!" Commander Leonard complained to Rolf Emerson after the press conference.

Emerson, soon to inherit two eight-year-olds, was every bit the commander's opposite, in appearance as well as ideology; but the two of them had nevertheless managed to maintain a working relationship. Major Emerson, handsome, clean-cut, and fine-featured, was, strictly speaking, RDF; but he had become something of a liaison officer between the general staffs of the military factions. Well aware of Leonard's xenophobia—and of the infamous "thigh wound" the field marshal had sustained during the Malcontent Uprisings—Emerson was willing to let the racial slur slide, even though he numbered several Zentraedi among his closest and dearest friends.

"It's unbelievable," Leonard was railing, the huge brass buckle of his uniform dazzling even in the dim light of Emerson's headquarters office. "A diplomatic mission . . . If it's a *diplomatic* mission, then why are they arming that ship with every Robotech weapons system we've ever developed?"

"It's called 'gunboat diplomacy,' Commander," Emerson replied, willing to concede the point. Lord Exedore and Breetai claimed that they had no real knowledge of what the Robotech Masters might possess in the way of a war machine now that their race of warrior giants had all but been erased from the galaxy.

"Well, stupidity's what I call it. It jeopardizes the very survival of this planet." Leonard paced in front of Emerson's desk. "Something stinks here, Major, and it's not in the ventilation system."

CHAPTER
TWO

In the midst of all the ironies and reversals, the struggles, treachery, conquests, and betrayals, the mad scramble for mutated Flowers and irradiated worlds, it was easy to lose sight of the war's central concern—which was not, as many have claimed, the Flowers of Life, but their deified stepchild, Protoculture. Even the Regis seemed to forget for a time; but it could hardly be said that the Regent's Invid, the Masters, or the Expeditionary mission, had anything other than Protoculture as their goal and grail. Protoculture was needed to fuel their mecha, to drive their war machines to greater and greater heights. And it was all but disappeared from the galaxy. What a trick it played on all of us!

Selig Kahler, *The Tirolian Campaign*

AS IT WOULD HAPPEN, COMMANDER LEONARD'S fears were justified, but eleven years would pass before the spade fortresses of the Robotech Masters appeared in Earthspace. And perhaps history would have vindicated Leonard if the man's misdeeds had not stayed one step ahead of his contributions. Fate offered him one consolation, though: he would be dead two years before the Invid arrival. Earth would fall, just as he had predicted; just as Tirol fell after the Masters had begun *their* long journey through space and left their homeworld defenseless.

The Invid, however, were less confident in those days. Optera—their native planet—and Tirol had been at war for generations, and the Invid especially were at a disadvantage in terms of firepower. They had, after all, been deprived of the one thing that had cemented the social structure of their race—the Flower of Life; and more importantly, they were novices in this game called warfare. On the other hand, the Masters were adepts, addicted to Protoculture, obsessed with control, and driven to transform themselves—not through any measure of spiritual evolution, but through sheer conquest of the material realm. Profligate, they lived for excess; cloned a race of warrior giants to police their empire, then, still not content, cloned an entire society they could rule at whim. They took the best specimens with them when they abandoned Tirol; all that remained were the three Elders of their race, several hundred imperfect clones—lost without their clone-masters—and Tirol's preclone population of humanoids, who were of no use to the ascended Masters.

Tirol, the third of Fantoma's twelve moons, was not the Masters' original homeworld; but they had successfully transplanted themselves on that utterly barren planetoid from one of the outer satellites. Tiresia, the capital, a blend of Tirol's analogue of Greco-Roman architecture and ultra-tech design, was the only occupied city; and as such was aware of the Invid's coming ahead of time.

Aware . . . but hardly prepared.

Early-warning sirens and howlers had the humanoid population scurrying for shelters beneath the city well in advance of the midnight attack. The clones wandered the streets in a kind of daze, while the Elders who were responsible for their reaction made certain to hide themselves away in specially-designed chambers the Masters had seen fit to construct before their mass exodus. But there were two who remained at their work while the alert sounded through the city: the scientist Cabell, and his young assistant, Rem.

"Whoever they are," Cabell was saying, while his fingers rushed a series of commands into one of the lab's data networks, "they've put down near the outpost at Rylac."

"Is their identity any doubt, Cabell?" Rem asked from behind the old man's chair. Video monitors showed a dozen burnt-orange oysterlike troop carriers hovering over a jagged ridgeline of mountains west of the city. The network spit out a data card, which Cabell immediately transferred to an adjacent on-line device.

"I don't suppose there is, my boy," the scientist said without turning around. Several of the ships had put down now, and were disgorging mecha from their forward ramps.

"Will the city's defenses save us?"

Cabell left the question unanswered; instead, he turned his attention to activation switches for the remote cameras positioned at the outpost's perimeter, his long snow-white beard grazing the control studs while he reached across the console. He was every bit a wizard of a man, portly under his tasseled robes and laurel-collared capes, with a hairless knobbed skull and thick white eyebrows, mustache, and beard. He was indeed old enough to be the young man's father, although that wasn't precisely the case. Rem was tall and slender, with an ageless, almost elfin face and a thick shock of slate-blue hair. He wore a tight-fitting uniform with a long cape of royal blue.

"We're defenseless," Rem said a moment later, reacting to Cabell's silence. "Only the old and the sick remain on Tirol."

"Quiet!" the scientist told him. The central viewscreen showed the transports lifting off. Energy-flux schematics scrolled across half-a-dozen lesser screens. "Now what could they have in mind?"

Rem gestured to a secondary video monitor. "Frankly, Cabell, I'm more concerned about these monsters they've left behind." Waves of armored, felinelike creatures could be seen advancing up and out of the drop zone.

Cabell leaned back from the console to contemplate the images, right hand stroking his beard. "They resemble drones, not monsters." One of the creatures had stopped in its tracks and seemed to be staring at the camera. Cabell brought the lens to bear on the thing, focusing in on the four-legged creature's razor-sharp claws, fangs, and shoulder horns.

"It spotted the remote!" Rem said, as the cat's eyes began to glow. An instant later a metal-shod claw swiped at the camera; the image de-rezzed, and the screen crackled with static.

The Invid were a long way from home—if Optera could still be thought of in those terms. That their strikes against the Masters' empire were fueled by revenge was true enough; but the conquest of worlds like Karbarra, Praxis, and Spheris had had a more consequential purpose, for all these planets had been seeded by Zor with the Flowers of Life—the renegade scientist's final attempt at recompense for the horrors his discoveries had inadvertently unleashed. But the resultant Flowers had proved a sterile crop, mutated at best; and so the search was under way for the one key that could unlock the mysteries of Zor's science: the Protoculture matrix he himself had hidden aboard the Superdimensional Fortress.

The legendary device had never been uncovered by Lang's teams of Robotechnicians, and now that ship lay buried under tons of earth, rock, and Macross debris far from where the Invid were directing their quest. But at the time they had no way of knowing these things.

The Flowers had been their primary concern—their nutrient grail—but that purpose had undergone a slight perversion since Zor's death at the hands of Invid troopers. For not only had he transgressed by seducing the Flowers' secret from the Invid Regis; he had also spread a kind of contagion among that race—a pathology of emulation. And within a generation the Invid had refashioned themselves, and, with a form of self-generated Protoculture, created their own galactic war machine—a fleet of disc-shaped starships, a strike force of bipedal crablike mecha, and an army of mindless battle drones—the so-called Inorganics. But this was chiefly the work of the Invid Regent, not their Queen, and a schism had resulted—one that would ultimately affect Earth's fragile hold on its future.

The Invid fleet was anchored in space above Tirol when word spread through the ranks that the Regent himself had decided to take charge of the invasion. Companies of Inorganics had already been deployed on the moon's surface to counter ground-force resistance. Now, aboard the fleet flagship, one thousand Invid troops stood at attention in the docking bay, backed by more than two hundred Pincer assault mecha.

The unarmored individual Invid was primate in shape. Bilaterally symmetrical, they stood anywhere from six to eight feet tall, and walked upright on two powerfully-muscled legs. Equally massive were the forearms, shoulders, and three-fingered hands, with their opposable thumbs. The bulbous head and huge neck—often held parallel to the ground—approximated that of a snail, with an eye on either side, and two sensory antennae at the snout. The skin was green, almost reptilian, and there was at this stage no sexual differentiation. The Regent himself was by and large a grander, nearly twenty-foot-high version of the same design, save for his purple hue and the organic cowl that rested upon his back like some sort of manta ray. This hood, which could puff like a cobra's at times, was ridged front to back with tubercle-like sensors that resembled eyeballs.

The commander of flagship troops genuflected as the hatchway to the Regent's ship hissed up, spilling brilliant light against the soldier's crimson body armor. Helmet snout lowered to the floor, the trooper brought its right hand to its breast in salute.

"My lord, the Inorganics have met only token resistance on Tirol," the commander reported, its voice distorted by the helmet filters. "So far there is no sign of the Robotech Masters."

The Regent remained on the shuttle's rampway, his bulk and flowing blue robe filling the hatch.

"Cowering beneath their beds, no doubt," the Regent said in a voice so deep it seemed to emanate from the ship itself.

The commander raised its head some, with a whirring of mechanical adjusters. "Our beloved Regis has expressed some displeasure with your strategy, my lord." It offered up a cassettelike device in its left hand. "She wanted this to be given to you."

"A voice imprint?" the Regent said dubiously. "How thoughtful of my *wife*." He snatched the cassette in his hand. "I can hardly wait to hear it."

He activated the device as he moved from the docking bay into one of the flagship's corridors. The commander and a ten-trooper squad marched in formation behind him, their armored footfalls echoing in the massive space.

"Do you truly believe that you'll find what you seek on this wretched planet?" the synthesized female voice began. *"If so you are even a greater fool than I ever suspected. This idiotic invasion of yours is the most—"*

"I've heard about enough of that," the Regent said, deactivating the voice. "Tell me, where is our *beloved* Regis?" he asked the commander after a moment.

"She has returned to her fleet flagship, my lord." When the Regent had reached his quarters, the commander thought to ask, "Shall I tell her you wish to see her, my lord?"

"Negative," the Regent said sternly. "The farther she is, the better I like it. See to it that my pets are brought aboard, and let the invasion proceed without her."

The Invid squad snapped to as the door hissed closed.

The humanoid soldiers at the Rylac outpost were easily overrun. Given the few weapons at their disposal, they made a valiant stand, but the Inorganics proved too much for them. The forward assault wave was comprised solely of Invid feline mecha; but behind these Hellcats marched companies of Scrim and Crann and Odeon—Invid robot analogues, which in some ways resembled skeletal versions of their own Shock Troopers and Pincer Ships, a demonic, bipedal infantry.

A schematic representation of a Scrim came to life on one of Cabell's monitor screens, rotating and shifting through a series of perspectives, as intact remotes from the Rylac sector continued to bring the action home to the lab.

"There is only one species capable of producing such a device," Cabell commented flatly.

"The Invid," said Rem. "It was only a matter of time."

"The strategy is typical of them: they won't descend until their fighting drones have cleared away the resistance. And after they've devastated Tirol, they'll leave these things behind to police us." Hellcat schematics were taking shape on the monitors. "These machines are puzzling, though. It's almost as if . . ."

Rem looked back and forth between the screens and the old man's face, trying to discern Cabell's meaning. "It's hopeless, isn't it?"

"I'm not saying that, my boy," the scientist replied, leaning in to study the data flows. "This feline drone is like its two-legged counterparts: computer-driven and incapable of independent action. Its functions, therefore, must be controlled by an external centralized power source of some kind." He swiveled around in his chair to gaze at his assistant. "That is its weakness, the one flaw in the system, and we must take advantage of it."

"Cabell—"

"Is it not easier to attack one target than a thousand? If we can locate that power source and disable it, then all these dreaded machines will be deactivated."

Alert lamps flashed in another part of the room and Cabell swung around to them. "The Inorganics are closing on the city. Now we'll see how they fare against real firepower."

"The Bioroids!" Rem said excitedly.

"They're our only hope."

Rick and Max had shuttled down to the surface simply to ride back up with Lisa, Miriya, Lang, and other members of the mission command team. Both men were aware that the short trip constituted their last visit to Earth for an indeterminate period of time, but neither of them made much of this. Max was still nursing some concerns about leaving Dana behind, but was otherwise fully committed to the mission. Rick, on the other hand, was so preoccupied with the wedding that he had begun to think of the mission as a simpler and more certain voyage. So it was during the return trip that he was paying almost no attention to the discussion taking place in the command shuttle conference chambers.

"I only hope this plan works," Jonathan Wolff was saying. "Coming in disguised as a Zentraedi ship . . . It could backfire on us."

"Oh, you're forgetting your own Earth history, Colonel," the Zentraedi ambassador told him. "The Greeks and their Trojan horse."

"I think you're confusing history and mythology, Lord Exedore. Wouldn't you agree, Admiral? Admiral?" Wolff repeated.

Rick surfaced from his own thoughts to find everyone at the table staring at him. "Huh? Sorry, I was, um, thinking about something else."

Wolff recapped the exchange: justification for the disguise had been something of an issue from the start. Exedore and Lang were of the opinion that Tirol's defenses would annihilate any ship that registered an alien signature. According to the Zentraedis, the Robotech Masters had been at war for generations with a race called the Invid, and any unannounced entry into the Valivarre system would be tantamount to an act of aggression. Wolff, however, along with several other members of the general staff, advanced the view that the Zentraedi themselves might no longer be considered welcome guests. After all, they had not only failed in their mission to reclaim the SDF-1, but had allied themselves with the very "Micronians" their armada had been ordered to destroy.

Wolff was a persuasive speaker, and while Rick listened he couldn't help but be impressed by the scope of the man's learning. Handsome, articulate, an inspired commander and deadly hand-to-hand combatant, the full bird colonel was considered something of a glamour boy; he favored wraparound sunglasses, wore his dark hair slicked back, and his mustache well-trimmed. But the leader of the notorious "Wolff Pack"was anything but glamorous in the field. Wolff had made a name for himself and his Hover-tank ground unit during the Southland's Malcontent Upris-ings, where he had first come to the attention of Max Sterling. When the Zentraedis who survived those days spoke of Wolff, one couldn't help but hear the mixture of reverence and dread in their voices; and anyone who had read the declassified documents covering the Control Zone mop-up ops had no trouble understanding why Wolff and Breetai were often mentioned in the same breath.

"I'm just saying that disguising the ship and loading it down with mecha only serves to undermine the so-called diplomatic thrust of the mission." Wolff snorted. "No wonder Leonard and the Southern Cross brass tried to make mincemeat out of you down there."

"What do they expect us to do?" Max wanted to know. "Go in there flying a white flag? At least we've got some bargaining power this way."

"Let's just hope we won't need to use any of it," Rick said at last, straining against his seat harness. "Without the Zentraedi, the Masters could be defenseless for all we know."

Exedore shook his head. "Oh, I wouldn't count on that, Admiral." Breetai had already briefed everyone on the mecha the Masters had been developing before Zor's death —Hoverships and Bioroids.

"Gentlemen, the time is long past for arguments about strategy," Lang cut in before Rick could speak. "We've all supported this plan, and it seems rather late in the day to be changing our mind."

"I agree," Max said.

"Look, *I* agree," Wolff wanted the table to know. "I'd just like us to agree on an approach. Are we going in with fists raised or hands up? The Masters aren't going to be fooled by our outward appearance—not for long, at any rate."

"Possibly not," Exedore answered him. "But if we allow *possibilities* to influence us, we'll never leave orbit."

"I've got as many doubts as anybody," Rick said from the head of the table. "But the time's come to put them behind us. We've made our bed, as the saying goes . . ."

Brave Talk, Hunter, he thought, listening to his own words. *And I'll keep telling myself that when I'm walking down the aisle*.

Two RDF officers were watching the approach of the command shuttle from a rectangular bay in one of the factory satellite's peripheral pods. One was a slim and eager-eyed young major who had recently been appointed adjutant to General T. R. Edwards; and the other was the general himself, his disfiguration concealed beneath an irregularly-shaped black-alloy plate that covered most of the right side of his face and more than half his skull. On the uncovered left side of his head, long blond hair fell in waves to the collar of his tight-fitting uniform. He was high-cheekboned and square-jawed, and might have been considered handsome even with the plate, were it not for the cruelty in his eye and downward-turning mouth.

"So tell me, Benson," Edwards said, while his one eye continued to track the shuttle's course, "what do you know about the illustrious vice admiral?"

"I know that Hunter's one of our most decorated heroes, sir," Benson reported to the general's broad back. "Leader of the Skull during the Robotech War, commander of the RDF after the destruction of the superdimensional fortresses, about to marry the admiral . . . That's about it, sir."

Edwards clasped his hands behind his back. "That's

right. The high command likes to award medals to people who end up in the right place at the right time."

"Sir?" Benson asked.

"Anything in your academy history books about Roy Fokker?" Edwards said nastily over his shoulder. "Now there was a real VT ace for you. I remember turning those blue skies red trying to nail his ass . . . But you're too young to remember the Global War, aren't you, Benson? The real heroes." Edwards leaned forward and pressed his fingertips against the bay's permaplas viewport. "Fokker taught Hunter everything he knew, did you know that? You might even say that Hunter is what Fokker would've been, Major—that Hunter *is* Fokker."

Benson swallowed hard, unsure how to respond, uncertain if he even should.

Edwards touched his skullplate, remembering, forcing himself back over tormented terrain—to what was left of Alaska Base after Zentraedi annihilation bolts had destroyed the Grand Cannon and made a hell of that icebound site. And how one man and one woman had survived. The woman was unharmed, protected where she cowered while her father had fried alive; but the man, *how he had suffered*! What agony he had endured, down on his knees shamelessly trying to push the ruins of an eye back where it belonged, fingers pinched in an effort to knit together flesh that had been opened on his face and forehead. Then the rapture he had known when a solitary Veritech had appeared out of those unnatural clouds. But it was the *woman* that VT pilot had come for, and no other. It was the *woman* who had been flown to safety, the *woman* who had risen through the ranks, while the man had been left behind to die, to rot in that alien-made inferno . . .

"Ah, what a wedding this will be, Benson," Edwards continued after a moment of angry silence. "Admirals Rick

Hunter and Lisa Hayes. Star-crossed lovers, if ever there were. Born and reborn for each other."

"Till death do them part," Benson returned with a uncomfortable laugh.

Edwards spun on his heels, face contorted, then erupting in laughter. "Yes, Major, *how right you are!*"

Most of the Zentraedi had been off scouring the galaxy for Zor's ship and its hidden Protoculture matrix when the Robotech Masters first perfected the Bioroids. Sixty-foot-tall nontransformable goliath knights piloted by low-level clones, they were meant to act as the Masters' police force on the remote worlds that comprised Tirol's empire, freeing the Zentraedi for further acts of conquest and continued warfare against the Invid. The Masters had never considered that Protoculture would one day be in limited supply, nor that their army of giant warriors would be defeated in a distant corner of the Fourth Quadrant by so simple a weapon as love. So it fell on the Bioroids by chance and Protoculture's own dark designs, to defend the Masters' empire against Optera's ravenous horde. But try as they might, they were no match for the Invid Shock Troopers and Pincer Ships, with their plasma weapons and energy discs. And as Protoculture grew more and more scarce, they could barely defend against the mindless Inorganics.

"It is sheer numbers," Cabell explained to Rem as they watched Tiresia's first line of defense fall. The clonemasters left behind to rule the Bioroid pilots were an inferior lot, so the fight was not all it should have been. *The Masters have thrown them our world*, Cabell left unsaid. Those massive spade fortresses with their clone populations were the Masters' new homes; they had no plans to return to Tirol.

Command-detonated mines took out wave after wave of

Hellcats, but this did little more than delay the inevitable. The Bioroids dug in, finding cover behind hastily-erected barricades, and fired until their cannons and assault rifles went red-hot and depleted. And when the Inorganics began to overrun their lines, they went hand-to-claw with the marauders, employing last-stand tactics worthy of history's finest. Cabell could feel no sympathy for them as such; but staring at the lab's central viewscreen he was overcome by a greater sense of pathos and loss. External mikes picked up the clones' anguished cries, their desperate utterances to one another in that raspy, almost synthesized voice the Masters so loved.

"There's too many of them!" the pilot of a blue Bioroid told his teammates along the front, before two Hellcats leaped and crashed through the mecha's visorlike face-shield. A second blue blasted the intruders with the last of his weapon's charge, only to fall an instant later, Inorganics ripping at the machine's armor in a mad effort to get to the pilot within.

Disgusted, Cabell stood up and reached across the console to shut down the audio transmissions. "The Flower of Life, that's what they've come for," he told his apprentice in a tired voice.

"But that plant hasn't been present in this sector for generations," Rem said, slipping into the padded con chair.

"Then they'll want the matrix. Or failing that, vengeance for what the Masters ordered done to their world."

Rem turned his attention to the screen. Scrim devils and Hellcats were tearing through the Bioroid base, eyes aglow like hot coals, fangs slick with the clone pilots' blood. "They'll rip the planet apart looking for something they'll never find."

"No one ever accused the Invid of being logical, my boy, only thorough."

"Then the city will fall next. Those drones are unstoppable."

"Nonsense," Cabell exclaimed, anger in his voice. "They may be intimidating, but they're not unstoppable."

Rem shot to his feet. "Then let's find their weak spot, Cabell." He drew a handgun from beneath his cape and armed it. "And for that, we're going to require a specimen."

CHAPTER
THREE

*Try as he might to offset the suffering his discoveries had un-
leashed, Zor's mistakes kept piling up, compounding themselves.
He'd sent his ship to Earth only to have the Zentraedi follow it
there; he'd hidden the matrix so well that the Masters had ample
time to wage their war; his seeded worlds had drawn the Invid
. . . What remained but the final injustice?—that by trying to replicate his very form and drives, the Regent and Regis should
become prisoners of appetites they had never before experienced.
Is it any mystery why even the Masters banished his image
throughout their empire?*

Bloom Nesterfig, *The Social Organization of the Invid*

BRIGADIER GENERAL REINHARDT, HAVING SHUTTLED
up to the factory earlier that day, was on hand to meet the
mission command team. He informed Lang, Lord Exedore,
Lisa, and Rick that things were still running on schedule;
the last shiploads of supplies and stores were on their way
up from Earth even now, and most of the 10,000 who
would make up the crew were already aboard the satellite,
many aboard the SDF-3 itself. Max and Miriya joined the
others by an enormous hexagonal viewport that overlooked
the null-gee central construction hold. They were joined
after a moment by Colonel Wolff and Jean Grant, who had
Bowie and Dana by the hand.

The view from here was fore to aft along the underside

of the fortress. Lisa often wished that the bow wasn't quite so, well, *phallic*—the euphemism she employed in mixed company. But the twin booms of the main gun were just that: like two horned, tumescent appendages that took up nearly a third of the crimson ship's length. If the weapon had none of the awesome firepower of the SDF-1's main gun, at least it had the *look* of power to it. Autowelders and supply shuttles were moving through the hold's captured sunlight, and a crew of full-size Zentraedi were at work on one of the sky-blue sensor blisters along the fortress's port side.

"How many kilometers out will we have to be before we can fold?" Wolff wanted to know. Everyone remembered all too plainly what had happened when the SDF-1 attempted to fold while still in the vicinity of Macross Island.

"Lunar orbit will suffice," Exedore told him. "Doctor Lang and Breetai concur on this."

"Speak of the devil," Lisa said, looking around the hold, "I thought he was supposed to meet us here."

Miriya laughed shortly. "He probably forgot."

"He's been pretty busy," Rick offered.

"Well, we can't wait," Reinhardt said, running a hand over his smooth pate. "We've got a lot of last-minute details to attend to and—"

Everyone reacted to Dana's gasp at the same moment, turning first to the child's startled face, then to the hatchway she had her eyes fixed on.

There was a giant standing here.

Half the gathered group knew him as a sixty-footer, of course, but even micronized Breetai was an impressive sight: almost eight feet of power dressed in a uniform more befitting a comic book hero than a Zentraedi commander, and wearing a masklike helmet that left only his mouth and lantern jaw exposed.

Before anyone could speak, he had moved in and one-hand heaved Lisa and Miriya atop each of his shoulders. His voice boomed. "So I'm not important enough to wait for, huh? You Micronians are an impatient lot."

He let the women protest a moment before setting them back down on the floor.

"I never thought I'd see you like this again," Lisa said, tugging her uniform back into shape. The only other time Breetai had permitted himself to undergo the reduction process was during the search of the SDF-1 for the Protoculture matrix.

"It takes a man to give away a bride," Breetai said in all seriousness, "not a giant."

Dawn marked Tiresia's doom. The troop carriers returned, yawning catastrophe; but this time it wasn't Inorganics they set loose, but the crablike Shock Troopers and Pincer Ships. They attacked without mercy, skimming discs of white annihilation into the streets, dwellings, and abandoned temples. The humanoid populace huddled together in shelters, while those masterless clones who had become the city's walking dead surrendered and burned. Left to fend for themselves, the old and infirm tried to hide from the invaders, but it was hardly a day to play games with the Reaper: his minions were everywhere, and within hours the city was laid to waste.

Cannon muzzles and missile racks sprang from hidden emplacements, spewing return fire into the void, and once again the Bioroids faced the storm and met their end in heroic bursts of orange flame and blinding light. From the depths of the pyramidal Royal Hall rode an elite unit on saucer-shaped Hovercraft outfitted with powerful disc guns and particle-beam weapons systems. They joined the Invid in an airborne dance of devastation, coupling obscenely in the city skies, exchanging thundering volleys of quantum death.

Morning was filled with the corkscrewing trails of angry projectiles and crisscrossed with hyphens and pulses of colored light. Spherical explosions strobed overhead, rivaling the brightness of Fantoma's own primary, low in the east behind clouds of debris. Mecha fell like a storm of blazing hail, cutting fiery swaths across the cityscape.

Here a Pincer Ship put down to give chase to an old man its discs had thrown clear from a Hoverchair. Frustrated, the Invid trained its weapons on Tiresia's architectural wonders and commenced a deadly pirouette. Statues and ornaments slagged in the heat, and five of the antigrav columns that marked the Royal Hall's sacred perimeter were toppled.

Ultimately the Invid's blue command ships moved in, forming an unbreachable line as they marched through the city, their top-mounted cannons ablaze. Inside the shelters the citizens of Tiresia cowered and clung to one another as the footfalls of the giants' war strides shook Tirol's ravaged surface, echoing in the superheated subterranean confinement.

Cabell and Rem had chosen a deserted, now devastated sector for their Hellcat hunt. With most of Tiresia's defenses in ruin, the fierce fighting that typified the early hours of the invasion had subsided to distant hollow blasts from the few remaining contested areas. A patrol of bipedal Inorganics moved past the alley where the scientist and his assistant waited. Rem raised the muzzle of the assault rifle he had slung over one shoulder, but Cabell waved him back.

"But it doesn't sense our presence," Rem insisted, peering over Cabell's shoulder. "Now's our chance."

"No," Cabell said firmly. "I want one of the feline droids."

They began to move into the street after the Inorganic had passed. Cabell kept them to the shadows at first, then grew more brazen. Rem understood that the old man was trying to lure one of the creatures out but he had some misgivings about Cabell's method.

"I hope we snare one of them and not the other way around," he said wearily, swinging the rifle in a gentle arc.

Cabell stopped short in the center of the street as a kind of mechanical growl reached them from somewhere nearby. "I have the distinct impression our progress is being observed."

"I was about to say the same thing."

"Perhaps our behavior is puzzling to them," Cabell mused, back in motion now. "They probably expect us to run in terror."

"And I forget, why *aren't* we?" Rem started to say when another growl sounded. "Guess they're not puzzled anymore . . . Show yourself, fiend," he growled back, arming the rifle.

"There!" Cabell said all at once.

The Hellcat was glaring down at them from a low roof not twenty yards up the street, midday light caught in the beast's shoulder horns, fangs, and razor-sharp tail. Then it pounced.

"On stun!" Cabell cried, and Rem fired.

The short burst glanced off the cat's torso, confusing it momentarily, but not long enough to make a difference. It leaped straight for the two men before Rem could loose a second shot, but he did manage to shove Cabell clear of the Inorganic's path. The cat turned sharply as it landed; Rem hit it twice more to no avail.

"Get away from it, boy!" Rem heard Cabell shout. He

looked around, amazed that the old man had covered so much ground in so little time—although the Inorganic was certainly incentive enough: it was hot on Cabell's trail.

Rem chased the two of them, firing wildly, and rounded a corner in time to see his mentor barrel-ass down a rubble slide and throw himself into the cockpit of an overturned Bioroid transport ship. Fixed on its prey, the Hellcat seemed unaware of Rem, and was busy trying to claw through the ship's bubble shield. Rem reached down to up the rifle's charge, only to find the thing depleted. He was busy cursing himself when he spied a fallen Invid command ship nearby, one of its cannontips still aglow with priming charge.

Cautiously, he approached the ship, the useless weapon raised. The command plastron was partially ajar, a four-fingered hand lodged in the opening. Rem clambered up and over one of the mecha's arms and gave the hatch a violent tug, forcing the rifle down into the invader's face as he did so. But the Invid was already dead, its bulbous head and stalklike neck split wide open. Rem ignored the stench and took a quick look at the cockpit's bewildering gadgetry. The alien's right hand was hooked around what Rem decided was the trigger mechanism, and from the looks of things the Hellcat was almost perfectly centered in the cannon's reticle. Rem grunted a kind of desperate curse, slid down into the cockpit—his legs going knee-deep into a viscous green bath of nutrient fluid—and hit the trigger.

A pulsed beam of crimson light threw the Hellcat clear from the transport and left it on its side thirty feet from the transport, stunned and enveloped by a kind of St. Elmo's fire. Cabell threw open the canopy and glanced back at the crippled command ship with a bewildered expression.

"Why did you save me?" the old man yelled in Zentraedi, *lingua franca* of the Masters' empire.

Rem heard the call and was tempted to stay put for a moment, but thought better of it. He showed himself and said, "Hello, Cabell. All safe and sound? You didn't really think I'd abandon you, did you?"

The scientist scowled. "You could have killed me, you young—" He bit off his own words and laughed, resignedly. "My boy, you amaze me."

Rem jumped to the ground and approached the transport. "Frankly, I amaze myself." He looked away from the alien ship he had fired, and gestured to the Hellcat. "Now all we've got to do is figure out how to get this thing back to the lab."

"My lord, we've found no trace of the Flower of Life anywhere," the voice of an Invid lieutenant reported to the Regent.

"But that's impossible, you *idiot*!" the Regent shouted at his monitor. "This is their homeworld. They must be here! Scan the entire planet."

The flagship throne room, like the Invid castle and hives on Optera, was an organic chamber, so given over to the urgings of Protoculture that its very bulkheads and sensor devices resembled living systems of neural-tissue circuitry. Visceral greens and purples, they pulsed to rhythms dictated deep within the ship's animate drives. So, too, the contoured control couch itself, with its graceful curves, the slender arcing neck of its overhead sensor lamp, its proboscislike forward communicator tube. The Regent did not so much sit as reshape his being to the seat's demands.

On either side of him sat a Hellcat larger and more polished than any of the standard versions, with collars encrusted with gems handpicked from the spoils of a score of conquered worlds. Elsewhere, in cages, were living samples from those same worlds: sentient prisoners from Karbarra, Spheris, and the rest.

"We have searched, my lord," the trooper continued. "The Sensor Nebula registers no presence of the Flowers. None whatsoever."

"Fools!" muttered the Regent, canceling the transmission. He could hear his wife's laughter behind him.

"Congratulations, husband," the Regis mocked him from across the room. "Once again you have impressed us all with your supreme stupidity."

"I don't like your tone," the Regent said, turning to her.

One might have almost mistaken her for a humanoid life-form; certainly she was more that than the ursoid and vulpine beings that populated the Regent's personal zoo. But at the same time there was something ethereal and insubstantial about her, an inhumanness that lurked in the depths of her cobalt eyes. Twenty feet tall and slender, she clothed her completely hairless form in a red full-length robe and curious, five-fingered tasseled gloves. Four emerald-green sensor scarabs that might have been facelike adornments decorated the robe's bracelike collar and neck closure.

"I told you the Robotech Masters were too clever to hide the matrix in their own back yard."

"Silence, *woman!*" the Regent demanded, rising from the throne.

But the Regis stood her ground. "If you hadn't been so desperate to prove yourself a great warrior, we might have sent spies to learn where they've taken it."

The Regent looked at his wife in disbelief. "Are you forgetting who got us into this predicament in the first place? *I'm* not the one who fell under the spell of Zor and allowed him to steal our Flower of Life."

"Must you keep *harping* on that!" the Regis screamed,

shutting her eyes and waving her fists in the air. "It happened a long time ago. And since then *I* have evolved, while you've remained the spoiled child you always were. You took his life; now you won't rest content until you've conquered his empire." She gestured offhandedly to the Regent's "pets" and caged life-forms. "You and your dreams of empire . . . Mark my words, husband, some day these beings will rise up to strike you down."

The Regent laughed. "Yes, you've *evolved*—into a pathetic imitation of the females of Zor's race."

"Perhaps so," she countered, arms akimbo. "But that's preferable to imitating the Masters' toys and bloodlust." She turned on her heel and headed for the door. "I'm returning to Optera."

"Stop! I forbid you to go!" the Regent told her, furious.

"Don't provoke me," she shouted from the doorway, "you spineless anachronism!"

"Wait!" the Regent demanded, cursing her. He whirled around as the door hissed closed, Tirol huge in the room's starboard viewports. "I'll show you," he muttered under his breath. "Tirol will feel my potency . . . and I'll win back your love."

"Toys," Dr. Harry Penn told Lang, an undisguised note of disapproval in his voice. "War toys, when we could be fashioning wonders." He was a large man with a gruff-looking exterior that masked the gentlest of spirits. The thick mustache and beard he had grown to mask the pock-marked, hooked-nose cragginess of his face had only ended up adding to the effect he had hoped to minimize. It was a scholarly, academic image he was after, and as the oldest member of the Plenipotentiary Council and one of Lang's top men he felt he deserved no less.

"There'll be time for that when this mission returns,"

Lang said evenly. "Until then we have to be sure of our strengths."

Penn made a disgruntled sound. "A peaceful mission, a diplomatic mission . . . Am I the only one who remembers the meaning of those words?"

The two men were standing by one of the factory's observation bays; in the blackness of space beyond, two Veritechs were being put through the paces.

These were not the first generation VTs the Skull and other teams had flown against the Zentraedi, but Alpha fighters, the latest prototypes from Lang's research department laboratories. The SDF-3's arsenal wasn't limited to these reconfigurable one-pilot craft—the last six years had seen the development of Hovertanks, Logans, and an array of new and improved Destroids—but the Veritech remained something of Robotechnology's favored child, weapon *extraordinaire* and near-symbol of the war. The Alpha VT had more armor than its older sibling; it packed almost twice the firepower and was equipped with ablative shields and detachable augmentation pods for deepspace flight. Moreover, it had the capability to link up with the so-called Beta VT—a bulkier, thin-winged variant that appeared to lack an appropriate radome—and thereby more than double its range and occupancy capabilities.

Lang indicated the blue fighter as it twisted through space, reconfiguring to Guardian, then Battloid mode. "I just wanted you to see for yourself the progress we've made, Harry."

"Sterling, here," said a voice over the ob deck's speakers. "The Alpha handled the last sequence beautifully. No sign of stress."

"Fine, Max," said Lang, directing his words to a microphone. "The prototype looks good so far. Now comes the real test," he added for Penn's benefit. "Max, Karen, move yourselves into position for trans-docking maneuver."

Max rogered the transmission; Karen Penn, Harry's only daughter, said, "We're on our way."

Lang risked a quarter turn and found Penn regarding him with a mixture of surprise and rage. "You're awfully quiet, Harry, is something wrong?"

"Have you gone mad, Lang! You know I didn't want Karen participating in this test."

"What was I supposed to do, Harry, refuse her permission? Don't forget, she volunteered, and she's one of our most able young pilots."

"But I don't want her to get mixed up in this, Emil. Can't you understand that? *Science* is her future, not warfare."

"Control," Max's voice squawked over the speakers, "we are in position at T-niner-delta. Standing by to reconfigure and align for docking sequence."

The maneuver called for each of the Veritechs to jettison and exchange their unmanned Beta modules, blue to red, red to blue. Max carried out his part without a hitch, imaging over to fighter mode and engaging the VT's retros for a solid linkup with its sister module. But Karen slipped up. Max couldn't tell at first whether she had been too heavy-minded, or had simply misread the VT's telemetry displays. In either case she was in trouble, the blue Beta off on a ride to eternity, and Karen in what looked like a planet-bound freefall.

Max tried to reach her on the net, through a cacophony of questions and exclamations from command—most of them from Dr. Penn himself. Karen wasn't responding, but there wasn't real cause for concern—yet. Assuming she wasn't unconscious or worse—something unseen, an embolism, perhaps—Karen had ample time to get herself into the Veritech's EVA suit; and failing that, the factory could bring its tractor beam to bear. But Max wanted to see Karen pull out of this one without an assist; she was bright and full of potential, and he wanted her for the Skull.

"Stabilizers are gone," Karen said suddenly. ". . . Power surge must have fried the circuitry."

Then Dr. Penn's panicked voice bellowed in Max's ears. "Sterling, do something! You've got to help her!"

"Karen," Max said calmly. "Go to Guardian and bring your thrusters into play. I'm right behind you if they fail."

"Roger, Skull leader," Karen returned.

On the factory ob deck, Penn muscled his way through a crowd of techs to get close to the monitor screen. He sucked in his breath seeing his daughter's red Alpha in a slow-motion end-over-end fall; but the next instant found the VT reconfigured, its bird-of-prey foot thrusters burning bright in the night. And in another moment she was out of danger and there were hoots and hollers ringing in his ears, tears of release in his eyes.

Lang and Penn were waiting in the docking bay when the VTs came in. Max missed the days of flattop touchdowns, the cat officers and their impromptu launch dances; but the *Daedalus* and *Prometheus* supercarriers were part of the SDF-1 burial mound now, and unnecessary in any case.

"Karen, thank God you're all right!" Max heard Dr. Penn call out as the blue's canopy slid open. "That little escapade nearly gave me a heart attack."

Guilt's his game, Max thought as he climbed out of Skull One.

"Well, if you were scared, imagine how I felt," Karen was telling her father. "I'm still shaking."

Penn waved a forefinger at her. "This proves once and for all you've no business being a test pilot."

"Don't overdo it, Dad." Karen removed her thinking

cap, spilling honey-blond hair to her shoulders. She had small delicate features, eyes the color of pre-Columbian jade. "I'm a professional. This stuff comes with the territory."

"I'll say she is," Max chimed in before Penn could get in another word. "That linkup wasn't her fault. Dollars to donuts you'll find some glitch in the guidance computers."

Penn glared at him. "I'm sure you mean well, Commander, but all this is—"

"Meaning well has nothing to do with it. I just don't want to see Ensign Penn's talents go to waste. She impressed me, Dr. Penn—and I'm not easily impressed."

Penn blanched some; he wasn't about to debate Sterling's words. But Karen was still his daughter. "Well, I'm not impressed," he told Karen after Max had walked off. "I have others plans for you."

She flashed him a look he remembered from way back and started to move off, but Dr. Lang put out his hand to stop her.

"Karen, a moment please."

"You gonna chew me out now?"

"Calm down," said Lang. "I'm going to recommend you for assignment to a Veritech team."

"Just a minute, Emil," Penn said, one hand clasped around Karen's upper arm. "Don't you think you're overstepping your authority?" He had already lost his wife, and Karen's joining the RDF had threatened to destroy what had once been a close relationship. Now Lang seemed bent on trying to scuttle what small joy he had left.

Lang pried his friend's fingers open and motioned Karen along. "I'm sorry, Harry, but she's old enough to make up her own mind. You can't hold on to her forever.

Besides, if this mission *should* encounter resistance, we're going to need experienced pilots."

"Resistance," Penn snorted, and began to storm off. But half-a-dozen steps away he swung around. "All the more reason to hold on to her for as long as I can."

CHAPTER
FOUR

Evidence points to the existence of a plethora of mystery cults in the years immediately preceding Tirol's so-called Great Transition (i.e., that period in which most of the moon's humanoid population were put to death and the Robotech Masters began their extensive cloning experiments). In fact, some of these cults survived well into the First Period . . . The labyrinth, apparently, was constructed for ritual use, and the Pyramidal Royal Hall added later as that subterranean cult gave way to one of stellar orientation. Several commentators have felt compelled to bring Minoans, Egyptians, and the Maya into the discussions but aside from certain structural similarities, there was little in common between Tirol and Earth's religions.

History of the Second Robotech War
Volume CCXVI, "Tirol"

WITH THE WEDDING ONLY A DAY OFF NOW, RICK SAT in his soon-to-be-vacated quarters aboard the factory satellite contemplating the future. Earth hung in the blackness of the viewport behind the desk. Around him were stacked boxes of personal items he had accumulated over the course of the last four years: photographs, citations—memorabilia dating back to his late father's air circus, the SDF-1 and New Macross before the storm. He came across a snapshot taken by a robocam unit of Minmei standing by the Macross park's fountain; poking out from the top of a shopping bag were two posters of the singing star from those early days: one an RDF enlistment ad, and the second a Miss Macross pinup. On the recent side, Lisa was equally well represented. But the more Rick pored through these things the more depressed he became. He had no doubts about his love for Lisa, but what would it mean to abandon all this space and free time he had grown accustomed to? Not that there had been much of either, given mission priorities and such, but the *idea* of personal time, the options. Rick's hand was actually trembling while he packed. He had begun to wonder whether a drink might help, and was reaching for the bottle he kept around for special occasions, when Vince Grant announced himself at the door and stepped in.

At just a shade under seven feet, Grant was the only man aboard who could come close to filling Breetai's shoes. He had brown skin and close-cropped tight curls, and a long face lent a certain nobility by his broad forehead and chiseled features. His dark eyes were bright and full of expression, and he was a man known to speak his mind, consequence be damned. Technically, he was Rick's adjutant, a commander, but he was also attached to rapid deployment's new all-terrain mobile base, the Ground Military Unit, or GMU. Grant had headed up a crackerjack Excaliber unit in New Macross, but Rick hadn't really gotten to know him until after the death of his sister, Claudia.

"Just wanted to see if you needed help with anything, sir," Vince said, offering a casual salute.

Rick turned a sullen face to the assortment of bags and boxes piled about. "Not unless you're good at juggling."

"What, these?" Vince said uncertainly.

"No, Vince, the past and future."

"Sir?"

Rick waved dismissively. "Forget it. What's on your mind, Vince?"

Vince took a breath. "Edwards, sir."

"General Edwards?" Suspicion rose in Rick's eyes. "What about him?"

"Would the general have any reason for acting against our best interests, sir? I mean, is there something I'm not privy to that might explain certain . . . *proclivities*?"

"'Proclivities'?" said Rick. "Say what's on your mind."

In a rush, Vince said, "It just seems to me that the man has some designs of his own. I'm not saying that it's anything I can put my finger on, but for starters there's his friendship with Leonard and that character Zand. You've been busy, sir, and preoccupied. You're insulated from the scuttlebutt—"

"If you have allegations," Rick broke in, "you'd better be prepared to back them up with some hard facts. Now, do you have any—yes or no?"

Tight-lipped all at once, Vince shook his head. "Only hearsay, sir."

Rick mulled it over after he dismissed Vince. The idea of going halfway across the galaxy with a divided crew was hardly a comforting thought. And in fact there was an underlying feeling of disunity that continued to plague the mission. Lang and Exedore on one side, Edwards and the political machine on the other, with the Southern Cross somewhere in between . . . Rick tried to put together what he knew of Edwards. Roy Fokker had often spoken of Edwards's self-serving allegiances during the Global Civil War, his later alignment with Admiral Hayes, Lisa's father, and the Grand Cannon project; but then, that was years ago, and a lot of good men had been lured over to the UEDC's side. In the decade since, Edwards had become a force to be reckoned with in Monument City, and a respected officer in the RDF. Presently, as leader of the infamous Ghost Squadron, he had what amounted to an unassailable power base.

It was with all this on his mind that Rick went in search of Max and some objective input.

But it was Lisa he found in the Sterlings' quarters.

She was standing behind the dummied gown he wasn't meant to see until tomorrow.

"Isn't this supposed to be bad luck or something?" Rick asked, looking back and forth between Miriya and Lisa.

"Don't go getting superstitious on me, mister." Lisa laughed. "Besides, I'm not *in* the dress." She stepped out from behind the dressmaker's dummy and saluted stiffly. "Now show some respect."

Rick played along, snapping to and apologizing.

"Impending marriage is no excuse for relaxing discipline."

I'll have to remember that, Rick thought as he approached Lisa and took her by the waist. "Hi," he said softly.

"I beg your pardon, Admiral, but aren't you exceeding your authority?"

Rick pulled her close. "I can't help myself, ma'am. So take away my star, throw me in the brig. But please, not until the honeymoon's over . . ."

Miriya made a sour face and turned to Max, who had entered unobserved. "Sounds more like a court-martial than a marriage."

Max allowed the lovers a brief kiss before announcing himself, and five minutes later he and Rick were on their way to the factory's combat-simulation staging area, where Max had a young ensign he wanted Rick to meet. En route they discussed Edwards, but Max didn't have much to offer in the way of facts or advice. Lang was the one Rick needed to speak with, Sterling suggested, and until then the less said the better.

Cadets underwent actual mecha and weapons training in

the factory's null-gee core, and out on Moon Base; but it was during sim-time that a cadet faced combat scenarios, and psychological profiles were established and evaluated. Robotechnicians took a good deal of pride in what they had created in the staging area, with projecbeam and holographic effects of such intensity that even veterans were sometimes overwhelmed. The object was not, however, to score bull's-eyes or dazzle the audience with space combat maneuvers, but to demonstrate that one could keep cool under fire and make prudent, often split-second decisions.

Jack Baker was the ensign Max had in mind. Rick watched him being run through one of the advanced scenarios, designed to place the trainee in a position where he or she would have to decide between adherence to command dictates or altruistic heroics. Rick had little fondness for the scenario, because it happened to feature him—a holo-likeness of Rick, at any rate—as the downed pilot, awash in a 3-D sea. For want of an actual enemy, cadets found themselves up against stylized ersatz Zentraedi Battlepods.

Baker's scores were well above average throughout the first portion of the scenario, but ultimately they dropped to standard after the ensign opted to go after his downed wingman, instead of following orders to reengage.

"Not the smoothest performance," Max commented, "but you have to admit he's got something."

"Yeah," Rick nodded. "But I'm not sure it's something I like."

Baker was ordered up to the control booth, and joined Rick and Max there a few minutes later. He was a slight but energetic youth, with thick, unruly carrot-colored hair and bushy eyebrows. Blue-eyed, pale, and freckled, he impressed Rick as something of a discipline problem. At the same time, though, Baker was forceful and determined; a seat-of-the-pants pilot, a natural.

"Sir, I know my performance wasn't perfect," Baker started right in. "But that test wasn't a fair demonstration of my abilities."

Rick wagged a gloved finger in the ensign's face. "In the first place, you went off auto-pilot, contrary to orders. Second, by doing so you endangered the rest of the team. And *third*, you didn't even manage to *rescue* me."

"Yes, but—"

"Dismissed, Ensign."

"But, sir, I—"

"You heard the admiral," Max chimed in.

Baker closed his mouth and saluted. "I appreciate the admiral's input, sir," he managed before he left.

"Funny, but he reminds me of someone," Max said, watching Baker walk away. "Flyboy by the name of Hunter, if memory serves."

"I guess he does have a certain reckless sense of style about him."

"And I suppose that's why you were so hard on him, huh?"

"Just trying to improve him as a team player, Max. Besides," Rick added with a laugh, "the look on his face was priceless."

Max accompanied Rick back to his quarters after they had watched a few more cadets and officers run through the simulator. Rick was in a reminiscent mood, so they talked about the first time they had set foot in the factory after *liberating* it from Commander Reno, and about baby Dana's part in that op. Max wanted to talk about leaving

Dana behind now, but Rick didn't seem to want to surrender his train of thought.

The factory was buzzing with activity; shuttles were arriving every few hours with supplies and personnel, and boarding of the SDF-3 was under way, with techs lined up for last minute briefings, assignments, and med-scans from Jean Grant's extensive med staff. In another area of the satellite, maintenance crews, carpenters, and caterers were setting up for the wedding.

"And it's not just the wedding," Rick was saying when they entered his quarters. "I keep thinking about the enormity and importance of this mission. Maybe . . . maybe we've taken on too much this time."

"I hope you're not going to start in about how you're the youngest admiral in the force, and how undeserving you are."

"The best and the brightest," Rick said to his reflection in the viewport. "That's me."

Just then the door tone sounded and T. R. Edwards strode in on Rick's welcome.

"Hope I'm not disturbing you, Admiral."

"What's on your mind, General?"

"Why, I just wanted to wish you good luck, Hunter."

Rick noted that Edwards's faceplate made it difficult to tell whether he was sincere. And it was just as difficult for Rick to put Vince Grant's suspicions from his mind.

"What d'you mean by that, Edwards?" Rick said defensively.

Edwards showed a surprised look and turned an uncertain glance to Max. "Well, the wedding, of course. What else would I mean?"

"Oh, oh of course," Rick said, getting to his feet. He extended his hand. "Thanks, Edwards."

"Admiral Hayes's daughter," Edwards mused while they shook hands. "Imagine that . . . The irony of it, I mean. No love lost between you and him back then, was there?"

Rick stared into Edwards's eye.

"Oh, I'm sorry, Admiral. I guess you don't like to remember those days." Edwards relaxed his grip and walked to the door. "Just wanted to say good luck. To you, too, Sterling."

Rick and Max exchanged baffled looks as the door hissed shut.

Cabell and Rem had managed to get the Hellcat back to the lab undetected; it was no easy task, but a little muscle power and an abandoned Hovercar did the trick. Cabell had the Inorganic on one of the scanner tables now. He had rendered it harmless by removing a transponder from the machine's flank. Having witnessed Bioroids blowing Hellcats to bits—literally—it came as no surprise to find that the thing was hollow, its entire circuitry contained in its thick skin. But if Cabell had discovered *how* it worked, the source of its power remained a mystery—one he hoped to solve by analyzing the transponder.

On the other side of the room, Rem was up to his ears in Pollinators. Explosions had loosed them from their cage and they were all over him, now, screeching up a storm, attaching themselves to his arms, legs, and neck, and trying desperately to bury themselves in the folds of his long cloak. They might have passed for small white, mop-head dogs, except for their muffinlike paws and knob-ended horns. For a long while Zor had kept their secret from the Tirolian elite, but eventually the Masters had discovered the crucial part they played in spreading the Flower of

Life. So Zor went a step further and hid most of the creatures, naming Cabell as their guardian.

"What's happening to these things!" Rem shouted in a muffled voice, pulling one from his face. "They're going crazy!"

"They have a biogenetic link to the Flower," the old man answered calmly, hefting the Hellcat's transponder. "The presence of the Invid is disturbing to them."

"And to me," Rem started to say, when something truly monstrous appeared on one of the viewscreens. It was an enormous ship, he decided at once—because nothing so ghastly green and hideous could live in the real world. Its central head and torso resembled a kind of armored, humpbacked slug with two mandibularly-horned lizard heads on segmented necks arising Siamese-like from where arms might have been. There were three tails, two of which were tapered with stinger ends, and eight legs protruding from a suckered belly more appropriate for a sea creature than a terrestrial behemoth.

Cabell narrowed his eyes at the screen and grunted. "Their Enforcer transport. It's meant to frighten us into submission. It's captives they want now, my boy."

His thoughts turned briefly to the three Elders, who had secreted themselves somewhere in Tiresia's labyrinthine underground. *What the Invid Regent would give for their fey hides*, Cabell thought. He began to consider using them as a bargaining chip for the release of Tirol's surviving populace if it came to that, but judged it best to let that decision rest until the moment came. Safety for himself and the boy was all that concerned him just now.

"Cabell, we've got to abandon the lab," Rem said, as renewed fighting shook the city. "We can't allow your research to fall into their hands."

"I've got what I need," Cabell told him, indicating the transponder. He began to gather up data cards and chips; then, as he activated a bank of switches above the main console, two floor panels slid open, revealing a stairway that lead to the labyrinth beneath the Royal Hall. In times prior to the Great Transition, the labyrinth had been used for religious rituals.

"What about the Pollinators?"

"Take them. We'll need them if we're ever to duplicate Zor's experiments."

Rem suppressed a curse as the Pollinators he had pried from his uniform reattached themselves, screeching their mad songs all the while. He hesitated at the top of the dark staircase.

"Do we stay down here until the Invid leave?"

Cabell laughed from the blackness deeper in. "Till they leave? You're an optimist, my boy."

From his quarters on the Invid flagship, the Regent watched the descent of the Menace with obvious delight. In a moment the hydra-ship was bellowing its arrival, three sets of jaws opening to belch forth squadrons of Enforcer troops, the invasion group's mop-up crew and police force. They rode one-pilot strike ships, golden-colored tubular-shaped crafts with hooded, open-air cockpits and globular propulsion systems. They picked up where the command ships left off, dispatching what remained of Tiresia's pitiful defenses. As scenes of death and destruction played across the viewscreen, the Regent urged his troops on, mouth approximating a smile, sensor antennae suffused with color. But follow-up transmissions from the moon's surface were enough to erase that momentary blush.

"Scanners continue to register negative on all fronts, my lord."

The ground troops had completed their sweep of Tiresia, but the Regent still wasn't convinced. "You're certain there's nowhere else the Robotech Masters might have concealed the Flowers?"

"Yes, my lord. We would have detected even the slightest trace."

The Regent leaned back in the control couch. "Very well," he said after a brief silence. "I wash my hands of this wretched world. Do what you will, my legions."

He had expected an immediate response, an affirmation of his command, but instead the lieutenant risked a suggestion. "Pardon me, my lord, but shouldn't we delay the extermination until they've told us everything they know?"

"Good point," the Regent replied after he had gotten over the soldier's audacity. "Have your units round up any survivors at once, and prepare them for questioning. We shall see if we can't persuade them to tell us where their Masters have taken the Flowers of Life. I shall conduct the inquisition myself. Inform me when you have secured the city."

"It is done, my lord." The soldier signed off.

The city's temples became prisons. Those Tiresians who survived the enforcers' roundup, who survived the plasma hell they poured into the breached shelters, were packed shoulder to shoulder in improvised holding zones. They were a sorry lot, these bruised and battered sackcloth-clad humanoids; but even greater indignities awaited them. Some knew this and envied the clones, all dead now. For the first time in generations no clones walked Fantoma's moon. Save one, that is . . .

"Are they bringing more in?" a man asked his fellow

prisoners as the temple's massive door was opened, admitting light into their midst. "These monsters mean to smother us alive."

"Quiet, they'll hear you," someone nearby said.

But the man saw no reason to remain still. "Invader, what do you want from us?" he shouted when the Regent's huge form appeared in the doorway.

The Invid looked down at them, his antennae throbbing and hood puffed up. "You know very well what I want—the Flower of Life." He reached out and plucked the man from the crowd, his four-fingered hand fully encompassing the man's head. "Tell me where it is."

"Never—"

"You fool," the Regent rasped as he lifted the man to shoulder height, applying pressure as he dangled him over the screaming prisoners. The man's hands flailed wildly against the Regent's grip. "Where are the Flowers?"

The Tiresian's responses were muffled, panicked. "We don't know—"

"Tell me, you insignificant little worm!" the Regent said, and crushed the man's skull.

"We know nothing," someone in the crowd shouted. "The Masters never told us of such things!"

"My friend, I believe you," the Regent said after a moment. He released the now lifeless body. "Enforcer," he added, turning aside, "reward these creatures for their honesty."

The lieutenant stiffened. "At once, my lord." While the Regent exited the hall, the enforcer armed a spherical device and tossed it over his shoulder before the doors shut, sealing the prisoners inside.

An old man caught the device and sadly regarded its flashing lights. "What does it mean?" someone asked in a horror-stricken voice.

The old man forced himself to swallow. "It means our doom," he said softly.

The explosion took most of the temple with it.

Returned to his flagship, the Regent met with his scientists. They were barefoot beings much like himself, although no taller than the soldiers, dressed in unadorned white trousers and sashed jackets suggestive of oriental robes. In the presence of their king, they kept their arms folded across their chests, hands tucked inside jacket cuffs.

"Tell me what you know," the Regent asked them, despondent after this brief visit to Tirol's surface. "Is this moon as worthless as it seems?"

"We have yet to find any trace of the Flower," their spokesman said in a modulated voice. "And most of the population is too old and sickly to serve as slave labor. I'm afraid there is very little of use to us here."

"Perhaps it will simply take more digging to find what we seek. Come," the Regent instructed their overseer, Obsim, "there is something I wish to discuss with you."

As they walked—through an enormous hold lined top to bottom with Shock Troopers, Pincer and Command ships, and inward toward the very heart of the flagship— the Regent explained his position.

"Just because the Regis is somewhat more *evolved* than I am, she treats me like I just crawled from the swamp. I fear she'll try to undermine my authority; that's why this mission *must* succeed."

"I understand," Obsim said.

"I'm placing you in charge of the search on Tirol. The Inorganics will be your eyes and ears. Use them to uncover the secrets of this place."

Obsim inclined his head in a bow. "If this world holds

any clue to the matrix's whereabouts, I will find it."

"See that you do," the Regent added ominously.

A transparent transport tube conveyed them weight-lessly to the upper levels of the ship, where the Invid brain was temporarily housed. The brain was just that, a tower-ing fissured and convoluted organ of Protoculture instru-mentality enclosed in a hundred-foot-high bubble chamber filled with clear liquid.

The Regent's attempt to emulate the Masters' Protocul-ture Caps: his living computer.

King and scientist stood at the chamber's pulsating, bubbled base.

"The invasion is complete," the Regent directed up to the brain. "I have brought Tirol to its knees."

A synaptic dazzle spread across the underside of the instrument brain, tickling what might have been the pitui-tary body, the pons varolii, and corpora albicantia. The brain spoke. "And yet your search for the matrix con-tinues."

"For a while longer, yes," the Regent confirmed in de-fense of his actions, the chamber effervescence reflected in his glossy black eyes.

"Find Zor's ship and you will have what you seek. Not until then." The brain seemed to aspirate its words, sucking them in so that its speech resembled a tape played in re-verse.

"You've been talking to the Regis again!" the Regent growled. "You expect me to search for a ship that could be halfway across the galaxy?"

"Calculations suggest that such a journey would consti-tute a minor drain on existing Protoculture reserves when compared to these continued assaults against the Masters' realms."

"That may very well be," the Regent was willing to concede, "but conquest is growth. *Conquest* is evolvement!" He turned to Obsim. "My orders stand: section the brain. Transport the cutting to the surface to guide the Inorganics. Bring me what I seek and I will make you master of your own world. Fail, and I will leave you to rot on this ball of dust for an eternity."

CHAPTER
FIVE

What with all the major players from the RDF and the South-ern Cross in attendance [at the Hunters' wedding], one would have expected at least one newsworthy incident; but in fact the only negative scene was one touched off by Lynn-Minmei's song, which provoked exclamations of disapproval from a few members of the Sisterhood Society. "We'll be together," the chorus went, "as married man and wife." Here was Lisa Hayes, first officer of the SDFs 1 and 2, admiral of the fleet, and commander of the entire SDF-3, suddenly reduced by Minmei's lyric to Rick Hunter's wife!

Footnote in *Fulcrum: Commentaries on the Second Robotech War* by Major Alice Harper Argus (ret.)

RICK WATCHED THE EARTH AS IT SWUNG INTO VIEW feeling a little like he imagined the starchild did in that old science fiction classic. He knew it was stretching things a bit to feel that way, but in a very real sense the future of the planet was in the hands of a council of ordinary men and women. *Human* beings, not superheroes or protectors, or starchildren who had already crossed over.

Earth looked unchanged from up here, its recent scars and still-open wounds concealed by a mantle of white swirls and dense fronts. But Rick had walked Earth's scorched surface for six years and knew the truth: his world would never be the same. And it took a new kind of strength to accept this fact, to overcome the inertia of age and surrender a host of childhood dreams.

"Penny for your thoughts," Lisa said from behind him.

He hadn't heard her enter, and swung around from the viewport with a guilty look on his face.

"Am I interrupting something?"

He smiled at her and shook his head. "A penny, huh . . . Is that all they're worth?"

"A nickel, then."

She came over to kiss him, and immediately sensed his remoteness. He turned back to the view as she released him. Sunlight touched the wingtips of dozens of shuttles ferrying guests up to the satellite for the wedding.

"'The stars my destination,'" he mused. "I can't help wondering if we've made the right choice. It's like a crazy dream."

Lisa pursed her lips and nodded; Max had prepared her for Rick's mood, and she wanted him to understand that her shoulder was the softest around. Still, she didn't like his waffling and sudden indecisiveness. "It's not a crazy dream," she told him. "If we succeed, we'll be insuring a future for ourselves."

"I know, I know," he said dismissively. "I'm not as mixed up as I sound. It's just coming down so fast all of a sudden. The mission, our wedding . . ."

"We've had six years to think about this, Rick."

Rick took her in his arms; she linked her hands behind his neck. "I'm an idiot."

"Only if you're having doubts about us, Rick."

"Not now," he said, collecting on the kiss Max had interrupted earlier.

In his small cabinspace aboard the SDF-3, Jack Baker was softly thumping his head against a computer console.

There was just *too much to learn*. Not only did you have to prove yourself in air combat maneuvers, you had to know all this extra *stuff*! Ordnance specifications, drill procedures, TO&E nonsense, *Zentraedi*! for crying out loud . . . If he'd known that mecha piloting was going to involve all this, he would have just gone to college or something!

The computer sounded a tone, urging him to enter his response to the question it had flashed on the screen.

"Plot a course from *A* to *B*," Jack read, "taking into consideration vector variants listed above . . ." Jack scanned the tables hopelessly and bellowed a curse at the ceiling.

At the same moment, the cabin door hissed open and a VT lieutenant walked in. He took a long analytical look at Jack, then glanced at the monitor screen.

"Troubles, Baker?" he said, barely suppressing a grin.

Jack reached over and switched off the monitor. "No, no troubles."

The pilot sniggered. "Here, this oughta cheer you up."

Jack took the envelope and opened it: inside was a handwritten note from Admiral Hunter inviting him to the wedding reception. "'I hope you can make it,'" Jack read aloud three times, trying to convince himself that the note was on the level.

"From Richard A. Hunter," Jack said to the pilot, gloating. "My buddy, the admiral."

The hold chosen for the wedding was on the factory's upper level, where a massive overhead viewport had recently been installed expressly for the event. The space could accommodate several thousand, but by three o'clock on the afternoon of the big day every seat was filled. Rick and Lisa had demanded a simple ceremony nonetheless, and in keeping with their wishes the hold was minimally outfitted. Two tiered banks of chairs had been set up to face a raised platform, behind which rose a screen adorned with a large stylized cross. The stage was carpeted and matched by a five-hundred-foot-long red runner that covered the center aisle. Large floral arrangements had been placed along the aisle and perimeter of the stage, and in the hold beyond sat two rows of gleaming Alpha Veritechs, red on the right, blue on the left.

The front rows had been reserved for close friends and VIPs, who sat there now in their finest gowns, pleated uniforms, service ribbons, and golden-epauletted dress blues. The hold was humming with hundreds of individual conversations, and organ music was wafting from a dozen theater speakers. Bowie and Dana, who were supposed to be waiting with the wedding party, were playing a game of tag among the rows, and Jean Grant was chasing both of them, asking her son if was too much to request that he behave himself just this once.

"Can't you act like a grown-up!" she screamed, at the end of her rope.

"But I can't, Mom," the youngster returned to the amusement of everyone within earshot, "I've got the mind of a seven-year-old!"

Seating hadn't been prearranged along any "familial" lines, but a curious breakdown had begun from the start. On one side sat Field Marshal Anatole Leonard and most of the Southern Cross apparat—T. R. Edwards, Dr. Lazlo Zand, Senator Wyatt Moran, and dozens of lesser officers and dignitaries—and on the other, the RDF contingent: Vince and Jean Grant, Miriya Sterling, Drs. Lang and Penn and the rest of the Plenipotentiary Council, Jonathan Wolff, the Emersons, and others. In a tight-knit group behind the council members sat Exedore, and Dana Sterling's three deathly-ill Zentraedi godfathers, Rico, Konda, and Bron. Breetai's micronized troops were farther back, along with some of the Wolff Pack, the Skull and Ghost Squadrons.

Up front, on the sunny side, were Lynn-Minmei and her singing partner, Janice Em. Lisa's response to Minmei's offer that day in the gown shop had been straightforward: she had asked her to sing at the wedding.

Janice Em was something of an enigma to the media. Word had it that she was Dr. Lang's niece, but rumor linked her to the wizard of Robotechnology in more intimate terms. In any case, she seemed to have appeared on the scene out of nowhere two years earlier, only to become Lynn-Minmei's much needed tenor and constant companion. She was a few inches taller than Minmei, with large blue eyes set in a somewhat pale but attractive face. Her hair color changed every few months, but today it was a delicate lavender, pulled back in a rose clasp behind one ear. She had chosen a yellow spaghetti-strapped gown to complement Minmei's blue halter and offset it with a necklace of ancient Egyptian turquoise.

"Did I ever tell you about the time Rick and I got married?" Minmei was saying just now.

Janice heard the sadness in Minmei's voice, but chose to react to the statement. "Maybe you should be telling Lisa," she suggested. "Or are you saving it for when the chaplain asks if anyone can show 'just cause'?"

Minmei reacted as though she had been slapped; then she let out her breath and laughed. It was so typically *Janice* to say something like that. When the press grilled her for the scoop on Janice and Dr. Lang, Minmei would often reply, "Well, if she's not related to him, she's certainly got his sense of humor."

"It was a fantasy wedding, Janice," Minmei explained. "When we were trapped together in a hold in the SDF-1."

"And here you are trapped with him in another hold."

Minmei ignored it. "I just can't stop myself from thinking about what might have been."

"'The saddest are: it might have been,'" Janice quoted. "But forget it, Lynn. The past is only an arrangement of photons receding at lightspeed."

"That's very romantic, Janice."

"Romance is for storytellers."

"And what about our songs—you don't call them romantic?"

Janice turned to her straight-faced. "Our songs are weapons."

Above the would-be chapel, on an observation balcony Max had christened the "ready-reaction room," Rick stood in front of a mirror trying to tie a knot. His tux was white with sky-blue lapels.

"The balloon's about to go up," Max enthused, bursting in on him.

"I can't do it, Max. You're going to have to do it for me."

It took Max a moment to understand that Rick was referring to the tie; he breathed a sigh of relief and went over to his friend. "Here, I'm an expert with these things."

Rick inclined his head to the view below while Max went to work on the tie. He felt as though his stomach had reconfigured itself to some entirely new mode.

"There," Max said. "It's a matter of finesse."

Rick thanked him. "A man couldn't have a finer best man or best friend. I mean that."

Max blushed. "Hey, I was saving that for the toast."

"Okay," Rick said in a determined voice. "Let's move."

He reached up to give a final adjustment to the tie only to have it slip and loosen up.

Max looked at it and shrugged. "Well, maybe you'll start a trend."

In the end you go it alone, Rick was saying to himself ten minutes later as he turned to watch Lisa come down the aisle. Breetai, in his helmet-mask and Ironman getup walked beside her, and Rick couldn't help seeing them as some kind of whacko father-and-daughter tag-team couple. Max's daughter was one step behind them. But as Lisa drew nearer the image left him, and so did the nervousness. She had roses and baby's breath in her hair, a choker of real pearls, and she looked radiant. Behind Lisa's back, Dana made a face at ringbearer Bowie and curled her fingers at her mom.

Max and Breetai left the platform soon after, and the chaplain began to read the short service Lisa had written. A few minutes later Rick and Lisa were joining hands, exchanging rings and vows, and suddenly it was over.

Or just beginning.

They kissed and a thousand strobe lights flashed. Cheers and applause rose from the crowd above a flourish of strings and horns; and outside the viewport, teams of Veritechs completed a series of slow-mo formation flybys. A fanfare sounded as local space came to life with starbursts, roostertails, and fountains of brilliant color.

Rick and Lisa shook a thousand hands and kissed a thousand cheeks; then they danced together to Minmei and Janice's song. Spotlights found them in the hold as they moved through gentle arcs and twirls across the floor. Rick held her lovingly and caught the glint of teardrops in the corner of her eyes. He squeezed her hand and felt a wave

of sadness wash through him. It was the song perhaps, a
love song to be sure, but one sung with a sense of implied
loss, an awareness of the ephemeral nature of all things.

> A world turns to the edge of night,
> the moon and stars so very bright;
> your face glows in the candlelight,
> it's all because tonight's the night . . .
> Now hold my hand and take this ring
> as we unite in harmony.
> We can begin to live the dream,
> the dream that's meant for you and me.

> To be together,
> For the first time in our lives,
> it's us together.
> As married man and wife, we'll be together
> from now on, until death do us part;
> and even then, I hope our love lasts forever.

"Oh, Rick," Lisa whispered in his ear, moved to tears
by the Voice that had conquered an army. "How I wish
Claudia and Roy could be here."

Rick led her through a turn that kept her back to the
guests. *And Ben*, he thought. *And Gloval and Sammie and
Vanessa and Kim and the countless millions sacrificed to
war's insatiable thirst . . .*

> I promise to be always true
> until the very end's in view.
> In good times and the bad times, too,
> I know that we can make it through.
> As one united we'll be strong;
> because together we belong.

If I could sing to you a song,
I'd sing of love that won't go wrong.

If we're together,
we'll make a brand new life for us together,
as married man and wife, we'll stay together . . .

Couples began to join them on the dance floor, and when the song finished, the party began in earnest. Happily, Rick found himself with some free moments while Lisa was off circulating table to table. Oddly enough, members of the Southern Cross and RDF were mingling without incident, and everywhere Rick looked he saw people having a good time. Except perhaps for Jean Grant, who was looking a little frazzled after having spent most of the ceremony chasing Bowie and Dana around.

A photographer brought Rick and Lisa back together for the cake cutting, but Rick drew the line at that, and refused to take part in any of the archaic dances the band insisted on playing. Instead, he wandered around with a smile frozen in place that misrepresented his true inner state. He had realized, as though waking from a dream, that there was only the mission now. No wedding to absorb his concerns, no higher priority than the SDF-3 and his command.

It was a frightening realization.

Elsewhere, Jonathan Wolff was zeroing in on Minmei.

"This has got to be the biggest reception I've ever played," Minmei was exclaiming to Janice as Wolff came over.

"You sang beautifully," he began on a confident note.

Minmei recognized a certain look in his eye and began

to glance around for an escape route. "Uh, thank you," she said in a distracted way.

"The name's Wolff. And do you know how long I've wanted to meet you?"

Wolff! Oh, terrific, Minmei was saying to herself, when Janice suddenly blurted out, "Try humming a few bars."

Wolff's smile collapsed and he began to look back and forth between the two women uncertainly. "I, uh—"

"Oh, right, you were talking to Minmei, not me," Janice said. "Look, I'll relocate and you can give it a second try."

Minmei and Wolff watched her walk off.

"Don't mind Janice, she's got a very peculiar sense of humor."

Wolff cleared his throat meaningfully and was about to say something, but Minmei excused herself and wandered away.

"There's someone over there I want to talk to," she said over her shoulder.

Undaunted, Wolff straightened his torso harness—in case anyone was watching. He saw Minmei talking to Exedore and three other Zentraedi men. But then Wolff noticed something else: a man about his own age standing nearby was also watching Minmei. Watching her with an almost palpable intensity. Wolff repositioned himself for a better view of the stranger, a maintenance tech by the look of his uniform. But there was something disturbingly familiar about him. Wolff was sure he had never met the man, but was equally certain he had seen him somewhere. As he studied the man's tall, lean figure and bearded face, an image began to form. The beard would have to go, Wolff decided, and the hair would have to be a lot longer and darker...But *where* had he seen him—in the Control

Zone, maybe—and why did martial arts and old movies come to mind?

Karen Penn, her father, and Dr. Lang were eating slices of wedding cake when a slovenly-dressed civilian joined them at the table. Lang introduced Karen to Dr. Lazlo Zand, a cold-handed man with eyes as pupilless as Lang's own.

"Good to meet you," Karen said, forcing a smile and wondering if Zand ran on ice water.

"Charmed," he returned. "That blond hair. You remind me of little Dana."

Karen felt a chill run through her, and something seemed to make her fork leap from the plate. She bent to retrieve it, but someone had beat her to it.

"Allow me," a red-haired ensign told her. "I'm pretty handy with hardware."

"Karen, Ensign . . . Baker, if I'm not mistaken," offered Lang.

She and Baker were both still holding on to the fork and locked in on each other's eyes.

"The pleasure's at least fifty percent mine." Baker smiled. He let go of the fork. "Consider me at your service, ma'am."

Karen's eyebrows went up. "I'll keep it in mind."

"And I'll keep *you* in mind," Baker said, excusing himself and moving off.

"Bit of a hotshot," commented Lang.

"That's the sort of person you'll be wasting your time with from now on," Harry Penn added gruffly.

Karen smiled. "I'm not so sure about that, Dad."

"But your father's right," Zand interjected, narrowing his eyes. "Scientists are more fun."

Karen couldn't hold the man's gaze. Absently, she tried

to raise a forkful of cake to her mouth. The utensil was twisted beyond recognition.

The party was still cooking eight hours later, but Rick and Lisa were ready to call it a day. They said their farewells from the balcony overlooking the hold; and Lisa got ready to give the bridal bouquet a healthy send-off.

At the last minute, Janice had thrust Minmei into the midst of the crowd of eligible women, but had herself taken off for parts unknown. Now Minmei was pressed tight in the center of that mass of supercharged youth, surrounded by officers, enlisted-rating techs, and cadets, most of whom were younger than she was. One honey-blond-haired ensign to her left couldn't have been more than seventeen.

On the balcony, Lisa was warning that anyone who hoped to remain single should stay out of the line of fire. Then she gave the thing a windup underhanded toss, and Minmei saw it coming.

She barely had to stretch out her hands, and what was stranger still, the women around her seemed *to give it to her*.

"See you all after the honeymoon," Lisa shouted, perhaps unaware of the bouquet's landing zone.

"Yeah, in about eight hours from now!" Rick added, tugging his bride away.

Minmei lowered her face into the flowers, then gave her head a quick shake when she looked up. *It's over*, she thought, recalling a sad song she used to sing. *Now I've got to get on with my life*.

"Good-bye, Rick," she said softly. *It is you I still see . . .*

* * *

On Optera, the Invid Regis learned of her husband's imminent return and made immediate plans to leave the planet. She didn't delude herself with thoughts that this might be some trial separation. Of course, it meant abandoning all the Genesis Pit experiments in evolution she had begun here, her progress in the Great Work of transmutation and freedom from the *base condition*; but what strides could she hope to make in his presence, what chance did she have to fulfill herself? No, he had held her back long enough. Further, it meant that she would have to decide what constituted a just division of their resources. He already had the living computer; but there were other Protoculture instrumentalities that would serve her as well as the brain once had. And she would take along half her active children, but leave him that sleeping brood she had not yet seen fit to awaken.

Their home on Optera, their *castle*, was an enormous hemispherical hive, once the sacred inverted chalice of the Great Work, but now a profane *dwelling* filled with his *things*——his servants and ridiculous possessions. He had claimed to be doing all this for her sake, and for a time she could almost believe him, pitiful as his attempts were. But she soon realized that he was merely nurturing himself with these conquests and acquisitive drives.

The Regent's ignorance and stubbornness had been enough to drive her mad. He was in every way her intellectual and spiritual inferior; and yet his will was powerful, and in his presence she could feel his sick mind reaching out for her, trying to smother her. She was certain that unless she left Optera, he would one day succeed in dragging her down to his barbaric level.

But she was free of him now, her mind clear on the path she had to take. No longer subservient to his dark demands, she would strike out on her own. If the matrix was to be found, it was she who would find it. Not by sanitizing the Masters' insignificant worlds, but by sending out her sensor nebulae to the far reaches of the galaxy to locate Zor's dimensional fortress. Then she would take the Flowers back from the thieves who had stolen them; she would liberate them from their matrix prison and find a new Optera for her experiments!

In the meantime the planet Praxis would suffice.

And woe to any who would stand in her way!

Actually, I've been thinking about it for months now, but I just didn't know how to ask, and I wasn't sure if you would understand my decision. Could you see me walking up to Lang or one of those council stiffs and saying, "Uh, do you think I might be able to go along on the ride?" And then have to tell you that I was going to be doing a tour by myself this time. Taking my act to Tirol—you would have brained me. I hope you'll forgive me, and I want you to know that we'll pick up right where we left off when the Expeditionary mission returns. I mean, who knows, maybe I'll have added a bunch of new stuff to our repetoire. Anyway, I'm certain the experience will be good for me.

Lynn-Minmei's good-bye note to her manager,
Samson "Sharky" O'Toole

THE ALARM WENT OFF AT 5:15 A.M. "RISE AND SHINE," said a synthesized, possibly female voice from the room's control deck.

Rick pulled the sheet over his head and buried his face in the pillow. He could sense Lisa stirring beside him, sitting up and stretching. In a moment he felt her warm hand on his bare back.

"Morning."

"What good is it being an admiral if you can't sleep late?" he asked without lifting his head.

She laughed and kissed the nape of his neck. "Not today, Rick."

"Then tell me why five-fifteen never seemed this early before."

"Maybe because bed never felt this good before," she purred, snuggling against his back.

Rick rolled over and put his arms around her. "That's a fact, ma'am."

The door tone sounded, ending their embrace. Rick muttered something and climbed out of bed, stepping into trousers before answering the door.

"Good morning, Mr. and Mrs. Hunter," a robo-butler announced. The thing was squat and silly-looking, with a rubber skirt that concealed its wheels; it was holding a full breakfast tray in its plasticized grips. "Dr. Lang wanted you to have breakfast in bed," the butler continued in the same monotone. "Please enter the appropriate commands."

Rick allowed the piece of Robowizardry to enter, but shut it down soon afterward, taking over the butler's program and conveying the tray to bed himself.

He bowed theatrically as Lisa sat up. "Service with a genuine smile."

They ate hurriedly and said little, famished all of a sudden. Then they showered together and began to dress. Rick watched Lisa in front of the mirror, smoothing her uniform and adjusting the collar of her jacket.

"Off to work," he said, looking himself over. "Do you realize that the next time we're in this room together, I'll be asking you what you did today, and you'll tell me that you commanded a starship across the galaxy. Does that sound a little *odd* to you?"

"Odd how?" she said, with a crooked smile.

"Odd like not something we do every day."

Lisa came over to tug his black torso harness into place. "Just think of it as a honeymoon."

Rick made a face. "I'll be sure and tell that to the Masters."

Jean Grant had cried at the wedding; those, however, had been tears of joy and remembrance, while the ones streaming down her cheeks today were anything but. Bowie was on the verge of tears himself, but was trying hard to be a *man about it*. Not that mom and son stood out any, though; the shuttle hold was filled with like scenes: tears, embraces, heartfelt exchanges. Wedding guests and family members would be shuttled home over the course of the next few days, but with the SDF-3 launch window less than four hours off, this was the crew's last chance for good-byes. Within a month, Human factory personnel would be transferred to new assignments on-planet, or at Moon Base or Liberty Space Station. No decision had been made concerning the satellite itself, but speculation was that the Zentraedi crew would remove the installation from Earth orbit—to where, no one knew.

Vince Grant bent down and put a hand on his son's head, giving it an affectionate rub. "It's going to be all right, Bowie. We'll be back before you know it."

"But why can't I come with you?" he wanted to know. "Other kids are going—kids not too much older than us," he added, including Dana. Bowie was thinking of one kid in particular he had met at the wedding, Dr. Lang's godson, Scott Bernard.

"That's true, sweetie," Jean said, smiling through her tears. "But you know you can't go." She touched Bowie's chest with her fingertips. "Your heart won't let you go."

Dana, who was bored and practicing spin kicks against a bulkhead, frowned and said, "Come on, Bowie. We don't want to go with them anyway. Space is no fun, anybody knows that."

Max and Miriya regarded each other and shook their heads as if to say, *where* did that one come from?

"Dana's right, Bowie," Jean smiled, tugging in a sob. "It isn't going to be any fun."

"Yeah, Dana, but you were in space already," Bowie pointed out. "*I've* never been there."

Rolf Emerson took advantage of a momentary silence to step forward and put his arm around the boy. "We're going to have a good time, Bowie. You wait and see."

Vince and Jean embraced Rolf. "Take good care of him for us, Rolf," Vince said with a serious look.

"You know I will."

Just then Lazlo Zand walked by headed for the shuttle ramp. Instinctively, Emerson hugged Dana and Bowie to his legs, a look in his dark eyes like he wanted to put a stake through Zand's heart.

Elsewhere in the shuttle boarding area, Janice and Minmei had received their seat assignments and were walking off in the direction of the VIP lounge. They were ordinary folk this morning, dressed in slacks and simple blouses. There was plenty of time to kill until the prep call, and Minmei wanted to get a drink.

"What's with you today?" Janice asked while they moved through the crowd. "The clouds are below us, so I don't see how you can have your head in them." When Minmei didn't respond, Janice took her by the arm. "Earth calling Lynn-Minmei. Please relay your hyperspace coordinates."

"Huh?" Minmei said, turning to her.

Janice made an exasperated sound. "What is it—Rick?"

Minmei looked away. "He always looked out for me. I just don't know if I can leave him like this."

"Look, Lynn," Janice began in a worried voice, "I don't

think Lisa is going to appreciate your cutting into their—"

"If I could just see him once more. *Both* of them. Only to wish them good luck."

"You already did that—about two dozen times!"

Janice could see that she wasn't listening; Minmei's eyes were searching the bay for something. "There!" she said after a moment, pointing to a small EVA vehicle near a secondary launch port reserved for maintenance craft.

"I'm afraid to ask," Janice said warily. But Minmei was already on her way.

"Admiral on the bridge!" a young enlisted-rating tech announced, snapping to as Lisa stepped through the hatch. She couldn't help remembering Captain Gloval constantly smacking his head on a hatch very similar to this one. And indeed he would have felt right at home on the SDF-3 bridge, which for all intents and purposes was identical to that on the SDF-1. Lisa had insisted it be so, even though Lang had tried to convince her of the giant strides his teams had made since reconstructing that doomed fortress. There were redundancies and severe limitations to the design, he had argued; but in the end Lisa had her way. It was her command, and this bridge was as much a tribute as anything else. To Gloval, to Claudia and the others . . . Of course, there were *some* changes that had to be allowed. The crew, for example: they were all men.

"At ease, gentlemen," Lisa told them.

She led herself through a tour of the now completed room, running her hands across the consoles and acceleration seats. Along the rear bulkhead were two four-by-four monitor screens linked to internal systemry and astrogation. Starboard was a complex laser communication and scanner console, crowned by a tall multiscreened threat board. And forward, below a wraparound forward viewport, were twin duty stations like the ones she and Claudia had manned for almost three years.

Lisa shook hands with her exec and crew—Forsythe, Blake, Colton and the rest. It was a formality, given the fact they all knew one another, but a necessary one. She wished each man good luck, then moved toward the raised command chair that was hers alone. She took a long time settling into its padded seat, but why not: the moment was six years in the making.

A terrible memory of her last short-lived command flashed through her mind, but she willed it away. She took a lingering glance around the room and declared in a determined voice, "Mister Blake, I want systems status."

If Lisa's new space was compact, tidy, and familiar, Rick's was large and impersonal. Constructed concurrently with its Earthside counterpart, the command, control, and communications center was an enormous room more than two hundred feet square and almost half as high. A fifty-by-fifty-foot screen dominated the bulkhead opposite Rick's command balcony with its half-dozen consoles and monitors. Below, a horizontal position board was surrounded by more than twenty individual duty stations, and adjacent to this forward, a bank of as many stations tied to the central display screen. Along the port bulkhead were peripheral screens, tech stations, and banks of sophisticated instrumentality, with a great Medusa's head of cables, feeders, and power relays running floor to ceiling.

"Quite a sight, isn't it, Admiral?" said someone off to Rick's right.

Rick turned, aware that he had been staring openmouthed at the room, and found T. R. Edwards regarding him analytically from the command balcony railing. "Uh, impressive," Rick returned, underplaying his amazement.

He had of course been here often enough, but still struggled in unguarded moments with the enormity of his responsibility.

"'Impressive.'" Edwards laughed, approaching Rick now. "Interesting choice. I think I would have said 'awesome,' or 'incredible,' or even 'magnificent.' But then, I didn't spend three years in space on the SDF-1, did I? Did you think the Grand Cannon *impressive*, Admiral? You did get to see it, didn't you?"

"Actually, I didn't, General," Rick said, wondering what Edwards was getting at. "I only saw it in ruins . . . where it belonged in the first place."

Edwards grinned. "Oh, of course. I forgot. *You* were the one who rescued the Hayes woman, uh, the admiral."

Rick caught a reflection of himself in Edwards's faceplate, then looked directly into Edwards's good eye. "Something bothering you, Edwards?"

Edwards took a step back, motioning to himself with elaborate innocence. "Me? Why, no, not at all. I suppose I'm just a bit overcome by this room of ours." Edwards folded his arms and stood at the rail, a prince on a battlement. He turned to Rick and grinned. "Has anyone ever had a finer War Room, Admiral?"

Rick's lips were a thin line. "I prefer Situation Room. I thought I made that clear at the briefings."

"Forgive me," Edwards said, throwing his hands out apologetically. "*Situation* Room." He swung round to the view again. "What an impressive Situation Room."

Belowdecks, Jack Baker cursed—the RDF, his commanders, his luck, himself ultimately. *It was because of that oversight in the simulator*, he decided. *That* was what had done it, that was what had turned off Hunter and Sterling. A-and that handwritten invitation to the reception—

ha! Richard A. Hunter indeed. Richard Anti-Baker Hunter was more like it. Or why else wouldn't he have pulled the assignment he wanted? Skull Squadron . . . that was where the fun was. Even Ghost would've done the trick, although he did have some reservations about that General Edwards. But, *hell*! to be stuck with Commander Grant! Grant was all right, of course, but his unit was ground-based, for cry'nout loud. And what kind of action could a guy expect to see on land on a mission like this! And what was an *ensign* doing there? Temporary duty or not, it just didn't make any sense, no sense at all.

"I shoulda gone to college," Baker muttered as he shouldered his way through a group of enlisted ratings to report in.

Most of his Expeditionary Force mates in the mecha hangar were marveling at the two transports that were central to the battalion's strength—the GMU, and the dropship that conveyed it planetside—but to Jack the devices were just modular nightmares: overworked, underpowered, and unimportant. Veritechs were what made it happen. One pilot, one mecha. Plenty of speed, range, and firepower, and nothing to drag you down. *Nothing extraneous in mind or body*, as Jack was fond of quoting, often fantasizing about what those early Macross days must have been like, pushing the envelope and *azending*! *Yeah!*

These . . . *monstrosities*, on the other hand, were about as sleek as an old-fashioned tank. Course there were plenty of good things inside—Hovertanks, Logans, and such— but he would have to get himself transferred to the Wolff Pack if he ever hoped to ride one of those.

Jack decided to circle the GMU and see if he couldn't find something, *something* he could get excited about. The thing was huge, maybe five hundred feet long, with eight one-hundred-foot-high globular wheels affixed to massive

transaxles, banks of superspot running lights, hidden particle-projection cannon turrets, and multiple-missile launch
racks. Up front were two retractable off-loading ramps,
and up top, behind blast deflectors, two external command
stations positioned on either side of the unit's real prize: an
enormous pulse-cannon, which, like a fire engine's tower
ladder, could be raised and rotated.

Jack was still appraising the unit five minutes later when
Karen Penn suddenly appeared on one of the ramp walk-
ways. The body-hugging RDF jumpsuit did things for her
figure that the dress hadn't, and Jack's scowl gave way to a
wide-eyed look of enchantment.

Karen saw him, smiled, and waved. When she was
within earshot she called brightly, "Hey, Baker, what are
you doing here?"

Jack smiled back and cupped his hands to his mouth.
"Luck of the draw!"

"I am beside myself," Dr. Lang confided to Exedore as
the two men completed their prelaunch inspection of the
fortress's spacefold generators and Reflex drives. They
were the same ones that had once powered Breetai's flagship, but Lang's Robotechnicians had spiffed them up a
bit. It had long been the professor's wish to cannibalize one
of the spacefold generators just to take a peek at its Protoculture core, but he knew this would have to wait till a time
when fold systemry could be spared. Presently, however,
Protoculture remained the most precious substance in the
universe, and Lang's teams had yet to discover the philosophers' stone that would enable them to create it. So chips
and sealed generators were transferred intact from ship to
ship or mecha to mecha. But even with all the energy cells
the RDF had managed to salvage from the Zentraedi war-

ships that had crashed on Earth, the supply was hardly inexhaustible.

How had Zor created the stuff? Lang was forever asking himself. He understood that it had something to do with the Flowers Exedore spoke of—the Flowers of Life. But Lang had never seen one, and how in any case had Zor gone from Flower to Protoculture? It was one of the many questions he hoped the Masters would answer once peace negotiations were out of the way. And then there were all the unresolved puzzles centering around Zor himself. But for the time being Lang was content with his own minor triumphs.

"It's more than I ever hoped for."

Exedore might have recognized the look on Lang's face as one often observed on the faces of children on Christmas mornings. The Zentraedi ambassador picked up on Lang's tone of anticipation as well.

"Well, can you imagine how I must feel, Doctor, to be going home after so many years?"

Lang looked at Exedore as though noticing something for the first time. "Yes, yes, I see what you mean, my friend. And in a strange way I, too, feel as if I'm returning home."

Exedore thought he grasped Lang's meaning, and shook his head. "No, Doctor. You will see that Tirol is not for you. Earth is your home, and ever shall be."

"Perhaps," Lang said with a glint in his eye. "But we have seen more radical reshapings in the past few years, have we not?"

Exedore was about to reply when a tech interrupted the conversation to inform Lang that all systems were go and the bridge was awaiting confirmation.

"Well, give the admiral what she wants, Mr. Price," Lang declared. "The moment has arrived."

A murmur of excitement swept through the crowds waiting in the shuttle boarding area. Suddenly people were moving in haste toward the viewports and breaking into spontaneous applause.

"Now's our chance!" Minmei said over her shoulder to Janice.

From the forward seat of the EVA craft where she and Janice had been hiding for the past few hours, Minmei could just discern the rounded, main-gun booms of the SDF-3 nosing into view from the satellite's null-gee construction hold.

"Now, Janice, now!" Minmei urged.

Janice bit her lower lip and began to activate a series of switches across the craft's instrument panel. Displays came to life one by one, suffusing the small cockpit with whirring sounds and comforting amber light. Abruptly, the small ship lurched forward as a conveyor carried it toward the launch bay.

Minmei searched for some indication that they had been spotted, but it appeared that even the techs' attention had been diverted by the unannounced emergence of the fortress. And before she could complete the silent prayer she had begun, the craft was lauched.

Minmei had nothing but confidence in her partner's ability to pilot the craft and position it in close proximity to the SDF-3; she had seen Janice do far more amazing things during their two-year friendship.

She frequently recalled the first time Dr. Lang had introduced her to Janice. He talked about Janice as though she were God's gift to the world; and later on Minmei under-

stood that Lang's hyperboles were not so far off the mark.
Minmei felt that Janice was somewhat cool and remote—
the only man in her life was that Senator Moran, and it
seemed a strange sort of relationship—but Janice could
fly, fight, absorb, and retain incredible amounts of information, speak a dozen languages, including Zentraedi. Her
considerable talents notwithstanding, however, it was Janice's *voice* that Lang had raved about; about how she and
Minmei could complement each other in the most perfect
way imaginable. And not solely for purposes of entertainment. What Minmei's voice had achieved with the Zentraedi, Minmei and Janice's combined voice could replicate
tenfold. And should the Robotech Masters decide to send a
new wave of bio-engineered warriors to Earth in the
SDF-3's absence, that *defensive harmony* might very well
prove the planet's saving grace.

Our songs are weapons, Minmei heard Janice saying.

Minmei was no stranger to grandiose dreams or grandiose purpose, and she had readily agreed to keep Lang's
secret. Janice, too, agreed, and the two women had become close friends as well as partners. But after two years
of that, dreams were suddenly a new priority, and Lang's
concerns seemed paranoid now. So as the EVA craft began
to approach the slow-moving fortress, Minmei told Janice
to hold to a parallel course.

"But we can't remain here, Lynn. The ship is going to
fold in a matter of minutes."

"Just do it for me, please, Janice."

Janice was quiet for a moment; then she said, "You have
no plans of returning to the satellite, do you?"

Minmei swung around in her seat and reached for her
friend's hand. "Are you with me?"

Janice saw the commingling of fear and desperation in
Minmei's blue eyes, and smiled. "Do I have a choice?"

Minmei looked down on Earth's oceans and clouds, and completed her prayer.

"Engineering confirms attainment lunar orbit," Blake updated. "We are go for launch, Admiral."

Lisa turned in her chair to study a peripheral monitor screen. There was a steady bass rumbling through the entire ship that made it difficult to hear statements voiced on the bridge. But at the same time Lisa was aware of the background blare of klaxons and alert sirens ordering all hands to their launch stations.

"Mr. Colton, start your count," Lisa ordered, hands tight on the command chair's armrests.

"T-minus-ten and counting," Colton shouted above the roar and shudder.

"Nine . . ."

"Admiral!" Blake said suddenly. "I'm showing an unidentified radar blip well inside the fold zone!"

"Five, four . . ."

Lisa craned her neck around. "What is it?!"

"Ship, sir—EVA craft!"

"Two, one . . ."

"Too late!"

"Zero!"

"Execute!" Lisa shouted.

And the mile-long ship jumped.

SEVEN

While the life expectancy of a standard Zentraedi mecha pilot had been determined by the Robotech Masters at three years, the life expectancy of a comparable Invid pilot was never even addressed. In effect, all Invid troops (save the sexually-differentiated scientists) could be activated and deactivated at a moment's notice—initially by the Regis only, and later by the living computers the Queen Mother helped create to satisfy her husband's wounded pride (after the "affair" with Zor)....A self-generated variety of Protoculture was essential to mecha operation, in the form of a viscous green fluid that filled the cockpit space. It was through this nutrient bath (liquified fruits from the mature Optera plants) that the living computers, or "brains," communicated with the ranks.

Selig Kahler, *The Tirolian Campaign*

"YES, MY BOY, I'VE BEEN MEANING TO SHOW YOU this place for quite a long time," Cabell confessed, gesturing to the wonders of the subterranean chamber. The scientist and his apprentice were deep in the labyrinth beneath Tiresia's pyramidal Royal Hall. "A pity it has to be under these circumstances."

It was a laboratory and monitoring facility the likes of which Rem had never seen. There were wall-to-wall consoles and screens, networktops piled high with data cards and ancient print documents, and dozens of unidentifiable tools and devices. In the glow of the room's archaic illumination panels, the place had a dusty, unused look.

"And this was really *his* study?" Rem said in disbelief.

Cabell nodded absently, his thoughts on the Pollinators and what could be done with them now. The shaggy creatures had become quiet and docile all of a sudden, huddling together in a tight group in one corner of the room. It was as if they had instinctively located some sort of power spot. Cabell heard Rem gasp; the youth was staring transfixed at a holo-image of Zor he had managed to conjure up from one of the networks, the only such image left on Tirol.

"But . . . but this is *impossible*," Rem exclaimed. "We're identical!"

Cabell swallowed and found his voice. "Well, there's some resemblance, perhaps," he said, downplaying the likeness. "Something about the eyes and mouth . . . But switch that thing off, boy, we've got work to do."

Mystified, Rem did so, and began to clear a workspace on one of the countertops, while Cabell went around the room activating terminals and bringing some of the screens to life. The old man knew that he could communicate directly with the Elders from here, but there was no need for that yet. Instead, he set about busying himself with the transponder, and within an hour he had the data he needed to pinpoint the source of its power.

"As I thought," Cabell mused, as schematics scrolled across a screen. "They are almost directly above us in the Royal Hall. Apparently they've brought some sort of command center down from the fleet ships. Strange, though . . . the emanations are closer to organic than computer-generated."

"What does it mean?" Rem asked over Cabell's shoulder.

"That we now know where we must direct our strike." He had more to add, but autoactivation sounds had suddenly begun to fill the lab, drawing his attention to a screen off to his left, linked, Cabell realized, to one of Tirol's few remaining orbital scanners. And shortly, as a deepspace image formed on the screen, it was Cabell's turn to gasp.

"Oh, my boy, tell me I'm not seeing things!"

"It's a starship," Rem said, peering at the screen. "But it's not Invid, is it?"

Cabell had his palms pressed to his face in amazement. "Far from it, Rem, far from it . . . Don't you see?—it's *his* ship, Zor's!"

"But how, Cabell?"

Cabell shot to his feet. "The Zentraedi! They've recaptured it and returned." He put his hands on Rem's shoulders. "We're saved, my boy. Tirol is saved!"

But the moon's orbital watchdogs weren't the only scanners to have picked up on the ship. Inside the Royal Hall—converted by Enforcer units to an Invid headquarters—the slice of brain Obsim had transported to Tirol's surface began to speak.

"Intruder alert," the synthesized voice announced matter-of-factly. "An unidentified ship has just entered the Valivarre system on a course heading for Tirol. Estimated arrival time: one period."

The cerebral scion approximated the appearance of the Regent's living computer, and floated in a tall, clear fluid bubble chamber that was set into an hourglass-shaped base.

"Identify and advise," Obsim ordered.

"Searching . . ."

The Invid scientist turned his attention to a spherical, geodesiclike communicator, waiting for an image to form.

"Insufficient data for unequivocal identification."

"Compare and approximate."

"*Quiltra Quelamitzs*," the computer responded a moment later. A deepspace view of the approaching ship appeared in the sphere, and alongside it the various memory profiles the brain had employed in its search.

"Identify."

"Zentraedi battlecruiser."

Obsim's snout sensors twitched and blanched. *The Zentraedi*, he thought, *after all these generations, returned to their home system*. He could only hope they were an advance group for the Masters themselves, for that would mean a return of the Flower, the return of hope . . .

He instructed the computer to alert all troopship commanders immediately. "Stand by to assault."

Much as spacefold was a warping of the continuum, it was a mind-bending experience as well. The world was filled with a thousand voices speaking at once, and dreamtime images of externalized selves loosed to live out an array of parallel moments, each as real and tangible as the next, each receding as swiftly as it was given birth. The stars would shimmer, fade, and emerge reassembled. Light and shadow reversed. Space was an argent sea or sky shot through with an infinite number of black holes, smeared with smoky nebulae.

This marked Lisa's sixth jump, but familiarity did nothing to lessen the impact of hyperspace travel, the SDF-3's tunnel in the sky. It felt as though she had awakened not on the other side of the galaxy but on the other side of a dream, somehow exchanged places with her nighttime self, so that it was her *doppelgänger* who sat in the command chair now. Voices from the bridge crew surfaced slowly, muffled and unreal, as if from a great depth.

". . . reports entry to Valivarre system."

"Systems status," she said weakly and by rote. "Secure from launch stations."

Some of the techs came to even more slowly than she did, bending to their tasks as though exhausted.

"All systems check out, Admiral. Dr. Lang is on-screen."

Lisa glanced up at the monitor just as the doctor was offering his congratulations. "I've taken the liberty of ordering course and velocity corrections. Hope you don't mind, Lisa."

Lang seemed unfazed by their transit through hyperspace; it was one of the strange things about a jump: like altitude sickness, there was no way to predict who would and would not suffer side effects. She was certain that a number of the crew were already being removed to sick bay. Surprised at her own state of well-being, Lisa shook her head and smiled. "We've made it, then, we've actually made it?"

"See for yourself," Lang said.

Lisa swung to study a screen, and there it was: a magnified crescent of the ringed and marbled jadelike giant, with its distant primary peeking into view—a magnesium-white jewel set on the planet's rim. A schematic of the system began to take shape, graphics highlighting one of Fantoma's dozen moons and enlarging it, as analytical readouts scrolled across an ancillary screen.

"Tirol," said Lisa. The moon was closing on Fantoma's darkside. Then, with a sinking feeling, she recalled the EVA blip.

"Still with us," a tech reported in an anxious tone. "But we're leaving it farther behind every second."

"Dr. Lang," Lisa started to say. But all at once alert signals were flashing all over the bridge.

"Picking up multiple radar signals, sir. Approach vectors coming in . . ."

Lisa's eyes went wide. "Sound general quarters. Go to high alert and open up the com net. And get me Admiral Hunter—*immediately*."

"We've got them," Rick was saying a moment later from a screen.

"Do we have a signature?" Lisa asked the threat-board tech. Her throat was dry, her voice a rasp.

"Negative, sir. An unknown quantity."

Lisa stood up and moved to the visor viewport. "I want visuals as soon as possible, and get Exedore and Breetai up here on the double!"

"Well?" Lisa said from the command chair, tapping her foot impatiently. Klaxons squawked as the ship went on alert. She had not forgotten about the EVA craft, but there were new priorities now.

Exedore turned to look at her. "These are not Tirolian ships, Admiral, I can assure you."

Breetai and Rick were with him, all three men grouped behind the tech seated at the threat board. "Enhancements coming in now, Lisa," Rick said without turning around.

The computer drew several clamlike shapes on the screen, pinpointing hot areas.

Breetai straightened up and grunted; all eyes on the bridge swung to fix on him. "Invid troop carriers," he announced angrily.

"Invid? But what—"

"Could they have formed some sort of alliance with the Masters?" Lisa thought to ask.

"That is very unlikely, Admiral," Exedore answered her.

Rick spoke to Lang, who was still on-screen. "We've got company, Doctor."

"The ship must be protected."

"Sir!" a tech shouted. "I'm showing multiple paint throughout the field!"

Rick and the others saw that the clam-ships had opened,

yawned, spilling forth an enormous number of small strike mecha. Pincer Ships, Breetai called them.

"I want the Skull scrambled."

"Ghost Squadron is already out, sir," Blake reported from his duty station.

"What!"

The threat board showed two clusters of blips moving toward each other. Rick slapped his hand down on the Situation Room com stud, demanding to know who ordered the Veritechs out.

"General Edwards," came the reply.

"Edwards!" Rick seethed.

Blake tapped in a rapid sequence of requests. "Sir. Ghost Squadron reports they're moving in to engage."

Cabell was puzzled. It was not Zor's ship after all, but some sort of facsimile. Worse, the Invid had sent its small fleet of troop carriers against it, and their Pincer Ships were already engaging mecha from the Zentraedi ship out near Fantoma's rings. Initially, Cabell wanted to convince himself that the Zentraedi had for some reason returned in Micronized form; but he now dismissed this as wishful thinking. It was more likely that the starship had been taken by force, and he was willing to guess just who these new invaders were. Presently, data from one of the network computers confirmed his guess.

He had pulled up trans-signals received by the Masters shortly after the destruction of Reno's fleet and the capture of the factory satellite. Among the debris that littered a vast area of space some eighty light-years out from Tirol were mecha almost identical to those the would-be Zentraedi had sent against the Invid. These invaders, then, would have to be the "Micronians" whose world the Masters had gone off to conquer, the same humanoids who had been the recipients of Zor's fortress, and with it the Protoculture matrix.

And while Invid and Terrans formed up to annihilate each other, a small ship was leaving Tirolspace unobserved. Watching the ship's trail disappear on his monitor screen, Cabell smiled to himself. It was the Elders, fooled like himself perhaps, into believing that the Zentraedi had returned. *For their skins!* Cabell laughed to himself.

So Tirol was suddenly Masterless. Cabell considered the battle raging out by the giant's ring-plane, and wondered aloud if Tirol was about to change hands yet again.

In the Royal Hall Invid headquarters, Obsim was thinking along similar lines. These starship troopers were not Zentraedi, but some life-form similar in makeup and physiology to the population of Tirol or Praxis. And yet they were not Tirolians either. By monitoring the transmissions the invaders were radioing to their mecha pilots, the brain had discovered that the language was not that of the Masters.

"Sample and analyze," Obsim commanded.

It was a primitive, strictly vocal tongue; and the computer easily mastered it in a matter of minutes, along with the simple combat code the invaders were using.

Obsim studied the communications sphere with interest. The battle was not going well for his Pincer units; whatever the invaders lacked in the way of intellect and sophistication, they possessed powerful weapons and mecha more maneuverable than any Obsim had ever seen. A world of such beings would not have been conquered as readily as Spheris, Praxis, and Karbarra had. But firepower wasn't war's only prerequisite; there had to be a guiding intelligence. And of this the invaders were in short supply.

"Computer," said Obsim. "Send the mecha commanders

new dictates in their own code. Order them to pursue our troops no matter what."

The starship itself was hiding inside Fantoma's ring-plane; but if it could be lured out for only a moment, the troop carriers might have a clear shot at it.

Obsim turned to face the brain. "Computer. Locate the starship's drives and relay relevant data to troopship commanders." He contemplated this strategy for a moment, hands deep within the sleeves of his robe. "And prepare to advise the Regent of our situation."

The tac net was a symphony of voices, shrill and panicked, punctuated by bursts of sibilant static and the short-lived sound of muffled roars.

"Talk to me, Ghost Leader," a pilot said.

"Contact, fifty right, medium range . . ."

"Roger, got 'im."

"Ghost Three, Ghost Three, bogie inbound, heading zero-seven-niner . . ."

"Ghost Six, you've got half-a-dozen on your tail. Go to Battloid, Moonlighter!"

"Can't get—"

" . . ."

Rick cursed and went on the com net. "Ghost Leader, do you require backup? Repeat, do you require backup? Over."

"Sir," the pilot replied an instant later. "We're holding our own out here, but it's a world of shi— er, pain, sir!"

"Can you ascertain enemy's weapons systems? Over."

Static erased the pilot's first few words. ". . . and some sort of plasma cannons, sir. It's like they're throwing . . . -ing energy *Frisbees* or something! But the mecha are slow—ugly as sin, but slow."

Rick raised his eyes to the ceiling of the bridge. *I should be out there with them!* Breetai and Exedore had returned to their stations elsewhere in the ship; and by all rights Rick should have been back in the Tactical Information Center already, but everything was happening so damned fast he didn't dare risk pulling himself away from a screen even for a minute. Lisa had ordered the SDF-3 to Fantoma's brightside, where it was holding now.

"Has anyone located General Edwards yet?" Rick shouted into a mike.

"He's on his way up to the Sit Room, sir," someone replied.

Rick shook his head, feeling a rage mount within him. Lisa turned to watch him. "Admiral, you better get going. We can manage up here."

Rick looked over at her, his lips tight, and nodded.

"Sirs, enemy are in retreat."

Rick watched the board. "Thank God—"

"Ghost is in pursuit."

Rick blanched.

"Contact them! Who ordered pursuit—Edwards?!"

Blake busied himself at the console. "Negative, sir. We, we don't know who gave the order, sir."

"Direct the Skull to go—*now!*" Rick raced from the bridge.

Lisa regarded Fantoma's ring-plane and remembered a similar situation in Saturn's rings. "Activate ECM," she ordered a moment later. "We're bringing the ship up. And, dammit, send someone out to rescue that EVA craft!"

Jonathan Wolff left the SDF-3 launch bay right behind the last of Max Sterling's Skull Squadron fighters. He was in a Logan Veritech, a reconfigurable mecha that would one day become the mainstay of the Southern Cross's Tactical Armored Space Corps. The Logan was often jokingly referred to as a "rowboat with wings" because of the bow-shaped design of its radome and the mecha's overall squat-ness. But if it was somewhat less orthodox-looking than the Alpha, the Logan was certainly as mean and maneuver-able—and much more versatile—than the VT. In addition, the mecha's upscaled cockpit could seat two, three in a pinch.

Scanners had indicated there were two people aboard the hapless EVA craft that had been caught up in the SDF-3's fold. And they were alive, though more than likely unconscious or worse. There had been no response to the fortress's attempts to communicate with the craft.

Empowering the fortress's shields had made use of the tractor somewhat iffy, so Wolff had volunteered for the assignment, itching to get out there anyway, even if it meant on a rescue op. Now suddenly in the midst of it, he wasn't so sure. Local space was lit up with spherical or-ange bursts and crisscrossed with blue laserfire and plasma discs of blinding light. Zentraedi Battlepods were one thing, but the ships the VTs found themselves up against looked like they had walked out of some ancient horror movie, and it was easy to believe that the crablike mecha actually *were* the XTs themselves. But Breetai and Exe-dore had said otherwise in their prelaunch briefings; inside each ship was a being that could prove swift and deadly in combat.

And that was indeed the case, as evidenced by the slow-mo dogfights in progress all around Wolff. Skull's VTs were battling their way through the remnants of the Invid's original strike force in an effort to catch up with the Ghost Squadron, who'd been ordered off in pursuit of the main group. Wolff watched amazed as Battloids and Pincer Ships swapped volleys, blew one another to fiery bits, and sometimes wrestled hand-to-pincers, battering each other with depleted cannons. Wolff watched Captain Miriya Sterling's red Veritech engage and destroy three Invid ships with perfectly placed Hammerhead missiles. Max, too, seemed to be having a field day; but the numbers were tipped in the enemy's favor, and Wolff wondered how long Skull would be able to hold out.

He was closing fast on the EVA craft now, and thought he could discern movement in the rear seat of the cockpit. But as the Logan drew nearer, he could see that both pilots were either unconscious or dead. Reconfiguring now, he imaged the Battloid to take hold of the small ship and propel it back toward Fantoma's brightside and the SDF-3. But just then he received a command over the net to steer clear, and a moment later the fortress emerged from the ring-plane and loomed into view. Inexplicably, the Skull Squadron was falling away toward Fantoma's opaline surface, leaving the ship open to frontal assaults by the Pincer units, but in a moment those ships were a mere memory, disintegrated in a cone of fire spewed from the SDF-3's main gun.

Harsh static crackled through Wolff's helmet pickups as he turned his face from the brilliance of the blast. But when he looked again, two clam-shaped transports had materialized out of nowhere in the fortress's wake.

Reflexively, Wolff went on the com net to shout a warning to the bridge. Secondary batteries commenced firing while the fortress struggled to bring itself around, but by then it was too late. Wolff saw the SDF-3 sustain half-a-dozen solid hits, before return fire sanitized the field.

A score of lifeless men and women lay sprawled across the floor of the fortress's engineering hold. Damage-control crews were rushing about, slipping in puddles of blood and cooling fluids, trying to bring dozens of electrical fires under control. A portion of the ruptured hull had already self-sealed, but other areas ruined beyond repair had to be evacuated and closed off by pocket bulkheads.

Lang and Exedore ran through smoke and chaos toward the fold-generator chamber, arriving in time to see one of the ruptured mechanisms vanish into thin air.

Lang tried to shout something to his team members above the roar of exhaust fans, but everyone had been nearly deafened by the initial blasts.

Just then a second explosion threw Lang and Exedore to the floor, as some sort of black, wraithlike images formed from smoke and fire and took shape in the hold, only to disappear from view an instant later.

Lang's nostrils stung from the smoke of insulation fires and molten metals. He got to his feet and raced back into the chamber, throwing switches and crossovers at each station. By the time Exedore got to him, Lang was a quivering, burned, and bloodied mess.

"They knew j-just where to h-hit us," he stammered, pupilless irises aflame. "We're stranded, we're *stranded* here!"

CHAPTER
EIGHT

I'm of the opinion that in this instance Lang (with regard to Janice) was emulating the Masters—or more accurately perhaps, serving Protoculture's darker side. Zand, and anyone else who conspired to control, was serving this purpose as well. Protoculture's bright side had yet to reveal itself, for what had it wrought so far but conquest, war, and death? Indeed, it could be argued that Protoculture's only bright moment came at the end, when the Regis wed herself to it and was transformed.

Mingtao, *Protoculture: Journey Beyond Mecha*

OBSIM WAS PENSIVE AS HE REGARDED THE COMMUN-icator sphere; four troop carriers and countless Pincer Ships had been lost, but he had achieved a good portion of his purpose: the invaders' starship was crippled if not destroyed. It had come into full view now from Fantoma's brightside, and was holding in orbit near the giant's outer rings. ECM had foiled Obsim's attempt to reach the Regent, but a messenger ship had since been dispatched and reinforcements were assured.

But what now? the Invid scientist asked himself. Surely the outsiders recognized that Tirol would soon be entering Fantoma's shadow. Would they then move the ship into orbit, risk some sort of landing perhaps?

Well, no matter, Obsim decided. The command ships would be there to greet them.

On the fortress, meanwhile, a mood of apprehension prevailed while the RDF licked its wounds and counted the dead. Unprovoked attack was one of many scenarios the crew had prepared for, but the Invid hadn't been seriously considered. Lang, for one, had thought that the Zentraedi had all but eliminated the race; and while he remembered the image of an Invid ship included in Zor's SDF-1 "greetings message," neither Exedore nor Breetai had been forthcoming in supplying him with any additional information. Moreover, the arrival of the "Visitor," and the subsequent Robotech War, had left the Earth Forces with the mistaken notion that *humankind* dominated the galaxy. Although the Zentraedi were giant, biogenetic clones, they were still in some way understandable and *acceptable*. But not so this new enemy wave. There had of course been prelaunch briefings that addressed the alien issue, but the Zentraedi's descriptions of the Invid, the Karbarrans, the Spherisians, might as well have been campfire ghost stories or horror-movie tribute—*War With the Newts*! So as rumors began to spread through the ship, everyone was left asking themselves why the mission had once seemed a sensible idea. And Lang had yet to tell everyone the really bad news.

In an effort to curtail some of the loose talk, Rick called for a immediate debriefing following the return of Ghost and Skull squadrons. Everything would have to be kept secret until all the facts were known.

He was pacing back and forth in one of the ship's conference rooms now, while the general staff and squadron commanders seated themselves at the U-shaped arrangement of tables. Livid, he turned to Edwards first, calling for an explanation of the man's motives in superseding command's orders regarding engagement. Edwards listened attentively while Rick laid it out, allowing a pregnant silence to fill the room before responding.

"The SDF-3 was under attack, Admiral. It was simply a matter of protecting the ship."

Rick narrowed his eyes. "And suppose those ships had come in peace, General—what then?"

Edwards snorted, in no mood to be censured. "They didn't come in peace."

"You risked the lives of your men. We had no idea what we were going to face out there."

Edwards looked across the table to the Ghost Squadron commanders. "My men did their job. The enemy was destroyed."

Rick made a gesture of annoyance, and turned to the VT pilots. "I want to know why your teams gave pursuit. Who gave those orders?"

Max stood up. "Admiral, we received orders to pursue."

"With the proper authentication codes?"

"Affirmative, sir," half-a-dozen voices murmured at once.

Rick knew that he could do little more than demand a report, because Edwards could only be censured by the Council itself. Where Rick and Lisa would ordinarily have had complete run of the ship, the dictates of the Plenipotentiary Council had forced them to share their command with Edwards and other representatives of the Army of the Southern Cross apparat. This was the arrangement that had been made to satisfy the demands of Field Marshal Anatole Leonard's burgeoning power base in Monument City. Edwards's presence, in fact, was an accommodation of sorts, an appeasement undertaken to keep the RDF and Southern Cross from further rivalries—the Expeditionary Mission's peace treaty with itself. The last thing anyone wanted was to have the SDF-3 return to a factioned and feudal Earth. Moreover, Edwards was the xenophobic voice of those Council members (Senators Longchamps and Stinson, chiefly, the old guard of the UEDC) who still felt that Captain Gloval and the SDF-1 command had been too soft with the Zentraedi during the Robotech war—granting asylum for the enemy's Micronized spies and suing for peace with Commander Breetai. And as long as Edwards continued to enjoy support with the Council, Rick's hands were tied. It had been like this between generals and governments throughout history, he reminded himself, and it remained one of the key factors that contributed to his growing discontent.

Rick glanced at Edwards. "I want full reports on my desk by fourteen-hundred hours. Is that understood?"

Again, Rick received eager nods, and talk switched to the issue of secrecy. Rick was listening to descriptions of the mecha the VTs had confronted, when a lieutenant jg entered with a personal message. It was from Lang: the EVA craft had been taken aboard and its passengers moved to sick bay.

Rick went pale as he read the names.

It was a terrible dream: there she was on stage all set to perform, and the lyrics just wouldn't come. And it seemed the hall was in space with moons and planets visible in the darkness where an audience should have been sitting. Then Rick was, what?—God! he was coming down the aisle with Lisa on his arm . . .

Minmei's eyes focused on Rick's face as she came around. She was in bed and he was leaning over her with a concerned look. She gave him a weak smile and hooked her arms around his neck.

"Oh, Rick, what a dream I had—"

"Minmei, are you all right?" He had unfastened her embrace and was holding her hands.

"Well, yeah," she began. "Except for that . . ." Then it hit her like a brilliant flash.

Rick saw the shock of recognition in her eyes and tried to calm her. "You're aboard the SDF-3. You're safe, now, and the doctors say you'll be fine."

"Where's Janice, Rick!"

"She's right next door." Rick motioned. "And she's okay. Dr. Lang is with her."

Minmei buried her face in her hands and cried, Rick's hand caressing her back. "Why did you do it, Minmei?" he asked after a moment.

She looked up and wiped the tears away. "Rick, I just couldn't let everyone leave. You're all so important to me. Do you understand?"

"You could have been killed, do you understand that?"

She nodded. "Thank you for saving me."

Rick cleared his throat. "Well, actually you'll have to thank Colonel Wolff for that. But listen, you better get some rest now. There's a lot I have to tell you, but it'll keep."

"Thank you, Rick."

"Go to sleep now," he said, standing up and tucking her in.

She was out even before Rick left the room, so she didn't see the orderly who entered, or the astonished look Rick gave the bearded man. It was a look of recognition, but one tinged with enough disbelief to render the first impression false. But as the orderly studied Minmei's sleeping form, he recalled how *he* had once protected her from giants and worse.

* * *

In the room adjacent to Minmei's, Dr. Lang was staring into Janice's blue eyes. Her skills had certainly saved Minmei's life, but why had Janice listened to Minmei in the first place? Their little stunt had destroyed all the plans he had taken such pains to set in motion; and coming as it did on the heels of the damage done to the fold generators and what that meant for the Expeditionary mission, it was almost more than he could bear.

"Janice," he said evenly. "Retinal scan."

Janice's eyes took on an inner glow as she returned Lang's all but forehead-to-forehead stare. But in a moment the glow was gone; her eyes and face were lifeless, and her skin seemed to lose color and tautness.

"Yes, Dr. Lang. Your request."

"I want you to replay the events prior to SDF-3's departure, Janice. I want to understand the logic of your decisions. Is that clear?"

"Yes, Dr. Lang," Janice repeated in the same dull monotone.

Lang laughed to himself as he listened. He had foreseen the *possibility* of such an occurrence, but to be faced with the reality of that now . . . That part of the android that was its artificial intelligence had actually developed an attachment, a *fondness* for Lynn-Minmei! The specter of this had been raised and discussed repeatedly by the Tokyo Center's team, but in the end Lang had rejected the safeguards they had urged him to install, and suddenly he was face-to-face with the results of that uninformed decision.

The android had taken more than a decade of intensive work; but when Janice took her first steps, all those hours and all that secrecy seemed justified. It was shortly after the destruction of New Macross that Lang had begun to think about teaming the android with Lynn-Minmei, and the singer had easily been convinced of just how important such a partnership might prove to Earth's safety. But defensive harmonies aside, Lang had chosen Minmei because of her undenied access to political sanctuaries Lang himself could not enter, the Southern Cross apparat especially. So Lang was understandably thrilled to learn that Senator Moran had taken an interest in Janice, the young sensation some people were calling his niece, some his mistress. But what good was his spy to him now, stranded as she was along with the rest of them light-years from Earth.

Lang uttered a resigned sigh as he reached behind Janice's neck to remove the dermal plug concealed by her fall of thick hair. The plug covered an access port Lang could tap for high-speed information transference. He had the portable transfer tube prepared, and was ready to jack in. But just then Rick Hunter came through the door.

Undetected, Lang dropped the tube behind the bed and voiced a hushed command to Janice. Hunter was staring at him when he turned from his patient.

"Uh, sorry, Doc, guess I should've knocked first," Rick said uneasily.

"Nonsense," Lang told him, getting to his feet.

Rick looked back and forth between Lang and Janice; he didn't know Minmei's partner all that well, but he was aware of the scuttlebutt that linked her to Lang. Janice was offering him a pale smile now.

"How are you feeling?" he asked.

"Homesick," Janice said. "And less than shipshape."

"Well I don't know what we're going to do about your homesickness, but I'm sure some rest will help the way you're feeling."

"That's good advice," Lang seconded. He switched off the lights as he and Rick left the room.

"She's . . . sweet," Rick said, uncomfortable with the silence the two men fell into.

At the elevator, Jonathan Wolff stepped out from the car, managing a salute despite the two bouquets of flowers he carried. "Thought I'd try and cheer up our new passengers," he said by way of explanation.

Rick and Lang traded knowing looks.

"Guess every SDF's meant to carry civilians, huh, Admiral."

"Does seem that way, Colonel," Rick said. "Minmei's in room eleven," he added, motioning with his chin.

Wolff moved off down the hall, and Rick and Lang entered the elevator. "I think our dapper young colonel has more than good cheer on his mind," Lang opined.

Rick felt his jaw. "Doesn't he have a wife and coupla kids back home?"

"Ask him."

Rich shrugged. "It's none of my business."

A second debriefing was held later that afternoon. In addition to those who had attended the earlier session were Commander Vince Grant, Brigadier General Reinhardt, Wolff, Lang, Breetai, and Exedore, along with various squadron and company commanders. Photo images and schematics filled the room's numerous screens this time; the crew was still on standby alert, and the ship would shortly reposition itself for an orbital shift.

Lang at last revealed that two of the spacefold generators had been destroyed during the assault. He explained that a fold might still be possible, but there was no guarantee the fortress would emerge in Earthspace, and anything short of that was unacceptable. The twelve-member Plenipotentiary Council had voted to withhold this information from the crew. But it was therefore imperative that the Masters be contacted as soon as possible.

"The Invid presence might prove a blessing in disguise

for us," Lang continued. "Because if the Masters are indeed being held captive on Tirol, the Expeditionary mission could well be their salvation."

Lang called up an image of the Fantoma system on the main screen. Like Uranus, the planet had been tipped on its side eons ago. It had an extensive ring system held in check by shepherd satellites, and numerous moons of varied size and surface and atmosphere. Tirol was the third moon, somewhat smaller than Earth, and the only one with an hospitable atmosphere. It was, however, a somewhat desolate world, barren, with much of its topography muted by volcanic flows. Just why the Masters had chosen to remain there with half the galaxy at their disposal was a question Lang had recently added to his long list. In a matter of days the moon would enter Fantoma's shadow, which could complicate things considerably.

"Surface scans and intensity traces have given us the picture of an almost deserted world," Lang added as a closeup of Tirol came up on the screen, "except for this one city located close to Tirol's equator. I have proposed to the general staff that we begin here."

Rick stood up to address the table. "There's evidence the city's seen a lot of nasty action lately, so we've got to assume the Invid have a strong presence down there. I think our best move is to drop the GMU to recon this entire sector and ascertain the Invid's strengths. The SDF will be holding at a Lagrange point, so you'll have all the backup you need in case we've underestimated their defensive capabilities. Any questions so far?"

The men shook their heads and grumbled nos.

"Has everyone received the new authentication codes?" Rick directed to Grant and Wolff.

"We have, sir."

"I've asked Lord Exedore—" Lang started to say when Breetai interrupted him.

"Exedore and I have decided that my troops should accompany Commander Grant's ground forces."

Rick regarded the Zentraedi with an appraising look. "You're not required to become involved with this, Commander Breetai. You're not under our command . . ."

"That has nothing to do with it, Admiral. You seem to forget that I have walked this world."

Rick smiled. "I haven't forgotten . . . Grant, Wolff, do you have any problems with this?"

Vince shook his head and extended his hand to Breetai. "Welcome aboard, Commander."

"Well, that's settled," Lang said, getting to his feet again. "I have one thing to add. It concerns the Invid ships." Perspective schematics of a Pincer Ship took shape while he spoke. "Their central weakness seems to be this scanner that looks like some sort of mouth. So direct your shots there if it comes to that."

"And I hope it won't," Rick interjected. "It's possible that our initial confrontation was a misunderstanding, and I don't want us going down there like liberators. This is still a *diplomatic* mission, and you are only to engage if provoked." Rick shot Edwards a look. "Is that understood?"

"Affirmative," Wolff and Grant answered him.

"All right, then," Rick said after a moment. "Good luck." *And I wish I could be down there with you*, he said to himself.

The dropship hangar bay was the scene of mounting tension, tempers, and liveliness when the word came down to scramble. Men and women ran for gear and ordnance while the massive GMU rumbled aboard the ship that would take it planetside. Jack Baker was among the crowd,

Wolverine assault rifle in hand as he lined up with his teammates for a last-minute briefing. Like the rest of them he had missed yesterday's EV action, but stories had spread among the ranks of an engagement with some new breed of XTs, who flew ships that resembled giant one-eyed land crabs. And now the GMU had been chosen to spearhead a ground assault on the Robotech Masters' homeworld. Jack would still have preferred piloting an Alpha Fighter with the Skull, but under the circumstances this op was probably the next best thing to that.

He looked down the long line of mecha pilots waiting to board the dropship and spied Karen Penn just as she was donning her helmet, blond hair like fire in the red illumination of the hangar.

"Karen!" he yelled, waving and hoping to get her attention above the sound of alert klaxons and high-volume commands. He was tempted to give it one last try, but her helmet was on now and he knew he wouldn't be heard. He did, however, lean out of line to watch her rush up the ramp.

At the same time, he peripherally caught sight of a captain taking angry strides toward him. Hurriedly, Jack tucked his chin in, steeled himself, and muttered a prayer that the line would get moving.

"Just what the hell was that all about, Ensign!" the captain was yelling into his face an instant later. "You think this is some kind of goddamned *picnic*, bright boy! You've got time to wave to your friends like you're off on some cruise! Well, let me tell you something, you deluded piece of space trash: it's no picnic and it's no cruise! You got that, you worthless little sublife protein! Because if I see you stepping out of line again, you're going to be sucking vacuum before we even hit!"

Jack could feel the woman's spittle raining against his

face, but told himself it was just a cooling sea spray washing over the bow. The captain continued ranting for a while longer, then gave him a powerful shove as the line suddenly jerked into motion.

Oh well, he reminded himself, *the worst she could do was chew him out, which didn't amount to much considering there were things down there waiting to kill him.*

In another part of the hangar, Minmei was saying thank-you to Jonathan Wolff. A personal note from Admiral Hunter had gotten her past security, and now she and Wolff were standing by the broad and flattened armored bow of the dropship. Several Micronized Zentraedi were gaping at the singer from a respectable distance, but Breetai soon appeared on the scene and hurried them to the ship with some harsh grunts and curses.

"I just had to thank you before you left," Minmei was saying. "Janice wanted me to tell you the same. You saved our lives, Colonel." She vaguely remembered him from the wedding; but then she had met so many men during those few hours . . . Still, there was something about Wolff that caught her attention now. Maybe it was the mustache, Minmei told herself, the man's swashbuckler's good looks and tall, broad-shouldered figure. She wished she had chosen some other outfit to wear. The RDF uniform just wasn't cut right for her shape.

Wolff didn't seem to mind it, however. "Actually the honor could have gone to anyone," he said, showing a roguish grin. "But I was lucky enough to volunteer."

Minmei liked that. "Janice and I were just trying to get a better look at the fortress, and all of a sudden . . . well, you know."

Wolff's eyebrows arched. "Really? That's strange, because I had your flight recorder checked, and it seems you two actually flew directly into the vortex of the ship's spacefold flash point."

Minmei's face reddened. "Well, whatever happened, I'm glad about it now."

"Me, too," Wolff said, holding her gaze.

Suddenly Minmei went up on tiptoes and kissed him lightly on the corner of the mouth. "Be careful down there, Colonel."

Wolff reached for her hand and kissed it. "Can I see you when I get back?"

"I'd like that, Colonel—"

"Jonathan."

"Jonathan." She smiled. "Take care, Jonathan."

Wolff turned and was gone.

"That little fool," Lisa said after Rick told her about Minmei. They were alone in a small lounge not far from the bridge. "What was she trying to do, get herself killed?"

"You have to see it from her side," Rick argued. "She felt like everyone she cared about was leaving her."

Lisa regarded him suspiciously. "No, I don't *have* to see things from her side. But I'm sure you were understanding with her, weren't you? Did she cry on your shoulder, Rick?"

"Well, what was I supposed to do? You know I'd send her back if we could."

"I wonder," Lisa said, folding her arms.

Rick made a conciliatory gesture. "Whoa . . . Look, I don't like where this one's going. She's here and there's nothing we can do about it, okay?"

Lisa looked at him for a moment, then stepped in to lean her head on his shoulder. They hadn't had a chance to say two words to each other for more than twenty-four hours, and their comfortable bed was beginning to feel miles away. They were both exhausted and still a little stunned by the events that had transpired since they'd *gone off to work*!

"Is it the honeymoon you hoped for?" Rick asked, holding her.

She let out her breath in a rush. "It's the nightmare I wished we'd never have to live through." She pulled back to gaze at him. "We came here to sue for peace. And now..."

"Maybe that doesn't exist anymore," Rick said, turning to the viewport as Tirol loomed into view.

In the nave of Tiresia's transformed Royal Hall, Obsim listened patiently to the computer's announcement. A flash of synaptic sparks danced across the brain section's fissured surface, strobing orange light down at the scientist and a group of soldiers who were gathered nearby. For the past several periods the starship had been trying to communicate with Tirol, but Obsim had elected to remain silent. If indeed they had come in "peace," why were they equipped with such a mighty arsenal of weapons? More confusing still, their ship and mecha were Protoculture-driven, a fact that linked them beyond a shadow of a doubt to the Masters' empire.

And now they were sending one of their transport dropships to the moon's surface, just as he had guessed they would.

"Tell the Command ships to prepare," Obsim instructed his lieutenant. "And have your units stand by for a strike-ship assault."

"And the Inorganics, Obsim?" the lieutenant asked. "Will the brain reactivate them now?"

Obsim came as close to smiling as his physiognomy allowed. "In due time, Enforcer, in due time."

I suppose I should have been surprised that it didn't happen a lot sooner. Rick never believed that he was cut out to command, and I can remember him already trying to talk himself into resigning his commission when work first began on the SDF-3. I wanted to get to the bottom of it, but he didn't want my help. Basically he didn't want to hear his fears contradicted. So I was left to puzzle it out like a mystery, and I was convinced that both Roy Fokker's death and Rick's continuing "little brother" attitude had a lot to do with his behavior.

Lisa Hayes, *Recollections*

IT WAS AN HISTORIC MOMENT: THE DROPSHIP'S ARRIVAL on Tirol marked the first occasion humankind had set foot on a world outside the Solar system. But it was business as usual, and that business was *war*.

The GMU rumbled down out of the dropship's portside ramp onto the moon's barren surface, and within minutes Wolff was shouting "Go! Go! Go!" into the Hovertank cockpit mike as his Pack left the mobile base. Their landing zone was at the foot of a towering black ridge of impossibly steep crags; but soon the Pack was moving across a barren stretch of seemingly irradiated terrain. The massive GMU dwindled behind the twenty-unit squadron as they formed up on Wolff's lead and sped toward Tirol's principal city—Tiresia, according to Breetai. It was late afternoon on Tirol.

The Hovertanks were ground-effect vehicles; reconfigurable assemblages of heavy-gauge armor in angular flattened shapes and acute edges, with rounded downsloping deflection prows. In standard mode, they rode on a cushion of self-generated lift, but mechamorphosed, they were either Battloid or guardian—squat, two-legged waddling mecha the size of a house, with a single, top-mounted particle-projection cannon.

Wolff called up the GMU on the comlink for a situation report, and Vince Grant's handsome brown face surfaced on the mecha's cockpit commo screen. A defensive perimeter had been established around the base, and so far there was no sign of activity, enemy or otherwise. "You've got an open channel home," Vince told him. "We want to know everything you're seeing out there."

Wolff rogered and signed off. There were no maps of Tiresia, but bird's-eye scans from the SDF-3 scopes had furnished the Pack with a fairly complete overview. The city was laid out like a spoked wheel, the hub of which appeared to be an enormous Cheops-like pyramid. Eight streets lined with secondary buildings radiated out from the center at regular intervals, from magnetic north right around the compass. Nothing came close to rivaling the pyramid in size; in fact, most of the structures were the rough equivalent of three stories or less, a mere fraction of the central temple.

Exedore had described Tiresia's architecture as approximating Earth's Greco-Roman styles, with some ultratech innovations that were Tirol's alone. This is precisely what Wolff found as his Pack entered the city; although hardly a learned man, Wolff had seen enough pictures and renderings of Earth's ancient world to corroborate the Zentraedi ambassador's claims.

"Um, fluted columns, entablatures, peaked pediments," he radioed back to the GMU. "Arches, vaults . . . buildings that look like the Parthenon, or that thing in Rome—the Colosseum. But I'm not talking about marble or anything like that. Everything seems to be faced with some non-porous alloy or ceramic—even the streets and courtyards."

But this was only half the story, the facade, as it were. Because elsewhere were rectilinear and curved structures of modernistic design, often surrounded by curious anten-nalike towers and assemblages of huge clear conduits.

And much of it had been reduced to smoldering rubble.

"I'm splitting the squadron," Wolff updated a few min-utes later. Straight ahead was the central pyramid, still a good distance off but as massive as a small mountain in Tirol's fading light. He switched over to the mecha's tacti-cal net. "A team will follow me up the middle. Winston, Barisky, take your team over to the next avenue and paral-lel us. But stay on-line with me. One block at a time, and easy does it."

"Roger, Wolff Leader," Winston returned.

"Switching over to IR scanners and moving out."

There was still no sign of the Invid, or anything else for that matter, but Wolff was experiencing an itchy feeling he had come to rely on, a combat sense he had developed during the Malcontent Uprisings, hunting down renegade Zentraedi in the jungled Southlands. He checked his cock-pit displays and boosted the intensity of the forward scan-ners. At the end of the broad street where it met the hub were a pair of stacked free-floating columns with some sort of polished sphere separating them. He was close enough to the pyramid base now to make out a stairway that ascended one face; the pillared shrine at the summit was no longer visible.

Just then Winston's voice cracked over the net, loud in Wolff's ears.

"We've got movement, Wolff Leader! Multiple signals all over the place!"

"What's your position, Boomer?" Winston gave the readings in a rush. "Can you identify signatures? Boomer, do you copy?"

"Nothing we've seen," the B-team leader said over a burst of angry static. "Bigger than either ship those flyboys registered. *Much* bigger."

"On our way," Wolff was saying when something thirty feet tall suddenly broke through a domed building off to his left. It was an inky black bipedal ship, with cloven feet and arms like armored pincers. The head, equally armored, was helmet-shaped but elongated in the rear, and sandwiched between two nasty-looking shoulder cannons. Wolff watched spellbound as orange priming charges formed at the tips of the cigar-shaped weapons. An instant later two radiant beams converged on one of the Hovertanks and blew it to smithereens.

Wolff gave the order to return fire as four more enemy ships emerged from the buildings and a fifth surfaced in front of him, *right out of the damned street*!

The Hovertanks reconfigured to Gladiator mode and singled off against the Invid, the streets a battle zone all at once, filled with heavy metal thunder and blinding flashes of explosive light. Wolff saw another of his number go down. On the tac net, Wilson reported that his team was faring no better.

"Go to Battloid mode. Pull back and regroup," he ordered. Then he tried to raise the GMU.

* * *

In the GMU's command center, Vince Grant received word of the recon group's situation: four, possibly five, Hovertanks were down and Wolff was calling for reinforcements or extraction. His Pack had been chased to the outskirts of the city, where they were dug in near the remains of what the colonel described as "a kind of Roman basilica."

"Tell him to hold on, help's on the way," Grant told the radio man. Then he swung around to the command center's tactical board. At about the time Wolff's Pack had been ambushed, Invid troops had begun a move against the mobile base itself. Deafening volleys were rolling in from the line, echoing in the sawtooth ridge at the GMU's back. Night had fallen, but it was as if someone had forgotten to inform Tirol's skies.

"Ground forces are sustaining heavy casualties in all perimeter zones," a com tech updated without having to be asked. "The enemy are employing mecha that fit yesterday's profiles, along with teams of one-pilot strike ships."

The commander studied a computer schematic as it turned and upended itself on the screen. Vince tried to make some sense of the thing. *A deadly kazoo*, he thought, *with forward guns like withered arms and an undercarriage cluster of propulsion globes*. Whatever they were, they were decimating the forward lines. He had already lost count of the wounded and dead.

"Wolff on the horn, Commander," a tech said. "He's requesting backup."

"Get his present location," Vince told the woman.

The tech bent to her task, but got no response. She tapped her phones and repeated Wolff's call sign and code into the net.

Vince leaned over the console and hit the com stud. "Go ahead, Colonel. We're reading you. Colonel."

"God, I don't believe it!" Wolff said at last.

"Colonel," Vince said more loudly. "Respond."

"They're . . . they're going after my men, pulling them out of the tanks . . ."

Several command-center techs turned to watch Vince at the com station. "Who is, Colonel?"

The net was silent for a moment; then Wolff added, "Cats, Commander. Some kind of goddamned *cats*!"

Grant lifted an ashen face to the room. "Notify Breetai that his Battlepod team has a green light."

"Bah," Cabell muttered, switching off the remote sensor's audio signal. "Our Bioroids were a better match for the Invid than these Earthers. It's a mystery how they defeated our Zentraedi."

Rem kept his eyes on the monitor screen while the old man swiveled to busy himself with other matters. Almost two dozen Human mecha had entered the city, but there was scarcely half that number now. They had successfully turned the tide against the Command ships that had surprised them, but Invid reinforcements had since appeared on the scene. The remains of countless Hellcats littered the streets the Humans had chosen for their last stand.

"But Cabell, isn't there some way we can help them?"

The scientist showed him his palms. "With what, my boy? We are effectively trapped down here." He motioned to the Pollinators who were peacefully huddled in a corner. "Would you drive these ferocious creatures against them?"

Rem made an impatient gesture. "We can tell the Humans about the Royal Hall."

"Break radio silence?" Cabell asked. "And draw the Invid right to us?"

"Would you rather the Invid inherit our world?"

Cabell stroked his beard and regarded the youth. "How like him you are . . ."

Rem beetled his brows. "Who?"

"Uh, why, your father of course," Cabell said, turning away. "He, too, would have thought nothing of such a sacrifice. But listen, my boy, how can we be certain these Humans are any better than the Invid? After all, we know the Invid's capabilities. But the Humans' ways are unknown to us."

Rem gestured to the screen. "Perhaps this will change your mind, Cabell."

Skeptical, Cabell faced the screen: a score of Battlepods had arrived to back up the Terran tanks.

"Zentraedi mecha," the brain announced. "*Regult* and *Glaug*."

"Yes," Obsim said, registering some surprise. "So there is a connection between these invaders and our old foes." He looked back and forth from the communicator sphere to the living computer. "Perhaps we are in some jeopardy, after all. Computer: evaluate and advise."

"Extrapolating from previously displayed battle tactics . . ." the brain began. "Defeat for our ground forces in seven point four periods unless reinforcements arrive from Optera. Substantial damage to aliens' mecha and casualties in excess of six hundred; but not enough to threaten their victory."

"Advise, then."

A bundle of raw energy ascended the floating organ's stem and diffused in the region of the midbrain. "Conserve our strength. Take the battle to the invaders' base. Sacrifice the troopers to keep the invaders from the city. And await the arrival of reinforcements."

Obsim mulled it over. "Is there more?"

"Yes," the brain added a moment later. "Protect the brain at all costs."

"Headless ostriches" was the term VT pilots had given Battlepods during the Robotech War. Bipedal, with reverse-articulated legs and a laser-bristled spherical command module, the pods had been designed for full-size warriors. There was just enough room for a single, fully expendable pilot, and little in the way of cockpit padding or defensive shielding. But Lang's teams had reworked the mecha, so that they could now be operated by two Micronized pilots with plenty of room to spare. RDF mechamorphs were trained in pod operation, but there existed an unspoken taboo that kept Humans to their own mecha and Zentraedi to theirs.

But there were no such lines drawn when Breetai's team leaped in to lend the Wolff Pack a much-needed assist. Battlepods and Hovertanks fought side-by-side hammering away at the Invid Command ships. Pulsed-laser fire and conventional armor-piercing projectiles split Tirol's night. An entire quadrant of the city burned while the battle raged, and friend and foe added their own fire and smoke to the already superheated air.

The Hellcat Inorganics had abandoned the scene, as though frightened off by the pods, and now the Command ships were suddenly turning tail.

Wolff sat in the mecha's seat, convulsively triggering the Hovertank's weapon as the enemy ships disengaged and began to lift off. The colonnade of a building collapsed behind him, sending gobs of molten metal airborne. He raised the GMU on the net to update his situation.

"We're being overrun," a panicked voice informed him in response. "Commander Grant says to pick yourselves up and get back here ASAP!"

Wolff ordered his few remaining tankers to reconfigure, and addressed Breetai. "We're moving out. The base is ass deep in pincers."

"At your command, Colonel," the Zentraedi responded, pleased to be taking orders once again, to have an imperative to follow.

Every bed and table in the GMU's med-surg unit was filled, and still the wounded kept coming. The mess hall was a triage area and battle dressing station now, and Jack Baker had found himself in the midst of it, pulled there from supply to lend a hand. All around him men and women were stretched out on the floor and tabletops in postures of distress and agony. A young woman with third-degree burns across half her body flailed her arms against the restraints a medic was attempting to fasten, while a nurse struggled to get an IV drip running. Elsewhere a man drugged beyond pain stared almost fascinated at the bloody stump that had been a leg less than an hour before. Some of the wounded groaned and called on God and relatives for help; but Jack saw others expire with no more than a whimper, or a final curse.

Jean Grant, the front of her surgical gown red-brown from blood and antiseptic washes, was moving from table to table checking wounds and shouting orders to her staff.

"Move it, soldier!" Jack heard someone behind him yell. He felt the edge of a stretcher smack against his hip, and turned as two women medics rushed past him bearing a lieutenant he recognized to surgery.

A warrant officer called to him next, waving him over to a bloodied expanse of wall, three bodies slumped lifelessly against it. "These men are dead," the officer announced, getting to his feet and wiping his hands on his trousers. "Get them out of here, and get yourself back up here on the double." The officer looked around. "You!" he said, finding another aide in the crowds. "Get over here and give this man a hand!"

Jack bent down to regard the dead, unsure where to begin.

"You take his arms," a female voice said over his shoulder. Karen Penn was beside him when he turned. She gave him a wan smile and wiped a damp strand of hair from her face with the back of her hand, leaving a smear of someone's blood on her cheek.

"I want to get out there," Jack grunted as he lifted the body. "Some paybacks are in order."

"Maybe that's what this guy said," Karen bit out. "Let's just do our job and forget the heroics."

"We'll see."

When they had eased the body down onto the floor in the next room, Karen said, "If I see your sorry face show up in here, I'm going to remind you of that remark."

"You do that," Jack told her, breathing hard.

The SDF-3 was still at its orbital holding point above Tirol. The general staff was kept informed of the situation below by continuous updates from the GMU. One such report was coming into the fortress now, and T. R. Edwards left the TIC's balcony rail to listen more closely. A tech loyal to the cause was making adjustments for reception, and punching decoding commands into the console.

"It's from Grant, sir," the tech reported, seeing Edwards peering over his shoulder. "The situation has deteriorated and is growing untenable."

Edwards glanced around the balcony area. Hunter and Reinhardt had gone off to meet with Lang and some of the council members. "Speak plainly, Lieutenant," he said, narrowing his eye.

"They're getting their butts kicked, sir. Grant is requesting air support from the ship."

Edwards straightened up and felt the stubble on his chin. "How do we know this isn't some enemy trick, Lieutenant? Did the GMU use the proper authentication codes?"

"Affirmative, sir."

Edwards was silent while the planetside transmission repeated itself. "But then they broke our code once already."

The tech risked a grin. "I think I understand, sir."

"You'll go far," Edwards told him, leaning in to dial the gain knob down to zero.

At the same time Edwards was gloating over having eliminated Vince Grant from his life, Minmei was fantasizing about how to get Jonathan Wolff into hers. It was the flower arrangement the colonel had had delivered to her cabinspace that kicked off the fantasy; obviously he had called in the order before he left, perhaps right after they said good-bye in the dropship hangar. She was toying with the flowers now, lost in a daydream, while Janice studied her from across the room.

"Keep fooling with those things and they're going to wilt before they have a chance to bloom," Janice said from the couch.

Minmei showed Janice a startled look, then gave the arrangement one last turn before she stepped back to regard it.

"You're thinking about catching that bridal bouquet, aren't you?"

Minmei smiled. "How could you tell?"

"Because sometimes I can read you like a screen," Janice sighed. She patted the cushion next to her. "Come over here, you."

Minmei fixed two drinks and sat down, kicking off her shoes and curling her legs beneath her. Janice sipped at her glass and said, "Now tell your partner all about it."

"Do you believe in omens?"

"Omens?" Janice shook her head. "First I'd have to believe that the future has already been written, and that's simply not the case. Reality is shaped and reshaped by our words and deeds."

"I'm not asking you *philosophically*, Janice."

Janice took another sip and glanced at the flowers. "You think destiny has thrown you and Jonathan Wolff together."

Minmei nodded. "Don't you?"

"No. Not any more than I think destiny brought you and me together. We have a tendency to highlight moments we wish to think preordained."

"I promised myself I'd never get involved with a military man," Minmei continued, as though she hadn't heard Janice. "Not after Rick. And now here I am worrying about Jonathan, just the way I used to worry about Rick." She met Janice's eye. "I don't want to lose him, Janice."

"Worrying doesn't change anything, Lynn."

"Then what does it matter if I worry? Maybe I just didn't worry *enough* about Rick."

"'They also serve . . .'" Janice mused.

"Huh?"

"Just something I heard once." She took Minmei's hand. "Go ahead and worry. We all have our appointed tasks."

"I'm sick of having to listen to everyone," Rick complained bitterly, sitting down on the edge of the bed. He and Lisa had taken advantage of a short break to rendezvous in their quarters. "The council has decided we should recall the GMU and leave Tirolspace. Suddenly they're all convinced this bloodshed has been a misunderstanding. They want to remove our 'threatening presence'—those are their words—and try to open lines of communication. Station a small unarmed party out here or something..." Rick exhaled forcibly. "War of the worlds...Even Lang has reversed himself. Ever since his teams started picking apart those Invid mecha we salvaged. All at once he's fascinated with these butchers."

Lisa rested her hand on his shoulder. "Don't do this to yourself, Rick."

He looked up at her, eyes flashing. "Yeah, well, I'm tired of being the one who has to walk around with his guts tied up."

"Rick, nobody's asking you—"

"My place is with the VTs. I just wasn't cut out for command."

Lisa kneeled down to show him the anger in her own eyes. "Maybe you weren't, if you're going to talk like that. But first tell me who we should have in command. And tell me what good you think you can do in combat?"

"Are you saying I'm rusty?"

Lisa's eyes went wide. "Stand down, mister, I'm not saying that at all. I'm asking you what good it's going to do to add another *combatant* to the field, when what we need is some enlightened decision making." She relaxed her gaze. "You're not thinking clearly, Rick. You need some rest, we're all frazzled."

"Maybe you're right," he allowed.

The door tone sounded just then, and Max entered.

"Rick, Lisa. Sorry to barge in."

"It's all right, Max," Rick said, getting to his feet. "What's up?"

Max hesitated for a moment. "Rick, why are we ignoring the GMU's requests for backup?"

Rick stared at Max blankly. "What are you talking about?"

"They've been sustaining heavy losses down there."

"Why wasn't I informed of this? Who's in the Situation Room now?"

"Edwards."

Rick cursed under his breath. He gave Lisa a brief kiss and grabbed hold of Max's arm, tugging him from the room.

The two men burst into the Tactical Information Center a few minutes later. Rick glanced once at Edwards and demanded an update from a tech.

"Colonel Wolff and Commander Breetai have pulled out of Tiresia with scarcely half their command, sir. Latest reports shows them in sector November Romeo—"

"Admiral!" a second tech shouted from further along the threat-board console. "Priority transmission from the GMU."

"Go ahead," Rick told him.

The tech listened for a moment, then swiveled to face Rick again. "They say they're receiving transmissions. From Tirol, sir—from somewhere in the city. The message is in Zentraedi, sir."

"Have they identified themselves?"

"Negative, sir, other than to say they are Tiresians, and that they have important intelligence for our forces."

"A trick," Edwards spat. "An Invid trick. They've been sending in false messages all morning."

Rick regarded him a moment, then turned to Max. "Scramble the Skull, Commander. Get down there and lend support."

"Aye, aye, sir." Max saluted, leaving the room in a rush.

"Tell Commander Grant to continue monitoring transmission," Rick instructed the tech. "I want them to patch us in so we can hear it for ourselves." Rick slapped his hand down on a mike switch. "Notify Exedore and Dr. Lang to meet me in the briefing room. I'm on my way now!"

Rick ran for the door, already considering the decisions he would have to make.

CHAPTER
TEN

Cabell's age was incalculable, as had been the case with Exedore, Breetai, and several other Zentraedis who'd permitted Zand's team to study them. But whereas the warrior clones had been "birthed" full-size and ageless, Cabell had enjoyed an actual childhood, adolescence, and adulthood. His decision to undergo the Protoculture treatments that fixed his age was a conscious one. It has yet to be demonstrated how DNA and Protoculture combine to allow this miracle to occur. Like the Micronization process, it remains a complete mystery.

Louie Nichols, *BeeZee: The Galaxy Before Zor*

"**M**Y NAME IS CABELL. I AM TIROLIAN SCIENtist. Our people are being held prisoner by the Invid in structures throughout the city. The Invid ships and Inorganics are receiving their orders from a computer that has been placed in Tiresia's Royal Hall. To defeat them, you must destroy the computer. And you must do this quickly. The Invid are many and merciless. Reinforcements will arrive if you do not take immediate action. My life is now forfeit; but I place the future of this world in your hands. Act swiftly, Humans, and be equally as merciless. For there is much more at stake than this tiny moon."

Cabell repeated the message twice more, then shut down the com device and turned to Rem. "Well, that does

129

it, my boy. We have compromised our location."

Rem answered him in a determined voice. "But we may have saved Tirol, Cabell."

The old man began to look around the room, his face a mixture of rapture and longing. He ran his long fingers over the console. "Such a waste . . . What wonders we had at our disposal, what miracles we could have worked in the Quadrant."

Rem raised his eyes to the ceiling, as a sound like distant thunder shook the lab. This was followed by the sibilant burst of faraway energy beams. "It's too late for dreams, Cabell."

"I fear you're right. Their search has commenced."

Rem reactivated the communicator and gestured to the console audio pickups. "Repeat your message. We have nothing more to lose."

"The transmission is being repeated," the Invid brain informed Obsim.

"Pinpoint the source, computer."

A wiggling current coursed over folds of computer cortex. "Below this very chamber. There are vaults and corridors, a mazelike complex."

Obsim swung to an Enforcer lieutenant. "I want the Inorganics to flush them out. Tell your troops to stand by."

The soldier saluted and left the nave for an adjacent room where several Invid were watching an armored Shock Trooper bring its annihilation discs to bear on a stretch of ceramiclike floor. Already a wide wound several yards deep and as many wide had been opened.

"Continue," the Enforcer's synthesized voice commanded. "Locate and destroy."

* * *

"What does he mean by 'Inorganics'?" Rick wanted to know.

Lang leaned back from the briefing-room table and steepled his fingers. "I think he must be referring to the fiendish drones Colonel Wolff faced in the city. Certainly the ships we salvaged are anything but *inorganic*."

Lang tried to keep the excitement from his voice, but he was sure Rick and the others caught it. He had passed the better part of twenty-four hours in the laboratory dissecting those ships and the remains of one of the alien pilots. And what he'd uncovered about the Invid had been enough to send him into a veritable delirium. Thinking back even now to those hours of experimentation and discovery was like some wild roller-coaster ride. The very shape and form of those beings! As though they existed outside any *rules* of evolution. And the incredible similarity their brain patterns had to the emanations of Protoculture itself! The green nutrient the pilots bathed in inside their crab-ships, the myriad mysteries of the ships' propulsion, communication, and weapons systems, the integrity of pilot and ship that rendered Robotechnology's advances primitive and childlike by comparison . . . It had all sent him running— literally *running*!—to the Council to sue for a course other than the warlike one they had embarked on . . .

"Dr. Lang," Rick was saying. "I asked you if this message will be enough to change the Council's mind about leaving Tirolspace."

Lang started to reply, but Exedore's late entry interrupted him. The Zentraedi ambassador apologized and seated himself at the table between Lang and General Edwards, who was plainly disturbed by Exedore's arrival. Rick had the transmission replayed for Exedore's benefit and waited for his evaluation.

Exedore was silent for a long moment. "I . . . hardly

know what to say," he began. Rick had never seen the Zentraedi so, well, *moved*.

"Cabell," Exedore uttered. "He was a contemporary of Zor, a *mentor*, I think you would say. And to me, as well. He . . . he *made* me."

Lang and Rick exchanged astonished looks while they listened to Exedore's explanation. This Cabell had apparently been instrumental in the creation of the first biogenetically engineered clones. "Then this message is on the level, Exedore?"

"No one would use the name Cabell to evil purpose, Admiral. Of this much I am certain."

"Bullshit," barked Edwards. "This is another Invid trick. They're trying to lure us to this . . . 'Royal Hall.' Why? Because they have some sort of weapon there. They're playing with us."

"What about it?" Rick asked the table.

One of Lang's techs spoke to that. "Scanners indicate the source of the transmission is subterranean—perhaps beneath the very structure we've identified as the Royal Hall. Colonel Wolff described it as . . ." the tech checked his notes, "'a flat-topped pyramid as big as a small mountain, crowned with some kind of columned shrine.' We've picked up intense energy readings emanating from the structure."

"A weapon," Edwards interjected.

Rick tried to puzzle it out. "Suppose it is legit. Would Cabell knowingly call a strike down on his own head, Exedore?"

"Without question, if Tirol could be saved by his actions."

"Then the Robotech Masters may still be alive. Is it enough to convince the Council, Doctor, yes or no?"

"I think they'll listen to reason. But if we can possibly achieve these ends without destroying—"

"Raise the GMU," Rick instructed one of his aides. "Inform Commander Sterling that I want a recon flyby of that pyramid. I don't want anybody trying anything stupid. Tell Grant to keep the GMU dug in and wait for my word to move in."

"And Cabell?" said Exedore.

"Yes," Lang seconded. "Surely a rescue team—"

"I'm sorry, Doctor," Rick broke in. "You, too, Exedore. But I want to know what we're dealing with before we send anyone in."

Edwards snorted. "We'll say some kind words over his grave," he said loud enough for Exedore to hear.

In the tradition of that apocryphal cavalry who were always arriving in the nick of time, the Skull Squadron tore into Tirol's skies from the shuttles that had transported them to the edge of the envelope, and fell like wrathful birds of prey on the enemy's Pincer Ships and Shock Troopers. Cheers from Hovertankers and mecha commanders filled the tac and com nets as the Guardian-mode VTs dove in for missile releases and strafing runs.

Captain Miriya Parino Sterling led her team of red fighters against a group of blue-giant Command ships that were going gun-to-gun with Breetai's Zentraedi cadre. The smoking remains of Battlepods and strike ships littered a barren, now cratered expanse of high plateau where the Invid had successfully breached the GMU's forward defense lines. Miriya's Alphas hit the massive twin-cannoned mecha where they lived, chattering undercarriage guns stitching molten welts across cockpit shields and torso armor, and red-tipped heat-seekers finding the ships' vulnerable sensor mouths. Explosions geysered fountains of white-hot alloy into the waning light as ship after ship fell, leaking viscous green fluids into the dry ground. Renewed, the Battlepods leaped to regain their lost ground, trading energy salvos with the larger ships, their orange and blue bolts cutting swaths of angry ionization through the moon's thin atmosphere.

Elsewhere, Max's blue team backed up the Wolff Pack's devastated Hovertank ranks, reconfigured to Battloid mode for close-in combat, while overhead, solitary Veritechs went to guns with the less maneuverable Shock Troopers. Ships boostered and fell, executing rolls and reversals as they engaged.

Even the GMU's main gun was speaking now, adding its own thunderous punctuation to the battle's murderous dialogue. A second and third wave of mecha burst from the base's forward ramps—Mac II cannons, Excalibers, and drum-armed Spartans—but the Invid would neither fall back nor surrender.

It was all or nothing, Max realized as he bracketed two of the alien ships in his sights. Missiles tore from the Battloid's shoulder racks and found their mark; the ships came apart in a dumbbell-shaped cloud of flame and thick smoke. In the end, once the RDF's debris was carted from the field, it would look like a slaughter had taken place; but in the meantime men and women continued to die.

Max ordered the Battloid into a giant-stride run, pulled back on the selector lever, and imaged the VT through to fighter mode. He went ballistic, instructing his wingmen to follow suit, and was about to rejoin Miriya when Vince Grant's face appeared on one of the cockpit commo screens.

"You've got new orders, Commander, straight from the top."

"Uh, roger, Home. Shoot."

"Your team's to recon the Triangle. Just a flyby with a minimum of sound-and-light. Do you copy, Skull One?"

"Can do, Home. Waiting for your directions."

"We're punching them in now," Vince said.

Max's onboard computer came alive, stammering vectors and coordinates across the display screen.

"And Max," Vince added. "Be sure to keep in touch."

Evening's shadow was once again moving across Tirol's face; a crescent of Fantoma loomed huge in the southern skies, its ring-plane a shaft of evanescent color. The battle was over—for the time being, forever, no one could be sure, any more than they could be sure who had won. If it went by the numbers, then the RDF had been victorious; but there was no known way of conveying that to the five hundred who had died that day.

Jack had been returned to his outfit and was out at the perimeter now, finally out on Tirol's surface, where he felt he should have been all along. There was a good deal of activity going on around him—mecha tows and transports and APCs barreling by, VTs flying recon sweeps—but he still wasn't content. He had been assigned to take part in a mine-emplacement op, which meant little more than observing while Gladiators planted and armed AM-2 Watchdogs across the field. (These anti-mecha mines of high-velocity plastique had been developed by one Dr. R. Burke—who was also responsible for the Wolverine assault rifles—and came complete with an Identification Friend or Foe targeting microchip housing a library of enemy ground signatures, even those recently cooked up by the GMU's computers to indicate Invid Scouts and Shock Troopers.) So instead of giving the Gladiator his undivided attention, Jack had slipped away to eavesdrop on a conversation that was in progress at one of the forward command posts. Jack understood that the enemy had been soundly defeated, but things were a still bit sketchy with regard to follow-up plans. He sensed that something important was up, and in a short time he had the astounding details.

A message had been received from Tirol's occupied city—sent by some sort of rebel group, from the sound of it—giving the location of the Invid's central command. The Skull had been ordered to recon the site, but nothing was in the works to save the rebels themselves, who were apparently holed up in the very same neighborhood. Having seen a crude map of Tiresia, Jack knew the place would be easy enough to suss out. And if a small team— even *one man*—could infiltrate, the rebels would be as good as free. All it took was the *right* man.

But chief among the things Jack *didn't* know was that his actions over the past hour had been observed at rather close range by Karen Penn. And she stuck with Jack now as he began to angle his way behind the command post and into the forward supply area. He waited until the sentries were preoccupied, then moved in and grabbed hold of a Wolverine and an energy-pack bandolier. Karen drew her hand weapon and decided it was time to confront him.

Taken by surprise, Jack swung around with his hands raised, prepared to assume the position. But realizing it was Karen, he simply shook his head and shouldered past her. Karen armed the handgun, which came to life with a short-lived but unmistakable priming tone. It stopped Jack in his tracks.

"Now, you want to talk to me, Jack, or the unit commander?"

"Look," he said, turning around carefully, "there's something I've got to do." He explained what he knew about the communiqué and the rebel group, and how a small group could get in and out unnoticed.

Karen listened without comment, then laughed shortly and deactivated her weapon. "You're certifiable, you know that?"

Jack made a face. "I'm going in alone, Karen."

"Oh no you're not," she said, grabbing a Wolverine from the rack. "'Cause I'm coming with you."

Jack showed her a grin. "I know where there's a coupla Hovercycles."

Karen pulled the bandolier's straps taut. "Lead on, hero," she told him.

Obsim peered into the trench the enforcers had opened in the floor of the Royal Hall. Fifty feet down they had broken through the roof of a narrow corridor, a stretch of the mazelike subterranean works the brain had discerned.

"The Inorganics will locate the Tiresians within the period," the brain informed Obsim when he reentered the Hall's central nave.

"I am pleased," Obsim said, trying on a regal tone.

"There are other concerns . . ."

"Prioritize."

"A group of airborne mecha are closing on our position."

Obsim glanced at the communicator sphere, where a holo-image of six blue Veritechs was taking shape.

"Advise, computer."

"Protect the brain. Activate the shield."

Obsim tried to calculate the resultant energy drain. "You are so instructed," he said after a moment of reflection.

Bubbles formed, percolating in the brain's tank.

"It is done."

*   *   *

Max had his team complete two high-altitude passes over the city before dropping in for a closer look. Schematics of Skull's topographical scans had revealed that Tiresia's Royal Hall was an enormous structure indeed, a truncated pyramid almost a thousand feet tall capped by a classical Roman-like shrine. It dominated the city, which was itself a kind of circular mandala set into Tirol's bleak surface. Scanners had also picked up dusk activity in the city's street; but whatever was moving around down there was smaller than the Invid ships the Skull had thus far gone up against.

"All right, let's stay alert," Max said over the net as the team followed him down. "Keep an eye on each other. Blue Velvet, you've got the number-one spot."

"Roger, Skull Leader, I'm on my way," the mechamorph responded.

Max watched him peel away from the group, roll over, and drop in for the run. They were all closing on the Hall, scarcely five hundred feet above it, when a translucent envelope of scintillating energy suddenly mushroomed up in front of them. The envelope expanded to encompass the entire Hall, and with it, Blue Velvet's lone Veritech. The rest of the team broke hard and climbed.

"It's a force field of some kind," Max said. "Blue Velvet, get yourself out of there!"

"No can do, Skull One, my systems are down! Reconfiguring and going for touchdown . . ."

Max was heading back toward the Hall again, and could see the Guardian-mode VT falling. But all at once there were three bizarre shapes on the shrine steps—headless, demonic-looking bipedal mecha, with dangling arms and orifice-dimpled weapon spheres.

"You've got company, Blue Velvet!" Max shouted the pilot's call sign twice more, but got no response. The

Alpha was preparing to land when the creatures opened fire and blew it off course.

Max watched helplessly as the Veritech grazed the edge of the pyramid and exploded, raining fiery debris down the Hall's steep side.

"Hit them!" Max ordered.

Missiles dropped from the Veritechs' undercarriage pylons and ripped in twisting tracks toward the Inorganics, only to detonate harmlessly against the Hall's repellent dome. But the enemy could fire through the shield and did, catching a second VT before Max could order the team away. He was trying to decide what to do next, when one of his wingmen came on the net. "Skull Leader, I'm picking up two friendly blips down below."

Max listened for the coordinates, tipped his Alpha, and leaned over to take a look. "You sure they're friendly?"

"Affirmative. The IFF says they're Hovercycles. They're approaching the Hall."

Hovercycles, now what the . . . Max said to himself. "All right," he said, "let's go down and see what's cooking."

"Wha-*hoo!*" Jack shouted, throttling the Hovercycle down a slope of arid ground and onto one of Tiresia's central spokes. "Life in the fast lane!"

"Idiot," Karen muttered to herself, goosing the handbar grip in an attempt to catch up with him. "He's going to get us both killed."

The cycles were face-effect vehicles, with conventional grips, right-angled bars rising up and back from a single shaft, and a front Hover-foot that resembled an old-fashioned carpet sweeper. The seat and backrest was a sweeping, padded affair, and although the cycles were built for one, the rear storage deck could accommodate a second rider if need be. They were fast, silent, and maneuverable, but essentially weaponless.

"What are you trying to prove?" Karen said, coming up alongside Jack's cycle. "Is this a rescue op or a joyride?"

Jack glanced over at her and began to lay out his philosophy about how self-confidence was what mattered most; but instead of listening she was just looking at him wide-eyed, and the next thing he knew, she had her handgun raised and aimed in his general direction—

"Duck!" she yelled, firing off two quick bursts that nearly parted Jack's carrot-colored hair.

"Jeez!" he said, when they'd brought the cycles to a halt. "Whaddaya think—"

"Take a look at that."

Jack twisted around in the seat and spied the Inorganic Karen's shot had neatly holed. Still on its feet and slumped against a wall, the thing reminded him of a character from an old cartoon. "Tasmanian devil," Jack recalled, snapping his finger, as the Crann slid to the smooth street.

"Is it alive?" Karen asked, looking around warily.

"Not any more."

"But what is it?"

"I don't know," Jack said, bringing the Wolverine off his shoulder, "but there's three more of them coming our way."

Karen reholstered her sidearm and followed Jack's lead. Suddenly, half-a-dozen blue energy bolts were zipping past her, impacting against a wall and sending up a shower of white-hot gunk. A blast of superheated air washed over her, stinging her eyes and nose while she brought the assault rifle to bear on the drones.

Jack was already firing; his rounds had managed to connect with one of the Inorganics, and Karen watched as the thing flashed out and crumbled, as though hollow. An instant later the other two went down, breaking open like ceramic figurines.

"Let's get out of here!" Jack yelled, as bolts began to rain down on them from surrounding rooftops.

Karen kept up with him, piloting the cycle one-handed while she loosed an arc of rear fire, dropping two more Cranns with well-placed sensor shots. "What now?" she said, her voice raspy from the heat, smoke, and all the shouting.

Jack motioned up the street, toward a small mountain of a structure. "Straight ahead. That's the Hall. The message originated from somewhere underground. I figure there's gotta be a way down."

"You figure," Karen said in disbelief. "I'm for turning back."

"Uh-uh. But I am for *turning*!"

Karen looked up: ten or more Inorganics were blocking the street. Their weapons were raised.

Perplexed, Cabell regarded the weapon Rem had given him; he fumbled with the rifle's selector lever. "Like this?"

"No, no, Cabell," Rem said, close to losing his patience. "Like this," he demonstrated, activating his own weapon.

Cabel mimicked Rem's movements. "Ah, I see . . . and you hold it like, er, you put your right hand, um, let's see, you—"

"Give me that thing!" Rem snapped, snatching the rifle from the old man's hands. Cabell was offering him a imbecilic shrug. "You'll probably vaporize your own foot."

"I wouldn't doubt it for a moment," Cabell agreed. "I'm sorry, I've never had any talent for the fine art of combat. Why, back when the Masters were first—"

"Save it, Cabell. Are we going or not?"

Cabell took one long last look around the room. Still-functioning remotes had permitted them to view the Humans' recon attempt, and later, their failure to breach the barrier shield the Invid computer had deployed. But with Inorganics closing on the subterranean lab now, there was no time for further monitoring of the situation. Cabell had insisted that they not be caught in the lab. The Pollinators would be his gift to the Invid; with them and some seedling Flowers, perhaps they could refoliate ravaged Optera, end this incessant killing . . .

"Well, what have we here?" Cabell said suddenly.

Rem came back into the lab, cursing, and found the scientist pointing to one of the screens. Here were two Humans just outside the force field, a male and a female, straddling strange-looking Hovercrafts.

"Could they be searching for us, Rem?"

"Don't flatter yourself," Rem answered him, tugging Cabell into the corridor. They could hear the Inorganics nearby, blasting through corridor walls and breaking into rooms.

"But they *could* be looking for us."

Rem continued to drag Cabell down the corridor. "Fine, fine . . ."

Cabell reached for one of Rem's weapons. "Then let's just go out and meet them."

CHAPTER
ELEVEN

Finally all the principal players had been introduced to one another: Masters and Invid, Zentraedi and Humans, Humans and Invid, Humans and Masters. Surely this was Protoculture's doing; but what would make the contest especially bizarre was the fact that not one of those players had all the puzzle pieces. It was a mad, mad, mad, mad world.

Dr. Emil Lang, *The New Testament*

THE REGENT WAS RELAXING IN HIS BATH WHEN OBSIM'S message finally reached him. The sunken tub in his private chambers was as large as a backyard swimming pool, surrounded by ornate fixtures the Regis had detested. *You have too many things,* she used to scream. *Things!*—when the very goal had always been to move away from such material trappings. Her goal, at any rate. *Freedom from this base condition . . .* her words to describe their world after the affair with Zor. After Optera, an Eden if ever there was one, had been defoliated by the Masters' warrior clones, robbed of the Flower that was infinitely precious to the Invid, so *essential.* They were like starving creatures now, feeding off what nutrients had been stored up in their flesh, but hungry, ravenous for sustenance only the Flower could provide.

The Regent sighed as he climbed from the tub, regarding the sterile green bath fluids with a mixture of sorrow and disdain. To be sure, the bath had been drawn from Flowers and fruits, but a mutated variety from Peryton that had to pass for the real thing, for absent, too, were the Pollinators, those shaggy little beasts critical to the Flowers' reproductive cycle. As a result, the Regent no longer bathed to empower himself, but simply to sustain a memory of brighter times.

Brighter times indeed, he told himself as a servant moved in to drape a robe over him. *You have taken a wrong turn*, the Regis had warned him. *A turn toward de-evolution and evil purpose*. She was already in Tiresioid form then, desperate in her attempts to emulate Zor's race. She had begged the Regent to join her in that novel guise, but he would hear nothing of it. His queen, his *wife*, had been defiled, his world contaminated, and still she would ask for such a thing. When his very heart was burning with a rage never before known to him. Was it any wonder then that he had chosen his own course? The goal—the goal, my *dear*—is conquest and consumption; and *things*—warriors and weapons and battle mecha—are pivotal to that end.

To hell with her if she couldn't understand his purpose!

And yet . . . and yet how lonely this place seemed without her. Surrounded by nothing but servants and soldiers now, he could almost miss the arguments of those final days. The passion. She had fled with half her brood to carry on with her mad experiments in transmutation, her quest for the perfect physical vehicle to inhabit while she completed her Great Work, a form more suitable for her wisdom and dreams, more supportive than his embrace.

"Curse her!" he seethed, taking quick steps toward the antechamber.

A messenger genuflected as he entered, lowering its head and bringing an arm to its breast. The Regent's Hell-cats were restless, pacing the room, sniffing and snarling. He put them at ease with a motion of his hand and bade the messenger rise and state its purpose.

The messenger handed over a voice-imprint and with-drew. The Regent activated the device and listened, run-ning it through again and again until satisfied that he had memorized Obsim's every word, every nuance.

Tirol under attack—by what Obsim had initially be-lieved were Micronized Zentraedi, but were now thought to be a coalition of Zentraedi and some unknown Tiresioid race. A race of beings with Protoculture-driven starships and mecha! *This* was the astonishing thing. Protoculture could only be derived from the Flowers, and the potent Flowers were indigenous to Optera, and Optera *only*. Look what had become of those seedlings Zor himself had tried to implant on Karbarra, Spheris, and the rest.

"What could it mean?" the Regent asked himself. An undiscovered world, perhaps, rich in the Flower that was life itself, ripe and waiting to be plucked.

He summoned the messenger to return. "Make haste to inform Obsim that reinforcements are on their way." He turned to his lieutenants next, his stingraylike hood puffed up, betraying his agitation.

"The Regis is not to learn about these matters. This new world will be our . . . our *present* to her."

But only if she agrees to listen to reason, he kept to himself. *Only if she accepts the path of conquest!*

The Regent's huge hand closed on the voice device, splintering it to bits.

*   *   *

Jack and Karen stood transfixed at the edge of the Royal Hall's shimmering shield, unsure of what they were up against. They had given the enemy drones the slip for the moment, but there was no time to dally.

"I say we try to go in," Jack was saying.

Karen gazed into the field's evil translucency. "And I say you ought to have your head examined."

"Maybe if I just touch—"

Jack reached his hand out before she could stop him, and in a flash was flat on his back unconscious.

Karen screamed and ran to him, kneeling by his side, wondering if there was anything she could do, her hands fluttering helplessly. "You stupid idiot!"

Jack came to and looked up at her stupidly, then shrieked as the pain caught up to him. His left hand flew to his right wrist, clutching it as though aware of the torment above. Karen pried Jack's fingers loose and pulled his hand to her. It was blanker than a newborn's, void of prints and lines. She told him to lie still, ran to the idling Hovercycle, and returned with a first-aid kit. She hit him with a pre-loaded syringe of painkiller and waited till it took effect.

Jack's face was still beaded with sweat a moment later, but the drugs had done their job; he offered her a weak smile and forced his breath out in a rush. "Now, what was that you were saying?"

"About you needing to have your head examined? Forget it." She showed him his effaced palm. "You're going to need a whole new personality."

"No big deal," Jack muttered. "The old one was about used up anyway."

"I'm glad you said it." Karen laughed, helping him to his feet. "Now let's get back to base."

They started for the cycles, only to swing back around to the sound of metal-shod feet. Five Hellcats came tearing around the corner, for some reason slithering to a halt instead of leaping. The drones fanned out and began to stalk the two Humans as they backed themselves slowly toward one of the Hovercycles. Karen had her blaster drawn.

"Nice kitties," Jack said in a calming voice. "On three we leap for the cycle," he told Karen out of the corner of his mouth.

"But—"

"Don't worry, I can drive. You keep those things away from us."

Karen thumbed the handgun's selector to full auto. "Ready when you are,"

"One, two . . . three!" he yelled, and they both bolted. Two of the Hellcats jumped at the same time; Karen blasted them out of the air, pieces raining down on the Hovercycle as Jack toed it into gear and took off.

A third Hellcat tried to keep pace with them, but Karen holed that one, too, right through the thing's flashing eyes. She had one arm around Jack's waist, loosing rear fire as he threw the cycle into a turn and raced down a side street.

"Where to?" she yelled.

"Left!" he answered, just as two more 'Cats leaped to the streets from the peak of a pediment.

Karen twisted on the cargo seat and laid down an arc that seared one of the beast's legs off. But others were joining in the pursuit; she stopped counting at eleven.

"How's our fuel?" she thought to ask.

"Going fast," he said, his bad hand up by his shoulder, comically mouthing the words. "Any suggestions?"

"Yeah. Remind me to let you go it alone next time something like this comes up!"

"I've got them, Skull Leader," one of the VT team confirmed. "They're both on the same cyc now, west of the

Hall on a connecting street between two of the main spokes. 'Bout a dozen drones behind them."

"Have they spotted you, Blue Lady?"

"Uh, negative. They've got their hands full. Some rough terrain up ahead—craters, devastated buildings . . ."

"Can you exfiltrate?" Max asked her.

Blue Lady fell silent, then said, "Think I see a way."

"Coming around to cover you."

"I'm going in," the woman announced to her Beta copilot. "Breaking hard and right . . ."

"Heads up, you two!" a female voice shouted from the Hovercycle's control pad speaker.

Jack thought he was hearing things and wondered if his brush with the force field hadn't damaged more than just his hand. Karen was discharging bursts from the cargo seat, but for every drone she killed another two would appear; it was as if some controlling intelligence was directing the chase.

Jack had been forced to take some bad turns back toward the Royal Hall, and was trying to puzzle out a way through the wreckage in front of them when that disembodied voice repeated itself.

"Heads up!"

Even Karen heard it this time, so Jack knew he wasn't imagining it. "An Alpha," she said, waving her free hand in his face. He looked up and saw the VT dropping in to match the Hovercycle's pace and course.

"Looks like you two are a long way from home," the pilot said. "I'm coming in for a pickup. Acknowledge."

"Fine with us," Jack said. "Hope she's not changing her mind?" he added when the VT didn't respond.

Karen interrupted her fire to peer over Jack's shoulder. She smacked him on the shoulder. "You idiot, use the net!"

Jack winced and opened the net, acknowledging the VT.

The Alpha dropped and let loose with two missiles that took out half the Hellcat pack; then the mecha split, its Beta hindquarters lowering a stiff ladder.

"Grab it," Jack told Karen.

They were near the central plaza again in an area of the city that had seen a lot of action, skirting the rim of a huge blast crater.

Karen holstered her weapon, got into a kneeling position on the seat using Jack's shoulders for balance, and took hold of the ladder, heat from the VT blasting her face all the while.

"Come on, Jack!" she was shouting into the wind a moment later.

Jack stretched out his bad hand, thought better of it, and took his good hand from the front grip. Karen curled herself on the ladder and leaned down to help him. But all at once, two Hellcats came tearing out of an alleyway making straight for the cycle. Jack caught sight of them in time, but forgot about his injured hand as he reflexively reached for the handlebars.

Pain like liquid fire shot up his arm. Out of control, the Hovercycle veered to the right and ramped up the rim.

Jack felt himself leave the cyc's contoured seat and go airborne. In an instant's passing, he was once again questioning his sanity, because floating out in front of him he saw some kind unanchored column—two of them, actually, separated by an equally free-floating featureless sphere. Jack impacted the uppermost column at the same moment he heard the Hovercraft crash in the smoky crater below him. His hands, knees, and feet tried to find purchase, but he soon found himself sliding . . .

He hit the sphere and clung there a moment, wishing he had suction cups instead of hands, then recommenced his slow slide, flesh squealing along the thing's smooth surface.

"Whaaaaa . . ." he sent into Tirol's evening chill.

Jack's fingertips somehow managed to catch the edge of the lower column. Breathless, he hung there, nose buried in one of the flutes as the Beta circled him. And all at once his hand began to remember something . . .

He screamed and let go, recalling the hotfoot he had given a cadet back in academy days, and hit the ground with enough force to instantly numb both his legs.

On his butt now, dazed and hurting, Jack directed some choice words against himself.

Muttering, he tried to stand up.

Six pairs of glowing eyes were approaching him out of the crater's groundsmoke.

"Can you see him?" Karen asked the Beta's pilot, as she threw herself from the ladder into the mecha's passenger space.

"Not yet," the pilot answered her with a hint of anger. "I've got a biosensor reading, but there's just too much smoke down there."

Karen tried to peer out the canopy. "We've got to go back."

"Suddenly you're not suicidal."

"Hey, look," Karen said, "we just went—"

"Tell it to the judge," the pilot cut her off. "I've got one of them, Skull Leader," she said over the net. "Number two's on his own. The cyc's a memory."

Karen heard Commander Max Sterling reply, "Reconfigure and go in. But keep it simple. First sign of big stuff and I want you out of there."

"Understood, Commander. Reconfiguring . . ."

*   *   *

Jack slapped his hip holster and gulped. He was weaponless, and the cat drones had effectively cut him off from whatever remained of the Hovercycle. Not that Jack was even sure he could find it in all the smoke. He turned through a three-sixty looking for some way out, and spotted the partially-ruined archway of an ancient-looking building. He ran for it without hesitation, ignoring the shock waves each ankle sent up his quivering legs.

Presently, he could discern broad steps in front of him, a short flight that led to a pillared platform, and beyond that the arch. Galloping, clanking sounds told him that the Inorganics weren't far behind.

But there was another sound in the midst of all that eye-smarting smoke: the sound of a Beta's VTOL flares. Jack realized that the mecha had changed modes and was descending. Trouble was, it was putting down on the wrong side of things. Six drones were standing between him and rescue.

Jack decided to try and wait it out; let the VT handle the drones, then show himself when the coast was clear. He limped his way up the stairs and hastened toward the building.

All at once a Hellcat landed in front of him. Jack dug his heels in and threw himself behind one of the columns as the creature leaped. He felt the closeness of its passage, and began to scramble around the column base, while the Hellcat turned and leaped again. It hit the opposite side of the pillar with a resounding crash, its clawed paws embracing the base and almost tearing into Jack where he stood. Jack jumped for the next column and the next, slaloming his way down the platform one step ahead of the infuriated drone.

He reached the end of the row and tumbled down a flight of steps. The Hellcat was above him snarling and preparing to pounce when he rolled over. Suddenly Jack heard a weapon discharge behind him; at almost the same moment the drone came apart in a shower of fiery particles. He tucked and rolled as heat and a concussive wave battered him.

Then someone's hand touched his shoulder.

It was an old man with a bald, knob-topped head and two-foot-long snow-white beard. Jack was certain he was dreaming now.

"Good work, my boy, good work!" the man was congratulating him in Zentraedi.

Jack shook his head to clear it. Behind the man was a youth his own age, a handsome lad with tinted hair and a long cloak. He was cradling an assault rifle.

"Are you the rebels?" Jack stammered, unsure if he had chosen the correct words.

Cabell stepped back, surprised that the Human knew the old empire's *lingua franca*. "Rebels? No. But we are the ones who sent the message. I am Cabell, and this is Rem."

Rem nodded and said something in a language Jack had never heard.

Cabell nodded and pulled Jack to his feet. "Your ship," he said quickly. "We must get to your ship."

"But—"

"Hurry! There's no time!"

Cabell and Rem put Jack between them and ran in the direction of the Beta's landing zone. Jack wanted to warn them about the drones, but pain was intercepting his words. Besides, the two Tiresians seemed to be aware of the things already.

Angry flashes of orange and white brilliance were piercing the groundsmoke up ahead of them. Jack heard the characteristic chatter of the Beta's in-close weapons, and follow-up explosions he hoped accounted for the last of the enemy drones. The old man, Cabell, had most of Jack's weight now; Rem was moving out front through a hail of white-phosphoruslike debris.

Then all at once the firing was over as quickly as it had begun, and Karen's voice echoed out of an eerie silence.

She called Jack's name, but he was too weak to respond. Rem and Cabell exchanged a few unintelligible sentences, got Jack between them once again, and hastened toward the call. They were close enough to hear the Veritech's whistling hum and feel the heat its thrusters were spreading across the bottom of the crater.

The glow of running lights brought out a low moan of relief from Jack. Cabell voiced a Zentraedi greeting; Karen picked up on it after a moment and instructed them to come out with their hands raised.

She was waiting in a combat crouch by one of the VT's backswept wings when the Tiresians appeared out of the smoke. Jack thought he saw a look of astonishment on her face before Cabell and Rem set him down on the ground. She uttered something he couldn't catch and directed a question toward the Beta's open canopy.

Cabell stepped forward and addressed her.

Jack heard her nervous laugh. She had lowered the muzzle of her Wolverine, and was repeating Cabell's words for the pilot.

"You've got to be kidding."

"No, I swear it," Karen confirmed. "He said, 'Take me to your leader!'"

■ ■ ■ ■ ■ ■ ■ ■ ■ ■ ■ ■ ■ ■ ■ ■ ■ ■

CHAPTER
TWELVE

Cabell impressed all of us as a kind, peace-loving man. And I knew he was one of us when he suggested that we might be able to rendezvous with the Masters in deepspace and give them what they were after (the Protoculture matrix). He'd just finished describing the horrors the Masters had spread through the Fourth Quadrant, and now he was telling us that we still had a chance to make our peace with them. Only a Human could think like that.

The Collected Journals of Admiral Rick Hunter

"I DON'T GIVE A DAMN ABOUT WHAT YOUR LITTLE escapade turned up!" Vince Grant was saying two hours later. "The only thing keeping me from throwing both of you in the brig is Admiral Hunter's request for leniency on your behalf. And when all the details of this are known, I'm sure he's going to change his mind as well. Do you read me?"

Karen and Jack swallowed hard and managed to find a collective voice. "Yes, sir; perfectly, sir."

Grant glared at them. He had his large hands pressed flat against the desk, but straightened up now and advanced to where the two former ensigns were standing at stiff attention. They had returned to the GMU scarcely an hour ago, just enough time for a pit stop at sick bay before being dragged off to Grant's office. Jack's right arm was in a sling, his head shaved and bandaged along his forehead. Karen had fared somewhat better, but perhaps because of that the commander was directing most of the flak her way.

"I would have expected as much from *him*," Grant continued, gesturing to Jack, "but I'd been led to expect better things from you, *Cadet* Penn. *Much* better things! Are you aware of the several *other* ways your self-appointed rescue mission could have turned out? Are you aware that *your* rescue endangered lives? Well?"

Karen gulped. "I am, sir. I apologize, sir."

Grant stared at her in surprise. "'Apologize,' Penn—*apologize*! That is the *least* of what you're going to be doing, believe me. Now I want to know which one of you came up with this bright idea."

"The cadet doesn't recall, sir," Karen said, eyes straight ahead.

"Really," Grant sneered, looking back and forth between Karen and Jack. "A conspiracy, huh?" Arms akimbo, he sidestepped, dark eyes flashing as he regarded Jack from his towering height. "And you, Baker... Born-to-be-a-hero, Baker." Grant motioned behind him. "I read you were looking for a VT assignment, is that true?"

Jack raised his eyes. "Yes, sir," he said weakly.

"You'll be lucky if you end up piloting a fanjet for the sanitation squad, mister!"

Jack blanched. "The cadet would consider it an honor to fly for the s-sanitation squad, Commander, sir."

"You bet you will, Baker."

Grant returned to his desk. "Where are the prisoners?" he asked one of his aides.

"In the holding area, sir. The shuttle and Skull Squadron are awaiting the commander's word."

Grant ran his eyes over Penn and Baker a final time. It was incredible that they had stumbled on the two Tiresians, that their joyride could possibly have resulted in just the break the RDF needed right now. But breaches of discipline couldn't be treated lightly, even when the results were more than anyone could have hoped for.

Vince knew Karen's father, and was aware of the friction between the two of them. Busted now, she would have little recourse but to follow Harry Penn's lead into research. Max, however, had appealed to Vince to go as lightly as possible; seemed that he and Rick had a special interest in Karen's fight for independence. And Baker's cause as well, although Vince couldn't quite figure it. Baker was too independent already.

"Get the prisoners aboard the shuttle, Captain. And as for these two," he said, twisting in his chair, "confine them to quarters. I don't want to see their faces. Understood?" Karen saluted, and Jack did the best he could.

"Sir!"

"Now get them out of here."

Jack followed Karen out of the office. "How about dinner in, say, six months, if we're out of this by then?" he asked under his breath.

Karen bit off a laugh. "Try me in about six years, Baker. Just maybe I'll be ready to talk to you."

Jack made a face. This wasn't supposed to be the way it worked out. But, then again, at least he had some great stories to tell over at the garbage dump.

Rick was hoping to have first crack at the prisoners, but the Council wouldn't hear of it. He had presented his case directly to Lang: the Tiresians were essentially military property; and if indeed they were the same group that had made contact with the GMU, their knowledge of the

Invid's command and control was of vital importance. "We will be certain to address that," Lang had told him. The Council had even found unexpected support from General Edwards, who still considered the Tiresian message suspect. Rick, however, had succeeded in limiting the interrogation committee to four members of the Plenipotentiary—Dr. Lang, Lord Exedore, Justine Huxley, and Niles Obstat—and four members of the RDF—himself, Lisa, Edwards, and Reinhardt.

The eight, along with security personnel, secretaries, and translators, were assembled in one of the Council's briefing chambers now, a long, narrow room with a single table and two rectangular viewports that dominated the starboard bulkhead. Tirol would be fully visible for the session, while the SDF-3's position had reduced Fantoma itself to little more than a slender background crescent. Presently, Cabell and Rem were escorted in and seated at one end of the table opposite Justine Huxley, a UEG Superior Court judge, and Niles Obstat, former senator and head of Monument City's regional legislature.

Rick heard someone gasp; when he leaned in to look to his left, he saw Lang half out of his chair.

"Is it you?" Lang was asking of the young Tiresian.

Lang's mind was racing, recalling a day more than twenty years before when he had stood in front of a data screen on the recently arrived SDF-1, and a face with elfin features and almond eyes had greeted Gloval's recon team. Then a robot with reconfigured wiring had walked into their midst, and while everyone was preoccupied, Lang had tried to activate that mainframe, had inadvertantly taken the mind-boost and altered his very life . . .

"Is it you?"

The caped Tiresian wore a puzzled look; he turned in

his seat, certain that Lang was speaking to someone behind him.

"Zor," Lang said, more shaken than Rick could ever remember seeing him. "You, you were the one . . ."

Cabell cleared his throat meaningfully and smiled, one hand on the youth's shoulder. "No." He laughed. "No, there is some resemblance—around the eyes and mouth, perhaps—but this is not Zor. Zor has been dead a long time."

Lang seemed to come to his senses. "Of course . . . I knew that."

Cabell followed Lang's gaze down the table, where it came to rest on a uncommon-looking man with dwarfish features, cropped red hair, and a thick brow ridge. The Tiresian's mouth dropped open.

"Welcome, Cabell," Exedore said evenly. "No, your eyes have not deceived you, as Dr. Lang's have."

"But, Exedore, how is this possible?" Cabell glanced from face to face, searching for other surprises, then returned to Exedore's. *The first of the Masters' biogenetically engineered clones!* The one whose very history Cabell had been forced to reshape and re-create after the Masters had turned their giant miners to warriors . . .

Little by little the story unfolded: how the SDF-1—identified by Cabell as Zor's ship—had crash-landed on Earth, and how some ten years later the Zentraedi had followed. And how a war for the repossession of that ship had commenced.

Cabell was on the edge of his seat, attentive to each added fact, and silent except when he interrupted to provide a date or refine a point.

"And the armada was actually defeated?" he said, as if in shock. "Almost five million ships . . ." Suddenly a maniacal expression surfaced. "Then, you have the *matrix*! You do have it, don't you!"

"It didn't exist," Lang answered him. "We searched—"

"No, no, no, no," Cabell ranted, shaking his head, white beard like a banner. "It does exist! You searched the fold generators, of course."

Rick, Lisa, Lang, and Exedore exchanged looks.

"Well, no," Lang said, almost apologetically. "We didn't want to tamper with the fold mechanism."

Cabell slammed his hand on the table. "It's there! It's hidden in the fold generators!"

Lang was shaking his head.

"What happened?" Cabell said, disheartened.

Exedore answered him. "The ship was destroyed by Khyron, Cabell. Its remains are buried on Earth."

Cabell grew strangely silent. He put a hand to his forehead, as though stricken. Rick recognized what he took to be a look of concern and abject terror.

"But . . . don't you see," he began. "No mere collision could destroy that device. It exists—the one source of Protoculture in the Quadrant—and the Masters have left Tirol to find it!"

"Left for *where*?" Rick demanded.

"Earth, Commander," Rem answered him.

"Oh my God," Lisa said.

Edwards and Rick looked at each other. The same names were on both men's minds, but for different reasons —Zand, Moran, Leonard. The field marshal's prelaunch warnings about Earth's vulnerability assumed a sickening immediacy. Rick suppressed a panicked scream that had seemed to lodge itself somewhere beneath his diaphragm.

"But you can overtake them," Cabell was saying. "The Masters' fortresses have superluminal drives, but there wasn't sufficient Protoculture reserves to permit a fold.

They have been gone for ten years in your reckoning. You could meet them and arrange an exchange for the device. Surely they do not want war with your world—not when there are so many worlds available to them." Cabell let his words trail off when he realized that no one was listening to him. It was at this moment that he decided to say nothing of the Elders who had left Tirolspace only a short while ago. *Let them be marooned in that cruel void*, he said to himself.

Brigadier General Reinhardt grunted sardonically. "This mission was undertaken to avoid just such a war. We came to tell the Masters that Earth didn't have what they were looking for."

"Unfortunately, we knew nothing of the situation here," Lang added. "The Invid's attack against us damaged our fold mechanism. We reasoned that by allying ourselves with Tirol . . ."

"You would have what you needed to return to your world."

"Precisely."

Cabell stared at his hands and said nothing.

"What about the message you sent our troops?" Rick cut in, anxious to return the interrogation to its central issue. "What's the situation down there?"

Briefly, Cabell explained the circumstances of the Invid's recent conquest of Tirol. He described and named the battle mecha the RDF had found itself up against: the Shock Troopers, Pincer Ships, Command ships, and the Inorganic drones—the Scrim, Crann, Odeon, and Hellcats.

"Their troops are known as Enforcers," he told the committee. "Essentially they have no independent will, save for certain evolved ones, who are thought of as 'scientists.' But the brain controls all of them."

"Brain?" said Edwards. "What is this idiocy?"

Cabell stroked his beard. "It is a computer of sorts—but much different than anything either of our races would fashion. We believe it is linked to a larger unit the Invid keep on Optera. But if you can get to the one they've placed in the Royal Hall, you will defeat them here."

"They've deployed some kind of force field," Rick said as all eyes turned to him. "So far we haven't been able to penetrate it."

"What about a surgical strike, Admiral?" Niles Obstat suggested.

Cabell stood up. "Please, Earthers, I know I have no right to ask, but our people are being held prisoner..."

Rick made a calming gesture to reassure the old man. "We're not going to do anything rash. But we do need a way in, Cabell."

"You can go in the way we came out," Rem said suddenly. "Cabell will map it out for you."

Cabell flashed his assistant an angry look. He had hoped to keep Zor's laboratory secret a while longer, but he supposed there was no hope of that now. "Of course I will," he told Rick.

Edwards was already in touch with GMU control. "Grant apparently had the same idea," Edwards reported. "He's sent the Wolff Pack in."

"The computer is invaluable," Cabell urged. "You must inform your troops that there are ways to deactivate the brain without destroying it. It could be of great use to all of us."

Edwards felt his faceplate and stared at Cabell obliquely.

It is invaluable, it controls all of them . . . It could be of great use to us. The words rolled around in his mind, settling down to a dark inner purpose.

"I want command and control," he said into the com while everyone's attention was diverted. "Get the Ghost Squadron ready for departure. I'll be down to lead them in personally."

Exedore and Lang met separately with Cabell and Rem after the committee session was dissolved. While the military faction was off deciding how best to deal with Cabell's revelations concerning the Invid brain, Lang, fully aware of the regulations he was violating, took the two Tiresians to the SDF-3's engineering section and eventually into the hold that housed the spacefold generators. On the way Cabell talked about the history of Tirol and the sociopolitical upheavals that had paved the way for the Great Transition and the emergence of Robotech Masters.

Lang and Exedore were as rapt as Cabell had been only an hour before. At last someone knowledgeable was filling in all the gaps of the saga they had tried to patch together from records found aboard the SDF-1 and the Zentraedi flagship. And how false those records were now proved to be! Even the misinformed scenarios Lang himself had worked out, the timelines he had spent countless hours assembling, the motives and explanations he had assigned.

Cabell spoke of Zor as one would of a demiurge, and in many ways Tirol's story was Zor's own—from his noble birth as a senator's only son, to his untimely death at the hands of the Regent's newly-evolved troops. Cabell told them of Zor's remarkable discovery on Optera, and of the subsequent development of Protoculture and Robotechnology; of the creation of the Zentraedi, and the growth of a new political elite; of the war that raged throughout the empire, and a renegade's attempts at rebalancing the scales . . .

Lang was given to understand that Zor, Cabell's one-time student, hadn't so much kept the secrets of Protoculture from the Masters as scattered them across the galaxy. There were still Flowers, on Optera and on many of the worlds Zor had seeded just prior to his death, but the Invid found them sterile and unusable because their Pollinators had also been taken. And while the Masters were in possession of these curious creatures, *they* no longer had the matrix that allowed for Protoculture conjuration from the Flowers. Zor had seen to it that no one could profit from his discoveries; and in the end he had driven himself half mad, convinced that he could somehow rule over all of it and parcel out to the universe the gift of everlasting life.

Exedore and Lang learned a little about Cabell, also; about how he and Zor and several other Tirolian scientists had deliberately refused to embark on the dangerous course the Masters had followed—the road to heightened powers and the toll that journey extracted. Ever since the Masters left, Cabell and his young assistant, Rem, had been trying to replicate Zor's achievements. But Cabell was now beginning to believe that the process was more one of mind than of matter, and that Protoculture would never be scientifically conjured from the Flowers—it had to be *willed* from them.

As Lang listened to Cabell's assessment of the Masters, he found himself growing weary and almost bemused by the Expeditionary mission's ironic accomplishment: in leaving Earth behind, they had left the door wide open for the Masters' arrival. It occurred to him that peace would never have been possible with such a race, and he could only shudder at the thought of Earth in the incapable hands of Leonard and the Army of the Southern Cross.

Once in the fold-generator hold, the language of pure science replaced the grunts and glottal stops of the Tiresian tongue. The computer was their interpreter now, and as

Cabell inspected the generators, he and Lang began to communicate with mathematics and schematic appraisals. Lang was amazed at how quickly the Tiresian was able to adapt and *reshape* his thinking to fit the demands of Human artificial-intelligence systems.

"But you have the necessary Protoculture reserves for a fold," Cabell said after a long while. "Enough for a flotilla of ships, in fact. All that's lacking is sufficient fuel for the Reflex drives." He saw Lang's bewildered look, and quickly created a program that could illustrate his ideas. Once or twice he called on Exedore to define a word or phrase.

Lang watched as a series of esoteric holographic displays took shape on the screen. He studied them a moment and offered Cabell a restrained smile. "Now I understand."

A fold required an all-important interaction between Protoculture and the fuels that powered the Reflex drives themselves, an interaction his teams would never had guessed.

"But what you have here would call for a magnetic monopole ore, Cabell."

The Tiresian looked impatient. "Well, of course. How else *could* it be done?"

"But we haven't the equipment necessary to create this much material," Lang told him. "And even if we did, it would require more time—"

"Nonsense," Cabell said dismissively. "You have all the ore you need right there."

Lang and Exedore followed Cabell's finger out the viewport.

"Fantoma?"

"You don't remember a time when the Zentraedi were miners, Exedore?" Cabell asked.

Exedore seemed almost embarrassed by the question. "I

do, Cabell. But we were never told what it was we were mining."

Cabell turned to Lang. "The base may be difficult for you to utilize since it was sized to suit the Zentraedi; but the ore is still there for the taking."

Lang stepped to the viewport and looked long and hard at the giant planet's jade-colored crescent. Then, as his eyes found diminutive Tirol, he recalled a premonition he had had long before the SDF-3's departure from Earth-space. He thought of the SDF-3's sizing chamber, and of Breetai's small team of Micronized Battlepod warriors.

Exedore was standing alongside him now. "But will we have enough time, sir?"

Lang said, "We have nothing but time."

The lights in the sky are stars, Jonathan Wolff told himself short of the tunnel entrance. He had dismounted the Hovertank and was gazing up into Tirol's incomparable night. But there was at least one light up there that wasn't a star, and he made a wish on it.

Minmei was somewhere on that unblinking presence he identified as the SDF-3, and the wish was meant to ascend to her heart. Wolff had hardly been able to keep her from his thoughts these past two days; even in the midst of that first day's battle he would recall her face or the fragrance of her hair when she had come to the dropship hold to wish him luck, to embrace him. He wondered how he had allowed her to take hold of him like this, and considered for a moment that she might have *witched* herself into his mind. Because it was out of control all of a sudden, a flirtation he had played on the off-chance, never figuring she would respond. And what of Catherine? he asked himself. Was she, too, staring up into evening's light, her arm around the thin shoulder of their only son, and sending him a wish across the galaxy? While he had already forgotten, broken the pledge he had promised to stick to this time, so they could have the second chance their marriage so desperately needed.

Odd thoughts to be thinking on such a night, Wolff mused.

"All set, sir," the lieutenant's voice reported from behind him.

Wolff took a quick breath and swung around. "I want it to go by the numbers, Lieutenant," he warned. "Two teams, no surprises. Now, where's our voice?"

The lieutenant shouted, "Quist!" and a short, solid-looking ranger approached and snapped to.

"You stick to me like glue, Corporal," Wolff told him. "Every time I put my hand out I expect to find you on the end of it, got that?"

"Yes, sir."

Wolff gave Quist the once-over. "All right, let's hit it."

The lieutenant got the teams moving through the smoke toward the subterranean corridors. It hadn't taken a genius to locate the entry once they had gotten a clear fix on where the Beta from Skull had touched down. And that crazy kid, Baker, had a good memory if nothing else, Wolff had to concede; his recall of the ruined buildings in the area bordered on the uncanny.

Wolff signaled for everyone to hold up at the entrance. He peered down into the darkness, then took a look behind him, where four Hovertanks were guarding the rear. The corridor was tall and wide, but not big enough to accommodate a mecha. Stairways, secondary corridors, and some kind of huge lenslike medallions could be discerned from up here.

Wolff found himself thinking back to the journals his grandfather had kept during a minor Indo-Chinese war few people remembered. Back then, Jack Wolff and a handful of tunnel rats used to go into these things with flashlights and gunpowder handguns. Wolff checked the safety on his blaster and had to laugh: his grandfather wrote about the booby traps, the spiders and rats. Today it would be mindless feline robot drones and a host of other stuff they probably hadn't even seen yet. But all in all it was the same old thing: a sucker's tour of the unknown.

"Bring those Amblers in," Wolff ordered.

Two squat, bipedal Robosearchlights moved up to throw intense light into the hole.

Wolff and his Pack began to follow them down.

CHAPTER
THIRTEEN

If Exedore had an Invid counterpart, it would have to be the scientist [sic], Tesla, for no other of the Regis's children was possessed of such a wide-ranging intellect and personality. It is interesting to note, however, that although fashioned by the Regis, Tesla had much more of the Regent in his makeup. One has to wonder if the Regis, taking Zor as her only model, mistakenly assigned certain characteristics to males, and others to females. Marlene, Sera, and Corg—her human child—immediately come to mind. Was she, then, in some sense culpable for fostering the Regent's devolved behavior?

Bloom Nesterfig, *The Social Organization of the Invid*

IT WAS TESLA WHO TOLD THE REGIS ABOUT THE TROUBLE on Tirol. He was one of the Regent's "scientists"—how she laughed at this notion!—and currently the commander of the Karbarran starship that was transporting life-forms back to the Regent's zoo on Optera. Tesla had been something of a favorite child, but the Regis had become suspicious of his ostensibly metaphysical strivings, and had nothing but distrust for him now that he had allied himself with her estranged husband. Tesla reminded her of the Regent; there was the same burning intensity in his black eyes, the same distention and blush to his feelers. He had no details about the situation on Tirol, other than to note that the Regent had dispatched two additional warships from Optera to see to some new emergency.

"So he's gotten himself into another fix," the Regis sneered.

"A possible entanglement, Your Highness," Tesla replied, offering her a somewhat obligatory and half-hearted salute. "A complication, perhaps. But hardly a 'fix.'"

The two were on Praxis, where a shuttle from the Karbarran ship had put down to take on supplies and specimens. The starship itself, a medley of modular drives and transport units from a dozen worlds, was in orbit near the Praxian moon; it was crewed by slaves, ursine creatures native to Karbarra, a world rich in the Protoculture Peat that fueled the ship.

A sentry announced that one of Tesla's lieutenants wished to speak with him. The Regis granted permission, and the lieutenant entered a moment later. Two Praxians, cuffed at wrist and ankle, followed. They were ravishing creatures, the Regis thought, appraising the duo Tesla had handpicked for the Regent's zoo. Tall, Tiresioid females with thick, lustrous pelts and strategic swaths of primitive costume to offset their smooth nakedness. The Regis confessed to a special fondness for the Praxians and their forested, fertile planet; but Praxis held even greater charms in its volcanic depths. Tesla, however, was unaware of the Genesis Pits she had fashioned here—her underground experiments in creative evolution.

"Shall I take these two to the ship?" Tesla's lieutenant asked.

As Tesla approached the females to look them over more closely, the taller of the two began to spit and curse at him, straining wildly against the cuffs that bound her. The Enforcer turned to silence her and took a bite on the hand.

Ravishing, the Regis told herself, *but warriors to the last*.

Ultimately the lieutenant brought a weapon to bear on the pair; stunned, they collapsed to their knees and whimpered.

Tesla nodded and adopted the folded-arm posture characteristic of his group. "Yes, they'll do fine," he told his soldier. "And see that they're well caged."

The Regis made a scoffing sound when the females had been led out. "My husband's need for *pets*. Instead of furthering his own evolution, he chooses to surround himself with captives—to bask in his self-deluded superiority." She glared at Tesla, finding his form repugnant, in so many ways inferior to the very beings his ship carried like so much stock. "So what are you bringing him this time, *servant*?"

Tesla ignored the slur. "Feel free to inspect our cargo, Your Highness. We have choice samples from Karbarra, Spheris, Garuda, Peryton, and now Praxis. A brief stopover on Haydon IV, and our cages will be full."

The Regis whirled on the scientist. "Haydon IV?" There was a sudden note of concern in her voice. "Have you given clear thought to the possible consequences of such an action?"

Tesla shrugged his massive shoulders. "What could go wrong, Your Highness? Haydon IV is our world now, is it not?"

Haydon IV belongs to no one, the Regis kept to herself. Captives aside, Tesla would be lucky to leave that world alive.

Her husband was about to make a serious mistake, but she could not bring herself to intervene.

* * *

The raucous sound of a static-spiced squawkbox woke Janice from dreams of electric sheep. One eye opened, she spied Minmei on her knees across the room trying to adjust the radio's volume.

"Too late," Janice called out.

Minmei swung around, surprised, fingertips to her lips. "I didn't mean to wake you."

Janice sat up and yawned. "I'm sure." She'd fallen off an hour ago, just after Lynn had left their new quarters for parts unknown. "What is that—a transceiver?"

"No one will tell me anything about Jonathan. This is a kind of, uh, unscrambler. I thought I could pick up some combat reports."

Janice stood up to get a better look at the radio and its decoder feed. "Where'd you get this, Lynn?"

"Promise not to tell?"

Janice looked around the room, calling attention to their confinement. "Who am I going to tell?"

"A woman who works for Dr. Lang got it for me. I explained the situation."

"Stardom does have its advantages, doesn't it?" Janice kneeled down next to Minmei and reached a finger out to readjust the radio's tuner. In a minute she located the com net's frequency.

"—neral Edwards and the Ghost Squadron are already on their way, over," someone was updating. After several seconds of static a second voice said, "That's good news, com two. We've lost Wolff—"

Minmei's gasp erased the next few words; then Janice succeeded in quieting her. "Listen, Lynn, just listen."

". . . had him for a while, but we're getting nothing now. Probably that force field. Everything was roses up till then. No sign of enemy activity."

"You see," Janice said. Minmei was still upset, but hopeful again. "It'll be all right, I promise."

Trembling, Minmei shut off the receiver and got to her feet. "I can't listen to it," she said, wringing her hands. "I just can't think about the horrible things he must be facing." She collapsed, crying, into Janice's open arms.

In the nave of the Royal Hall, the Invid brain looked as though it might succumb to a stroke at any moment. Cells were flashing out one after another as power continued to be shunted to the force shield and energy reserves were depleted. A dozen or so soldiers stood motionless, awaiting the brain's command.

Obsim, too, was on the verge of panic, convinced now that the Regent meant to abandon him there. Looking frightened and desperate, he paced back and forth in front of the brain's bubble chamber under the expressionless gaze of his Enforcer unit.

"Don't watch me like that!" he shouted, suddenly aware of their eyes on him. "Who let the Tiresians escape? It wasn't me, I can tell you that much. Don't I have enough to do already? Do I have to do *everything* myself?" He waved a four-fingered fist at them. "Heads are going to roll, I promise you!"

Obsim tried to avoid thinking about the punishment the Regent would have in store for him. A one-way trip to the Genesis Pits, perhaps, for quick devolvement. Nothing like a little reverse ontogeny to bring someone around. Obsim had seen others go through it; he recalled the sight of them crawling from the pits like land crabs—obscene representations of an evolutionary past the Invid had never lived through, a form that existed only in the shape and design of the Pincer Ships and Shock Troopers.

Obsim stopped pacing to confront the brain.

"Situation," he demanded.

The living computer struggled to revive itself; it floated listlessly in the middle depths of the tank, dull and discolored. Obsim repeated his command.

"Intruders have entered the subterranean vaults and corridors," the brain managed at last.

"Show me!" Obsim barked, fighting to keep his fear in check. "Let the Inorganics be my eyes."

An image began to take shape in the interior of the communicator sphere; gradually it resolved, albeit distorted, as if through a fish-eye lens. Obsim saw a small group of armed invaders moving through the corridors on foot. There were males and females among them, outfitted in helmets, body armor, visual and audio scanners. The Inorganic remained in its place of concealment and allowed them to pass by unharmed.

"There is a second group," the computer announced. "Closer than the first. In the area where the Tiresians' transmissions originated."

That place had not been found; the Inorganics had instead given chase to the Tiresians themselves.

"They entered the way the others left," Obsim speculated. "Could they be in league?"

The brain assessed the probability and flashed the results in the communicator sphere.

Obsim made a disgusted sound. "As I feared. They must be stopped."

"Activating the Inorganics will substantially weaken the shield," the brain said, second-guessing Obsim's command.

"Do it anyway." The scientist straightened his thick neck, allowing him to regard the room's distant ceiling.

"Let them waste their firepower battering us from above, while we destroy their forces below."

"Puppies?" Wolff repeated, exchanging puzzled glances with the radioman. "Ask him to clarify."

Quist listened for a moment. "She says they look like little sheepdogs, sir, except there's something funny about their eyes and they've got some kind of horns. Sounds like there's a whole bunch of 'em."

"You can hear them?"

"Yes, sir."

Wolff pressed the headset to his ear and heard a chorus of shrill barks. "Sounds like they're crying," he commented. "Verify their position. Tell them to sit tight."

Aware that the external links were down, Wolff sent a runner back to the entrance, then gave the signal for the team to move out. His group had encountered nothing but mile after mile of corridor and serviceway, with the occasional cavernous room to break the monotony. By all accounts they were well beneath the Royal Hall, but they had yet to locate a way up. The B team, however, had wandered into a tight maze of even smaller tunnels, and were now in what their lieutenant described as a database lab. That's where they found the puppies.

Half an hour later the two teams reunited.

It was indeed a computer room, consoles and screens galore, but the lieutenant's "puppies" were anything but. The creatures remained huddled together in one corner of the lab, screaming their sad song, loath, it appeared, to leave their spot.

"Sir, I tried to pick one of them up and it just seemed to disappear right out of my arms," the lieutenant told Wolff.

He gave her a dubious look and was about to try for

himself when the voice of one of the corridor sentries rang out.

"We've got movement, people! From all directions!"

Wolff studied the motion-detector display briefly. There was a wider corridor two hundred yards left of the lab that led almost straight to the entrance, with a two or three jags thrown in. He dispatched a second runner with instructions for the tankers, and began to hurry everyone along toward the corridor.

"The . . . *things*, sir, do we leave them?"

Wolff glanced into the room at the Pollinators' white-shag pile. "They're probably just Tirol's way of saying 'rat.' Now let's move!"

Delivered into the upper reaches of Tirol's envelope only moments before, the Ghost Squadron dropped out of Tiresia's dawn like brilliant tongues of flame, half to batter away at the Royal Hall's evaporating shield, while Edwards's elite rushed in to follow the Wolff Pack's trail. Edwards had Cabell's map of that subterranean maze in hand now, and was determined to get to the Invid brain before anyone else.

The commander of the Hovertanks waiting by the crater entrance to the corridors didn't know what to think as he watched General Edwards leap from VT's cockpit and commence what looked like angry strides in his direction. He jumped down from his own turret cockpit and ordered everyone to attention. But it was obvious in an instant that Edwards wasn't interested in formalities or honorifics.

"What's Wolff's position?" Edwards demanded, pulling off his helmet and gloves.

A lieutenant ran forward and produced the sketchy map Wolff had sent back with one of the runners. Edwards snatched the thing away before the officer could lay it out.

"They're about half a mile in, General," the lieutenant said, while Edwards began comparing Wolff's map to the one Cabell had drawn.

"Who was the last man in there?" Edwards asked, preoccupied.

A young corporal presented herself and articulated a summary of the present situation. "The colonel has pulled back to a position . . . here," she said, indicating a corridor junction on the cruder map. "The colonel hopes to lure the enemy along this corridor—"

"It's plain what the colonel proposes to do, Corporal," the squadron commander said before Edwards could turn on the woman.

Edwards studied the maps a moment longer, then grunted in a satisfied way, and began to suit up in the gear one of his number brought over. "I want you to see to it that no one follows us in there, Captain—*no one*, is that understood." Menacingly, Edwards flicked his rifle's selector to full auto and all but brandished the weapon.

"Understood, General, we'll hold them here," the captain responded, trying his best not to have it come out sounding confused.

Edwards tapped the man roughly on the shoulder as he stepped past him. "Good for you." He waved his twelve forward and they disappeared into the floodlit entrance.

Five minutes along, Edwards pulled Colonel Adams aside to give him special instructions. Again they consulted the Tiresian's map, and Edwards pointed out the tunnels that would lead directly to the heart of the Royal Hall.

"Wolff is closer to the Invid brain than he probably realizes," Edwards began. "And if he can break through whatever it is they're throwing against him, he's going to find the way in. Detail three men and make certain that doesn't happen. Give him rear fire if you have to, anything that'll pin him down." Edwards showed Adams the route he would be taking. "I'm going around him, but I need some extra time."

Adams glanced at the corridor's smooth walls and ceiling. "Maybe we can arrange a cave-in for him."

"Do whatever it takes," Edwards said harshly, repocketing the map. "It'll be no one's loss if he doesn't make it out of here."

Elsewhere in the corridors, Wolff had ordered his Pack to open fire. They couldn't see what they were shooting at, but the energy hyphens the enemy was returning were similar to the drone bursts they had faced on the surface. There was nothing in the way of cover, so everyone was either facedown on the floor, or plastered flat against the walls, retreating by odd and even counts through stroboscopic light, blasts of heat, and earsplitting explosions.

Backed around the first jag in the maze, they had a moment to catch their breath, while a horizontal hail of fire flew past them down the central corridor. In response to a tap on the shoulder from the radioman, Wolff raised the faceshield of his helmet. They had reestablished traffic with the Hovertank command.

"We must be outside the field already," Wolff said.

"Negative, sir. Command reports the barrier is softening. The Ghost Squadron's hammering it to death."

"Edwards, huh? Guess we shouldn't be choosy."

Quist smiled. "No, sir. The rest of his team—"

"We got troubles, Colonel," the team's point interrupted breathlessly, motioning up the corridor. "I'm picking up movement. They're boxing us in."

Wolff shifted his gaze between the storm off to their left

and the corridor ahead. "But how . . . They would've had to pass the tanks—"

"Incoming!" someone yelled, and the corridor ceiling took two oblique hits.

Wolff and his team tried to meld with the floor as fire and explosive debris rained down all around them. The ceiling sustained two follow-up hits before he could even lift his head. Then he heard Quist say, "It's coming down!" just when everything began to crumble . . .

"It's no use," Rick announced in the dark, sitting straight up in bed.

Lisa stirred beside him and reached out a hand to find the light pad. He was already out of bed by the time the ceiling spots came on, hands on hips, pacing. Lisa said nothing, deciding to wait until he had walked off some of his frustration. She was exhausted and in no mood for a midnight support session, let alone an argument. Even so, she had managed only an hour of half sleep herself, expecting this very scene.

Rick had been impossible since the Tiresians' capture, and his behavior seemed to be having a kind of contagious effect on everyone around him. Suddenly there was an atmosphere of hopelessness, a sense that the situation had become untenable. Lives had been lost, the spacefold generators had been damaged, the very Masters they had come so far to meet were on their way to Earth . . . For Lisa the events of the past few days had given rise to a peculiar mix of thoughts and feelings; it was not unlike a time ten years ago, when the crew of the SDF-1 had been thrust overnight into a whirlwind of terror. But she refused to permit herself to relive those moments of dread and anticipation, and was determined to steer clear of behavioral ruts. And much to her surprise, she found that she had discovered the strength to meet all the fear and challenges head on, some inner reserve that not only allowed her to *maintain*, but to conquer and forge ahead. She wanted to believe that Rick had made the same discovery, but it was almost as if he had willingly surrendered to the past, and was actually desirous of that retro-gravitation. This from the man who had been so take-charge these past six years, who had devoted himself to the SDF-3's construction and its crucial mission.

"Rick, you've got to get some rest," she said at last. "This isn't doing either of us any good."

It seemed to be the only conversation they could have anymore, and she knew exactly what he was about to say.

"You just don't understand, do you? I *need* to be doing more than just standing around waiting for things to happen. I have to get back where I belong—even if that means resigning my command."

She met Rick's gaze and held it until he turned away. "You're right. Maybe I don't understand you anymore. I mean, I understand your *frustrations*, but you're going to have to tell me why you need to risk your life out there. Haven't you proved yourself a hundred times over, Rick?" Lisa threw up her hands.

"It's my duty to be with my team."

"It's your duty to *command*," she said, raising her voice. "It's not your duty to get yourself killed!"

Rick had an answer ready for delivery when all at once Lisa's com tone sounded. She leaned over, hit the switch, and said, "Admiral Hayes."

It was the bridge: scanners had picked up two Invid troop carriers closing fast on the fortress.

Rick saw Lisa blanch; agitated, she pushed her hair back from her face. He was about to go over to her when his own intercom erupted.

"Tell General Reinhardt to meet me in the Room," Rick

said, responding to the brief message. He switched off, and rushed to the wardrobe, pulling out one of his old flight suits.

"I'm on my way," he heard Lisa say into the com.

She watched him suit up in silence; there were tears in her eyes when he bent over to kiss her good-bye.

"I have to do it," he told her.

Lisa turned away from him. "Expect me to do the same."

CHAPTER
FOURTEEN

*We have a desperate new mission: to mine enough of Fan-
toma's mysterious ore to rebuild the fortress's damaged spacefold
generators, and journey to the other side of the galaxy to save our
beleaguered world from destruction at the hands of the Robotech
Masters. If this mission sounds suspiciously like the old mission,
it's because it is the old mission, played backwards. I am growing
weary of the ironies; I am growing weary of the whole thing.*

The collected Journals of Admiral Rick Hunter

THE CLAM-SHAPED INVID TROOP CARRIERS REMANI-
fested in Fantoma's brightside space, using the giant's
rings for ECM cover and yawning more than a thousand
Pincer Ships into the void, while the Earthforces' superdimensional fortress raised its energy shields and swung itself from stationary orbit. As the fortress's secondary
batteries traversed and ranged in, teams of Alpha and first-
generation Veritech fighters streamed from the launch
bays. Inside the mile-long ship, men and women answered
the call of klaxons and alert sirens, racing to battle stations
and readying themselves in dozens of command posts and
gun turrets. Scanners linked to the Tactical Information
Center's big boards swept and probed; computers tied in to

those same systems assessed, analyzed, executed, and distributed a steady flow of data; techs and processors bent to their assigned tasks, requesting updates and entering commands, hands and fingers a blur as they flew across keyboards, decks, and consoles.

On the enemy's side, things were much less complicated: pilots listened and obeyed, hurling themselves against the Humans' war machine with a passionless intensity, a blind obedience, a violent frenzy...

"Are you sure you want to go through with this?" Max Sterling asked Rick over the tac net. Rick's image was on the VT's right commo screen. Miriya was on the left one. There was still time to turn back.

"Positive, Skull Leader," Rick responded. "And I don't want either of you babysitting me."

"Now, why would we want to do that?" Miriya said.

Rick made a face. "Well, that's what everybody else is trying to do."

Max made light of his friend's plight, but at the same time was fully aware of the concern he felt. He had no worries about Rick's combat skills—he had kept his hand in all these years. But Rick seemed to have forgotten that out here stray thoughts were as dangerous as annihilation discs. *Nothing extraneous in mind or body,* Max was tempted to remind him. Any pilot, no matter how good he or she might be, had to keep those words in mind; it was as much a warning as it was a code. Mechamorphosis was a serious matter even under optimum conditions; but in space combat it meant the difference between life and death.

Max took a long look at the cockpit displays; the Invid crab-ships were just coming into range. The field was so packed the enemy registered as a white blur on his radar screen. Signatures and targeting information came up on one of the peripherals.

"Block party of bandits," Max said evenly, "nine o'clock clear around to three. ETAs on closure are coming in . . ."

"Roger, Skull Leader," Rick radioed back. "Talk about your target-rich environment. They're going to be all over us."

Max could hear a certain excitement, an *enthusiasm*, in Rick's tone.

"We've got a job to do," he advised. "Let's just take them as they come. Nothing fancy. Go for target lock."

Rick acknowledged. "Ready to engage."

Max tightened his hand on the HOTAS. He had visuals on the lead ships now, pincers gleaming in starlight.

An instant later the cold blackness of space was holed by a thousand lights. Death dropped its starting flag and the slaughter recommenced.

Jonathan Wolff had yet to see a finish line for the hellish race his team was running in Tiresia's cruel underground. Four had died instantly in the corridor's collapse, and two more had been pinned under the superheated debris; the rest of the team was huddled on top of each other at the junction, throwing everything they had around the corner. But there was something to be thankful for: the cave-in had only partially sealed off their escape route. Moreover, while the drones were continuing their slow advance, whatever had hit them from behind was gone.

"I'm not picking up any movement, sir," the pointman was shouting above the clamor of the weapons.

Wolff wiped bits of cooled metal from his bodysuit and regarded the mass that had almost buried him. It was the same smooth, ceramiclike material that made up Tiresia's surface streets and many of the city's buildings. Some ferrocrete analogue, he guessed.

A corpsman was seeing to the wounded.

Wolff motioned to Quist and asked in hand signals if they still had contact with the tanks.

The radioman nodded.

"Advise them of our situation and tell them we need support," Wolff said into Quist's ear. "I want to see a fire team down here in ten minutes. And I don't care if they have to blast their way in with the tanks."

Quist crouched down along the wall and began to repeat it word for word. Wolff moved to the medic's side. The wounded soldier was a young woman on temporary duty from one of Grant's units. She couldn't have been older than eighteen, and she was torn up pretty badly. *Powers*, Wolff recalled.

He reached down to brush a strand of damp hair from her face; she returned a weak but stoic smile. Wolff gritted his teeth and stood up, infuriated. He spoke Minmei's name in a whisper and hurried to the junction, his handgun drawn.

Deeper in the maze, Edwards had had his first glimpse of the enemy; but he hadn't stopped to puzzle out or catalog just what it was he had killed. His team was simply firing its way through corridor after corridor, stepping over the bodies and smoking shells their weapons leveled. Hellcats, Scrim, Crann—it made no difference to Edwards; he was closing on the access stairway to the nave of the Royal Hall, and that was all that mattered.

Colonel Adam's splinter group had rejoined the main team after throwing some red-hot rear fire Wolff's way. If they hadn't been entirely successful in burying the Pack alive, Adam's team had at least seen to it that Wolff was no longer in the running for the grand prize, the Invid brain.

Edwards, at point with a gun in each hand, was the first to see the jagged trench Obsim's enforcers had opened in the floor of the Hall. He had no notion of its purpose, but he guessed that the narrow band of overhead light was coming from a room close to the nave, perhaps even adjacent to it. He waved the team to a halt and spent a moment contemplating his options. Surely the brain was aware of their presence, unless the Ghost's bombing runs had given it too much else to think about. Even so, Edwards decided, the enemy was down to the dregs of its force. The things he killed in the corridors were easy prey, and if the Tiresian's word could be trusted, that was all the more reason to assume the brain was preoccupied.

He asked himself whether the brain would expect him to come up through the breach. It would be a difficult and hazardous ascent. But then, why would they have trenched the Hall's floor if they knew about the stairway? He forced any decision from his mind and fell back, allowing his instincts free reign.

And something told him to push on.

Five minutes later the team was creeping up the steep stairway Cabell had described, and Edwards's hand had found the panel stud that would trigger the door. He gave the team the go sign and slammed the switch with the heel of his fist. They poured up and out of the tunnels wailing like banshees, rolling and tearing across the nave's hard floor, lobbing concussion grenades and loosing bursts of death.

Two rows of Invid soldiers who were waiting for them to come through the nave's front entrance were caught by surprise and chopped down in seconds. But two Shock Troopers stepped out of nowhere and began dumping annihilation discs into the hole, frying a quarter of the team before the rest could bring the ships down with a barrage of scanner shots. One of the ships cracked open like an egg, spilling a thick green wash across the floor; the other came apart in an explosion that decapitated the lieutenant.

The nave was filled with fire, smoke, and pandemonium now, but Edwards moved through it like a cat, closing on the brain's towering bubble chamber while the team mopped up. Two seven-foot-tall sentries came at him, spewing bolts of orange flame from their forearm cannons, but he managed to throw himself clear. At the same time he heard the simultaneous discharge of two rocket launchers, and covered himself as the projectiles found their mark.

Edwards was on his feet and back on track before the explosions subsided. Out of the corner of his eye he caught sight of an unarmed robed figure making a mad dash for the brain. The alien started babbling away and waving its arms in a panicked fashion, as if to plead with Edwards to cease fire. Edwards held up his hand and the nave grew eerily silent, save for Obsim's rantings and the crackle of fires.

"What's it saying?" Major Benson asked.

Edwards told them all to keep quiet. "Go ahead, alien, make your pitch."

A rush of sounds left Obsim's mouth, but it was the brain that spoke. In English.

"Invaders, listen to me: you must not destroy the brain. The brain lives and is a power unto itself. Your purpose and desires are understood, and the brain can see to your needs."

Again Edwards had to tell everyone to cut the chatter. The tall Invid continued to mouth sounds from its snaillike head, which was bobbing up and down at the end of a long, thick neck.

"Behold," the brain translated, as the communicator sphere began to glow. "Your people are at this very moment battling our troops near the rings of Tirol's mother-world."

The communicator showed them a scene of fierce fighting, Pincer Ships and Veritechs locked in mortal combat.

Obsim made a high-pitched sound and swung around to face Edwards, hands tucked in his sleeves. "The brain can put an end to it."

Edwards stared at the alien, then leveled his weapons at the bubble chamber. "Showtime."

From the command chair's elevated position on the SDF-3 bridge, Lisa had a clear view of the battle's distant light show, countless strobelike explosions erupting across an expanse of local space like so many short-lived novas. The Veritech teams were successful at keeping most of the Invid ships away from the fortress, and those few that had broken through were taken out with the in-close weapons systems. But the silent flares, the laser-array bolts, and annihilation discs detailed only half the story; for the rest one would have to turn to the tac net and its cacophony of commands and requests, its warnings and imprecations and prayers, its cries and deathscreams.

Lisa had promised to keep it all at arm's length, to maintain a strategic distance, much as she was doing with the fortress. Resolute, she voiced her commands in a clipped, almost severe tone, and when she watched those lights, it was with a deliberate effort to force their meaning from her thoughts.

An update from one of the duty stations brought her swiveling around now to face the threat board: the two motherships had changed course. Lisa called for position and range.

"Approach vectors on-screen, sir," said an enlisted rating tech. "They're coming straight at us."

"The Skull team requests permission to engage."

Lisa whirled around. "Negative! They're to pull back at once."

She turned again to study a heads-up monitor and ordered a course correction. Reinhardt's voice was booming through the squawkboxes, his bearded face on one of the screens. He asked for a second correction, a subtle maneuver to reposition the main gun.

"Coming around to zero-zero-niner, sir. Standing by..."

"Picking up strong EV readings. We're being scanned and targeted."

"Get me Lang," Lisa ordered.

Lang addressed her from a peripheral screen; he had anticipated her question. "We've shunted power from the shields to the main gun, but we're still well protected." At the same time, she heard Reinhardt say, "Prepare to fire on my command."

"Has the Skull pulled out?"

"Uh, checking..."

"Quickly!" she barked.

"Affirmative," the tech stammered. "They're clear."

"On my mark—" Reinhardt started to say.

Suddenly two brilliant flashes flowered into life in front of the ship, throwing blinding light through the viewport. Caught in the grip of the exposions, the fortress was shaken forcefully enough to toss techs from their stations and send them clear across the bridge.

Lisa's neck felt as though it had snapped. She put one hand to the back of her head, and asked if everyone was all right. Sirens somewhere off in the ship had changed tone; the fortress had sustained damage.

"What happened?" Lisa said as reports poured in.

"No trace of the ships, sir."

"God, it's like something *vaporized* them . . ."

Lisa watched in awe as the light show began to wink out.

"What's going on out there—has the enemy disengaged?"

The threat-board tech scratched his head. "No, sir; er, yes, sir. That is, the VT teams report all enemy ships inactive. They're dead in space."

The tech on the SDF-3 bridge wasn't the only one scratching his head. In a corridor fifty feet beneath Tiresia's Royal Hall, Jonathan Wolff was doing the same thing.

"They just stopped firing," one of the Pack was saying.

Certainly no one was about to argue with that or be anything less than overjoyed, but the question remained: *why*?

Wolff poked his head around the corner of the corridor like some of the others were doing, and saw half-a-dozen bipedal Inorganics stopped not ten years from the junction. And not simply stopped, but shut down—frozen. Presently, everyone who could stand was out in the middle of the central corridor gaping at the silent drones; it was the first time any of them had had a chance to inspect the things up close, and they found themselves relieved enough to comment on their remarkable design. Wolff, however, put a quick end to it.

The requested fire team had arrived without incident from the other side of the collapse. Wolff sent the wounded back, along with most of the original squad—it was looking better for Powers—and pushed on toward the Royal Hall. The field command post had yet to hear word one from Edwards's team.

They remained cautious and alert as they regained the ground they had surrendered. Wolff led them past the computer room and on into a confusing warren of tunnels and ducts. Along the way they passed dozens of Inorganics in the same state of suspended animation. But at last they came to the trench Edwards had seen earlier, and instinctively Wolff knew they were close to reaching the center.

"It's blue smoke and mirrors," Edwards sneered as the image in the communicator sphere de-rezzed. He had seen the explosions that wiped out the two troop carriers, but remained unconvinced. "You could be running home movies for all I know."

Obsim made a puzzled gesture and turned to the brain.

"You have a suspicious mind, Invader." The synthesized voice had a raspy sound to it now, as though fatigued.

"That's right, Mister Wizard, and I'm also the one holding a gun to your head." Edwards half turned to one of his men. "I want immediate confirmation on what we just saw. See if you can raise anyone."

The radioman moved off and Edwards continued. "But if you *are* on the level, I've got to say I'm impressed. The brain is certainly far too valuable to destroy—but then again, it's far too dangerous to remain operative."

Obsim showed Edwards his palms, then fumbled to open a concealed access panel in the bubble chamber's hourglass-shaped base.

"The brain can be deactivated. It can be yours to command."

Interested, Edwards stepped forward, brandishing the weapon.

"Go ahead, alien."

Obsim pulled two dermatrode leads from the panel and placed them flat against the center of his head; his fingers meanwhile tapped a command sequence into the panel's ten-key touchpad. At the same time, the brain seemed to compress as it settled toward the bottom of the chamber. After a moment Obsim reversed the process, causing an effervescent rush inside the tank as the brain revived.

"Again," said Edwards, and Obsim repeated it. Then it was Edwards's turn to try, while Colonel Adams held a gun to Obsim's snout. Edwards got it right on the first take; the brain was asleep.

Edwards shut the panel and stood up, grinning at the alien. "You've been a most gracious host." Without taking his eyes off Obsim, he yelled, "Do we have that confirmation, soldier?"

"Affirmative," came the reply.

"Waste him," Edwards said to Adams.

The burst blew out the Invid scientist's brain; the body collapsed in a heap, Obsim's once-white robes drenched in green.

"Wargasm." Adams laughed.

Edwards regarded each of his men individually; the gaze from his single eye said much more than any verbal warning could.

Just then, Human voices could be heard on the staircase. Edwards and his men swung around, weapons armed, only to find Jonathan Wolff crawling cautiously from the hole.

Wolff took a look around the room, as his team followed him out. There were two devastated Shock Trooper ships and twenty or more Invid corpses. Wolff had seen the charred remains of what looked like four men on the steps. Now he focused his attention on the bubble chamber.

"This the thing the Tiresians were talking about, sir?"

"That's it, Colonel," Edwards said.

Wolff glanced down at Obsim, then at Edwards. He had questions for the general, questions about what had gone on in the corridors and what had gone on here, but he sensed it wasn't the right time—not with Edwards's team looking as though they weren't full yet. Ultimately, he said, "Too bad I didn't arrive sooner, sir."

"You're lucky you didn't," Adams told him with a sly smile. "It was a real horror show."

"Yeah," Wolff mused, watching Edwards's men trade looks, "I can imagine."

Edwards broke the subsequent silence by ordering his radioman to make contact with the ship.

Edwards was jubilant. "Tell them the mission was a complete success."

Without warning, he slapped Wolff on the back.

"Smile, Colonel—you're a hero!"

CHAPTER
FIFTEEN

It was without question a mind-boost for [Edwards], comparable to the one Dr. Emil Lang had received while reconning the SDF-1. And in the same way Lang became almost instantly conversant with Zor's science, Robotechnology, Edwards became conversant with the lusts and drives of the Invid Regent. This, however, was not engrammation, but amplification. Edwards and the Regent were analogues of one another: scarred, vengeful, and dangerous beings.

Constance Wildman, *When Evil Had Its Day: A Biography of T. R. Edwards*

THE BATTLE WAS OVER AND AN UNEASY CALM PREvailed; no one aboard the SDF-3 was sure how long the lull would last, but if the Robotech War had taught them anything, it was that they should make the most of tranquil interludes.

None dared call it peace.

One by one the inert Invid ships were destroyed, after it was determined that the pilots were all dead. Dr. Lang and Cabell speculated that the living computer, in addition to vaporizing the troop carriers and shutting down the Inorganics, had issued some sort of blanket suicide directive. Many among the RDF found this difficult to accept, but the explanation was strengthened by Cabell's recounting of equally puzzling and barbarous acts the Invid had carried out. On the moon's surface, a building-to-building search was under way, and most of Tiresia's humanoid population had already been freed. The hundreds of drones that littered Tiresia's subterranean passageways remained lifeless; one day soon that labyrinth would be sealed up, along with the Royal Hall and the sleeping brain itself. But that would not be before Cabell had had a chance to show Lang around, or before the Pollinators had been rescued and removed.

There was something of a mutual-admiration society in the works between Lang and the bearded Tiresian scientist. And while it was true that the Expeditionary mission had "liberated" Tirol, it was questionable whether that could have been achieved without Cabell and Rem's intelligence. More to the point, Cabell's importance in the work that lay ahead for the mission's robotech teams was beyond dispute. Lang had taken every opportunity to press him for details of the mining operation, and was eagerly awaiting the RDF's clearance for a recon landing on Fantoma. Earth's survival depended on their being able to mine enough ore to rebuild the SDF-3's damaged engines, and to fold home before the Masters arrived.

During the course of the discussions, Lang learned something of Tirol's gradual swing toward militarism in the years following Zor's great discoveries. Cabell spoke of a short-lived but wonderful time when *exploration* had been his people's main concern. Indeed, the Zentraedi themselves were originally created to serve those ends as miners, not as the galactic warriors they would eventually become. The defoliation of Optera, the Invid homeworld, had been their first directive under the reconfigured imperative. There followed a succession of conquests and police actions, and, ultimately, warfare against the very creatures whose world they had destroyed.

Then they had traveled halfway across the galaxy to die . . .

As Lang listened he began to feel a kind of sympathy for the Invid; it was obvious there were mysteries here even Cabell had yet to penetrate. But what also gripped Lang was a sudden existential dread, rooted in the fact that war was not something humankind had invented, but was pervasive throughout the known universe. It brought to mind the rumors he had been hearing, to the effect that General Edwards was already pressing for the construction of an entire *fleet* of warships. According to his camp, the return mission had to recognize a new priority: the idea of peaceful, preventative negotiations was no longer viable— not when war against the Masters was now viewed as a certainty.

Oddly enough, Cabell took no issue with Edwards's demands. It was not so much that he wished to see the Masters of his race obliterated—although he himself would have gladly put to death the cloned body politic they had created—it was his unassailable fear of the Invid.

"Of course I applaud this victory and the freeing of my people," Cabell told him. "But you must believe me when I tell you, Doctor, that the greatest threat to your planet is the Invid. Put aside your sympathy—I know, I saw it in your face. They are not the race they once were; they are homeless now, and *driven*. They will stop at nothing to regain their precious Flowers, and if that matrix exists— they will find it."

Lang wore a sardonic look. "Perhaps it would be better to do nothing—except pray that the Masters find the matrix and leave."

"I fear they will not leave, Doctor. They have all they

need with them, and your world will be nothing but a new battleground."

"So what choice do we have?"

"Defeat them here, Doctor. Exterminate them before you face the Masters."

Lang was aghast. "You're talking about genocide, Cabell."

Cabell shook his head sadly. "No, I am talking about *survival*. Besides," the old man thought to add, "your race seems to have a penchant for that sort of thing."

Rick was among the dozens of VT pilots who had ended up in sick bay. There was no tally of the dead and wounded yet, but the hospital was already overcrowded and shuttles were still bringing up men and women from the moon's surface.

When Lisa first received word of his injuries she thought she might faint; but she was relieved now, knowing that his condition had improved from guarded to good, and that he had been moved out of ICU and into a private room. But she wasn't exactly rushing to his side, and couldn't help but feel somehow vindicated for her earlier remarks. At the same time, she recalled the last visit she had paid Rick in sick bay. It was shortly before the SDF-1 had left Earth for a second time—ordered off by Russo's council—and Khyron's Botoru had been waging a savage attack against the fortress. Rick was badly wounded during a missile barrage Lisa herself had ordered. She remembered how frightened and helpless she had felt that cool Pacific morning, seeing him in the throes of shock and delirium, his head turbaned in gauze and bandages . . . It was a painful memory even now, eight years later, but she was determined not to let it soften the anger that had crept in to replace her initial dismay—an easy enough challenge when she found him sitting up in bed and grinning, well-attended by the nursing staff.

"Here you go, hero," she said, placing a small gift on the sheet, "I brought you something."

Rick unwrapped the package and glanced at the audio disc it contained—a self-help guide that had been a best-seller on Earth and was enjoying an enormous popularity on the fortress. He showed Lisa a confused look. "*The Hand That's Dealt You* . . . What's this supposed to mean?"

Lisa sat on the edge of the bed. "I think it's something you should hear."

Rick put the disc aside and stared at her a moment. "You're still angry."

"I want to know what you intend to do, Rick."

He looked away, down at his bandaged arm. "I'm going to meet with the Council tomorrow."

Lisa couldn't believe what she was hearing, but managed to keep her voice even and controlled. "You're making a big mistake, Rick. Can I talk you out of it?"

He reached for her hand and met her gaze. "No, babe. I know where I belong. I just want you to respect my decision."

She let go of his hand and stood up. "It's not a matter of respect, Rick. Can't you understand that you've picked the worst possible moment to resign? Who else has your experience? This ship is as much yours as anyone's, and Lang is going to need you to supervise the recon—"

"I don't want to hear it."

Lisa huffed at him. "Edwards will be taking over. Doesn't *that* mean anything to you?" Lisa paced away from the bed and whirled around. "You haven't heard the latest, have you?"

"And I don't want to. I'm a pilot."

"You're a disappointment," she said as she left the room.

On another level of the fortress, Jean Grant was crying in her husband's arms; Vince, in his usual fashion, was trying to be strong about it, but there were tears in his eyes. They had just shuttled up from the GMU, their first time offworld in days, and fatigue and intensity finally had had a chance to catch up with them. Perhaps in a last-ditch effort to escape this moment, Jean had tried to run off to sick bay to assist the med teams, but Vince had restrained her. Max and Miriya were present in the couple's spacious cabin.

Max handed them both a drink. "Medicine for melancholy," he said, forcing a smile.

Max, too, wore his share of bandages under his uniform; there had been more than the usual complement of close calls, at least one of which could be traced to his protective attitude toward Rick. Max had suffered some minor burns because of it, but Rick had nearly gotten himself killed. That he saved Rick's life was all that mattered —a secret only he and Miriya shared.

Jean thanked him for the drink and wiped her cheeks with the palms of her hands. "What are we going to do?" she put to all of them.

"We're going to pitch in and make it happen," Vince said, knocking back the drink in one gulp. "It can't take forever to get the generators back in shape."

Max and Miriya traded looks. "Five years," she said.

Jean gasped. "Miriya, no!"

"That's just Lang's first estimate," Max added hurriedly, trying to be helpful. "And I'm sure he's playing it well on the safe side."

"But *five years*, Max . . . The kids . . ."

Vince put a massive arm around his wife's trembling shoulders and quieted her. "They're both better off where they are."

"With war on the way?" Jean's face flushed with anger. "Don't patronize me, any of you!" Distraught, she sighed and apologized.

Miriya said, "Even if it takes five years we'll reach Earth ahead of the Masters. They abandoned Tirol ten years ago, and Cabell's guess is that it will take them another ten."

"Estimates," Jean said. "Is that how we'll explain it to Bowie and Dana—that we guessed wrong in thinking the Masters would be here?"

No one had an answer for her.

"So *this* is all that remains of Tirol's children."

Arms akimbo, Breetai drew himself up to his full Micronized height and made a disappointed sound. All around him Tiresia's humanoid citizenry—the weak and aged fringe who had taken to Tirol's wastes during the Great Transition—were being cared for by med-staff personnel from the GMU, which had been moved from its LZ to an area near the center of the ruined city. Elsewhere, Destroids and Hovertanks patrolled the streets, continuing their search-and-sweep and cordoning off restricted areas, including the Royal Hall's vast circular plaza.

Exedore, who had shuttled down to the surface with members of Lang's Robotech team, heard the anger and frustration in Breetai's words. And he knew that Breetai spoke for all the Zentraedi under his command.

"You would no doubt have preferred a face-to-face encounter with the Masters, Commander."

"I won't deny it." He looked down at his companion. "I feel . . . what is the word, Exedore?"

"*Cheated*, my lord."

Breetai inclined his head knowingly. "Yes. Although . . ."

Exedore raised an eyebrow.

". . . on some level, we failed."

To recapture Zor's ship and return the matrix, Exedore completed. It was the Imperative reasserting its hold, the Masters' cruel imprint. He was tempted to point out that the matrix would only have made it as far as Dolza's hands in any case. But what was the use of contradicting Breetai? Besides, Exedore had more pressing concerns on his mind.

"Commander," he said at last, "have you arrived at a decision yet?"

Breetai grunted. "You have become quite the diplomat, Exedore." He turned to regard Fantoma's sinister crescent in the skies behind him, thinking, *Zarkopolis, where my real past lies buried*. To be returned there after so much space and time . . .

"We will comply with Lang's request."

Exedore smiled. *An even older imperative*. "It was meant to be," he said, eyes fixed on the living remnants of the Masters' fallen empire.

T. R. Edwards studied his reflection, leaning in toward the mirror in his quarters, fingertips playing across the raised and jagged devastation of his face. The scars could easily have been erased by microsurgical techniques, but a *cosmetic* solution was the last thing Edwards desired. In their raw ugliness, they were a constant reminder of the deep-seated injuries spread through the rest of his body and soul—areas no laser scalpel could reach or transform.

He was feverish, and had been so since the incidents in the Royal Hall; it was almost as if his brief contact with the Invid brain had stirred something within him. Beneath the fever's physical haze his thinking was lighting-quick and inspired; his goal was clear, and the path to it well-marked. He realized now that he had been guilty of a kind of reductionist approach to both purpose and destiny. He had convinced himself that Earth was the star—a Ptolemaic sin—when actually the planet was little more than a supporting player in a much grander drama. But he was finally beginning to understand that *there were worlds for the taking*!

He rationalized his failures, however, blaming fate for having kept him Earthbound while the SDF-1 had spent two years of cosmic journeying.

Let Zand and Moran and Leonard play their little games on Earth. Edwards laughed to himself. *And let the Masters arrive to* soften *things up*. In the meantime he would construct the fleet to conquer all of them! It was going to require a good deal of manipulation to wrest the Council from Hunter and Lang's control, but he suddenly felt more than up to the task. Perhaps if Hunter could be fooled into setting off on some secondary mission . . .

Edwards savored the thought. Lang would be preoccupied with overseeing the mining project, Reinhardt was no problem, and the Zentraedi would be offworld. That still left Max Sterling and that troublemaker Wolff, but how difficult could it be to undermine them?

Edwards struck a gleeful, triumphant pose in front of the mirror. "No more demolished man," he said to his reflection. "Let the games begin."

A week went by, then another, and still there was no sign of the Invid. The high command began to wonder if the battle for Tirol hadn't been won after all. With the Masters gone and no trace of the Flowers of Life, the Invid had little use for the world; so perhaps they had simply disregarded it. Cabell spoke of other planets the Invid were thought to occupy—worlds that had been seeded by Zor. Surely those constituted more than enough to satisfy them; and moreover, what quarrel could they possibly have with Earth at this stage of the game?

With all this in mind, a gradual transfer of personnel, stores, and equipment to the surface of Tirol had commenced. Refortified, Tiresia would serve as the RDF's tactical and logistical headquarters. The SDF-3, with a substantially reduced crew and half the VT squadrons, was to remain in stationary orbit, protecting both the moon and the soon-to-be-operative mining colony on Fantoma.

Hope and optimism began to find their way back into the mission once everyone accepted the conditions of the extended stay, and it was only a matter of time before a certain celebratory air took hold. Terrans and Tiresians worked side-by-side clearing away the horrors of the recent past, and the city seemed to rejuvenate. Both sides had known death and suffering at the same alien hands, so there was already a bond of sorts. The Council, hoping to enlarge in this and at the same time take advantage of Earth's New Year's Day, finally scheduled a holiday.

A rousing set from Minmei and Janice accompanied by their newly-formed backup band kicked things off. The superstar of the SDF-1 performed with an enthusiasm she hadn't demonstrated in years, and dug into everyone's collective past to blow the dust off songs like "We Can Win" and "Stagefright," classics for most of the crowd, nostalgia for some. After the set she danced the night away with heroes and rear-echelon execs, but spent most of that time in the embrace of Jonathan Wolff. No one was surprised when the two of them disappeared together halfway through the festivities.

Nor was Dr. Lang surprised to see that his AI creation

had zeroed in on Rem, whom Lang, despite Cabell's claims to the contrary, seemed desperate to accept as Zor incarnate. He had been meaning to urge Janice to move in just that direction—for who knew what secrets Rem and Cabell might be hiding?—but Lang's personal encoding of the android had made that unnecessary: Janice was as attracted to Zor's likeness as Lang was. Cabell, unaware of Janice's laboratory origins, seemed positively delighted by the fact that she and Rem had coupled off; round midnight he was even out on the dance floor executing a Tiresian clogging step that looked to some like an old Geppetto jig straight out of *Pinocchio*.

Elsewhere in the crowd, Jack Baker and Karen Penn were talking; when Vince Grant had rescinded the order that had kept them both confined to quarters, Karen had reversed her own decision never to speak to Jack again.

"Come on, Karen—just one dance," Jack was saying, tailing her as she threaded her way across the floor. "One dance is gonna kill ya?"

Karen stopped short and whirled on him; he brought his hands up expecting a spin kick, and she began to laugh. "I'm talking to you, Jack—isn't that enough?"

"Well, no, dammit, it's *not* enough." Karen was back in motion again. Jack ignored a bit of razzing from friends and set out after her.

"All right," she said, finally. "But just *one*." She held up a finger.

"My choice?"

"Anything you want. Let's just get it over with."

He waited until the band played a long, slow number.

"You gotta admit," he said, holding her, "it was a good ride while it lasted."

She held him at arm's length for a moment, then smiled. "The best . . ."

Not everyone was dancing, however. Or smiling. Years later, in fact, some would say that the "New Year's" celebration showed just how factionalized the Expeditionary mission had become in less than a month out of Earth-space. At the center sat Lang, Exedore, and the Council, joined now by Tirol's unofficial representative, Cabell; while the fringe played host to two discreet groups, Edwards's surly Ghost Riders, and Breetai's Zentraedi, on what would be one of their last nights as Micronized warriors. And separate from any of these groups were certain RDF teams, the Skull Squadron, the Wolff Pack, Grant's GMU contingent.

Rick Hunter, recovered from his wounds, seemed to occupy a middle ground he and Lisa had staked out for themselves. They had been trying hard to make some sense of their dilemma, slowly, sometimes painfully. But at least they were lovers again, back on the honeymoon trail, and confident that things would work themselves out. The Council had yet to rule on Rick's request, and for the time being the topic was shelved.

"Home, sweet home," Rick was telling Lisa. He put his arm around her and motioned with his chin to Tirol's star-studded sky. "We'll have to draw up a new set of constellations."

Lisa rested her head on his shoulder.

"Which way's Earth?"

Lisa pointed. "There—our entire local group."

Rick was silent a moment. "Whaddaya say we dance, Mrs. Hunter?"

"Thought you'd never ask."

They walked hand-in-hand toward the center of the floor, and were just into their first step when the music came to an abrupt stop. Murmurs swept through the crowd and everyone turned to the stage. Dr. Lang was at a mike stand, apologizing for the interruption.

"Listen to me, everyone," he was saying. "We have just received a dispatch from the SDF-3. An unidentified ship has just entered the Valivarre system. It is decelerating and on a probable course for Tirol. General Reinhardt has put the fortress on high alert, and suggests that we do the same. Skull and Ghost Squadrons are ordered to report to the shuttle-launch facilities at once. CD personnel are to report to their unit commanders immediately. Admiral Hayes and Admiral Hunter—"

"Lisa, come on," Rick shouted, tugging at her arm.

She resisted, hoping she would wake from this, so they could continue their dance—

"Come on!" Rick was repeating . . .

The war had come between them again!

The following chapter is a sneak preview of DARK DEBUT—Book II in the SENTINELS saga.

All I have learned of the Shapings of the Protoculture tell me that it does not work randomly, that there is a grand design or scheme. I feel that we have been brought here, kept here, for some reason.

Yet, what purpose can there be in SDF-3's being stranded here on Tirol for perhaps as long as five years? And during that time will the Robotech Masters be pursuing their search for Earth?

Because many tempers are short, I do not mention the Shaping; I'm a little too long in the tooth, I fear, for hand-to-hand confrontations with homesick, frightened, and frustrated REF fighters.

Dr. Emil Lang's Personal journal of the SDF-3 Mission

ON CAPTURED TIROL, AFTER A FIERCE BATTLE, THE Humans and their Zentraedi allies—the Robotech Expeditionary Force—licked their wounds, then decided it was time to mark the occasion of their triumph. It was, as nearly as they could calculate, New Year's Eve.

But far out near the edge of Tirol's system, a newcomer appeared—a massive space-going battleship, closing in on the war-torn, planet-size moon.

Our first victory celebration, young Susan Graham exulted. *What a wonderful party!* She was just shy of sixteen, and to her it was the most romantic evening in human history.

She was struggling to load a bulky cassette into her sound-vid recorder while scurrying around to get a better angle at Admirals Rick Hunter and Lisa Hayes Hunter. They had just stood up, in full-dress uniforms, clasping white-gloved hands, apparently about to dance. There had been rumors that the relationship between the two senior officers of the Robotech Expeditionary Force was on shaky ground, but for the moment at least, they seemed altogether in love.

Sue let out a short, romantic sigh and envied Lisa Hunter. Then her thoughts returned to the cassette which she was tapping with the heel of her hand. A lowly student-trainee, Sue had to make do with whatever equipment she could find at the G-5 Public Information shop, Psy-ops, Morale or wherever.

At last the cassette was in place, and she began to move toward her quarry.

In Tiresia, the planet-moon's shattered capital city, the Royal Hall was aglow. The improvised lighting and decorations reemphasized the vast, almost endless size of the place.

The lush ballroom music remained slow—something from Strauss, Karen Penn thought; something even Jack Baker could handle. As she had expected, he asked her to waltz a second time.

And he wasn't too bad at it. The speed and reflexes that made him such a good Veritech pilot—*almost as good as I am*, she thought—made him a passable dancer. Still, she maintained her aloof air, gliding flawlessly, making him seem clumsy by comparison; otherwise, that maddening brashness of his would surface again at any second.

They were about the same height, five-ten or so, he redheaded and freckled and frenetic, she honey-blonde and smooth-skinned and model-gorgeous, and long since tired of panting male attention. Jack had turned eighteen two months ago; Karen would celebrate her majority in three more weeks.

They were like oil and water, cats and dogs, Unseducible Object and Irrepressible Force, ever since they had met. But they had also been battle-comrades, and now they swayed as the music swelled, and somehow their friendly antagonism was put aside, at least for the moment.

The deepspace dreadnought was a bewildering, almost slapdash length of components: different technologies, different philosophies of design, even different stages of scientific awareness, showed in the contrasts among its various modules. From it, scores of disparate weapons bristled and many kinds of sensors probed.

With Tirol before it, the motley battle-wagon went on combat alert.

On the outer rim of the ballroom, members of General Edwards's Ghost Squadron and Colonel Wolff's Wolff Pack traded hostile looks, but refrained from any overt clashes; Admiral Lisa Hunter's warnings, and her promises of retribution, had been very specific on that point.

Edwards was there, a haughty, splendidly military figure, his sardonic handsomeness marred by the half cowl that covered the right half of his head.

Per Lisa's confidential order, Vince Grant and his Ground Mobile Unit people were keeping an eye on the rivals, ready to break up any scuffles. So far things seemed to be peaceful—nothing more than a bit of glowering and boasting.

Hanging in orbit over the war-torn ruin of Tirol, Super

Dimensional Fortress Three registered the rapid approach of the unidentified battleship.

SDF-3 had been tardy in detecting the newcomer; the Earth warship's systems had been damaged in the ferocious engagement that had destroyed her spacefold apparatus, and some systems were still functioning far short of peak efficiency.

But she had spotted the possible adversary now. Following procedure, SDF-3 went to battle stations, and communications personnel rushed to open downlinks with the contingent on Tirol's surface.

Perhaps the strangest pair at the celebration were Janice Em, the lovely and enigmatic singer, and Rem, assistant to the Tiresian scientist Cabell.

Janice was Dr. Lang's creation, an android, an Artificial Person, though she was unaware of it. Rem was the clone of the original Zor, the discoverer of Protoculture, creator of miracles and holocausts, and also unaware of it.

Lang shook his head and reminded himself that the Shapings of the Protoculture were not to be defied. He was really quite happy that the two were drawn together.

He turned to Cabell, the ancient lone-survivor of the scientists of Tirol.

What was once the gorgeous cityscape of Tiresia, and magnificent gardens surrounding the Royal Hall, was now only a blasted wasteland.

Above was a jade-green crescent of Fantoma, the massive planet that Tirol circled. Its alien beauty hid the ugliness that Lynn-Minmei knew to be there in the light of Valivarre, the system's primary. The green Fantoma-light cast a spell with magic all its own. How could the scene of so much death and suffering be so unspeakably beautiful?

She shivered a bit, and Colonel Jonathan Wolff slipped his arm around her. Minmei could feel from the way he had moved closer that he wanted to kiss her; she wasn't sure whether she felt the same or not.

He was the debonair, tigerishly brave, good-looking Alpha-Wolf of the Wolff Pack—and had rescued her from certain death, melodramatic as it might sound to others. Still, there was a danger in love; she had learned that, not once but several times now.

Wolff could see what was running through Minmei's thoughts. He feasted his eyes on her, hungered for her. The Big, Bad Wolff, indeed—an expression he had never liked.

Only this time, the Big Bad was bewitched, and helpless. She was the blue-eyed, black-haired gamine whose voice and guileless charm had been the key to Human victory in the Robotech War. She was the child-woman who had, unknowingly, tormented him with fantasies he could not exorcise by day, and with erotic fever-dreams by night.

She hadn't moved from the circle of his arm; she looked at him, eyes wide as those of a startled doe. Wolff leaned closer, lips parting.

I love her so much, Rick thought, as he and Lisa went to join the dancing. His wife's waist was supple under his gloved hand; her eyes shone with fondness. He felt himself breaking into a languorous smile, and she beamed at him.

I can't live without her, he knew. *All these problems between us—we'll find some way to deal with them. Because otherwise life's not worth living.*

The music had just begun when it stopped again, raggedly, as Dr. Lang quieted people from the mike stand. The ship's orchestra's conductor stood to one side, looking peeved but apprehensive.

Everyone there had already served in war. Something in side them anticipated the words. "Unidentified ship... course for Tirol... Skull and Ghost Squadrons... Admiral Hayes and Admiral Hunter..."

The war's come between us again.

Rick started off in a dash, but stopped before he had gone three steps, realizing his wife was no longer with him. Fortunately, in all the confusion, only one person noticed.

He looked back and saw Lisa waiting there, head erect, watching him. He realized he had reacted with a fighter jock's reflexes, the headlong run of a hot-scramble.

It was the argument they had been having for days, for weeks now—tersely, in quick exchanges, by day; wearily, taxing the limits of their patience with one another, by night. Rick was a pilot, and had come to the conclusion that he couldn't be—*shouldn't* be—anything else. Lisa insisted that his job now was to command, to oversee Flight Group ops. He was to do the job he had been chosen to do because nobody else could do it.

Rick saw nothing but confidence in his wife's eyes as she looked at him, her chin held high—that, and a proud set to her features.

Sue Graham, wielding her aud-vid recorder, had caught the whole thing, the momentary lapse in protocol, in confidence—in love. Now, she rewound the tape a bit, so that the sight of Rick Hunter dashing off from his wife would be obliterated, and began recording over it.

Just as people were turning to the Admirals-Hunter, Rick stepped closer to Lisa. In that time, conversation and noise died away, and the Royal Hall itself, weighted by its eons of history and haunting events, seemed to be listening, evaluating. Rick's high dress boots clacked on an alien floor that shone like a black mirror.

He offered her his arm, formal and meticulously correct, inclining his head to her. "Madam?"

She did a shallow military curtsy, supple in her dress-uniform skirt, and laid her hand on his forearm. The whole room was listening and watching; Rick and Lisa had reminded everyone what the REF was, and what was expected of it.

"Orders, Admiral?" Rick asked his wife crisply, loudly, in his role as second-ranking-officer-present. By speaking those words, he officially ended the ball and put everyone on notice that they were on duty.

Lisa, suddenly their rock, gazed about at them. She didn't have to raise her voice very much to be heard. "You all know what to do—ladies, gentlemen.

"We will treat this as a red alert. SDF-3 will stand to General Quarters. GMU and other ground units report to combat stations; all designated personnel will return to the Dimensional Fortress."

Already, there was movement as people strode or hurried to their duties. But no one was running, Lisa had given them back their center.

"Fire control and combat operations officers will ensure that no provocative or hostile acts are committed," she said in a sharp voice. "I will remind you that we are *still* on a *diplomatic mission*.

"Carry on."

Men and women were moving purposefully, the yawning hall quickly clearing. Lisa turned to an aide, a commo officer. "My respects to the Plenipotentiary Council, and would they be so gracious as to convene a meeting immediately upon my return to SDF-3."

The aide disappeared; Lisa turned to Rick. "If you please?"

Rick, his wife on his arm, turned toward the shuttle

grounding area. REF personnel made way for them. Rick let Lisa set the pace: businesslike, but not frantic.

When the shuttle was arrowing up through Tirol's atmosphere for SDF-3 rendezvous, the two studied preliminary reports while staff officers ran analyses and more data poured in. Rick paused for a moment to look at his wife, as she meditated over the most recent updates.

He covered her hand with his for a moment; squeezed it. "We owe each other a waltz, Lisa."

She gave him a quick, loving smile, squeezing his hand back. Then she turned to issue more orders to her staff.

To Rem, the Humans and their REF mission had been bewildering from the beginning, but never more so than now.

With this news of a unidentified warship, he and his mentor Cabell—who had been a father to him, really, and more than a father—were chivvied toward the shuttle touchdown area, to await their turn to be lifted up to the SDF-3. Their preference in the matter wasn't asked; they were an important—perhaps crucial—military intelligence resource now, even though they were just as mystified as anybody else.

There were confused snatches of conversation and fragments of scenes as Rem guided Cabell along in the general milling.

There were the two young cadets Rem had come to know as Karen Penn and Jack Baker. They had been pressed into service as crowd controllers and expediters of the evacuation. Jack kept trying to catch Karen's eye and call some sort of jest or other; she just spared him the occasional withering glance and concentrated on her duties

Rem couldn't blame her. What could be funny about a

situation like this? Was Jack psychologically malfunctional?

Then there was the singer, Minmei, Janice Em's partner, possessed of a voice so moving that it defied logic, and a face and form of unsettling appeal. The one they called Colonel Wolff seemed to be trying to usher her along, seemed to be proprietary toward her, but she wasn't having any of it. In fact, it appeared that she was about to burst into that startling and alarming human physiological aberration called *tears*.

The Ghost and Skull and GMU teams were cooperating like a mindlinked triumverate, though Rem had seen them ready to come to blows only a short time before.

He looked about for Janice Em, Minmei's partner and harmony and, in some measure, alter ego, but couldn't see her. She had been with Lang only moments before, but now Lang was gone, too. Rem tried to push troubling thoughts from his mind, such as the rumors that were rife about Lang and Janice. Lang was supposed to be like an uncle to her, though some said he was "much more."

But *what*? Rem barely understood the concept "uncle," and had no idea what "much more" might mean. Yet his cheeks flushed, and he felt a puzzling rage when he thought of Jan having some nebulous relationship to Lang that would make the old Human scientist more important to her than, than . . .

Then all at once Rem and Cabell were being rushed into a shuttle, and a sliding hatch cut off the haunted nighttime view of ruined Tiresia.

214

ABOUT THE AUTHOR

Jack McKinney has been a psychiatric aide, fusion-rock guitarist and session man, worldwide wilderness guide, and "consultant" to the U.S. Military in Southeast Asia (although they had to draft him for that).

His numerous other works of mainstream and science fiction—novels, radio and television scripts—have been written under various pseudonyms.

He currently resides in Ubud, on the Indonesian island of Bali.

She turned her head. Leon Cooley sat hunched on
the stool at the end of the bar, nursing a longneck.
Not bad-looking, for a murdering piece of convict
shit. Rosy brown, bald, long eyelashes, with a gap
between his two front teeth. He looked almost
sweet; that threw you off if you didn't know his
history. Or if you weren't a cop.

Cooley was on death row for two counts of murder. He might have beat the first count eventually.
He killed someone while driving drunk—arguably
an accident. But there was the matter of the second
count: He murdered a prison guard. Killed him
with those gappy teeth. No way an incompetent
public defender could claim *that* was a tragic error
in judgment.

Now Cooley had a date with the needle in two
years and change; and he and Grace shared Earl in
a sort of spiritual ménage à trois—so Earl could
teach them how to stay out of hell.

"You know how what feels?" Grace asked him
coldly. "Facing an execution? Have you got disciples,
Leon? Or have you already been put to death?"

Cooley was drinking a beer. Sweaty rings of condensation gleamed on the varnished wood—maybe
like planets, God's vast universe. Earl wanted everything to be so cosmic, but when you were slogging
around in the humanity, it really wasn't.

Also by Nancy Holder

The Wicked series: *Witch, Curse, Legacy, Spellbound,*
   and *Resurrection*
Pretty Little Devils
Possessions
Buffy the Vampire Slayer: Queen of the Slayers (and many
   others)
Angel: The Casefiles (and many others)
Smallville: Silence and *Hauntings*
Athena Force: Disclosure
The Pretty Freekin Scary series (written as Chris P. Flesh)

SAVING GRACE

CRY ME A RIVER

NANCY HOLDER

BALLANTINE BOOKS • NEW YORK

Saving Grace: Cry Me a River is a work of fiction. Names, characters, places, and incidents are the products of the author's imagination or are used fictitiously. Any resemblance to actual events, locales, or persons, living or dead, is entirely coincidental.

A Ballantine Books Mass Market Original

© 2009 Twentieth Century Fox Film Corporation

All rights reserved.

Published in the United States by Ballantine Books, an imprint of The Random House Publishing Group, a division of Random House, Inc., New York.

Ballantine and colophon are registered trademarks of Random House, Inc.

Fox logo and *Saving Grace* TM & © 2009 Twentieth Century Fox Film Corporation

ISBN 978-0-345-51594-0

Printed in the United States of America

www.ballantinebooks.com

9 8 7 6 5 4 3 2 1

To all those who embrace their Grace

Nothing is to be preferred before justice.
—SOCRATES

SAVING GRACE

CRY ME A RIVER

CHAPTER
ONE

Feathers and braids in her blond hair, gray tank top clinging to her wiry frame, flared jeans slung low, Grace was throwing 'em back at Louie's and the jukebox was blaring "Born to Be Wild." It was past closing time and the windows were dark, except for the occasional flash of lightning. She couldn't hear the thunder, only the song, which, she supposed, made a great sound track for a girl like her. The pulsing beat egged her on. She bobbed her head and mouthed the words, letting the deep bass course through the soles of her cowboy boots as she pushed them against the rung of her bar stool.

The place smelled like stale beer, cigarettes, and a whiff of cooking oil. Louie kept it as nice as he could but a bar was a bar. Be it ever so humble, there was no place like Louie's when it came to getting shit-faced.

Thunder roared and the mirrors caught the lightning, reflecting light around the room. From somewhere in the ceiling, raindrops splashed on the bar—plink, plink, plink—like the echo of shell casings during a shoot-out. Grace dipped her forefinger in the water and pressed it against the varnished surface. *Grace was here.* The next raindrop washed her print away.

"Maybe it's time to build an ark," she said to Earl as she hoisted a shot of fine tequila to her lips. Saltshaker and lime wedge stood at the ready on a soggy paper napkin to her right.

Her burly cowpoke last-chance angel was hunkered on the stool beside her; he smiled a tad and said, "You'd need a little help with that."

"Naw." She threw back the tequila and it went down sweet. She shook salt straight onto her tongue and squeezed lime juice down her throat. She slammed the empty shot glass on the bar a little too hard. She loved getting wasted. She loved a lot of things Earl didn't approve of. "I don't need help with anything."

He cocked his head. Tousled salt-and-pepper hair framed his grave weathered face. His teeth weren't the best, which made him seem more real; nothing of God's was perfect, not even His angels. If you rolled that way. Thinking about God and so forth.

"That so?" he asked. "No help?"

"Not much," she said.

Instantly the jukebox song changed: *I get by with a little help* . . .

"Don't start with me," she said as she pulled a cigarette out of her pack.

"I started with you awhile ago," he drawled. "I just haven't gotten much of anywhere."

She grinned and pulled in smoke, let it linger, blew it out. A roll of thunder rattled the bar. She looked for Louie or someone like him to pour her another; then Earl was behind the bar, fulfilling her wish like a genie.

"Noah had help." He handed her the shot glass. "Building the ark."

"Yeah, and then God drowned their helpful asses." He knit his brows; he knew she was getting the story wrong on purpose. Noah's sons had helped with the ark and they were saved. Grace was not above redecorating the truth to make a point.

"And *everybody* ditched Jesus," she went on. "His disciples couldn't even stay awake on that stakeout the night before his execution."

"Man, I know how that feels," said a familiar voice.

She turned her head. Leon Cooley sat hunched on the stool at the end of the bar, nursing a longneck. Not bad-looking, for a murdering piece of convict shit. Rosy brown, bald, long eyelashes, with a gap between his two front teeth. He looked almost sweet; that threw you off if you didn't know his history. Or if you weren't a cop.

Cooley was on death row for two counts of murder. He might have beat the first count eventually. He killed someone while driving drunk—arguably an accident. But there was the matter of the second count: He murdered a prison guard. Killed him with those gappy teeth. No way an incompetent public defender could claim *that* was a tragic error in judgment.

Now Cooley had a date with the needle in two years and change; and he and Grace shared Earl in a sort of spiritual ménage à trois—so Earl could teach them how to stay out of hell.

"You know how what feels?" Grace asked him coldly. "Facing an execution? Have you got disciples, Leon? Or have you already been put to death?"

Cooley was drinking a beer. Sweaty rings of condensation gleamed on the varnished wood—maybe like planets, God's vast universe. Earl wanted everything to be so cosmic, but when you were slogging around in the humanity, it really wasn't.

"I started dying the day I was born," Cooley replied, grinning at her.

"Spare me," she snapped.

"That's what I'm trying to do, Grace," Earl said, back on the stool beside her. He put in a fresh piece of chaw between his lip and his gum. There was a plastic soda bottle in his lap for the spit. "Also, Jesus was not executed the morning they took him into custody at Gethsemane. He went to trial."

"Yeah, those Romans, they got 'er done," Grace said.

She winced; that was pretty blasphemous, even for her. She wrinkled her nose at Earl to show that she was just being . . . herself.

"You're upset because all those criminals you've been catching are going free," Earl said.

"Damn straight." She made a "gimme-gimme" motion at the sparkling bottles of hooch arrayed behind the bar, and her angel frowned.

"I think I'd better cut you off," Earl said. "Have you ever given any thought to the condition of your liver?"

"I don't need an ark. I know exactly when I'm dying," Cooley bragged.

"You're such a dumb shit," Grace said, taking another drag, feeling the smoke wind inside her like a slow-motion, benevolent tornado; holding it as it bestowed a millisecond of calm; blowing it slowly back out into the troubled world.

"Or your lungs?" Earl added.

"I'm a dumb shit because I know?" Cooley asked, shifting on the stool. "And you don't have a clue when and how you'll go?"

"I'll go out fighting," she assured him.

"That's what I'm afraid of," Earl said as a golden glow spread across her face and his feathery wings flared open. She stared at him, awestruck for just one instant—and then he, Cooley, and the bar vanished.

And Grace woke up in her bed in her house. Alone. She winced and touched her forehead. No, not alone. She had a hangover, unfortunately. She didn't think it was a result of the dream tequila; probably the actual Jacks and beers she'd sucked down last night. The squad's most recent case had gone south in court. That was six in a row. Another asshole was walking. There was no justice. . . .

The rain was pouring down and thunder rumbled above her. She wanted to stay in bed, but it was time to rise up, protect, and serve. With a yawn, she blew wispy blond bangs off her forehead and grabbed her bathrobe. Her mind kicked over as she considered where she'd dropped yesterday's clothes, and where her gun and badge were— nightstand drawer, good—and hustled barefoot into the kitchen/front room, where Bighead Gusman sprawled on his doggie bed.

"Hey, Gussy; hey, Piggy," she said as he lifted his head and panted at her. She opened the door and gestured for him to go on out. The raindrops beat a staccato rhythm on the cement, and Gus made a sound like a foghorn, plopping his massive head back on the soft padding.

"Don't blame you," she said. "It's raining like a son of a bitch. Let me know when you're ready."

She made kissy noises at him, grabbed a cigarette, a pack of matches from Toby Keith's bar in Bricktown, a bottle of extra-strength aspirins from the cabinet to the right of the stove, and took everything with her into the bathroom.

Her neighbor wasn't up yet so there was no one to flash. Popping the top off the container with her thumb, she tossed back a couple-four tablets as she turned on the shower and let it run hot. She climbed on in and let the water sluice down over her aching head, opening her mouth and gulping down some more relief. Her hangover would go away. It always did. She just had to work through it.

Grace put thoughts of her persistent headache on hold as she finished up her sausage sandwich from the drive-though and pushed through the glass door marked OCPD MAJOR CRIMES. She had on boots, jeans, a faded plum Henley shirt, and her sheepherder jacket, but she'd forgotten an umbrella. She was damp and she was chilly. And queasy. Maybe that greasy sausage sandwich wasn't such a good idea.

The familiar morning bouquet of acidic coffee and jelly donuts, breakfast burritos, and wet leather blasted her nose. Her stomach lurched again. Fluorescents cast the desks and swivel chairs in a pasty gloom. Phones rang; file cabinets slammed. The squad room at a quarter past her hangover wasn't a drowsy and slow joint to wake up in like some more civilized places of business; you got dropped back into the pinball machine the minute you showed up. And that was the way Grace liked it.

There was some anxiety in the air, though, and determination; Grace could smell it. Everyone was pissed off about how the D.A. kept losing their evidence-rich, loss-proof cases. Grace wanted to kick his ass. Since that was not an option, she wanted to kick someone else's ass—a bad guy's, maybe. Make that definitely. Next asshole who gave her attitude was going to be sorry.

Butch Ada was on deck, walking past the interview room where Grace had broken some felonious broncos in her day. Such as Six-Pack Johnson yesterday afternoon, when he gave up the bastard who was selling guns out of his pickup across the street from Webster Middle School. Johnson copped a plea for his part in that delightful business model; no big surprise, everybody would probably walk anyway. Shit.

Hand-rolled Stetson off, all-American haircut gleaming, Butch moved with an easy gait like he was herding some longhorns across the prairie. He held a cell phone to his ear, and gave her a wave as he said into the receiver, "Let me know when tox comes back."

Grace responded to his morning greeting with a salute. She dry-swallowed some more extra-strength aspirin and resolved to drink lots of water today. From the desk facing Butch's, Bobby Stillwater nodded in her direction, glossy black hair pulled back Native-American style, his reading glasses pushed down his nose. He looked grim and thoughtful as he studied a color photo on his desk. She could see it from where she stood: Backed by pine trees, a mangled arm extended from a pool of blood. A head lay beside a boulder.

Homicide, it's what's for breakfast, Grace figured. Maybe it was a new case.

She began optimistically reordering the day's priorities; like any other OCPD detective, she had too many open cases already. But a brand-new case—fresher than forty-eight hours—had a much better chance of closing than any of the lukewarm and cold cases piled sky-high on her desk. Everybody wanted a shot at the hot ones. Captain Perry was very fair about divvying them up, even if she loved Grace best.

And there she was, Kate Perry, walking out of her private office. Kate was Grace's relatively new boss, although they'd worked Vice together, making them job friends with some tight history, but they weren't going shopping together anytime soon.

Kate was wearing a dove-gray linen jacket and dressy jeans, silk T-shirt and some turquoise jewelry. As she sipped coffee from a white OU mug, her gaze rested on Butch for a second; she narrowed her eyes and looked back at Grace.

"So what've we got?" Grace asked the captain.

"A uniform caught a body in the Oklahoma River, near the Bricktown Canal," Kate replied, as Ham Dewey pushed through Major Crimes's front door. His honey-blond cowlicks were smoothed down; he had on a dark blue jacket, white shirt, and black trousers. Black shiny cowboy boots. Grace multitasked, giving most of her attention to Kate while checking out Ham's ass as he ambled up beside her. Her partner cleaned up great, and Grace's hormones appreciated the effort. Tasty as he looked, though, she liked him better naked.

Before Captain Perry could clear her throat in a pointed

and meaningful way, Grace swiveled her head back to her and blinked, pledging her complete and total attention.

"DB. River," Grace recapitulated.

"Lena Garvin's doing the autopsy," Kate continued. "Henry took his mother to that reunion in Wichita."

"*There's* a hot time," Grace drawled, privately reminiscing about the night she'd gotten wasted and seduced Henry on her floor. He'd just lost his old cat Molly, and Grace's family had revealed yet more dysfunction. That was reason enough to get drunk together; the screwing had seemed like a good idea at the time, but Henry had started sniffing around in hopes of a relationship. She'd let him down as easily as she could.

But she'd let him down.

"Lena Garvin," Ham grumbled. "Not the best." Henry was the best OCPD had, and he had the awards and dusty bottles of champagne to prove it. "Morning, Grace," he added, his voice a little warmer. His gaze rested on her face, and she looked away. There was a reason she didn't let men spend the night, not even Ham. Especially not Ham.

"Hey." Her head was pounding. Maybe if Ham had come over last night she wouldn't have drunk all that Jack and taught Gus how to twirl around in circles.

Maybe she would have drunk even more.

"Lena Garvin's who we have," Kate said neutrally. "The lab's checking out the deceased's personal effects. Right now he's a John Doe."

"How's it look?" Dewey asked the captain.

"Like a body in a river. That's all we know, Detective," Kate answered without a trace of sarcasm. In police work, there was a difference between connecting the dots and jumping to conclusions. Kate hadn't become the first female captain of Major Crimes by being sloppy. She handed Grace the case file and took another sip of coffee. "Not enough to go on yet. Young male, late teens, fully dressed. No note."

Grace flipped it open. Big colorful pictures of a bloated corpse pushing out of jeans and a flak jacket. Parts of the clothing were gone. So were parts of the body itself.

"Maybe a suicide, maybe a homicide, maybe he got drunk and fell in," Grace said. "Ham and me. We on the clock for this one?"

Kate raised a skeptical brow. "I seem to recall a solemn oath to get some of that paperwork off your desks. You've both got case folders piled so high, you'd be crushed to death if they fell over."

"We'll do it at lunch," Grace promised. Ham nodded. Who wanted to screw with forms in triplicate when there was work to be done?

"We got prints?" Ham asked, assuming it was a done deal.

"Not yet," Kate said, grinning faintly. Maybe she thought they were like little kids, demanding more candy and ice cream. Or maybe she saw herself before she got her own office, preferring the action to department meetings and budget bullshit.

"I'll get the prints," Grace said. "Ham, you check in with Rhetta. See what kind of forensic evidence she's got."

"On it." He turned to go.

"When's court?" Kate asked him pointedly.

"On it after court," Ham replied without a beat.

"We've got to win this one, if it belongs to us," Kate reminded Ham. "D.A.'s off his game."

"You got that right," Butch said as he disconnected his call. Ticking his glance from his crime-scene photos, Bobby blew air out of his cheeks, mirroring everybody's collective frustration.

Officially, their job ended when the D.A. took the case to trial. The police department gathered the evidence, caught the bad guy, handed him over to the court, and testified. It was the job of judge and jury to mete out justice. That was the party line. Inside the squad room, Major Crimes was extremely pissed off at the bad outcomes of their last six cases. Walk, walk, walk, probation, plea bargain down to practically no time, and another walk. Bullshit. Gang violence was way up in OKC, and the bad guys were laughing at the cops. Why not? At the end of the day, the D.A.'s office was going to let them back on the streets to do it all over again.

"We'll win this one, if it's a case," Grace swore. In her mind, she had already talked to Lena Garvin and was running the prints through IAFIS. Matching 'em in record time. With what? Butcher? Bomber? Bookmaker? Her headache vanished and her senses sang. A new case. A new day.

And tonight she was going to ride Ham until she dropped. *Cuz I'm a cowgirl, baby.*

"And I want your desks cleared—and I mean cleared—as in, there is nothing on said desks, at five o'clock today. *Not* like Longhorn Benny Arnold's trashy temple to his lost days of glory." Kate said it loudly enough for Butch to overhear, and Grace grinned over her shoulder to see if the barb hit home.

At his desk now, on another phone call, Butch half-smiled and tapped the oversized head of his Longhorn bobblehead. High noon in the bullpen. Grace knew it was incomprehensible to Kate that Butch had opted to quarterback for the University of Texas when he woulda, coulda, shoulda been a Sooner. Grace was on board with that; she didn't get it, either, and she'd slept with the guy. Repeatedly. In their long-term committed relationship of three months. Butch was good at pushing.

Like Earl said, life was full of mysteries.

*   *   *

Twenty minutes later, Grace entered the autopsy room. She was all duded up like a sci-fi movie extra in a gown, booties, gloves, cap, and mask, shivering in the cold. Cold kept bacterial growth down in the cutting room, same as in the big body fridge behind them. In other words, it let you rot slower.

Lena Garvin stood over the body, gowned, masked, gloved, her hands busy. Her gaze flickered up at Grace but she remained silent.

Grace had always been fascinated by the autopsy room. The tile walls held a large clock, shelves, books and paperwork, and human-anatomy charts—maybe in case the cutter got lost in all those organs and cavities, needed a road map. There was a scale to weigh the internal organs, which currently held John Doe's lungs. It had also held alcoholic livers, punctured hearts, shot-up spleens, and the fabulous detached penis of a porn star. Average human head weighed around eight pounds, same as a bowling ball. Porn star's penis . . . not quite eight pounds.

Bottles lined the shelves like patent medicines at an old-time travelin' show. In the drawers beneath, there was a hacksaw—no shit—and a whole passel of scalpels. Henry could take apart a body like a chef at Benihana's and look for clues the same way Rhetta could dissect a crime scene. But Lena was no Henry. She was a mediocre recent hire, and no one had warmed up to her much.

Grace joined Lena at the autopsy table and stared down at the bulging, battered corpse. The victim looked like a badly rotted balloon from Macy's Thanksgiving Day parade. The river current had dragged him along, and the fish had definitely been biting. There wasn't very much skin left on his face; his right eye was gone, and his left, intact, was glassy. Consistent with drowning as primary cause of death. In other words, he'd been alive when he'd gone into the river. But Grace wanted the deck stacked. She wanted conclusive evidence.

There was lots of head trauma that could go either way, pre- or postmortem. Lena hadn't opened up his skull yet, so his brain was not available for inspection. Drowning victims could bleed from head injuries even after death, because they died with their heads down and blood flow was subject to gravity.

Henry's stand-in had still said nothing by way of greeting. The room felt a couple of degrees chillier. Grace wondered what her deal was, but tried to stay loose and friendly.

"Hey, thanks for letting me come in," she said, even though it would have been unreasonable for Lena to refuse her request to observe.

"Sure." Hark, she doth speak.

"Did he hold his breath?" Grace asked. That would, of course, further indicate that the victim had been alive when he'd been thrown in the water.

"I've got froth," the other woman answered. "But you know that could happen from a drug overdose. Lungs were hyperinflated." She nodded at her scales. They looked like normal lungs to Grace. "I'm going to screen for diatoms. We'll see what the lab finds."

"You're screening for drugs, too?" Grace said carefully, not wanting to tread on her toes but unsure how far Lena would go to establish cause of death. Henry had once told her that screening for diatoms—algae—was an unreliable test for drowning. He usually ran it anyway, as well as a tox screen for drugs. Drug overdoses could look like drownings and vice versa.

Boil it all down, the only literal cause of death was oxygen deprivation. Starve tissue of oxygen, it died. But that was like saying the cause of death was dying. Grace liked all the answers that led to *the* answer. She liked as much evidence as she could collect. It was a form of ammo. She wanted to keep shooting until she hit the target.

"I'll do a full screen," Lena assured her. But there was full and there was full. "There's a lot going on with this corpse," she added, gesturing to the skull. Patches of fish belly–white skin puffed from the bone.

"You can see how glassy his eye is." Lena pointed to it; it gleamed like someone had put a shiny silver dollar on it for the ferryman. "More telling is the amount of water in the lungs. Classic wet drowning. You're right; he tried to hold his breath, which caused laryngospasm, but at some point he exhaled and drew another breath. Or tried to. Diatoms will tell us if he drowned in the same body of water he was discovered in."

Not according to Henry, Grace thought.

"Got it," Grace said. If he'd been alive when he went in, he wasn't a dumped body. It could still be a homicide, if somebody forced him in.

"Any sign of restraints?" She scanned his wrists, a combination of bone and shreds of flesh.

"None so far," Garvin said, shaking her head. "What with the bloat and the fish, it might be hard to tell."

"There might be metal particles or rope fibers embedded in the skin."

"Yes, Detective," the woman said in a clipped tone.

Whoops. Grace knew she'd better ease off. She moved ahead mentally to forensic evidence. Rhetta had his clothes and any other personal effects. Sometimes people who committed suicide put stones or other heavy objects in their pockets. A few tied their legs together, too. They knew that their instincts for self-preservation would likely overtake them, and if they could save themselves, they would. Grace understood that kind of anguish, but it was cowardly to kill yourself.

I'd never do it, she told herself. *No matter what happened to me.*

The average civilian thought drowning was a peaceful death. Yeah, about as peaceful as being waterboarded or suffocating with a pillow smashed over your face. If you asked a dozen people in a bar if they'd rather fall into an erupting volcano or drown, eleven of them were idiots unless you were asking the question in a cop bar like Louie's. Cops knew the score.

Cops *kept* score. She already wanted to win this one, if it was a real case. And she would. She'd do whatever she had to. Hell, yeah. That might bother Earl, but it sure as hell didn't bother her.

"How long was he in the river?" Grace asked.

"I'd say nearly a week," Lena replied. Grace heard the hesitation in her voice. "Degloving has commenced."

Lena gestured to the victim's extremities. The hands and feet were skeletal, with bits of flesh hanging off them. When a body was left in water for only a couple of days, the palms and soles looked wrinkled and/or covered with goose bumps. Longer than that, and the fat in the planes of tissue began to slough off the extremities like baggy socks and a pair of gloves. Hence: degloving.

"There's still some skin on the right forefinger," Grace observed.

Lena frowned at the body. "Yes," she said, flushing as if she realized she should have caught that. "We could slip that off, put it on someone's finger, and get a print that way."

No shit. That was what Grace had just said, wasn't it?

"Great. I'll wear it," Grace offered. "My hands are small. Like his."

A sharp nod. "I'll prep it and give you a call when I'm ready."

"Prep it?" Grace echoed uneasily.

"I think I need to dehydrate it in acetone overnight."

"Oh?" Grace blanched. She didn't want to lose that much time, and she wasn't sure this woman would get it right; maybe Lena herself wasn't sure either, so she didn't want any witnesses watching her screw up the whole thing.

Lena had her back up, that was for sure, stiff-necked and tight-shouldered: practically tapping her toes in impatience for Grace to get the hell out. Grace didn't move.

"Maybe we could try it first," Lena ventured, not looking at her. "Let me take another look at it." *Alone*, she meant.

"You got it," Grace said with a bright smile. She exited the autopsy room, took off her robe, gloves, and mask, and tossed them in the biohazard can. The squad needed a win. And with Lena Garvin on their team, someone should run interference.

She's gonna screw it up, Grace thought. As she passed by a window, the rain came tumbling down.

CHAPTER
TWO

After Grace left the autopsy room, she went to see Rhetta in the crime lab. Rhetta wasn't there, and by all appearances—the banker boxes on her exam table labeled with case numbers—she had evidence to process from six million other cases ahead of the floater. Ham was still in court, and if Grace went back into the squad room, her only alternative was her paperwork, which meant that it was time for a smoke in the stairwell.

Out she sailed, facing the concrete stairs where she'd had some of her best thoughts, stolen private displays of lust from Ham, and arguments with Earl. Her pointy-toed cowboy boots clanged on the cement as she climbed up; she stopped to pull a pack of Morleys out of her pocket and light up. Then, sitting down on a step, she drew in the sweet smoke, held it, let it out, and tipped back her head. Her temples were throbbing and she was dehydrated. Water, water, everywhere, so drink some, girlfriend. She thought about the day, and the dead thing on the table that once had been a kid. Thought about how badly it stank. That *thing* had once had hopes and dreams. Went to birthday parties, looked up at the stars and wondered.

Her mood darkened and she took another drag, trying to quiet her mind as it plotted and planned how to run the case. If there was a case.

She closed her eyes and picked a piece of tobacco off her tongue.

Then she felt a kind of sweet joy wash over her, and she smiled; there was Earl's wing tip, brushing her cheek.

"Hey, man," she said. She was grateful for the company.

He sat beside her with a spit bottle cradled on his knee. He was wearing jeans, leather walking shoes, a T-shirt that displayed what looked like an advertisement for a beach in a language she didn't speak, and a loose, unbuttoned work shirt over that. He inclined his head by way of greeting.

"Morning, Grace. Bet you ain't feeling so good," he drawled.

"I feel fine," she said, looking up at the ceiling as she took another drag.

"Half a bottle of Jack and a six-pack says otherwise," he countered. "Not enough sleep, fast food for breakfast . . ."

"Are you my mother's angel, too?" she asked him, sliding a mock-suspicious glance toward him.

He shrugged easily. "All I'm sayin', it's hard to do your job when you've got something else going on. Maybe you need to cut that gal some slack. You don't know what she might be dealing with herself."

Grace's dark eyes flashed. "First of all, I'm doing my job just fine. Second, Lena Garvin's this close to incompetent. Not because of some shit going on in her life, but because she doesn't know what she's doing."

"Oh, she don't?" he asked calmly, spitting into his soda bottle. "Seems to me she was following procedure."

"Oh, I see." She cocked her head, not exactly angry with him but maybe a little bit raw. Because he obviously had no idea what he was talking about. "I didn't realize there's a medical school in heaven and that you went to it. You want me to start calling you Dr. Earl?" She thought a moment. "Do angels have last names?"

"I don't," he replied. "I am aware, however, that

you've called me a whole string of names on occasion."
If he was offended, he didn't show it.

"I never have." She rose and tamped out her cigarette.
Then she squatted down to collect the remains.

"You don't know all the things you do when you're
drunk. And you were drunk last night, Grace. And you
have a hangover today. And if you have to run after some
crazy young kid who's got a gun and a grudge, you just
might have a little trouble doing it."

"Listen, Earl," she said, looking up with the shredded
cigarette in her hand. Then she paused. "Are you telling
me that's going to happen?"

But he was gone.

Of course.

The big Oklahoma sky dropped buckets of water on the
gussied-up brick buildings of Bricktown, the flower beds,
and the ducks bobbing in the deserted canal—no tours in
the driving rain, so no tour boats. The windshield wipers
of Bobby's four-by-four fwapped back and forth as Butch
popped a stick of spearmint gum into his mouth and offered one to his partner. Bobby shook his head.

"We found a leak in the living room last night," he told
Butch. "It's been raining down inside the wall for who
knows how long. We were moving the furniture out for
the carpet. Big patch of black mold."

Butch grunted sympathetically. Bobby and Marissa had
been saving up for new carpet for months. Bobby wasn't
big on buying things on credit. If something happened to
him, he didn't want Marissa stuck with a bunch of bills.

"I'm going to open up the wall myself, save some money
that way," Bobby said. "Maybe we'll get lucky. Could just
be some sheetrock, drywall, that kind of thing."

"Could be," Butch said. "Let me know if I can lend a
hand."

Bobby inclined his head. "Thanks."

Butch didn't say anything. He and Bobby were partners, and as far as he was concerned, that meant you helped out. He'd take a bullet for Bobby. When he'd partnered up with a married man, he'd wondered if Bobby would have done the same. Bobby had a wife and kids to think about. If Bobby stepped into the line of fire, he might leave behind a widow and two orphans. Might make a man hesitate when his partner needed an assist.

There was a fortune-cookie fortune in Butch's wallet, one from a first date about seven months ago: *He who travels light moves faster*. First date, last date. Stephanie had been a sweet girl, but there hadn't been any fireworks. She'd given him the fortune even though it had been in her cookie; made some comment about how she owned way too many shoes and never traveled with fewer than four suitcases; and smiled at him when he put the slip of paper in his wallet. She thought it was a memento. It was actually a friendly reminder.

Over the months, Butch had come to learn that he had nothing to worry about where Bobby was concerned. A man with family was a man hardwired to protect people. A man who didn't take unnecessary risks. Besides, when Bobby was on the job, he was no longer just a husband and a father. He was a cop, and a damn fine one.

"While we're in the area, I'll check in with October," Butch said. "See if he knows anything." October was one of Butch's informants. He called himself October because it was the month of his daughter's birth. His real name was Patrick Kelly, and he was their eyes and ears in a local gang led by a scumbag Butch had been after since before he became partners with Bobby. With all the squad's recently lost cases, Butch felt more motivated to go after loose ends. And October's big boy, Big Money Martinez, was loose as a goose.

They parked over by the ballpark and started canvassing the shops and restaurants for information on their waterlogged John Doe. Nope, nope, and nope, and couldn't they *please* do something about the homeless people who wandered into Bricktown at night?

"I think they come from that shelter," said a woman at the counter of an upscale fudge store. The store was decorated in egg-yolk yellow and cream, yellow wooden shelves holding stacks of white and yellow striped candy boxes. She wore her strawberry-blond hair in a geometric bob like Victoria Beckham's. "They deal drugs out of there, you know."

"Would you like to file a complaint?" Bobby asked her, looking attentive and polite.

She kept looking at Butch. Her cheeks got rosy. "Just . . . could you shut them down or something?"

"We'll look into it," Butch assured her.

"Thanks." Her voice was breathy and soft.

"So you didn't see anything, hear anything?" Butch prompted, keeping it professional.

"Like a *splash*? The thought that someone would have jumped into the water, just across the street . . ." She made a little "eek" face. "Scary."

"This area is heavily patrolled," Bobby reminded her. Bricktown was a prime tourist attraction, and OKC wanted visitors to feel safe to spend their money while they were there.

"Maybe so, but those homeless people still wander over here. And someone still managed to jump into the river," she argued.

"That's not confirmed yet," Butch said. "It could have been a boating accident."

She cocked her head. "Oh. I hadn't thought of that. Still, to think that there's been a dead body near my store . . ."

"Thanks again for your help," Butch told her. The

way he saw Oklahoma City, there were dead bodies near a lot of places. "Here's my card. Please give us a call if you think of anything."

She smiled, glancing from Butch to the card and back again. He knew that look on her face, what she was thinking. *Maybe I'll just call you anyway.* He stayed neutral. He wasn't seeing anyone at the moment, but he was enjoying the time off. If he could find a woman who understood what it was like to be a cop . . . a woman like Grace . . .

Cowboy down, he thought, with a soundless chuckle. *Travel light.*

"Would you both like a piece of fudge? On the house." She started to open the display case.

"That's very kind of you, but we're not allowed to accept gifts," Bobby said, finally stepping in to smooth things over for Butch.

She laughed as she shut the case and spread her palms on the counter, almost like someone about to be frisked. "Are you serious? What do they think, that I'll try to bribe you with a piece of rocky road?"

Something like that, Butch thought. *Give us some truffles, maybe a couple pieces to take home, next thing you're asking us to fix a parking ticket. The Big Rock Candy Mountain has some slippery slopes.*

"Maybe you boys can come in on your off hours sometime. Then you'd be regular customers, right?" Her hand strayed to her hair; she touched the ends. Butch wondered if she was aware that she was doing it. He kept his smile easy and let his partner—his *married* partner—do the talking.

"The next time I'm in Bricktown with my family, we'll be sure to stop in," Bobby assured her.

A little bell tinkled over the threshold as the two detectives exited the shop. Bobby gave Butch a look, and Butch didn't react.

"What do you *do* to these women?" Bobby asked.

"I didn't say anything, man," Butch protested.

"It must be pheromones. They smell that you're single."

Butch cricked his neck and moved his shoulders. "Maybe they just look down at my hand and see that there's no ring."

"You could wear a wedding ring. If you really wanted to fend them off."

"I don't like to wear jewelry. Specially not on the job," Butch said.

"What about that thing?" Bobby asked, gesturing to Butch's large UT belt buckle. A gust of wind flapped at Bobby's long blue-black hair, held away from his face with a silver clasp. Droplets smacked the pavement.

"Rain's going to mess up the crime scene," Butch said, ignoring Bobby's jibe, as he always did. "Wish we could find it first. If there is a crime scene."

Bobby nodded. "With you." He stepped over a puddle from the last batch of rain. "Let's see what October has for us. Day won't be a total waste."

"Day ain't over yet," Butch agreed.

One hour a day in the yard, five days a week. One hour of fresh air. Leon Cooley wanted to tip his head back and let the rain wash down over his forehead and cheeks. Rain made the world smell good.

But he didn't go. Word was the White Freedom gang had a hit out on him. It was about something he was supposed to have said a few days ago about some white prisoner's woman. He hadn't; he didn't give a shit about no white woman. Except maybe Grace Hanadarko and that fine friend of hers, Rhetta Rodriguez. People were skittish around him, assumed he had some kind of network of homeys outside to do his bidding. Like he might send one of his friends around to rape their girlfriends and burn down their houses. Shit.

Okay, so he knew one or two guys.

He'd messed up once—okay, twice, second time was an actual murder—and now it was the needle for him. Now he was counting the days, not because he was impatient—hell, no—but because he just wanted to know where he stood. Still, there was no sense rushing things, and he didn't want to go before he and Earl were finished with each other. Earl was trying to help him get right. Leon wasn't sure what exactly that meant, but he figured that as long as Earl was around, he hadn't gotten right yet. That scared him, bad. What happened if he got killed before Earl signed off on him?

"Hey, Leon," Earl said. He appeared, just like that, no wings of glory, wearing his jeans and shirt. He had on a T-shirt that read JUST SAY NO.

Leon realized only then that he had been pacing back and forth like a cheetah at the zoo. He stopped.

"Hey, Earl, did you bring me some smokes?" he asked.

"Smoking's bad for your health," Earl drawled, spitting tobacco juice into his soda bottle. "It'll kill ya."

"Okay, what is it today, some sermon, some lesson?" Leon asked, tensing up even worse. "You going to make me have another one of those dreams?"

"The one where Grace Hanadarko runs you over? Or the one where you two fly kites?"

"Shit, man." Leon huffed. "I thought you were supposed to teach me about God. So I can repent. And go to heaven."

"My job's to get you right with God," Earl concurred. "If you're in the mood to repent, you'd better take that up with him. I'm just FedEx—"

"—delivering the message. I know." Leon leaned against the wall. "So what are you here to tell me?"

Earl moved his head toward the frosted window. Bastards didn't even let Leon have a view. "You've stopped exercising."

"Some asshole's ordered a hit on me," Leon informed him, dull resentment boiling up in him. "Some Aryan-gang son of a bitch."

Earl shrugged. "Okay, then, so that's why you stopped exercising in the *yard*. But you can exercise in here. You used to. Doing all them push-ups."

Leon stared at Earl as if he had lost his mind. "I've got less than three years to live. Why should I bother?" He ran his hands over his bald head and dropped his hands to his sides. Even after all this time, caged up, it spooked him when Earl simply materialized inside his maximum-security cell.

"Well, you're alive *now*." Earl sat on Leon's cot. "What if you have a stroke? You want to spend the rest of your life drooling and peeing on yourself?"

"Earl," Leon protested. "C'mon, man. I'm not going to have a stroke." A chill ran down his spine. "Am I?"

Earl spit into his bottle. "I don't know, Leon. But I do know that God gave you a body to live in. You just have to do a few simple things to keep it in tune. Like a guitar."

"It's a lot of damn work," Leon protested.

"You want to be transferred to a prison ward where they leave you in shitty pajamas for a week at a stretch?"

"Who cares?" But when Earl put it that way, maybe he did.

"Life is sacred," Earl said. "It's the best thing God had to give you. Isn't it? Is there something better than life itself?"

Leon dropped his head, shook it. "I *knew* it. I knew you'd get around to that Jesus stuff one of these days." He blew out air. "God loved us so much He gave us His only Son."

"Today is not that day." Earl tapped his fingers on the

sides of the bottle. "Besides, you and I have been through all that. God doesn't care if you're a Muslim or a Jew or a Buddhist. He just wants you to have faith."

Leon huffed. "I *do* have faith, Earl. So why am I *here*?"

"Those two people you killed, well, you took away their gift. God sure didn't put you in here."

Leon began to pace again. "Then she should be here, too. Hanadarko. She hit me with her Porsche, killed me dead."

Earl spit in his soda bottle. "That was a dream. Didn't really happen."

"Yeah, it was a dream *you* set up so you could save her from going to hell. Bitch would have killed someone sooner or later. Then she'd be in here, same as me."

"That how you see it?" Earl asked, sounding genuinely curious.

Leon nodded.

"We don't know that, neither one of us. And as for not killin' someone, she has killed people. In the line of duty."

"Yeah, she does it, it's legal. But if you hadn't scared her—"

Earl crooked his eyebrow. "If I hadn't appeared to you, maybe you'd have killed another prison guard. Like I said, life is sacred to God, Leon. Everybody's life."

"You always got an answer for everything, don't you?" Leon began to pace again. He was edgy, pent up.

"I sure don't, and you know it. I'm just—"

"Don't say it!" Leon whirled on him. He balled his fists and clenched his teeth. He was so *angry,* so white-hot—

"Careful there, son," Earl said, his smile fading. "Your temper could get the best of you. It did before, didn't it? And I mean business about that stroke. You need to get your blood pressure checked."

"If God loves me so much, why doesn't he just take me

now?" Leon demanded. "How come I got to suffer like this?"

"Tombs come in all shapes and sizes," Earl said, making a big show of inspecting Leon's bare cell. Like it wasn't that bad. Like it wasn't four bare walls and a few pathetic pictures from magazines taped to the walls, instead of a living room with a plasma TV or a mall or even an alley full of garbage cans. "Stones roll away when you least expect them."

A flare of hope shot through Leon; just as quickly, he smothered it. Earl was a damn smart son of a bitch. He probably knew that part of Leon—a large part of him— had made a silent bargain with him. *I accept God, God lets me out of here through the front door. A free man with a long life. Hallelujah.*

"Whatever, man," Leon said dully. Then he narrowed his eyes and peered through his lashes. "Why did you come to see me today?"

"No special reason." Earl smiled. "Maybe I just missed you."

"Bullshit."

Earl shrugged. "Maybe God misses you."

"Hey, I haven't gone anywhere. I've been praying and all that shit."

"With your mouth," Earl said. "But not your heart."

"What, I'm getting grades in prayer now?" Leon scoffed. "I'm not praying right?"

Earl nodded. "God can't hear what you're saying. Not the way you've been praying lately."

The condemned felon turned his head. "I haven't felt like it."

"Leon, you got to have a connection with God. Prayer's like working out, only with your soul. You're getting flabby." Earl pursed his lips. "There's gonna be a white light and a tunnel. I'll be there to stretch out my hand.

But if you don't have the strength—the *faith*—to grab on . . ."

"Okay," Leon muttered. Earl was scaring him. "I'll pray." Earl said nothing. Leon looked up at Earl and blinked. "What, *now*?"

"No time like the present," Earl said. All traces of humor faded from his face. "It may be later than you think."

CHAPTER
THREE

Lena Garvin finally called Grace to tell her she was ready to get the print, and Grace called Ham. They didn't need him, but Grace wanted a witness regarding how well or how badly it went. He was out of court and in a surly mood when he met her in the autopsy room, thin little card strip for the single print and ink pad in hand. He told her that he had a bad feeling that court hadn't gone the right way. Again. The jury didn't seem to like what Ham was saying. It felt like they had already decided to let the defendant go.

"It's like we're cursed," he complained. "Like the juries all think we entrap these poor innocent citizens and work 'em over for false confessions."

"Assholes," Grace agreed. "Next case we catch, we'll boldface and underline it for them."

"Jesus," he grunted. "Civilians."

Pursing her lips, Lena slipped the cap of flesh from the corpse's forefinger over Grace's latex glove. Dead skin from a dead guy. *Tell me your name, kid,* Grace thought.

Then she let Ham roll her finger over the ink pad, then over the strip. Clear whorls. A good print. Go, Lena.

"Thanks, Detectives," Lena said briskly as Grace handed her back the dead guy's fingertip. They took off the clinical gear and left.

"So where'd it go wrong at court today?" Grace asked as they headed together back to Rhetta's.

"It wasn't just that." He glowered. "D.A. told me Joey Amador got probation at his sentencing hearing."

She stopped walking. "Shit, Ham. That asshole beat that old lady."

"But he's real sorry about it. And the judge bought it." He clenched his jaw and rubbed his right fist with his left hand.

"That was our win. You and me." She scowled. "We got a solid confession."

He gave his fist a punch. "Amador had better watch his sorry ass. The minute he violates probation, he's ours."

"Damn straight," she said. "We'll sic the beat cops on him, too. I'll bet he screws up by Christmas."

"Thanksgiving." He grinned at her, perking up. "Caught you staring at my ass while Captain Perry was filling us in."

She smiled to herself, saying nothing. Let him dangle. So to speak.

"You want to grab a beer after work?" he asked, his voice as warm as bourbon. "At your house?"

"Sure." She grinned at him. Good. *There* was a win.

Back-burnering her irritation with Lena and her disappointment over the Amador case, she spotted Rhetta through the glass of the crime lab and waved. Bustling Rhetta didn't see her. Grace's best friend since grade school had on white latex gloves and a white lab coat. Her chocolate-brown hair was up in a messy bun held back with a black headband, and she was wearing her big, thick glasses. Gold glinted in the light; Rhetta was a good Catholic, and she always wore a cross around her neck on a thin gold chain.

Ham's phone went off. He opened it. "Yes, Captain," he said. "On my way." He turned. "Captain Perry's got something for us. I'll check it out."

"Okay," Grace said. "I'll stay with Rhetta."

He handed her the print card and headed down the

hall. She admired his ass again, and then she went into the crime lab.

"Hey," she said by way of greeting, running her gaze over the shredded jeans jacket that Rhetta was scrupulously measuring. Rhetta was the best. Several objects were arranged in a straight line—a roach clip, four pennies, two quarters, and an unfolded piece of wet paper with seven numbers. That might be a phone number. Also, the initial *J*, but very elaborately drawn, in a sort of scrollwork. The ink hadn't smeared a bit, and the paper was in excellent condition.

"Was that on my vic?" she asked Rhetta. She took in the banker boxes, which had been moved to Rhetta's shelf, next to her picture of her kids in their Halloween costumes. A soldier with a fake plastic but no less impressive gut-shot wound, and a cowgirl. "You *did* give me cuts in line. Thanks, Rhetta."

Rhetta set down her ruler and beamed at Grace, the way she did when she was so excited she could barely stand it. She took the print card and laid it down next to the tattered denim.

"I did give you cuts and these are his clothes. Look at this, Grace." She tapped her boot heels on the floor, the Rhetta happy dance. "That piece of paper was in his pocket. He was in the river for what, a week?"

"Aren't you supposed to tell me?" Grace asked. "You're Forensics."

Rhetta jabbed her forefinger at it. "Grace, that's plain notebook paper. That should be a little ball of mush. And the ink should have run. It's cheap ink." She fluttered her lashes. "Don't you find that the least bit suspicious?"

"Suspicious, hell, yeah," Grace said. She gave Rhetta a wary look. "But I have a feeling our definitions of suspicious don't match up."

"Maybe Earl's involved," Rhetta said, leaning toward her Best Friend Forever. "Maybe it's another message."

Grace snickered and showed Rhetta the print card, which she set down next to Rhetta's microscope. Then she leaned sideways, examining the scrap of waterlogged paper without touching it. It was definitely in better condition than the cadaver it rode in on.

"Earl doesn't work that way. He told me police work isn't in his job description." Grace straightened up and smoothed her braids out of her eyes. "He couldn't even help me find Gus when he was lost."

"He *did* help you find Gus," Rhetta countered. "He helped you put up flyers, and how do you know he wasn't responsible for bringing him home?"

"Because my neighbor brought him home," Grace replied.

Rhetta let that go. "But you can't deny that he gave us all those clues to find Father Patrick Satan Murphy." Rhetta came down a notch when she mentioned the shithead's name. Father Murphy had started molesting Grace when she was nine years old; and he was dead now, which was a good thing.

But the man who had killed Father Murphy was dead, too—a suicide, no less. That weighed on Grace's conscience. She'd tried to give the guy a break, let him get out of town before the cops closed in to arrest him for the murder. Instead, he had a meltdown and shot himself. Wrong of her, and he had paid. No one knew, except Earl.

"No," Grace said emphatically, shaking her head. "Earl insisted he wouldn't be doing any crime busting." Still, who knew? Earl was an unpredictable devil of an angel, coming and going and flying her out to the Grand Canyon and the Parthenon. Serving her and Leon Cooley dream-booze and then lecturing her on drinking and smoking too much.

She punched the number on the paper into her cell phone. It didn't go through; the mechanical phone lady informed her it was not a working number. "I'll check this out," she said. "What else have you got?"

Rhetta pointed at the tatters of jeans jacket. "This is a men's small. There are fibers in the pockets, but not much in the way of personal effects. Except for that piece of paper."

"My brothers always had all kinds of shit in their pockets," Grace mused. "Maybe it's a jacket he didn't usually wear. Or someone else's jacket."

Maybe even the killer's. Maybe that was the killer's piece of paper, and his handwriting. And that number was John Doe's phone number, or the killer's number. Killer calls him to chat, tosses him in the river. . . . Grace started crunching the possibilities. Maybe there was no killer. No killer, no case.

"Get me whatever you can, Rhetta," she said. "See why that paper is in such good condition. If you stay on it . . . I'll make you spaghetti."

"Get thee behind me," Rhetta said, groaning with pleasure. "I still say it's divine intervention."

Grace pressed her lips together thoughtfully. "I think you're onto something." Rhetta's answering smile was smug. "I think God threw that kid into the river so you could get that phone number."

Rhetta's face fell. "You're mocking God."

"No, I'm not." Grace smiled sweetly. "I'm mocking *you*. Who knows? Maybe someone found the body and stuck the phone number in his pocket to help us out. Then threw him back in, like a fish. Catch and release." She'd have to reread the statement of the officer who had discovered the body to see if that was remotely plausible. She'd seen a lot of weird behavior in her life.

"Right. That's what I'm saying," Rhetta insisted. "Someone like Earl."

Grace sighed. "See, this is what Catholic school does

to people." She held up a hand. "Okay, I'll keep an open mind."

"Me too," Rhetta promised. And Grace was too much of a good friend to snort at her. Rhetta was a good Catholic. In Grace's opinion, "open mind" did not fit in that definition.

Bricktown.

Butch and Bobby sloshed past the fountain and the restored brick buildings, watching another straggle of tourists scurry into restaurants and shops to get out of the rain. The partners climbed back into Bobby's truck and drove east. Landscaped frontage roads and banks of flowers gave way to chain-link fences, tires, and a dark blue couch on the side of the road with a hand-lettered sign on it that read GRATIS.

They reached some old warehouse buildings sided with aluminum. No landscaping here, just weeds. Bobby rolled over gravel and parked on a rise in front of the one with the sign above the rusted metal door that read JEHOVA'S MINISTRY. The shelter featured boarded-up windows and a guy outside in an Army jacket everyone called the Count. All the scruffy man did all day was count the sections of the cracked sidewalk, and number them with a piece of chalk. Not in sequential order or any other pattern. He just wrote numbers on them. In spite of the rain, he was out there, shielding his piece of chalk and muttering to himself.

"I'll send October out if I see him," Bobby told Butch as the door of the shelter squealed open. They'd agreed that Bobby would canvass the homeless guys and the staff about the floater. Butch would stay out of it in case October wanted to meet. October was a sort of trustee at the shelter, had longer-term bunking privileges in return for keeping the place clean and doing odd jobs. He'd see

Bobby and get the message that Butch was waiting at their prearranged rendezvous point.

Bobby shut the door himself, and Butch sauntered past the Count toward the warehouses and Dumpsters on the east side of the street. The Dumpsters were collecting rain, creating sloshy garbage stew inside their rusting bodies. Staying in the shadows, Butch found an overhang and folded his umbrella. Checked his cell phone for the time of day and put it on vibrate. Then he waited. Rain puddled around his boots and he looked for higher ground. A rat scurried past. People thought detectives spent their days chasing down guys with guns. A lot of the game cops played consisted of avoiding garbage.

Storm clouds darkened, melting together to drive away the sunlight. It was a late afternoon like this one when he'd been driving, hydroplaned, and had the accident. He'd walked away and his buddy was paralyzed for life. Butch put that aside and stayed alert. October might want to be a good guy, but he was living a bad guy's life. Time would tell if he really could change.

Butch's patience was rewarded when he detected the telltale rhythm of October's walk. October had a limp—industrial accident, denied workman's comp; he let his temper get the best of him and trashed the foreman's office, and the foreman, too. Did a bit of time for it, and he could have come out of it just fine.

But once released, he moved onto the streets, and no amount of counseling or recidivism-program assistance could convince him to give straight life another try. Butch wondered what else had happened to October to drive him to such an extreme reaction, but Butch wasn't a social worker and October was a good informant. So.

Lightning flashed, and October appeared at the southern end of the alley. The short, leathery, twentysomething guy was a pulsar of compact muscle, tattoos, and acne scars. He was wearing a faded white T-shirt with a cross on it, an Army jacket over that, and a pair of jeans. He also had on a soaking wet red and black rag—his gang colors—that concealed his red hair.

"Yo," October said in his husky voice. He looked pretty good, for October. His gang, the Sons of Death, had set him up at the shelter to trawl for recruits. Butch had recruited him as well. Should Butch have told the guy who ran the shelter? Probably.

Butch nodded at the informant. He had a twenty in his left hand by then, and October ticked his gaze down at the money the way some men stared at heroin.

"Here's the deal," October said. "I'm moving up. I'm answering direct to Jorge. He reports to . . . you-know-who." Despite his nervousness, October thrust back his shoulders, proud of his accomplishment. Jorge was the number-two man. October had gotten a significant promotion.

Butch smiled grimly, not exactly able to congratulate him. The gang's number one was Big Money Martinez. One of Big Money's victims had been a thirteen-year-old girl named Priscilla Jackson. She refused to follow in her older sister's footsteps and hook for him. So he cut her into pieces. And fed them to his dog.

Butch knew Big Money had done it, but he didn't have hard proof. He had sworn that someday he'd bring that bastard down.

"Big Money," Butch said, and October swallowed hard. He licked his lips and glanced over his shoulder. Butch kept his right hand on his service weapon, holstered on his belt.

"Yeah, him." He looked down at the twenty. "That's for my little girl," he said. "Merrie. You'll give it to her momma, same as always." He adored his little girl.

"I will," Butch promised him. "If you help me out."

October frowned and crossed his arms. Uncrossed them. Shifted his weight. He was hopped up. "I am helping you out, man. I'm way in now, okay? I'm *connected*. So . . ." He pointed to the bill. "That should be a fifty."

Butch said nothing. He just waited.

"Merrie needs money," October said, gesturing to the twenty. "She's going to *have* things." His eyes blazed.

Who could explain the chaotic logic of the criminal mind? October loved his six-year-old daughter more than anything on the planet. But rather than get a real job, and find a way to reconnect with Merrie's mother, Janaya Causwell, October stayed on the streets. Then he endangered his own life to inform on his fellow gang members, including a man he feared so much he couldn't even say his name, because Butch threw some cash his way. For his daughter.

"Listen, here it is, okay? Jorge is moving me out of the shelter," October continued. "We aren't finding any good guys here."

"That's a shame," Butch deadpanned.

"I'm going to live with four other guys in an apartment. I'm going to give you intelligence on—on Big Money. You'll be able to take him down with the shit I give you."

"That remains to be seen," Butch said. If October could ever actually deliver. And didn't get himself killed first.

October took a long breath and licked his lips. Butch wondered what he was on. His eyes were jittering. "I'll get you what you need, Butch. So we'll need a new way to meet. And you're going to have to pay me a lot more money."

"You got something in mind?" Butch asked.

"Hundreds instead of twenties." October scratched at a scab on his cheek.

"About how we meet?"

"You don't come to my new place, ever," October said. "They see you, I'm dead."

"How're they going to connect you to us?"

"They see cops around any of us, they'll kill us all. Jorge already told us that."

"Does he suspect you?"

"No. That's what he tells everybody." October stuck out his chin in a way that reminded Butch of Grace's bulldog. "But he means it. I am risking my life, working with you."

Why the hell are you doing this? Butch wondered. But he just nodded.

"You can't come to me," October said. "And I can't call you at work anymore. So I'll need your home number." He pulled out his cell phone.

Like hell, Butch thought. He had a separate phone with its own number for people like October. He recited the digits, and October punched them very slowly into his phone.

"There's a message on there for a fake pizza delivery," Butch said. "If anyone tries it, they'll get the recording or else I'll answer as Tony's Pizza and Pasta."

"Let me try it." October dialed, listened, nodded. "Okay. Good." His eyes narrowed as he put his phone back in his pocket. "So if I need help . . ."

"I have caller ID. If you can leave a message, say the words 'stuffed crust.' I'll try to get you out," Butch said. "But no guarantees, October." Butch stayed straight with his informants whenever possible, trying not to promise more than he could deliver. Some cops led guys like October on, painting pretty pictures of a new start with WitSec—witness protection—and then dumped them like a bad date.

"Stuffed crust. Okay. And a backup signal, right?" October said, ignoring Butch's warning. Butch wondered what crime October had committed to advance in the ranks as he had. Made his bones, murdered someone? Someone else's son or daughter?

"Okay," Butch said. "Backup signal."

"If I can't call, or I can't talk, once I'm settled in I'll tell you where the nearest Dumpster is that you can see from the street," October told him. "I'll put a white towel on the handle."

There were 157 ways in which that could not work, but Butch didn't point that out. Instead he fished in his wallet for another ten. Then, as October started bouncing on his heels and cleared his throat, Butch brought out the real prize: Merrie's first-grade school picture. October had given it to Butch for safekeeping a month before. Wordlessly he handed it to October, who grabbed it from him.

"It's too dark out here," he whined. "I can't see it."

Two little piggy-tails, a missing front tooth, blue eyes, and mocha skin. Freckles. She was wearing a yellow T-shirt from Frontier City. Butch had given Merrie's momma some free tickets.

"C'mon, Butch," October said.

Sighing, Butch pulled a flashlight out of his jacket pocket and shined it overhead. So much for secrecy. He stood witness as October studied the picture, shifting his weight, and gave a sad little sigh that was totally at odds with the rest of his life. Tears glistened on his lined, pocked cheeks. Butch could see the love on his face, the yearning that softened him. That softness was Butch's secret weapon.

"Merrie." Even October's voice sounded different. "Only thing that keeps me going," he whispered. "She's it for me."

The do-rag gangsta man handed the picture back to the cop and stared at the wallet while Butch replaced the picture. October had explained that he didn't want anyone in his gang to know about his daughter. No shit, given what Big Money had done to Priscilla Jackson. For a gang informant, October was not traveling light, and that was how Butch really controlled him.

"Janaya knows the money comes from me?" October asked him. When Butch nodded, he added, "And . . . does she say anything?"

She sure did, but Butch was not about to repeat it. It was going to take more than a few dollars here or there for her to speak kindly about "that prick."

"She puts the money to good use," Butch reminded him.

"Yeah. Yeah, good," October said. "When you have kids, you'll see what it's like. Your heart lives outside your body. They become *everything*." He pinched the bridge of his nose. "She's the one thing I'm proud of. If anything happened to her . . ." He raised his face, unashamed of the tears that streamed down his cheeks.

"You'd help her, right, man?" he demanded. It was a question he always asked. "If anything happened to me, you'd step up?"

"Yes." It was the answer Butch always gave. And it was the truth.

"You're not lying to me?" October searched Butch's face. "I trust you, man."

"I'm not lying to you," Butch said. He checked on Merrie a couple times a month. She and her mother were doing pretty well. They were on welfare, but Janaya was hoping to get a job now that Merrie was in school. Janaya was erratic, but so far she had a handle on her weaknesses for men and drugs. At least both Merrie's parents cared about her. There were a lot of kids who didn't have that going for them, including kids who lived in the best parts of OKC.

Butch's cell phone went off. He checked the caller ID. Grace. He couldn't help grinning.

"Yeah," he said, turning away from October.

"Hey, Butch. Got a match on a phone number the floater had on him," she said. "Helping Hand Teen Crisis Hotline. I'm going to go check it out with Ham. What about you guys?"

"Nothing," he said. "So far."

" 'Kay," Grace said, and hung up.

"Time to shove off?" October asked him, trying to sound affable. Butch couldn't figure out how he could possibly have become one of Jorge's lieutenants. His mistrust of October increased exponentially. It had been a long time since Butch believed more than about 30 percent of what anyone on the streets told him. "Okay, let me go first. Give me a few minutes," October said.

And as usual, Butch wondered if this entire scripted meet-and-leave was some wackadoo maneuver laid down by October, if someday a herd of homeboys was going to jump Butch in the alley. Maybe even today.

"When are you moving out?" Butch asked him.

"I'm not sure," October replied. He could be lying; he could have forgotten. Or he could simply not know.

"Okay," Butch said. "Call me."

"I will." October looked hard at Butch, as if it might be the last time they saw each other. That was always a possibility.

Then the informant turned and melted back into the rain. After a couple of minutes, Butch ambled back toward Bobby's truck. Hand on the gun, eyes on the landscape. Watching, alert, owning the street, just in case.

The Count jumped out in front of him. His crazy eyes spun beneath bushy brows and above hollow cheeks; he waved his hands back and forth, demanding his attention.

"The world is coming to an end," the Count informed him with stinking breath. "God is going to flood the earth and wash away the unrighteous." He wiped his nose with the back of his hand. A wet smear of chalk smeared his upper lip like a plaster mustache.

"Seems like it," Butch said. "Thanks for the warning."

As Butch headed for the truck, Bobby appeared, shutting the shelter door. He shook his head as the two climbed into the vehicle.

"No one knows anything. A guy ODed in the shelter bathroom yesterday. The minister who runs the place swears no one's wandering over to Bricktown." Bobby started the truck. "It'd be a long walk."

"October's moving into an apartment with four other foot soldiers," Bobby said. "He got a promotion."

"He's going to get himself killed." Bobby turned on the defrost and increased the speed of the windshield-wiper blades.

"They all do, sooner or later," Butch agreed. "It's a suicide mission." He looked out the window. "It's not going to let up."

"No, it's not," Bobby replied.

CHAPTER
FOUR

"Okay, here's the weird thing," Grace said as she fished her hamburger out of the Johnnie's bag. She was talking to Ham on her cell while she was driving. The rain was heavy, so it was probably not a good idea to be doing so many things at once. "The phone number on the paper in the floater's pocket was written in a code. It took Tech about an hour to crack it."

"Why would someone do that?" Ham said. "I mean, it's a phone number on a piece of paper. In his pocket. Why bother with a code?"

"I guess he didn't want anyone to know he was calling a crisis line," Grace surmised. "Kids can be real paranoid." She took a big succulent bite of burger. Extra cheese, extra sauce, and onion rings as a side dish, too. It amazed her that she had had a hangover that morning, because it was all gone. Johnnie's was a bona fide holy grotto.

"Maybe he had a good reason," she added, downshifting as she reached a red light. The storm drains on either side of the street were overflowing, water churning against the curbs as pedestrians hugged the building side of the sidewalks. "To be paranoid, I mean. Maybe we're dealing with someone whose parents are high profile."

"So maybe they didn't file a Missing Persons," Ham said, following her train of thought. "We got no BOLO, nothing in the system to ID him. If their kid goes missing, they might send out someone private to pick him up and take him back to rehab and we never would know."

"Right, except the kid winds up in the river instead." She chomped a greasy onion ring in two and one half fell in her lap. Thank God she was wearing jeans. She slurped soda through her straw. Yeah, she was going to order a pizza for her beer session with Ham in a couple of hours, but she was hungry *now*.

"How'd it go with Captain Perry's lead?" Kate had ordered Ham back to the office because someone had called in a suspicious man wandering along the river.

"Turned out the guy was a jogger. Choctaw heritage. The caller thought he was a Middle Eastern terrorist."

Grace grunted. The way she looked at it, people in Oklahoma City deserved to be jittery. Timothy McVeigh and 9/11 loomed large in everyone's minds. But the hypervigilance did make for some interesting police work. She tried not to take the mistaken identity personally, as she herself was part Choctaw.

"By the way," Ham said, trying to sound casual, "I told her we'd both go in early tomorrow morning to get some more of those files off our desks." As usual, they had failed in their sworn oaths to get the paperwork under control. Captain Perry was not amused.

"Fine. You can go in *extra* early and do mine, too," she said.

"Yeah, bullshit."

"Hey, sucker, you're the one making bullshit promises." Grace took another swig of soda. "So I'm already at the address," she went on. They were in a race to see who got there first. Not very mature but oh, well.

"Liar. I am," Ham retorted.

"You are not." She grinned. "You're so full of shit. First one there gives the other one a blow job."

"You're on," he said.

The light turned green, and she was about to gun it when she caught sight of a kid about Clay's age walking a puppyish black Lab about Gus's size from beneath the shelter of an umbrella. She watched for a second, wondering about anyone voluntarily strolling around in this rain. Kid and pup looked reasonably happy. A horn beeped behind her.

She disconnected and paid better attention to the road.

Helping Hand was located in a strip mall off North Robertson. A nondescript two-story brick building with double rows of horizontal windows featured an ice-cream parlor; a deli; a combination cellular-phone and photocopy shop; and finally, Helping Hand, on the northeast corner. There was a tiny sign on the plain wooden door that you would miss unless you were really looking for it. Which was probably the point.

Ham pulled in nearly two minutes after Grace. As she leaped out of Connie the Porsche and dashed beneath the building overhang, she wagged her Johnnie's bag at him like a trophy and licked her lips suggestively. He laughed.

Then she tried Helping Hand's door, and found it locked. There was a buzzer set into the brick on her right; she pushed it. Ham grabbed her bag and ate the last onion ring, then wadded up the bag and expertly pitched it at a cement trash receptacle behind him. It went in.

"Yes?" someone said through the intercom.

"We're Detective Hanadarko and Detective Dewey," Grace said. She had called ahead.

They were buzzed in. Grace went first up a dingy, narrow flight of stairs. There was some graffiti on the wood paneling; someone had attempted to clean it off but hadn't succeeded. That was it, no pictures or plaques with uplifting slogans or anything.

"Cheerful place," Ham murmured.

"Yeah, no shit," Grace said. "If you didn't feel like killing yourself *before* you got here . . ."

There was another door at the top of the stairs; as they reached it, it opened. A thin, middle-aged man in a charcoal-gray sweater and a pair of gray trousers stood on the threshold. His graying beard was closely trimmed. A fluffy white-haired cat sidled up beside him and me-owed at the visitors.

"Hello, Detectives," the man said pleasantly. "I'm Evan Johnson. And this is Ragdoll. I hope neither one of you is allergic."

They both shook their heads and entered a postage stamp–size foyer with a plain oak desk, a multiple-line phone system, and a desktop computer with a printer. An upholstered light blue chair was pushed back. White cat hairs dusted the desk. A cup of tea wafted peppermint in the chilly air. There was a framed needlepoint picture on the wall that said YOU ARE NOT ALONE. A framed business license: First Church of the Savior, Oklahoma City DBA Helping Hand Teen Crisis Hotline. Church-run, then.

Grace noted the lack of extra chairs, a couch, just the little office setup. It reminded her of her insurance agent's office. No frills.

"We're not a walk-in service," Johnson explained as he watched her take in the surroundings. He pointed at a door on his left. "Just phones. Our hotline volunteers work in two rooms through there. We have extra staff today. The rain makes it difficult for some kids." He smiled sadly.

"As I explained on the phone," Grace began, "we're trying to ID a drowning victim. He had your number on a piece of paper in his pocket, written in code. With the initial *J*." She handed him a printout of a picture Rhetta had taken of the miraculous item in question. "Is there anything you can tell us about this?"

Johnson took the paper and studied it. "Well, obviously, my last name starts with a *J*." He knit his brows. "As for the code . . ." He shrugged his shoulders.

"We think whoever did this, didn't want anyone to know he'd called you," Grace filled in. "That must happen fairly often."

"Yes. We get a lot of whispered calls. That's why we guarantee anonymity. On both ends of the line." He cocked his head. "I don't recognize this handwriting."

"So . . . when the kids call you, they don't know who they're talking to?" Grace prompted.

"We'll give them a first name, yes," Johnson said. "We try to connect with the caller."

So maybe the needlepoint line was a talking point for the volunteers, and not just some sentimental bullshit on their wall.

"Do you ever answer the phones yourself?" Grace asked.

He shook his head. "Not really. I do administrative work, fund-raising. We're nominally supported by a church, but they don't really have the funds."

"So it's unlikely a caller would refer to you as 'J.' Since your first name begins with an *E*."

"Unlikely," he agreed. "We have a roster of volunteers. Our phones are open twenty-four hours a day, seven days a week." As if on cue, a phone trilled through the door.

"It must be tough to find that many volunteers," Grace said.

"We go through thick and thin," Johnson replied. "Somehow it all works out."

For you guys, yeah, Grace thought, seeing the image of the floater.

Johnson went over to his computer and moved the mouse on its pad. "Here," he said, hitting a button. "I'll make a list of volunteers whose names begin with *J*. James Tallbear . . . Joe Varisse . . . Juanita Provo . . . I won't be able to give you their private information, but I can ask them to get in touch with you."

Ham looked at her. She translated his expression: *We can try to get a warrant if we need to.* She gave him a brief nod.

"We may wind up interviewing everybody," Grace said. "Or this may be resolved another way."

"Of course," he said. A piece of paper printed out and he handed it to Grace. Five names.

"And they won't mind talking to us?" Grace pushed gently.

"Not at all." He smiled at her. "We cover that eventuality in training. Our volunteers are highly altruistic. They really want to help troubled youth." He pointed to the sheet. "Joe's here now," he said. "Juanita comes in at two a.m. James is taking a break from working for us. Jackie's tomorrow at midnight."

Noted, Grace thought. "Lots of late-night shifts," she said.

"As you might imagine, our busiest time is late night through early morning. After the bars close and everyone else is in bed."

Grace was no stranger to underage drinking. "Of course." She folded the paper and eased it into her jeans pocket. "Can we check in with Joe?"

"I'll see if he's on a call," Johnson told her. "Excuse me."

He left them there and walked through the door. Grace scooted over to the window on the computer screen he'd left open, grabbed her little notebook out of her jeans pocket, and jotted down Joe Varisse's home address. Ham moved closer to the door Johnson had closed, listening. Footsteps warned her to scoot back over to Ham.

The door opened. A tall dark-skinned man stood on the threshold. He looked at them both with faint apprehension, then entered the room.

"Evan's taking my calls," he told them. He had a deep, melodious voice, like warm honey over warm oatmeal. Or something else warm. "What would you like to know?"

Grace blinked at the sound of his voice. She knew that voice. Then she broke out in a wide smile as it came to her. "You're Freeway Joe. You do the early-morning traffic on the radio."

He grinned at her. "That's me."

"I can't tell you how many times you have saved me from being late to work." She held out her hand. Looking amused, he took it.

Then he looped his thumbs in the pockets of his jeans. Sensing her unasked question, he said, "I volunteer because my little sister committed suicide about five years ago. She was eighteen. I figured if I could stop someone from doing the same thing . . ."

"I'm sorry," she said. There was a moment of uncomfortable silence, then she moved on to business. "I'm Detective Grace Hanadarko. This is Detective Hamilton Dewey. We're trying to establish the identity of a drowning victim. We think he called the hotline and talked to someone whose name begins with *J*. We're running a print and we're getting a sketch. So far, what we have is mid- to late teens, about five-seven, slight build."

Varisse tsked and lowered his head, as if taking a moment for the deceased. Grace liked that. "We only talk to them on the phone," he said. "We never meet face-to-face. The anonymity helps them open up."

He was talkative. Grace liked that, too. While she engaged him, Ham glanced through the doorway that Varisse had left open.

"We figured our victim died about a week ago," Grace said. "Anyone talk to you about drowning himself around then?"

"Most of our potential suicides plan to OD. Or they've got a gun," Varisse told her. "Mostly they want to go out listening to rock music. Something a little closer to home than drowning. So they can talk to us."

"They could take you with them on a cell phone," she pointed out. "Do you get many jumpers?"

"Funny thing about a hotline," he said. "A lot of experts argue that people who really plan to kill themselves won't call us. They'll just do it. We just keep them talking. As long as they're talking, we've got a chance."

"Speaking of talking," she said. "Maybe there's a room we can go to?"

"Maybe the deli downstairs," Varisse suggested. "It's a little crazy back there. . . ."

"That'd be great," Grace said.

"I'll check with Evan," Varisse replied. "See if he's cool."

Evan was cool. Grace filed away that maybe Evan did take the occasional call. In the deli, Varisse asked for hot tea with lemon, to pamper his voice. There were some neon-green flyers for Helping Hand beside the cash register. And some grape-colored ones for gastric-bypass surgery. Grace got some tea as well, and ordered everything bagels with cream cheese all around. Ham opted for coffee, and the three sat by the window. It was still raining; neon signs bled pink, blue, and red through the glass. Tires whooshed; the door opened and closed many times as people came in out of the rain.

"So what do you tell them when they call you?" Grace asked Varisse. "The ones who are threatening to commit suicide?"

He took a nibble of his bagel and chased it with tea. "That they'll probably fail. The majority of people who try to commit suicide survive the attempt. They wake up with pumped stomachs or a mental-health hold. Or severe internal injuries, brain damage, facial disfigurements from the gunshot. With lots of medical bills for their parents, legal problems, and freaked-out friends and relatives."

"And whatever's been bothering them is still there," Ham said.

"Yes." Varisse nodded. "Only they're even less equipped to deal with it because they've compounded the problem. We try to refer them to some real help."

"Still, it's pretty harsh to tell them that they're going to fail," Grace led.

"I take them past the point of suicide. Make them see that oblivion is highly unlikely. Tell them that if they've swallowed a bunch of pills, they're probably going to vomit before they lose consciousness. That they might go into a coma and get put on life support, and that their relatives might have to decide if they're going to pull the plug."

Grace nodded, encouraging him to continue.

"I ask them about their families. How they'll react to their death, or even a failed attempt. If they think they'll go to hell for committing suicide."

"Do very many believe that? That they'll go to hell?" Grace asked. She remembered the DBA on the wall. Christian organization.

"Some. Sometimes all they've got is me, on the phone." He sipped some more tea. The cup looked like a toy in his grip. He had muscles; he worked out. "They've passed their breaking point. They don't see any reason to go on. I try to make them see that it's just temporary."

"Do you tell them they might go to hell?" Grace asked.

"No. I'm not a religious person," Varisse replied. "We're funded by a church, but Evan has made it clear that we don't have to be believers. They're a pretty cool group."

"Do you go to their services, things like that?" Ham ventured.

"I don't even know where the church is," Varisse replied.

"If someone's ODing on the line, do you dispatch the paramedics if you can get a trace?" Grace asked.

He nodded. "And most of the time, the caller's pissed off at me when he finds out they've shown up. Callers like that are usually loaded—drunk or high. They're embarrassed. But once they sober up, a few have called back to thank us. Or their parents do. Make a donation."

"Do you record the conversations?" Grace added another packet of sugar to her second cup of tea.

He shook his head. "We don't have the resources for that. But each volunteer keeps a log of calls."

We could also subpoena that, Ham's look told her.

"Do they ever stop by? To thank you or leave a donation?" Grace shook in a third sugar packet. Ham watched her stir in creamer. More creamer. She smirked at him and added another packet of sugar.

"Evan discourages that kind of thing." Varisse looked down at his teacup. "Ongoing relationships. We try to help with an immediate crisis. We're not therapists."

Which wasn't exactly a *no*. And why did he break eye contact just then?

Ham had noticed, too. Grace knew it without even looking at him. After all, they were partners.

"So, say I'm thirteen and I call during your shift and you intervene," Grace said. "I decide not to kill myself. But what if I change my mind and call back? What if I get scared again? Will I get to talk to you?"

He looked back up at her. "Maybe, if I'm still on my shift. But I might be on another call."

"So if I ask for you?" she pressed.

"Sometimes there's two of us. Even three. We try to rotate the calls. But when it's just me, then you'll get just me."

"What if you find out I'm thirty-seven?" she asked. She was a tad older than that.

"That's about what I figured," he said, grinning at her. She sat up straighter. "We don't turn anybody away, of course. Youngest caller I've ever had was ten. Her step-father was abusing her."

"Yeah, it can start early," Grace said in a low voice. She took a sip of her tea. It scalded her tongue. She took another sip.

"Do you guys ever listen in on each other?" Ham asked. "Say, you've got a tough call or you don't know what to say?"

"Not usually. When we're training, yeah."

"Are most of your calls people who want to commit suicide?"

"No. Less than half. Some people just need a connection. They don't know how to reach out to anyone real. We're at a safe distance. On the phone."

"E-mail?" Ham asked.

"No. There are some agencies that do that. IMs, chat rooms, texting. We're old-fashioned."

Time to double back. "So *do* you think they go to hell?"

Varisse shook his head. "I think we make our own hell. Right here." He pulled out his cell phone and looked at it. "I don't want to keep Evan."

"Of course not." Grace took one more sip of tea. Ham just left his coffee. They got up and hustled through the rain with Joe back to the door of the crisis center. Grace noticed that he had a key; he didn't need to be buzzed back in.

They went upstairs, finding Johnson back in the foyer. He told them another volunteer had arrived—Shirley Maxwell. She was already fielding a call in the back room. Joe Varisse had another hour, and Johnson was going to go home for the day.

"I'll put out an e-mail to all the volunteers and ask them to contact you," Johnson told Grace and Ham.

"Thanks. Anything they've got, any leads, would be appreciated," Grace said as she and Ham put down a quarter-inch stack of their business cards.

Johnson walked out with them, opened an umbrella, then headed toward a Dodge Caliber and got in. Through force of habit, Grace checked his plates. Oklahoma. He had a Sooner bumper sticker. No religious stuff.

"Damn," Grace said as she wiped some sugar off her fingers and fished out her keys from her jeans pocket. "There's not much accountability. Working alone, door keys floating all over the place. I mean, what if I was some sociopath who decided to tell every third guy who called me that he was better off dead? Ted Bundy worked on a hotline. How many women did he murder back in the day?"

"What if Joe's dealing drugs out of there? Or he hooks up with some vulnerable woman?" Ham looked up at the dripping overhang. "Something was going on with him," he added. "People like that, do-gooders, sometimes they have questionable boundaries."

Grace smirked. "Yeah, no shit, Detective."

He frowned. "Be nice, Grace."

She touched the buzzer without pressing it. "I'm just pushing your buttons, Dewey."

CHAPTER
FIVE

"Push harder," Grace whispered as Ham did his thing. They'd wrapped up at the office—no hits on the print, nothing from Butch and Bobby—and called it a day.

Now it was dark and rainy and sweet, in a raunchy kind of way.

There were wine bottles and booze bottles and cigarettes and pizza remnants all over the floor of her bedroom. They were writhing on their old stomping grounds, aka her bed. Grace's clothes were strewn from the refrigerator to the bedroom and back again. Ham's were in a pile in the bathroom. Nice long soak, a few bottles of wine . . . now he was on top of her and she was half out of her mind, it was so good. It was always so good. She died two, three times a night when she was screwing Ham.

And went straight to heaven.

"Oh, Grace, oh, God," Ham groaned. She knew that catch in his throat, felt him tense, and let her head roll back in the cradle of his palms. He spasmed hard. He was done.

And she was, too. Done and done in. The night had been glorious, candles and pearls, fluffy handcuffs and just a tiny bit of rough. Just fun rough.

Ham let out all the air, sighing hard, and she smiled. He gathered up her hair and kissed the side of her face, nibbling on her ear, and sighed again. Kissed her temple.

"Grace," he murmured, as if he couldn't say her name enough. He was getting awfully sentimental, so she slid out from his embrace and sat up. He reached a limp hand for her, easily dodged, and flopped his arm in the warm spot she had just vacated. Buck naked, she wandered into the living room.

"Where are you going?" he called.

"Gus has to go out," she replied. "Don't you, Gusman?" she whispered.

Gus was fast asleep. She nudged him with her toe and he didn't move a muscle. Didn't even blink. And damned if it wasn't still raining.

A blast of cool air kissed her as she opened the fridge and surveyed her beer supply. With a grin, she reached for a longneck just as Ham's hands slid around her waist. She felt his sex, still half tumescent, pressing against her back.

"That was nice," he said.

"That was hot," she corrected. She didn't do nice. They didn't do nice. Sex was sex, not a sashay through the tulips. Not even for Ham.

She left the beer in the fridge and shut the door. Since Ham had moved out on Darlene, it was harder to get him to leave at night. He'd promised things weren't different between the two of them, but they were. Moving out meant moving on or moving in, and she was nervous.

"Hey," she said, glancing at the clock on the microwave, "it's almost two."

"Yeah," he replied, sounding tense, as if bracing himself for the boot.

"Time for *Juanita's* shift on the hotline." She turned around in his arms, draped her wrists over his shoulders, and bumped against him suggestively. "We could call her."

"Dry run?" he asked, arching his pelvis against her. "Pretend to be strung out, scared . . ."

"We probably shouldn't mess with her. Don't want

any sort of entrapment dirtying our case. We gotta win this one." Grace rocked to their rhythm.

"If it is one."

They nodded in unison and stopped the sex dance. She left the warmth of his beautifully cut body and rooted around for her cell phone. It was tangled up in her bikini underwear. How come would remain one of life's mysteries. She found the hotline number and punched it in while they walked together to the couch. They sat down naked.

"Helping Hand," said a woman's voice, thick Hispanic accent. "This is Juanita. I'm here."

"Hello, Juanita, my name is Grace. Hanadarko," Grace said, giving Ham a nod. He sat back on the couch, putting a pillow behind his back. He had no idea that, on many other occasions, an angel had sat in that exact spot, chewing tobacco and munching on pizza with extra jalapeños and no mushrooms. "I'm a detective with OCPD. I'm sorry to disturb you like this, but I'm working on a case. My partner, Detective Dewey, and I left our business cards there at the crisis center."

"Yes," Juanita said, her voice rising a little. A bit nervous, talking to a cop. That was normal for most civilians. "I saw it. Evan left me a note and asked me to call you." She laughed shyly. "I'm sorry. I didn't realize he meant tonight."

"No. I'm just . . . up anyway, and he mentioned that you worked this shift." Ham snaked his foot under her thigh. She raised her leg so he'd have better access. "I have an unidentified drowning victim, and he had the center's phone number on a piece of paper. So I'm interviewing the volunteers to see if anyone can tell me who he is."

There was a pause. Grace didn't know if that was significant, or if Juanita was just thinking. It was so much easier to read body language than to speak to someone over the phone. Maybe they should have waited.

"We get a lot of calls," Juanita said. "Lately, I've been talking to more girls than boys. Unwanted pregnancies, boyfriend problems. A lot of their parents are losing their homes. That seems to be harder on the girls."

"It all seems so insurmountable when you're tired and scared," Grace said. "I'm not preventing any calls from coming in, am I?"

"No, we have call-waiting," Juanita assured her. "I don't think I've talked to anyone who threatened to drown himself."

"This kid was maybe sixteen, but he was small for his age. We're doing a composite based on forensic evidence." That was a polite way of saying based on his skull and pieces of skin and hair. "Once it's completed, we'd appreciate it if you'd take a look at it."

"Of course." There was another pause, and then she said, "Evan mentioned there was a *J* on the piece of paper."

"Yes." Grace cocked a brow. Ham looked at her. She held up her finger, and he got up and got two beers out of her fridge. She let the silence grow. Juanita was probably used to pauses on the phone. But maybe she filled them herself when they grew too long.

"I have another call," Juanita said.

"Okay, well, thanks. We'll be in touch." Grace hadn't heard any telltale beep, but that didn't mean anything—she might have missed it. She reached her hand straight up, and Ham put a cold beer into it. She clicked off her cell phone and set it on the coffee table. Lightning flashed. Rain fell.

Ham plopped down and took a swallow, looking over at her. She shrugged and started on the beer, while Ham started in on her, lazing his free hand over her breast.

"I'm not sure, but I think J-for-Juanita's a little nervous," she said. "We should stay on her."

"First, I'll stay on you." Ham's hand traveled to her

other breast, rough, warm fingertips on chilly, puckering skin.

"I need to get some sleep," she said, taking another drink.

"So . . . we can sleep."

"You need to go home," she insisted. "Those rats in the walls of your apartment will miss you."

"It's not that bad of a place." She heard the edge in his voice. He didn't want to leave.

Gus raised his head from his bed and told her in his Scooby-Doo way that he had to go weewee. Finally. Grateful for the opportunity to move away from Ham without seeming like she was moving away from Ham, Grace walked over to the side door and opened it. She made a little bow.

Gus flopped his head back down.

Thanks for nothing, Bighead.

Grace frowned. "Are you sick, man? Have you peed at all today?"

"He's fine." Ham started to reach for her. Then he sighed and set down his beer, scarcely touched. Wordlessly, he got up and walked past her; she smelled the yeasty scent of sex and hops as he went into the bathroom. After he peed, he didn't come out. He was getting dressed.

It is what it is, Grace thought as she watched the rain come down.

About three hours after Ham left, Grace's cell phone rang. She was asleep, fumbled, got it.

"Detective Hanadarko," Grace said.

"It's . . . Juanita. I hope I didn't wake you up."

I knew it. I knew something was up with her. Despite the low-grade hum in Grace's gut, she stayed neutral. "No, not at all. I keep crazy hours when I'm working on a case." She was trying to make Juanita think she was just like her. They were the same kind of people—people who would normally talk to each other, share confidences. Police work was a lot like working a crisis line: If you got people talking, you were getting somewhere.

"I . . . I thought of something." Juanita sounded shaky.

Stay easy, Grace. "That's great. Anything you can do to help me—"

"And I need to talk to you."

Bingo. Mucho bingo. *You are talking to me. But that's not what you mean, is it? You've got something. You know something.*

"Sure. You want me to come over there?" She waited a beat.

"I'm . . . no." Juanita's voice was low, breathy, as if she didn't want anyone to hear her.

"Or . . . you could come down to the office," Grace said, as if she was struck with sudden inspiration. She made her voice grow warmer, tinged it with a bit of excitement. "We might have a sketch today. I could show you the deceased's personal effects." *And interview you, with Ham or one of the guys behind our observation mirror, make sure I got our asses covered.*

"I sleep during the day." Juanita was losing her nerve.

"That's no problem," Grace said. She heaved a frustrated sigh. "I have a mound of paperwork to do. I'm so busted. I'm going into the office in a little bit to get it done before anyone comes in."

"Oh," Juanita murmured.

C'mon, c'mon, Grace silently urged her.

"Joe and I went down to that deli you've got there," she chattered on. "That's probably where I screwed up. I drank so much coffee I got wired. That was really dumb of me. I have enough trouble sleeping as it is."

"I know what you mean," Juanita said. "That's one of the reasons I don't mind the late shift." She took a breath. "Maybe I could bring you some coffee." Then she backtracked. "What am I saying? There's coffee at a police . . . at your work."

"Are you kidding? Our coffee is like battery acid. No one ever drinks it. We all bring in our own."

"Then . . . I could bring some, and maybe a couple of bagels. Or if you'd rather have a donut . . ."

Grace made herself not do her version of the Rhetta happy dance. But she did smile at Gus, who had opened one eye and was gazing steadily at her.

"Y'know, I've got the worst sweet tooth," Grace confessed. "I try to stick to the healthy stuff, like bagels, but you get what you want. Oh, hell, if they've got maple bars—"

"They do," Juanita said. "And chocolate ones, too." She waited.

"Damn. How about a couple of each? We can share. I just went to the ATM and—"

"Oh, please," Juanita said. She sounded almost cheerful. "Don't worry about *that*."

"Well, thanks, Juanita. So, see you in . . . maybe half an hour?" Grace pressed. She carried the cell phone with her into her bedroom and gazed at the tornado of clothing. Shook her head and opened a drawer. Clean bikinis, cool. Clean bra. Two for two.

"Yes," Juanita replied. Given a task and a chance to be helpful, and committed to showing up with food.

Grace hung up and dialed Ham.

"Yeah." His voice was early-morning husky; it got her where she lived.

"It's almost seven. Juanita's coming in," she informed him. "And you have to do my paperwork."

He groaned, then laughed silently. So, no hard feelings for kicking him out. At least, none he was sharing.

CHAPTER
SIX

Tired but alert, Grace showered, dressed, and microwaved yesterday's leftover coffee. As she braided her hair, she looked around for Earl, to show him she damn well *could* wake up without a hangover, but he was probably off eating tabouli in Iraq.

The streets were slick, but Connie knew how to hug the corners. Grace got to 701 Colcord Drive in plenty of time and winced when she saw, really saw, all the folders on her desk. Poor Ham. Whistling under her breath, she scooped up the first five hundred pounds or so and hefted them onto his desk.

"Hey," said Bobby as he walked in. He was carrying a large brown paper shopping bag. She raised a brow. He said nothing, just walked over to Butch's desk and set the bag on his partner's chair. He opened the top drawer to the desk and pulled a colorful box out of his sack and stuffed it in the drawer. Pulled out another box.

Intrigued, Grace wandered over. The entire bag was full of various boxes of candy. Fudge, specifically.

She opened another one of Butch's drawers and placed the box inside. Bobby nodded his thanks.

"What're we doing this for?" she asked, grinning her lopsided grin.

"Butch broke a heart while we were out canvassing," he said. "She either owns or works in an upscale fudge shop."

"Fudgepacker?" she quipped as she examined one of the boxes. It seemed a little light to be a one-pound box of truffles. "This is an expensive joke, man."

"Sweet tooth," he said. "It would be if I'd bought candy at the store we went to," Bobby replied. He flashed her a smile. "And if there was fudge in any of those boxes."

She began to open the box in her hands, then stopped. She'd save the surprise for its intended target.

"I got someone coming in," she said. "Scared, I think. From the hotline."

Bobby folded up the bag and stashed it in his own desk. "Coming in willingly?"

"I think she wanted to meet me somewhere else. But after our string of bad luck around here, I don't want to screw it up, you know?" She jerked her head in the direction of the interview room. "You think you could observe?"

"Sure."

"Thanks, man."

Grace took the next pile of case files and transferred them to Ham's desk. Then she thought a moment and took back a stack, opened one, put on her glasses, and sat down. She had to reassure Juanita that she really did have to come in. Lessee, lessee. ADW. Assault with a deadly weapon. Black on black. She remembered the perp. Stared into his mean, dull mug-shot eyes and saw nothing there but a serious need for a time-out. In solitary.

"What time is she coming in?" Bobby asked her.

"Not sure. Soon," Grace replied. She checked the time on the face of her cell phone. It was coming on seven forty-five. "Maybe about now."

"I'll go get some coffee," said Bobby, leaving her alone in case her anxious citizen arrived.

"Thanks, man," she said. Added, "But don't drink it, y'know? That shit'll kill you."

They shared a smile and Grace called Ham on his cell.

"I'm almost there," he said.

"I'm here now. I think you owe me something." She liked his dirty chuckle. "She's not here yet, but let me do some girl talk with her."

"Got it." He sounded tired. "Grace, maybe *we* should talk."

"Shit, Ham, we talk all day." She hung up.

"Not now, Earl," she said, just in case he felt like giving her a little morning pep-talk-slash-lecture about her situation with Ham before Juanita showed up. But her admonition was greeted with silence. She huffed, wishing for a distraction so she could close the file folder.

And God answered her prayers, as Juanita Provo hovered on the other side of the glass entrance to Major Crimes. She was Hispanic, early forties, with a few curves; bronze lipstick and eye makeup; wearing a navy blue raincoat over jeans, heeled boots, and a white blouse. She cradled a cardboard take-out box in her arms loaded with coffee and frosted donuts. Not a bagel in sight.

Grace caught the door and speed-dialed Ham. Juanita smelled like roses. She smiled at Grace with big white teeth.

"Hi," Juanita said. Yep, same voice.

"Hey. Wow, thanks," Grace said warmly. "Is this one mine?" She eased the nearest coffee out of the container. It was a strategic move: Juanita still had something to do with her hands, and Grace had taken command of the situation. She stood aside to let Juanita in. Watched her assess her surroundings. Judging from Juanita's level of curiosity, it appeared that she was new to the inside of a police station.

"Hmm, that's good," Grace said, taking a sip. *Gack,* where was the sugar? "We can go in here," she said, indicating the interview room. "It's not all that comfortable," she added, "but it's private."

"Okay," Juanita said, still happy to be helpful. Her gaze strayed to Grace's and Ham's desks, which faced each other. "Wow, is that the paperwork you mentioned?"

Grace smiled. "Don't worry. I've got all day to deal with it. I'm grateful to you for the excuse to put it off for a little bit. So if you feel like, y'know, *chatting* for a while . . ." She raised her brows: *please, please, please?*

Juanita's face clouded, as if she was being brought out of a warm bubble of girl-to-girl camaraderie into the colder reality of why she had called Grace. If people thought Grace would play nice because she was a girl, Grace was happy to let them think that. She officially did not notice Juanita's change in demeanor and walked her into the interrogation room. Pushed the button to make the light go red, signaling that the room was occupied, and shut the door behind the two of them.

She set her coffee cup on the table. Juanita blinked at the handcuff ring in the center while she put down the carton. At the two-way mirror.

"It's not much," Grace agreed. "Would you be more comfortable at my desk?"

"Oh, no, this is okay," Juanita assured her. She brightened. Falsely. "Do you want chocolate or maple, to start?"

Grace's cell phone vibrated inside her jeans. She guessed that Ham had arrived.

Grace took a chocolate frosted bar and sampled it. Fat, sugar, and cocoa. You couldn't go wrong with that. She gave a little moan and pulled back her chair. Juanita sat down, but she didn't take a donut. Grace pretended not to notice as she flashed Juanita a guilty little grin and took a maple bar, too.

Juanita smiled a little, and picked up the other maple bar. She broke off a little bit and put it in her mouth. A tentative sort. Grace would be gentle.

"You must be tired, after your shift." She drank some coffee.

"I . . . there was a boy," Juanita began.

Here we go. Grace took another sip of coffee. Then she looked at Juanita.

"His name was Zack. He called . . . a lot." She looked at her maple bar as if it might tell her what to say next.

"And did he mostly talk to you?" Grace asked her.

She nodded. "Evan doesn't want us to form attachments. We're not therapists and we're not always there. So if someone calls expecting to talk to the same phone volunteer, but can't, it adds to their sense of powerlessness."

"Makes sense." Grace tore off more maple. No, wait, it was time for some chocolate, no, for both. God, she was hungry.

"But . . . he was so . . . ," Juanita trailed off.

So you broke the rules. Told him your schedule. "Trouble at home? Drugs?" Grace asked.

"The thing is, if it's not him," Juanita said, "I don't want to violate his privacy."

Or get in trouble. "That's perfectly understandable," Grace said calmly. "People take a big chance when they open up to you. I respect that."

She waited. Juanita sat quietly.

"So . . . was it drugs?" Grace asked, trying to set up a scenario. That's what cops did, built up a picture, a scenario, for the interviewee to participate in. So the subject could add detail or correct the officer. And then, eventually, some of the interviewees realized they had tipped their hand or outright confessed. Juanita dipped her head.

No, Grace translated.

"Bad home life?"

"He stopped calling about a week ago," she said, gazing up at Grace with a stricken look.

Grace's cell phone vibrated again. She debated. Juanita was maybe about to have a breakthrough. Maybe the call was urgent. Maybe the best thing was to let Juanita take a moment.

"Excuse me," she said, pulling out the phone. It was a text message from Ham: SKETCH.

Wow, that was fast, she thought approvingly. *Maybe Earl is helping us.*

"Juanita," she said, "I know that at Helping Hand you talk to people on the phone. But maybe you saw someone hanging around in the parking lot, or sitting in the deli. We have a sketch. I'd like to show it to you."

Her eyes got huge. "Of the . . . does he look? . . ."

"No, no, it's what our John Doe looked like before," Grace said. She leaned forward slightly. "You'd be helping us out if you could tell us if you ever saw him around."

"Okay." Juanita cleared her throat. "Yes."

"Excuse me," Grace said, pushing back her chair. "I'll get the sketch and I'll come right back."

The woman crossed her arms and nodded. "Okay."

Grace left the room and saw no one in the bullpen. On a hunch, she entered the observation room. Ham was sitting in the chair nearest the door with an open folder in his lap, revealing the sketch. Kate, Bobby, and Butch were there, too. Grace took the sketch from Ham. Wide, light eyes, big forehead. Sharp nose, weak chin. Long hair, no particular style.

"Hi, Zack," Grace tried experimentally.

"Look at her," Butch said.

Grace looked through the mirror at the drab, unfriendly room. Juanita's head was bowed and her fists were clenched.

"She's praying," Grace said. "For this Zack? Or for herself?"

"Go find out," Kate told her, looking serious and determined.

"On it."

Grace strode back toward the interrogation room, then forced herself to slow down. She took a deep breath and put on her game face: sympathy, hope, sorrow. She gave the door a little knock and went on in.

Juanita raised her head and slid her hands into her lap. Straightened her shoulders. Licked her lips.

"Now, this is just our best guess," Grace began. "But we've got a young man in our morgue with no name, and we'd like to know who he is."

Gently, she placed the sketch down in front of Juanita Provo. The woman sucked in her breath and sat back in her chair. Her eyes widened, welled.

"Oh," Juanita whispered.

Hello, Zack, Grace said to the sketch.

"Does he look familiar?" Grace ticked her gaze to the observation mirror.

"I . . . yes," Juanita ground out, farther back in her seat. "He . . . are you sure . . . he's dead?" she rasped. Then she touched the center of her forehead with a trembling hand. "I mean . . . I don't know what I mean. . . ."

She covered her mouth with her hand; Grace was afraid Juanita might throw up, and she glanced around for the metal trash can, which they mostly kept in the room to slam down on the table and scare the living bejesus out of the hard cases.

"Zachary. He went by Zack." She made a choking sound deep in her throat. "Oh, God, we . . . I . . ."

Had phone sex? Robbed a liquor store? "You met," Grace began. "It was against the rules, but you saw him. You know that this is Zack." She flickered with triumph as Juanita shifted in her chair. Score for Hanadarko.

"He had no one," she said. She began to cry. "He was so lost."

"That's okay," Grace said. "You take your time." Grace grabbed one of the paper napkins from the deli and handed it to her. Juanita took it and wiped her eyes.

"Terribly lost," Juanita said, sobbing hard, once. Then she caught herself. "I told him to pray."

"That's good," Grace said.

"Pray for it to go away."

Say what? Grace waited. And waited.

"Pray for it to go away," Grace echoed. "It" what? Their love for each other? His heroin addiction? "Juanita, what was wrong?"

"He thought he might be a homosexual." Now the words ran together, as if she had to get them out quickly or she might never say them. "So I told him if he lifted his heart up to Jesus Christ, he could be healed. He could be *normal.*"

Grace's blood pressure rose. *So this kid comes to you, confides in you, looks to you for help. And you give him a line of fundamentalist bullshit?*

She clenched her jaw. "How'd that work out for him?" she bit off, then shut her eyes—because of course that was the wrong thing to say. She tried again. "Is that the policy of the crisis center? To pray with the callers?"

Juanita wept. Grace was afraid she was going to lose her. She opened her mouth to assure Juanita that she, Grace, prayed six times a day and most especially at noon for troubled youth, when Juanita spoke again.

"No. We're funded by a church, but it's nondenominational." Then she amended. "I mean the hotline's supposed to be secular. If they ask to pray on the phone, we do it, sure, anything to give them some time to cool down. But I . . . I knew this was against their policies."

Their policies. She was already putting distance between herself and the center. Probably assumed Evan would boot her ass.

"So when Zack called because he was confused about his sexual orientation, you indicated to him that being gay is not okay?" Grace gritted. Wrong thing again. She hadn't had any sleep. "I'm sorry," Grace began, but Juanita spoke over her, moving her anguished gaze from somewhere in time to right here, right now, and Grace's face. She flared a bit.

"It's *not* okay. It's a sin. And I wanted to save him. Jesus could have lifted that burden from him, if his faith was strong enough."

Then she dropped her head again, as if she knew she shouldn't even bother trying to justify her actions. The crown of her head gleamed under the fluorescents. Grace wanted to smack her, balled her fists beneath the table. *I have to be like her. She'll open up.*

"You were trying hard to help him. You must have met with him, prayed together," she said, her training winning out over the big red blur of anger fuzzing her mind.

Juanita nodded. "Yes. We met."

Grace picked up her maple bar, trying to remind Juanita that they'd had some good times here in the interview dungeon confessional. "At church?"

The woman shook her head. She was biting the lipstick off her mouth. Balancing-act time; Grace had to get the most bang for her questions until Juanita melted down or stopped talking.

"He didn't want to go to a Catholic church," Juanita said.

"And you're Catholic?"

"*Sí.*"

Grace caught the code switching—moving from English to Spanish—and knew Juanita was starting to lose it. The more stress she was under, the more likely she was to really put it out there. Or fold up her tent. But there was more. Grace was certain of it.

"That must have bothered you," Grace said, getting out of her chair. She walked around the table. "I'm Catholic.

I've got a brother who's a priest." *Who is a sanctimonious asshole.*

Juanita looked dubious. Grace very much regretted her outburst about praying away the gay. For that she assigned herself four folders of paperwork. No, two. She cleared her throat and perched on the corner of the table. "And I have a sister who's a lesbian," she said. She was lying of course, she needed to stack the deck so that Juanita would show her hand. "I've got some tough family dynamics."

"Oh." Juanita nodded. She wrapped her napkin around the forefinger of her left hand. Grace noted the absence of a wedding ring.

"He . . . people at school made fun of him," she said. "He was small, and girlish. He talked about being more macho. He really wanted to change."

"But . . . he couldn't," Grace said sadly, going for the cheese-out manipulation. "Not in time, anyway." A beat. "Did you suspect he was going to do it?"

Juanita jerked. "Suspect? . . ."

"That he was going to commit suicide." Grace crossed herself. "The one unforgivable sin."

"Oh, Dios *mío*," Juanita whispered brokenly. "Zack, *mijo*."

"You shouldn't blame yourself," Grace said. *Even though I sure as hell do.*

"I—I didn't get through to him." Juanita sniffled. "He died in a state of sin."

Grace shook her head slowly. "Sometimes people are so broken that we just can't fix them. But at least you tried."

"People don't fix other people," Juanita said. Her quavery voice suddenly became very firm. "Only God can fix them. But they have to offer themselves to Him to fix."

"You're right. I didn't say that well," Grace allowed.

She put a hand on Juanita's shoulder. "This must be so hard on you. When you say he had no one else, are you saying he had no family? Do you know his last name?"

"No," she replied. Too quickly.

"Please think hard," Grace urged softly. "We need to find his next of kin. Arrange for his burial."

"Oh." She chewed off more lipstick. Tightened the napkin around her finger like a noose. Grace figured Juanita was trying to dodge the aftermath, put some space between her and the boy she had failed to save from going to hell. And the crisis center, which would probably give her hell.

"We've sent his prints out," Grace said. "They'll come back sooner or later." That was probably a lie. There were about 150,000 cases listed in the ViCAP system. Victims, perps, suspects. There were over 300 million people in the United States.

"I—I think his last name might be Lacey," Juanita blurted. "He said it once to me."

Yes. Grace nodded thoughtfully. "You've got a good memory. Do you remember if he talked about parents? A brother? Sister? Someone with a name? Do you remember the name of his school?" It wouldn't be too hard to track him down now.

"His father is a truck driver," she said. "He's gone a lot."

"What's his mother's name?" Grace asked her.

"I don't know." She started to cry. "*Por favor,* please. This is all I know. I've been up all night." The tears came harder. "Please, let me go home."

Grace had no choice. She couldn't charge Juanita with anything. Accessory to suicide, yeah, maybe.

"Thank you so, so much for coming to me with this," Grace said, keeping the door open for Juanita to come back. "I know it was hard. But what you did today is going to help us."

Juanita sobbed. "He is gone from God. He's gone from God."

"We don't know that," Grace soothed, squatting beside her chair and rubbing Juanita's arm.

"He didn't die in a state of grace. I—I thought I could do some good. I thought . . ."

Grace's anger built again. Juanita was more concerned with her own complicity than the fate of Zack's immortal soul. *Typical Catholic bullshit,* she thought.

"Talk to your priest," Grace said, taking Juanita's hand. *Confession is good for the soul. He'll probably make you feel even guiltier, and you can wallow in it. That'll take your mind off being fired from the hotline.*

Juanita nodded. "Thank you," she said.

"Oh, and here. For the donuts," Grace said, handing her a ten. "Please."

"No, no," Juanita said, but she took it and stuffed it in her purse. She left, still crying.

As Grace shut the squad-room door, Kate, Ham, and Butch filed out of the interview room, grim-faced and angry, like her. Grace kicked a trash can.

"Zachary Lacey, whose father drives a truck," Captain Perry said.

"I'll contact the schools. The Oklahoma Department of Public Safety can get a match against the commercial driver's license records," Bobby said, heading for the phone. Grace checked the wall clock. Nine straight up. Offices were open.

"God, she might as well have pushed him in," Grace said.

"You call a help line, thinking you're safe from judgment," Kate concurred. "If they had a religious agenda, they should have advertised it." Her look took in Grace and Ham. "Did you get a sense that this Joe Varisse was on the up-and-up about that place refraining from spiritual counseling?"

"Maybe," Ham said. He turned to Grace.

"They're like that, those religious groups," Grace bit off. "Pull you in, then once they've got you . . ."

Then she turned away. Turned back, and looked at Ham.

"Once we find out which school he went to, let's talk to the kids who were mean to him. Shitheads."

Ham nodded. "Got it."

And Butch opened his top desk drawer. Saw the candy box and opened it. A sound chip activated and the room was filled with a woman's voice shrieking, "Butch, oh, Butch, oh, my God!"

Everyone started cracking up as Bobby darted over and opened the other drawers and the other candy boxes. More women joined the ecstatic chorus. Then a sheep baahed and a cow mooed, long and low and contented.

As laughter joined the cacophony, Butch just shook his head. Then Bobby reached into a box under his desk and said, "Who wants fudge?"

CHAPTER
SEVEN

Pizza, popcorn, a pound of sour gummy candy, and two liters of root beer.

Let the games begin.

Grace popped in the DVD of the horror movie Doug would probably not want Clay to watch while Clay settled in. They were both wearing their pj's. Clay's were a faded T-shirt from the Cowboy Hall of Fame and a pair of gray sweats. Grace had on baggy white men's flannels with blue stripes.

Gusman nosed at the pizza box on Clay's lap. With a giggle, Clay pulled off part of the crust on his double-super-triple-extra-meat-worshipers' pizza slice and let Gus hoover it in. Clay's giggle became a full-throated laugh, and Grace smiled fondly at the two of them. She sat down next to boy and dog, and Clay handed her a piece of pizza. They were using paper towels for plates.

Grace picked up the remote. "So, previews or no previews?" she asked.

"Previews. There will probably be a lot of cool gross ones," Clay said. His dark eyes, so like his dead mother's, sparkled with anticipation. He still had his baby dimples. He was so cute.

She grinned. "Previews it is."

They watched in silence as a zombie chewed the top off a woman's skull. With a roar, he began to eat the screaming chick's brains.

Zachary Lacey's autopsy's done, Grace thought. *Cause of death, drowning. Shit.*

"Does it ever bother you when you see dead bodies in real life?" Clay asked her. "Like, all mangled?"

Like your mother was when I found her?

"Yeah," she said. She glanced over at him. He was rapt. "But it's worth it, Clay. It helps me catch the bad guys."

He processed that. She narrowed her eyes.

"Are you going to have nightmares over this movie?"

"No way," he said, blanching. "I've been waiting for months for this to come out on DVD."

She reached out to tousle his hair, but he was getting to an age where that was a patronizing gesture, maybe. Instead she jostled him with her hand and chomped down on sausage and spiced taco meat.

"Your dad say anything about this movie?"

Clay looked even more worried. "He doesn't even know it exists."

"Good." She picked up the remote and turned up the sound. "Let's keep it that way."

He laughed. "You're cool, Aunt Grace."

Ripping open the bag of sour candy, she moved her shoulders and cricked her neck. "Yeah, well, that depends on your definition, Clay."

"You're fun. And you listen to me."

The image of Father Patrick Satan Murphy, her priest and her molester, bloomed in her mind's eye. He had taken her for ice cream and to the movies, and a dozen other "fun" places. And he'd listened to her in the confessional. Murphy was the man her entire family trusted with not only her physical safety, but the care and nurturing of her immortal soul. Her direct line to God the Father and the Blessed Virgin, mother of all. Father Murphy took Grace's virginity when she was nine years old.

Nine.

So this kid Zack calls for help, and some bitch tells him he's got to pray for God to change him so God can love him. Sweet.

"Clay," Grace said, "you've got a lot of people who care about you, man. And if there was something that was bothering you, *anything,* you could go to one of those people and tell them about it, right?"

He crammed some popcorn and gummy candy into his mouth. "Sure, Aunt Grace."

Right. And your uncle, the priest, would tell you it was bad to be gay, and your grandmother would change the subject, but at least I can teach you to tell someone. If I'd told someone, I would have stopped Father Murphy.

Or maybe . . . no one would have listened to me. Maybe they would have blamed me. Look at all those other kids the Church betrayed. All those damn bishops. They didn't just turn the other butt cheek. They looked the other way.

Her stomach lurched as she glanced at Clay, safe in her house, eating a bunch of crap, watching a movie. So many people loved him. Wanted the best for him. But . . . would they be able to give it to him?

She caught her lower lip as her chest tightened and she was filled with something that made her tremble. How on earth would she help him make his way to adulthood? Become a man?

"He's got a father for that," Earl said. She jerked her head up. Clay was curled up beside her, and Gus was snoring against her thigh. Earl lounged in her easy chair with a bag of microwaved popcorn in his lap. An old re-run of *Law & Order: SVU* was on.

"What happened to the movie?" she asked.

"You both conked out and it was giving me the willies, so I popped it out and turned this on. But it's pretty gruesome, too." Earl made a face.

"I recorded the game," she told him. "You could watch that."

He raised a brow. "Which game?"

She laughed silently. "You are clearly not from Oklahoma." She gathered up her hair and let it fall. Dropped her head back against the sofa.

"A father," she said. "You mean Doug, his dad." She looked over at him. "Right?"

He changed the channel. Yet more crime-scene investigators were hunkering down around a dead body. Sighing, he surfed on. "You don't know what I mean, Grace."

"Maybe I do. Maybe that's the same father who lets airplanes crash into buildings and sixteen-year-old boys drown in rivers because they're gay."

"God's real sorry about Zachary Lacey," Earl said, looking hard at her. "I am, too."

"Sorry because he was gay so he went to hell?" she tested. If Earl could confirm Zack's sexual orientation, she was one step closer to the finish line.

"Grace, please." Earl was aggrieved.

"Well, people *can* do things that send them to hell. You said I was going to hell."

"Zachary Lacey was a sweet kid," Earl said. "Or so I've been told."

And I'm not. "Then why did you guys let this happen to him?"

Earl sighed. "You just don't get it, do you, child?"

"No. I don't, Earl. I sure as *hell* don't." She snaked her way off the couch and stood. Gus and Clay remained as they were. "I'm tired."

"No, you're thirsty." Earl turned off the TV. "You're thinking of going to the fridge and grabbing a beer."

"So? My ranch, my rules, man." She bowed her back, stretching out the muscles and staring up at the ceiling.

"And a bottle of tequila," Earl added. "That's on your mind, too."

Grace huffed and straightened, prepared to give him a stink eye. "Again I say . . ."

But he was gone.

"Good," she said aloud, sounding petulant and immature even to herself.

She went into her bedroom and came back with a soft cream-colored blanket that she arranged over Clay and Gus. Gus's legs pumped and he wheezed; he was doggie dream-jogging. Then she closed up the box of leftover pizza, walked into the kitchen, and opened the fridge. There were the lovely beers. Screw him. She crammed the pizza box on top of a brick of cheddar cheese and reached her hand in for a nice longneck.

Then she looked at the clock on the microwave, its red eye beaming behind the receipt for the pizza and some packets of Parmesan cheese. Damn. It was four a.m.

She shut the fridge not because Earl had shamed her but because she didn't feel like drinking a beer this close to starting a brand-new day. With her luck, she'd catch another FBI's Ten Most Wanted and get busted down for drinking on the job.

Taking another peek at Clay, she stomped into her bedroom and climbed into bed. She rolled over on a pack of matches and got them out of her way. Wondered who was talking to whom at Helping Hand and if they were doing more harm than good. She'd tried to talk a kid out of jumping off the bleachers at his school. Failed.

They were mean to him at school.

Grace ruminated on that awhile. She had to get some sleep. She fluffed up the covers and closed her eyes, but they popped back open. She tensed all the muscles in her body, hard, and relaxed them one at a time.

She sat up and lit a cigarette. She wondered who else couldn't sleep at four—make that four thirty—a.m. Maybe Rhetta was up, milking Holy Cow, worried about how to pay for the farm. Making lunches for her kids. You couldn't call moms with kids at four thirty a.m. It scared 'em. And it woke up the kids.

Grace tamped out the cigarette and lay back down again. Counted sheep.

"Maybe you'll do better if you count your blessings," Earl said.

They were back in Louie's, and the water was rising around her ankles. It was icy and it made her bones ache.

"Shouldn't we start bailing?" she asked him. "This place is filling up fast." She squinted against the lightning that flashed in the window. "And it's still raining."

"It's always raining someplace on Lifeboat Earth," Earl said.

The alarm woke her up and she realized she'd had another dream. No Leon Cooley in this one, thank God. No hangover, either. She never had too much to drink in front of Clay. *Bleah*. Too much popcorn and sour candy, though.

She got up and made her signature rubbery pancakes. They stuck to the pan but, hey, she'd cooked breakfast. Clay got up and took a shower, put on his Catholic-school uniform, and took a few bites of pancake.

"Can I have cold pizza instead?" he asked her.

"Sure. I'm having that, too," she replied.

She picked up a cup from the pile of dirty dishes, rinsed it out, and poured coffee in it. She took a slug and then got the pizza out of the fridge. Flipped open the box and gestured for him to help himself.

"Can I have a cup of coffee?" he asked.

"No." She glanced at the clock on her microwave. "Uncle John should be here in about ten minutes. Be sure to brush your teeth." She poured him a glass of milk. Then she took a slice of pizza. "And you might not want to mention our choice of movie to him, either. Even though we fell asleep before the really good parts."

"How do you know?" he asked.

"How many horror movies do you think we've watched together?" she demanded. "You don't know the best gory stuff comes later?" She showed him her teeth and chomp-chomp-chomped.

"Chmp, chmp, chmp!" Clay tried to be a zombie while at the same time not chewing with his mouth open.

They smiled, coconspirators.

The best gory stuff.

It was difficult to say which was harder on the friends and family of missing persons. Sometimes when you told them their loved one was dead, they thanked you. They had to face the fact that Cousin Mo was gone, but at least they knew. It was the not knowing that made it so hard. It was hell not knowing. That was why so many people had risked their lives to retrieve all the bodies out of the Murrah Building as fast as possible.

Time to meet the Laceys.

Grace entered the interview room and looked at the seated couple. She felt the tension rise as she came in and sat down. Ron Lacey was a burly man with a full beard, and he kept his Owens Field ball cap on. His eyes were too close together, and Grace reminded herself that just because that made him look kind of stupid, it didn't mean he was. His jaw was tight and he had that flat, resentful expression some people got around cops. It didn't matter if she could help him. He detested her just because. Maybe to underscore that point, Monsieur had chosen to wear a faded Harley-Davidson T-shirt. Harley bikes went for around fifteen grand, for starters. She sincerely doubted he owned one.

Cherie Lacey, his wife, sat huddled beside him with the long scarlet fingernails of her right hand wrapped around his bicep. Younger, with blond hair straightened into a stylish cut. She had on way too much makeup, and was wearing large hoop earrings with hunks of glass or maybe cubic zirconium dangling from them. She wore a leopardskin-print tank top and spiky black boots decorated with loose boot bracelets studded with brass roses and more sparkles. Her eyes welled with tears, and she was holding an unlit cigarette between the slender fingers of her left hand, which was shaking.

"Hello, Mr. and Mrs. Lacey," Grace said in a soft voice. The couple was facing the two-way mirror. "I'm sorry to have to call you down here like this."

Cherie Lacey glanced at her husband. He stared stonily at Grace. Cherie licked her lips and toyed with her cigarette. "Where's Zachary?" she asked. Her voice twanged pure Texas. Grace should have made Butch do this one.

Ron Lacey stayed quiet. Waves of hostility rolled off him like body odor. Despite no match on the print, Grace was fairly certain that his son's body was lying in the morgue; Grace wondered how Daddy would react when he found that out.

For the time being, the mom was the one who was more engaged, so Grace concentrated on her. "When was the last time you saw your son, Mrs. Lacey?"

"He's my stepson," she replied. "It's been about a week."

A week. Potential match, Grace thought. She kept her face neutral. "Did you file a Missing Persons report?"

Cherie blanched. "Well, I—"

"No, she didn't," Lacey interrupted, "because he runs away a lot. Little shit."

Beneath her coat of makeup, Cherie's forehead was wrinkled, as in maybe she was a little older than she first appeared. "He usually comes back after a couple of days. I didn't want to get him in trouble at school, so I . . . I called him in sick." She blanched. "Was that, um, illegal?" She swallowed hard and grasped her husband's arm tightly. The frown lines on his face softened as he laid his hand over hers. She didn't look back at him.

"Maybe not if you call him in for a couple of days," Grace replied. "But he's been gone a full week, ma'am."

She swallowed, contrite. "I know. But Ronnie was on the road, and I wasn't sure what to do."

"You're a trucker," Grace said. "Long haul. You were in Nebraska." It would be easy enough to verify if she needed to.

His too-close, stupid eyes practically crossed. He must be fun in a bar fight. "So?"

"Just sayin'," Grace said evenly. "Making sure I understand the big picture."

He glowered at Grace. "There is no picture here, cop. This is family business. We'll raise him our way. They only care if he's in school so they can get money from the government."

"Sir," Grace said, then forced herself to take a breath, "we have reason to believe that your son is dead, sir. We have a body in the morgue, and there's been a positive ID of a composite sketch by someone who knew him."

"No," Cherie whispered. "Oh, no, dear God, no."

Grace opened her file folder and laid the sketch faceup on the table. There were also color pictures of the bloated horror they'd fished out of the river, but she kept those facedown and out of sight.

If she was looking for some grief from the man, or shock, she didn't get it. Although Cherie Lacey caught her breath and covered her mouth, Lacey's expression never wavered.

"Zack," Cherie whispered. "Oh, my God, that *is* Zack. Ronnie, oh, no, *no*." She burst into tears and he patted her, almost reflexively, as he waved his free hand dismissively at the sketch.

"That's just a drawing," he said. He gestured to the folder. "What else you got?"

"I have very disturbing pictures," Grace replied. "It's possible we have the wrong person. As you say, this is just a composite sketch, done by a police artist with a computer. But whoever it was, he drowned, and he was in the river for a week."

"Oh, no, no," Cherie moaned. "*Ronnie—*"

"We don't know it's him," Lacey said, sounding impatient. "I want to see the other pictures. The *real* ones."

Grace considered. She could not let her instant dislike of this man color the way she treated him now. It was highly likely his son was dead, and the photographs would stay with him for the rest of his life, unless his heart was coated with Teflon.

"I need a positive ID, but I need to warn you that you may not be able to do that from any pictures that we took of the body." Grace looked down at her folder. "The body is not in good shape," she underscored. "We could try other ways, a DNA match." Unless the kid wasn't his. Where was Zack's natural mother in all of this?

"I can take it." Lacey started to reach across the table. Like he was in charge. Grace placed her hand on the folder.

Cherie hiccupped. Her face was dead white.

"Mrs. Lacey," she said, "you're not obligated to look at these pictures. Since Zachary was your stepson, I suggest I show them just to your husband. So if you'll kindly look away."

"Can . . . can I go out of the room?" she asked.

"Yes," Grace said. "If you want some coffee, just ask someone. They'll be glad to help you."

Cherie hurried past Grace in a cloud of drugstore vanilla cologne, probably the next aisle over from where she got her blond hair.

"Mr. Lacey, may I ask you where Zachary's biological mother is?"

"No idea. She split on us when Zack was nine. We got a few postcards at first, birthday cards, that kind of bullshit. Then they stopped coming." He glared at her. "And I *did* file a Missing Persons on her, and you people came up dry. You can check all that."

Maybe that was why Ron Lacey hated cops. Although Grace doubted it.

"Just show it to me, goddamn it," he bit off at her.

Grace took her hand off the back of the first picture— the close-up—and flipped it over like the bottom card in a game of blackjack. She felt she was being brutal and she didn't want to be; she didn't want to make this man pay because he was a redneck asshole who didn't seem concerned about his son at all. He was looking at her, not at the picture, and she realized he was staring at her breasts.

"There," Grace said, sliding the photo toward him with her forefinger.

He had the decency then to stop leering at her and glanced down at the picture. He went white. Stared. Kept staring.

"Is that your son, sir?"

He was silent for a long time. Grace wondered if he'd gone into shock. Then he bobbed his head once.

"I think so. Yeah."

She wanted his voice to sound raw with emotion. She wanted to be able to say someday that in that moment, he aged ten years. But he didn't. She reminded herself that grief did funny things to people. Juries had convicted innocent people because they didn't behave "right" during their trials. And she was not here to convict him. Just to figure out how and why Zack Lacey had died. Maybe in the process she could figure out how and why his mother had disappeared.

Circumstantial, she reminded herself. *I'd run away from this asshole, too.*

"Where'd you find him?" he asked finally.

At last. Some interest, Grace thought. "I'm so sorry for your loss," she said. She meant it. "A police officer on patrol found him in the river." She didn't disclose anything more than that.

He frowned at her. "A week ago? And it took this long to let us know?"

"He was found two nights ago, sir." Grace picked up the photograph. "There was no ID on . . . with him. Just a phone number for a teen-crisis hotline. He's called it a number of times. Do you know why, sir?"

"He called a *what*?" The man stared at her.

"A crisis center." Grace made herself sound soft and confused. "Do you have any idea what he was upset about?"

"No." He was back to stiff-jawed. And by the pink in his doughy cheeks, she was pretty sure he was lying. "What now? You send his body . . ."

He trailed off, and she got the feeling he was more embarrassed that he didn't know the term for "funeral home" than he was freaked out that his kid was dead.

There was something going on here. Something she did not like. At all.

"We have a few more tests to run," she said. Henry was back tomorrow, yes. "We want to make absolutely certain that no crime was committed against your son."

"A crime," he echoed. He frowned again, and then his lips parted. "Someone killed him?" He sucked in his breath. She couldn't tell if he was bullshitting. Or if he knew someone killed him.

"We don't know that, sir," Grace said. "We're trying to determine that. So we would like to keep his . . . remains . . . here for just a little longer."

He looked past her shoulder. Grace guessed that

Cherie was looking at him through the window. "Are there . . . storage fees? If you keep him for more tests?"

No way, she thought, incredulous that that would be his first thought. *No effing way. I thought I'd seen and heard it all.*

"No, sir."

"Then . . . I guess . . ." Now he did look down. He sighed and wiped his face with his hands. His shoulders rounded. Grace made no sound. Even though no clock was ticking, she heard one; maybe it was her heartbeat. Maybe Lena Garvin would give the body up. She'd say she'd done all the looking necessary and they needed the room in the morgue. And she'd be right. But Henry would be there tomorrow.

"I guess he's not going anywhere," the man said.

"Thank you, sir."

She got up and put the photograph in the folder. "I'm sorry," she said again, turned, and left the interview room.

Cherie was perched on the edge of Butch's desk, wiping her eyes with a tissue. Butch was leaning back in his chair with his hands wedged under his armpits. Classic body language.

Then Cherie turned and saw Grace; her lips parted and her eyes widened. Grace pursed her lips, and the woman burst into tears.

"It's Zack, isn't it?" she wailed.

"We believe so, ma'am," Grace replied. She was aware that Butch, like Grace herself, was watching Cherie closely as she sobbed.

"I need to ask you to step back into the interview room, just for a few questions," Grace said, gently and sadly.

The woman nodded and slid off Butch's desk like a snake. Grace walked her back in, and Cherie hurried over to her husband and threw her arms around him.

Lacey kind of sagged as he held her. Grace gave them some time and then she broke it up.

"I'm so sorry, but I have to ask you a few things," Grace said. "We want to know why this terrible thing happened to your child."

"I'm going to sue that damn shrink," Lacey blurted.

Grace blinked. "Your son was seeing a psychiatrist?" *And you thought it was odd that he called a help line?*

"So he could get his meds," Lacey said. "Antidepressants." He threw the word like a punch.

"So he had a problem with depression," Grace said.

"I read up on those things. They can make kids go crazy, commit suicide." Lacey's right eye twitched. "That's what you think happened, isn't it? That he killed himself? God*damn* it. Damn it, damn it to hell!" He made a fist and slammed it hard on the metal table. Again and again, as Cherie cried harder. Grace was glad to see some big emotion out of the man. It was better than pussyfooting around.

"Do you know why he was depressed?" Grace asked. "Did it have anything to do with being gay?"

"*What?*" Lacey froze. "Shut up," he snapped at Cherie, who was still crying. To Grace, "What the hell are you saying? My son is not a faggot."

"That's why he called the crisis line," Grace told him, her voice low, her expression sympathetic. "He was afraid he might be a homosexual."

"No way. No way," Lacey yelled. He jumped out of his seat. Grace half-expected him to launch himself over the table at her. Jeez, no wonder Zack had kept it to himself.

"Ronnie, please. Oh, God, Zack," Cherie wept.

He turned on Cherie. "Shut the hell up!"

Grace observed, waiting to see if he went physical on his wife. Or if she flinched in fear that he might. No action. Grace kept watching. The veins on Lacey's neck were bulging. The stepmom's emotional behavior hadn't altered since Grace had dropped the bomb. Cherie was devastated over his death. Pure and simple.

"How did you hear this?" he demanded.

Grace had a feeling that if she told him, he'd storm over to Helping Hand with a bazooka. So she said, "We have some privileged information at this time."

"I am suing them," he said. "Turn my boy into a faggot—"

"We have no indication that your son was gay, sir," Grace cut in. "Only that he was very distressed."

"What else did he tell them? They're liberals, right? Goddamn—"

"We are doing everything we can to figure out what happened to him," Grace said. "Please, Mr. Lacey, let us do our jobs."

"I want to see him," Lacey said, swinging his attention back to Grace. "Let me see him. He's my only son."

And my only son is not a faggot, Grace supplied.

CHAPTER
EIGHT

"So is that the deal, Earl?" Grace asked her angel as they shared a cigarette and a chaw in the stairwell. The Laceys were gone. And Lena Garvin wanted to get rid of Zack's body, just as Grace had predicted. "God doesn't want us to, y'know, be bad because of His ego? *His* kids can't be screwups? Talk about conditional love."

"God wants you to be happy, Grace," Earl said.

"Christians aren't perfect, just forgiven," she intoned.

"Something like that." He spit into his soda bottle.

"Well, that must be such a relief. For the Christians." She stomped out her cigarette and put it with the rest of its buddies on top of the ledge. Then she flung open the door.

Two more hours on the day shift. She sailed into the autopsy room and hovered on the perimeter, to find a new body lying on the aluminum table, female, cuts across her face; and Lena Garvin speaking into a transcription microphone. Busy girl.

"I'm releasing Zachary Lacey," Lena said, making a point of switching off the mic. "Does the next of kin have a funeral home picked out?"

"Tox screens come back?" Grace asked.

Lena shrugged. "Not yet, but what does that matter? We don't need the remains any longer. Is that all?"

"Actually, no," Grace said. "He was on antidepressants. Can you check for that, too?"

"Sure. But there's no need to keep the body. We've got plenty of samples to work with."

Samples.

"But there might be *other* things," Grace pressed. "Things we haven't thought of yet."

"I have completed the autopsy," Lena insisted, shooting Grace a dirty look.

Grace took a deep breath. "Can't you keep Lacey in the fridge one more night?" she asked, bracing herself for a blast. "I got a feeling. I really do."

I got a feeling that you missed something, and Henry will be back tomorrow. And you know that is what I'm saying, and please, Lena, God, you have to know this is not personal but I want to, I don't know, make sure this kid, this dead kid, gets justice. So, yeah, I am asking you to give me permission to let Henry take a look.

Lena looked from Grace to the cadaver on the table and back to Grace. Then past her. For a second, Grace had the sense that Earl was in the room. Maybe he was Zack's last-chance angel, too. Maybe he'd help her out with the investigation for once.

Maybe every time a pig snorts an angel gets his wings.

Then Lena narrowed her eyes and said, "Okay."

"Thanks," Grace said, startled. "Thanks so much." Without realizing she was going to say it, she added, "Come to Louie's tonight. We go there after work."

Lena sighed. "Fine."

Grace smiled at her. Really smiled. "You can follow me over."

Zachary Lacey had been a student at Franklin High. The final bell had just rung and the kids were all filing out. It wasn't raining, but battleship-gray clouds hung as low as they could go. The streets were wet. Water dripped off bushes and trees.

The kids who were racing toward the parking lots—texting, putting in their earbuds—were just a handful of years older than Clay. Grace realized with a start that when she imagined Clay in her mind's eye she still saw him much younger. Would he sustain any more major trauma in his young life? If anyone ever hurt him, she hoped she got the same judge who gave Joey Amador probation when she got put on trial for assault and/or murder one.

She and Ham couldn't do any searching without a warrant, which they didn't have, but they could ask questions. All the kids carrying enormous backpacks that made them look like hunchbacks. Which ones had been mean to Zack? Who wasn't mean in high school? *Rhetta*.

Grace and Ham visited with Ms. Miller, the well-groomed principal, but it was obvious pretty soon that she didn't really know who Zack Lacey was. The sketch didn't ring any bells. After she checked his schedule, she lined up some of his teachers for interviews. Zack was: quiet, an underachiever, absent a lot, sweet. Everyone was shocked. No one saw it coming. Of course not, because they were mandated reporters: If they saw signs of abuse or distress, they were legally obligated to let someone know. And no one had.

Somehow, the word got around that there were cops on campus and that Zack Lacey was dead. Word always got around. Kids walked slowly past the window that looked into the principal's office, where Grace and Ham were conducting their interviews. Lookiloos, into the drama.

Except for maybe one kid, who appeared and then reappeared in the window. Five-five, maybe a hundred twenty sopping wet, purple-black with long eyelashes and West Indian features. He had a cap on rally style and jeans probably as loose as was allowed. Gold necklace, baby gangsta wannabe. Grace saw that Ham saw him, too; and her partner took over when she excused herself from their interview with Mr. Tranh, the vice-principal.

She trotted down the hall with its diversity mural and a pretty good painting of a mustang, Franklin's mascot. Then she zoomed outside and raced up to the kid while he was still watching the window. When he saw her, he started to bolt. But he had on a big-ass backpack, which probably slowed him down.

"Hey, man," she said, pulling back her jacket so he could see the badge at her waist. "I'm Detective Grace Hanadarko. Did you know Zachary Lacey?"

He stopped. His back was to her. She saw kids looking and figured he wanted the ground to swallow him up. Just as she was about to repeat the question, he turned around, nodded. His lips were trembling. Zack's death mattered to him. A lot.

"Listen, I'm really sorry," she said. "You two were close, right?"

He looked left, right, superanxious.

"Can we go someplace, sit down?" she asked. "I need some help. People want to close the lid on this, say he was just some redneck kid with problems who jumped in the river—"

His mouth dropped open. He blinked at her. There were flecks of gold in his eyes. She caught the merest whiff of marijuana. Noticed it but let it go. For now.

"Is that . . . is that how? . . ."

All she had to do was reach out one finger and push him; he'd fall right over on his ass. A stiff wind blew, nearly doing the job for her. She put her hands in the pockets of her sheepherder's jacket.

"Yeah, that's how," she said. "I'm sorry, man."

She watched him tense, working against tears. "A coffee shop," she suggested. "A place where we can just talk, you and me."

"I got nothing to say to you." He took an unsteady step backward. He wasn't just upset. He was *scared*.

"I won't use anything you tell me against you," she promised. She saw his stony refusal and pulled out her business card. "At least tell me your name." He remained silent. "All I have to do is describe you to your principal." She crossed her fingers that he would care.

He reached out a hand for the card. "My name is Antwone."

Yeah, baby. Go, baby. "Antwone . . ."

"Yeah." He turned his back and strode away. Her card was in his right fist. She kept watching, her concentration on that fist. He was close to the gutter; if he threw it . . .

He still had it in his hand when he loped across the street.

"Could be nothing, could be something," Grace told Ham as she drove toward the station. "Kids are skittish. Like colts. But he was definitely afraid."

"You smelled weed on him. Maybe he was afraid you could tell he was stoned."

She shrugged. "Maybe he was afraid I'd assume he was Zack's boyfriend." Her cell went off. It was Butch's ringtone, so she said to Ham, "Grab it."

"Yeah, Butch," Ham said. "Huh. Okay. Yeah, we'll take it. Give me the address." He whipped out a three-by-five notebook with a pen stuck through the spirals from his jacket pocket. He pulled out the pen with his teeth and pressed the phone against his ear so he could write. "Yeah, yeah, got it."

He hung up and looked over at Grace. "Butch and Bobby went to see Zack's shrink. Doc knew about as much about him as the school principal."

Grace let Connie cling and squeal as she took a corner. "In other words, nothing."

Ham tapped his pen against the notebook. "The way they saw it, the psychiatrist—Dr. Metzner—would just rubber-stamp his prescription renewal for Prozac. But Metzner did mention that Zack's family is Catholic. Their parish priest is named Pepera. Butch set up an appointment with Pepera in his parish office in twenty minutes, but he just got a call from an informant. I said we could take it."

"Sure," Grace said, revving Connie's engine. "Where's he located?"

"Back across the river. Take the Forty."

Grace took the big bridge, passing over near where the North Canadian River became the Oklahoma River, which fed into the Bricktown Canal via a lock. They were near Del City.

"There's the turn," Ham said.

She roared into the parking lot and sat a minute while Ham got out. She wasn't a big fan of Catholic churches. Earl said that was okay. Johnny, her priest brother, said it wasn't. She was a baptized Catholic. Accountable, then, for lack of team Holy Spirit.

She got out and locked Connie. Raindrops pelted the top of her head, and she thought about dashing back to the car for her umbrella. Her beloved Porsche 911 sure was clean from all the rain.

Father Pepera had an office in the parish hall. A modestly dressed middle-aged woman wearing a crucifix—might have been a nun or just a secretary—checked in with him by phone from her desk and told Ham and Grace she would escort them.

Ham and Grace walked on terra-cotta tile through a Navajo-white hallway. They passed a statue of the Virgin Mary and a painting of Jesus walking on the water while the apostles sat in their fishing boat, looking frightened. Ham jerked his head at it.

"This rain keeps up, we'll be getting to work in rowboats," he said.

"I had a dream I was building an ark," she told him. He chuckled. "I didn't let the D.A. on the thing," she added. "He drowned."

"No lawyers on the ark," he agreed.

Or priests, she thought as the woman rapped sharply on a door with a nameplate that read FATHER PEPERA. *Except maybe Johnny, if he asks nice.*

The door swung open. The man was sitting behind his desk. He was pale, and there was a blotch on one of his sagging, lined cheeks, looked like a melanoma. He was almost bald, and had very bushy white eyebrows. Grace spared a second glance at his jowls and his droopy earlobes. Here was a man beloved by gravity.

"Yes, Detectives," he said in a flat voice.

She flashed her badge. "Hello, I'm Detective Grace Hanadarko and this is—"

"I know. We spoke," he said.

He'd spoken to Butch, not to either of them. She figured there was no need to correct him. A detective was a detective. But she did have to make sure they did things by the book, so she introduced Ham.

By their lack of interest shall ye know them: A detective was still a detective. There were over ten thousand recognized saints in the Catholic Church. Pepera probably knew all their dossiers. But cops? Interchangeable.

"We have a drowning victim named Zachary Lacey," she continued.

"The suicide." She could have chiseled words into a stone tablet with his voice.

She stopped, glanced at Ham. He remained pokerfaced. That was the right way to go, for sure, so she did, too. But she was beginning to have a funny feeling at the base of her spine. Like her vertebrae might pop out, she was holding things in so tightly.

"We're investigating the situation, Father," she said. "We don't know yet if he took his own life."

Father Pepera did not defrost. "I thought that was what Dr. Metzner was told. If he did kill himself, I won't say Mass for him."

Grace's lips moved but she couldn't make a sound. She was stunned down to her toes. "But . . . the Church—"

"The Church has left it up to the conscience of the parish priest," he replied, folding his hands and laying them on his desk. "And I will not say Mass for anyone who commits such an atrocity."

He gazed up at her. There was a defiant gleam in his eye, like he was enjoying being an asshole. Like he was daring her to say he couldn't run his own show. *My parish, my rules.*

Ham took over while Grace fought for composure. "Father Pepera, this is a juvenile. He was only fifteen, and he was under psychiatric care."

"He was sixteen," the priest countered.

Are you shitting me? Grace wanted to yell at him. But she didn't. She licked her lips. "We've spoken to his parents. He was taking antidepressants, and sometimes they have side effects. Suicidal thoughts—"

He shook his head. "They are only nominally members of this parish. I haven't seen any of them in church for months. We take care of our own, Miss . . ."

"Hanadarko," she said, fighting to keep the sharpness out of her tone. "Father . . . sir, as I said, we haven't determined if he took his own life."

"Well, if he didn't, then I'll bury him," he replied. As cold as that.

Grace stayed on target. She had lost it with Juanita. She wouldn't lose it here. "If you could remember anything that might help us. Was he in Faith Formation, was he—"

His phone rang. He looked at Ham and Grace. "I can't help you. His grandmother might be able to offer you some insight. She was a parishioner here until a few years ago. Still sends me a Christmas card every year."

"Do you have an address or a phone number for—" Grace began, but he picked up the phone, giving her a look that indicated her dismissal.

Grace turned her back and marched stiff-legged out of his office. Ham followed, shutting his door.

"Stay cool, stay cool," he urged her as she strode down the hallway. Her boot heels rang on the terra-cotta tile as she marched into the office of their escort. The woman was typing. She had the radio on low, classical music.

"Hi," Grace said, sugar sweet. She smiled at the woman. "Father Pepera suggested we get in contact with Zachary Lacey's grandmother."

"Lovely woman," the secretary said, beaming. "She used to run a prayer-quilt group. She made the most beautiful quilts."

"How long ago did she move?" Grace asked.

"Oh, it's been at least ten years," the woman said.

When Zack was six. "Would you by chance have her phone number? Address?"

The woman hesitated. Grace smiled harder. "It's all right. We're investigating the death of her grandson, Zachary."

The woman knit her brows and peered up at Grace through her lashes. "Did that boy . . . do himself in?"

"We don't know. We need to ask Mrs. Lacey a few questions to help us understand what happened." Grace waited. Cops did a lot of waiting.

"Well . . ." The woman brightened. "I'll get in touch with her and ask her to call you. How's that?"

Less direct, but better than nothing, Grace thought. "That would be great," Grace said. "Let me give you my card. Ham?"

He pulled a card out of his wallet. Grace took it and handed it with hers to the secretary. She was amazed at herself, masking her fury, playing nice. Nice would get them so much further. But as soon as it was safe to, she was going to rip Father Pepera a new one.

"Thank you," Grace added, as the woman pulled out the center drawer beneath her keyboard, pulled out a paper clip, and clipped their cards together. Then she placed them beside a coffee cup with an image of a stained-glass window on it and words written in flowery lettering: *When God closes a door, He opens a window.*

Grace flushed, said nothing. *What if God locks all the doors and sets the building on fire?*

"We're in a little bit of a rush on this," Grace said. "The family wants a Mass and, well . . ."

The woman looked grim. "It's all this divorce and easy living," she said in a low voice. "People don't have a sense of responsibility anymore. Sin is very real."

"Yes, you're right," Grace said evenly, bouncing her head like Butch's Longhorn bobblehead. "But we want to straighten this out for Zachary and his family."

"Of course." Now Church Lady was the one who sounded insincere.

When they got out of earshot, Grace let loose. After she ran out of names to call Father Pepera, she invented new ones. She called Johnny and demanded that he come to Louie's, then changed her mind and asked him to meet him at her home instead. Ham looked a little crestfallen—her priest-brother at Grace's house equaled no booty call—but he said nothing as they climbed into Connie.

They returned to the station and Grace slammed out of the car. She was seething with a burning, white-hot mighty fury that was made no better by the sight of a dozen little pamphlets hanging from the ceiling above her desk. They had been attached on lavender gift-wrap ribbon, and they had titles that read *GAY? NO WAY! I WAS SAVED BY JESUS: I WAS GAY; HEALED BY JESUS; HOMOSEXUALITY: LOVE THE SINNER, HATE THE SIN; ARE YOU SAVED?* And the best one, to which were attached aluminum foil "wings" on either vertical edge: *LUSTFUL THOUGHTS: PRAY!*

Made no better at first, until she corked the fury with an appreciative snort. Their elaborate prank did what cop practical jokes did best, took the edge off, and she grinned at Bobby, who was seated at his desk, talking on his cell phone as she and Ham cracked up. She half-expected there to be a strap-on in her drawer, but in these days of sexual-harassment worries, probably not.

"You won't believe what happened," she began, but Bobby held up a hand as he stood. He wasn't smiling.

"I just got a call from Butch. He's got an informant named October who has a little girl."

"Merrie. Yeah, I know about that, man," she said, waving her arms so her mobile of religious tracts would flutter around. Ham picked up a purple feather boa from the seat of his chair. And a tube of hemorrhoid cream.

"Hey, my brother's gay," Ham protested mildly.

"And we love that about him," Grace assured her partner. Although at the moment, Nick kinda detested her for sleeping with his married brother.

"Merrie's missing," Bobby went on, patting himself down, digging into his jeans pocket for his car keys.

Grace turned. "Missing as in . . ."

Bobby shook his head. "Mom went to pick her up from school and she wasn't there."

"What?" Grace and Ham traded looks. Looks that said, *Oh, shit.*

"I got a call about another case, had to come in; Butch is out there now, looking for her," Bobby said. "I'm going, too."

Grace glanced at her cell phone. "Hell, we're off the clock in ten minutes," she said. "All I had left was to check in with Evan Johnson about Juanita's extracurricular, off-the-books spiritual-counseling service." She raised her brows at Ham.

"I'm in," he told her.

"You call Butch for the plan. I have to make a quick stop," Grace said.

She left the squad room and went to the autopsy room. Lena was there, bent over another corpse. With a start, Lena jerked away from the body and moved her gore-covered, latex glove toward her face, then dropped her arm to her side and averted her head. But Grace saw what she was trying to hide: Lena was crying.

"Hey, man," Grace said. "What's going on?" For a split second Grace put Merrie on the table, but that didn't make any sense. She looked down at the body. It was a black man, maybe thirty. Didn't look so good. Looked dead. She wondered who would get the case. She looked back up at Lena.

"Nothing," Lena said, not meeting her gaze. "I can't go to Louie's."

"Good," Grace replied. She gave her head a shake. "I mean, that's why I'm here. I can't go, either. I came to let you know."

"Okay." Lena stepped closer to the autopsy table. Possessively. "I'm doing this one on overtime. Captain Perry asked me to."

And so . . . is that why you're crying? Is your boyfriend pissed because you blew him off?

But Grace didn't ask those questions. She just nodded and left the room. And felt even less confident of Lena's corpse-side manner.

CHAPTER
NINE

Ham checked in with Butch—no change in Merrie's status—and he and Grace got into separate vehicles. Bobby was already gone. Grace found a pack of cigarettes under a circular for the local big-box pet store and lit up as she screamed down the darkening streets of OKC. She called Butch herself because she needed friendly voices at a time like this, plus she was hoping for miraculous good news. He was at the shelter where October lived.

"October's not here," Butch told her. "He moved out this morning. I'm questioning the other residents, to see if anyone knows where he went."

"He's missing, his kid's missing. You think he took her and split?" Grace asked. "Who's with Merrie's mom?"

"I went over there first but I didn't stay long. Maybe you could go talk to her, see if you can get anything." He paused. "Something's up over there. Her place is a mess."

"On it," she promised him. "Where's Ham?"

"He's going to Merrie's school, to check out if anyone saw her leave," Butch said. "Teachers are supposed to wait for the parents, make sure the kids are accounted for. I was closer to the shelter."

Triage.

"Bobby's going over to Big Money's territory, see if he can turn up anything." Butch's voice sounded tight.

"Got it. We'll find her, Butch." She knew what he was worrying about: that Big Money had discovered October was a traitor. Bowel Movement had cut up a thirteen-year-old, and he'd never gotten called on it. Stupid D.A. No one was afraid to do anything to her town. Goddamn it—

Calm down, she told herself, as she barreled on over to Merrie's blasted-out hovel of a building; trash, condoms, and urine in the hallways, graffiti everywhere. Jesus God, what a place to raise a kid. Her thoughts flew immediately, as they often did, to Clay.

"Hey," she said, when Merrie's mother, Janaya, opened her door. Janaya took one look at Grace and broke down.

"Oh, my God, my baby, my baby," she wailed.

In a movie, Janaya's place would be spotless and she would be wearing humble if modest attire. She would work as a waitress and go to church every Sunday. But Janaya's boobs were hanging out of a V-neck sweater, and her jeans were so tight Grace could see the outline of her sexual parts. Her F-Me heels were so high, Grace half-expected her to fall forward on her massive chest and bounce back upright.

Grace shuffled through half-dressed Barbies and big brightly colored plastic toys and trash and dirty paper plates that smelled like rot and cat urine; and high heels and some makeup; and her boot heel came down on something that broke like glass. Maybe a crack pipe. Maybe a plastic syringe.

"He took her, I know he took her," Janaya said, sobbing.

The remains of some Mexican fast food littered a threadbare couch. Grace cleared two spots and flashed her badge, gestured for Janaya to sit down. Janaya stayed on her feet, nominally. Grace remained standing as well.

"I'm Detective Grace Hanadarko," she said. "I was sent over here—"

"Butch," Janaya said. "He's looking for her." She nodded, vigorously.

"You didn't pick her up from school," Grace began, pulling out her notebook. "You got there a little late and she was gone."

"Oh, my God, all right, I was a few minutes late!" Janaya shrieked, taking a step away from Grace. She teetered on her shoes. "But no one's supposed to take her. Don't you know anything, bitch?"

Grace lifted a sticky towel off the couch and set it on the floor. Didn't drop it. Tried to show respect. This was a frantic citizen. "I know you're upset—"

"*Upset?* Patrick takes my baby and you think I'm *upset?* I'll kill that son of a bitch. I will do it."

Grace held back what she was thinking: that the best-case scenario was that Merrie was in October's possession. No. Best-case scenario was some playdate Janaya had forgotten about and Merrie was at a friend's house, eating cookies and watching a Disney movie.

"Butch was getting him out of that life," Janaya said. She swayed; Grace reached out a hand and grabbed her forearm. "He was going to help him find a job."

Is that what Butch told you? Grace wondered. She set that aside. It wasn't important right now.

And then her cell phone rang. Civilian ringtone. Still supporting Janaya with her right hand, Grace grabbed the phone out of her jeans pocket with her left. "Detective Hanadarko."

"It's Antwone," a hushed voice confessed.

Shit. "Antwone," she said. "Hey, man. I'm glad you called." She waited. Janaya went completely still and stared hopefully at her, and Grace fought her instinct to shake her head, tell her no, this had nothing to do with her baby.

Kept waiting for Antwone to speak.

"Antwone?" Grace pressed. "You still there, man?"

"Yeah." His voice was muffled. "I'll meet you. I—I have a job at a bowling alley. I get off at eleven."

"Cool. Gimme the address." She waited some more.

"Maybe we can meet a few blocks away," he said. "There's a taco stand."

"I won't act like a cop," she promised him. "At your bowling alley."

"They saw you at school."

"Okay." She had no idea if she could keep the appointment, but she wrote down the name of the taco stand. Janaya kept watching her. "Listen, Antwone, I'm on a case and I may not make it. Can I call you at this number?" It was blocked, but that would not be a problem.

Janaya wilted and turned away. Grace stayed with Antwone on the phone.

"Um," he said, "I guess."

He was scared and he wanted to talk. Her crime-dar was blaring. But Zack was dead, and so far, a six-year-old named Merrie was not.

She hung up and said, "Janaya, have you gotten calls on your cell phone? Who's called you today?"

Janaya was going glassy and dazed. Her light brown cheeks turned bright red and she broke eye contact. "I lost it. I don't know where it is."

So what was the truth? She pawned it? Stole the one she had had but the battery wore out?

"Do you have a phone line here?" Grace looked around the room.

"It's, um . . ." She licked her lips, sandpaper on an emery board, stared at Grace as if Grace herself knew the answer and might be willing to share. As Grace blinked *No clue,* Janaya started crying again. "It got cut off. This is not the way it's supposed to be!"

No shit, Grace thought.

* * *

Butch had canvassed the shelter, down among the gray men. The director of the shelter informed him that October had left with a duffel bag in his arms, apparently walked down the street, and got picked up elsewhere. Then the director took Butch to task for concealing October's "criminal affiliation," and Butch humbled himself as expediently as possible. That done, he walked out the squeaky front door.

Wearing a trash bag as a rain poncho, although it was not currently raining, the Count was scribbling away on the sidewalk, and Butch could still smell him from ten feet away.

Butch had just pulled out his cell phone to check in with the rest of the squad when the Count looked up at him and said, "Oklahoma plate." He had rheumy alcoholic eyes and if he had six teeth he had half a dozen. He tapped the wet sidewalk with his chalk. Butch looked down at the smear of letters and numbers. He pulled out a notebook and jotted them down.

"Did you catch the make of the car?" Butch asked him.

The Count started writing on the pavement again. Butch watched.

123456789987654321.

"Was it a big car? Was it white? Red?" Butch prompted.

246810121416.

No matter. He could call it in. His cell phone rang. It was Bobby.

"Nothing yet," Bobby shorthanded.

"I have a license-plate number," Butch told him. "I'm going to run it. I'll call you back."

· "The car's a '64 Chevy Impala. Lowrider classic," Butch told Grace. "Registered to Lawrence Shimoda, who reported it stolen almost exactly a year ago. Mr. Shimoda is not answering his phone and I went by his place. There's a For Rent sign on the front door."

"Okay," she said.

The five detectives in the Major Crimes squad were all cruising like sharks through the chum of Big Money's kingdom. It did not look as run-down and scummy as the part of town where Janaya lived, or the environs of the shelter, even. You had your basic graffiti on the mailboxes as well as a few signposts, trashy alleys, but the cars were not the worst and the yards were not the grossest. Why go into a life of crime if the best you could hope for was what you already had?

So . . . it was nondescript. Forgettable. Lacking the high drama of, say, shooting heroin under your tongue or your first murder. Tired old houses and middle-aged apartment buildings. No *CSI: Miami* here, baby. No sound track. Still a '64 Chevy Impala done right could be a classic, collectable automobile. High end, *muchacho*. She thought about Ron Lacey and his Harley T-shirt. Most gang members didn't even make minimum wage. But they might wind up with a stolen Electra Glide.

Grace called Captain Perry to bring her up to date. Then she called Butch again. "There's an APB out on Merrie," Grace told him. "No BOLO on October because what if his gang doesn't know about his kid?"

Butch grunted, thanked her, and hung up. She knew he knew that moving cautiously with the media made sense. So was Butch wrong, mixing it up with a guy with a little girl? Would she have done it?

"Yeah," she said aloud.

She called Johnny to tell him not to show at her house. She also told him what Father Pepera had said.

"That's not Church policy," he said. "I've said Mass for a suicide victim myself."

She hadn't known that.

"Well, he's insisting that it's up to his conscience."

"I'll talk to him."

"Put the fear of God in him," she advised him. "Plus, Johnny? He's an asshole."

He ignored that. "I'll get back to you," he said.

She and Ham checked in on some of Big Money's known hangouts—a strip club, a coffee shop, a chop shop. But again, they couldn't really lay it out there, either, because they were still stuck with not wanting BM to make the connection between October and his daughter. No one had anything, not even in exchange for money or get-out-of-jail-free passes.

Thanks to Captain Perry, Downtown put a lot more cops on the streets to search for the little girl. Nothing plus nothing still equaled nothing, and Grace and Ham kept the pressure on as best they could. But some nights the bad guys were like bits of mercury, dribbling away if you pushed on them at all.

After wasting money on food they didn't eat, the two left Noodletown, a Korean restaurant. Hepped up on green tea, Grace checked the time. It was ten thirty. She was supposed to meet Antwone at eleven.

"You know what I'm not liking?" she said to Ham as they headed for their cars in the little parking lot. "I'm not liking that Janaya lost her cell phone. And she didn't have a landline. So no one is able to contact her. I mean, I called all the people on the list she made for me." She stepped over a puddle. "And I called the number she gave me as the one for *her* cell phone. But I had to suggest that we do that."

"Yeah," he said. "That's bullshit. But she's high, scared." He ran the scenario. "She's sitting in her apartment, and her kid is missing, and she's not asking friends to make calls, check around." He looked at her. "It's wrong."

"I'm going back over there," Grace announced.

"No. I'll go. You go meet up with Antwone." He put his hand on her shoulder. "Grace, we're doing everything we can for Merrie."

She hated her feeling of defeat. Hated it. Raindrops smacked the top of her head, and she batted at them angrily, as if they were doing it on purpose.

"I'll call you if something breaks," he promised her. "I'll go over to Janaya's now."

She nodded. Although she had concerns over Lena's handling of Zack's autopsy, she had full confidence that Ham would do it right. She flooded with deep, sincere gratitude that he was her partner.

So she drove to the taco stand, driving by first to make sure there was no posse waiting to jump her or any other surprises. She saw Antwone sitting at a picnic table by himself; a couple sat at the next table, making out. He was studiously avoiding them.

Shadows slid over Connie as Grace got out and walked calmly toward the kid. He raised his head and saw her. She saw his back go up. Another raindrop plopped on top of her head, and she half-raised her hand to signal to him that she saw him and she was cool.

Yeah, right. Like he thinks I'm cool.

Deer, meet headlights. She revved up her cop brain because something was going on and she was not leaving until she found out what it was.

"Hey," she said. "Thanks for coming."

He didn't reply. Pot fumes rolled off him. Damn, not the sharpest tool in the shed. Maybe he'd had to build up his nerve to talk to her.

"Let's just make it easy on us both," she said gently. "I know you want to tell me something. So tell me. Please."

Antwone hung his head.

"Antwone," she prompted, and then she realized he was whispering. She leaned forward, and she had a flash of déjà vu, sitting in the confessional at church, telling Father Murphy she'd lost her temper at Paige during dinner, all the while knowing he was going to screw her when she finished.

"Zachary was my . . . my boyfriend." He whispered it in a rush. "We had to be so careful. We couldn't tell anyone." He glanced up at her. His eyes fluttered shut as if he were fainting; his brows knit together into one unibrow of torment. His chest rose and he took in a ragged breath, punctuated by a high, agonized gasp as his lower lip trembled. Grace had seen a lot of hurt in her day, an awful lot of pain, and this kid was in hell.

"They hated him. And *I* loved him. I was the only one, but I was . . . we . . ." He crumpled forward, resting his arms on the picnic table and pressing his forehead against the backs of his hands. "Oh, my God."

Grace waited, a witness to his agony. She would watch him cry all night if it would help her figure out what happened to Zachary Lacey. She would do whatever it took. But she wouldn't let herself feel what he was feeling. A cop had to carry a chip of ice in her heart, observing, assembling the clues. Now would be a perfect time for a full confession, or for Antwone to unknowingly dump a treasure trove of useful information on the table.

"How much did they hate him?" she asked. *Enough to kill him?*

Antwone cried awhile longer. Grace waited. *C'mon, c'mon,* she pushed. *Tell me the thing that will break this case.*

She stayed detached and watched, trying to decide if his grief was genuine or if he had killed Zack and was putting on the sobfest of his life. She doubted option number two. He was here, after all. He had come to her for help.

"Hey, man, you'd be surprised how many people I know who are secretly gay," she said, placing a comforting hand on his arm. He pulled away. "I mean, they told *me* they're gay, but they're keeping it a secret." *Stupid, Hanadarko.* "You got to give me something to work with, Antwone. What do you know about Zack that we don't know?"

"Man, if my daddy knew I was here sitting with you . . . ," he began.

If Daddy knew you were gay . . .

"He was going to this church, this crazy, big-ass church," he told her. "That place scared the shit out of me, all the rolling around and shaking. He said it was working, that he didn't think he was gay anymore . . . that he was . . ."

Going to stop loving you? So you killed him? Grace thought.

"Did you go with him?"

"Hell, no." He pushed his fists against his eye sockets. "But he wanted me to." He licked his lips and took a deep breath. She kept watching. There was more.

"Can you give me the name of the church?" she asked him. "Was there anyone there he hung out with?"

"Pastor Marc, the youth pastor. That dude's gay. I'm sure of it."

"How sure?"

The taco-stand lights went out. In the darkness, Antwone stared at his fingernails.

"I—I didn't know I was . . . that way . . . until I met Zack. We were partners and then . . ." He trailed off as if he realized he'd just said too much. "I gotta go." Pushing the flats of his hands on the table, he began to rise. This was it. She was going to lose him. She thought fast and furiously.

They were partners. They had something going on? Were they in a band together? Business? Debate team? Grace's heart sped up, like a big cat after a kill. Moving from the prowl to running it to ground.

The truth.

Now she had to be careful. He just might outrun her. She had to corner him.

"You were new at it," she said. "You didn't know how the streets work."

"I don't know what you're talking about." He took a step back and crossed his arms over his chest.

But he didn't walk away.

"Was it just to friends, at first? A little bit of weed?"

He shook his head hard. "We—I'm not into that."

"Give me the name of your connection," she said. "A first name will help. We watch most of them. We may already have you on camera buying from him." She was lying. "But if you tell me yourself, I'll help you, man. I swear it." She kept her face open and honest, in case he could see her in the oily murk of the taco stand. "If this guy hurt Zack . . ."

Clouds scuttled; the moon came out and kissed his dark downy cheek. Her heart broke a little for him but she kept herself in check.

"I gotta go," he said.

Shit.

"If this guy hurt Zack . . . ," she repeated.

He turned and began to walk away. She started seeing his future in front of her eyes: dropping out of school to avoid arrest; hitting the streets full-time. Hustling, stealing. It was like watching him die. Like losing him to hell.

"Antwone, Zack wouldn't have wanted—"

"How do you know?" he demanded, whirling around. He burst into tears. "He had *nothing*. His dad beat the shit out of him."

New data point.

"And something was weird about his stepmother. He was onto her. He told me he was going to prove that she was lying." He added all this in a rush.

Yeah, Antwone, keep going. Gimme clues. Gimme ammo.

"What about the gay youth pastor?" she asked. "Marc. He in on any of that?"

Antwone's face hardened. "*He's* an asshole. Zack thought he was so great."

She tensed and tried not to show it. "Did Marc try to make a move on Zack?"

"I don't know. I just know Zack started acting different after he started going to that church. He kept telling me Jesus could fix everything." He narrowed his eyes. "I don't think Jesus can fix shit."

"No argument here," she agreed. She could almost hear the flapping of Earl's wings. "Did you know he was on antidepressants?"

"He threw that shit away after he accepted Jesus as his personal savior."

"But . . . was he still depressed?" Her cell phone vibrated. She let it go. "Depressed enough to kill himself? Or do you think he might have accidentally fallen into the river while he was stoned? Maybe . . . fishing?"

"Shit," he said. "Zachary and me never went fishing in our whole lives. I gotta go." Before she could protest, he fixed her with a look. "I have homework."

"Please. Stay." She raised her chin. "Listen to me. You're telling me stuff, good stuff. I'm going to use it. But I'm not going to use it against you." As his lips parted, she raised her left hand out, gang style. No weapons here. *Cuz you got nothing, too. I take what's left, you'll be dead in five years.*

He licked his lips and looked left, right, as if someone might be there with a lifeline to provide his final answer.

"Zack died," she said. "Maybe he did it himself, but maybe not. And if he didn't, I want to find out who did."

"You don't understand," he muttered. "You're a *cop*."

She held out her hands. "Man, who understands better than me? I live in the same world. I know the rules. I just don't play by them. Is your father in a gang?"

He stiffened. "My father went to prison for a crime he didn't commit."

Yeah, tell me another, Antwone Senior. "That happens," she said. "I took down one of the FBI's most wanted and then someone falsely reported I was drinking on duty. She was a chick who was pissed off at me." Maybe that was not so clever, proving that it was hard to trust authority figures.

His lips parted. "That sucks."

"Tell me about it. But it got put right. At least for me. I want to put it right for Zack."

Tick . . . tick . . . tick . . . She thought about checking her cell phone. But she sensed that, this time, she shouldn't break eye contact. She looked him straight in the eye.

Finally, Antwone's shoulders sagged. "Flaco," he said, and told her the story of how he and his "partner"— what a word for a gay teenage drug dealer—had bought drugs from a known OKC dealer. His face went blank and sullen the way Ron Lacey's had; he was defiance incarnate, daring her to leap across the picnic table and cuff him. But there were tears in his eyes, and she knew it was all bullshit. He was still sweet, still hopeful, still . . . good.

"I know him," she said. "He's an asshole."

Antwone smiled a little, very tentatively, and the sun came out. Maybe he could crawl out of the pit. Maybe she could give him a hand up.

"He was cool with us," he said finally.

Ya-huh. Probably gave you all the weed you could smoke in return for selling it to your classmates. But never any money.

"I may have more questions," she said. "Give me your address." Before he could refuse, she added, "The school will give it to me if you don't." She pulled out her notebook, glancing at her cell phone at the same time. Ham.

"I'm only doing this for Zack," he said.

"That's cool, man," she said. *Whatever works.*

Antwone gave her an address and left. Grace called Ham back.

"October doesn't have her," he said. "He called Butch with some information, and Butch could tell he doesn't know she's missing. And Butch didn't fill him in."

Shit. "You tell Janaya that October doesn't have her?"

"I think she knows," Ham said. "I think she's involved with the disappearance."

"Are you still with her?"

"We've got a uniform watching her place. I need to get some sleep." He hesitated.

My house is not a hotel. And bed warmers don't sleep over.

"Walk me through it," she said. "While it's fresh."

"It was the lack of interest in staying connected. She doesn't seem focused on finding out where Merrie is. She kept insisting October had her, and she wouldn't entertain any other possibility."

"Well, addicts can be like that," she said. "Glom onto something and work it to death. God, Ham, did you see her apartment? Where's Social Services in this? Did Butch ever contact them?"

"Merrie's school was watching Janaya, she was late a lot to pick Merrie up, but there were no signs of abuse. Butch said he never saw her place look so bad. You know how addicts are. They do okay for a while and then something sends 'em over."

"Like killing their kid because their new boyfriend's jealous, doesn't like sharing Mom's attention."

Ham took over. "Or she tried to make her stop crying a little too hard. Freaked out. So we search the Dumpster for empty bleach bottles and get a cadaver dog."

Grace's stomach lurched. That could not happen to little Merrie.

Oh, but it could.

"Butch is sure October doesn't know she's missing?" she asked.

"October called to tell him he was moved in, but he was afraid to give him the address."

"That's helpful." She actually meant it. Any new information was helpful. "Antwone was Zack's boyfriend. They were dealing."

"You think it got Zack killed?" Ham asked.

"It usually does, sooner or later," she replied. "Henry's coming home tomorrow. I'm going to ask him to take another look at the body."

He sucked in his breath. "Lena Garvin's not going to like that."

"We had a meeting of the minds," she said. "Something's up with her, though. She was crying in the autopsy room. Not over that. She was already crying when I came to tell her we couldn't meet up at Louie's tonight."

"Well, it could be a woman thing," he ventured. Grace made a sound like a snorting pig. "C'mon, *you* get moody."

"I never do," she said gleefully, raising the decibels on the snorts.

"God, I hope we find that little girl." She heard the tension in Ham's voice. "I'm thinking about all those mothers who kill their kids. There's gotta be a special place in hell for them."

"Do you think she's capable of it?" Grace asked him.

"No one surprises me anymore. Except you."

"I'll see you in the morning," she told him, and disconnected.

CHAPTER
TEN

"Okay, listen," October whispered into the phone.

Seated inside an all-night coffee shop in a booth all by himself, Butch listened. Hard.

"You-know-who is going to a buy on Saturday night. It's gonna be big. So he's going himself. Here's where it's going down." He rattled off an address and Butch blinked, hard. It was on the same street as the shelter, in the row of warehouses where Butch had waited for October so many times. Damn.

"Are you going to be there?" Butch asked him.

"I don't know yet."

"What's your new address?"

There was silence. October cleared his throat. "I'm not sure."

October's reluctance made a kind of sense. Big Money was not going to be on October's turf when and if he went down. But if the cops came into October's house, there was a good chance dots would be connected. Conclusions would be drawn. And October would get a bullet to the back of the head. If he was lucky.

"Did you give the money to Janaya?" he asked Butch. "The eighty bucks?"

"It was thirty." Butch closed his eyes. He still wasn't going to tell October that Merrie was MIA.

"Okay. But you know this is my big score, this information on the buy," October declared. "I am giving him to you. That should be worth at least . . ." He took a deep breath. "Five hundred dollars."

So cheap, Butch thought. Less than two weeks' salary, even at minimum wage. Was that why guys like October went south? They couldn't even imagine themselves making it in the everyday world? It had to be hell or heaven, but never life on Earth?

"Butch? Am I right? Five hundred?"

"Yes. I think you're right." Butch waved away the tired waitress as she trudged toward him with a coffeepot. He was the only customer in the entire restaurant.

"No shit?" October blurted. "And you'll give it to her?"

"I think, for that much, I'll put it in a savings account for Merrie," Butch said. From the looks of things, Janaya could cook five hundred dollars in five minutes.

"Hey, wait a minute," October protested.

"Or if you'd rather I give it to Janaya, I will."

"Yeah. So give it to her before Saturday, okay?" In case Butch got killed, he meant. "And bring lots of friends," October whispered. "*He* will."

"Got it." Butch thought, *This could be it. The time I finally nail Big Money to a tree.* It was supposed to be his quarterback moment. Goal line in sight, his team had the ball . . .

But it felt like that night when he'd walked away and his buddy hadn't.

He hung up, stood, and dropped five bucks on the table. Merrie's school picture came out with the five-dollar bill, and he gazed down at the snapshot before picking it back up. Then he got in his car and took a drive.

Grace had hung up with Ham, but she hadn't gone home to her bed. She'd stopped in a grocery store and bought a cup of caffeine at the coffee bar and a chew toy for Gussie in the pet aisle. Then she drove the streets of Big Money's hood, looking for the lowrider Impala. Shapes and shadows moved and blended in the alleys and darkened windows: gangbangers, thieves, and other criminals. Kids looking to belong to something, anything. Anyone. Silhouettes of lives disintegrating before her eyes. And when the dawn came and the sidewalks rolled back out, the husks of their bodies would turn to dust in the sun.

No Chevy, no Big Money. She thought about calling Butch, but he had her number if he wanted to talk; and maybe he was catching some z's, although she doubted it. After a time, she returned to Janaya's building and chatted with the uniforms assigned to watch the woman. The wind smacked her cheeks to help her stay awake; she walked the block, feeling her heart spinning in her chest.

The rain began to pour down, and Grace leaned back her head as she patrolled, getting soaked clean down to the bone. There had to be something she could do for Merrie. There was always something to do.

And you wonder why I drink, she thought, picturing Earl. Wet and shivering, she kept walking; hell with the storm, the darkness matched her, black on black. Trees shifted in the wind. Bushes shook, as if some gigantic invisible monster crept among them. Crime and evil and death. Where was St. George the dragon slayer when they needed him?

The uniforms were in their car, drinking coffee and watching. She walked past them again, giving them a wave; then across the street, squinting up at the apartment she figured for Janaya's and saw that the lights were on. Was Momma pacing the floor, or was she getting high?

"This is bullshit," she said aloud, and she walked up

to the graffiti-covered front door of the building. Once upon a time it might have been orange; now it was air-brushed layers of colors outlined in black. Everyone on the planet had tagged it; so sad that this was their Iraq, Afghanistan.

The door was locked and she wasn't about to break and enter. She waited about thirty seconds before a black guy stumbled through the door. He blinked and smiled, revealing gold teeth, about to say something when Grace showed him her badge. He muttered a few choice expletives and gave her a wide berth as he staggered out into the rain. He looked so stoned, she wondered if he even knew it was raining.

Janaya lived on the third floor; Grace made a lot of noise on the concrete stairs so the dealers and hookers could take it elsewhere if they felt like it. One tender-loving couple didn't feel like it; on a mission, she moved past them wordlessly.

She banged on Janaya's door. Sure enough, there was loud hip-hop music, and it took a long time for said door to open. Janaya was higher than a kite.

And when she opened the door, there was a cell phone in her hand.

Grace lifted her badge off her belt and felt the jangle of her handcuffs without bringing them into play. Part of her mind was playing the scenario before a court of law—child abandonment, endangerment—but it was more important to find the kid than bust her mother. Not invited, she did not enter Janaya's home.

"We know everything," she said. "We tapped your cell phone. That you don't have."

The woman crumpled and began to cry. "It just happened, it happened and I . . . I didn't know . . . what to do."

Someone came up behind Grace; she turned to find Butch behind her. He was as wet as she was, and beneath his low-slung cowboy hat, his eyes flared as he took in the situation. She gave him a sharp nod.

"Janaya, may we come in?" he asked calmly. Warmly.

"LaKeisha has her," Janaya said to Butch. "I got there to the school and I . . ." Her knees went out from under her and, as before, Grace held her upright. "I was a little late and, well, I've been late before, so LaKeisha got her. I couldn't find the phone and now I got it and she called me all screaming 'Where the hell you been, girl?'"

Grace wanted to do the Rhetta happy dance. She wanted to break into a rebel yell. Butch's shoulders straightened.

"Are you going to take her away and give her to Patrick?" she asked fearfully. Her eyelids fluttered and her words were slurred. She was flying. "Because he's straightening out his life?" *And I'm not,* the unspoken ending went.

Grace slid a neutral look at Butch. He whipped out his cell phone, ready to make the calls that would get them to Merrie, and Social Services would take it from there.

"We need LaKeisha's phone number and location," Grace said to the weeping, addled woman.

"Am I going to jail?"

For possession at the very least, Grace thought, but she said, "We need to find your baby."

"Merrie," she ground out, as if she were dying. Which she was, inch by inch.

Good, Grace thought. *Die faster.*

"Butchy," Merrie said against his shoulder as he carried her out of LaKeisha's apartment. She smelled like cookies. She had fallen asleep watching *Lilo & Stitch.* LaKeisha's older daughter had given her a little stuffed dinosaur she had named Cherry. Janaya often told Merrie she was as sweet as cherry pie. She was half asleep, with Cherry in the blanket with her, waving tiredly at

LaKeisha and her four daughters, two of whom were crying.

The teacher at Merrie's school—a white teacher—had mistaken LaKeisha for Janaya when LaKeisha came by from picking up her own daughter at the same school. LaKeisha had realized that Janaya hadn't shown up. Her friend was already on thin ice with the school for showing up late a few times too many. So LaKeisha put her arms around Merrie, and the white teacher didn't say a word, just waved.

After she left the school, LaKeisha had called Janaya, who hadn't answered. Figuring Janaya was too high to talk, she took Merrie home and kept trying to reach her momma. For hours. She sure didn't call the cops because that was not what folks did.

When she and Janaya finally connected, Janaya didn't tell her about the police search; and when the authorities came by, to her place, LaKeisha was infuriated. She had asked Butch if Patrick was going to get custody of Merrie, and he'd told her he didn't know. Social Services was involved now.

"Well, he should get her," LaKeisha had informed him while one of her daughters took Merrie to go potty. "She a junkie bitch ho, and that's all I got to say about her."

When Butch had carried Merrie out of the house, he'd put her into the car of a social worker who'd promised the little girl that she could see her momma real soon. The social worker assigned to the case looked a lot like Michelle, the girl he'd taken out one time, who had pretended to hang herself at work out of unrequited love for him. Everyone had been in on that one, too.

Butch hadn't wanted to hand Merrie over. He didn't want her with strangers. He knew Grace was appalled at what she'd seen at Janaya's, and he had been, too. Last time he'd been there, the place was pretty good. Not perfect, but not the disaster it was now. Janaya would be evaluated, and maybe there were some programs for her that would enable her to retain custody and maybe there weren't.

Saturday was three days away, and he needed to tell his captain that Big Money was within his sights. But if October got wind of what was going down with his baby and his former woman . . .

Butch had Janaya's cell phone. Janaya had agreed to give it to him. He'd checked the calls and was taking the SIM card to Tech in the morning to see who she'd been talking to. What a tangled web . . .

He stripped down and got in the shower, let the stress and the frustration and, yes, the guilt, sluice off with the soap and the hot water. The guilt stuck.

Ham got a call from Grace that Merrie had been found. He'd been lying in the bed in his apartment, running scenarios for new searches for the six-year-old when his cell rang. They shared the joy and then she hung up; and he thought very briefly about phoning Darlene. But it was late and he was tired. So he lay down and ran scenarios for how to solve the Zachary Lacey case. If they had a case.

Grace spent the first part of the morning driving around South Rob looking for Flaco. She didn't find him at any of his old haunts, which raised alarm bells—maybe he'd left town because he'd committed a murder. But maybe he was in bed, asleep. It had stopped raining and the early-morning birds started trilling; dawn was close at hand, and you couldn't squeeze blood from a turnip no matter how hard you tried. In other words, even Supergrace needed to rest.

She went home and gave Gus his new chew toy. He was properly appreciative, even taking it outside when he went weewee. She took a hot bath, complete with candles and bubbles, and thought about calling Helping Hand to see who was doing what.

Merrie was found; her parents were nonfunctional; but the research indicated that kids did better in their families of origin pretty much no matter what. She smiled her wry, crooked smile at the thought of her own family of origin and gave props to Johnny for his reaction to Father Pepera's bullshit.

Then she dozed off. Just as her nose slipped beneath the layer of bubble-bath foam, she woke up and almost leaped out of the tub. A little weirded out, she wondered if Earl would have popped into the bathroom to wake her up before it was too late.

Four hours later, she sailed into the autopsy room. Henry was there, and she did a little two-step by way of greeting. It was just the two of them, no body on the slab. He was staring at a digital X-ray, and he lowered it and looked at her as she beamed at him.

"I'm so glad you're back," she said. "I have this vic—"

"Lena left me a note," Henry broke in. Then, pointedly, he added, "With her letter of resignation." She blinked, but he went on. "But you were right to keep Zachary Lacey, Grace. I noticed that his left ankle was bent at an angle, so I ran an X-ray. Fracture dislocation of the talotibial joint."

She parsed. "Meaning that his ankle was broken when he fell into the river? Or that he caught it on a rock?"

"I'm leaning toward that the ankle was struck by a blunt object before he went in. And that someone wielded that blunt object."

"Ha. Gotcha," she blurted. "So someone hit him, and he fell into the drink and couldn't swim." She pondered that. "Or someone made certain he would drown before they threw him in."

"I've got quantitative tox results, too," he continued. "Lena put them in stat for you before she cleaned out her desk. Negative for antidepressants but positive for rohypnol. Roofies."

"Date-rape drug."

"Good thing Lena ran the tox screen as fast as she did." Henry set down the X-ray but he kept scrutinizing it. "That stuff breaks down fast."

She detected more than a hint of disapproval. "You liked her," she observed. "You think I had anything to do with her quitting?" She touched her chest. "Henry, I invited her to Louie's. She was going to follow me over."

He peered at her over his glasses. "You also asked her to retain custody of a body so I could check her work."

"You're senior to her," she insisted.

"And how would you feel if the tables were turned?"

"They're turned all the time," she shot back. "Between Captain Perry and IA, I get checked and double-checked." She stuffed her hands in her pockets. "And I was right to do it. She didn't catch the ankle."

"It would have been difficult, with all the bloat," he began, and then he pursed his lips. "I could have trained her."

"We're not here to train people." She was incredulous. "We're here to put away bad guys and protect innocent citizens."

He huffed, as if she'd opened a valve and his slow leak was showing. She wondered if his mood had anything to do with taking his mother to the family reunion. Probably all the relatives his age had spouses and families. They were on their second or third sets of kids from different marriages. And Henry still lived with his mother. And she had turned down all his attempts to repeat their cat-pity sex.

"I'm sorry, Henry," Grace said. "We're losing all these cases, man." She raised up on tiptoe and kissed his cheek.

He softened, mollified just a smidge, and his cheeks went pink.

"Is everybody going to Louie's tonight?"

"Absolutely," she declared. "Butch had a missing kid but we found her last night."

"Oh? That's great," he said, warming up a bit.

"Yeah." She smiled at him. "Thanks for the catch on the ankle."

"It's my job." His face softened a bit more, as if he just couldn't stay mad at her. Good to know. Plus, she really liked Henry.

She patted his arm and went to visit Rhetta. Rhetta had fibers consistent with the interior of a Chevy truck manufactured after 2000, and she was interested in the report of rohypnol. If they could match fibers and traces of roofies to a specific vehicle . . .

"Yeah, I'm loving that thought," Grace said. "Hey, we're going to Louie's tonight. Right?"

"One drink, sure," Rhetta said. "Then I have to go home and muck out stalls. All this rain is turning the whole farm into a mud pit."

Grace nodded. "I think it's God's wrath for all the sin and easy living. I think our days are numbered."

"You're always so cheerful," Rhetta drawled.

About an hour later, Grace and Ham were canvassing Flaco's haunts on foot, showing Zack's picture and offering rewards for information. It was a chilly day; the smell of coagulated oil warred with that of wet newspaper and trash pressed against the cyclone fence along the street. There were parts of OKC that were breathtaking; this was not one of them.

It appeared that Flaco had not left town. He'd been seen at the minimart; he'd been at the bus stop. But he was never where they were. The information on his driver's license was bogus, and a water bill in his name turned out to be listed for a residence he did not reside at.

The streets cleaned up as they hit a row of gay bars on West Thirty-ninth. Flaco was known to sell coke and meth to the barbacks and dancers on the circuit. But it was the same deal: He'd been around, just wasn't there today. Flaco was like the Elvis of Oklahoma City.

Grace's bad mood was getting worse. She had started out their canvass miffed because Kate had refused her request to get a warrant for the Laceys' property. A man like Ron Lacey surely owned a truck. Grace had asked Records for the file on Zack's absent mother, and had been told it would be awhile. No one wanted to help her out.

"Perry's right," Ham told her as they entered a gay bar called Pan. The black lights were on, revealing a pretty good facsimile of Elvis, naked, holding a phallic microphone. Vibey techno music thrummed low, and a couple of pretty young men in red satin basketball shorts and silver jerseys carried oval black lacquer trays above their heads, setting up for the night ahead. But it was too early for more than a table or two of patrons. Grace smelled no weed, but there were furtive scramblings throughout the place as people cleaned up for a visit from the po-lice.

"It's only hearsay that Ron Lacey beat the shit out of Zachary, and there's nothing that puts Zachary in a vehicle of his prior to the kid going into the river," Ham went on.

"Bullshit," she grumped. "Daddy practically pounded on me when I suggested his son was gay."

"But he didn't." Ham moved his shoulders. "Sure didn't seem to care much about Zack."

"Poor Zack. Mom goes missing, Dad resents him. That's how I see it, anyway." She thought of Clay, also motherless.

"Dad remarries, Zack's still in the way," Ham said.

"Hi," a waiter in pancake makeup, eyeliner, and crimson lipstick sashayed up and vogued for Ham. "Whatcha lookin' for, cowboy?"

Grace and Ham flashed their badges and introduced themselves. The waiter was even more excited to meet them, which was refreshing.

Ham showed him Zack's school picture. "You seen this guy?"

The waiter aimed a pencil flashlight at the photograph and studied it. He raised his brows and slowly nodded. "Why, yes, I believe he was in here about a week ago. I know because I had to ask him to leave." He batted his false eyelashes. "Very cute but highly underage."

"Was he with anyone?" Grace asked. She pulled out a picture of Flaco. "Like this guy?"

The waiter pressed his fingertips against his chest. "Wow, Detective, are you psychic? That's Flaco, and, yes, they were here together."

"I'm just lucky," Grace said. "Finally. So, Flaco was here with him. Did they have drinks? Do anything else? Smoke some weed in the back room?"

"Detective, shamey-shame-shame," the waiter admonished her. "Smoking marijuana is illegal."

"Yeah, okay," Grace said. "We know Flaco is a dealer."

"Well, he's been banned. For trying to bring that young man in here," the waiter said, rolling his eyes at the mere thought of such a dastardly act.

"You're sure that Flaco brought him here?" Grace repeated.

"Let me get my manager," the waiter offered. "Oh, Janet!" He bustled off.

"See, Grace?" Ham drawled. "We do it right, we get rewarded."

"Remind me to hit you at an inopportune moment."

"Harder. Harder," he mock-begged her.

But when they interviewed Janet the manager (who was a guy), they didn't get anything new—just corroboration that Flaco had tried to bring Zack Lacey in and they'd both been booted. No one had seen Antwone with them, though. Zack-plus-Flaco had been a private date.

"So much for praying away the gay," Grace said as she and Ham left. "So Flaco sells to gay bars not just because there's a steady stream of customers, but because he likes the scene himself."

"And he's a chicken hawk. Likes 'em young," Ham spun as they walked down the street. "And something goes wrong. Zack's going to tell because he's got religion now. Zack's underage, so it's statutory rape. They're doing drugs and getting it on. Flaco's on probation from the last time—"

"Let's hear it for the OKC justice system," Grace muttered.

"Flaco's been giving Zack roofies; hell, maybe Zack likes it that way so he can let Flaco do what he wants without taking any responsibility for it."

"So Zack doesn't remember any of it," Grace agreed. "Doesn't have to come clean in confession. Or whatever they call it in the non-Catholic world."

"But God tells Zack to come forward. So Zack tells Flaco he's going to tell. Bam. Dead Zack." Ham nodded.

"Sounds good," Grace said. In its way.

"Or Antwone finds out they've been together, and Antwone kills him," Ham said. "You like him for that?"

"I don't know," Grace replied. She stuffed her fingertips in the pockets of her jeans. "We need to talk to Flaco. Maybe Antwone knows where he lives. If he wants out of this he'll give Flaco up."

Ham ran his fingers through his hair, then dropped his hands to his sides. His face was sweaty, his eyelids heavy. Grace glanced over at him, wondering if he was okay. He had a lot on his mind. But she knew Ham Dewey. There was every chance that if she asked him if he was okay, he would clam up and tell her that he was. Take umbrage.

"Plus, we can go *talk* to the Laceys," she continued. "Just because we don't have a warrant doesn't mean we can't question them at their home. About various subjects including why Karen Lacey ran off. And how soon Ron and Cherie got together after Karen disappeared."

"We have to be careful," Ham reminded her. "If we see anything, we can't use it as evidence until we return with a warrant. And even though I think they both cheated on their IQ tests to hit a hundred, they might be smart enough to remove a murder weapon from the premises."

"Or their bottle of street drugs," she said.

"So we dot the *i*'s, cross the *t*'s," Ham reiterated. "We make sure we are bulletproof. Once we get the case put together, the D.A. can lose it for us."

"Yup," she agreed. "But we won't lose it for us." At his nod, she took a breath. "And I guess one of us will have to go to Zack's freaky church."

He grinned at her. "Guess so."

She licked her lips. "How badly do you want a blow job?"

CHAPTER
ELEVEN

Louie's, half an hour after the squad's quitting time. And it was raining.

Grace sat at a booth waiting for Rhetta while Ham shot pool with Butch and Bobby. Ham had actually turned down her bribe of oral pleasure and insisted that they should both go to the holy-roller church. He was drinking a longneck, but Grace had gone with a beer and a tequila shot. For starters. She needed to brace herself. As luck would have it, there was a nine o'clock healing service at the church that very night.

Antwone would get off work at the bowling alley at eleven. So much for quitting time. Not that she was complaining. There wasn't much on TV, and it was no fun to watch horror movies without Clay. She'd keep the DVD until the weekend. Clay was coming over again on Saturday night.

The jukebox was playing "It Wasn't God Who Made Honky Tonk Angels" when Rhetta walked into the bar. She was wearing jeans and that plaid blouse with the ruffles at the neck. Her hair was in a ponytail, and she had on dangly earrings and her glasses. She saw Grace and headed for her.

Grace threw back her shot of tequila so she could get another one when Rhetta ordered her white wine. Rhetta scooted into the booth with a happy groan.

"This day is over," Rhetta said.

"Hey, man," Grace said, picking her cigarette up from the metal ashtray and taking a drag. "Wait until you hear this. Zack's priest told me if it was up to him, Zack couldn't be buried in hallowed ground."

Rhetta looked startled. The waitress came over.

"Chardonnay, please," Rhetta told the woman. Grace held up her empty shot glass and the waitress nodded. "You mean because it looks like suicide?"

Grace said nothing, just took another drag on her cigarette. "You agree with him?" Grace asked her. "Suicide's the greatest sin there is if you're a Catholic. And we keep track of our sins. Big ones, little ones. Is that the one that God cannot forgive?"

Rhetta leaned toward her. Her face kind of shone. "I have faith, Grace. And I place that faith in a God who wouldn't punish a person when he is at his lowest. That priest is totally wrong. Totally."

"That's what Johnny says, too." She grinned and nodded as Rhetta's brows raised. "I haven't fully discussed it with Earl."

"That's pretty progressive for Johnny," Rhetta said.

"I'm not saying what I'm thinking about my brother," Grace informed her, blowing out smoke. Then she grinned. "It is pretty progressive of him. He told me he said Mass for a suicide victim himself."

"Wow." Rhetta was clearly startled. The waitress arrived with their drinks, and Rhetta took a moment to stare into the chardonnay. If that had been Grace's glass, the wine would be gone by now. The second tequila shot sure was.

"I'm supposed to look to my own soul." Rhetta took a sip of wine. "And my soul needs something else to talk about. I am beat." She took another sip and closed her eyes for a moment. "Dear God, thank you for wine."

"At happy-hour prices, amen," Grace added, crossing herself. "You get anything else on Zack?" Not exactly changing the subject, but it was just about the best she could do at the moment. Maybe it was no accident that her sweet puppy Gussie was an American bulldog.

"Fibers, rohypnol," Rhetta said. "River water. Pathology found diatoms."

"Diatoms are bullshit. Any semen?"

Rhetta shook her head. "He was semen-free."

"Henry didn't say anything about marijuana, either."

"No cannabis residue," Rhetta confirmed.

"That's weird. He and his boyfriend were dealers."

"Maybe after he accepted Jesus, he stopped using." Rhetta took another sip.

"I'm going to his church with Ham tonight," Grace said, smirking. "Pentecostal type of place." She lifted her fingers in the air and wiggled them. "Praise the Lord."

"And pass the ammunition," Henry said, coming up beside them. He looked very happy. Grace assumed the King of Darts had hustled an unsuspecting citizen for beer money, shameless Corona coroner guy. "*You're* going to church?"

"Gee, yeah, except I'm a little worried the holy water will boil when I walk in," Grace drawled.

"They don't have holy water," Rhetta said. Henry nodded.

"Holy shit, no holy water?" Grace said. "That's also weird."

Rhetta grimaced, mildly scandalized. Henry chuckled. Over at the pool table, Ham raised his cue over his head with a shout. His resemblance to a baboon was startling.

"Creamed 'em," Ham crowed. "Praise the Lord." He walked over to the booth and high-fived Grace.

"Are you practicing for tonight?" Grace asked him.

"I am," he confirmed. He turned to the others. "Please feel free to join us."

Grace grinned at Rhetta. "When we were in school, the nuns told us it was a sin to go inside a Protestant church. Having a friend who was a Protestant was like consorting with a known felon."

"This is true," Rhetta agreed. "Johnny threatened to tell my parents when I went to a dance at the Methodist church."

"Horrors," Grace said, widening her eyes and touching her cheeks. "He *did* tell my parents when I went to the drive-in with a hot young Lutheran. Of course, I don't think it was his religion that flipped them out."

"I'm going to go back to my place and take a shower," Ham announced.

"Cleaning up for church?" Grace asked, startled. She looked down at her light blue, long-sleeved leotard top, jeans, and muddy boots. "Is this okay to wear to a healing service?"

"It's a working-class church, right?" Rhetta asked, assessing her. "I think you look fine."

"You look great," Henry agreed jovially.

"Okay, so I'll meet you in the church parking lot at about ten to nine," Ham said. Off he went, him with his fantastic, sorry ass. Grace wondered if they could get some sexual healing in before they called it a night.

Henry was still smiling. "Henry, is something up?" Grace asked.

He smiled more broadly, all mysterious. She and Rhetta traded looks, shrugged, and looked back at him. He didn't give it up, whatever it was. Then he trotted back to his special moneylender zone in the den of iniquity.

"I should go, too," Rhetta announced, leaving more than half her glass of wine as she gathered up her purse. *More than half.* "We've got a mountain of rotting hay because of all this rain."

"That's a drag," Grace said sincerely. "Maybe Earl can

ask God to turn off the faucet. Well, I have time before I'm saved to go home and feed Gus." And to fortify herself with a little more alcohol for the coming ordeal.

"Shall we?" Rhetta asked her.

She rose and sauntered toward the exit with Rhetta.

"What is up with Henry? I haven't seen him smiling like that since . . ." Grace blinked. "Shit, Rhetta, do you think Henry's getting some?"

"Hmm." Rhetta considered. "That would be nice, wouldn't it?"

Grace chuckled. Rhetta opened the door to Louie's and they both stared at the rain. The parking lot was a minefield of puddles, even though that was a mixed metaphor at best. Rhetta would have put it better.

Their umbrellas were in the stand to the right of the door. Rhetta fished around for hers, then handed Grace's over.

"Thanks, man," Grace said, popping it open. She hopped over the transom like a skydiver leaving the plane, followed closely by Rhetta. She heard some laughter inside the bar, caught sight of Rhetta waving goodbye to her, and jogged on over to her beloved Porsche. She snapped the umbrella back into its compact size and dumped it on the floor of the passenger side. Connie awoke with a purr, and Grace zoomed home to her dog.

Earl was loitering at her breakfast bar, examining what was left of the pizza she had shared with Clay. He smiled as she tore off her sopping wet jacket and she gave him a nod.

"You're soaked through. Where's your umbrella?" he asked her.

"Left it on the porch to dry." He gazed at her with humor twinkling in his eyes. "What?" she asked.

"You're going to church."

"Undercover. For a case."

"You're going to church," he repeated.

"You said you don't care if I go to a church. I can go to a tree if it brings me closer to God." She leaned over to give Gus some love. Gus yodeled and snuffled and looked back at Earl. Earl smiled at him. As she scratched Gus between his ears, she remembered the brown, long-tongued dog that had appeared in her backyard and elsewhere upon occasion. Maybe that dog was not actually God, but Gus's last-chance dog angel. Not that Gus had ever done anything that would send him to dog hell.

"All dogs go to heaven," Earl said.

"Stop reading my mind, man," she retorted, but she felt a bit uplifted. "I'm going to put on some warm clothes."

"Get *gussied up* for church?" He chuckled.

"Oh, and you're the first person who's ever come up with that," she salvoed over her shoulder.

"I ain't a person, Grace," he called after her.

"Wanna jump in the shower with me?"

He smiled and shook his head. "How *do* you put up with her, Gus?" he asked the dog.

"Hey, I heard that," she called.

"Funny how she only hears the things she wants to," Earl said to Gus. Gus made happy panting noises; he tap-danced on the wood floor and Earl escorted him to the door. Gus looked up at him expectantly and Earl shrugged.

"Much obliged, Gus. I don't really have to eat, and I never have to take a piss," Earl informed him. "But you go right ahead. Enjoy."

Gus scooted across the threshold—as much as a big dog like that could scoot—and Earl cocked his head, listening.

Stepped outside after all, and furled his wings.

Leon was sitting in his cell, less likely to do any exercising now that he'd gotten the news: His boy would not be visiting him that week. Leon's ex, Tamara, and her fiancé were taking him to visit the fiancé's family. Taking Benjamin out of school and everything.

It was a blow, and Leon was not taking it well.

"Bitch," he muttered between his teeth. "My son is all I live for. She knows that."

"I'm sorry, Leon," Earl said, appearing in front of him. "You want to play some cards, pass the time?"

"I want to get rid of that son of a bitch." He clenched his fists. "Stole my wife."

"No, you don't," Earl said. "Leastwise, I hope you don't." Then he lifted his head. "I gotta go to France," he announced.

"I just wish I could go . . . anywhere," Leon said. He flopped down on his cot and covered his eyes with his hands. Earl knew Leon wanted to break down and cry. Earl really wished he would. It would do the bitter convict a world of good. Jesus cried so hard in the garden of Gethsemane that he wept blood. But the hard shell Leon had put around himself was one of the reasons he, Earl, had been assigned to him. Plants couldn't grow in cement. They sprouted out through the cracks. Same thing with the souls of men. And women. A broken heart was often God's best garden.

Grace spent so much time detesting Leon for murdering people that she failed to see how alike they were. She had to see that, someday.

If she wanted to see the light.

You live your entire life in a place and you assume you had seen it all. But somehow a large white temple with a sloped roof and white marble stairs leading to four big white columns had passed Grace by. She parked down the street and walked with the crowd streaming into the church, greeting each with hugs and "praise Jesus's."

It was drizzling, but she left the umbrella in the car

because it was *not* her umbrella; Rhetta must have been in on the switcheroo for the one that was now folded and dripping on the floor of Connie's passenger side. The wording on its outside surface read FOR A GOOD TIME CALL JESUS. 1-800-JCHRIST. Ha. Payback, when it came, would be sweet.

Scanning for Ham, she reached the double doors of the Ark of the Covenant Pentecostal Tabernacle. Two men in dark suits with carefully arranged white hair were handing out programs, saying, "God bless you" to each person as they took one and filed into the church. They had on blue tags with USHER written on them in white letters, followed by a white cross.

Grace had a brief, sharp moment when she remembered being dragged to church with her mother and father, and all six of her siblings. She felt herself tense up, and reminded herself that Father Patrick Satan Murphy was definitely in hell now. Or so she hoped.

"We hope you'll receive the Lord tonight," another usher said as she passed the two older guys with the programs. This one was much younger and cuter. He grasped her hand, squeezed it, and gazed into her eyes as if he wanted to propose marriage to her.

"Thanks," she said, moving on in the steady stream of people entering the church. Most of them wore shiny, expectant smiles, but a young woman to Grace's right, with auburn hair pulled back in a ponytail and wearing a navy blue peacoat, was crying. Instantly, an usher in a chambray shirt and a pair of dark brown trousers broke ranks and came over to her.

"Are you troubled, sister?" he asked the woman, taking her arm and gently pulling her out of line. "Let's pray about it together."

A lady with blue hair was riding in a wheelchair pushed by another young usher. They were chatting amiably. There were a hell of a lot of ushers.

Past the double doors, a foyer with a vaulted ceiling that belled heavenward in an inverted lily shape. An enormous crystal chandelier sparkled like a comet. Prisms danced on a large oil painting of Jesus standing on a mountain with His arms wide open—no marks of the Crucifixion in His palms. Large sprays of lilies arced out of white vases embossed with crosses.

A drum, a guitar, and voices raised in jaunty song wafted beyond a second set of doors as a woman near Grace's own age greeted her. She was wearing a red and pink floral-print blouse, a black jacket, and a matching skirt. She took one of Grace's hands in both of hers. She had an usher tag, too. Janet.

"Are you new tonight? Do you have a special need that you would like Pastor Andy to pray for?"

Yeah. I would like Zack Lacey's case to be solved. If he was murdered, I'd like the sacks of shit who killed him brought to justice.

"No, thanks," Grace replied sweetly.

"Praise Jesus," the woman said, giving Grace's hand one last squeeze before Grace walked through the next set of doors into the sanctuary.

It was massive, with stairways that led to seats way up in the nosebleed section. Dozens and dozens of rows. Hundreds of seats. Maybe a thousand. And the pews were crammed with people chatting, laughing, embracing. Ushers were directing, escorting, and handing out slips of paper and stubby pencils. People were handing them back the pieces of paper, which went into white cans labeled PRAYER REQUESTS.

The main attraction was a huge stage dominated by an enormous white cross banked with pots of lilies. On either side of the cross, a golden church candelabra gleamed with long white tapers. Stage left, on a dais sat a band of six men dressed in suits, and one woman in a ruffled white gown. She was banging a tambourine against her palm. Two of the men were playing guitars; two were singing into a mic; one was beating the tempo on a full drum kit. And the last one was playing a sax. The song was familiar, yet not. Maybe she'd heard it on the radio.

Then she raised her head to see a screen, and the words of the song appeared, line by line, as scattered members of the congregation began to sing.

Washed in the blood of the Lamb, I am.
Washed in the blood of the Lamb, I am.

It wasn't really a song; it was a chant. More of the worshipers joined in as a full choir in white robes marched from stage right, waving their arms. Applause thundered through the dome. Some congregants raised their hands, threw back their heads, and closed their eyes. They smiled. Others began murmuring to themselves. Praying.

"Jesus, we give you the praise. Oh, Lord, Jesus, come into my heart."

The choir turned and sang. An organ joined in, vibrating through Grace's feet.

Teenagers gathered in clumps on the risers, getting into it, swaying, murmuring. One kid started to cry. Another took note, and *he* started to cry. The first crier upped the ante, swaying and murmuring as tears streamed down his face. The second guy sank to his knees. Whether they realized it or not, they were egging each other on, competing over who was more filled with the Holy Spirit.

This was *so* not like Catholic Mass. It was more like a pep rally. She could sense the rising emotion, as manufactured as a designer drug, and gave her head a little shake.

The band and the organ played faster and louder, and the lights started to dim. She broke into a grin as the cross on the stage lit up. She'd figured that would happen. The praising increased in fervency, need, urgency; the drummer and the organ player found a special pulse and tapped into it. More voices chanted the endless refrain. Hands raised in the air. Folks swayed, wept.

Grace whipped out her cell phone. "Hey, Ham, where the hell are you?"

"Sister, I'm sorry, but you need to turn that off," said the usher she'd seen pushing the wheelchair as he darted toward her. His name tag revealed that he was Luke, and he practically had to yell at her to be heard. "We have some wonderful seats close to the cross. If you feel led to answer the call tonight, you won't have far to walk."

"Yeah, sorry," she said. "Thanks, but—" Then she saw Ham standing up to wave at her. Third row from the stage. Good job; he was about fifteen feet away from a mahogany podium that at that very moment was rising out of the stage floor like a magician's trick. The congregants began to cheer. The cross on the stage blazed; she half-expected fireworks. Or a fog machine. Or both.

"My, um, significant other's over there," Grace said, nodding at Ham. "He saved me a seat, God bless him. I've been saved." The usher looked both confused and crestfallen.

"I'll take you to him," the usher said. "Is this your first time with us tonight?"

Then a trim, middle-aged man walked out from the wings, carrying a cordless mic. He had a muscular build and military posture; he was wearing a dark blue suit but it was a nice suit, adorned with a white carnation boutonniere. The crowd went completely batshit at the sight of him.

"Bless you! Bless you tonight!" he shouted. He held up a hand and the love intensified. People were practically doing the wave. Grace looked up at the seats, stupefied. Wow.

"Is that Pastor Andy?" she asked her escort.

The man beamed at her. "No, sister, that's Pastor Jimmy, our music director."

"Washed in the blood of the Lamb, I am," Pastor Jimmy sang, and then he held the last note. The band copied him; they hung there, drawing it out. Then he signaled for a downbeat and sang:

I am God's loving Son; He is my only One.

They all started singing the new line, her usher included, as they finally reached Ham's row.

"Thanks," she said.

The usher reached into his pocket and handed her a printed form the size of a three-by-five card and a little pencil. "If you write down your name and a prayer request, I'll get extra points," he told her. He looked so excited.

"Really? Well, shoot, okay." She scribbled a few words down and handed it and the pencil back to him.

"Praise Jesus," the usher said.

"You got that right." She smiled and winked at him, then scooted into the row. Half the people she stepped over didn't seem to realize she was even there.

Then she sank down next to Ham. He was wearing court clothes—jacket, dark jeans, and his black boots. He smelled great, of soap and a hint of something spicy. She saw water droplets on the ends of his hair. He had shaved. She wanted to go home, watch TV, and jump him.

"Oh, my God, Ham," she said. "This is just . . . nuts." She gazed around. "No wonder the Catholic Church is losing people. This is way more fun."

"I used to go to revivals with my great-uncle when I was a kid," he said. "The kind in the tents."

She was impressed. "Were there snakes?"

"Naw. I always hoped."

"Well, you should have filled out a prayer request," she said. "Tonight might have been your lucky night."

"I saw you fill one out." He raised a brow. "What did you ask for?"

"I asked Pastor Andy how long he's been practicing

medicine without a license." She fluttered her lashes. "Telling kids to dump their meds."

It was obvious he wasn't sure if she was kidding. She made a show of looking around.

"Do they sell refreshments at these things?" she asked.

"Is your soul singing?" Pastor Jimmy asked the crowd.

"Amen!" the congregation shouted.

"Is your soul lifted up to the Lord?"

"Hallelujah!"

"Are you ready to stand before the Master?"

"Yes, Jesus! Hallelujah, amen, sweet Lord. I give you the praise, oh, my sweet Jesus." They were shouting loud and strong, bellowing and hollering.

"Poor Zack," Grace murmured. "He didn't stand a chance."

"*Hallelujah!*"

CHAPTER
TWELVE

In yellow rain boots, a raincoat, and an old cowboy hat, Rhetta slipped and slid in the mud as she trudged toward the barn. She was cold, wet, and very worried. They were already behind on payments and now the barn roof was leaking in two new places, and her daughter was coughing and talking about feeling hot. Rhetta took her temperature, slumping with relief that, so far, it was still 98.6. If she had to stay home from school tomorrow, she and Ronnie would have to flip a coin to see who stayed home from work. If the Zack Lacey case broke, there would be more evidence, and Rhetta wanted to be the one to process it. For Grace.

But now . . . warmth.

Happiness.

She stood at the entrance to the barn, loving that she owned a barn (well, along with the bank) and loving that there were animals inside it that she raised and fed and named. She put the worry away as she silently counted her blessings. Her life was filled with life. There were homeless people all over the country, all over OKC, and she and her family had one another. And their menagerie. And Grace.

She smiled faintly at the thought of Grace at a holy-roller church service and slogged through the damp to the first bucket catching the rain from the barn. It wasn't as full as she expected it to be, so there was some more good news.

Holy Cow lowed.

"How are you doing this fine evening?" Rhetta asked her as she ran a hand down Holy Cow's flank, admiring the markings that looked like Jesus. "Would you like to be milked?"

Holy Cow mooed. Rhetta smiled at her. "It's going to be okay," she said. "We just have to have faith."

And from the hayloft, Earl smiled down on Rhetta.

"Praise God! Miracles are happening here tonight," Pastor Andy shouted, king of all creation. He smiled like he was high as he gazed down on his flock. The woman beside Grace was sobbing. "Miracles everywhere. Behold the power of Jesus!"

The old lady who had been wheeled in was walking on her own steam across the stage. Four men in suits stood with white blankets in their arms. Pastor Andy high-stepped toward the woman as she shuffled toward him.

"Satan took away her power to walk, but Jesus gave it back! Hallelujah, sister!" He darted forward and tapped his fingers on the woman's forehead. "You stay out of there, devil. This sister belongs to the Lord!"

The woman stiffened. Then she began to shake all over. The band thrashed in an acceptably religious manner. The organ pumped like it was time for the kickoff. On your mark, get set . . . Boomer Sooner!

The entire auditorium was thrilled as the old lady flung her arms straight up, jerked back her head, and fell backward. Two of the men with the blankets broke her fall and laid her gently on the floor. The preacher man strutted backward as the crowd cheered. The woman kept on convulsing and thrashing.

"That's what I'm talking about!" the weeping woman beside Grace shrieked. "Oh, my dear Lord Jesus, hallelujah!"

"Holy sh—" Grace blurted, covering her mouth with her hand. She looked at Ham, who grinned in a superior way. *Been here, done this.*

It went on and on, as the ushers brought up their white coffee cans filled with requests and Pastor Andy went through them by the handful. Arthritis, hallelujah! Chronic fatigue syndrome, we give you the praise! No job, you're gonna get a job. Who has a job right here right now for this sinner? Will work for soul food, yessir, I hear you, brother.

After a while it got boring, because it actually got predictable—if you knew how to play against the house, and Grace did. Pastor Andy called out a malady; the ushers had the afflicted ready to hop onto the stage; Andy zinged them on the forehead, and they went into convulsions. It was quite orgiastic, and it reminded Grace of the previews for the zombie movie she had seen with Clay.

"There's not much point in sticking around," she said to Ham.

"Grace, it's just getting started," Ham told her. "We could be here hours until it's time to see Antwone."

"Hours? And you *knew* this?" she said. "Why didn't you warn me?"

"There is someone here tonight who has lost someone. That person died by his own hand," Pastor Andy announced. "He was lost, and alone, and he did not know that God had a plan for his life, a beautiful, unfolding plan."

Ham raised a brow at Grace. She raised one back. "I'll bet you there's a dozen people who fit that description," she said.

Then, Pastor Andy bounded to the edge of the stage and pointed at Grace. A spotlight fastened on her.

"Come up here, Sister Grace. We know you loved him, and we know you are grieving for him. Let God heal your heart!"

"Praise Jesus!" the congregation roared.

"Undercover," Grace gritted, as Ham slapped her on the back. "*Ham,* stop it."

"Hey, you wrote it down. And you used your real name?"

"Yeah, that was genius," she said. "I thought maybe they'd keep track of me, ask questions so I could—"

"Sister Grace!" Pastor Andy yodeled.

"How the mighty are fallen." Ham reached into his jacket pocket and pulled out his cell phone. He shot off a couple of pictures as the usher, Grace's best friend forever and ever, hallelujah, beckoned her from the end of the row to come on up. His face was shiny with perspiration and his cheeks were apple-rosy. He was on the verge of doing his own happy dance. His sinner had been picked. God was good. All the time!

"Put that camera away, Hamilton, or I swear I will never—"

"Ssh, ssh, Grace," he urged her. He started laughing. "Don't make a scene."

"You guys set this up," she hissed at him. "I don't know how you did it—"

He held up his hands, protesting his innocence, but he was laughing so hard that tears were streaming down his cheeks. She wanted to belt him one, and she would have, but the usher had maneuvered his way down the row and was eagerly grasping her hand. *Break the case, break the case,* she reminded herself as she succumbed and allowed him to parade her toward the stage. Floodlights surrounded Pastor Andy's head like a halo as he held out his arms like Jesus, urging her to come forward and testify.

Last time we testified, the guilty got probation, she thought. Her mind was racing as she clattered up the steps in her cowboy boots. Pastor Andy started doing his chicken walk toward her and she pulled back her jacket, flashing her badge. His smile didn't falter and he just kept hopping toward her.

"It's all right, sister," he said into his headset mic. "God loves everyone." He swept his arm to include the coliseum of onlookers. "Isn't that right?"

High up in the nosebleed seats, Earl waved at her. "I am going to kill you," she gritted through her teeth. Then she had the hopeful notion that all this was one big stupid dream and she was going to wake up any second.

"You lost a brother, a friend," Pastor Andy said, "through a death of his own choosing." His eyes welled. "How that must tear at you."

Only because I have to—

Without warning, a wave of grief washed through her. It wasn't sadness; it was something deeper. It descended on her like a stone, pushing her down. She was suddenly drowning in it, almost unable to catch her breath.

"Psalm 18:2," Pastor Andy intoned. "The Lord is my rock, my fortress, and my deliverer; my God is my rock, in whom I take refuge. He is my shield!"

He stomped the floor on the word "shield." The choir began to sing. *The Lord is my Shepherd, no want shall I know!* The audience joined in.

"And the horn of my salvation! He is my stronghold!" the pastor bellowed. "Hallelujah!"

Then he started toward her, his hand raised up as if he were about to smack her on the forehead. She glanced over her shoulder to see the guys with the blankets ready to catch her.

And she narrowed her eyes at Pastor Andy.

He kept coming.

"Back off," she gritted, certain he couldn't hear her; he probably couldn't see her lips, either. She hoped— *prayed*—her body language would keep him from making a scene.

"Praise Jesus," he cried.

And then, as she braced herself for a head rap, he slowly laid his hands on her shoulders, and gazed into her eyes. "It's all right," he said in a low voice. "God knows your heart. He knows what you need."

There was a hushed moment, just one heartbeat in all the nuttiness, and then he threw back his head and yodeled, "Jesus, Jesus, Jesus!" and all the other lunatics did, too.

Lights blared at her; the music was deafening as her escort led her back toward her seat. People reached out their hands to her, squeezing her fingers as she stumbled past them. They said, "Bless you, sister; praise God, sinner," patting her, touching her.

Grinning from ear to ear, Ham waited for her to plop down. Then he leaned over and whispered, "Can I have your autograph?"

She didn't answer him. She seethed privately for a few seconds, and then she turned around to look at where Earl had been sitting. The seat was empty. Figured.

"Did you write down Zack's name?" Ham asked her.

She shook her head. "Figured he wouldn't know who Zack was, either. I just asked if people who commit suicide go to hell."

"He assumed you were talking about a guy."

"A black guy. A brother," Grace drawled, but the joke didn't go anywhere.

There was a lot more swaying. The woman next to Grace started jabbering—speaking in tongues—and the man behind her took it up. The energy in the room reached a fever pitch; ushers started running up and down the aisles checking on the people who were rolling around having fits. They handed out some water bottles but let most of the holy rollers roll on.

"Come up and receive the Lord!" Pastor Andy shouted. "He is waiting to save your soul from Satan! Stand on the conviction that you are His beloved!"

Streams of people rushed to form lines. They descended the stairs, guided by the ushers, hands in the air, murmuring, swaying, yelling. Ushers stood at the head of each line and held both the hands of the convicted. They fell to their knees at the foot of the stage while the choir sang and the band played and Pastor Andy bounced forward, shouting, "You are saved, brother! You are saved, sister!"

Grace's usher looked over at her. She smiled at him and nodded, and stayed planted.

"I'm going up," Ham said breathlessly, and then he grinned at her to show her that he was kidding.

"You'd better pray that someone is going to save your ass," she shot back. "From *me*."

The parade kept marching forward. Grace started checking the exits and planning a strategy in case there was a riot. There was an incredible amount of energy, pressure, and high, high emotion. This was how people died after soccer games in England, or on Black Friday, the shopping day after Thanksgiving.

Then somehow, miraculously, it was over. The old lady who had walked across the stage was back in her wheelchair. Some people were drooped over the backs of the chairs in front of them, like pews, weeping and smiling or shaking their heads. There was a powerful eau de B.O. hanging in the air. And relief. And joy.

On the way out, Grace's usher caught up with her. Color crept up his neck and across his cheeks. He smiled at her shyly and dropped his gaze.

"I, um, hope you'll come back," he said. He smiled at her, and then at Ham. "With your husband."

"Thank you." She resisted the impulse to wink at him. *I could take you to heaven, baby.*

"Your husband?" Ham asked, jostling her arm. "Is that what you told him?"

"These guys make assumptions," she shot back.

Out into the fresh air. Ham breathed it in and pointed upward, at the ring around the moon. "It's gonna rain. Some more."

"Bobby's got mold."

"I know. He's really worried about it."

"Maybe we can have some kind of work party, help him out." Grace glanced at the church. "We should have prayed for him." She pulled out a cigarette. "Not mocking prayer, man."

"Did you feel anything when you went up there?" Ham asked her. "Some kind of spirituality? I thought your hair was going to stand on end." His mouth twitched. "And that you were going to bite him if he tried to hit you in the forehead."

"Right. Assault a beloved minister in front of six hundred witnesses." She struck a match, for which she received some glares from others in the multitudes headed for their cars. "God deliver me from this filthy habit." After she lit her cigarette, she blew out her match and carried it in her hand. "Your church isn't like that, is it?" She wiggled back and forth.

"Much more sedate," he assured her. He was waiting.

"Naw," she said. "I didn't feel anything. Not a damn thing."

CHAPTER
THIRTEEN

Ham's truck was parked closer to the church. Grace let him drive her to her car and described how to get to the taco stand. Antwone was due there in twenty minutes. Just enough time to get there and park.

As Ham followed her over, she checked her messages. Evan Johnson. Very distressed, wanting to discuss the "situation" with Juanita. A message from Juanita, ditto. And then, an older, halting voice:

"Detective Hanadarko, my name is Emily Prescott. I'm Zachary Lacey's grandmother. Father Pepera phoned me. Please, call me back. It doesn't matter what time it is." Hard, wracking sobs ended the call. Deep grief. Grace was sure Father Pepera had proved to be *such* a comfort.

She passed the taco stand, scoping it out as she left her message system. She'd call Emily Prescott later. If she was Zack's maternal grandmother, maybe she knew where Zack's mom was.

A streetlight caught the chrome on Ham's wheels as he slid in ahead of her around the corner. They both got out and walked toward the tables where she'd met Antwone the night before. They were right on time, but he wasn't there.

They waited a few minutes. Grace grabbed a taco and started crunching away like a starving woman. Ham got a soda. A man collected a to-go order and a lowrider slithered past. Not their Chevy Impala.

"Maybe he has overtime at the bowling alley," Ham said.

"Or else he chickened out and bailed," Grace countered, talking with her mouth full as she snaked out her cell phone. She called Antwone's cell. No answer. She disconnected and polished off her taco, thought about ordering another one, decided against it as she wadded up the trash and threw it out. She nodded at Ham.

"You go to the bowling alley. I'll wait here."

He nodded and jogged across the street to his truck. Grace stretched her back, then walked the perimeter, scanning for people and things that shouldn't be there— like bad guys dealing dope on the corners, bad girls waiting to be picked up by bad guys—but all was calm. No misdemeanors, no felonies.

Then she heard something farther down in the alley behind the taco shop. She froze. A scuffle; the sound of a fist hitting a body; a low moan. Silently, swiftly, she drew her weapon and darted into the shadows, pushing her spine against the wall. She peered deep in the darkness, making out nothing past the tips of her boots.

Another blow. "Faggot . . . ," a male voice said.

Shit. Antwone.

Keeping her gun out and up, she glided soundlessly into the blackness. The gray began to shift as she waited for her eyes to adjust; for the moment, she focused on listening. She needed both hands for her gun; otherwise, she would have slid her fingers into her pocket to demon-dial for backup. Draw out her pencil flashlight. Thank God her phone was on vibrate.

The alley reeked of rotten lettuce and dog shit and maybe a whiff of dope. Pieces of darkness began to thicken into shapes. Possibly two individuals bent over something on the ground. Make that some*one* on the ground. Probably Antwone. One of the guys arced back his foot and kicked. Hard. The shape on the ground grunted.

She gathered in all the details she could. The kicker was around six feet tall, two hundred pounds. It was too dark to make out the other guy. She was not seeing a gun on Kicker, but that didn't mean no guns were present. For all she knew, the guy on the ground wasn't Antwone and he was just biding his time until he could pull out his Glock and blow somebody's head off. She couldn't just sail into the situation expecting impunity because she wanted to help. On the streets, you got extra points for taking out a cop, especially if someone else was kicking your ass.

Then No Kick separated himself from Kicker. He was much smaller, definitely a kid. Damn. Grace kept her weapon aimed at Kicker.

"Someone's here," No Kick announced. He started sprinting in the opposite direction, sloshing through puddles, stumbling around a trash can. It fell with a clatter-clatter-crash.

Kicker swore under his breath and took off after him.

Grace wanted like anything to pursue. She strained like Gus when he was watching the stick fly end over end through the air. But she had a mandate to protect and serve. So she raced over to the prone figure, sweeping with her gun, then fanning with her flashlight over the muddy army jacket and Antwone's swollen, bruised face.

"Antwone, it's Detective Hanadarko," she said. "Are you armed?"

"Ow," he said, gasping. "No."

"What hurts?"

He was silent. She shook his shoulder. No response. She flipped her cell phone open with her teeth and dialed the dispatcher, identified herself, and requested an ambulance. She got confirmation that one was on the way just as Antwone tried to sit up. She dropped to one knee and helped him, slowly. He looked like he'd been in a prizefight. His lips were bleeding. One eye was swollen shut.

"Can you see me, man?" she asked him. "How many fingers—"

"Shit," he hissed. "Shit."

"Who were those guys?" she asked him. She demondialed number three, which was Ham. "He's here. He was jumped. Beat up. I called for a bus."

"On my way," Ham told her.

"I don't need an ambulance," Antwone said, wiping blood away from his nose.

"Maybe you do," Grace countered. "You got kicked pretty hard. Who were those guys?"

"I don't know." He wouldn't look at her.

"You definitely do. Were they guys from school?"

He hung his head. Stayed frozen that way.

"Guys beating you up because you're gay?"

He did the sullen thing like a pro.

"Antwone, don't wuss out on me now," she told him. "Guys you sold weed to?"

Nothing.

"Guys from Flaco?"

"No," he said stonily. He was mad, blaming her for getting in his face, more afraid of legal trouble than physical pain. She got that a lot. She didn't care. She just wanted him to talk to her.

"Did they go after Zack? Beat him up for being a faggot, too?" Was his death a hate crime?

He sniffled. She felt in her pockets for tissue. Found a paper napkin from Louie's with a phone number on it. Another UPS guy. Oh, well. She handed it to him while she found another one and folded it over, preparing to dab at his cuts.

"Don't touch me," he said. "I'm bleeding."

"Are you HIV positive?" she asked matter-of-factly.

"Hell, no." And then, "I don't know. I don't want to go in an ambulance. I'm okay." He stared up at her. "Please."

She held up two fingers. "How many?"

He grinned tiredly and flashed her his middle finger. She stifled a guffaw. The kid had guts. Maybe he didn't want to go to the hospital because drugs would show up. She had promised to leave him out of it as best she could.

"Walk back and forth," she said, watching him. He did so, well. No weaving or stumbling.

"Okay. Maybe you're going to live." She called back in, canceling the bus and the backup. She could feel the weight of more paperwork descending on her weary shoulders.

She walked him back to the taco stand and made him sit at the picnic table. She bought a Sprite and asked for an extra cup of ice. Dumping the ice in a wad of napkins, she pressed it against his forehead. He jerked; she grabbed his chin and made him stay still.

"Tell me their names. I need to question them," she said.

He clenched his jaw and she huffed at him. "Do you think if you don't tell on them they won't hurt you again?" Then she thought a minute. "Are they customers? Dope customers?" A bigger, brighter lightbulb went off. "Or did they front you the cash for a drug buy?"

His eyes flared. Bingadero. She made a mental note, leaning toward him. "Were you and Zack going to make the big buy together? From Flaco?" She waited. "Were you moving up the distribution chain? Were you going to buy something else? Something stronger?" *More expensive?*

"They're just asswipes," he spat. "I was going to take them out." She gave him a look. "I *was*. I was just—"

"Resting up first," she interrupted. "Give me their names and I'll stop bugging you." She moved her makeshift ice pack to another bruised spot on his face.

"Ow. Drew Covel. Brian Bradford."

"Which one was the shrimp?"

"Drew."

"Do they go to your school?" When he clamped his mouth shut, she ran her free hand through her hair and dropped it to her side. "Antwone, you already told me their names. I can find out if they go to your school. Save me the effort, okay?"

He was still silent, and she cursed the idiocy of idiots everywhere. "They didn't see me. They won't know you talked to me," she said.

"Yes, they go to my school," he ground out. "Brian's on the football team."

"Figures. Guess Brian is the quarterback."

"Yeah, but second string," Antwone said.

"There's a tiny bit of justice, there." She smirked; he smirked back. "I hated high school, man."

He balled his fists. He hated high school, too, oh, yeah. High school was such a weird disconnect—you weren't an adult yet, but you could get beat up like one.

"How did they find you tonight?" Grace asked him. "They come along, see you, pull you out of your car? Where is your car?"

"Around the corner. They must have followed me from the bowling alley. They go there a lot." He lowered his voice. "Mess with me while I'm working."

"Did they mess with Zack, too? Call him a faggot?"

He nodded.

She held up her fingers and counted off suspects. "Lots of people messed with Zack. His father. Guys at school." *How do I detest thee? Let me count the ways.*

"Yeah." Antwone's voice was mournful, angry. He jutted out his swollen lower lip and exhaled.

"Do you know where Drew and Brian live?" Had to be in the school district. "Have they helped you buy drugs before?"

He hesitated. She wanted to smack him upside the head and tell him just to tell her, goddamn it. His boyfriend was *dead*. Antwone was a juvenile; she didn't have to read him his rights because she wasn't charging him with anything. He could ask for a lawyer. He probably wouldn't. And she needed to keep him talking.

"It was going to be a bigger buy than usual," he said at last, praise God, hallelujah. "Oh, God." He twitched, beginning to panic, realizing he was unburdening himself to an actual police officer. Grace had facilitated the process many times, and she couldn't help the satisfaction that warmed her heart against the cold night. And the colder reality that this sweet, mixed-up boy was mixing it up in bad shit. He was just like Zack: He never had a chance.

"It's cool, Antwone. We're good here, you and me. Like what? Like when?"

"I don't know now. It was supposed to happen a week ago. Then Zack . . ." He took a ragged breath. "I guess they have their own customers who want their shit. Drew and Brian took their money to help me make the buy. Now no one's got shit."

"They called you a faggot."

He nodded wearily. Warily. He looked up at the moon and Grace wondered what he saw. How old and how bad did you have to be to have a last-chance angel? Was there a shortage? What happened if you needed one but they were all out of them? Did God wave his magic wand and, lo, there were more?

Birds cackled in the darkness. A lowrider spray-painted with a mural of a Hawaiian sunset drove past playing *norteño* music, maybe Los Tigres del Norte. A brown masculine face stared out from the driver's side, checking Grace out. He whistled at her. She ignored him.

Eventually, Antwone stopped bleeding.

A few minutes later, Ham showed up. Grace filled him in on Antwone's run-in with his investors, culminating in their kicking the crap out of him and calling him names. Ham pursed his lips and blew out his cheeks.

"Same thing happened to my brother," Ham told Grace and Antwone. "Guys at school used to hassle Nick. Me and my brother Rafe, we looked out for him. Bashed some heads."

"You have a gay brother?" Antwone asked.

"Are you kidding, man? The dude owns an art gallery," Grace said.

Ham nodded, and Antwone smiled a little, then winced and touched his mouth. Grace lit a cigarette, offering her pack of Morleys to Antwone, who shook his head.

She blew out smoke. "We started looking for Flaco today. Hit a string of gay bars, and it turns out he and Zack went to at least one together. What do you know about that?" She looked back at him.

Grace saw a world of hurt in Antwone's beautiful eyes. "I hate that dickhead," he said. "We should've never gotten involved with him."

Ham walked over to the taco stand, got a refill on the soda, and handed it to Antwone, who guzzled it thirstily.

"He the one who get you started in all this?" Ham asked.

Antwone nodded. "We thought we could make a bunch of money, save it up . . ."

Escape, Grace finished silently.

"We need to get you to the doctor," Grace said, grabbing his chin and scrutinizing his face. Cuts, contusions, but now that she could see him in the light, nothing permanent-looking.

"I'm not going. You can't make me go," he said, pulling back. "You're not my mother."

Yeah, what about your mother? Where is she in all of this? "Get some onion rings before they close, Ham," Grace told her partner. He nodded and walked back to the take-out window.

"There was so much shit in Zack's life," Antwone said, as if there were none in his own. "He had this laptop he carried around all the time. There were stickers of metal bands all over it, like he was trying to be cool." He shook his head. "He said he was going to bust his stepmother with what was on it. But he wouldn't tell me what it was. He said when the time came he'd share it with me."

Ooh-la-la. "What do you think he knew?" Grace asked.

Antwone reached for Grace's pack of cigarettes after all. She let him take one, handed him her lighter. The doofus thing about smoking was that it did make you look older and cooler. He looked *great*. Blame it on the media.

"I think she was cheating on his old man," Antwone opined as he blew out the smoke. "I think Zack found her e-mails to and from the other dude."

"And what, like, copied them onto his laptop?" Grace asked. "As evidence?" Antwone nodded. "Where did you last see this laptop?"

"I don't remember." Antwone fell silent. He lowered his head, and Grace raised her brows at Ham as he returned with the onion rings. Because it was obvious that Antwone sure did remember. Maybe he had it.

"Did you keep it for him?" Grace asked, as she dipped an onion ring in ketchup. "Do you have it?"

"I just *told* you—"

"You kept it for him, and those guys who beat you up took it from you," Grace spun. "You sold it so you could buy more supply from Flaco."

"No," Antwone bit off, frowning at her. "I would never do that. It was Zack's."

"Do you think his stepmother found out and took it?" *And killed him over it?*

He looked sick. Maybe the streets were a bit too . . . streety for him. Battered, minus his boyfriend . . . it had to suck to be him right now.

"I don't think she's that bad," Antwone ventured. "Mrs. Lacey. I don't know her that well, but she's always been nice to me. Her son is a total asshole."

"She's got a son?" Grace repeated. No one had mentioned anything about a son.

"Paul. He's on the baseball team at school." Antwone was getting tense again. "I steer clear."

A blunt object, Grace thought. *Like a baseball bat?* From the way Ham's brows shot up, she deduced he was thinking the same thing. *Warrant. Warrant, warrant, warrant.* But it wasn't enough to go on, and she knew it.

"Are you sure you don't want to go to the doctor?" Grace asked him. "Do you have a place to go home to?"

He got quiet. Then he nodded. Grace took note. She wondered if he, a juvenile, was living on his own. Decided for the moment not to press too hard about that. Ham was on her wavelength; she watched him watching Antwone and felt a rush of pure joy. They were good at this; they were good at this together. That was what made the sex so great.

"I gotta go," Antwone insisted.

The three rose. Ham moved to one side of Antwone and Grace shifted to the other. Antwone noticed but he kept walking. Grace offered him another cigarette, and he refused it, like a bitter, condemned man headed for the gallows.

"We went to Zack's church tonight," Grace said as he led them to a beat-up Corolla. No gangbanger's car for

Antwone, no sir. He was leading the life—minus the dealing—that Grace might have imagined for Janaya—humble but respectful. Minus the dealing. Yeah, there was that. She glanced at his license plate. Oklahoma. She'd check who the car was registered to.

Antwone looked at her expectantly. She quirked up her mouth in a lopsided grin. "That church was weird, man. Jesus, Jesus, *Jesus.*" She shook all over, and he smiled sadly.

"They told him he would go to hell unless he changed. He was so scared of hell."

So, suicide not likely, unless going off his antidepressants got him all jumpy, so to speak.

"That totally sucks." Grace shook her head. "We're going to ask you for your help some more. Are you still willing to help us? After getting beat up tonight and admitting that you sell drugs?"

His eyes narrowed. "I'm more willing. If someone killed Zack . . . you know they do shit to—to *faggots.* Tie them to car bumpers, hang them."

"Drown them?" Grace asked softly.

Antwone put his hand on the door handle. His knuckles were skinned; bloody red tissue glistened on chocolate-brown in the overhead streetlight. "Did he . . . was he in pain when he died?"

"We don't know," Grace said. "Help us find out."

"Yeah," he said.

"I'm serious. I want you to help us. We'll try to keep the dealing out of it. I can't promise . . ."

Ham gave her a look. She avoided his gaze.

"I . . . whatever." Antwone's hands were shaking. With some difficulty, he unlocked his car, opened the door, and slid in. Grace let him shut the door and stood back from the curb, beside Ham. With a squeal of tires, Antwone peeled out. The air was damp and smelled of Oklahoma crude. And trash and dashed hopes.

"Maybe he's a flight risk," Ham said as they watched the night swallow up Antwone's car.

"Maybe he's not," Grace murmured.

He turned to her. "About the dealing. Grace, we know what we know."

"We didn't charge him, didn't read him his rights." At his frown, she sighed heavily. "He's got so many strikes against him, Ham. Black, poor, gay. If those guys turn out to be good suspects, we'll use it. If not, let's let him go. We've done that before."

"D.A.," Ham said.

"Shit, look at Butch's informant. Lowlife piece of crap has actually *bragged* to Butch about some of the stupid shit he's done."

Ham nodded. He stuffed his hands in his pockets. "Speaking of stupid shit, how about that holy-roller church telling Zack he's going to hell because he's gay?"

"Catholic Church says the same thing." She waggled her shoulders and smiled. "Come to heaven with me?"

"Yeah," he said, as though the sun had broken over his face. Ham happy was a beautiful sight. "Let's go."

Blastoff, baby.

CHAPTER
FOURTEEN

It was pouring buckets by the time Grace and Ham arrived at Casa Hanadarko, Grace twirling her Jesus umbrella, then tossing it onto her porch and letting Ham chase her into the house. She tripped through it, threw the side door open, and charged back out into the rain, in the privacy of her own soaked yard. Gus was on her bed; he came to see what was going on and barked with joy as Grace yanked off her boots and ripped off all her clothes in the freezing rain and twirled in a circle, laughing her head off.

"Jesus, Grace," Ham cried as he darted back inside. She taunted him, swinging her ass at him, while he stripped down. "Are you crazy? It's freezing out there."

She pushed into the house, laughing, and flung her soaking wet self into his arms. He picked her up firefighter style, and she whooped like a siren as he carried her into the bedroom. Thrilled by all the activity, Gus followed them back in and scooted under the bed.

Ham flopped Grace down onto the mattress, and she rolled back and forth to dry herself off, then over onto her stomach to grab a condom out of the nightstand. Like most men, Ham wasn't fond of rubbers; like all of Grace's men, he wore one because she wanted him to.

"Put that on your Jesus umbrella," she told him, biting her lower lip and making waggly Groucho eyes at him.

He did as he was told; then he kissed her, lacing his fingers through hers and pushing her arms over her head. He straddled her. Her skin was covered with goose bumps, and he blew on her neck as she laughed and rolled her pelvis beneath him. His fingers moved down her leg.

"Grace," he whispered. She writhed, throwing back her head in sheer abandon. Sweet release was on its way, courtesy of OCPD Major Bangs.

"Oh, God, Ham," she murmured. His fingers zoomed to the sweet spot, and she opened up to it, all of it; sex was so amazing, especially with him. Sex was the best. Ham Dewey was the best.

He was rock hard, and he wanted to move to the main event, but he pleasured her until she was soaring. Then he anchored her down to the bed with his sex, stroking, building, heating her up. They flew together.

"Oh, Grace," Ham whispered, and then a low, gut-deep moan escaped him as he climaxed. She came soon after, uninhibited, joyful, satisfied.

For a while, they lay like spent animals, while Gus remained under the bed. Grace was a puddle. Ham looked like he had died.

She decided they needed to top off the evening with some bourbon, and traipsed naked into the kitchen to grab her bottle. She spotted the flyer for Helping Hand, and her cop brain began to rev up. She gave her head a serious shake to prevent the synapses from synching. Took a quick swig of booze to confuse them even further. The cold pizza was still there; she grabbed the box and the bottle and sailed back into her bedroom. Ham was under the covers, and it looked like he might fall asleep.

So she hopped onto the bed and wafted the bourbon bottle under his nose. He chuckled.

"I'm toast," he moaned. "I can't move a muscle."

"Then I'll eat the rest of this delicious pizza myself," she announced. She took a huge mouthful. "How much of what Antwone told us is true, do you think?"

"I can't believe you got him to admit that he sells drugs," Ham said into the pillow. He rolled over onto his back. She loved his hairy chest, flat stomach, fine equipment. "Is he really that naïve?"

"He's really that grief-stricken," Grace said, holding out her pizza slice to him. "Completely off his game."

"Yeah," Ham replied quietly.

He lay back down, snuggling into her damp sheets and started looking too comfortable. Grace glanced at her radio alarm clock. It was after one. Tomorrow was a workday. There'd been a lot of tough, late nights this week. Tomorrow was Friday.

"You can take a shower if you want," Grace said. "I'm going to go check on a few things." She had a copy of the coroner's report and Rhetta's lab findings. And the pictures of what used to be Zachary Lacey. Nothing new, probably nothing that would give her anything new, but it would get her out of her bed. Hopefully, it would do the same for Ham.

She heard his sigh but didn't respond to it as she stuffed the rest of the pizza into her mouth, slid to the edge of the bed, and got up.

Grabbing her robe, she belted it around her body, using the edge to dry herself off. Gussie came, too, leaving Ham alone in her room. Point made, perhaps, that neither of the Hanadarkos were interested in the afterglow thing.

She plopped down onto the couch with the bourbon and opened the case files on her lap. It was so obvious to her that they needed a warrant, to go looking for blunt instruments and Zack's laptop. She just needed something that would get her past a judge with her golden ticket in hand.

Her eyelids fluttered. Maybe she was too tired to do this after all.

She and Earl were treading water so clear that when she looked down, she could see her toes. Both of them were fully dressed, except that she was barefoot.

"Hey, it's a wet T-shirt contest," she said to him. His light blue T-shirt was silkscreened with a couple of red Chinese characters in a rectangle.

"All you have to do is dunk your head under," he replied.

She gave him a look. "Dunk my head? . . . So I'll be baptized or something? Earl, I've already been baptized Catholic." She moved her hands. "It's a life sentence." She splashed water at him. "Or a death sentence, if you're gay. Are angels gay?"

"I have no idea," he replied.

"Do people who kill themselves go to hell?"

His features sagged. "People who kill themselves are already in hell, Grace."

The warm water cradled her. "What about this unconditional love you keep talking about? God stops loving us if we commit suicide?"

"Suicide is about annihilating the self," Earl replied. "God can't love you if there's no you to love."

"That's bullshit." She floated on her back. "It's about stopping the pain."

"Maybe direct suicide. But what about indirect suicide? Dying slowly. Smoking, drinking too much, bringing home guys you don't even know."

She bobbed on the water as wavelets massaged her backbone. "Hey. When did this become about me?"

"Having a death wish, being too fascinated with death," he continued. "Maybe being a firefighter. Or a cop."

Her mouth dropped open, and water poured into it. Sputtering, spitting it back out, she glared at him. "Hey, what the hell are you saying? That a cop . . . that Kane . . . committed suicide because he died in the line of duty? That is totally screwed."

"It's not how, it's why," he said. He looked at her. "You lied tonight. Again. Because you *did* feel something at that service."

She scowled at him. "Earl, it was a manufactured experience. Those guys are experts at crowd control. Group psychology."

"Most abuse victims numb out during sex," he said. "You let yourself enjoy it. Revel in it. But you numb out during religious experiences."

"That wasn't a religious experience. It was bullshit."

She followed his gaze. Zachary Lacey, intact, swayed beneath the water like a piece of seaweed. He was dressed in the clothes they'd found him in, undamaged. His eyes were incredibly shiny; and tears, like bubbles, swam toward the surface.

"That bullshit religious experience killed him, too," she said. "He needed someone. He trusted them. And once he let down his guard, they threw him in the deep end. That poor kid didn't know how to swim."

"Maybe they did their best," Earl said.

"Maybe the diocese knew Father Murphy was screwing all of us, and looked the other way. Maybe Evan Johnson told Juanita to send her callers to church." She stared down at Zack, watching the fish approach. Watching death claim him. "Maybe I have never had a religious experience in my entire life."

"And I'm just a brain aneurysm, waiting to pop."

"I don't know, Earl," she said. "Are you?"

Then Zack tipped back his head and stretched up his hands toward her. She couldn't tell if he could see her. A couple of deep breaths to oxygenate herself, and she dove beneath the surface. The water charged with golden light, and it was as warm as sunshine. The sensation reminded her of something, but she couldn't quite place what it was.

Down she went, deeper; beginning to feel the pressure on her lungs as she clasped Zack's wrists and swam back toward the surface. But the boy was too heavy; he was dead weight. She began to sink. She held fast, blowing out air bubbles a little at a time, emptying herself out. She knew how people drowned; they couldn't stop themselves from inhaling. It was a reflexive action and, of course, what they inhaled was water, not air. That was how Lena had known that Zack was alive when he went in.

She was going down, and the water remained golden and warm. Should be colder, should be darker. God, she wanted to take a breath. Her body was straining, her stomach contracting.

If she let go of Zack, she could go back up, get a breath. But as she released his right wrist, he slipped away, sagging downward as if pulled by gravity. Which was wrong. The dead floated.

I gotta let you go, man, Grace thought. But just as she loosened her grip on his left wrist, he began to struggle. *Damn, he's alive.*

She couldn't let go if there was a chance of saving him. Her stomach convulsed, and she bit her lips to keep herself from trying to breathe in. Her lungs screamed at her and her legs kicked. She had to let go of him.

No, goddamn it. I won't.

Then Earl appeared beside her. He took Zack's other hand, and he and Grace began to swim together. Zack was waterlogged; he weighed a ton.

When they broke the surface, Zack was not there. Grace gasped in oxygen, on the verge of throwing up or passing out. Once she stabilized herself, she looked back down through the water. The boy had vanished.

"Where is he?"

"Stone's rolled away, I reckon," Earl said. He wore a T-shirt that read LIFEGUARD. His hair was slicked back and his eyelashes were wet.

"What the hell are you talking about? What stone?"

He shrugged. "Actually, that was something I was talking about with Leon Cooley. But it could just as easily have been you. You two are alike. You just don't know it."

"Don't even start that shit."

He held up his hands.

"So where were you when Zack went in the river?" Grace demanded. "Was anyone with him?"

"God was with him," Earl replied. "The whole time. Even when the needle went in."

"What are you talking about?" Grace asked. She looked down and saw—

She *saw*—

Grace jerked awake on the sofa. Her front door had just shut and her phone was ringing. She grabbed the phone as she walked to the door and checked the peephole. Ham, leaving.

She took the call. There was weeping on the other end.

"Miss Hanadarko, I'm so sorry," the caller hiccupped. "This is Emily Prescott, Zack's grandmother. I'm sorry to call you but I can't, I just can't stand this."

"It's all right, Mrs. Prescott," Grace said. "I was going to call you first thing in the morning. I was just waiting for the sun to come up."

"Oh, please." Mrs. Prescott wept for a good, full minute. "*Please* tell me what happened to Zachary."

I wish you could tell me.

"How did he die? Did he—did . . . Father Pepera said . . ." She dissolved into more weeping. "That father of his. He scared off my daughter and then . . ." She sobbed. "I should never have left. I wanted to stay for Zack, but, oh, my God . . ."

"We're trying to determine what happened," Grace said gently. "Mrs. Prescott, can you tell me where your daughter is?"

"We lost contact. Karen told me she was leaving Ron, and I—God forgive me—I told her divorce is a sin. Marriage is one of the holy sacraments and she had married Ron Lacey. She had a child with him. She told me she hated me because I wouldn't support the divorce. She said I would rather have her be good than be happy. And—and she was right."

Sounds like God, Grace thought.

"Were there any letters between you and Karen?"

"After a while, they stopped coming. I haven't heard from her in at least eight years."

"What about Zack? Did Karen stay in touch with him?"

"No, and it tore my heart out. A child needs his mother."

"Was Ron Lacey abusive?"

"I don't know. I knew Karen was unhappy with him." She lowered her voice. "They had to get married. She was pregnant." Grace could hear the humiliation in her voice, even now. "You know, you try to raise a child to be God-fearing and . . ." She started to cry again. "Father Pepera won't say Mass for Zachary if he took his own life."

"There are other priests who will," Grace told her.

"No. Church law is clear," she said hoarsely. "He'll go to hell. Or he . . . he's in hell."

"Ma'am, with all due respect, my brother's a priest, and, and he says that the Church's position on suicide has changed."

"Zack, Zack," she moaned.

"My brother," Grace tried again, but the woman was crying too hard to listen. She made herself some coffee, listening to Mrs. Prescott until she wore herself out.

"Listen, Mrs. Prescott, I have to go now. I need to go to work. I'll do everything I can to solve this case . . . mystery." She winced. Zack was not a case. Zack was a person. Or a lost soul, according to some.

"Thank you," the old lady said, calmer now, if no less sorrowful. "Thank you with all my heart."

Grace hung up and stared at her phone. "So what do you want me to do, fabricate evidence?" she said aloud.

She squinted at the side door. No rain, and a rosy dawn. Everything smelled fresh from the rain. It was the kind of Oklahoma morning that made her grateful to be alive, and she smiled as she let the moment wash over her, wash right over her, like a baptism.

She couldn't remember what she had seen in her dream, but when she tried, darkness moved inside her, and chilled her to the bone.

She went into the bathroom. Her neighbor was up, so she let him see her boobies. They waved at each other in a neighborly way, and then she took a hot shower, sluicing away Ham's scent. As Gussie ate his breakfast, he told her a few things about life. He was so cute that Grace had to get down on the floor and wrestle with him for a few minutes.

As he slurped up water, she tossed back coffee and took some aspirin. She didn't have a headache yet, but she had a feeling it was going to be a stressful day.

A deep calm washed over Butch as Captain Perry gathered the squad in the interview room. Everyone took seats except for her. Bobby gave Butch a thumbs-up, nodding soberly as he drank his morning coffee. Off to one side, listening intently, Ham reminded Butch of a hunting dog watching a duck fall from the sky. This was the work they loved, not paperwork and desk jockeying. This was the real deal, OCPD style.

Although she wasn't late, Grace was the last to show,

looking mighty fine in a damp sand-colored top and tight flared jeans. As Captain Perry announced the mission— they were going to October's alleged drug buy accompanied by the mighty forces of Tactical—Butch watched a huge grin spread across Grace's mouth—those lips he had kissed so many times, her thumbs hanging off her pockets as she rocked back on her heels. Sassy cowgirl ready to jump on that bull and ride him well past the eight seconds you needed for a win. That woman had thighs on her.

A map of the warehouses and their alleys had been blown up and hung against the whiteboard. Blueprints of the interior of one warehouse in particular flanked the map. Tactical's names were written on the whiteboard on the perpendicular wall. Butch thought back to a time when that list included Kane, the cop who hadn't made it when they'd gone against Big Time Reynolds. Big Time, Big Money. Big sleep. Bullshit.

Butch took a moment in prayer; his shoulders began to tighten, but he did not let himself react to the memory of Grace herself taking a hit, her flak jacket bearing the lifesaving brunt; still, the round had stopped her heart. He made himself stand down. He would protect her with his life, but he sure as hell wouldn't get in the way of her doing her job.

"We're going tomorrow night," Captain Perry said, inclining her head at Butch. "Butch has someone on the inside. Not entirely reliable, but he's the best we've got."

"He might have been given disinformation," Butch warned them. "They might be testing him to see if he's loyal. In which case there might be no deal, or it's a trap. For him and for us."

"We've got people watching the warehouse," Captain Perry went on, holding up a picture taken from behind the steering wheel of a car. "About an hour ago, this black man in his midtwenties, bald, about six-two, unlocked the warehouse door and went inside. He spent forty-five minutes there, exited, and got into the same car you all were searching for last night." She smiled as the squad shifted in their chairs. "If Big Money was trying to thumb his nose at us, I'm thinking he did a pretty good job."

"Or if he's trying to bait us." Grace moved her shoulders as if she were trying to stay loose. "I mean, c'mon, the *same* car?"

"Sixty-four Impala, I'd drive it every chance I got," Butch said. A beat passed. "If I was a scumbag lowrider."

"Listen to me. I know you've been wanting this guy since way before I came on board." Perry walked over to the big whiteboard and put up the surveillance photo with a magnet. "But we got to be careful."

Nods all around from the Careful Posse.

"We let them go in. We set up a parabola microphone if we can get close enough to a window and listen in on them. We wait. For as long as it takes to get a clear signal."

"What about wiring October?" Bobby asked.

Kate turned to Butch. "Butch and I talked about a wire, but we've decided not to risk it."

"And I'm not sure I could get October out of there long enough to get it on him," Butch added.

"When's the last time you heard from him?" Grace asked. "He call you today?"

"Not since the night before last," Butch said. "But I wasn't expecting him to."

"So we're not going in with guns blazing," Captain Perry said. "We're going to take every precaution. If it looks wrong, we are backing off. I don't want any dead heroes."

Looks went around the room. Everyone wanted that son of a bitch, and they knew Butch wanted him most of all.

"When's your birthday, man?" Grace asked him. He told her. "Well, happy early birthday, Butch. I'm going to wrap this asshole up in ribbons just for you."

"What did I just say, Detective?" Captain Perry gave Grace the stink eye.

"No more dead heroes," she said. "Yes, ma'am."

They ran down the operation repeatedly. Discussed things that could go wrong—and there were a lot of them. The longer the briefing lasted, the more Butch thought about Merrie, and when he hit a full tank of uncertainty, he asked to see Captain Perry in her office.

She was sympathetic. To a point. She sat behind her desk and glanced through a dozen phone messages, took a sip from her OU cup, and sat back in her chair.

"Butch, we've been over this. She's in foster care. Her mother is in custody. The court's not going to release her to her father."

But she might have relatives. October and Janaya have families somewhere.

She grabbed her cell phone and flipped it open. "Tell you what. Leslie Jones, that family court judge? I'll run it by her. If she concurs that Merrie's safest where she is, I'll see if she can assign placement for the next twenty-four hours. We'll proceed as planned tomorrow."

He took that in.

"Then Social Services will have time to evaluate the situation. I sure as hell would not hand that child back to either of her folks." She peered up at him through her lashes. "Would you?"

"No," he allowed.

"You know that if you tell Patrick Kelly what's going on, it'll just rattle him. So let this happen, Butch. We all want Big Money. He butchered that little girl." Captain Perry's eyes flared; she reached for something on her desk and held it out to him.

He took it. It was a photograph of Priscilla Jackson in

a maroon and cream cheerleading outfit. Her dark brown hair was pulled back into a ponytail, and a sprinkling of freckles dusted her brown skin. She had heavy eyebrows and she was wearing braces. Enamel rubber-ducky earrings completed her outfit.

"Thirteen," she said. "Gang-raped. First Big Money cut off her feet. Said she would never need them to give him a hand job. I have the crime-scene photos here, too," she said, her nicely manicured nails scooping up another photo that Butch had memorized and that haunted him in his sleep. Or his nightmares.

He gave his head a quick shake.

"So, we both know where we stand," she concluded.

"Yes, ma'am." A muscle jumped in his cheek and he stood up. Slung his thumbs in his belt.

"Something else bothering you?" she queried, making a steeple of her hands.

"No. Just thinking about what kind of man could do something like that."

"A walking dead man." She gave him a hard look. "We'll get him. If not this time, then the next."

His silence was his agreement. And his vow. And his thanks.

"Okay, then," she said. "We'll meet with Tactical in an hour and break down the op." She looked down at her desk—reports, case files, more reports.

He returned to the bullpen, to discover his desk decorated with the October pages from several copies of a charity calendar for an animal shelter in Norman. Little kitties and puppies gazed up at him. Everyone knew about Merrie. There was a 4-H calendar, too, featuring pictures of kids and their livestock. The picture was for March but someone had crossed that out and written OCTOBER. One of Butch's colleagues had drawn a dialogue balloon above the head of a big-eyed calf. It read LONGHORN!

He didn't say anything, just cleaned it all up and turned the Longhorn magnet on his file cabinet right-side up. Captain Perry was right.

Maybe he could get October out of this shit with a job and some counseling. Maybe Janaya would put it back together. She was in custody, shrieking that she had been denied her rights and insisting that Merrie be brought to her at once.

Travel light, cowboy.

The squad shelved a lot of plans for the day, including a lunch trip to Home Depot for Bobby's mold problem. Grace had to back-burner her kid case, and Butch knew that hurt her heart. He decided that once this was over, he'd do some more canvassing around Bricktown and along the riverbanks to see if he could help her out. Even if it was on his own time.

They met with Tactical and went over and over their plan of attack. There were no new calls from October. If there was no new information, there was nothing to say.

Except maybe good luck. Or good-bye.

CHAPTER
FIFTEEN

After the squad's meet-up with Tactical, Grace and Ham made the time to follow up on the information from Antwone. Grace watched from the bleachers at the baseball field as Cherie Lacey's kid, Paul Finch, came up to bat.

He curled back his lip and stepped away from a bad pitch. He was a big kid, almost fat; he had thick lips and really short hair. Piggy eyes. He had on sweatpants and a sweatshirt. It was really football season, not baseball yet. But these guys were serious ballplayers, determined to rout anyone who dared to play against them. Grace understood that this was "independent P.E.," meaning that teams were allowed to hold practice and have it count toward their grade. A few heads turned her way—*cougar!*—but she didn't react and, eventually, they gave up trying to figure out who she was.

Another pitch. Too low. Grace would have let that one go, too, but Paul took a swing. He missed it, of course, and hoots and howls of protest rode the crest of his little defeat. Paul slammed the bat down on home plate in frustration. But he didn't say anything, which spoke to his self-restraint.

"Hey, Finch, don't swing at the shit ones," one of the guys in the dugout called. He was tall, skinny, red-headed.

Paul didn't respond. He set his jaw and got into position. The batter's helmet gave him a bizarrely mechanical look, like he was a cyborg. Grace wondered how he was taking his stepbrother's death. That was on her list of questions for him.

Batter up. Next pitch. Low again. Finch swung again. Moron. The dugout protested, whooping and catcalling.

"Shit!" Finch shouted, slamming his bat on home plate again. "Gimme something to hit!" His piggy eyes narrowed.

Grace watched. Something to hit. Could she see him smacking his stepbrother on the leg, breaking his ankle? She sat back, resting her elbows on the riser behind her, letting the watery sun hit her face. The bleachers were wet; she'd dried off a spot and plopped her scrawny ass down. Evan Johnson and Juanita were still on the list of things to do.

Another bad pitch. Paul started swearing like crazy, and the pitcher grew pale and held up his hands as if to placate him. Grace wanted to smoke. She wanted to smack Paul upside the head and tell him to behave like a human being. On the other hand, his anger issues might make her job easier.

Ham was off checking out Brian and Drew. Antwone's mom had called him in sick from school. Grace was going by his house in a bit.

Paul struck out but he was saved by the bell. Literally. Last period of the day, Friday. The whoops of joy and hand slapping made her grin as the players broke it up and headed for the showers.

Paul walked with a couple of guys, heads bent together as they made batting motions. Paul nodded, and one of the other players slapped him on the shoulder. So Paul Finch had friends.

Her gut told her that now was not the time to detain him for a little chat. She'd keep him fresh, and use him later.

She trotted down the bleachers and dropped onto the wet grass. With a quick call to Ham to let him know what she was doing, she hopped into Connie and drove on over to Antwone's house.

His sad, sad house. Cracked brick shack, weeds in the yard, the driveway just one pothole after another. The windows were covered over with aluminum foil. Evidently the drug trade was not the lucrative side business one might expect.

She climbed two steps made of dry rot and rang the bell. A dog started barking. That cheered her up a little. At least he had a pet—

Holy shit!

Racing from around the back of the house, a Doberman slobbered and growled at her. The dog had to be at least as big as your average mastiff—i.e., enormous. It showed her its big mean teeth, all the better to rip off her hand with, as she hissed at it to back off, shouting for Antwone to open the frickin' door.

The dog ran for her; its eyes gleamed; ropes of drool bungee-jumped out of its massive jaw. Its growl was a preparatory windup; he was going to leap at her any second. She'd be damned if she'd shoot it, but she wasn't going to stand there and get mauled. With tremendous misgivings, she unholstered her service weapon and pointed it at the animal.

"Antwone!" she bellowed. "Get the hell out here or I'm going to have to shoot your dog!"

The front door burst open and Antwone stood there, yelling, "Obama! Get your ass in here!"

Grace grinned at Obama's name; then took four giant steps backward as the dog raced on over to Antwone. Antwone dropped to his knee and Grace made a face, wondering where those ropes of drool were going to land.

Ewww.

Wiping his cheek, Antwone straightened, and guided Obama into the house by the collar. The dog whimpered and panted, but he went willingly. Antwone shut the door behind himself and stood on the rickety porch. He had a bit of five o'clock shadow. He was wearing a black T-shirt and ripped-up jeans. No shoes. It was cold today.

"Did you stay home from school because you're hurt?" she asked him, peering around him at the closed door. "Can I come in?"

"No," he said quickly. "No, you can't."

"Maybe if I looked over your stuff, things Zack gave you, it might help me understand—"

A shadow crossed his face. He was conflicted. He knew she had a point. And yet. He lowered his gaze and shook his head.

"Do you live alone, Antwone?"

"No. My mother is at work." He said it too quickly and he crossed his arms. What was in there, a goddamn meth lab? His mummified mom drinking gin?

"Right. Heard she called in for you today," she said, and turned to go.

"Hey. Wait."

She turned back around.

"Thank you," he said. He didn't smile, so she didn't, either. But she wanted to.

"You're welcome," Grace replied.

At the school, Ham caught up with Drew Covel and Brian Bradford as they walked out of the main building together; and when he identified himself, the guilt on their faces was a joy to behold. He got them to give him cell phone numbers for their parents. He called both sets and told them that an OCPD detective had witnessed Brian and Drew beating a juvenile the night before, and that they were going to be charged with battery. No mention of the drug deal for the moment. He and Grace could use it later to add some pressure if they needed it.

Drew's mother agreed to drive him down to the station. She sounded frightened, but maybe a bit relieved, too. Brian's father said they would only speak to the police if they could have a lawyer present, and Ham told him that was just fine.

Grace was busy with Antwone, so for the moment, Ham was on his own. As he prepared for his meet-and-greet with the Covels, his stomach clenched in a weird way and the beginning of a headache knocked at his temples. His thoughts flew to tomorrow's raid. He could not get sick.

Massaging his forehead, he walked into the interview room, where Bobby had already seated Drew and Mrs. Covel. Drew was hunched over in his chair, sitting on his hands. He was about five-six, maybe a hundred forty. Close-cropped hair, almost like a skinhead. He had on a dark blue hoodie and a pair of baggy jeans. He didn't particularly look like a thug. He just acted like one in alleys.

Mrs. Covel was dressed in a dark gray raincoat over a pair of dark green cords and some brown leather boots. Her red hair was pulled back into a ponytail and she had on minimal makeup. She had pierced ears but she wasn't wearing any earrings. When Ham walked in, she absently touched her hair and let out a ragged breath. Her folding chair was placed farther away from her son's than Ham would have expected, given the circumstances. And she wasn't interacting with him. In fact, she was unconsciously leaning slightly away from him, as if he frightened her.

She knows, Ham thought. *She knows her kid's a volatile asshole.*

With another tight stomach cramp, Ham set Zack's case file on the table, close to the handcuff ring so Drew would be sure to glance at it—a subtle reminder of who held the power in the room. He bobbed his head at Mrs. Covel, who nervously returned the gesture. Drew didn't look up at him.

Ham sat down and placed his fingertips along the bottom of the file. His head hurt worse. Drew's gaze ticked up at the manila folder, then back down to the square inch of table in his line of sight.

"I think you know why you're here," Ham said. He waited. He made as if to open the file, then didn't. "A witness placed you in an alley last night on South Newcastle Road. You were assaulting Antwone Abboud. Do you want to talk about that?"

"No." Still no contact. Ham could feel the anxiety pouring off the kid. He was scared shitless that Ham knew more than he was saying.

"The witness heard you calling him a faggot."

"Oh, my God, Drew," Mrs. Covel said, covering her mouth. "No."

"I watch TV," Drew informed the dull surface of the table. "You have to give me a lawyer."

"And I have to read you your rights," Ham said, "and charge you with a crime, if you want to roll that way. Let me tell you something else first. Your classmate, Zachary Lacey, was found dead a few days ago."

"I know that. Everybody knows that," Drew flung at him.

"It was discovered during the autopsy that he was beaten prior to drowning. Badly." It was admissible and legal for cops to lie to get other people to tell the truth. He waited. "And Zack was a 'faggot,' too."

Mrs. Covel jerked hard and swiveled her head at her son. Ham pitied her; her expression said, *You finally did it, you monster.* How did a mother and son get to that place?

"Badly beaten," Ham said, sliding his finger inside the

folder, as if he might flip it open at any second and show Drew the horrific pictures of a dead boy. "Just last year, a gay teenager was tied to the bumper of a truck and dragged—"

"I didn't do anything to Zack Lacey," he said.

"I talked to some of the kids at school. They said you harassed him and Antwone a lot. Cornered them in the gym, rammed their heads in the toilets and flushed. Called them names like fudgepackers—"

"Everyone did," Drew cut in, leaning forward and wrinkling his nose. He looked proud, not contrite. Ham was amazed that he was so forthcoming. At the very least, he could be expelled for this shit. "Those two fags were so obvious about it. They, like, pushed it in everyone's face."

Mrs. Covel was shriveling up. Shame, disgust, and horror waged war on her face; she bit her lower lip and her shoulders silently shook as she began to weep. Ham figured her total ignorance of the situation was part of the problem. Drew didn't have to answer to her. Maybe he figured he didn't have to answer to anybody.

"I thought your school had a no-bully policy," Ham said.

Drew snickered. "No one would have done anything to them if they'd kept it to themselves. It was so gross."

"If you want gross," Ham said, tapping the file, "I can give it to you."

"I want a lawyer," Drew said. "I'm supposed to get one, right?" He glared at his mother. "Don't just *sit* there."

Her face went dead white. Her eyes seemed to fix on a point above Drew's head—maybe back to happier times, when he was still a sunny little boy and not the monster beside her. Ham let the moment expand to fill the tension; he thought of a time when Rafe and he caught up with five guys who had been hassling Nick.

Rafe held them and Ham doled out their punishment. Luckily it was football season; the pricks told everyone they'd gotten hurt during practice.

There'd been a lot of that, watching Nicky's back. Making sure he was safe when he walked home from school, or worked the late shift at his job at Tacoville. For Nick and Zack, Ham was going to hold this dirtbag to account. So he stared at Drew, who was twisting in his chair.

"Get your phone out and call someone, for Christ's sake!" Drew yelled at his mother. She burst into tears and began to dig in a brown leather hobo bag. You wake up; get your kid off to school; work a job; go to the police station; call a lawyer.

"Hate crimes are up in Oklahoma City," Ham went on. "Juries are tired of them. They convict fast."

Weeping, Mrs. Covel pulled out her cell phone. She stared at it as if it were a grenade. As if . . . maybe . . . she should put it back in her purse.

"Jesus, Mom, get it together!" Drew shouted.

"Please," Mrs. Covel said in a rush, "I—I don't know anything about hiring a lawyer." She looked up at Ham with her big brown doe eyes, and he wished he could help her, really help her. Take her kid outside and beat the living shit out of him. Ship him off to military school.

"We can give you a phone directory," he said. "You can stay in here to make the call, if you want. I can step outside."

Ham picked up the case folder and exited the room. Left alone, maybe Mrs. Covel could get through to her son. Make him realize he was about to jump off a cliff and there was no water to break his fall. But probably not.

"Hey," Bobby said from his desk. "Brian Bradford, his

father, and Hunter Beaumont are waiting in B. Captain Perry wants to observe. I'll babysit this one for you."

Ham nodded. He was loaded for bear. If these two dirtbags hadn't directly contributed to Zack's death, then they'd made his short life miserable. Hunter Beaumont was a well-known defense attorney who cost serious bucks. And caused serious trouble for the department— one of the most recent six cases that went south had been a Hunter Beaumont special, coached testimony loaded with innuendo and false witness that got the job done.

Ham's head throbbed. He shoved open the door to Room B and slapped down the case file, letting it fall open so Mr. Bradford, Beaumont, and Brian could see the post-mortem photograph of Zachary Lacey. Beaumont narrowed his eyes at Ham, an acknowledgment that the gloves were off on both sides this time, not just his. Brian paled, and Mr. Bradford said, "I object to your showing my son this picture," as if they were in a courtroom TV drama.

Ham left the picture faceup on the table. "Drew Covel told us that you and a bunch of other guys used to beat up on Antwone Abboud and Zachary Lacey every chance you got. That you drove by their houses late at night and left shit on their porches. You broke their car mirrors and spray-painted their lockers. There's lots more."

Brian's eyes were huge. Ham had scored a direct hit in this game of Battleship.

"You don't have to respond," Hunter Beaumont said. "Have you read this young man his rights, Detective?"

Ham reached in his pocket to get his wallet, where he kept his Miranda card. "You have the right to remain silent."

"Drew's a lying sack of shit," Brian announced.

This was going to go well.

*   *   *

"Brian Bradford gave me over a dozen names of kids who bullied those two guys," Ham told Grace as she came in from her interview with Antwone and another fruitless search for Flaco. "And 'bullied' is a goddamn politically correct word for what they did. Beat them, stole their shit, texted them hundreds of messages every day."

"Who can afford that?" Grace wondered aloud. "Texting that much?"

"I've got lists of suspects," Ham said. "I'm thinking hate crime, Grace."

"Hate crime, whether they did it to Zack himself or drove him to it," she agreed.

"I wonder if he told Juanita or Pastor Marc about any of this."

"Well, we'll have to ask them," Grace said. "Evan Johnson asked us to come in. He's going to talk to Juanita." She blew air out of her cheeks. "I just want to go to Louie's and unwind."

"There are other ways to unwind," he said. Then he winced.

"You okay?" she asked him.

"I've got some stomach thing," he admitted. "Headache." He pressed his teeth together.

"Shit, Ham, the raid's tomorrow. You should pack it in." She knit her forehead and peered at him. "You look bad."

"Not yet," he said. "I want to bust this open."

He was the best partner in the world. That was one blessing she would count, time and again.

CHAPTER
SIXTEEN

Evan Johnson was staying late to talk to Juanita Provo, and he wanted Grace there. Despite not feeling well, Ham said he would go with her to Helping Hand, so that made it a better deal. They drove over separately. The sky was dark and the clouds were low; were Rhetta and Bobby ever going to catch a break?

Grace got there first and licked her lips invitingly as Ham got out of his truck. Without consulting each other, they both made for the deli. Some coffee and maple bars might ease the tension they were about to experience upstairs—the court-martial of Juanita Provo, Meddler Extraordinaire. But it was nearly six at night, and the donuts were long gone. Grace substituted bagels and cream cheese; she carried the white plastic sack while Ham got their coffees.

"More cream. More sugar," she ordered him as he slaved over a hot condiment table.

Then they headed over to Helping Hand, and Grace rang the bell; they got buzzed in and went up the tottery, gloomy stairs. As before, Johnson stood there in nice clothes with Ragdoll, the cat, circling his ankles.

"Detectives, hello," he said kindly, but without his previous warmth. She and Ham both said their hellos and Grace handed him the bag of bagels. "Let's go into one of the phone rooms. We'll have a little more privacy."

They followed him into a softly lit hallway covered with kid-style artwork, photographs of gatherings, and some framed thank-you letters. There was a white-board with names and hours. The shift lineup. Grace scanned it. No Juanita.

They went past a door on Grace's right, which was cracked open. Grace made a show of drinking her coffee but in actuality, she was listening hard.

"Annie," a male voice said, "you *do* matter. You matter to me."

Good luck, Annie, Grace thought fervently.

"Here." Johnson moved in front of Grace and opened the second door, which was on her left. A couch faced her, and Juanita sat on it with her hands around her knees. Her expression was guarded. There was a cheap seventies-style oak coffee table in front of the couch, and on it, piles of notebooks and a Yellow Pages. Also, a laptop and a phone.

And a Bible.

And a rosary.

Oh, brother, Grace thought. Clay was studying martyrs in Faith Formation; looked like Juanita was hoping for a little reprieve because she was so tortured and God-fearing.

"Hey, Juanita," Grace said.

"Why did you tell them?" Juanita snapped. It took Grace a minute to realize that Juanita was speaking to her about her inappropriate interactions with Zack. Grace figured she had confessed, but apparently some-one had narced on her.

"Didn't. Not a word." There was nowhere else to sit, so she and Ham stood side by side inside the door, drinking their coffees.

Juanita looked at Ham. "Did you tell them?"

"Nope," Ham replied.

Silence fell. No one was eating any bagels. *Antwone,*

Grace thought. *Maybe he told Evan Johnson. Or maybe Pastor Marc the gay youth leader made the call.* Zack might have confided in either one of them. Maybe he coded the Helping Hand phone number for his asshole father.

Grace hadn't met Marc yet. If he'd been at the pray-o-rama last night, she hadn't seen him. She had a lot of leads. People she wanted to talk to. But first they had to catch Big Money. There was always too much to do.

And then . . . paperwork. She was going to do more illicit sexual things to Ham to make sure he did hers for her.

"So . . . we didn't tell on you," Grace said. "We didn't tell Evan here that you met privately with Zack Lacey and told him that being gay was a sin. We didn't tell him that you prayed with him to remove his homosexual orientation so he could go to heaven. Possibly to be with his mother, who has been missing for ten years. And we also didn't tell him that you encouraged Zack to go off his antidepressants." Grace mentally crossed her fingers, hoping she was right.

"*What?*" Johnson cried, staring at Juanita. "You did what?"

"I did not," she bit off. "I didn't tell him to do that." Her eyes strayed to her Bible, as if it were a teleprompter. "But I told him . . . I told him that if he had enough faith and he prayed, God could cure anything."

Including war and world hunger, Grace thought, but that was an old joke between her and God, har.

"So *Zack* screwed up," Grace said. "He didn't have enough faith. So he died."

Now Juanita looked a little less sure of herself. A little more likely to reach for her rosary, although she yanked her hand back and clenched it in her lap. She swallowed hard. "I didn't mean it to sound that way. I meant that if God hears, really hears your prayers, then He can make miracles."

Unless God's not listening.

"But Zack might have thought that you meant it was up to him, Zack, to somehow prove himself to God," Ham said. Grace was grateful he was there. This was excruciating. She wanted to punch that woman out. She'd rather be doing paperwork than this.

"I didn't mean that. I didn't want him to think that." She pressed her fingertips against her forehead. "I wanted to give him hope."

What you gave him was more pressure. Another way he wasn't measuring up. You stupid bitch.

Grace remained tight-lipped and silent.

"Do I need a lawyer?" She glanced up at Johnson. "I—I'm sorry to drag Helping Hand into . . . this." She looked at Grace and Ham. "What's going to happen to me?"

"Juanita." Johnson perched on the arm of the sofa. "Why did you do this? Why didn't you come to me, tell me what was going on? None of this was in your log."

Juanita sniffled. Grace dug in the bagel bag for a napkin. She didn't give it to Juanita.

"She didn't come to you because you would have interfered," Grace said. "And she knew best." Grace cocked her head. "How many other kids have you done this to?"

"None," she said. She kept her gaze focused on her hands, so Grace assumed she was lying. "*Ay, Dios*, Zack was special. We had a connection."

Lucky Zack.

Grace sipped her coffee. Her hand was shaking, and her stomach was tight. She was pissed off. Ham must have felt it; he glanced over at her with a neutral face, but she knew he was checking in with her.

I was special, too, she thought. *That's what Father Murphy told me.*

"*Did* you know he was taking antidepressants?" Ham asked Juanita. She shook her head.

"That he was a loose cannon?" Grace finally managed to say. "Someone you had no business getting involved with? I downloaded the Helping Hand volunteer handbook. You violated nearly every rule you agreed to follow when you signed on here."

Johnson moved off the sofa arm and stood, a protective gesture. "I know Juanita didn't mean to do any harm. If there's a lawsuit . . ." He blinked.

It was sinking in that there might be a lawsuit. And a scandal. Headlines. TV. Bad juju for Helping Hand and its leader, one Evan Johnson. Grace wondered how far he'd back up his volunteer. She ruined kids' lives in her spare time, but this was his *job*.

"We're not here to talk about a lawsuit, sir," Ham said. "We're investigating the death of Zachary Lacey. We have established the cause of death as drowning. But we don't know if he committed suicide, or if there was an accident, or foul play."

"Foul play?" Juanita said. Her eyes got huge. "Like murder? Who? . . ."

"That's why we're here," Ham continued. "We're detectives with Major Crimes."

"I didn't kill him," Juanita said quickly. She reached for Johnson's hand. "Evan, you *know* that, right?"

"Yes." Grace heard the hesitation in his voice. The poor guy didn't know anything anymore.

"We have a list of minors who harassed Zack. Beat him up, bullied him. Did he mention anything like that to you?" Ham asked.

Juanita looked at Johnson as if for permission to speak. He looked back at her encouragingly, but Grace could see the love was gone between them. Maybe Juanita could get a pet to take care of.

"He told me that some boys hassled him," she said. "Made fun of the way he walked. Things like that."

Things like that.

Ham nodded. "Did he give you any names?"

"Drew, I think. And someone named Kathy," Juanita told him.

"Any other names?" Ham asked. "We have a list but I'd rather you told me yourself." That way, the department couldn't be accused of leading her.

"Brian, I think. Paco, and someone they called the Fatman."

Ham wrote the names down. "Did the school do anything about it?"

"I—I don't know," Juanita said.

If you wanted to help him so badly, why didn't you contact the principal? Do something that would really help him, instead of telling him to pray? Grace stared at her. *Or do you believe that God helps those who help themselves?*

"Did he talk about running away? Ending it all?"

"Most kids who call us talk like that," Johnson put in. Grace gave him a sharp look but said nothing. She was chewing the inside of her lower lip to keep herself from losing her temper. For his part, Ham was rubbing his forehead. He didn't look good.

"I'll be right back," he said, handing the list to Grace. To Johnson, "May I use your bathroom?"

Johnson pointed down the hallway. Grace faced off against Juanita and Johnson alone.

"Did Zack mention drug use to you?" she queried. "In any form? Did he tell you that he used drugs? Or sold them?"

"No," Juanita said, but her cheeks reddened and her mouth pulled tight. So she was lying, or she had guessed and never confronted Zack. If she'd pursued it, maybe she could have suggested something he could do to help himself. Do some real good.

"I am not a therapist," said Juanita, glancing over at Johnson. Grace was pretty sure it was too late to get his approval. At least, she hoped so. "I just wanted . . ." She trailed off.

Yeah, what did you want? Grace asked silently as Ham came back into the room. *Did you pray to God for it? Did you get down on your knees and make a bargain? Or did you doze off every night reading Bible verses, marking your place with a little bookmark that said God's angels are everywhere—and you were one of them? And you knew, just knew, that God would provide?*

Tell me about wanting. Tell Zack Lacey.

"I'll tell you what Juanita wants," Grace said aloud as she pulled over to the side of the road, got out, and began to walk one of the many trails along the Oklahoma River. Ham was clearly ill, so she sent him on home minus the booty call. "She wants him to've been murdered."

"Then he's a victim," Earl said, picking up a stone and skipping it over the gray churning water. It was actually the North Canadian River; the part that ran through Oklahoma City had been renamed. The sun was going down on another day.

"And God just loves victims," Grace replied. "That's why there are so many of them."

"What I mean is, if he was killed, that means he didn't take his own life. Being murdered is not a sin in any religion I know of." Earl brushed his fingertips together to clean off the grit. He could fly to Morocco in the twinkling of an eye, but he had to wipe dirt off his fingers just like a human. "It's hard to keep up with 'em all, though. The religions, I mean. You guys seem to invent a new one every week."

"We should throw the book at her." Grace lit a cigarette. "Sanctimonious Bible-thumper."

"Let's just walk a spell." Earl skipped another stone,

then put his hands in his pockets and strolled along, gazing at the water. Grace looked at his graying hair, the careworn lines in his face, and wondered why God had made him look that way. The ozone whiff of night fog lay over the busy water; the staccato tat-tat-tat of a woodpecker echoed the rapid-fire rhythm of her angry heart.

Earl kept walking, deep in thought. She wondered what he was thinking about. It drove Rhetta crazy that Grace didn't ask him very many questions. He turned his head slightly.

"Don't say anything," she warned him. She didn't want to hear any of his answers.

He pulled his hands out of his pockets in a gesture of innocence.

And the two kept walking.

Grace's little sister, Paige, was having a Bunco party, and she'd invited Grace to attend, which surprised Grace and Earl both: Paige was a middle-class PTA-book-club-French-manicure kind of girl, and Grace was a rebel slob. Nothing sounded more hideous than playing a soccer-mom dice game with a bunch of, well, soccer moms. It was the antithesis of Grace's perfect Friday night: Her original plans for the evening began with going to Louie's to get a head start on the evening, then bringing Ham home to finish the evening off with a great big bang. But Ham was MIA. She hoped whatever was wrong with him got cleared up fast. They needed him for the warehouse raid, to be staged in a little over twenty-four hours. Some weekend sex would be nice, too.

Then she'd realized that because of the raid, she was going to have to cancel out on her Saturday night movie sleepover with Clay. She'd found out that Doug had dropped Clay at Paige's because he had a date, so she'd called over there to see if Clay could spend the night tonight instead. And that was when Paige realized that Grace had the evening free, and insisted she come to her party. It amazed Grace that she, Superdetective Hanadarko, had been so clueless.

Grace would rather vomit, seriously, but Clay was over there, and, strangely, she actually wanted to see Paige, if not her Bunco posse. Wanted to be near her. There was no way to explain that aberration, but Grace went with it. She even put on a dress that Paige might approve of, and wrapped her hair into a chignon.

Paige had a nice middle-class house in a great school district. She also had a husband who was cheating on her, and Paige knew it. Such a good Catholic woman, keeping up her end of the deal.

It wasn't until Grace had parked and rung the door-bell that she noticed her mother's car parked on the street. She groaned inwardly. Paige plus Mom was a bit too much family, thank you very much.

Her retreat back to Connie was cut short as Paige yanked open the door. She was wearing an ice-blue cash-mere sweater and a pair of black knit pants. She had a cocktail glass in her hand.

"Grace, come in," she said warmly. "We're having mojitos."

Oh, God, just shoot me, Grace thought. But what she said was, "Cool," and walked on in. She thought she felt the warm fuzziness of Earl's approval brushing against a shoulder. But when she looked for him, she was alone.

"Butch, how could you do this to me?" Janaya demanded, as he visited her in the county jail on Shartel. They were sitting in a grimy, sad little room at a table. Gray metal table, gray cinder block walls. The matron was standing by the frosted-glass door.

Janaya was dressed in an orange jumpsuit. She was

coming down off her addictions, and her jailers weren't giving her anything to help her along. Her hair was wet and she was sweaty and, Lord, if Butch ever thought about doing drugs, all he would have to do is remember how bad Janaya smelled tonight.

And see the vomit splashed on her cheek.

"Everything was going well for you, girl," he said to her. "What happened?"

The whites of her eyes were yellow. "There was this guy," she began, licking her lips over and over.

Wasn't there always, in these kinds of scenarios?

"Does Patrick know about this guy?"

She shook her head. "I ain't talked to him for months."

"I have a hundred bucks for you from him," Butch said, throwing in a few because, after all, Janaya was Merrie's mom. "Once you get out of here, I—"

"God*damn,* I feel like shit." She ran a trembling hand across her forehead. "I feel . . . oh." She doubled over, her head curling toward her chest, her shoulders rising up. The matron went on alert as Janaya groaned and fell forward, her head about to hit the table until Butch raced around and grabbed her.

The matron hit a button and ran over to them. Together they held her, or tried to; Janaya writhed and convulsed, falling off the chair onto the gray linoleum; and she began to foam at the mouth. The stench of urine hit the air.

The door buzzed open and two prison guards blasted in. Things began to happen fast: Medical was called, rushing in as Butch relinquished his hold on Janaya and became a passive onlooker. The team hustled her onto a gurney, and he followed as far as he could, but his part was over. Janaya'd been doing so well, just a week ago—relatively speaking, for a woman who'd started turning tricks when she was fourteen and knew deep in her soul that when things started to get better they'd wind up much worse than they were before. Self-fulfilling prophecy, or the law of the street?

Flat and sad, he checked in with Captain Perry and told her what had happened. God knew what Janaya's street drugs had been cut with; it could've been anything from Ajax cleanser to flour. One step forward, sixteen back. In many depressing ways, Janaya and October were well suited.

Butch thought about calling Bobby and offering to help with his mold project. But it was the night before the raid, and Bobby might want some time with Marissa and their kids.

So he drove on down to Louie's to have a beer and listen to the jukebox. He was seated at the bar when a tousle-headed cowboy sat down next to him and ordered a longneck. He seemed vaguely familiar, but Butch couldn't place him.

"Evenin'," the man said. Butch returned the greeting with an incline of his head. "So, looks like the Bowl Championship Series is going to put the Sooners and the Gators up for the big one."

"You're crazy," Butch shot back. "Better check the scoreboard. The Longhorns will be there."

"I don't rightly understand the BCS system," the man said. "I heard there's a computer program you can buy to decipher it. Used to be football was easier to figure out than women."

"All you need to know is that Texas is going to take the whole thing."

Butch sipped his beer and smiled faintly as he thought of Grace. He figured she was off screwing Ham; he wondered if Ham had ever made breakfast for her, like he had: Texas omelet, homemade waffles. Grace told Butch she wasn't a breakfast person. Her code for "Back Off."

He'd learned the vocabulary during the short stay of his boots under her bed.

Butch thought of Janaya, who had been climbing out of the pit; some dickhead had grabbed her hand and pulled her back down. If anybody had ever made her breakfast, it was probably by tossing her a breakfast burrito into a bag after she paid for it at the drive-through.

"You look troubled, if you don't mind my saying," his bar buddy went on. "It's Friday night, time off the clock. Life is good."

Butch shrugged and made rings on the bar with his beer glass. He stared into the foam and pushed the beer away.

"Someone I had hope for . . . well, it's not working out so good for her," he said.

"I had me one of those," the man said. "But I think she's turning around." He tapped the bar with a finger. "Least, I *hope* so." He grinned at his little joke. "It can get overwhelming, pulling for somebody when their heels are dug in deep."

"Yeah."

"Feels like it might be easier not to care at all. Just saddle up and mosey on."

"Don't think I can do that," Butch said.

"Then there's hope for *you*," the man replied. He held out his hand. "My name is Earl."

"Yeah." Butch smiled. "I think we met before." They shook hands.

"Think so. Well, it's been a pleasure."

The man gestured for his check. "Be seeing you around," he said to Butch. Then he left.

After a few minutes, Butch paid and headed for the door just as Henry walked in. There was a woman with Henry—Lena Garvin, the short-hire who'd quit. Butch hadn't really met her; mostly he'd listened to Grace complain about her incompetence and kept her on his radar, hoping she wouldn't catch any of the bodies in any of his own cases. Henry was beaming at her, and she was laughing. Then Henry saw Butch and he grinned like a cat-eatin' canary.

"Henry. Ms. Garvin." Butch tipped his cowboy hat. "We haven't met but I saw you around at the station."

"I saw you, too." She smiled neutrally, probably wondering what he'd heard about her.

"Hi, Butch. Where is everybody?" Henry looked around the bar. Probably he wanted to introduce Lena, show her off.

"We got business tomorrow night," Butch said. "Everyone's resting up." *You might want to plan for some overtime.*

"Excuse me," Lena said. "I need to use the ladies'. It was nice to meet you." She gave Henry's arm a squeeze, a pleasant smile at Butch, and left the two men.

"Nice, Henry," Butch said sincerely.

"Yeah." Henry was beaming. "Grace insulting her . . . it was the best thing in the world for me. Lena wouldn't date anyone from work—"

"And now she doesn't work there," Butch finished.

Henry grinned. "Right." He looked toward the bathrooms. "She just broke up with some guy. . . ."

Oh, no, rebound, Butch thought, his happiness for Henry deflating a bit. This date came equipped with all sorts of baggage.

Henry must have caught his expression. He pushed up his glasses and his cheeks went a little pink. "Butch, I go home to my mother and a twenty-one-year-old *cat.*"

"Got it." Butch said. He was going home to . . . what? Maybe he'd do that canvassing for Grace tonight. "Good luck."

"Thanks," Henry replied.

Butch left the bar, called in and checked on Janaya,

and drove on over to Bricktown. Heard the wind crying across the little canals and the refurbished buildings, warrens of stylish bars and restaurants filled with good food and Blood Alcohol Content readings above 6 percent, the magic number for criminal penalties in the great state of Oklahoma. Kiddieland for big people.

Janaya was in bad shape. The doc Butch talked to on the phone said that her drugs had been very dirty and a war was on inside her body. Butch called Merrie's foster care but his call went straight to voice mail.

You are not a social worker, he reminded himself.

The fudge store was still open, and a middle-aged couple was peering into one of the cases. The clerk with the Victoria Beckham hair was waiting on them, and Butch thought about getting something for his sister Nell and his mother. But who was he kidding? He was really thinking of getting something for himself. And he was here to help out on the case.

His boots rang on the pavement as he crossed the tidy street and studied the green metal bridge attached to the Miller Jackson Company Building, his gaze traveling a line from the bridge to the canal. Even though this was the off season for the canal boats, someone would have seen something. Maybe the body didn't start out here, as they had assumed. Maybe it had started on the other side of the lock from higher up on the Oklahoma River.

He got back in his car and went farther upriver, by Regatta Park. The sky was black, the moon ringed with prisms. More rain was on the way. The drug raid would likely take place in the rain; one more variable to contend with.

He pulled over to a more secluded spot of the river, moving past the berms of rocks to the dark waters. Looked up, down, thinking, assessing. Walking farther back up onto the grass, he pulled a flashlight and studied the sloshy mud. Not even Rhetta would be able to ferret out clues from these washed-out banks. Plus, there were seven miles of river to examine. It wasn't even a needle in a haystack; it was the memory of a needle in a haystack that had long since scattered.

He continued on, weaving his flashlight in arcs. The moonlight kissed the brim of his Stetson. There, a shape.

Beside a large cardboard box, a man was bundled up inside a sleeping bag, reading by flashlight. As Butch approached with the light full on the reader, the man looked up warily from his book and squinted at him. A skel—short for skeleton, a homeless man so thin and wiry it was amazing he was still alive.

The man put up his hand to block out the light, and Butch lowered it to the man's other hand. Empty. Then Butch flashed his badge.

"I'm a police officer. Please get out of the sleeping bag, sir," he said.

"I will, I am," the man said in a tremulous voice, setting down his book. "I don't have a gun. Please don't shoot me."

"I won't," Butch assured him as the man snaked out. He got onto his knees and crawled toward his hands, flat on the gritty earth, pushing himself to a standing position like someone doing yoga. He was wearing a filthy, shredded OU baseball cap, a flak jacket, a pair of mud-caked sweatpants, and tattered running shoes.

Butch ran his flashlight over the sleeping bag. The title of the book the man had been reading was stamped on the cover in plain white letters: *Being and Nothingness* by Jean-Paul Sartre. Heavy reading for somebody in a place like this.

"I'd like to ask you a few questions," Butch said.

The man looked up at Butch. Rheumy eyes, gray dying skin. "Hell is other people," he said in a nasal New Jersey accent. He raised both his brows as if he'd just delivered the code word, and Butch had to respond appropriately before he would reply. Butch had been down this road a hundred times, maybe a thousand: The other guy wanted you to play by his rules. Butch was okay with that.

"That's from *No Exit*," Butch said. "Also by Jean-Paul Sartre."

The man blinked. "A cop with a soul."

"So I hope," Butch replied.

"What do you want?" the man asked.

"We're looking for information. A teenage boy might have jumped in the river, or been pushed in. We don't know."

"A kid," the skel echoed.

"Have you seen anyone go into the river?" Butch asked. "About a week or so ago? It was raining very hard."

The man licked his lips. He looked very tired. "I have seen way, way too much. That's how I wound up here."

"But did you see someone go into the river? I might have something for you if you did."

The man drew himself up, looking insulted. "I don't need money. I live off the grid."

An owl hooted. Butch thought about those two jerk-water kids Ham had interviewed today, loaded with entitlement and cruelty. He looked at this filthy man, and sighed.

Don't even try, Butch warned himself, but he was fresh from his philosophical chat with the cowboy in the bar. *To protect and serve.*

"There's a shelter near here," Butch said. "It's run by a church. You might have to listen to a sermon." *And try to avoid our drug raid.*

"I'm very comfortable here," the man informed him succinctly. "And I have a lot of reading to do."

"They have showers and two hot meals a day," Butch added. The man stared at him as if Butch were speaking Swahili.

Damn it. Come back on into the world. Start over, he willed.

"It's going to rain some more," Butch said, his last gambit.

The man shrugged.

Defeated, Butch turned to go. His boots crunched. Thunder rumbled.

"I might have seen *something,*" the man declared.

CHAPTER
SEVENTEEN

I gotta stop chugalugging these wimp-assed drinks, Grace thought as she topped off her mojito glass from the pitcher in the kitchen and opened Paige's fridge. She was starving. Every single one of Paige's girlfriends was on a diet, and Paige had refrained from serving much in the way of snacks so as to "empower" them.

"Grace, what are you doing?" her mother said sotto voce as she came into the kitchen with an empty salsa dish.

"Paige said it was fine if I raided the fridge," Grace lied. She emerged with a package of sharp cheddar cheese and carried it to a cutting board. She grabbed a knife and whacked off a hunk. "Want some?"

Her mom looked over her shoulder in the direction of the festivities and gave a barely perceptible nod. Smug, Grace carved two healthy slabs from the rectangle and handed one to her mother. Her mother blanched at this breach of protocol. No plate, no doily, just cheese. Then she made a guilty little "oh-what-the-heck" face and toasted her wild child with it.

Together they gobbled them down.

"Paige is so happy you're here," her mom said, wiping at the corners of Grace's mouth with a manicured fingernail. She was all rosy and joyful. Maybe it was part hooch, but mostly it was her delight that her daughters were both accounted for, and under the same roof. With smooth jazz playing, even, like a movie. She picked up a cocktail napkin decorated with shoes and handbags that said GIRLS NIGHT IN! "You should spend more time with her."

"I have a very demanding job," Grace reminded her mother. "Stakeouts, double homicides . . ."

"Johnny told me about that suicide." Her mother cut herself another piece of cheese. Aha, a fellow starver. "The parish priest doesn't want to say Mass for the boy."

"He's *refusing*," Grace corrected her. "Says that kid is already in hell." She looked over at her mother, leaning against Paige's immaculate counter and draining her most recent drink. "What do you think?"

"I think . . ." Her mother took a deep breath. "The Church has so much more to contend with these days. When I was your age, we didn't have many other influences. Everyone I knew was a Catholic. We all understood what that meant. We had the same values." She smoothed errant strands of Grace's hair away from her face. "It's a lot more complicated, now that we . . . mix."

"Why?" Grace asked, cutting off more cheese for herself. Between them, they'd wolfed down almost half. "Why should it be more complicated?"

"It just is," her mother said.

"It just is," Johnny said, his voice tinny on Grace's cell as she curled up in her pajamas on her couch. After the ordeal by Bunco finally ended, she'd hung out with Clay for a few. But he had his cousins and the Wii, and although he loved her dearly, she knew she should make a clean getaway. Accordingly, she'd gotten out of Paige's house as fast as she possibly could. She'd won the Bunco game, and was now the proud owner not of a pot of money, but a trio of scented candles and matching hand lotion. The Bunco money would be donated to Catholic Charities, and who knew *that* when she was playing like a gunslinger at high noon? For the love of Christ.

"The Church is eternal," Johnny continued. "From one age to the next, we have abided by the commandments set down by the Savior. There are rules that govern the behavior of Catholics that are consistent no matter where he or she lives."

Grace nodded. She was smoking. Gus was sniffing at the little gift bag brimming with her scented candles and hand lotion. She picked the bag up off the floor in case he decided to pee on it.

"Right. No birth control even if you live with your sixteen kids in a Brazilian slum. No women priests even though you don't have a priest in your parish because there aren't enough to go around. Oh, and no screwing kids."

"Grace . . ."

"And suicide is a sin. Only maybe if you're, like, possessed by mental illness, you might get a Mass out of it."

There was a silence. She smiled sourly, glad she was pissing him off. Call her petty. Call her bitter. Call her someone who wished she'd never even heard of the Catholic Church.

Then he surprised her, Johnny did, as happened on occasion.

"That's actually fairly accurate," he said. "And Grace? Zachary Lacey being gay? God loves the sinner, hates the sin. If Zachary didn't indulge in homosexual acts, then he didn't sin."

"Well, thank God you cleared that up," she said wryly. "Tell that to his grandmother. She's losing her mind."

She heard a beep. "I got another call. I really do, Johnny. Thanks for the catechism lesson." She switched over.

"Guess what I have in my hand." It was Ham.

She slid down on the couch a little, grinning to herself. "You must be feeling better."

"Yeah. Maybe it was a bad bagel. But I'm okay now." A beat. "Want some company?"

She calculated. If he came over now, he might try to spend the night. That was starting to occur too often, that pushing toward an actual relationship. Men could be so needy. Ham tried to stay over; Butch had made her breakfast when she was injured on the job. She took another draw of her cigarette and watched the smoke rise toward the ceiling. Her house was a one-seater.

"I'm going to bed," she told him. "But we could have phone sex. Guess what I have in *my* hand."

His laugh was amused, lusty.

Hang 'em high, sheriff.

Then she got another beep. She checked the number and groaned. She had completely forgotten to call Mrs. Prescott. She told Ham who it was, and he sighed long and hard. *Long* and *hard*.

"Night," she said regretfully. And then, "Hello, Mrs. Prescott. I'm so sorry I didn't get back to you today."

"Miss Hanadarko," she said. Her voice was slurring, like maybe she'd had a bit too much to drink. "I spoke to Father Pepera this evening, and he said that Ron hasn't requested a Mass. Is Zack . . . has Zack been . . ." She sniffled.

Jesus. Mrs. Prescott didn't know if Zack had been buried. For her part, Grace wasn't sure if Henry had released the body or not. They were kinda done with it. Henry had taken more X-rays but all he had found was the one broken ankle.

"Ron hasn't returned my calls," she said. "And I—I want to know . . ."

"Would you be coming into town for the service?" Grace asked.

"I'm disabled, Miss Hanadarko. I have severe fibromyalgia and I live with an aide. My husband died last year."

"I'm so sorry," Grace said sincerely. She made a fist and lightly pounded her forehead, her mea culpa that she hadn't phoned earlier. Gus snuffled at her feet; he loved her no matter what, especially if he could have hand lotion for dessert. "I'll find out what's going on for you."

"Oh, would you, please?" Her voice cracked. "God bless you, child."

They disconnected and Grace put out her cigarette. She shooed Gus away from the gift bag, dug inside for one of the candles, and plopped the bag on the breakfast counter. Then she blew french-fry bits off the nearest plate, placed the candle on it, and carried it into her bedroom.

Grabbing a book of matches from Louie's, she lit the wick and put the plate on her nightstand. Brushed her teeth, and lay down on her crimson sheets. Her twinkle lights glittered like stars.

She watched the flame. A kid who thought it was his fault, whatever it was. All over Oklahoma City, children were trying to atone for things they'd never done . . . and never would.

Dying because of the lies their parents told them. And the biggest liar? God the Father.

This little light of mine . . .

She was going to let it burn all night, in memory of Zachary Lacey. Keep vigil for justice. Make the wrong go away. Her lids flickered; she forced them open and shifted in the bed to keep herself awake. Weariness sank her more deeply into the mattress, as if she herself were being lowered into the earth.

After a time, her eyelids closed; and she was unaware of Earl standing at the foot of her bed, watching her in the candlelight, moved by the kind thing she had done by keeping the boy alive in her heart.

"Yes, God bless you, child," he told her.

As she slept.

They walked through the Garden of Allah, Leon Cooley and his son, Benjamin. Nightingales sang in pomegranate trees on the banks of a gently flowing river of honey, which was festooned with rushes and overhung with date palms. The sky glowed.

"You didn't die, did you?" Leon asked Benjie, gazing at his boy's dark skin, his big brown eyes, his nappy head. His kid through and through. A little bit of Tamara in him, too, but Benjie looked like his father. "You're not here because—"

Benjamin smiled at him. "I'm always with you, Dad. I'm part of you." Then his expression changed and he pointed to the river. "You have to save her."

Leon looked. Grace Hanadarko lay facedown in the honey-water as it burbled past them. She was wearing jeans and her sheepherder jacket. Her hair floated around her head like yellow seaweed.

Leon took a step toward her, then looked back at Benjamin—or where Benjie had stood. His son had vanished. The pomegranate trees swayed; incense and orange blossoms permeated the air. He was alone on the riverbank.

"Benjie, where are you?" he yelled. He whirled in a circle. "Son!"

The waters pushed Hanadarko past him. If he ran he could catch up with her.

"Benjie!" he screamed.

Then he heard Benjie shout from the river. "Dad, help me, save me!" And it wasn't Hanadarko in the water. It was his boy.

Leon Cooley stood rooted to the spot. He clenched his jaw and balled his fists. And before he knew it—before he realized what he was doing—he was jumping into the water to keep that bitch from going under.

"Stop messing with me, Earl," he said when he woke up. He stared up into the blinding golden light filling his cell, forcing his eyes to stay open as he searched the brilliance for his last-chance angel. "That dream was bull-shit."

"I didn't give you a dream last night," Earl said as the light died down. "Whatever you dreamed, it came from somewhere else."

In the morning, Grace rolled out of bed, drank a lot of water and coffee, and took Gus for a run. Then she called the Laceys and got Ron, asked if she might come out to their place to take a look around. She had the perfect excuse—Mrs. Prescott's desire to know about the arrangements—even though she didn't need one. And even though it was a bullshit excuse. Cops didn't go around doing crap like this. At least she didn't. Very often.

"We're still investigating his case," she reminded Daddy Lacey.

Lacey agreed, even though it didn't sound like he wanted to. People who resented cops could be defiant one minute and acquiescent the next. You never knew which way the wind would blow, but the weather was on her side that morning.

Grace called Ham and asked him if he would come with her. She repeated their mantra. "We won't do anything stupid. We don't have a warrant. But if we get permission . . ."

"Amen. Hallelujah," Ham said.

He drove over to her place, looking like a night alone had done him some good. Jeans, blue shirt, jacket. He smelled great. It was clear he wanted to take some personal time in the sack before they went to the Laceys'. Maybe he was feeling sentimental because, with a raid tonight and all, one of them might get killed in the line of duty. But Grace was ready to roll in a totally different direction.

They took Ham's truck. On the way over, Butch called and said he had a possible witness. A homeless guy had seen a kid standing at the river's edge, staring down into the water. Three nights in a row. They were working on a description but so far his witness was erratic.

"So maybe it was Paul, planning to throw Zack in," Grace said to Ham as they zoomed along the Forty. "Or Zack, planning to jump in."

"Or another kid altogether," Ham suggested.

They got to the Laceys', not half as bad a bastion of right-wing paranoia as Grace had anticipated. Beneath the gigantic American flag on a flagpole, a cyclone fence separated the Lacey property from all comers. NO TRESPASSING PRIVATE PROPERTY THIS MEANS *YOU* hung in several places on the chain link. Also I HUNT AND I VOTE. There was razor wire along the top.

On the private property sat a light blue ranch house with a composition shingle roof, maybe three bedrooms and two baths. Wild grass and verbena grew in profusion. Across a blacktop roundabout was a detached garage with a closed door painted buff brown. Grace crossed her fingers that there was a truck in there.

Ham pulled off the road and parked next to the fence gate. Grace hopped out, missing a muddy berm, and discovered that the padlock was hanging open, possibly in anticipation of their visit. She pushed on the gate and Ham drove in.

Lacey himself opened the front door. Grace scrutinized him. Flannel shirt, work boots, canvas pants. Coffee cup in hand. He hadn't shaved. He looked beyond irritated.

"Good morning," Grace said. "Thanks for having us over."

Lacey scowled at them both and gestured for them to come in. Grace and Ham scanned the entryway as they kicked the mud off their boots. There was a free-standing oak hat rack loaded with baseball caps and surrounded by muddy shoes. The floor was hardwood, and while it had seen better days, it wasn't in bad shape.

In the living room, there was too much furniture—a sofa and a settee both, two overstuffed chairs, a coffee table and three side tables, all of it on the appalling side, wooden curlicues and Granny Smith–green velvet; God, where did you even *buy* shit like that? Thomas Kinkade knockoffs lined the walls—lighthouses glowing in the fog, English cottages. Lots of pink, red, and purple silk flowers in cut crystal vases with doilies underneath them. There was an oversized shopping bag from Crossroads Mall on top of an oak sideboard, but Grace couldn't exactly paw through it without asking. Still, she sidled over and tried to peer in. Looked like black jeans.

Lacey sat down in one of the Granny Smith–green chairs. He didn't invite them to do the same, but Grace took a spot on the sofa and Ham sat in the other chair. This was not a guy to tower over. He would be especially infuriated that a woman was the instrument of his intimidation.

"I called Cherie," Lacey said. "She's shopping for clothes. She don't wear much black." He looked at them as if they would catch his drift.

"For the service," Grace supplied. His silence was her answer. "So you've made plans."

"We haven't made shit," he countered, settling back into his chair with his coffee cup. "So what did you find out? Did he do it or not?"

Grace realized that he thought that was why they were there: to deliver the verdict. "We're still trying to find that out, sir. We thought if maybe we could talk to you, and your other son, Paul—"

"My stepson." A tiny flash of pleasure washed over his face. Hmm, liked the stepson better than the dead son. Heartless bastard. "He's in his room." Then he bellowed, "Paul! Get your butt out here."

After about a minute, Paul Finch emerged from a hallway to the left. He was wearing gray sweatpants and a white T-shirt. White socks. He looked muzzy, as if he had just awakened. He stopped short when he saw Grace.

"Hey. You were at school yesterday," he said.

Lacey raised his eyebrows at Grace.

"Yes." She stood and showed him her badge. Ham did the same. "We're investigating the death of your stepbrother."

"I thought he killed himself," Paul said blandly. He was definitely not broken up over the idea.

"We don't know." Grace turned back to Lacey. "Mrs. Prescott called. Father Pepera contacted her."

Lacey's face soured. "It was her fault Karen left me. And she babied Zack something fierce. She probably turned him gay."

Ham stayed cool. Grace struggled to do the same. These were data points coming out of the mouths of parties they were interested in, nothing more.

"When was the last time she saw Zack?" Grace asked as she sat back down.

"Couple of years. She lives in Kansas. He'd stay over there for a couple of weeks."

"Was that before she became disabled?" Grace asked.

Lacey guffawed. "That old witch is not disabled. She just wants to get a free ride. Me, I'm a workingman. Paying for her lazy ass." He looked at Paul. "Isn't that right? I work hard to put food on this table."

Paul said nothing, and looked over at Grace and Ham. "Why were you watching me at school?"

"Procedure," Grace said. "We have to interview the victim's relatives. But I didn't want to disturb you in front of your friends. School was out for the day. I didn't want to hold you up."

Some of the wariness left his face. She decided to press her advantage.

"That pitcher, man." She shook her head. "I hope he's not the best you've got."

Paul laughed. "He sucks."

"He sure does. I'll bet it's hard to win games with a loser like him on the team."

"We do okay. At least, we did last year."

"League champions," Lacey said. "Kid's got trophies, ribbons. MVP . . ."

"Oh, could I see that?" Grace asked.

Paul looked at his stepfather. Lacey shrugged. Grace would take that as consent if it came to trial. Lacey was a lot less hostile on his I-HUNT-I-HAVE-A-GUN-I-VOTE-I-DON'T-PAY-STORAGE-FEES-FOR-THE-CORONER'S-FREEZER home turf. And he wasn't acting like a murderer who was afraid of getting caught.

"Okay." Paul headed back down the hall. Ham and Grace followed him.

His was a typical messy boy's room, with pennants and baseball posters on the walls; computer game CDs piled around an unmade oak twin bed with scratched bedposts and a half-eaten banana on a napkin; and dirty clothes scattered like autumn leaves all around. Grace noted a black baseball-equipment bag and wandered over to it.

"What kind of bat do you use?" she asked him.

"I had a brand-new Plasma Gold, but someone stole it," he said. "I'm just using my old shit Easton until I get some bucks scraped together."

Blunt instrument. Grace forced herself not to look at Ham. She could feel that he'd made the connection, though, via their partner ESP. "How long ago did it get stolen?"

"A couple of weeks. My mom was so pissed."

"We had words over that," Lacey said from the doorway.

"Where was it stolen?" Grace continued. She knew Ham would stay silent and let her run the questioning. If they both chimed in, it would rattle their subject. Paul would know it was a big deal to them.

"I don't know. Just, one day, it was gone." He opened the bag and pulled out his glove. "This is a Nokona. Walnut leather."

"Cool," Grace said admiringly as she slipped it on. It dwarfed her hand. She took off the glove and handed it back to Paul, aware that Ham had been surreptitiously snooping around as only the best could snoop.

"Would you mind if we looked in Zack's room?" Grace said to Lacey. "We might learn something useful."

Lacey hesitated. Grace took note. Then he said, "I talked to Father Pepera today. He said Zack never came to him about any gay stuff. Zack told that shrink those tranquilizers were making it hard for him to sleep. I think I'm going to sue that Jew doctor."

Antidepressants, not tranquilizers, she wanted to say, but that wasn't the point, was it? *And* of course Zack never talked to Father Pepera. The good father was an asshole.

"I knew he was gay," Paul said. "It was so obvious."

Grace swung her head around to look at him. "Did that bother you?"

Paul glanced at his stepfather, then back to her. "Hell, yeah. How would *you* like to have a faggot stepbrother?"

"Who is dead," Grace reminded him.

He didn't say anything. Wow, cold.

"Did you talk to your priest about having a funeral Mass, Mr. Lacey?" Ham asked.

Lacey looked down and away. "Yeah, well, we're having a disagreement about that at the moment."

"Mr. Lacey," Grace said, "my brother is a priest. He told me that the Church does not refuse Mass to people who commit suicide. Especially minors. And we're still investigating what happened to him. For all we know, it could have been a tragic accident."

Lacey's lips parted and he started to say something, then turned and led the way farther down the hall. Paul came, too. The door was shut, and Grace mentally crossed her fingers.

Laptop, she thought. *And he lets me take it.*

In they went, into the catacomb. While Paul's room was All-American Boy, Zack's was a dark, stinky altar of death-metal love: outsized posters for Megadeth and Carcass covered the otherwise plain white walls. His sheets were nondescript white and his blanket was dark brown; on the floor, a jumble of black T-shirts and jeans. There was an old PlayStation, but it was covered with dust. It was almost as if he had never actually lived in his room, only unpacked a duffel bag in preparation for a short visit.

His closet door was open. *Laptop, please.* Grace said to Lacey, "May I?"

"It smells in here," Lacey announced, as if he had just noticed it. "He used to eat in here. Didn't eat with the rest of the family."

"He was so frickin' weird," Paul muttered.

Grace waited. Lacey ignored her and looked at Ham, as if he was the go-to detective on the case. The *man.* Grace let it roll off her; if she ever let sexism bother her, she was in the wrong line of work. The only thing she did with it was try to figure out how to use it to make progress in their investigations. So she let herself go innocuous and invisible while Ham nodded and walked in front of her, placing a hand on the sliding door of the closet.

"This okay?" Ham asked him.

"I guess," Lacey grumped.

Ham pushed it back and bent down, examining a pair of Doc Martens and a more prosaic pair of muddy black Converse slip-ons. An Army jacket and a heavy black winter coat. A white dress shirt that seemed remarkably out of place.

Grace moved to a battered oak dresser covered with band stickers and opened the drawers. On top of some rather gray tighty whities was an amber plastic prescription bottle for Prozac. Grace rolled it with the edge of a pair of white underwear so she wouldn't get prints on it: ZACHARY RONALD LACEY. His prescription, definitely. Filled in September, two months ago, and it was close to full.

Suicide remained the front-runner theory.

Ham moved from the closet to peer under Zack's oak bed. Grace heard Lacey huff but he did not withdraw permission, so she kept combing through the chest of drawers. School track shorts. A receipt for one admission at the group rate to Frontier City, dated twelve days ago. A Sunday. The psychological profile they had put together of Zack didn't include Oklahoma City's premier amusement park. She tried to form a mental image of him screaming his head off on a roller coaster. Nope.

She left it there and turned as Ham searched a free-hanging shelf beneath an Iron Maiden poster. There was a jumble of old paperback books, many of them fantasy novels, which puzzled her; and then Ham lifted *The Lord of the Rings* and retrieved a pamphlet that said *GAY? NO WAY! SAVED BY JESUS!* It was identical to one of the ones the boys had hung like a mobile from the ceiling above Grace's desk.

Ham showed the pamphlet to Lacey. Purple rushed up his neck. He balled his fists and sucked in air. If looks could kill: BLAM-BLAM-BLAM-BLAM-BLAM.

"What's that shit doing in my house?" Lacey said. "Gimme that."

Paul snickered.

"It might prove useful," Ham began, but as there was no warrant, they had to do as he asked.

Lacey ripped it into tiny pieces and Grace had to swallow down her whimper. Ham looked from the shelf to Grace and back again, signaling that there were more pamphlets, and she kept her face neutral as she went back to her chest of drawers.

"I think you both better leave," Lacey announced. He looked as if he was about to stroke out. Paul stood beside him, gaze wandering back to the bookshelf. He headed for it; maybe he realized Zack was not coming back for any of his stuff and he could help himself to whatever he wanted.

Grace was disappointed but not very surprised. She wanted like anything to ask Lacey if he owned a truck, but she kept her mouth shut, aware that he was hovering behind her and that he wanted them off his property because they knew the horrible secret of Dysfunction Drive.

"Thanks for having us out," Ham said, as if it had been Lacey's decision.

"This is bullshit," Lacey shot back. "This whole thing." And Grace could see that Ron Lacey was waking up to the fact that the bullshit he was referring to was his life: He marries a woman who disappears; he fathers a homosexual who commits suicide. No wonder he preferred bat-swinger Paul and Paul's hot if somewhat dim and trashy mom to Ron Lacey the Prequel.

"We're trying hard to figure this out," Grace said, like the rodeo clown deflecting the bull after the rider falls off. "We're real sorry to bother you."

He glared at her as if he wasn't sure if she was being sincere or sarcastic. Paul was watching his stepfather as if he was trying to figure out how to act—what the family stance on all this was—and said, "He was real weird. None of my friends liked him."

Oh?

"I can see why," Grace said, shaking her head. "I've

got a nephew into goth stuff. He's in the vice principal's office every other week."

Ham didn't react to her blatant lie. He never did. He lied, too, if he thought it would help their work. How come if he was an adulterous liar *he* didn't have a last-chance angel?

"That's the kind you have to look out for," Lacey opined. Then he fell silent again.

They walked back down the hall. A bathroom door hung open, and Grace took a lightning-fast inventory: a pile of flat packing boxes and a couple rolls of packing tape. For Zack's belongings? That would not be good.

"Thanks again for your time," Ham said as the front door closed in their faces. Don't ask, don't tell, don't bother us again.

"Shit, Ham," Grace said as they walked back to Ham's truck. "Did you see all the packing boxes in the bathroom? What if he throws out all the good stuff?"

"Paul's missing a bat," Ham said, and she grinned.

"Yeah. Maybe we should have asked outright about the laptop." She shook her head. "Then the evil stepmom would know we were onto her. That we know Zack was collecting shit about her."

"She might not be evil at all," Ham said. "She might just be horny, picking up guys when Ron goes on the road." He smiled faintly. "I mean, would you want to sleep with Ron Lacey?"

"I would rather die of horniness." She smiled. "Paul's missing a bat. We have found missing murder weapons all over this great city in the past, Ham. In Lake Hefner, even."

"Zack gets hobbled and can't swim. Drowns."

"Murder in the first degree," Grace concurred. "And we will find that bat."

"Let's go to your place and celebrate."

Even if they fell asleep, they had to get up to go on the raid. Plus it was daylight. So technically, it would not qualify as staying over.

"Gotta take our victories where we find 'em," she said.

CHAPTER
EIGHTEEN

Butch worked out and showered. It was six p.m. They were due to rendezvous a few blocks from the warehouse at eight. October had told him the buy was set for eleven.

Two phone messages came in while he was cooking mushrooms in butter and fajita seasoning for the steak he was broiling. The first was from Captain Perry. The other was from October, on Butch's fake-pizzeria cell number.

As long as Butch had known Captain Perry, she hadn't pulled any punches, and she didn't do so now. Straight and direct, and he was grateful to her for it.

"Janaya Causwell didn't make it," she told him. "She had a heart attack about two hours ago."

Damn, girl. He spared a moment of silence for the tragic, wayward woman. Another for her daughter.

"I have a call from October," he reported. "I haven't checked it yet."

"If he doesn't know about Janaya, you shouldn't tell him."

"Yeah," he said, stirring the mushrooms.

"Butch, we have a chance to get Big Money tonight. If your informant freaks out, he could blow this entire operation sky-high. Get someone killed. Maybe one of our own."

"I know," he said. "I'll see what he wants."

"Let me know. Call me back," she ordered him.

Butch checked the message.

"Hey, Butch, it's all set. But after this, I want out," October said. "Janaya's friend LaKeisha got a message through to me that Janaya wants to talk to me. We're going to make it work. You can help with that, right? Help us?"

Butch's heart pounded. What the hell was this? Was LaKeisha setting October up?

He called Captain Perry and repeated the message. She grunted, sighed.

"How did he sound?" she asked.

"Happy." It was the happiest Butch had ever heard him, in fact. "Eager to get out."

Captain Perry swore. "This is a surprise, and surprises are not good."

He agreed. His mind raced. The scent of steak and baked potato filled the room, but he was losing his appetite.

Surprises were not good.

"Let me think this over," she said. "I'll call you back."

She hung up and he called Grace. Since she was a woman, she might have a take on this.

Her voice was muffled, as if she had been asleep. He imagined her in bed, then turned that channel off and took a sip of water.

"Shit, that's weird. But it sounds like high school," Grace suggested when he told her what LaKeisha had done. "Girls did shit like that, pretending to help a guy get back together with his girlfriend when the one pretending was really after the guy. And all these people are definitely stuck in high-school land."

"Janaya died a couple of hours ago," he told her.

"Shit." Grace was quiet for a moment. He heard the strike of a match.

"Maybe LaKeisha's in with Big Money and it's a trap," Butch said.

"Trap for October," Grace said. "Not us." She exhaled. "He knows he's one step away from a fatality, being in a gang."

Not really. October tuned out the parts of reality that he didn't like. Always had.

"Yeah," Butch said. Butch knew the score; he wasn't some rookie cop working his first informant. And if this went south for October, he wouldn't be the first one Butch had lost, either. He thought of Merrie Kelly.

"Butch, you okay, man?"

"Yeah." And he was. He put his heart elsewhere and kept his cop blood beating. "Captain said she was going to think it through and get back to us."

"She'd better go for it," Grace said. "I'm ready to rock and roll." She giggled a little, and her voice moved away from the phone. He heard a smack. If Ham wasn't with her, someone else was. Not his business.

"Me too," he said.

"See you at eight."

"This is a no-knock warrant," said Marston, tonight's Tac lead. "We will move into place at one and two." He flashed a laser light on the plans of the warehouse and adjoining alleys, showing a large one at the front door of the warehouse, a two at the rear. "Red goes in first. Blue activates once there is activity in the rear."

Yeah, baby, activity in the rear, Grace thought, sharing a smirk with Ham.

Marston nodded at Grace when he concluded. "Detective Hanadarko?" he said.

"Everyone standing here knows what kind of scumbag Big Money is," Grace began, addressing Major Crimes and Tac both. "He cut a thirteen-year-old girl named Priscilla Jackson into pieces and fed them to his dog. He's recruited kids as young as eight to courier weapons and drugs to his gang and serve as lookouts." She passed out copies of Big Money's surveillance photo. Tac examined it more closely than her team, since he was not as well known to them.

They put on their amulets and good-luck charms. Bobby kissed a picture of his wife and kids. Butch slithered into his Longhorn shirt. Ham fastened his St. Christopher medal to his chest with black duct tape. Grace placed a wrapped paper tube of white sage in her boot.

"Sound check," she announced. She and Ham jumped up and down for Bobby and Butch. No jingling. All was silent.

"Sound check," Butch said next, as he and Bobby did the same. Ham and Grace gave the all-clear.

Grace glanced at Ham as she adjusted her type-three body armor. He was looking at her with a dangerously soft expression. She tipped her head back and he gazed down on her. "Are you feeling okay, Ham?"

"Butch is worried about his informant," he said. "And I'm fine."

"I know, man. It is what it is." Then, chuckling, she added, "Whatever the hell it is." A beat. "Show me an informant who's not a squirrel, and I'll show you a dead informant."

"Yeah," he said. His smile widened. "Baseball bat."

"Laptop." She shimmied.

"Pastor Marc."

Grace's smile fell. "Yeah, about that. The youth group meets at nine a.m., and I was thinking, you know, that you're more of a morning person than I am." She waggled her brows hopefully.

He laughed. "You're so full of shit. C'mon, Gay Youth Pastor is our main attraction."

"Speak for yourself. I'm liking Dad. *Storage fees,* can you believe it? And he goes ballistic when all we find is one pamphlet. God, I hope he leaves the other ones alone. Maybe Rhetta can get prints. Clues. Leads."

"We push the right domino, everything collapses," he agreed.

Butch and Bobby approached. Ham and Grace nodded at them. Bobby was quiet, focused. Butch looked loose, but Ham could tell he was on his guard. It was Butch's guy who'd brought them here tonight. And nobody on the squad wanted Big Money worse than Butch.

"It's gonna happen, man," Grace said, patting Butch's forearm. He nodded.

"Captain Perry said if we get done in time, she'll buy us a round at Louie's." He grinned. "I told her to ask Louie to stay open late. Just in case."

"I went to Paige's last night and drank mojitos," Grace informed them all. Ham and the others cracked up. "I played Bunco and I *won*. Candles. And hand lotion." She held out her hands. "Gardenia."

"Mmmhmm," Butch said appreciatively.

Ham figured Grace was not going to mention that they'd used up half the bottle during sex. Grace's sheets were a mess. But his ass smelled like a flower garden.

"Okay, let's roll," said Marston.

Tac drove them over to the warehouse district in their van, and everyone silently climbed down, MP5's in hand. Ham let go of everything in his life but the op. Grace was his partner. Butch and Bobby were on his squad. Tac had the parabola mic and the battering ram.

He, Grace, Butch, and Bobby were part of the Red Team. Red was going to sneak down the alley and assemble around the back door. Their deficit was the fact that the alley was narrow and crowded with Dumpsters and garbage. The warehouses were covered with aluminum siding, which could cause ricochets, but everyone was packing heavy shit, so that wasn't too likely. Rounds would just tear through. They'd made as sure as they could that no one else was inside those warehouses.

The Blue Team would take the front of the warehouse. Their deficit was that they were vulnerable to attack from late arrivals and/or reinforcements. Although Tactical had already swept the area for bad guys hiding in adjacent warehouses or staked out on the roofs, they might have missed someone.

"Make sure your clips are loaded," Marston said by way of parting.

Grace's team moved silently into position and waited for the signal from Blue. Blue would be the first to act; they would hoist up the parabola mic and confirm that the players were in place, and that something actionable had occurred—i.e., the buy. Or a murder. Whatever.

Grace and the boys crouched into position, helmets on, guns up, waiting. Grace listened to her heart, sure and steady, a little trippy from adrenaline. She was as focused as an eagle. No one spoke. No one moved. A bomb could have gone off but if it wasn't their bomb, no one on the Red Team would so much as blink.

There was a white towel on the Dumpster. Butch shifted his gaze to it, staring at it as if it were a snake about to strike. October's signal. Trouble. Danger. For Butch's team? Or for October?

Shit, he thought. He nudged Ham, who looked questioningly at him. Butch looked at the white towel. Ham got it—Butch had told him about it—and he pursed his lips. There was nothing to be done now. You planned and strategized and practiced, and you had procedures you were not to violate, and then there was a white towel. And you didn't know what the hell to do. Being a police officer was not like being an accountant. It was mostly about winging it. Shooting from the hip.

And not dying if you could help it.

So what did the white towel mean?

*   *   *

There were sounds inside the warehouse, muffled and echoing. Grace kept track of them in case they got louder near their door. She didn't look at anyone; she stared at the door. She was as motionless as a statue; her mind was clear of chatter; and rarely had she felt so alive. This wasn't just what she was born to do; it was what she was. The tornado and the calm eye; the whirlwind and the silent aftermath of the blast. No one else existed because everyone on Red Team was one being: Justice. If Big Money died tonight, it was Justice. If any of those scumbag assholes went with him, Justice.

And then:

"GO! GO! GO!" roared inside her helmet speaker.

Grace aimed her MP5 as the door burst open. Blurs of dark skin, brown skin, sallow skin; do-rags and guns. Bullets blazing past her helmet; she was rolling to one side without conscious awareness of doing so. Propping herself up on her elbows. Scooting back and racing around a trash can.

Rounds from a submachine gun threw up mud, splattering her face. Bullets tore into the siding above her head. Buffeted by the wall of sound, her ears filled with cotton and her headset crackled in her helmet: *eleven guys count them officer down armed dangerous they are exiting toward Red go go go . . .*

She was coated with mud; it began to rain and a big mofo wove in the doorway, then barreled back into the warehouse, squirting blood. She got up on one knee and stood her ground. Blue would chase them through; she was supposed to stay in the alley, and mow the bad guys down when they tried to escape, rats from the *Titanic*. She waited, her finger on the trigger; and she aimed her gun right into the chest of some scrawny guy who was crying—

—*October*, she thought—

and she hesitated.

And Scrawny Gun shot right at her.

BLAM-BLAM-BLAM-BLAM-BLAM! replied her teammates.

Something stung very, very badly, and everything went away.

White light, white light, white light.

Got you, now, Earl thought as he extended his hand in the white tunnel. *Girl, I got you—*

Grace woke up in the hospital, surrounded by loved ones: Rhetta, Butch, Bobby, Johnny, Ham. And Paige. She groaned. Not because Paige was there. Well, okay, *maybe* not.

"Not again," she muttered.

"A bullet grazed your left thigh. You weren't hurt badly," Rhetta said. "But you got knocked out. So you're under observation for a concussion."

"Shit," Grace said. "I love those jeans."

"I'll patch them for you," Rhetta promised.

Standing apart from the others, hovering on the threshold of her room, Earl smiled the sweetest smile at her, so not like any other smile of his she'd ever seen, and walked—or vanished—into the hall. Her last-chance angel had come for her again, as he had before.

Maybe God just doesn't want me to die, she thought.

Then she looked up at Ham, who waved a catheter back and forth like a hypnotist with a pocket watch. She grimaced at him, then smiled gently at Butch.

"Hi, Scarecrow," she said. "Where's Toto?"

"October's gut-shot," Butch said, coming to the bed and taking her right hand in his. "They're not sure he's going to make it."

"That's a bitch, man," she said sincerely, even though she was fairly certain it was October who had shot her.

She gave Butch's hand a squeeze. "Johnny, maybe you should go see him," Grace said to her brother. She let go of Butch's warm big hand and tested her forehead. Her fingertips came away clean, meaning that Johnny hadn't performed Last Rites on her. Johnny didn't say anything. Maybe October wasn't a Catholic—i.e., one of the lucky ones.

"Who else?" she asked. "Did we get Big Money?"

Butch looked grim. He shook his head. "Big Money didn't show. We got everybody else, though. Two fatalities for them, but we caught them in the middle of the buy, so they've all been put away wet. Couple of injuries on our side, but you're the worst."

"That's something, Butch," Grace said. She was so sorry. And so pissed. "We got some poison off the streets."

His jaw was clenched. Now Big Money would be more cautious than ever, sinking into the sludge like a sewer gator. They might never see him again in their lifetime . . . or in their city. If he'd just leave . . . he'd still carve little girls up in someone else's town.

When Henry's cat died, I slept with him, she thought. *Hell, I'd sleep with Butch just because, but I would also do it to ease his pain.* She looked over at Ham. *Well, that sure would complicate things, wouldn't it?*

"Hey, guess what," Ham said. "Joey Amador was in the warehouse. We shot him. He had a gun in his hand when he went down."

"Are you shitting me?" Grace cried.

"Shit, no," Ham replied.

"No shit." Grace chuckled. Paige rolled her eyes at the language, and Grace filed that away under "Ten Ways I Can Prove My Sister Is a Superficial Tightass." "Did we shoot him dead?"

"No," Ham said. "My aim was off."

"Hey, I shot him," Bobby said.

"No way. It was me," Butch insisted.

"Well, it probably wasn't me, because I've got good aim," Grace said. "And you know he'll just get probation again, because of all the police brutality." Grace made her hand into a gun and fired it at Ham. He fired back.

"It's really not funny to talk about killing someone," Paige announced, distressed.

"We're just taking the edge off," Grace told her. She had explained police humor to Paige before. "We don't really mean it." *Except for all the time.*

"Well, I hope you don't talk like that around the kids." Paige gave Johnny a look, as if the moral authority of the Hanadarko clan should use this as a teaching moment.

"I almost died again," Grace told Rhetta, who was blowing her nose.

Rhetta shook her head. "No, this time they said you were going to be fine. We all knew it. It was just a graze. And a concussion."

Grace paused. Rhetta stopped honking, and Grace locked gazes with her very best wonderful friend in all the world. She looked at her hard and nodded: *I am telling you that I saw the white light again. And Earl.* Grace had described her first near-death experience during the squad's failed assault on Big Time Reynolds's crack house.

Rhetta's eyes widened, and she covered her mouth with both her hands and slowly sat down in a brown plastic chair. Message received.

"Well, God does work in mysterious ways," Grace said to Ham, as he came up beside the bed. "Looks like you get to interview Pastor Marc alone tomorrow."

"I'll get them to discharge you," he promised, picking up a bedpan and making as if to place it on her head like a hat. They grinned at each other.

Paige cleared her throat, clearly ill at ease with their juvenile antics. "I can stop by your house and feed your dog."

The thought of her fussy sister seeing her dirty dishes and possibly her sheets and floor slathered with prized Bunco gardenia hand lotion made Grace wince. Paige was already gathering her purse and Grace half-heartedly raised her head off her pillow in protest.

Ham stepped up and said, "I have to go by Grace's for the case file," which was a damn lie, but Grace nodded vigorously.

"It's on the counter. You know," she said, yawning. "He has to go anyway, Paige." She yawned again.

"Okay." Paige modeled her signature expression of mild frustration, one that had taken Grace years to understand: She was being spared the hassle of doing the errand, and yet her will had been thwarted.

"On the counter," Grace repeated to Ham.

Everyone took that as their cue to leave. Rhetta, Butch, Bobby, and Ham kissed her good-bye. Her own two siblings did not. Hanadarko family weirdness. Grace, however, was an equal-opportunity smiler as the gang filed out. She was about to turn out her light when Doug and Clay walked in. Clay's face was dead white, and his eyes were swollen.

"Hi, Aunt Grace." He looked up at his father, who put a hand on his shoulder.

"Hey, Clay," she said, reaching out her hand. "It's so nice of you . . ."

A big tear rolled down Clay's cheek.

"Clay, I'm all right," she said. "I'm fine. It was just a scratch."

He lowered his eyes and nodded. "I know."

Doug sighed, and Grace saw the resemblance to Clay around his eyes. Clay's grandpa and mom, both gone. His aunt . . . make that *favorite* aunt, damn it, back in the hospital with another bullet wound. So *was* being a cop a form of indirect suicide?

"This is getting kind of old," Doug said. "Do you always have to be such a hotshot?"

I hesitated, she thought. *I wasn't a hotshot at all.*

She said, "Hey, I'm getting out of the hospital tomorrow. Can Clay come over and spend the night? You could give him Monday off. Call the nuns and say he's sick." *Lying to nuns. A hellfire offense for sure.*

"Oh, *wow,*" Clay breathed. "Dad, please?"

"Not on your life," Doug said, shaking his head at both of them. "But he can come over next weekend."

"Damn, I'm spending a fortune in video-rental fees," she muttered as she smiled at Clay. "Cool, man." She lowered her voice. "We'll eat so much crap we'll puke."

"Yeah." He grinned at her, shiny eyes and white teeth. "Chomp!"

You had to take life's pleasures where you found 'em.

CHAPTER
NINETEEN

It was almost nine when Butch stopped by October's hospital room. There was a guard outside who let him in, and a young nurse inside who informed him visiting hours were over . . . until she saw his badge and gave him an excited little smile. She was a short little blonde, very cute. Her name was Terri.

October looked terrible. He looked like Butch's homeless Sartre-reading philosopher, only dead. There was a cannula in his nose and grizzled beard on his sunken cheeks. As Butch turned to go, October's eyes drifted open.

"You got me out," he whispered.

Butch swallowed back whatever he might have said, and nodded. "Where was Big Money?"

October coughed lightly. His breathing was shallow. "He had a fight with his girlfriend." He took another short breath. "She's a bitch."

Damn. If only Big Money had traveled light, too . . .

"Sorry," October said.

"I saw your towel on the Dumpster. Your signal. I wasn't sure what it meant. If you were warning us to abort." *Caused a bit of confusion, and Grace got shot.*

October shook his head. "Wasn't mine."

Butch took that in. Had someone else known about October's signal? Was it some kind of coincidence?

"LaKeisha said Janaya wants to make up," October said.

Cold certainty washed over Butch. He couldn't lie to this guy anymore.

"October . . . Patrick," he began.

But October's eyes rolled shut, and his mouth dropped open. Butch looked at Nurse Terri, who checked the read-outs on October's heart-rate monitor.

"He's just very tired," she said. "We're giving him morphine for the pain."

"He probably loves that," Butch said as he turned to go.

She was studying him. When he caught her eye, she dimpled slightly. "So, you're a cop."

"Yeah."

"He's your prisoner? From a shoot-out?"

He nodded. *At the Not-Okay Corral. Grace got shot.*

Her eyes got a little wide. "Wow."

All that, and I cook, too, he thought. But that was the little head talking.

"I have a break," she said, smiling. "They'll watch Mr. Kelly from the nurse's station. Want to go to the cafeteria for a cup of really bad coffee?"

"Sure," he replied, and told himself that was the little head, too. But maybe . . . it was a little cold and a little dark back at his place, right about now.

Ham was sitting in Pastor Marc's office at twelve thirty on Sunday afternoon while Pastor Marc himself buzzed around like a meth addict. The walls had posters of Christian rock groups and one of those Not of This World logos against a sunset. There was a stained-glass rectangle hanging in the window, which depicted a cross against a rainbow. Rainbows could be symbols of diversity and/or gay pride. Ham could hope.

Morning services were over, and the youth group was

meeting back at the church in an hour. They were going to the rez to build a house. Ham had called Bobby, asked him if he might also wander over once they hit Native-American property. Butch was over at Bobby's, helping him with his mold.

Pastor Marc had some nachos with ground beef and a soda on his table. He offered some to Ham, but Ham passed. Now the detective sat in a wooden chair backed with a few inches of blue fabric, observing the whirlwind, all the time looking for clues regarding Marc's sexual orientation. Weak chin, check.

His gay brother, Nick, would kill Ham if he knew he was thinking like that. But hell, sometimes you *could* tell.

"So to answer your question, yes, we *are* an inclusive church." Pastor Marc's last name was Grayhill. He had chubby cheeks, a low forehead, and a sort of mullet hair-cut Ham could not believe. He wished Grace was there to see it. She had gotten discharged, wasn't even limping, but she'd made him go by himself. Payback would be sweet.

He smiled at Ham with capped teeth. "Jesus really does love everybody."

"So . . . does the church allow commitment cere-monies?" Ham asked.

Pastor Marc didn't miss a beat. "By 'inclusive,' I mean that we accept all who have sinned against the will of God. That includes you, and that includes me. No one is worthy of the glory of the Lord. But He gives it to us if we are truly repentant and live clean, just lives."

"And Zachary Lacey went to Frontier City with the youth group," Ham said. "Two weeks ago."

Something washed over Pastor Marc's face. His jaw tightened; the blood rose in his cheeks. Ham remained neutral, letting the clues come to him.

Old joke: So there were these two bucks in the forest, an old one and a young one. They were standing on the crest of a hill, looking down into a meadow filled with does. And the young buck says to the old one, "Let's run down there and screw one of those does!" And the old buck says, "Let's *walk* down and screw *all* of 'em."

Ba-da-dum. A younger Ham would have started asking questions right then, to see what was ailing the good minister. But the older Ham remained patient. Partnering with Grace had taught him the wisdom of patience. A little.

"Yes, Zack went with the group." He was speaking carefully, his back turned to Ham as he rooted through a red metal toolbox identical to the one Ham's mom owned. Virginia Dewey had walked Ham through his first oil change when he was still in elementary school.

"How'd he seem?" Ham asked. "At Frontier City?"

"Where's that hammer?" Pastor Marc muttered.

Blunt instrument.

"He seemed . . . detached." Pastor Marc turned around and huffed with his hands on his hips. *Gay.* "He said things weren't going well at home."

"We have a witness who told us he had an altercation with his father shortly before he died. Did he talk about that? Did you notice any injuries?"

"He was a private person." Pastor Marc wasn't looking at him. Ham could just feel the anxiety rolling off him and remained calm, steady as she goes, but the sounding notes of the "William Tell Overture" were on him like a fever. "I respected that. I hoped that, in time, he would feel free to open up to me. He had only been coming to the youth group for a couple of months."

"Did he bring anyone to Frontier City? Hang out with a particular group of kids?"

"He came by himself, and the group hung out together," Pastor Marc reported. He was getting superbusy with his search for the hammer. "If he was troubled, he didn't share that with us."

Us.

Pastor Marc looked up at Ham. He picked up a nacho, scooping up a dollop from the sour cream on the side of the cardboard plate. "I'm sorry, Detective, but I need to get ready."

Dismissed. "Sure, of course. Thanks for your time," Ham said, getting up as Pastor Marc grunted and held up a ball-peen hammer. Thing like that would have shattered an ankle. Henry hadn't said anything about shattering. "I'll walk myself out."

Pastor Marc nodded, clearly done. Ham went out the side door into a busy courtyard decorated with a white statue of Jesus in the middle of a rock fountain. Mexican paver tiles were inscribed with the names of donors and in memory of various people. He surveyed the names as he walked: PATHI, ATKINSON, BRAUN. People in their Sunday best chatted in groups. A few smiled his way. A friendly bunch on a Sunday morning. He used to go to a church in Chandler. He hadn't picked a new one yet, but this one was not it.

He walked out of the courtyard to the back parking lot just as three guys piled out of a truck. One of them looked familiar. He was wearing a football jersey and as he ran around to the truck bed, Ham read off his last name on the shirt, above the number 22: COVEL. He wasn't Drew Covel, the jerk kid Ham had interviewed. Had to be a brother or a cousin.

Covel scrambled into the truck bed and grabbed up a medium-sized Styrofoam cooler. Then he scrabbled back down and trotted toward the courtyard.

"Hey," Ham said, closing the space between them. The other two guys had climbed into the bed, gathering up more supplies for the trip, Ham supposed, to the reservation. Neither saw Ham approaching their friend.

Ham's badge must have caught the light; Covel glanced down at it first, then up to Ham's face. He blanched and looked back over his shoulder. His two friends were busy.

"Is your brother Drew Covel?" Ham asked.

"I wasn't there," the boy said quickly. "I had nothing to do with it."

"Well, I'll be damned," Grace said as she carried some extra-superlacy bras toward a dressing room. She was at the Crossroads Mall, in the Victoria's Secret store.

And so was Cherie Lacey, just coming out of a dressing room. Cherie was dressed in a pair of tight jeans with rhinestone swirls down the sides, a pink belt studded with gold roses, and a dark pink sort of a peasant blouse. Her nails matched her blouse. She had been trying on black bras to go with her grieving-stepmom black dress. Or else she did a little pole dancing in her spare time.

It took Cherie a minute to figure out who Grace was.

"Oh, hi. Detective . . ." Cherie was at a loss.

"Hanadarko." Grace pulled a sympathetic smile. "How you doing, Ms. Lacey?"

Cherie shrugged, hefting another big Crossroads Mall shopping bag over her shoulder. It had the black dress in it. To match the dark circles under her eyes.

"I guess I'm okay, considering what's going on. Ron said you came out to the house yesterday. Did you find what you were looking for?"

Laptop. "We weren't looking for anything specific," Grace replied. "Just anything that could help us figure out what happened." A beat, and then, "Zack's grandmother is all torn up. She's afraid Father Pepera won't say Mass for Zack."

Cherie fingered the black bra on the top of her little pile. The cups were see-through. So maybe she was cheating. Or maybe she just liked to keep the home fires burning.

"I'm not a very good Catholic," Cherie confessed. "I don't really get all that stuff."

"My brother will say Mass for him," Grace said. "He's a Jesuit. Priest. They're more liberal." She nearly choked on her words. "Hey," she said brightly, "you want to go get a cup of coffee or something in the food court? I really shouldn't be spending any money on stuff like this." She wrinkled her nose. "Mortgage payments."

"I hear you. Ronnie would kill me if he saw the bills for this stuff." She paled. "I mean, he wouldn't *really* kill me."

"I know what you mean," Grace assured her. "I don't have a man, so no one's looking over my shoulder except the bank and my credit-card company." She set down her bras on the nearest table as Cherie headed for the nearest cash register. Grace started to follow her empty-handed; then on second thought, she grabbed the black thong from her selections and followed her on over. What the hell.

Cherie paid in cash, then Grace handed over her plastic; they headed to the food court. Cherie grabbed a diet soda, and Grace ordered onion rings; they sat down at a table for two. Cherie had a sizable number of purchases inside the catch-all big bag, given that she had only one special occasion on her calendar. At least that Grace knew of. Grace had only just located her when she was buying the dress, and followed her on over to Vicky's.

They settled in, almost like girlfriends; Cherie with her pink nails and makeup—her lips were lined in a dark pink, then filled in with a lighter one—and Grace, still kind of slaggy from being in the hospital. Her thigh hurt but she wasn't even limping. Paul was the one who had answered the Lacey phone and told her his mom was shopping. Grace had remembered the Crossroads shopping bag at their house, and hit it lucky.

Lucky being a relative term. She wasn't sure what was worse, interviewing Pastor Marc or going to a mall.

Dipping an onion ring in ketchup, she gestured with

her head for Cherie to help herself. Cherie waved her hands no-no-no.

"Have to watch my figure," she said with a little wink. "It's harder to take it off the older you get. And I'm getting up there."

"Get out." Grace guffawed. "You can't be older than . . ."

"I'm nearly thirty-five," Cherie confided.

"Wow, I guess you'd have to be," Grace said. "But still." So she'd had Paul around the age of eighteen. She wondered where Dad was.

"Ya gotta stay out of the sun," Cherie told her. "And moisturize." She made a little face. "And you shouldn't smoke."

"Keeps the weight off," Grace countered. "Ron told us that Zack ate in his room a lot. Didn't eat with the rest of the family."

Cherie tapped the end of her straw with each of the fingernails of her left hand. "I never felt like I knew him very well," she said. "I married Ron when Zack was fourteen. Just a couple of years ago. I think he had these dreams that his mom would come back." She sighed and slid her hand down the side of her cup.

"Does Ron know what happened to Karen, just doesn't want Zack to know?" Grace asked.

"She really did just disappear," Cherie said. "Which makes me think . . ." She hesitated, then shrugged and took an onion ring. "I think she did herself in, too. I think it runs in that family. Ron gets these dark moods." She shivered.

"They say that mental illness has a genetic component," Grace agreed. "Do you worry about Ron out on the road, by himself?"

"No, it's almost . . ." She looked pensive.

". . . a relief?" Grace filled in.

"Oh, no, I wouldn't go that far," Cherie said, nibbling

on the very edge of the onion ring. "We're newlyweds, after all."

"You came from Texas," Grace said. She grinned. "Or at least, you sound like it."

"El Paso," she said. "Such an armpit."

"Won't argue with you there." Grace felt her cell phone vibrate. "Excuse me." She checked it. It was Ham.

MEET UR HOUSE 1 HR?

She texted back a yes and put the cell phone bag in her pocket. Cherie had taken the opportunity to glance at her cell phone, too. She jerked her head up when she realized Grace was looking at her.

"I should go," Cherie said. "Ron's got a short run tomorrow, and we need to decide what to do about the funeral." She pressed a paper napkin against her lips. "Is there any chance you will be able to declare or say or whatever it is, about if Zack's death was an accident or if he—he killed himself?"

Grace pursed her lips and shook her head. "Can't say yet. And it could have been a murder." She picked up another onion ring and bit down hard.

Cherie looked a little sick. A lot of people did when they heard the word *murder*.

"Oh, God," she murmured, sliding back her chair. "Well . . ."

Something told Grace to go for it. There and then. "Have you seen Zack's laptop? Kid at school said he always had it with him. It had these stickers on it, death-metal bands . . ."

"Laptop," she said slowly, as if she had never heard the word before. "I didn't notice. . . ." Her hands trembled as she picked up her shopping bag.

"And Paul's missing a baseball bat," Grace added.

Cherie brightened. "*That* I knew about." As if she were actually pleased he'd lost a two-hundred-dollar piece of sports equipment.

"Is it possible one of the guys on his team took it by accident?"

"The bat, you mean? I don't see how, with his initials and all," Cherie replied. "And those are nice boys."

"Except for ganging up on Zack, of course," Grace said. "That part . . . not so nice."

She looked confused again. "Ganging up? . . ."

"Calling him a faggot, that kind of nice stuff." Grace cocked her head as if to say, *Well?*

"Oh, no, you must be mistaken. Those are good boys," Cherie insisted. "Back in Texas . . ." She stopped herself. "They're very nice," she concluded. "Oh, my God, if they hassled him . . ." Her eyes welled.

She started to cry in earnest. She was good at it. In fact, Grace couldn't even tell if she meant it or not. She grabbed more napkins and dabbed at her eyes, blotting eyeliner and mascara. Again, as the layers came off, she looked older than thirty-five.

"Did he open up to you? Tell you anything about what was going on with him? When was the last time you were together?"

"I took him to the grocery-store pharmacy to get his prescription renewed. About three weeks ago."

But he had stopped taking his meds, and there was nearly a full bottle in his underwear drawer. The date was September, nearly two months ago. Maybe Zack had faked her out, told her he needed more.

"What did you two talk about?" Grace prompted.

"He wanted to know what I wanted for my birthday." She wept harder. "He said he wanted to get me something nice because he had saved up a bunch of money."

From dealing drugs?

"People think just because he was my stepson, I'm not all that upset. But I *am*."

"I can see that," Grace said.

"I want to know what happened to him." She blew her

nose. "I cared for that boy. Losing his momma and all . . ." She took a deep breath. "Ron's so angry, but that's his way. He gets angry when he cares. I've been trying to hold it in because, well, I wasn't really family. But this is all the family I've got."

He gets angry when he cares.

"Cherie, we were told that Ron and Zack had a bad argument shortly before Zack's disappearance. That blows were exchanged."

Cherie sucked in her breath and stared at Grace with real fear in her eyes. Grace felt that frisson of electricity that told her she'd hit the right nerve, square on. She waited.

"Oh, God, please don't think that way about Ron," she begged. "I was so afraid it would get out . . . because then y'all would be thinking the way you are thinking."

"You don't know what I'm thinking," Grace said.

"I do. I knew as soon as you started talking to us in that room that if you found out about that fight . . ." She covered her mouth to keep the nightmare from pouring out. "Ron wouldn't do that. I know that man."

"Did they fight over him being gay?" Grace asked.

She shook her head. "We didn't know. It was over me. Zack didn't like me. Ron didn't tell me what Zack said about me. But . . . he did hit Zack."

"A lot."

"A lot," she said brokenly. "And I haven't done anything wrong. I swear it to you."

"If I found that laptop, what would I find on it?" Grace asked her.

"I don't know," she said, "but I wish you would find it. Then that would clear Ron, and maybe I could find out what Zack had against me."

"Ron hasn't been charged with anything," Grace reminded her.

"Okay," Cherie said, bobbing her head as the tears

came. "Right, I know that but I'm so scared. . . ." She bit her lower lip. "We honestly didn't know that Zack was worried about being a homosexual. No one ever told us that."

"Dr. Metzner didn't catch it?" Grace asked.

Cherie shook her head. "Maybe he wasn't supposed to tell us. We're plain people, Ronnie and me. I don't even know any gay people."

"Except Zack," Grace said.

"Oh, my God, why did this happen to us?" Cherie whispered.

She sank back down in her chair, rested her head in her hands, and sobbed.

CHAPTER
TWENTY

"Gay-orcism?" Grace echoed, as Ham paced in her living room. She had just returned from her talk at the mall with Cherie, to find him pacing, livid, in her driveway. They walked inside, and he slammed her door so hard the windows shook. One look at him and Gus had retreated to her bedroom.

"Yeah. After Frontier City the youth group goes back to the church, and Pastor Marc leads them all in prayer and he leaves to get pizzas. Alone."

"Leaving them alone, bad boy," Grace said, grabbing two beers out of the fridge. Ham needed to cool off.

"So while he's gone, these guys get this great idea to have an exorcism for Zack to stop him from being gay." Ham ran his hands through his hair. "They put him in a chair and tie his hands behind his back and start screaming Bible verses at him."

"Are you shitting me, man?" Grace waited for the punch line. Because Ham wouldn't be this angry about a few Bible verses. She didn't get that riled up about Bible verses, and she was the one with the religious issues.

"And Pastor Marc's not coming back from his pizza errand. So they get really into it. Someone saw this James Bond movie so they get *another* chair, only they yank the seat out of it, and they take off his jeans and his underwear and they sit him down in the chair. And they start asking him if he's gay, and when he doesn't confess, someone hits his balls from underneath the chair—"

"*What?*" Grace nearly dropped the longnecks.

"With a pool cue. They've got a pool table in their rec room, and they're smacking his balls with it and shouting at him. And Pastor Bullshit is not there. And he *should* be. He was gone for over an hour."

Grace's mouth dropped open. "He's giving them time to do it?"

"And Zack is not saying a word, not a frickin' word, and his head falls forward, so they get spooked and let him go." Ham made fists and punched the air. "And after he's gone, Pastor Marc comes back with their pizzas."

"Jesus." Grace gaped at him.

"Marc knew. He did. He acted guilty when I was in his office today."

"Another adult dangles him over the pit. God*damn* it," Grace said. She slammed down the beers. She was pissed. Really pissed.

It's a fierce white-hot mighty love.

This was such pure and utter bullshit. Unbelievable. It was so incredibly stupid that she couldn't even believe it.

"I want," Grace said, "I want to bring that asshole down to the morgue and let him see Zack Lacey now. We're all supposed to rise from the dead in our mortal bodies, Ham, so *pure.* . . ." She clenched her teeth so hard she could almost hear them crack.

"Grace, Grace," Ham whispered, taking her gun out of the holster, then her badge, laying them on the counter. Ham walked to the side door and opened it, taking Grace with him.

The world smelled like ozone, and oil refineries, and cow manure. It smelled like incense.

I hate men of God. I hate how they screw with kids and ruin their lives. If we have souls, they just tear them out.

Through the side door, the rain poured down in buckets, by the river-load. Grace stared at it, understanding the impulse to drown the whole screwed-up mess. God saying, *To hell with this.*

Ham shut the door in some parallel universe where life was normal, and carried her down the hall into her bedroom. She curled up in his arms and wished they could skip some steps and be joined now, right now; she let him roll her onto the bed and undress her. Zippers, buttons, bra hooks. He tore it off and then shot out of his own clothes like a comet. He was ready and he parted her legs and she arched her back with her teeth showing.

Gimme, she thought, as her most basic, demanding self. Nothing let her forget better than Ham inside her. She snapped into the moment, fully awake, aware, and alive; other men could do this but no man could do it like Ham. He thrust and she bucked, and there were no priests and ministers and no bullies, nothing but the amazing delight of sex with the man who played her like a screaming guitar. Liquid heat and fierce, white-hot mighty pleasure. She clung and she moved and he did the things he knew she loved. And that was the only love involved; love of the flesh, and of being alive.

"Oh, Grace, oh," Ham moaned.

And it quieted her body, if not her mind. One out of two wasn't bad. Three, if you counted her soul. Her stormy soul, bothered and incessant.

But her body, for the moment, rested. In peace. Ham lay still and quiet beside her like a dead man. Someday, one of them would die first. Maybe they wouldn't even know each other anymore, when that happened. She took comfort in the idea of not knowing when Ham died.

The rain came down in torrents. She listened to it for a while. Then Ham shifted his weight with a slow, long sigh.

"Cherie didn't seem to know about a laptop." Grace told him. "Said Paul's initials were on his bat. She confirmed that Ron beat Zack for talking trash about her."

"These are good things to know," Ham mumbled. His breathing changed, and she knew he was drifting off to sleep. Lucky bastard.

She thought about reminding him that there were no sleepovers. But it was only four in the afternoon. He'd wake up long before bedtime.

"Oh, hello again," said the coy cocktail waiter in Pan, the bar with the black-velvet Elvis singing into a penis. "How is the crime business, Detectives?"

"Can't complain," Grace said as she and Ham scanned the perimeter. Empty booths, a few scattered patrons at the tables. The jukebox was on low, more background noise than music. Sunday night in a gay bar was about as dead as Sunday night in a straight bar. "Got a question."

"Fire away." The waiter posed. *Hit me with your best shot.*

"When you saw Flaco in here with our underage guy, did our guy have a laptop with him? That he maybe left?"

The waiter shrugged. "I don't know anything about laptops. Lap dances, yes." He smiled at Ham. "I would even give *you* a discount."

Ham wondered if Nicky ever did this kind of shit. Then he said, "This laptop was covered with stickers from heavy-metal bands."

"Death metal," Grace elaborated. "Megadeth."

"Ick." The waiter splayed his long, buffed fingernails over his chest. "But let me ask Janet to check Lost and Found." He darted away.

A few minutes later, Janet came back with him. Dressed in a woman's black business suit, a black silk tank top, and big-ass stilettos, Janet was probably presurgery, but his voice was high for a man's. Grace figured he was taking estrogen. He seemed perfectly at ease with having two detectives in his place.

"Yeah, I remember that laptop," Janet said. "Flaco was carrying it and the kid kept trying to hold it. Flaco was giving him shit."

Grace wanted to kiss him, but thought better of it. So she simply nodded like Detective Sergeant Friday on *Dragnet* and tried to get more details. There weren't any. Flaco and Zack came in with a laptop, Flaco was hogging it, the end.

"You've been a big help, Janet," Grace said.

"My man is a cop," Janet replied frankly.

After Grace and Ham left, they had a great time going into hysterics and trying to decide who Janet's man was. They invented an elaborate story that starred Bobby because that was the most ludicrous choice they could come up with, except for Grace.

They canvassed the Lost-and-Found boxes of the other five bars they had visited on Thirty-ninth before. There were no laptops in any of them. There were sunglasses, cell phones, handcuffs, whips, vinyl underwear, and very expensive condoms in individual boxes—unused, thank God.

Ham got a call requesting he go back to the station to talk to Pastor Marc's attorney about the torture-ring bust. Shortly after he took off for that fun task, Antwone called. He wanted them to come over. Grace was alone, but that worked for Antwone, too.

She took Connie to his dump of a house, and who should open the door but Antwone himself. With a new black eye and a fresh cut on his lip.

"Who did this to you, man?" she asked, and this time he let her in. His dog must have been in the backyard. The living room was shabby but tidy. An old orange sofa, a leather recliner. Athletic shoes on the floor. A TV and a DVD player. A plastic tablecloth with bumblebees printed on it covered a dining-room table. Car keys, a soda, a few bills, some schoolbooks. A minor could not give his consent to search; she didn't have a warrant. She reminded herself of these facts.

"Some guys in Zack's church group," he said. "They said I told what happened. I didn't even know what they were talking about."

"They messed with him big-time," Grace said. "He didn't mention the gay-orcism?"

"The *what*?" He stared at her.

"I'll tell you later. I swear," she said. "Why'd you call me?"

"Flaco texted. He wants to set up the buy."

Oh, God. Grace's eyes widened. *Here we go.*

"On my BlackBerry," he added, pulling it from his pocket.

"Can I take this from you?" she asked, making sure he was relinquishing possession. She took it and opened up the messages.

FLACO: U READY?

"What did you tell him?"

"Nothing," Antwone said. "As soon as it came in, I called you. What is a gay-orcism?"

"It's bullshit. The church kids tried to de-gayify Zack. I'll tell you later, man."

"No. Now," Antwone said.

Grace sighed, frustrated. His dump, his rules. She sat him down and tried to go easy, but he was crazed by the end of it. Maybe even ready to kill someone.

"Antwone, I'm sorry. I really am," she said. "But you gotta stay focused with me. The last person who was seen with Zack's laptop was Flaco. If he has it, and we can get it . . ." She let the last sentence trail off to its obvious conclusion. But he was still back with the revelation that good Christian Jesus-fearin' folk had tortured the boy he loved.

"Why didn't he tell me?" Antwone moaned, doubling up his fists. He looked left, right, as if for someone to hit, something to destroy.

"To protect you," she said. "Because he cared about you."

He broke down sobbing, his abject, animal cries coming from the hole in his life. Grace sat quietly, a witness, and anger boiled up inside her. The whole situation was so wrong. So . . . unjust.

"Zack," he mourned, "oh, Zack."

She felt his BlackBerry vibrate in her hand. Looked down and saw that it was Flaco again. Shit.

"Antwone, listen, it's Flaco. I'm going to tell him you'll make the buy," she said. Antwone kept crying. She wasn't sure he heard her, but she texted Flaco back anyway.

OK.

That was all she said; then Flaco responded CALL and the phone rang. Grace looked from Antwone to the faceplate—CALLER ID BLOCKED and texted Flaco again.

POS—shorthand for "Parents Over Shoulder," which was a catchall for not being able to answer a call, among other things.

Flaco texted OK. CALL L8R.

OK, Grace texted back. GTG. Got to go.

She hung up. Antwone was going down the lonesome meltdown road; she tried to wait him out, took a seat and bore witness. She had never seen anyone cry so hard in her entire life, and she had seen a lot of tears.

The phone rang. CALLER ID BLOCKED.

POS, she texted.

No reply.

Antwone kept crying. Grace was getting so antsy she thought she might break out in hives. She checked the time on his cell phone and told herself she would wait fifteen more minutes before she tried to get him to stop.

Or twenty.

The phone rang. CALLER ID BLOCKED. She took a deep breath and said, "Antwone, if you want justice for Zack, we need to move on this. You need to answer the phone."

He just looked at her, so ragged and spent and miserable that she felt her cop self shut down. She detached and went on automatic. Her walls went up, the shell around her heart hardening, so she could do her job.

She held the phone out to him. For a second, she thought he was going to throw up.

"Yeah," he said, connecting. "Yeah, Flaco."

Grace closed her eyes and heaved a sigh. Nodded. She pulled out her notebook and wrote, "Get specific address."

"Yeah, okay, where?" he asked, then gestured for Grace's notebook. She handed him her pen. He wrote down an address on Reno.

Then he hung up. He took a deep, ragged breath. "He says this is his house. He wants me there at ten."

"Good, Antwone. I'm going with you. You go in and make the buy and I'll come in after you."

He frowned at her. "That's entrapment, man."

Grace shook her head, even though it was. "It's not. It's not at all. We think he has Zack's laptop. And we need it. We need to see what's on it."

When he didn't say anything, she folded her hands and rested her elbows on her knees. "Antwone, Flaco is an asshole. At the very least, you can help me get him off the streets. That's one less—"

He whipped his head up. "There's too many assholes. Every time I see you, you tell me about someone else who hurt Zack. And *I* get hurt. And it will never, ever stop." Tears rolled down his cheeks. "I only wanted to love him, you know? And now he's dead."

"I know," Grace said, "and you have cause, Antwone. You have cause. But you've been dealing drugs. *You're* one of the assholes. It's the truth. And you know it."

He wrapped his hands around his head. "We just wanted to make enough money so we could get away—"

"It doesn't matter why," she said, scooting her chair closer to his. "It matters that you did it." She wrapped her hand around his forearm; he tried to jerk away but she wouldn't let him. "Flaco might have murdered Zack. You need to stay with me, and help me find out what happened."

Grace left a couple of messages for Ham and followed Antwone's old Corolla. Grace realized they were back in the same part of town where they'd searched for the '64 lowrider Impala. She had a moment's pause where she tried to put Flaco together with Big Money—they both had drugs in common—and she called Antwone on his cell phone. Suddenly she felt very wrong about what they were doing. She should have called her captain, tried to get a warrant.

"When we get there, drive past," she said. "I'll call you."

They glided over wet streets, past blasted-out tenements and then one or two gentrified streets. He made a right and she stayed close behind. They were on North Twenty-third; there was a little frontage road; and they passed the street number. It was a small brick house surrounded by what appeared to be azalea bushes. The porch light was out.

She called Antwone. "Pull over now," she said.

He complied, and she felt a tightness in her chest. He was a kid. She was considering putting him in harm's way. So she could figure out why another kid was dead.

This is wrong.

She sat behind the wheel and clenched her teeth. Then she got out of Connie and walked over to the Corolla. She rapped on the driver's-side window and he rolled it down.

"Go home," she said. "Go now."

He frowned. "Hey, what?"

"I'm going by myself," she said. "You can't go in there. It's too dangerous."

"But you said," he began, and when she didn't change her expression, he shook his head. "I have to go in. He's not expecting you."

"Go home," she said again. Then she turned away and walked toward the little house. Drew her weapon. She shouldn't go in alone. She knew it. She was doing it anyway.

Antwone pulled away from the curb. Good.

Her cell phone rang. It was Ham.

"I'm going in," she said.

"Grace, no. We need a warrant," he said. "If you get the laptop without a warrant, we can't use it."

"We don't have enough for a warrant," she said. "We have no proof that the laptop has got anything we need or that it's inside Flaco's house."

"If Antwone goes in to make the buy, you can go in," he said. "It's a raid. You can do a search."

"No. I sent him home," she said.

"Grace, Flaco's a dealer. He knows Antwone."

"Zack knew him, too."

"At least wait for me," he said. "Please. Tell Antwone to call him and say he's running late."

"That's bullshit, Ham," she replied.

Her phone vibrated. It was Antwone. "Hold on," she said to Ham, switching over to Antwone's call.

"I'm at his back door," he whispered. "I'm there now."

She gripped the phone. "Shit. No. Get the hell out of there."

"Hey, man," a voice said. "I told you to use the front door."

"I'm sorry, Flaco," Antwone replied. He disconnected his cell phone.

Shit, shit, shit. She switched over to Ham. "Antwone's inside. I'm going in."

"On my way. I'll bring backup."

"No lights, no sirens." She disconnected and ran like the devil, straight up to the windy, wet bushes to find a five-foot-tall chain-link gate behind them. Praying that Flaco had no confederates posted, she climbed it—no razor wire, thank God—and landed as softly as she could in slippery mud, to one side of a cement walk. She crawled on her hands and knees past the front of the house; then rose and hunched over, wiping her hands on her jeans, drawing her weapon again, and moving, swift and deadly.

She went past a dark window and then a brick chimney; then she saw the two of them framed in a window with diamond-shaped panes, recognizing Flaco from his mug shots. He was true to his nickname—*flaco* meant "skinny" in Spanish—addict-thin, bald, with a hooked nose, and a long bandito-style mustache. He was wearing a black sweatshirt and jeans, and there was a Glock in his hand. He was patting Antwone down. The two looked to be alone.

And the back door was still open. It was a wooden door with a square of glass bounded by white wrought-iron grates.

Sucking in her breath, Grace tiptoed on the balls of her boots around the south corner and plastered herself against the side of the house directly beside the door. Her heart was pounding, and she held her breath so she could at least hear what they were saying. And then she realized she could see Flaco reflected in the glass in the door. He had the gun, had it, still had it; they were moving to a glass-and-wrought-iron kitchen table.

"Did you bring the money?" Flaco asked.

"Yeah, man," Antwone said.

Grace had no idea if that was true. All this time, she

had never asked Antwone if he could actually make the buy.

Gun up and cocked, she watched Flaco's reflection. His smile showed gaps where teeth were missing. He was not a very attractive man.

But she could have kissed him when he put down his gun to examine an envelope that Antwone had apparently handed him—an envelope she had not seen on him when they'd left his place.

Wait for it, she told herself; since Antwone was going through with the buy, she might as well make as good use of it as she could. Slowly she let out her breath and stared as Flaco held out what looked to be a brick of marijuana wrapped in plastic wrap. He pulled the film off and showed it to Antwone with the air of a waiter allowing a guest to inspect a bottle of wine before he decanted it.

"Want to try it out?" Flaco asked, breaking off a corner and handing it to Antwone.

"Stop! Police!" Grace shouted, bursting through the door. She headed straight for Flaco's gun and grabbed it before he had a chance to. Aimed her weapon at his head, placing herself between him and Antwone.

"On the floor, get on the floor *now,*" she ordered him, advancing on him but staying far enough out of range that he couldn't touch her if he decided to launch himself at her.

But he knew the drill; he went down to his knees and then lay facedown, spread-eagling himself as Grace stood over him, her gun aimed at his head.

"You bastard," Flaco said to Antwone. "You are *dead.*"

Grace patted him down. Finding no more weapons— *moron*—she cuffed him.

She looked at Antwone. "You okay?"

He nodded, but he didn't look very steady. She lowered her voice. "Take a look around."

For the laptop, she meant, and he understood. He walked past the kitchen table farther into the kitchen itself, and started opening drawers and cabinets.

"Hey, what the hell?" Flaco said. "I got rights, man."

"That's right," Grace said. She reached into her pocket and pulled out her copy of the Miranda. She began to read it. "I am Detective Hanadarko, OCPD. You have the right to remain silent—"

"Screw you," he said.

"Anything you say can and will be used against you—"

"Screw you!"

"—in a court of law."

Antwone shook his head. Grace said, "Have you ever used a gun?"

He shook his head again. She gestured him over. "See how I'm holding it? Hold it like that. Flaco, on your rights? Hold that thought."

She handed the gun to Antwone. Crossing her fingers that there would be no incidents, she moved from the kitchen into a dining room packed with boxes of what appeared to be small appliances—toasters, waffle irons, juicers. Add up enough petty theft, you might reach larceny territory, but it would be a stretch.

She passed that room up. "You okay, Antwone?" she called.

"Yes," he called back.

She opened a door and found herself in a darkened room. She felt for a wall switch and found it. Turned on the light. Flaco slept on a mattress on the floor, which didn't surprise her in the least. His pillowcase was smudged and dingy. There was a crack works and a bag of marshmallows beside the mattress. Dirty clothes, muddy boots; a little TV and a DVD player. He'd been watching either porn or *Die Hard*. Had to love that irony.

There was a desk pushed against a wall heaped with clothes and an empty hamster cage. A shotgun. Loaded.

A dresser. Filled with ammo and whack magazines . . . and a laptop. With stickers. Zack's laptop.

"Oh, my God," she blurted, because most of the time, it wasn't that easy. "Earl?" she called, glancing around.

She grabbed it up and slid it beneath her jacket. Came back out to Antwone and smiled at him.

"Where've you been? What did you do?" Flaco bellowed, still facedown on the floor.

"Used your bathroom," she said. She took the gun from Antwone. "Thanks, man," she said. Then she mouthed, *Go home now.*

He shook his head, and she narrowed her eyes at him. She pulled up a chair and sat down, keeping the gun aimed at Flaco. She let Antwone see the laptop. His face broke into a smile and he swallowed hard.

Then he left.

CHAPTER
TWENTY-ONE

"You two played this one awfully damn close to entrapment," Captain Perry said as she, Ham, and Grace sat with the guy from Tech who was opening up the many locked files on Zack's computer. "You've made a mountain of paperwork for yourselves, too."

"Not me," Grace said. "Ham's doing mine." She smiled at him. Captain Kate grunted.

"I don't want to know how you struck that bargain."

"Arm wrestling," Grace told her.

What they found on Zack's laptop was mostly video games, MP3 files, and tons of e-mails between Zack and Antwone. *We'll get some money and we'll get out of here. We'll go to California. I have a cousin in Fresno.*

"*Fresno*. Have you ever been to Fresno? Oh, dear God, they might as well have stayed in Oklahoma City," Captain Perry murmured.

"This is bullshit," Grace announced. "What on earth was so great that—"

"Look," the tech guy said.

A short movie began to run: Darkness, and then a light going on. Grace recognized the bathroom where the packing boxes had been stashed, seen from the counter pointing toward the toilet. Cherie stepped into view. She was wearing a floral nightgown, and she turned and shut the door; from the forced perspective, her arm looked enormous.

Then she walked toward the toilet.

"Okay, this is getting weird," Ham said.

She lifted the lid off the tank and laid it on the counter. Reached inside and pulled out a fifth of what appeared to be gin. She uncapped it and put it straight to her lips.

The four watched in silence as she sat on the toilet seat and kept drinking. Then the movie ended.

"That's it?" Grace asked. "That's what he had on her?" She looked at Ham. "Do you think Cherie would kill Zack because he knew she was boozing in secret?"

Ham made a face and shrugged.

"Can we have a warrant?" Grace asked the captain. "There were roofies in Zack's tox results. Rhetta found fibers consistent with a truck. If the Laceys have a truck—"

She sighed. "If you can manage to talk a judge out of one, you can use it."

"Hot damn." Grace grinned.

"Ron's on a short run today," Grace said as she and Ham pulled up to the gate in front of the Lacey compound. It was midmorning, and they'd taken Connie. The American flag was not flying. Ron was probably the one who raised her every morning. "Paul's probably at school. So maybe Cherie's home alone. Maybe she's passed out cold in the bathroom."

Naturally they hadn't called ahead: *Hello, can we come over and serve you with a warrant? We're looking for anything you don't want us to see.* It didn't matter if anyone was home. They didn't need consent to search. The warrant was their ticket in.

Ham got out and pushed on the gate. Open, as before. Ham walked it wide so Connie could drive on through. Then together he and Grace went to the front door.

Grace had just rung the doorbell when the garage door opened and a big, shiny black four-by-four not unlike Ham's roared out of the garage and screamed down the driveway. Cherie was behind the wheel, and Paul Finch sat beside her, staring out of the window straight at Grace. The tires squealed as it took the corner from the driveway to the road too hard, but Cherie righted it and floored it with the finesse of a NASCAR driver.

"Shit!" Grace yelled as she and Ham slammed back into her Porsche and took off after her. Ham put her light on the roof and called Dispatch. He read the Laceys' license-plate number off the warrant and advised that they were in pursuit, and their subjects might be armed.

"Ham, she killed him," Grace said.

"Or Paul or Ron did."

"I say it's her. Blow job."

"You're on."

She burned rubber.

"You made it through Visiting Day," Earl said to Leon.

Leon grunted. "Man, I don't have that many more visiting days. Tamara knows that."

"Kinda hard for them to have a life and spend every Sunday down here, I reckon." Earl pulled a harmonica from his jeans pocket and handed it to Leon. "You can play the blues, if you want."

"Don't make fun of me," Leon snapped at him. "Or—"

"Or what? You ever wrestled with an angel, Leon?"

Leon's shoulders slumped. He dropped the harmonica on the floor; the clatter echoed as if he'd thrown it down a well.

"He's all I got to live for," Leon said.

"That's not true," Earl said. "You've got God to live for."

"So is God punishing me? Keeping my son away from

me so I'll pray better? Exercise?" He said the last word
like it was the dirtiest word he'd ever spoken.

Earl looked aggrieved. "How many times do I have to
tell you? God don't work that way."

"What if I don't believe you?" Leon flung at him,
stomping to the opposite side of the cell.

"Well, who else are you going to believe?" Earl asked
him, making a show of looking around the cell for a
third party. "I mean, I think I'm it."

"It's not fair. She took him from me and it's— Not.
Fair."

"Life's not fair," Earl agreed. "But life is good. Even
your life. That's what God wants you to believe. If you
could find just a smidge of joy—"

"Are you crazy? I'm sitting on death row."

"But you ain't dead yet," Earl said. He looked hard at
Leon. "That's the gift. You have to accept that gift before you make any more progress. Or else . . . we're at a
roadblock."

"Oh, my God, Henry," Rhetta said as they ate lunch
together. She was having leftover tuna casserole. Henry
had a ham sandwich. Grace's squad were all in the field.
"A gay-orcism, can you believe it?"

Henry sighed. "It's going to be all over the news."

"That's a huge church," Rhetta said. "Grace told me
they have over a thousand members."

"It fills a need." Henry drank his diet soda.

"Past tense, I'm thinking. Unless Pastor Andy can distance himself far enough from Pastor Marc. Do you
think Pastor Andy knew?"

"I don't know," Henry said. "It sounds like the Spanish Inquisition."

"Part of my church's not-so-illustrious past." She took
a bit of tuna casserole, sighed, and set down her fork.

"And your church survived it." Henry picked up his ham sandwich.

"Yeah, but we're not a cult of personality. Our teachings are what unite us." She thought a moment and fingered the gold cross around her neck. "I guess that's not true."

Henry smiled kindly at her.

She blew air out of her cheeks. "That poor baby, cold and alone in your cooler. I hope they find out what happened to him. My God, I would go crazy. You'd have to just lock me up forever."

"I need to make room in there. I'll have to release him to a funeral home this week," Henry said.

"Yeah." She adjusted her glasses. "How's it going with Lena?"

He sighed, too. "She's moving to Albuquerque. They had an opening there. And . . . it turns out that the guy who broke up with her . . . is going to Albuquerque, too."

"Oh, Henry, I'm so sorry." She laid her hand over his.

"I still have my cat." He gave her a weak smile, and took another bite of his sandwich.

Now they were reaching the Forty, and the bridge that crossed the North Canadian River. Ham requested a 10-52—roadblock—and any minute, Grace expected to hear the whum-whum-whum of a department chopper. Then suddenly, Cherie yanked off the main drag and raced over a frontage road that swooped down toward the riverbank.

Grace ticked her gaze from the back of the truck to the river water and *knew* the way she knew sometimes that this is where Zachary Lacey had come to die.

"This is where she did it, Ham. She dumped him here. The current carried him down into the lock, toward the canal."

It began to rain. Grace flipped on the wipers without

missing a beat. The black truck remained in her sights. She braced herself for shots, for a standoff, a confrontation. They were going to run out of road sooner or later. Ham had his service weapon out. She kept her boot against the floor, and Connie loved her for it.

"Maybe Ron gave her some kind of ultimatum," Ham said. "If she didn't stop drinking, he'd leave her. And she told him she did stop. But Zack caught her so she had to get rid of him."

"He tried to tell his father but he wouldn't believe him. So he caught her on camera," Grace continued. "It's nuts." But they'd seen people get murdered over parking spaces.

The frontage road emptied into a turnaround, with some posted signs about fishing licenses and noodling—catching catfish bare-handed. The truck screeched and slid to the left. The passenger door flew open and Paul Finch jumped out.

Then Cherie flew from the driver's side, wearing a pair of jeans and a Windbreaker. The rain was pouring down on her, and she covered her head as she staggered off the blacktop into the tall grass leading to the river. There was a small wooden pier jutting out over the river with a couple more signs and a trash can.

Grace kept driving until she almost touched the truck's back bumper. Ham opened the door and crouched behind it with his gun drawn. Grace whipped out her weapon and did the same, praying that Cherie was not armed.

"Stop," Grace called.

Ham and Grace both broke into a run. Ham was closer to Paul Finch; he got him down on the ground while Grace kept after Cherie. Cherie leaped onto the landing, and Grace swore under her breath. If that bitch jumped in the water—

"Shit!" Grace yelled as Cherie went in.

Grace lowered her gun and placed it on the pier, tore off her jacket, and jumped in after Cherie. The river was high because of all the rain; in the summer, sometimes it was too shallow for boating. And it was damn cold. She hoped backup came with blankets and hot chocolate. She broke the surface and saw Cherie's head about fifty feet away. She was going down.

Grace got to her and wrapped her arm under Cherie's armpits lifeguard style. She started swimming against the current while Cherie struggled.

"If you don't stop it, I'll knock you out," Grace promised her.

"Just let me drown, let me drown." Cherie sputtered and choked.

"Wish I could," Grace gasped. She saw Ham at the very edge of the pier. "No!" she shouted at him. "We're on our way in."

She heard the blades of a chopper above them. The shriek of sirens.

"Praise the Lord," she said.

Ham sloshed along the bank and helped her pull Cherie out. The woman was sobbing. Paul Finch, in handcuffs, looked down from the pier, and his eyes were bulging from their sockets.

"Mom!" he shouted. "Don't say anything!"

"I didn't mean to do it," Cherie said to Grace. "I just wanted him to loosen up and tell me how much he knew."

The roofies, Grace filled in. "Knew about . . . what you'd done," Grace filled in.

"She didn't do anything!" Paul said.

"It's okay, honey," Cherie told him. Then she began to cry.

"Back in Texas . . . ," Cherie Lacey whispered in the interview room at the station. She was dried off and cuffed to the ring in the table. She had waived her right to an attorney. D.A. would probably have a shit fit. "He hit me. Raped me."

"Your first husband," Grace said. "Back when your name was Charlaine McAllister. You were married to Tom McAllister. You killed him when Paul was six. Drugged him, cuffed him, and set the bed on fire. Allegedly."

She hung her head. "It was self-defense. Paul knew it. He protected me. Never said a word to anyone for eleven years."

"You ran. Committed several counts of identity theft. Then you met Ron. Wanted a shot at a normal life. But you had this weird stepson, Zack."

"And Zack . . . he told me he was onto me. And I . . . I panicked." She started to cry. "I gave him a roofie to make him talk. It wasn't working. I thought. So I gave him another. And it was too much."

"He was overdosing. You forced him into the truck." Rhetta was collecting fibers from that very truck even as they spoke.

"You can't know what Texas was like. The things Tom did . . . it was a nightmare . . . hell . . ." Tears streamed down her face. "He abused Paul. He threatened to kill me so many times."

"Cry me a river," Grace said. "Zack didn't know shit about Texas. He wanted Ron to know you were hiding bottles in the toilet."

Cherie stared at her for a full ten seconds. Her face drained of all color. "Oh, my God." She threw back her head and screamed.

"She thought Zack was dead," Grace told Gus, as she came home from the world's longest day on the job. She was chilled straight down to the bone. "That she'd made him OD on the roofies. So she decided to dump him in the river. But he woke up and tried to get away. Tried to save his own life."

"Brf," Gus said, sitting down so she could properly scratch him behind the ears. But she felt so tired and drained she could hardly lift her hand.

"Paul's baseball bag was in the cab and she went after him. And you know what she told me? 'He didn't struggle for very long.' As if that was a good thing."

She took off her gun and her badge. Stumbled into her bedroom and took off her boots. Lay down fully clothed. Gus hopped up next to her and put his head on her feet.

"Oh, Jesus, Gus," she whispered.

The rain came down and she floated in exhaustion and sorrow, her bed her ark, Gus and the ghost of Zack Lacey her two-by-two companions.

Cry, Earl urged her as she stared into the darkness. *Cry me a river, Grace.*

Two days later. The rain poured down on the cluster at the grave site, umbrellas open, faces sad and lost or maybe a little bored. The casket was shiny dark wood. Grace had sent a funeral spray of roses. Zack's dad was there, looking shell-shocked. Grace wanted to hate him for all the misery he'd put his boy through. He'd beaten Zack and rejected him. Then he'd married a pitiless lowlife murderess who killed his only child.

You had him, she thought. *You had him, and you practically forced him into that river yourself with all your bullying and your stupidity.*

But here he was, in the rain, wearing an ill-fitting, cheap navy blue suit. The pants pooled over the tops of his scuffed black work boots, and the jacket hung on his wide shoulders. His suit was too large for a large man like him, and that struck her as kind of . . . sad. He'd made the attempt, still couldn't pull it off.

He held a dirty khaki ball cap between his hands. His head was lowered, and he was staring at the casket. He was stone-faced, and Grace couldn't read his expression.

She felt dull and heavy and weighed down, as if every muscle in her body had atrophied.

O, God, by whose mercy the souls of the faithful find rest, mercifully forgive the sins of your servants and handmaids, who here and everywhere repose in Christ, that, released from every bond, they may rejoice with you forevermore. We ask this through Christ our Lord.

In his black clerical suit and white collar, Father Pepera was putting his final seal of approval on Zack's funeral. As the group began singing "Salve Regina," Grace shifted her attention to him. It must be driving him crazy, knowing he was burying a gay kid who had neither confessed nor repented, at least as far as he knew.

Ham, Butch, and Bobby stood silently, hats off and heads bowed beneath umbrellas in the heavy rain. Rhetta couldn't come; her daughter was sick. Grace had called Zack's grandmother and given her the fantastic news that her grandson had been murdered. She was grateful.

Antwone stood with a woman who was an older, shorter version of him, without an umbrella; he looked small and alone, beat up and scared. Flaco was in custody, but there were always the assholes at school and the customers Antwone would be unable to satisfy. Grace thought that he and his mother should move to Fresno, or at least get the hell out of Oklahoma.

Janaya Causwell was already in the ground. Patrick Kelly was going to recover, and Butch had agreed to sponsor him in a rehabilitation program. The goal was a job, structure, and possibly, someday, full custody of his daughter.

Big Money had disappeared. For the moment.

At the end of the hymn, the mourners began to depart. Bobby, Ham, and Butch shook hands with Ron Lacey, then hugged Grace. Ham lingered.

"Yeah," she said to his unspoken question. "Come over in about an hour." She needed some alone time first.

"I'm sorry for your loss," she said to Ron Lacey. He looked at her as if he had no idea who she was. Then he nodded. Wife in jail, kid dead. What the hell was he supposed to do with Paul Finch?

She turned to go, and saw, through the rain, the forlorn figure of Juanita Provo, standing with Joe Varisse. Maybe that was why Varisse had acted strangely during their interview; he had a thing with Juanita. As Grace walked toward them, he squeezed Juanita's hand, then hung back as she approached Grace alone.

"I'm so sorry," Juanita said.

Grace looked at her.

"Sorry I couldn't do more for him. That terrible church . . . if he'd come to *my* church . . ."

Grace's lips parted. Juanita still didn't get it. She walked past her, and Juanita started crying.

"Detective," she called, running up to her. "I wanted to help him. You know I wanted that."

Grace stopped, but didn't turn around. "You didn't," Grace said coldly.

She headed for Connie without looking back . . . until the last second, when she began to climb into the driver's seat. At the head of the casket, she saw Earl, wings unfurled, his head dipped low. She couldn't see his face, but was certain, somehow, that he was crying.

When she got home, Earl was there, too. He was wearing a T-shirt that said "Masada," with a silkscreen of a cliff. He glanced down.

"Masada's a holy place in Israel," he told her. "In 37 BC, a bunch of Jewish rebels and their families took their own lives, rather than be taken captive by the Romans."

She blinked at him. "They committed suicide?"

He nodded.

"And that's holy."

"You were pretty rough on Juanita Provo," he said. "She wanted you to forgive her. Absolve her."

"That's your boss's job, not mine."

She heard Ham's truck in the driveway. "All this worrying about forgiveness. Zack never needed forgiveness. He needed justice. And I got him that," she said. "That's what I risk my life for, every goddamn day. And if your boss thinks that's a suicide mission, He can stay on His side of heaven."

She went to let Ham in.

The rain poured down into the river, where Butch's homeless skel had seen someone else stand at the water's edge for three days, and then leave. That one didn't go in. That one chose a different way.

The rain poured down on Grace's house, where she lay in a sleeping tangle with Ham, another candle burning for Zack Lacey. She was dreaming of Leon Cooley. He was walking on the water, like Jesus. And she was sitting in a little boat, bailing like crazy.

"Come on in. The water's fine," Leon said.

Grace jerked awake. She raised her head, listening to the hard patter of the rain. She grabbed her cell phone, and walked into the hall. Dialed a number.

"Hello," said a sad, tired voice.

"Juanita," she began, "it's Grace Hanadarko."

In the living room, Earl was having a chat with Gus. "Squirrels can be fast," he explained. "You gotta ambush 'em. See, when you bark, you warn 'em. You need to be sneaky."

Like you, Grace thought, as she finished her call and walked into the living room. Gus's tongue was hanging out as he listened intently to Earl. Grace smiled faintly, wondering if Earl and Gus really did communicate in some special dog-angel language. God might have appeared on her porch a few times, posing as a reddish brown dog with an enormous tongue, matching a tattoo on Earl's back. Or if it wasn't God, Earl might have a future in law enforcement, if he could stage such elaborate practical jokes.

Earl turned to her. "That was a nice thing you did, calling Juanita."

She shrugged. "Talk's cheap." She walked to the door and watched the falling rain. "He'll never see another rainstorm," she murmured.

"Oh, I think you're wrong about that," Earl said, coming up beside her. "Zack's got a lot to look forward to. And so do you, Grace. God's got big plans for you."

She pursed her lips. Then warmth bloomed behind her, and the rain stopped. It was three a.m., but golden light poured down from the sky and made the rectangle of her door glow. Made her hands glow. She turned to Earl, and he was washed in a blaze of glory so bright she couldn't see his face.

"Why do you have to fight so hard?" he asked.

"Because that's me," she replied. "That's who I am, Earl. A fighter."

The brilliance faded, and Earl smiled at her. "You got me there."

"Sorry to disappoint you." Although in all honesty, she wasn't sorry. She really didn't give a damn what he thought. God could take her or leave her.

"I'm not disappointed," Earl replied. He chuckled. "And neither is anyone else." He cocked his head. "It's going to be okay, Grace."

"It's okay now." She shrugged. "I'm going back to bed."

"Sweet dreams."

She pointed at him. "*No* dreams. I just want to sleep." She moved past him, waving at him. "Good night, Earl."

"Night, Grace."

Gus's toenails clattered as he followed her down the hall. Ham murmured in his sleep as Gus hopped onto the bed and snuggled up to Grace's feet. She looked at the candle, and felt the beginning of a tear welling in her eye. She swallowed it away and stared, long and hard. Silent.

In some religions, what she was doing was praying. And, Earl noted with true angelic joy, she was good at it.

Earl thought of a quote by Antoine de Saint-Exupéry, one of his favorite writers: *If you want to build a ship, don't herd people together to collect wood and don't assign them tasks and work, but rather teach them to long for the endless immensity of the sea.*

Longing was praying, Grace style. Longing for life, and justice, and the whirlwind. Longing as Earl had rarely seen, in his long and endless life.

And so . . . there was hope for Grace, God's beloved lost and ever-so-wild child.

And that was enough.

For now.

ACKNOWLEDGMENTS

My deep and humble thanks to Nancy Miller, Holly Hunter, Everlast, and the cast and crew of *Saving Grace*. I am in awe. Thanks also to my fantastic agent and dear friend, Howard Morhaim, and his assistant, Katie Menick. To my editorial squad: Keith Clayton, Liz Scheier, and Kelli Fillingim, my deepest gratitude. My appreciation as well to Debbie Olshan. Thanks to Katharine Ramsland, Lee Lofland, Jonathan Hayes, Phyllis Middleton, and Wally Lind of crimescenewriters. And thanks to Dave Lindo of OKC Kayak.

Thank you, my Grace-daughter, Belle. You are a cowgirl, baby. Shake it up.

Read on for an excerpt from Nancy Holder's

SAVING **GRACE**
TOUGH LOVE

Published by Ballantine Books

"Fight," Grace told the dying boy.

Definite drive-by. Probable DOA—dead on arrival. Sixteen, maybe, and his life was nearly over.

Not yet, though. He had backup: Grace Hanadarko and Ham Dewey, OCPD Major Crimes. They were busting their humps to keep him alive. While Grace tried to stanch the flow of blood from the grievous, life-sucking wound, her partner talked to 911. Ham spoke calmly but loudly into the phone, running down the pertinent information: location, location, location; victim's condition. By Ham's questions and answers, Grace knew a squad car was en route for backup—lights and sirens—and an ambulance was practically there. But help wasn't there yet, and it might not come soon enough.

The pitch-black alley stank of rotten food and dog shit; it was a terrible place to die. Wind pitched grit, gravel, and fetid newspapers against Grace's face. The knees of her jeans were soaking up blood and rock chips as her bare hands slipped in and out of the hole in the kid's chest. The hole. The big, gaping, fatal hole that was expelling blood like an Oklahoma gusher.

He can make it, she told herself.

The hole that was too big—

He will make it. He will.

She had violated procedure by not taking the time to snap on a pair of latex gloves before she went to work. Maybe someone else would lose focus and fret about that, spin a mental mini-drama about getting a positive result on the subsequent HIV test they would take. But she wasn't someone else, and right now she had this kid's whole world in her hands.

Despite the buffeting wind, Ham held the long black flashlight steady while he stayed on the line with dispatch. Grace's world was reduced to a circular yellow glow, a spotlight. The boy's complexion was very black, almost purple-black; she couldn't tell if he had gone cyanotic, which would not be a good sign. But if this murder came to trial she was saying that there had been enough light for the shooter to see this short, scrawny boy, this unarmed teenager who was gurgling and dying. Plenty of illumination for the bastard to hit what exactly what he'd been aiming for: a one-way ticket to hell.

"Live," Grace ordered him. Then something happened to his eyes: they fluttered open, and she felt a thrill down her back as they focused on her. "Come on. You can do it. You can—"

His eyes widened. She saw him seeing her. He was aware, and with her. Ham's flashlight shone like a halo.

"Yeah," she said. "Good. Stay with me."

Then they went dull and glassy, and she knew he wasn't seeing anything. Her hands slid in the wound, and she set her jaw. If they got him to a

hospital, got a transfusion going, got a team working on him—

"Grace," Ham said softly. "Grace. He's gone."

She was silent a moment, aware that she was panting and that icy sweat was sliding down her face.
Her back muscles were spasming. Her knees felt like
ground glass was embedded in them.

Pain. Hurt. World of hurt. The boy, gone . . .

Then she said, "To hell with that," and pressed her
hands over the boy's wound again.

And she didn't let go until the ambulance came.

Around eleven that night, Grace blew into her
house along with the fierce, near gale-force winds,
her long, curled blond hair brushing the shoulders
of her black suit jacket as she shut the front door
and leaned against it, her head back, her dressy
boot heels flush. Overcome with exhaustion, she
wiped her eyes. She was wearing the change of
clothes she kept in her locker at the office: black
trousers, white shirt, matching jacket—like the
damn FBI.

A few drinks at Louie's had done nothing to dull
the knife of the condolence call she had made to the
overcome, overwhelmed, meth-addicted mom of the
victim. He had a name now—Haleem Clark—and
from the looks of it, he had bled out in that alley
after being shot while making a drug buy for his
mother. Some kids get sent to the store for a loaf of
bread. Haleem died fetching a chunk of crystal for
Mommy Dearest.

This was how Grace and Ham figured it went
down: The dealer met Haleem and they began to

conduct their business. Then Mr. Dealer saw something he didn't like, and took off down the alley. They guessed that would have been the vehicle carrying the shooter. Maybe it was someone he owed money to. Or sold bad drugs to. Or maybe he just saw the glint of a weapon.

Whatever the case, he was smart to run because someone in the vehicle shot at him. At least once. Rhetta Rodriguez, head of the crime lab and Grace's best friend since kindergarten, had extracted a bullet from the exploded remains of a pile of dog shit, and it sure looked like it had come from a Sig P220 to the two of them. Grace and Rhetta were both assuming Haleem's gut shot came from the same weapon. Rhetta would get back to Grace after ballistics made their report.

Despite the Sig's reputation as an accurate weapon, the shooter still missed the dealer. So Mr. Killer made another pass in his vehicle, leaving nice deep tire tracks in the mud that Rhetta's lab was already working on. Also, by tracing Haleem's shoe prints through the mud and garbage, Grace surmised that Haleem had run toward the vehicle, maybe assuming the occupants would recognize him, or else spare an innocent bystander.

Maybe the shooter didn't like Haleem. Maybe he didn't like black kids buying drugs. Whatever the motive, he—or she—took out Haleem on a second attempt, the vehicle hanging a U and driving by him again. They couldn't quite figure out why he hadn't been shot in the back—why he hadn't dashed headlong back into the alley to get out of the line of fire. It was almost as if he had stood waiting to take a bullet while the vehicle took the time to drive past him one more time.

That second pass was Grace's judicial ace in the hole. Coming back around implied intent and premeditation. That invited stiffer penalties, including the needle. If praying for an execution would get it done, then Grace was all for praying.

Okay, then, maybe just crossing her fingers.

Someone called in the shooting (though of course no witnesses came forward during the subsequent canvass), and dispatch sent Grace and Ham over, as they were already in the vicinity, working on a liquor store burglary. As first on the scene, they rendered assistance. The victim strangled on his own blood anyway.

At sixteen.

Grace went to the mom's while Ham attacked their shitpiles of paperwork; afterward, they went for drinks at Louie's. With their first toast—two longnecks chased with tequila shots—Grace swore she would find the shooter, find him and strap him to the same gurney in the same death chamber where Leon Cooley had died, unless someone else got him first.

As for Haleem's mom, she'd wailed like a banshee when family services came for her three other kids, screaming that she'd just lost one baby, and how could they do this to her? High as a kite, and there was no food in the house, and the littlest one was wearing nothing but a filthy diaper and some flea bites.

"She might as well have pulled the trigger herself," Grace muttered. She felt a million years old.

Then toenails clattered, and Bighead Gusman, her

white bulldog, greeted her with his nose against her kneecap and a low, happy moan. Without lifting her head or opening her eyes, she gave him a good scratch and a pat. Some of the storm clouds dissipated as he chuffed in response and led her toward the kitchen, where he knew that his five-star dinner sat waiting for him in a family-size can. Grace remembered only then that she had a fresh rawhide bone shaped like a barbell out in the car. With a couple of snorts, Gus assured her that he was happy to see her even if she never brought him home another chew toy in his life. He was always happy to see her. She smiled very faintly.

Okay, so maybe there was life after death, and dogs were in charge of it.

"Evenin', Grace," Earl said, as she grabbed a beer out of the fridge. One minute she and Gus were alone; the next, her last-chance angel was standing beside her in the kitchen. Earl did that, just showed up; it used to be the sight of him was enough to set her teeth on edge. Now, as with her Gussie, she was glad Earl was there.

By all appearances, Earl was a fifty-something workin' man with straggly teeth and tousled brown and gray hair. He was wearing a gray jacket with a couple of militaristic-looking badges over a plaid shirt, which was itself over one of his signature T-shirts—a photograph of a tornado and the words OKLAHOMA'S FIFTH SEASON. Ha, got that right. Jeans and black athletic shoes completed his ensemble. But he also had a pair of golden, feathery wings that he kept tucked away, unless he had to fly off to France or Milwaukee, or hold a dying child in his arms.

When even one feather brushed Grace, it made her feel stoned and orgasmic. Blissful. She needed some bliss, just about now. Haleem Sampson Clark had not died in a state of bliss.

"Hey, Earl." The fridge door hung open; she raised her brows and paused, in case he wanted one, too. Earl nodded. She grabbed three beers and checked the level on the tequila bottle that was sitting next to an opened box of pancake mix. The bottle was nice and full. Grace was counting her blessings.

Earl took one of the longnecks and held it up, toasting. "To Haleem."

They clinked, threw back. One of the things Grace loved about beer was that the seventh one tasted as fantastic as the first one. Every time.

"Where is he now?" she asked him, pushing coils of hair away from her eyes. "There a ghetto in heaven, too? Angels fly by now and then, and wave, then go hang out in the nicer neighborhoods?"

Earl smiled at her sadly with world-weary eyes. "You know heaven don't work that way, Grace."

"I don't know shit," she retorted, as she crossed to the side door and forced it open against the stabbing wind. She made kissy noises at Gus. "Go wee-wee, Gusman."

As her housemate trotted happily past her, she said, "I take that back. I do know shit. I know that kid is dead."

"Dead in this world," Earl concurred. "But in the next, he's only dead to pain and sorrow."

"Like I said." A frustrated sigh escaped her. She didn't think every single word coming out of Earl's mouth was bullshit anymore, but she also wasn't quite sure how much was lifted from the in-house marketing memos God circulated every morning, versus how much was stuff Earl made up on the spot. Or maybe some of it might actually be true.

"And Haleem knows his mama loves him, in her way," he added.

"Yeah, loved him to death." Grace grabbed the tequila bottle. "Just like God and Jesus, huh? God loved His only begotten Son so much He let Him hang there, suffering . . . " She trailed off, as tired of her own cynicism as she was sure Earl was.

"You should close that pancake mix," Earl said. "It's going to spoil."

"Clay's coming over tomorrow night. We'll finish it off." Still, she set down the tequila bottle and crimped the edges of the plastic bag together. Then she opened up Gus's can of wet food and thwunked the massive, chunky cylinder into his bowl. Broke it up nice with a spoon and then set it on the floor as she opened up the side door again. The wind slammed it wider; she jumped; Earl did not. Equally unruffled, Gus sashayed in, harrumphed his thanks, and dug in.

"Good thing he ain't a Chihuahua," Earl drawled, and Grace grunted.

"Yeah, he'd be long gone by now." She smiled affectionately at her puppy guy. "Gone with the wind."

She leaned against the breakfast bar, awash in weariness. The last of her street-induced adrenaline had long ago burned off, leaving her to crash, hard. Crashing was difficult to take, so cops pulled brutal practical jokes and swore and drank too much and had libidos to match the need to stay alert so they could stay alive. Ham got that—the prime directive to mix it up—or rather, he used to, until he started feeling sentimental about her instead of simply lustful. Now he was muddying the waters of their firecracker partnership with buzzkill feelings.

Did Earl understand that she had to drum it up to keep it up? She had a demanding profession; she had to stoke her fires to keep burning bright. Tonight he just smiled his pleasant, accepting smile and drank with her in silence. Her mind went over and over what she had done, and what she had failed to do. If they'd gotten there sooner, if she'd tried harder to stanch the wound. It was such a bitch when her best still wasn't good enough.

She should have saved that kid.

"Sto... *plating*... *underst... Interrupt* ... *the mess... of you. It's so very, very easy to lose yourself this way."*

She still couldn't breathe or think properly. She was furious that she needed to leave one hand against him to steady herself. She was furious at him for being right. And for being so bloody self-righteous.

And for being steady on his feet as he regarded her.

And then she realized he was trembling. She could feel it beneath her palm.

He was a seasoned rogue, and that kiss had shaken him.

Suddenly this unnerved her more than the kiss itself.

"Is that why you do it?" she asked softly. Ironically. "To lose yourself?"

Swift anger kindled in his eyes. "Have a care."

She took her hand away from him finally, slowly, as if he were a rabid dog and would lunge at her if she made any sudden moves. She was steady on her feet now. Her breathing had nearly resumed its usual cadence. She couldn't yet back away; he maintained a peculiar gravitational pull. She could still feel the warmth of his body on her skin. She wondered distantly if she always would. As if she'd been branded.

"What if I want to be lost?" she whispered.

By Julie Anne Long

Julie Anne Long

Between the Devil and Ian Eversea

AVON

An Imprint of HarperCollinsPublishers

AVON BOOKS
An Imprint of HarperCollins*Publishers*
10 East 53rd Street
New York, New York 10022-5299

Copyright © 2014 by Julie Anne Long
ISBN 978-0-06-211811-0
www.avonromance.com

First Avon Books mass market printing: April 2014

10 9 8 7 6 5 4 3 2 1

Acknowledgments

MY DEEPEST GRATITUDE TO my darling editor, May Chen; my stalwart agent, Steve Axelrod; the talented, hard-working staff at Harper Collins; and all the wonderful readers who let me and everyone else know how much my books mean to you.

Between
the Devil and
Ian Eversea

Chapter 1

IF INNOCENCE HAD A color, it was the rain-washed silver-blue of Miss Titania Danforth's eyes.

Her spine was elegantly erect against the back of her Chippendale chair, her hands lay quietly in her lap; her white muslin day dress was as spotless as an angel's robe. She would have in fact been the picture of serenity, if not for her lashes. They were black, enviably fluffy, and very busy. They fluttered up. They fluttered down. They fluttered up again. Then down again. As if she could only withstand the potent gaze of the Duke of Falconbridge in increments.

A bit the way a virgin might sip at rotgut gin, the duke thought dryly.

Then again, even grown men found him disconcerting. Disconcerting was what the duke did best, without even trying.

Two hours earlier Miss Danforth's companion hired for the ocean voyage to England—a redoubtable barrel-shaped woman of middle years whose name the duke had promptly forgotten—had delivered her along with nearly a dozen trunks, and with an irony-tinged "Good *luck*, Yer Grace," departed with startling haste. No teary, lingering good-byes between her and Miss Danforth. But then, long ocean voyages could play havoc with even a saint's nerves, and familiarity was a well-known breeding ground for contempt.

And now that Falconbridge had seen his cousin's daughter, he was certain no luck was necessary. Her faultless breeding was in every word she spoke. Her voice was pleasant, low and precise, with a very becoming husk to it.

But her beauty astonished.

As if to affirm his conclusions, a great sheet of afternoon light poured in the window and made a corona of her fair hair. She might as well have been wearing a bloody halo.

On the whole, however, sheltered women irritated him. He never knew what to say to them. They taxed his patience. But the future of this particular sheltered woman was now his responsibility, thanks to an almost-forgotten promise he'd made many years ago.

A promise his cousin had seen fit to immortalize in his will.

The surreptitious press of his wife's knee against his stopped him from sighing aloud or muttering under his breath or any of the things she knew he was tempted to do. He reflected for a moment on the multitude of glorious things that could be communicated with a knee press. That he was known, loved, fortunate beyond all reason, and could afford to be charitable when the beautiful, gloriously kind young woman at his side on the settee was his. Genevieve was never dull. She'd never had a prayer of being dull, having been raised an Eversea.

Fortunately, he'd done most of his underbreath cursing when the succinct, ever-so-faintly harried letter from Miss Danforth's solicitor had arrived two months ago.

Genevieve said brightly, "I understand the crossing from America can be . . ."

She paused as two footmen appeared in the doorway, their knees wobbling under the weight of a profusion of brilliant hothouse blooms stuffed into an urn.

"For Olivia?" Genevieve said this almost with resignation.

"Yes, my lady."

"I think there might be a little room on the mantel."

The footmen shuffled into the room and hoisted the urn up with little grunts. Miss Danforth followed their progress to and fro with wide, wondering eyes.

The long stems continued quivering for a time after they departed.

"I was saying," Genevieve continued smoothly, "I understand the crossing can be grueling indeed, but the sea air seems to have agreed with you. You look radiant, Miss Danforth. What a delight it is to meet such a pretty cousin!"

Miss Danforth glowed. "You're too kind! Truly,

the crossing from America was mercifully un-eventful. I understand I come from hearty stock."

The lashes went up again and her eyes were limpid. She looked about as hearty as a blown dandelion. He humored this transparent attempt at flattery with a faint smile. "Certainly, Miss Danforth, our stock, as you say, has withstood any number of buffetings over the centur—"

"... *aaaaannnnnnnn* ...!"

He swiveled his head. High-pitched, very faint, very sneaky, a sound floated into the room. It was impossible to know from which direction it came. It waxed and waned, a bit like the whine of a diving mosquito.

He glanced at his wife, who was sporting a faint, puzzled dent between her eyes.

Miss Danforth, on the other hand, remained unruffled. She gave no appearance of having heard a thing, unless one counted a slight further straightening of her spine. Her eyes were bright with curiosity now. Perhaps she thought men of his advanced age—he had just turned forty—naturally acquired twitches and tics, and she was prepared to be sympathetic and tolerant.

"Your home is remarkably beautiful," she said. "And so very grand."

"We're so pleased you think so," Genevieve said warmly. "I loved growing up here. Falcon-bridge is indulging me in a hunt for another home nearby, so we can live near my family for at least part of the year. But I cannot wait to show you the grounds! Though I'm certain it will all seem rather tame compared to America, Miss Danforth."

Miss Danforth's laugh was like bells. "I daresay it isn't as exciting as you might think, though it certainly is different from England. Oh, and I do hope you'll come to call me Tansy! All my friends do."

Both Genevieve and the duke paused. There *was* a bit of American expansiveness to her manners, as if all those wide-open spaces across the ocean caused them to stretch indolently, the way one slouches in a chair when no one is about to impress. The duke smiled faintly.

"We'll have such fun introducing you to society, Tansy," his wife indulged. "How exciting New York must be, but oh, we do manage to have a lovely time here! Do you enjoy dancing? We've a splendid array of activities planned for you."

"Oh . . . well, I fear I'm a bit of a wallflower. Life has been a bit . . ." She cleared her throat. ". . . a bit quiet, you see, for the past year or so."

The lashes stayed down and there passed a little moment of silence. For they did see. Her parents had been killed in a carriage accident a little over a year ago, her older brother had died in the War of 1812 before that, and that left Miss Danforth alone in the world. Save, of course, for the duke, who was now charged with marrying her off to a title spectacular enough to match the girl's fortune, which would only be released to her in its entirety when the match was made. Her future, essentially, was in the duke's hands.

So dictated her father's will.

His cousin had decamped from Sussex to America when the girl sitting before him was only eight years old. The duke had always hoped to see him again, for they'd been close, and the duke's close friendships were few.

"... *aaaaaaannnnforth* ... !"

Bloody hell—there the sound was again. So eerie, nearly ghostly, it almost stood the hairs on the back of his neck on end. He whipped his head about again. But not before he saw Miss Danforth's eyes fly open wide, then give an infinitesimal guilty dart toward the window and back again.

He narrowed his eyes at her.

Her smile never dimmed. Her hands remained neatly folded in her lap. She met his gaze bravely.

"Perhaps a sheep fell into a drainage ditch?" Genevieve suggested into the ensuing silence. "Poor thing."

"... *oooooooove you* ... !"

The sound was quite discernible as a voice now.

A *man's* voice.

"Per ... perhaps it's the wind?" Miss Danforth had tried for casual, and almost but not quite succeeded. "Wind" was more a squeak than a word.

Miss Danforth jumped when the duke stood abruptly.

"I'll just have a look, shall I?" He crossed the room in three strides. He pushed the window open and a stiff breeze hoisted the curtains high, like a villain brandishing his cape.

He peered out. On the green, far below the window, a man was down on his knees, his hands clasped in the universally understood gesture of beseeching, his head thrown back so far his mouth looked like a little dark O. And from this O issued howls of what sounded like tormented passion.

"Miss Daaaaaanfooooorth! I loooooooove you! Please just one word, I beeeeeggg of you! Do not forsake me!"

The duke eyed this pathetic scene for a moment.

And then he turned around very, very slowly, and stared at the now silent and very wide-eyed Miss Danforth.

He was silent for so long that when he launched his brows upward in a silent question she jumped. "Does that voice sound familiar, Miss Danforth?"

She cleared her throat.

"Oh . . . dear. That does sound like Mr. Lucchesi. He was a passenger on my ship, and I fear he may have nurtured a . . ." Pretty color flooded her face. ". . . a *tendre* which I assure you I do not return, though I took great pains to ensure I was all that was polite and my behavior was all that was appropriate. He must have . . . he must have somehow followed me from the ship."

Probably her open American manners were at fault. Although, admittedly, Lucchesi wasn't bellowing "Tansy!"

". . . *pleeeeeeaaaaase* . . ." The forlorn word drifted into the window.

"He's Italian," Miss Danforth added into the ensuing dumbstruck silence.

"Ah," said Genevieve sympathetically, as if that explained everything.

Miss Danforth shot her a look of gratitude.

"These things happen," Genevieve embellished.

At this, her husband's eyebrows shot upward again.

"Not to *me*, of course," she hastened to add. "But my sister Olivia . . . well, you've seen the flowers." She waved in the general direction of the mantel. "Men have always thrown themselves at her feet. They're forever sending flowers. They make embarrassing wagers about when she'll be married in the Betting Book at White's and . . ."

She trailed off when she saw what was no doubt incredulity writ large on her husband's features.

"Careful, my dear," he said. "It's beginning to sound like an endorsement."

She grinned at that and he grinned back, and there passed an infinitesimal moment during which they were the only two in the world.

Miss Danforth's voice intruded.

"I am so terribly sorry to inconvenience you, when you've been so kind and welcoming!" Miss Danforth's hands wrung. "I never dreamed . . . that is, I could not anticipate . . . to follow me onto your grounds! I am *appalled* that—"

The duke held up a hand. "Do you wish to speak to Mr. Lucchesi, Miss Danforth?"

She shook her head so vigorously the two blond curls flagellated her cheeks like a cat-o'-nine tails.

"Do you wish *me* to have a word with Mr. Lucchesi?"

"No! That is, I'd rather you didn't. That is . . . Oh, I wish he would just go away." She ducked her head again. And said nothing more.

He did sigh then. Mother of God, but she was the veriest babe. The girl was a danger to herself. The sooner he could hand this one off to an appropriate husband, the better. It ought to be a simple enough matter to accomplish, but he would need to keep her out of trouble until that happened. That sort of thing shouldn't present too much of a challenge. Intelligent rogues were afraid of the Duke of Falconbridge and the stupid ones could be dispensed with easily.

One particular rogue, however, warranted a personal warning.

He turned to his wife. "My dear," he said idly, "do you suppose your brother is in Pennyroyal Green at the moment?"

She didn't need to ask *which* brother.

IAN EVERSEA ROLLED over and opened one eye. Mercifully, he'd awakened before the usual dream could really get his talons in, which was one reason he awoke in a cheerful mood.

As he always did after that dream, he stretched his legs and flexed his arms, grateful he still pulled air, grateful he still possessed all his limbs.

Not to mention *another* appendage.

He sighed a long, satisfied sigh and opened his other eye.

The window next to him framed a perfect half of a moon and a few stars. It was evening.

Which meant he'd better leave soon, or he'd ruin his unbroken record of never staying an entire night through.

He rubbed at his ear. "Funny," he muttered.

"What is funny, *mon cher*?" came a sleepy, French-inflected purr next to him. She was the other reason he'd awoken in a cheerful mood.

"My ear is hot."

Monique propped herself up on one elbow and peered at him through her great cloud of auburn hair. A position that mashed her large and delectable breasts together and reminded him of the pleasures of pillowing his head there. An embarrassment of riches, those, just inches from his nose.

"What is it they say when your ear is hot? Someone must be talking about you." She reached out a finger and trailed his ear with it.

"Someone," he murmured with satisfaction as he rolled over to Monique to pull her into his arms and continue the marathon of lovemaking, "is *always* talking about me."

Chapter 2

❧

POOR GIANCARLO.

It was now nearly midnight and Tansy couldn't sleep. She shoved aside an explosively colorful flower arrangement—they seemed to be *everywhere* in this house, apparently thanks to Olivia Eversea—dominating a little table near the window.

She stepped out onto the little balcony into the star-strewn Sussex night. She tried to imagine him down on his knees on the green. He'd likely have been scarce more than a speck of white linen seen from the distance of the third floor window. Mother of God, what a terrible moment—sitting very still, beaming like a loon at the duke and duchess, while the words *bloody hell bloody hell bloody hell* clanged over and over in her head as realization set in. She'd never dreamed he'd *follow* her from the docks, let alone appear beneath the Duke of Falconbridge's window to bellow things like "forsake," of all words. Wherever had he *learned* it? His chief attraction, apart from his liquid brown eyes, had been his mellifluous

murmured Italian (which he never suspected she
mostly understood) interspersed with charm-
ingly fractured English. He must have been reading English poets or some nonsense when he
wasn't romancing her on deck. She didn't know
how reading poetry could ever lead to anything
good.

The Duke of Falconbridge had done little more
than flick an eyebrow and—poof!—Giancarlo had
somehow been spirited away. She'd been assured
she would never have to worry about him again,
and the duke and duchess (the duchess primarily)
had gone on to talk about other things and other
people, so very many people, all family members,
in a voice of such warmth, and she'd been spared
any queries about her association with Mr. Lucchesi.
Because the duke was likely confident he'd ended it.

A speck, indeed. That was what Giancarlo was
to someone like the duke.

The duke. She suspected the duke accomplished
more with a flicked eyebrow than most men did
in a lifetime of toil. He'd been polite, of course,
welcoming, of course, but a bit . . . unyielding. A
bit impervious to her attempts to charm. She'd felt
a little winded after the conversation, as though
she'd been attempting to scale a slippery wall for
an hour only to do nothing but slide down again
and again. It was probably best to nod and agree
a good deal around him. Her father had known
what he was about when he consigned her fate to
the Duke of Falconbridge.

Tansy supposed he could be considered handsome, but he must be forty years old at *least*. So astonishing, given that his wife was so very pretty and was hardly older than she was, and she was twenty.

She recalled the glance they exchanged.

It had reminded her of looks exchanged between her parents. Those looks had always felt like a door ajar on a world she'd never be invited to visit.

She'd loved her parents very much and had been loved, too, she knew, but she also known precisely where she fell in the hierarchy of affection in her family.

She suspected the duke considered her a speck, too. A temporary problem to be handed off to another man, whose problem she would then become. A baton of sorts, in the eternal marriage relay.

So be it. She wrapped her arms around herself and gave a little shiver of anticipation. She *wanted* to be married. Imagine what all of her erstwhile friends in New York would say if she became the Duchess of this or the Countess of that. And if someone could find her a duke for a husband, surely it was another duke?

Likely she'd never see Giancarlo again.

She did feel a minute pang of regret. She'd never anticipated it would all reach such an . . . untidy . . . crescendo. It had begun with a variety of glances—fleeting and lingering, sidelong and direct—sent and intercepted. And then, experimentally, she'd timed a pretend slip on the foredeck just as he was passing; her hand had curled over his arm as he helped her to right herself, and as she stammered thanks, standing a bit too close, his pupils had gone huge.

This closeness had evolved into an invitation to stroll on the deck.

She understood enough Italian to know that Giancarlo (his bicep tightened beneath her grip when she accidentally-on-purpose breathed his name for the first time—"*Giancarlo*"—as he helped her to her feet again) was saying things no gentleman should say to any proper lady—reckless, stirring, often baffling things. He would like to kiss her. Her lips were like plums. Her lips were like roses. Her ass was like a peach. Her skin was like a lily. All manner of flora and fauna were represented in his compliments. He would like to do other things besides kiss her. She wasn't familiar with Italian slang, more's the pity, because she expected she'd have gotten quite an education.

She'd even mulled allowing him to do one or two of the things he professed to wanting to do. And with each passing day on the ship the lips of her hired companion, Mrs. Gorham, had gone thinner and thinner and thinner and her underbreath muttered warnings grew darker and darker. But Tansy couldn't stop. She was a virtuoso of flirtation who'd been denied an opportunity to practice her art for far too long, and the whole episode had acquired the momentum of a driverless carriage rolling downhill.

It was probably a very good thing the ship had docked when it did.

She ventured out onto the little balcony outside her window and searched the English sky, but she couldn't find the particular constellation she wanted to see. And though she knew it was ridiculous, it was this more than anything that made her feel bereft all over again, as if she were spiraling aimlessly through the heavens, like so much dandelion fluff, inconsequential, destined never to land.

Somewhere out there in the Sussex dark was the home she'd once known and loved fiercely as a little girl. Lilymont. Sold when her father had taken his family off to America. She wondered who owned it now. Her home in New York had been sold, too, as dictated by her father's will, and though she missed it, in a peculiar way it was also a relief. After her parents died, nearly everything once familiar and beloved—from furniture to flowers in the garden—had seemed foreign, even a little sinister, like props in an abandoned theater.

She needed a home of her own. And she wouldn't have a home, a *real* home, of her own again until she was married.

And now the silence seemed total and fraught, like the aftermath of a gunshot, and the dark outside wasn't the dark of thick woods frilling the edges of the New York estate. Even the stars seemed strange and new viewed from this side of the Atlantic. They called the constellations by different names here in England, she recalled. The Big Dipper was called instead the Starry Plough. She was uncertain about the rest of them, but it wasn't as though she'd learned the Queen's English the way she'd learned Italian.

All she knew for certain was that she didn't like the dark, and she didn't like quiet, and she didn't like to be alone.

She reached for a night robe, thrust her arms into it and tied up the bow at the neck, shoved her feet into a pair of satin slippers, seized her lit lamp and tiptoed down the long marble stairs.

Her surroundings were so unfamiliar it was like moving through a dream, and she liked it. It seemed to carry as little consequence; it seemed as though anything could happen, as though anyone or anything could appear, monsters, dragons, princes, ghosts. She almost wished something would appear, simply for novelty's sake. She'd stopped being afraid some time ago.

She found herself in the kitchen by instinct, as if it was the heart of the house and she'd followed the sound of its beat. A slice of bread, perhaps a cup of something hot. She knew her way around a kitchen well enough to heat a kettle.

Unsurprisingly, a vase of flowers going limp from the heat of the kitchen was in the middle of the kitchen table. For heaven's *sake*. She gave her head an imperious little toss. Not too long ago she'd collected bouquets as effortlessly as she collected beaux.

A boy on the hearth snored softly, and stirred and muttered in his sleep. She supposed his job was to turn the grand haunch suspended on a spit over the fire. The haunch was near to being licked at by low flames. It would burn.

"Pssst," she said.

He shot upward, all limbs flailing like an upturned spider for a moment until he righted himself, thrust his fists into his eyes and ground them a bit.

"Cor! I nearly pissed meself, ye scared me so."

"I'm sorry."

He stared at her for a moment. "Are ye an angel?" was his conclusion. He sounded almost accusatory.

"Far from it."

"Was I asleep?"

"You were."

"You be an angel then, m'lady, if you saved me from burning the haunch."

She laughed softly at that. Something about him—the sense of barely repressed mischief, no doubt—reminded her of her brother, who had been everyone's darling. "I imagine you need your rest, and if you give it a crank now it should be fine. I'm Miss Danforth, a guest in the house. I was feeling a bit peckish and—"

"Jordy! I *thought* I heard voices!"

Both the boy *and* Tansy jumped this time. The voice belonged to a small woman who looked as soft and plump and homey as a loaf of rising bread. Rust-colored curls sprang from the confines of her nightcap and were still shimmying on her forehead. Clearly she'd hurried to the kitchen.

"Oh, miss, ye must be Miss Danforth." She curtsied, clutching her voluminous white night robe in her hands. "Mrs. Margaret deWitt at yer service, miss. I be the cook."

"I *am* Miss Danforth, and a pleasure to meet you, Mrs. deWitt. I'm so sorry to disturb you! It's just that I felt a bit peckish, and I—"

Miss deWitt lit up at those words. She *lived* to vanquish hunger and to fuss over young people. "Here now, Miss Danforth, you just sit down and I'll make ye a cuppa and summat to eat. You're a slip of a thing, ain't ye? You ought to have rung and we'd have brought it up."

She was kind. Tansy knew this instinctively; her face, her voice, belonged to a woman who knew her place and liked it well. She felt a temptation to lean toward it, like a flower into the sun. It somehow seemed a safer sort of kindness than the exquisite welcome of the duke and duchess.

"Oh, I couldn't have rung. I didn't want to disturb anyone and the house was so quiet and peaceful and—"

"'Tis no trouble at all to be awakened. Some of us are a bit restless nights, aye, like mice? Shame on ye, Jordy, for botherin' Miss Danforth."

head was lolling, before thunking her own solid behind in a chair across from Tansy.

"Thank you so much, Mrs. deWitt. It was just what I wanted."

Miss deWitt's smile was triumphant. "I knew it! I know a girl who likes chocolate, m'dear. The prettiest ones do."

Tansy felt her pride settle into place again. "Have you worked for the Eversea family long?"

"I've known Miss Genevieve—Her Grace—since she was a wee thing. She was Miss Genevieve Eversea then. Mind ye, now, Genevieve is a beauty, but she's always been quietlike; ye be pretty as an angel yerself," the cook hastened to reassure.

"So I've been tol'—er, that is, you're much too kind."

Tansy rotated her cup of chocolate on the table abstractedly, then stopped. She prided herself on her ability to remain in control of any circumstance, whether it was a ballroom flirtation or an Italian shouting "forsake" up at the window, or reading a message about a carriage accident while the messenger, a curious stranger, looked on and waited for her to regain her ability to speak and breathe and to find a shilling to pay him for delivering the news of the end of her world.

"But 'tis the duchess's sister, Miss Olivia . . . talk about a beauty! She does have a way of turning men into fools for her. And she'll make a grand, grand match, too."

Tansy's pride yanked at its tether. She was used

to stopping conversation when she entered a ball-room. She was used to dropping jaws. *Can you do that, Olivia Eversea?*

It seemed an awfully long time since she'd been in a ballroom.

"Miss Genevieve spoke so affectionately of her brothers and sisters."

"Oh, aye. There's Master Marcus, married to Louisa, and Colin, settled and raising cattle but no babies yet. Miss Olivia, she may be married to a very grand viscount before the year is out, at long last, bless her poor sore heart. And then there's Master Ian . . . Ah, goodness, that is quite a bright moon out the window!" she said abruptly.

Tansy swiveled her head. It was bright, all right, but such was the nature of the moon.

She half suspected the distraction was deliber-ate. Who had Mrs. deWitt just mentioned? Some-one who hadn't been mentioned by either the duke or the duchess earlier today, she was certain of that.

The cook appeared to have abandoned that thread of thought. "'Twill be a simple thing for a young lady such as yerself to make a splendid match. Perhaps even as fine as Miss Genevieve."

She wished people would cease talking about her as if she were simply a shoe missing a mate. If it were *that* easy, surely she would even now be exchanging meaningful world-excluding looks of her own with one of those smitten swains from New York? Many of them had vowed eternal love, and many of them were at *least* as handsome as poor Giancarlo, and one of them had kissed her, because he was bold and she'd dared him. She had liked it, and stopped it immediately because she possessed more sense than her father had no doubt credited her.

Apart from an accelerated pulse, there really had been no consequence. He hadn't captured the whole of her imagination, let alone her heart, for more than a day. And she was certain the man she married should be able to capture both.

Fortunately, she'd made a list of requirements for a husband. She thought the duke would find it helpful.

"You flatter me, surely, Mrs. deWitt," she said.

Mrs. deWitt turned to look at Tansy, speculation written over her soft features. She studied her a moment.

Then she surprised Tansy by reaching over and patting her hand, a familiarity perhaps brought on by the fact that they were all wearing night robes.

"Dinna ye worry about a thing, Miss Danforth."

It was probably a platitude, but it felt, in the dark kitchen, with Jordy somnolently turning the haunch at a soothing rhythm, that Mrs. deWitt had seen into her soul. Suddenly Tansy's throat tightened and her eyes began to burn.

Probably just the steam from the chocolate.

Chapter 3

❧

THE NIGHT WAS JUST beginning to give way to
dawn when Tansy's eyes popped open.

The cloudlike mattress beneath her wasn't
swaying with the motion of the sea. The elegantly
furnished room was all slim lines and dark woods
and gilt and shades of blue. Not America. Not a
ship. *Sussex*. Pennyroyal Green, to be precise.

A stripe of inviting rosy light was pushing its
way through a crack between the curtains.

She drowsily slid out of bed, rubbed her fists in
her eyes, heaved her heavy braid over one shoulder and followed the road like the road to certainty across the deep Savonnerie carpet.

She gently grabbed a fistful of the curtains,
which were gold velvet and soft as kittens, and
peered out the window.

The horizon lay before her in strata of colors:
first the soft manicured green of the Eversea parklands, above that a dark line of trees both fluffy
and pointy, which must be a forest, beyond that
a broad expanse of darker green, mounded like

a tossed blanket, of what had to be the Sussex downs, and finally a narrow strip of silver. Probably the sea.

The sky was just taking on a maidenly blush. She watched as the rising sun gilded mundane things one by one, as if allotting each of them a turn at glory. First a tall, neat shrubbery, then a white stone bench, then a fountain, then a man—

She sucked in her breath so quickly she nearly choked.

A *bare* man.

Bare from the waist up, anyway.

He was standing on the little balcony next to hers, just feet away.

She ducked back into her room and dragged the curtain over her face, leaving just her eyes exposed, like a harem girl, and leaned forward for a better look. She could only see his back: a glorious burnished expanse of shoulders, a lovely trench of sorts along his spine, dividing two ridges of hard muscle, all of that narrowing into a taut waist.

Suddenly he thrust his arms up into the air, arched backward as though he'd been struck by lightning, and made a sort of roaring sound, like a pagan god calling down the morning. Though she doubted whether a god would sport fluffy black hair in his armpits.

He promptly disappeared back into his room, just as though he'd been a cuckoo popping out of a clock to announce the time.

His roar still echoed faintly.

All in all, not an inauspicious start to a day.

She climbed back into bed. If it was a dream, she wanted it to continue.

CAPTAIN CHARLES "CHASE" Eversea swept into the Pig & Thistle, seized a chair, turned it around backward, straddled it, reached for Colin's ale and took a gulp before lifting a hand to call over Polly Hawthorne, the Pig & Thistle's barmaid.

"Thank you," he said belatedly, gravely, to Colin, dragging the back of his hand over his mouth.

Colin scowled but it was more a formality than indignation. Of them, Chase was older, Colin the youngest, and the Eversea brother hierarchy was an unshakable thing. He wouldn't even dream of protesting.

"Is . . . *regular* sitting passé now, Chase?" Colin asked mildly. "Afraid you can't hold your increasingly aged torso up without the assistance of a chair back?"

"His baubles have grown three sizes now that the East India company has promoted him," Ian said. "He needs the additional support."

"If you accept that position with the company offered to you in London, you, too, can have enormous baubles, Ian. When did you get home?"

"Late last night. Too late for my own room to be ready, apparently, as I'm ensconced on the third floor. Rode in from London. And you know my plans, and not even the lure of a bauble-swelling promotion will change them. I'll be gone soon enough. You'll just have to savor my presence while you can." He'd mapped out five ports of call, and he finally had precisely enough money saved—through scrimping and clever investments—to do it. China, India, Africa, Brazil. He'd pored over his map of the world so often, sometimes he thought it was singed on his retinas. He could see it when he closed his eyes.

"Ian probably needs to put his baubles on ice after the week he spent with Mademoiselle—"

Ian kicked Colin silent. Polly Hawthorne had suddenly appeared at the table.

Pretty thing, dark and slim and young, graceful as a selkie, Polly had nurtured an unrequited youthful yearning for Colin, and never forgiven him for having the unmitigated gall to get married. She still refused to acknowledge his existence, but Ian suspected that at this point it was partially out of habit. You had to admire the way the girl could hold a grudge, he thought. He admired consistency. The women he'd known tended toward the fickle, and though he'd definitely benefited from that more than once, he still didn't like it. It was probably hypocritical, but there you had it.

Ian had watched Polly grow up here at the pub her father owned—the Hawthorne family had owned the Pig & Thistle for centuries. He was protective of her, and of Culpepper and Cooke, and everyone else who made Pennyroyal Green the home he'd known and loved his entire life. Perhaps unfairly, he wanted to be able to come and go as he pleased—to war, to exotic countries—and arrive home again to find all them still here, exactly where they belonged, if a little older.

He smiled at Polly, and she flushed and began fidgeting. Such was the power of an Eversea smile. He wasn't stingy with them. Watching women smiling and flushing never got tiresome.

"Three more of the dark, if you would, Polly."

"Of course, Captain Eversea."

"Mademoiselle *who*?" Chase prompted immediately, when Polly had slipped away again.

"LaRoque." Ah, Monique. He remembered rolling out of bed, her fingernails lightly trailing his spine, as she tried to persuade him to stay. He *never* stayed. With any of them. It was one of his rules. He had another rule about giving gifts—he simply didn't. He wanted a woman to feel persuaded by him as a man. Not to feel bought.

"You haven't a romantic bone in your body," Monique had pouted as he dressed. "Merely a bone of passion." Her command of English was often tenuous, but she'd still managed to more or less sum him up accurately. He wasn't insulted. She still wanted him. Because he did know how to give a woman exactly what she needed.

"Monique LaRoque. The actress?" Chase wondered.

"Impressive, or should I say, unseemly, knowledge of London gossip you have there, Chase. Yes. The actress."

"I've heard of her. My wife once saw her perform."

It was a casual enough sentence. But the words "my wife" were faintly possessive and Chase delivered them as if they were a benediction.

They fell on Ian's ears like an accusation. Colin did the same damn thing with the same damn words. When he wasn't talking about cows. He shifted irritably in his chair, as if dodging a lowering net.

"She's uniquely talented, Mademoiselle La-Roque," Ian said. Perversely. To induce a reverie in the two recently married men.

There fell a gratifying hush.

Colin had always been more innately a rogue, and Ian enjoyed prodding at him to see if the rogue in him was dead, killed by matrimony, or simply dormant. Then again, surviving the gallows could inspire any man to seek refuge in an institution like marriage. Or perhaps he'd gotten a little too used to Newgate after his notorious stay there to ever adapt fully to freedom again.

Finally, Colin asked hopefully, on a lowered voice: "*How* unique?"

Ian simply, cruelly, smiled enigmatically.

Monique *was* talented, but not particularly uniquely. Maneuvering her into bed had been a game involving copious charm, his very best innuendos, and outflirting other men. But not gifts. Never gifts. The conclusion had been nearly foregone, but they had both enjoyed it up to and beyond the moment she capitulated. She was skillful and nimble and soft-skinned and gorgeous and . . . showing distressing signs of devotion.

Which was why Ian was relieved to have an excuse to return to Pennyroyal Green—he'd promised his cousin Adam, the vicar, that he'd lead a crew of men—many of them admittedly a bit motley in character if willing in spirit—in much-needed repairs to the ancient vicarage. If he stayed in London too long, the mamas would remember how eligible Ian Eversea was. But if he stayed in Pennyroyal Green too long, *his* mama might remember how eligible he was, instead of devoting all of her attention to the matter of his sister Olivia. Who was, at last, submitting to a semblance of courtship from Lord Landsdowne, and in fact appearing to enjoy it.

Appearing. One never knew with Olivia.

All of the Everseas had been holding their breath ever since. And the flowers from the hopeful—or masochistic—continued to arrive for her.

The bloods who had voted against her in the Betting Book at White's were beginning to perspire a little. No one thought Olivia Eversea would wed ever since Lyon Redmond had vanished, taking, it was said, her heart with him.

Funny, but he hadn't given Monique a thought since he'd returned last night from London. Which was likely ungracious, at the very least. Given that she'd been all he thought about for weeks before that.

If he stayed in Pennyroyal Green long enough, Monique would probably forget about him. He wondered whether this was a relief.

Until he returned to London, that was. And the game began again.

If he wanted it to.

The notion of *that* made him restless, too.

Polly returned with ales and thunked them down.

"Chase is paying," Ian told her. With a brook-no-argument eyebrow lift in Chase's direction.

Chase gamely produced the proper coinage.

"To large baubles and willing actresses!" Ian toasted his brothers cheerfully.

They hoisted their tankards "To large bau—"

Their smiles froze. Their gazes locked on a point over his shoulder.

"What?" Ian swiveled his head to look.

"To large baubles!" the Duke of Falconbridge said easily.

Bloody. Hell.

How did *he* get in here? It was a wonder the entire pub hadn't fallen silent, the way singing birds do when a stalking cat is spotted in the garden. But no: everyone was drinking, talking loudly and making broad, ale-fueled gesticulations, as usual, and Culpepper and Cooke were at the chessboard, and Jonathan Redmond was throwing darts at the board with his usual alarming precision. No one had noticed that an infamous duke wended his way into the Pig & Thistle.

Ian knew firsthand that the man could be stealthy.

His sister Genevieve loved Falconbridge, that much was clear. She had married him, throwing over Lord Harry in the process. And Ian loved Genevieve.

But it was damnably awkward to be tangentially related to someone who had once ordered him at gunpoint to climb out of his erstwhile fiancée's window.

At midnight.

Naked.

It was a testament to Ian's fortitude and general pleasure in risk that he was able to walk all the way home wearing only one boot (the duke had thrown the other one out the window, along with his clothes) and the shreds of his dignity and one half of his shirt, the only other clothing he was able to retrieve in the dark. His turn on the battlefield had prepared him to stoically confront an infinite number of eventualities.

Then again, Falconbridge ought to *thank* him for climbing into this fiancée's window if it stopped him from marrying the wrong woman and brought him to Genevieve.

He was fairly certain the duke didn't see it that way.

He wasn't known as a forgiving man—nobody liked him, apart, it seemed, from Genevieve—and he was known to have a long memory for any perceived wrongs perpetrated against him and for righting the balance no matter how long it took. Genevieve had fervently assured Ian the duke hadn't murdered his first wife, as popular rumor had it, and though in all likelihood he would refrain from murdering Ian for Genevieve's sake, one just never knew.

Ian was hardly proud of the episode. If he'd known he'd wind up related to the man, he would in all likelihood have never climbed that tree to Lady Abigail's window.

The three Eversea men clambered to their feet and bowed to their brother-in-law, with cheerful and polite greetings, and then when they sat again, Colin extended a leg and used it to push out the empty chair next to Chase in an invitation.

Ian shot him a filthy look.

Colin fought back a grin.

Colin, who was the only other person (besides perhaps Genevieve) who knew about his midnight exodus from the window at gunpoint.

The duke settled into the chair, his shoulder within inches of brushing Ian's.

Ian contracted all of his muscles.

Polly appeared as if by magic.

"Try the dark, Falconbridge," Chase recommended.

Chase claimed to actually like the man. But

then Chase enjoyed a number of things Ian found questionable, including goose liver, and puppets made him nervous. He might be a fellow war hero, but his judgment wasn't sacrosanct.

Polly slipped away to do His Grace's bidding.

"What brings you to our humble pub?" This came from Colin.

"I was out for a stroll and when I saw the Pig & Thistle, I seized upon it as an opportunity to see my brothers-in-law in their native habitat."

They all laughed politely, giving him the benefit of the doubt that it was meant to be a joke.

"Chase has been promoted," Ian told him.

"Congratulations, Captain Eversea," the duke said. "Rising in the ranks there, are we? Aiming for a governorship?"

"I don't think my wife would like to live in India, but it's not out of the question."

"I don't think they have any puppets in India, so it's safe," Ian reassured him, and Chase kicked him under the table.

The duke either didn't notice or chose to ignore this non sequitur.

"And Ian has been offered a promotion as well," Chase said. "You did know his rank is Captain, Falconbridge?"

"Ian," Ian said, "is taking a trip around the world, and will be booking passage very soon. And will be gone for quite some time."

"Ah. Around the world you say," the duke mused. "Coincidentally, we have a guest lately arrived from across the ocean. I'm not certain whether Genevieve has told you about my young ward, Miss Titania Danforth, and her imminent arrival from America."

She had. But they'd all forgotten until now. A relative of the duke's, who was to be married off apace to a title approved of by the duke. Something of that sort.

"Miss Danforth arrived yesterday."

"Safely and well, I hope?" Colin said politely.

"Quite safe and well. And a more unspoiled, well-bred, impressionable young woman you'll never meet. It's my sincere hope that, while she's here, you will consider her welfare in the same light with which you consider Genevieve's, and treat her accordingly."

No matter how obliquely stated, Ian knew at once it was a warning.

The man had a lot of bloody nerve. As if he couldn't resist mounting any female in his vicinity. He had *criteria*.

There was a silence at the table, roughly akin to the sort that follows an invitation to duel.

Don't say it, Ian. Don't say it. Don't say it.

"Or you'll . . . what?"

Colin and Chase were motionless. He knew they were each holding a breath. In the silence that followed, Ian imagined he could hear the condensation trailing the glass of ale.

The duke said nothing.

"I would die for Genevieve," Ian added into the silence. Grimly.

It was only what was true. He'd put his life on

the line for others more than once. And it was one of the reasons his sleep, for years, had hardly been a peaceful one.

He didn't do it lightly.

The duke finally moved, lifting and sipping at his ale leisurely.

"Well," he said, "let's hope you won't need to die for Miss Danforth."

He drained his ale in a final gulp, then raised his eyebrows in approbation. "Excellent brew. Perhaps I'll have to visit the Pig & Thistle more often."

And with that horrible threat he bowed and took his leave.

"She must be magnificent if the duke thought he needed to *warn* you." Colin was thrilled.

"Nonsense. She sounds dull," Ian said idly. "The innocent ones generally are."

Chapter 4

❧

THE DUKE SENT FOR Tansy that afternoon, and she smoothed absurdly clammy palms down her skirts before hurrying to a room with a large polished desk in it. He sat at it as though it were a throne, but then, nearly everywhere he sat would seem that way, she thought.

"In all likelihood I don't need to remind you of the terms of your father's will, I'm certain, Miss Danforth, but I'll state them thusly: the entirety of your fortune will be released to you upon your marriage to a man of whom I approve."

Why did he sound like a lawyer? Perhaps that was why her father had entrusted her fate to this man. Perhaps he was capable of communicating only in orders, or by flicking that formidable eyebrow. It was difficult to argue with that eyebrow.

"Thank you. I'm aware of them."

There was an awkward little silence.

"The last time I saw you, you weren't any taller than . . ." He held his hand a few feet above the floor. "You hid behind your mother's skirts. It was at Lilymont."

She smiled politely. If she'd hidden behind her mother's skirts, it was, in all likelihood, the last time she'd ever been shy. He'd probably been intimidating even then. His wife—he'd had a different wife then—had been so pretty, she'd thought. She'd laughed so easily. She'd loved the sound of her mother and the duke's wife laughing together in the garden.

The very word "Lilymont" had started up an ache again. She could see it clearly: the walled garden half wild, colorful and surprising and tangled, like something from a fairy tale, at least from her perspective at three feet tall.

And then she remembered the duke had lost that pretty, merry wife quite some time ago. Which was how he had come to be married to Genevieve.

She stared at him curiously, as if she peered hard enough, she might see some sort of give, something that might indicate that life had battered him a bit. She saw nothing but a sleek, older, inscrutable duke.

"I'm given to understand that you *would* like to marry." He said this somewhat stiffly.

"Yes, thank you." *Of course*, she almost added. She felt herself begin to flush.

When he paused, she saw an opportunity to intervene.

"I thought it might be helpful to make a list of qualities I should like in a husband."

There was a pause, which she thought might be of the mildly nonplussed variety.

"You've made a list," he repeated carefully.

She nodded. "Of qualities I might like to find in a husband."

Another little hesitation.

"And . . . you'd like to share this list with me?"

She couldn't tell whether he was being ironic. "If you think it might be helpful."

"One never knows," he said neutrally.

"Very well." She carefully unfolded the sheet of foolscap and smoothed it flat in her lap, then cleared her throat.

She looked up at him, and he nodded encouragingly.

"Number one: I should like him to be intelligent . . ."

She looked up again, gauging the result of her initial requirement.

He gave an approving nod. "Half-wits can be so tedious," he sympathized.

". . . but not too intelligent."

She was a little worried about this one.

"Ah." He drummed his fingers once or twice and seemed to mull this. "Do you mean the sort who goes about quoting poetry and philosophers? Waxes rhapsodic about works of art? Uses terms like 'waxes rhapsodic'?"

It was precisely what she meant. She hoped the duke wasn't the sort who went about quoting poets and philosophers. She rather liked the term "wax rhapsodic," however. She silently tried it in a sentence. *Titania Danforth waxed rhapsodic about the balcony man's torso.*

"I think I prefer him to be . . . active. To enjoy the outdoors, and horses and shooting and such. I enjoy reading. But I'd rather not pick apart what I read. I'd rather just enjoy the pictures stories make in my head."

And now she was babbling.

She hoped he didn't think she'd sounded ridiculous. It had, rather, in her own ears.

"Do you?" She couldn't tell whether he was amused or thoughtful. "I'm not one for reading a good deal myself. My wife, on the other hand, enjoys it very much. I tolerate the habit in her."

Genevieve did have the look of the sort who would enjoy reading very much, Tansy thought glumly. He did, however, sound a little ironic.

"What's the next item on your list, Miss Danforth?"

"Ah. Number two: I should like him to be of fine moral character."

In truth, she'd added that one because she hoped it would impress the duke. She wasn't entirely certain how he would interpret fine moral character. She wasn't even certain how *she* would interpret it or whether she in truth possessed it. It sounded dull, but necessary.

"Of fine moral character," he repeated slowly, as if memorizing it. "This is helpful in terms of narrowing the field," he said gravely. "Thank you."

When he said nothing more, she looked down at her foolscap again.

"Number three: I should like him to be handsome."

She said this somewhat tentatively. She glanced up. *He* was handsome. Even with the frost of gray at his temples. But perhaps he'd think looks were unimportant when moral fiber was critical.

"Rest assured, I wouldn't dream of binding you to a gargoyle, Miss Danforth."

Excellent! She smiled, relieved. "I wasn't terribly worried, since all of the men I've seen so far in Sussex have been so . . ."

Gorgeous, she'd nearly said, in her rush of enthusiasm. Thinking in particular of the balcony man.

". . . pleasant," she completed, piously.

He was silent a moment. She thought the creases at the corners of his eyes deepened. Was he combating a smile?

"Many of them are," he said somewhat cryptically. "The next item would be . . . ?"

"Ah, yes." She returned her eyes to her list. "Number four: Enjoys . . ."

Damnation. This was another delicate one. She looked up at him again. The duke had fine lines around his eyes, which made her think that he might *occasionally* laugh. She'd seen no evidence of it yet. She wondered if he actually enjoyed it when he did, or if he felt it was a social requirement, like bowing and the like.

"A good brandy? Brisk walks at the seaside? Embroidery?" he prompted. She could hear the barely contained patience. A speck, she thought. I am an irritant, a speck, and he is scarcely tolerating me.

". . . laughing."

She said it faintly. Almost apologetically.

"Ah," he said thoughtfully. "Well, I fear we may have a conflict between requirement number two and this particular requirement. I'm afraid I'm going to need to ask you to choose only one of them."

Her lungs seized so swiftly she nearly coughed.

Bloody hell. Well, she had only herself to blame for this.

A fraught silence ensued, her breathing suspended as she mulled the consequences in her mind.

And then he brought his palm down with a smack on his desk so hard it made her jump and burst into laughter. He threw his head back and laughed with it.

"Oh, Titania. You look so *stricken*! I am *teasing*. You see, I, too, occasionally enjoy 'laughing.' But I do believe I now know what you would choose if you had to."

His laugh was marvelous, so infectious that she rapidly recovered from being incensed and found herself laughing, too. Though she hadn't quite forgiven him for shaving a year or two from her life with his little joke. She'd imagined her doom a little too vividly.

"Your father was a good laugher," he said when they were both quiet again.

"The best." She dug her fingernails into her palm when she thought tears might prick at the corners of her eyes. They came at the oddest times. Even on the heels of laughter.

"He had a remarkably nimble mind, too. He could debate me into a corner on occasion. We enjoyed it, rather. And I'm very difficult to defeat, mind you."

"I don't doubt it," she said sincerely. But she was half teasing, too.

He smiled.

The laughter seemed to have loosened him, and Tansy recognized something: he was simply a bit stiff, as uncertain of her as she was of him. And he'd experienced a loss, too, when her father died. Someone to whom he'd been close, and she doubted the duke had many bosom comrades. Knowing this aroused her sympathy. She suddenly felt—and this seemed ridiculous, and yet there it was—protective of him.

"He called you 'Titania' in his letters to me."

"The name was his idea, and Mother never could refuse him anything. Then again, it was Mother who persuaded him to return to America. I always thought my name was a bit cumbersome. A bit much to live up to."

"I think you've quite grown into your name."

"Thank you. I think. It was Mother who called me Tansy. Father eventually capitulated."

He smiled again. And it looked so natural, she was relieved to believe he did it often, and not just because an occasional smile was expected of everyone. "But you certainly look like your mother."

"That's what everyone says."

A silence, an easier, softer one, ensued.

"I always hoped to see all of you again," he said gently. As if he knew too much discussion all at once would be unwelcome.

"I do remember you," Tansy told him, a bit shyly. "Just a very little. You were married to someone else then. I remember thinking she was so very pretty, like someone from a fairy tale. And she had such a lovely voice."

"Oh, she was. She *was* pretty. She passed away some years ago."

"I know. I am so sorry."

He nodded shortly.

There had been a baby, too, she recalled, and now she was sorry she'd mentioned it. She remembered her father receiving the letter from the duke. He'd told her mother about it in a few short, devastating sentences, and then repaired to his study, closing the door. As if by being alone he could share his friend's grief.

"But you should know, Titania, that I cannot recall ever being happier than I am now."

She knew it was true. There was really no mistaking it. She would never be able to describe happiness in words, she thought. It was something one witnessed.

And he'd said it because he wanted her to know she could be happy, too.

"I'm glad," she said softly. "Thank you for telling me."

He cleared his throat. "Do you have any more requirements on your list?"

She did.

"Number five: I should like him to be kind."

She looked up, a little worried about that one, too, but less worried than she had been when he first entered his office. She knew now, no matter what was said about him, that the duke was kind. Impatient, perhaps, more than a bit arrogant, perhaps, but one rather expected that of a duke. She felt he was fundamentally kind.

"And that's all I have for now."

He smiled faintly. "Is the list a work in progress?"

"I haven't yet decided."

"Do keep me apprised of critical changes in its content," he said somberly.

She suspected he was teasing her again.

"I shall." She smiled.

"I think we have an excellent chance of finding a match meeting your requirements. Your father was one of the most sensible people I've ever known, and he trusted my judgment. I imagine you'll be spoiled for choice. But I will know which young men are worthy of you, Titania . . . and which ones most definitely are not. But if you have any questions, you may feel free to confide in me."

"Thank you," she said, while thinking, *Good try*. He might be kind, but she also suspected he knew how to curtail fun, and she wasn't *that* naive.

"I'd like to chat a bit again, if you're amenable to it," he added, as he stood, signaling for her to stand, too.

"I would like that."

This, she found to her surprise, *was* true.

THE INTRODUCTION OF Miss Titania Danforth into Sussex society was to begin with a dinner, a little aperitif of a party before the ball—a *modest* ball, is how the duchess described it—to follow that evening. The most amusing people in Sussex had been invited, Genevieve had assured her, and a portion of London, too, and then she'd recited a list of titles both major and minor, both married and unmarried. When Tansy pictured them, they were all attractive. Funny the sort of magic the word "lord" could confer upon a person when it preceded a name. Privately she was now convinced the only way her own name would ever sound anything other than cumbersome would be if the word "duchess" came before it. Duchess Titania. Countess Titania? Lady Titania?

It was only a matter of time, she told herself stoutly.

The modest ball would be followed in a month or so by what Tansy was tempted to call an immodest ball, but which Genevieve referred to as a Grand Ball.

Tansy had been told she needn't do a thing but emerge from her chambers looking beautiful, "which you could accomplish wearing only sackcloth, if you preferred," Genevieve said with her usual generosity and graciousness. "Not that wearing sackcloth is a custom in Sussex."

"Ha ha!" Tansy laughed.

She'd decided to take looking beautiful tonight with the seriousness of blood sport.

And because her own American maid had been terrified at the very idea of making the crossing into a new country with her, Genevieve graciously sent over her own, a girl named Annie who was quiet, competent, and eager to please.

But Tansy was not in a mood to be pleased.

"Not the green. The blue."

The abigail pulled the blue from the closet.

"Not that blue. The *other* blue." The girl pulled it into her arms and turned around halfway when Tansy said, "No, perhaps the pale green silk?"

"I think you'll look beautiful in any of them, miss," the poor abigail said desperately.

Tansy nearly stamped her foot.

"Tell me, Annie," she demanded. "Have you a beau?"

Annie blushed. "Aye, miss. He works in the stables."

Tansy softened, genuinely curious. "How lovely! Is he handsome, your beau?"

"Aye, if I do say so myself. His name is James. We're to be married, but—"

"Oh, *are* you to be married? How lovely!" She beamed.

Annie glowed. "Oh, it is, it is. And yet we must

wait, for we haven't enough money to set up housekeeping, you see. James would like to build a little house for us to live in, so we needn't always live-in, and . . . surely I shouldn't bore you with this, Miss Danforth," she said desperately.

"I'm not bored at all. It's terribly important to have a home of your own. I should like one, too, you see. For I haven't one anymore. Or a family, you see."

And in that moment the hopes and concerns of womanhood transcended their societal roles and bound them fast in a subtle accord.

"You've a home here and we'll look after you," Annie said firmly. "If ever you need anything, Miss Danforth."

"Thank you," she said, quite touched.

There was an awkward, warm little silence, and Tansy turned away again, toward the wardrobe.

She'd never worried so much about a ball gown. Along with every young woman in New York society, she had taken her ability to captivate utterly for granted, regardless of what she wore. This was why the sympathy calls had been shot through with a subtle, yet unmistakably morbid glee. The queen had at last been nudged from her throne. It had taken disaster to do it, but still.

The balls had gone on without her while she dealt with solicitors and the like. And only a very few of those young women ever called on her again.

Tansy hated to admit it, but her confidence was

not as ironclad as it once was. Though perhaps all it needed was a little exercise in the proper context. Such as a ballroom full of men.

"Now . . . think about it this way," she said. "If you were me, and you wanted your beau to look at you and forget that anyone else in the world existed, which dress would you wear?"

Annie looked captivated by this notion, then turned and perused the dresses hanging there. "The white with silver ribbon," she said decisively.

Now they were making progress.

"Why?" Tansy pressed.

"Because you'll look like an—"

"Please don't say angel!"

Annie smiled. "A pearl what stepped from an oyster. A mermaid. A nymph."

A pearl! A nymph! A mermaid! Tansy liked all of those. She held the dress beneath her chin and studied herself in the mirror. With her hair down about her shoulders, she supposed she *did* look a bit like a mythical creature. The silver ribbon reflected the silver blue of her eyes, the white made her skin glow nearly golden, and her lips were blush, the color of the inside of a shell.

It would do. She exhaled.

"You see, Annie, it's just that I've only the one chance to make a first impression. And it's been so very long since I've been to a party like this."

"I will make certain you'll be unforgettable, miss."

Tansy gave a short nod. "Thank you."

The white dress it was. She slid it over her head like a gambler choosing the card that would decide the game.

AT DINNER SHE was introduced to myriad Everseas.

Her first impression was of a forest of tall, darkly appealing men, all white smiles, magnificent cheekbones, and exquisite manners, with manly, very English names: Colin, Marcus, Charles. They were so clearly of a piece, variations on a theme begun by their parents, who were two very handsome people. All of the boys were taller, just a little, than their merry-eyed father. The mother had the same heart-shaped face as Genevieve.

If they'd been bonbons in a box, she thought she might have first selected the one called Colin, the tallest of them, the only one whose eyes, she could have sworn, were more green than they were blue. And they sparkled.

She smiled at him.

He smiled back, and almost, not quite, winked.

And then his body convulsed swiftly as if someone had stabbed him with a fork.

He frowned, and the frown wavered and became a smile aimed at the woman across from him.

Her coloring was striking, her hair black, her skin fair, her dark eyes enigmatic. She had the air of permanent confidence of one who knows she is loved, and she was wearing a little private smile for her husband.

His wife. Madeleine. The other wives were named Louisa and Rosalind.

For alas, every last one of the Everseas was married.

Everyone, apart, that was, from Olivia.

And at the first sight of Olivia Eversea, Tansy's confidence wavered just a bit.

It was easy to see why she'd inspired the men of greater Sussex and beyond to turn the house into a thicket of flowers. Where Genevieve's beauty was warm and calm, Olivia glittered, like a diamond or a shard. Her eyes were fiercely bright and she was thin, perhaps a bit too thin, but it suited her; there was no angle from which Olivia Eversea's face wasn't somehow fascinating. Tansy found herself admiring the way she held her shoulders, and how graceful her slim arms were when she reached for the salt cellar.

"How very interesting to have an American in our midst, Miss Danforth," she said. "You hail from New York?"

"I do. I was born here, and I remember it fondly. But I love New York." A wave of longing for her previous life crashed over her so suddenly that her hand stilled on her fork. She'd once sat around a dinner table with her own family, laughing and bickering, and had once taken it for granted.

She reapplied herself to her peas. She needed stamina for the evening ahead. She hoisted the fork up again.

"Now, the south of your country in particular is populated by slave owners, is it not, Miss Danforth?"

Tansy's fork froze on its way to her mouth.

Oh, Hell's teeth. It sounded like a trap.

And she strongly suspected Olivia Eversea was a reader of the sort that she and the duke were not.

"I suppose some might say that," she said very, very cautiously.

"Do you know anyone who—"

Olivia suddenly hopped a few inches out of her chair and squeaked.

"Mind the stockings," she muttered darkly.

Or at least that's what Tansy thought she'd said. Tansy frowned a little.

"Olivia works so hard for excellent causes." This came from the matriarch, Mrs. Eversea, and she managed to make it sound both like pride and a warning.

Ah, *that* was likely why Olivia hadn't yet married. Tansy couldn't imagine a man in the world who would tolerate that nonsense for long. Suddenly she was far more certain she'd be able to usurp Olivia's flower throne.

She smiled at Olivia, as a way of apologizing for that unworthy thought.

Olivia smiled back at her, as if she'd heard every word of that thought and wasn't the least bit worried about her supremacy.

"Where is your brother?" the matriarch, Mrs.

Eversea, asked the handsome Eversea next to her. Marcus?

Brother? She looked up the table at all those handsome faces. There were *more* of them?

Which one of these men was the balcony pagan? she wondered.

A surge of optimism swept through her. Perhaps men like the Everseas were commonplace here in England. Perhaps finding a beautiful titled husband would be as simple as shaking an apple from a tree.

"Last I saw of him he was out with Adam repairing a paddock fence or a roof or something somewhere," the one called Chase said. "And they'll be at the vicarage repairs for days."

The duke looked up and said dryly, "As a form of penance for his usual—"

His face contorted in a wince. She knew a ferocious twinge of pity. Possibly when one got to his age, which was forty at least, many things made you wince. Gout, heart flutters, capricious digestion.

"Our cousin Mr. Adam Sylvaine is the vicar here in Pennyroyal Green," Genevieve said to Tansy. "He's always helping the Sussex poor. We're so very proud of him."

"How lovely to have a vicar as part of the family. Have you another brother?"

"Aren't we fortunate to have such wonderful weather at this time of year?" This came from the duke, a question posed to the table at large, as if he hadn't heard her question at all. Perhaps he hadn't. Perhaps she'd underestimated his age and he was beginning to need an ear trumpet to hear voices over a distance of several feet.

"IT'S LOVELY. DO YOU NORMALLY HAVE INCLEMENT SPRINGS?"

She had a sudden impression of the whites of eyes as they all widened.

"Our springs are so beautiful, Miss Danforth. You'll love them," Olivia volunteered, softly, carefully, as if demonstrating the proper indoor tone.

"Have you another brother?" she tried, more softly, a bit suspicious now.

"What are your interests and pursuits, Miss Danforth?" This came from Colin. It was a subject change, but his eyes held a promising sparkle.

"Oh, I've become a bit of a wallflower, I'm afraid. I'm looking forward to learning what the natives of Sussex enjoy."

Colin recognized this as flirtation, she could tell. This one was a rogue, or once had been.

"Colin likes cows," Chase said abruptly, irritably. "Very, very much."

"Cows . . ." Tansy mused. "Well, I can think of few things more fulfilling than raising a bovine to adulthood," she said.

There was an astonished hush.

Colin looked as though he was torn between thinking this was balderdash and wondering whether he cared whether it was or not, since it was precisely what he wanted to hear.

"Miss Danforth, have you ever traveled to the East Indies?" Chase interjected. It sounded almost experimental.

She swiveled her head toward him. "I haven't had the pleasure yet, but I imagine working for the East India Company is so *dashing*. The two of you must be very talented. I hope you'll tell me more about it during my stay."

She beamed at them.

And everyone could see the moment when Colin and Chase surrendered to the big eyes and eyelashes and the smile and they glowed.

There was another almost palpable hush.

And then Chase and Colin began talking over each other about cows and the East India Company until the footman brought in the blanc-mange.

Chapter 5

"Wallflower my eye!" Olivia said to Genevieve after dinner. She perched at the edge of Genevieve's bed and rubbed her ankle. "So much kicking and poking going on beneath the table tonight! Will we need to edit our conversation forever while she's here? 'I can't think of anything more rewarding than raising a bovine to adulthood.' *Honestly!* And it's not like she won't *see* Ian at some point. We can't disguise his existence forever. She may not find him in the least appealing when she does. She's such a young thing, and Ian can be such a jade."

Genevieve hesitated. The ironic parting words of Tansy's paid chaperone, "Good *luck* yer Grace," echoed in her mind.

She judiciously decided not to share this with Olivia. Not yet, anyway.

"Well, we shan't be sharing every meal with her. I think she's charming. She's alone in the world and I think she's only trying to please. She's just as charming to everyone, including me, and she'll be that way to you, too, if you give her a chance."

Genevieve was magnanimous in happiness and love and prepared to be blinkered and loyal to a reminder of something her husband cherished from his past.

"We shall see," Olivia said to the mirror. Love had been less kind to her, and she would never trust easily again.

AFTER A BRIEF dash to her room to pinch her cheeks and bite her lips and shake out her dress after sitting for dinner, Tansy ventured toward the ballroom.

She arrived on the threshold just as an excellent orchestra launched into a reel. And suddenly it felt as though her heart had been lifted up and twirled.

Lively music was very close to perfect happiness. Her life for so long had been full of movement, none of it particularly pleasant, none of it her choice. Tonight she would love to lose herself in one dance after another, like a butterfly flitting from flower to flower.

She took another tentative step into the room.

It wasn't yet crowded. None of the faces she immediately saw were familiar. It was odd to think that by the end of the night they likely would be.

She took another step into the room. A bit like wading into cool water and becoming accustomed to it, bit by bit.

She took another step, smiling.

And then she froze.

Something terrible happened.

Her breath left her abruptly, as if she'd been dropped from a great height. Her vision spangled. She gave a half turn and peered over her shoulder, as if expecting to see the assailant who had taken a shovel to her head and utterly scrambled her senses.

She slowly, cautiously, turned her head again back toward ballroom. Toward that wall.

Alas, she already knew it wasn't a shovel assailant. It was much worse.

It was a man.

A disturbing, delicious heat rushed over her skin. The entire world amplified inexplicably. Suddenly everything seemed louder and brighter and she was terribly conscious of her limbs, as if they were all newly installed and she would have to relearn how to use them.

For heaven's sake. It wasn't as though she hadn't *seen* handsome men before. She'd routinely managed the affections of handsome men with the skill of a puppeteer. And it wasn't a result of being out of the game, as it were. Giancarlo, handsome as he was, had scarcely raised her pulse.

What on earth was the difference here, then? Was it the way he held himself, as though the world itself was his to command? The faintly amused, detached expression, as if he intended to use everything and everyone he saw in it as his plaything, and make them like it? The sleek fit of his flawlessly tailored, elegantly simple clothes, which only made her wonder, shockingly, about what he looked like under the clothes? The arrogant profile? His delicious, nearly intimidating height?

It was all of those things and none of them. All she knew for certain was that it was new, and suddenly she was as blank-minded as a newborn.

Conscious that she was gawking, she forced herself to look in some other direction, which turned out to be, for some reason, up.

The only thing of interest on the ceiling was the chandelier, so she feigned wonderstruck admiration.

When she looked down again, the man was watching her. Clearly puzzled.

Her heart kicked violently.

His mouth tilted slightly at the corner, his head inclined in a slight nod, polite, a little indulgent.

His gaze kept traveling across the room, idly.

He'd skimmed her. As if she'd been a chair or a chandelier, or, *unthinkably* . . . a plain girl.

For the second time in minutes she experienced the shovel sensation.

A horrifying thought occurred to her: what if she wasn't considered attractive in England? What if there was something about her features the English found comical? What if golden hair was considered passé? She felt as though the sword had suddenly been flipped from her hand.

She nearly leaped out of her slippers when someone touched her elbow. She'd forgotten there were other people in the world.

She whipped her head around again and found Genevieve next to her.

"Oh, there you are! Good heavens, don't you look beautiful! Do come with me, Tansy. We'll have your dance card filled in moments, I *assure* you." Genevieve looped her arm companionably through hers and pulled her determinedly away. "And please don't feel shy. Everyone will be delighted to meet you, I promise you."

Tansy allowed herself to be led away, far away, from that man, and as she did, she aimed a smile radiantly, recklessly, across the room, into the crowd. The young man who happened to be standing in the path of it went scarlet, and then his face suffused with yearning and she knew, she *felt*, him watching her walk away.

And as she and Genevieve wended through the ballroom, she sensed male heads turning, one by one, like a meadow full of flowers bending in a summer breeze.

Before the night was over, she'd make that man take notice, too.

GENEVIEVE LED HER through the crowd, making introductions to young men and young women. A gratifying number of eyes went wide; conversation was stammered; dances were begged. In short, everything was as it *should* be, and she began to relax and enjoy herself. Stingily, strategically, she gave away just one waltz to a randomly chosen young man, so that all of the others would wonder why she'd chosen him, before she told Genevieve, "All of this conversation has made me a bit thirsty. Do you think we can visit the punch bowl?"

She began heading in that direction before Genevieve could reply or effect another meeting.

The man was still standing alone against the wall, observing the ballroom at large. Time seemed to slow as she approached.

She watched as if in a dream he straightened, turned, and said, "Well, good evening, Genevieve. Where are you off to in such a hurry?"

He was on first name terms with the duchess!

Tansy's heart was now pounding so hard it sent the blood ringing into her ears.

Genevieve said, "Miss Danforth, I'd like you to meet my brother, Mr. Ian Eversea. Captain Eversea, since his promotion."

Her *brother*! The brother no one would expound upon!

Ian. Ian. Ian Ian Ian.

It wasn't Lancelot, but it would do.

His bow, which was graceful, seemed unduly fascinating. She suspected everything he did would be fascinating—yawning, scratching, flicking sand from the corners of his eyes when he woke up in the morning. She found it difficult to imagine him doing anything so very ordinary.

Up close his face was a bit harder, a bit scarier, and more beautiful. Cheekbones and jaw and brow united in an uncompromising, faceted, diamondlike symmetry. His mouth was elegantly sculpted. His eyes above cheekbones as steep and forbidding as castle walls were blue, amused, ever-so-slightly cynical. He was older than she'd originally thought. He was even larger than she'd originally thought. He had shoulders that went on for eons. And he was able to look at her without scarlet flooding his cheeks, unlike so many other young men.

All of the things she felt in his presence felt too large to contain, too new to name. And it was this, perhaps, she'd been waiting for her entire life.

Could *this* be the balcony man?

"It's a pleasure to meet you, Miss Danforth."

His voice was so baritone, resonant, she fancied she could feel it in the pit of her stomach, like a thunderclap. Aristocratic. Warm but not too enthusiastic. Good. Fawners could be tedious.

And she would see what she could to amplify that enthusiasm.

It occurred to her then she hadn't spoken yet. She steeled herself to dazzle.

"I hope you'll call me Tansy."

Funny. Her voice had emerged sounding surprisingly small.

He smiled faintly down at her. "Do you?"

The English all seemed to find this amusing.

To her shock, she could feel a fresh wave of heat

rushing into her cheeks. He was likely looking at a literally scarlet woman.

She tried a radiant smile. It felt unnatural, as though suddenly twice the usual number of teeth were wedged into her mouth.

What was the *matter* with her?

"My friends do. And I hope we will become friends."

"Any friend of my sister's is a friend of mine."

Said with pretty, impartial gravity.

And the faintest hint of what she suspected was, again, amusement.

Genevieve made a small sound in her throat. Tansy glanced at her curiously. It sounded almost like skepticism. Perhaps a warning.

"We're on a quest to fill Tansy's dance card with the most splendid dancers, Ian."

It sounded very like Genevieve didn't want to include Ian in that number.

"I've been a bit of a wallflower, I'm afraid."

Tansy lowered her gaze demurely. Which gave her a clear view of his hands. Big hands, long straight fingers. A prickle of interesting heat started up at the back of her neck. "I'd be honored if you would dance with me, Mr. Eversea."

Very, very bold of her. Quite inadvisable, and yet, she could blame it on American manners, and she knew no English gentleman would be able to refuse.

She suspected that hadn't been Genevieve's intention at all, for whatever reason, but even so.

She looked up again to find Ian exchanging an unreadable look with Genevieve and mouthing words. They looked like: *Must I?*

The. Nerve.

"It would be my honor and privilege if you would share a waltz with me," he said solemnly, but with a glint in his blue eyes, which he probably thought was devastating.

The fact that it *was* devastating was beside the point. So devastating she nearly forgot he'd just been insufferable.

As nearly as insufferable as she'd been.

"I shall look forward to it greatly, Mr. Eversea," she said just as gravely, as Genevieve towed her away again.

Chapter 6

❧

MISS DANFORTH WAS DANCING a quadrille with Simon. The young man looked dumbstruck by his luck, and frequently stumbled over his own feet. Ian would warrant young Simon had danced that particular reel a hundred times in his life if he'd danced it once. Miss Danforth smiled radiantly at him each time he stumbled, as if he'd done it on purpose for her entertainment.

Ian frowned faintly.

His sister appeared at his elbow.

"Good evening, again, Genevieve. Did the dancing exhaust your husband?"

She rolled her eyes. She was so confident of her husband's vigor that insults and jests regarding his age rolled off her. "He was pulled into an impromptu meeting. Something regarding an investment he'd like to make." She paused. "It's thoughtful of you to be . . . kind . . . to Miss Danforth, Ian."

He smiled a slow, grim smile. "So thoughtful of your husband to warn me not to corrupt her."

"Oh. Did he?" She didn't sound surprised, however. "You can see where he might be sensitive on the topic, however."

She was teasing him. Mostly. He tried to work up righteous indignation, but it was difficult to remain self-righteous when it came to Genevieve. Especially since she was so *happy* with the duke that she all but walked about glowing like a medieval saint.

And also because he wasn't exactly proud of cuckolding the man with his former fiancée.

He sighed. "I'm not a corrupter of *innocents*, Genevieve." The implication being that the duke's erstwhile fiancée had hardly been an innocent, and had been rather complicit in the whole episode.

Genevieve made a noncommittal sound.

And said nothing for a time.

And then, "She's very pretty, Miss Danforth," she said carefully.

He sighed. "I suppose she is. Then again, so many women are, to my everlasting gratitude."

And, he was certain, Miss Danforth was quite accustomed to being called pretty, quite taken with herself and quite accustomed to wielding her eyelashes and big eyes to get what she wanted from men. Yet she was the veriest child, for all of that. The blushing. The blinding smile. The awkward conversation. He had seen it before, a million times it seemed, and now it distantly amused him, and when he wasn't in the mood to humor it, it irritated him. It posed no challenge. He had no use for it.

"How very blasé you are, Ian."

"Yes," he said simply, not in the mood for a lecture.

He looked about for his brothers, or his cousin Adam or someone who could be persuaded to sneak up to the library to join him in draining his father's brandy decanters in order to make whatever dancing ensued more interesting for them. He didn't see any of them. He supposed he'd have to settle for ratafia in the short term.

"I wish you trusted me, Genevieve."

"I wish I did, too," she said lightly, with a playful little tap of her fan.

And it wasn't until then that Ian was certain that she didn't. Not really.

It stung a bit, but he supposed he ought not be surprised. He hadn't earned his reputation as a rogue by not applying himself to the task.

"Falconbridge is charged with finding a match for her," his sister said. "Preferably a titled or at least spectacularly wealthy one. Those were the terms of her father's will."

"Dukes are hardly thick on the ground, though, are they? Though the Duke de Neauville's heir is of age, and could use a wife, no doubt. As all heirs do. I've spoken to him at White's. Fine manners. Not too much of an ass. He's perfectly inoffensive."

Genevieve laughed. "I suppose one can do worse than perfectly inoffensive."

He shrugged. "My felicitations to Miss Danforth and the poor devil she *does* marry. Speaking of which, here comes *your* poor devil."

But Genevieve had stopped listening to him, because she'd already seen her husband moving across the crowded ballroom, aiming for her like a ship aims for shore.

HAVING ABRUPTLY ABANDONED Genevieve for the punch bowl, he gave a start when he saw a pair of eyes peering through a tall potted plant. He leaned closer.

"Oh, good evening, Miss Charing."

"Good evening, Captain Eversea." Miss Josephine Charing's china-blue eyes blinked. She was a pretty, garrulous young lady with a big heart and a brain comprised primarily of feathers and air. She was lately engaged to Simon Covington.

"Is aught amiss? It's not like you to hide in a corner."

"It's what *you* do, isn't it, Mr. Eversea? When too many girls want to dance with you."

"Er . . . I may have done, on occasion," he said carefully, a bit startled. "Sometimes one just likes to take a bit of a rest."

"It's challenging to be beautiful, isn't it?" she said with an air of wistful authority.

"I suppose it is." He was amused. And he was fairly certain Miss Charing had been at the ratafia a bit too enthusiastically. "Why are you behind the plant? Is something troubling you?" He regretted asking immediately. Confidences were the baili-wick of his cousin Adam Sylvaine, the vicar. But Adam wasn't here. Feminine confidence in par-ticular invariably panicked and baffled Ian. The things women fussed over!

"Is some*one* troubling you?" he added, almost hopefully. He could easily dispatch any rogues who might be a little too free with their hands or words. He almost hoped that was the case. He was feeling restless and irritable and wouldn't have minded taking it out on someone who de-served it.

"It's just . . . well, I'm afraid," she confessed on a whisper.

"Who are you afraid of?" He was instantly alert. He scanned a practiced eye over the ball-room but saw no one who appeared unduly men-acing. Unduly drunk, certainly.

"Have you seen Miss Danforth?"

He blinked again. "Yes. Are you afraid of Miss Danforth? She didn't appear to be armed when I saw her."

She hesitated.

"My Simon is dancing with Miss Danforth."

Ian peered in the direction she was looking. And so he still was. Serious Simon Covington, with his long sensitive face, who was so walking-on-clouds smitten with Miss Charing, was indeed dancing with Miss Danforth.

"Isn't she pretty?" Josephine said querulously.

Attempting to be magnanimous. But sounding panicked.

"Yes. But so are you."

"You are kind," she said distractedly, the second time he was accused of such a thing tonight, and neither time had been entirely sincere. It was a testament to how much in love she was with young Simon that she didn't even look at Ian when she said it, when he knew that in days of yore the compliment would have enslaved her.

"Whenever he dances with someone else, he always looks for me. Not rudely, mind you. Otherwise he might trip over his dancing partner. And he hasn't looked for me once since this waltz began. Not once," she repeated mournfully.

"To be fair, you're hiding behind a plant at the moment," he pointed out.

"It was an instinct, I fear, after he'd gone round and round with her and seemed to have forgotten I existed."

Ian turned to scrutinize the happily rotating couple. Miss Danforth was beaming up at Simon as though she'd never seen or heard anything quite so fascinating in her life. So convincing was it that even Ian wondered if perhaps Simon possessed hidden depths he'd so far failed to see.

He frowned thoughtfully.

"Don't worry, Miss Charing. You see, I'm given to understand that Miss Danforth is a bit timid.

And Simon is mad about you. If she should make eyes at him, I'll call her out."

Miss Charing laughed. "*I'm* not timid at all," she said, sounding relieved. "Simon says he's happy to let me do all the talking for the both of us. He says it's a relief."

"A match made in Heaven, surely."

"Thank you, Captain Eversea."

"At your service, Miss Charing. Will you step out from behind the plant now, so Simon *can* see you? Perhaps you ought to have a sandwich?" He reached behind him and surreptitiously shoved the punch bowl out of her vision to take her mind off it and gestured with his chin to the sandwiches.

"I do love sandwiches!"

As she busied herself with the selection of one, he took a look at Miss Danforth and Simon again.

He couldn't help but notice that Simon seemed to be doing all of the talking.

SIMON COVINGTON RETURNED Miss Danforth to the waiting cluster of friends, and like a shred of iron sucked into a magnet, immediately attached himself to Miss Charing's side. Ian couldn't help but notice he looked contemplative, however, and a bit wonderstruck, as though he'd just had a religious experience he was struggling to interpret.

What had *gone on* during that waltz?

He took a step toward them, tempted to investigate, when a flash of red at the corner of his eye spun him around with an unerring instinct.

A lush, dark-haired beauty appeared to be pe-rusing the sandwiches.

He knew precisely what she was actually pe-rusing.

He smiled, and as he spoke, aimed his gaze nonchalantly out over the ballroom.

"Good evening, Lady Carstairs. Are you look-ing for something to satisfy your appetite?"

He turned slightly, saw her swift little enigmatic smile without turning fully around to look at him. And she bent, just a little, to select a sandwich, which allowed him to admire the curve of her der-riere outlined in garnet silk, which of course had been her intent. She was a widow and a friend of the family of the late Lady Fennimore, and she di-vided her time between Sussex and London.

"Presuming my appetite *can* be satisfied," she said lightly. "You see, I've a taste for the unusual."

"One need only make a special request to have it met," he said gravely. "I'd be honored if you'd discuss your unique appetites with me during your visit to Sussex."

And as she returned to her friends—without looking him in the eye—Ian reflected that it was a bit like five card loo.

If the Duke of Falconbridge was said to never lose at that game, Ian Eversea could be said to never lose at this one.

"MR. COVINGTON WAS telling me of the plans he has to build a house on the land near the . . . oh, what did you call it? The Academy of . . . the School for . . ." She paused, flustered, looking searchingly into his face, as though the answers to all of the world's troubles could be found there.

"Miss Marietta Endicott's Academy for Young Women," Simon completed breathlessly, as if she'd said something too adorable.

Upon the conclusion of the waltz, Simon had escorted Miss Danforth back to where Ian stood with Miss Charing, and now the two of them were reminiscing about it.

Miss Danforth beamed at him. She swung her head to include the gathering at large. "Is he often like that, Miss Charing? Does he finish sentences for you?"

"No!" Miss Charing said, with something like alarm.

"But he's so very clever! How *do* you keep up with him?"

Simon was scarlet with pleasure.

"I sometimes wonder myself," Miss Charing said, studying Simon as if he was a stranger who'd just donned a Simon costume.

"I enjoy all of Miss Charing's sentences so thoroughly I'm happy to let her do most of the talking," Simon maintained stoutly. Mollification transformed Miss Charing's features.

Momentarily.

"I must say, your gift for conversation must be contagious, Miss Charing, for I found Mr. Covington to be positively scintillating. I hesitated to say one word lest I miss one of his." Miss Danforth smiled at him.

Simon beamed and croaked quietly, gleefully, wonderingly, to the gathering at large, "I'm scintillating!" Like a drunken parrot.

"You see, I've been a bit of a wallflower for some time, and it's very helpful to me when someone guides the conversation along, for I fear I'm a bit out of practice." She lowered her eyelashes.

"You did very well!" Simon defended. "Very well, indeed! Isn't she doing well?" he demanded of the gathering at large again, swiveling his head to and fro.

"*Very* well," Ian said dryly.

Miss Charing darted a panicked glance at Ian.

Miss Danforth looked up at him, saw the frown, and that pink rushed into her cheeks again, and she jerked her head abruptly away toward the ballroom floor. Away from him. A peculiar little thing, given to blushes and gushing, it seemed, and thoroughly intimidated by him. Such a child! Where had she been kept before she was sent across the ocean to England? Surely she hadn't been raised in a convent?

Just then his sister Olivia, stunning in willow green silk, limped toward them, leaning on the arm of Lord Landsdowne, whose face was a picture of somber solicitousness, as if Olivia were breakable.

"What happened, Liv? Did you kick a ne'er-do-well a bit too hard?"

"So witty, Ian. It was a rather too enthusiastic turn in the reel, I fear. My ankle went one way and I went the other. I shall live to dance again. I simply need to rest it a bit. Which sadly leaves Lord Landsdowne partnerless for the next reel."

Landsdowne promptly said, "It will be my honor to sit by your side and *will* your ankle to recover. I can be very persuasive."

She smiled at Landsdowne.

And then Landsdowne turned slightly, seeming to remember his usually impeccable manners, and saw Tansy.

A moment of silence and stillness ensued as Landsdowne's eyes settled on her in a bemused way. Ian could almost read the man's thoughts: *Surely she can't be as pretty as all that.*

"I haven't yet had the pleasure," he said slowly to her. Landsdowne was a grown man and a fairly formidable one. He wouldn't goggle or stammer. No. He would mull. And plan.

"Forgive my manners," Olivia said immediately. "Viscount Landsdowne, this is our guest, Miss Titania Danforth, of America."

Miss Danforth's lashes lowered and she curtsied, slowly and gracefully, for all the world like a petal drifting from a tree.

And Ian watched Landsdowne's eyes follow her all the way down. And all the way up.

"How fascinating to have an American in our midst, Miss Danforth," he said.

Landsdowne hadn't yet blinked. Bemusement

had evolved into something like wonder. His tone had gone a bit drifty.

"Oh, I'm the one who's fascinated! To be among such esteemed company. You are the very first viscount I have ever met." She cast those eyelashes down again.

Landsdowne smiled at this, obviously disarmed.

"And I'm the very first baron you've ever met!" the formerly silent Simon declared, elbowing into the conversation.

She turned, happily. "Oh, *are* you a baron, Simon? How *very* delightful."

"Not yet, he isn't," Miss Charing said somewhat churlishly, which made Ian eye the level of the ratafia cup she held. "His father has to die first."

"Do you attend many balls and parties in America, Miss Danforth?" Landsdowne asked smoothly.

"Not so many lately. I fear I've been a bit of a wallflower." Those fluffy dark lashes went down again.

To his credit, Landsdowne looked somewhat skeptical. "Well, we certainly must remedy that, mustn't we? I assume a round of gaiety is planned in order to introduce Miss Danforth to Sussex society? This party is only a beginning, Miss Danforth."

"Miss Danforth has been taken under the Duke of Falconbridge's wing," Olivia explained, and Landsdowne hiked an impressed brow.

"I've not yet danced a reel this evening. I

wonder if I remember how! I should be so embarrassed to try it in front of all of these people after such a long time."

"I'm a patient teacher, I'm told, if you'll allow me," Landsdowne said. "Will you?"

"Oh . . ." Miss Dansforth cast her eyes down, then up again. "I don't know if I dare subject you to the caprices of my dancing."

There was an odd little silence, as if everyone thought Olivia's blessing needed to be bestowed.

"Please do dance with him, Miss Danforth," Olivia urged finally, graciously. "He dances beautifully and we oughtn't deprive the assembly of the pleasure of watching him."

This, though ironic, was positively gushy for Olivia, and Ian knew it.

Landsdowne looked wry. "Then of course I shall dance for Your Majesty's entertainment," he said with mock gravity, and bowed low, very low, one leg extended, to Olivia, who nodded regally, accepting the fealty as her due.

SIMON AND MISS Charing wandered off to the garden, where a kiss or two might be stolen, or Miss Charing might vomit. It could easily go either way, Ian thought.

"You ought to be dancing," Olivia said to him.

"I like sitting with you." Which was true enough. He was less fond of reels than of waltzes, and he recognized that it was more or less his duty as a single man to dance, but he'd decided that Olivia needed the company.

Olivia snorted.

They were watching Miss Danforth and Landsdowne dance the reel. For an alleged novice, she certainly learned the steps very quickly. She was light on her feet and danced with every evidence of joy.

"He looks almost . . . playful." She said the word as if it were foreign and she was uncertain of its pronunciation.

Ian laughed. "Is he normally a somber chap? He seems it. Though a good one," he added hurriedly. "I like him a good deal."

"No, he has wit. The quiet, dry sort, however. I quite like it. He *is* a good one," she said absently. "I like him."

There was a pause.

"You like him. How torrid."

She shot him a wry sideways glance. But didn't expound.

His sister was passionate about nearly everything. The abolishment of slavery. The protection of the poor. The preservation of cherished historical landmarks. The color of clothing. Her tastes in nearly everything were very specific and impassioned and cleverly, usually wittily, reasoned, which was part of her charm. She was challenging and often exhausting, but never dull.

She was very guarded about Landsdowne.

And he had never once heard her utter Lyon Redmond's name since he'd vanished. He had often thought there would always be only one man for Olivia. And that one man had disappeared more than three years ago.

Landsdowne threw back his head and laughed at something Miss Danforth, the wallflower, had said.

"What do you think of her?" Olivia asked.

"Very pretty and vapid and uninteresting. An awkward ingenue. Ought to excel at being a spoiled wife of a rich aristocrat. And no doubt will be given the opportunity to be one soon enough."

Olivia mulled this. "I might agree with all of those words save one. I'm less convinced of the 'uninteresting' part. I wonder if she's . . . strategic. The bit with the lashes. All of that."

"I think when one is presented with a cipher, one can assign all sorts of meaning. The way we try to see shapes of things in clouds."

"You're likely correct."

Another silence ensued. Miss Danforth was smiling. Her complexion was creamy, faintly gold in the chandelier light, a luxurious, pearl shade. She moved lithely, and it was strangely a pleasure to watch her hop and clap the steps of the reel. She danced as though the music was part of her, and Ian felt something in him lighten as he watched. As if joy was her native emotion.

Landsdowne laughed again when she crashed into someone and was forced to apologize profusely.

"I don't know whether he laughs a good deal when he's with me," Olivia said.

Ian wondered if his sister, accustomed to being the toast of all of Sussex, and London as well, was worried.

"He's probably too busy being fascinated by you, Olivia."

"That *must* be it." Olivia smiled at that.

Chapter 7

LANDSDOWNE RETURNED MISS DANFORTH to them at the end of the reel, both of them flushed and happy looking. Then he settled down next to Olivia; rather like a regal, faithful hound who would never leave his mistress's side, Ian thought.

Which left him with Miss Danforth. Who wasn't smiling, or fluttering her eyelashes, but who had suddenly gone still.

When the strains of the Sussex waltz started, he bowed, and extended his arm to a girl whose dress was so white and gossamer she might as well have written "I'm a virgin" across her fore-head. Ian thought of the widow in red across the room and let his thoughts stray in her direction, half resenting the opportunity robbed from him by this little girl. He suppressed a sigh.

Miss Danforth gave her hand to him almost portentously, slowly, as if she were pulling the sword from a stone. Lucky me, to be presented with such a gift, he thought wryly.

He took it with a certain ironic gravity, and placed his hand against her waist.

He felt her breath hitch in the jump of her slight rib cage.

Suddenly, he wondered how long it had been since his touch had felt new, surprising, exciting, to a woman, and a little of that was communicated to him, too.

A rogue, fierce surge of protectiveness swept in, startling him, and then swept out again.

He looked down. Into eyes of such a singular crystalline silver-blue color he fancied he could see himself in them. The eyes of a woman who had no midnight trysts or any other stains of any sort on her conscience.

They *really* would have very little in common.

He eased them into the one, two, three of the other whirling waltzers the way he would ease his horse through the traffic on Bond Street.

She hadn't yet said a word. She was staring as though she was from one of those distant islands Miles Redmond wrote about and had never before seen an Englishman in the flesh.

He was tempted to lead off with *Boo.*

"How are you enjoying England, Miss Danforth?" he said instead.

"I like what I've seen of it so far very much indeed."

It was delivered with such fervor, he widened, then narrowed his eyes briefly. If he hadn't known better, if a different woman had issued the words, he would have considered that an innuendo. That, combined with the "I'd be honored to dance with

you, Mr. Eversea" and the "I hope you'll call me
Tansy." Perhaps all Americans were just a bit too
forward.

But now she was looking up, gazing limpidly
back at him. He was a connoisseur of women's
mouths, and hers was a work of art, he was forced
to concede. The bottom lip a shell-pink pillowy
curve, the top shorter, with two gentle little peaks.
A bit like a heart. Both whimsical and sensual, one
was tempted to trace its contours with a finger.

Her face was rather heart-shaped, too, and the
heat of the crowded ballroom and the vigor of
dancing had made her rosy. It was the sort of color
a good bout of lovemaking put into a woman's
cheeks.

He contemplated telling her this, just to shock
the living daylights out of her.

"Is something amusing, Mr. Eversea?" She said
this with something like strained gaiety.

"Oh, something is always amusing. I suppose
that's my motto, if one must have one. What is
yours, Miss Danforth?"

"Never surrender," she said instantly.

He was a bit taken aback.

"That *is* a pity," he tried. Murmuring. Half-
heartedly sending out the innuendo as a smug-
gler would send a signal with a lamp from the
coast, but not expecting much by way of response.

Something did twitch across her cloudless
brow. Irritation? Confusion? Indigestion?

"I beg your pardon?" she said politely.

He didn't expound. "That's a much better motto than the one for, oh, Leicestershire: 'Always the Same.'"

This elicited a burst of loud laughter from her that made him suppress, just barely, a wince.

She modulated it instantly, then fell abruptly silent. A moment later she cleared her throat.

"Then again, there's a measure of comfort in sameness," she said, to the man who thrived on risk and newness, especially new women. "Why did you mention Leicestershire? Is there something special about it?"

She seemed to be waiting with bated breath. As if *everything* hinged on the next thing he said.

"It's where Richard the Third was buried. Or so they say." That was nearly all he knew about Leicester. That, and the motto.

"Richard the Third? The kingdom for a horse king? The poor bent chap? Are you very interested in history, then?" It was a rush of barely contained eagerness.

"One and the same. Are you very interested in history, Miss Danforth?"

The answer was important. If it was affirmative, it would encourage him to avoid conversation with her altogether in the future. Not even an opportunity to play red flag to the Duke of Falconbridge's bull would tempt him to endure conversations about ancient history.

The present was so much safer than the past, as far as Ian was concerned, and the future was a concept he'd only begun contemplating with excitement. It would be his refuge, all those ports on that map of the world. He would run like a river, never stopping. He suspected, after all, it was his nature to keep moving.

He looked out over her head at the ballroom, and saw Olivia sail by in the arms of Lord Landsdowne, who looked possessive and proud. So she'd either walked off her sore ankle or decided she'd better dance with Landsdowne on the heels of his reel with Miss Danforth. Olivia looked . . . one never knew with Olivia. She'd perfected the art of appearing as though everything was perfect. And there was a certain defiance to her lately. As though she thought Lyon Redmond was actually looking on when she went walking with Landsdowne, and when she danced with him, and suffering over it.

"I'm interested in some periods of history. Perhaps I'll go to Leicester one day." Miss Danforth sounded a trifle desperate.

He returned his attention to her.

"Perhaps you will," he humored. And as if this entire conversation was rudderless and he could not be blamed if he failed to stay the course, he looked out over her head again . . . There she was. Lady Carstairs dancing with some other fortunate soul.

He knew her quick sultry smile and that little head toss were all for him, and he wondered which of the alcoves he ought to attempt to maneuver her into before the night was through. For at least a little more charged conversation.

Now that *was how one flirted, Miss Danforth*, he was tempted to instruct.

"Have you an occupation, Mr. Eversea?" Miss Danforth tried, a trifle sharply.

"I do. Primarily it's scandalizing decent people."

He had the grace to regret it. It was a terribly unfair thing to say. Glib and arrogant and more impulsive than he normally was. It was just that life suddenly seemed too short for waltzes like this one.

Color flooded her cheeks. Again. The girl blushed as regularly as the tides moving in and out. And he knew he'd neatly cornered her: asking him to expound would be tantamount to wanting to hear scandalous things, which would of course mean she was indecent.

She clearly hadn't the faintest idea what to say.

It was poor form to punish the girl for being innocent and sheltered and inexperienced, and uninteresting to him because of it.

"Why do people call you Tansy?" he said, as if he hadn't just been unthinkably rude.

"Well," she said thoughtfully, "nicknames are usually shortened names, are they not? For instance, if the diminutive derived from the first syllable of the name Jonathan is Johnny, what would my nickname logically be given my name is Titania?"

"Well I suppose one would call you Tit . . . sy."

An infinitesimal moment of horror passed.

He was halfway into the word before he fully realized what he was saying, and momentum carried him all the way through it.

He stared at her as if a mourning dove had just sunk fangs into his hand.

Had . . . had this delicate well-bred "wallflower" actually led him right into saying "Titsy" to her?

Surely that hadn't been her intent?

But now he was thinking about her breasts.

Really wondering about them.

He would be damned if he would look down at them.

Perhaps quite *literally* damned.

She gazed back at him evenly. He thought, though he could not be sure, he detected a glimmer of triumph or defiance there, but that may have just been the light of the chandelier glancing from her clear, innocent eyes.

"You see, one can hardly call me that, Mr. Eversea," she said somberly.

"I suppose not," he said shortly.

The final moments of the waltz were passed in utter silence between them.

And as he bowed farewell, he did look at them on his way down.

They were excellent, indeed.

TANSY RETURNED TO her chambers late, late, very late, quite foxed on ratafia, champagne, and compliments, both given and received.

She stood motionless for a moment in the center of the sea of carpet, riffling through memories and moments, smiling softly over each little triumph, each glance, each laugh won. Until she got to the only one that truly mattered.

And then her smile slowly dimmed.

She groaned and covered her face in her hands and rocked it to and fro.

She had been grace personified with everyone else. With him, she'd brayed like a mule with laughter and enthused over everything he'd said with the force of an animal released from a trap. Graceless and appalling. She'd watched it happening, as if she were floating over her body in the ballroom, and there was nothing, nothing at all, she could do to stop it. What was *wrong* with her? If this was love, it was dreadful.

The difference, primarily, was that she'd never before needed to really try for a man's attention. Or try *very* hard, anyway. More specifically: she'd never before wanted a man's attention the way she wanted his.

"Titsy!" she moaned. "I made him say Titsy!"

It wasn't as though he hadn't deserved it.

She yanked off one satin slipper and hurled it across the room. It bounced very unsatisfactorily off the thick carpet, soundlessly.

"He's a *boor*," she said aloud to the room and the great arrangement of flowers, now drooping.

So few good opportunities existed to use that word.

And then she yanked off her other slipper, looking about for something to throw it at.

She threw it at the wall.

She fancied she heard a grunt on the opposite side.

Excellent.

She exhaled at length, and then settled at her desk, stabbed a quill into some ink, unfolded her sheet of foolscap and carefully added to her list:

Makes you feel like you're the only woman in the world when he's with you.

It seemed a terrible character flaw. A terrible, terrible character flaw to look past her shoulder at a brunette who, while certainly pretty, was also getting on in years. But then, if she was a widow, that meant she possessed the freedom to do whatever she liked—including all of those things Giancarlo had suggested in Italian slang—with Ian Eversea. Who wasn't a duke, who would never be a duke, who did not even have a title, even if he had those blue blue blue eyes that made her breath snag . . .

Tansy flung herself backward on her bed. Just for a moment. Just for one, long, lovely moment. She would close her eyes for just a moment. Her feet were sore and it would be lovely to . . . lovely to . . .

Chapter 8

*A*ARGH!

The moment her eyes fluttered open, her hands flew up to cradle her head. Cannons were firing in there. Last night's champagne and ratafia seemed to have re-formed into a boiling ball of lead and situated itself behind one eye.

BOOM. BOOM. BOOM. BOOM.

She lay as still as she possibly could to avoid jarring anything overmuch. No effigy installed in Westminster Abbey had ever lain quite so motionless. She was fascinated by, and a little proud, of the gruesome pain. She felt very worldly. And nauseous.

She glanced down. She was still entirely dressed. Apart from her slippers. Where were her slippers?

But it was just about dawn . . .

Curiosity was stronger than nausea.

She slipped out of bed and very, very gingerly, as though her head was a grenade balanced atop her neck, carried herself to the window by following that beam like a tightrope. She gingerly parted the soft curtain.

Aargh!

Ghastly punishing light!

Even though the sun was just a suggestion on the horizon, like half of a peach rising from the water.

She recoiled and gripped her head.

But instinct forced her forward again, and she tentatively cracked her eyelids.

She was rewarded for enduring pain. The man was standing on the balcony!

The sun had just reached him, and he was part in shadow, partly gilded. A pagan harlequin.

For one merciful moment pain ceased.

All of her senses were marshalled to the job of seeing him, like spectators rushing a fence at a horse race. She breathed and she felt him everywhere, again. As though her entire body wanted to participate in his beauty.

But then even in her incapacitated state something about him . . .

Something about the height . . . something about the way her breath stopped . . .

Could it be a certain insufferable in-love-with-himself Eversea?

He arched backward again, thrusting sunburnished gorgeously muscled arms high into the air like an acrobat landing, and he roared— though this time the roar tapered off into what sounded suspiciously like a hungover groan.

And then he broke wind, scratched his chest, and ducked back into his room.

She snickered.

"Ow ow ow ow ow ow!" And was immediately punished by the return of the booted battalion in her head.

She stumbled and fell upon the servants bell-pull as a lifeline.

She would have happily traded all the blood in her veins at that moment for coffee.

"HAVE YOU ANY books on Richard the Third? Bent fellow, the kingdom-for-a-horse chap?"

It seemed a miracle to be ambulatory, but after her second well-sugared cup of coffee and two and a half fluffy scones, Tansy and a similarly fortified Genevieve set out for a walk into town, on the theory that the fresh air and exercise would do them good and that Tansy would naturally like to get a closer look at Pennyroyal Green.

The fresh air *had* done them good. It smelled faintly of the sea and green things, and she liked it. She could scarcely remember anything about it, though she'd lived here as a child, but the landscape of Sussex, as far as she could tell, was subtle. Modest. The hills were mild swells and the trees a humble height, unlike the arrogant, craggy-faced mountains and unruly forests of America. Sheep dotted the hills and clouds dotted the blue skies, like puffy white reflections of each other.

The church and the pub were opposite each

other, which surely must be good business for both, and she craned her head as they passed an intriguing shop called Postlethwaite's Emporium, which featured an enticing selection of bonnets and gloves in the window.

The dark of the bookshop was a blessing to her still faintly pounding head after the bright light. She enjoyed horrid novels, and she'd read a novel by a Miss Jane Austen which she'd quite liked, but lately she'd become fascinated by adventure stories. Specifically, stories of survival. Robinson Crusoe had lost everything—how had he managed to get on after that? That sort of thing. She'd acquired a tome written by a Mr. Miles Redmond, who had a series of adventures in the South Seas and was nearly eaten by cannibals. He'd lived to tell the tale. Surely she could prevail over the upending of her own life if others had triumphed over odds and humans who ate other humans.

The bookseller, a wiry older gentleman called Mr. Tingle, beamed approvingly at her and fidgeted with his spectacles, which was, she suspected, what he did when he flirted—the equivalent of a lash bat.

So she rewarded him with a lash bat.

"I aver, Mr. Tingle, this may be the finest bookshop I've ever set foot in! I've never *seen* such a fine selection. You must be very discerning, indeed."

Mr. Tingle's face suffused with happiness, and he did more fidgeting with his spectacles.

"We have the play of Richard the Third set forth in a collection of works by our own Mr. William Shakespeare. Perhaps you'd be interested in reading it? Or would you prefer to read a history of the man?"

"The latter, if you please."

"Ah, a *scholar*!" He clasped his hands with such glee she hated to disagree with him.

"*Are* you interested in history, Miss Danforth, er, Tansy?" Genevieve was perusing a biography of Leonardo da Vinci, rapt. Turning pages over, slowly, one by one.

She hesitated.

"A sudden fascination swept over me," she decided to say.

This much, at least, was true.

"I suppose new places can inspire new interests," Genevieve said.

"Truer words were never spoken," she agreed vehemently.

"Well, I'm delighted to be of service to such a fine mind," Mr. Tingle declared. "In fact, I'd like to make a present of this volume, Miss Danforth, as long as you choose another one to purchase."

"You are too, too kind, Mr. Tingle! You are a generous man, to be certain."

"Oh, bosh." Color moved into his cheeks. "It's a pleasure to do business with such an avid reader." Avid was a bit of a stretch, but she suspected he'd be mightily disappointed if she disabused him of the notion. "Can I interest you in another period of English history? Perhaps something about William the Conqueror?"

"Well, let me think . . . have you any books written by Mr. Miles Redmond?"

Mr. Tingle's hands froze on his spectacles. His eyes darted toward Genevieve and back again.

Tansy felt, rather than saw, Genevieve go motionless.

A bewildering, indecisive little silence followed.

At last Mr. Tingle cleared his throat. He lowered his voice. "We *do* have a selection of Mr. Redmond's books," he said, as carefully as if he were confessing to a collection of pornography.

"I enjoyed one of his books on his adventures in Lacao. I would love to read more about that particular journey."

Mr. Tingle lowered his voice to something like a discreet whisper.

"I'll just go and fetch the one that follows for you, will I?"

THEY'D EACH ACQUIRED a new book, each one very much representative of their own personal fascinations and who they were as people, though they didn't know that, and they clasped them to their bosoms as they walked. Genevieve reminded her of the Sussex landscape: subtle. She wasn't prone to chatter or untoward confidences, she was intelligent and measured, her wit quiet but quick. When she spoke. The emphasis was on the *quiet*. And Tansy felt a bit tethered. Her own personality, in general, was decidedly buoyant. A bit more impulsive.

"May I ask you a question, Genevieve?"

"Certainly."

"How long have you been married?"

"Nearly a year now."

There was silence, as they trod side by side, coming abreast of the ancient cemetery surrounding the squat little church. Tansy stopped, mesmerized by the stones. The newer ones were upright, the older ones reclining a bit, sagging, as everything is wont do with age. A huge willow rose up and sheltered most of it, like a hen fanning its wings out over her chicks.

The English all seemed very restrained, and she told herself she probably ought not ask the next question.

"How did you . . . know? About the duke, that is. Or . . ."

Or *did* you know? was what she wanted to know, but it seemed far too presumptuous. And given the looks she'd seen Genevieve exchange with the duke, she was certain the question was unnecessary. He'd said he was happy. She knew he was happy. But how did one know?

Genevieve smiled. "You'll know when it happens to you, if that's what you're worried about. There's really no mistaking it."

She did have a little of that married woman superiority Tansy generally found *infinitely* irritating.

"Did you by any chance ever lose your powers of speech around him?" she asked, half in jest.

Genevieve looked amused, yet puzzled. "I daresay I rather found my powers of speech when I met him."

Alas. Tansy suspected her own particular affliction might very well be unique. Ian Everseaitis.

He was unpleasant and rude and beautiful and scary, and she wondered hungrily if the book she held would somehow hold a key to him. How did an interest in Richard III reveal him, or would it? It was all she had at the moment, so she clutched it to herself like a map.

"Do you mind . . . do you mind if we walk through?" She gestured at the gravestones.

"Not at all."

She silently wove through the yard, which wasn't so much sad as it was peaceful and wistful. She rather liked the idea of the graveyard surrounding the church. Dead was dead; there was no getting around it, really. She of all people ought to know. Perhaps the location of the graveyard served as a reminder of those who were bored with attending church that it was all dust to dust, and they ought to see to their souls if they wanted to proceed through the pearly gates after a tombstone was erected on top of them.

She silently read the names on the stones as she strolled through.

"Quite a few Redmonds," she said. "And Everseas. Is Mr. Miles Redmond a part of the Redmonds of Pennyroyal Green?"

"He is, indeed," Genevieve said politely.

Interestingly, she didn't expound.

Tansy didn't press for more information. The Everseas were not as subtle as they thought they were. She would get to the bottom of that particular mystery in time, she knew.

And then she stopped and knelt near a particular stone. A certain Lady Elizabeth Stanton had passed a good thirty years ago at the age of twenty-one. Did Lady Elizabeth marry her title, or was she born with it? Why did she die so young? Was it childbirth or a fever or a fall from a horse or . . . ? Had she ever lost her powers of speech when a boorish man stared down at her as if he could read every thought in her head and found them criminally mundane?

She didn't have any flowers on her grave, but she was flanked by graves that were freshly adorned, and this struck Tansy as wholly unfair.

"There aren't any flowers on this one."

Genevieve sympathetically studied Lady Elizabeth Stanton's stone. "I suppose over the years families move away, or the last of them expires, and sometimes stones are forgotten."

"Well, they ought to have flowers, don't you think?" She felt urgent about this suddenly, as if she were the naked one, not the grave. "*Someone* ought to remember. We can't have flowers on some and not all."

It didn't sound remotely rational even to her, but Genevieve didn't appear to have an argument for this.

Tansy scanned the churchyard, and Eureka!

She found one little blue wildflower, poking through a fence.

"Sorry!" she whispered to it. "And thank you," and she gave a little yank.

She transported it to the grave and lay it gently down.

That was better.

"Blue is your color," she whispered to the late Lady Elizabeth, just to amuse herself.

Tansy turned to see if Genevieve was watching, but she was looking upward and waving at something.

There, at the very top of the vicarage, was Ian Eversea, hands on his hips, watching the two of them.

He was significantly smaller at that distance, but she still knew. Her body seemed able to sense him. She fancied she could feel his blue eyes from where she stood, like the beams of two little judgmental, cynical, gorgeous suns.

She could practically feel all of her native charm and polish evaporate the way sun evaporated rain. What *was* it about the man that made her feel so very gauche?

He lifted a hand—there appeared to be a hammer in it—in a sort of salute.

"He always was an excellent climber, my brother."

Genevieve sounded a bit ironic.

But Tansy barely registered this. Suddenly he was all she could see, delineated against a blue sky. And her heart had struck up a sharp beating, like a hammer against a dulcimer.

She stood abruptly, brushed her hands down her skirts and mutely followed Genevieve around the corner.

Only to abruptly encounter a cluster of men deep in conversation, gesticulating in that universal language men shared when something needed to be built or repaired. Each of them seemed to be clutching a tool of some sort—a spade or hammer or saw. *How* men loved tools, she thought.

Then turned abruptly when the ladies rounded the corner.

They stopped talking and gesticulating.

Their eyes rapidly tracked from Genevieve to Tansy and back again.

And they stalled on Tansy, as motionless as pointing hunting dogs.

She gave them a demure smile. And fluttered her lashes.

And then they all bowed, and when upright again, commenced variously gaping, toeing the ground, or fidgeting with their hair.

Which was just as well, because she couldn't speak, either. Because she'd watched Ian Eversea clamber down from the roof and now he was striding ever closer. For a moment he seemed to use the air she needed to breathe. Her lungs had stopped moving.

She tipped her head a little back, as if the air were clearer there, and took a long breath.

Genevieve made the introductions as Ian drew ever closer.

"Gentlemen, this is our guest, Miss Titania Danforth. Miss Danforth, this is my cousin Reverend Adam Sylvaine. You met Simon last night at the ball, Miss Danforth, and Lord Henry Thorpe has returned from abroad and is kindly helping with repairs to the vicarage."

Lord Henry was young enough to still have a few pink spots sprinkled on his cheeks. His hair was closely cropped.

The man leaning on his shovel found his voice first, and didn't wait for the niceties of introductions.

"Mr. Seamus Duggan at your service, Miss Danforth." He had curly black hair and green eyes and his Irish accent was a beautiful thing. It leaped and lilted like a jig. He bowed low, keeping one arm suavely slung around the shovel as if it were a spare lover. "I do mean that. If ever you need anything, and I do mean *any*—"

"We try to keep Seamus too busy to get into too much trouble," the vicar interjected pleasantly.

"Ha ha," Seamus laughed, in a hail-fellow-well-met way, but he shot a faintly aggrieved look in the direction of the very tall vicar.

The vicar was clearly from the Eversea mold of stunning men. He exuded an air of lovely calm and strength, and Tansy suspected it was the sort he'd earned the hard way. Because she knew a bit about learning things the hard way.

But she wasn't interested in "calm." She was

interested in that spiky, breathless, ground-is-shifting-beneath-her-feet feeling she'd only felt for the man who was . . . now right upon them.

IAN HAD AN unerring instinct for excellent examples of the female form; like a weathervane, he invariably spun toward it. He'd been pounding a nail into the roof when something made him pause, and slowly rise to his feet, and . . . watch. His breath suspended. Something purely carnal touched its fingertips to the back of his neck and communicated with his nether region. All of his senses had marshalled to witness whoever she was.

Two women had entered the churchyard, and the way she moved—it was intangible, really, something about the line of her spine, the subtle sway of her hips—issued a call, and his body responded. His heart picked up a beat or two in anticipation of discovering her identity.

He shaded his eyes.

One of them was Genevieve—he recognized the color of the ribbon she'd used to trim her favorite bonnet.

The other one then must be . . .

. . . could it be Miss Danforth?

Alas, he feared it was. *Titsy* Danforth.

He gave a short humorless laugh at his own expense.

Still, he shaded his eyes and watched. He did like the way she moved. He frowned faintly as she plucked a flower from between the fence posts and knelt and laid it on a grave. Genevieve looked up at him and gave a surreptitious shrug.

And then she waved her arm in a great arc of greeting.

His manners drove him down off the roof.

Unsurprisingly, he could *hear* Miss Danforth well before he was upon the group of men.

"I'll *definitely* keep you in mind, Mr. Duggan," Tansy was saying as he approached. A bit like an actress trying to reach the back of the house. Perhaps she was a bit hard of hearing? She *had* laughed rather more heartily than a lady ought to the other night when they'd danced. "Thank you *so* much for your kind offer."

What offer had Duggan made?

"Oh, please *do* keep me in mind, Miss Danforth," Seamus said gravely.

And she smiled at that, slowly, and with great satisfaction.

And despite himself, her smile had an interesting effect on Ian, too. He was tempted to look away, and yet it was as though she'd flung a handful of fairy dust at them. He'd seen similarly dumbstruck, biddable expressions on a man subjected to a mesmerist's pendulum.

"Good afternoon, ladies," he interrupted politely. "I assume all introductions have been made?"

"They've been made," Seamus affirmed fervently, "and I shall never forget this day for as long as I draw breath."

Miss Danforth rewarded this stream of blarney

with another dazzling smile. Not the least non-plussed.

She hadn't yet looked Ian in the eye.

He frowned again, then caught himself just in time and arranged his face in more neutral planes.

"Will you be attending the Sussex marksmanship competition, Miss Danforth?" Simon wanted to know. "And my lady," he hastily appended, including Genevieve as an afterthought. He'd known Genevieve his entire life. Calling her "my lady" had been a bit of an adjustment for everyone.

Genevieve shot Ian a wry glance.

"A marksmanship contest! How exciting! *May* we attend?" Miss Danforth clasped her hands beseechingly and turned to Genevieve. And then she swiveled back to the men. "Will all of you be shooting in it? You all *look* like marksmen. I'm absolutely certain each of you wield your tools with skill and precision."

Ian's eyes widened again and he intercepted a darted glance from Seamus Duggan, who was a dyed-in-the-wool rogue and a bit of a ruffian, and who could be counted on to hear that sentence precisely the same way he had.

"Of course. I think Ian is one of the judges this year," Genevieve said. "Aren't you, Ian?"

He gave a little grunt of confirmation and swiped a hand across his brow where perspiration had glued his hair to his forehead.

"It's archery *and* shooting," Genevieve volunteered. "And Adam took home the shooting trophy during the last competition."

Adam, the vicar, shrugged modestly.

"Good heavens! A shooting vicar!" Miss Danforth seemed awestruck. "How *very* impressive. Remarkable skill and control are required to properly aim a musket, isn't that so?" Her dark lashes flickered up and her blue eyes peered up at Adam through them.

"I suppose there is," Ian heard his usually brutally pragmatic, utterly unpretentious cousin say, after what could only be interpreted as a moment of dumbstruck admiration.

Ian shot him a look, and Adam gave his head a rough little shake and turned. "If you'll all excuse me, I need to finish writing a sermon. A pleasure to meet you, Miss Danforth. Good day, Genevieve."

Everyone else seemed to ignore the departure of the vicar.

"But I came in fourth in archery," Lord Henry hastened to brag. "And this year, I vow, I'll take home the prize."

She swiveled toward Lord Henry. "Oh, if there's something I admire more than a man who is confident about repairing things with his hands, it's a man who's competent with a bow and arrows. So elegant! So primal! It calls to mind Greek gods and that sort of thing, don't you think, Genevieve?"

Genevieve was startled to be called upon. She'd seemed bemused by the entire exchange.

"It wasn't the first thing that came to mind," she said, quite diplomatically. "But I suppose one might view it that way."

"There's nothing more impressive than men up on the vicarage roof for repairs," Ian tried. Just to amuse himself.

No one heard him.

They were all muttering "mmm-hmmm" and nodding vigorous agreement with Miss Danforth, though in all likelihood none of them would have been caught dead calling themselves Greek gods in any other circumstance.

"I *love* to shoot," Simon claimed wildly. "Guns, arrows, everything I can!"

Miss Danforth aimed the rays of her attention at him. "Oh, I often feel that nothing is more masculine than excellent aim. Such a useful skill." She gave a delighted little shiver. "I suspect you're very good at it."

If a man could be said to preen, Simon—quiet, levelheaded Simon—preened.

And the expression on the others immediately darkened, and shifted.

Suddenly they began speaking over one another all at once, describing their prowess with weaponry. And her head turned to and fro between them, shedding upon each of them in turn the radiant beam of her attention.

If he didn't know any better, Ian would have thought Miss Titania Danforth had played all of them as skillfully as an orchestra conductor.

And at last her eyes met his, and hers were as clear and innocent as ever.

Unless . . . well, surely that glint in them was just the sunlight.

"And how is *your* aim, Mr. Eversea?" she asked. Seemingly emboldened.

He met her gaze evenly.

And said nothing.

In seconds color crept slowly back into her tawny cheeks.

She cast her fluffy lashes down. And looked away from him.

He sighed.

"All right, back to work, gentlemen," he ordered in a brook-no-argument voice. "The roof and fence won't repair themselves, and I know some of you are going to need a few more points in your favor in order to get into Heaven . . . Seamus. Good day, ladies, and we'll see you at home this evening."

TANSY DID WHAT amounted to brooding on the way home. Genevieve attempted conversation once or twice and then fell politely silent, too.

At home they took two steps into the foyer and stopped short.

"Please tell me no one died!" Genevieve blurted at the footmen.

There were flowers *everywhere*. Or it appeared that way. Vases stuffed full of them were scattered about the foyer.

"I am pleased to tell you that everyone lives, Your

Grace, to my knowledge. Two of these arrangements are for Miss Olivia, and the other . . . three," and the footman smiled fondly, "are for Miss Danforth. The mantels of the house can scarcely accommodate *two* such popular young ladies. How you do brighten up the house. We haven't yet found places for all of them, and I thought Miss Danforth would like to see hers and decide where they should be placed."

Tansy circled them with awe.

Three different admirers! After only just one ball! Her heart began to take up a steady beating. Dare she hope that one of them was from . . . ?

But it was a foolish hope.

She perused the cards. From two young lords and another young man she could scarcely recall, to her slight embarrassment. Boys. They were all boys.

The copy of Richard III seemed to glow like a little coal in her hand.

"And the table is set for luncheon if you ladies would care to go through," the footman told them.

And when they did go through, Tansy found a small paper-wrapped, string-bound package next to her plate. She picked it up with delight and hefted it. "What could it be?"

She unwrapped it gleefully while everyone watched.

She laughed merrily and held her gift up to the assembled.

The Dancing Master, by John Playford.

She read aloud from the sheet of foolscap enclosed.

" 'Please don't construe this as a criticism of your dancing, but I've an extensive library, and I could spare this one.'

"It's from Landsdowne. How very thoughtful of him! He did so graciously tolerate my clumsiness the other night."

"Yes," Olivia said politely and very carefully. "He is generally very thoughtful."

Her grip, Genevieve noted, was a bit white on her fork.

Chapter 9

❧

SINCE HE WAS ALREADY dirty from working on the vicarage roof and was too late to join everyone for a meal, Ian visited Mrs. deWitt in the kitchen for a chunk of bread and cheese, and decided to clean his old musket, the very first one he'd ever owned, an activity he found meditative. He thought about what manner of weapons he ought to bring with him on his journey, and the kinds of women he might encounter, and the opportunities to make money and friends, and he had the thing taken apart and was busy with oil and rags when Genevieve wandered in.

"Good afternoon, sister of mine. What do you want?"

"How did you know I . . . Never mind. Ian . . . what do you think of Miss Danforth?"

He paused mid-wipe. "Are you asking because of that interesting conversation outside the vicarage? Or because you're gauging whether I'm merely biding my time until I ravish her?"

"Conversation? The word 'conversation' implies

I was included. And if you wanted to ravish her, you'd have to plow through a thicket of other men."

Ian laughed. "Ahhhh, Genevieve. Are we jealous?"

"Hush. Of course not. It's just . . . does she seem to you . . . well, a trifle too . . . effusive?" She'd chosen the word delicately, Ian could tell, which amused him.

"Are you worried because not one of those men gave you a second glance, Genevieve, when usually they go misty-eyed at the mere sight of you? You've already landed *your* duke."

She gave him a playful push.

"I think she's a bit awkward, Genevieve. And young. And American. They seem a bit louder and brasher, Americans. But yes, pretty. She's just accustomed to attention, no doubt. And knows how to get it." He shrugged with one shoulder. "We're on the whole, simple creatures, men are, and some women discover this sooner rather than later."

Genevieve gaped at him. *"Awkward?* Are you mad? Are we discussing the same girl? She charmed Tingle at the bookshop—and you know what a skinflint he can be—into *giving* her *two* books for the price of one. I would wager poems celebrating her delicate grace and big eyes and the like will start arriving any day. She's a bit . . . I do *wonder* if . . . well, she talked to a flower today when she was pulling it. She apologized to it, and then thanked it."

"She apologized to the *flower*?"

"And then thanked it."

"Sounds downright pagan. Perhaps she *is* a witch, and she's casting a spell on all those men." He waggled all ten fingers in Genevieve's face like a conjurer. "One never knows what Americans get up to. Perhaps she wanted to visit the graveyard for a bit of graveyard dust, which I hear is useful in spells."

Genevieve snorted softly. "I don't think *magic* has anything much to do with it. Unless she can disorient men by batting her lashes and then— abracadabra!—transform them into glazed-eyed fools."

Ian was pensive. "I do wonder something . . . she might be a bit hard of hearing. She seems to lose control over the volume of her voice rather regularly for no discernible reason. And does she have a tic? She tips her head back at odd times."

"I've noticed the bit with the volume! Not with the head. Poor dear, to be so afflicted."

"Yes, let's pity the poor dear who has men eating out of her hand," he teased Genevieve. "That should make her more tolerable to you and all the other women."

She pushed him again.

"I knew a bloke like that at Cambridge who was subject to twitches and shouting. You'd be in the middle of a deep conversation, say, about economics or the Peloponnesian war, and all of a sudden his head would jerk violently to the left and he'd shout 'Bollocks!' Or something more profane than even *I* am comfortable saying aloud to you. All in all, a capital bloke, however. One got used to it. He said it was because he was dropped on the coal hod when he was a baby. But I doubt Miss Danforth is mad, or was dropped on the coal hod."

"Conversations with you are always so edifying, Ian."

"You're welcome," he said cheerily.

"Olivia doesn't like her."

"Olivia doesn't like anyone easily," Ian said shortly.

"Landsdowne sent Miss Danforth a book of country dances today."

Ian went silent and his hands stilled momentarily on his musket.

"Did he?" he said disinterestedly.

He pictured his sister watching Miss Danforth dance with Landsdowne, his proud, proud sister who would never grovel or maneuver her way into a waltz the way Tansy Danforth had, who had already lost enough, and something cold and hard that didn't bode well for Miss Danforth settled in his gut.

Ian was in fact considerably more skeptical of Miss Danforth than he was willing to reveal yet to Genevieve. Or to anyone. He was willing to watch and bide his time.

"And I know you aren't preparing to ravish her, Ian, because I'd never speak to you again, and I know you'll miss my conversation."

"Nonsense. You aren't *that* interesting," he said easily.

But temper tensed his muscles, tightened his grip on his musket. He had only himself to blame; he wasn't entitled to righteousness in that regard. He didn't like the reminder, however.

"Are you any closer to buying a house in Sussex?" he asked.

"Falconbridge is most interested in Lilymont. It was Miss Danforth's home as a girl, did you know? As charming a place as you'll ever see. Rather compact for a duke, however." She smiled.

He went still.

Lilymont. He knew the house. It *was* small. From its hill one could see the downs rippling outward and a generous silver wedge of the sea. Large windows and gracious simple lines, and weathered stone walls, amber in the sunlight. An ample, but not too ample, garden of fruited and flowering trees was enclosed by a high stone wall with wild vines of flowers growing up it. It would need a little taming, but only a little. He liked things a bit wild, a bit disheveled. He liked things to be themselves, when at all possible.

He'd never seen a more perfect house, in its way.

It was interesting to hear Tansy had once lived there. Oddly, he could picture her as a flaxen-haired girl little girl, performing pianoforte pieces for the guests or playing in the garden. He wondered if she missed it, or even remembered it.

"It's a wonderful house. It deserves an owner who loves it," he said.

"ARE YOU ENJOYING your stay, thus far, Miss Danforth?"

While Genevieve and Ian were chatting about her, the duke had called Tansy into the study for another chat, and they were sipping tea together.

"I'm having a lovely time, and everyone is so very kind and generous."

"I saw the flowers sent to you. I think your father would have been proud. And worried."

She smiled at that. "Oh, I'm certain it's nothing but generosity. The people of Sussex are just being kind."

The duke's eyebrows went up skeptically at that. "The male people."

This made Tansy laugh. "And the Everseas are such a lovely family. Everyone is so warm and kind. And charitable, it would seem."

She crossed her fingers in her lap over this little lie.

"Charitable?" This word bemused him.

"We stopped into town, and I met the vicar, Reverend Adam Sylvaine, and Mr. Ian Eversea was on the roof, hammering. It seemed a charitable pastime for a wealthy gentleman." She said this as innocently as she could muster.

"Was he." The duke had, rather quickly, gone so cold and remote it was like being thrust out of a warm cabin into a frigid winter. "I'm not surprised he was on the roof. Ian Eversea excels at climbing."

She wasn't certain what to say about this, but it definitely sounded ironic.

And hadn't Genevieve said something very similar in the churchyard?

"I was surprised to see him at work with the others . . . not of his station."

"I suppose it would be surprising."

She sensed their conversation would rapidly end if she continued her Ian Eversea fishing expedition. It was all *very* interesting.

"My brother was a soldier," she said.

The duke softened.

"As many of the Eversea men were. You must miss your brother."

"He was irritating and bossy and protective and quite funny."

"He sounds just about perfect."

She dug her nails into her palm and smiled.

She would *not* cry. She could feel the urge pressing at the back of her throat. She was tougher than she looked, and she would not. She simply nodded.

He seemed to know it. How she liked him, even though he still frightened her just a very little.

"After my first wife died, I was a bit . . ." He seemed to be searching for just the right word. ". . . lost."

He presented the word carefully. As if he was handing her something a bit delicate and dangerous.

It was a gift, she knew, this confidence of his. She was honored by it.

She knew precisely what he meant. But looking

at him now, it was nearly impossible to imagine it. He radiated power; he seemed so very certain of himself, so rooted to the earth, it was difficult to imagine him feeling the way she did frequently now, like a bit of flotsam floating on the air.

"I know what you mean." Her voice had gone a little hoarse. Close to a whisper.

"But I knew, because of my first wife, that I would make a good husband and a good father and that it was what I wanted to be. I didn't want to make my life a monument to loss. In some ways I think the losses make us better at knowing how to be happy. And at knowing how to make others happy."

It was a lovely way to put it, and she never would have expected it of him. Which hardly seemed a charitable thought, but there you had it.

"Do you think so?"

He smiled slightly. "I know so. And I think losses help you to understand who deserves your attention, too. For life is too short to spend the best of ourselves on, shall we say, people who will not appreciate it or return it in kind. People who do not deserve you."

The duke fixed her with a gaze that seemed benign enough.

Tansy returned his gaze innocently, though she wanted to narrow her eyes shrewdly and study him.

Ah, but she was clever. All of this talk of knowing who deserves whom, she was fairly certain, was an oblique reference to Ian Eversea and implied a certain intriguing . . . unworthiness. But why? Because of glances exchanged with a wanton widow?

Then again *everything* since she'd seen Ian Eversea felt like an oblique reference to him. He had become the story, and everything was a footnote for now. She didn't necessarily like it that way. But she would need to read it to the end.

"I shall remember that," she said solemnly. "Thank you."

He gave a short nod and turned toward the window, and she knew she was dismissed.

She didn't see Ian again until evening, when most of the family gathered in the parlor after dinner.

His shirtsleeves were rolled up and he wore snug trousers and Hessians, and while she pretended to read her book about Richard III, she peered up at him and tried to imagine him without his shirt.

She looked down again quickly when warmth began to rush over the backs of her arms.

"Plan to stay in Sussex long, Ian?" This came from Olivia, who was stabbing a needle in and out of a hoop of cloth. Flowers were blooming in a violent profusion on it. As if there weren't enough flowers in the house already.

Genevieve sat next to her, feet tucked beneath her on the settee, a book fanned open in her hands. The duke had gone off on some matter of business, apparently.

"Bored with me already?" He said it abstractedly, however, as his eyes were on the chessboard.

"It's so very difficult to be bored when you're around, even if one tries."

The corner of his mouth lifted. He nudged a piece forward, and Colin, who had stopped in to borrow something from his father and was talked into a chess game, swore something beneath his breath.

"What did you ladies do in town today?" Olivia asked the two of them.

Tansy knew an opportunity when she heard one.

Her heart, absurdly, began to thud with something like portent.

"I've obtained a new book," she said. "You may be interested in it, Mr. Eversea."

All the Mr. Everseas present looked up, until it became clear she was looking at Ian. Too late, she remembered he was a captain now.

"Have you?" He glanced warily at the thing in her hand, as if to ascertain whether it was indeed a book.

"It's a fine history of Richard the Third."

His smile was small and polite. "Ah."

Not a conversation encourager, the word "Ah."

"You mentioned him the other night," she prompted. "Whilst we were dancing."

"Did I?" He looked bemused.

"He's buried in Leicestershire?" she pressed, a bit desperately.

"Ah, yes. I recall." His brow furrowed faintly

in something like concern, as if studying her for signs of witlessness.

Everyone seemed to have arrested what they were doing in order to hear this conversation.

The backs of her hands and her neck began to heat.

"It's fascinating. The book."

It wasn't. She'd read a chapter or two, gamely, but the author had contrived to make what was probably a fascinating or at least quite violent and bloody subject seem like a punishment.

"Are you about to tell us about it?" Ian said this pleasantly, but he sneaked a look at the clock over the mantel. And back at her. As if he were formulating an excuse to escape.

"What's this about Richard the Third?" Colin asked. "Ian hasn't willingly set foot in our library since he got in trouble for sneaking peeks at father's anatomy books. Ian enjoys climbing trees," he added, "and riding."

Ian flicked an amused warning look in his brother's direction before returning his gaze to her.

Another of those references to *climbing*.

Tansy felt her eyes burning with mortification. He could at least have the decency to look away while she flushed, slowly, to the roots of her hair, and while her face slowly caught on fire, or so it felt.

But no. Instead he watched, with mild dispassionate interest, much the way he might watch the sunset or the sunrise.

Boor, she reminded herself.

Still, she found herself saying, "You can have it, if you like."

"The . . . book?" He looked mystified.

She nodded, mutely. Slowly extended it.

His hands reached out. He took it gingerly.

"Thank you, Miss Danforth," he said gravely.

"You're welcome."

He stared at her a moment longer, and when it seemed she'd say nothing else, he returned his attention to the chessboard.

The alps. Ice skating. Snowbanks.

She tried to think of very cold things in the hopes that the flames in her cheeks would vanish.

Ian Eversea's heart.

Ah, how about that? That was working.

LATER, MUCH LATER, after everyone retired one by one and she had waited because she didn't like to be alone, Tansy returned to her bedroom and was startled by the sight of flowers in a vase.

Ha, Ian Eversea! Take that! Evidence that she was, indeed, appreciated. Desired, even! By not just one man, but by four! That she *did* possess grace and charm and *could* captivate. She stared at the flowers, waiting for a certain triumph to build.

She groaned and dropped her face into her hands and rocked it to and fro. It was no use. She relived the moment, as if it had stretched torturously in time: her hand stretching out the book to

him and his baffled face as he took it. Indulging
her, as if she were a foolish little girl.

She blew out a breath, and then yanked off her
slippers. One at a time.

And then she hurled them at the wall.

Wham.

Wham.

" 'You can have it if you like,' " she mimicked
herself to herself. "Oh, good heavens, what a fool
I am!"

But throwing the slippers had made her feel
marginally better.

Then she stalked over to the desk and settled in.

She fanned out the sheet of foolscap and read
it to herself as if it were a spell she could conjure
right then and there.

How would *anyone* come to know her? To see
her? To love her?

She dipped the quill into ink and wrote.

Has known a loss or two.

She'd begun to suspect it mattered.

Chapter 10

SOME KIND OF THUMP made Ian struggle to the surface from sleep, choking like a half-drowned man, thrashing at his sheets as if he were digging out from an avalanche.

He lay still again.

His lungs sawed greedily for air as he fought his way to the surface of consciousness.

Bloody. Hell.

As he always did, he waited for his breathing to steady, for his heart to quit hammering away like an inmate beating on the bars of a cell.

He peeled the sweat-soaked sheets away from his torso, let the blessed cool air wash over his bare skin. He touched his fingers to the scar at his abdomen. It rather resembled the path that meandered to the Pig & Thistle from the Eversea house, right down to the way it was raised more at the end, like the little hill where the Marquess of Dryden had been shot not long ago. Chase had pointed out the resemblance to the road when they compared scars. Ian figured he could always follow it like a map back to the Eversea house if he drank a bit too much at the pub.

If he didn't stretch regularly and often enough, it drew all the muscles around it taut as a miser's purse strings and he could count on a day or so of agony, solvable only by hard liquor and a soft woman and a hot bath.

It had been dug there by a bayonet on the day of his greatest triumph and his greatest failure.

There were other scars, too, but this was the only one that liked to make its presence known, as surely as if it were another organ. His heart pumped blood, his lungs moved air in and out, and the scar's job was to never let him forget.

The room still felt too close—it was smaller than his own room, and the curtains were heavier—so he heaved his body out of bed and was at the window in a few strides. He shoved it open.

He peered out the window.

And one balcony over . . .

. . . well, damned if that wasn't Miss Danforth.

And how had no one noticed he was sleeping in the room next to *hers*? Surely the duke would have made sure one or the other of them had been removed to a room at the opposite side of the house posthaste.

He decided then and there, however, that he wouldn't request his room be moved. He would stay right where he was.

Lamplight poured out the open window, and she had brought a lamp with her onto the balcony.

Her chin was propped on her fists and she was gazing out over the Eversea grounds, which from her vantage point rolled almost as far as the eye could see. She looked smaller than usual, rather slumped in a manner that was almost defeated. For the first time it occurred to him that the sparkle she seemed to bring everywhere with her resulted from some effort, rather than some supernatural source of charm allotted to her in exchange for selling her soul to the devil.

She tipped her head back, like a bird gulping water. She seemed to be scanning the skies above, for a sign, perhaps, from Heaven. It *was* entirely possible she had some sort of nervous tic. She'd been doing that in the ballroom, too. Or perhaps she was subject to nosebleeds.

And then she lowered her head again, and her shoulders dropped, and her hands disappeared for a moment as she appeared to rummage around somewhere out of sight.

She produced a small pouch and propped it on the edge of the balcony.

And then she removed from the pouch a scrap of something.

What the devil . . . ?

It couldn't be.

Oh, but it was.

It was a *cigarette* paper.

He watched, fascinated and appalled as she expertly ran her tongue down it. Then she flattened it on the balcony edge, shook a little tobacco in a slim line down it. To his wondering eyes . . . she rolled it as adeptly as any soldier.

She held it beneath her nose, closed her eyes, and her shoulders rose and fell as she inhaled deeply.

Holy Mother of—

Ian gave a start when someone knocked on his chamber door. He swore under his breath and ducked back from the curtain.

Yanking the door open, he found a footman there, holding a tray bearing the brandy he'd rung earlier for, as well as a sheet of folded foolscap on a tray. "A message for you, Mr. Eversea."

He flipped it open so quickly he nearly sliced his fingers.

" 'I will in all likelihood take rooms at the Pig & Thistle whilst I'm in Sussex,' " he read aloud.

It was signed *LC*.

Who the devil was . . .

Lady Carstairs.

He'd nearly forgotten about Lady Carstairs.

Beautiful. Brunette. Unusual tastes.

"Yesthankyouverymuchgood-bye."

He shut the door in the startled footman's face and, message in his hand, bolted to the window and peered out.

Surely he'd dreamed that. But she was gone, and the wind was sweeping away a few stray flakes of tobacco.

IT WAS NO use. Just past midnight Tansy threw off her blankets with a long sigh, rolled from her bed and shoved her feet into her slippers. Then she knelt to fish about in one of her trunks and came up with a pair of painted tin soldiers that had once belonged to her brother. She held them gently, and smiled faintly. As much as she cherished the memory of playing soldiers with her brother, she was certain he would rather they saw active duty, so to speak, rather than languish an eternity as mementos. He would have teased her for her sentimentality, anyway.

Soldiers in hand, she seized a candle and progressed down the shadowy hallways to the kitchen.

It was time, if at all possible, to obtain a few answers, or she would likely never sleep a night through again.

Mrs. deWitt was sitting at the table, spectacles perched on her nose, poring over a book of what appeared to be accounts, muttering to herself. ". . . beef for Thursday . . ."

She looked up and shoved over a plate of scones, as if she'd been anticipating Tansy's arrival, and stood to put the kettle on.

Tansy settled in. "Are you going over the accounts?"

"Aye. 'Tis a fine bit of balancing, doin' the budget, though it's generous enough. What's that ye've got in yer 'and, there, Miss Danforth?"

"I thought Jordy might like to have these. They were my brother's."

She pushed the soldiers over to her.

Miss deWitt's eyes went wide with surprise and

then she beamed meltingly. "Ah, the boy ought to 'ave some toys. Ye've the heart of an angel, Miss Danforth, to think of a wee servant boy."

Tansy regally waved away the compliment, but she blushed with pleasure. "I did the accounts after my parents passed away."

"Did ye now?" Mrs. deWitt looked up, sympathy written all over her face.

"I liked it, I discovered."

" 'Tis a bit like a puzzle, isn't it? Deciding what you ought to buy and how much you'll need and so forth?"

"Oh, it is." She'd needed to pension off some of the servants and decide who would remain as a small crew to keep the house open. She'd held difficult conversation after difficult conversation. She'd expected to be overwhelmed, it had instead been a respite. The quiet moments in the kitchen, discussing the day-to-day running of the house with the small staff, was nearly meditative, and she'd found comfort in their voices and company.

"How are you getting on, Miss Danforth?"

"Everyone is quite wonderful." She said this with the same ceremony as she would have said "Amen." It was precisely what she ought to say, she knew.

This made Mrs. deWitt beam.

She bit into the scone. "Heaven on a plate, Mrs. deWitt! I could eat these every day of my life."

"Thank you, my dear. You know how to warm

an old soul's heart. Now, are you enjoying your time with the family?"

"Oh yes! They're all very charming. And there are so many of them and I'm still trying to remember everyone's names. Let me see. Now . . . Colin is married to Madeleine, yes? The lovely dark-haired woman?"

"He is indeed, and a dear girl she is, so clever and kind and quiet."

"And Marcus is married to Louisa? She's so pretty, isn't she?"

"Oh, my, yes, indeed! And two people more perfect for each other cannot be found anywhere on the face of this earth!"

"And there's Genevieve married to the duke . . ."

Mrs. deWitt sighed happily. "Such a love story, that one, and what a grand man."

"And then there's Ian and . . ."

Mrs. deWitt's gaze drifted. "Well, would you look at that time? We ought to be in bed, the two of us."

She stood up and began bustling about, pushing utensils and crockery around the kitchen rather aimlessly.

"And then there's *Ian and* . . ." Tansy repeated stubbornly.

Mrs. deWitt went still in the midst of shuffling.

And then at last she sighed heartily and turned, slowly, in resignation.

"Now, child, I can tell you this: ye dinna want your head turned by that one."

"Ha!" Tansy laughed unconvincingly. "Ha ha! My head turned! I ask you! My head is on straight, thank you very much. I was simply curious."

There was a long hesitation during which the cook regarded her shrewdly and Tansy reflected back nothing but bland innocence. She'd perfected the look when she was a little girl.

"God love 'im," the cook sighed at last. "The boy is trouble."

Tansy's heart stood still. This was going to be *good*.

Or awful.

"He's not a boy," she said thoughtfully, before she could think better of it.

Mrs. deWitt looked at her sharply.

"Aye, that he ain't. 'E's a man, and he's been to war and back, and to London and back, and men are shaped by the things they find in both places, aye? For good or for ill. I've seen it time and again. Ye've only to look at the lad, and . . . well, my own old heart turns over when he smiles, and that's the truth. He gets what he wants just that way. 'E's good at heart but 'e's a restless one, and any woman who pins her hopes to him is asking for heartbreak, or my name isn't Margaret deWitt."

Tansy suspected the cook's name really was Margaret deWitt.

She remembered again the look Ian had exchanged with the lovely dark-haired woman at the ball. All silent, understood innuendo, swift and expert and sophisticated, as if Tansy wasn't even there and didn't matter. And a hot little rock of some nameless but deeply unpleasant emotion took up residence in her stomach. Jealousy. Or shame. Definitely from the same family tree as those two emotions.

She didn't like to think of herself as one of legion.

She didn't like to think of Ian Eversea bedding and breaking the hearts of a legion.

Or of anyone, for that matter.

She didn't want to think of herself foolish enough, ordinary enough, to fall just like any other woman.

Nor had she ever in her life thought of herself as a fool.

She risked the question anyway, even though she didn't really want to hear the answer.

"*Has* any woman pinned her hopes . . . ?"

"Oh, a host of them, I daresay. Beginning with poor Theodosia Brackman back when the boy was just fifteen. Then there was—"

"A list won't be necessary," Tansy said hurriedly. Her imagination filled it in, anyway. She expected the list of names all began with *poor*. "Poor Theodosia Brackman, poor Jenny Smith, poor Tansy Danforth . . ."

She'd never been *anyone's* poor *anything*.

". . . and one hears things about—" Mrs. deWitt lowered her voice to a whisper. "—certain kinds of women in London."

She wasn't *that* sheltered. She was certain she knew what "certain kinds of women" meant.

Worse and worse.

Mrs. deWitt probably ought not say such things to her, but probably thought she needed a powerful warning.

It was unpleasant to hear, yet she indeed needed to hear it, the way she needed cod liver oil on occasion. It would do her good. Perhaps it would cure her of what was in all likelihood a passing condition, which, given that it made her charmless, stuttery, and given to blushes, had nothing at all to recommend it. And given that he was indifferent to her charms, was really rather a waste of time. And her talents.

Besides, she was destined for a duke, wasn't she?

She wanted a husband, a family and a home, and it was time to cease wasting her time on thoughts of Ian Eversea.

She returned to her bedchamber filled with scone and resolve, yet her legs and heart felt heavier, somehow, as if she were returning to walking on the ground after a little sojourn in the clouds.

SHE OPENED HER eyes just before dawn again, wondering, before memory set in, why she felt low-spirited.

Then she recalled her figurative dose of cod liver oil from the night before.

And sighed.

The little rosy strip of light lay where it usually did, beckoning her to walk it.

She debated breaking herself of the habit. It would be the mature and sane thing to do. But the gentle little sunbeam road lay there on the carpet, and she found herself sliding from the bed to follow it, the way an animal has no choice but to follow an intriguing scent. She gently parted the curtains.

He was already standing on the balcony. A moment later it occurred to her he was standing unusually still. Staring out over the strata of Sussex colors as she had, only he'd likely seen them countless times before. When he turned to look out over the morning, she thought she saw, but couldn't be sure, darker hollows beneath his eyes. Probably from staying up all night counting the women he'd seduced, the way other people counted sheep. He turned his head, and it seemed to her he was a trifle tense and white about the mouth. Perhaps he'd been at the Pig & Thistle until very late, or romping with a widow, and now his head was pounding.

And at last he stretched as he always did, bending backward, thrusting his arms into the air, and the beautiful line of him arching pulled something taut in her, too, like a bowstring drawn back. She could feel that pulling, tightening sensation inside her.

He began to roar, as she'd heard him do before in the morning, but stopped abruptly and winced.

Then he rested his hands on the edge of the balcony and breathed, his big shoulders moving slowly, deeply. As if something hurt and he was breathing through it.

She could vouch for how hangovers hurt. She wasn't utterly devoid of sophistication.

Perhaps all that heartbreaking he went about doing had worn the poor soul out.

Cod liver oil, she reminded herself. And gave a haughty sniff.

She backed away from the curtain.

Chapter 11

❧

"ARE YOU SURE YOU wouldn't like to come along?" Genevieve hovered in the doorway, pulling on her gloves. "You could accompany Olivia to the meeting of the Society to Protect the Sussex Poor. They would love to have you, I'm certain."

Tansy very much doubted Olivia would love to have her. And besides, she had other plans, and they didn't include spending the day with the frighteningly beautiful Olivia Eversea, whom she had begun to think of as her competition, or, more specifically, the bar above which she planned to rise in Sussex. Because every woman needed a goal. Four bouquets and counting, she thought. And a book.

As if summoned by her thoughts, a footman appeared in the doorway, bearing a great vase full of pink and white flowers. "For you, Miss Danforth. Where would you like me to put them?"

More flowers! She clapped her hands together. "Thank you so very much! How delightful!"

She peered at the note attached and read it

aloud. " 'Because their brightness and purity reminded me of you.' Henry Thorpe, Lord Lester."

Purity, was it, Lord Lester? What on earth had
given him that impression? Still, it was meant to
be a compliment and so she was pleased.

"That's five bouquets for you this morning, and
four for Olivia," Genevieve said, somewhat wickedly. "Good heavens, I never did think anyone
would give Olivia any bouquet competition."

"Oh, I would *never* dream of counting!" Tansy
said, staring down at her note. "What a generous
lot the young men of Sussex are."

"I suppose they are."

She turned to the footman. "Perhaps we can
distribute the flowers a little more widely? If you
would take a bouquet to Mrs. deWitt, and then
perhaps send one down to the vicarage for anybody buried in the churchyard who might need a
flower or two?"

The footman was clearly enchanted, too. He
beamed at her. "Anything you like, Miss Danforth."

Genevieve watched the footman depart, the
corner of her mouth quirked wryly. "Will you
be all right on your own today, Tansy? We'll in
all likelihood be gone until this evening, at least.
With luck we'll be home before dinnertime."

Genevieve sounded genuinely worried. Tansy
reached impulsively for her hands.

"Oh, you're so very kind to invite me along
with the two of you, but I've so much correspondence from home to attend to—a few matters of

business, you know—and it would be a wonderful opportunity to see to it. And tomorrow, with the marksmanship contest, will be so very social and lively. But perhaps I can persuade a groom to accompany me on a short ride? I do so love to ride!"

"What a wonderful idea! Of course! I'll have them saddle my mare for you! She's lovely. And the groom will be happy to accompany you."

Tansy also had no intention of taking a groom, and had every confidence she could concoct a story to convince the groom to stay put and not make a fuss. Why *should* she take someone? She rode like she was born to the saddle, which she nearly had been, and she was accustomed to riding alone over her property at home, or with her papa at her side. She wasn't going far. She could, in fact, see her destination, if she peered hard enough through her bedroom window. It wasn't as though she would be set upon by brigands. There was no place for them to hide in this mild little landscape, unless perhaps they dressed all in green and leaped out from the shrubberies. A brigand would get bored indeed waiting for someone to trundle by, and would likely fall asleep before someone did.

And she just didn't want anyone to witness what she wanted to do today. Not even a groom, who likely wouldn't say a word, given that servants were paid for their discretion.

She told the groom she was off to meet a friend

at the end of the drive and kicked the little mare into a trot before he could say anything.

She had her eye on the fluffy knot of woods beyond the stream and not far off the road she'd walked with Genevieve into town.

The air was delicious; both she and the mare gulped great winey draughts of it, and tossed their heads. She would love to have undone her bonnet and let her hair fly free.

She drew the mare to a halt.

A girl was sitting next to the stream, arms wrapped around her knees. A long apron covered a brown walking dress decorated only with a narrow band of lace at the sleeves.

"Oh. Good morning," Tansy said cautiously.

"Good morning," said the girl, just as cautiously. Very politely.

It seemed that no other conversation would be forthcoming. They continued to study each other.

Until the girl asked, "Are you Miss Danforth?"

"Why, yes, I am." In a small town, doubtless nothing remained a secret for long, and this girl probably knew everyone there was to know.

"How do you do, Miss Danforth. I'm Polly Hawthorne. My father owns the Pig & Thistle. The pub."

"Oh, of course! I've seen it. Seems a lovely place. I hope to visit while I'm in Sussex."

It was the right thing to say. Polly smiled. She was a pretty thing, almost elfin, small and slight with big dark eyes, a pointed chin, and black hair wound up in a braid.

The two wordlessly eyed each other a bit longer. Tansy sensed no one knew Polly was here, either. While at the same time, the girl doubtless knew that well-bred young ladies didn't ride alone, unless they were up to something.

"I just like to have a bit of a think here, when I get a moment away from the pub," Polly said by way of explanation. "About life, and the pub, and the Everseas, and the like."

Tansy shrugged, as if this went without saying. "It's hard not to think about the Everseas, I daresay. There are so many of them and they're everywhere you look. And admittedly they are easy on the eyes."

Polly grinned at that. "They do brighten up the Pig & Thistle. And to think so many of them almost died."

This was startling. "You don't say?"

"Well, I was just thinking about it this morning, you know, because I hear Captain Ian Eversea will be traveling again, and on a dangerous trip, for all of that. Master Colin, he nearly lost his life at the gallows, until there was an explosion and he disappeared. And Master Chase—the other Captain Eversea—his leg was injured. And Master Ian nearly lost his life in the war, I'm told. It's livelier at the pub when they're all home, and they do leave generous tips. And they're so kind. Sometimes I think Master Ian is kindest of all."

It was quite a fascinating litany. Colin had gone to the gallows? *Had* Ian nearly lost his life? Tansy's heart clutched at the thought. To think she might have never seen him from across a crowded ballroom and lost so many things: her ability to think, to speak, to charm.

And he was *leaving*?

When would that be?

Her gut felt hollow at the thought.

She tossed her head. It mattered not at all to her.

Well, so be it. She'd sworn off him, anyway, and it was so much more pleasant to be celebrated rather than ignored.

"It's a pleasant spot for a bit of a think. I was looking for one of my own," she said to Polly, tentatively.

"I won't keep you."

Tansy nearly laughed. She liked this strangely regal young girl, for no real reason except that she seemed utterly self-possessed. And she was convinced Polly wouldn't say a word about seeing her here.

"Perhaps I'll see you at the Pig & Thistle, then."

Polly nodded politely, and Tansy drew her horse around and set a course for the trees. And presumably Polly resumed pondering Everseas. Polly, who would likely live and die in Pennyroyal Green, and might never even see London, and so the Everseas, such as they were, comprised the weather of her days.

There was a lovely hush in this little wild portion of the woods; some of the trees seemed as old as time itself, through birches and hawthorn, over a little rise, until she saw a clearing.

It was small, mossy, surrounded by a number of large oaks and a horseshoe of shrubbery, but it would get enough light, and one day, perhaps next spring, anyone meandering by would think they'd stumbled across a fairy bower, if everything went according to plan.

She would have to hurry, as the sun was growing higher and she didn't want to perspire through her muslin.

She dismounted and tangled the reins in a hawthorn, then unwrapped a bundle of things she'd brought with her.

An hour or so of dirty, satisfying labor later her work was nearly done. She stood back, peeled off her work gloves, and surveyed her handiwork. Then sprinkled it all carefully with water from the two flasks she'd brought with her.

Then she led her horse over to the fallen tree and settled herself in the saddle again.

Polly was gone. Back at the Pig & Thistle, no doubt.

On the way home, Tansy indulged in loosening her bonnet and letting it dangle behind her so the breeze could run its fingers through her hair. Surely she wouldn't brown in just the few minutes it took to ride from the forest back.

She rode blithely back to the stables at Eversea House, confident no one would have witnessed a thing.

She was blissfully unaware of Ian Eversea standing at his window, frowning, watching her golden head bobbing like a guinea atop Genevieve's mare, scandalously, well-nigh incriminatingly, alone and looking a trifle disheveled.

SOME KIND OF thud in the wall had awakened Ian from a perfectly satisfactory nap. It was the second night in a row that such a thing had happened. Were the rodents brawling for territory in the walls? Perhaps they ought to get a few cats.

He rolled from bed and was instantly, mercilessly, humbled by the fact that he was no longer twenty years old and able to abuse his body in all manner of ways without consequences. His muscles had tightened after all that bending and hammering on the vicarage roof. He needed to stretch and bend all his limbs and have a good scratch before he could move with any sort of grace.

He settled in at his desk and bent again over his map. He'd marked his ports of call with a neat little star. China. India. Africa. South America. America. He could keep moving just like this for years, if he wanted to. And something in him eased when he looked at that map. Whenever he felt like a dammed river, whenever he felt caught between Sussex and London, whenever Chase or Colin said the word "wife" in a way that made him want to kick both of them, he found the map a great comfort. The day was coming when he would set foot on the ship and it would move over the ocean and not stop moving. It sounded perfect. He had no doubt about what and whom he would miss. It was just that he suspected moving would feel like a relief, and that whatever dogged him might finally be left behind somewhere on the South Seas.

He looked down at the book on his desk. He hefted it in his hand, idly ruffled the pages, and quirked his mouth wryly. Why in God's name would Miss Danforth give him a bloody book? And blush scarlet while doing it? In all likelihood for the same reasons Landsdowne had given *her* one. Perhaps she had a cat's talent for crawling into the lap of the one person who could scarcely tolerate it. Miss Danforth was likely the sort who couldn't rest until everyone worshipped her. It was wearisome and irritating, yet admittedly faintly amusing.

All in all, however, the very notion of her made him tired. The girl wasn't quite who she wanted everyone to think she was, and that troubled him.

Still, the book had been a gift. And as he remembered her face flushing scarlet, he laid it aside again with a certain tenderness he couldn't quite explain.

He looked up.

It was nearly twilight, and a stiff breeze was beginning to sidle in through his window, which was open a few inches.

He crossed to it to pull the curtains closed and peered out, then ducked back in, hiding behind the curtain.

Miss Danforth was out on the balcony, and

her blond hair down about her shoulders—good Lord, she had miles of it— almost created its own light, so brilliant was it beneath the half-moon. Soothing stuff. His hands flexed absently as he imagined drawing his fingers through it.

He watched, mystified, as she leaned slowly forward and assumed something like an awkward arabesque. Her night rail filled like a sail in a passing breeze, and he was treated to a glimpse of very fine white calf before it deflated. She tilted her head at an impossible angle, and her hair fell in a great sheet down her back. Soothing as watching a river move.

But what the devil was she *doing*? Perhaps it was some sort of interpretive dance? Was she bowing toward America the way Muslims bowed in the direction of Mecca?

He winced as she gracelessly righted herself again, her arms seesawing. He could rule out dancer.

She slumped again, propped her chin on her fists on the rail of the balcony and returned to gazing out at the black of the Sussex hills, as if she expected something to emerge from it, or something had vanished there. Perhaps expecting some beau to come and climb the balcony, à la Romeo Montague.

It was funny, but he'd done that more than once, too: stare off into the dark as if it were a crystal ball, as if the dark could reveal to him as much as it concealed.

And then she dropped her hands and rummaged about again at something he couldn't see. He held his breath, as he waited for the pouch of tobacco to appear.

She emerged with a bottle.

Of what appeared to be . . . Mother of God . . . *Liquor.*

Surely not.

Surely he was *dreaming* this.

It was followed by a little glass, which she settled with a little clink on the edge of the balcony.

She yanked the cork and splashed just a drop or two into the bottom of it.

Clear liquor, which meant it was either gin or whisky.

Or water. Perhaps she found English water intolerable? Perhaps she'd imported American water.

But then she toasted the darkness and bolted it, and there was no mistaking the wince. God knows he'd winced just like that countless times in his life.

And like a diva leaving the stage after a second act, she backed into her room again.

Chapter 12

THE SUSSEX MARKSMANSHIP TROPHY gleamed on a little podium like a grail.

Which it was, for every man gathered. The contest would begin with archery, progress to shooting, and end with winner carrying away a tall silver cup, theirs to keep until the following year.

The row of targets were arrayed, waiting to have their hearts pierced with arrows.

The Everseas and Redmonds took turns hosting the contest, and this year the honor fell to the Everseas. Ian was the Master of Ceremonies, graciously bowing out of the competition, having taken home the cup twice in previous years.

Nearly everyone in Pennyroyal Green and Greater Sussex appeared to be present, including a few Gypsies and a regiment of soldiers, resplendent in red coats. The Pig & Thistle had been closed for the duration, and Ned was there with Polly.

Most years, the men would arrive and stand, eyes shaded, admiring the silver cups and fantasizing about victory, while exchanging advice and playful insults about prowess.

This year fully half of the men were gazing at another sort of grail.

Off on the sidelines, Miss Danforth, in a pale blue walking dress with a darker blue ribbon trimming it, had managed to find a place in the sun where the satin trim gleamed, setting her off like a beacon. She was surrounded by a crowd of admirers that ebbed and flowed a bit like the tide, according to whomever she was bestowing her attention upon. Lord Henry was among them, as was Simon Covington and Seamus Duggan, and Landsdowne was on the periphery, though he was at least proximate to Olivia. Ian saw his sisters, Genevieve and Olivia, Evie Sylvaine—his vicar cousin's wife—Josephine Charing, Amy Pitney, and a few other worthy ladies of the Society to Protect the Sussex Poor. But they stood in a knot that looked decidedly judgmental. A murder of crows, a pride of lions, a judgment of ladies, he amused himself by thinking. Still, he might need to revise it to a murder of ladies, given some of the expressions.

They were to take the competition in several sets; the contestants would have three shots each at different distances.

"Set one!" he called. "Take your places, please!"

The men filed onto the field, Simon among them, and he smiled and saluted in the direction of Miss Danforth.

"Good luck!" she called cheerily.

Seamus Duggan, who'd been too busy being poor and then a bit of a roustabout for most of his life, wasn't an archer, and so he was able to watch from the sidelines. Very close to Miss Danforth. He waved at Simon cheerily, ironically, too.

"READY!" Ian called.

The archers hoisted their bows and selected their arrows.

"AIM!"

The bowstrings were drawn back in near balletic unison, and targets were skewered with steely gazes.

And just then Seamus Duggan stepped in front of Miss Danforth and she reached out to touch his elbow, reflexively.

When Seamus Duggan turned to smile at her, Simon reflexively rotated toward the two of them as if he were helpless not to, as though it were a crime in progress he needed to arrest immediately.

And that's when he shot the arrow into the crowd.

Time seemed to slow as it whipped through the air toward the masses of people.

"RUN!" Somebody—many somebodies—screamed.

The crowd scattered in all directions like flushed birds, screaming for their lives, shedding handkerchiefs and bonnets and shoes in their haste to flee.

And when they had retreated and checked their persons for arrows, there was a murmur of relief and congratulations.

Which tapered off into a hush when it became clear one man remained behind.

Quite conspicuously behind.

Almost as though . . . he'd been skewered in place.

A brief ominous silence ensued as all eyes turned Lord Henry's way.

He was still upright.

He was white as a flag of surrender.

"I . . . think I've been shot," he said, bemused.

Alas, nobody disagreed.

The hush seemed to gather density, like a thunderstorm about to break.

"Yes, I do believe I've been shot." He said this louder.

Then louder, as shock gave way to clarity and, presumably, to pain. "*Help!* I've been shot! Help! Help! Murder! *Murder!* Murderer!" He pointed a quivering finger at Simon, who looked as though he wished the ground would swallow him.

There was a great murmuring in the crowd.

"Unless yer 'eart is in your arse, Henry, I think you'll live to see another day," someone shouted.

Henry whirled vainly trying to get a look, like a dog chasing its tail.

The arrow had entered his left buttock cheek. Everybody could see that except him.

"He shot me on purpose! *Scoundrel!*" He lunged

for Simon, just as Ian lunged for him, to seize his arm and pull him back.

"Calm yourself, lad. You oughtn't move over-much."

The arrow was well and truly in there, piercing right through the nankeen.

"Aye, 'ave a rest, milord. Ye might not want to sit down to rest just yet, though," someone called, to general laughter.

"Don't laugh!" somebody else shouted. "'Tis a tragedy! He needs 'is arse for horse riding and sittin' at the pub chairs!"

"'E looks a bit like a weathervane, don't 'e, wi' that thing stickin' out o' 'im?"

"That's a fine tail feather ye got there, m'lord! Ye look like me prize rooster!"

"That there be a mighty funny-looking grouse ye've bagged there, Simon! Are you going to serve him up tonight?"

Simon was wretched and white-faced with shock. His hands were trembling. "Stop it!"

"Wot's it feel like, m'lord?" somebody asked the wounded Lord Henry.

"It hurts!" he said, sounding surprised and martyred. And a bit intrigued. "Quite a bit, actually." He was doing an admirable job of not weeping, though it certainly looked as though he wanted to. And Ian knew the look of a man who would faint at any moment.

"All right. That's enough," he barked. "Behave yourselves, gentlemen. And ladies," he added ironically with a swift and pointed look in Tansy Danforth's direction, whose gaze fled from his. Having been skewered before, though admittedly not with an arrow, Ian had a good deal of sympathy for it. "Is your father at home, Miss Pitney?" he called.

Miss Amy Pitney's father was the town doctor.

"The next town over, delivering a baby," she said regretfully.

Ian sighed. His shoulders slumped. "Very well. I need ten tall and preferably wide volunteers . . ."

AND THAT'S HOW, thanks to Miss Danforth, Ian found himself on his hands and knees carefully extracting an arrow from the large white hindquarter of a whimpering man.

He was laid out, facedown, on a blanket. Rather like a grouse at a banquet, in fact. Ian's volunteers surrounded poor Lord Henry in a circle, backs to him, shielding him from the crowd. Nankeen was trimmed away neatly with a knife. Ian thrust his flask at him and instructed him to drink. He was given a rag with which to muffle his screams. And when the arrow was extracted, he was bandaged adroitly, because Ian had needed to do it dozens of times before during the war.

Lord Henry didn't faint, but it was a near thing.

"See the doctor this evening, if you can," Ian instructed the unfortunate, punctured Henry.

Simon was white and wringing his hands, hovering on the outskirts of the circle. "I'm sorry. I'm

so sorry, I'm so sorry, I'm so sorry. I didn't mean it,
Henry, I'm so sorry."

"No hard feelings." Harry was clipped but
magnanimous in martyrdom. "Do you intend to
shoot Duggan next?"

Ian seized Simon by the elbow and pulled him
aside.

"How in the bloody hell did that happen?
You're a better shot than that, Simon. Not as good
as I am, naturally, but . . ."

Ian knew how it had happened. Or why it had
happened. He wanted to hear it from the man
himself.

Simon drew in a long breath and exhaled miserably, thrusting his hands deep into his pockets.

"It's just . . . Ian, it's well . . . it's just . . . well,
look at her," he said with muffled anguish. "I don't
want to think the way I think, Ian. I really don't,
but . . . *look* at her."

Miss Danforth was wringing her hands, and
a small crowd of young men were jostling each
other for the honor of comforting her. From where
he stood he could see the sun glance off the tears
glittering in the corners of her big eyes. Her lush
lower lip was trembling. She looked convincingly
distraught, for someone so skilled at fomenting
mayhem.

Instantly, a half-dozen handkerchiefs were
thrust out to her. She looked up, limpidly grateful.

"Oh, she's pretty, all right," Ian said grimly.

Behind them was a small knot of females, all of

whose mouths had gone hard and horizontal and whose arms were crossed across their chests. Ian was reminded of wasps about to swarm.

"Pretty? She's an *angel*!" Simon corrected, on an outraged hush. "So delicate and kind."

"I'm not certain 'flattery' and 'kindness' are synonymous, Simon."

"You can simply tell she has a heart of gold. Like her hair . . ." he said dreamily.

Ian snapped his fingers beneath his nose, and Simon looked surprised.

"You shot Lord Henry because she's an angel? I think you have your winged beings confused. It's *Cupid* who supposedly shoots arrows at people."

"It was an accident! I was distracted. She was . . . she did . . . she did something to distract me, let's just leave it at that. She said archery was her favorite sport of all. That no one looked more like a Greek god than with a bow and arrow. And . . ."

"And you . . . wanted to be a Greek god?"

"Of course! Wouldn't you?"

"But Cupid is the deity with arrows, and he's a fat little baby."

Simon sighed with exasperation. "I think you're missing my point, Captain Eversea. What *wouldn't* you do for a woman like that? I care for my Josephine with all my heart. And yet . . ."

Ian looked over there again, and found Miss Danforth looking his way, her eyes bright and silvery even from that distance. As if she wanted to see his opinion of her performance.

He raised his hand in a subtle, sardonic little salute.

She gave her head a little toss and graciously waved away the handkerchiefs thrust at her. Tilted her head up and offered up a tremulous smile to the crowd of men.

On the outskirts of which stood Josephine Charing and Amy Pitney, who looked very willing to shoot her with an arrow. Ian was confident their aims would be terrible, and confident Miss Danforth would somehow escape, because if ever there was a survivor, she was one.

It was an interesting question, however, that Simon had posed. Ian had done a lot to *get* a woman. Doing something foolhardy *for* a woman, in order to impress a woman, however, or earn her regard . . . never. Never had he made a fool of himself for a woman. Most of his family failed to recognize he had a pragmatic streak a mile wide. He'd never called anyone out and he'd never yet been called out, though the duke had cut it very fine. He'd never lost his mind over a woman, though he'd nearly lost his life over one and had certainly lost his dignity once.

He'd never lost his mind to the point where he'd shot anyone with an arrow over one, that much was certain.

"I think *you* need a drink, Simon. I think we all need a drink. And you best make sure Henry truly forgives you. Because the next competition is shooting, and I saw enough carnage during the war."

PERHAPS IT HAD been all the stiff drinking they'd done to settle rattled nerves after the arrow incident, or perhaps it was because not enough drinking had been done in the wake of the arrow incident, but otherwise skillful marksmen were shooting shamefully wide of the mark. Over and over and over.

And the mark target was an apple, glowing like a beacon at one hundred paces.

They stepped up, one by one.

Shot, one by one.

And missed, one by one, again and again and again.

The apple remained mockingly smooth and whole and gleamed improbably in the sunlight.

"I don't know what the trouble is," Ian muttered. "At this rate, if we all needed to shoot our food in order to survive, we'd starve."

He would have loved to shoot it. It was such an easy target, and he was such a skillful shot, and he felt trapped in a moment that was both dull and embarrassing. The apple needed shooting, for God's sake.

Yet another hapless contestant stepped up to fire, and missed.

"Oh, for heaven's *sake*," Tansy Danforth muttered.

He swiveled toward her in surprise.

Her eyes flew innocently wide. She bit her lush bottom lip. Which instantly made him wonder what it might be like to sink his own teeth gently into it.

Which surprised him, and made him frown more darkly than he intended.

She at least blinked at the frown. "May *I* . . . have a go?" She said it tentatively. Very shyly. The lashes went down.

He almost sighed.

This posed a bit of a dilemma, as within days of meeting her the men of Sussex had decided they wouldn't dream of depriving Miss Danforth of any whim.

The gentleman currently holding the musket turned to her.

"It's a very heavy gun," he apologized, as if he'd forged it himself and should have anticipated her need to shoot it.

"I'm sturdier than I look."

This brought a rustle of chuckles and the choked, helpless words, "Like gossamer," from somebody.

Ian rolled his eyes.

"Very well," the man said. "It's a bit unusual, but as you're a guest, perhaps we can make an exception for Miss Danforth . . . Captain Eversea? What say you? May we have a ruling?"

All the men in the crowd were nodding encouragingly.

Ian was torn between genuine concern that she would sneeze or topple beneath the weight of the musket and shoot someone in the crowd, and he was more or less fond of, or at least used to, everyone in that crowd, and wanting to see what would happen when she fired that thing.

Because he had a hunch about Miss Danforth.

"Nobody move, nobody say a word when she pulls the trigger, are we clear? I want no undue distractions. I want everyone to hold as still as they possibly can. Pretend it's the aftermath of Pompeii and you'll never move again. Are we clear?"

Heads bobbed up and down.

And then they dutifully froze.

After all, the truly undue distraction, Miss Danforth, would be the one holding the musket.

"Allow me." Ian took the musket from the previous shooter, who promptly froze into position. "Now, allow me to show you how to hold it, Miss Danforth."

She cleared her throat. "Oh. Good idea."

Suddenly Miss Danforth was blushing again. She untied the ribbons of her bonnet slowly, carefully, and something about that motion— the undoing of a ribbon, a sort of ceremonial undressing—again touched soft little carnal fingers to the back of his neck.

What the devil was it about her? There was just . . . something innately sensual about the girl. He remembered watching her emerge from the woods, her bonnet bobbing behind her, and wondered if this seeming innocent might have come by her sensuality by taking a secret lover. But no; everything else about her was virginal.

He realized he was staring, and she was staring back at him, her bonnet now dangling from her fingers. She lowered it gently to her feet.

He gave himself a shake.

"Very well, Miss Danforth. You heft the musket up to your shoulder just . . . so . . ."

He stood behind her, and heft it up just so. Her hands went up and expertly closed around the weapon.

He was close enough now to feel the heat from her body. She radiated warmth like a little sun. Close enough to see the little arc of pale nape, and the scattering of fine golden hairs there. The temptation was to brush a finger over them, or to apply a slow, hot kiss on that little secret strip of skin. He knew from experience it was a splendid way to get nipples to go erect.

He realized he hadn't moved in some time, mesmerized, in a bit of a reverie, and it might have been seconds or hours. He looked up. Everyone was still frozen in place. But some incredulous glares were aimed his way.

He cleared his throat.

"You hold it like this . . ." he said, then realized he'd already said that.

Ian braced himself as a good portion of the crowd tensed and bristled and stirred.

"I wager she shmells like rainbowsh," someone near him surmised on a murmur. Someone who had been at his flask all morning, from the sound of it.

She didn't. She smelled faintly of something floral, perhaps lavender, but he was no expert on flowers. The sweetness and tang of fine milled soap rose from her warmed skin. It was as if suddenly someone had flung open a door onto a sylvan meadow. He could feel a sort of delicious torpor stealing in, as if he could easily melt into her. Surely the temptation to close his arms around her and pull her into his body was nothing more than a reflex. That was what one *did* when women were just this close, after all.

When a beautiful woman was this close.

A beautiful woman who smelled like a meadow.

So he made sure she had it hoisted correctly and then stepped back abruptly and lifted his arms in the air, as though held at gunpoint or as if she were a hot stove, so the crowd wouldn't rush him with pitchforks and torches.

Interestingly, that musket nestled into her arms like a long lost pet.

Ian had a hunch they were looking at a ringer.

He folded his arms over his chest.

"Now, this thing has a bit of a recoil, Miss Danforth."

"I've been watching, thank you," she said primly. "I think I may be prepared."

The crowd obeyed their orders.

The silence was, in fact, so taut, Ian thought he could have bounced a guinea from it.

And just when it seemed no one could hold their breath any longer, she pulled the trigger.

She flew backward into Ian as the apple exploded.

He levered her upright. He felt his fingers linger on her shoulder blades. They were delicate, and there was another moment where her fragility caught him by surprise. That rogue surge of protectiveness swept in again. And swept out.

Such a joyous roar arose you would have thought she'd negotiated armistice after a long and bloody war.

She stood holding the musket, still aiming it, wearing a look of grim satisfaction, but, interestingly, not surprise.

She smiled modestly.

"A fluke, surely," she insisted demurely, again and again, as all the men surged forth to congratulate her. "Beginner's luck, of a certainty. Americans. We're born knowing how to shoot things, I suppose. All those bears and wolves and Indians from which we need to defend ourselves."

"I'll defend you, Miss Danforth!" came a voice from the crowd.

"I would *never* be afraid if I were protected by an army comprised of the men of Pennyroyal Green and Greater Sussex. I've never known such gallant, thoughtful men."

For God's *sake*. Surely at least Seamus Duggan, who was Irish, would recognize blarney for what it was.

And yet they all seemed like hounds, pushing their snouts into her hand for more strokes every time she said such things.

She was no beginner, he'd wager. At shooting, or at creating a mythology for himself, or at getting men to eat out of her hand.

Wallflower, his *eye*.

He ought to know. He conducted his own seductions with the finesse of a fine conductor.

"Well done, Miss Danforth," he said quite cynically.

She turned her gaze upon him. He felt himself brace against the impact of it, which surprised him. He blinked. There were times he forgot—or would like to forget—just how very pretty she was. He was accustomed to beauty. But hers was stealthy; his body reacted to it before his mind could dismiss it.

And for a moment he could have sworn he might have blushed.

It made him strangely angry; he felt tricked, somehow. He did not want to find a woman he distrusted so thoroughly appealing.

To his surprise, scarlet rushed into *her* cheeks again.

"Thank you, Captain Eversea. The compliment means a good deal coming from you."

"Does it?" he said so abruptly, so ironically, she blinked. "Why?"

One never knew whether she meant what she said.

She apparently had no answer for that—she stared wide-eyed up at him as if her wits had abandoned her, or as if he'd caught her in the midst of some heinous act. And that flush migrated into her tawny cheeks and spread down her collarbone, and he watched its progress.

And for a moment he found himself simply staring back, as if he'd been given an opportunity to observe a rare wild creature.

Their mutual stare was interrupted by two men chuffing over, ferrying the trophy between them.

"We've all between us decided you deserve the trophy this year, Miss Danforth."

"Oh, my goodness! Surely I don't warrant the trophy for shooting one little apple!"

"It would be our pleasure. What say you, Captain Eversea?"

Miss Danforth stared up at him, and her white teeth sank into her bottom lip.

He could have sworn she was holding her breath.

"Miss Danforth may have the trophy."

The trophy came nearly up to her hip.

And there was no shortage of volunteers to haul it back to the house for her.

Chapter 13

THE ENTIRE MARKSMANSHIP COMPETITION crowd migrated to Eversea House, thrown open for the purposes of a party, and happy villagers and competitors milled over the lawn—admittedly, some did more staggering than milling—as well as in and out of the larger parlor, and a long table had been dragged out to the green, covered with a cloth, and piled with an assortment of little cakes and fruit. Ned Hawthorne had been persuaded to part with a few kegs of his light and dark for a price ruthlessly haggled by Mrs. deWitt. An impromptu orchestra of sorts was recruited—really, two fiddles and an accordion. Dancing commenced on the lawn.

IAN WANDERED INTO the house and paused on the periphery of the parlor, studying the scene before him.

He gave a short laugh. The light loved Tansy. He would have sworn it deliberately sought her out like any other lovesick swain, and bathed her in glow.

It could, of course, be the other way around. She in all likelihood had a stage diva's knack for finding the best light in any given room. Regardless, it was easy to imagine her as the lamp in a room and all the young men as moths, circulating, moving in closer at their peril. Each of them secretly soldiers in the game of love, plotting strategies.

They hadn't a prayer. Titania Danforth was Napoleon.

She could possibly even outshoot Napoleon.

She held court on a settee, accepting a plate of cakes and a glass of ratafia from one swain, smiling up at another. Like the sun, the rays of her attention seemed to effortlessly include all of them while leaving each both convinced and uncertain whether he was her favorite. Or whether she had one.

It might have been more amusing—he might have admired the sheer mastery and showmanship—if one of the men circulating hadn't been Lord Landsdowne. Granted, Landsdowne wasn't quite as obvious as the younger men about it. But then, he wouldn't be. Ian watched him, as he'd watched him the other night, and recognized the look on his face. Not rapt, per se. But a certain inscrutable thoughtfulness. He was a patient man. Older. Wealthy. Titled. Utterly confident, quite solid. He'd courted Olivia in patient, persistent, inventive ways that kept her intrigued, and had lured his notoriously capricious sister into something close to an understanding. And that was by no means an unimpressive feat, given that no man in three years had come near to anything of the sort.

And the trouble was, he'd seen that look on Landsdowne's face when he'd looked at Olivia.

And when he thought of Olivia—his proud, difficult, brilliant, charming, beautiful sister—the idea of her sustaining yet another blow to her heart made him suck in his breath, as if he was sustaining that blow right now.

A cluster of women were arrayed opposite. One of them was Olivia, and she was pretending not to notice. And yet he was somehow certain she was suffering.

Suddenly Colin was next to him, a seed cake in one hand and a glass of something that looked like the Pig & Thistle's dark in the other.

He followed the line of Ian's gaze.

"So . . . what do you think of our Miss Danforth?"

"She's horrible." Ian presented the word absently, with a sort of reverent hush.

Colin's head jerked around to stare at him. "What on . . . Did you sustain a blow to the head? How on earth did you draw *that* conclusion?"

"It all began when she didn't blink at all when I said the word tits. And you just did, and you're a jaded roué. Or were, before you were married."

"Insults and blinking aside . . . I'm struggling to imagine the context in which one would say 'tits' to Miss Danforth."

"She dared me." Ian said this on an awestruck hush. "That . . . that . . . *wench* actually led me right to it. Or rather, she led me into saying 'Titsy,' but the difference is the same."

Colin was examining him thoughtfully, with concern, as though searching for signs of fever.

"Assuming this is true," he said, "and I'll allow that it's a trifle unusual, given her wealth and background and youth, and so forth . . . you didn't have to take that dare, now, did you?"

Ian launched an incredulous eyebrow. *How long have you known me?* "Furthermore she goes about collecting hearts as blithely as if she's picking blueberries, Colin. Without thought to the consequence."

"Hmm. Now, who does that remind me of?"

"She smokes and drinks! Hard liquor!" Ian insisted wildly.

Colin snorted. "I'm starting to think *you've* been smoking and drinking hard liquor."

Ian hesitated, and then presented his coup de grace on a hoarse whisper: "I think she may even have a secret *lover.*"

It was quite an accusation, and he knew it.

This drew Colin up to his full height. He fixed his brother with a hard, searching stare. For one wild instant Ian wondered if he was about to be called out.

Then Colin's face cleared as if he'd clearly reached a conclusion.

"How long has it been since *you've* taken a lover? A good week or so? No wonder you're losing your mind."

Excellent sarcasm.

"I'm telling you, Colin, she's Beelzebub in a bonnet. Satan in Satin."

"The devil in damask?"

"Precisely," Ian agreed fervently. Deliberately ignoring Colin's irony.

"Ian . . ." Colin's tone was placating. "I wonder if this isn't all wishful thinking on your part, because you know the duke will murder you sooner or later and Genevieve would never forgive you if you . . . shall we say . . . went near the girl. Or through her window, to be more specific."

"For God's sake, Colin, I'm not *mad*. You know me. I've never lost my mind over a woman in my life, and I see them all quite clearly, thank you very much. I'm only telling you the conclusions I've drawn upon observation. Just watch her."

As Colin was a good brother, he humored Ian and did just that.

"For heaven's sake, Ian . . . I mean . . . just look at her." His voice went a trifle drifty over the last three words.

Ian turned very, very slowly and glared at Colin. "And?" he said tightly.

"Ian . . . her eyes are so . . . may I tell you something?"

"Go on," Ian said sourly.

"You know I love Madeleine with all my heart. She *is* my heart. I would die for her, etcetera. I've never been happier."

"Very well."

"When I get to Heaven?"

"The 'when' presumes rather a lot."

"I think the color of the skies in Heaven are precisely the same shade as Miss Danforth's."

Ian stared at him. "Et tu?" he said sadly at last. "Et tu, Colin?"

He flung himself back against the wall and banged his head against it, slowly, rhythmically. Similar to the rhythm of a drum playing a man to the gallows.

"Have a drink, Ian, or have a woman. Surely you've one or two on the dangle. Just keep away from *that* one, if she troubles you so. How difficult can it be?"

Sage advice delivered, Colin gave him a thump on the back and peered out toward the garden. "Croquet!" he said happily. "What a splendid idea. Come out to the garden with me and Madeleine. I know hitting something with a mallet will make you feel better."

Ian shot him a weary, wry look. "In a moment."

"Suit yourself."

He watched Colin aim for Madeleine, who was sitting across the room in conversation with Marcus's wife, the way a man in a desert headed for an oasis. But then he always aimed for Madeleine that way.

"A FINE PAINTING I think you'll enjoy hangs in just the other room, and I've long wished to get a look at it. Would you care to accompany me? I'd be honored to hear your opinion."

Sergeant Sutton was dashing, though much of it had to do with the uniform, she was certain. And it was something about the uniform, something about the word "Sergeant" in front of his name, something about his gray eyes, that reminded her a bit of her brother. A bit. But she liked the look of him. He wasn't Ian Eversea handsome, of course—honestly, who was?—but he was handsome enough, and *certainly* considerably friendlier. They'd chatted quite easily about a number of things, and it was this easiness she found a balm after Ian Eversea's eyes on her—judging, searching, and . . . something else had been in his eyes, something darker and more confusing and a bit knowing. Something both thrilling and frightening.

Then again, there was something about being utterly unwilling to let any dare—and this felt a bit like that—go unaccepted.

So she followed Sergeant Sutton down the hallway—quite a ways, it seeemed—until they paused at a painting.

It was a painting of a horse. It struck her as unremarkable, though in all likelihood a fine one, if she had to guess, but she wasn't a student of art. She was fond of horses, and this one was lovely, but then again she couldn't think of a single reason why the Everseas might hang a homely horse on the wall.

"It's an excellent rendering," she decided to say. "It looks very much like a horse."

He didn't say anything. It had suddenly gotten

very quiet. So quiet she could hear Sergeant
Sutton breathing unnaturally loudly.

"Miss Danforth . . . as you've no doubt concluded yourself, we have a spiritual accord."

This was startling information.

"Have we?" she said cautiously.

"Oh yes. Believe me. I have a sense for these
things. I realized it when we both admired the
painting. And do you know what must necessarily become of spiritual accords?"

Having never knowingly experienced a spiritual accord, Tansy answered truthfully, "No."

"They must find release in, shall we say, physical expression."

"Must they?" Damnation. She shot a surreptitious glance over her shoulder, to see if anyone
was in the vicinity. Not a soul. She could no longer
even hear the voices of the revelers. Blast.

She took a step backward. The click of her heel
echoed ominously on the marble, as if to empha-
size just how alone the two of them were.

"Oh yes. It is nature's law. And you're not a
scofflaw, are you?" he teased.

"Not as of yet, I don't believe," she said cautiously. "Although if it's nature's *law,* as you say, I
feel a little lawlessness coming on now."

"Oh, we can fight our desires all we wish, but
nature always wins. Nature knows what's best.
And why shouldn't we give it a little assistance? I
feel that we should."

"*Our* desires, Sergeant Sutton?" He'd stepped

closer. She stepped back. "I *feel* you should have used a different preposition."

He laughed at that.

She took another step back. Another step or two and she would be able to make a reasonably graceful escape without lifting her skirts in her hands and running for it.

But that's when he reached out a hand and closed it around her wrist, brought her hand up to his mouth and pressed a hot kiss into her palm.

"Did you feel that down to your toes, Miss Danforth?"

"Truthfully, I felt it more in the pit of my stomach."

"That's excitement," he reassured her.

"That's revulsion," she corrected, and pulled back on her wrist.

He held fast. "It takes a moment for the effect to take hold. Sometimes it takes more than one kiss to get the job done."

He used her own arm as a lever to pull her closer, and even though she dug in her heels, her slippers slid across the marble as if she were on skis. The dark little caverns of his nostrils loomed and time seemed to slow as the dark maw slowly opened in preparation to latch over hers. The stench of cheap tobacco smoke permeating his coat stunned her senses, and she was just about to spit on him when—

"Unhand her."

The voice was lazy. Offhand. Quiet.

But something about it stood all the hair on the back of her neck on end.

She'd never heard anything more menacing in her life.

Sergeant Sutton dropped her arm as if it were a snake and spun around.

"Captain Eversea!"

Ian Eversea was indeed standing there, towering, his posture gracefully indolent. But his face was granite, apart from the faint curve of a very unpleasant smile.

Tansy reclaimed her wrist jealously and rubbed at it.

She wondered if she could get away with kicking Sutton now that his attention was diverted. She eyed the back of his trousers.

Ian Eversea took her in with a glance, ascertaining that nothing more than her dignity was hurt, and warned her against violence with the slightest shake of his head.

And he said nothing to her.

"'Physical accord'? 'Spiritual accord'?" His voice was still nearly a drawl, as if he couldn't be bothered to raise it over a toad like Sutton. But his scorn made each word crack like a whip. "I have never heard such a steaming load of shite. Get out of here, Sutton. Go. Before I make it impossible for you to move. And if you ever bother Miss Danforth again, I will make certain she's the last female you ever bother."

Sutton's jaw was tense. A swallow moved in his throat.

The air crackled with suppressed violence, like the prelude to a thunderstorm.

For the first time in a very long time, a surge of genuine fear swept her.

"And you'd know a bit about killing, wouldn't you, sir?" Sutton finally said. It sounded a bit like an insinuation.

Ian smiled at this. Swiftly. It was like watching a saber being unsheathed.

His voice went silky. The voice a cobra might use, Tansy thought, to mesmerize its prey.

"Enough so that one more wouldn't make a damn bit of difference to me, Sergeant."

And before her eyes, Sergeant Sutton blanched. She'd never actually seen someone do precisely that before.

Sutton stared at Ian a moment longer, then muttered some oath under his breath and spun on his heel.

They watched him until he walked down the hallway and disappeared back into the party.

She cleared her throat. "Thank you," she managed, with a certain amount of dignity. Her voice was a bit frayed.

He said nothing. He was staring at her as if he couldn't quite decide whether she deserved killing, too.

"Killing?" she queried. "Done a lot of it?" she said, just to interrupt the stare.

The stare continued.

He still said nothing. He just studied her with those blue eyes, and she felt them on her like cinders.

"May I ask you a question, Miss Danforth?" His voice was still quiet, almost lazy.

She nodded permission.

"What the bloody hell are you playing at?"

Ah. Suspicions confirmed. He *was* angry.

She bit her lip a moment. "You don't have to curse."

Good God. Even she thought that was inane.

She could see he *almost* laughed.

"Oh, my *stars*. I do apologize for my rough ways."

She almost laughed at that. She sensed that would be unwise indeed, because he hadn't yet blinked. There was the sense about him of a coiled spring. Or a primed musket. Whatever anger he'd felt at Sutton—or at her—hadn't yet entirely spent itself. And here she was alone with him.

"Answer me, please."

He was probably a bloody good captain, if she had to guess. Scared the life out of his soldiers by just talking in a quiet voice.

"I'm not sure what you mean," she hedged, though she was pretty certain that she did.

"Flirting with men, encouraging their attentions with wild, insincere, yet strangely effective flattery, generally causing an uproar, all so you can have all of them eating out of your hand, and then recklessly finding yourself in a compromising, even dangerous, position as a result."

Oh. That.

You noticed! she was tempted to say.

"All of them except for you," she pointed out.

She couldn't *believe* she'd said it.

It was fairly clear this had brought him up short. He was staring at her with something like amazement now.

"Or perhaps you're . . . jealous?" she suggested hopefully, weakly. Half jesting.

Her own recklessness amazed her. But in for a penny, in for a pound.

And she wanted to jar a way past that stare.

She was sorry she'd said it when the next expression to take up occupation on his face was incredulity.

He shook his head slowly to and fro.

"I've watched you, Miss Danforth . . . in the midst of your games. And it's so very clear you know little to nothing of the . . . shall we say, matters between men and women. I would wager my entire inheritance on it. And I find game playing combined with ignorance tedious. I'm not a boy."

She was badly stung.

"The matters between men and women! Do you mean sex?"

A heartbeat of utter silence followed.

"I suppose you think you're being very bold," he said quietly.

She was fairly certain she had succeeded in shocking him.

Perhaps even rattling him.

She said nothing, because she'd shocked herself by saying it and needed a moment to recover.

"Have you ever even been kissed before, Miss Danforth?"

She contemplated which answer would incriminate her the least and impress him the most, though why she should want to do the latter eluded her. She *had* been kissed, but it hadn't caused a single unusual physical response.

Whereas simply looking at Ian Eversea seemed to cause her senses to riot.

"Perhaps."

She wouldn't have blamed him if he rolled his eyes.

Perhaps mercifully, the incredulity was simply amplified a bit.

"It's a risky game you play, *Tansy*. Why do you do it?"

She was angry now. "Because. I. *Can*. And because they like it."

"I suspect you mean because they like *you* when you do it."

This brought her up short. A tense little silence followed.

"Why do *you* do it?" she countered. *Ha!*

His eyes flared in surprise, then anger swiftly kindled in them.

Splendid. She was certain she'd at least startled him. *Yes, Captain Eversea, I know about your alleged exploits.* She imagined saying that aloud. She discovered she wasn't *that* brave.

But he ignored the question.

"I won't always be lurking around corners

when you face the consequences of your actions, Tansy. Not every soldier is born a gentleman, and not every gentleman understands the word no. Men are fundamentally brutes. Some just wear better clothes and have more money. You ought to be more afraid."

He was undoubtedly correct. She *ought* to be.

"Come now, Captain Eversea, surely you of all people know that a little risk makes life less dull, altogether."

He gave a short laugh. She suspected she'd surprised it from him.

"*My* risks are calculated, Miss Danforth. And informed by experience."

"And you can't possibly know that I know *nothing* about, as you say, 'such matters.'"

He inhaled deeply, exhaled at length, sounding oh-so-long-suffering. "Oh, you know how to make them yearn, I grant you. You know how to get *attention*. There's a look experienced women have, that's all. A demeanor. And you haven't the look."

This was news. How on earth would an experienced woman look? Shocked? Tired? Wicked? Reflexively, she tried an expression that she thought might incorporate all three.

He laughed again, genuinely. "I've seen that expression on one of Colin's cows, after she'd eaten something she ought not."

Torn between laughing and scowling, she frowned.

"You don't *need* the look. It isn't something to aspire to, Miss Danforth. You're going to marry someone with a title and all the money you'll ever need, isn't that so? Aren't you destined for a duke or something of the sort? So don't even think about practicing. Like I said, I won't always be around to rescue you."

"I imagine you've benefited from that 'look' any number of times, haven't you, Captain Eversea?"

She was out of her depth with him, which made her even more reckless than usual. She was like a kitten with tiny sharp claws crawling up his trouser leg. She suspected he would indulge her only so long before he shook her off abruptly.

"Miss Danforth," he said patiently. "It's clear you want to goad me into saying scandalous things to you that you can take back to your room and savor, pore over at night like found treasure. You want my attention. You don't want the consequences of that attention. You don't even know what the consequences *are*. And for me, it's just . . . it's well, just rather dull," he added with an attempt at kindness, and an intolerably condescending lift of one shoulder. "And in some circumstances, it might even be hurtful. And if someone I care about might be hurt as a result of whatever game you're playing . . . I simply can't allow you to do it."

Dull!

Someone he *cared about*!

Oh, the *infuriating* humiliation. Her eyes burned.

For some reason all of this hurt mortally.

"You don't know me at all," she said, her voice a rasp, her face hot. She could only assume it was a scorching, unflattering red.

"I know you some," he said easily, sounding bored. "And some is enough."

He leaned back against the wall of the terrace, struck a flint against the box and lit a cheroot without asking whether she minded. He sent the smoke up into the air and aimed his gaze out over the landscape he likely knew the way he knew his own face in the mirror.

His own damned handsome, unforgettable face.

"Well, I suppose you're right," she said. "But you ought to know, isn't that true, Captain Eversea? Because you of all people know it's all about the *getting* of someone or of something. Everything you do. Everything else is a waste of time. God forbid a woman should evince an interest in you first. I'll wager you'll run like a frightened little girl."

She couldn't seem to control what came out of her mouth when she was around him. Surely this was inadvisable.

He turned his head sharply then, eyes wide in surprise, then hot with a real fleeting anger. She took a step back, as though he'd lunged at her with a lit torch.

Then something speculative settled into his gaze. He studied her long enough for her heart to flop hard in her chest, painfully, like an obsequious mongrel. Eager to be patted or kicked, whatever he preferred. And she was angry that she was so very inexperienced that she couldn't stop her heart from doing otherwise.

At least she felt *seen* by him for the first time.

Oh, how she wished she knew what he saw.

"Know a bit about being a frightened little girl, do you, Tansy?" he said softly.

Oh.

She felt pinned like a butterfly to a board.

How, how, *how* she wished she had something to throw.

She opened her mouth. But she couldn't speak. Her voice had congealed.

She simply turned and . . .

Well, she didn't precisely run.

But she walked rather more swiftly than she might have done.

And as her footsteps echoed, making her feel as though she was chasing herself, he called after her, dryly, "You're welcome."

Chapter 14

Hɪs ᴛᴇᴍᴘᴇʀ sᴛɪʟʟ ᴏɴ the boil, Ian found himself charging in the opposite direction from the festivities.

As it turned out he was on his way to the kitchen, which he hadn't realized until he arrived. By the time he did, a certain fascination had begun to edge its way into his rather complicated anger, which flared bright and fresh every time he pictured Sutton's hand closed around Tansy Danforth's wrist as she struggled to pull it away. His gut knotted. What a pleasure it would have been to flatten Sutton. She could have been hurt. Or at the very least, quite inexpertly kissed against her will, and no woman should endure that.

How dare the girl put herself at risk like that? How stupid did one have to *be*?

He stopped abruptly and pulled in a long deep breath. He was fair enough to realize his anger seemed all out of proportion to the circumstances.

Is that why you do it?

Ah. And there he had it. What in God's name had the girl heard about him? Or had that just been a guess aimed as skillfully as she'd aimed that musket?

This, perversely, amused him.

And at this thought he could feel something else sneaking in on the heels of his indignation. Something that felt a bit like . . . could it be . . . admiration?

Very, very reluctant admiration.

She *was* quick. He'd give her that.

When she wasn't trying so bloody hard.

He paused in the kitchen. It was mercifully dimly lit and peaceful at the moment. Much to his delight, arrayed on a tray like the crown jewels as if awaiting his arrival, was a solitary fluffy, golden scone. Just the thing for his mood. Surely it was fate.

He reached for it.

From out of nowhere a blur appeared and spanked his hand lightly.

He yelped.

It turned out to be Mrs. deWitt.

"Ow! Why the beating? You hurt my feelings gravely, Mrs. deWitt."

She laughed softly. "As if anyone could ever do that! Ach, dinna touch that, Master Ian. That there be for Miss Danforth."

Even *scones* were held in thrall for the girl?

"That *particular* scone is for Miss Danforth? *Why*, pray tell?"

"Yes, 'tis 'er favorite, and one does like to spoil 'er a bit, now, ye see."

"One *does*," he said, but Mrs. deWitt missed the irony. "Surely, then, there's another very similar scone for me."

"Not until after the baking this afternoon."

"I'll give you a shilling for this one," he said childishly.

She snorted. " 'Ave some cheese."

"I want a scone. I want *that* scone."

"Ah, now, Master Ian, and will *ye* be marryin' a duke, now, or some such, someday? Are ye all alone in the world now? Did ye win a trophy today?"

"Probably not, no and no," he conceded.

"Well then," she said, as if this decided everything.

Imagine that. Defeated by the cook. He wasn't child enough to snatch it from her anyway, though he was sorely tempted.

"Let me find ye a lovely piece of cheese, Master Ian," she pacified.

"Very well." He'd decided to be gracious in defeat. He settled at the table and irritably shoved aside a vase full of flowers.

"Those be for Miss Danforth," the cook said proudly, as if it were her own accomplishment.

"Shocking," Ian said.

He eyed them critically. They were from someone who possessed a hothouse, which could be nearly anyone with money in Sussex.

He was irritated suddenly, wondering precisely who it was.

"But she gave them to me, sweet girl she is. And she had the rest taken down to the churchyard. And she gave toy soldiers to little Jordy! She has a heart of gold, she does."

It was all Ian could do not to choke.

Then again, he didn't suppose he'd given much thought to Tansy Danforth's heart. Or hearts, as he should say, given that she'd gone on a campaign to steal them from nearly every man she encountered, including possibly the one he would not allow her to have, and that was Landsdowne's.

What went on in her heart? She *could* be hurt, that much he knew. She'd reacted like a wild thing prodded with a spear when he insinuated she might be hurting someone he loved.

He felt a little minute jab in the region of his solar plexus then. Sympathy, or guilt, he wasn't sure. Suddenly he wished he could unsay it. He found the notion that he might have hurt her feelings surprisingly distasteful.

Mrs. deWitt slid cheese and a slab of bread slathered in honey in front of him. The honey was a peace offering.

"How did you know this scone was Miss Danforth's favorite?" he asked.

"We have a visit of nights, and we've a bit of a bite to eat when we talk."

He nearly choked. "You . . . 'have a visit'?" He

was bemused. "Of *nights*? You and Miss Dan-forth?"

"Aye, Master Ian, she's but a young woman still and I think she's a wee bit lonely. We chat a bit in the kitchen sometimes at night. Not every night. Sometimes very late. I leave one out for her, and if it's gone in the morning I know she had trouble sleeping. She's a young girl alone in the world. And here you all be, a big comfortable noisy family, and you know everyone you see and all the land, too. She's a bit lonesome, aye?"

"She's lonely because she's alienated all the women in Sussex and bewitched all the men into injuring themselves and each other on her behalf."

Mrs. deWitt laughed indulgently. "Ah, now, surely you exaggerate Master Ian, and wouldn't that be just like you."

"No, I mean it!"

Mrs. deWitt just chuckled some more at what she likely suspected were his antics. "Ah, ye always did have a fine wit, Master Ian. Think of it. "

"Lonesome? Her constitution is made of iron. If she'd been born another gender, she'd give Napo-leon a run for his money in terms of campaigns. She's shameless."

But even as he said it he could feel doubt en-croaching.

"Of *course* her constitution is iron, Master Ian. She's alone in the world, what choice has the girl? I dinna ken about shameless. I for one believe she's as sweet as an—"

"Don't say angel!"

"Oh, I suppose she's just not for the likes of you, Master Ian. Ye never did take to the angels."

But she winked at him with great affection.

Ian sighed. "No, I never did."

Lonesome. He recalled her expression when he'd asked her whether she knew a bit about being a frightened little girl. As if he'd seized the collar of her dress and yanked it clean off. Stripping her of some critical disguise.

And yet it had all been for her own good, of that he was certain.

Why, then, did he feel a sudden uncomfortable urge to apologize?

His curiosity got the better of him.

"But what do you *talk* about?"

"Aye, just a bi' of talk between women, right? Budgets and cooking and the like. It wouldna interest ye in the *least.*" She said this quite inscrutably.

Just a day ago she would have been absolutely correct.

TANSY MANAGED TO convincingly sparkle through the rest of the afternoon.

But the day had gone on too long, and the supreme effort it took to charm had given her a headache, as if she'd drunk too much champagne, which she hadn't. She suspected it was a bit of a spiritual hangover, which had rather a lot to do with Ian Eversea's brutally accurate summary and dismissal of her.

She sat down hard, propped her chin in her hands and tried hard to hate him, but all she could muster was a sort of resigned, honest misery. She felt rather like a shoddy magician whose secrets had been exposed. She couldn't fault him, not really. She in truth rather admired it, which added a bit to her misery, given that she was fairly certain he now didn't like her at *all*, if he'd liked her just a little before.

But . . . though there had been a moment when he helped her shoulder the gun, where the air seemed to go soft and dense as velvet, and she could have sworn their breathing had begun to sway at the same rhythm, like two rivers joining, and she'd strangely never felt safer or more peculiarly imperiled. And she'd wanted time to stop then, to freeze the two of them the way the entire crowd had frozen, so she could lean against him, because that's where she'd always belonged, or so it seemed. And to just see what that moment was all about.

And at the recoil he had pushed her upright as if she'd been something aflame.

She thought about this. And decided she unnerved him, too. At least a little.

It cheered her, but it made her uneasy as well.

You mean because they like you when you do it?

Aargh. Her cheeks went hot again.

Know a bit about being a frightened little girl, Tansy?

She dropped her hot cheeks into her hands. But then she raised her head slowly and took a long steadying breath. Because regardless of what he thought of her, it was strangely a relief to be *known*.

Oddly, she wasn't tempted to throw her slippers at the wall this time.

The thing was, there were things she now knew about Ian Eversea that he probably didn't even know he'd revealed. That he might not even know about himself. There was a certain advantage to being underestimated, at least for a time, and the advantage was that she could surprise him into a flare of anger—disconcerting as it had been to be in the path of those blazing eyes—because she'd prodded some sore place in him. She took no pleasure in hurting him, but there was still a little bit of a thrill.

And despite her resolve, she found that the hunger to know him had in no way diminished.

He might not have the slightest interest in Richard III, but she'd found a way into Ian Eversea, anyway, quite inadvertently.

Tansy gazed at the wall.

She unfolded her sheet of foolscap and spread it out neatly and read it to herself. And then, because she was fundamentally honest, she added to the bottom:

Fiercely loyal to those he loves.

THE NEXT AFTERNOON Ian stopped in at the Pig & Thistle for a pint of the dark, which he'd been dreaming about for the last hour as he hammered nails into a decrepit paddock fence. Surely he'd purchased his way into Heaven with all of this work lately. Though his cousin the vicar assured him it didn't work quite that way.

He pushed open the door of the pub and saw Landsdowne sitting by himself, enjoying what appeared to be a steak and kidney pie and a pint of the light. Landsdowne looked up, saw Ian and beckoned him over.

Ian pulled out a chair and reflexively raised a hand. When Polly didn't appear in a heartbeat, he swiveled his head to look for her.

He didn't see her, but Ned noticed him and without asking brought Ian a pint of the dark.

"I give Polly a bit of time off during the day, Captain Eversea. She goes off for a bit, but she should have returned by now."

"I'm certain she'll be here any minute, Ned. She's a good girl."

Ned brightened. "Aye, that she is. That she is."

Polly Hawthorne was quite simply Ned's heart, Ian knew. And he reflected again on the dangers of loving. *Anyone*. The thing that allegedly made life worthwhile quite had the power to destroy you, too. Interesting irony, that the thing that made you strongest was also what made you weakest. Altogether more dangerous than war, love was.

"How goes it, Eversea?" Landsdowne offered laconically.

"It goes quite sweatily. But we're close to having a new roof on the vicarage."

"Admirable. Every building deserves a roof."

Ian gave a short laugh.

There was a silence between them. Ian drummed his fingers, wondering how to begin.

"What else is on your mind?" Landsdowne said politely, with a certain dry amusement.

"My sister . . ." He hoped Landsdowne would pick up the thread.

". . . is magnificent." Landsdowne completed this almost grimly.

Ian launched his brows and waited for more.

It wasn't forthcoming.

So he decided to be blunt. "Do you still think so?"

Landsdowne gave a soft laugh. "Ah. Did you come here to ascertain my intentions, Eversea? I should have thought my intentions are quite clear by now."

"And your intentions remain . . . unaltered in their course? Despite recent gifts sent to another young woman?"

"Are you perchance alluding to a certain blond angel who has lately alit upon Sussex?"

Good God, even Landsdowne talked like a fool about her.

Angel, my left hindquarter, he thought. He had enough of the gentleman left in him that he thought he would leave it unsaid, and he wasn't about to enumerate what he considered her secret vices.

Unbidden came an image of that bare, vulnerable little crescent of fair skin between the collar of her walking gown and her bonnet, and the delicate blades of her shoulders, and her clear eyes staring back at him, wide and as shocked as if he'd struck her when he demanded the reason his opinion meant anything at all to her.

That peculiar impulse toward protection rushed at him again. Fierce and quite irrational.

He understood then that she was only truly awkward around *him*.

No. He would keep her secrets. Though he could not say quite why.

Landsdowne sighed. "It was merely a friendly gift, Eversea. I meant nothing by it, truly, other than hoping to make her feel more welcome in Pennyroyal Green. But . . ." He leaned back in his chair. ". . . can you imagine what your life would be like, Eversea, if you awoke to her every morning? To eyes full of admiration instead of challenge? To simplicity and charm and innocence and that restful beauty?"

Ian nearly choked. This, however, was too much. Simplicity? *Restful?*

It was a moment before he could speak.

"If you intend to divert your attentions from Olivia in order to court Miss Danforth, you may find yourself part of a stampede," was all he said. Very carefully.

Landsdowne smiled a little. "I'm aware." He sounded entirely unaffected. After all, he was the man who had found a way into Olivia Eversea's seemingly impenetrable good graces and turned the ton's betting world on its ear. "And *you* don't intend to join the throng?"

Ian gave a short humorless laugh. "Ah, no. I'll be sailing soon for a half-dozen exotic ports of call. I can think of very few women who'll consent to be dragged along on a journey like that."

"Well, then. What would you do if I did tell you I intend to abandon my suit? To throw over Olivia for Miss Danforth? Will you call me out? What would that accomplish?"

"It would accomplish," Ian said thoughtfully, "the setting of an example. For if I shot you, odds are very good no one would throw over Olivia again."

Landsdowne grinned swiftly at that. "You're likely right."

A brief little silence felled, during which Ian silently compelled Landsdowne to explain himself. He certainly wasn't obliged to do it, but he was a man of honor.

"Here is the thing." Landsdowne sighed. And then his mouth quirked humorlessly. "I don't know if Olivia will ever love me. And yet . . . the more time I spend with her the more I can't do without her."

Lyon Redmond was indeed fortunate he'd disappeared, Ian thought. Because he would have strangled him on the spot had he reappeared just now. He'd left so much unhappiness in his wake, and the unhappiness rippled out to include people like Landsdowne, who didn't deserve it.

"And yet . . . I often think I would be happy to settle for simply her . . . esteem. To live with only that for the rest of my born days. For her. Olivia Eversea's mere esteem is worth more than the love and devotion of a dozen women. I cannot currently imagine a day without her. And it isn't my intention—I give you my word of honor—to pursue Miss Danforth. Does that answer your concerns with regards to your sister?"

He said it flatly.

It was as raw a declaration of love as Ian could imagine, and he felt a brief twinge of shame for cornering Landsdowne into it. He nearly pitied the man. He knew a brief surge of anger for his stubborn, prideful sister. He was a good man, a worthy man, and he deserved better than esteem. Olivia's pride had surely caused at least some of her own unhappiness.

But Ian's loyalty was to his sister.

He nodded shortly. "Thank you, Landsdowne, for telling me. Rest assured you have my utter discretion. And my apologies if I seemed intrusive. But I imagine you understand."

"I do. I, too, have sisters."

"I hear Miss Danforth is all but promised to de Neauville's heir, anyway."

It was a lie.

Because he'd just decided right then to write to the Duke de Neauville's heir to tell him about Miss

Danforth. He was young, a good shooter, handled the ribbons well even if he drove a bit recklessly, wanted the best of everything, was an otherwise inoffensively uninteresting young man, and the de Neauvilles owned property in Sussex. Surely if anything could turn Miss Danforth's head and *keep* it turned, it was a handsome, fledgling about-to-be-a-duke. And that was the sort of marriage she was destined for, anyway, wasn't it? He would be doing everyone a good turn in writing to the duke's son.

"Far be it for me to intrude upon another man's territory," Landsdowne said wryly.

Which was when Ian noticed his ale still hadn't arrived.

And it looked as though ales hadn't arrived at many of the tables. Woebegone faces were craning toward the bar, gesturing with empty tankards. Murmurs were beginning.

Ned rushed over to him.

"Captain Eversea, I'm worried now. Polly would never leave for this long without asking or without telling me where she's gone. I'm afraid something's amiss."

"Do you want me to help you look for her? Do you have someone to mind the pub?"

"I've been meaning to hire someone for some time, but things are so busy I just haven't yet gotten round to it. Jemmy can do it in a pinch, but he's a bit slow. We'll have a riot on our hands if we're gone long."

Perhaps an exaggeration, but not by much. They looked around at the yearning faces of the men in the pub, all very unused to being denied Ned's light or dark when they wanted it.

"We best hurry, then. Far be it for me to cause a riot."

Chapter 15

IT HAD BEEN DAYS before she was able ride out on her own again, but Tansy had seized the opportunity the minute the duke and Genevieve departed to inspect another property available for purchase, a good two hours carriage drive away. A little too far for Genevieve's preference, and just far enough from the Everseas, as far as the duke was concerned, and this was a source of more or less good-natured bickering.

Tansy had charmed the groom—who surely knew better, but had just as much trouble refusing her anything she wanted as nearly every other man in Pennyroyal Green—into saddling her mare and allowing her to ride off alone again, since it was to be such a very short ride on such a beautiful day.

She wanted to take a look at her handiwork.

She was parallel to the stream when she pulled her horse to a halt.

Someone was staggering toward her—a woman, she saw, when the wind whipped out a long dark skirt—who then dropped again to her knees with a squeak.

Tansy's heart lurched.

"Polly!"

She trotted over, scrambled almost gracelessly down from her horse, dashed over and knelt next to her, placing a hand on her arm.

"What's happened? Are you hurt?"

Polly seemed a bit embarrassed.

"Oh, I'm sound enough, except me ankle . . . oh, blast, but I've twisted it, Miss Danforth, in a blessed vole hole, I believe. I can't seem to get far. And oh, my dress! I've dirtied it! My papa is going to *kill* me."

Tansy understood full well the distress of dirtying a dress and worrying a father.

"If only I could find a stick to help with the walking . . ." Polly fussed. She furrowed her brow and looked toward the Pig & Thistle, as if she could will herself back into the pub.

"A stick! What nonsense. You'll wait here and I'll fetch help if we need it. But first, may I have a look? Here, let us take off your shoe, just . . . so."

Polly extended her leg without question, and Tansy carefully unlaced the worn, serviceable walking boot and handed it to Polly to hold.

"Oh, it's swollen! You poor thing. Now, if only we had something to wrap it . . . you see, I've done this before! My brother and I used to play together, and I would run after him. I never could catch up. He was older and his legs were longer and I tripped in holes in the pasture."

Polly laughed at that. "I always wished I had a brother."

"Mine was both wonderful and a great trial to me. He died late in the War of 1812."

"I'm so sorry, Miss Danforth. The men do love to go and be soldiers, and leave us at home missing them and worrying."

"Please do call me Tansy."

She wondered which Eversea in particular Polly had missed and worried over.

"Tansy. Thank you, Tansy. Papa will be so worried. I'm all he has, you know, and I only have the few memories of Mama. And I canna serve at the Pig & Thistle with a limp. How could I be so *foolish*?"

"Oh, we're all foolish at one time or another. We'll worry about that later. Let me see if this will help . . ."

Tansy fished out a handkerchief and was able to wrap it around Polly's slim ankle twice and tie it neatly. She bounded to her feet and hauled Polly gently upward.

Polly tried to put a little weight on it, leaning heavily on Tansy. She brightened. "Oh! It's a bit better." She tried another step and yelped. "Bloody *aitch*, Tansy! I'm afraid I can't do it all the way back to the Pig & Thistle like this. Oh, my papa will be so upset with me!"

"Well, he will be at first, but if I know papas, he'll be happier to see you alive than he will be angry that you hurt yourself. Here, lean on me and we'll settle you back down again. I'll go and fetch help straightaway."

Tansy managed to get herself into the saddle, which was a bit of a struggle, and she was afraid she'd showed Polly her stockings and part of her chemise in the process. Then she kicked her horse into a decidedly unladylike gallop and tore across the downs in the direction of town.

She was shamelessly enjoying the excuse to ride at breakneck speed when she saw two men riding toward her across the green.

She pulled her mare to a halt and stared. Then threw a glance over her shoulder at the woods. She really was quite in the middle of things and didn't see any refuge.

Ah. She wondered if this was the sort of thing she ought to have considered before she rode out alone.

She wasn't armed, more's the pity, for goodness knows she could have shot either of them from horseback where she sat.

If they wanted to abduct her and sell her into slavery on a pirate ship, she would put up a struggle, but there really was no doubt about who would eventually win.

She watched, and said a little prayer, and a moment later . . . something about one of the men . . .

. . . something simply about the way he occupied space . . .

She knew it was Ian Eversea.

Her relief seesawed with alarm for a moment before nerves settled in to stay.

Nerves and guilt.

And her heart, of course, took up that disorienting jig it normally did in his presence. Even when he was still at a distance.

He sat a horse so beautifully, her breath snagged in her throat. She decided to try to take pleasure in that before the berating began.

She saw the moment he recognized her, because he drew to an abrupt halt, too.

He kneed his horse into a canter and was beside her in seconds.

"Miss Danforth," he drawled, sweeping his hat from his head. "*Imagine* seeing you where you shouldn't be. And alone, too, which you also shouldn't be. Or are you?"

"And good day to you, Captain Eversea. I was riding into town to fetch Mr. Hawthorne. Polly Hawthorne was . . . out for a walk . . . and has twisted her ankle and she can't put her weight on it. I discovered her."

He transformed before her eyes. His face went brilliant with relief and joy. "*You* found Polly? Where is she?" He turned to shout over his shoulder. "Ned! We've found Polly!" He turned back to Tansy. "Is she otherwise sound?"

He sounded so worried, she found herself soothing him. "She's fine. She's turned her ankle and can't put her weight on it but she's otherwise well and cheerful enough. And worried about her father worrying about her."

"Ned! Polly turned her ankle but she's sound otherwise."

Ned's head dropped to his chest in relief and he kicked his horse into a trot.

"Where is she?"

"Follow me," Tansy said. Enjoying the opportunity to order him about.

"Miss Dan—"

She tugged her horse around and kicked it into a gallop again.

Catch me if you can, Captain Eversea.

POLLY'S LITTLE ELFIN face lit when they galloped into view.

Ned all but threw himself down from his horse and ran to her, then turned to Ian, wordlessly, who was next to them in a moment. Tansy watched as Ian scooped Polly up as if she were weightless. Together he and Ned gently situated her in the saddle of Ned's horse.

And if I were Polly, Tansy thought, *I would never forget the feel of his arms around me, and how it felt to be lifted gently, as though I were precious. Almost worth turning an ankle over.*

With a tip of his hat to Ian and Tansy and a heartfelt, "My thanks," to both of them, Ned Hawthorne urged his horse forward again. From the sound of things, Ned was clearly fussing and berating, and Polly protesting and placating.

She smiled. Lucky Polly, to be so missed.

She turned toward Ian.

He was smiling, too, at the two of them as they retreated.

Tansy's heart squeezed. It was a beautiful smile.

Warm, wholly satisfied and relieved, utterly unguarded. It made him look very young.

That's what he looks like when he cares about
people, she thought, wistfully.

That smile faded when it turned her way, alas.

"How did you happen to find her, Miss Danforth?"

He could have at *least* congratulated her. Or
thanked her.

She hesitated.

"I've seen her near . . . here. Whilst I was riding.
It's a lovely spot, isn't it? Very quiet by this stream."

"What were *you* doing here by *yourself*? Burying bodies? Meeting a lover?"

She pressed her lips firmly closed.

And when he refused to blink, she sighed.

"Nothing remotely as interesting. Would you
please, please, please stop being so bloody curious
and overprotective? I said please. *Three* times."

He studied her a moment, clearly fighting a
smile.

"No need to curse," he said mildly. "Are you
going to stamp your foot? You've that look about
you."

"Are you giving me permission to do it?"

He did grin again, and the grin evolved into a
laugh. He had a beautiful smile, even more beautiful when he aimed it at her.

A little silence followed, and he swiped a hand
over his hair, almost self-consciously.

"You ride very well," he volunteered. "Then

again, why wouldn't you? Every 'wallflower' rides like a hellion."

"Of course I ride well. This soft little country is nothing compared to rugged American terrain. I frequently rode by myself. And I have to dodge Indians and bears and the like when I do it."

Judging from the look on his face, he was thoroughly enjoying this bald-faced lie.

"Miss Danforth, I'm not ignorant of geography, you know. I'm familiar with your part of New York."

Oh.

"But doubtless you need to gallop hard to elude your suitors and incensed women," he added.

"I leave all of them in the dust," she said gravely, her hand over her heart.

And he laughed again, sounding delighted, and the laugh evolved into a happy sigh, as if she were part of something amusing being performed on Drury Lane.

Could it be that they were actually *enjoying* each other?

If she thought about it too much she would likely revert to gawking and stammering.

There was a silence that threatened to become awkward.

"Is that where you learned to shoot?" he asked. "Like a bloody marksman?"

"My father and brother taught me. I rather took to it. I don't very much like to shoot animals, however."

"But you have no compunctions over murdering apples."

She laughed. "That apple deserved to die. I know how to *load* a musket, too, you know. I should one day like to shoot a rifle."

"I have an excellent rifle," he said. "A Baker. Shot it during the war."

He stopped short of volunteering to allow her to shoot it, she noticed. And it seemed like those silent words filled the little pause that followed.

"From when you were in the army," she prompted.

"Yes."

He didn't expound. She imagined he'd shot a good deal when he was in the army, and seen a good deal, and suddenly she didn't want to remind him.

"You don't really like Richard the Third, do you?"

He looked startled. "I don't dislike him. I would have to say I have no powerful feelings about Richard the Third. Have . . . *you*?" He said it with great trepidation.

"No. I like stories of people surviving things. I'm rather fond of Robinson Crusoe."

He looked a bit taken aback by that. "Robinson Crusoe is a marvelous story," he said on a hush. "*Quite* tolerable for a novel."

"Isn't it?" she said eagerly. "I've also quite enjoyed the books by Miles Redmond about his South Seas Travels."

Amazement flickered across his face. "Mr.

Miles Redmond's stories have inspired me to take an ocean voyage around the world."

"You might be eaten by a cannibal," she warned.

"They'd have to catch me," he said soberly. "And I'm an excellent shot. Not as good as *you*, of course. Apple killer."

They regarded each other in another peculiar little silence. Somewhat alarmed by their accord. And by the fact that they appeared to be very much enjoying a conversation.

With each *other*.

She suddenly wondered if Ian Eversea—who allegedly was so expert and blasé about women—felt a trifle awkward around *her*.

His horse snorted encouragingly into the silence. Growing a little restive.

And yet he didn't suggest they leave yet.

"Do you miss your home in America, Miss Danforth?"

The question sounded almost tentative coming from him. As if he thought it were a delicate question, or was afraid it would result in a torrent of unwanted information. Men could be so amusing.

Then again, he could actually be trying to know her.

"Yes," she said, mimicking his taciturn answer of a moment ago.

The corner of his mouth lifted, appreciating this.

"Genevieve said you used to live at Lilymont."

She inhaled sharply in surprise. It was a bit like hearing the name of a loved one out of the blue.

She turned away, reflexively; she didn't quite realize it, but she'd aimed her body in the general direction of Lilymont. "I did."

"A charming house. I remember how much I liked the garden when I saw it last."

"I loved the garden. My mother planted so many of the flowers there. I had such a wonderful time helping her. And my brother would chase me around it, pretending he was a British soldier and I was an American. The joke was on both of us when we went to live in America and we couldn't decide who would be the enemy."

Ian laughed. "Brothers are experts at torment."

"I suppose you would know. You're fortunate to have so many."

"I suppose I am. Did you know Lilymont is for sale?"

"*Oh.*" It was a syllable of pure yearning. "How fortunate the new owners will be. I wonder if you can still see my name on the wall where I scratched it there with a little knife. Underneath the ivy in the corner next to my mother's favorite apple tree."

Ian was quiet. His hat remained in his hand, and the wind ruffled the hair away from his forehead. He had the eyes of a rifleman, she thought.

And there was a look of contemplative assessment in them, the same look her mother would get when poring over the kitchen budget looking for errors. As if he'd needed to erase an impression of her and start over at the beginning.

Suddenly his eyes focused at some point on the top of her head, flicked to and fro.

Where they stopped.

And then he slowly grinned.

"*Now* why are you grinning at me? It can't mean anything good."

He seemed to love it when she was riled. He did it very easily, riling her.

"It's . . . well, you should see your hair. It's every which way."

"*No!*" Her hands flew up to her head, aghast. "Is it? Well, I'm certain it's nothing compared to yours."

He gave her a look of pity. "Good try. As if I mind what my hair looks like."

"You *should*," she muttered darkly.

She could see him struggling mightily not to laugh again. "And where the devil is your bonnet? I assume you went out wearing one."

She felt around the back of her neck but already knew it was gone. "Bloody—that is, *drat*."

"Left it behind, did you, while you were burying victims, eh? Or trysting?"

She rolled her eyes. "I *thought* I felt it fly off. It was such a pleasure, you know, to ride like that, and I suppose I didn't . . ."

He craned his head behind them. "I don't see

it. Perhaps you left it . . . wherever you were. Why don't we go and fetch it?"

She rolled her eyes at him again. "Good try. But . . . I'll need to repair my hair before I return." She was fussing now. "I can't go home looking like I've been ravished."

She slid him a tentatively minxlike sidelong look.

He just shook his head slowly.

"Leave it be, Miss Danforth. I like it this way. It makes you look as wild and disreputable as you truly are."

"At least you like *something* about me."

A curious silence ensued.

He looked a bit taken aback. And thoughtful.

If she'd hoped he'd launch into a list of all the things he liked about her, she was sorely disappointed. He remained quiet, watching her, with a look that started a little ballet of butterflies in the pit of her stomach. She sensed there *were* other things he liked about her, but he couldn't say them aloud. At least not to her.

"I wish I had a mirror," she said finally.

He appeared to give serious consideration to her dilemma.

"Perhaps you can see yourself in my eyes."

She blinked.

And then went very, very still.

The words had been issued oh so offhandedly.

She had no doubt he would see the impact immediately, because he was watching her.

It was a dare. Suddenly, out of nowhere, without warning . . .

Was Ian Eversea at last flirting with her?

Or . . . testing her?

Or some interesting combination of both?

Chapter 16

SHE PONDERED THIS CONUNDRUM.

He maintained a neutral expression.

How many times had he said this sort of thing to other women?

Surely *she* of all people would be able to call his bluff.

"Perhaps I *can* see myself in your eyes," she said cautiously.

She took a step toward him.

And then another.

And another.

She saw his mouth begin to curl at the corners at her cautious progress.

At last she was close enough to catch just a whiff of what she suspected was bay rum and starch. Her head swam. Her heart lurched.

And then she subtly squared her shoulders and tipped her head back and looked into his eyes.

It was only marginally less difficult than looking into the sun, for different reasons.

His eyes were so blue she felt them like an ache

inside her, and she felt her fingers curl into fists, withstanding the impact. It seemed such an intimate thing to know about a person, that a darker ring of blue surrounded the lake of his iris, that his eyelashes were black but burnished a sort of russet at the tips, that his pupils had gone large and dark and his breath seemed to have stopped and—

Her nerve failed.

She exhaled, which is how she knew she'd stopped breathing, in a long shuddery breath, and ducked her head. And took a step backward.

He was deep water, and she was in over her head, as he never tired of pointing out.

She thought she could hear him breathing. How very still he'd gone. There was a suppressed energy about him. She was reminded of a fox patiently waiting for just the right time to pounce on a vole. She did indeed feel like the only woman in the world just then.

"No. I can't see myself very well in them," she said, her voice gone small.

On the contrary, she saw herself there very well indeed.

A peculiar prickling started up at the back of her neck. The butterflies were now performing a vigorous reel.

As he'd implied before, she didn't know quite what to do about it.

Which made her feel young and gauche again.

And a little angry. He never seemed to tire of

pointing out her naive inadequacy to her in all manner of ways.

There was an odd little silence as they perused each other from a safe distance.

He cleared his throat.

"Ah. Well, there's a stream, nearby, Narcissus." His voice had gone gruff. "I think you can see yourself reflected in it. Have a look, if you must."

They rode over to a likely place, and he dismounted, produced a handkerchief, and spread it out along the ground at the bank, which was mercifully not too damp. He gestured with a flourish for her to kneel.

Just like Sir Walter Raleigh. Well, almost like Sir Walter Raleigh.

Like an empress, her nose exaggeratedly in the air for effect and just to make him smile, she strode over and gracefully knelt, and bent to see if she could indeed use the surface of the stream as a mirror.

She could. And he was right. If they were going to reference the Greek myths, she would have to go with Medusa.

She set about pulling out the pins which were askew. A swift run of her hand over her head told her she'd lost a few of them. She thrust her fingers up through it and gave it a good raking, an attempt to tame it.

She was so preoccupied with the reconstruction of her hair it took her a moment to realize he'd been absolutely silent for quite some time.

She turned to make sure he hadn't disappeared.

An expression she couldn't decipher fled from his face as she did.

She might have called it "rapt," but it was gone far too quickly for her to be sure. Perhaps it had just been gas.

"What are you doing?" she asked.

"Just engaging in the time-honored pastime of suffering the loss of precious minutes of my life for the sake of a woman's vanity."

"Oh, you poor thing, to be so very ill-used. You're fortunate you're passable looking, Captain Eversea. Because if you actually possess any of that vaunted charm, I've yet to witness it."

This, as she'd suspected, just made him laugh. "Hurry," he said ungraciously, just to prove her point.

She managed to twist and tame her hair and jab pins into it, and she was satisfied with the result.

"How did I do?"

He studied her, wearing a faint frown, so long and in such a way that it suddenly became a bit more difficult to breathe.

"Less interesting, but more presentable," was his cryptic verdict.

She eyed him suspiciously for signs of mockery. None was evident.

He looked a little preoccupied himself, in fact.

He hadn't blinked in quite some time. Unnerving.

She felt a bit like prey.

And again, she wasn't quite certain what to do about it. The butterflies did a slow orbit in her stomach. This is why I oughtn't ride alone, she thought.

She stood without his assistance, plucked up his handkerchief, and he took two steps toward her horse in preparation for hoisting her up again.

And then—

Later, she would find it ironic that she hadn't actually thought to feign a stumble before then.

All she knew was that she was upright one moment and on her way down the next. She saw the ground coming at her and thrust her hands out with a muffled shriek and—

She hit what felt like a wall.

Which turned out to be Ian, who had lunged for her with lightning speed. Her head thumped his chest, and her hands latched into his shirt and pulled as he levered her smoothly upright again, as if they were performing some sort of awkward tango.

When she'd oriented herself again she realized she'd managed to yank open his shirt and her hand had slipped between the buttons.

It was a moment before she realized:

She was touching his *skin*.

Instantly she felt the leap and tension of his muscles.

She stopped breathing.

Judging from the tension in him, so had he.

The moment seemed suspended in time.

Her fingers fanned out, tentatively, just a little.

She just couldn't help it. She wanted to touch a little more of it, while the opportunity presented itself. She wanted to imagine the rest of him unfurling from just that spot.

And a beat of held-breath silence ticked by before he spoke.

"Don't," he said gruffly.

It was too late. She couldn't have moved her hand if he'd aimed a pistol at her.

His skin was hot and silken over a chest that was frighteningly, fascinatingly, hard. She was a little afraid now, but she could not have pulled away if she tried. "Tansy . . ." His voice was a soft warning.

He didn't pull away from her, either.

Time suddenly seemed to slow, to thicken, to soften, like . . . like . . .

Lava.

His voice was softer now. The edges husked. It stroked over her senses like rough velvet.

"You try too hard, Tansy. Do you know what you remind me of?"

"A dream come true?" she whispered it. *I'm touching Ian Eversea's skin I'm touching Ian Eversea's skin.*

"Someone who always grabs the soap too enthusiastically, and finds it flying out of her grasp over and over."

"Imagining me in the bath, are you?"

He laughed. Shortly, though. A distracted laugh. Somewhat pained.

"I think you come at everyone before they can come after you, Tansy. You're afraid to be—"

He stopped abruptly.

Vulnerable, she completed silently in her head, astonished. Certain that's what he meant.

It was astonishing for a number of reasons.

Because it was true.

Because he'd been unnervingly insightful.

And because she realized he'd stopped because . . .

He'd been talking about himself.

She didn't dare say *that* out loud.

She turned her face up to him.

He must have seen the wondering realization in her face, because his eyes almost *literally* shuttered. Cool, inscrutable. If it was a color in an artist's palette, she would have called it "Warning Blue." She'd have to be a masochist to want to breach that defense. He'd immolate her with a few drawled words.

"What happened to you?" she whispered, before she could stop herself.

Because after her parents died, she'd stopped knowing when to be afraid.

Something had made him the way he was. Just as something had made her the way she was.

Somewhat distantly she was aware of his heartbeat quickening beneath her palm. A glorious feeling. How incongruously soft and warm his skin was in contrast to those cold, guarded eyes. Her imagination wandered. Would his skin be

like this everywhere on his body? Would she find
different textures, curling hair, more muscle . . .
his hands were on her thighs.

His hands were on her thighs!

She'd been so distracted by her own reverie, she
hadn't noticed, and now it was too late. They'd
landed softly, stealthily. And now he was drawing
his fingertips up along them, up over the curve of
her hips, lightly and achingly slowly, as if pointing out to her precisely how female she was, how
he saw her, how ensnared she was.

Because she certainly was.

The hairs stirred upright at the back of her neck
and over her arms; her nipples were suddenly
almost painfully alert, and his dragging fingertips over the fine, fragile muslin sent rivulets of
flame fanning out through her body. It was so exquisite and fascinating, she forgot to draw breath.

In seconds he'd knit a net for her out of her own
desire.

Then, with the speed of a wolf seizing a hare,
he scooped his palms beneath her buttocks and
pulled her hard against him. And held her. He
looked down into her eyes, his pupils large, black.
He waited, it seemed, just long enough for her to
feel the beginning of what would undoubtedly
prove to be a very fine erection. For her body to
soften, to yield, to fit to him. For her hands to slip
around his neck and clasp him.

What followed wasn't a kiss so much as a siege.
When his lips landed against hers—magically,

her head was already tipped back to receive them—she tensed. An instant later it seemed the rightest thing in the world, the fit of his mouth over hers. Suddenly, it was the answer to everything. Ah, and too late she understood, *here* was the danger of which he spoke. Firm, warm, sinuously clever, he brushed his lips over hers, introducing her to the universe of pleasure that could be had from her lips alone.

Before he plundered.

Her mouth parted beneath his with a sensual knowledge as old as time and stronger than sense. Her hands slid down and she clutched at his shirt for balance as layer upon layer of new pleasure was revealed to her in the stroke, the dive, the twining of his tongue with hers. And somehow what began as a proving kiss of near violence evolved into something different. Something sensual, depthless, heady, drugging. She could feel him slow, his body ease. She was spiraling in some place where gravity didn't apply. She would fall forever if she didn't hold on to him; the kiss was her world now.

She moaned softly, her pleasure, wonder, spilling into sound. His body tensed as he pulled her more tightly. She could feel the outline of his hard cock at the crook of her legs, and a shocking pleasure cleaved her. She pressed herself closer still, and he ground himself against her, and it hurt, and it felt wonderful. She wanted to disappear into him.

"Tansy," he breathed hoarsely. "God."

And suddenly she knew that he could take her right here, right now, and she would not have minded. She wanted something from him with a savagery she'd never known. His hands moved up over her back, slid upward to cradle her head, to hold her at her mercy as his mouth took and hers gave, and he hoarsely whispered, "*Sweet.*"

He gently dragged his fingertips over the bare skin of her throat, leaving fine little fiery rivulets of sensation that traveled, shockingly, boldly to her breasts. Lightly, one of his fingers hooked into her bodice and he dragged it roughly over her nipple.

It was exquisite and terrifying.

"*Ian.*" A raw gasp. She wanted more. And she was afraid.

He tore his mouth from hers, dropped his forehead against hers. His breath was hot, swift, ragged, against her face. And like that they breathed together, her breath so tattered it sounded nearly like sobs.

She would never be the same, she was certain.

And then he abruptly released her and stepped back.

Which seemed an unthinkable cruelty.

The two of them stood and stared and breathed like pugilists backing into their own corners again.

Her senses were in utter ruins. She would be ages collecting them again. Perhaps she'd never get them back in the proper order.

It could have been an eternity or seconds later when he spoke again.

"Many, many men wouldn't have stopped, Miss Danforth." He said it quietly.

Ah. So this was yet another lesson. Or at least that was what he wanted to pretend. How altruistic of him.

She gave a short, bitter little laugh.

And still she couldn't speak. She'd once possessed the skill, she was certain of it.

He could.

"Please stop playing at things you don't fully understand, Tansy. It will be the undoing of you. It's so very, very easy to lose yourself this way. "

She still couldn't breathe or think properly. She was furious that she needed to leave one hand against him to steady herself. She was furious at him for being right. And for being so bloody *self-righteous*.

And for being steady on his feet as he regarded her.

And then she realized he was trembling. She could feel it beneath her palm.

He was a seasoned rogue, and that kiss had shaken him.

Suddenly this unnerved her more than the kiss itself.

"Is that why *you* do it?" she asked softly. Ironically. "To lose yourself?"

Swift anger kindled in his eyes again. "Have a care."

So he didn't care for having *his* secrets unraveled, did he?

She took her hand away from him finally, slowly, as if he were a rabid dog and would lunge at her if she made any sudden moves. She was steady on her feet now. Her breathing had nearly resumed its usual cadence. She couldn't yet back away; he maintained a peculiar gravitational pull. She could still feel the warmth of his body on her skin. She wondered distantly if she always would. As if she'd been branded.

"What if I want to be lost?" she whispered.

Something wild and dangerous flared in his eyes. An almost incinerating longing. It was there and gone.

"You don't know what you're saying."

His hair had fallen down over his brow, and he looked faintly ridiculous, and never more beautiful.

Despite the fact that his face was suddenly granite.

"I know one thing. I know that you want me."

She didn't say, *As much as I want you.*

His head went back sharply. And then he froze. He was utterly motionless apart from the spirals of hair the wind was lifting. Did he look like this when he took aim at a target with a rifle? She suspected he did.

She would love to wind her finger in one of his spirals, let it unfurl.

At last he ducked his head into his chest and

dropped his shoulders. Then he spun on his heel and strode to her horse. He wordlessly held the stirrup for her, and with a jerk of his chin beckoned her over.

He helped hoist her up as if she were a sack of flour, and not a woman he'd just kissed witless. Then he mounted his horse and stared down at her, wearing a faint frown.

He gave his head a rough shake. "It's time we get back."

He wheeled his horse around and urged it forward.

She thought she heard him mutter a single bemused word under his breath.

She wasn't certain, but it may have been "devil."

Chapter 17

IAN CLOSED HIS EYES.

Two birds were calling a leisurely, liquid sounding duet to each other across the enclosed garden. The hush had a waiting quality, perhaps because the plants had been allowed to flourish with abandon and muffled any sounds that might want to enter or escape.

He opened his eyes again, and slowly—the sound of his footsteps almost an intrusion—followed the inlaid stone path, which was tufted with grass and determined flowery weeds in some places and completely overgrown in others. The loosely serpentine walkway meandered through birches and oaks, walnut and apple and cherry trees, old and solid now, leafed out and healthy. A few lucky flies buzzed over fruit that had plopped to the ground.

The flowers were clearly planted according to a plan, but now every variety had run amuck, brilliant and fighting for room, like a crush at a ball. He didn't mind it, really. He liked a little chaos.

In the corner, the ivy was dense and inches thick. A peculiar sort of anticipation ramped in him as he approached it. He hefted it like a curtain and it released its grip reluctantly, its dry little fingers scraping against the wall.

He peered.

And there, ambered in the morning light, laboriously scratched into the stone, was one word: *Tansy.*

He put his finger on the word, tracing each letter. It had taken determination and a *knife* to do that. He gave a short laugh. A "wallflower" who wasn't afraid of guns and knives or riding at breakneck speed.

He wasn't certain why he'd wanted to come here today. It had something about how she'd looked when he said "Lilymont." Something brilliant and raw and very real had suffused her face, and then she'd tamped it. She'd uttered the word "Oh" with the rawest yearning he'd ever heard when he told her the home was for sale.

In so many ways she remained a walking question mark.

But this was real to her.

And he supposed he wanted to see why.

Because he thought he had tasted all of those things when he kissed her. Desperation and abandon, an unnerving, thrilling, recklessness, a fierce joy, a devastating depthless sensuality. She tasted of endless, endless pleasure and possibility.

It had shocked him badly.

And so he had taken refuge from it all by couching that kiss as a lesson. A dexterous bit of reasoning on his part, he thought.

And it *had* been a lesson.

For him, anyway.

After that kiss, he wasn't certain he'd ever truly kissed anyone before in his life.

Is that why you *do it?*

He hadn't fooled her.

She knew that he wanted her. Had likely known it before he did; the want of her stealthy, creeping into his blood over a series of days.

It infuriated him to be seen through, to the point where a red haze nearly crept over his eyes. It was fury, primarily at himself, for becoming ensnared.

And it also filled him with a sort of helpless, reluctant, very amused admiration.

He sucked in a long breath, held it in for a punishingly long time. Released it slowly, as if she'd been opium he'd inhaled into his lungs and he could expel her.

She would be better served by indignation and hurt pride and by at least attempting to believe that he'd meant to teach her a lesson, and by staying far, far away from him.

He'd been doing his part and avoiding her rather successfully ever since by rising very early and disappearing into good, wholesome, consuming physical work with hammers and boards and the like and taking his meals at the pub and lingering there over the chessboard with Culpepper and Cooke and retiring to his rooms very late at night, too late to peer out his window and catch Miss Danforth in the act of some new vice. He'd managed to allow an *entire* week to go by in just this fashion. He hadn't thought about her at all.

And yet here he was at Lilymont, as if he'd been driven there with no choice in the matter.

He did want her.

But that was neither here nor there. And while he normally got what he wanted when it came to women, he was sensible enough to know that the danger here wasn't in the getting of the woman but in the woman herself.

He dropped the ivy, watched her name vanish behind it.

Symbolically dropping the curtain on the entire episode.

The sun was higher now, and he could feel it on the back of his neck.

He wasn't certain whether it was this that made him turn suddenly. Only that something about the hush in the garden seemed to have shifted slightly, as if to accommodate another presence.

When he swiveled.

The Duke of Falconbridge was standing at the entrance.

There was an absurd moment when he actually wondered whether his conscience had spoken aloud and summoned the duke. Or perhaps he was dreaming, for dreams certainly had a way with presenting one with the worst scenarios possible. He ought to know.

The two of them froze and stared at each from across the silent, woolly garden.

And Ian, as he always did when he saw Falconbridge, felt a certain amount of shame. They had both shamed each other, on that fateful night, and really, it was hardly conversation kindling.

"Good morning," Ian said politely.

"Good morning."

Their voices echoed absurdly in the cool morning air.

A silence. Ian supposed it would be just a little too ironic if he scrambled up a fruit tree and clambered over a wall instead of walking past the duke, back to where he'd tethered his horse.

"Interested in Lilymont, Eversea?" The duke asked it idly.

"Yes," Ian said simply.

"Why?"

A presumptuous question.

It deserved a curt answer. "Curiosity."

The duke looked around at the trees. He strolled deeper into the garden, and Ian took a subtle step away from the ivy-covered wall, as if it would incriminate him. "I thought I'd stop by to have another look around. Genevieve likes it. It's a bit on the small side. Needs a good deal of work."

And it's a bit too close to where the rest of our family lives, no doubt.

"I can see why she likes it," Ian said instead.

Another silence. Not even a bird obliged them with a song. They were all collectively holding their little avian breaths, apparently.

"This was Miss Danforth's childhood home," the duke volunteered casually. He strolled deeper still into the garden, but not toward Ian. He took a sideways route, as if the apple trees and cherry trees were of critical importance to his decision whether to buy the house.

"It has a good deal of charm."

The duke turned to look at him. "You aren't interested in purchasing the property, too." More of a statement than a question.

"No. I'm departing for a long ocean voyage in a matter of weeks. Every penny of my savings will be devoted to that."

The duke nodded politely, as if none of this was of any true interest to him. "Ah. Yes. I recall. Your trip around the world." He paused. "Sometimes movement is precisely what a man needs."

Ian stared at him. He imagined the duke would be delighted that in a matter of weeks he would be moving inexorably farther and farther away from him. And given the caprices of sea travel, not to mention foreign cultures and food, could very well never return.

The duke simply turned, reached out, gripped a fine branch and pulled it down as if to inspect it. "And sometimes what he needs is someplace and someone who feels like home."

Ian fought a frown. Why was Falconbridge philosophizing about what a man needed? The duke knew nothing at all about him, apart from what he looked like naked and in the dark, and the fact that he was an excellent climber.

"I imagine you're right on both counts," Ian said politely.

The duke paused in front of a cherry tree, his profile to Ian, who could see the deep lines at the corners of his eyes.

My sister loves this man.

And suddenly he knew a moment of regret. A wish that he could turn back time and know him, too, to see in him the things Genevieve valued in him.

"I'll be off then, Falconbridge. My cousin expects me at the vicarage. Repairs, you know."

"Of course. Good day, then." The duke nodded, but didn't quite look at Ian.

They subtly skirted each other at a safe distance, like tomcats too conscious of each other's strengths to make even a token fuss about territory. Falconbridge going deeper into the garden, and Ian heading for the arched gate.

Once he'd seen the hem of Ian's coat whipping around the corner, the duke moved swiftly toward the ivy in the corner. He'd been watching Ian a little longer than Ian knew.

He lifted up the ivy and shaded his eyes. It was a moment before he saw the word.

Tansy.

He went still.

Ian Eversea had caressed that word with something like . . .

The duke could only describe it as reverence.

He pivoted slowly and shaded his eyes, stood listening thoughtfully, grimly, as the hoofbeats of Ian's horse tore away, like a man trying to escape something.

THIS AFTERNOON THE duke had asked Tansy to pour during their visit, and she was delighted with the ritual and the comforting sounds: The *tinks* of cubes of sugar dropped against porcelain, the bell-like music of the tiny silver spoons against sloped sides as they stirred.

"I've had word Lord Stanhope will be visiting his properties here soon. He's the Duke de Neauville's heir."

A duke!

The word jolted her pleasurably, and a bit of tea splashed into the saucer.

She couldn't help it. Duchess Titania de Neauville. She tried on the sound of it in her head. Good heavens, it was almost the only time the name Titania seemed appropriate.

Clearly she was *born* to be a duchess.

Would he be handsome? Clever?

Would he try to kiss her until she forgot her name?

Would he try to pretend it was all her fault that he'd kissed her, and that it had been a lesson, then dodge her for a week, when she knew better?

Oh, how she knew better.

She bit down on her back teeth against a little surge of righteous anger.

And to squelch the sensation again, which she found, both to her delight and dismay, she could conjure at will, of his fingertips trailing her throat then sliding into her bodice.

She looked down into the tea and remembered the hot demanding sweetness of his mouth, and a wave of weakness swamped her. And she didn't dare look up at the duke.

Ian Eversea was infinitely more sensible than she had credited. For he had made himself scarce after that kiss. Then again, she was not eligible for a complete seduction, unlike a certain attractive widow, for instance, and what use was she to him in that regard?

Although she suspected the reason for his absence was quite different, she couldn't help but regret his wisdom in keeping his distance.

Her face was heating, and she looked up, to find the duke's eyes on her speculatively. Perhaps he thought she'd gone rosy over the idea of a fledgling duke. The notion of whom had been introduced not a moment too soon.

"I thought *you* were the only duke."

He smiled faintly, indulging her. "We're a small club, to be certain. His son is a decent fellow. Pleasant, well-bred, educated, not a shred of controversy associated with his name. I daresay even handsome, and possessed of a certain amount of moral turpitude."

"Kind of you to remember my list."

He smiled again. "And wealthy. Very wealthy."

She hadn't listed wealth, oddly enough, because she would possess her own once she married. She certainly had nothing at all against it. She imagined the carriages, the gowns, the servants, the parties, the horses.

The home. The family. The children.

"He has a beautiful home here in Sussex," the duke added, when she didn't speak. "About twice the size of Lilymont."

The word, as it always did, made her stop breathing for just a moment.

"Lilymont always struck me as a very good size," she said. "But then, I was very small when I lived there. It's for sale, I understand," she added tentatively.

"Genevieve is interested in it. But we haven't yet made a decision about it."

A ferocious, rogue little surge of envy took her, and then she tamped it.

"How lovely it would be to keep it in the family." It would be lovely to know she would be welcome there, at the very least.

She did like saying the word "family." It occurred to her then that she was glad they were her family: the duke and his wife.

"The gardens were quite lovely, then, when you were a little girl. You used to run about there with your brother."

"I did," Tansy said faintly, smiling. "We used

to play at being soldiers. And then he went off to be one."

She didn't say, *And didn't come back*. The duke knew that.

"So often the ones that return . . . never really leave war behind. In so many ways. War changes a man irrevocably. There's a roughness and a recklessness that can . . . sink in, become integral to his character."

She regarded him guilelessly.

Or what she hoped was guilelessly.

"But doesn't life change you, too?" she asked. "Rather inevitably? One can hardly predict what will happen, isn't that right?"

The duke hesitated, then slowly nodded in concession, raising a brow.

"But I think sometimes it's like setting a broken arm," he said. "If it isn't done quite right, by someone very skillful and knowledgeable, it fuses in a particular shape and can never be quite right again."

Tansy fought to keep from narrowing her eyes. She suspected she was being warned in some fashion. Again. About Ian Eversea.

"Sometimes things are broken in such a way to fit with other things, are they not? Like the pieces of a puzzle or of stained glass?"

The duke drummed his fingers on the desk. A silence drifted by, and it lasted so long that the chink of a melting sugar cube against the side of a teacup was startlingly loud.

"You certainly are your father's daughter," he finally said.

GENEVIEVE WAS ALREADY in bed, reading, her hair roped into a dark braid, when he slid in and wordlessly reached for her.

She abandoned her book and went willingly, sighed while nestling into his chest as he burrowed his face into her hair. They lay in silence for a time, humbled by how fortunate they were, humbled by the miracle of loving and being loved and by how vigorous lovemaking really seemed never to lose its novelty.

"I've heard from the Duke de Neauville," he said. "His heir is arriving in Sussex to visit."

"Ah. I imagine you'd like to introduce him to Miss Danforth."

"How restful to know that I need never speak again, since you read my mind so perfectly."

She laughed.

He loved the feel of her laugh vibrating against his chest.

"Miss Danforth's brother was a soldier. Decorated. Lost in the war. Bayonet got him, I recall."

"Ah," Genevieve said softly. "Poor Tansy. Ian was decorated, too. For valor, I believe. He'd saved a life. He has quite a terrible bayonet scar."

"I've seen it," the duke said simply.

The two of them were silent at that, because Genevieve knew full well when the duke had seen it.

She nestled a little closer into her husband. Both because she knew he didn't like to remember that, and because she was grateful that whatever happened had ultimately brought the duke to her.

"Is he really leaving on a long sea voyage?" he asked.

"Ian?" Genevieve said sleepily. "Sometimes I feel like he's already on it. But yes. He is."

"Good," the duke said.

Chapter 18

A STEAMING BATH HAD CHEERED Ian immensely after a long, long day of physical labor, and Ned had to nearly push him out of the door of the Pig & Thistle, but he was sober enough by the time he arrived home.

He paused in the middle of his room. The bath, the pleasure of it, had made him unduly aware of his skin and his body and his muscles and his senses, and what a glorious pleasure it was to possess them. To be alive. To be able to feel and taste and . . .

And now his muscles tensed again. He slowly flattened a hand against his still warm, damp chest.

How . . . new . . . her hand had felt against his skin, the tentative unfurling of her fingers, that discovery of him, brave and reckless and innocent and yet somehow not.

She didn't kiss like a virgin. She kissed like she was born to do only that, with only him.

He wanted to touch her again.

He wanted to feel his skin against hers again.

He wanted to taste her. Everywhere.

And the need he'd been holding at quite sensible bay for over a week rushed over him like a bonfire.

He'd avoided his window for a week. He would not go to it now. He would not.

He told himself this all the way to the window.

When he got there, he peered out. A wedge of light emerged from her windows. His heart gave a lurch. For there she was, out on the balcony, doing . . .

What in God's name *was* she doing?

She was leaning far out over the balcony edge, one leg out behind her, and her arms had begun windmilling. His heart shot into his throat until she seemed to find a certain balance. Still, she remained in a precarious position.

Ian bolted from his room and flung open her chamber door, which mercifully wasn't locked, and was out on the balcony in a few steps.

He managed to keep his voice calm. "What the bloody hell are you doing? Everyone was speaking euphemistically when they refer to you as an angel. You haven't any wings, Miss Danforth. You'll hit the ground with a thud when you fall. And you will fall, if you maintain that angle."

She froze. There was a heartbeat of silence before she spoke.

"Oh, good evening, Ian. Aren't you funny."

"Step back from the balcony, Miss Danforth. I'm not worth jumping over, believe me."

"Ha. Believe it or not, I don't spend every waking minute thinking about you."

"Just most of them?"

She merely slowly, gracefully, straightened again, stepped back from the edge of the balcony, turned and looked up at him. It wasn't with reproach, necessarily, but she didn't say a word.

And suddenly he didn't think that was very funny, either.

"Then we're back to my original question—what the bloody hell are you doing?" He lowered his voice.

She hesitated. Her lips worried over each other.

And then she heaved a defeated sigh.

"It's just . . . well, I can't find the stars I need." She sounded abashed.

"The . . . stars you need? Are you an astrologer? Is that why you can read into my soul? Or perhaps you intend to use them to navigate a ship all the way back to America?"

"No, and I know you'd pine yourself right into the grave if I did navigate all the way back to America. I'm looking for the Seven Sisters. Or whatever it is you might call them in this country."

He was already smiling, damn the girl, and it was suddenly very clear to him, alarmingly clear, that her presence made everything better, colors brighter, the air more effervescent, and her absence over the last week had muted his experience of life altogether. It was like breathing air again after being trapped in a box.

Very, very alarming.

"Ah. The Pleiades. You can just see them from this side of the house if you crane your head . . . so. No need to risk life and limb by leaning over the balcony. See that very bright star there?"

"Where?" She leaned backward, far enough that her shoulder blades brushed his chest.

He suspected it was calculated.

He ought to move away.

He really, really ought to move.

He didn't move away.

"Oh! I see it! I see them! Or part of them." She sounded so delighted and relieved, he gave a short laugh.

She startled Ian by settling back against him as if it where the most natural thing in the world and stared up at the sky. And the thing was, it felt natural. In his weary state, the faint lavender sweetness and soft warmth of her made him dizzy. And he suddenly thought he might know what it would be like to be a planet, endlessly, gracefully spinning through the solar system. He couldn't, for a moment, think of why he hadn't held her just like this before.

"Why the Seven Sisters?" his voice had emerged somewhat huskily.

Hers was soft, too, when she replied. "My mother used to tell me a story about how they got up in the sky when I was a little girl. I loved it. It changed a bit, each telling." She gave a soft laugh. "That's why I liked it so much. She used to say to look for her in the sky when she was . . . gone. She said she'd be at a tea party with the Seven Sisters. And I guess I never thought she . . ." She hesitated. ". . . well, do you know how gone 'gone' is, Ian?"

He was struck dumb by the hollowness in her voice. He knew that sound. It came from the absence of someone you loved.

And oddly, he knew exactly what she meant. All the talk of living forever in Heaven wouldn't change the fact of *gone*.

"I do know," he said gently. "It's as though . . . death is merely a sort of theory, until it takes someone you know. Let alone someone you love. I was a soldier. 'Gone' was my daily way of life there, for a time. One never, never really gets used to it."

He'd never said anything of the sort to anyone else before.

"My brother was a soldier," Tansy confided. "And he died in the War of 1812. Bayonet got him."

Gone. Everything she'd been a part of was gone. And the enormity of that left him speechless. There really were no words to describe it. The simple ones would have to do.

"I'm sorry."

She knew he meant them. It was in his voice.

They didn't speak for a time. She leaned gently against him, and he allowed it, and silently they thought about "gone" and each other.

"My sister Olivia," he began, "she won't say anything about it, truly, but I believe—we all believe—she was in love with Lyon Redmond. He's heir to the Redmond family, and Mr. Miles Redmond's brother. And he disappeared a few years ago. I don't know what's worse. Knowing for certain whether someone is gone forever, or always wondering what became of them."

He felt her go still as she took this information in thoughtfully.

And then she sighed and moved a little away from him, just shy but not quite of touching him, as if she'd only just realized she was leaning into him for comfort, and was uncertain of her welcome.

His regret was a little too powerful.

Which was when he realized he'd been taking comfort in her, too.

"Forever," she drawled disdainfully, softly. "I hate the word 'forever.' It's hard to really imagine the concept isn't it? And then you *know*. When someone is gone forever, you finally understand what it means."

"I don't much care for the word, either. Especially with regards to matrimony, and staying in one place, and the like."

She laughed at that and turned around, and . . .

She might as well have aimed a weapon at him.

Her night rail would have been demure if it didn't drape the gorgeous lines of her so lovingly, so nearly tauntingly. The bands of muscles across his stomach tensed in an effort to withstand the impact of the sight. Her hair was plaited in a large, messy, golden rope slung over her shoulder and pouring down the front of her.

And an absurdly large, girlish bow closed the neckline.

He couldn't help but smile at that.

"Why are you grinning?" She sounded irritable.

"You look like a gift, tied up with a bow."

"Like the gifts you give to your mistresses?"

"Like the *what*?"

"Shhhh! Lower your voice!" She was clearly delighted, stifling a laugh. She'd achieved precisely the effect she'd wanted.

"I haven't 'mistresses,' for God's sake. There aren't a *host* of them. And I certainly don't buy them gifts."

"All those experienced women wearing experienced expressions. What do you call them?"

"There aren't 'all those' . . . It's not as though I . . . You make it sound as though I've a harem."

The woman was maddening. It was like jousting with a weathervane. And what in God's name *had* she heard about him?

Clearly, enough that was close to the truth. Or she was an excellent guesser?

"Poor women, who never get gifts," she mourned wickedly.

"Tansy . . ." he warned.

"It might be interesting to be part of a harem," she said wistfully, softly. "Never knowing whether one might get a visit from the maharajah . . . the anticipation . . . it would be . . ."

He held his breath, waiting on absurd tenterhooks for what she thought it might be.

". . . delicious," she finally said thoughtfully.

Oh, God. Oh God Oh God. She was going to be the death of him.

He couldn't speak for a time. They were teetering on a precipice here more dangerous than her balcony arabesque of a moment ago.

"What if . . ." His voice was hoarse. He cleared his throat. "What if the maharajah never comes?" His voice was hoarse.

"With all those wives? I'm certain he comes often."

He stared at her. Had she *really* said that? Did she know what it *meant*?

He gave a short astonished laugh.

"*Shhhhh!*" she said again.

"You would *hate* being part of a harem, Tansy. All those other women competing for a bit of attention. *Just* imagine."

"But it wouldn't be lonely."

The words startled him into momentary speechlessness. And he remembered what Mrs. deWitt had said.

How was it he hadn't realized before that she might be lonely? She was so *effervescent*; she could attract company the way a bloom attracted bees.

But he supposed it wasn't the same as belonging to someone. Or to somewhere.

But she *was* alone. He felt utterly chagrined that

he was only now realizing it. He'd been quite an ass, in many ways.

Then again, she wasn't entirely without fault in the matter. Captivating all the men in the town was one way to ensure that the women wouldn't thrill to your company.

"And I would be the favorite wife in no time," she hastened to add, before he could think about it any longer.

"If the maharajah didn't kill you first. I hear they use scimitars when their wives irritate them." He drew a finger across his throat.

She laughed at that. The throaty, delighted sound landed on his heightened, roused senses like fingernails gently dragged down his back.

And that's when he knew: he'd waited too long. He'd somehow missed the moment when he could have, and really should have, made a sensible retreat. The night rail, the night, the girl, the lavender, the laugh—he was now in thrall to his senses. *Everything* served to titillate them. He was theirs to command. And anything that happened next was a foregone conclusion.

And something would happen. Oh, something would.

"Do you know something, Tansy?" he said softly.

"Mmmm?" She'd been watching his face in the dark, as if she were searching for a particular constellation there, too.

"It's always been deucedly difficult for me to resist unwrapping gifts."

Her breath hitched in surprise.

She wasn't the only one who could be a devil.

Anticipation. It was the whetstone against which desire was honed. No one knew this better than he did.

The earth turned, the stars twinkled, the shadows swayed, as he waited to hear what she would say, which in the moment seemed the most important words he'd ever hear in his life.

"Is that so?" She'd tried for "casual"; instead she sounded breathless.

"It is, indeed," he said softly, as solemnly as a judge.

Anticipation could be delicious. It could also be torture. Often the two were one and the same.

He simply waited, and allowed her to anticipate.

He couldn't quite read her eyes in the dark, which he liked, too, because risk was part of the thrill. The risk of defeat. Was she deciding whether to flee?

Perhaps *he* should take this opportunity to flee.

It was silent, apart from the sound of her breathing, growing ever swifter.

And when he could have plucked the tension between them like a harp string, he watched, as if in a dream, his hand, so very, very inadvisably, slowly reach across the foot or so of safe distance between them and grasp the end of the ribbon.

That catch in her breath was one of the most carnal sounds he'd ever heard.

And then, tormenting the two of them, he

pulled the satin through his fingers and watched the bow unravel very, very slowly.

"There's the bow undone," he whispered.

And then he wound the ribbon in his fist and tugged her gently forward, until she stood just shy of touching his chest.

And for a space the shock of being close silenced both of them.

And then:

"I'm not a mule to be tugged about by reins," she whispered against his chin. With unconvincing indignation.

"True enough. A mule would have bolted away before I could have captured it. That is, unless the mule *wanted* to be captured."

She gave a short, nervous laugh. Her breath was uneven now. Excitement, or fear, or both.

He waited.

Anticipation. The seducer's best friend.

Or so he told himself.

He released the ribbon, and slowly, gently, pushed aside the folds of her robe.

He suppressed a groan of delight. She was nude beneath that robe, and he'd known she would be.

He slid his palms around her waist, took his fingertips on a leisurely slide along her rib cage, felt her belly leap. She was trembling. Her breath was hot and ragged on the vee of skin exposed by his open collar. Her skin was a silky miracle. He glided his hands across her belly, heard her softly breathed, helpless, "Oh," as delicious sensation coursed over and through her, and savored the decadent pleasure of knowing he was likely the first man to touch her like this.

He should stop. He should stop. This was madness.

He could feel the blood in his veins heat and thicken as if she was a drug, a powerful liquor. He filled his hands with her breasts. The full, silky give of them made him groan softly. He could hear his own breath now, a soft roar in his ears. And the tiny catch and stutter of her breath, and then the ragged intake of air as he caressed them.

Her head went back at the pleasure of it.

He drew his thumbs leisurely over her nipples. They were already ruched into hard knots.

She arched into his touch as though lightning struck.

He did it again. Harder. He wanted to take one into his mouth.

How quickly this had escalated.

"Ian," she whispered. Half afraid, half drugged with yearning, half plea. "It's . . ."

"I know," he said. "I know so many things, Tansy. So very, very many things about you, and how you feel, and what you want . . ."

He ducked and gently, just a little, flicked his tongue over her nipple.

He realized then he was playing roulette with his own desire. It was time to back away before he was too deep in. Just this taste of pleasure for her now, and then he could leave. He was always the one to leave women, anyway; like an actor who followed an excellent script, he'd always known precisely when to do it. Self-preservation was an instinct.

Why then, did he say: "I can make you see stars, Tansy." On a whisper.

She looked up into his face as if he were the universe.

He *had* to kiss her then.

Her mouth was as yielding as a feather bed; he sank into it with a sigh, a moan, that made him realize what a relief kissing her again was. That every moment he'd spent up until now not kissing her had been a shameful waste. And it began just that way, languid and wondering, a slow exploration, each of them taking unguarded pleasure in the textures and taste and perfect fit of each other. She gave and took in that kiss with a sensual grace and abandon that made him want to shout hallelujah, that nearly dropped him to his knees.

But he only took that kiss deeper, and his tongue dove and stroked, her hands clutched as they slid up over his chest and latched around his neck for balance, and she opened herself to him.

His fingers trailed her bare thighs, up to delicate, sheltered skin between them, up to the silky vee of curls. She ducked her head and buried it against his chest; her breath gusted hot and rapid on his collarbone.

The want of her shook him; his limbs felt stiff and clumsy. He could taste lust, peculiarly electric, in the back of his throat. His cock strained against his trouser buttons.

He skated his fingers between her thighs and found her slick and hot. Wet. So ready for the taking.

Her breath caught on the word *"Oh."*

He did it again. A tease, a feathery slide of one finger, and she jerked. "Ian . . ."

He did it again, harder.

She arched into it on a choked gasp, circled her hips against him, her hands clutching his shirt. How he wanted her hands on his skin. Her breath had begun to come in shallow little gusts against his throat.

He did it again slowly, tantalizingly.

He stopped. Testing.

"No," she begged softly on a whisper. "No, please don't stop . . ."

"Keep your eyes on my face, Tansy."

He wanted to witness her pleasure.

And so he was able to watch her eyes go heavy-lidded, and her head tip backward, and the cords of her throat go taut, and her head thrash forward again, and the air come shredded between her parted lips as he played with her desire like an orchestra conductor. And this was how he knew when to stroke harder, when to circle and tease, when to slide a finger deeper into her so that she moaned softly, gutturally, against his chest. A sound that nearly made him come right there and then.

With hands clumsy and shaking he unbuttoned his trousers, and his cock, thick and erect, sprang free, and he lifted her thigh with one hand, as high as his waist, and slid his cock against her wetness, tormenting himself, tormenting her. Once . . . twice. Three times. A dangerous, dangerous game, the most dangerous he'd ever played, when in one thrust he could be inside her and chasing his own pleasure, his own release, and he knew it would be explosive. His every cell cried out for it.

And yet the two of them did seem to seek risk. They would take it too far, he knew that now. It was inevitable. Perhaps not now, perhaps not tonight.

"Ian . . . I'm . . . *help me* . . . I'm . . .

He pressed his palm hard against her and circled, and she choked a sound of bliss, and her body bucked.

He pressed her head into his chest just in time to muffle her scream. And he held her close and felt triumph as he felt her body shake like a rag, over and over with what was likely her first ever release.

Silence apart from the ragged tide of breathing. Cool air over heated skin.

She shuddered.

He pulled her night rail around her, wrapped her in his arms and pulled her close. A little closer than his erection would have preferred. He felt quite martyred, in a way, and blessed in another.

He waited for her breathing to regain normal rhythm.

"*Shooting* stars." The words were muffled against his chest.

He gave a short, almost pained laugh. "I'm a man of my word."

He was afraid now. In a way he'd never before been. He didn't know how to extricate himself from this. Because he knew another woman couldn't possibly be the answer; nor was avoiding Tansy altogether. For this was a different kind of want. It wasn't mere sensual hunger. He knew how to sate that kind of hunger. He suspected the correct word for it was "need." There was a first taste of opium, or gin, for every addict, after all. This strange, wild, reckless, beautiful girl could very well be the end of him. He might as well throw himself off the balcony now.

How very ironic. The duke would finally have his revenge then.

He could feel her heart beating.

He savored it, as if the heartbeats ticked off the minutes they had left together.

She tipped her head back and looked up at him. For a long time, in silence. "Are you going to lecture me now? About how very dangerous all of this is, and so forth?"

How strangely fragile she felt now in his arms. His arms went over her shoulder blades. Suddenly it seemed to him that it did feel as though wings could sprout there.

"No," he said softly. "I think you know. This can't happen again, Tansy."

Her head jerked back and she looked up at him. He heard her breath catch.

And so the words had landed hard.

He'd meant it to sound like an order. It was difficult to shake the habit of issuing orders.

Knowing her, he suspected she'd interpreted it as a dare.

God help him if she did.

And it really was a prayer to God for help. If she dared him again, it would be all or nothing.

He looked down at her, and traced her lips with a single finger the way he had traced her name on the wall of Lilymont.

He dropped his hands abruptly from her.

"Go inside before you take a chill."

He suspected his tone had already gotten the chill started, which was just as well.

He backed away from her and didn't turn around until he was in his room again, the door closed behind him, the window firmly locked, and yet he knew he was hardly safe.

SHE DIDN'T EXPECT to sleep, but she finally tumbled over the edge into a deep, black dreamless one.

She was disappointed about the dreamless part. Her senses had just been thoroughly, properly used for the first time ever, and until she slept they'd reverberated like a thoroughly strummed instrument. She'd lain there and felt her body humming a hallelujah chorus. She wouldn't have minded reliving the evening again and again and again in her sleep.

For, as he'd said, it couldn't happen again. Not in waking life.

So that's what bodies were for, she'd thought, drifting back into the house from the balcony, realizing her feet were chilled. And that's what lips, and fingertips, and breasts, and nipples, and skin, and arms, and cocks, were for. And that's what men were for, and women were for. Suddenly, as bliss echoed all through her, everything else humans were capable of seemed superfluous.

I know so many, many things.

He *would* say that and then go on to say it couldn't happen again.

He was right, of course.

And when she awoke in the daylight, she had the sense to feel a certain reprieve. As though she'd escaped something. Daylight was slightly less conducive to madness, and she did not intend to be among the legion of women Ian Eversea had seduced and abandoned. A woman ruined because of a weakness for a beautiful man with a legendary way about him, and therefore useless to anyone, and a disgrace to the duke and his family, not to mention her own family.

She found the notion of that unbearable.

And yet . . . he kissed her as though he . . . *needed* her.

Only her.

As though he was searching for something and finding it . . . some solace, some ease, some answer. She'd felt his kiss in the soles of her feet, the palms of her hands, from the top of her head on down.

Through every part of her. He'd trembled when he kissed her, and his hands had been skilled and reverent, and she knew he'd been . . . lost.

Seducer. Seduction. She knew he was known for this, and the words implied calculation, process. It might have begun a bit like a chess game, but it had taken on its own momentum, and owned both of them.

It made her want to give and give. She had never thought of herself as an inherently generous person. But it worried her that she wanted to give him anything he wanted when he kissed her.

She would not believe he kissed every woman that way. He would have been worn to a nub by now.

Then again, how ever would she know? Perhaps it was all part of his magic.

And what if . . . well, he certainly wasn't a duke. He didn't even have a title. What would it be like to be married to Ian Eversea? Surely there was no harm in imagining it . . . surely a man like him would take a wife *one* day . . . She woke in time to find the stripe of light leading to the window. How would he look this morning? Any different than he had? How did she look?

She followed the little light road and peeked out.

But he wasn't there.

She waited a bit, the speed of her heartbeat ratcheting up a bit.

And he didn't appear.

And when the light was finally high enough, she knew he wasn't going to, which, she supposed, was all for the best.

Deflated, resigned, feeling quite martyred and mature, she flung the braided rope of her hair over her shoulder and settled in at her desk. She smoothed out the foolscap, and decided she would need to write smaller if she wanted to confine her list to a single page. She reached for her quill and wrote:

Kisses me as though his very life depends upon it.

Chapter 19

"We set sail in a little less than a month, Captain Eversea. Will you be on board? We could use a man like you. Pirates, you know. Le Chat is still sailing, or so rumor has it."

"I thought I was embarking on a pleasure jaunt, and you intend to put me to work?"

"Men like yourself live for it," the captain said dryly.

Ian couldn't argue with that.

He inhaled deeply. They were so close and yet so far from the sea in Sussex, and here the smell of it was primordial and thrilling. A heaving glassine green-blue stretching for as far as the eye could see. The ship seemed a behemoth at the dock but would be a speck on the chest of the sea. They would be at its mercy. He found the notion peculiarly soothing.

"I'll be aboard."

He thought of Tansy Danforth standing on deck, her bright eyes reflecting the seas and skies. She'd probably enjoyed that voyage, the risk, the danger, the newness. And how fun it would be to banter with her, to share the sights, to protect her from the goggling men on board and to watch her attempt to rein in those flirtatious urges.

And at night . . . in a narrow little bunk . . .

Something tightened in his gut again. He wanted her with a ferocity that bordered on fury. And it was this he needed to outrun, too.

He remembered the archery competition, and he thought sometimes he was like that: ever since the war he was like a bowstring pulled too far back for the arrow to do anything but overshoot every target. What he wanted and needed was to keep moving, until somehow his restlessness had run its course.

He watched the ship and dock activity idly a moment. The crew was working ceaselessly, repairing sails, scrubbing and sanding decks, bringing on cargo and supplies, checking the manifests as they grew person by person.

He'd apologized to his cousin Adam and begged leave for a day or two in London so he could put a deposit down to hold his place on this particular ship. It would sail as far as Africa, but he could step off in any port he chose along the way, or take another ship bound for anywhere. Anywhere at all. As long as his money lasted. And he'd saved enough money to keep moving for years, if he so chose.

"Eversea!"

A delighted voice spun him around.

"Caldwell!"

It was Major Caldwell who had suggested him for the East India Company promotion.

"A pity you won't be working for the company here in London, Eversea. Not only would we have a splendid time, we could use a clever sort."

"I'm flattered you'll miss me, sir, but this is something I've long wanted to do. Before I'm too decrepit to do it, mind you."

"Well, make your fortune and gather a few stories and bed a few brown maidens and return to us full of enviable stories, if you must."

"I must."

He said.

Meaning it.

HE RETURNED LATE enough that the entire house was asleep, and so he stripped off his clothes and flung himself, smelling of horse and the sea, into his bed, and fell too quickly asleep.

And in moments, it seemed, he could feel Jeremiah Cutler's little body tucked beneath his arm, plump and squirmy, vibrating with sobs. But he couldn't hear him over the screams of horses, the ceaseless roar of artillery, the guttural cries of men cut down. He handed Jeremiah back into the safety of his father's arms. He turned and lunged, dodging through chaos. He had only seconds to get to—

Ian broke through to consciousness with a gasp and a hoarse inarticulate cry.

He sat bolt upright, breathing as though he'd actually been running. He dropped his face into his hands and breathed through them.

The dream was potent; it was as if he'd lived it all over again.

He lifted his head at last.

Tansy was sitting at the foot of his bed, knees tucked under her chin, arms wrapped tightly around them, watching him.

He nearly yelped.

"What the bloody . . . *how* did you . . ."

"I think you were having a terrible dream," she said somberly.

"Am I *still* dreaming?" he asked wildly. "This isn't usually part of it. But if it is, I should warn you, it never ends very well for women."

He fell back against the pillow, hard.

Bloody hell. He threw a beleaguered arm over his eyes and sighed a sigh of despair.

Tansy slid from the bed, walked across his room to his bureau and sniffed the pitcher suspiciously. She poured some water into a glass, brought it back and held it out to him.

Ian reflexively took it and gulped it down. "Thank you."

"You're welcome."

He wiped the back of his hand across his mouth and clunked the glass down on his night table.

"How did you know I was home?"

"I saw your light."

A horrible suspicion struck.

"Wait . . . How did you get in here, Tansy?"

"Your window was open. Just a little."

"My wind— Oh God. Tell me you didn't climb from your balcony onto mine. *Tell me you didn't climb from your balcony onto mine!*"

"It was easier to do than I thought."

He opened his mouth. Only a dry squeak emerged. He tried again. "You can't *do* that. Mother of God. Do you want to die? You're going to marry a title and a fortune, remember? And live happily ever after." His words were still frayed. "Finding your broken body on the ground below my balcony would ruin my morning view."

"Shhhh," she said soothingly.

He closed his eyes. His breathing seemed deafening in the room, now that he had an audience.

He felt the mattress sink next to him and opened one eye.

She'd stretched out along the length of the bed, dangerously close to him but not touching, close enough that he could smell the sweetness of her, and now she was nestling her head into his other pillow.

Then she reached over and gently lifted his hand from his chest. Slowly, gently, carefully, as if stealing a bird egg from a nest.

"What are you doing, Tansy?"

"Comforting you."

He snorted softly.

She took the hand back with her to her side of the bed and held it companionably.

And because he couldn't think of a reason to pull away, he allowed it.

And it *was* comforting, strangely enough. He couldn't remember the last time he'd held anyone's hand.

They lay side by side, flat on their backs, in silence.

"I couldn't sleep, either," she said, after what seemed a long time.

He gave another short humorless laugh. "Bad dreams?"

"Sometimes. And very disturbing good dreams, too, about the man in the room next to mine."

He half smiled. "Tansy." A drowsy warning.

He could almost *hear* her smile.

They were silent again.

"Ian?"

"Mmm?"

"What was your dream about?"

He stiffened.

The thing was, he'd never told a soul. Oh, he'd told the story behind the dreams. It was part of the war stories men shared with each other. But he'd never confessed to being haunted by it at night.

And while he waited and said nothing, the fire said quite a bit. It popped and crackled and a log flopped over.

"Did you hear me say anything in my sleep?"

He'd always wondered. He dreaded the answer.

"It sounded like 'Justine.'"

Ah, bloody hell.

He sighed a long sigh of resignation and swiped his free hand over his face. "I wish you hadn't heard that."

"I've heard worse. I heard you break wind the other day on the balcony. Just a little."

"You *what*?" He was *not* going to blush.

And now she was laughing.

"Leave. Leave now. Or I'll do it again." But now he was laughing, too, and bit his lip to stop it. "Lower your voice, for God's sake."

But he didn't let go of her hand so she *could* leave.

"Have you been *spying* on me, Tansy?"

Though he was aware any indignation was hypocritical, given that he'd essentially spied on her, too.

"I wasn't *certain* it was you, until only recently. I just thought it was a man with a beautiful torso."

The words ambushed him. Beautiful torso?

He'd truthfully never been so disarmed by a woman in his entire life. She was one of a kind.

Don't leave yourself so open to hurt, Tansy, he wanted to tell her. *You shouldn't say those sorts of things to me.* He knew the power of words and flattery, because he'd used them strategically. And so did she, for that matter. But she was so *sincere*.

What was the matter with him when sincerity unnerved him completely?

He could tell her that he thought she was beautiful, too. That her lips were paradise. That her hair was a symphony of color. That her skin . . . oh, her skin.

But he wouldn't, because words like that bound another to you. Everyone wants to know how much they matter. He never used them lightly.

And in the wake of those words, he considered it might be sensible to drop her hand.

Perhaps . . . perhaps not just yet.

"Who is Justine?" she wanted to know.

"A bit of the war that won't let me leave it behind, I'm afraid. That's all."

"Were you in love with her?"

He made an exasperated sound. "God. Women and *that word*. They bandy it about so freely and I doubt half of them know what it means."

"In other words . . . no?"

He sighed, pretending extreme exasperation, which made her smile again. "Very well. Since you're relentless. Justine was . . . she was someone for whom I felt responsible, and she died in the war. I was too late to stop it. And I suppose I regret it every day."

He glanced over to find her clear eyes not on him but on the ceiling.

He smiled. She always seemed to be looking up.

His smile faded when he remembered she looked up for her mother.

"I'm sorry," she said softly, at last. As if she'd pictured the entire episode and genuinely mourned it along with him.

She knew what it was to mourn, too.

And strangely, there was a sudden easing in him, as if someone had finally played a note that harmonized with the one he sounded every day.

So as the words came for the first time, he aimed them at the ceiling, too, his voice abstracted.

"She was the wife of my commanding officer. Pretty, vivacious, very kind. I was close to both of them. We tried as best we could to keep women away from the battlefield but she traveled with our regiment and she wanted to be near her husband. She was intrepid as well as foolish, I suppose. But none of that matters. I was able to get to her child in time, but I couldn't get back to her—I took a bayonet in the gut, which rather slowed me down—and she got caught in cannon fire. I saw it. I never knew whether he would have preferred to have his wife or child alive because I spent the rest of the war recovering in a farmhouse in Flanders."

Her grip on his hand grew tighter and tighter as he talked. As if she walked the whole thing through with him.

"Oh, yes. I've medals and the like," he said dryly. "I'm brave as brave can be, so they said. I just wasn't fast enough to get back to her without getting myself skewered. And so I saved her child, but watched her die. And I get to watch her die in my dreams on occasion, too."

Tansy was quiet for a long while, taking this in.

"Well, as long as you have medals," she said thoughtfully.

He threw back his head and laughed, and had to bite his lip to stifle it.

And she laughed, too.

It was the *perfect* thing to say. *Well, you did your best,* or *It wasn't your fault*—it didn't matter how true those things were. It didn't matter how you tried to rationalize it away. The dreams would come anyway.

She knew it.

"Do you know . . . what's coincidental about that, Ian? My parents wished *I'd* died, instead of my brother."

It was such a ghastly thing to hear, his mind blanked for a moment. It was almost as though she'd confessed to murder.

He almost stammered. "Surely you're mistaken—"

"I heard them say it." She said this matter-of-factly, but he heard the steeled nerve in her voice. "Overheard them, I should say. My mother said, right after my brother died, 'If only it had been the girl.'"

It was like someone had punched him in the heart.

He was shocked by how literally painful the words were.

And a sort of furious flailing helplessness followed. As if he'd been once again one second too late to prevent someone from being cut in two by cannon fire.

"People say terrible, misguided things when they're in pain, Tansy. Things they don't mean."

"But sometimes you just know, don't you? *You* have so many siblings. *You* must know. They loved me but they loved my brother more. He was their pride and hope and the heir and so forth. And I was just a girl. I loved him, too, you know. I suppose I've always wanted to matter more than I did."

Love.

He didn't say, *There's that word again.*

He supposed it explained a good deal about Miss Titania Danforth and her quest for attention.

He'd always suspected Colin was his mother's favorite. And that Genevieve and Olivia were his father's. He didn't suppose he'd cared. There was always enough affection—and affectionate contempt—to go around in their household that it didn't matter to him. For selfish reasons, he would have happily gone to the gallows in Colin's place. To spare himself from having to watch Colin die, and to spare his mother from having to witness Colin's death.

Every day Colin had spent in Newgate had been a torment, though Ian had made sure Colin never knew this. He'd kept up the gallant nonchalance.

The fact that Colin had *escaped* the gallows was very like Colin.

"Your parents loved you, Tansy." Surely this much was true. He felt as though he could make it true with the force of his words. "Perhaps they simply worried more about you than your brother."

"Of course they loved me," she said absently. "I know they did, don't worry. Enough to threaten me—in their will, no less—with the loss of everything I've ever known or loved, unless I marry an amazing title and I'm taken care of for the rest of my life. And they didn't quite trust me to get it right on my own. Thought I might do something rash."

"I suppose they must have known you pretty well, then."

A smile started up at one end of her mouth and spread to the other, crooked, wicked. Then she laughed. Pleased with herself. Her laugh was wonderful. It was mischief made musical.

And then she sighed contentedly. "It's nice to be known," she said wistfully.

"You lost them in a carriage accident?"

She nodded.

"What were they like?"

He wouldn't know where to begin answering a question like that if anyone had asked it of him. And what she said would reveal as much about her as it did about her parents, he was sure.

She was quiet a moment, apparently giving it some thought. "Mother was always laughing. She loved to sing. She loved wildflowers. Columbine—I don't know if they grow here. They look like little paper lanterns? And aster, the purple ones. Like purple stars. Chicory, buttercups, Queen Anne's lace. The blue ones reminded her of my father's eyes. When I have a home, a permanent home of my own, I want to plant all of them in my garden to make it feel like home again. I promised Mama I'd bring a little of them home to England should I ever visit. She used to talk to them to make them grow." She was smiling now. "She thought of them as her children, in a way."

Suspicion dawned.

"Did your father smoke, by any chance?" He asked it almost disinterestedly. "Cigars, cigarettes?"

"He did! And my father . . . his laugh was the best sound you ever heard. My mother could make him laugh, but I was the best at it. His coat smelled of his tobacco . . . he rolled his own cigarettes with a particularly pungent brand he'd somehow gotten a taste for. My mother hated it." Tansy smiled faintly. "And at night he'd sneak just a bit of whisky. She hated that, too. Or pretended to. He rather liked being scolded, I think. It makes you feel cared for, doesn't it, sometimes?"

"I suppose it does," he said softly. As in his head the tumblers of a sort of lock clicked into place.

What it must have been like for her.

She *was* lonely. And, given the circumstances, resilient as hell.

He reflexively squeezed her hand a little tighter, unconsciously sending some of his strength into her.

She squeezed it back.

"I dealt with the solicitor to take care of a few stray ends of business," she said, "and I helped close up the house and pension off the servants, all but a few. A few to care for the house, a staff to care for the stables. I'd trust all of them with my life. But after that . . . do you know what it's been like, Ian? It's a bit like going to the theater. And the play we've come to see is my life. A wonderful play. But then it ends before you expect it to, and you're forbidden to leave, you're locked in the theater, and you're left to stare at an empty stage. And for all you know, you'll just sit there forever. Terrible word, forever."

"They ought to ban it from dictionaries," he concurred.

She smiled at that.

"And for quite some time it has felt like . . ." She turned to him earnestly, and he was treated to how her silvery eyes looked by lamplight, warm and hazy. ". . . It's hard to describe . . . I've been to school and learned everything there is to learn, and nothing has the power to surprise me anymore. Or to scare me."

He was stunned to realize that she was essentially describing what it was like to come home from the war.

He remembered returning . . . it was as if he'd used up every emotion he ever had, because he'd felt nearly everything there was to feel at such a pitch for so long that ordinary life felt rather flat and muted and painfully slow. He'd been willing to do nearly anything to *feel* something. And to forget.

Fortunately, Ian thought, God created French actresses and young women with flexible morals.

That rather took care of the forgetting. Climbing up trees and through windows and being ushered out of those windows at pistol point took care of the excitement part of it.

"It's a bit like that when you come home from war, too," he said slowly. He'd never said such a thing aloud to anyone. "Your senses are so accustomed to being constantly engaged and abused . . . that real life seems, for a time, inadequate and unreal and very dull. Almost stifling."

She was watching him in a way that made his heart turn over strangely. Soft and sympathetic and ever-so-slightly shrewdly.

"Is that why you have a host of mistresses?"

She was teasing.

He laughed drowsily. "*Never* a host. They're *far* too much trouble to deal with them in quantity."

She laughed softly, and suddenly he was suffused with an admiration that was almost painful. That she should *see* so clearly. That she could laugh and not judge. That her heart was accepting. That she'd confronted the utter destruction of her life with relative grace and looked forward with hope, not bitterness, not regret.

And there was a moment when he couldn't breathe, because he suddenly wanted to be worthy of her, and he quite simply didn't know how that was possible.

He'd been . . . such an ass.

"There will be a new play, Tansy." How ridiculously inadequate it sounded.

"When I marry and have my own home and family." It almost sounded like a question.

"Yes. Then." He made it sound like a promise. As if it were up to him, he'd make it happen.

And if it were up to him it would.

He was suddenly violently, irrationally yanked between two poles: The wish that she should have everything she ever wanted. To be safe and loved best of all by someone.

And the wish that she wouldn't, so this particular moment could be suspended in time. So this particular play, whatever this was, would never end.

They were silent for a time. And then she glanced down at his bare torso—his "beautiful" torso—and with a single finger, tentatively traced that scar. Delicately. Following it down, down, down, to nearly where it disappeared beneath the sheets.

He ought to stop her.

His muscles tightened with the pleasure of her touch, and with imagining what he could do to her, where he would touch her, how he would take her, how he would begin. His cock stirred. She *must* know what she was doing to him. She was still a devil, still a taker of risks, for all of that.

"I'm sorry this happened to you," she said softly. Her finger was so very near the border of the sheet, and in a moment his arousal would elevate that sheet. How he wanted to turn to her. Peel off her night rail. He could see the shadows of her nipples pushed against it, and he imagined drawing one into his mouth, imagined the little helpless sound of pleasure she would make when he sucked.

His cock stirred a little more.

"Tansy," he whispered. He slipped his fingers through her hair and drew it out, luxuriating in the silk of it, in the colors, every shade of gold there was, as her gentle fingers traced his scar. "Tansy."

"Yes?"

"You need to leave."

"Leave?"

"Out the door, and not out the window."

"Are you certain?"

"I'm certain."

"They're both dangerous routes."

She didn't need to tell *him* that. "Staying is far more dangerous than either of those. I meant what I said the other night. If you don't leave, Tansy, I *will* make love to you. It will be all, or it will be nothing. And I cannot warn you again."

The hush that fell was velvety and taut. Her wandering finger froze.

She studied him, gauging his mood, and whether to test him, and whether it was what she wanted. She had only an inkling of the pleasure that could be had. If only she knew what a razor thin line of control he walked. Knowing her, she would have risked pushing him over the edge. Because she'd just endured her own personal war, and risk and sensation were helping her to forget.

He would give nearly anything to kiss her right now.

And if he kissed her, he wouldn't stop until he'd taken everything he could.

Stay. It took every fiber of his control not to say it. It took every fiber of his control not to tear that night rail right from her body and lose himself in her.

"Because men are brutes?" She said this almost lightly. On a whisper.

He looked down at her. At the soft point of her chin, at her clear eyes, the generous mouth.

No, he realized. Because I want to make love to you. To *you*. Not just for surcease. Or to chase pleasure to its ultimate peak. Because I want to give *you* pleasure, to hear *you* cry out, to be inside *you*, to talk to *you* when we're quiet and spent.

On the heels of that came an even more alarming realization.

He suspected he wouldn't mind settling for simply holding her hand all night.

That was an . . . interesting . . . notion.

A very, very *unwelcome* notion.

"Yes," he agreed softly. "Because men are brutes."

She sighed and stretched. "Very well."

She slipped her hand out from his.

She shoved her hair out of her face, slid off the bed and treaded delicately as a fawn across his soft carpet, apparently enjoying the feel on her bare feet, which made him smile.

"But you can leave the night rail," he called softly after her.

She laughed softly.

She winked and blew him a kiss.

He watched her open the door, peek out, and disappear.

He'd never hated the sound of a door closing more.

He groaned and dragged the pillow over his face. It was cool. Perhaps it would lower the temperature of his feverish thoughts.

Unconsciously, he closed his fingers, as if he could capture and hold the sensation of her touch in his palm.

And that's how he fell asleep.

Chapter 20

"You're all looking unusually dazzling this morning, ladies."

His sister and Tansy and Olivia were dressed in what he recognized as their finest. Colors that set off their eyes and hair and presented bosoms and arms and the like in their best possible light. He was the brother of two sisters, and he'd known myriad women; he knew *far* more than he wanted to about such things and had been tortured by questions about fashion more than once.

"Why, thank you. You're looking remarkably alert this morning, Ian."

"You flatter me, surely," he said dryly.

"Why are you still in Sussex?" Genevieve was shrewdly suspicious.

"I've business," he said smoothly. "And I promised Adam I'd help keep the motley crew of workers organized while we finished the repairs to the vicarage. Where are you off to? Because I gather from your finery that you are off to someplace other than town."

"We've been invited to tea. Lord Stanhope is a guest of Lord Henry's family."

Stanhope.

The Duke de Neauville's heir.

The one said to be looking for a wife.

Clearly, Ian's message had been successfully conveyed and enthusiastically received.

Which ought to have made him rejoice.

And yet somehow his mind blanked, as if he'd heard news of a murder.

He realized he'd gone still, fork hovering in the air in the vicinity of his mouth. He'd forgotten whether he intended to put it in his mouth or set it down. He decided to set it down.

"Ah, the Duke de Neauville's heir. I'd forgotten there were other dukes besides yours."

"Ha," Genevieve said.

Tansy hadn't yet looked at him. She was stirring the marmalade pot as if it were one of the witches in Macbeth. Slowly, and with great focus.

"What are you hoping to find in there, Miss Danforth? I haven't heard whether you can read marmalade the way you can read tea leaves."

She stopped, looked up. There was a peculiar clutch in the vicinity of his heart when her eyes met his.

She blushed.

Slowly, beautifully.

It didn't irritate him in the least.

Which worried him a good deal.

THEY DEPARTED, AND Ian paced to and fro, feverishly, for a time.

And then he found himself heading toward the stable. He saddled up and rode out through the woods along the little tributary of the Ouse, back the way they'd come the other day. He followed the stream she'd knelt next to, slowing his horse to a walk.

He scanned for hoofprints and footprints and brush and shrubbery that might have been pushed aside or crushed. He didn't know quite what he was looking for. Anything unusual. His father had taken all of his sons out hunting at an early age, and tracking was second nature to him.

A glint caught his eye. He pulled his horse to a halt.

Something lavender and shiny.

He swung down from his horse, looped the reins into a hawthorn, trod toward the glint and stopped.

Thoughtfully, he plucked up a bonnet; trailing from it were lavender satin ribbons. He held it gingerly. He shouldn't doubt her.

Why did it matter so very much?

He strode forward, ten, twenty feet, and came to a little clearing he hadn't ridden through since he was a boy. A nondescript place, but it had inevitably changed over the years; one of the old oaks had been split by lightning and now lay on its side, and the others had grown into behemoths around their fallen comrade.

He rotated slowly, scanning the place, for . . . what, he wasn't certain. Flattened grass, from lovers rolling about? A man's footprint, a woman's footprint?

But the clearing was mostly dirt; no moss grew. It wasn't the sort of place one could comfortably tryst. Then again, he'd managed to tryst up against trees. Where there was a will to tryst, there was always a way.

Perhaps she came here the way Polly did. To contemplate nature's wonders in solitude. It didn't really sound like something she would do; then again, he'd had the blinkers ripped from his eyes recently.

Suddenly he stopped. And peered.

What appeared to be two little stakes were poking up out of the ground.

Next to two little mounds.

As though something *had* been buried.

Good God.

Even though he'd jested about it, now he was ever-so-slightly worried. He was beside the mounds in two steps.

He crouched and peered.

The earth was dark and disturbed, but in an orderly way. Not as though an animal had dug for something or churned it with hooves.

As though something had been planted.

A scrap of what appeared to be foolscap was affixed to the first stake.

In exquisite, copperplate handwriting was written the word: *columbine*.

And on the other: *asters.*

He sat back on his heels.

She'd likely planted them as a tribute to her mother.

"Damn."

The word was really more of an exhale.

He closed his eyes as a wave of something roared through him, like a dam broken.

It felt like a torrent of sunlight, and it hurt, and it felt glorious.

He knew then that the punching sensation he'd felt in the vicinity of his heart last night was really the locked gates of it being kicked open.

THE FIRST SURPRISE about the heir to the Duke of Neauville was that he wasn't *very* handsome.

Oh, he was handsome enough. He was appealing in an even-featured-possessed-all-his-limbs-and-teeth way. He was tall and long-limbed. His hair was a sandy color and his gray eyes twinkled and his complexion was free of spots. His manners were as exquisite and polished as the silver—ancient silver, passed down through generations and worth an untold fortune, no doubt—upon which they were served luncheon. Everything in the room gleamed: crystal, porcelain, utensils, upholstery, his admirably complete set of teeth.

He possessed the sort of subtle remote self-consciousness of those who knew they were very important and who were accustomed to stares.

Until he really took a good look at Tansy.

Gratifyingly, he gawked like any green lad.

Which made her cast her lashes down. Then up again.

It was a reflex, really.

"A p-pleasure indeed to meet you, Miss Danforth."

Ah, a bit of a stammer. She loved it when she made men stammer.

He was charming, really. Or really, it was what she should have been thinking.

Somewhere along the line she'd begun to interpret charm a little differently.

As challenge. Impenetrable confidence.

Occasional charmlessness, even.

He bowed low, very low, over her hand, and held it like a Frenchman, and slowly righted himself again.

"Everything I've heard about you is true."

Ah! So she was a legend already.

One day she might even be as talked about as Ian Eversea.

"WHAT THE DEVIL are *you* doing here?"

Ian whirled. Colin was standing in the doorway of the family's library with his mouth agape.

Ian surreptitiously tucked the book he'd pulled from the shelf and tucked it under his arm.

"Is it really such a shock?"

"The last time I can remember you coming in here voluntarily was when Father acquired a book featuring medical illustrations, and you thought there might be a naked woman or two inside."

"There *was*," Ian pointed out. "I was right. My suspicions were rewarded. Even though her internal organs were sketched inside her. And I never forgot how inspiring the experience was."

Now go away, he silently bid Colin.

No such luck.

"What are you holding, Ian?"

"Nothing."

"It appears to be a book."

"If you knew what it was, why did you ask?"

"Is it an anatomy book?"

Ian snorted.

Colin flung himself down in a chair and peered out the window. "I'm glad Genevieve will be living close. They've about settled on purchasing the estate. I'm certain you're glad your nemesis will be close, too."

"He's not my nemesis," Ian said. Rather to his own surprise.

"Inconvenient reminder that you possess a conscience, then."

"Perhaps," he said curtly.

He didn't want to continue looking through his book until Colin left. And he very much wanted to continue looking at the book. He'd visited a section of the library shelves he'd never before seen, and it had taken him quite some time to find it.

Oh, but he had, and treasures lay within. At least they were treasures to him.

Colin showed no signs of leaving. He swung a

booted leg, gave the empty brandy decanter a dis-
consolate shake.

"Well, then."

"Colin, may I ask you a question?"

"Why on earth are you asking permission to
ask a question?"

Ian steeled himself.

"Why do you love Madeleine?" He asked it casually.

But Colin's mouth dropped open.

Even when Colin was in Newgate, pale and
shackled, they'd never discussed life or death or
love or loss. Ian had brought the best of the broad-
sheets to him. In one issue, Colin had been depicted wearing a pair of horns. He'd had it framed
for Colin. Because that's what brothers were for.
Every other memory was too precious to be aired
in that prison cell.

So obviously Colin was surprised. "I see. I
assume there's a context for this question?"

"Consider it . . . research."

Ian could see that Colin was skeptical. He could
feel his brother's eyes on his back speculatively. A
strange little silence passed, and Ian went still, his
heart beating with a deeper thud.

"Well . . . she's the strongest person I've ever
known." Colin sounded as though he was thinking about it for the first time. "She's fascinating
and fearless, but she's fragile, for all of that. She
sees right through me and loves me anyway and
has from the first, though I'm not certain she'll

ever admit to that. Because she's not as strong as she thinks she is, but she'd needed to be strong for so long that it made me want to be strong for her, a better person for her. She's so beautiful to me it hurts, sometimes, to look at her. And no one has ever before needed me, and she does. She really does."

And no one has ever before needed me, and she does. She really does.

It was quite a speech.

Ian stood motionless, moved and, truth be told, astonished, beyond words.

In the ensuing awkward silence, he realized there was a world of knowledge and experience his younger brother possessed that he did not. Just as Colin would never know what it was like to nearly die on a battlefield, as he had. Colin had survived unscathed. Then again, nearly going to the gallows had likely shaved years off his life.

"*And* she's as interested in the raising of cows and sheep as I am lately," Colin added.

"I guess someone needed to be. Are you sure she isn't pretending just to make you happy?"

Colin snorted. "Miss *Danforth* is interested in cows."

"If she said that, Miss Danforth was lying."

"I know, but at least she made an effort to do it, which is flattering."

There was another little silence.

"Did you come to the library today for a reason, Colin?"

Go away now, Colin.

"I was looking for you. I'd like to buy a mare for Madeleine as a surprise for her birthday and I'd hoped to persuade you to come with me."

"Here's my advice: if you're not buying the horse from the Gypsies, then your judgment is probably sound."

Colin gave a short laugh.

And still he didn't leave.

"Why don't you tell me why you're wondering these things, Ian?"

Bloody hell. His younger brother rivaled their cousin Adam for the ability to peer into his soul.

Ian was torn between wanting to talk and not knowing precisely how to articulate what there seemed to be no words for, primarily because it was new. A big amorphous knot of emotions and impressions, one of which was panic, another of which was glory, and there were dozens of subtler ones in between. He wouldn't even know where to begin unraveling it.

He tried.

"Colin . . . do you believe in destiny?"

"Certainly." Though Ian suspected this was a lazy answer to avoid a philosophical discussion.

"I think my destiny might be to be murdered by the Duke of Falconbridge."

Colin lifted a dismissive hand. "He can't murder you. He's family. Family doesn't do that sort of thing. At least knowingly," he added after a moment, somewhat cryptically.

"Tell that to Othello."

"A Shakespearean reference, Ian? Did you . . . actually *listen* at school?" He sounded aghast.

"Perhaps I had a knack for remembering only the things that prove enlightening later."

"Why do you think the duke will . . ."

He stopped, frowned faintly, as a suspicion began to form.

"Noooooo . . ."

"No?"

"No. No no no no no. Tell me you didn't . . . not Miss Danforth! Tell me you weren't that mad!" Colin leaped up and reached for Ian's lapels and gripped them. "Tell me you're not that suicidal! What is the *matter* with you, when there are so . . . many . . . women in the world?"

"Get off." He pushed his brother away. "Calm yourself. Of course not. It's not like that at all."

To his knowledge, it was the first time he'd ever lied to Colin in his life.

Colin was still staring at him. "Because you know Genevieve will never forgive you. And the duke may *not* kill you, but you'll always wonder, won't you? What a fun way to go through life."

He was about to say, *The duke's not a murderer.* But then cuckolding a man really was a matter of honor, and Ian wasn't certain he'd blame the duke for wanting to exact revenge . . . and if he should ever suspect that Miss Danforth had crawled into his bed last night . . .

"All right, then," his brother said. "If you *are*

worried about the duke with regards to that girl, I wouldn't lose sleep over it. After all, it's what *everyone* sees when they look at her. I imagine you're only now coming around to seeing it. And in time it'll go the way of your other, shall we say, passing fancies, no doubt."

"I see." It almost sounded like sacrilege to hear it described that way. "Well, then."

"And by passing fancies, I mean women."

"Thank you. I knew what you meant."

He was quiet.

Go away, Colin.

Colin regarded him with some sympathy.

"You know, marrying someone—anyone, practically—would solve the problem."

"Of Miss Danforth?" For she needed solving, as far as Ian was concerned.

"Of you."

He snorted.

"Don't marry someone dull, though," Colin hastened to add.

"Can't marry someone dull if I never get married at all."

"Forget what I said about family. Mother *will* murder you then," he said easily. "Now, come with me."

Ian sighed, and hurriedly slid *Native Flora of North America* back into place on the shelf. He would be back to study it later.

But he didn't push it *all* the way in. And when the Duke of Falconbridge entered the library a little later, specifically because he'd seen Colin and Ian departing it, he scanned the room thoughtfully. When he noticed the spine of one book poking out from the otherwise neatly aligned books, he immediately aimed for it and pulled it from the shelf.

He read the title.

And he straightened slowly and stared after where Colin and Ian had disappeared.

Chapter 21

When she bounded downstairs for breakfast the following morning, Tansy was greeted by a footman who was just taking receipt of more bouquets! How she loved flowers.

"These arrived for you, Miss Danforth," he said, smiling as she began to lunge forward enthusiastically.

But she stopped short.

And backed away two feet. As if instead of flowers, she'd been given one of the plants that eat animals, the sort that Miles Redmond had documented in his book.

At last she stretched out her hand for them, slowly, disbelieving, and the footman relinquished a colorful, casual bundle, tied with a blue ribbon.

And then her hand began to tremble as she took an inventory of the flowers:

Columbines. Asters. Marigolds. Wild roses. Bergamot. Lupine.

And the thing that stopped her breath: a trumpet-shaped flower called "shooting star."

It was like looking across a spring meadow in bloom back home.

Shooting star!

They could only be the gift of one person. The person who claimed he never gave gifts. At least not to women.

How had he . . . how on earth . . .

"A message accompanied them, Miss Danforth."

The message was sealed with a blob of wax but no press of a signet. She slid a finger beneath to crack the seal, and read: *I apologize if I've ever behaved like an ass.* It was the most romantic message she'd ever received.

All other messages would strive to live up to it for the rest of her days. She was convinced of that in the moment.

"And these have just arrived for you, too, miss, with the vase as well. Where would you like me to put them?"

He gestured to an exquisite alabaster vase stuffed with tasteful, towering, flawless, hothouse blooms. Roses, crimson and erect, looking like scepters, white lilies like trumpets. A triumphant arrangement only one man could have sent.

An arrangement, in fact, fit for a duchess.

Both arrangements stole her breath, for different reasons.

She opened the note that accompanied it.

These reminded me of you. I hope you don't think me forward, but I would be honored if you

*and Falconbridge would join me for an afternoon
picnic today.*

"I think someone is smitten." Genevieve was
smiling.

Which someone?

And which one was scarier?

SHE FOUND HIM sitting in one of the parlors, perusing a book he tucked behind him the moment she
entered the room.

"Good afternoon, Captain Eversea."

"Good afternoon, Miss Danforth."

He remained seated. His long legs were
stretched out before him, his arms folded behind
his head, and the sun was behind him, giving him
a little corona of glowing auburn. Like the embers
of a fire.

As befit a devil.

"Thank you for your very kind gift," she said.

"You're welcome."

"And for the apology."

"You're welcome."

"That must have been torture for you to write.
The apology."

He was silent.

"I can just imagine you sitting there, beads of
perspiration popping out all over your brow, your
pride writhing in torment as you selected just the
right words . . ."

He gave a short laugh. "Enough."

She smiled at him.

"Aren't you going to stand for me? Gentlemen generally do, when a lady enters the room."

And at that he drew himself slowly to his feet, and somehow the unfurling of his great length and height effectively blotted out the sunlight pouring in the window. He took two steps toward her.

As usual she felt at a loss.

"Is that better?" he said softly.

It was and it wasn't.

He was so very, very tall.

She was always so very tempted to allow him to engulf her.

"I remained sitting," he said thoughtfully, "because I liked how the sunlight poured over you as you entered the room and lit you up, and I quite simply couldn't move for enjoying it."

Oh.

Now he'd done it. He'd stolen her breath completely.

She was the arch flatterer, and she hadn't the faintest idea what to say. Like his message accompanying the flowers, this particular observation meant more than every single compliment she'd ever received in her life. She knew it was sincere.

And she once again had a sense for how he could so easily captivate women.

She didn't like the idea of him captivating women. Women.

And then she remembered: he never gave gifts.

"Thank you," she said, almost timidly.

He smiled, a slow crooked smile that ended in a short laugh, because he knew, he knew, just what he did to her.

Beast.

"Aren't you going to flatter me, Miss Danforth? Don't I look manly, and so forth? Don't I give the best compliments you've ever heard?"

"I'm certain you have that conversation with your mirror every morning."

He laughed again, that surprised, delighted sound. "So what are you going to do today?" He flicked a glance over her striped muslin morning dress, and she felt the heat start up at the back of her neck and her arms, her nipples perk to attention, and she knew from now on every time she stood in a room with Ian Eversea she might as well be wearing nothing, because she'd feel naked regardless.

"I've been invited to a picnic with Lord Stanhope. And Genevieve and the duke."

"Have you, now? Back to visit him so soon? And how did you find his lord, yesterday?"

"Amiable."

"Amiable," he said slowly, as if rolling an unfamiliar wine about in his mouth. "Now, given that I know you're prone to hyperbole, 'amiable' sounds like a veritable indictment."

"It's not. Did you hope it was?"

"Of course not. Amiable is all anyone can hope to be. The absolute pinnacle of personal achievement."

"And if *you* keep striving, I know one day you'll reach that pinnacle, too, Ian," she soothed.

He grinned at her.

A funny, soft little silence ensued.

"Ian . . . I've been wondering . . ."

"Yes?"

"Will you tell me more about lovemaking?"

He blinked. "Tansy. Mother of God. You have to stop *doing* that."

"Doing what?"

"Ambushing me with questions of that nature, and the like."

"It is the one way I get the better of you, and it's very, very funny to alarm you, so no, I won't."

This amused him slightly. "I did have to at least ask."

"But regarding my question . . . Don't you think I ought to be educated before I take any risks?"

Truthfully, it was a deliberate provocation. A red cape shaken out in front of a bull. She wanted to hear him talk about it.

She knew he wanted her, and knew *all* the power lay in her hands.

Too late she realized he would of course know exactly what she was doing.

He didn't like it.

His eyes went flinty. "I'm certain your husband will do it for you, when the time comes. It's his duty . . ."

Husband. She blinked. The word landed with a sort of thud between them. A funny little silence followed. She observed him through narrowed eyes.

She didn't like the sound of the word "duty," either, and suspected he knew it.

". . . *and* it will be your duty to please him."

She suppressed a wince. "Perhaps it will always feel like a pleasure, not a chore," she said bravely.

"Perhaps," he said idly. "You could very well be right. But it isn't always a pleasure, you know. Not every man is a skilled lover. Not every man will make you feel as if your blood is on fire and your knees are water, and like you can't breathe for wanting him."

She froze.

Speaking of ambush.

Interestingly, as if he were a conjurer, her blood was now on fire and her knees like water, and she'd stopped breathing.

How did he do that? How did he know? It was desperately unfair that he knew so much more than she did. And he'd said it so easily. He stepped a little closer. Just an inch or so. She could breathe now. She was doing it admittedly faster, however.

He wasn't finished.

"Not every man will make you want to do anything he wishes because the moment he touches you your body is his to command. Not every man is capable of making you scream with bliss in every imaginable position, or knows where to touch you, or listens to your breath and your sighs to know precisely *how* to touch you, so that the pleasure you experience is the most intense. Not every man will make you see stars every . . . single . . . time."

With every word her temperature seemed to rise another degree. Her senses seemed to understand that he was calling to them, like a charmer coaxing a snake from a basket, and it was true . . . she couldn't breathe for wanting him.

How in God's name did he know exactly what he did to her?

More importantly, what on earth did he mean by "every imaginable position"?

"There are many positions?" was what she finally said, her voice a whisper.

"Yes." A curt answer.

She was speechless.

"Is that what you wanted me to say, Tansy? Is that the sort of thing you want to know about lovemaking?"

Really, he was a relentlessly cruel bastard, and yet she'd asked for it and he'd quite turned the tables on her. It really was impossible to toy with the man. She could not maneuver him in any of the usual ways.

And then she had a suspicion, which blossomed into a realization, when she looked at his hands. They had curled, involuntarily, and his knuckles were white. As though he was digging his nails into his palms to maintain control.

He was able to describe it in such detail, but he was describing how it felt for him, too.

Not in general.

With her.

With *her*.

And this seemed immense.

Mainly because she thought it might even

frighten him. The man with a bayonet scar across his abdomen who suffered over a life he couldn't save while unthinkingly nearly sacrificing his own.

"Thank you for that. It was quite edifying." Her voice was frayed, as though she'd been locked in a heated room. Which, metaphorically speaking, she was. "And *I* . . . well, I suspect that not every woman will turn your blood into lava, or haunt your every waking thought, or make you tremble when you kiss her, or lose your mind and do things you never dreamed you'd do. Like track down just the right hothouse so you could send her a bundle of wildflowers native to a very specific region. When you make rather a point of never giving gifts to women."

He went utterly motionless. Like an animal caught by a predator in a clearing.

Something like reluctant admiration flickered across his face. It was chased by something else, too: fear, or hurt, there and gone. She almost reflexively reached out to touch him, to apologize . . . for what? For seeing through him? For angering him? For subjecting him to something new?

She didn't want him to ever feel more hurt. She never wanted this brave man to be afraid of anything.

It wasn't her *fault*. It wasn't something she'd done to him deliberately, after all.

Well, not entirely.

His voice was steady. "I can assure you, some

women never know that kind of pleasure. Take a survey of your friends. You'll doubtless discover most of the married ones are mulling their household budgets whilst their husbands busy themselves on top with the act of getting an heir. And young spoiled heirs never need to learn how to pleasure a woman."

This did make her instantly flush scarlet. "You're awful."

"You don't know the half of it, I'm afraid. I'm no hero, Tansy."

She suspected she knew at least part of it. She suspected he was at least partially wrong. He was allegedly an inveterate rogue, and she'd witnessed nothing to dispel the notion. She thought of a certain sloe-eyed brunette widow and exchanged glances, and about what Mrs. deWitt had said.

It ought to matter to her more than it did.

And that was the danger of kisses, and seeing stars on a balcony at night. Her senses suddenly seemed to have dominion over her brain.

"We can limit our conversation to the weather, if you prefer," he said, when it seemed she would say nothing. "Wouldn't that be more sensible?"

"It's hot today," she said instantly.

He smiled, a slow, delighted smile. Then shook his head.

Damnation, but she liked him.

The tension loosened.

"I meant every word I said the other night. Do not play roulette with me, Tansy." He said this gently, almost apologetically. "It will be all. Or it will be nothing."

She backed away two steps. Back into the sunlight, inadvertently.

And he stood and watched her. "Like watching an angel return to Heaven."

She snorted at that. "Now *that* was blarney."

He grinned.

"Comfort yourself with the knowledge that it's all in your hands. But then, I know that's precisely where you like men to be."

He reached for his hat, lying next to him on the settee, and settled it on his head.

"And enjoy your picnic."

Chapter 22

"Has anyone ever told you that your eyes are the most singular color?"

They were walking along, side by side, across parklands that seemed never to end. Green as far as the eye could see. Once, when she was a little girl, she'd thought Heaven might look like this, but now she hoped it didn't. It was rather dull, all told. A bit safe.

And the fact that it seemed endless suddenly made her nervous. A bit like a marriage. The endless part. The "until death parts us" part.

She was somehow suddenly less certain about the safe part with regards to marriage.

"Not in so many words, no."

"They are. And when you smile . . . they're like stars."

Stars.

Seeing stars.

He *would* have to say stars.

Would Lord Stanhope make her see stars? Could he? She glanced down at his hands surreptitiously. Beautifully groomed hands. Had he ever hammered a nail with them? Defended anyone with a weapon? Had they ever trembled when he touched a woman? Did he listen to a woman's breathing in order to ascertain the kind of pleasure he could give her, and . . .

He interpreted her silence and her sudden pink color as bashfulness. "I do apologize, Miss Danforth. I hope you don't think I'm being too forward."

"Not at all. How could I object to such a thoughtful observation?"

She slid a sidelong look at the well-made young man. No lines at the corners of his eyes from squinting down a rifle or riding into the sun. His laugh was surprisingly hearty, and just a trifle irritating. Perhaps because it seemed too easily won, which seemed a very unfair thing to think. He laughed a good deal, too. Life was good to him; why shouldn't he laugh?

He'd shown himself to have a rather literal sense of humor. Better than none, she supposed. But it had thus far been difficult for her to strike a spark from it when he was so very amiable. It was only in walking and talking with him that she realized how the past few years had shaped her, carving out unexpected nooks and crevices in her character. Surprisingly, she wasn't as easy to navigate now. She wasn't as easy to persuade.

One really only discovers one's true self in contrast to other people, she realized.

Which is the only way one discovers one's true needs.

She was tempted to ask Lord Stanhope if he had any scars that told the story of his life.

Scars. Which, coincidentally, rhymed with "stars."

She drew in a sharp breath, remembering how she'd drawn a finger along the hard torso of a man, tracing a bit of his history, an event carved into his soul, while his fingers combed through her hair almost reverently, as though it was made of rare silk.

Have you ever put yourself in harm's way for another person without thought for your own safety, Lord Stanhope? She was tempted to ask him.

"Where did you go, just then, Miss Danforth?"

Blast. Lord Stanhope might be a bit tedious, but he was observant.

Which she supposed spoke well of him.

And he was going to be a duke.

The word definitely still held its glamour. Fanning out from it was a world of possibility beyond this stretch of banal, tamed greenery.

"I was imagining my eyes as stars. Such a lovely thing to say."

"You must hear that sort of thing all the time."

She smiled enigmatically. "Not as prettily, I assure you."

"Speaking of pretty, I have had the good fortune of purchasing a very fine gray mare. I think you and she would be beautifully matched."

He was matching her to a horse?

Was he about to *give* her a horse?

God help her, she wouldn't mind having her own horse here in Sussex.

Was he looking for a *wife* who would match this horse? This was a bit more troubling.

"Would you care to go riding some morning very soon?" he asked.

"I would love to, thank you. I enjoy it very much."

She peered over her shoulder. In the distance, Genevieve had kicked off her slippers and appeared to be reading to her husband, who had removed his hat and was playing, idly, with the ends of a long ribbon that circled her dress just below her breasts. Catching it, releasing it, as the breeze fluttered it.

She smiled, but felt a sharp stab of envy. Genevieve was married and she was in love with a man many people probably considered unknowable.

Then again, one might describe Ian Eversea in just that way, too.

But he possessed the key to her senses. He was waging a campaign to have her that included no promises and no future. He was likely, as the duke had implied, broken in a way.

And as she smiled up at the future Duke of de Neauville, she wondered why it didn't matter as much as it should.

ONCE AT HOME again, she sorted through the bouquets sent to her—five, this time!

She opened her mouth to ask the footmen to take a few of them down to the churchyard so the Ladies of the Society to Protect the Sussex Poor could distribute the bouquets again over naked graves.

But then she paused. And she thought about Olivia and Lyon Redmond and the loss of him, and she knew, suddenly, that the Olivia she now saw wasn't the Olivia she'd been before he'd disappeared.

And that was what Ian had been trying to tell her. Ian loved his sister, and Ian knew what "gone" felt like and he'd trusted her with that information because he'd known she would understand. And oh, how she did.

She carefully removed all of the cards from the bouquets.

"Would you please tell Olivia Eversea that all of these have come for her?"

The footman nodded as if this were an ordinary request.

She made her way up the marble staircase, thoughtfully.

And then she settled in at the little writing desk and retrieved her list of requirements, which was beginning to look a trifle worn and dirty at the edges from all the handling it had endured. Then again, she'd learned a good deal in a short amount of time.

On the surface of things, Lord Stanhope seemed to meet many of the requirements.

Funny how each day revealed a few more that seemed absolutely critical.

But the quill called to her, so she picked it up, and twiddled it between her fingers, before carefully adding two new, quite essential points.

Must have a few interesting scars.

Makes me feel more alive than anyone ever before has.

And it was this last, above all, that was significant. She'd valued very little in the past year, but Ian Eversea had both brought her down to earth abruptly as well as shown her the stars.

On the surface of things what she was about to do couldn't be more reckless. It was hardly the act of someone who had both feet planted firmly on the ground.

But it was one of the more reasoned decisions she'd made in a very long time.

Chapter 23

IAN DIPPED IN AND out of sleep like a bit of flotsam tossed on a shallow stream.

She should not come to him.

He *prayed* she wouldn't come.

He woke again. Lay there in the silent dark. And felt like a bastard. An utterly worthless, lustful bastard. Who wanted what he wanted and had applied every trick of persuasion to get it.

The night stretched on.

And now he feared she wouldn't come.

He hadn't any right to do that to her. To use her own sensuality as a weapon to seduce, to persuade. To instill doubt in her future when he did, truly did, want her to be happy and to have what she wanted.

Surely he wished her a lifetime of happiness more than he wanted to make love to her.

He wasn't certain.

But if he could have one night with her. Just one night. He would have a lifetime to repent his methods. From across the sea, of course.

And the irony was that this could very possibly be the duke's revenge. To want beyond reason the one woman he shouldn't, and couldn't, and might never, have.

And as one of the longest nights he'd experienced since the war inched glacially by and she didn't come, the heaviness of disappointment finally carried him off to sleep like a stone hurled into the deep.

Sometime later—it was still dark—he awoke again and stirred. He tilted his head to the side; the wick of his lantern had burned low.

He turned his head again toward the window and froze.

She was sitting on the foot of his bed.

They stared at each other a good long time in silence.

"Am I dreaming?" he asked.

An eternity, which was likely only a few seconds, passed before she spoke.

"No." In a whisper. Hesitant. A trifle fearful. A trifle amazed.

She was there.

Wordlessly, very slowly, he pushed the blankets away from his body. He moved to her, silently. And without preamble reached for her night rail and slowly lifted it off over her head.

Her arms went up, assisting him, fell again.

She sat nude before him, her heart beating so loud the blood whooshed in her ears.

And he eased her backward, slowly, to the bed.

Her arms went around his neck. And oh, the glory of his skin touching hers. Of the heat and strength and weight of his body. She clung to him, savored the chafe of her nipples against the coarse hair scattered over his chest. He buried his face in her throat and sighed, placed a soft, hot kiss beneath her ear, and she felt herself begin to melt, to surrender utterly. And then he moved his lips to the delicate bones at the base of it, and she arched back and threaded her fingers through his incongruously soft, fine hair. She found his ears and traced them, trailed her fingers over the immense hard curve of his shoulder. Rejoicing in the fact that there was so much of him to discover.

And a sort of wildness overcame the two of them, as if nudity had turned them into the first man and woman and sex was their very first discovery.

There was to be no narration, no finesse, no coddling. He covered her as if she were a long-time lover, and she surrendered, as if in a dream, not knowing where it would lead, only that she would go wherever he wanted to take her. And in the dark silence it only seemed right, to make sense.

He found her lips, and the kiss was savage and hungry and deep, almost punishing, as if he'd waited a lifetime for this very kiss, as if she'd deprived him of the very thing he needed to survive. She cupped the back of his head with her hands and yielded to the heady dark sweetness of his mouth, stroked his hair, to soothe, to gentle him, and the kiss eased into something more languorous, more penetrating, more profound. Somehow she felt it everywhere in her body, stealing into her veins like opium. Slow, slow. As if in slowing it they could make time itself their slave, and it would stop for as long as they wanted this moment to last.

He gently pulled his mouth away and rested his forehead against hers. His breath rushed out hot and hoarse. She felt the rise and fall of shoulders.

"How I've wanted you." Half whisper, half groan, against her mouth.

He slid his lips down along the arch of her throat, lower, lower, until his mouth found her nipple and circled it hard, with a sinewy tongue.

She gasped and arched, and he did it again, then closed his mouth over it and sucked.

"Oh, God, Ian." A ragged whisper.

He did it again, moving to her other breast, and then his mouth went traveling, down, down, down the seam that divided her ribs, his lips and tongue and breath stopping just long enough to set every cell in its path on fire.

He was shockingly skilled. Every bit of the swift, sensual assault was deliberate, new, devastating. With his tongue, his fingertips, the slide of his palm, sensation built upon sensation, buffeting her, ensnaring her, turning her into a creature whose only purpose was to accept pleasure. She writhed beneath him, moaning softly.

He dipped his tongue into her navel, slid his hands over the soft curve of her belly, lifted her up and then parted her thighs with his hands and touched his tongue to the silky hot wetness between her legs.

She jerked at the sensation; a glorious shock.

But he didn't stop. His fingers played lightly, lightly, on the delicate skin inside her thighs as his tongue delved and stroked and circled, quickly and lightly, then slowly and hard.

She whimpered. Dear God, it was like no pleasure she'd ever before imagined. She rocked her hips in time to the thrusts of his tongue. And she could feel herself hurtling headlong into the unknown. Her words came in raw desperate sobbing shreds.

"I can't bear it . . . oh please . . . I need . . ."

She shattered in a hoarse cry, bowing upward from the force of it, and she nearly blacked out as her body bucked in the throes of it.

He raised himself over her with his arms, and with one hand guided his cock into her.

The shock of him filling her threw her head back on a gasp. He pulled her thigh up around his waist and thrust again, slowly. He dipped to kiss her, gently; he licked her nipple as he thrust and dove, almost languidly.

He withdrew. And then filled her again. The rhythm built, and with it that indefinable insistent, delicious pressure, beginning on the periphery of her senses. And with each thrust it gathered, banking, into something so almost unendurably blissful she knew it could only be released in a scream.

And then their bodies collided hard as his hips drove his cock swiftly, deeply, into her, the rhythm of his thrusts swift and pounding, his hoarse breathing and muttered oaths and her own soft cries mingling as she dug into his shoulders with her nails and their bodies raced toward release.

She threw her head back. "Please, Ian . . . please . . . I'm . . ."

He went rigid over her, and she heard his ragged cry of something almost like triumph as his release rocked his body.

HE LOWERED HIMSELF carefully. Rolled to the side of her, then collected her in the crook of his arm. Her skin, its silkiness, undid him.

"You are beautiful," he murmured.

"A compliment," she murmured. "Wonders never do cease."

He breathed into the sweetness of her hair. He pushed the silky mass of it aside and kissed her neck, and she sighed. He wrapped his arms around her body, and for a time they lay quietly. He savored the rise and fall, rise and fall, of her rib cage beneath his hands. They said not a word.

Inevitably, his hands began to wander. A leisurely journey, sliding over the soft mound of her belly, then delicately up her rib cage to her breasts. He cupped them in his hands and feathered strokes over them. Again, and again. Like a man fanning flames. Reveling in the satiny texture of her skin. Reveling in the tension he felt in her spine as desire tightened her muscles, shortened her breath, then made tatters of it. Reveling in the way she arched like a cat into his hands. She was devastatingly sensual and abandoned; she took to receiving pleasure with the instinct of a beautiful animal, and it only made him want to give her more and more and still more, and to take her every way he could.

And soon she was rippling beneath his touch, her buttocks circling hard against his hard cock. He slid his hand down over her spine and slipped it between her thighs, and his fingers slid into her silky wetness. She groaned with the pleasure of it and parted her thighs a little more, begging for more.

His hunger for her seemed fathomless. The more he took, the more he wanted.

He nipped the back of her neck and moved gently away from her, tipping her onto her stomach.

He dragged his palms down her back, then raised her hips, and unquestioningly she moved with him, trusting. He pressed a kiss at the sweet dip of skin at the base of her spine and slid his hands over her arse. He nipped one cheek gently, as if it were a peach.

And then he rose up and slid his cock between her legs, teasing her, teasing himself.

"You feel . . . so good, Tansy."

She moaned softly, and he could feel her flesh throb against him.

He did it again, sliding slowly, gently. Another tease.

She jerked from the pleasure, her fingers curling into the counterpane.

"Ian, I will *die* if you don't . . . please . . . more . . . *faster* . . ."

And then he slid into her, quickly and deeply, and he could feel her gasp, and tense. And then he withdrew, slowly, so slowly, allowing her to feel every inch of him.

She moaned, and hissed in a breath, and swore something softly.

"Beg me, Tansy," he whispered.

"*Please*, Ian. Please. *Faster*, please."

He drove himself into her, pulling her hips up hard against him, burying himself to the hilt, then sliding slowly from her.

"Please . . ." She rocked her hips against him. Nearly sobbing from the pleasure, from the sensual torture. "I'm so *close* . . ."

He did it again. Slowly. A sensual sadist.

And again.

And then he could no longer tease her, because desire had him in its teeth now. He was rigid and shaking and perspiring from the effort of control.

And so he freed them both.

He drove into her, swiftly, his hips rocking hard as he pulled her hips up against him, burying himself deeply in her faster and faster still, a relentless pounding, a mad, greedy hunger.

"Oh God . . . Oh God . . ."

She screamed her release into the counterpane, thumping it with her fists as he drove himself toward his. His release ripped him from his body, nearly blacked his consciousness. He heard his own guttural cry as if from another planet. He thought he may have said her name.

"IF I HAD known . . ." she whispered, tangling her fingers in the fine hair scattered over his chest. Then trailing her fingers toward the hollow of his armpit. He had one arm thrown over his head.

"If you had known . . . ?" he prompted softly.

Her cheek was against his chest, and she could feel the steady thump, thump, thump of his heart beneath her cheek. An oddly precious, intimate sound. And there was the scar, the reminder that he was human and vulnerable and someone had nearly killed him.

She tensed at this, and tightened her grip a little, pulling a few of his hairs.

"Ow," he said softly.

"Sorry."

"Finish your sentence."

"How good this was . . ."

"You might have skipped being a well-bred heiress and gone straight onto being a scarlet woman?"

"Then again, perhaps not. I have it on good authority that not every man is as good at this sort of thing."

"A lot of men just climb on top and go at it."

"What a waste of so many marvelous body parts."

He laughed softly.

She kissed him on his chest. On his *beautiful torso*.

"That feels good," he murmured. Encouraging.

She drew her tongue down the seam that divided his ribs, and let her hands trail after, remembering how he'd done it to her, and how it had lit her every cell on fire.

He stirred and sighed, his fingers stroking through her hair.

"That's good," he confirmed on a murmur. "Don't stop."

She continued her progress to his flat stomach, stroking over it with delicate fingers. Lingering. Teasing. Watching, as he did, for the tension of his muscles, for the change in his breathing, in order to know exactly how to pleasure him.

She dipped her tongue into his navel, tasted salt.

His breathing was beginning to come short. His cock stirred and leaped a little as it grew harder.

And so she moved her mouth there, and drew her tongue hard and slowly down along it.

"*Christ . . .*" and then he swore something considerably more filthy than that.

She circled the head of it with her tongue and drew his cock into her mouth. And sucked.

He moaned softly, and his hands went down to tangle in her hair.

And the power to give him pleasure stirred again the desire in her. It seemed fathomless. Insatiable.

"Again?" she teased.

"And again and again," he ordered.

And so she did.

And as his cock thickened, dragging her lips and mouth and tongue over it, now swiftly, now slowly, she reveled in watching him shift restlessly, his thighs falling open, his body bowing upward, his hands curling into the counterpane, his breath short and harsh. His head thrashed back and he swallowed; the pleasure seemed well nigh unendurable, and it banked her own pleasure.

"Tansy . . . I want you to ride me."

She straddled his body, flinging her heavy mass of hair over her shoulder wantonly, and gazed down at him. The cords of his neck taut, his chest was burnished by firelight, his eyes burning.

Together they guided him into her.

He bracketed her hips with his hands and urged her to move her body up and then down again, until she understood the rhythm. And at first she moved to watch his eyes darken, to hear him beg her hoarsely with her name. And then she moved to please herself, as she had no choice: instinct drove her blindly toward it.

They rocked together until the two of them, one right after the other, saw shooting stars.

JUST AS THE light was going pearly and gray in the sky, and she knew she should return to her room, Tansy sighed and moved out of his arms. She reached for her night rail and drew it on over her head.

She sat for a moment, watching him, Ian's arms crossed behind his head, his hair tousled, his eyes drowsy and warm, a faint smile playing on his lips as he gazed back at her.

Her heart lurched.

What if . . . what if she woke up every day of her life to this view? Was it really so unthinkable? Surely no man could remain an alleged rogue for the entirety of his life? Surely Ian wouldn't mind waking up just like this, either?

But there was something on the periphery of her awareness, some little warning voice. It sounded, unsurprisingly, like the Duke of Falconbridge's. She said nothing.

She just smiled at him.

His smile grew wider, and a little more wicked, and her heart squeezed. She could feel herself blushing. Despite being clothed, and despite every delightfully wicked thing she'd done last night.

And at last Ian rolled over and sat up on the edge of the bed with a little grunt. He straightened to standing somewhat gingerly.

"It goes a bit tight if I don't stretch every morning," he said apologetically, gesturing to that scar.

She watched him arch his back and thrust up his

arms and bend backward, as he fought a grimace, and she felt her muscles tense along with him.

Not a God, then.

Or a pagan roaring to greet the day.

Just a beautiful, wounded man.

Chapter 24

Tansy clapped a hand down on her bonnet as Stanhope's high flyer careened around a bend in the road at reckless speeds. He was a brilliant driver and the horses were beautiful, copper colored and shining like new pennies, and the sun struck sparks off their haunches and manes.

"You're a brilliant driver!"

"Beg pardon?"

It was impossible to speak over the thunder of their hooves.

"YOU'RE A BRILLIANT DRIVER!"

"YOU LIKE MY HIGH FLYER?" he guessed.

She gave up. "Yes!"

He beamed at her, certain of their accord.

But when they stopped, and the horses tossed their heads and shifted restlessly in their harnesses, and the moment was no longer distractingly terrifying, and they were alone, certain dullness settled into her chest.

He was a relentlessly cheerful presence, talked only of himself but so good-naturedly that she indulged him. He certainly laughed a good deal. Something about his laugh made her feel more alone than if she were standing on a high cliff at the end of the world, shouting her name into the void to hear it echo back at her.

In all likelihood he knew he'd been born fascinating, by default, because he was going to be a duke when his father died, and he considered the ceaseless talk of himself a bit of beneficence on his part.

But better a cheerful sort than a surly sort, she supposed.

He helped her down and beamed with the pleasure of being able to do that for her, and then offered his arm to escort her back to the house.

As she moved, she could feel the night before in the stiffness of her legs. And as Stanhope led her back toward the house, she surreptitiously brushed the back of her hand against her chafed and still kiss-swollen lips, and heat rushed over her skin, just like that. In the mirror this morning she had looked alarmingly, intriguingly, thoroughly wanton, her hair in wild disarray, her eyes brilliant, her cheeks flushed; on her breast was the mark of a vigorous, lingering kiss, and remembering it now made her knees sag a little.

She'd resented the need to dress and bathe so soon, in time for Stanhope to take her out in his high flyer; she wanted to lie still, while the feel of Ian's hands and the warmth and scent of his body still lingered on her skin. Lie still and savor it until it faded like the very last note in a symphony. Lie still and try to decide what it meant to her.

And now last night had seemed real, and this jarringly cheerful, reckless outing with an heir seemed like a dream.

"I must say, Miss Danforth, I may always cherish the letter I received from Captain Eversea. I may even have it framed."

They would have that in common, she thought. They both wanted to frame missives from Captain Eversea.

"You received mail from Captain Eversea? Which Captain Eversea?"

"The one who will be embarking upon an ocean voyage soon? Within the month, I believe. Captain *Ian* Eversea."

Shock momentarily destroyed her ability to speak.

"An . . . ocean voyage?" She choked on the words. Suddenly, the ribbons of her bonnet seemed too tight.

"Oh, yes, 'round the world he's going! The sort of voyage to rival Miles Redmond's travels, from the sounds of things. He could very well be gone for *years*. With luck, a cannibal won't eat him. He looks a bit stringy to me, ha ha! Not an ounce of fat on the man."

Tansy couldn't feel her hands or feet. "Years?" she said faintly.

"One can't experience Africa and China and

India and the like in less time than that," he said knowledgeably. "So certainly, years."

"Wh-What did he say in the letter?"

Her teeth were chattering as though someone had dropped an icicle down the back of her dress.

"He suggested I might want to hurry to Sussex to meet the 'American Paragon,' as queues to meet you were long and rivals were shooting each other with arrows and the like over you. He's not given to gushing. So I knew you must be special, indeed. The man is an excellent judge of things, from horseflesh to shooting to women."

The world seemed to tilt on its axis. She stumbled.

Lord Stanhope flexed his arm and quite capably kept her from falling.

"Slippers are hardly practical for walking," he said fondly.

A faint ringing started up in her ears. Her voice sounded to her as if it was coming from a far, far off land. Africa or China, even.

"He . . . *summoned* you to Sussex? For me?"

Stanhope looked a bit worried now. "Perhaps I shouldn't have said anything at all to you. It's just that it seemed like a wonderful stroke of good fortune, and I felt as though gratitude were in order, since he did encourage me to come."

"He . . . summoned you to Sussex to meet *me*?"

She sounded like a demented parrot. She didn't care. The shock was gruesome.

"I do want to thank him, though, for aren't we having a wonderful time? I don't think he'd object overmuch."

"A wonderful time," she repeated, faintly, after a moment, like a broken cuckoo clock.

HE'D HAMMERED HIS final nail into the vicarage roof today, and after they all stood back, hands on hips, and admired their handiwork, he'd taken the crew of workmen along with Adam down to the pub to congratulate and celebrate with them.

He was surprised to see a young man named James who worked in the Eversea stables competently waiting tables.

"Captain Eversea, what can I bring you?"

"James! What a pleasant surprise to see you here. Helping out while Polly's ankle heals?"

"Aye, and it was your Miss Danforth we have to thank for it, too."

His heart stopped. He fought to keep his eyes from shifting guiltily.

"Er . . . *my* Miss Danforth?"

"The Miss Danforth who lives with the Everseas," he said, smiling. "The one who won the Sussex marksmanship cup."

"Oh, that Miss Danforth. Yes. How kind of her."

For now, Polly remained behind the bar, the better to flirt with all the customers at once. Ned, Ian decided, was going to have his hands full with her suitors in no time.

As one by one all the vicarage workmen, Seamus and Henry and Adam included, departed the Pig & Thistle for other obligations and destinations, Ian lingered. He called for another ale and nursed it more slowly than he normally would.

As he'd watched her slip out the door of his room this morning, he'd had to stifle a protest. He'd wanted nothing more than to pull her back, curl his arm around her, fold her into his body and lay there quietly on the bed, tracking the hour of the day only by the length of the sunbeam through the slit in the curtains and the color of the shadows in the room. And they would watch the sun go higher and then slowly sink again, while they made love, and slept, and made love, and slept, and talked and laughed and made love and slept.

Possibly with her hand clasped in his.

The world seemed . . . roomier . . . and kinder and more colorful and funnier today. He wasn't unfamiliar with the effects of excellent sex on a man's temper. This was like that, and yet different somehow. He felt fundamentally altered. As if he'd been sitting in a dark room for ages, and someone had casually strolled in and lit a lamp.

The only thing that would make the day even better, he thought, was if she were sitting across from him right now.

An alarming thought.

Your Miss Danforth.

My. Mine. He was beginning to understand the

appeal of that preposition with regards to women, and why Colin and Chase brandished it as if it were a medal they'd each earned.

And as the sun sank lower, he was aware that he was postponing returning home because he felt almost . . . shy. He recoiled from the word. *Surely* not. Very well, then: he did feel uncertain. And he'd been so very certain about everything not very long ago. There was no longer any reason for him to remain in Sussex, and it was time to return to London to complete preparations for his voyage.

And he just didn't know what would happen next. For there *would* be a "next," the awkward, fraught time between now and the moment his ship left shore.

All he knew for certain was that he wanted to see her.

And he wondered what he would read in her face when he did. Welcome? Desire? A firm and yet closed resolve to never be alone with him again, as a result of a sudden onset of regrettable sense? Regret? Would they make love again?

The bands of muscle across his stomach tightened at the thought. Of *course* it wasn't wise. But the laws of physics had been upended for him; the harder he pulled away from the notion of making love to her, the deeper and more desperate the need for her seemed.

He got up abruptly and went home.

Fittingly enough, he arrived in that neither-day-nor-night in-between hour.

His heart picked up speed the closer he came to his chamber. Once inside, he stared at the now neatly made bed.

And then he inhaled deeply, exhaled at length, and almost tenderly lifted the curtain away from the window. As if he were pushing her hair away from her face in order to kiss her.

Twilight was purpling the horizon.

She was standing on her balcony, holding a perfectly rolled cigarette and trying, in vain, to light it.

He frowned.

He would warrant she'd never actually lit a cigarette in her entire life. Rolled, certainly.

"You don't smoke," he called softly.

She froze. But she didn't turn toward him. It was a moment before she spoke.

"How would you know?"

She said it so bitterly, it shocked him.

She refused to meet his eyes. But her hands were trembling now, he saw, and she nearly dropped the cigarette.

Bloody hell. Something was terribly wrong.

He ducked back into his window, and then went through the door of her room out onto her balcony.

"May I?" he said gently.

She shrugged almost violently with one shoulder.

He took the cigarette from between her fingers.

He lit it with a flint.

A strikingly pungent smoke curled out of it, and he coughed. Her father's blend.

And she coughed.

She didn't attempt to smoke it. He handed it back to her, and she just gripped it between her fingers as if it were a spear she'd like to jab into him.

And not once did she look at him directly or say a word to him. She seemed as remote and cold as a locked room.

And then she looked up reflexively at the stars, as if seeking comfort and home, and his heart broke just a very little. Or kicked. It was hard to know for certain, because the pain was sweet.

Little things she did would always break his heart open, he felt. Always. His heart would forever be like a pond frozen over in winter cracking with the thaw.

"When were you going to tell me?" she said finally. Sounding weary.

"Tell you . . . how to light a cigarette?"

"That you're leaving. For good, essentially. More or less. In a fortnight, isn't it? Or were you just going to disappear, and hope that I considered you a figment of my imagination? A sort of fever dream?"

Oh. Hell.

"Ah. I thought you knew I was leaving."

"No." She said it flatly.

"Yes. I'm sailing soon, Tansy." He said it gently. "I did say I would be off around the world."

"You did say." She said it with faint mockery. "You just didn't say *when*."

Silence.

The ash was lengthening at the tip of the cigarette, heading for her fingertips.

"Are you going to smoke that, or . . ."

She suddenly tamped the cigarette out with great violence and whirled on him.

"And you wrote to Stanhope to tell him to hie his way here to Sussex to see me. Solving the problem of me, weren't you? Neatly disposing of me. Wave the shiny heir in front of Miss Danforth's eyes to distract her from her ridiculous *tendre* for *you*. Keep her out of the way of Landsdowne. Because she's just that shallow and just that fickle and anyone and *anything* can distract her, and here, have yourself an heiress, Stanhope, so she doesn't get in the way of anyone I actually *care* about."

In the force of her fury and hurt, he found himself becoming very, very calm, and very, very clear. It was what made him a good soldier, and why he never seemed able to stop being one.

"I of course didn't say that in so many words. And you know it isn't how I feel."

His calm seemed to make her angrier.

"Do I? How *do* you feel, then, Ian?"

He was silent. He couldn't choose from any of the words he knew, because none of them were sufficient. Of course, a single word would do the trick. But he wasn't going to say that to her now. Because he was about to lose her, and he didn't think she would believe him, and he would be gone anyway, and what good would it serve either of them?

She snorted softly when he stood there and said nothing.

"What did you do to the Duke of Falconbridge?" Her voice was bitter. "Because I know it was something. He doesn't like you."

Ah. So her goal this evening was to find as many ways to hurt him as possible.

"Did he say as much?" Not surprising, really. But it seemed unlike the circumspect duke to state it baldly.

"He implied, and I'm not as stupid as all that, Ian. Something about 'climbing' seems to come up rather a lot with regards to you. And I doubt it means anything good."

Her bitterness was knife-edged.

He didn't have the right to be angry. And so he found himself going calmer and calmer. The eye of the hurricane around them.

"What did I do to the duke?" he said musingly. "Very well. Since I have never lied to you, Tansy, and since you asked, here is what I did to the duke: I attempted to seduce his fiancée. The woman he was to marry before he met my sister. She was, in fact, quite willing. We had, in fact, been planning to tryst for some time; I climbed a tree to her chamber window, where he was lying in wait in the dark in her bedroom, unbeknownst to her. I had just climbed into bed with her, and I hadn't yet touched her when he . . . when he . . . suffice it to say he ushered me out of the window at gunpoint. Naked."

He'd delivered the words baldly, unleavened with compassion, tenderness, or apology. She *had* asked. It had happened precisely that way.

Let her do with the truth what she would.

She now knew more about him than most of the people he'd known his entire life.

Tansy had gone utterly silent, listening.

Utterly still.

He couldn't even sense her breathing.

He saw the curtains rise a little at her window, which were open just an inch.

Windows seemed to play an inordinate role in his fate.

"You . . . *knew* she was his fiancée?"

Her voice sounded scraped raw. As if she could scarcely speak in the wake of that confession. She was aghast.

"Yes."

More glacial, ominous silence.

"Why? Why did you do it?"

And suddenly the fury broke through.

"Because she was beautiful. Because she wanted me. Because I wanted her. Is that what you want me to say, Tansy? Because the duke was rumored to be a dangerous man, and I liked the idea of risk. Shall I quote *you* on the subject of risk, Miss Danforth? Shall I remind you that you climbed in my window, and that you allowed me to lay you back on my bed, and allowed me to lift your night rail from your body, that you slid your hands into my shirt, that you—"

She'd jerked away from him as if he'd thrust a torch into her face.

"*Stop* it. Don't you know, Ian . . . the duke is a *person*. He'd lost his child. He'd lost his wife—"

"Don't you know he was rumored to have *killed* his wife? The rumor didn't arise from nowhere. No one is suspected of that unless people have reason to wonder. He's no saint, Tansy."

"What utter shite, and you know it! Of course he's no saint! Who *is*? Certainly not you. And it's hardly an excuse, and you know that, too. But he'd hoped to marry again and rebuild his life. And you *took* that from him. No wonder he thinks you're *broken*. You took it because you *could*. You took it simply because you wanted it."

Broken? He supposed he was.

He gave a short, dark laugh.

"It wasn't quite as simple as all that, Tansy. Nothing ever is. And if you take a deep breath and think it over, you'll know I'm right. You knew who I was before you came to me. I have *never* lied to you. Never. And I have never promised a thing."

But she wasn't in the mood to listen. She was in a mood to hate him, and she needed the hate to distance herself from him. Like a boat she could leap into and push away from a dock. As if that would make any of this less painful.

"You always do get what you want, don't you, Ian? You wanted me, and you in all likelihood did exactly what needed to be done to *have* me. Was it the risk that made me so appealing? Or did you want to shame the duke again?"

He was silent. Long enough for her words to reverberate, long enough to allow her to hear what she'd just said, and to shame her just a little. She knew they weren't true. She was just flinging shards of words. She hoped a few of them struck him. She wanted to hurt him.

She succeeded.

But he knew better than she did how to withstand pain.

"I never *wanted* to shame anyone," he said quietly.

She was breathing quickly now. She gave her head a rough shake.

"Look me in the eye and tell me you're proud of everything you've done, Tansy. Look me in the eye and tell me you thought about the hearts you might be stealing or breaking with flattery and flirtation. Look me in the eye and tell me that you carefully thought through the consequences of every one of your actions. Particularly the actions of last night."

She didn't turn to him. "Yes, damn you," she said brokenly. Sounding furious. "I thought last night through. Did you?"

"Yes," he said tersely.

The break in her voice nearly undid him.

They regarded each other unblinkingly, from a distance of just a few feet. There might as well have been an ocean between them.

"Tansy." He tentatively stretched out a hand. He wanted desperately to gather her to him.

"Please don't touch me."

His hand dropped.

"You always do get what you want, don't you, Ian? You wanted me, and you in all likelihood did exactly what needed to be done to *have* me. It's all about the *getting* of someone, isn't it? God forbid you should *give*." He couldn't believe she thought any of these things were true. She just wanted to lash out.

He waited again, and though he was certain nothing he said would matter at this point, he chose his words carefully, succinctly. So perhaps she would remember them later, when her anger had ebbed.

"I will tell you a few things that I know to be true. I wanted you, Tansy. I want you now. I will want you until the day I die. I never promised or implied a thing other than that. You wanted me, too. The duke will never allow me to marry you. And I am leaving."

He could feel her take each word as a blow. And he'd delivered them that way. Irrefutable facts, all incompatible with each other.

She stood, utterly motionless, her face peculiarly set, and yet peculiarly crumpled, as if she was made of melting wax.

"And *you* . . . are probably going to marry a future duke. Take comfort in that, Miss Danforth. And you're welcome for that, by the way."

He could do bitterness well, too.

She jerked her head away from him. Stared off toward America, or Lilymont, or someplace that felt like home. Someplace that wasn't him.

And if he wasn't broken before he set foot on the balcony, he felt broken now as he left.

Chapter 25

As usual, it didn't take long for word in Sussex to spread: Miss Titania Danforth was being courted quite determinedly by Lord Stanhope, and wagers were being made over how long it would take him to make her his bride. If the way he drove his high flyer was any indication of his courtship style, those that had "before the month was out" stood to win.

It was generally understood that the competition, which was considered legion, didn't stand a chance, and that sending flowers to her and the like was a quixotic exercise, and yet they continued to straggle in, for one just never knew. It was the same philosophy the ton at large took to Olivia Eversea. It was like an investment. Best to keep a hand in. The winds of fate were fickle.

So flowers still abounded in the Eversea house.

Which meant the Everseas saved a good deal of money on decorations for the Grand Ball.

Tansy stood with Annie in front of her wardrobe and scrutinized her row of dresses as though

Tansy was queen and she was choosing her ladies-in-waiting.

The abigail's face was radiant and abstracted. And at last she turned to Tansy and blurted, "Oh, there's something I just must tell you, Miss Danforth. We're to be wed in a week! My James and I!"

"Oh, Annie! That's wonderful, wonderful news!"

She turned and gave the abigail a swift little hug, which made both of them blush.

"It has made all the difference, the money from waiting tables at the Pig & Thistle. Ned Hawthorne thinks James is ever so good with the customers. We cannot thank you enough for recommending him."

"So lovely to hear. I hear 'Titania' makes a fine second name for girl babies," she teased.

Annie blushed scarlet at this, and she seemed momentarily speechless with pleasure.

"Well, we should dress you tonight as if you're already a duchess, Miss Danforth," she finally said.

Tansy went still.

But then, naturally, gossip had entered the bloodstream of the Eversea household, and of course the servants would know about Stanhope's attentions.

She immediately squared her shoulders, as if the courtship was a lead-lined cloak.

She'd scarcely made an effort to charm anyone in the last fortnight or so, but it wasn't as though Stanhope or anyone else had noticed. He chattered happily when they went out walking, or drove recklessly in his high flyer, or he rode alongside her.

Meanwhile, she hadn't seen Ian at all.

She supposed he was busy with preparation for his round-the-world journey. She tried very hard to be very philosophical and mature and sophisticated, to think of her time with him in terms of fleeting, startling beauty—a sunrise, a sunset, that sort of thing. When that failed to console her, she tried to poke the embers of that righteous, incinerating anger with which she'd driven him off the balcony the other night. But that failed, too, because that particular fire was dead. Because he'd been absolutely right, of course, and it was ridiculous to be angry with *him* for something (granted, remarkably stupid and selfish) he'd done before he met her. To be angry at him for being who he was. She understood what drove him, perhaps better than anyone ever had. She'd already forgiven him.

And she didn't think he was that person anymore, either.

It seemed, then, that all that was left to her was to suffer, silently, for as long as . . . well, until she no longer did. Presumably at some point in the history of her life she no longer would suffer, or at least she'd arrive at some effective way to manage what right now seemed gruesomely unfair and nearly intolerable.

The two of them would just have to join the

annals of star-crossed lovers, she supposed. Tristan and Isolde. Romeo and Juliet.

Olivia Eversea and Lyon Redmond.

It was far more romantic-sounding in books.

In reality, it was ghastly.

And besides, he certainly hadn't said that he *loved* her. *I will want you until the day I die.* He'd said *that*, but not a word about love.

Would it be better if he'd said it?

Yes, she'd decided. It would have been. She wasn't certain whether he *did* love her, or whether he would even recognize it if he did, and it was this that gave her a spine, and this that got her through the ensuing fortnight of Stanhope's courtship, and this that propelled her from bed each morning since that night on the balcony, and this that made the notion of life without him just an infinitesimal fraction more bearable.

It was, however, a mercy that Ian was leaving the country. Because to marry someone else while they shared the same continent, breathed the same air, looked up and saw the same stars, seemed . . . ridiculous. Counter to natural law.

And yet to *not* marry, and marry brilliantly, seemed not only a betrayal of her parents' wishes, but of the duke . . . and herself. Her parents had wanted nothing more than for her to be safe and cherished and settled. To have a home and family and permanence once more.

And God help her, it was what she wanted, too.

But tonight . . . in all likelihood, she would

have to see him tonight. At least out of the corner of her eye.

She shook herself from a reverie and turned to Annie, who was watching her with a disconcerting look of sympathy, which fled instantly.

"What would you wear, Annie, if you were going to see a man for the very last time, and you wanted him to never forget you, and for every woman he ever saw after that to pale in comparison to the memory of you?"

Annie's expression then made Tansy realize that yes, servants observed everything. They knew who slept where, and how crumpled the beds were in the morning, and she realized that footmen who moved silently through the house must notice glances exchanged. They must know.

The abigail suddenly reached out impulsively to squeeze her hand.

And then she whispered: "It won't matter what you wear, miss. He will never, ever forget you."

IAN DIDN'T WANT to go to the ball.

He didn't want to watch Tansy dance with other men and he didn't want to dance with any other woman. But he was no coward, he generally had very fine manners and a sense of duty, and so he shaved and dressed scrupulously and went and stood in the ballroom. His mother had insisted; if he was going to go off again on an around-the-world trip, she wanted to see as much of him as she could before he did. He never could deny his mother what she wanted.

So he managed to smile and bow and say appropriately banal things to the people who passed by. He'd been through worse evenings, by far; he would survive this one. He would just keep moving through the ballroom, smiling, nodding. That way, if anyone were to say, "Have you seen Ian?" many were bound to nod yes, and assume he was dutifully participating. He was nothing if not a strategist.

And then tomorrow he could leave for London. Distance would help. Like opium, it wouldn't eliminate the pain, but it would certainly help to muffle it.

The glittering ranks of ball-goers swelled. Everyone he knew, clad in finery he'd seen event after event, poured in. After all, everyone wanted to be present when it was rumored that the duke's ward, Miss Titania Danforth, who had been such a disturbance upon the calm waters of Sussex society, would become engaged to someone who would *also* become a duke. What marvelous symmetry, some sighed. Certainly it was destiny.

Ian hadn't yet seen her.

He hadn't, in fact, seen her for almost a fortnight.

Or for twelve days, four hours, thirty-two minutes, and forty-one seconds, to be precise.

He'd looked at his map this evening, but then

shoved it aside and whiled away some time doing those particular calculations instead.

During that calculated time, he had returned to London and begun purchasing supplies and commissioning clothes appropriate to a trip to Africa and all the points in between. And during that time, he supposed she'd been whisked about in a high flyer and taken on picnics and walks and the like. He hoped, quite uncharitably, that she was bored, and that she thought about him constantly, because if she was going to forget him, there was time enough to do that *after* he sailed away.

And then he hoped—and the very nature of the selflessness amazed him—that she wasn't too bored, because the very idea of her unhappiness, of her sparkle dimmed for any reason, filled him with something close to panic. As though his own life was imperiled.

"What the devil are you glowering at?"

Colin, one of the circulating ball attendees, stopped in front of Ian and stared.

"I wasn't glowering," he said reflexively.

"I beg to differ. You've quite frightened all the young ladies standing across from you."

Ian blinked. There *were* young ladies standing across from him. And each of them had wide eyes and pale faces. Well, then.

"Ah. I think I need to visit the loo," he said bluntly to Colin, who made a sympathetic face as Ian stalked off down the hallway, toward where he'd interrupted Sergeant Sutton in the act of trying to persuade Tansy of their spiritual accord. Not toward the loo, just away.

And then someone stepped out in front of him.

He froze.

A beautiful brunette with a decidedly pouting lower lip. Alarmingly, it took him a moment before he recognized her.

He'd nearly forgotten about her altogether.

And there really was no reason to avoid her now.

"My apologies, Lady Carstairs, for not writing to you earlier. I've been unavoidably detained by business both in Sussex and London. But I am so pleased to find you here."

"I shall endeavor to forgive you. Some things are enhanced by anticipation."

Anticipation.

She *would* have to say anticipation.

It was as though someone had thrust an arrow into his gut.

He froze for a moment.

"Is something amiss, Captain Eversea?" Her hand went up to touch his arm.

"No. Not at all." He managed a smile. He stared down at her hand resting on his arm, and he was tempted to flick it away. It was a lovely hand, elegant, well-tended. It looked wrong there, somehow, like a spider. "Why don't you tell me where your rooms are."

"The second floor. The third from the stairway."

They heard footsteps then, clicking down the hallway.

A woman's footsteps.

Lady Carstairs ducked away. "Until then," she murmured, and slipped with the skill of someone who was accustomed to slipping away, her fingers trailing his arm.

Ian turned abruptly, toward the sound of the footfall.

And went still.

Tansy stood there.

She'd been watching him.

Her face was white.

They simply stared at each other for some time. The pleasure in simply looking at each other, being in each other's presence, was barbed with unspoken things.

She had no right to that expression of betrayal.

And yet . . .

At last he spoke.

"And what can I do for you, Miss Danforth?" he said quietly. Curtly.

It felt strange. As though he were speaking his native language for the first time in a long time, after speaking another to everyone else.

For twelve days, four hours, thirty-two minutes, and forty-one seconds.

And it was a relief just to be near her. Suddenly, gravity seemed much less oppressive.

She didn't say anything for a time. She was apparently mustering nerve. How unlike her to need to muster nerve.

"Are you going to make love to her?"

He nearly swore. Damn her and her penchant for ambushing him with questions.

He'd do nearly anything to take that expression from her face, and yet . . . And yet he wanted to shout at her for being naive. Things were as they were.

"Are you going to marry a future duke?"

The voices of the partygoers echoed like the remnants of a dream. One of those voices was that of the future duke. The young man with the lofty fortune, the influence, the money, the title. A young man who had likely never cuckolded the Duke of Falconbridge.

"Probably," she echoed, her voice frayed. Ever so faintly anguished. Defensive.

And angry.

His head went back hard. Then came down in a nod.

And then he shrugged.

There they had it, after all.

More relatively absurd silence ensued.

And Lady Carstairs was waiting for him in her room, and in minutes, in all likelihood, she would be tapping a satin slipper in impatience. He imagined the lush white curves of her body beneath his practiced hands. He imagined the moans and sighs he knew how to elicit. He would wrap one of her thighs around his waist and take her swiftly against a wall or in a corner. That glorious pleasure and forgetting could be had in burying himself in her body. Temporary surcease.

Tansy didn't move, didn't speak.

He moved so abruptly, toward her, she flinched.

"What do you want from me, Tansy?" His voice was low, furious, urgent.

She clasped her hands in front of her. He looked down at the little white knot of her fists and up at her white face. Two hectic spots of color appeared high in her cheeks.

He wanted to touch her to soothe that color away.

He didn't dare.

He waited.

And waited.

And when her voice came, it was whisper thin.

"I don't want you to make love to her."

He sucked in a sharp breath. He took the words like an arrow. The sort that murders.

And the sort that Cupid shoots into its victims.

There were so many things he could say. He could point out hypocrisy and futility and fairness and rightness. He could point out, yet again, that while she was wise in some ways, she was naive in the ways of the world and that men had needs and all that nonsense, and she had no right, no right, to stand there with that look on her face. That everything said about him was true, and she knew it. He could say that she had driven him to it. She had no right.

Too bad for you, Tansy.

It was the most merciful thing to say. It would allow her to go her way and him to go his, which was as it should be. Allow her to loathe him a little, and then a little more, and then finally forget.

It was what he meant to say, anyhow.

"Then I won't."

Is what he said instead. Very gently.

It was tantamount to a confession.

He didn't know who he was anymore.

All he knew is, he wanted her to have whatever she wanted. No matter what it was. No matter what the cost.

And having just sealed his fate, he spun on his heels and left her just as her lovely face suffused with a nearly celestial light, because he didn't think he could bear to look at that, either.

DURING A LULL between dances Stanhope sidled up to him, his handsome young face open and shining. He had a petulant chin, Ian decided, with a surly lack of charity. There was just something about it, the way it sat there, unblemished and square, that bothered him immensely.

"I just wanted to thank you, Eversea, for your letter informing me about Miss Danforth."

"No need," Ian said curtly.

"Oh, please don't deny me the pleasure of my gratitude," he said quite grandly, looking pleased with the choice of phrase.

"You're going to be a duke. Far be it for me to deny you a thing."

Stanhope looked momentarily a little uncertain at this, and then he nodded, missing irony completely. Then again, irony is a defense for those who are at least occasionally disappointed, Ian thought, and surely the young lord hadn't yet experienced anything of the sort.

"I do think my courtship of Miss Danforth has gone well. Very well, indeed."

"Has it?" Ian grit his teeth.

"It was easy, old man. Really, there was nothing to it." He snapped his fingers. "A few bouquets, a few compliments about her eyes and the like, a few rides in the old high flyer, and she's mine! She's a simple thing, really."

"That easy, was it?"

"Certainly. She's young yet, and so her personality is still forming. Though she's cheerful and agreeable. I suspect she can be molded."

"Ah. So she's that malleable, is she?" He wasn't aware, but his volume was increasing exponentially with each sentence he uttered. No mean feat when speaking from between clenched teeth.

"Oh, of a certainty, sir," Stanhope said gravely, on a confiding air. "Oh, she isn't perfect. She's a bit vain and frivolous. A bit vapid, I think, and a bit shallow. But that's due to youth. A few babies will change all of that. And Lord, but she *looks* perfect."

Ian spent a moment in blank, furious speechlessness.

"Vain? Frivolous? Vapid? Shallow?" Ian hissed the words as if they were darts he were hurling into a board. Stanhope blinked at each one. "Have you . . . seen a mirror lately, Stanhope?"

"Ha ha!" Stanhope laughed. He did laugh an inordinate amount. "Oh, ha ha, Eversea! Witty. But she is beautiful," he pointed out. "She'll be a *marvelous* ride, and my heirs will be incredible looking, don't you think?"

"Did you just call Miss Danforth . . . a marvelous ride?"

"Yes."

"A . . . marvelous . . . ride," Ian repeated slowly, flatly. As if learning new vocabulary.

A red haze was moving over his eyes.

"Yes?" Stanhope was a little confused now.

"And you think she's vapid, shallow, and frivolous. *She* is." He said this as if he were trying to record the duke's words for posterity. As if he wanted to get them precisely right.

"Well, yes," Stanhope hastened to reassure him. "But then most women are. The dears. What would we do without them, right, Eversea?" He gazed out over the ballroom at all the other women he might have had so easily, given his title. "And I know you *never* do without them."

Ian stared at him the way he would stare at a cobra he intended to shoot to smithereens.

For a good long time.

Without blinking.

Stanhope looked at him, began to turn back toward the ballroom, and then recoiled when he really got a look at Ian's expression.

"You're worrying me a bit, Eversea. You haven't blinked. You're a bit young yet for apoplexy, aren't you?"

"You *should* be worried, Stanhope," Ian said pleasantly.

Stanhope looked down and noticed that Ian's hands were clenched into knots. The better to launch into the jaws of young lords.

"Did you think . . . Oh, I meant no insult. She's a grand girl. Splendid. I was certain I made that clear." He gave a short nod. He seemed to think this took care of it.

"That's all you can say? She's a *grand* girl?"

And now Ian was shouting.

And conversations in the periphery ceased as people craned to hear.

Stanhope was now clearly baffled, and his feet shifted uneasily. "What higher compliment can I pay? What else is there, really?"

"What else is there? WHAT ELSE IS THERE?" And suddenly he was breathless and hoarse. "She . . . apologizes to flowers. She talks to the stars. She rolls a perfect cigarette. She *thinks* about the servants. She smells like a bloody meadow. She shoots like a rifleman. She rides like a centaur. Just being able to make her laugh is like . . . winning a *thousand* Sussex marksmanship cups. *Better* than that, you pompous, *whinnying*, RIDICULOUS *ARSE*."

He was distantly aware that it sounded almost as though he was speaking in tongues, in a series of non sequiturs. That he was gesticulating incredulously and possibly somewhat threateningly. That Stanhope was staring wide-eyed at him, and that the brightening he detected in the room around him might just be the whites of dozens of eyes as they widened, too.

He didn't care. They were visions of her, memories, all queued up at the exit of his mind, every last one of them significant, like linked dreams, and he couldn't stop them. And yet none of them were adequate. None of them added up to the girl.

Stanhope took another step back.

"Er . . . the whites of your eyes are showing, Eversea . . ."

"She has a wit that can cut right through a man. She's . . . oh, God, she's gentle. She's more forgiving than she ought to be and kinder and braver and wiser and more loyal than you'll ever be, you worthless, mewling, OVERBRED, *FATUOUS* . . ."

He trailed off when he realized that he had quite an audience.

All silent.

All utterly rapt.

"Eversea," someone muttered in resignation.

"What a pity the syphilis has gone to his brain," someone whispered. "That must be it."

"I haven't lost my mind!" He said this a little too loudly. And then added, "And I don't have syphilis!"

He *had* lost his mind.

And to the end of his days he would regret shouting "I don't have syphilis!" in a crowded ballroom.

His brothers would never, ever let him forget it.

The silence that followed was laden with doom.

Young Stanhope stepped toward him and said quietly, "I say, Captain Eversea, perhaps you ought to retire for the evening? I'll overlook the insult if you apologize. She's enough to addle any man's brains. Just look at her in that dress. Like an angel, she is."

Ian almost sighed.

How very pleasant it would be to shoot this man, he thought idly. How easy it would be to say, "Name your seconds." He *would* kill him. There was no question about it. But Stanhope's only fault was that he'd never *needed* to develop character, and likely never would. Stanhope was the most important thing in Stanhope's world, and that was the lens through which he saw everything and everyone.

And yet Stanhope had enough breeding to forgive him, and this was nearly intolerable.

Ian looked across the crowd and his eyes met Tansy's wide blue-gray ones. And immediately he felt her everywhere in him.

The expression in them nearly buckled his knees.

And yet . . . if he did kill the young heir, he would destroy her reputation and future, not to mention his own.

He sought out other pairs of eyes. Genevieve was staring at him with two hot spots of disbelief high on her cheekbones.

She shook her head just a little, to and fro.

Falconbridge was watching him, too.

Ian met his eyes evenly. He'd thought to read murder there.

But he saw nothing of the sort. He in fact couldn't read the duke at all.

For a moment he held that fixed gaze. Unapologetically. Defiantly.

And suddenly he knew what he had to do.

It was as clear, almost painfully clear, as if a blind had been yanked up in his bedroom on the morning of the worst hangover of his life.

But then it was exhilarating. And so very, very simple.

But first things first.

"I apologize, Stanhope."

He turned on his heel and walked out of the ballroom, and that was a sound he would never forget, either: his boot heels echoing on the wooden floor as everyone watched him walk away.

"MADNESS. THAT'S ALL it was. You know how old soldiers can be. And you can inspire anyone to madness. You're very lovely, my dear."

He'd taken to calling her "my" this and "my" that, and every time he did, Tansy wanted to swat him, which surely wasn't the way she should feel about someone who was allegedly about to propose to her.

"He's not old," she said sharply.

"Old*er*," Stanhope indulged placidly. Amused with her, apparently.

There was a certain peace in knowing she was about to be proposed to. It would mean that years of upheaval would end. Life would take on a certainty it had lacked for too long. She would acquire a husband who could be managed. She would obtain what remained of her parents' fortune. She would never want for anything. He hadn't yet tried to kiss her, but she knew, thanks to a waltz or two, that he smelled of starch and almost nothing else, and she suddenly had grave difficulty imagining him naked or breaking wind or roaring in the morning.

Or kissing her.

Or making love to her.

The night had continued after Ian's outburst, and the dammed conversation had flowed again to fill in the brief shocked silence, and then everyone had drunk and danced enough to mostly forget about it.

Ian, she was certain, had left the ball entirely. She knew he wasn't in the ballroom as surely as she was certain she would know if the sun suddenly disappeared from the sky.

She'd stayed. For a short time.

She was certain she'd held conversations and danced dances and fielded and issued compliments, but she couldn't remember any of them when she returned to her chambers. She'd begged a headache, and allowed Stanhope to believe it was nerves.

And Stanhope had parted from her, telling

her he'd arranged to call upon the duke at eight o'clock the following morning.

When she was in her room again, she leaned her cheek against the wall as if she could hear Ian's heartbeat right through it.

He was leaving tomorrow. Or so she'd heard.

She finally made herself undress and crawl into bed, but she didn't sleep at all.

Finally, when it was just past dawn, she tipped herself out of bed and followed the little road of light to the window.

But he wasn't outside on his balcony.

And so she sat down and took out her list of requirements one final time.

She emphatically crossed out *of fine moral character* and carefully—and very painstakingly in even, small letters, smaller now, because she was running out of room—wrote something else there instead.

She blew on it impatiently, waiting for the ink to dry.

Then a tear plopped on it, and she was forced to carefully blot it, and wait even longer, which was maddening.

And then with a sort of blind purpose she snatched it up and carried it down the hall to the office where the Duke of Falconbridge liked to conduct business.

She gave a sharp rap on the duke's door. Sharper than she'd intended.

"You may enter," he called. Very alert for that hour of the morning.

He looked up and began to rise.

"Titania." He sounded surprised.

She curtsied, but otherwise wasted no time on the niceties.

"This is my revised list, Your Grace. I wanted you to have it."

He reached out and gingerly took it. She supposed it was starting to look a little disreputable.

"From the looks of things, it's grown quite a bit."

"As have I."

She had the satisfaction of seeing the duke blink.

She whirled and left without being dismissed.

Falconbridge's eyes fell to the item that was clearly the newest.

Defends me in a crowded ballroom at the risk of his own dignity, because he knows me and loves me better than anyone ever has and ever will, even if he can't say it.

Yet.

Chapter 26

By eight o'clock in the morning, Ian had already been awake for four hours, accomplishing something that would surprise a good many people.

He immediately took himself up to the room Falconbridge had been using as an office during his stay.

The duke's door remained shut. The clock had yet to strike eight.

"What ho, Stanhope."

For there Stanhope already sat, just as a footman had told Ian, jouncing one leg nervously.

When he saw Ian he shot to his feet and then staggered backward a few steps.

"Eversea."

He looked nervous. As well he might. For numerous reasons.

Ian, however, was all soothing contrition.

"I'm sorry again about last night, old man. I drank a bit too much, and you know how it is when you've worked a bit too hard . . ."

He was utterly certain Stanhope hadn't worked a day in his life.

"Certainly, certainly."

"Nervous?" Ian smiled enigmatically.

"Well, of course. Ha. I'm about to ask for Miss Danforth's hand in marriage." He *was* decidedly green about the mouth.

Ian whistled, long and low. "Marriage is forever."

Forever. A portentous word, forever.

"Ah, yes. I know. Long time, forever."

"It is, indeed. It is, indeed. Listen, old man, I was sent to tell you that the duke isn't actually in—he's waiting for you instead at the vicarage. He's there on a bit of parish business and the notion took him—he'd like you to meet him there."

"The vicarage?" Stanhope was confused. "The Pennyroyal Green vicarage? I was certain he would have liked to speak to me here. We made an appointment last night, you see, and when the footman admitted me I was directed to wait right here."

"Ah. I think it was an impulsive decision on Falconbridge's part, and perhaps word hasn't yet reached all the servants," Ian improvised smoothly. "I think he thought the vicarage would more accurately reflect the gravity of the event. Confer a little more of the sacred upon it."

"Ah. Certainly, certainly. I can see that, I suppose. Very well, then. Thank you for conveying the message, Eversea. No hard feelings about the night before?"

"None at *all*." Ian smiled.

Stanhope glanced at the door of the office uncertainly.

He glanced toward the stairwell.

"You'd best hurry. He dislikes tardiness. Considers it a character flaw."

"Thankfully I have my new high flyer."

"*Thank*fully." Ian sounded relieved.

"Good day, Eversea, and thank you."

He turned and hurried past him, jamming his hat down on his head.

"Thank *you*, Stanhope."

And Ian settled into the chair to wait, and put his hand over the pistol in his pocket.

THE DUKE'S MOOD was edging toward foul, because he'd just opened a message this morning from the solicitor responsible for Lilymont's sale. It had been sold just that morning.

Bloody hell. He knew Genevieve would withstand the disappointment, but there was nothing he loathed more than disappointing her.

Deciding Stanhope had in all likelihood marinated in his own nerves long enough, and that he could probably expend a little of his mood upon the boy, the duke called him in.

"Enter, please," he said irritably.

A clean-shaven, crisply dressed, white-faced, granite-jawed Ian Eversea slowly walked in, clutching his hat in one hand.

And a pistol in the other.

Ian strolled deliberately over to the desk and lay the pistol on it.

"I'd like you to be able to make an informed decision, Falconbridge," he said, "after you hear what I have to say. We will settle everything between us here and now. And then if you wish to shoot me, I'd like you to have that option."

The duke stared at him. Ian had the satisfaction of knowing he'd at least nonplussed the man a little.

Something darkly amused twitched across the duke's face. Then he gave a subtle nod. "Very well. What can I do for you, Eversea?"

The tone wasn't . . . warm. To say the least.

"I'm here to speak to you about Miss Danforth."

There was a silence.

Ian fancied it was the sort of silence once experienced before the guillotine dropped.

"What about Miss Danforth?" His tone was deceptively casual. But the vowels were elongated. Nearly drawled. It was the duke's way of warning him. His eyes flicked over to the pistol.

"I would die for her," Ian said simply.

Drama was as good a place to begin as any.

The duke blinked.

Ian didn't wait for the duke to speak. "But it will never come to that, because I, more than anyone, am uniquely qualified to keep her safe all of her born days. Because I love her. And I know her. I know her heart. No one will ever love her better. I will endeavor to deserve her every day of my life."

The duke's fingers took up an idle, slow drumming on the edge of his desk.

He said nothing. He hadn't yet blinked.

"I know you've cause to despise me, Falconbridge. I know you've cause to doubt my honor. To apologize for my past offenses against you only now would seem self-serving. But I *am* sorry. I was driven then by motivations I can scarcely explain to myself, let alone you. But one reckless night should not define a man for a lifetime. If you can look me in the eye and tell me your soul is stainless, I'll leave now. And if you can look me in the eye and tell me that you don't think I deserve happiness, I'll leave now. And if you truly believe I cannot make Tansy happy, I will leave now. I don't know if she loves me. But I love her. And I would die for her."

The duke listened to this with no apparent change in expression. The silence was a palpable thing. Brittle as glass.

"I thought you were leaving, Eversea." He sounded pensive. "A trip around the world."

"*She* is the world. She is *my* world."

Something glimmered in the duke's eyes.

"And what about your savings?"

"I think you may have already guessed what I've done with them."

Falconbridge gave a short laugh. Surprised and seemingly perversely impressed.

"Very well. What do you want from me now?" The duke's voice was a little abstracted. He sounded, in truth, fascinated.

"I've come to ask you for the honor of Titania's hand in marriage."

There ensued a silence so long and painful it was as though time itself had been stretched on the rack. Ian worried for a moment that he'd given the duke apoplexy, and would now have his death on his conscience, to boot.

And then the duke stood up slowly.

Ian didn't budge.

He moved deliberately around the desk. Not quite in a stalking fashion. More of a careful one. As if giving himself time to change his mind about what he was about to do.

Ian consoled himself that the man hadn't snatched up the pistol.

He stood directly in front of Ian, eye-to-eye.

Ian stood his ground. He didn't like knowing that he could count his brother-in-law's eyelashes if he so choose, but he didn't blink.

Which is why it took him a moment to realize the duke was holding something in his hand.

The last time the duke had slinked toward him like that he'd been holding a pistol.

This time he was holding what appeared to be a sheet of foolscap.

"Titania delivered this to me this morning. It's a list she made of requirements for a husband. She thought it might be . . . helpful . . . to me."

He handed the sheet to Ian. Urged him to take it with the launch of one eyebrow.

Ian eyed him skeptically.

He took it between his fingers.

The duke gave an impatient jerk of his chin, urging him to read.

So Ian bent his head over it.

His heart lurched when he saw that her fingerprints darkened the edges. And that it was stained faintly by what he suspected were tears. Despite this, he could read it well enough.

And by the time he'd read all the way to the bottom, the foolscap was rattling.

Ian's hands were trembling.

He took a long, slow breath and looked up at the duke. "I think it's fair to say she loves you, Eversea." Falconbridge sounded ever-so-slightly resigned. But surprisingly, his voice was gentle.

Even amused.

Ian found he could barely breathe.

"And our accounts?" he managed finally.

A hesitation. "Are even."

Ian gave a short nod.

"Very well. My life is in your hands again, Falconbridge. What will you do with it this time?"

"TANSY, WHY DON'T we go for a drive?"

Tansy jumped. She'd managed to dress herself, and had taken a single cup of tea in her room, and picked the scone Mrs. deWitt had sent up into powdery smithereens. It now lay untouched on a plate. And she had stayed put, jumpy as a prisoner about to be led to execution, which was hardly the way she ought greet the day she might very well become engaged.

"But . . ." Suddenly, she didn't have an excuse.

And going out seemed better than staying in. And movement better than not moving.

Movement. Ian was likely on his way to London, anyway. He could even now be standing on the deck of the ship.

Genevieve looped her arm through Tansy's and tugged. "Come. It's an *excellent* day for a drive. Some might even say a transformative day for a drive."

SHE STARED LISTLESSLY out the window as Penny-royal Green scenery unfurled.

Genevieve pointed out landmarks.

"Look, there are the two oak trees entwined in the town square! There's a legend about them, you know."

Tansy didn't care.

"Doesn't the vicarage look lovely with all the new repairs? And look, there's Miss Marietta Endicott's academy. They've added a wing since you were a little girl. Do you remember it?"

She shook her head noncommittally. She remembered it. Vaguely. She just didn't want to *discuss* it.

"Now we're passing the O'Flahertys' home. It certainly has improved over the past year or so. They've a new roof and paddock fence."

Who were the O'Flahertys'? Why should she care about their paddock fence?

She began to wonder where on earth they were going. It had begun to feel less like an idle drive meant to distract her and more like a means to a destination.

But then Tansy straightened as the scenery began to look a trifle more familiar. Just something about the jut of the rocks to the left . . . the slight rise and curve in the road . . .

A peculiar tingle started along the backs of her arms.

"Where are we going, Gen—"

When the house came into view, she gasped.

"And look. Here we are at Lilymont," Genevieve said quite unnecessarily. "It occurred to me that you hadn't seen it since you were a girl."

"No," Tansy managed.

She was helped down from the carriage by a footman and began drifting toward the house, reflexively. It looked the same, if a bit in need of paint and a bit of weed-tugging. The mellow stone walls still glowed amber in low sunlight. The windows all glinted at her, like smiling eyes. She could almost imagine her five-year-old self and her brother gazing down from one of them.

Genevieve remained next to the carriage.

"And look," she said, "the garden gate is open." She pointed at it.

Tansy turned. The wooden gate was ever-so-slightly ajar. As if it had been anticipating her arrival.

"Do you mind?" Tansy turned to Genevieve eagerly. "May we?"

"Yes! Let's do have a— Oh, drat! I've just

dropped my glove in the carriage . . . you go on ahead, Tansy, I'll be right on your heels. I know you're eager to see it."

Tansy gave the little gate a push to open it wider, and stood motionless at the entrance.

Her childhood came back at her in a rush that gave her vertigo. Everything had gotten larger and woollier, but the path was still there, obscured as it was by tufts of grass, and all the beloved trees, and the ivy still spilled over the walls, and there was a man standing in the garden.

There was a *man* standing in the garden!

"Ian."

Her hand flew to her heart. It was more a gasp than a word. It had leaped into her throat so swiftly she thought it would choke her.

He didn't say anything for a good long time. They stared at each other like witless people who had never before encountered another human.

"Am I dreaming?" she said finally, softly.

"No."

She jumped and swiveled around at the sound of the carriage pulling away at a swift clip. She took a step toward the gate, and froze.

And turned around again.

Her heart began to hammer.

"Please don't leave without hearing me out, Tansy."

"Well, I can't leave," she pointed out, practically. "I do believe I've been abandoned here."

He began to smile.

She turned away from it, because his smile was almost too beautiful to bear.

And restlessly she began to move.

She could scarcely hear her own footfall, or the birdsong, as she wandered wonderingly into the garden over the woolly overgrown ground. She touched a flower. And another. She stretched out an arm and lovingly drew her fingers along the warm stone of the garden wall. She set one foot in front of another along the path. And yet she couldn't look at him. She didn't dare look at him. Not yet.

What if it *was* a dream? Tears began to prick at the corners of her eyes. To have everything she wanted, and only to wake up, would be cruel.

But she was no coward, and so she stopped and turned.

The expression on Ian's face turned her knees to water.

"Why are we here, Ian? Shouldn't you be preparing to board a ship?"

His voice was gentle. "First, I want you to know that Lilymont is yours. It belongs only to you. If you want it. No matter what you decide your future will be."

Her heart stopped.

"You bought this house . . . for *me*?"

"I bought the house for *us*, but if there is no us, it belongs only to you."

She stared. "I don't under—"

"I love you." He sounded almost impatient.

He delivered the words like a musket shot.

Time seemed to stop. The birds ceased singing. The words echoed in the quiet garden.

Magic words, those words: she felt them everywhere in her body, slowly, like tiny candles lit one by one in every one of her cells. And then suddenly she couldn't feel her limbs, or the ground, and she would not have been surprised to look down and see a cloud beneath her slippers.

"What did you say?" she whispered.

Only because she wanted to hear him say it again.

"I love you. I love you. So much it amazes me I've managed to live this long without you. I used to think that in order to find peace, I needed to keep moving, to keep searching, until I'd exhausted every corner of the world. But . . . Tansy . . . *you* are the world to me. *You* are my home, and, quite ironically, my peace, though I haven't truly known a moment's peace since I've met you. Which I quite like. And if you would do me the honor of being my wife, I will always love you better than *anyone* in the world, until our children come, and then I will love all of you more than life. I will devote the rest of my days to doing my best to making you happy. You must marry me, unless, of course, you'd like to see me perish. Will you?"

She couldn't yet speak. She was memorizing his beautiful face, and the way the light and shadows were just so, so she could savor the memory the rest of her days.

"That was quite a pretty speech, Ian," she said finally.

"Thank you."

He looked quite apprehensive now.

"Much more coherent than the one you gave at the ball."

"Thank you," he said again, sounding clipped and tense.

Ah, but she shouldn't tease him.

"What if I said I didn't love you?"

"I would say you were lying," he said, and produced her list with a flourish. He dangled it in front of her.

She stared at it openmouthed.

And now she was blushing.

"Falconbridge gave it to me. I have his blessing. So you might as well say it, Tansy."

She inhaled deeply, reached out and took his hand.

His was shaking a little, but then, so was hers.

Now that he had her hand, he pulled her abruptly close. Up against the sheltering warmth of his body. Wrapped his arms around her. Slid his hands down over her back, as if to claim her, as if to prove that she was real and she was his.

"Say it," he whispered.

"I love you," she whispered. "I will be honored to be your wife. And I think the only way my name will ever make sense is if the name Eversea follows it."

He kissed her to seal that promise. It was gentle, that kiss, and slow, and deep, and it bound the two of them, soul to soul.

When he lifted his mouth and rested his forehead against hers, she whispered, "I think I saw stars."

"Of course you did. And I will make sure you do. Every. Time."

IAN OBTAINED A special license so they could be married in spring in a modest clearing in the forest that had nothing much to recommend it apart from the profusion of brilliant wildflowers, all of them American expatriates. He had referred to the book in the library and planted even more of them than she had, as a surprise for Tansy.

And all those American flowers made her feel as though her parents and brother were there with her.

A crowd of townspeople gathered to witness the marriage, as did innumerable Everseas, including Sylvaines who rode into Pennyroyal Green for the occasion, and the servants. Reverend Adam Sylvaine conducted the service, and even he couldn't get through it without pausing to clear his throat suspiciously.

Everyone wept, for different reasons. Really, said the magnanimous, it was very big of Ian Eversea to take Miss Danforth out of circulation, as she'd caused a temporary insanity.

And every man who acted like a fool was forgiven, since Ian Eversea had clearly acted like the biggest fool of all, and in doing so had won the equivalent of—as he legendarily said—a thousand Sussex marksmanship cups.

"BEAUTIFUL SCENERY, DON'T you think? Such astonishingly colorful flowers. Such a lovely day for a wedding. So warm and bright and clear. Didn't she look beautiful? I never thought I'd see the day when Ian would agree to be legshackled. He even took the promotion for the East India Company, so he'll be in London part of the time. But she certainly is lively. He's unlikely to be bored."

Olivia was nervous. She was prattling inanely, and she *never* prattled, let alone inanely. Landsdowne was so quiet, and it was a full sort of quiet, the quiet of the preoccupied. The quiet of preparation. He was either going to tell her that they were through, that it was no use. Or . . .

"By rights it ought to rain right—"

"Olivia."

She stopped. And took a deep breath.

"I know you don't love me," he said.

She nearly choked. Shocked. "I . . ."

He saved her. "But I think that one day you will. And until then, I would be content to devote my life to making you happy. For your happiness is mine."

"Oh . . ." And now her breath was lost completely.

He paused and turned.

"Olivia . . . my dear, beautiful, Olivia . . . would you do me the honor of becoming my wife?"

She stared at him as if she'd never seen him before. Her hands went up to her face.

And fell again.

It wasn't as though she hadn't known this might happen.

She looked up at Landsdowne.

He had become dear, or he had become familiar, and sometimes those two things were one and the same.

She told herself this.

She didn't know anymore.

She wondered if she ever *would* know.

It was only one word, she thought. A word upon which her entire future would turn. The word would decide whether or not she had a future. She need only open her mouth and say it.

It was simple as the flip of a coin. She told herself that.

Her heart pounded like a fist against a wall.

"Yes," she told him softly.

She laid the word down. It felt strangely weighted to her. Like a monument.

Or a tombstone.

He closed his eyes and mouthed, *Hallelujah*.

And he took a long, shaky breath. His face was brilliant with happiness.

And there was that at least: she had the power to make someone else supremely happy, and it was as close to happiness as she'd felt in a very long time.

And maybe one day she wouldn't be able to tell the difference.

"I should like to kiss you now," he said.

"I should like that, too."

She found that this was true.

He gathered her into his arms.

And in that moment she felt like a girl. It had been a long time, a very long time, since she'd been kissed. And if a tiny corner of her heart where she kept a memory in a dungeon howled betrayal, she ignored it. Lyon wasn't here, and Landsdowne was, and she was still young.

DROWSY, THOROUGHLY SPENT, happier than any two people on the planet had ever been since time began, or so Ian emphatically claimed, he and Tansy twined their limbs and rested after the fourth bout of married lovemaking in their new home.

"I wanted to give you something when we were alone, Tansy. Close your eyes and hold out your palm."

"Very funny, Ian. It's so large I'd have to hold out two palms to hold it."

He laughed. "Just do it, please."

She closed her eyes, and he trickled something that felt like a very fine chain into her hand.

"Open your eyes."

She gazed down into a fine little pool of gold. She used her little finger to scoop it up, and lifted. It was a necklace.

Dangling from it was a tiny gold star.

He was rewarded when her eyes began to shine with tears and then she laughed.

"A gift! Of all things, yet *another* gift from Ian Eversea."

"I've discovered I've developed a taste for giving them."

Wonderingly, she ran her thumb over the tiny, simple, exquisite little star. Not expensive. But perfect.

"It's etched!"

"Turn it over, Tansy, and read it."

She turned it over and read it aloud: *"Forever."*

"My favorite word!" she said delightedly.

"Mine, too. It's *our* word now."

At Avon Books, we know your passion for romance—once you finish one of our novels, you find yourself wanting more.

May we tempt you with . . .

- **Excerpts** from our upcoming releases.
- Entertaining **extras**, including authors' personal photo albums and book lists.
- Behind-the-scenes **scoop** on your favorite characters and series.
- **Sweepstakes** for the chance to win free books, romantic getaways, and other fun prizes.
- Writing **tips** from our authors and editors.
- **Blog** with our authors and find out why they love to write romance.
- **Exclusive content** that's not contained within the pages of our novels.

Join us at
www.avonbooks.com

An Imprint of HarperCollins*Publishers*
www.avonromance.com

Available wherever books are sold or please call 1-800-331-3761 to order.

FTH 1013

RAVISHING ROMANCE FROM
NEW YORK TIMES BESTSELLING AUTHOR
ELOISA JAMES

The Ugly Duchess
978-0-06-202173-1

Theodora Saxby is the last woman anyone expects the gorgeous James Ryburn to marry. But after a romantic proposal, even practical Theo finds herself convinced of her soon-to-be duke's passion . . . until she suspects that James desired not her heart, but her dowry.

As You Wish
978-0-06-227696-4

Includes *With This Kiss* and *Seduced by a Pirate*, two stunningly sensual stories in which gentlemen who rule the waves learn that true danger lies not on the high seas, but in the mistakes that can break a heart . . . and ruin a life forever.

Once Upon a Tower
978-0-06-222387-6

Gowan Stoughton, Duke of Kinross, is utterly bewitched by the emerald-eyed beauty, Lady Edith Gilchrist. But after Gowan's scandalous letter propels them to marriage, Edie realizes her husband needs a lesson and locks herself in a tower. Somehow Gowan must find a way to enter the tower and convince his new bride that she belongs in his arms.

Three Weeks With Lady X
978-0-06-222389-0

To marry a lady, the newly rich Thorn Dautry must acquire a gleaming, civilized façade. Lady Xenobia India vows to make Thorn marriageable in just three weeks. But neither Thorn nor India anticipate the forbidden passion that explodes between them.

Give in to your Impulses!

These unforgettable stories only take a second to buy and give you hours of reading pleasure!

Go to *www.AvonImpulse.com* and see what we have to offer.

Available wherever e-books are sold.

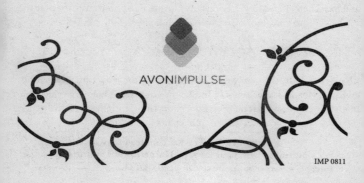

AVONIMPULSE

IMP 0811

Reaper was pushed back into the seat by the acceleration of the Checker. The engine roared out a solid wall of sound though the muffler cutouts. The speedometer climbed as Reaper hung onto the wheel. He no longer needed the handgun laying on the seat next to him. He was at the wheel of a huge projectile, a guided missile, one he was able to aim very precisely.

As the sound of the nitrous-boosted engine boomed out, Reaper watched as Arzee went onto the gravel shoulder and lost control of his car. As the distance between the two vehicles closed, he saw the Vette spin out and stop sideways across the road. Reaper could now see Arzee sitting at the wheel struggling to draw a weapon. That wasn't something Reaper was going to allow to happen.

Indecision was not something a SEAL could tolerate. Neither could he afford to be reckless. Reaper knew that Arzee was his best lead to finding his family. But if Arzee killed him, he couldn't do his family much good. He would just have to be very careful and precise.

Avon Books by
Dennis Chalker & Kevin Dockery

THE HOME TEAM: UNDECLARED WAR
ONE PERFECT OP
HELL WEEK

Avon Books by
Kevin Dockery

FREE FIRE ZONES
THE TEAMS
POINT MAN
SEALS IN ACTION

THE
HOME
TEAM

UNDECLARED
WAR

Command Master Chief
DENNIS CHALKER, USN (Ret.)
with KEVIN DOCKERY

AVON BOOKS
An Imprint of HarperCollinsPublishers

AVON BOOKS
An Imprint of HarperCollins*Publishers*
10 East 53rd Street
New York, New York 10022-5299

I dedicate this book to a legend in the Teams, Timmy "Ho Ho" Prusak. He has brought so much value, knowledge, and camaraderie to the Teams, especially to the men that worked under him. I know, because I was one. I also dedicate this to his lovely, supportive wife Ingra and the rest of his family. Some day we will meet again at the Pearly Gates. He will be waiting with a hot dog or two, a six-pack, and of course his small telephone pad. He is one of the best. To you, Ho Ho!!

THE HOME TEAM

UNDECLARED WAR

Chapter One

"It was a dark and stormy night; the rain fell in torrents—except at occasional intervals. . . ."

"Just what in the hell are you talking about?" Edward Ward said from his place in the driver's seat of the M998 series High Mobility Multipurpose Wheeled Vehicle (HMMWV), commonly called a Humvee. The heavy military vehicle was moving slowly through the rain, hardly an unexpected weather situation in northeast Bosnia-Herzegovina. The wide military vehicle bumped and jostled the passengers as it passed over a rough and rutted road that was little more than a cart path.

There were some better roads on the northeastern slopes of the Majevica mountain range, but these men were intentionally avoiding them. The vehicle rolled along quietly, hidden in the dark on a path few other people would choose to travel even in full daylight.

The passengers in the wide, boxy vehicle stood out as much as their ride did. The men had an unearthly, alien look about them as most of them wore AN/PVS-14 night-vision devices on their faces. The single large extended eye tube of the PVS-14, along with the frame that strapped to their faces, gave them a bulging cyclops look.

The only one inside the vehicle who was wearing a different style of night-vision device was Ed Ward, the driver. He had a set of AN/TVS-7 night-vision goggles on his face—the goggles giving him excellent depth perception. Ward had no trouble driving the Humvee in almost complete darkness, even with the vehicle's headlights turned off.

"Just thinking about the beginning of a book I heard about," Chief Ted "Grim" Reaper said from the front passenger seat. From the backseat of the vehicle, Titus "Bear" Parnell spoke up.

"You know, when I first got to Team Two, Mike Boynton was the master chief," Bear said. "He always said that back in Vietnam, rainy nights like this one were great to operate in."

"That's because no one in their right mind would be going out in this shit," Mike Martell, the fourth SEAL of the group, said from where he sat in the back, listening carefully to the radio over the headset he had clamped over his left ear.

"So, that must be why we're out here," Ward said.

"Ho, ho, ho," Bear chuckled. His teammates were used to the fact that the big SEAL actually laughed like Santa Claus. That laugh usually drew a second look from anyone else who happened to be around when his deep voice boomed out. One look at Bear would tell you where his nickname came from, and evaporate any thoughts of Saint Nick. None of the

SEALs were small, but Bear looked like a beer keg with legs and arms—thick, muscular legs and arms.

At his place in front, Chief Ted Reaper continued to look out of the window of the Humvee at the driving rain of Bosnia-Herzegovina in the early spring. The snows were gone, but that just made the poorly kept, muddy country roads a quagmire. He and his fellow SEALs made up the Navy contingent of their detachment from the Joint Special Strike Force (JSSF). They had been attached to the U.N.-mandated Stabilization Force, the SFOR, that was trying to maintain stability in the war-torn area of the Balkans. The JSSF was put in place to react quickly to any situation. They could rapidly evaluate a problem and either decide to deal with it themselves or call in a greater strength force from the SFOR assets scattered around the country.

The men of JSSF also conducted classic special operations missions: special reconnaissance operations to locate potential rogue groups or war criminals, direct actions in the form of strikes against designated sites or personnel, and civil affairs, where they tried to develop good relations among the civilian population of an area.

To secure maximum flexibility in conducting these operations, the Joint Special Strike Force had been put together from the Navy, Army, and Air Force special operations forces. The Air Force contingent of this JSSF detachment were two combat controllers, who were the best field air controllers in any of the services. The Army contingent of six Special Forces troopers made up the bulk of the JSSF detachment. In overall command were two professional Intelligence officers who had a great deal of experience running covert paramilitary operations for the CIA.

Chief Reaper was the senior noncommissioned officer (NCO) of the detachment, which didn't always sit well with the Army guys but didn't cause any real friction. The SEALs bumped heads and cracked jokes with the Army troopers on occasion, and both groups of men made fun of the Air Force contingent. The jokes came from years of traditional rivalry between the services.

Underlying the gags was an unspoken respect the men had for each other. The operators were all professional warriors and knew the skills and capabilities each man brought from his branch of the service. The only real unknown factor was their commanding officer.

There were two officers in the detachment, Lieutenant Mark Franklin, who was the executive officer and Captain Cary Paxtun the commanding officer. Both men had been in the Army Special Forces before changing their career paths and going into intelligence work. Franklin had remained in Army Intelligence while Paxtun had gone on to operate directly with the CIA.

Both men had spent years working in Afghanistan and other parts of the world, Paxtun as part of the paramilitary forces of the CIA and Franklin with the Army. Between them, they spoke seven languages including Arabic, Serbo-Croat, Pushtun, Afghan, Persian, and Russian. They had both come back to Special Operations because that was where the action was now, and Reaper was of the opinion they should have stayed where they were.

Neither man's skills were in question as far as Reaper was concerned, but their attitude very much was. In the SEAL chief's opinion, both of the officers had forgotten what it meant to work as part of a team, something that the SEALs take very seriously. Paxtun acted as if he just considered the men under his command to be tools for his own advancement. Franklin wasn't much better but at least tended to stay with the Army members of the unit and left the SEALs alone.

Besides directing the JSSF detachment, the two officers had been working hard at setting up an intelligence network among the many different groups in the area. They were often away from the headquarters the group had established in a house in the small town of Argulak. As far as Reaper was concerned, both officers could be out chasing goats in the mountains, that would be fine with him. All he wanted was for the officers to do their jobs and allow him the leeway he wanted to make sure his men were protected and that the mission was accomplished.

Neither Paxtun or Franklin told the men of the JSSF who they had talked to, what had been discussed, or even why they would be talking to a particular person in the first place. The specifics of who the agents were and how the intelligence was developed wasn't a question that Reaper or the rest of the men felt that they had to know. The information that the two men did learn, they held very close to their chests. That was something Reaper was concerned about. If there was information regarding a target, a location, or forces in an area that could affect his men or his mission, Reaper wanted to know about it.

Information—good, reliable intelligence on an

area or enemy—could be more important than ammunition on an op. Since he felt that his leaders couldn't be completely trusted to tell him everything they knew, Reaper fell back on an old SEAL tradition. As the Teams had done in Vietnam, Reaper and the SEALs developed their own intelligence sources among the locals.

The SEALs' mission that night was intended to help increase the good relations that had been developing with some of the displaced locals—at least that's what Lieutenant Franklin had said. When Yugoslavia had broken up years earlier a whole bunch of old tensions and hatreds, nursed for years among parts of the population, had lifted up like a bunch of serpents tasting the air.

Ethnic cleansing was a new term for an old idea, hate people for their religion/race/background/whatever. One of the missions of the JSSF was to prevent any further atrocities from being committed against anyone. Presently, they were helping a group of Muslim refugees who had moved into an abandoned village in a resettlement area at North Sapna.

The people had been badly mauled by the Serb forces over the last several years but were finally coming to trust the men of the SFOR, and especially the SEALs of the JSSF detachment, and listening to what they had to say. The lives of the Muslim refugees had been as hard as could be imagined. Almost no families were left intact by the ravages of ethnic cleansing. Few husbands were around, and the haunted eyes of many of the younger women answered questions that the SEALs never asked.

There was a meeting that night in the local village schoolhouse, the biggest building in the area that still had walls and a roof. That was where the remaining elders of the refugees would make their final decision about staying. Paxtun wanted the SEALs to be in attendance to observe the meeting and give a show of support.

"Things have been pretty calm among the Serbs for the last couple of months," Bear said from the back of the Humvee.

"Yeah," Reaper agreed, "but something is in the wind over this relocation of the Muslims. There haven't been any reports of recent Serb movement in the area, but some of the locals are nervous as hell. Can't blame them given the way they've all been treated in the past.

"Those fundamentalist Muslims who claim to be in from Pakistan have been preaching around, trying to stir things up. Personally, I think they all are ex-mujahideen fighters from Afghanistan, not just the few Paxtun says are part of the group. At any rate, none of the villagers want to have anything to do with them. They've all had enough war to last them the rest of their lives.

"But it's going to be a few years yet before there's any kind of really stable government over here. Even with the fighting having at least died down, things are more political than ever. Everybody wants to be in charge. And those Muslim fundamentalists are the worst of the bunch. They're offering protection to the villagers from the Serbs claiming we can't do our jobs. It looks like just another old-fashioned shakedown racket.

"The last thing we need around here is a Serb attack in a protected area. With all the different factions in the area, this whole region is like a pot just barely simmering. It could boil over at any time. We've worked too hard to take care of these people to let them down now. I want to keep a close eye on things."

"I still think Paxtun's going to be mightily pissed when he sees you took his Humvee," Bear said.

"Well," Reaper said, "his idea to conduct a lightly armed, low-provocation, high-presence recon is a bunch of crap. Just because things have been quiet does not mean they're going to stay that way, no matter how much we'd like them to. If anything happens, I want the firepower to say—go the fuck away—loud and clear."

The firepower Reaper was referring to was in the form of the Mark 19 40mm grenade launcher attached to a ring mount on the roof of the Humvee. The big weapon was the size of a box that would hold a large pair of cowboy boots. On the back of the this "box" were two vertical handles for aiming, and a piece of wrist-thick pipe sticking out of the front.

The barrel of the grenade launcher could spit out half-pound 40mm high-explosive grenades at a rate of around 350 a minute to a distance of over 2,000 meters. The Mark 19 was a formidable piece of hardware by anyone's measure.

"Paxtun wanted us to stick to the main roads," Ward said as he guided the heavy vehicle through another deep set of muddy ruts in the roads. "If he isn't pissed about our taking his vehicle, he will be if we bring it back with a busted axle."

"Then you just pay attention to your driving,"

Reaper said. "If we're going to do a recon, we'll stick to the same roads that any Serb forces would use. It's not like you guys don't know the rule. . . ."

"Never take the easy way in," Ward, Bear, and Martell said in rough unison.

"I don't think even the Serbs would try this goat path in the dark," Ward said. "There aren't even any goats on it. It is a hell of a lot shorter than that paved road around the mountain, though. We're going to get to the village a couple of hours earlier than planned by the looks of things."

"The goats heard Bear was in the area and made a run for it," Martell said from the back.

"Speaking of making some odd friends," Ward said, "Captain Paxtun has been pretty friendly with the Russians up in Uglyville. Maybe he knows nothing is going to happen."

"Or he knows something is coming down and just doesn't feel like telling us," Bear said.

"Belay that talk," Reaper growled, "Paxtun's our CO and knows our mission. He talks to a hell of a lot more people than the Russian SFOR contingent up in Ugljevik. I don't like those Afghan mujahideen he meets with, but he built a rapport with them while they were fighting the Russians in their own country. And they hate the Russians. If the Serbs were planning something in the Russian sector, we'd know."

"Oh, yeah, he's buddies with the mujahideen all right. He's about the only source of human intelligence we have on those people, it's not like Lieutenant Franklin knows a bunch of those mujahideen by their first names. But the only information we really have on Paxtun is based on rumor. And rumint has it that he became a hardcore Muslim himself in Afghanistan," Bear said. "He may have been hot shit against the Russians over there, but I still don't like him."

"Rumor intelligence is worth what you pay for it," Reaper said. "It's nothing more than military gossip. You don't have to like him. You only have to follow his orders. Basing your opinion on nothing better than rumint doesn't make you look any better. I don't care what he has to do, or did, as long as he can keep a lid on those Afghans."

"Besides," Martell said. "Isn't he from your home state, Bear? You guys should be asshole buddies by now."

"Shit," Bear said. "He's from Dearborn. That city has the largest Arab population outside of the Middle East. I didn't exactly spend a whole lot of my life there. You even told me that he made you itch, Reaper when . . ."

Bear stopped in midsentence as Reaper put up his left hand in a fist to signal that he had spotted something. No one spoke as each SEAL instantly snapped into sharp attention. The rain had stopped and the early evening air was clear. "I have lights moving to the east of the village," Reaper said.

Just past the crest of a rise, the Humvee eased quietly to a stop, facing partly downslope. All of the occupants of the vehicle could see the few moving lights to the east of the village a few hundred meters away.

The third-generation light-amplifying tubes of the night-vision devices the SEALs were wearing showed everything in shades of green. The lights

Reaper had seen were invisible to the naked eye, but were plain to see through the electronic tubes. The dimness of the lights suggested that they were probably screened in some way, like the red lens used on a military flashlight. That was not something a group of refugees would be using.

The outskirts of the small village weren't more than a few hundred meters away, starting at the foot of the hill the SEALs were stopped on. The schoolhouse was just a few meters farther on down the single village street. It was in the woods beyond the village, approaching the schoolhouse, that the scattered lights moved in closer.

The kerosene lamps lit in the schoolhouse gave a soft golden glow to the light pouring out the few windows of the building. That light was magnified to a brilliant level in the night-vision devices. The drawback the devices had was that they robbed the users of natural night vision when they were taken off. The very new AN/PVS-14 NVDs eliminated that problem by being a monocular design. Only a single tube was placed in front of one of the operator's eyes. The other eye just looked out into darkness. The effect was a little strange before you got used to it, but the extensive training the SEALs did to prepare for any of their missions made these men well practiced in using their equipment.

"Bear, with me," Reaper said, "Ward, get on the Mark 19, Martell, contact Paxtun and give him a sitrep."

Not another word was spoken, it didn't have to be. Mike Martell turned to his radio to send the situation report that the unit was investigating a possible contact. Ed Ward secured the Humvee and reached up to unlock the hatch cover above and between the two front seats.

As Ward was opening the half-moon-shaped hatch cover, Reaper and Bear pulled up the black balaclava hoods they had been wearing around their necks. Their faces and heads were now completely covered except for their eyes and the gleaming monocle of the AN/PVS-14s. Without a further word, the two SEALs opened their doors quietly and slipped into the moonless night.

The hillside was wet and slick, but the two SEALs moved smoothly and quietly over the rocks and mud. Behind them, Ward stood up in the weapon platform mount on top of the Humvee. There, he pulled the cover off the Mark 19 40mm grenade launcher and removed the travel retaining pin to release the mount.

The sixty-two-pound box of ammunition on the feed bracket of the weapon only held a single forty-eight-round belt of grenades. Even a big SEAL would be hard put to quickly manhandle a fresh box of ammunition that size into reload position. An accurate gunner wouldn't waste ammunition—and Ward was a very accurate gunner. With two careful and quiet pulls on the charger handle, Ward prepared the big weapon to fire in support of his Teammates out in the darkness.

Moving carefully from cover to cover, neither SEAL had a need to speak as they approached the village. Constant training had almost removed the need for words between them. The two men had worked together so long that each knew what the other would do in any situation. They were a shooter pair, and they had done this kind of target approach a hundred times in all kinds of terrain. Holding their M4 carbines out at the ready, the SEALs stealthily moved and froze in concealment to assess the situation.

———

As they came closer to the village, the two SEALs could make out more and more detail through their night-vision devices. The village was made up of a number of cottagelike homes of white walls and tile roofs, the same as could be seen in thousands of European countrysides. The houses faced a central street, which the SEALs' Humvee would have reached if it had continued on its way. At the far end of the village was the larger schoolhouse. The rubble of a small mosque was near the school, the house of worship having been destroyed by the Serbs and not yet rebuilt.

Beyond the school were open fields interspersed with woods, and it was in those woods that the SEALs had seen the moving lights. But it was more than just their eyes that gave the two SEALs information about their surroundings.

The rain had stopped, but the night was still wet. The musty, earthy smell of the rain covered a lot of the night's odors, but Reaper could still pick up the sharp tang of wood smoke from some of the village's chimneys. And there was the slightly sweetish stink of the decomposing grass and leaves that had been uncovered by the spring thaw. The bite of the still-cold night air dulled some of the SEALs' sense of smell, but they could still notice odors well enough to file away the information.

The one smell that was not consciously noticed by each SEAL, but would have been of immediate concern by its absence, was the smell of his partner. They knew each other's smell in the dark. They had worked and trained that intensely together.

Both SEALs had sharp hearing. The men heard the burring sound of the light wind as it pushed away the storm clouds. There was a slight rustle of cloth as each SEAL moved through the night, a slight rubbing of their Gore-Tex jackets or trousers against the hard nylon of their assault vests and body armor. In spite of this being planned as just an observation mission with no action expected, each of the SEALs was wearing a full loadout of weapons, equipment, and ammunition. The gear included an assault vest filled with ten loaded thirty-round magazines for their M4 carbines, a SIG P-226 pistol in a low-slung assault holster secured to the right thigh, three spare fifteen-round magazines to their pistols, and a knife. This was in addition to a first aid kit, signaling flare, Motorola MX-300R radio, throat mike and earpiece, and tactical Level IV B/C hard body armor that could stop a standard bullet from an AK-47 or M16.

In spite of all of their equipment, the most valuable thing the SEALs had with them was their training and experience. There was no noise from their gear. Each piece of equipment had been examined, taped, and padded as necessary until nothing made any unintentional noise. The rustle of their clothing was so faint it couldn't have been heard more than a few feet away. The loudest thing that the two SEALs could hear was their own breathing, but they knew that couldn't be heard by anyone else around them—if there was anyone there.

Both men quickly slipped past the schoolhouse and into the woods beyond. The question of who might be out there was partially answered by the sounds of metallic clicks and bangs as loose pieces of equipment and rifle slings tapped against each other in the darkness. There were probably armed men in the woods, not more than a few hundred meters away. Almost that same distance behind the SEALs were their Teammates at the Humvee.

Suddenly from the dark came a sound that confirmed the SEALs suspicions, the sharp metallic clack of an AK-47's safety being clicked into the firing position. A unique sound that was instantly recognizable to anyone who had heard it in serious circumstances. And both SEALs knew that the villagers were not armed.

Taking cover behind a tree, Chief Reaper partially covered his mouth with his hand. Keying the throat mike to his MX-300R radio, Reaper whispered, "Smokestack Four this is Smokestack One. Contact, I say again, contact. We have an unknown number of hostiles in the woods to the east of the schoolhouse."

The response from Martell back at the Humvee astonished both Reaper and Bear who heard the answer over his own radio.

"Smokestack One this is Smokestack Four, return to the ride. I repeat, return to the ride."

———

There was no question but that Reaper and Bear would get back to the Humvee as quickly as they could, while still maintaining a silent movement. They slipped through the woods and village area like two shadows. Martell wouldn't have called them back unless the need was serious. It was only a matter of minutes before the two SEALs were back inside the vehicle.

"What's the problem?" Reaper said not seeing anything out of the ordinary.

"Chief," Martell said, "it's Engine One. Captain Paxtun said we are to immediately cease operations and return to base."

"What?" questioned Reaper. "Get me Paxtun on the box right now."

As Martell started calling out on the radio, Bear just looked at his chief and shrugged his shoulders. As Reaper was going to say something, Martell reached forward and handled him the microphone from the radio and clicked on the speaker.

"Engine One, this is Smokestack One," Reaper said as he pressed in the bar at the side of the microphone.

"Smokestack One, this is Engine One," Reaper and the rest of the SEALs in the Humvee heard. "Have you started back to the train?"

"That's a negative, Engine One," Reaper said. "I don't think you understand the situation here. We have hostiles closing in on friendlies. I suggest a full tactical response."

"Negative on that request Smokestack One," the speaker replied. "I have put out a cease-action order on all operations in our area of responsibility effective 2000 hours today. You are to immediately proceed to the train. Restricted rules of engagement are in effect and you may not fire unless fired upon and in imminent danger."

"Sir," Chief Reaper said as he began to lose his temper. "We have friendlies in danger from a hostile group of eight to ten . . ."

"Stand down, Chief," came out of the speaker. "You have a direct order to return to base and cease all actions immediately. There are no hostile forces known to be in the area."

"Sir," Chief Reaper spoke angrily, "I'm looking at the hostiles! I wish to immediately refer this up the chain of command to headquarters in Tuzla on an Emergency Flash Priority."

"That is a negative, Reaper," Captain Paxtun's voice came over the speaker. Anger could now be heard in the officer's voice. He must have been shaking with anger as Paxtun had just committed a serious breach of communications protocol by using the chief's real name over the air. "There is an electrical storm over the Majevica mountain ridge that is breaking communications with higher command. You will immediately return to base or face charges under the . . ."

Martell, observing Chief Reaper's knuckles grow white as his hand clenched the microphone, suddenly reached over and twisted a dial on the faceplate of the radio, then he flipped a switch.

"Sorry, Chief," Martell said with a grin, "it must be all of that electrical interference. When those electrical storms hit the mountains, radio reception just goes to shit and . . ."

Gunfire suddenly erupted to the east of the

Humvee's position. Immediately Martell stopped talking and everyone looked toward the school-house. The sound of gunfire was slightly muffled, but there was no mistaking the deep stuttering boom of an AK-47 fired on full automatic. Between the shots could be heard the screams of the refugees. Whoever those troops were, they were attacking the schoolhouse and slaughtering the unarmed refugees inside.

"Bear, with me," Reaper said. "Martell, try to get command at Tuzla on the horn."

Before actions could be put to the chief's words, there was the sound of glass breaking in the distance and a wail cried out as a small body was thrown from the schoolhouse. The cry of the little boy was cut short as the child struck the stony ground near the schoolhouse.

The limp form of the child lay still. In the green glow of the night-vision devices, the pitiful body looked like little more than a discarded bundle of rags. Even at a distance, the child was so small he could not have been much older than Reaper's own six-year-old son back in the States.

A cold fury settled in on the occupants of the Humvee. Without a word being spoken, Reaper and Bear exited the vehicle and headed for the school-house in a low, crouching run. In spite of their haste, the two SEALs would alternately stop as one covered the other's advance. As the leading SEAL knelt in a crouch and covered with his weapon, the trailing SEAL would move forward and pass the other.

The practiced leapfrogging movement was quick and efficient—eating up the meters between the

Humvee and the far edge of the village where the schoolhouse was. The gunfire increased as the SEALs grew close, then suddenly tapered off. As they came close to the side of the schoolhouse, the SEALs passed the small, still form of the child who had been tossed out onto the rocks.

There was no time to feel anything for the child, or even to stop and see if he was still alive. There were others in immediate danger inside the schoolhouse—if it wasn't already too late to save them.

Reaper did not feel rage. Even the anger he felt against the astonishing orders of his commanding officer had melted away with the need for sudden, precise and controlled action. Only a cool head would prevail in such a situation, and Reaper could be as cool and hard as old bone if the situation warranted. It was one of the reasons he had long ago received the nickname "Grim" Reaper.

Other figures were slipping away into the woods as Reaper and Bear moved up to where they could see the door of the building. As a figure came out the door, Reaper could see that the man was wearing the same mottled, gray-and-brown camouflage uniform that so many of the mixed regular and irregular forces in the war-torn country used.

On the man's head was an odd thing, a flat round cloth hat with a rolled brim. It was a Pakol, the traditional Afghan hat. But it was the objects in the man's hands that seized Reaper's eye. In his right hand was an AK-47, held away to shield the man from the smoking-hot barrel. In his left hand was a child's rag doll. The man was laughing and saying something in what sounded like Arabic to Reaper. Coming out of the well-lit schoolhouse, the man probably never even saw Reaper standing nearby.

The gap-toothed smile on the raider's face was enough to heat the SEAL's cool resolve. And the weapon in his hand registered as a threat. Reaper didn't even consciously think of his action as the muzzle of his shouldered M4 carbine settled on the center of the man's chest. The short stutter of a three-round burst was quick justice for a single individual's action of ethnic cleansing.

Just to the right side of Reaper's field of vision, he saw the orange-white flower of an AK-47's muzzle blast bloom in the night. Before Reaper's mind could do more than register the light, there was a smashing pain against his chest. A thundering blow knocked the big SEAL down to the ground. Multicolored lights danced in front of Reaper's eyes as he tried to just draw in a breath. As he fell back, the rest of the rounds fired from the AK-47 passed over him.

His hands tingled oddly as Reaper pulled up his M4 and fired back. Or at least he tried to fire back. When he squeezed the trigger, the M4 refused to fire. Without conscious thought, Reaper let go of the M4, which dropped to his chest, and he reached for his SIG P-226. In a smooth movement, his right hand grasped the pistol, his thumb releasing the restraining strap of the holster as his fingers closed around the rough, checkered finish of the plastic grips.

As the bearded face of the man who shot him came up from the darkness, Reaper was already pulling his pistol up and thrusting it out. As he pulled the trigger and double-actioned the SIG, time

seemed to change in its natural flow. As if in slow
motion, Reaper could see his pistol come up even as
the hammer was going back for the shot. The
bearded man appeared to be moving very slowly as
he started to point his rifle. There wasn't much of a
question that there wouldn't be a second place fin-
isher in this race. The winner would be the only one
who lived.

Reaper noted the thick, bushy black beard of the
man who was trying to kill him. There were broad
black eyebrows above eyes that were widely open.
As the man opened his mouth, Reaper could see
teeth stained from years of neglect and tobacco use.
Then the face dissolved in a mask of red as Reaper
won the race and the SIG in his hand bucked and
roared.

With the immediate threat neutralized, the passage
of time went back to its normal rate of flow. There was
the sharp report of another M4 being fired as Bear took
down one of the other armed men who had come to
wreak havoc among the unarmed villagers. Then
Reaper heard the slow knocking, spaced-out, thunk . . .
thunk . . . thunk . . . of a Mark 19 being fired. It took a
moment for the fist-sized 40mm grenades to travel
from the muzzle of the weapon to the target. Just a second or two after the sound of firing rang out, the spaces
between the trees bloomed with the flowers of high-
explosive grenade detonations.

Back at the Humvee, Ward fired the Mark 19
grenade launcher in a long burst, tracking the
grenades so that they would explode in the woods
beyond where his Teammates were fighting. The
blasts would convince the raiders that rapidly going

someplace else would be a very good idea.

Thousands of ripping steel fragments from the exploding grenades slashed through the trees and brush of the woods. As the razor-sharp steel cleared the area, Reaper quickly picked himself up from the ground and shook off the effects of the blow to his chest. His M4 carbine, dangling across his chest on its sling, was not going to be of much help to him. Even without the night-vision device strapped to his head, Reaper would have seen the large dent and hole in the receiver where the weapon had stopped the first round from that AK-47.

"Well, fuck me," he said quietly to himself.

His SIG pistol had served him well enough and would have to continue to do so. As Bear ran up to his chief, neither SEAL could see any sign of more activity on the part of the raiders. Whoever they had been, they had cut and run, leaving their dead behind. They didn't have the stomach for a protracted fight when what they had thought would be a soft target had suddenly turned very hard.

The open door of the schoolhouse was behind the two SEALs. As Bear maintained watch, Reaper went up to the door and looked inside. Light was pouring out of the door, bathing the two SEALs in a golden glow, as fires started from the broken lamps in the building spread their flames.

Reaper pushed his AN/PVS-14 NVD up on his forehead. The light from the fire was more than enough for him to see the scattered bodies of nearly

twenty villagers—men, women, and children—
scattered around the room. The torn and limp bodies
told Reaper all that he needed to know. There would
be no refugees accepting the offer of a safe haven by
the SEALs, the JSSF, or anyone else.

Chapter Two

A subdued Humvee full of SEALs returned to the "train," the radio code name for their headquarters established in a house near the city of Rastosnica. The large house was isolated enough from other buildings for security's sake, and large enough to comfortably hold all of the JSSF detachment.

The unit's two officers, Captain Paxtun and Lieutenant Franklin, had their quarters on the upper floor of the house, but only Paxtun was waiting when Reaper returned with his men. Two of the unit's other Humvees were missing when the men pulled up to the house. Their vehicle was still parked where they had left it.

The results of the night's actions weighed heavily on the SEALs. They had gone out with the intention of simply supporting a "hearts and minds" campaign to help win over some of the locals who had suffered so much. A show of strength and solidarity to show the refugees that they were finally safe in an area they could call home.

The SEALs' mission had been a complete failure. It wasn't because of any lack of action on their part. But the people they had been trying to help were dead, and there wasn't anything that could be said to make that result easier to accept.

One of the things that had been bothering Reaper during the entire drive back to their headquarters was just who the hell the village attackers had been. The bodies that the SEALs had searched revealed very little—but what they did find looked important.

The Afghan Pakol hat the one raider had been wearing was odd, but the really significant find had been the pocket copy of the Koran that had been on the body, the small book neatly wrapped in waterproof cloth. There was no way that a Serb raider would have been carrying a copy of the Koran. A Serb might have considered the Muslim holy book to be a source of paper at most. He certainly wouldn't have been carrying it carefully wrapped and protected as its owner had been. No, the raiders had been Muslims—and they had killed their own people.

As the SEALs entered the house, Captain Paxtun was waiting in the front room. It was immediately obvious to Paxtun that his orders had not been obeyed—the tear in the front of Reaper's vest and the damage to the weapon hanging across his chest were plain to see. It wasn't the kind of thing that could happen to a man who was in a vehicle accident. Reaper had been in combat, against direct orders.

"Chief Reaper," Paxtun said, "are any of your men casualties?"

The tone in Paxtun's voice gave Reaper the impression the captain would have preferred that all of

the SEALs were casualties. There probably would
have been less paperwork for them than for the kind
of attack that he and his men had witnessed.

"No, sir," Reaper said. "My troops and I are fine.
I would like to dismiss them to stow their gear and
grab some chow."

"Fine, Chief," Paxtun said, "dismiss them. You
and I have to have some words about the incident
this evening."

"Yes, sir," Reaper said.

Turning to Bear, Reaper continued, "Clean yourselves and your gear, get something to eat and grab
some sack time."

"Chief . . ." Bear started to say.

"Belay that," Reaper said, "you have your instructions."

Reluctantly, the SEALs left the front room, leaving the two officers and their chief behind them.

"Where is Lieutenant Franklin and the rest of the
men?" Reaper asked.

"They're out on another scouting mission," Paxtun said. "I don't expect them back for some time."

"I hope their operation goes a lot better than ours
did," Reaper said.

"Chief," Captain Paxtun began, "there are cause-
and-effect situations here that you have no knowledge of. The political situation is at a critical stage
and we cannot afford another Serb incident making
the news for . . ."

"Serbs," Reaper exploded. The frustration and
shock he felt since almost being killed that evening
evaporated in a wave of anger and rage. "How the
hell can you jump to that conclusion? Those weren't

any Serbs who killed those people. Those raiders were Muslims themselves. No Serb would ever be caught with this in his pocket."

With that statement, Reaper threw the Koran that he had in his pocket down onto a chair next to where Paxtun was standing.

"And just where in the hell do you think a Serb would have gotten this?" Reaper said and he threw the Pakol hat into the captain's face.

Ducking to the side, Paxtun dodged the cloth hat and allowed it to fall to the floor behind him. The officer was almost shaking with rage at the SEAL chief standing in front of him.

"Chief," Paxtun snapped out. "You will get hold of yourself right now, soldier."

"Wrong, sir," Reaper growled, "I'm a sailor."

Being corrected by the SEAL chief enraged Paxtun even more. "You will stand at attention when addressing me . . . sailor," Paxtun snapped. "I don't care what service you're in, you can be brought up on charges of insubordination and assaulting an officer right now. This minor material you've brought in from somewhere could come from anywhere, and mean anything."

Taking a moment to get control of himself, Paxtun looked at the SEAL chief and the hat on the floor.

"Chief Reaper," Paxtun said in a much calmer voice, "there has been no Serb activity reported in this area for some time. It was just the villagers' bad luck that an incident took place while they were all in the same building. It's possible that the Serbs heard of the meeting and decided to stage a raid disguised as Muslims. Maybe we were simply due for some action breaking out in this area again. Any thought that there was a group of rogue Muslims attacking their own is just supposition on your part. The present political situation among the local Muslim groups is far too sensitive to allow such inflammatory suspicions to be voiced without solid proof."

Reaper just looked at Paxtun with astonishment. He was denying the evidence that was right there in the room. Just what in the hell was going on here? Reaper thought.

"Suspicions?" Reaper said. "Just what do you mean, suspicions? How the fuck can you deny what happened tonight? That wasn't a raid, it was a planned slaughter of those refugees and the villagers who were putting them up.

"Those raiders knew where everyone would be and surrounded most of the area. That wasn't a schoolhouse—it was a killing zone. If you hadn't called me back to the vehicle, my men and I might have been able to save a few of those poor people. As it is, they're dead and the bulk of the raiders got away. If we had taken the route you originally planned for my patrol, we wouldn't have gotten there until well after . . ."

Reaper paused at the realization that Paxtun's intent may have been just what he was about to say— he had wanted the SEALs to miss the incident. They were just supposed to have shown up and count the bodies.

"That's it, isn't it, sir?" Reaper said as he closed the distance between himself and Paxtun. "You made some kind of deal with those assholes. We were never supposed to have ever even seen them, were we? My men and I were just to be witnesses to the aftermath of another Serb slaughter."

"That'll be enough of that shit, Reaper," Paxtun almost shouted. Paxtun rarely swore and that told the big SEAL chief that his words were hitting home.

"Just what is it," Reaper said, "you have cooked up with the people who sent those raiders? Just what were you supposed to get out of the deal? Intelligence? Some kind of information that would make your career?"

Reaper looked deeply into Paxtun's eyes as he spoke. He didn't see enough of a reaction to tell him that he had guessed right yet. Paxtun was angry, but the captain remained cagey and in control.

"If not intelligence, what?" Reaper said. "Money? Guns? Drugs? Just what the hell could someone offer you that would be worth the lives of all those people?"

"Take control of yourself, Chief," Paxtun said sharply.

"Sir," Reaper said as he drew himself rigidly to attention, "I respectfully request permission to report to SFOR headquarters in Tuzla. I will personally deliver a full report on the incident this evening to the authorities there. The relocation project is their responsibility and they can make the final determination of the situation and which parties might be held accountable."

Paxtun looked shocked as he realized just how close he was coming to losing control of the situation. It was now obvious to anyone who may have seen them standing there that he didn't want Reaper reporting anything to anyone. There was suddenly near panic showing in the officer's face. Whatever the situation was, Reaper knew from looking at Paxtun that something was wrong and he was up to his asshole in it.

"Just a moment, Chief," Paxtun said in a reasonable tone. "Any reports coming from this unit will be made by myself or my executive officer. It is obvious that you are too upset by the action today to think clearly. The accusations you are making are outrageous. I'm sure you'll see just how wrong they are after a night's sleep. You make out your report tomorrow and I will see to it that it reaches the proper people."

"I will be making my own report to Warcom, my own Navy command, sir," Reaper said with a special emphasis on the last word. "And I will make it tonight. I do not require your permission to do so."

The anger that washed through Paxtun showed plainly on his face. As the big Navy SEAL turned to leave the room, the shorter officer said, "This is my command, Chief, not yours. And I am the intelligence professional. Any reports that come from this unit will come directly from my desk. I will inform command in Tuzla of the situation—and of your part in it."

"My part in it?" Reaper said.

"Obviously, Chief," Paxtun said, "the strain of working under these conditions was too much for you. Something at the refugee village must have simply set you off and you opened fire on them. I would of course expect your men to say whatever they had to in order to cover for their chief, but you have obviously lost control of yourself. That is what

I will tell both the Tuzla command, and your own people."

Relief swept across Paxtun's face as he thought that he had taken control of a situation that had threatened to get completely out of hand. The blame for the slaughter would be put on the head of what he could say was an undisciplined SEAL who had lost control. He had disobeyed specific orders as to how he was supposed to have approached the village and what path he was to have taken. What other standing orders may he have ignored? Their story would fit the facts well enough to confuse the issue badly. A small smile slowly spread across Paxtun's face.

For a moment as he stood there, Reaper no longer could see the smirking face of the officer in front of him. What he saw was a small bundle of rags being tossed through a schoolhouse window. And all he heard was a child's whimpering cry suddenly cut off. He had to get out of that room now, before he did something he would regret.

"The hell you will," Reaper said very softly. "I'll be making my own report, and it will be going through Navy channels."

Reaper turned to leave the room without another word. The soft tone of voice Reaper had used had a lot in common with a quiet wind blowing through a graveyard—they both were heard mostly by the dead. If the intelligence officer had learned more about the Navy SEAL chief, he would have known to be afraid of that voice. What Paxtun did realize was the seriousness of what Reaper was threatening to do.

The smirk that had been on Paxtun's face just a

moment before had been replaced with something that looked a lot like sudden fear. Paxtun wasn't a big man, just a little over five feet six. And he certainly didn't have the build of the six-foot-tall, 215-pound Reaper. But he still tried to physically stop Reaper from leaving the room.

"Don't you turn your back on me, mister," Paxtun said. "I am not done talking to you yet!" He grabbed at Reaper's left shoulder and tried to twist the big man around.

An iron-hard right fist, toughened by years of exercise, salt water, and rough use—the same hand that had rubbed the short hair of a six-year-old son back in the States months before—shot up from behind the SEAL's right hip and smashed squarely into the officer's jaw. Paxtun flipped over backward and landed flat on the floor. The angle of his jaw was anything but natural as the nearly unconscious officer groaned from where he lay sprawled. The broken jaw would keep the man from eating solid food for some time—and it spelled the death knell for Reaper's military career.

Chapter Three

Months after the JSSF incident in Bosnia, a blue Pontiac Firebird sped along the northbound lanes of I-395, heading in to Washington, D.C. At the wheel of the car was Navy captain Alan Straker. For a high-ranking officer, Captain Straker's deeply tanned skin and heavy muscular build made him stand out as someone who hadn't spent his career behind a desk.

The brilliantly shining gold Trident, the Naval Special Warfare breast insignia, in plain view on the upper right side of Straker's uniform, was a big giveaway as to just how he developed that tan and those muscles. The Trident could be worn officially only by men who had passed through training and been accepted as active SEALs by their peers in the Teams. That symbol on his chest proclaimed him to be a Navy SEAL operator—no matter what his rank or assignment.

Not all of his muscles came from having been in the SEAL Teams. Straker's bright blue eyes had looked out from under a sweating mass of thick black hair at a number of opponents during his days on the wrestling team at the U.S. Naval Academy. He had always accepted a challenge, and reveled in overcoming them. The challenge he was facing right now was simply the irritation of having to maneuver through D.C. traffic.

Straker decided on parking at the Pentagon and grabbing a ride in on the subway. He could make his appointment at the huge Department of State building between Twenty-first and Twenty-third Streets by just getting aboard the Metro at the Pentagon and getting off at the Foggy Bottom stop south of Washington Circle. The walk was only about half a mile down Twenty-third Street, and the late September weather in D.C. wasn't so bad that he would arrive in a sweat-soaked uniform. Besides, finding a parking spot at the Pentagon was going to be one hell of a lot easier than conducting a parking search in downtown Northwest D.C.

While standing at the subway stop at the bottom of the very long escalators at the Pentagon, and during the ride itself, Captain Straker maintained a pensive look. At only slightly over five ten, but carrying 245 pounds on his broad-shouldered frame, Straker wasn't jostled a lot by the other passengers on the subway. Certainly no one poked at the big SEAL to see if there was a soft spot indicating flab instead of muscle. Only his six-year-old niece would ever think of doing such a thing anyway. A small smile slipped onto the face of the SEAL as he thought of his sister's youngest, the smile evaporating as his mind went back to his mission at hand.

At present, Captain Straker's assignment in the Teams was a general one. He was working TAD (temporary assigned duty) at Special Warfare Group Two at Little Creek, Virginia. His present position was only to last until the confirmation of his promotion to rear admiral (lower half). Once at flag rank, he would go on to the Special Operations Command in Tampa for a tour of duty there.

With the temporary duties at Group Two, also came a job that no SEAL ever wanted—investigating the possible wrongdoing of a fellow operator. Straker had been ordered to investigate the incident of a SEAL chief petty officer being accused of willfully disobeying orders, assaulting a superior officer, and the murder of foreign nationals. The charges were seriously inflated in Straker's opinion, and the situation a foul one.

Only the classified seal the State Department had thrown over the whole affair had so far kept it out of the hands of the Judge Advocate General's office. Somebody at State wanted a SEAL's ass as a sacrifice over this one—and they wanted all of their ducks in a row before final charges were brought. Straker intended bringing the situation to a close before the JAG's office became inextricably involved. State wanted a straightforward guilty plea, and Straker was going to play that desire for all it was worth.

As he walked south to the State Department Building Straker reflected how, at his rank, politics had become another battleground. In this fight, words did more damage than any bullets ever could. If the present situation burst in his face, that admiral's star was going to go back into the box. But no SEAL had ever been left behind, living or dead. Even if all you could do was go back and bring out a body, if that's what it took that's what you did. It had been a mantra in the Teams since well before Lieutenant (j.g.) Straker had gone through training. He certainly was not going to be the first one to break that tradition by abandoning a Teammate to the military-hating cookie-pushers at the State Department.

It took some time to travel through the huge building to locate the conference room that Straker had been told to report to. Already in the room and busily shuffling papers was Martin Rosacrantz, the midlevel State Department bureaucrat who was pushing ahead with the case against Ted Reaper. Rosacrantz was a tall, thin individual with a receding hairline and a superior attitude. Straker wasn't surprised. He had yet to meet any people from State who didn't feel they were superior to the military. Even though it was the military who had to keep cleaning up the messes or carry through the ideas of the moment for the present administration.

"Thank you for being prompt, Captain Straker," Rosacrantz said. "Please have a seat and we'll get right to business."

Without waiting for Straker to sit, Rosacrantz began talking.

"This meeting should be little more than a formality before formal charges are brought against Chief Petty Officer Reaper," Rosacrantz said.

"I hardly think that the decision to bring capital charges against anyone should be considered simply a formality," Straker said.

Rosacrantz looked at Captain Straker with surprise showing on his face.

"But you can hardly argue against the evidence

and the gravity of the situation. You have a highly trained operator who had a serious failure of judgment that resulted in the murder of two native Muslim defenders of a refugee group. It's quite possible that his slaying of the militia members directly resulted in the slaughter of the villagers.

"The situation in Bosnia-Herzegovina is very unstable right now. The peace accords have been kept in place by very careful diplomatic maneuvering by State with both the local governments and NATO. The U.N. has a direct interest in just how well we handle the situation. This incident must be handled properly."

"If by properly, you mean railroad an enlisted man who has given fifteen years of exemplary service to his country," Straker said more than a little heatedly, "then you will not have the cooperation of the Navy or of Naval Special Warfare."

Straker continued before Rosacrantz could get over his shock at the SEAL's blunt manner of speaking and hard tone of voice.

"I have personally examined the reports of the incident and interviewed the bulk of the personnel involved. Additionally, I have gone over the service records of everyone involved in some detail. More than that, I put Chief Reaper's history under a microscope. Nothing, and I mean absolutely nothing, in his record indicates anything but exemplary behavior on his part along with the utmost professionalism in the execution of his duties."

"The situation in Bosnia-Herzegovina was a combat environment," Rosacrantz said, "with severe stress on everyone stationed in the area. It would have certainly affected the judgment of a man not used to the intricacies of operating with foreign nationals with their own set of morals and ideals."

Straker swallowed the expletive he almost burst out with. "The level of stress you seem to think so extreme is exceeded on a regular basis during our normal training in the SEAL Teams," Straker said. "And Reaper had been in combat before. His conduct under fire with a detachment from SEAL Team Four during Operation Just Cause in Panama demonstrated coolness under fire. He was able to absorb severe hardship without complaint and without wavering from the objective at hand.

"After his combat experience, he went on to be a First Phase instructor at the Special Warfare Training Center in Coronado. Again, he showed proficiency and competence in his job while also looking out for the welfare of the students placed in his care. He is a completely professional military man.

"The same can't quite be said in regards to Captain Paxtun. I find his military records interesting for their brevity. In fact, he doesn't seem to have existed except perhaps in a vacuum before more than a few years ago. It's been a few years but I've seen this kind of military record before, back when I was a young officer in Vietnam. This is the record of an intelligence operative seconded to the military and given a protocol rank. This man isn't a commissioned officer or even really a soldier, he's a spook!

"I don't know just how deeply you've looked into the backgrounds of this officer—and I use that term with reservations. Maybe you're just working from a limited briefing. But with one of my SEALs' career on the line, you can be sure that I've looked deeply into all the backgrounds of everyone involved.

"Did you even know that Paxtun had been captured by the Soviets while under deep cover in Afghanistan? After being disavowed by our own government, he was finally rescued by members of a local mujahideen faction. For months, he stayed at the Amir Muawia camp in the Khost province of Afghanistan. That place was originally set up by the CIA and the ISI, the Pakistani military intelligence service. Now, it's nothing more than an Islamic fundamentalist base—a training camp for terrorists. On top of that, the ISI is corrupt as hell and ass-deep in the opium trade and gun running.

"That man should never have been allowed back into a combat zone. Certainly not put in charge of a special operations unit. And most emphatically not put into an area where Islamic fundamentalists were trying to gain a political foothold among the Muslim refugee population.

"We've traced at least one of the Islamic fundamentalist factions operating in that part of Bosnia directly back to the Khost region of Afghanistan. If I can find that out just from my contacts in the intelligence community, how in the hell did you guys here at State miss it completely?

"Those Islamic fundamentalists could give lessons in enthusiasm to Baptist missionaries. Don't you think the men who rescued Paxtun from the hands of the Soviets just might not have a bit of influence over him?"

Having visibly wilted under Straker's verbal onslaught, Rosacrantz quickly recovered his composure and spoke back to the big SEAL.

"Captain Paxtun was fully debriefed after his unfortunate problems in Afghanistan," Rosacrantz said. "It was to his credit that the man never broke under the enthusiastic interrogations of his Soviet captors. At that time, the Soviet military would have liked nothing better than to have had a U.S. intelligence officer taken prisoner from that particular part of the world. It is to Paxtun's credit that he was able to immerse himself deeply in the local Muslim culture and prevent his cover from being blown.

"Paxtun was considered more than able to command the special operations people of that JSSF contingent. His special knowledge of the customs and culture of the Muslim people was expected to be a great asset to the mission. It is unfortunate that the men from your command did not seem to be able to take their direction from a capable and well-trained officer."

"Are we reading the same reports?" Straker said. "Do you really have any idea just what the true situation is over there?"

"You are hardly qualified to judge the . . ." Rosacrantz began to say.

"Oh, but I am qualified to judge this situation," Straker interrupted in a menacing tone. "I have been put in very bad situations in the past by self-serving intelligence operatives who overreached themselves and wanted someone else to blame when things went bad. And I will not stand by and allow it to happen to the men I serve with.

"The idea that the Serbs conducted the slaughter at the relocation village has nothing to support it. There were no Serb forces operating in the area that

SFOR knew of. There were no Serb forces that the Russians knew to be operating in the area. And the Serbs themselves say they had no units within miles of that village during the time of the attack."

"You could hardly expect the Serb forces," Rosacrantz said, "who are themselves suspect in a number of criminal atrocities, to admit that they were the ones who conducted this action."

"No, I would hardly take their word for it," Straker said. "But it is significant that their information correlates with everything we can get from other sources. And there is the evidence that was recovered by Chief Reaper after the incident that points the finger at Islamic extremists doing the killing."

"You cannot accept as evidence the described finding of a minor piece of clothing and some religious tracts," Rosacrantz said. "The materials simply don't exist."

"That in itself is interesting to me," said Straker. "The only evidence described by Chief Reaper never made it up to higher headquarters. But the funny thing was, all of his men who were questioned separately about the incident described exactly the same things. And Captain Paxtun had been conducting extensive contact ops on his own accord without informing his men, or anyone else that I can locate right now."

"If Paxtun is the experienced intelligence operative that you describe," Rosacrantz said, "you could hardly expect him to give out sensitive information when there wasn't a need-to-know."

"I saw a number of Intel people try to hide behind the sensitive information shield before," Straker said. "That may have worked on a naive young officer twenty-five years ago, but it won't work now. You try and push these swollen charges forward and I will make it my responsibility to uncover everything that was going on in that particular piece of the world.

"Chief Reaper is not going to plead guilty to anything at this point. He will not roll over and play dead no matter how badly the State Department wants him to. Reaper has told me his suspicions regarding the situation over there and Paxtun's involvement in it. It does not make a very pretty picture.

"Paxtun could have been just trying to gather intelligence on the situation in that area of Bosnia-Herzegovina. He could easily have been cooperating with an Islamic group he felt he owed something to. Or he could have been going behind everyone's back to just line his own pockets. Smuggling guns, drugs, whatever, has been going on in that part of the world for decades. Some of the Islamic organizations are raising their operating funds by selling opium out of Afghanistan. It wouldn't be the first time an intelligence officer took advantage of being in the middle of the situation to add to a personal retirement fund.

"Accusations are easy. There is no hard evidence as yet to support these suppositions—only the words of several SEALs who I trust. But if JAG was to become involved in an official investigation, I'm sure corroborating witnesses and evidence could turn up.

"And before you tell me that security classifications will keep me from learning what I want to know, I should tell you that the Special Warfare community is a very tight one. We have been in the business of gathering intelligence for this country for a very long time.

"The Teams were working for the intelligence community since before the CIA even existed. There are a lot of ex-Team guys in the Intel world right now. This thing stinks and I will find out just what is rotten. I think that some very bad judgments were made in regards to our allies in that part of the world. And there are some extremist groups around there who have their own agendas. Agendas they have every intention of following no matter what they have to do or who they have to kill.

"I don't know who, or to what extent, Captain Paxtun was involved with over there—and I don't particularly want to find out unless I have to. And if I do, you can rest assured that it will become part of the official record."

Martin Rosacrantz was stunned by the tone of the big SEAL's words as much as their content. As the bureaucrat sat back in his chair and stared at the SEAL, Straker considered it time to take a new tack. Now it was his turn to play diplomat and push a cookie across the table. Chief Reaper couldn't get out of this situation unscathed. The bit about exposing some kind of possibly unsanctioned ops or corrupt activity had hit the bureaucrat harder than Straker expected. Offering an alternative punishment for Reaper, and making it sound worse than it was, could give the State Department, or just Rosacrantz, a means to save face.

"There is the fact that Chief Reaper struck a superior officer," Straker said. "Even one who may not have been a true commissioned officer. That is a serious breach of military discipline. There are no witnesses to the incident, but Paxtun's jaw being broken in two places speaks for itself.

"Making Reaper face charges under the Uniform Code of Military Justice would bring a great deal out during a court-martial—some of which the State Department may not like shown even to a secure court.

"I think I could convince Chief Reaper to accept one option. He could leave the Teams and return to the fleet, maintaining his rank as a Navy chief petty officer. That would keep him under military control and he could retire as soon as his twenty years were completed."

Straker had no real expectation of Rosacrantz accepting his first suggestion of punishment for Reaper. The people at the State Department had the reputation of being bargainers and Rosacrantz was no exception. What he wasn't saying to Rosacrantz was that Reaper had already admitted to having struck Paxtun. That the SEAL chief was ready to stand up for what he had done and accept whatever punishment would be due him for his actions was one of the factors that put Straker solidly on Reaper's side.

"No," Rosacrantz said emphatically, "Chief Reaper will leave the service entirely. Paxtun has been stripped of all rank and relinquished all claims for any benefits he may have accrued. He has been expelled both from the military and the intelligence community. Your chief will not receive any more lenient treatment for his involvement in this affair."

"Chief Reaper is up for reenlistment within a few weeks," Straker said. "As a career military man, he has to put in his twenty years before he becomes eligible for any retirement. If he was not allowed to reenlist, he would have to just leave the service. Any actions taken by him after he left the Navy could jeopardize any benefits that would come to him down the road. His discharge is already in the works." Straker neglected to mention that the discharge would be an honorable one. "I'm certain Chief Reaper can be shown the benefits of ending his career."

Captain Straker had a bad taste in his mouth even as he said the words. They could keep Chief Reaper from facing any kind of trumped-up charges. The fact was that a number of Balkan-area Islamic groups that had been supported by the State Department had turned out to be terrorist organizations. That was something that State didn't want talked about. The situation in the Balkans was a mess, and the present administration didn't seem to be able to do anything about it as things got worse. Getting Reaper the hell out of the line of fire would be the best Captain Straker could do. He would just have to get by in the civilian world.

Chapter Four

In the years following the massacre of Muslim civilians at the village, the story never left the immediate area of Bosnia or the halls of the U.S. State Department, Intelligence agencies, or military. Coming from a land that had seen the worst of war for years, the story of a handful of villagers being slaughtered didn't make even a footnote in the international news.

The loss of a few personnel to the Intelligence community and the Navy, even the small ranks of Naval Special Warfare, were absorbed without notice. Lives were changed in major ways, without directly affecting the U.S. government in the least. In other parts of the world, the policies of the U.S. administration of the 1990s, especially those of the State Department and Intelligence community, were going to affect the government, and the world.

A large part of the operating funds that al Qaeda and other organizations depend on came from their involvement in the illegal drug trade. Growing opium poppies had always been part of the Afghan farming scene. When Iranian drug merchants came into Afghanistan, fleeing revolutionary justice in Iran, they helped set up drug processing labs inside the country to convert opium first into morphine-base and then into heroin. The high-quality heroin produced was quickly slipped into the drug pipeline.

The Balkans had been developed by al Qaeda and others into a southeastern approach into Europe. The drug pipeline stretched from Afghanistan and central Asia, through the Middle East, north to Bosnia, and on to Italy and beyond.

Heroin flowed by the metric ton from al Qaeda labs in the mountains to addicts in Germany, Norway, and England. These were productive markets and money poured into the coffers of al Qaeda as Afghan heroin saturated Europe. That money helped to finance a number of extensive operations by Islamic extremist groups.

In spite of the success of their narcotics trade, what was desired above all by al Qaeda and their brother organizations was a secure connection into North America and the United States markets. Having returned to the States while still maintaining his contacts in Afghanistan and elsewhere, Cary Paxtun was happy to supply that connection.

Paxtun had come from the large Arab and Muslim community in southeastern Michigan. His ethnic Middle Eastern background had served him well when he had been working as an intelligence agent among the mujahideen in Afghanistan. But he had been out of the United States and away from his home area for a long time.

What Paxtun needed was a local contact to help him set up a major drug distribution network. He found that business partner in Steven Arzee, a younger Muslim who had been running a small nightclub in Detroit. Out of his club, Arzee had also been conducting some drug deals and other illegal business with the assistance of a number of his extended family members.

The fastidious Arzee was not a soldier, in spite of the airs he gave himself. But he was a dedicated Wahhabi Muslim with a good deal of street smarts and some very loyal and trusted men with him. With Paxtun's knowledge and connections and Arzee's manpower, their illegal and legal businesses quickly grew.

Creating private secured bank accounts, money laundering techniques, surreptitious transport of materials across international borders, and other such skills had been part of the trade craft that Paxtun had learned during his time in the intelligence community. This knowledge base, combined with the contacts Paxtun had in the mujahideen brotherhood, helped both Paxtun and Arzee to become very successful.

———

North of the center of Detroit exist a number of smaller factories surrounded by tract houses and old neighborhoods. A loss of jobs had caused most of the factories to close down years earlier. Both the local neighborhoods and many of the factory buildings fell into a bad state of decay.

One old manufacturing center had undergone a

resurrection of sorts, though not to make cars as it had years before. The Factory, as it was known, was now a nightclub for the adventurous in Detroit. Built on the first floor of the old auto plant, just off the intersection of two major highways, the Factory was a modern playground for the clubbing youth of both the city and the surrounding suburbs. Young Canadians from across the Detroit River in Windsor also came to taste the night life at the Factory.

The Factory had been organized along the lines of a permanently located rave. It had proven itself popular as a rave in spite of the protests of the hardcore rave devotees who insisted that such an event had to remain portable and underground to be a true rave.

With its grittiness and progressive electronic music, the Factory won over even the hard-core ravers. A rave was a place to go to release tensions and burn off excess energies. The subculture who flocked to raves preferred a place that offered them their distinctive style of techno music, dress, dance, and visual effects. It also would allow them to combine the atmosphere with open sexual behavior and consumables that included alcohol and psychedelic chemicals.

What neither the suburban upscale clubbers or the ravers knew was that the Factory was just another means of feeding their decadent habits and taking their money in the process. Many things went on in the six-story old building, besides the frenzied dancing and sexual antics of the clubbers. Those who wanted to could find that there was more than alcoholic drinks and exotic cocktails available to them. Various top-quality drugs were available on the floor of the Factory.

Sales of such things remained inside of the building and a very hard force of security goons saw to it that any entrepreneurs who sought to sell their own wares on Factory grounds quickly chose another line of work, once they had healed. Those who continued to sell never had the chance to heal after dealing with security a second time. The bulk of the security force had been recruited from the Arab community in Dearborn and surrounding areas.

Speaking among themselves mostly in Arabic, the security people distanced themselves from the customers even as they watched them. All the security force were deeply committed believers in Wahhabi Islam, as such they considered themselves immune to the entreaties of even the prettiest of the clubbers.

Local drug gangs let the Factory alone as long as it kept its retail share to itself and didn't extend into their turf. If any of the dealers thought that their wholesalers might be supplied from the Factory, they kept that theory to themselves.

Police and drug enforcement agencies never had any proof to substantiate a search warrant for the Factory. Informants knew better than to even consider dealing any information on the Factory to the authorities. The few who had tried had never been found, except as some unidentified parts left as private examples to others.

The most modern scanning techniques and shielding kept listening devices from ever transmitting from inside the building, and wiretaps turned up nothing useful. The police and DEA never connected more than rumors to the Factory, and that wasn't enough to get a warrant. Not that any authorities expected to get past the first floor of the place with any real chance of finding anything. The huge plant was small only by automotive manufacturer's standards. The block-long edifice was a nightmare to a police agency.

On the first floor, there were still remnants of the conveyor system and frames that had assembled cars decades before. The place could be a whirling flux of gyrating bodies during peak hours, and just a huge area to cover during slack times. All attempts to infiltrate undercover agents into the club had failed. Without having hard intelligence on what was going on inside the building on the upper floors, the police could do nothing. The only thing that was known was that the public owner had his offices on the sixth floor at the east end of the building.

The owners of the Factory according to official documents was a consortium of investors. The listing of investors consisted of other businesses, holding companies, even mutual funds. Following the line of ownership would only result in running up against a blank wall as the paper trail disappeared into foreign finance laws. Liquor licenses and such were all in line with the necessary requirements, no legal details had been missed.

A very stylish Steven Arzee showed himself on the club floor on occasion. He was listed as the executive manager of the club, but he reported to the real manager regularly.

Cary Paxtun had opened the club several years earlier with funds from his overseas investors. He did not maintain quarters or offices in the Factory. The money from the legal aspects of the club were quite lucrative though they were small change in comparison to the profits from the drugs, money laundering, and other activities.

Part of that money had gone through more fronts and businesses to pay for several very major land purchases. Two whole islands in Lake Michigan had been purchased almost outright by Paxtun through cutouts. He now maintained his quarters between a luxury high rise in downtown Detroit and the mansion of a private hunting club on South Wolverine Island in Lake Michigan. Paxtun's privacy was very important to him, and so was the maintaining of cutouts between himself and his trusted lieutenant Steven Arzee.

But in spite of his security and distance between the illegal activities of the Factory and himself, Paxtun was anything but a relaxed man. He had his own bosses that he had to satisfy. The overseas investors who not only had supplied him with funds, but were also his source of high-grade narcotics, had made demands on Paxtun. These demands were ones that he could not refuse, and must not fail to satisfy, and he was in the process of failing them now.

———

". . . officials said that the quantity of arms seized was the largest ever taken in Canada. Elsewhere in the news . . ."

A thumb punched down hard on the remote control. The TV screen across the room immediately faded to black with a dull "snap" as the sound clicked off. Cary Paxtun looked up from the desk and snarled at Steven Arzee standing nearby.

"How the fuck could this have happened?" Paxtun said. "That route was supposed to be solid. The weapons had been built into the bottom of the shipping container itself and shouldn't have even been detectable through the insulation. There was no reason for anyone to have even been looking at that shipment—we spent a bucketful of money to make everything seem as legitimate as possible."

The fact that Paxtun was cursing indicated just how angry he was—a fact not lost on Arzee. He knew that the situation was a serious one. The seized weapons were intended for people who expected them. They wouldn't have accepted the shipment even being delayed. The fact that the authorities had found them was a disaster.

"It was just blind, stupid, bad luck they were ever discovered," Arzee said. "The Toronto port authorities had asked for a demonstration of a new mobile scanning system. They were trying to meet the demands of the Homeland Security Border and Transportation people. The damned system uses some kind of new X-ray technology called Z(R) Backscatter. It was set up at the exit gate and it checked every container that was going out of the port. The truck driver couldn't have turned around even if he had known about the system.

"I checked with our people in Toronto. None of them knew the system was going to be demonstrated that day. The setup that was being demonstrated was packed in a van that just parked next to the exit. It was just bad luck, there was no way to have foreseen it."

"Bad luck, huh," Paxtun said. "Everything's fucking gone. The guns, the grenades, the missile launchers, the ammo, explosives, everything. A few hundred thousand dollars worth of ordnance just gone with no decent explanation for its being missing, at least not one that Ishmael will be willing to hear. Or do you want to tell him that he won't get his shipment because of bad luck?"

Arzee's face blanched at the idea of telling the terrorist leader any bad news at all. Paxtun could see in his lieutenant's face that he wanted nothing at all to do with Ishmael, that he was terrified of him. And Paxtun couldn't blame Arzee for his fear.

Ishmael was not the man's real name. It was a kunyah, an Arabic pseudonym adopted from the names of the Companions of the Prophet and other heroes of Islam. A kunyah was used to disguise the name of a faithful while he was on a mission.

No matter what this man's real name was, he was dangerous to anyone who blocked his path. As the leader of a major terrorist cell infiltrating into the United States, Ishmael would kill anyone he saw as a threat to his mission. And he would kill them quickly and without hesitation. Paxtun knew the man well because it was Paxtun's organization that was bringing the cell members into the United States and Ishmael had been one of the first men brought in.

The demand to bring in the terrorists had been made of Paxtun by people that he could not refuse. It wasn't a matter of money, or even of stopping the very lucrative flow of drugs he was receiving. You refused al Qaeda only once, and that was when you felt tired of living. Failing them was a quick ticket to Paradise.

After the events of 9/11, the Afghan drug traders there expected U.S. reprisals against targets in their country. That fear caused them to dump their stockpiles of heroin and opium before they could be destroyed by U.S. military action. Accepting a low profit margin was considered better by the traders than a complete loss of their stocks.

A large amount of these drugs found their way into Paxtun's hands. And he took advantage of the situation to build up his distribution network, and profits. The heroin out of Afghanistan was an 80 percent pure narcotic. It was known as Heroin No. 4, or White Heroin, by the addicts who craved it.

Al Qaeda didn't mind the increase in business by Paxtun, they also benefited from the profits of his drug sales. The drugs were simply considered another sign of the decadence of the infidels, another means of attacking them. Osama bin Laden liked destroying the West through its own sins and indulgences. He had specifically financed the development of a new liquid heroin, the "Tears of Allah," to help corrupt the population of the West even faster.

Paxtun, Arzee, and their people had accepted al Qaeda's help, and their money. Paxtun had proven himself trustworthy by his deeds in Afghanistan and his later actions in Bosnia and finally the United States. He had proven himself so trustworthy that his organization was considered a hawala, part of an ancient form of money exchange. A hawala used trusted people around the world as a way to transfer millions of dollars in cash without documents. Money was left in a hawala and the responsible person was simply told who to give it to.

At the moment, Paxtun was holding over several million dollars in cash in an al Qaeda hawala. But that would mean little if he failed to supply Ishmael with what he needed. And Ishmael wouldn't speak to an underling, even one as highly placed as Paxtun's second in command. Arzee was a fellow Muslim, but he hadn't proven himself in the jihad. That meant Arzee was off the hook in telling Ishmael the bad news. It was going to be Paxtun's task, and that had him thinking quickly.

"There were just too many things that could go wrong with the shipment," Paxtun said, "and a number of them did. Delays due to plain bad weather made the ship late. But we planned for that possibility. Now, we've just run out of time. Ishmael has told me to expect the time schedule to change again. He won't tell me the operation, but he's probably going to move the timetable ahead again."

"He's probably never told you his real schedule anyway," Arzee said. "The man is more than paranoid about security. If anything, he's gotten worse about holding back vital information until damned near past the last minute. He even kept the arrival schedule of his men to himself until they were practically waiting at the border. Ever since Khalid Shaikh Mohammed was captured in Pakistan back in March, Ishmael and his bunch have become even tighter about keeping things to themselves."

"We have to accept the situation for the time being," Paxtun said. "We're in way too deep for there to be any way out for us now. There's nothing we can do but carry on supporting Ishmael and his people. Besides, we owe them our lives and they have no problem in reminding us of that fact."

"Well," Arzee said, "at least the money has been good the last couple of years."

"Yes," Paxtun agreed, "there's no question of that. But that's not going to help us. He wants firepower, a lot of it. And he's going to want it right now."

"Supplying something like that's going to be next to impossible," Arzee said. "It's not like anyone advertises heavy firepower and we can't just buy the weapons he wants. Maybe if we had enough time to go out into the underground market. . . ."

"What did you say?" Paxtun asked.

"Go into the underground market?" Arzee said. "I mean the contacts are there. But Ishmael didn't want to trust any kind of black market to supply his needs. And to get what he wants would take time we don't have."

"No, no," Paxtun said with excitement rising in his voice. "What you said before that."

"What?" Arzee said. "Just buy the stuff? There's no way to really do that. It's not like you can just walk into a gunshop and they'll have the kind of hardware we need. Nobody carries that kind of military weapon, no matter what the movies say. And Ishmael is going to want the real deal. Full automatic fire and lots of it."

"So what if we had a source of the guns and someone who could build what we wanted?" Paxtun said.

"Around here?" Arzee said. "Where?"

"Something Nicholas was talking about a while back," Paxtun said.

Raising his voice, Paxtun called out, "Nicholas, get in here."

Nicholas Murat was a cousin of Arzee's. As such, he and his brother Amman, held positions of high trust in the organization. This wasn't a matter of simple nepotism. It was very common in the Arab community for a business to use many members of an extended family. Blood counted for a lot, and loyalties inside of a family were strong.

At first glance, Nicholas and Amman Murat didn't look like brothers at all. Amman was taller than his bother as well as being a bodybuilder. Heavy muscles covered Amman's frame, and he liked to use his strength to solve problems. His mean streak was satisfied when he helped enforce his cousin's directives. And he knew that Paxtun was in charge.

Nicholas Murat was the physical opposite of his brother, but no less mean. His smaller size was balanced out by being much faster than most people. Nicholas hadn't put his speed to use learning a martial art. Instead, he had developed a taste for and skill in the use of firearms. Taste would be something of an understatement. Nicholas was fascinated by guns, all kinds of guns. He made up for his slight stature by using large and powerful weapons. And he kept up on the latest developments in the firearm market.

Moving into the office from his usual position near the outside door, Nicholas came to see what

Paxtun wanted. Not being one to speak a lot, the gunman waited quietly for his boss to speak to him.

"Nicholas," Paxtun asked, "what's the hottest piece of firepower on the market at this moment?"

"That would depend on what you mean, boss," Nicholas said, "hand-held, vehicle mounted, what?"

"Something an individual could use for an assault."

"Well, there's an outfit down in North Carolina that's making a pump-action 40mm grenade launcher. They're reproducing one from the Vietnam War."

"A grenade launcher?" Paxtun said. "No, that would have too many ammunition supply problems for what I'm thinking of. Besides, North Carolina is too far away to consider. Anything made closer to here?"

"There's just been an article published in *Small Arms Review* about a full-automatic shotgun going on the market," Nicholas said as he warmed to his subject. "It was demonstrated earlier this year down in Florida at the SHOT show. It's called the Jackhammer. Ten-round magazine and a really short overall package. Hottest piece of hand-held firepower there is right now, and the company making it isn't more than an hour's drive from here, somewhere up near Port Huron."

"Do you have that magazine available?"

"Yes," Nicholas said, "I was just reading it a while ago."

"Could you get it for me please?" Paxtun said.

As Nicholas left the room, Paxtun sat with a pensive smile on his face. "A machine shotgun," he said. "That would be just the weapon for a fast raiding party. Its effective range would be pretty short compared to a rifle, but close-in, it would rip a target apart."

Quickly returning with an issue of *Small Arms Review* in his hands, Nicholas laid the magazine down on the desk in front of Paxtun. Pointing to the cover, he said, "They must have thought a lot about this weapon themselves, they mentioned the article right on the cover. I marked the page for you there."

Flipping the magazine open to the indicated page, Paxtun just looked at the picture that led off the article. It showed a large man holding a very futuristic-looking weapon. Nicholas took Paxtun's intent look at the article as showing interest in the weapon.

"This was written by Matt Smith," Nicholas said, "he says he was at the demonstration firing. That's it, the Jackhammer Mark 3-A3 shotgun. It's only thirty-one inches overall length. That's barely more than an inch longer than a military M4 carbine with the stock collapsed. And the bullpup design puts the firing mechanism behind the trigger group, that lets the weapon have nearly a twenty-one-inch-long barrel and still be very compact. It's short enough to hide under a coat.

"That big drum at the rear holds ten rounds of twelve-gauge ammo. With magnum 00 buckshot, that's twelve pellets downrange for each shot. It fires on full automatic at four rounds a second—that's sixty-four pellets downrange in one second. That swarm of buckshot can rip a house down. And you reload just by dumping out the drum and slapping a new one in place."

Looking up from the magazine, Paxtun had a strange look on his face.

"You don't have to sell me on this, Nicholas," Paxtun said. "I acknowledge your greater expertise."

Nicholas positively beamed with pride at the unaccustomed praise.

"Where can we find this weapon?" Paxtun asked.

"The address of the shop is at the end of the article," Nicholas said as he pointed back to the magazine. "It's near Marine City north of Lake Saint Clair. The article does say that the Jackhammer is only made as prototypes right now. But it's been months since the SHOT show and they may have gone into production by now."

"Thank you, Nicholas," Paxtun said, "would you excuse us for now?"

As Nicholas left the office, Paxtun looked down at the magazine open in front of him and the smile grew across his face.

"Oh," Paxtun said, "this is too good."

"What?" Arzee said. "The weapon?"

"No," Paxtun said as he turned the magazine around on the desk. Pointing to the picture of the man holding the Jackhammer he said, "This man is Ted Reaper, late of the U.S. Navy. I now believe that this is indeed a very small world."

"Reaper?" Arzee said puzzled. "Reaper? You man that guy who screwed up your deal in Bosnia five years ago?"

"The very same," Paxtun said with a smile. "Allah works in interesting ways. He's not only set the tools we need into our hands, he delivered an old enemy to me. This man crossed me badly once, he will now learn just how foolish that was."

"But you can't imagine he'll sell us what we want?" Arzee said. "And what the hell is he doing in Michigan?"

"Making guns, by the looks of things," Paxtun said. "And no, I certainly wouldn't expect this man to sell us anything no matter what we offered. He's as upright as a Boy Scout. But he will have a weakness, everyone does.

"I want you to find that weakness. Find out everything you can about this man and his business as quickly as you can. And you have to keep it quiet. I don't care what it takes, costs, or what favors you have to call in—you find a handle that we can use to control this man.

"It would be very sweet to force this particular individual to break the law in order to help us. But it will take something very solid to make him hand us over the weapons. If there aren't enough of them available, he can just make more of them. This article lists a shop address and phone numbers. You find out if he has a family, parent, kid, girlfriend, whatever it is that brought him to Michigan or that he has around here. The records are out there, you just have to find them.

"This man tried to take me down once," Paxtun said with hatred in his voice. "Which makes using him all the better."

Chapter Five

A loud buzzing roar filled the small room as the big man in the dark blue shop apron held the long steel bar against the wheel, the flexible cloth buffing wheel spinning at more than 1,700 rpm. With his feet spread out for stability, the big man leaned close to the buffer and ran the long steel bar across the face of the wheel. The buzz increased in volume as the rapidly moving cloth stripped dark, cloudy layers of buffing compound off the surface of the steel—leaving a bright shining surface in its wake.

His face hidden behind the rubber and cloth of a respirator mask and his eyes behind safety goggles, the man leaned into his work, concentrating on the path the steel took as he guided it across the surface of the buffer. His hands were covered in Kevlar gloves, the fingers of which were wrapped in layers of worn tape to insure a good grip. A solid grip was important not only to make sure that the steel was guided properly across the rapidly moving cloth wheel, but also necessary for safety as any observer could quickly see that the object being so carefully buffed and polished by the man was the long blade of a broadsword.

In his dark blue shirt, jeans, and black boots, the man was almost completely still except for his hands guiding the steady passing of the blade back and forth across the wheel. His concentration was on keeping the shape of the blade distinct, smooth, and even— while not allowing the sharp edge to dig into the cloth wheel. The power of the spinning wheel would tear the blade from his hands and drive it into the floor, wall, or possibly something that could bleed quite a bit.

Watching silently from the doorway, the stocky, gray-haired man sitting in a wheelchair knew not to interrupt the man standing at the buffer. He waited quietly until the man at the machine stopped and straightened up. After looking along the edges and body of the blade to be certain he hadn't missed polishing a spot or blurred the lines of the blade's edges and corners, the man switched off the buffer and the wheel whined down to a stop.

Pulling down his respirator, the man turned to the doorway and noticed the individual sitting there. "Oh, didn't know you were there," Ted Reaper said as he pushed the safety goggles up to his forehead.

"Somehow, it didn't seem to me to be a really great idea to bother a man either while he was buffing, or holding a yard of sharp steel," Keith Deckert said with a big grin spreading out under his bushy white mustache, his teeth splitting the features of his face. "But you did want me to remind you when it was coming up to lunchtime."

"Thanks," Ted said as he looked at the watch on

his left wrist. "I've got just enough time to clean and box this thing and get back to the house before Ricky gets home."

"You might want to take a moment to wash up as well," Keith said with a chuckle. "You look like a reversed raccoon."

Catching a glimpse of himself in the glass front of a cabinet, Ted could see that the goggles and respirator had protected his eyes and lungs, but the greasy residue from the buffing wheel had spattered the exposed parts of his face with gray muck. The only parts that were clean were his mouth, mustache, nose, and eyes.

"Here, give me that pigsticker," Keith said. "I'll get the tape off the grip and pack it while you clean up."

"Thanks," Reaper said as he handed over the blade, hilt first.

Deckert turned his powered wheelchair and ran it over to a tall workbench on top of a large parts cabinet where he laid the sword down on a carpeted surface. Turning the armrests inward across his chest, he moved a control and his LifeStand Compact Model LSC wheelchair began to unfold and extend the back and seat upward. In a moment, Deckert was in a standing position, secured to the chair by the armrests, which had formed a padded brace against his chest. In an almost straight up-and-down standing position, the muscular arms of the man could reach the top of the workbench and manipulate the materials there easily and skillfully.

"And a mighty big pig you could stick with it, too," said Keith as he started stripping off the dirty masking tape that had been protecting the finish of the blued-steel cross-guard and wire-wrapped grip.

Reaper stepped away from the grinding room and walked to a small workbench where he kept his own toolbox and materials. He unclipped the small Uncle Mike's pocket holster he had in his right front pants pocket and placed it and the stainless steel Taurus Model 445 five-shot .44 Special concealed-hammer revolver it held into a large central drawer in the toolbox.

Since he had been in the civilian world and not in the military, Reaper had to have a need to go armed. Security was always something you had to think about in a gunshop, even one frequented by customers who were in law enforcement. The shop hadn't always been a gathering place for cops, and civilian customers still came in. It would take a fairly stupid crook to rob a gunshop, but dumber things had happened.

Moving across the workshop, Reaper went over to the opposite wall where a large utility sink stood next to a long, shallow, steel tank with a tight-fitting cover.

There was a smell of solvents coming up from the covered cleaning tank, but the smell would have been a lot worse if the shop had been hot. The tall, barnlike shop building was well insulated against the winter cold or summer heat, both of which could get pretty extreme in southeastern Michigan. But even if it wasn't as heavily insulated as it was, there would be little enough to hear in the way of noise this far out in the country.

The steel building was attached to the back of a

two-story brick farmhouse and sat on twenty-five acres of land less than five miles from the Saint Clair River and the border between the U.S. and Canada. The location was closer to Port Huron than Detroit, both cities being less than an hour's drive away. The area was open countryside with stands of trees separating fields. The house and barn were set back from the main road, a quarter-mile of black-topped driveway leading to a semicircular drive at the front of the house, with an extension leading out to the back shop building.

It was an out-of-the-way location for a business, but that's what the farmhouse and steel barn had been converted into. The front part of the first floor of the house was a gunshop, the barn a well-equipped machine shop with facilities for polishing and finishing metal and wood.

D & R POLICE SUPPLIES AND GUNSMITHS was all it said on a small sign on the white siding at the front of the house. The sign was a fairly new one, the paint on it being much fresher than that of the tan-painted twin doors leading into the house. The doors were at the top of a long ramp, allowing the owner's wheelchair easy access to the building.

There would be plenty of room for additional workers once business picked up. The gunsmithing and small gun shop had been at the farm for a number of years, but the police supply business was new. So for now, there were just the two men living and working in the building.

The farm and buildings were both owned by Keith Deckert, a big, gray-haired ex-Army sergeant who had lost the use of his legs several years earlier in a racing accident. Outside of the limitations on his mobility, the only thing remarkable about Deckert's body was that his arms, shoulders, and chest were even more muscular than when he had been an Army Ranger.

As Reaper was scrubbing his face and arms, Deckert was polishing the grip and hilt of the sword with a soft cloth.

"Damned big for a knife," Deckert said with a chuckle. "This from some movie or something? One of those Harry Potter books? Conan?"

"Sort of," Reaper said from across the room. "Ricky saw one like it in that Hobbit movie, *Lord of the Rings: The Two Towers.* Apparently, there's a sword like it in some role-playing game he's into with his friends."

As he was drying his face and hands on a wad of paper towels, Reaper walked over to where his friend was placing the sword in a long, wooden box. The shining blade, diamond-shaped and double edged, was thirty-six inches long with a simple blued-steel cross guard. The round disc pommel was also blue steel and secured an eight-inch grip that was covered with twisted steel wire. The pattern of the wire seemed to almost flow in an optical illusion as you kept looking at it.

"Hopefully, he'll like it," Reaper said as he tossed the wad of towels in a trash can. He looked with a critical eye at the blade lying on a bed of red velvet in the long, polished wood case, but could see no flaws in it. "I made it real, not a toy. It'll be something that can stay with him forever if he wants, maybe better than his old man did."

"Things haven't improved between you and Mary?" Deckert asked quietly.

"No," Reaper said with a note of sadness in his voice. "And I'm not sure they ever will. But I have to make certain that Ricky knows it isn't his fault and that I still love him. So I made this for him, something from my own hands."

"Well, it's a little big for him now," Deckert said. "But I'm pretty sure he'll grow into it. You'll have to get him fencing lessons so he knows how to swing one."

"You don't learn how to wave one of these around in classical fencing," Reaper said. "He's getting into something called the Society for Creative Anachronism, SCA they call it. Bunch of kids, some adults, too, get together and re-create the knights of old. They stage sword fights with padded fake blades and other weapons."

"Uh-huh," Deckert said, "sounds weird as hell. But at least it doesn't seem like something that would keep him sitting in front of a computer all day."

Reaper closed the lid on the long wooden case and secured it in place with two brass latches. Picking it up by the leather handle, he turned to the nearby door that led into the house.

"Nope," Reaper said, "the boy does like his activities. Gets out and moves around, better than a lot of kids today. He's smart enough to like getting on his computer and playing games with his friends. But he doesn't spend all day sitting in front of a computer or game console."

"Sitting down all the time isn't necessarily all bad," Deckert said as he pushed a control and his wheelchair started to slowly collapse back into a sitting configuration. Chuckling at his friend's mild embarrassment at what he had said, Deckert turned to the doorway and started to roll toward it.

"So, you hear that news out of Canada?" Deckert said, to let his friend off the hook and change the subject.

"What news?" Reaper said. "I've mostly been in the grinding room the last few days and the noise level isn't the best for listening to the radio."

"There's these great new inventions called headsets," Deckert said as he rolled through the door Reaper was holding open. "You should look into them. At any rate, seems that Canadian customs up in Toronto found some container ship with a bunch of guns and ammunition on it. At least they found one container with a load of hardware hidden in the walls—you know how the news exaggerates these kinds of things."

"Yeah," said Reaper following Deckert out of the shop and into the house. "They find a couple of boxes of shells and two weapons in a takedown and the guy had an arsenal of guns and ammunition. So what did they find really? Did you hear?"

"Seems it really was a bunch of small arms," Deckert said. "Real bad-guy stuff. Military AK-47s, RPG-7s, ammunition, even grenades and explosives."

"Shit," Reaper said surprised. "Sounds like they

busted a supply run for some terrorist cell. Did they get any leads on where the stuff was going?"

"Not that I heard," Deckert said. "According to the news, they didn't know if the stuff had arrived for some Canadian group or was headed somewhere else. It was close enough that it could have been heading here to Michigan, Chicago, or maybe that big ship terminal down in Toledo. The Canadians made a great big deal of finding the stuff, not a hell of a lot of guns in the Great White North."

"They would have made a big deal of finding that kind of stash even here in Detroit," Reaper said. "Good to see that the security is starting to work."

"Yeah, well you better change into something a little cleaner than those clothes before you head to see Mary and Ricky," Deckert said as he rolled past the kitchen of the house and into the office that had originally been the dining room.

"There's an idea," Reaper agreed as he laid the sword case on the kitchen counter and headed to the stairs leading to the second floor. He had been living in the shop/house for some months now—ever since he had separated from Mary, his wife of fifteen years. Times had been hard since he was forced to leave the service, and he knew that he hadn't treated his family the best way that he could in the intervening years.

Losing his career and being forced to leave without any retirement or benefits had been hard—both financially and emotionally. He had gone out with his buddies from the Teams a few too many times while the family lived down in Imperial Beach in Southern California. It was when his old friend and

Teammate Bear, who had now retired from the Navy, had looked him up that things had seemed as though they would improve.

Bear had said that there was a friend of his back in Michigan who could use some help. Being that Reaper had spent more than a little time working in the armory, and had learned metalworking in high school, Bear thought he would be a great addition to his friend's gun shop. It was the chance for a good job doing something Reaper would like.

Going out to Michigan, Reaper met Keith Deckert for the first time and the two men hit it off well. Mary and Ricky were tired of moving across the country as they had so many times when Reaper was in the Navy. But he had sworn that this would be the last time. The bulk of the family's savings had been spent in making the move.

Things had improved a bit in Michigan for the Reaper household, at least the cost of living was a hell of a lot better than it was in Southern California. Mary had been able to do part-time teaching, which she had always loved. Ricky was making friends in school now. He even was starting to like winter sports, not exactly the sort of thing he could have done in the San Diego area.

In spite of the good things, there was still a lot of hardships. Reaper wasn't making much money at the gun shop. It was grating against Reaper that his family was living more on what his wife made as a substitute teacher than on his earnings. The lack of his retirement pay was keenly felt at least once a month. But he was working hard to change that.

Months earlier, Reaper had put forward the idea

of making his friend's small custom gunsmithing shop into a larger business. The production rights were available for the Jackhammer assault shotgun and Reaper felt he had the contacts to make it a successful seller. The big growth in Homeland security, customs, and police response units looked to be a good source of revenue. Deckert agreed and had put in his savings to expand the business. They secured the rights to the Jackhammer shotgun and had built a number of prototypes. These had been displayed and demonstrated by Reaper at a number of police, military, and trade shows.

The new shop had missed out on the market that had boomed just a few months before with the outbreak of the Iraq war. The Jackhammer had not been picked up by any of the services yet. Losing that business had put Ted Reaper back in the dumps, especially since his friend Keith Deckert had risked his farm and home as collateral to expand the shop.

That depression had resulted in more than one argument in the Reaper household. Finally, he had separated from Mary, moving into one of the mostly unused upstairs bedrooms at the farmhouse. Deckert had told him that the rooms weren't a lot of use for him right now, he had already converted the downstairs family room into a bedroom to keep from having to use a lift to get up and down the stairs.

So Ted had moved out of his home, leaving his wife and twelve-year-old son living in the small house they had bought with what they got out of the place they had sold in Imperial Beach. The house was in a nice, old neighborhood south of Mount

Clemens—and only a relatively short ride from the farm on Ted's Harley. His 1983 Electra-glide was a holdover from his Team days.

Deckert had a hell of a nice garage, fitting for an old Detroit-area gearhead. He still had the hot rod that was built up from an old Checker cab, and his customized 2001 Chevy Venture van. The van had a power lift installed on the driver's side rear door that Keith could strap his wheelchair into. Once in the van, he locked his chair in place and could drive the van with its modified controls. There was still room in the garage for Reaper's bike. Even some space left over for a good collection of weights and workout gear.

After changing into a clean pair of Levi's and a thick black sweater—it could still get cold in Michigan on a bike, even in mid-May, just the month before there had been a winter snowstorm—Reaper placed the sword case in a green canvas barracks bag to protect it and strapped it to the back of his bike. Slipping on his leather jacket and helmet, he climbed onto the bike and started up the engine. Hitting the remote secured to his handle bars, the overhead door opened up behind him. He pushed the bike back out of the garage and roared off on his way.

Chapter Six

The ride wasn't a long one, and the spring air made it a pleasant run. There were long stretches of open country roads between the shop and where Reaper's home had been. The earthy, wet smell of the marshes that lay along some of the roads helped clear away the gloomy thoughts that Reaper had about coming from where he lived now rather than going home.

The trees lining the street that his old home was on were growing leaves fast, and the bud husks all around the ground crunched under his wheels as he turned up the driveway of a modest single-floor, ranch-style house in a working-class family neighborhood. In spite of the bright promise of new life on the sunny day, pulling up to the house just didn't feel like coming home anymore.

Ricky hadn't come barging out of the house as the bike pulled in, so he probably wasn't home from school yet. Mary was standing in the doorway, an unreadable expression in her brown eyes as she watched Reaper set the kickstand on the bike and climb off the seat. The sight of the slender, blond woman still stirred feelings in Reaper, but the lack of greeting in her face told him that the feelings probably were not mutual.

"Hello, Mary," Reaper said as he walked up to the door. "Is Ricky home from school yet?"

"No, not yet," Mary said as she stood to the side and opened the door. "He wanted to stop by a friend's house on the way home to see some new game or other. He should be home any moment now. You know you're late, don't you?"

As Reaper stepped into the house, his shoulders slumped a little at Mary's accusatory tone. A feeling of fatigue crossed through him was he walked into the living room, carrying the barracks bag that he had taken from the bike. The home was small, but it was clean and tastefully furnished. He knew that was all Mary's doing. His tastes were what she considered "military spartan" when she was being polite. And it did make for a good place to raise a boy, in spite of the chill Reaper felt in the air.

"And what's that?" Mary said as Reaper drew the long wooden case from the barracks bag and laid it down on a low cabinet along the wall of the living room.

"Something I've been making for Ricky," Reaper said as he unlatched the case. "It's a sword from that movie he liked so much, *The Two Towers*. There's some reproductions of the movie blades on the market, but this is a lot more like the real thing."

"A sword?" Mary said with exasperation in her voice. "That's what you consider a present for him?

Just what is he supposed to do with it? He's a twelve-year-old boy and you made him a weapon an adult would have a hard time handling."

Suddenly, Mary stopped talking and just looked at the floor. When she lifted her head, she looked as if she hadn't slept in a day.

"You said things would change," Mary continued in a tired voice, "I waited after you had to leave the Navy, and things didn't change. You went through job after job and things didn't change. No job was good enough, or exciting enough if you really want to be honest about the situation. You spent your time training and staying in shape in case something came through that would let you strap a holster on again—and it never did.

"You never spent enough time with Richard. You still call him Ricky. He prefers the more mature name Richard now. Instead of learning what your own son liked, you were always trying to make things better for us, and just succeeded in making them worse. You weren't there for us when you were in the Teams, and you aren't there for us now. Instead, you try to buy your way back into a boy's heart with gifts—long, sharp, deadly gifts."

"It's not all that sharp," Reaper said.

"And that means what coming from a SEAL?" Mary said sharply. "That you can't shave with it?

"Oh, Ted," she continued in a sad tone of voice, "don't you see that nothing has changed really? I know that your heart's in the right place, but your judgment is still flawed. This is just an example of that. He's just a twelve-year-old boy, and not even that until his birthday next month.

"Now you go and make him this extravagant gift. It's not a toy, or something he can safely play with. It's not even something that he can show his friends outside of the house. It's a weapon. One made for a man, not a young boy. If he was to take this to school to show the class what his father had made him, do you know what they would do? They would expel him for bringing a weapon onto school grounds!"

Reaper made a strong effort not to raise his voice or get angry. He was not going to let his boy come into the house just to hear his parents having another argument, a habit that they had been seeming to fall into every time they got together over the last months. But he was getting heated up, Mary knew instinctively which of his hot buttons to push, even when she didn't seem to intentionally want to. This lecturing-schoolteacher mode of hers was one that had always grated on him.

This was what their marriage had become, one long set of arguments. Sometimes the fights had been about money, a lot of the time it had been about work, or his drinking, or his going out with friends until all hours of the night. Sometimes, the reason for the arguments just seemed to be to have a fight. It wasn't how two people were supposed to live with each other, certainly not while trying to raise a young son. It was the constant fighting that had finally driven Reaper out of the house, officially separating the marriage, months before.

He knew that a lot of what was wrong came from his frustrations at trying to start up a new career. He had been exercising hard, working out with weights and running, to try and burn out some of the stresses he had been feeling. But here he was with his wife again, and she had made him feel inadequate and stupid within minutes of his entering the house. And what she had to say next made him feel worse.

"I just can't keep going on like this, Ted," Mary said, "and I won't. It's not healthy for either of us or for Richard. I've contacted the lawyer and told him to go ahead with the paperwork for the divorce."

"You didn't have to go through with that," Reaper said. "We said we would give it some time and try to get things back together. This," he pointed at the sword, "this was just what I could do right now. I'm not trying to make up for anything by giving him this. I thought he could put it up on his wall and think of his old man. I'm trying to make it better, the shop, the work, it all has a chance of getting better. It will just take some time. . . ."

"I did give it time, Ted," Mary said cutting him off. "And things haven't gotten any better. You know it scares me when you come home sometimes now. I never know if you've gone out and tied one on again. And Richard is afraid, too. The lawyer told me that if I had a restraining order put out on you, it would cost you your job. That the new gun laws would make it illegal for you to have firearms if there was a restraining order in force against you. So please, just listen to what I want and leave. You can see Richard some other time."

Reaper just stood there for a moment frustrated at the situation and the fact that he couldn't do anything about it. He wouldn't take it out on this woman, whom he had loved deeply and was the mother of his son. This wasn't a fight he had been trained for—though the situation was common enough among the men of the Teams. Right now, it would be better if he left rather than say something to make the situation even worse.

"Please let Ricky, I mean Richard, have the sword when he gets home," Reaper said tightly as he kept a grip on himself. "You can always just put it away until he's older. Tell him that I love him and I'll see him later."

"All right," Mary said, "I will. But please call first before you come over. I'll let you know what the plans are for his birthday next month."

"Thank you for that much," Reaper said as he turned to the door. Seething with anger but keeping it tightly under control, he went to his bike and kick-started it hard. He backed out of the driveway and roared down the street. His anger at the situation was clouding what would otherwise be a constant alertness to his surroundings. He never noticed the Ford van parked down the street with its engine running, with two men sitting in the front seats of the van and watching his house. As he turned the corner a block away and sped on, he never saw the van start moving forward toward his house.

———

During the ride back to the shop, Reaper considered just keeping going for a while. The words of Bob Seger and the Silver Bullet Band's song "Roll Me Away" ran though his head. He was more than "tired of his own voice" in the words of the song. But he wasn't going to be feeling free for a while, he had responsibilities to others and headed back to the shop. But the thought of heading to the mountaintops sure sounded good at the moment.

Once back at the shop, Reaper put his bike back on the kickstand and went into the house. Without looking for Deckert, who had already heard the garage door slam behind the big SEAL, Reaper headed back to his workbench in the shop. He slipped his Taurus back into his pocket, securing the spring clip that held the holster in place more from habit than from really thinking about it.

Pulling a stock Springfield Armory M1911A1 .45 automatic from the work rack next to his bench, he began to strip the weapon down in preparation to doing some custom work on it as ordered by a customer.

As he manipulated the parts of the pistol with an ease from long practice, Reaper found that he just couldn't concentrate on his work. After a few minutes of doing basically nothing with the gun, Reaper put the box he had placed the parts in back into a rack next to his bench and went up into the house to find Deckert.

"Keith," Reaper said as he entered the front showroom of the shop, "I'm going out for a run around the block."

Looking up from where he was bent over a log book on the front counter, Deckert just said, "okay," and went back to what he was reading. Deckert knew that Reaper was angry about whatever had happened back at his old home. Probably had another argument with Mary, was Deckert's thought.

The situation was too bad, he had hoped the couple would be able to get their problems behind them.

But Reaper was going out for a run, so things hadn't gone well.

An old habit from the Teams: when you felt bad, go for a run, when you felt good, go for a run. Hell, when it was raining, sunny, hot, or cold—you went for a run. And considering that the "blocks" in their part of the country tended to be one mile on a side, at least if you only counted the paved roads, Reaper was probably going to be gone for a while.

Reaper hadn't done anything more to prep for the run other than take his shop apron off and leave it by his bench. Trotting off down the road, the SEAL set out at an easy pace. Passing up the first side road, Reaper continued on with his feet steadily eating up the distance. The warm sun, clean air, and sounds of the spring peeper frogs in the ditches helped clear his mind. As he turned onto a one-mile run to the next major road, he was starting to feel better.

There wasn't anyone talking, there weren't any life decisions to make. There was just the steady effort of putting one foot in front of the other, the sound of his own easy breathing in his ears, and the country road stretching out in front of him. Keith Deckert referred to Reaper's penchant for working out as "getting his endorphin fix." The ex-Army sergeant was probably right, though Reaper would always say that he had to stay in shape for the training contracts they hoped to get for their new business.

Reaper had spent a tour of duty in the Teams as a First Phase instructor at BUD/S, the basic Underwater Demolition/SEAL course, teaching land warfare among other skills. Combined with his other experiences in the Teams, he could be a real asset to a police or security organization, training their people to face the new threats in the post-9/11, Operation Iraqi Freedom and Operation Enduring Freedom, United States. That was what he had convinced his friend Keith was a real business opportunity.

So they had extended themselves in the shop. They now had their Type 07 federal firearms license and had paid for their special occupational tax stamp.

All that expensive paper meant that they could deal in any kind of firearm, including National Firearms Act (NFA) weapons such as automatic weapons, suppressors, short shotguns, and the like. That was how they had legally obtained the license to produce the Jackhammer. Now they could stock additional NFA weapons, such as they could afford, in order to demonstrate them for possible sales to police departments. Along with the guns, they were carrying a select line of police and security equipment.

Even with the possible divorce, maybe Reaper could still make things work out between himself and Mary—for the sake of their son if not for themselves. He had stopped drinking almost altogether—the exercise had helped with that. Besides, he didn't have his Teammates around at all hours as they had been in San Diego. Which was actually something that he missed from time to time.

As he started approaching the shop, Reaper's mind was calmer than it had been when he set out for his run forty-two minutes earlier and six miles ago. As he approached the shop, he could see two cars in the driveway in front of the house. One of the cars was a black 2000 Pontiac Grand Am GT. A nice enough car and not the usual thing that was parked in front of the shop.

The other car in the drive was a real classic, a 1972 silver Corvette Stingray hardtop, complete with the chrome bumpers, the last year they had produced the car in that style. The fiberglass-bodied sports car looked like a low, flat shark with a bright silver grin. As Reaper trotted up to the front door of the shop, he figured maybe he was spending too much time talking about cars with an old-school Detroit gear-head like Deckert.

The overall good feeling Reaper had from his run evaporated instantly as he stepped through the doors of the farmhouse and turned into the retail showroom of the shop. He quietly took in the stunning scene without showing any surprise or emotion. Deckert was sitting in his chair at the far right corner of the customers area of the showroom. He was on the public side of the counters, but that was the least of what was wrong in the room. Reaper immediately accessed the situation as a combat equation—and the factors of that equation were three other men in the room.

In the center of the room was a slender man of medium height and slightly swarthy complexion. In his light brown camel's hair blazer, gray woolen trousers, light blue silk shirt with a silver silk tie, and black leather kidskin gloves, Arzee looked like a country gentleman who might be trying out top-grade double shotguns prior to going out on a grouse hunt. The Jackhammer shotgun in his hands looked like anything but a graceful hunting weapon. Still, the open breech of the weapon told Reaper that it was empty and the man wasn't an immediate threat.

The tailored suit and styled haircut did not disguise the oily nature of the man underneath it all. His highly polished black oxford shoes looked as if they were replaced immediately if they were ever scuffed. From all of the man's carefully crafted style, Reaper figured he knew who drove the Corvette, the man he was identifying as Suit.

The glass display case on the wall behind the Suit was empty. That was where the four prototype Jackhammers had been racked up. The long boxes of ammunition cassettes that had been on the bottom of the case were missing along with the other three guns. These three thugs did not appear to be running a simple gun robbery, otherwise they would have probably just shot Reaper as he came in the door. No, they had been waiting for him to return from his run. There was something more they wanted.

Reaper's training and experience had him immediately identifying the levels of threat in the room, assessing the situation, and quantifying his response. For all of its complexity, his reactions spanned barely seconds before he had completed his judgments. He didn't know the threat's names, and didn't care. Reaper quickly put his own identifiers, as good as a name to him, on the strangers in the room.

Immediately to his right, barely a step away, was a thug who Reaper categorized as little more than a musclehead. Maybe five feet ten, 235 pounds, with swarthy skin and buzz-cut black hair, the thug was heavily muscled with almost no neck showing. The tan sports jacket and black turtleneck sweater were probably intended by the man to maximize the visual impact of his size.

The muscles looked to have come from hours of pumping iron, but their appearance told Reaper that this was a vain man. Although his workouts were the kind that increased the size of his chest and arms, the musclehead didn't look like he spent as much time on his legs, building up his size in a more symmetrical manner.

The man also moved stiffly, musclebound from all of his exercise. In spite of a more limited range of motion in his arms and legs, the big man was fast enough. Stepping up behind Reaper, the musclehead grabbed the SEAL from behind, securing a solid grip on both of his upper arms. The thug held no weapon and probably thought with his muscles and little else. But at that moment, he didn't need a weapon.

To the left, standing behind the Suit so that he could clearly cover both Reaper and Deckert, was a gunman who was pointing a massive Desert Eagle semiautomatic pistol at Reaper. The gunman had covered the SEAL from the moment he had entered the room. The muzzle of the big pistol looked to be about a .44-magnum caliber.

The gunman was only about five four in height, slight in build with tan skin, black hair, and a bushy mustache, wearing a loose brown sports jacket, unbuttoned over a black shirt and black pants. Reaper classified him as a gun weasel—he had the look of a little man who had something to prove with a big gun. That big gun made him the most immediate visible threat in the room.

He may have been slight in stature, but the gun weasel held the Desert Eagle in a steady hand. The hammer was back on the big pistol. That fact cut back on the possible openings for Reaper to secure the gun.

But who in his right mind would carry such a massive piece of hardware? The gun was impractical to carry concealed for someone even Reaper's size, and it was heavy to drag around as well. For all of its weight, the power of the Desert Eagle made it a real handful to control. But that same power was probably why this gun weasel carried such a piece—compensation for his stature and build.

The little man had the only two threatening weapons visible in anyone's hands in the showroom. The Desert Eagle remained steady in the man's right hand while his left kept covering Deckert with an M1911A1 .45 automatic. By the look of the smoldering hate combined with frustration in Deckert's face, the gun weasel was probably adding insult to injury by threatening him with his own weapon.

Reaper noted the location of everyone in the room and cataloged their probable threat level. He just watched as the man snapped the thumb safety on to the M1911A1 and slipped the pistol into the waistband of his trousers. As the gun weasel approached Reaper, he pulled the big Desert Eagle back against his right hip, keeping it out of the way of a chance grab. Reaper didn't move at all as the other man used his free left hand to snatch the Taurus revolver from Reaper's right front pocket.

After slipping the Taurus into his own pocket, the gun weasel conducted a cursory pat-down. With a curt "he's clean," the gun weasel stepped back away from Reaper. The little man didn't realize just how serious a mistake he had made in his poorly done search. He had taken the obvious weapon, but hardly the only one the SEAL had.

In Reaper's right front pocket, clipped behind the holster and along the rear seam of the Levi's, was a green G10-handled Emerson CQC-7BW folding knife. The 3.3-inch-long chisel-ground Tanto-style blade was razor-sharp. Not exactly a sword, but better than nothing in the hands of a trained man. And Reaper was a very well-trained man.

Chapter Seven

Turning to the counter to his right, Arzee casually set the Jackhammer shotgun down before turning back to Reaper.

"Mister Reaper, I presume," Arzee said with a small smile, "so good to meet you. I've read excellent things about your work here."

"You'll have to excuse me if I don't shake hands," Reaper said. "And you are?"

"Yes," Arzee said, "well, I thought it would be necessary for my friend there behind you to restrain your enthusiasm lest it get the better of you. And I think we can forgo the formality of names for now."

Reaper could see the reflection of the man he now thought of as Musclehead, in the glass of a display case. The big thug smiled broadly at Arzee's words and squeezed down hard on both of Reaper's upper arms. Reaper showed no reaction to the crushing of his arms. His hands started turning dark red and then Musclehead lightened up his grip after a sharp word from Arzee. Gun Weasel, the SEAL's name for the little man, just kept watch on Reaper and Deckert, no smile, no reaction, and no wavering of the big Desert Eagle in his hand.

Sure of his own strength, Musclehead was holding Reaper in what he considered a firm, unbreakable grip. But Reaper knew half a dozen ways he could disable Musclehead and break free in a moment. Gun Weasel was another matter entirely. After he had put away Reaper's and Deckert's guns, he had moved to a spot on the other side of the room where he would watch both men without having to turn his head. He knew the weapons he was holding gave him range, and he was using that distance as a safety measure.

Gun Weasel was more than six feet from Reaper. If the range had been four feet, Reaper may have had a chance. But more than six feet was too far away. One thing Reaper had was patience. The Suit wanted to talk about something. If this had been a robbery or some kind of straightforward murder, Reaper and Deckert would already be dead. So the SEAL stayed very alert, watching for his opportunity to show itself. It would come, and he could wait for it while listening to what Arzee had to say.

The thugs did not know how hopelessly they were outclassed. But Arzee knew, or at least suspected. The specter of sudden death was fluttering its leathery wings around the room, and that was making Arzee nervous. In the final analysis, Arzee was nothing more than a street thug who had made good. Now, he was looking at someone who was truly dangerous— a cleaned-up junkyard dog was looking at a timber wolf.

"I wouldn't want anything to happen to you until we concluded our business," Arzee said to Reaper.

"This is not the way people normally conduct a business meeting," Reaper said. "Besides, what possible business could I have with you?"

"Why, the gun business, of course," Arzee said. "It seems I'm in need of someone with the proper materials. This weapon of yours is just the thing to aid some associates of mine. We already have the others packed away outside, I was just admiring this specimen as you came in."

"You have got to be out of your fucking mind," Reaper said. "What kind of crack-brained raghead idea is that? You catch something that affected your mind while out there butt-fucking these girls you brought with you?"

Reaper was speaking with deliberate crudity. If he could get this character to lose his temper and get in the line of fire between himself and Gun Weasel, that could make the opportunity Reaper needed to begin his move. But Arzee wasn't taking the bait.

"Please, Mr. Reaper," Arzee said. "You are much more intelligent than that. I realize that you are not going to do business with me openly—you never would. I couldn't offer you enough money to do so. And these men aren't going to be what it takes to convince you to supply what I want. They could break you into pieces and you would try to spit in my eye with your last breath—and by the looks your partner there is giving me, he would do the same if not more."

Deckert just sat in his chair and looked at Arzee. He also had lots of patience and would wait as long as needed. Deckert knew the limitations his wheel-chair gave him, but he also knew that if he could force an opening, Reaper would react to the chance. He didn't know these people from Adam, but it was obvious that at least the snappy dresser had history with Reaper. Suddenly, a cellular phone began to ring.

"Excuse me for a moment," Arzee said with exaggerated courtesy as he reached into his pocket. Pulling out a phone, he snapped it open and listened to it for a moment.

"Ah, as I expected," Arzee said. "It's for you, Mr. Reaper."

Reaching out, he set the phone down on the carpet-covered counter and slid it to within reach of Reaper. Musclehead turned Reaper toward the counter and released his right arm.

"Careful now," Arzee said to Reaper as Gun Weasel pointed the Desert Eagle and pulled up the M1911A1 with his left hand. "I'm certain that this call will be very important to you."

Reaper's face showed no expression as he reached for the phone. He was puzzled as to just what might be going on, but he was also still watching for his opportunity. The voice at the other end of the phone caused Reaper's blood to run cold for a moment. A buzzing seemed to fill his ears as he heard a quavering voice at the other end of the line. A very familiar voice.

"Hello?" said Mary, with stark terror obvious in her tone. "Ted? Is that you?"

"Mary," Reaper said with a catch in his voice, "are you all right?"

"They haven't hurt me," she said. "Two men

wearing masks barged in just after you left. They waited until Ricky came home and took us both from the house. They put blindfolds on us and made me make some phone calls after driving us somewhere.

"Oh, Ted," Mary said as her voice started to break down completely. "I'm so scared. Why is this happening to us? What do they want? Who are these peop . . ."

And the phone was cut off at the other end of the line.

"Before you make any unnecessary threats of retribution," Arzee said, relaxing now as he felt he fully had the upper hand, "let me tell you that nothing is going to happen to your family as long as you do what I want."

He reached forward and took the phone from the SEAL's unresisting hand. Folding it, Arzee slipped it into Reaper's shirt pocket.

"You will be contacted on that phone with further details," Arzee said. "It's completely untraceable so there's no use trying to track me down with it. Only I have the number to it, so only I will call you on it. Please do not feel beholden for the small gift, I have another I assure you," and he patted his inside jacket pocket.

"Do as I say and complete our business, and the last call will be directions for you to meet up with your family. Oh, and I really wouldn't bother calling in the police or FBI. It seems your wife called some people and told them that she was leaving the area with your son for a while. She didn't feel quite safe what with a pending divorce and all. So she took your son out of school, made herself unavailable for work, and, for all intents and purposes, has disappeared for a while. Seems having an ex-SEAL for a husband makes a woman being frightened for herself quite understandable to some people.

"So, even if you go to the police," Arzee said with a broad smile, "the chances are that they will blame you for her being missing.

"And the words of a fellow veteran," Arzee said as he turned to Deckert, "would at best be discounted. If not, well, I'm sure you can figure out that very little evidence will be found. And you can't be sure just where that evidence would point."

"It seems you have all the bases covered," Reaper said calmly. "What do you want me to do?"

If Arzee had known the big SEAL at all, he would have recognized that soft tone of voice as being the warning of a very dangerous situation. Paxtun hadn't known that in Bosnia, and Arzee didn't know it now. Reaper was fluid and smooth, and ready to explode into action, with nothing showing as a warning at all.

"I will be leaving first," Arzee said, "just so there are no misunderstandings. Neither of my two companions here know where your family will be staying, so they couldn't tell you anything if they wanted to.

"After I am safely away, you and your partner here will set to work making more of these nasty pieces of firepower. You have three days, seventy-two hours from now, to produce four more of these weapons along with a half-dozen of these ammunition cassettes for each of them. I have been told that is a reasonable number and shouldn't be any problem for you to make.

"And I assure you, if any problems do arise, you

had better solve them instantly or someone else very dear to you will pay the penalty. You simply deliver the weapons and we will have concluded our business. Your family will be returned to you and we will go on our way."

"How do I know I can trust you to return my family no matter what I give you?" Reaper said.

"You don't," Arzee said with a nasty smile. "But your options are very limited. I suggest you and your partner plan on some long work days. Make a big pot of coffee."

With that, Arzee headed toward the door. Even Gun Weasel was more relaxed as he let Arzee pass through the line of fire between him and Reaper, dropping down the Eagle's muzzle as the man went by. But he still had the .45 aimed at Deckert, so that was not the opportunity Reaper was looking for.

Musclehead was still holding Reaper by the arms, though his grip on the SEAL's right arm was very light. Arzee went out the door and the men all heard the sound of a 454 cubic inch Big Block V-8 fire up a few moments later. The rumble of the engine's 270 horsepower quickly faded as the Corvette moved up the driveway and turned west down the main road.

"So, little man," Deckert said as he looked at Gun Weasel. "Your boss left you holding the bag while he made sure of his getaway?"

Gun Weasel turned and looked coldly at the big man in the wheelchair.

"Feels neat doesn't it?" Deckert said. "You come along just so that you could look down at somebody shorter than you? That must be it. Little man, great big gun. You probably need such a stupid gun because you hit like a pussy. I wonder just what you're trying to compensate for? Short stature or short something else?"

With a sudden movement, Gun Weasel stepped forward and snapped out with his left hand, backhanding the steel slide of the .45 across the left side of Deckert's head. The blow rocked the big man in his wheelchair as blood spurted from a cut on his left ear. It was just by luck that the cushioning of the ear had kept the blow from breaking the squamous portion of the temporal bone of Deckert's skull.

As the big man slumped in the chair, Gun Weasel suddenly laid the .45 down on the counter to his right and grabbed the armrest of the chair. Twisting and lifting hard, Gun Weasel flipped up the chair and dumped Deckert to the ground. Deckert lay slumped and unmoving as Gun Weasel panted at the exertion. It had been a much heavier chair than he had expected. Turning, he faced Reaper—less than four feet away.

Without a single outward sign of preparation or tension, Reaper exploded, suddenly snap-kicking Gun Weasel square in the groin. The top of Reaper's foot drove Gun Weasel's scrotum up into his pubic arch, the testicles just missing being crushed against the juncture of the ossa innominata bones of the pelvis.

The intense pain of the blow drove a cloud of blackness through Gun Weasel's brain as green and yellow lights flashed in front of his eyes. The small man wasn't dead, but he was going to wish he was when the blessing of unconsciousness wore off. He slipped to the ground as the huge Desert Eagle pistol fell from his nerveless fingers.

As part of the same action with which he snapkicked Gun Weasel, Reaper shoved back with his left leg, forcing himself back against Musclehead. The SEAL's powerful leg smashed Musclehead's back against the shelving units on the wall behind him. A steel reloading press extending out from a shelf smashed into the thug's back, bruising his right kidney and forcing him to throw up his right hand in shock.

Reaper smashed back with an open-fist backhand blow from his right arm, striking Musclehead above his right eye, splitting open his eyebrow. Reversing the motion of his hand and arm, Reaper snapped his right hand into his right front pants pocket.

A practiced grip secured the Emerson CQC-7BW between the thumb and first two fingers of Reaper's hand. Continuing the motion, Reaper smoothly drew the folding knife back, pulling it out and down while dragging the back of the blade against the rear seam of the pocket. The Wave, a small semicircular notch on the back of the blade—the *W* in the identifier of the knife—completed its intended purpose by snagging against the rear seam of the pocket and forcing the blade to open against the resistance. The blade pulled open and was secured by the liner-lock snapping into place.

Reaper pulled his hand forward and up, still holding the blade between his thumb and two fingers, allowing the weight of the open blade to pivot the knife into a point-down position. Grabbing hold of the handle in a hammer grip with his thumb over the pommel for additional leverage, Reaper pivoted on his left foot while pulling his left arm away from Musclehead's weakened grip.

Grabbing the injured man's arm, Reaper slammed it down on the carpeted top of the counter to his left. In a continuing motion, Reaper drove the knife down in an icepick stab—right through Musclehead's forearm.

The angular Tanto point and slicing chisel edge of the blade slipped through skin, fascia, and muscle—missing the major blood vessels and tendons though it nicked the posterior interosseous vein as it passed between the radius and ulna bones. The tip of the blade sliced through the carpet that padded the top of the counter and sank deeply into the wood beneath. The knife had penetrated so deeply that part of the grip was driven into the wound.

For such a large man, Musclehead made a very high-pitched scream as he sank to his knees, stopping short as his arm pulled against the embedded knife. The entire action, from the start of the snap kick to the blade sinking into the wood, had not lasted two seconds.

Musclehead was not going anywhere for a while, certainly not until someone removed the pinning knife. The pain of the wound, and the fact that the side of the blade was pressing against a branch of his median nerve, would keep Musclehead from even considering trying to pull the blade out himself.

Continuing with the circular motion of his body, Reaper turned to face where Gun Weasel lay on the floor. The Desert Eagle was to the man's side, where Reaper stepped over and picked up the huge weapon.

Gun Weasel was unconscious, though breathing raggedly. He was not an immediate concern.

Turning back to Musclehead, Reaper took a quick glance at his handiwork with a knife. He could see that there was no arterial spurting from the wound around the blade, the hilt of which was deep into the arm. It wasn't that he was at all concerned for Musclehead's welfare, but he might need information from him later. The thug probably wouldn't bleed to death, though falling into shock was a very real possibility. Reaper grabbed Musclehead's right hand and slapped it down against the thug's inside upper left arm.

"Hold it or die," Reaper said grimly. Then he turned to where Deckert lay on the floor.

His friend's eyes were open and he was aware of what Reaper had done—he had been only feigning unconsciousness to try and give Reaper his chance.

"You about done now?" Deckert said.

"Yeah," Reaper said as he pulled his friend up and righted the wheelchair. Helping Deckert back into the chair, Reaper grabbed the M1911A1 lying on the counter and put it in his partner's hand.

The situation was moving fast and Reaper didn't notice the mistake he had just made. His immediate concerns were for his friend and his family. And the only certain source of information about Reaper's family was getting farther away by the moment. Snatching up a rag from the counter, Reaper pressed it against the side of Deckert's head where he was still bleeding.

"Okay, enough," Deckert said, "I'll be all right.

You have to get after that asshole in the suit. Take the cab, I can hold these two."

Deckert waved to the key cabinet underneath the cash register behind him. "Get the keys and move you slow-ass squid," he growled. "Leave this mess to me."

His friend was hurt but functioning. And Reaper knew that his family was in real danger. Reaper accepted the situation and dashed around the counter, slowing only long enough to grab the indicated set of car keys as he headed back to the garage.

But just as Reaper was leaving, he heard Musclehead, still in his pained voice, futilely scream at the unconscious Gun Weasel, "Get up. We've got to stop that crazy Marine from going after Arzee!"

Now Reaper knew who he was chasing—this Arzee character could expect a lot of pain unless Reaper found his family, safe and alive, soon.

Chapter Eight

Closest to the house door of the garage was Keith Deckert's favorite vehicle. Even if he wasn't able to drive it as he had in the past, he meticulously maintained the stealth hotrod he had built, keeping it ready to go at a moment's notice. As Reaper dashed into the garage, hitting the garage door opener on the wall, he lowered the hammer on the Desert Eagle that he was still holding and stuck the big pistol into his pants pocket. Then he started pulling the protective tarp covering off the car as the door started to rise.

Removing the tarp revealed nothing more exciting-looking than a 1972 model Checker cab. The square, boxy front end of the cab, with its two pairs of headlights held in oval chrome metal frames at the upper corners, had the styling of a 1950s-era family sedan. The vehicle even had the white plastic roof light with the name CHECKER on it in block lettering. The whole body of the cab was bright yellow with a white-and-black checkerboard stripe running along either side of the body and doors. The outside of the vehicle was purely just a Checker cab, but a lot of the inner workings no longer were.

The car was a "sleeper." What you saw was not what you got. Keith Deckert had built the Checker cab over years as a pet project. The only time the Checker was really seen in public was during what was called the Woodward Dream Cruise in the summer where the sound of the vehicle was a popular favorite.

Under the hood of the Checker was a 454 Chevy Big Block V-8 engine bored out oversize to 505 cubic inches and fitted with forged extra-strength pistons. The engine had large diameter custom-formed headers and a big single 2x4 Holley four-barrel carburetor giving it a base horsepower of 550. A precharger kept the engine's oil up, lubricating the system and eliminating warm-up oil problems. The Checker could move out at top speed very soon after starting.

The power of the engine went through a rebuilt heavy-duty Turbo-Hydramatic 400 transmission with a Griner aluminum billet racing valve-body and a 3.73:1 differential gear on the rear axle. The suspension of the cab had been beefed up with extra control arms with solid bushings. A remote cutout in the exhaust system allowed the muffler to be by-passed by the driver at the flip of a switch.

With the muffler cutout operating, the roar of the engine could deafen people standing close by. More than just a noise producer, the cutout system added a few more horsepower to increase the speed of the cab. That wasn't the only trick under the deceptive body of the Checker. The vehicle and engine had been fitted with a Holley Cheater nitrous oxide system (NOS).

In the trunk was bolted down a twenty-pound bottle of nitrous oxide. The gas bottle had a Holley NOS remote bottle control so the driver didn't even have to open the trunk to turn on the main valve. Turning a switch on the dashboard would remotely open the gas bottle and charge up the system.

After Deckert had tuned the big Chevy engine and knew what he wanted, and what the V-8 would accept, he had fitted the carburetor with his choice of the metering jets that finally bled the nitrous oxide into the air/fuel flow. A remote key switch on the dashboard would arm the NOS system. Lifting the red safety cover and flipping the lighted blue toggle switch underneath it would open the electric solenoids that released the nitrous oxide into the engine.

With the nitrous going, the roar of the Chevy V-8 would sound like it belonged on the deck of an aircraft carrier as the exhaust cutouts would automatically open if they hadn't already been set that way.

It was a lot more than sound that resulted from dumping nitrous oxide into a carburetor and an engine system tuned for it. For a maximum of thirty seconds, the engine would suddenly have 250 extra horsepower. The top speed of the Checker was over 130 miles an hour with the tricked-out V-8. Pushed by 800 horsepower, the Checker would top out at over 160 miles an hour as it accelerated from the nitrous. The Checker became a huge, blunt steel missile.

The weakness of the system was that the vehicle

just couldn't maneuver well. At speed, the cab had a huge turning radius, and even then it risked flipping free of the road surface. In a straight line, the vehicle was in its element. The main limiting factor of the Checker was that it couldn't push the air out of its way any faster.

Opening the door and climbing into the cab, Reaper pulled out the Desert Eagle and tossed it down on the seat next to him. He pulled up the seat harness with its double shoulder straps and locked it in place around his waist. Sticking the key into the ignition, he fired up the big engine and it caught on the first crank.

The interior of the garage echoed with the sudden roar of something that was definitely not your average car engine. The sound quickly settled into a muted rumble as the muffler of the exhaust system suppressed the sound of the engine. Stopping for a moment, Reaper used both hands to disconnect the NOS safety key from the key ring. Sticking the key into its socket on the dashboard to the right of the ignition key, Reaper turned it and the light came on under the NOS switch. The red safety cover of the nitrous switch now glowed like a spot of blood on the dashboard, the lettering that said ARMED easily visible.

Reaper quickly backed out of the garage and started after the Corvette. The expression on his face was one of grim purposefulness, one you would not want to see if you were the reason for it in the first place.

Being way back in the country now worked very well in Reaper's favor. There was only one way back to the highway, the main road to Detroit. The chance that the Corvette had turned north was minimal. The only thing for miles in that direction was more open country and then Port Huron thirty miles away. To the east was the Huron River and Canada on the other side. But the Corvette had Michigan plates on it. Reaper followed his instinct and turned in the direction of the highway.

———

Having lived in the city for most of his life, Arzee did not spend much time in the country. Having grown up in the dirt and squalor of the industrial areas around Detroit, he hated the dirt fields and mud of the country. He did find the open rural areas had one advantage that appealed to him. While traveling over the country roads, Arzee had been speeding, but not by very much.

He barreled through a long S-curve in the road and felt the Vette stick to the ground like it was running on a track. Traffic seemed to be nonexistent on the well-maintained long country road. There was a huge stretch of marshland to his left and just the occasional farmhouse, barn, or outbuilding breaking up the trees and fields to his right.

Coming out of the turn, he was looking down a several-miles-long stretch of empty road that had no stops, turns, or traffic, very little even in the way of crossroads except for one every mile or so. It was a big temptation to let the classic Corvette stretch out a bit, a temptation that Arzee indulged himself in.

The 350 cubic inch V-8 under the long, low hood growled louder as Arzee fed more fuel into its four-barrel carburetor. Two-hundred horsepower pushed the streamlined sports car down the road as the speedometer swept past sixty miles an hour, on its way to seventy.

Arzee was a few miles from the gunshop and well satisfied with the way things had gone. Paxtun had told him that Reaper was an ex-Navy SEAL, as if that was supposed to frighten him. Reaper may have helped force Paxtun out of the service, but that hadn't meant anything to Arzee when he met Reaper. Sure, the guy looked like he could be a hardcase, but you didn't always judge things just by looks. This tough SEAL crap was just a bunch of Hollywood hype and TV bullshit. When it had come right down to it, Reaper had just stood there and done nothing while Arzee had told him exactly what was what and how things were going to be done. So much for tough looks.

As far as Arzee was concerned, it didn't take much in the way of brains to pull a trigger for the military, and Arzee had little respect for those men who had joined the Army, Navy, or whatever rather than try to make it on the outside as he had.

The plan Arzee had put together to secure the guns and maintain a tight leash on Reaper looked as if it would work fine. If Reaper went to the police and complained about his family's disappearance, he would have to convince the officers that his wife had been kidnapped, and that might take some doing.

It was far more likely that the authorities would think Reaper had done in his family himself—the idea of a rogue ex-SEAL committing such a crime wouldn't be hard to swallow. The phone call the wife had been forced to make to the local police saying she was in fear of her life would reinforce that idea.

When Reaper supplied the guns they wanted, their firepower should be enough to satisfy Ishmael that Paxtun's organization was doing all that it could to support their Islamic brothers in their struggle. If the guns were recovered down the line after Ishmael had used them, they could only be traced to Reaper—who would have already committed "suicide" in his remorse over killing his wife, and then his business partner. At least that would be the way any carefully planted evidence would point.

The problem about the lost weapons looked to be under control. Arzee was very glad he had found the information about Reaper's family and was able to put it to immediate use.

His men would be leaving the gunshop about now, if they weren't already gone. Arzee expected little trouble from that quarter. The hardware would be secured. He was certain that Reaper and his partner would work their asses off to turn out more of the exotic shotguns over the next three days—just as they had been told to.

From what Paxtun had said, Chief Reaper's weakness for children and families had been demonstrated in Bosnia. The kids there hadn't even been his brats. With his own wife and child being held hostage, he couldn't risk any harm coming to them.

Arzee was quite proud of the way his plan had unfolded. There would be loose ends, but those could be made to disappear. With Reaper as a cutout, any investigation leading to him would stop there. What specifically was to be done with him, his friend, and his family could be decided later after his usefulness was at an end.

The S-curve wasn't much more than a quarter mile behind Arzee when he noticed another vehicle coming up behind him in the rearview mirror. Whatever it was, it certainly wasn't a cop car unless he was passing by Mayberry out here in the sticks. His radar detector hadn't gone off and it didn't look like any cop car he had seen outside of an old movie or TV show. It was some kind of boxy, vintage design, with a front grill like an old Plymouth or something. Still, the old beast was catching up to him. He'd let it get closer and figure out what it was before bolting away in a real performance car.

When he looked in the mirror again, Arzee could see that the old car was noticeably closer. He could make out some details now and was astonished to see that it was a cab of all things that was catching up to him. His surprise caused him to let up on the gas, slowing slightly, allowing the cab to close up even more.

Just what was a cab doing way out here? Some farm clod needed a ride? That was going to be some fare. This was not the area where you could expect a cab to just be passing by. The driver must have had the gas pedal pushing through the floorboards to be catching up to the Vette the way it was.

Then the cab was close enough that Arzee could make out real details, and what he saw caused his blood to freeze. There was a sudden buzzing in his ears as his blood pressure skyrocketed and his skin itched from muscular reaction. Behind the wheel of that cab was Reaper! And his expression made him look like death itself was driving that horrible yellow car.

Arzee was suddenly so scared that he whimpered a little, though he couldn't hear himself do so. In fact, he would have found it almost impossible to make any coherent sound given the fact that his mouth and throat had suddenly gone as dry as a sun-pounded beach in August. He pressed down on the gas pedal, trusting in the power of his classic car to run away from the devil in a box that was right behind him. Slowly, he started to pull away.

Chapter Nine

Reaper watched the Vette start to accelerate. Whatever was under the hood, it was a sure thing that the Vette could outmaneuver the Checker. For the moment, the straight stretch of road they were on took away that advantage. Now they were in a race that the Checker could win—if he could stop the speeding sports car.

Reaper reached down to the seat next to him and put his hand on the Desert Eagle. For a moment he considered opening fire with the big pistol, which he had confirmed was a .44 magnum with a fresh round in the chamber. The Vette was low and fast, but Arzee wasn't moving around the road much at all. He was just trying to outrun the Checker. His mistake.

The fiberglass body of the Corvette Stingray wouldn't offer very much resistance to the 240-grain jacketed hollow points loaded in the Eagle. They would barely be slowed as they smashed through the body of the sports car. Of course, that was also the problem. If Reaper misaimed or one of the magnum slugs was deflected off a metal component, he could end up hitting Arzee. And that could cost him the only solid source of information that he could be sure knew where his family was.

No, the pistol wasn't going to be the answer, and Reaper lifted his hand away from it. Instead, he reached to the dashboard and flipped the switch that operated the muffler cutout solenoids. The exhaust pipes were now blowing straight out into the open air. The sound of the big V-8 roared out unabated. A flock of ducks in the marsh to the left jumped into the sky, flying away quacking and protesting the violent noise. The drop in back pressure inside the exhaust system gave the Checker more horsepower and increased its speed.

———

The reaction inside of the Vette was close to being the same as that of the ducks. There wasn't any quacking, but Arzee was starting to feel a little panic. He could hear the sound of the Checker's engine even over the roar of his own 350 V-8. That yellow beast was going to catch him. He would have to try to outmaneuver it.

Coming up in the distance, Arzee could see a road sign that showed he was approaching a T-intersection. According to the sign, another road would be going off to the right. If he could make the turn, the Checker couldn't at the speed it was going. It would either have to slow down to make it, or it would miss the turn entirely and have to come back to it. Either way, it would put a lot of space between the two cars and give Arzee a better chance of getting away, or maybe even ambushing the Checker himself. It was going to be a desperate gamble, but Arzee knew his driving was up to the challenge.

Arzee allowed the Vette to drift over to the left side of the road. The extra space would give him a better chance of making the upcoming turn. The gravel shoulders of the road would be a danger, but that was something he knew so he could watch out for it. Just as he was committing himself to the turn, a horrible blasting roar sounded out from behind him when the Checker cut out its muffler.

Startled by the sound, Arzee made the mistake of making the Corvette fishtail slightly as he jerked at the wheel. That was his undoing as he started to lose control of the car.

The rear of the Vette swung to the right, and Arzee twisted the steering wheel to compensate. The rear of the sports car then swung back to the left, going past the hard road surface and slipping out onto the gravel of the shoulder. The wheel on the gravel lost traction and spun, increasing the sideslip of the Vette. Overcompensating, Arzee pulled the wheel hard over to stop his skid—but it was far too late.

The back end of the Vette came back onto the roadway much harder than it should have. The car was now in a full spin and it was going to keep going until it lost speed or Arzee brought it under control. The side road Arzee wanted so desperately to take went past as the back end of the Vette skidded past it. The car was sideways across the road and still turning. It did a full turn and a half, finally coming to rest on the left side of the road, sideways across both lanes with the nose of the car pointed out to the marsh. Arzee was stunned, but he had the presence of mind to draw his weapon.

From underneath his jacket, Arzee fumbled trying to pull his SIG Pro automatic from his Galco Miami Classic shoulder holster. The handgun was hanging horizontally underneath his left arm and his hand finally grabbed the grip as his thumb popped free the safety strap. There was a reassuring feeling to the weapon and Arzee's hand started to pull it from the holster. The ten rounds of .40 Smith & Wesson ammo that were in the weapon would take care of Reaper. And there were two more full magazines under his right arm to help if he had to reload. Then Arzee looked out to the left of the car, toward the approaching sound, and his own scream was lost in the noise.

————

The two cars were almost evenly matched as far as top speed went. Reaper knew the area and turns were coming up where the Corvette would have the edge over the powerful but heavy Checker. This race had to end fast so Reaper decided to play his ace in the hole. Reaching over to the dashboard, he flipped up the red safety cover over the NOS switch. Bracing himself, Reaper flipped the switch.

Solenoids popped open and, from the rear of the Checker, nitrous oxide flowed forward into the carburetor and the combustion chambers of the engine. Suddenly, it was like the big V-8 was running on rocket fuel. Originally invented in order to give piston-engined fighters during World War II a source of emergency power, nitrous had been almost forgot-

ten during the age of jet aircraft. Racers had redis-
covered the advantages of the additive during the
1970s. Now, there were speed records held by cars
that had been running with nitrous oxide boosts.

Reaper was pushed back into the seat by the acceleration of the Checker. The engine roared out a solid
wall of sound through the muffler cutouts. The
speedometer climbed as Reaper hung onto the wheel.
He no longer needed the handgun lying on the seat
next to him. He was at the wheel of a huge projectile, a
guided missile, one he was able to aim very precisely.

As the sound of the nitrous-boosted engine
boomed out, Reaper watched as Arzee went onto the
gravel shoulder and lost control of his car. As the distance between the two vehicles closed, he saw the
Vette spin out and stop sideways across the road.
Reaper could now see Arzee sitting at the wheel
struggling to draw a weapon. That wasn't something
Reaper was going to allow to happen.

Indecision was not something a SEAL could tolerate. Neither could he afford to be reckless. Reaper
knew that Arzee was his best lead to finding his
family. But if Arzee killed him, he couldn't do his
family much good. He would just have to be very
careful and precise.

Moving his steering wheel only slightly, Reaper
lined up with the rear of the Vette. He saw Arzee's
mouth open in a scream just as the juggernaut that
the Checker had become smashed into the Vette.
Reaper had carefully aimed the cab to impact on the
right side of the Vette's back end. The heavy truck
frame of the Checker absorbed the energy of the
crash with ease. The bodywork crumpled a bit at the

left front fender, but that would be repairable. What happened to the Vette was not something that looked even salvageable.

The whole back end of the sports car had disappeared in a cloud of glass fragments and shattered fiberglass. The chrome back bumper flew off to land somewhere in the marsh, twisted and unrecognizable. From behind the front seat back, the Corvette Stingray ceased to exist. The front part of the car spun around completely before going off the road and partially sinking into the marsh. The huge noise of the impact terrified a large gaggle of Canadian geese who took off deeper into the marsh, the large birds honking in panic as their flapping wings and running feet took them across the top of the water.

The terrified flight of the big birds tore up the reeds and cattails in their way. The plants grew in huge patches all over the marsh. Now there were dozens of open paths ripped through the green plants radiating away from the crash site.

Chapter Ten

Arzee was spun about in the crash. Dizzy and disoriented, he realized that he had lost his weapon. That was the least of his worries for the moment. The recognizable portion of the Vette had slipped into the shallow water and he now was in real danger of drowning. What was left of the car was lying parallel to the road it had just left, the driver's door facing into the marsh and already half underwater. Clawing at his seat belt release, Arzee freed himself and pushed at the door. It wasn't latched, there wasn't anything left for the door to latch to—the rear door post was gone.

Scrambling out of the wrecked car, Arzee could hear the Checker screeching to a halt. He only had seconds before Reaper would come back for him. Now in a full-blown panic, Arzee half-crawled, half-swam, out into the marsh. Ducking under some plants and mulch, he clawed at the mud to pull himself forward. An almost primitive instinct to hide from the predator was all that directed his motions.

Covered in mud, slime, weeds, and dead brown cattails, Arzee pulled himself to the far side of a
muskrat mound and stuck his face down into the
stinking mud to hide.

———

Reaper flipped the safety cover down, shutting down
the NOS system once the smashed Vette was well
behind him. Pushing hard on the brakes, Reaper
made the Checker's tires smoke as he brought the
cab to a stop. Quickly shifting into reverse, Reaper
again tore rubber off his tires as he backed the vehicle up to where the remains of the Vette lay sinking
in the marsh.

Bits of the car's body were scattered all around.
The rear axle was down the road from the impact
site, mangled and barely recognizable as part of a
power train. Only the single wheel still in place
identified the axle for what it was. The other wheel
was nowhere to be seen. It had probably been
thrown a good distance and had sunk into the dark
waters of the marsh.

On the shoulder and facing into oncoming traffic
on the wrong side of the road, the Checker came to a
stop. Reaper rolled down the driver's window and
looked over the wreckage. The Desert Eagle was in
his hand, the hammer back and safety off. Reaper
carefully looked for any signs of a possibly armed and
uninjured Arzee. There were no signs of the man and
nothing but the slowly sinking front half of a smashed
and smoking car to show he had even been there.

Opening his door and stepping out of the
Checker, Reaper went down to where the wreckage

of the Vette lay. Stepping into the water, the SEAL looked for the missing man. There was no sign of Arzee, or of any blood indicating an injured man had been in the driver's seat. Reaper's best source of information was gone.

In spite of possibly not being injured, Arzee had to have been badly shaken up by the crash. Normally, Reaper would be in his element tracking a man across a plant-filled marsh. But it seemed as if nature itself was going to take that ability away from him.

The dozens of paths torn through the marsh's weeds and plants from the panicked dashing of the geese extended far from the shore. The birds were gone but the damage they had done prevented Reaper from being able to identify any specific trail that Arzee may have made as he crawled through the marsh. There was nothing to be seen of the man anywhere in the water. His body could be sinking into the mud, or the man could be hundreds of feet away hidden in the luxuriant growth of the marsh.

———

Gritting his teeth in frustration, Reaper turned to the remains of the Vette. Reaching into the smashed car, Reaper pulled out a briefcase he spotted sticking out from under the passenger seat. The wet case had probably been thrown under the seat during the violent maneuvers of the crash. Arzee was too smart to have left anything incriminating in the case, but it might hold a clue of some kind about where he might go next. Pulling open the glove compartment with more than a little difficulty, Reaper grabbed up all of the papers inside and stuffed them into his shirt. That was all Reaper could get from the wreck that looked at all valuable from an intelligence standpoint.

Time was slipping away. Reaper realized that his only remaining sources of information about his kidnapped family were the two thugs back at the shop. He had to wring out anything they knew about the location of his wife and son before they might be taken farther away or worse. Whoever was working with Arzee was going to be expecting him. How long it would take for the man to be missed couldn't be known.

Anyone else involved might just decide to cut their losses and kill Mary and Ricky, an option Reaper refused to accept. He had to tell Deckert not to call the police or do anything until he had come back and talked to the two thugs.

He would have to move fast to get back to the shop before Deckert did anything. With a reluctant final look around the crash site, Reaper stepped back into the cab. Starting the car up, he spun it through a tire-smoking U-turn. As the roar of the engine blasted out, he flipped the cutoff switch and put the muffler back into the exhaust system. He needed some speed, but he did not want to attract any more attention than he would just by driving down a country road in a yellow Checker cab with a damaged left front end.

As he was driving, Reaper remembered the cell phone Arzee had slipped into his shirt pocket. Pulling it out, he flipped back the cover and held the phone up so that he could see the road as well as the face of the phone. It was just a cheap phone, one of those prepaid models that couldn't be traced to a specific owner.

Working the phone was easy enough. Punching up the shop's number one-handed, Reaper hit the send button and waited. The first three rings at the other end of the line seemed to take forever. Never before had Reaper noticed just how long it took a phone to ring. Finally, on the fourth ring, Deckert picked up.

Chances were, Deckert was using the phone on the wall behind the cash register. "Keith," Reaper said. "It's me, Reaper."

"Yeah, Ted," Deckert said. "I'm still here playing babysitter."

Deckert's voice sounded strained, probably an effect of getting slapped upside the head with a .45 automatic. He would have to be taken to an emergency room and get checked out for a possible concussion.

"I caught up to the Vette but lost Arzee," Reaper said, "I tried to track him through the marsh but couldn't find him. He could be dead or just hiding for all I know. So those two you have are the best . . ."

Reaper heard a rapid pair of loud shots roar out from the phone. Then there was a grunt and a thump and clatter as if the phone had been dropped to the floor.

"Keith," Reaper shouted into the phone. "Keith!"

There were a few more sounds over the phone that Reaper couldn't make sense of. Then the line went dead as the other phone was hung up. Reaper snapped the cell phone closed and slipped it back into his pocket. His full concentration was now on just getting back to the shop.

The trip took longer than Reaper thought he

could stand. First his family had been hurt, now his friend and partner was in trouble, probably shot, maybe dead. The nitrous wouldn't do him any good in this race, he would never have been able to negotiate the turns in the road if he were going too fast. Every driving trick he had learned as a SEAL stuck with him as he barreled back to the shop. He cut through turns as if he were a professional race car driver.

Pulling up to the house, the first thing Reaper noticed was that the black Grand Am was missing from the driveway. Somehow, Gun Weasel or Musclehead had managed to get hold of a loaded weapon and had overcome Deckert. Reaper jumped from the Checker and ran into the house, not certain of just what he would find.

Coming into the showroom with the Desert Eagle at the ready, Reaper could see no one standing or attempting to conceal themselves behind the glass cases of the counters. What Reaper could see was Deckert's body lying on the other side of the counter, next to where the phone hung on the wall. Gun Weasel and Musclehead were gone. There was also a big chunk of the carpet missing that had been covering the counter. A drying pool of blood where the carpet had been showed where Musclehead had been pinned.

But all of those details were unimportant compared to Deckert lying on the floor. Reaper could see two bullet holes in the back seat of the wheelchair. Somebody, Gun Weasel most likely, had punched two rounds into Deckert while he was speaking on the phone. Reaper had been right, his friend must have been a little dingie from the blow he had taken. If he hadn't been injured, the ex-Army Ranger would never have turned his back on the two thugs.

Kneeling down next to Deckert, Reaper immediately noticed that there wasn't any blood on the ground. As he touched his friend, he could feel him stir and then a low groan came from the prostrate figure.

"Take it easy, Keith," Reaper said. "You took two good ones in the back."

There wasn't much question of where Deckert had been shot. As close as he was, Reaper could now see the two dark holes in the back of his friend's shirt, holes that matched up pretty well with the two in the seat back of the wheelchair.

"Oh, Christ!" Deckert groaned out. "Lord save old men from their own stupidity. I am way too old for this shit."

Reaper helped his friend turn over and sit up a bit. Now, with his hands on him, Reaper could feel the body armor that Deckert was wearing under his work shirt. Under the two holes in the back of the shirt, Reaper could feel the lumps of the bullets that had been fired into, and stopped by, the vest Deckert had been wearing.

"Oh, damn," Deckert said. "I will never bitch about going to the bank again."

"Huh?" Reaper said, puzzled at the odd remark.

"I had been planning on going to the bank this afternoon," Deckert explained. "So I had my vest on since getting dressed this morning. A fat old man in a wheelchair makes a tempting target and body armor helps give you an edge. It sure proved its worth today. Now help me up into my chair."

Reaper knew his friend's self-depreciating humor was just how he dealt with life in general. As he lifted the big man up, he could feel little in the way of fat under the hard layers of muscle that made up Deckert's back, shoulders, and arms. His legs might not have been of much use to him, but there was nothing the matter with his strength.

"You all right?" Reaper asked as Deckert settled into his chair.

"Not particularly," Deckert said sarcastically, "I've been pistol whipped, shot, and dumped on the ground twice so far today. Right now, I feel like Nolan Ryan hit me in the back with two fastballs. I've had better days."

"You want me to get you to a hospital?" Reaper asked.

"No, I'll be fine," Deckert said. "Besides we have to get on to the trail of whoever those clowns were."

As he settled into his chair, Deckert gasped as his back hit the seat back.

"Oh, that wasn't fun," Deckert said as he leaned forward.

"Your back is probably a bruised mess and I'll bet the slugs are still in your vest," Reaper said as he stood over Deckert. "Get your shirt off and let's at least get those slugs out of there."

Deckert winced as his arms were pulled back to clear the shirtsleeves.

"Any idea what the hell happened?" Reaper asked as he helped his friend get out of his vest.

"Not much I can say," Deckert said. "I gave the

big one a rag to help him stop the bleeding after you
had left. Tried to pull the knife out but he screamed
as soon as I touched it. The little bastard was still
laying curled up on the floor so I figured he wasn't
worth bothering with—besides, my head hurt like a
bitch.

"Then you called and I answered the phone. Not a
lot to say after that, the room went boom and the
next thing I knew, you were kneeling there."

While Deckert was talking, Reaper had been examining the back panel of the vest. He pulled a
SwissTool from underneath the counter and unfolded it into its pliers configuration. With a little
digging, Reaper pulled out a flattened lead slug.

"Motherfucker," Reaper said. "I'll bet that little
bastard still had my Taurus on him when I left. This
is a .44 Special semiwadcutter bullet, or at least
what used to be one. The same thing I keep in my
weapon. I forgot to search that sucker before I left.
He must have pulled it out and nailed you when you
answered the phone. God damn, Keith, I'm sorry. I
screwed the pooch this time."

"How the hell do you figure that?" Deckert said.
"I'm the stupid one who turned his back on the little
fucker. It's not like you didn't have something else
on your mind at the time. What the hell is my excuse? There's a whole rack of handcuffs over there
and I didn't think to put a pair on him."

"Shit, mistakes all around, I guess," Reaper said.
"I lost the Vette at Saint Joe's Marsh. The car was
chopped in half so I know that overdressed asshole
couldn't drive away, but I couldn't find him before I
called you."

"Nothing to be done about it," Deckert said as he winced and held his head. "How's the cab?"

"Good enough to get you to a hospital," Reaper said.

"I'm fine," Deckert protested.

"You won't be any help to me if you pass out from a concussion or start spitting blood from a broken rib," Reaper said. "I'll report the accident to the sheriff's officer when we take you in."

"But your family," Deckert said. "Those ass-wipes were pretty sure of themselves. We have no proof that they were even here. Before you came in, the snappy dresser had sent the gun handler into the office. They pulled the tape from the surveillance cameras."

"Shit," said Reaper. "I'll think of something."

———

The two men put together a fast story of how Deckert had been hit by some falling steel stock in the shop. Falling out of his chair, he had struck his head on a workbench. The story was enough to satisfy the people at the hospital. The emergency room doctor said that there were no broken bones or a concussion, but that they wanted to hold Deckert overnight for observation. Deckert's protests overrode the doctor's suggestion and the two men headed back to the shop.

When Reaper called in the accident, he acted as a passerby who had just seen the Vette in the water. There was a surprising answer from the sheriff's deputy. There was some wreckage still near the intersection by the marsh, but no car was anywhere around. It looked to the deputy as if someone had just lost a load of junk and not bothered to pick it up. With no car and no one hurt or complaining, there wasn't anything to interest the department.

Calling around to the other local emergency rooms Reaper learned that no one had come in from a car accident that day—seriously injured or otherwise. Returning to the crash site, Reaper further searched the area. There was even less to examine now than there had been before. The front end of the Corvette had completely sunk into the muck bottom of the marsh. The only thing new that Reaper found was what looked like a trail where someone had staggered out of the marsh and up to the road. If the man who had taken his family had a cell phone, it appeared that he could have just called someone to come and pick him up.

Chapter Eleven

Physically, Arzee had not suffered anything more serious than some bruises and abrasions from his accident with the Checker cab. His pride and nerves had taken a severe beating. His favorite classic Corvette was nothing more than a scattered pile of parts in a marsh. The actions of the day before had put Arzee's nerves into little better shape than his vehicle was in.

He had been in firm control of the situation and it had still gotten away from him. How had that happened? It was unbelievable that Reaper would risk anything happening to his own wife and child. They were his own family. He had lost his career over children that weren't even his own in Bosnia. How could he put his own in jeopardy?

Everything that Arzee knew told him that Reaper should have done exactly what they wanted, let go of the weapons and delivered more, all to get his family back. The plan had even accounted for the police or other authorities, removing any support for

Reaper from that source. The situation should have completely subjugated Reaper to their control, and it hadn't.

That Reaper's family would be the control for the ex-SEAL was something that Arzee had been counting on. Paxtun had approved of his plan, indeed had been enthusiastic about it. It would not only replace the weapons they needed—there was a delicious irony about using the man that had cost Paxtun so much, and costing him even more.

Paxtun had been so certain of the plan that Reaper's family had been sent on to the facilities on South Wolverine Island. It was the most secure site they had available to them and was where Paxtun could keep a personal eye on the hostages. Paxtun was already on the island and Reaper's wife and kid had arrived there the night before.

Arzee had already contacted Paxtun that morning—calling him over a prepaid cellular phone that had been part of a bulk purchase made elsewhere in the country. Speaking in Arabic and in coded phrases added security to a point that seemed extreme. But nothing was too extreme for the group of operatives that had been sent over by the overseas investors that were backing Paxtun's and Arzee's enterprises.

Just the existence of the operatives, and especially their leader, had been kept a very closely guarded secret. Amman and Nicholas were Arzee's cousins and he trusted them for his most sensitive operations. Along with two more family members, his cousins Hadeed and Joseph, they were the only ones who had a direct hand in the kidnapping of Reaper's family and the extortion of the guns. But his cousins knew only that the operation had been done partly for revenge—something they could understand very well. But they hadn't been trusted enough to know the significance of Ishmael or his men.

The leader of the action group had taken the kunyah Ishmael for his name during the operation. Historically, Ishmael was the son of the biblical Abraham and Hagar. Hagar was the handmaiden of Sarah, Abraham's wife. According to Islamic heritage, Ishmael was considered the father of the Arab people. It was a fitting name for someone who felt that he was going to help lead the true believers of Islam into a new world free of the infidels and their influence.

This modern Ishmael considered his planned operation to be a sacrifice to Allah. He had a twelve-man crew of hand-picked men to help him complete his mission. For their kunyah names, the men of Ishmael's group had taken names of the sons of the legendary Ishmael. The whole group was known as the Sons of Ishmael and preferred to be addressed as such by Paxtun, Arzee, or anyone else in Paxtun's organization.

The Sons of Ishmael were an action cell of al Qaeda, and they had a significant operation coming up in the United States. Arzee knew none of the details of the mission, target, or timing of the operation, and he didn't want to know any. The eyes and faces of every member of Ishmael's cell that Arzee had met had shone with a dedication that bordered on the fanatical. It would not be safe to cause any difficulty at all to such people.

The only thing that Arzee was certain of was that Ishmael was terrifying. He considered his mission to be like the sacrifice of his namesake, the biblical son of Abraham. According to Islamic legend, it was Ishmael who Abraham had been going to sacrifice on God's order, not Isaac. Legend further stated that Ishmael had been spared through God's intervention, and that his sons and their descendants became the first true Arab people.

Ishmael had told Paxtun and Arzee that he felt he was going to help re-create the Arab people as a major power in the world. The United States would be forced to leave the Islamic world and the Middle East. Free of the influence of the infidels and the Great Satan, the Islamic world would soon grow to become the dominant culture of the entire planet.

That level of fanaticism was hard to face. If Ishmael considered someone a threat, or even a possible threat, to the cell or their mission, he would kill them without hesitation. Right now, Ishmael was up at the mansion on the island with Paxtun. The more than 250 miles that separated Detroit from that island in Lake Michigan still felt far too close for Arzee's mental comfort.

Both Paxtun and Arzee had converted to Muwahhidan, what the West and many Arabs called Wahhabism, in Afghanistan. The austere, conservative form of Islam was what their rescuers had believed and it had appealed to Paxtun over the months he had spent in the mountains of that desolate country. Paxtun had in his turn convinced Arzee that conservative Islam was the way, though Arzee may have also been swayed by the appeal of the huge amount of money offered by Paxtun and his proposals.

Arzee considered himself a true believer in Islam. He knew that the path to righteousness required adhering to the dogma of his chosen faith. But he was not a religious fanatic. His years on the streets of Dearborn and Detroit had influenced him greatly. His religious convictions were not as solid as he thought they were.

There was an unbelievable amount of money to be made in the various criminal activities of Paxtun's organization. The drug distribution network Paxtun and Arzee had developed was making huge profits with relatively little personal risk to either man. The money had proven worthwhile to everyone involved. Even the Taliban had been happy to take a cut of the profits from the product of the Afghan poppy fields.

Now the military actions of the United States had taken the Taliban out of the picture. But it had not eliminated al Qaeda as a functional organization. Paxtun and Arzee had been told that they would support Ishmael and his men—and the demand could not be refused.

So the organization had been hard at work bringing in Ishmael and his men to the United States. A training and staging area had been prepared and set up at the private island in Lake Michigan. The most recent group of cell members, Ishmael's "sons," had been sent up north to the island some days earlier. Not having them hiding out at the Factory, acting as janitorial and maintenance staff for any onlookers, was the only good thing that had happened to Arzee in the last few days.

The loss of the weapons shipment looked to have been a disaster for Arzee and Paxtun. Paxtun was going to have to explain to Ishmael how new security procedures were being put into place by the Of-

fice of Homeland Security. Those procedures and
new technologies were intended specifically to find
such shipments of weapons and ammunition as the
one that had been seized. It was while Paxtun was
explaining that to Ishmael that Arzee was supposed
to be arranging for new firepower.

Right now, Arzee had their resident drug chemist
hard at work making high-quality explosives to replace some of what had been lost. As far as the guns
went, they already had the weapons from the gun
shop. They still had Reaper's wife and son as prisoners and could force the SEAL to do what they
wanted. So more of the new weapons should be
available by Saturday afternoon.

Paxtun had suggested that Arzee call Reaper and
tell him that the clock was still ticking on the deadline for more of the Jackhammer shotguns. Arzee
wouldn't admit it to anyone, not even himself, but
he was more than afraid of the SEAL who had
chased him down. He wasn't going to call the cell
phone he had left with Reaper. His reason was to
make the big SEAL sweat over the fate of his family
even more by not hearing anything. The truth was,
Arzee didn't know how he would react if he heard
the man's voice on the phone any time soon.

Arzee believed that once Reaper realized he
could do nothing about the situation, he would do
what was demanded of him. But the pain Arzee felt
in his muscles and bones lessened his faith in the
plan. And his most trusted men, his cousins, were in
much worse condition than he was.

Nicholas wasn't too badly injured by his introduction to SEAL close-quarter combat. The private

doctor had said that Nicholas should refrain from doing whatever it was that had caused his groin injury. He was lucky there was no permanent damage. But the small man was still walking very gingerly—and sitting very carefully.

Amman had been another matter. His left forearm had been severely damaged by the knife that Reaper had used to nail him to that counter top. It had taken both hands for Nicholas to pull that knife out of the table, and he had done more damage to his cousin's arm in the process. If Nicholas hadn't used that same knife to cut a chunk of carpet to wrap around the wound, Amman might have bled to death before he had gotten back to the Factory.

As it was, Amman had a large bandage wrapped around his left arm and was taking pills for the pain. The two cousins were only good for standing guard around the offices until they healed up. But at least they could be trusted to watch the new project that was moving along well. The project looked as if it would be yielding a profit soon.

The offices and quarters Arzee used were on the sixth floor of the old auto plant. The bulk of the sixth floor, at the top of the building, had been the paint shop. That was where a clandestine laboratory had been set up in one of the old paint booths. The ventilation and filtering system prevented any of the fumes from the lab escaping into the atmosphere in a detectable form.

Fazul Daoud, the graduate student in organic chemistry from a local university, had been cultivated by Arzee and Paxtun in order to manufacture designer drugs for the organization. Having the young chemist and the laboratory available had proven a possible lifesaver when it had been able to produce a large amount of sophisticated explosives for the Sons of Ishmael.

Ishmael had thought that the ability to manufacture the explosives he wanted had been a very professional backup put in place to fulfill his possible needs. Now that the immediate demand for explosives had been satisfied, the lab was already back to producing more financially lucrative items.

Leaving his offices, Arzee went out the door and across the hallway to the old paint shop. Stairs led up to the offices, the entrance to the stairway being heavy steel fire doors secured with chains and padlocks. The building's elevators could only be operated with a key—and all but one of them were kept shut down between floors for security.

The only other way to the top floor was to go up a ramp along the north wall of the building. A very heavy steel bar and lock sealed the ramp door. By the time a police raid unit could force access to the floor, any evidence would have been long destroyed. There were five such ramps, originally put in place to move racks of parts from floor to floor while constructing cars. At the top of each ramp were thick steel fire doors. Each door had to be penetrated before finally reaching the sixth floor.

Near the middle of the huge floor at the top of the building, surrounded by racks, conveyors, and the other refuse of heavy manufacturing, were several large steel rooms. The boxlike rooms had wall-sized doors at either end. The doors were kept as securely sealed as every other entrance to the floor. Whole car bodies had been moved in and out of the rooms on racks. Some of the rooms had been set up for painting, others serving as large ovens to bake the paint.

Amman sat outside of a standard door in the side of one of the steel enclosures. He was looking a bit the worse for wear from the expression on his face, and by the sling on his left arm. The big man stood a bit unsteadily as Arzee approached. Then he unlocked the door and opened it for his boss without speaking a word.

Arzee passed into the room, and listened to the sound of the air being sucked through the area by the ventilation system. Along one wall of the enclosure was a rack of bubbling laboratory glassware, tall assemblies of glass, rubber tubing, and metal clamps, all held to a framework of steel rods. There were a dozen of the same apparatus setups all running at once. The tall glass rigs were filled with liquids that bubbled and flowed. On top of each setup was a glass condenser, water flowing through the cooling jacket. The condenser was the only piece of apparatus that Arzee could name, the rest was a complete mystery to him.

But the bubbling mass was not a mystery to Fazul Daoud, the white lab-coated wizard who managed the illicit laboratory. He turned as Arzee came in and raised the protective plastic shield he had over his face.

"Nothing dangerous going on that I should be concerned with, is there?" asked Arzee seeing the shield.

"Not really, sir," Fazul answered. "It was much

more dangerous when I was turning out that pentaerythritol tetranitrate you wanted."

"The what?"

"I'm sorry sir," Fazul said. "The PETN high explosive you asked for. The worst part of that was working with the formaldehyde and acetaldehyde to form the precursor. I had to wear a respirator for that. The nitration and purification was straightforward enough."

"Speak English, Fazul," Arzee said, "talking like this does not impress me and I don't have time for it. Now is this procedure going ahead smoothly?"

"Yes, sir," Fazul said. "Right now, this is just a straightforward extraction. The hydride and ether being used could be very dangerous if mishandled. They are quite flammable, even explosive."

"You are trusted to prevent any mishandling from happening," Arzee said. "Now, how long is the process going to take, and how much are you estimating the yield to be?"

"The extraction takes about sixty hours," Fazul said as he warmed up to his subject. He was completely in his element talking about his laboratory work. "The balance of the process should be completed a day after that. Since this is being done in a laboratory and not on an industrial scale, these Soxhlet Extractors only hold a relatively small charge. I expect the yield to be about thirty-five grams per unit, so between 400 and 450 grams of pure Methylenedioxy-n-methylamphetamine."

"That is pure MDMA?" said Arzee. "Raw Ecstasy?"

"Yes, sir," Fazul said. "The process is much the same as that used by some of the biker gang cookers to crank out their crystal methamphetamine. But their process is crude at best. Our system is much more sophisticated and efficient. The product here is of much greater purity than any other brands available on the street. Once I have diluted the final product down with a buffer and pressed it into tablets, they will be ready for sale. The customers should be well satisfied."

"These clubbers will pay well for their Ecstasy tablets," Arzee said. "How long do you expect to take to manufacture the pills themselves?"

"Each thirty-five-gram batch should make about 580 tablets at the popular dosage," Fazul said. "Using the press and dies does take some time to actually form the final pills. I expect to have several thousand tablets available for you in four days. They'll be marked and shaped as double-stack white Mitz, a very popular underground brand."

"Excellent," Arzee said. He was happy something was working out according to plan for a change. "Do you need any relief or other support?"

"Nothing I can think of, sir," Fazul said. "The process is pretty straightforward for the extraction. As you can see, the extractors run themselves for the most part. I can get what rest I need well enough as they run."

Arzee looked at the rows of glassware bubbling away. The liquid would rise in the Soxhlet Extractors until it reached a certain level, then quickly be siphoned off into a large round flask nesting in an electric mantle heater. Each setup would make a quantity of Ecstasy, the popular club and rave drug, that would have a final street value of more than

$11,000. And there were twelve setups running at once. Over $130,000 profit would be a good return for a few thousand dollars investment in chemicals and glassware.

Even wholesaling the drug would be more than profitable while minimizing the risk. Maintaining a pure product is how they had cornered the heroin trade. This would be no different. And the process, chemical, and equipment, could even be sold to some of the biker gangs that they worked with on other projects. Arzee had a smile on his face for a change as he headed back down to his offices.

Chapter Twelve

In northern Lake Michigan, almost twenty miles from the closest point of the mainland, is South Wolverine Island. About five miles to the northeast is North Wolverine Island. Covering more than 3,300 acres of ground, South Wolverine Island is shaped like an inverted fat banana with the stem end pointing due south and the other end curved over to point northwest. The island is a little over five miles long and about a mile and a half wide. North Wolverine Island, shaped like a straightened comma mark, is two and a half miles long and barely over a mile across at its widest point.

Both islands are covered with trees, brush, and grasslands. There are wide sand beaches at several points along the shoreline of South Wolverine, while North Wolverine is almost completely surrounded by a thin border of sand beach. The grasslands and trees offer good cover and grazing to the herds of deer and other game on the two islands. The only industry that had ever come to the islands was logging, as it had on most of the islands of Lake Michigan during the late 1800s and early-to-mid 1900s.

The logging camps were long gone, but there were still traces of man on both islands. North Wolverine Island had a few cabins along its west shore. On the widest part of the northern end of the island was a 1,000-meter-long grass landing strip for aircraft. The island was covered mostly with grasslands, broken up by patches of scrub brush and low trees. Some small hills rise up from the relatively flat island at its southern end.

South Wolverine Island holds a large area of trees and brush in the rolling ridges that cover over two-thirds of the island. At the southernmost point, separated from the main part of the island by 400 meters of sand, stands a single automated lighthouse. Near the metal-framed light are the remains of an old brick lighthouse along with a single-story structure that had been the living quarters of the lighthouse keeper almost a century earlier.

The decaying structures at the southernmost point of South Wolverine Island are not the only buildings on the island. A mile almost due north of the old lighthouse is a huge two-story mansion built decades earlier. Seeing the island as a summer refuge, a lumber baron had established a large estate on South Wolverine.

Years after the lumber baron was gone, the estate was bought up and improved by an automobile magnate from Detroit. He had a two-story summerhouse built on the island. The mansion-sized house held six bedrooms, each with their own bathrooms, a maid's room with bath, and a rambling first floor. This floor included a billiard room, music room with a separate chamber for the pipe organ, a library, and a twenty-by-forty-foot indoor swimming pool.

Built on a hillside, the summerhouse had a walk-out basement foundation with over a dozen rooms and chambers including a photographic dark room, several walk-in refrigerators, a coal cellar, four huge cisterns holding thousands of gallons of water, and even a single-lane regulation-sized bowling alley that runs along the east side of the pool structure. At the opposite side of the pool is a collection of utility pipes that lead to a six-foot-wide tunnel connecting to a powerhouse two hundred meters away.

The powerhouse holds large diesel-electric generators that supply power to the house and other structures and facilities on the island. The powerhouse is part of the hangar facilities and garage that stand at the southern end of a 1,200-meter landing strip. At the west shore of the island, directly across from the large rise that the mansion stands on, are the boat docks and landing facilities.

The offshore waters teem with fish at different times of the year. Shallow water shoals extend for more than three miles to the north of the main island. The South Wolverine Island Shoals, a long expanse of treacherous shallow waters, extend for more than nine miles to the south of the island. Thirty-foot-deep channels separate the different parts of the southern shoals. The three most dangerous areas of shallow water are marked with lighted buoys. It was to warn boats from this stretch of water and the hidden dangers there that the lighthouse was designed to do.

The geography and location of the South and North Wolverine Islands made them excellent places for sportsmen. But, except for the small spit of land above the sand that holds the inactive lighthouse, the islands are private property. Even the lighthouse was not open to the public, so very few people landed on the posted property of the islands.

The islands were a huge, private playground for the rich of several cities, lying roughly 250 miles equidistant from either Detroit or Chicago. The auto magnate and his family had long since left the area. The properties had gone through a number of hands, each trying to make something more of what was available at the remote location. The previous owner had established a hunting lodge on South Wolverine Island, surrounded by thousands of acres to support exotic imported game.

The owner of the hunting lodge had failed to see his private club become a successful concern. He had fallen on difficult times, both personal and professional, something Paxtun had been able to take advantage of. Obtaining both North and South Wolverine Islands for under market value, Paxtun now had a very large, very isolated facility available to him. That was something his investors had ordered him to obtain for their use.

Now, the hunting preserve and lodge were listed as being closed to the public for renovation and upgrading of the facilities. That explained a large number of workers going to and from the islands whenever the weather permitted. One thing that had not been announced publicly was when the hunting club would reopen, if ever.

Having finished leading the morning prayers with his men, the man called Ishmael sent them out of his suite of rooms. The main room of his sumptuous quarters at the mansion was easily large enough to hold all of his men. Ishmael was a tall, medium-built, intense man. His close-cropped, thick black hair, beard, and mustache framed an oval face with a very high forehead. Shaded by thick eyebrows were bright, intense, dark brown eyes.

Ishmael had been with al Qaeda since its beginnings and had spent his share of time sleeping on little more than rocks. His quarters now were what had been called the "Owner's Chamber." The suite had an almost thirty-foot-square room with an attached semicircular enclosed sleeping porch and two separate large combination dressing rooms and baths. Ishmael thought it shameful that just the cupboard space and closets of one of the baths were larger than what many families called a home back in his adopted Afghanistan.

Not that he hadn't been used to luxury at one time in his life. Ishmael had been born into a privileged family in 'Ajman, in the United Arab Emirates. He had been educated and raised a devout Muslim, and remained so even when studying abroad in Europe and England. He spoke a number of languages, including English, German, French, and Arabic.

When the Soviet Union had invaded Afghanistan in 1979, the young man who would become Ishmael went to fight the infidel invaders. He joined the mujahideen and took part in the jihad.

The fighting hadn't stopped with the Soviets abandoning their actions in Afghanistan. The occupation of holy Muslim soil by the infidels from the United States had incensed Ishmael as it had many other fundamentalist Islamic Muslims. It had been obvious to any devout true believer that the U.S. had been bent on driving Iraq from Kuwait solely for its own benefit.

The defeat of Iraq had only been the United States' opening gambit into the Arabian peninsula as far as Ishmael and his contemporaries were concerned. The justice that had been brought against the United States by the Prince, bin Laden, had been used by the infidels as an excuse to destroy what had become Ishmael's new home in Afghanistan.

Planning had been going forward for several years for a new strike against the Great Satan, deep in his own homeland. That planning had been modified by the horrendous invasion of Iraq by the U.S. forces as they went forward with their intent of occupying the Middle East. But Ishmael and his men were now in the United States itself, deep in the heart of their enemy. And they would very soon be striking fear in that heart—fear that would reverberate throughout the world and let their Muslim brethren know that the fight was not over.

———

Paxtun retained his office down the second-floor main hallway from what had been his personal quarters now used by Ishmael. For his own sleeping quarters, he had moved into what was called Chamber 4, part of an extended suite of rooms. From

Chamber 4, he could pass through a dressing room and vestibule and be in his outer office.

Made from one of the major sleeping chambers of the original mansion, Paxtun's office had a large central chamber, sixteen-by-twenty-five-feet in size, as well as an attached bath and separate dressing room. The main chamber was his outer office, that Paxtun used for meetings and such. The enclosed semicircular sleeping porch just off the main chamber was where he kept his private inner office.

Sleeping arrangments were not of major concern to Paxtun at the moment. Since Ishmael's arrival weeks earlier, he had done little in the way of sleeping. And what sleep he did get was restless and unsatisfying. Ishmael was a demanding taskmaster. Nothing short of perfection was acceptable to him in support of what he considered his holy duty.

Paxtun had yet to be fully informed of the details of the operation. The only thing that he knew was the code name of the attack, Operation Shaitan's Blessing. That could mean anything and take place anywhere. It made for a situation that he had a hard time accepting. It wasn't that his conscience bothered him about being responsible for a possible major terrorist attack in his home country. It was the fact that he didn't know enough of the details to insure that he was protected from possible discovery.

Inside his inner office, Paxtun still felt safe and relatively in control. His extensive knife and sword collection was in cases and racks both on the walls and several glass-topped tables. On the table between the two doors that connected the inner and outer offices was his most recent acquisition. The long, flat wooden case that Hadeed, one of Arzee's cousins, had brought to him didn't hold an antique or foreign blade. It did hold the sword made by Reaper's own hands. Arzee's relatives had known of Paxtun's passion for blades, and they had brought him the sword as well as a real prize—Reaper's family.

The wife and son of the man who had forced him to relinquish his military and intelligence career were in his complete control. For the time being, he had them secured in a storage room in the basement. It amused Paxtun to have the woman and child secured in the windowless, concrete-walled room. Twice a day, they were taken out to make use of the toilet facilities. All the rest of their time was spent in their prison room. Even their meals were brought to them there.

Paxtun hadn't quite decided what to finally do with the two hostages yet, but he had time. They had to be kept alive to insure Reaper's cooperation—for the time being.

As Paxtun was contemplating the good parts of his situation in his inner office, Ishmael strode in from his room down the hall. His arrival instantly brought Paxtun out of his reverie. The news had come in from Arzee that he had secured four of the Jackhammer shotguns. Any additional weapons would be available in two days. The exotic weapons would help replace part of the firepower confiscated by Canadian customs. Additional weapons would take longer to obtain—there just weren't any more immediately available.

This was not the news Paxtun wanted to give Ishmael. That the man was a fanatic went without question. Causing him difficulties could set off what Paxtun had quickly learned was a violent hair-trigger temper. Ishmael and his superiors had proved a very profitable group of partners for Paxtun's enterprises. Now that the time had come to pay back some of those investments with interest, Paxtun was having some second thoughts about the arrangement. It was one thing to very profitably distribute narcotics and build an infrastructure to support activities in the United States. It was quite another to actively take part in a terrorist action within the continental United States itself.

Paxtun had little choice in how events moved forward now. The last group of Ishmael's men were coming into the country that night. They would be at the island base the next day if everything went according to plan. That was another bit of good news that Paxtun could pass on to Ishmael. But even that news had a bad taste to it for Paxtun.

Once all twelve members of the Sons of Ishmael had joined with their leader, the group would greatly outnumber Paxtun and his handful of men on the island. Ishmael had insisted that there be as few support people as possible on the island to insure security for himself and his men, an insistence that Paxtun had to go along with.

Even the cook and caretaker staff had been removed from the island more than a month earlier. Paxtun had one of his junior men doing the cooking, something that was wearing thin over the weeks. Coming to the island was a strain now, especially after the fare they had been used to from their usual expert cook. He was tired of food that was microwaved or had come from cans. There was no wine at the meals either. Drinking alcohol would be a sin in the eyes of Allah. More importantly, it would piss off Ishmael and his men.

Ishmael entered Paxtun's office unannounced and without knocking. The arrogance of the man was just another bitter pill that Paxtun had to swallow.

"Good news, Ishmael," Paxtun said, "the final group of your men have arrived in Windsor. They'll be brought across the border tonight."

"You are certain that your procedures will work?" Ishmael said in flawless English. "And that their papers will stand up to the closest scrutiny?"

"No problem whatsoever," Paxtun said. "The crossing procedure is the same as we used for yourself and the other four groups of men. The papers are the very best available. Each man will have an authentic U.S. government passport with his picture in it as well as a Michigan driver's license.

"We used the photographs of your men you forwarded to us. The driver's licenses are as authentic as anything issued by the State of Michigan. No police officer or customs agent would be able to tell them from the real thing. The passports are of the same quality.

"Before they cross the border, each man is given pocket litter to go along with his papers—money, random documents, receipts, and ticket stubs. Those items would mark him as just another tourist out of the thousands that cross the border every day."

"I will not accept any errors at this stage of the

game, Paxtun," Ishmael said. "There is far too much at stake and the timing is becoming critical."

"It might help if you let me know what part of the mission timing is tight," Paxtun said.

"That is of no concern of yours," Ishmael said firmly. "You are simply to make sure that there are no flaws in the support that is asked of you."

"No flaws at all," Paxtun said, trying to steer the conversation away from the delicate matter of Ishmael's mission. "We have men of the one faith in a number of different areas who have been brought into the plan but have no knowledge of their specific part in it."

There were more details on how Paxtun had obtained the identification papers that he had told Ishmael. But he did not feel it necessary to tell the terrorist leader all of his secrets.

"The actual border crossings," Paxtun explained, "were planned to take place at the times of the highest traffic volume. The vehicles used all had multiple passengers and were known to frequently visit the gambling casinos on both sides of the border. Once in Canada, your men were issued the passports with their photos and descriptions inside and their original documents were taken away. For all intents and purposes, they were U.S. citizens from that point on.

"They would cross back into the States by another route than the one the vehicle had originally crossed over by. As far as the customs people were concerned, they were looking at U.S. citizens coming back from a good time across the river. The passports were just a backup, the driver's licenses alone have proved enough for each crossing so far. The driver knew what to say and coached each person in the van as to just what answers to give at the border.

"Your people came into the country without ever even raising a blip on the radar of customs. The Immigration and Naturalization Service wouldn't even think to look for them. By the next day, they are on their way here to the island."

In spite of the detailed and methodic nature of Paxtun's techniques, and the fact that they had worked flawlessly so far, Ishmael still felt it necessary to prevent his subordinate from feeling too full of himself.

"The loyalty of your people is something I question," Ishmael said. "You simply buy it, which is not the same thing as true loyalty at all. My men have loyalty unto death for our cause. Your people are less than mercenaries. They betray their own country for mere monetary gain."

The rebuke was directed at Paxtun and the line about money was intended to sting him. The mild insult didn't mean anything to him. He had been listening to such for weeks now anyway. But what he had to tell Ishmael next did worry him.

Finally, Paxtun told Ishmael the news about his missing hardware behind the closed doors of his office, quickly adding the news about the new firepower that had been acquired. The reaction of the big terrorist leader was everything Paxtun had expected and feared.

The fact that his mission might have been put in jeopardy by another's incompetence filled Ishmael with rage. The tall, slender man stalked back and forth across the room like a caged tiger. He paused for a moment and gazed quietly at Paxtun who stood next to his large wooden desk that faced away from the four large windows in the curved outer wall. Then Ishmael crossed his arms and lowered his head as if in deep thought, walking past the desk and near where Paxtun was standing.

As Paxtun took a step closer to Ishmael, the bigger man suddenly turned and viciously backhanded Paxtun across the face. As Paxtun staggered and almost fell, Ishmael lashed out with another stunning backhand with his opposite hand. The smaller man reeled and fell against the heavy desk. Only his hands gripping the edges of the desk kept Paxtun from collapsing to the floor in a heap.

"You think some new toys would cover up your incompetence?" Ishmael snarled. "There is no tolerance for failure. We cannot afford to let mistakes hinder our cause. The only reason you are not dead now is that you may still be able to serve the cause—an arrangement that has paid you very well.

"You have served us well in the past," Ishmael continued in a deceptively softer tone. "That is why you reap the benefit of our compassion. You brought us weapons when we needed them to drive the Soviet invaders from our country. Perhaps it was too much for me to expect you to be able to do so again on such short notice.

"Others who I respect told me that you were once a warrior. You have been living here in this decadent country for too long since leaving Afghanistan. You were once hard, but these surroundings have soft-

ened you and made you easy. Your own country
proved itself false to you and your faith when it
abandoned you once. Then it so unjustly turned you
out after your service in Bosnia. We are the only
ones who have accepted you fully and made you a
trusted brother of ours.

"It was arrogant and stupid of you to assume that I
did not know of the lost shipment of arms the instant
that it happened. Do you consider me so slovenly
that I would leave a detail as important as the delivery of such a thing solely up to you? I know that you
had to put together a plan for obtaining replacement
weapons in a very short time. And that woman and
her child that you brought to the island last evening
are part of that plan.

"Let me assure you," Ishmael said in a soft, dangerous tone as he leaned in close to where Paxtun
still held himself up at the desk. "That woman and
child had better not turn into a threat against us. If
anything you do risks me, my men, or our mission,
you will be the first one to die. I agree they make
good hostages no matter what your original plan
may have been. The Americans are soft that way
about their own women and children.

"Not that they extend that compassion to anyone
else in the world," Ishmael said as he started pacing
the room. "They have bombed our women and children, attacked us out of the sky, and out of our
reach. When the much-vaunted U.S. military finally
came down to the ground, they did so in their heavy
tanks and armored vehicles—smashing everything
in their way."

Paxtun now realized with certainty just how great

a fanatic Ishmael was. His fate was inextricably intertwined with this madman who walked about the room, ranting as if he were giving a speech to his men. It was as if the man wanted to keep convincing himself.

"In their arrogance," Ishmael said, "they overthrew our governments and killed our leaders. They defiled our holy places of worship, robbed us of our antiquities, our heritage, our past. They claimed we had weapons of mass destruction. That was the reason they used to justify their actions in the eyes of the world.

"But we are here now," Ishmael said as he came close to Paxtun again and stood facing him. "Here in the very heart of the United States. We had not yet obtained such weapons as we had been accused of. But we can take such things from the infidels themselves. We will turn the poisons of their own making back on them."

Realizing that he was saying more than might be prudent, Ishmael had a very serious look come over his face as he stood straight and faced Paxtun.

"The importance of our mission was not allowed to rest on a single shipment of arms and materiel," Ishmael said. "There have been other arms shipments sent to various action cells throughout the United States. Those cells have already been made aware of our needs and are sending materials to us as we speak. They should begin arriving tomorrow. Whatever additional plans you have to replace the lost shipment may go forward as necessary. Those arms will have to replace those sent to us from the other cells.

"It is a pity that we lost the U.S.-made Stinger

missiles that were in that last shipment. Obviously the existence of such weapons frighten the authorities. They neglected to tell the public of their seizure when they took the shipment. No matter. We have other Soviet weapons that will be available to us. But there would have been a certain irony in using the U.S. weapons against their own people.

"My experts have been examining the guns that came in last night. They say the firepower they represent may replace some of what was lost through your incompetence. At least they are devastating in a close assault. They have helped buy your life back—for now."

Switching to a very commanding tone, Ishmael said, "I have been told to expect the first arrivals of equipment tomorrow. You will have your people pick them up and transport them here when you bring in the last group of my men. The explosives your chemist made have been judged as adequate by my technicians. They will be of use in replacing some of the more specialized pieces that were in the shipment that was lost. Their delivery was another saving grace for you. It would be best if there were no other errors or delays on your part."

"There shouldn't be any difficulties," Paxtun said as he finally found his voice. "Everything is ready. You tell us where to pick up what and we'll do it. Another truckload coming in here will not be a problem."

"It had best not be a problem," Ishmael said, and he strode out of the room.

Ishmael's violent manner almost made Paxtun angry enough to have the man killed immediately. He had the sudden urge to grab a blade and chase the terrorist leader down in the hall before he even reached his own room. But Paxtun knew that Ishmael's men would kill him long before he could leave the island. If he did get away, al Qaeda had a long memory, and an even longer reach. Paxtun wouldn't live out the year. That thought stayed his hand as it inched toward a weapon, Paxtun knowing that it would be suicide to take on the man physically.

On top of the ingratitude of the terrorist leader for everything Paxtun had done to replace the lost weapons with some of the best hardware available was the shock that the whole thing had been unnecessary. Ishmael had put his own backups in place, showing just how important he considered his mission to be. By not telling Paxtun about more weapons being available, he had forced the man to use extreme measures to obtain guns. The satisfaction Paxtun had felt in holding Reaper's family hostage had evaporated—it had never been necessary.

The ex-Army officer and drug lord just accepted Ishmael's insults and orders. Paxtun had no choice in the matter. Ishmael would eliminate him just as soon as he stopped being useful. It was good that he had been paid a lot of money and lived well at the old resort—he was going to be earning every penny of it. He only hoped he would have time later to enjoy his gains.

Chapter Thirteen

The situation for Reaper was quickly becoming the worst he had ever endured. His career in the SEALs and Special Warfare had exposed him to levels of stress that could bring the average man quickly to his knees. But none of his training or experience had prepared him for a direct threat to his wife and child.

His family was missing and no one was able to tell him where they had gone. It was only the morning after they had been taken, but the hours that had passed were the longest that Reaper had ever lived through. There was so little that he could do, and a feeling of helplessness was not something he was used to. He couldn't go to the police; the only ones he could turn to were his friends. But the kind of people that Reaper could call his friends were a very competent group of individuals.

Reaper and Deckert were in the office of the house, converted from what had been the dining room. They were working from the one slim lead they had. The name "Steven Arzee" had been on the car registration papers Reaper had taken from the Corvette's glove compartment. Deckert had been conducting a search for information on Arzee over the Internet. Like everything else that had been tried by the two men so far, the search had proven fruitless. Reaper leaned back from his seat at the side of the desk and stared into space thoughtfully as he drank from the cup of coffee in his hand.

"Ted," Deckert said as he pushed himself back from the computer desk, "I've called in every favor I know. Every cop or detective who's ever come through that door and left his number has gotten a call from me. No one knows anything. In fact, no one even suspects anything. When the kidnappers had your wife call her school and say she was going away, they believed her.

"The two of you have had trouble in the past. If she felt threatened and told a bunch of people that you were the cause, they believed her. Being a SEAL has worked against you here. Hell, man, even her sounding nervous over the phone was considered understandable by people who think you guys should be kept under glass and only taken out in time of war.

"That Arzee asshole covered all the bases. We're not even sure that's the name of the guy who was here. Whoever he is, he's probably still alive, maybe not even hurt very badly. No hospital or emergency room in the area had an accident victim brought in. And if he is still alive, he's got you by the short hairs."

"Damn," Reaper said, "I know you're right, but what the hell am I going to do about this? Even if we wanted to give them what they want, he hasn't

called on this damned cell phone to demand anything more. I have never felt so fucking helpless in
my life."

Deckert didn't know what to say to his friend. He,
too, felt helpless to do anything to affect the situation. Reaper had been working with Deckert for
some time now, and the two men had become close
friends. In the military, you learned how to judge
and who you could trust. It was a skill you needed
when your life could be on the line at any time.

As the two men sat thinking about the situation,
they heard the sound of a motorcycle coming up the
driveway. Without saying a word, Reaper and Deckert separated to be able to cover the maximum area
inside the house.

Reaper headed into the kitchen where he could
see down the hallway leading to the front doors of
the house. Deckert moved into the retail area, and
took up a position behind a counter. He extended his
chair so that he was able to look out over the display
case. Underneath the counter top, he held an eight-
shot 12-gauge Remington 870 police shotgun with a
folding stock. The shotgun was loaded with Tactical-
brand #4 buckshot and had been fitted with a Duck-
Bill choke on the muzzle.

The shot spread through the special DuckBill
choke would completely cover the front door from
Deckert's position. The twenty-seven copper-plated
.24-inch hardened lead pellets in a single Tactical
round could easily deal with most targets. The stock
was folded up over the top of the receiver and barrel
for compactness and ease of movement in a con-

fined space. With his hands and arms powerful from work and rolling his wheelchair for years, Deckert could handle the big weapon as if it was a pistol.

In spite of his favorite Taurus revolver having been taken, Reaper was far from unarmed. In his hands he held a SIG P-220 semiautomatic pistol. The blued steel, double-action weapon was chambered for .45 ACP, the same round that Deckert preferred for his M1911A1.

There were eight Federal 230-grain Hydra-Shok hollowpoints loaded in the SIG's magazine, with one chambered and ready to fire. The special Hydra-Shok ammunition would expand as it struck a target, penetrating deeply and leaving a rat tunnel-sized hole behind it. Even if the man was wearing body armor, he would feel as if he was hit with a thrown cinder block. Neither Reaper nor Deckert intended being caught as they had the day before.

The sound of the approaching motorcycle stopped as the bike reached the house and the rider shut off the engine. A few moments later, the front door opened and a burly biker in dusty black leathers and heavy boots stepped into the house. He wore a helmet that completely covered his face and head. Pulling off his gloves, the man turned to the right and entered the retail shop.

Pulling his gloves off occupied the man's hands for the moment. But Reaper wasn't going to take any chances. For the moment he was going to stay at his more centralized location. There was no window behind Reaper's back and he could see the front door while still covering the other two entrances to the house from the garage and the shop. He knew that Deckert would be more than ready to deal with their new customer.

In the retail store, Deckert watched the big man move easily and confidently into the room. He didn't recognize the man in his biker outfit and the shop was pretty out of the way for walk-in traffic. If they hadn't been waiting for something to happen, like somebody just walking in the door, he would have solidly locked up the front.

"Can I help you?" Deckert asked from his place behind the counter.

"Yeah," the stranger said in a gruff voice still muffled by the helmet, "I'm looking for Ted Reaper. I was told I could find him here."

"He's not available right now," Deckert said. "What's your business with him, maybe I can help?"

"I don't think so, I'd just like to see him. It's kind of personal."

"I'm sure he wouldn't mind if you told me," Deckert said.

"No, I'd like to speak to him first," the stranger said. As he spoke, he reached up to his jacket pockets with both hands.

As soon as the stranger's hands went up, Deckert raised his shotgun above the counter. He didn't have to turn the barrel, the weapon had been leveled at the biker from the moment he had come through the door.

"Stand real still," Deckert said. There was a sharp twinge of pain across his back as he raised the Remington—a reminder of the two big bruises from the bullets of the day before. The muzzle of the shotgun looked even larger than it normally did with the big DuckBill choke on it. The inch-wide V-slot of the choke added even more to the intimidation factor of the weapon.

But the big biker didn't seem intimidated to Deckert. He just froze in his movement.

"I wondered just what kind of cannon you had under that counter," the big biker said. "I should have known an Army guy would need a big gun to make up for something."

As Deckert stared at the man, the biker started to chuckle quietly. The sound quickly grew to a loud laugh, a very distinctive loud laugh.

"Ho, ho, ho," the man roared. "You should see your face Deckert. Having that mean old squid working for you making you a little bit jumpy now?"

The sound of that laugh snapped Reaper's head toward the front of the shop. The voice had sounded a little familiar but muffled by the helmet, he hadn't been able to place it. But that laugh was something he would never forget.

Reaper strode down the hall and into the retail shop. He looked at the back of the biker, who had not moved since Deckert had raised the shotgun.

"Can I take my helmet off now?" the man asked.

"Go ahead," Deckert said, not lowering the shotgun an inch.

As the black helmet came off the man's head, Reaper stepped to the side and looked into the face of an old Teammate and friend.

"Damn," Reaper almost shouted, "Bear! What the hell are you doing here? God damn, but it's good to see you."

"Damn, I should have known it was you," Deckert

said as he lowered the weapon. "Sorry about that."

He laid the shotgun on the counter top, the muzzle pointing away from Bear, but with the weapon still within reach.

"Hey, no problem, man," Bear said with a big grin on his face. "I figured if you were just going to shoot me, you would have done it when I came through the door."

Bear turned to Reaper while still holding his gloves and helmet in his hands. The two men wrapped their arms around each other in a powerful embrace, slapping each other's back as they did so. Standing back, Reaper took a look at his old partner.

"It is good to see you, Teammate," Reaper said. "But you really picked a time to finally come around. I invited you out here last summer."

"Well, I couldn't make it then," Bear said. "I've been traveling around a lot since I retired from the Teams. But when Keith here gave me a call yesterday, I rode all night to get here."

"So, Keith called you did he?" Reaper said looking at Deckert. "Did he tell you what was going on?"

"Just that there was trouble and you could use some help, was all," Bear said. "It was not the most detailed phone call I've ever gotten, but it didn't have to be. He said you needed help and here I am. Things must be interesting. Or do you two greet all of your customers with guns in your hands? If you do, this place isn't going to be staying open long."

With that, Bear stepped over to the counter and laid his helmet and gloves down. Sticking his hand out to Deckert, the two men shook hands with a strong grip.

"Real good to see you, man," Bear said. "I hope having this old Navy chief here is working out for you."

"He keeps life interesting, that's for sure," Deckert said. "And just what in the hell were you reaching for a minute ago anyway?"

"Reaching for?" Bear said puzzled. "Oh, you mean when I was going to put my gloves in my pockets?"

"Yeah, with a gun pointed at you," Deckert said.

"Just what in the hell is that thing on the end of that barrel anyway?" Bear said as he looked down at the shotgun on the counter. "It looks like something the Teams carried back in the Vietnam days."

"It is, sort of," Deckert said as he laid his hand on the weapon. "A reproduction, anyway. It's a Duck-Bill choke. Some friends of mine make them now, they're copies of the ones the SEALs carried in Vietnam. Change the pattern from a circle to an oval four times as wide as it is high."

Deckert picked up the Remington and hung it by its sling from the back of his wheelchair. "Kind of turns the gun into a big chain saw. Makes it hard for us old guys to miss."

"Not bad, even for an old guy," Bear said.

Turning to Reaper, Bear continued. "Shoot man, if we're done handling guns, you got a beer around here someplace? I've got enough road dust in my throat to cover a highway."

Reaper went over and locked the front door and Bear followed him to the rear of the house. Bear and Reaper sat down at the table in the dining nook next to the kitchen. Deckert had passed through the office and into the kitchen, stopping at the refrigerator to pull out three long-necked bottles of Corona Extra beer. Wheeling himself over to the kitchen table, Deckert paused to take a bottle opener off a peg next to the refrigerator. He set the bottles and opener down onto the table.

"Hey," Bear said as he reached for a bottle and the opener, "classy. All the modern conveniences. Bet you've even got indoor plumbing."

"Well, it is a bit better than some of the places we've stayed at," Reaper said as he opened a bottle. "Warmer at least. Dryer, too."

"Okay," Bear said. "We've said all the nice things and you showed me the wrong end of a great big gun. You officially have my interest. Now just what in the hell is going on here?"

"What did Keith here tell you?" Reaper asked.

"Nothing much," Bear said. "Only that you were in trouble and needed some help. That was enough to bring me in. As far as details go, I don't know a damned thing."

"And you didn't think to ask?" Reaper said.

"You would have?" said Bear.

"Okay, I can't argue much with that, brother," Reaper said. "Well, the short version is that a guy showed up yesterday along with a pair of goons. They tried to strong-arm me into giving them a bunch of new guns that we've been developing here. Keith got caught up in the fallout."

"Some butthead came in here to strong-arm you?" Bear said a little incredulously. "How the hell did he expect to get away with that?"

"He had some of his boys grab up Mary and

Ricky," Reaper said quietly. "When he came out here, he already had them secured someplace. I went after him to try and get him to tell me where they were. I took out his wheels but he got away."

"He's got Mary and Ricky?" Bear said with surprise evident in his voice. "So why don't you get the cops or the FBI on his ass? This place should be crawling with detectives right now."

"The son of a bitch had Mary contact her boss and tell him that she was taking Ricky and getting out of town for a while. Seems everyone was able to believe that she would be afraid of an ex-SEAL husband."

"Sorry, brother," Bear said. "I had heard that you were having some family trouble—not that that's too unusual with Team guys. But why don't you go find this guy and beat the intel you want out of him?"

"Because when Reaper here tore the ass off that guy's Vette," Deckert said, "he ducked into a marsh and disappeared. We're not even sure he's alive. The last thing he said to us was that we had seventy-two hours to build him some more guns. Since then, there haven't been any more demands made, no calls, nothing. When Reaper here thought I had been shot, he quit looking for the guy and came screaming-ass back here."

"You got shot?" Bear asked. "You look pretty good for a dead guy."

"I was wearing a vest," Deckert said disgustedly. "But while Reaper was heading back here, the two guys who had come in with this guy got away. I really owe something to the small one who got the drop on me."

"Don't beat yourself up," Reaper said. "I'm the

one who didn't do a good shakedown on the guy."

"I seem to remember being the one to tell you to get out after that guy," Deckert said. "And now all we have to show for it is a damaged hot rod, a single name, and a beat-up briefcase."

"Damaged hot rod?" Bear asked.

"You should see what a souped-up Checker cab can do to the fiberglass back end of a Corvette," Reaper said. "Like hitting dry wood with a splitting ax."

"Okay," Bear said. "I'm sure there's more to that part of the story. But what about the briefcase?"

"It was just a briefcase I found in the front end of the Vette," Reaper said. "There wasn't anything else in the car but the case and what I grabbed up from the glove compartment. None of it was anything incriminating—not a damned thing we could go to the police with. The only name we've got is Steven Arzee, and we're not sure that's his name.

"What we found in the case was mostly business correspondence and paperwork about some kind of bar in Detroit called the Factory. All of it looked legitimate, invoices for booze, food, things like that. The most interesting thing was a bunch of business cards for the place with Arzee's name on them. The cards have the title Executive Manager on them."

"I've been looking on the Internet and found some interesting stuff on this Factory club," Deckert said. "It seems to be a pretty popular place with the young crowd, at least its Web site shows a bunch of bands rotating through the place."

"You don't know about that place?" Bear said. "I've never been there myself but a bunch of the local bikers know about it. It's built in an old auto plant, that's why they call it the Factory. From what I know about it, it's a great place to pick up chicks. Some of the guys have said you can score just about anything you want there, too."

"It looks like our only solid lead on this Arzee guy, or whoever he may be working with," Reaper said. "Those cards say manager, not owner. So there must be somebody up the line from him. Maybe we can learn something from them."

Bear looked over at his friend. "You wanna go for a visit?" he said as a big smile split his face.

Chapter Fourteen

The situation had changed for Reaper. Now he had something tangible to direct his energies against. Reaper's family probably wasn't being held at the Factory club. It wouldn't do to assume that Arzee was stupid. He wouldn't keep kidnap victims at his own place. He would have them stashed somewhere else, or at least that was the way to plan. The Factory looked to be the best chance of getting a lead on Arzee's location. If Arzee was the guy they wanted, once he had his hands on him Reaper was sure he could convince the man to talk to him.

There was an unknown factor to the equation—who might Arzee be working for? Did he have a boss? If he did, they had yet to show themselves.

To act on the situation, they needed intelligence: they had to gather information on Arzee and the best lead they had for now was this Factory club. A reconnaissance of the club would have to be conducted, a straightforward urban sneak-and-peek.

Conducting covert recons of an area and then setting up a concealed observation post was something Reaper was very experienced at. His friends Bear and Deckert were not going to allow him to go that mission alone. One very good thing about the situation: if Reaper had to go into a bad area with minimal support, Bear was the Teammate he wanted at his side.

The location of the Factory club was easy enough to find. The street and Web-site addresses had both been on Arzee's business cards. Specific information on the place wasn't any harder than looking it up on the Internet. They even showed a map to the club's location.

The Web site told about how the Factory was a modern techno music club with all of the amenities. What wasn't mentioned on the site or anywhere else, was Steven Arzee by name or as the executive manager. More hours of research on the Internet, combined with a number of phone calls, uncovered nothing more useful than a bewildering morass of company names, limited liability corporations, and a lot of dead ends.

Deckert's police connections in Detroit knew about the club, but that was about all. The place had its share of trouble in the past but nothing unusual, nothing that made it stand out as more than a bar or dance club. The Factory just didn't raise any particular red flags on the police radar.

While Deckert and Reaper were doing their research, Bear made some calls of his own and then left on his Harley. About an hour later, Bear returned driving a nondescript Chevy van with his bike in the back. He just said that he had borrowed the vehicle from an old friend, figuring they would need something low-key to operate from. Reaper could only marvel at how Bear seemed to know somebody everyplace he went. The man had more contacts than a politician.

Transportation was laid on and the target had been located. It was time to gear up and head out. When Bear came into the house, Reaper was back at the kitchen table packing a bag with gear. Reaper was using a Camelback HAWG backpack. The green backpack had a number of attachment points for gear on its outside surfaces. There was also room for 1,100 cubic inches of gear inside it.

All the space in the backpack would be needed for the camera gear Reaper was laying out on the kitchen table. There was the camera itself, and a single telephoto lens that was almost half a foot long. A huge black-and-white cylinder with a number of bars and posts attached to it sat on the table. The big cylinder was over a foot long and half that dimension thick. A compact folding tripod, a small pair of Carl Zeiss 8x30 binoculars, and several other small bags and packages made up the balance of the gear going in the backpack.

Reaper had already filled the 100-ounce flexible liquid reservoir that fit in a special pocket in the backpack. The water that filled the reservoir was available simply by biting on a mouthpiece and sipping at the end of a tube that went over the shoulder strap and into the pack. You could wear the pack and never need to pull out a canteen.

"Damn," Bear said. "You got enough to take a few snapshots there?"

"Just the essentials for a long surveillance," Reaper said. "I've got another one here for you."

He reached down to the floor and picked up a second backpack from a different manufacturer that their shop had started carrying. The pack was a Hydrastorm Tsunami and also had a 100-ounce water reservoir inside a special pocket. A delivery tube went over the shoulder and had a bite valve on the end.

"I gotta carry all that shit as well?" Bear asked.

"No, just what you think you'll need for a twenty-four-hour observation post," Reaper answered. "We may not have the OP set up that long, but that's the way I want to plan. I recommend you fill that reservoir with water and toss in something solid to eat. There's some oatmeal bars in the drawer over there."

"Oatmeal bars?" Bear said, now recognizing several of the brown-wrapped rectangular chunks lying on the table. "You mean MRE oatmeal bars?"

"Yeah," Reaper said as he continued to check through his gear, "Keith likes them and bought a couple of cases from a supplier a while back."

"Never trust an Army guy to have good taste in food," Bear said as he dug through the drawer. He pulled out several of the oatmeal bars, as well as a handful of chocolate bars. Going back over to the table, he dropped his pile and picked up the Hydrastorm Tsunami. As he held the pack, he took a closer look at the sophisticated camera gear on the table. The huge black-and-white cylinder with the protrusions all over it turned out to be a short, fat telescope.

"Just what is that rig anyway?" Bear asked.

"This?" Reaper said pointing to the telescope.

"This is a Celestron C5 Schmidt-Cassegrain telescope set up with a T-ring adapter so that it can act as a 1,250 millimeter f/10 telephoto lens. Basically, it's a five-inch diameter reflecting scope with lenses. You get really fine details with it so you can blow up the shots as big as you want."

"Uh-huh," Bear said, "and this is?"

"This is a Nikon D100 six-megapixel D-SLR digital camera body along with a 75- to 300-millimeter telephoto lens spare battery pack and a one gigabite Lexar compact flashcard—digital film. There's a spare charged ENL3 battery-pack battery and another Lexar flashcard in the boxes."

"Right," Bear said. "Do you really have any idea of what you just said?"

"Not really," Reaper said with a grin. "Mostly I just read all that stuff from the box."

"This kind of thing is just laying around a gun shop?" Bear asked.

"No," Reaper said. "This rig belongs to Keith. He uses it to take pictures of birds. Puts them up on his computer."

"He watches birds?" Bear said a little incredulously.

"Yeah, birds," Reaper said. "Said he had a pair of peregrine falcons nesting near here a few years back. When you shoot on the range next to the shop, hawks start circling downrange watching for any game you scare up."

"Bird-watching," Bear said. "Chief, I'm worried about the two of you. You guys have got to start getting out more."

Reaper grinned at his friend, then looked back

down at the gear. He remembered the reason he was packing it and the grin quickly faded.

"With this kind of camera rig," Reaper said, "we won't have to develop any film before we can see the pictures. Keith has all the computer programs and stuff he needs to make us any kind of enlargements or hard copies *we* might need. This rig eliminates a possible security leak because we don't have to go out and get film developed. Pack whatever you want to take, we're leaving soon."

Bear knew that the joking was over and set to work. Besides the packs, there were two bundles of cloth rolled up and secured with line. In addition to the camera gear and other materials, Reaper was stuffing a towel into the HAWG pack to pad out the camera and lenses. Since Reaper had a concealed carry license for Michigan, he was taking his SIG-220 secured in a Galco leather PLE paddle holster set behind his right hip. Over his left hip he wore a Galco double magazine case with two spare magazines to the SIG.

In the right front pocket of his Levi's, Reaper carried his older Emerson Commander-BTS folding knife. The five-inch black G-10 epoxy handle held a 3.75-inch-long black-T coated blade. The knife was larger than the CQC-7BW that Reaper had been carrying, but that blade had disappeared along with Musclehead and Gun Weasel—the names Reaper was now using for the two goons from the day before. The value of a good Emerson pocket knife was well proven. Reaper wasn't about to go out without one.

As far as Bear was concerned, all he needed for the recon was a folding knife. They weren't planning to do an assault on the Factory, not even penetrate it for a sneak-and-peek. With nothing in particular on him, Bear could possibly slip into the club with the crowd. No one had seen him with Reaper so there was no reason to connect the two men.

The two SEALs were going to conduct a drive-by to check out the area. If things looked good, they would then set up for a longer observation post. It was a mission they had done dozens of times, both during training and on real-world ops in the field.

The only thing that Reaper was certain about as they headed down to the Factory was that the place was popular. The Web site had listed a number of upcoming events, both raves and several concerts. That could put innocents into the line of fire, another reason to keep that portion of the operation low-profile—a soft probe.

The Factory may have been popular and doing well as a club, but it sure wasn't doing anything for the immediate area around it as far as Reaper and Bear could tell. Their first impression of the neighborhood around the Factory was that of urban decay. In a several square block area, the Factory was the only place that looked as though it wasn't about to fall down or rot away.

Located near the crossroads of the Chrysler and Ford Freeways, two of the major highway arteries in Detroit, access to the Factory wasn't a problem. Moving around the area freely might be. The east end of the block-long building was the only part of the structure that had a good coat of paint on it. That, and the big sign that said THE FACTORY in huge block letters, pretty much showed which end of the building was the main entrance. The other three sides of the six-story structure had been tagged frequently, gang and just plain street graffiti covering every accessible surface.

In their beat-up van, Reaper and Bear drew no particular attention as they drove around on the surface streets near the Factory. Bear needed little in the way of disguise to blend in with the locals, his biker jacket, heavy boots, and faded Levi's did not stand out any more than did his beard and sunglasses. Reaper also wore Levi's over work boots, and had a long black nylon jacket zipped up over a gray sweatshirt. Dark glasses and a knit cap completed his street outfit.

The men did not want to stand out in the neighborhood around the club. Red and gray brick houses that had seen their heyday more than forty years earlier made up the neighborhood that surrounded the Factory to the south and west. To the north and east were smaller factory buildings, most of them vacant and empty. Just as empty were the boarded-up houses that used to hold the workers who manned those factories.

Both SEALs felt as if they were traveling through a war zone. The occasional pair of suspicious eyes that looked out a window just reinforced those feelings.

"Damn," said Bear, "we saw better areas in Bosnia."

Reaper just grunted in agreement as he watched the Factory building looming up in front of the next street corner. They were going to do a drive-by on several sides of the Factory. Then they would head up one of the surface roads and cross a bridge over the highway. There was an industrial storage building directly across from the plant.

The south face of the Factory building had been the loading docks and storage area when it had been an active auto plant. There were still stacks of steel frames and piles of industrial debris along the fence line—too open to make good cover during a penetration. The fence wasn't in the best of repair, but it was all standing with no holes or gaps in the fifteen-foot-tall wire mesh. Three strands of barbed wire on top of the fence extended into the yard on angled supports. The wire was tight and clean with no breaks or missing strands. There were a number of large rollaway gates in the fence, all but one secured with heavy chains and padlocks.

The only gate that looked used was at the far southeastern corner of the property. As the van passed the gate, Reaper took a number of pictures of the gate, fence, and yard area behind it. A draped towel covered and hid most of the camera from prying eyes during his pass—Reaper aiming and shooting the camera by feel. Lots of pictures would help make up for any misaimed shots. The telephoto lens showed a good view of the power system for pulling the gate open and closed with a chain drive.

At the center and southwestern corner of the main building were rectangular concrete extensions that looked as if they held stairways and big freight elevators. The elevators would have moved the cars up and down through the floors.

"Bear," Reaper said, "look at those two big elevator stacks. See the square chimneys between them?"

"Those bolted-together ones?" Bear asked.

"Yeah," said Reaper. "See any problem in climbing up them?"

Several of the stacks were very close together—only a few feet apart at most. Reinforcing bars and flanges stuck out from all sides of the stacks. To experienced climbers like Reaper and Bear, those stacks were as good as a stairway or ladder—only a lot better for concealment.

"Nope," Bear said agreeing with Reaper. "All of that stuff sticking out from those stacks will give us as many foot and handholds as we could need. It has to be strong enough to support us or those chimneys would have collapsed of their own weight long ago."

The two men drove on past the Factory and the side street along the west side of the building. Half of the block to the west of the Factory was a huge parking lot. The lot had a few standing double streetlights, and scattered weeds growing through the blacktop. A fifteen-foot-tall chain-link fence stretched around the lot, the fence brown with rust.

The west wall of the Factory had four rows of green glass windows on the upper floors. The windows along the bottom two floors had been bricked over. The few windows that remained were glazed with thick, wire-reinforced glass in steel frames. There were no doors on this end of the building and no cover in the open parking lot.

Brown brick industrial buildings extended for several blocks north across the street from the Factory building. There were no cameras mounted on telephone poles or any surveillance gear that either SEAL could see anywhere around. No one seemed to care about the area, and no one was on the streets at all. Even the fire hydrant next to the Factory had a yellow circular sign hanging off one of the pipe caps reading OUT OF SERVICE.

Rather than pass the factory again, Bear turned the van left onto a side street as Reaper lifted his camera and took a rapid series of pictures of the north face of the Factory building. Just the same as they had seen on the western wall of the building, the north side of the Factory had four rows of windows along the upper floors. But there were no windows at all along the bottom two floors. Those areas were filled in with what looked like steel paneling.

There were three sets of steel fire doors spaced out along the first floor of the building. In addition to the door openings, there were two sets of fire escapes extending up from the second floor to the sixth floor. These were the obvious ways into the upper floors and would probably be alarmed.

There was no graffiti on the north face of the Factory above the sidewalk level, the upper wall was clean. If none of the local artists felt like going up those inviting fire escapes, then Reaper and Bear weren't going to climb them either. Going in the easy way to a target had never proved to be the safe way.

Going north along a side street away from the Factory, Bear turned right and then drove the van across a bridge to the eastern side of the highway. At this point, the Chrysler Freeway was eight lanes of divided highway at the bottom of a man-made valley.

Facing the east end of the Factory building from across the highway was a five-story storage warehouse. Half-filled dumpsters and scattered construction vehicles were the only signs that the place was still active. The dumpsters had a lot of cardboard boxes in them that were unweathered. Since it had rained just the week before, the condition of the boxes told Reaper and Bear that somebody had been working around these dumpsters recently.

Trash had to be generated by somebody, and that meant there was probably activity in the building, something neither of the two SEALs were particularly pleased to note. The storage building had a clear view of the east side of the Factory on the other side of the highway. It was from the roof of this building that Reaper wanted to set up their observation post.

Chapter Fifteen

Reaper and Bear were conducting their mission as if they were well behind enemy lines with no support. They had no backup on call, no emergency extraction, no fire support. Everyone in the area of the Factory or the chosen observation post (OP) location would be assumed to be the enemy, with no exceptions. The rules of engagement were simple, there would be no engagements. Contact would be avoided—period.

The two SEALs had worked on operations like this before, but never where the stakes had been so high. It wasn't their own lives the two men had to be concerned with, it was the lives of Reaper's wife and son. If discovered, they could expect no mercy from the kidnappers. And if they were caught by the police, the only thing they could reasonably expect would be for the kidnappers to cut their losses, and eliminate any witnesses.

There was no question that Bear would support his Teammate in any way that he was capable of. But the real cost of their success or failure would be held by Reaper alone. The only way he could operate under this much pressure was to cut it off, shut out personal feelings, and deal with the task at hand. This was something they learned in the Teams, you could either compartmentalize your life and concentrate on your job, or not remain an operator.

The ability to ignore the pain, the distractions, and keep going, was something Reaper needed very badly right now. For the time being, those aspects of his personality that made him a father, a husband, a lover, were closed off. The compartments in his psyche that were left open were the ones that made him an experienced, efficient, Navy SEAL chief.

But he was not alone on this operation. His Teammate being with him meant a very great deal to Reaper. SEALs didn't operate alone, they were always part of a Team, even a team as small as two men. Bear and Reaper had trained together, frozen, sweated, and ached as one unit. In the field, one would know what the other was thinking automatically. In any situation, they knew what the other man would do, how he would react.

So Reaper was not completely alone; he had Bear and Deckert to work with. Deckert had proven himself a very valuable resource. From his desktop computer, Deckert had come up with hard intelligence that was proving very valuable right now.

Besides detailed maps of the area they were traveling in, Deckert had located aerial and satellite photos on the Internet. These shots gave a lot of information about the Factory and the area surrounding it. The drive-by that the two SEALs had completed confirmed the intel Deckert had developed.

The east end of the Factory faced another fenced-in parking lot. Then there were the lanes and ramps of the highway intersection. There was nothing close-in that the two SEALs could use for cover, no place where they could park a vehicle overnight without drawing attention. It was the building complex across the highway from the Factory that looked good. Behind the storage building were a number of areas where vehicles were parked and construction equipment stored. They would launch their mission from that area.

Up close against the side of the warehouse was a large billboard mounted on tall posts. The billboard would supply cover for the two men as they climbed up to the roof of the main building. On top of the roof were two huge elevated billboards, plainly visible from the highway and the area across the street. It was there, at the base of those huge signs, that the SEALs would set up their hide, their camouflaged hidden position, and establish their observation post.

Bear's bike was secured in the back of the van along with the rest of their gear. Some of the equipment was very high tech. Other pieces were from the much lower end of the technology scale. Two sets of generic dark coveralls would cover the two SEALs and help them to blend in with any workmen in the area. In the pockets of each of the coveralls were a pair of FOGs (Fast-rope Operator Gloves) and a Hatch balaclava hood made of lightweight black Nomex. Two five-gallon plastic buckets with lids, some rolled-up dark cloths, a couple of sections of carpeting not much bigger than medium-sized throw rugs, and a few coils of parachute cord made up the bulk of their equipment.

Two additional pieces of gear would look odd to anyone but a SEAL: a pair of extendable aluminum painter's poles. The top of each pole had a two-pronged steel hook attached to it, the prongs of the hooks well padded with heavy tape. With a line that was fixed to it, the hook slipped down into the hollow pole. Catching the tines of the hook on an object would pull it from the pole, securely attaching a climbing line to the target.

The modifications had converted the painter's poles into climber's extension poles, the same kind of tool that the SEALs used to board ships with. Normally, a coiled caving ladder was used with the hooks. Instead of the ladders, Reaper was using lengths of 9/16-inch tubular nylon webbing. The flat nylon webbing took up little space and was very strong. Using it to scale a building wall took a lot of upper-body and grip strength, something Bear and Reaper had plenty of.

Bear pulled the van around and parked it among some trucks and other vehicles. The van was beat up enough that it didn't stand out in the lot. A little maneuvering parked the van so that the back end was clear and Bear's bike could be rolled out. The area in front of the van was clear so that it could be driven forward and onto the road quickly.

The two SEALs were now in their element. They were operational on a hot op. It didn't matter that they were in civilian territory. Working together as they were was like putting on an old coat. They were

comfortable and at ease while also working at a
heightened state of awareness.

The two men changed into their coveralls, gathered up their gear, and left the van. Both men had a
set of keys to the van and to Bear's Harley. The devil was in the details. Little things like spare keys
was something that couldn't be missed. Eventually,
your luck would run out. Mr. Murphy was always
prepared to screw over you and your mission.

Anyone who noticed the two men leaving the parking lot would only see another pair of workers. An
observer would have had to look fast to see the two
workers disappear next to an old and faded billboard.

While Bear kept watch, Reaper scrambled up the
side of a ladder attached to the billboard. The bottom
of the ladder was slightly out of reach overhead, but
Reaper just jumped and started up the ladder using
the strength of his arms. A platform surrounded the
billboard and that was where Reaper stopped. The
gear buckets came up next on the ends of the nylon
lines. Bear clambered up the ladder not as gracefully as Reaper had, but with just as much obvious
strength.

The five-story storage building that Reaper wanted
to reach was at the northwest corner of a block of four
structures. They were now within reach of the top of
the two-story building at the southeast corner of the
block. This place seemed a little newer than the others in the area. It did have more security than the others. Someone had secured concertina coils of shiny,
sharp new razor wire along the edge of the roof
coaming to block possible burglars.

Razor wire was sharp, it was nasty, and it was

something that Reaper and Bear had seen a number of times during their training and while out on missions. They had faced much more sophisticated barriers during some of their training when they penetrated classified Navy installations to test security.

This was the only avenue of approach the SEALs could use to get on the roof in broad daylight. The upper part of the billboard stuck up past the edge of the roof, protecting it from view.

The billboard was not going to be enough to protect the two SEALs from the observation of anyone who was on the roof of any of the buildings in the block. The aerial photos that Deckert had located showed plain, flat tar roofs on two of the structures they would have to cross. The two men would have to get on the roof and cross it quickly to avoid being seen.

Both men quickly set to work without a word being spoken between them. They broke out and secured the gear, then left the buckets on the platform. As Bear extended a climbing pole and attached a webbing coil to the hook, Reaper undid one of the cloth bundles. Wrapped around the outside of the bundle was one of the sections of carpeting.

Using the extended climbing pole, Bear set the hook on the edge of the roof. Reaper secured the carpet section to his belt with a piece of nylon webbing. Then he grabbed the webbing leading to the hook, stepped out, and walked up the side of the building, ignoring the three-story drop below him. Grabbing hold of the edge of the roof, Reaper pulled himself up enough to peer out across the flat tar.

No one was there. It was just a flat expanse of roof with about sixteen inches of wall surrounding it. The only movement was the fluttering of some plastic shreds where discarded bags had stuck to the razor wire coils. A quick glance across the other roofs didn't uncover any possible observers to Reaper.

Pulling the carpet section up, Reaper tossed it across the razor wire. Pulling himself up and over the carpet, Reaper made climbing onto the roof look easy.

Now that one of them was exposed on the roof, speed became essential. Bear quickly got onto the roof and pulled up the climbing pole. Crouching low, the two men crossed over to the next building they had to climb. This roof only went up a single story above the one they were on and part of the structure blocked anyone's view of the two SEALs.

No fancy climbing technique was used to get to the next roof. Reaper secured one end of the nylon webbing to his belt. Then Bear cupped his hands and Reaper stepped into them. Bear lifted Reaper up to where he could look out over the next roof. No razor wire or observers could be seen, only the dark, dirty windows of another wall.

Pulling himself up to the roof, Reaper pulled the web line off his belt. Bracing his feet against the wall, Reaper leaned back with the webbing tight in his hands. A quick yank on the line and Bear climbed up to the roof.

Crossing to the last wall, the two SEALs repeated their technique and within a minute, both men were on top of the building where Reaper wanted to set up the observation post. It was a good location and both men could see the Factory plainly on the far side of the highway.

There were two huge billboards on top of the

storage building. Reaper wanted to set up their OP at the base of one of those billboards. A small shacklike building up against the western side of the roof topped a stairwell to the inside of the building. The doorway of that shack was where any guard or observer could be expected.

A worn fiberglass and metal tubing chair next to the stairwell door was a bad sign. The chair was flipped over and leaning against the stairwell top, just as it would be if someone used it regularly and didn't want rain to be caught in the seat. For the moment, the roof was empty of people except for the two SEALs.

Chapter Sixteen

Now that both men were finally on the target roof itself, they moved fast to get into a concealed position—what they called their hide. The huge billboards were set on top of steel columns that were secured to the roof by a heavy girder and mesh frame. There was almost two feet of space between the steel mesh on the frame and the tar and gravel surface of the roof itself. Reaper intended to set up their observation post in the space under the frame.

The billboard structure stood right next to the stairwell. With Bear next to him, Reaper crouched low and ran to the platform. Ignoring the sharp edges of the gravel, both Reaper and Bear lay down and scrambled underneath the edge of the frame. Crawling up to where they could look out over the roof coaming, they began to set up their observation post.

Their first move was to secure the observation post from the view of anyone looking from the Factory. To do that, they unrolled a length of Hessian screen and hung it up in front of what was now their hide. Hessian screen was nothing more than plain, rough-woven jute cloth—simple burlap. The weave of the dark brown cloth was open enough to easily see through it if you were on the shaded side and looked out toward the light. Looking in from the lighted side, you couldn't see past the cloth.

The billboard platform was a heavy steel grid welded onto a framework of I-beams. The whole platform was raised above the surface of the roof on a bunch of short steel legs. The legs ran around the edge of the platform as well as down the middle the long way. To hang up the cloth screen, Reaper and Bear clipped it to the bottom flange of one of the I-beams with wooden spring clothespins. Once the screen was up, the rest of the observation post, now a camouflaged hide, could be completed.

The two collapsed painter's poles were used to support a dark drop-cloth cover over the hide. With the cloth in place, it would be very hard to see the two men in the shadows even if someone were standing on the grid. The poles leaned in against the front I-beam with their back ends on the gravel roof. The open end of the tentlike hide was covered with the Hessian screen.

The carpet sections now proved additionally useful as Reaper and Bear pulled them up and rolled the strips out across the gravel. They would protect the men from some of the coarse chunks of rock as well as cut down on any noise they might make. A quick look around the outside edges of the hide didn't show any light, so if the two SEALs couldn't see out, no one could see in. The hide was secure and they were in place.

Both men started to assemble their cameras and

observation equipment. The Celestron C5 scope that Reaper was using was so big it sat on its own small folding tripod. There was a T-ring adapter on the back of the scope that connected it to the Nikon D100 digital camera.

Bear had brought Deckert's spare camera, a Minolta Dynax 7000i 35mm film camera. The film camera was a backup in case something went wrong with the digital system. The dozen rolls of film Bear had in his pack shouldn't even need to be used on the mission.

There was an old adage in the Teams regarding mission-critical gear. "Two is one, one is none." If one piece of important gear was all you had brought with you and it failed, then so did the mission. And this mission was far too important for any details to have been overlooked.

Picking up his binoculars, Reaper looked out across the highway to the Factory building about 275 meters away. He cupped his hands across the top and sides of the binoculars. With the sun still high in the midafternoon sky, Reaper's hands protected the lenses from flashing in the light. The simple precaution was second nature to the man. To his right, Reaper could feel Bear setting out the spare camera and telephoto lens as well as his own binoculars.

Not a word had been spoken between the two men since they had left the van. Now they settled in for a long vigil. From any side of the roof and even through the steel grid of the platform, all that could be seen was a dark pile of loose cloth, as if a tarp had been shoved up underneath the platform, or blown there by an errant wind.

With their black balaclavas pulled over their heads, the two men disappeared into the shadows of their hide. There was no way that anyone from ground level could see up into the area five stories above where the SEALs lay. From the Factory, even a person using a powerful telescope and who knew where to look would have seen nothing more than shadow.

The basic infiltration of the target area had been completed. Now the two SEALs would take careful note of all activity around the Factory. This would be a long, painstaking operation. They were on the military equivalent of a police stakeout, only Reaper and Bear didn't have anyone to come and relieve them. They could only lie still and watch.

Through his binoculars, Reaper could see the entire east wall of the Factory building, the parking lot that lay between the building and the highway, and the fields to the north and south of the empty lot. Running along both the south and east sides of the fields were major multilane interstate highways.

The Ford Freeway passed over the Chrysler only a few hundred meters south of where Reaper and Bear lay. The intersecting highways made for a mass of bridges and curved ramps crossing over one another. The ramps, lanes, shoulders, fences, and excavated area put a no-man's-land more than a hundred meters wide between the hide and the beginning of the parking area to the east of the Factory.

The east parking area of the Factory was a huge, square, fenced-in area of concrete—one hundred meters on a side. It appeared to have regular activity as the concrete surface was in fairly good repair. There were no signs of the weeds and grasses that broke through the surface of the parking area to the west of the Factory.

Light poles stood in the parking lot and it was surrounded by a fifteen-foot-high chain-link fence topped with barbed wire. At each corner of the lot were closed-circuit TV cameras on top of tall poles.

South of the parking area, across a two-lane road, was a weed-choked vacant lot. The most prominent feature of the lot was another massive billboard raised up on a steel framework. The advertising sign was huge, more than eighty feet wide and almost a third of that tall. The bottom of the billboard was raised up nearly a hundred feet into the air so that it could be clearly seen from both the northbound Chrysler and westbound Ford Freeways.

There was a much smaller billboard next to the massive one, the smaller facing to the southwest and connected to the larger at its southern corner. The larger billboard had a wide platform around its base with a ladder leading up to it along one of the support pillars. These billboards could be seen a long distance away along either highway. They also had a direct view into the front windows of the Factory.

Reaper and Bear examined all of these details through their binoculars. In spite of the cameras available to them, both men each carefully sketched out a map, a panoramic view, of what they saw. They would compare the two sketches later to see if either man noticed something the other had missed.

His area sketch finished, Reaper turned his attention to the Factory building itself. It was the east-facing wall of the factory that Reaper studied through his binoculars. Then he attached the Nikon to the back of the Celestron scope and carefully photographed every feature of the wall.

Almost the entire eastern face of the building was made up of windows. It consisted of six floors of windows, each floor having seven panels of glass separated by white columns. The window panels were made up of dozens of glass panes held in a steel frame.

The huge front of the building was half a block wide and twenty-five-meters tall. Thick blinds were on the inside of the hundreds of windows to block the blinding morning sun. Now, with the sun past noon and lowering to the west, the windows remained covered on the inside—not a good situation for outside observation.

It was only midafternoon and there was still a full day to go.

Chapter Seventeen

By 3 P.M., 1500 hours in Reaper's log, the traffic on the highways increased considerably as the local rush hour began. By 1530 hours, the traffic on the highway ramps below the SEALs was bumper-to-bumper. Traffic was heavy, but nothing was going on at the Factory that Reaper or Bear could see.

At 1613 hours, Reaper was watching as a brown UPS truck pulled up to the front of the Factory. The driver stopped on the street and walked up to the two sets of double doors underneath the big Factory sign. With his clipboard in hand, the delivery driver knocked at the doors and waited.

Reaper was watching the driver through the Nikon camera attached to the big Celestron scope. As Reaper continued to watch, the delivery became more interesting as the man just kept standing at the doors. Even after repeated heavy knocks, it was a few minutes before someone finally came to see who was there. Either the cameras in the parking lot couldn't see the front doors or the person on watch didn't care that anyone was there. Sloppy security was something that particularly interested Reaper. He continued to take pictures and watch the scene.

Whoever had come to the door wasn't the man the driver wanted to see. The doors closed in his face and again, the driver just stood there. The little show in front of the Factory was at least something to watch and helped keep Reaper's attention up. Then there was some action at the door that grabbed Reaper like a hand at his throat.

The front door of the Factory had opened and Steven Arzee was standing there in what looked like a fancy bathrobe.

"Son of a bitch," Reaper said quietly.

Bear had been watching the delivery through a pair of binoculars. The limited magnification of the glasses did not give him as clear a view of the man standing in the door as Reaper had through the big Celestron.

"What?" Bear said softly.

"That's him," Reaper said. "That's Arzee signing the clipboard."

"That's him?" Bear said. "Sure doesn't look like much, does he?"

Reaper continued to concentrate on the action and ignored Bear's comment. Bear looked over at his friend and could see Reaper taking pictures. The concentration in the SEAL's face was obvious as he watched Arzee walk back into the building. As the front doors closed, Reaper snapped a last picture of the scene, his finger steady and firm as he applied pressure to the shutter, the same firm pressure he would have used to pull the trigger of a rifle.

"We found him, Bear," Reaper said. "We've got him."

"What do you want to do now?" Bear asked. "Go after him or what?"

"We maintain surveillance," Reaper said. "Let's see what else shows up."

Bear could tell that his friend was hoping for a sign of his family. It was going to be a long night.

Bear took over the watch at the bottom of the hour. The UPS truck was long gone and there hadn't been any more action at the target. Then, at 1645 hours, a white passenger van pulled out of the single-story structure at the southeast corner of the Factory.

Swinging the big Celestron scope over on its tripod mount, Bear aimed it toward the corner of the Factory fence that had the powered gate. Twisting the deeply knurled silver focusing knob on the back of the scope brought the scene into sharp clarity. Centered in the middle of the scene was the van that had pulled out of the garage and stopped.

Lying to Bear's left, Reaper could also see what showed on the bright LCD screen in the back of the digital camera. Every little detail of the van was in clear view as it stopped at the electric gate. Bear snapped a number of pictures of the van, paying particular attention to the vehicle's license plate, the driver—who couldn't be seen through the darkened window except as a slight silhouette—and a magnetic sign stuck to the side of the van's door. It didn't look as if anyone else was in the van except the driver.

"Check this out," Bear said in a quiet whisper. "They're running some kind of bus service."

Reaper had his binoculars pulled up and focused on the van.

"What does the sign say?" Reaper whispered.

"Golden Casino Tours," Bear said. "What the hell does that have to do with a nightclub for the young crowd? They don't go to casinos for the most part."

"Sounds like something they might be running on the side," Reaper said as the van passed through the now open gate and turned to the west. "Did you see anyone get out or use a hidden touch pad outside the van to open that gate?"

"Nope," Bear said.

"So they must either use a remote control opener or someone inside the garage used a switch," Reaper said.

"Can't see into the garage door from this angle," Bear said. "But it could be a pressure plate or hose on the ground."

"Don't think so," Reaper said. "That van had to sit there for a while, as if someone had to try to find a remote. A pressure switch would have opened the door much faster and started as soon as the van approached."

While the two SEALs whispered their conversation, the powered gate began rolling shut. As the gate closed, other cars started arriving and pulling into the fenced-in parking area to the east of the Factory building.

"Looks like someone is starting to show up," Bear said quietly.

Most of the half-dozen vehicles that arrived over the next fifteen minutes only had a single person in them. Several older sedans had a pair of women stepping out of the doors, one had three ladies leave it. Both Reaper and Bear figured that they were looking at the wait staff arriving for work. The fact that most of the people who got out of the cars were young women reinforced that thought.

"Maybe just a bartender and a bunch of waitresses," Bear said.

"Probably," Reaper replied. "But that guy who drove the Mustang looks a little big to be a bartender. I figure either a front door screener/greeter or maybe a bouncer."

A quiet grunt was all that came back from Bear in the way of an answer.

Time in the hide went by, as did the local traffic on the highways. A few more vehicles had pulled into the Factory parking lot. Arzee may have left in the van, but Reaper didn't think so. Deckert's research and contacts had not been able to come up with a home address for Arzee. Even the address on his Corvette's registration was given as the Factory. Arzee probably had his living quarters someplace in the old auto plant and didn't leave them. It didn't make a difference now, Reaper knew that he was going to have to raid the place they were watching.

To stage a covert raid, they had to continue the surveillance. How things worked at the Factory, who went where and what went on when the place closed, would be vital information. So Bear and Reaper kept their position and watched. Rotating on a thirty-minute schedule kept alert eyes on the target—one of the men watching while the other rested.

They drank sparingly from the backpack containers. Staying hydrated was something both SEALs had learned a long time ago. The oatmeal and chocolate bars would be enough to keep the hunger pangs at bay. Movement had to be kept to a minimum. So they had no chance to get up to take a leak, and no place to do it anyway. Peeing on the side of the building might not seem like much, but the smell could easily catch the attention of a curious guard. The only option remained to simply gut the situation out.

Watching the action at the target helped Reaper and Bear ignore their discomfort. Customers had started to show up, at least cars came in and mixed couples of young people got out and headed into the Factory. Each car was noted and photographed. The same procedure applied to each couple. Then, at 1845 hours, a vehicle showed up that hadn't been expected.

"Hey, Reaper," Bear whispered. "check this out. That casino van is back."

Reaper was already looking at th ig white passenger van as it pulled up to the ga he van rolled into the driveway, a clear view blocked by the closed gate. It sat there for a few moments without either the gate moving or the van doing anything.

"Look, the sign is gone," Bear whispered.

Reaper had noticed it, too. The sign about "Golden Casino Tours" wasn't on the side of the van. When the vehicle had left only a few hours earlier, there had been signs on both front doors—the side away from the SEALs visible for a short time as the van drove west. Now, the sides of the vehicle were clean.

As both SEALs watched, the driver's side door of the van opened and a man got out. He walked up to the gate and yanked at it. The gate jerked and started to roll open.

"Somebody needs to do their preventative maintenance," Bear said.

"Be sure to get shots of the side windows of that van," Reaper said.

"Already on it, Chief," Bear said.

When the driver opened the door and got out of the van, the interior dome lights came on. The van was in the shade of the building and the inside light made it possible to see through the screened windows. Inside the van, people filled every seat. Checking the screen of the digital camera after the van passed into the garage and the gate closed, Reaper and Bear were able to count four silhouettes for certain, with a possibility of one or two more.

"Now why would they try to slip people into the club though the side door?" Bear asked.

"And why take the signs off the van to do it?" Reaper said.

"Curiouser and curiouser," Bear replied.

The two SEALs returned to their vigil over the front of the Factory building. As the sun set, it became possible to see lights on through the windows on the east side of the building. Only a few lights shone through the upper floor windows, but the shades kept any details from being seen.

The only other activity after the arrival of the white van was an increase in the number of customers. By 2045 hours, it was dusk and the sun had just set. An hour later little had changed, although now some couples were leaving as more arrived.

"You know, Reaper," Bear said as he stood his

watch on the Factory, "there's only one way to really get more information on that place."

"And what is that?" Reaper said in a soft voice.

"One of us is going to have to go in there," Bear said.

"I know, but it isn't going to be the safest thing in the world to do," Reaper said. "Neither of us look like the average customer."

"No," Bear agreed, "but there have been a few bikers in the crowds going in. I could blend in pretty well with them."

"You're volunteering?" Reaper asked.

"You already said that Arzee knows you," Bear said. "So you sure as hell can't be the one going in, and I'm the only other one up here from what I can tell."

Reaper knew that Bear was right. One of them had to go in to gather information from inside the place and Bear was the logical choice. Even though Reaper didn't like the thought of letting his friend face possible danger without immediate backup at hand, he had to agree with Bear's logic.

"Okay, you go," Reaper said finally. "But you get back out and up here by 2300. If you don't, I'll come in and get you in spite of them recognizing me."

"Don't worry, Sweetie," Bear said with a grin. "I'll be back before the streetlights go on."

"Just get the fuck out of here," Reaper said with a smile.

Bear slipped out from under the tarp and went back off the roof by the same route they had used to climb up. Inside of fifteen minutes from Bear's leaving, Reaper heard a Harley's powerful engine being started and driven away. As the engine noise disappeared, Reaper was left alone in the darkness with his thoughts.

After about ten minutes, Reaper noted the arrival of a big motorcycle at the Factory. The bike slowed at a corner, then roared up to the entrance to the parking lot, turned in and stopped. As Bear climbed off his bike, he signaled Reaper that he was all right in his own personal style—he scratched his ass and then waved his hand in the air.

"Clown," Reaper said quietly to himself, smiling as he did so.

No new customers showed up after Bear went into the Factory. Two couples left the club, one at 2150 hours, the other at 2207 hours. Neither couple appeared rushed in any way, so Bear probably hadn't raised a ruckus inside the place.

The last couple to leave appeared in anything but a hurry. They openly showed their feelings toward each other while in the parking lot. When they finally got to their car and climbed inside, the vehicle sat there for a while.

Reaper resisted the urge to swing the big scope around and see exactly why the windows of the car began to fog up so heavily. He didn't think that Bear would have done the same thing on his watch.

The silence of the night was broken by the crunching, grating sound of a steel door being opened—the steel fire door at the head of the stairway leading down into the warehouse underneath him. Someone was coming out of the warehouse and onto the roof.

Reaper could do nothing as he listened to footsteps crunch in the gravel. Then the footsteps clanged as they moved onto a steel grate. The sound was coming from hard-soled shoes on iron steps, and the only iron steps on the whole roof led up to the billboard platform, the platform that Reaper lay hidden beneath.

The steps grew louder as they clanged across the steel grid, then stopped. The tarp over the hide muffled the sound somewhat, but whoever paused up there had to be only a few feet away. Reaper heard the click of a lighter being flicked to life, then the sound of someone taking a drag and exhaling loudly. Somebody was taking a smoke break while looking out over the highway. And they were standing directly over Reaper's hide.

Reaper forced himself to relax and settle down and resumed his watch on the Factory. Now it became urgent that he spot Bear before he tried to return. Reaper's watch read only 2220 hours. Bear still had forty minutes to go before he was supposed to be back at the OP.

The minutes dragged by slowly. There was a "tink" sound and then a tap on the tarp almost on top of Reaper's head. Reaper thought the smoker must have finished his break and tossed away his cigarette. The sound of the shoes once more clanging across the grate and down the steps proved he was right. The door once more crunched shut and it left Reaper alone on the roof.

Ten minutes later Reaper saw Bear leaving the Factory. The only odd thing Reaper could see was that another big guy was escorting Bear to the parking lot. The man just stood at the gate while Bear got on his motorcycle and roared off.

Half an hour later, Bear was back in the hide.

"A guard came out on a cigarette break right on top of here not forty minutes ago," Reaper whispered.

"Yeah, that must be the guy I had to drop downstairs," Bear said.

"What!" Reaper questioned.

"Relax, I'm just fucking with you," Bear whispered. "I stayed below the edge of the roof and listened, then looked, before I came up. There's no one around."

"So why did that guy follow you to the parking lot?"

"You mean Ashel?" Bear whispered as innocently as he was able under the circumstances.

"You know his name?" Reaper whispered.

"Yeah," Bear said. "I've got an appointment with his boss tomorrow night to see about a job as a bouncer."

Reaper shook his head in admiration. "You've got the watch," he said.

Most of the vehicles had been long gone by 0230 when the last of the staff left. The door guard, Ashel, had escorted a number of the ladies to their cars as the club closed for the night. Then the last of the lights on the first floor were turned off and even Ashel left.

Lights were still glowing on the sixth floor of the Factory building, but only in a few windows. By 0245, those lights were off. It seemed odd that not even a single police cruiser had passed by during closing time. That had always been a prime time to bust drivers who had too much to drink before they were able to get out on the major surface streets. But no cops had showed, not one at all.

The morning rush hour picked up around 0500 hours. Both Reaper and Bear had become wet and cold from the morning dew by this time, a condition they had grown used to over the years. What you couldn't change or control, you endured, a basic truth of SEAL operations.

Movement at the garage end of the Factory caused both Reaper and Bear to forget about their uncomfortable surroundings. The white van had made another appearance. This time, the gate opened smoothly and the van exited, turning north. The casino signs still weren't on the van. The dark windows prevented any view of the inside or any occupants.

Normal traffic, both vehicular and on foot, took up the rest of the morning. People came to work and suffered through a Friday morning rush hour. By noon, Reaper announced himself ready to abandon the OP. The two men carefully policed the area. Outside of some scuffed gravel, not a sign showed that the SEALs had even been there. Reaper even tossed the cigarette butt that he found on top of the tarp back underneath the billboard support grid.

Climbing down the walls, the two men headed back to their van. Bear had already secured his bike in the back and they were ready to go. After almost a full day in a camouflaged hide, Reaper had something urgent to attend to. Standing in the cover of the van, Reaper relieved himself into the weeds.

Chapter Eighteen

The ride back to the shop was a somber one for Reaper and Bear. Outside of locating Arzee, they hadn't seen a single positive sign of Reaper's wife or son. Now reaction was setting in from their long mission. A numb, dead tiredness hung over them from being up for more than a day manning their observation post.

During the trip back to Deckert's, Bear had dozed off while Reaper drove. He only woke up as they pulled into the driveway leading to the farm. Bear leaned forward in his seat and stretched out with a wide jaw-cracking yawn and deep growling groan. Reaper thought Bear suddenly resembled his nickname even more than usual.

"You need a tree to scratch your back against before you crap in the woods?" Reaper asked as they pulled up to the house.

A loud fart was Bear's first response.

"Arrgh, me mouth tastes like a she-cat littered in it," he said.

"What?" Reaper said as he pulled the van back around to the rear of the house and parked out of sight of the main road.

"My favorite line from an old Viking movie," Bear said. "It was a Richard Widmark flick called *The Long Ships*. It had lots of great tits in it, too."

As Bear turned to look at his staring friend, he explained. "Hey, I just had the music going through my head okay? I used to think about it during those long swims back in the Teams."

"Whatever works for you," Reaper said with a grin and a shake of his head.

Inside the house, the two SEALs carried their packs with the camera gear into the office where Deckert was waiting.

"Here you go," Reaper said as he handed Deckert the memory card from the Nikon camera.

Without a word, Deckert started downloading the digital photos into his desktop computer. He had software that would let him easily manipulate the pictures the two SEALs had taken during their observations of the Factory. Important shots could be printed off as hard copies for further study.

While Reaper hovered over his friend's shoulder as he worked, Bear sat down at a desk and went over his notes and logbook. He added details and scribbled notes on the margins as he looked at the sketches he had made of the interior of the Factory club floor. There was little talk and no joking as they began to analyze the raw intelligence data gathered during their long vigil.

Looming over Deckert's shoulder got old fast for Reaper. He gathered up the logs, printouts, and other materials, and went out to the kitchen table where they had room to spread out a little. All types of information lay across the table top; satellite and aerial photographs, hard copy photos from the computer, maps, logbooks, sketches, even street maps, newspapers, and Detroit magazines. None of it told Reaper the location of his family. But it did show him the size of their target in graphic detail.

Bear stepped into the kitchen and poured himself a cup of coffee. Carrying his steaming mug, he walked around the counter to the table where Reaper sat. As Bear approached, Reaper put down the pair of dividers he had been measuring a map with. Pushing himself from the table, Reaper leaned far back in his chair and stretched, rubbing his face with both hands as he did so.

"So," Bear said as he sat down at the table, "figured out anything yet?"

"Yeah," Reaper said as he ran his fingers back through his hair, "it's big, really fucking big. That damned factory building is more than 480 feet long, 130 feet wide, and over ninety feet tall. That's more than 62,000 square feet per floor—and there are six floors. That's a whole lot of area for just two guys to cover."

Bear picked up a picture from the pile on the table as Reaper sat back straight in his chair. The picture Bear looked at showed the full east face of the Factory building.

"The first floor is pretty much a wash for anyone being there," Bear said. "It's mostly a big open space broken down into dance pits and band stages. There are a couple of bars and some areas with tables, but no place there could be much in the way of an office. The whole front area near the doors was the kitchen—at least that was where the food came from. There's a coat check on one side of the doors and that's about it. On the southeast end is a stairway going up. It's behind a set of steel fire doors and the guy working at the front door keeps a close eye on it."

"That stairway must also open up on the garage," Reaper said. "It's at that corner of the building."

"Makes sense," Bear said. "The only other way up to the other floors was by a ramp on the north side of the building, and that was closed off behind the main bar. There are three different freight elevators on the south side of the building, but the gates to those are chained and locked. Except for the smallest one up near the front, none of them even looked used. The two main elevators had their platforms up on the second floor, blocking them off."

"During the night," Reaper said, "the only floor that showed any activity besides the first floor was the top floor, the sixth. That one had lights on. Everything I've seen indicates that there's offices only on the eastern end of the building."

"That matches up with some of the stories Deckert came up with about when that was an active auto plant," Bear said. "All of the admin offices and white-collar work went on at that end of the building. The plant manager had his office somewhere on the top floor. Everything else was assembly lines. They even left some of the line machinery as decorations around the main floor—it separated some of the dance pits and stages."

"That makes the east end of the top floor the priority target," Reaper said. "By 0235 hours, all of the cars in the parking lot were gone. Even the working staff had left by then. But that enclosed garage at the southeast corner is an unknown factor."

"So," Bear said, "I'll watch the hallway and stairs while you search the office."

"I wasn't asking you to go in with me on this one, Bear," Reaper said. "This isn't any kind of sanctioned op. I'm going after my family and I can't ask someone to break the law and go in with me."

"Don't remember you asking," Bear said as he tossed the picture he had been examining back onto the table. "You figure you can keep me out of this, brother?"

Reaper looked at the man for a moment, unable to think of anything to say.

"You've been up what, thirty, thirty-six hours straight?" Bear said. "Small wonder you can't see what's right in front of your face. Get a couple of hours of sleep and we'll hit it again."

"Can't afford the time," Reaper said. "They are going to call for more weapons by tomorrow afternoon. We have less than twenty-four hours to find my family and stop this."

"What you can't afford is to make a mistake, Chief," Bear said. "Deckert is going to take some time to finish up processing the pictures anyway."

Reaper had to admit the logic of what his friend had said.

"Okay, you're right," Reaper said. "I'm going to grab a couple of hours of sleep, then look at all of this again."

"Sounds good to me," Bear said.

The insistent buzz of the alarm awakened Reaper after what felt like only a few minutes of sleep instead of a few hours. Years of iron-hard discipline had him turn off the alarm clock and swing his feet off the bed while the rest of his body still wanted to sleep. He was a little rested now, though not much. His eyes felt thick and gritty. If his breath smelled half as bad as his mouth tasted, he'd better be careful about where he breathed or he'd blister the paint on the walls.

A quick, scalding hot shower did a great deal toward clearing out the rest of the cobwebs in his brain. Reaper again was able to concentrate on the tactical problem of just him and Bear hitting the Factory. He knew that Deckert would want to help, but the practical questions regarding his mobility would keep him from an active role. Not really polite, but it was the truth.

A raid on the Factory had to be done quickly. The longer he waited, the greater the risk grew for Mary and Ricky. There was a good chance that they had not been kept at the Factory. If that were true, he had to eliminate that possibility quickly. The Factory was their best practical source for more intelligence and a way of developing further leads. Getting their hands on Arzee was a top priority. Reaper was more than willing to wring the man dry and toss him away like a paper towel.

Hitting the Factory and not finding his family, successfully snatching up Arzee, or even getting any new leads . . . that wasn't something Reaper found acceptable to think about.

Going back into his room, Reaper pulled on fresh jeans and a sweatshirt. Feeling a damned sight more human, he turned and opened the door to go downstairs. Voices could be heard speaking from what sounded like the kitchen area. And there were more people talking than just Deckert and Bear. A quick look out his bedroom window showed Reaper no police cars, but two new vehicles sat out in the driveway. There was a silver 4x4 pickup truck with the paint on the hood peeling and an older model Buick Century sedan. These certainly didn't look like the kind of vehicle Arzee's people drove.

Stepping back to his bedside table, Reaper picked up the SIG-P220 he had lying there and checked the load. Fresh brass shone back up at him as he drew the slide partway back. Lowering the hammer with the decocking lever, Reaper slipped the SIG under his belt at the small of his back, then pulled his sweatshirt over the weapon. Now armed, he went downstairs to check out the voices.

Pausing for a moment on the stairs, Reaper could now better make out the voices in the kitchen and what was being said. The conversation astonished him and he knew that he wouldn't need his SIG.

"So he came charging in from the sea with some maniac at the wheel of a PBR and pulled us out," one voice clearly said. "When I finally asked him how he found us, he said that he got a position fix on our last radio transmission before our commo went down. It was a good thing he did too because he showed up just as the ragheads were closing in on Kafji. If he hadn't shown up, my spotter and I would have been the first ground losses of Desert Storm.

That would be a hell of a way to make the history books."

Reaper came down to the kitchen to see a sight he never would have allowed himself to hope for. Deckert sat in the kitchen making something while around the table were Bear and another man Reaper immediately recognized.

"Well," Reaper said. "If you hadn't been a normal hardheaded Marine, you would have abandoned that hide before the Iraqis had gotten too close. Goddamn, Max, it's good to see you."

The slender younger man Reaper was speaking to stood up and embraced the SEAL chief in a fierce bear hug. As they broke the embrace, Reaper stood back and looked at the shorter man.

"You're looking good, Warrick," Reaper said, "but the grunge look has been out of style for years, or have they stopped letting you have anything sharp since you left the Corps?"

Max Warrick let a wide grin spread over his face as he rubbed at the week-old stubble across his chin. Chuckling, he ran his left hand back through his unkempt, stark white hair.

"Naw," he said, "I was just coming back from transporting a bail jumper to Kansas City when I got a call last night from Bear here. He said that you needed help and it was important—so I just kept rolling past Chicago and headed on here. I've been on the road over a week chasing that jumper down. So I just figured I'd show up and see what the party was. Maybe I'll have time to make a run across the river to Canada and get some Cuban cigars while I'm here."

"It's damned good to see you here," Reaper said, "but I don't think there's going to be much time to make any smoke runs across the border."

"Just like a jarhead to become a bounty hunter to keep the blood moving," a second new arrival said from off to the left. "Must be the jazz, just like that A-Team character you look so much like."

"That's Bail Enforcement Agent to you Air Force pukes," Warrick said.

Reaper turned to face the new person coming into the room.

"Damn," Reaper said, "if they aren't coming out of the woodwork. Good to see you Ben."

He reached out and grabbed the smaller man's outstretched hand, pulling the slightly built speaker in close for a strong hug. The new individual on the scene was noticeably short, only a few inches over five feet tall, and very slight of build. To look at his craggy face, glasses, and thin brown hair, one would have first thought of either a drowned rat or a really skinny lawn gnome. But Ben MacKenzie, the ex-Air Force pararescue jumper—PJ for short—had fooled many people who had made the mistake of judging him by his outward appearance. The smaller man was engulfed by Reaper's embrace, but he hugged back just as fiercely.

Stepping back for a moment, Reaper stood to the side as Ben walked over to the table and sat down.

"It's not that I'm disappointed to see the two of you," Reaper said, "but what the hell are you doing here? I haven't seen you, Ben, since we left Bosnia, and that was what, five—six years ago? And it's probably been even longer than that since I've seen you, Max."

"I've been working as a paramedic in Indianapolis off and on at least up to last night," Ben said. "That's when I got the call from Bear that you needed help."

"And what's your story, Max?" Reaper said. "Ben operated with Bear and me over in Bosnia, but you never did. How the hell did he know he should call you?"

"I met him at a shooting competition and gun show down in Kentucky a year ago last fall," Max said. "He was wearing those motorcycle leathers of his with a Trident on them. One thing led to another and we spent a long night swapping lies at some redneck bar south of Louisville. My memory is a little hazy about the general details of that night."

"And you just took it upon yourself to call these guys in?" Reaper said as he shot a glance at Bear, who sat at the table and tried to look innocent.

"Well, yeah," Bear said. "I phoned them last night after I had left the club and headed back to the hide. Both of them demanded to know where and when after I told them you needed help, and why."

"Your family is involved," Ben said bluntly. "You don't go after a man's family, no matter what. So why don't you sit the fuck down and tell us what you need?"

Reaper stood for a moment looking at the table and the men surrounding it. He understood the brotherhood of warriors, how those who had shed blood together shared a bond that outsiders would find almost impossible to understand. But Reaper had never been someone who liked asking for help. He hadn't even thought of contacting men like these, his friends, to share danger with him. It took another member of that brotherhood to recognize the situation and put the call out. That would be something he would owe Bear for a long time to come, one of those debts that are shared between close friends but are never really spoken about.

Coming to a decision, Reaper sat down and started to brief his friends on the situation.

"Short version," Reaper said, "we have an unknown number of hostiles who have taken two hostages and are holding them at an unknown place. Our only suspected location of the hostages is at a nightclub in a converted six-story factory building near downtown Detroit.

"The building is in a poor neighborhood with a limited civilian population nearby. My intention is for Bear and me to conduct a penetration of the target building to either locate the hostages and bring them out, or develop further intelligence as to their location."

"How do you expect to develop that intelligence?" Warrick asked.

"I intend making a prisoner of the man in charge of the organization who took the hostages in the first place," Reaper said with a cold stare at Warrick.

"Do we have identification on this individual?" Ben asked.

"Yes," Reaper said, "he was positively identified at the target last night. His name is Steven Arzee. If he's not the top man in charge, he can tell us who is."

"I think he may still be pissed about Reaper ripping the ass off his favorite car," Bear said

"Always thought a Vette was a pussy-ass car," Ben said. "Count me in."

"Took your family, huh?" Max said. "Sounds like a good guy to mess with. I'm in. When did you want to take him down?"

Reaper looked at the men around the table. Bear leaned back in his chair with a soft smile across his face. Max and Ben both looked committed to action and intent on Reaper's every word. He felt a sudden surge of pride in the trust these men put in him.

"Time is something we don't have much of," Reaper said. "We go tonight."

Chapter Nineteen

Having made the decision to go ahead with the operation, Reaper lost no time in bringing Deckert, Max, and Ben up to speed on what he and Bear had observed the day before. All of the men around the table were experienced professionals. They knew the risks in conducting an operation—especially a clandestine one with no official support.

In fact, there was far less than official support for their proposed actions. What they were planning to do sitting around that kitchen table was just plain illegal. Even just talking about what they had in mind would be considered conspiracy to commit a criminal act. In spite of that, they committed themselves to the action without reservations. They knew Reaper and trusted his judgment.

And Reaper trusted the men he was briefing. Each of them would be able to recognize specific strengths and weaknesses in the tactical situation or in his plan according to their own experiences. The specific plan of assault on the Factory was something Reaper still had to work out in his mind. A bull session with his friends would greatly help him finalize that plan.

"Here's the target," Reaper said as he laid a large sheet of paper on the table. The sheet was an aerial view of the Factory and the area surrounding it. It had been made up by Deckert, taping together sheets of printouts from an Internet Web service to make a single large picture. The warped-diamond shape of the highway intersection stood out as the main feature at the bottom of the shot. Near the middle of the sheet was the roof of the Factory building. The angle of the shot showed some of the south side of the building but the detail was limited by the one-meter resolution of the original picture.

Pointing to the Factory building, Reaper continued.

"The basic structure was originally a small-scale auto plant. On the east end of the building were the administrative and engineering offices. They were separated from the construction floor by cinderblock walls. On the construction floor there are concrete support pillars every twenty feet the length and breadth of the building.

"This is a great big son of a bitch and the location of the building is an interesting one. It borders two major highways, so there are very limited avenues of approach from the south and east. It's right on the border of three different police districts but lies inside the Thirteenth District. It isn't known if the owner has paid off the local police or has some kind of arrangement with them, but during our time in the observation post, we didn't see a single police cruiser anywhere near the building.

"We can't have any contact with the local police or fire personnel. If they come into the area, we either have to withdraw or lay up until they leave. They're friendlies, whether they know it or not, so this isn't a permissive environment. We can't open fire on our own.

"So we'll have to keep it very tight, people. No firing whatsoever unless it is absolutely necessary and you are sure of your target. We are going to operate as if it's a hostile environment—but the rules of engagement are solid and there isn't any room for mistakes."

Reaper went on describing the building and what he and Bear had seen during their long vigil. Bear pointed out details of the exterior of the building where he had seen them, and he carefully described the interior of the first floor and the layout of the club facilities there.

A single huge band and dance area dominated the western end of the building, the stage stretching half the width of the building. Four additional smaller band stages and dance areas stretched along the rest of the floor. Scattered about were sections of tables being served from the bar that ran along the northeast wall, and the kitchen area in the first floor of what had been the admin offices.

Bear had seen no sign of Arzee or the two goons that Reaper had carefully described. The briefing/planning session continued with more and more details being brought forward and described. The photographs that Reaper and Bear had taken had been cleaned, cropped, and printed by Deckert. Reaper brought these out and handed them around. In addition, Deckert had been doing research on the Internet about the plant and its history. Through that source, he had come up with a number of photos of what the inside of the plant used to look like.

An unusual feature of the cinder-block and steel construction building was that the floors were covered with thick blocks of wood. These blocks helped dampen vibration from the various machines when they had been running. Bear said that it made a very interesting walking surface.

But the biggest question couldn't be answered from the information they had in front of them—where was Reaper's family? Nowhere could they find a specific area where hostages would probably be taken. The only real clues they had came from the observations taken by Reaper and Bear.

"The only floors that were lit at all," Reaper said, "were the first and sixth floors. The first floor was lit up because of the club. The sixth floor had some of the offices on the eastern end of the building lit up during the evening, even past the 2 A.M. closing time of the club. That's a pretty good indicator that nothing much happens on the four middle floors of the building."

"Unless they just shield the lights," Ben said. "That's a pretty big floor area to try and search."

"No arguing that," Reaper said. "But we did see some lights being used in the middle area of the sixth floor. According to the information Keith came up with, there are no rooms or walls to speak of on almost any of the construction floors. So any rooms that we do see had to be added after the place was turned into a club—and we search them. But the main target I see is the sixth floor."

"There were ramps, a big stairway near the front door, and several elevators going up to the rest of the floors," Bear said. "But they are all either locked up or closed off. There's only one set of stairs near the front door that aren't secured with a lock and chain—and they have a guard, or at least a big goon acting like a bouncer, stationed right in front of them."

"Looks like the upper floor is it then," Ben said.

"Yes, I think it is," Reaper agreed, "besides, we have no other real choice."

"You know," Max said, "if I could climb up on this billboard to the southeast of the building, I could control the entire eastern face of the place with a good rifle. The trick will be getting up there with something like that without being spotted for what I am."

"Oh, I think we can find you something suitable for the job," Deckert said with smile. "There's some stuff in the vault downstairs that just might fit the bill perfectly. You leave that stubble on your chin in place, dirty up a bit, and wear some old clothes, and you could pass for a street person just wandering around. No one would even look at you twice."

"That's a hell of an idea," Reaper said. "We scrounge up an old shopping cart and fill it with crap and make up our own street person. We could hide a rifle easily enough with a little work."

"What I have in mind won't take a little work," Deckert said. "I'll be back in a minute."

With that, he rolled away from the table and went over to the door to the basement.

"Bear," Deckert said, "could you give me a hand bringing some gear up?"

"Not a problem," Bear said as he got up and walked over to the stairs.

A lift device had been bolted to the wall that combined with tracks on the stairs to let Deckert travel to and from the basement of the building. As soon as Deckert had cleared the stairway, Bear followed him down and the two men disappeared under the house leaving Reaper, Ben, and Max still sitting around the table planning.

While Bear and Deckert scrounged around down in the basement, Reaper and the others continued to detail out their assault on the factory. Max would provide fire support from his billboard sniper hide while Reaper and Bear went into the building itself. Ben would have the hardest job on the site. He would provide transport and maintain security around the outside of the building while Bear and Reaper conducted the assault. Deckert would remain at the shop where he could coordinate communications over cell phones.

By the time Deckert and Bear had come back up from the basement, Reaper and the others had worked out a basic plan. When Reaper saw the packages, cases, and boxes that Bear and Deckert had brought up from the security vault in the basement, he couldn't hide his surprise. He recognized what the men were carrying. This was more than he could have honestly expected.

"Keith," Reaper said, "you can't do this. These are the most expensive parts of our inventory. I can't let . . ."

"Shut up, squid, and give us a hand," Deckert said as he cut Reaper off. "It's not up to you to say what I can and cannot do with the inventory. I may not be able to go out and operate with you guys because of these wheels of mine, but I can damned well still be a supply sergeant if I choose to!"

Deckert and Bear quickly laid out the materials they'd brought on the kitchen counter. Deckert started opening up some of the boxes while Bear went back down to the basement for another load.

"I think you may find this to your liking, Max," Deckert said as he set out on the countertop what looked to be a soft-sided laptop computer case. D-ring attachment points were sewn into the back side of the black Cordura nylon case, making it able to be secured a number of ways for carrying. As Deckert unzipped the sides of the case, he folded back the top to display the contents.

Inside the case lay the components of a tactical sniper rifle—broken down so that no single part was more than sixteen inches long.

"Holy shit," said Max, impressed by what he saw, "just what the hell is it?"

"It's an Arms Tech Limited Model TTR-700 rifle," said Deckert. "That's their Tactical Takedown Rifle. It looks like something out of Hollywood, doesn't it?"

"I should say so," Max said.

"Well, this ain't from the movies," Deckert said. "This is the real thing. That's a modified Remington 700 bolt-action fitted and bedded to a custom Choate folding stock. The Schneider match-grade stainless steel fluted barrel is sixteen inches long with a recessed muzzle crown. It's also threaded for an MD-30 muzzle suppressor which is in the bottom of the case. There's a Leupold VARI-X IIc three to nine power, 40mm variable tactical scope on quick release mounts guaranteed to hold their accuracy. And there's room for two twenty-round boxes of ammunition. The whole weapon goes together in thirty to sixty seconds from the time that you open the case. It's chambered for 7.62 NATO and is black oxide-finished for protection and cutting down reflection."

"Is it accurate?" questioned Max.

"Fires to half an inch, a half-minute of angle, with the proper ammunition," Deckert said. "And we have the proper ammunition. There's Federal 308 Winchester Match, 168-grain boat-tail hollowpoint ammo in these white boxes. In this blue box may be something you're not used to. It's Engel Ballistic Research Incorporated's 7.62mm Thumper ammo. That's match-grade 220-grain subsonic ammo. With the suppressor in place and using EBR's Thumper ammo, that gun isn't much louder than a mouse fart."

Max looked like a kid in a candy store as he professionally examined the weapon in the case, and started to assemble it. Bear had brought up the rest of the boxes from the basement and Deckert was displaying more materials and weapons. The next weapon Deckert laid out proved to be just as impressive as the take-down rifle in its case, only this weapon was much smaller still.

"That is the smallest shotgun I have ever seen,"

Ben said as he looked at what appeared to be a giant pistol.

"That's a Serbu Super-Shorty 12-gauge shotgun. That front operating handle folds down and locks into place so that you have something to hold onto when you fire it. And you need something to grab, this gun does not play nice. It's a modified Mossberg pump-action shotgun, fitted with a pistol grip and a folding front grip. The whole gun is only 16.5 inches long with a 6.5-inch barrel and weighs 4.5 pounds empty. It holds three rounds, two in the magazine and one in the chamber, but those are full-sized 12-gauge rounds.

"Right here," Deckert said as he opened up a cardboard box, "is from SKI Industries. It's the first holster made for the Serbu Super-Shorty. It's a black nylon CQB-style drop-down leg holster with a partial break-front that holds the shotgun with its forward grip folded. It has straps to hold it to your thigh, and an elastic restraining strap for the gun. The loops on the outside of the holster hold an extra three rounds and the whole rig is ambidextrous. You could fast-draw this thing if you wanted to. Makes it just about the biggest handgun you could ask for."

"Pretty much answers the question about whose gun is bigger, doesn't it?" Ben said.

"A manly gun for manly men," Bear said with a grin.

"Yeah, and a pretty special one with the ammunition I have for it," Deckert said, picking up a smaller ammunition box from a larger case. "This is Mark II Aerodynamic, drag-stabilized, expandable-baton shotgun ammunition. And it will feed and fire in that Serbu Super-Shorty."

"You sure you don't have a job with the company making this stuff?" Bear asked. "You sound like an ordnance salesman."

"Yeah, well it's not like I expect you to pay for it," Deckert said.

"Bear," Reaper said, "will you shut up? I think I know what he's leaning towards with this one."

"You got it," Deckert said. "These are really good bean-bag rounds. You load up the Super-Shorty with these and it'll give you a less-than-lethal option. These shells throw a forty gram nylon bag with a stabilizing tail at about three hundred feet per second from a standard riot gun. That stubby barrel on the Super-Shorty will cut way back on that velocity, but they still should be effective to at least twenty yards. It'll be like hitting the guy with a Sunday punch—while wearing brass knuckles."

"What else did you have me drag up from down there anyway?" asked Bear.

"An H&K MP5K-PDW," Deckert said picking up the small submachine gun. The folding stock that helped identify the weapon as the personal defense weapon model lay to the side of the almost pistol-sized 9mm sub gun. "And a Gemtech Raptor muzzle suppressor for it. This model uses the tri-lock system that Gemtech patented to lock the suppressor on the HK 3-lug barrel. Reduces the sound of each shot by thirty decibels.

"That other box there has a Beretta Model 92-F pistol in it. The barrel of the pistol is threaded for the Whispertech 9mm can in that long skinny box. The can's seven inches long and one and one-eighth inches in diameter. It's covered with a black moly-coat to kill reflections and it won't change the zero of the pistol or interfere with its operation.

"To really cut back on sound," Deckert said, "there are a couple of hundred rounds of EBR 9mm Hush Puppy ammunition in that last box over there. That ammo has a 147-grain bullet that fires at about 980 feet per second, even out of a submachine gun barrel. It will help make the sound of any shots from either the Beretta or the MP5K as quiet as possible by eliminating the sonic crack.

"Just as an added bonus, I put in some work in the shop last night while you guys were partying it up downtown," Deckert said as he pulled a black nylon case up from the floor. "This is the last one of these we're going to have for a while."

Opening up the case, Deckert drew out what looked like a futuristic rifle.

"Damn," Reaper said, "you finished one."

"Yeah," Deckert said, "and I used the last of the prototype parts to do it. This, gentlemen, is the Jack-hammer Mark 3-A3 assault shotgun. It is a bullpup-style, selective fire 12-gauge shotgun loading from a ten-round cassette magazine. The bullpup design puts the firing mechanism behind the pistol grip. That makes the weapon thirty inches long with more than a twenty-inch barrel length. It can be fired one-handed on full automatic. That long handle on the top of the weapon holds the sights. You can rip down a house with this gun—and those bastards who have

Reaper's family took the only other four guns in existence. I want them back."

"Keith," Reaper said after Deckert was done describing all of the gear and the Jackhammer, "I can't let you do this. What we're doing is illegal as hell. You'll lose your federal license at the least if anything happens to this gear."

"So, don't let anything happen to the gear," Deckert said simply. "Now go and get your family."

Reaper didn't have anything more he could say. Deckert's mind had been made up and, if he wanted to be completely honest with himself, Reaper had to admit he was damned glad to have the help.

Chapter Twenty

There was a hard time limit on how long Reaper and his men had to conduct their operation. Arzee had said that the additional weapons had to be ready by Friday afternoon—that was seventy-two hours after his raid at the shop. That time was only twenty-two hours away. The cell phone he had left had never rung.

Reaper had no way of knowing that Arzee was simply too scared to call before the time had run out. If he and Bear hadn't seen the man at the front door of the Factory, they would have thought he had been killed in the car wreck. Why he hadn't called wasn't important right now. The fact that he still held Reaper's family was.

While Max, Bear, and Ben caught a little sleep, Reaper sat down and worked out the details of a plan of assault for the Factory. When he had the operation sketched out to his satisfaction, he called everyone down to the kitchen and laid it out for them. The basic plan was simple, as all good ones should be. It called for Deckert and Bear to penetrate the building while Ben and Max acted as support. With all the men around the kitchen table, he described what he wanted to do.

"Max," Deckert said, "you'll be going in first to scout out the area and report to us. We'll stay in the area with the insertion vehicle. If you run into anything that you can't just walk away from, we can come in and get you out fast. After that, you'll establish your sniper hide in the southeast quadrant on the upper deck of this billboard."

Reaper pointed out the indicated billboard with his pen on the large aerial photo they had used earlier.

"Now, you're sure you don't see any problems in getting up to that deck?" Reaper said.

"No," Max replied, "none at all. Your pictures show two different ladders to get up there. The bottom rung is only about ten feet off the ground. I shouldn't have any trouble climbing up to it with a short length of rope and a grappling hook."

"We may be able to do you one better on that," Reaper said with a smile. "Dressing you up as a homeless person and giving you a shopping cart full of crap will blend you in so that no one will notice you at all. We'll just stick a hard-sided box or milk crate in your cart. Since you're going to have the cart with you anyway, you might as well make use of it. Climbing up on that will put you within reach of the lower rung. That'll be a lot easier that tossing up a line, less obvious, too."

"Sounds good to me," Max said, "but I'll take the hook and line anyway."

"We'll drop you in the area of this railroad bridge underpass a half-hour before sundown," Reaper said indicating the bridge on the print. "Under the bridge is dark as hell, no one will be able to see us from the target. Sundown is at about 2045 hours tonight. That should give you a good hour of light to make your way past the Factory to this field where the billboard is. You can scout out the target from as close as you feel comfortable, but remember, the bouncers are right there at the front door. They'll put the bum's rush on you if you try and go by the eastern side of the building."

"No problem," Max said, "I'll work my way over to the field and set up my nest for the night at the bottom of the billboard or at whatever cover looks best. The only problem I might run into is if another homeless guy is already there. If the bouncers see me, I'll only be another guy looking for a place to sleep. By the looks of these bridge overpasses here on the highway," Max pointed to the highway inter-section and ramps just to the south and east of the Factory, "there's probably already a fair-sized homeless population up under them."

"We didn't see any during our OP," Reaper said, "but that doesn't mean they aren't there. So you set up as you see fit. But I want you up in the billboard by 2200 hours. That's well enough after dark for you not to be seen and you can relax in place a bit.

"We'll use your truck for the insertion vehicle. Keith's got a camper top behind the shop that we can mount up and use for moving you and your shopping cart into position without being seen. Bear and I can remain in the camper until we insert at 0230 hours. The raid itself is going to go down at 0300 hours.

"Bear and I will leave the camper here in the neighborhood just to the southwest of the target. There's almost no traffic to speak of in that area during the day, and in the middle of the night we'll probably be the only ones walking around at all."

"So you think," Ben spoke up. "What about gang-bangers or just street punks?"

"If we run into any," Reaper said, "it'll be a bad thing—for them. Both Bear and I will have suppressed weapons if anyone wants to push the question of our being on their turf."

The men around the table went silent for a moment. The situation was an extremely serious one. Reaper's comment did more to drive that point home than anything that had been said all day. Somberly, they continued listening to Reaper's plan.

"There are a number of large chimneys and ventilation stacks on the south side of the building. Several of them near the southwestern corner have reinforcing rods bolted to the outside of the stacks; some of them run right up along the corners. For Bear and me, those will be like a stairway to the roof."

"Yeah," Bear said, "a stairway with no landings—no place to stop and rest or look around. How high did you say that roof was?"

"About 120 feet," Reaper said. "We'll have two loops of line with each of us. If we need to rest or stay secured, we'll just wrap them around the pipe or rods with a prussic knot and stick a foot in the loop."

"Okay," Bear said. "I only wanted to see if you had accounted for my frail old bones."

"Right," Reaper said with a grin. "You'll outlast me."

Turning back to the photo printout, Reaper didn't notice the lopsided smile that Bear had on his face. He also missed the sharp look that passed between Bear and Ben MacKenzie. Whatever it was that the two men shared, they weren't willing to talk about it just then.

"So we go in from the roof and make the hit on the admin offices," Reaper said. "It should take us about a half-hour to forty-five minutes to make the climb and get onto the roof. That puts us on the target at 0330–0345 hours. We penetrate the building and search the offices. Anyone there, we secure them and continue the search. If we recover the hostages or Arzee is one of the prisoners, we leave by the stairs. If not, we extract the same way we came in with all the intelligence material we can find. Any questions?"

"I'm going to remain with the extraction vehicle?" Ben asked.

"Yes," Reaper said, "that will give you the fastest means of pulling us out of the area if the shit hits the fan.

"If we do have to abandon the target," Reaper continued, "our emergency rally point is here," he pointed to the print, "just north of the railroad bridge where we dropped off Max. There is no contact with the police, and as little contact as possible with anyone around the target. Guns are tight on this op, the rules of engagement have no slop in them."

All the men nodded their assent with what Reaper had just said. There could not be any danger to innocent bystanders on this operation. It was going to be as surgical a strike as anything they had ever done in the military. And the personal costs could be higher than any of them were willing to pay.

Speaking up, Bear broke the uncomfortable silence that followed Reaper's pronouncement. "You know, if we throw some mud on the camper and pickup, dab a little rust-red or primer-colored paint on it, it'll look just like a jarhead's paradise. No one will even want to look at it with that peeling paint it already has."

"Hey," Max said, "don't dis my truck, man. And don't get that damned silver paint GM puts on their trucks. I've seen it peel a bunch of times—so that's not my fault. She may look a bit worn, but my baby's mechanically as sound as anything on the road."

"Just as long as it's dependable," Ben said.

"As anything on the road," Max replied, "I'd stake my life on it."

"I think you are," Ben said.

The warriors had no further questions about the basic plan Reaper had laid out. Everyone now had his own preparations to go through to get ready for the operation. Only the fact that they had all gone though extensive training and had a wide pool of experience between them even allowed for the possibility of a raid on the Factory being staged at such a short notice.

Reaper continued to go over everything they had in the way of intelligence to see if he had missed anything. Deckert left in his van to shop for some communications gear. Ben MacKenzie had brought a variety of medical gear in the trunk of his car, the tools of his everyday trade as an emergency medical technician, and was checking over his trauma bag.

Bullet wounds were not something anyone liked to think about at any time, and especially right then, but Ben made certain to be prepared to deal with anything that he could. His skills as a combat medic were considerable and he felt that he could prevent anyone on the team from having to answer the uncomfortable questions a hospital would ask regarding the treatment of gunshot and other wounds.

For Bear, he dealt with the tools that made gunshot wounds. Behind the house and along the side of the shop, a measured range had been laid out for test firing and sighting in guns. Carrying all of the weapons both he and Reaper would be using, Bear headed to the range. Before they left for the op, Reaper would check out his own hardware himself, firing the weapons to refresh their characteristics to him.

Bear had it in mind to check out all of the guns at once to make sure that there weren't any mechanical problems at all. If any glitches arose in the guns, he still had time to fix the problems before they left for the op.

For his own primary weapon, Bear had picked the Jackhammer shotgun. The short, nasty piece of firepower appealed to him. And using the gun on the people who had gone to such lengths to get them just seemed fair. The ten-round capacity of the shotgun combined with its cyclic firing rate of 240 rounds per minute made it a very powerful and compact chunk of firepower.

For a secondary weapon, Bear would carry the Beretta 92-F with the Whispertech suppressor. Reaper would be using the H&K MP5K-PDW as his primary weapon That was a chunk of hardware that had always been a favorite of his back during his active Team days. Instead of a sidearm, Reaper would pack the Serbu Super-Shorty in the SKT thigh holster. The compact little pump-gun would be loaded with the Mark II beanbag rounds in case Reaper had to deal with someone he'd rather not kill.

There were only three ammunition cassettes ready for the Jackhammer that Bear could take with him on the op. If he had to get into a firefight, the thirty rounds of 12-gauge ammo would have to be enough for him. Switching cassettes in the Jackhammer was easy and fast. But removing the fired casings and then reloading the cassettes themselves was a slow process. All of the cassettes would be loaded with magnum Winchester OO buckshot, a heavy combat load Bear knew well.

This model of the Jackhammer would fire three-inch magnum 12-gauge ammunition. Deckert had told him that the other guns, the ones that had been taken, would only fire the standard 12-gauge shells. The fifteen .32-caliber pellets in these three-inch, 12-gauge loads could deal with people, as well as the locks or hinges of any secured doors they had to pass through. Reaper had a set of lock picks, and the skills to use them. But there could easily come a time during the operation where speed would be a lot more important than silence—such as if they had to blast their way out of the place with Reaper's wife and son in tow.

In the event that they ran into something really resistant, Deckert had some other Law Enforcement ammo from the same MK Ballistic Systems people who made the beanbag rounds he was using. The ammo was QB-slugs, antivehicle/antimaterial tacti-

cal ammo. As near as Bear could tell, the rounds
were loaded with plastic-coated gray steel slugs.
Deckert said they would tear through nearly anything, especially a steel fire door inside a factory.
Firing those rounds through the Serbu Super-Shorty
would not be fun, their recoil would be terrific.

Neat stuff all in all. They didn't have a lot of material to work with, yet no one could have found
fault with Deckert's selflessness. He generously offered up everything he had available, despite the
fact that the shop didn't quite have the same size
budget as the U.S. Navy.

As Bear approached the shooting bench, he almost stepped on Max Warrick, who lay prone on the
ground. Either the ex-Marine scout-sniper hadn't
been shooting, or the ammunition and suppressor on
his rifle constituted the best combination Bear had
ever "not" heard.

Max had the TTR-700 rifle assembled and laid
out across the rolled-up carrying case as a rest. As
Bear stood directly behind Max, the TTR-700 quietly put out a round of EBR subsonic Thumper ammunition downrange. The bullet "clanged" into the
steel gong target Max had set up behind the paper
target holder. The shot had been incredibly quiet, almost undetectable as a suppressed gunshot.

The ringing of the target was much louder than
the shot had been. After leaning over and looking
through a sixty-power spotting scope he had set up
on a small tripod next to him, Max carefully jotted
down a note in the data book he had lying out open
on the ground. After he had finished writing, Max
turned and looked at Bear standing behind him.

"You need the range?" Max asked.

"Not if you still do," Bear said. "How much longer will you be?"

"I'm just about done here," Max replied. "I'm only confirming the final zero of the scope with this subsonic ammunition. A few rounds of 168-grain match ammunition to confirm where it hits and I'll be done."

"Why are you going to use the louder match ammo if that quiet-ass subsonic is so good?" Bear asked as he set his burden of weapons down on the range table.

"Might need the range of the 168-grain on the op," Max said. "This EBR Thumper stuff is tits, it fires to about one minute of angle, only half an inch bigger than the best groups from that Federal Gold Medal match ammo. But it has the trajectory of a thrown brick—all subsonic ammo does. With a one hundred-meter zero, the bullet is hitting the exact point of aim each shot with the Thumper ammo. With that zero, I have a drop of fifteen and a half inches low at 150 meters. The drop is forty-two inches low at 200 meters."

Settling back behind his weapon, Max snugged it into his shoulder. "According to the scale on that aerial photo you guys came up with," Max said, "the shortest range I'll have to deal with from the billboard to the southeast corner of the building will be 122 meters. The longest range will be 165 meters to the far northeast corner. Since I'll be so high up in the air on the billboard, my aim into the sixth floor will be a flat shot."

Raising his head, Max slipped several 168-grain supersonic match rounds from a ten-round red plastic holder into the magazine of the opened bolt action of the rifle. He closed the bolt and chambered a round in the rifle. He fired a shot that had a much louder, sharper "crack" to its report than the soft thuds of the EBR subsonic. The "clang" from the target sounded much louder when the bullet impacted an instant later.

"Why the steel target?" Bear asked.

"In case I have to put a round into somebody," Max said as he looked up with a blank expression on his face. "Deckert said that he could make a new barrel for this rifle within a couple of hours, and destroy the old one completely. As long as I police up my fired brass either here or at the target, there won't be anything to use as forensic evidence to connect this gun to this shop. That steel gong makes sure that there's not going to be any fired bullets laying around that could be matched up to something the police find."

"It's a weird mission having to look out for the legal end," Bear said thoughtfully.

"Yeah, it is," Max said as he settled back down behind his weapon. With a smooth, practiced motion, he eased back the bolt of the rifle and caught the ejected empty brass from his last shot before it sprang from the receiver.

"From what I can tell, Reaper's between a rock and a hard place," Max said as he looked at the brass cartridge case he held between his fingers.

"I figure that I wouldn't be around if it wasn't for him and what he did for me back in Storm," Max continued. "He has whatever help I can give him. If it takes a big chunk of my time afterwards because of some legal bullshit—so be it."

The ex-sniper punctuated his comment with another shot. The muffled crack of the bullet, immediately followed by another loud clang from the steel gong, took less than a second. The deformed slug fell to the ground among the others that had been fired that day.

"I think I'll just wait until you're done," Bear said thoughtfully. "Maybe I should use that same steel target."

"Maybe," Max agreed.

As Max finished up with his weapons, Bear drew out the Jackhammer from its case. The gun looked like something from a science fiction movie but was reasonably light and easy to handle. He had one cassette locked in place in the weapon and was ready to fire. Deckert had told Bear that the new Jackhammer had been test-fired and operated properly. But Bear wanted to familiarize himself with the firing characteristics of the very odd gun.

"Okay, Bear," Max said as he got up from his firing position, "the range is all yours."

"Great," Bear said and he stood a little to the side of where Max had been. The Jackhammer didn't eject fired cases. The ammunition stayed in the chambers of the cassette through the firing cycle. With no ballistic marks being left on shotgun pellets when they were fired, he didn't have to worry about leaving traceable projectiles lying about. So Bear just tossed an empty can downrange as a target. Before the can hit the ground and bounced, Bear snapped the Jackhammer up to his shoulder and pulled the trigger.

Boom . . . Boom . . . Boom roared out as Bear fired a three-round burst in under one second. Gouts of dirt erupted into the air as the shot loads smashed into the backstop. The empty can was nowhere to be seen—it had almost disappeared when the first swarm of buckshot smashed into it. Even Bear was startled by the power and sound of the Jackhammer. Max just stood there for a second, stunned.

"I think you got it, Bear," Max said.

"Yeah, it does look that way," Bear said with a big, wide grin across his face. "You know, I think I may like this gun."

Chapter Twenty-one

Preparations for the operation moved forward rapidly and smoothly—a reflection on the level of professionalism of everyone involved. Reaper wanted the team ready to launch at 1900 hours. That would give them time to transport to the area, including a cushion in case something went wrong, something as simple as bad traffic. Reaper wanted to put Max and his gear on the street by 2015 hours at the latest.

It had been an incredible rush to get everything together. When the preparations were done and they stood ready to go, there was plenty of time to do one final briefing and a brief-back. For now Reaper declared them good to go, with only the final details to be worked out.

Deckert had proven himself more than capable, even without the use of his legs. He had almost literally stripped the shelves of their fledgling company to make certain that they all had what they needed for the mission. When the gear he wanted turned out to be something they didn't have, he simply went out and bought the stuff. Reaper knew he owed a deep debt to these men. Not only did they risk a lot, including their freedom, to help him get his family back, some of them had emptied their wallets out to pay for it.

Some of the setup for equipment had just been funny. For the op they would employ the weirdest insertion platform any of them had ever even heard of before. Max's pickup truck had been fitted up with a well-used camper shell that Deckert had behind the shop building. Keith had said that someone years back had given him the camper as a deposit on a high-level gun that the guy never came back for. After a few years had passed, he considered the camper abandoned and thus his property.

The only trouble with the camper was the fact that it had been up on cinder blocks and the lifting jacks had been torn off years ago when the camper fell over during a windstorm. Watching two SEALs, a Marine, and an Air Force PJ trying to lift the camper onto the pickup truck would have been a good video for one of those "funniest moments" shows.

Eventually, with much grunting and a liberal amount of cursing—Bear could swear in five languages besides English—they finally mated the camper with the truck. They adopted Ben's suggestion and applied copious amounts of dirt, mud, and a little rust-red spray paint, effectively matching the splotches of bird shit and peeling paint that already streaked the silver truck.

Removing the screws allowed the window between the camper and the truck to be fully removed, so that now any of the guys could crawl through from the cab of the truck to the camper and vice-versa. Ben and Max made bets as to just how long it would take Bear to crawl through the window—Bear declining to take up that particular challenge, arguing it was beneath him.

Pulling out the central convertible table/bed combination inside the camper made room for Max's shopping cart disguise prop. Deckert had spotted a reasonably rusted shopping cart sitting in a ditch behind a shopping mall while out buying commo gear for the team. He and Bear had driven back out and grabbed up the cart, as well as an assortment of milk crates, boxes, and general junk.

Max draped himself with some of the worst clothes that could be found, along with rubber boots that had seen better days. He had a pair of rubber-soled boat shoes with him that he slipped into the pockets of the very ratty overcoat Ben had pulled from his car trunk. The shoes were for climbing up the ladder to the billboard, the coat had been the one MacKenzie put on when changing a tire in bad weather.

With his cleaned, tested, and zeroed TTR-700 rifle in its case underneath his filthy fisherman's sweater, Max was now one of the best equipped and most dangerous street people soon to haunt the corridors of downtown Detroit. Max didn't carry a sidearm, but he did have a razor-sharp Gerber Command II combat knife in its scabbard hanging pommel-down underneath the left side of his sweater. A strategic hole in the sweater made the knife quickly available.

When slid silently from the black nylon of the scabbard, the nearly seven-inch-long blade with a serrated back edge at the tip made for an intimidating tool. Its appearance alone would make anyone Max might run into on the street pause before accosting him further.

To take care of communications, Deckert located several sets of Motorola "Talkabout" T5420 radios. The little transceivers, not much bigger than the average cellular phone, were about as secure as the Motorolas Reaper and Bear had used back in the SEAL Teams. The little hand-held radios had fourteen available channels and thirty-eight quiet codes to cut back on interference. Those same codes would help add to the communications security of the team. A two-way boom mike and earphone setup helped complete the communications rig. The voice-activated transmitter made it possible to use the radios hands-free.

A little discreet tinkering with the radios by Deckert deactivated the call tone that announced an incoming signal. It wouldn't do to have a radio beep, no matter what the tone, while Reaper and Bear tried to silently infiltrate what could be considered an enemy stronghold. Rechargeable batteries were abandoned since they just didn't have the time to charge up enough sets to use before Reaper wanted the operation underway.

Fresh batteries were installed in all of the radios and carefully tested. The little sets had a two-mile range over flat terrain; they would do extremely well over the limited distances of the mission site. Deckert taped a set of tested spare batteries to the back of each radio—just in case.

"It's amazing what one can buy at RadioShack," Deckert quipped lightly.

Ben MacKenzie wore his normal clothes, a long-sleeved denim shirt and dark Levi's. He would maintain the watch on the operation from inside the cab of the pickup truck. Deckert reprogrammed the police scanner that Max had installed long ago to make certain that they were matched to the local Detroit police and emergency frequencies. He set up a second scanner for State and Federal frequencies. For weapons, Ben had his own pump-action Remington shotgun, one with a standard five-shot magazine and an eighteen-inch barrel. A pistol grip replaced the stock of the Remington to make it more manageable in the close confines of the truck cab. The shotgun was Ben's primary vehicle weapon and he had clips installed under the front seat of the truck that held the shotgun securely and concealed.

Underneath the dash of the truck, Max had a second weapon secured, a blued-steel Smith & Wesson six-and-a-half-inch barreled Model 29 .44 magnum, the Dirty Harry gun itself. The big revolver showed signs of long, but careful, use. And the cylinder, filled with Federal Gold Medal 250-grain metal-cased slugs, gave it a deadly look. After showing it to Ben and Bear, Max slipped the magnum revolver back underneath the dash into a hidden holster accessible by the driver.

"Why drag such a huge thing around, even if you do carry it in a truck?" Bear asked.

"Full metal-jacketed loads," Max said with a smile, "high velocity. They kill cars dead."

"Uh-huh," was Bear's only comment.

For his personal weapon, Ben used what he had brought with him, turning down Deckert's offer of anything in the shop. Ben slipped a 9mm Glock 19 into a concealed holster in the Bianchi K.O. 200 fanny pack secured around his waist. Two spare magazines rested in the pouch of the fanny pack. The magazines and weapon were loaded with Winchester 125-grain silvertip hollow points, a load Ben said had served him well for years.

As a backup weapon, Ben wore a Brauer lightweight ankle holster holding a simple five-shot Smith & Wesson Chief's Special revolver. The compact little snub-nosed revolver had been modified by having the spur of the hammer removed. Other than that it remained a stock gun. Loaded with Federal 125-grain .38 Special jacketed hollowpoint Hydra-Shok ammo, the little gun could still be a potent stopper.

When Bear asked Ben why he carried such a small weapon in such an outdated holster, the smaller man answered simply, "You can draw it easily when sitting in a car, or an ambulance."

Giving the statement a little thought, Bear realized the logic of the man's choice. Sitting in a car, you could reach an ankle easily. When sitting, it would actually be faster to draw from than a belt or shoulder holster—something that made a lot of sense given Ben's job as an emergency medical technician, riding around in ambulances all day long.

The time had come for Reaper and Bear to gear up and make ready for the operation. Bear had tested all of the weapons, and Reaper had made time to check-fire them himself. Everything was mechanically fine and operating properly. Bear winced a bit as they finished up on the range. When Reaper asked him about it, Bear said that it was nothing, only a headache. After going back in the house to get ready for the op, Bear reappeared his old smiling self again after taking what he said was a handful of aspirin.

The gear both men would wear on the operation had been spread out across their beds. Everything they had was new, unworn, and unexposed to their everyday environment. There would be no isolated hairs, fibers, or anything else to give forensic people something to track. One couldn't seal off everything, but Bear and Reaper were determined to make sure they left as little as possible behind.

Black Royal Robbins 5.11 range pants, the choice of the FBI and other agencies, had also been the choice of Reaper and Bear on the op. A set of PACA Thunder concealable body armor went over their brown T-shirts. The Level IIIA vests, made of a hybrid Zylon fabric over 0.200-inch thick, had proven capable of stopping a 9mm full-jacketed slug moving at 1,639 feet per second.

Wrapping the waist straps around the flexible black vests snugged them in tight to their sides. Neither SEAL would be wearing the hard trauma plate that would have given them additional armor protection. The plates would have reduced their range of movement and they had a hard climb ahead of them to get on top of the Factory building. Armor couldn't protect everything, no matter how much of it you wore, so you simply had to decide when enough was enough and go with what worked for you.

Generic long-sleeve black cotton shirts went on over the vests. The shirts could be bought all over the country at department stores, but still they removed the labels from them. Slipping on the black Bates Spyder Sidewinder leather/nylon boots, both SEALs pulled the laces tight. The soft-sided flexible boots had a deeply formed rubber outsole that gripped well and made climbing a little easier.

A BlackHawk CQB/Emergency rescue rigger belt went on over the pants. The heavy belts were made of 7,000-pound tensile strength black-nylon webbing and had a 5,000-pound test black-anodized aluminum nonlocking snap carabiner snapped through the parachute-grade adapter that was part of the belt's construction. If they had to, both SEALs knew that they could hang by the belts and trust them to support their weight.

Pouches and holsters went on the belts. Reaper had the special thigh holster on his right side to hold the Serbu Super-Shorty shotgun. On his left side, he secured an Omega TalonFlex MP5/Flash Bang thigh rig pouch. The pouch held two spare thirty-round curved stick magazines for Reaper's MP5K-PDW. Each magazine was filled with a full thirty rounds of EBR 9mm Hush Puppy ammunition. With the magazine in his weapon, Reaper would have ninety rounds for the entire op—and he planned to come back with most or all of them.

What Reaper wouldn't be carrying on this operation was any flash bang distraction grenades. He had chosen his specific ammo pouch so that he could carry a half-dozen spare Mark II bean bag 12-gauge rounds, three in each flash-bang pocket. The Serbu Super-Short was a handy little shotgun, but it had a very limited magazine capacity.

In his right front pants pocket, Reaper slipped in his Emerson Commander-BTS knife—clipping it to the pocket so that its Wave feature could snap open the blade if needed. Reaper made a mental note to himself to keep an eye out for his Emerson CQC-7BW. That knife had disappeared along with Musclehead and his injured arm. He would have to try and get it back, while maybe discussing philosophy with Musclehead along the way.

Over his shirt, Reaper secured a Chalker sling, designed and patented by a fellow SEAL some years before. The Chalker allowed almost any shoulder weapon to be carried by a single attachment point. The weapon could then be shouldered without breaking the seal on a gas mask—something that wasn't a consideration for Reaper on this mission.

The sling also allowed a weapon to be dropped immediately so that a secondary weapon could be drawn—the dropped weapon hanging down from the center of the wearer's chest. Lastly, it was just a very good sling to climb with, and there was going to be a lot of climbing on this operation.

A Chalker Hi-port weapons catch was secured to the upper left shoulder strap of Reaper's Chalker sling. He clipped the standoff adapter at the back of the MP5K-PDW's receiver to the brass snap shackle on the center front of his chest. The snap shackle was rated at five hundred pounds breaking strength, so Reaper felt it could securely hold his submachine gun.

The Gemtech Raptor suppressor was attached to the barrel of the MP5K-PDW, the suppressor secured to the three lugs on the H&K weapon's barrel. The Hi-port adapter had a quick-release Velcro strap to it that wrapped around the suppressor on the weapon and secured it to the upper part of Reaper's left shoulder. The MP5K-PDW was so short that even with the nine-inch-long black Raptor suppressor installed, it still didn't stick up past Reaper's left shoulder. It would be well out of the way while climbing.

A pair of inner shells from a set of FOG—Fastrope Operator Gloves—went on Reaper's hands. He didn't need the protection of the normal heavy leather padded outer FOG shells for this operation. But the glove liners would protect his hands, and help keep him from leaving any fingerprints around. Under the front of his belt, Reaper tucked a black Hatch Nomex balaclava hood.

The Nomex hood would protect his face from the flash and heat of a fire or explosion, not something Reaper expected to need. But it also covered his face with a nonreflective black cloth, all but his eyes. The hood prevented either SEAL from requiring black face paint. Black camouflage makeup was something that would be hard to get off quickly if they had to shed their gear and blend into a group of civilians.

In each of his back pockets, Reaper slipped a four-foot length of 7mm black Kernmantle nylon climbing rope. The two ends of the line were tied together with a fisherman's knot—making the rope a single big loop. The two loops would be used to make prussic knots if they needed them.

Prussic knots were a climbing aid that could slip along a rope or pipe. When pressure was put on the loop of rope hanging from a prussic knot, the knot tightened up and wouldn't slip down. Taking the pressure off loosened the knot and it could again be slipped upward. Using the knots, a climber could hold position easily and free his hands for other work.

Reaper strapped a black Casio G-Shock watch to his left wrist. Finally, he slipped the black Motorola Talkabout radio into his upper-left shirt pocket. The wire for the two-way boom headset went underneath Reaper's Chalker sling strap and was secured to his shirt with a simple safety pin. The EarGel earpiece had been fitted to Reaper's ear only a hour earlier, and it now slipped in snugly. After checking out his rig, jumping, twisting, and turning in it to see if anything shook loose, rattled, or snagged, Reaper signaled the others that he was ready to go. He pulled the earpiece out and let the light headset dangle from its wire.

Bear rigged up essentially the same as Reaper. He wore the same clothes, boots, belt, rig, and sling as his partner did with changes to fit his weapons. For a thigh holster, Bear wore a BlackHawk Omega VI assault holster with the bottom opened up to allow the passage of the Whispertech suppressor attached to the barrel of the Beretta M92-F pistol he carried. Bear carrying the Beretta gave both men a suppressed weapon for quiet shooting. Two straps secured the holster to Bear's thigh and a spare magazine went in the pouch on the front of the holster body.

On his left thigh Bear secured an Omega shot shell pouch. Each of the two pouches on the thigh rig held ten rounds of 12-gauge ammunition secured in place under inch and a half-wide elastic strapping loops. The Chalker sling and standoff adapter did fine for holding Bear's Jackhammer Mark 3-A3. With the adapter mounted just behind the pistol grip of the Jackhammer, the weapon balanced easily and hung freely in the muzzle-down position.

The same style of Hi-port adapter that Reaper had used held Bear's Jackhammer muzzle-up with the flash hider of the gun secured to his left shoulder. The two spare ammunition cassettes Bear had available fit into Blackhawk shotgun shell pouches. The pouches were intended to hold twenty-five rounds of 12-gauge ammunition, secured under an elastic strap, but each would secure only one of the thick, round ammunition cassettes. Bear secured the pouches to the front of his belt, one on either side of the buckle.

In spite of his different load of ammunition and equipment, Bear could move as well as Reaper in his rig. Now both men stood armed and ready to operate.

Putting on long, black overcoats covered up their gear with only a few bulges suggesting that the two men might not be all they seemed. The ammo pouches and thick action of the Jackhammer made Bear look almost potbellied under his coat. Anyone mistaking the SEAL for a jolly fat guy would have been in for a serious surprise. As Bear looked at Reaper, he broke out with a laugh.

"Ho, ho, ho," Bear laughed. "All you need are a pair of dark glasses and you would look like a Neo-wannabe from *The Matrix*."

"The what?" Reaper asked.

"A movie. You don't get out much, do you?"

"Not enough to go see a movie," Reaper said. "Now let's go down for the brief-back."

"And more," Bear said as he grabbed up a paper bag.

Reaper shook his head for a moment about his

friend's antics. Over the last day, Bear could be up or down depending on the moment. Yet he couldn't fault his friend for loyalty, and he felt incredibly grateful for his assistance.

Everyone else was already sitting around the kitchen table when Reaper and Bear came down the stairs, except for Max, who had been relegated to the kitchen counter, as close to downrange as he could be placed in the room. Part of Max's disguise as a street person included the wafty aroma of his dirty and somewhat moldy clothes. Basically, he smelled like a wine-soaked compost heap that someone had slipped something into that shouldn't be there. Simply put—he stank.

"Wow, nice disguise," Bear said as he exaggerated a swallow and twisted his head around.

Max refused to be goaded by the SEAL and simply sat and waited for Reaper to begin.

"Okay, brief-back time," Reaper said. "Each man tell his part of the plan. You go first Max."

"I get dropped off with my cart underneath this railroad bridge here," Max pointed at the map Reaper had spread out over the table, "at 2015 hours. Sunset is at 2045 hours. I have about an hour of light to get to the bottom of the billboard and nest-up. I'm to be in position on the billboard platform and good to go by 2200 hours. I have freedom to fire in support of the op but only with positive target identification. My time for drive-by extraction is 0445 hours. And I should bring my cart along if I have the opportunity."

"Okay, Ben," Reaper continued, "your turn."

"I drive the truck and maintain radio watch on the

scanners and our own commo throughout the op," Ben said. "If there's anything coming across the police or emergency net, I notify everyone and head for the emergency rally point. When possible, I maintain communications with Deckert here over a cell phone, keeping the net secure. After off-loading Max and his cart under the bridge, I park over in the industrial area across the highway where you and Bear did for your OP.

"Driving back into the target area, I drop you and Bear here in this neighborhood at 0230 hours. This is as close as I can approach to the target without chancing being seen. It only gives you and Bear a few blocks to walk to get to the target, most of that distance can be covered through the alleys. After dropping you off, sorry, inserting you . . ."

"You make it sound so kinky," Bear said.

"Knock it off, Bear," Reaper said, wondering what had gotten into his friend. Bear had never before wisecracked during the final prep for an op.

"Okay, after I drop you off, I park here." Ben pointed to a spot on the photo printout they had used during their planning. "If there's any foot traffic or I feel compromised, I move over to here and park." Ben pointed to another spot. "If I really don't like the area, I head back across the highway to the original lay-up point.

"If the shit hits the fan and we can't make the rolling exfiltrations, I drive around, passing through the emergency rally point at 0500, 0530, and 0600 hours. Extraction at 0600 hours puts us to within twenty minutes of sunrise so things are going to get noticeable after that. If no pickups at 0600, I head back to the shop."

"That's right," Reaper said, "and I don't want you hanging around trying to pick us up later. If we get in trouble and miss the last extraction at 0600, each man is to cache his gear and make his way back here as best he can. Everyone will have a hundred bucks cash on him and a calling card Keith bought this afternoon. If you can't make your way back here, call in. Okay, Bear, now you."

"You and I insert in the neighborhood to the southwest of the target at 0230 hours. We walk into the southwest corner of the structure, avoiding all possible contact. We then go over the fence at the corner of the building and climb up to the roof of this single-story structure." Bear pointed to what looked like a material-handling dock for taking away finished cars at the southwest corner of the Factory.

"We go across the roof and decide which means— a chimney, corner, or pipe—we'll use to climb up to the top floor of the building. We've planned for it to take fifteen minutes to get to the garage rooftop and across to the chimney area and a half-hour for the climb to the main roof.

"Once on the main roof, we'll make our way into the structure and check out any rooms or secure areas we find on the factory-floor areas. The primary target is the offices at the far eastern end of the building. We move fast and quiet. No contact. This is a sneak-and-peek and we'll pick up the hostages if and when we find them. We extract and climb down by 0430 at the latest. If we find hostages or have prisoners, we come down by the stairs at the southeastern corner or the fire escapes on the north face of the building, depending on the circumstances. We call for emergency extraction at point Alfa, Bravo, or Charlie—the stairs, fire escape east, or fire escape west—respectively. Drive-by extraction is at 0440."

Reaper could find no fault with his friend's rendition of the plan. Still he had a funny feeling about hearing his own family be referred to as hostages. That was exactly why they were called that, to make it a little easier to concentrate on the task at hand and not the people involved.

"The only part left to assign is call signs for everyone to use over the net," Reaper said. "Any suggestions about something we're not likely to forget?"

"Okay, our leader here has long been known as the Grim Reaper," Bear said.

"Only by you and a handful of guys in the Teams, Bear," Reaper said. "I always hated that nickname."

"Well, you're really going to hate this one then," Bear said with a wide grin. "Gentlemen, I give you the four horsemen of the apocalypse. Our marine sniper friend is War. This rather diminutive Air Force PJ is Famine. I shall be Pestilence, since I make such a pest of myself anyway. And the Grim Reaper shall of course be Death."

"That sucks, Bear," Reaper said.

"Yeah, but it fits," Bear said, "and there aren't enough of us to be the apostles."

Reaper sighed, "Okay, if there aren't any other ideas," he said, "we go with Bear's suggestion."

No one else made a sound.

"So I guess that's it, we're good to go," Reaper said as he stood up.

"Not quite," Bear said as he stood up and walked over to a cabinet. "We still have one more thing to do."

He pulled out a dark brown bottle of Canadian Club whiskey and five shot glasses. Setting them out in front of everyone, Bear set down the bottle and then picked up his paper bag. He pulled out five slim aluminum tubes, each less than an inch in diameter and about six inches long.

The tubes contained Romeo y Julieta, Romeo No. 1 cigars from Havana, Cuba.

"What can I say," Bear said. "It was illegal for me to run them across the river so we'd better burn the evidence. Besides, I had to get Max his Cubans."

"I'll get some of my own after this is over," Max said with a smile.

"Not bad, Bear," Reaper said as he lifted the bottle and filled everyone's glass, then he set the bottle down, picked up his glass, and held it out to his friends. A feeling of esprit de corps filled the room.

"A toast," Reaper said. "I've never had a mission mean more to me, or knew a group of people I would rather have with me on it. So here's to the start of it. Once we go, there's no turning back. So we go—and everyone comes back."

"Everyone comes back," they all said, Bear loudest one of all. Each man gathered the last of his gear and left the room. The cigars remained on the table, to be smoked after the mission had been completed and everyone returned home again—including Reaper's family.

Chapter Twenty-two

Heavy traffic still filled the main highways around Detroit as Reaper and his men headed into the northern downtown area. The next weekend would be the Memorial Day holiday so the streets would be more or less deserted by the same time on the next Friday. Reaper couldn't look that far ahead, in fact he made an effort not to anticipate anything at all.

Reaper, Bear, and Max sat in the back of the pickup truck, riding in the camper along with Max's shopping cart. The only member of the four horsemen who hadn't dressed to draw a second glance was Ben, who sat up front driving the vehicle. In the back, Bear got a chuckle out of the idea that Famine was driving around the streets of Detroit in a 4x4 GM pickup truck.

In spite of the traffic, the men made good time and arrived in the area of the target less than forty-five minutes from leaving the shop. They couldn't cruise the area around the target, the possibility of gathering any new intelligence was greatly out-

weighed by the chance anyone would notice the
camper going by several times during the evening.
Reaper made the decision to go ahead with the first
insertion of the operation.

As Ben passed along the side road leading to the
railroad bridge, the top floors of the Factory building rose less than half a mile away. Looking through
the back window into the cab and the windshield beyond, Reaper watched the road and the area around
them. He suddenly made a decision and told Ben to
stop the truck.

"Go past this driveway and back into it," Reaper
said, "back up close to those bushes in the rear
there."

Reaper had seen a small industrial parking lot next
to the bridge. The flat, dirt and gravel lot had scraggly
grass, bushes, and scrub trees growing thickly along
its borders. The squat masonry bridge itself blocked
any view of the parking lot from the Factory, and at
that time of day no vehicles were present in the area.

With the truck backed up to fair cover, Bear
opened up the back door and took up a position behind the camper, where he could watch out for anyone who might be around them. Max and Reaper
manhandled the shopping cart out of the back of the
camper. Their practice sessions with this maneuver
back at the farm now paid off. The cart originally
hadn't fit easily though the rear door of the camper.
Removing the inside screen door and the liberal application of a heavy hammer had adjusted the cart to
more easily pass through the door.

Without a word spoken, Max slipped back up in
the bushes as Reaper and Bear climbed back into the

camper body. Reaper simply said "go," and Ben pulled out, leaving Max behind.

Inserting Max and his cart had taken well under a minute from the time that Ben started to back the truck into the parking lot to when they pulled out onto the road. Max saw no signs that the action had been noticed by anyone around the area, and only a few windows in any of the industrial buildings nearby allowed anyone to look out in the first place. The operation had now begun and there was no turning back.

The truck and the rest of the team had a long wait ahead of them before Reaper and Bear could insert for their penetration of the Factory. Their synchronized watches read twenty-hundred (2000) hours, eight o'clock on a Thursday night. From where the Horsemen watched, the crowd for the Factory club seemed light, but they soon started to build up in spite of the weekday night.

It would be dangerous for the pickup to remain in the area. Somebody could see it and connect it to another appearance later that night. One choice was to drive around—but that could expose them to a chance encounter with the locals or, even worse, a police cruiser. It could also put them out of radio range with Max in case War called for help or an emergency extraction.

Staying in the area while under some cover or blending in somewhere seemed the safest bet. The quiet area they had parked in before seemed good, and Reaper told Ben to drive over to where they had put the van during their observation-post vigil. The big open area still had a lot of industrial machinery parked about, as well as a number of vehicles. If the place had a guard that did the rounds, neither Bear nor Reaper had seen him. Among the other vehicles, the pickup camper rig didn't stand out at all. With the truck parked and hidden, and Ben remaining up on radio watch, Reaper and Bear did the only practical thing they had open to them—they settled in for some sleep.

Neither of the two SEALs would insert for six hours yet. Not only had Reaper and Bear been running on little sleep for the past several days, they had another reason to get some rest. Nerves can build up while waiting to launch an op, no matter how well trained an operative is.

That same nervous energy that can help keep you sharp and alert also saps your body's reserves. It can wear you down just as much as if you had been running a marathon, even though you were just sitting still. It was far better to try to relax and follow the soldier's rule—sleep wherever and whenever you could because it might be a long stretch before the chance for some sleep came around again.

So Reaper and Bear crashed. Ben remained in the front cab where he settled in comfortably and expected to make a night of it. With his police scanners running softly, Ben set his Motorola Talkabout on the dashboard, just behind the steering wheel. He could hear everything he had to and could function well enough as the sunset started to color the sky.

The bed pads still left in the camper didn't smell as springtime fresh as they could have been. Reaper and Bear considered them a hell of a lot more comfortable than some of the places they had slept during ops in the Teams. From where he lay in the bunk over the cab, of all things, Bear started singing softly.

"So we'll raise up our glasses against evil forces," the rough baritone voice growled out, "singing—whiskey for my men . . ."

". . . And beer for my horses," a surprisingly deep bass voice finished from up front in the cab.

"Great," Reaper sighed quietly, "two fruitcakes."

"Let me guess, Death, old friend," Bear said using Reaper's call sign, "you don't listen to the radio much either, do you? Country-western, Toby Keith, the *Unleashed* CD, any of those things sound familiar to you? Famine, old boy, our grim friend here simply has no culture."

Ben simply remained silent in the front and listened to his radios. They ran on power from the spare battery in the camper body, so he didn't worry about running the truck's battery down.

The noise from the scanners wasn't much to listen to, mostly static. But Ben made up plot lines to go along with the fragments of stories he heard over the scanners, something he had learned to do years ago. Soon, only deep, slow breathing came from the camper.

The evening went on and turned into the early morning hours without incident. Ben had occasionally called up Max to get a situation report, sitrep, on what was going on at the Factory. Outside of the ebb and flow of customers, the Marine sniper had seen nothing out of the ordinary. War was now well settled into a sniper's hide up on the billboard. He could look around the edge of the smaller billboard and see the entire front of the Factory building.

Using a Bushnell Yardage Pro Scout laser range finder he had accepted from Deckert before leaving on the op, Max had confirmed his ranges to the Factory—122 meters to the near corner, 164 meters to the far corner. He lay almost level with the fifth floor and still could have a good shot into the top floor if the blinds opened.

Then, at 0200 hours the time came to get ready to move out. As Ben prepared to wake Reaper, he turned and looked back into the camper. He could barely make out two eyes staring back at him. Either Reaper had been awake, or his internal alarm clock kept very good time. Reaper rose and moved to where Bear slept over the truck's cab. Bear remained sound asleep, but he came silently awake at Reaper's touch.

"Time to earn your whiskey and meet those evil forces," Reaper said quietly to Bear. Then he leaned forward and said through the window into the cab, "Move on out, Ben."

The night had turned chill, yet not too cold at about fifty degrees. So Reaper wouldn't have to worry about Max stiffening up. The sky had remained only partly cloudy, and a bright first-quarter moon still shone down on the area intermittently. The light could be a blessing to the climbers once they started on their way up the side of the building. But it would quickly become a curse if it revealed them to someone before they even got to the target.

The Factory had its last call at 0200, so the customers had mostly left by the time the camper truck eased its nose into the nearby neighborhood. A short radio call from War in his hide told the rest of the team that the coast was about as clear as it was going to get.

Patting themselves down one more time, Reaper and Bear made certain of the location of every piece of gear by touch. The balaclavas went over their heads and they pulled them down to bunch around their necks like a collar. Walking the streets wearing a ski mask was not the way to keep from drawing attention.

A large red clay brick three-story home had once been someone's pride. Now the abandoned building stood mute, almost all of its windows and doors covered with plywood. The attic windows of the old house looked down on the dirty silver and white camper truck as it stopped in front of the alley the house bordered. The mute eyes of the blank windows were the only witnesses to the two black-garbed men who quickly exited the back of the camper and darted into the alley.

The alley they ran through did not lead directly to the Factory, or the approach angle they wanted to make to the building itself. The alley did lead across the street and continue down the block. Only half a block from the street, the narrow passage crossed over a second alley that ran east and west. This second passageway ended directly across from the corner of the Factory where Reaper and Bear wanted to start their penetration.

The old Teammates recognized the danger in following the alleys. Some of the few occupied homes could have dogs standing watch in their backyards. That danger had to be weighed against the risks of two men walking the streets so early in the morning. Reaper had decided that he would rather take a chance on barking dogs that they could run away from than of being possibly caught in the open, away from cover, by someone in the street. In spite of his love of animals, Reaper would not have hesitated to use his suppressed weapon against someone's aggressive animal—he had far too much at stake to worry about the niceties of the situation.

Luckily, neither Reaper nor Bear ran into any dogs along their approach to the target. When they reached the passage leading to the Factory itself, their cover ran out. To their south sat a line of decaying homes. Directly in front of them stood the Factory, not much more than a hundred meters away. But to the north they had the open area of the abandoned parking lot.

No vehicles remained in the lot, nothing but the grass and broken blacktop they had noted earlier when the two SEALs did their original drive-by. Only now, they had to walk down the alley with no cover to their left, just the open spaces of the chain-link fence that surrounded the parking lot. But when an obstacle finally appeared, it didn't come from their open side, or even the Factory.

Jerome Slaneal had been given the brush-off by his girlfriend Lateasha. The fifteen-year-old now looked at a long summer ahead without a lady to help comfort him. Of course, if any of his friends suggested such a thing, Jerome would have had to introduce them to his blade. The young man considered himself an expert in knife fighting and close-quarter combat—even if he had never heard that particular term.

So Jerome had a mad on, and the two strangers he saw walking down the alley were just what he needed to take out his frustrations. There were two of them, but he had his favorite blade with him. Besides, the two strangers were white—he reasoned that they had to be lost or had parked in the wrong place. They might be headed toward the club, and Jerome knew well enough not to bother anyone who was a customer there.

The information on the streets was that anyone who caused trouble for the guys in the club soon turned up missing. But Jerome was high on the arrogance of youth, and the forty-ounce bottle of malt liquor he had finished just an hour earlier had given him the false bravery of alcohol. He could tell the two men walking by so silently weren't headed toward the club anyway, they weren't taking a direct route there. That made them fair game according to his rules.

The blade Jerome took so much pride in was a wicked-looking hook-nosed folding knife made of stainless steel, with a four-inch serrated blade. The young man had no idea that what he held was only a cheap knock-off of a Spyderco Civilian. He just knew that he could slice the clothes, or the skin, right off of somebody with that blade. And he could snap the knife open with a practiced flip of his wrist.

If the two outsiders gave up and surrendered to Jerome what he believed was his due, he would probably let them go with just a good scare—probably.

Both Reaper and Bear realized that someone lurked behind them at almost the same instant. Years of training and experience caused them to automatically spread farther apart so as to not get in each other's way. Both men had pulled up the bottom part of their balaclavas to cover the lower halves of their faces. It would have taken both hands to pull the back of the hoods over the tops of their heads. They wanted to keep their hands free, but not to have any trouble. Maybe they could just outwalk whoever was behind them. If he had intended to shoot, he would have done so already.

Then Jerome commanded, "Freeze, mufa."

Damn, this is not what we need right now, Reaper thought as he recognized the youthful crack in the voice behind them. Both he and Bear looked at each other as they just kept walking. They remained out in the open and needed to get across the street and to the wall of the building only a few dozen meters away.

Then Jerome almost shouted, "I said freeze, motherfuckers!"

The sharp click they both heard behind them sounded like a knife locking open. They had no way around it now. This gate crasher was probably armed. Reaper stopped and looked at Bear, gave him an almost imperceptible nod. Then the two SEALs turned away from each other, rotating around smoothly until they faced their young opponent.

Even for a street tough, Jerome could get nervous when facing something he didn't understand. These two didn't move like normal sheep did when they saw his blade. And their eyes looked anything but scared as they bore into the younger man's gaze. The black masks only covered the bottom half of the men's faces, but that was enough to intimidate him. The fear only helped to make Jerome angry at himself.

"Give it up, you mothers," Jerome said, brandishing his knife.

Reaper had had enough of the young punk and he was tempted to give him what he asked for—even if he didn't know it. Instead of raising a weapon, Reaper slipped his hands into the pockets of his overcoat—the same overcoat that Bear wore, a style that covered them to their ankles.

"I don't think you want any part of this," Reaper said, and he pulled the front of his coat open.

Jerome was suddenly looking at more hardware than he had ever seen even in the hands of SWAT cops. Then the other dude opened up his coat and he had an even bigger gun strapped to his chest than the first one did.

Even youthful enthusiasm loses ground when a young pup looks at the growling teeth of a pair of wolves. Standing his ground, but only because he was frozen with fear, Jerome completely forgot about the knife in his hand as it dropped from his nerveless fingers.

"Go your way," the big, bad dude in black said. Then the two of them turned back to the direction in which they had been moving and started to step away.

Jerome voiced one last burst of reckless bravado, in spite of feeling the results of his fear trickling down his leg in a warm flow.

"You say what, moth—" he started to shout.

Then the taller man in black, the one who had spoken, turned around sharply. His movement caused the long coat to fly open. His hands were no longer in his pockets, but were holding that horrible-looking gun strapped across his chest. Jerome knew that if he uttered one more word, that awful weapon would start talking to him—and it would be the last thing he would ever hear.

Jerome never looked back as he turned and ran

away. At any moment, he expected to feel slugs stitch across his back. It was something he would never mention to anyone. The two men he had just faced had to be stone-killers—the taller one looked and sounded like Death himself. Jerome would never know just how right he had been.

Chapter Twenty-three

With a quiet sigh, Reaper turned back to the task at hand and both men moved quickly to cross the last few meters to their target. Along the way, the two SEALs fully pulled up the hoods of their balaclavas, completely covering their heads in black Nomex cloth, and shed their black overcoats. They stashed them nearby, where the coats could be picked up later during the extraction. If they had to be abandoned it wouldn't matter; they had been purchased from a thrift shop and were effectively untraceable anyway.

The western side of the Factory towered above the two SEALs as they ran up to the wall. The facade of the building was the last place they wanted to hang around. The red clay bricks had been painted years ago with a now-peeling coat of white paint. In spite of the gang graffiti along the first-floor wall, the two black-clad SEALs stood out in stark contrast against the white surface.

Reaper prepared to go up the corner of the chain-link fence when Bear grabbed him by the shoulder. Pointing, Bear indicated a corner of the building only fifteen feet away. The loading dock or garage building, had two fifteen-foot-high roll-up overhead steel doors, set about three feet back from the edge of the sidewalk. The main structure came right up to the edge of the sidewalk.

In the shadows of the corner caused by the setback, a four-inch-diameter steel pipe was strapped to the walls and extended up two stories to the upper roof, to the point where a number of the chimneys, stand pipes, and ventilation stacks started. Plans had to be fluid to meet a changing situation. Climbing up the fence and dealing with the barbed wire wasn't set in stone as being the only way up the side of the building.

The big steel pipe looked like a staircase to two men with Reaper and Bear's climbing skills. Grinning under his balaclava, Reaper went over to the pipe and started to climb. He placed a hand to either side of the pipe and pulled back hard on the steel to make sure it was still anchored solidly. When the pipe didn't move, Reaper set his feet on either side of it and, in a crouching stance, walked up the side of the building, pulling with his hands to maintain traction for his feet.

When Reaper gained the first roof, he unhooked the Hi-port weapons catch on his Chalker sling and swung the MP5K-PDW into position for use. Bear followed up the pipe. Even though the tube had been sturdy enough for one man to climb it, two men on it at the same time might have put too much stress on it. So while Bear ascended, Reaper held his position and maintained an overwatch.

Now the big climb loomed up in front of the two

SEALs. From their present position, they had to go up more than four stories to gain access to the roof of the factory building itself. The photos they had taken combined with their inspection during the drive-by only gave them so much information about the pipes and stacks. Seen up close they looked like a viable means of assaulting the building. But only a thorough inspection would tell Reaper and Bear which pipes were sound, and which stacks had walls thick enough to not echo like giant drums when they climbed them.

The first two stacks proved far too exposed for comfortable use by Reaper. And they turned out to be little more than sheet metal when examined. Putting your feet on the sides of these stacks would have caused the stacks to boom like dull cannons.

The rest of the stacks rose on the far side of the freight elevator housing. To cross around the structure, Reaper and Bear had to crawl out on a foot-wide ledge and make their way more than twenty feet to get to the far roof. The tar of the very short overhang roof had been cracked and pebbled from years of winter freezing and summer heat. The surface of the roof looked like wet alligator hide in the faint moonlight—and felt about as slippery, too.

But both men reached the other roof with little more than a fast heartbeat to show for their exertions. Reaper immediately went to a set of four large square stacks near the center of the building. The two middle piles had been shoved tightly together, while the outside stacks left a good two-foot space between themselves and the center ones. Best of all, the sheet-steel sides sounded solid, as though they were filled with insulating cement.

At the corners of the smoke stacks were steel shafts, pipes really, about an inch in diameter. The shafts were part of a support structure for the stacks that extended all the way up to the roof. By 0315 hours, the two SEALs had confirmed their means of reaching the roof and were still on schedule. Their alleyway incursion hadn't slowed them much, despite Reaper's sense that they had taken far too long just to reach the Factory.

Now they climbed up the side of the inner two stacks. Both men remained covered from almost any observation by the smoke stack on the outside of each of them. The shadows in between the sets of stacks concealed them from all but the closest inspection. No casual observer would be able to watch them make the climb.

The climbing technique to go up the stacks used both the sides of the structures and the pipes up along their outsides. Reaper and Bear would jam their toes into the space between the pipe and the stack. Performing a lay-back maneuver, they leaned back and pulled with their arms and practically walked up the side of the stacks.

Going up the stacks became a long and tedious climb. Only men in exceptionally good shape could even attempt such a feat. Reaper felt gratified that he had kept himself in top condition and Bear had always held up his end. The other SEAL may not have exercised to the point that Reaper did, but he had never, ever, let his partner down.

Both men had their loops of rope for prussic knots to rest with while on the way up. The climb went easily enough and no rest was needed by either man so the rope loops stayed in their pockets. Once they got to the top of the climb, the rope loop climbing aids came in handy for another purpose.

The tops of the smoke stacks were surrounded by a two-foot-wide steel grid catwalk. On top of the catwalks, guardrails made of steel pipe ran around them. Reaper saw no easy way up to the roof beyond the top of the stacks; the catwalks were in the way. They would have to use climbing techniques to get around the obstructions.

Taking one of his loops of rope, Reaper slipped it around the pipe and then put the end of the loop through the knot he had just made. Pulling the loose prussic knot up as high as it would go, Reaper snugged the knot down. Now he had a loop of line that he could place a foot into and it wouldn't slip down the pipe.

Reaper lifted one leg up and stuck his foot into the loop. He stepped on the loop and leaned far out into the air. He didn't look down, and he didn't think about the hundred-foot fall to the ground. Instead, Reaper worked to place his second prussic knot loop around the pipe stanchion at the corner of the catwalk that held up the guardrail. Once that knot was secured, it was a simple matter, though still a physical strain, to put his other foot into the loop. Now he could stand up and climb onto the catwalk, passing underneath the guardrail.

Being the faster and more experienced climber, Reaper made the top of the catwalk well before Bear did. But his partner followed almost exactly the same steps to reach the top of the catwalk. No more than a minute later Reaper bent over and helped Bear up to the grid. Now the two SEALs stood on the roof of the Factory, and their real mission could begin.

Like all of the other industrial roofs the two SEALs had seen, the top of the Factory roof consisted of a poured tar surface covered in rough gravel. The gravel looked old and thin in spots. The same thing could be said for the hundreds of pounds of bird droppings that covered the roof, the only difference being that the layer of guano wasn't thin in spots.

It had only taken the two men about twenty minutes to make the climb, putting them on the roof at 0342 hours. They had forty-five minutes to make their search of the interior and begin their exfiltration. If they had to climb down the outside of the building, it would be a lot easier and faster than coming up had been. If they found Reaper's family and got pinned down, as a last resort, they would call in the police and just hunker down until they arrived. But all of this depended on their getting inside the building, and doing it fast.

There was a central structure that ran the length of the Factory roof. It looked like a long, low building raising up from the gravel and tar. There were doors, windows, and vents in the structure, that was a skylight and ventilation system for the sixth floor paint shop.

One of the doors stood ajar and Reaper could feel a draft moving through it. The door had been tied off to a guardrail on a set of steps leading down into the building. It must have been propped open for ventilation when someone didn't want to run the big blowers. Peering around the frame of the open door, Reaper could make out a dim light inside, just enough to see by. He wouldn't need the red-lensed pilot's penlight he had clipped to his shirt pocket.

It looked like the best way in. Reaper could not see any alarms or trips around the door, so he signaled Bear and set up to enter. Bear snugged up behind Reaper, who was kneeling low to the ground in preparation to going in as the point man on the entry. With his Beretta up and pointed forward Bear squeezed Reaper's shoulder in the go-ahead signal. Both men rapidly went through the door and down the stairs, breaking to the right and left as they came to the floor.

It was pucker time: that moment when they first entered the building and were the most vulnerable. They raised their suppressed weapons ready for use, but found no one there to use them on. The floor spread empty before them, the lights they had seen came from a few bare lightbulbs standing up on floor fixtures. The lights were too few and too dim to really illuminate the football field-sized floor area. But they were enough to allow Reaper and Bear to see details of the interior.

The far eastern end of the building comprised the office area. That was Reaper's primary target. The two SEALs moved out across the floor to get up to the southern wall. Once near the wall, Reaper maintained a watch forward while Bear covered the way they had come. Both men trusted the other completely. This was their element, the darkness and danger made them feel at their most alert, their most alive. Reaper considered the reason for being here the worst he had ever known. Now that he had gone into action, the feeling of helplessness that had dogged him for days was gone.

Tracked areas on the floor and overhead showed where the car bodies had been moved along for work. Dominating the middle of the floor, several long sheds had tracks going in one end and out the other, had the look of paint booths or drying ovens to Reaper—something that they could come back and examine after they had covered the primary search area: the offices.

One of the booths had its big doors closed and plastic chemical drums were stacked up around most of it. If the light had been better, Reaper would have seen that those drums appeared much cleaner and brighter than anything else in the huge room. The drums were new and held the solvents used in the drug lab, the lab hidden behind the closed doors of the booth. The black booth walls and doors combined with the bad lighting to make it look as if the doors didn't even exist—no light leaked out from the drug operation inside.

The floors felt weird to walk across. Then Reaper remembered that the whole factory had been paved with wooden blocks to cut down on vibration. The concrete support pillars that had been noted by Bear during his visit to the first floor were up on the sixth floor as well.

The pillars blocked a clear view of the whole production floor. Piles of machinery, mostly abandoned flexible belts for the assembly lines and mounds of steel matting, grids, and wires, lay scattered around haphazardly. Yet, pathways appeared in places around the floor. Reaper and Bear used these paths to skirt along the edges of abandoned factory parts as they crossed the big room.

At the far end of the room a cinder block wall separated the production floor from the hallway beyond and the offices beyond that. Big doorways penetrated the wall at three points that Reaper could see. The biggest one was a double-wide opening near the southern side of the building. Lights remained on in the hallway, more than in the main floor area. The lights were not bright enough to make the area well illuminated, but they did show that no shadows could be cast across the floor. That became the deciding factor for Reaper to choose the right-side entrance as his way into the office area.

Normally, Reaper would have acted as the point man for a stack of at least four SEALs to go through the doorway and take control of the hall beyond. But since Bear was his only Teammate, they didn't have the manpower to work the doors and halls as securely as their training demanded. Reaper adapted their tactics to fit the situation. He and Bear crossed over to the far (north) side of the big door area and set up their short stack of two men to go through the doorway. The need for additional manpower became immediately evident as Reaper took his squeeze signal from Bear and swung around the end of the wall, straight into Musclehead who sat there on a chair.

The two men ended up right on top of one another, too close for Reaper to even bring his MP5K-PDW into play. In spite of his surprise, and the big bandage on his left forearm, the man in the chair responded amazingly quickly. The powerful man stood and grabbed the Raptor suppressor of the

MP5K-PDW in a single motion. He wrenched the weapon around, forcing the muzzle away from him. Reaper responded with the only action that made sense to him—he let go of the submachine gun.

In spite of his trying to wrench the weapon from Reaper's control, Amman was surprised when his opponent suddenly gave it up. As he pulled the weapon back and away from Reaper, Amman saw that it was attached to the other man by some kind of strap and buckle. Unable to free the weapon from its strap, he pulled even harder to yank the other man off balance.

As the strong man tried to pull Reaper over by yanking on the MP5K-PDW attached to the Chalker sling around his chest, the SEAL snapped his left hand up and yanked on the release. That feature of the sling was intended for exactly the situation Reaper was in.

When Reaper pulled the release, the shackle instantly let go of the submachine gun. With no resistance to his pull, Amman fell backward with the weapon in his hands. Normally, the action following an operator's release of his primary weapon from a Chalker sling was to immediately draw his secondary weapon. But since no real noise had been made yet, Reaper wanted to keep the penetration from being compromised.

Stepping forward into Amman before he could turn the submachine gun around, Reaper snapped up his right hand in a hard palm smash to the muscleman's face. As the big man's head snapped back, the upper and lower lateral cartilage in his nose was driven deep into his face. The shock drove the air out from Amman's lungs, spraying blood from his shattered nose out over his face.

Reaper had to quickly follow through on the big man and put him down for the count. He stepped forward, lifting his right leg in a hard knee butt into Amman's groin, barely missing smashing the testicles up into the pubic arch of the pelvis. The pain of the knee smash brought the musclebound Amman almost to his knees, bending him forward at the waist and exposing the back of his neck.

Seeing the target, Reaper brought down his right arm in an elbow smash, knocking Amman down and putting his lights out with a hard blow to the sixth and seventh cervical and first thoracic vertebra of his spine. The shock of the blow traveled almost directly into Amman's nervous system, causing immediate unconsciousness. If Reaper had struck his blow with a pointed elbow on a single vertebra, Amman would have died instantly from a severed spinal cord.

The fight had only lasted a few seconds, an eternity for Bear who hadn't been able to get a clear shot around Reaper. As Reaper recovered his MP5K, the doorway on the south wall, the one they had missed in the darkness and confusion of the sudden assault by Amman, slowly eased open. The muzzle of an M4 carbine slipped forward just an inch past the door frame and moved to center on Reaper's back.

Out of the corner of his eye, Bear saw the movement and recognized the threat. Snapping up his Beretta, Bear fired two quick rounds into the door. The heavy steel door stopped the subsonic EBR Hush Puppy rounds, but the impact of the bullets startled Nicholas. As he tried to dodge the bullets he thought were coming through the lavatory door, Nicholas pulled the trigger on his M4.

The stuttering burst of fire impacted next to Reaper who dove away from the stream of 5.56mm projectiles. Lying on the ground unconscious, Amman wasn't able to roll away and he took the impact of half a dozen rounds. He never felt himself die.

Missing his target and shattering the noise discipline of the op, Bear dropped his suppressed Beretta, allowing it to dangle at the end of the Pistol Leash lanyard connecting the butt of the weapon to his belt.

As the Beretta hung at the end of its stretched coiled lanyard line, Bear released the Hi-port velcro strip with the thumb of his left hand. His right hand solidly held the pistol grip of the Jackhammer as he lowered the weapon down and into firing position.

Nicholas recovered from his surprise at the impact of Bear's bullets. Swinging the muzzle of his M4 around, Nicholas knew that he had only fired a handful of rounds from the M4. He had loaded his carbine with a 100-round double drum Beta C-mag. Inside the magazine were more than eighty rounds of green-tipped M855 ball, the slugs having enhanced penetration from their steel-cored design. He knew it was more than enough ammunition to easily take out the interlopers.

Nicholas opened the steel door to the men's lavatory only enough to see a good target. His sense of time seemed to slow down, causing the whole action to seem as if it was in slow motion as he aimed his M4. Through the barely four-inch-wide open slit of the doorway, Nicholas saw that the black-clad man in front of him had a Jackhammer! Where the hell did he get that from?

That became the last conscious thought Nicholas

ever had as he watched a bright orange-red flame belch out of the end of the gun in front of him.

Bear knew that he would only have a small chance of hitting his target with any of the fifteen 0.33-caliber hardened-lead pellets in a shotgun load. But a burst of fire from the Jackhammer would make up for that by saturating a small target area with shot. As he saw the barrel of the weapon in the doorway swing toward him, Bear lined up his shot. As soon as he saw the silhouette of the man holding the gun, he squeezed the trigger.

The Jackhammer roared out a solid wall of noise, echoing in the huge room. The pellets smashed into Nicholas, penetrating his body up and down his torso and into his skull. Reaction to the shock caused his hand to clench on the trigger to his M4. Set on full automatic, the carbine ripped out a long burst of spinning death.

The unaimed bullets stitched across the room as Nicholas fell backward. The stream of slugs ripped open several of the plastic solvent drums on the other side of the room. The stench of ether and alcohol now started to fill the area as volatile liquids gushed from their pierced containers.

Inside the paint booth where he had been keeping a sleepy watch over his bubbling glassware, the young drug chemist Fazul Daoud was terrified by the sudden roar of gunfire. Diving under a lab table, Fazul heard the glassware above him shatter from the many steel-cored slugs tearing through the sides of the paint booth. Squealing and trying to cover his head while hiding under the table, Fazul never noticed the ether fumes thickening the air of the lab. The mewling sounds of fear in the small room faded and finally stopped as Fazul slipped into unconsciousness.

Fazul wasn't the only one to respond to the sounds of gunfire on the sixth floor. In his apartment just off his offices, Arzee sat up in bed. He had no idea what had happened, but the cracking roar of a 5.56mm weapon, possibly Nicholas's favored M4 carbine, had been followed by the deep booms of what might have been a shotgun fired unbelievably fast. Neither Amman nor Nicholas carried a shotgun. Aside from Fazul Daoud in his laboratory, they were supposed to be the only other people in the entire building at this hour.

Ishmael and his men had forced Arzee to send away the men who normally stood guard in the building. Only those men who were most trusted, Arzee's own family, had been allowed on the upper floors. Down in the club, where Ishmael and his men had refused to go, just the bouncers had been enough to keep watch. It had been a mistake not to put the guards back on duty as soon as possible.

Getting up, Arzee picked up the AKMS-47 folding stock assault rifle that he kept at the side of his bed. Now that the last of the Sons of Ishmael had been sent to the island, he had felt that he could finally get some sleep and recover from the beating he had received in the car crash. His left arm pained him at the thought, the twinge deep inside the cast on the broken limb. He still couldn't hear very well because of the ringing in his ears. He had even been forced to leave the office lights on, as a child might. His injured arm made him so clumsy that he now bumped into things if he got up during his restless nights.

Outside the offices, Reaper picked up his MP5K—

PDW and snapped out its stock. The time for the quiet approach had ended. Reaper and Bear would now have to go through the offices as quickly as they could. The first target would have to be the office in the center of the far wall, the only one with light streaming out underneath the door. He turned to see if Bear was back on his six and covering his back. Reaper saw his partner stop and pick up the smoking M4 carbine and sling it across his back. Then he grabbed something else from the body of the man inside the doorway and slipped it into his pocket.

A quick look at the pile of meat on the floor told Reaper that the musclebound thug he had fought would never bother anyone again. He spared the second it took to bend over and pull out the familiar folding Emerson CQC-7BW he saw sticking out of Amman's pocket. Bear came up to his side and silently squeezed his shoulder. The two SEALs moved forward to go through the door indicated by Reaper's pointing finger.

Panicking inside the office, Arzee opened the combination lock on the secure filing cabinet and was trying to pull out the large salesman's case in the bottom drawer. In his near terror, he twisted the case around and jammed it in the drawer. As he struggled to pick the case up, the door to his office shattered and two black-clad men stormed in, each of them heavily armed.

To pull at the drawer with his one good arm, Arzee had set his AKMS-47 down on the floor next to him. Now, while looking up at the cold, unblinking black eye of the suppressor pointing directly at his head, his own weapon seemed to be miles away instead of just inches. When he looked up past the muzzle of the unwavering gunbarrel, the eyes of the man holding it truly glowed more frighteningly than the muzzle of any gun. His gun simply promised a quick end to life. The smoldering orbs of the man holding it told of a long, lingering death for both Arzee's body and soul.

The eyes of the man holding the weapon darted around the room before settling back on Arzee—who had as much chance of looking away as a bird did when facing a king cobra.

"Clear," boomed a voice from across the room.

"Clear," shouted the voice of the man in black in front of him, his voice muffled by the black hood he wore.

Someone out of his field of vision passed by without getting near Arzee or the man in front of him. Whoever it might be completed searching the room and moved on.

"Clear," came the other voice, this time from behind where Arzee knelt. Whoever the owner of that other voice might be, he must have just gone through to his apartment. The only other door in the office, on the other side of the room, led to the barracks room where the Sons of Ishmael had rested.

"Wh-wh-whhoooo are you?" Arzee finally managed.

Without a word, the man in front of him did something strange. Instead of answering, he stepped over to the window, grabbed the line, and pulled open the blinds. He then reached out and flipped open the window. Finally, the black apparition spoke, and Arzee wished that he hadn't.

"War, this is Death," the man said. Then he seemed to listen and finally said, "Roger that."

After he returned to Arzee, the man in black reached up with his free hand, the muzzle of his weapon never wavering for an instant, and he pulled back the hood covering his face.

It was Reaper! In his entire life there had never been a man whom Arzee wanted to see less than the one standing in front of him.

"Where's my family?" asked a voice as cold as death.

Pushing the muzzle of his weapon underneath Arzee's chin, Reaper repeated, "Where's my family? I won't ask you nicely again."

"Th-they're not here," Arzee said with rising panic in his voice. "No one's here. But they're safe. I swear they're safe. No one has done anything with them. I can lead you to them. They're up at the . . ."

———

In the smashed laboratory, Fazul Daoud was breathing the heavy ether fumes that filled the small room. The ether was gradually depressing Fazul's breathing more and more. Ether fumes not only acted as an anesthetic, they were highly explosive.

Some of the smashed glassware had been filled with the ether solvent. Other parts were filled with water to cool and condense the solvent back into the extraction system. One of the smashed Freidricks condensers, a complex piece of expensive equipment that was now just glass shards, lay in a growing pool of water. The water crawled across the lab table, wetting down what it touched before dripping off onto the floor. Exposed wires torn from an electric heating mantle were touched by the pool of water and suddenly sparked.

The accumulation of volatile ether fumes were ignited by the spark. A huge roiling ball of flame exploded outward with a loud roar, engulfing the room and shattering the remaining glassware. The broken glass released even more ether to feed the explosion. The steel walls of the paint room tore away like cardboard from the force of the blast.

———

The office area was shielded from the bulk of the explosion by the cinderblock wall that separated it from the production floor. Tossed back by the explosion, Reaper escaped most of the blast. Glass shattered and sprayed from the door frame. Seeing what might be his only chance, Arzee snatched up his AKMS-47 and started to swing it one-handed over toward Reaper. Before Bear or Reaper could recover enough to fire, they heard a quiet thud.

Arzee dropped his weapon and staggered back against the filing cabinet. Before Arzee fell against the wall, a second thud was heard. From his sniper position, Max had fired as soon as he saw Reaper threatened with the weapon. There wasn't time to make the shot a wounding one and the open window provided a perfect line of fire.

"No!" shouted Reaper, as he watched the man who could tell him where his family was fall against the wall. Then a second blast thundered through the building as more solvent drums caught fire.

In spite of the damage from the two suppressed

shots, Arzee still had a single action left to him. He reached up with his uninjured hand and pulled down on what looked like a fire alarm switch on the side of the cabinet. Reaper dove forward to pull the man back from the wall, but his effort came too late. With a sudden pop and an acrid cloud of smoke, the M1A2 cryptographic document destroyer in the top of the filing cabinet ignited.

Reaper knew the device and the destruction its twenty-eight pounds of Thermate filler could do to the contents of a cabinet or a safe. The Thermate would burn for about a minute, producing a pound of molten iron and slag every two seconds. It would eat through the four drawers of the heavy steel cabinet—but with the top drawer closed, the papers in it would actually insulate the drawers below them for a few moments. The Thermate burned at four thousand degrees, but the paper still needed air to burn up completely.

Reaper thrust his hand in the open bottom drawer and tore out the heavy case jammed there, tossing it over to Bear. Bear threw a wastebasket at Reaper while he grabbed another one and turned to the big mahogany desk that dominated the center of the room. With no time to talk both SEALs collected every piece of paper they could and stuffed them into the plastic bags inside the trash cans. Reaper pulled open the drawers of the filing cabinet even as molten iron started to burn though the sides of its top. Files, papers, books, whatever he found got stuffed into the bags. They had lost their best source of information. Now they prayed they'd find some intelligence from around the room.

"Death," Bear shouted, "it's time to go!"

Bear twisted the top of his bag shut. Picking up Arzee's AKMS-47, he unsnapped the hook that held the front of the sling to the weapon. He stuck the rifle through the hand loops on the salesman's case that Reaper had tossed to him and snapped the sling back in place. Now able to hold it with a long cloth strap, Bear slung the case across his back and out of his way. The case must have weighed nearly fifty pounds but Bear handled it easily.

"Death, the fire," Bear shouted. "We have to go—now! You can't do Mary or Ricky any good if you burn to death!"

His partner's shouting finally got through to Reaper as he desperately gathered everything that he could. Crushing the neck closed on his stuffed garbage bag, he took one last look at Arzee's body lying on the floor then turned to Bear.

When they left the office, they could see the glow of the fire through the open doorway into the production area. They had no way to get back to their climbing site. The two SEALs turned to the stairs in front of them. As they ran down the dozen flights of stairs, Reaper shouted into his mike.

"Famine, Famine, Famine," he said, "Evac, evac, evac."

"Death," came back over the earpiece, "Famine, I'm with War. Evac, evac, evac."

What Reaper and Bear learned later was that Ben had seen the fire start to break out on the upper floor of the Factory and had decided to come up to the building. When he received Reaper's radio call, he was positioned next to the billboard and ready to pick up Max. When Reaper and Bear burst out of the front doors of the Factory, Ben moved to pick them up. They swung into the open door of the camper and Max grabbed their arms, pulling the two men in.

As the truck moved away from the Factory building, the upper floor exploded outward in a ball of flame. The entire top of the building became a huge conflagration as the remaining intact solvent containers burst apart from the fire. The ether and alcohol explosion engulfed the building. Fire truck sirens could be heard approaching from off in the distance.

There would be nothing that the fire department could do to save the building. By the next day, the old auto factory would have collapsed into a pile of smoking ashes and rubble. The wooden block floors, soaked for decades in oils and lubricants and augmented by drug solvents, burned with a fierce, hot flame. The strong factory building acted as a furnace before collapsing in on itself. The flesh of the bodies of Arzee and his men were consumed in the heat, burned more completely than if they had been professionally cremated. The final fragments of bones had been crushed to powder and mixed with the rubble when the walls collapsed.

Chapter Twenty-four

The four horsemen didn't hold a celebration or homecoming at the farm later that morning. The victory cigars still lay in their aluminum tubes—intact and unlit. The feelings of disappointment hung thick in the room as the men sat around the kitchen table. The group should have been rejoicing at the recovery of Reaper's family. Instead they sat in quiet silence while they decided on their next move.

A subdued Reaper got up from the table, went into the kitchen and started to get himself another cup of coffee. As he tried to pour the hot, black liquid into the mug, he sloshed some over the side and it spilled onto the counter. Only a little thing, nothing at all, really. But Reaper's nerves were frayed to say the least.

"Goddamnit all to hell!" Reaper cursed as he picked the mug up and smashed it down on the counter. The porcelain coffee cup was strong, but not indestructible. It cracked and shattered under the impact, splashing coffee over most of the countertop.

None of the people around the counter even

started at the outburst. It wasn't as though they
didn't feel the same way. A major operation conducted with minimal support, too few personnel,
and at lightning speed from conception to execution. They should have been proud, but they didn't
have the hostages. And the one among them who
had every right to feel the worst was Reaper.

"Did you get it?" Bear asked calmly.

"Get it?" Reaper almost snarled. "Get what? I
didn't get anything."

"The spider," Bear continued in the same calm
tone. "Did you get it?"

"What spider?" Reaper demanded. "What in the
fuck are you talking about, Bear?"

"I figured you must have seen a spider there on
the counter," Bear said. "I know you don't like them.
And I would never think that you just wanted to
smash up Deckert's crockery."

For a moment, Reaper stood there stunned at his
friend's words. Then he looked down at the busted
coffee mug and the mess he had made of the
counter. As he smiled, Reaper shook his head at his
own reactions. Taking a deep breath, he blew it out.

"Okay, Bear," Reaper said in a normal tone of
voice. "I'm back."

"Never really thought you had left, Brother," Bear
said.

"Okay," Reaper said, "we have to start up again.
Only this time we might try not to burn the target
down to the ground behind us."

"It really hasn't gotten all the way to the ground
yet," Deckert said. "That building is a real inferno. I
watched the news this morning and that fire is the

big story. Apparently, the local water hydrants weren't working or somebody turned them off. Either way, the fire departments who responded couldn't do a damned thing about the blaze. They stood by, controlled traffic and made sure the fire didn't spread to the surrounding neighborhoods. Then they pretty much broke out the marshmallows and hotdogs for a barbecue.

"I'll tell you one thing," Deckert continued. "You guys would have a lot more to worry about if any of the locals knew you had a hand in that fire. The police can only arrest you, maybe shoot you. But most of the workers in downtown Detroit want to lynch you. That fire is right on the corner of two of the biggest highways in the city—and they shut them down a couple of hours ago because of the smoke and ash. You guys seriously fucked-up the Friday morning rush hour."

"Well, at least it'll be a while before they can pull out any bodies," Max said. He had already dumped his street-person clothing and taken the first hot shower. Now he sat at the table with his hair still wet and a towel draped over his shoulders.

"I don't think there's going to be any bodies to concern anyone with," Ben said knowingly. "I've picked up many a fire victim, and that furnace isn't going to leave much behind. Bodies, bones, bullets, brass, even teeth, they're all going to be part of a football field-sized pile of slag."

"The news said that the fire chief suspected that chemicals or paint had been stored on the upper floors," Deckert said. "They might consider the whole thing nothing more than an accident. No one has said arson out loud, or much of anything else really."

"Well," Reaper said, "what we have to do is go over every piece of material that we pulled out of that place before it went up. There's two stuffed garbage bags full of Intel that we need to digest. Bear stripped out the desk and I grabbed everything I could from the filing cabinet. That cabinet had a destruct charge on it—Arzee wanted it gone more than anything else. He was dying when he pulled the switch and that's pretty hard core for an asshole like that.

"So we'll start with that bag. Try and keep everything as separate as you can from the two bags. Anything from the desk or the filing cabinet may be significant. We'll go through the filing cabinet papers here. Keith, why don't you work on the counter and sort out the desk materials there."

"As soon as I clean up the mess somebody left behind here," Deckert said with a grin.

More than an hour later, the men were still sorting through the papers they had now separated into reasonably neat stacks. Before anyone had touched anything, Reaper had them all put on a pair of disposable plastic gloves from a box in the shop. The documents they had found still came from a crime scene and would be considered evidence by any police agency that got hands on them. It would be best if none of the men around the table left their fingerprints on any of the materials. Both Reaper and Bear had been wearing their FOG glove liners during the operation and had been the only people to handle the documents. They hadn't left any fingerprints anywhere so far.

After an hour of sorting and examination, they separated the papers into two sets of stacks. One set was from the desk, the other was from the cabinet.

Where the papers had come from might be important in figuring out what they were. Most of the documents didn't really mean anything. They were regular business items such as the utility bills, UPS shipper receipts, and bar supply lists. The desk had given up most of those items.

The next stack contained documents that the men couldn't read. These papers, maps, and booklets had been written in Arabic for the most part. Reaper now suspected that a hell of a lot more was going on than just what involved his family. The rest of the men also put two and two together and came up with the likely idea of terrorists operating on U.S. soil.

The situation could be a very serious one. Yet the primary mission was still locating Reaper's family. That was all that concerned Reaper for the time being. Once his people were safe, then the rest of the materials would be sent on to the right hands.

The undecipherable documents made the biggest pile from the filing cabinet. The last mound in both sets of papers turned out to be things whose use no one could figure out. Doodles, notes, phone numbers, everything that came from the drawers of the desk or filing cabinet had ended up in the bags of Reaper and Bear.

"There's something missing here," Reaper said.

"How can you tell?" Bear demanded as he looked up from a pamphlet he had been reading. The booklet had been extolling the virtues of a hunting lodge on a private island in Lake Michigan. It was an odd thing to find and had perked his interest.

"Because there's nothing on the Factory here,"

Reaper said. "By that I mean the company books, the records of their cash flow. Things like that."

"Maybe they kept them in that top drawer of the filing cabinet," Max suggested as he looked up from the table. "You said that you had to leave it shut to keep the papers from burning fast."

"True enough," Reaper said, "but that doesn't fit the rest of this stuff. These Arabic documents look important. I can't read the stuff, but the layout resembles some of the military materials we got hold of in Desert Storm and later in Bosnia. Why would they put the company books in the top drawer of a destruct-rigged cabinet?"

"They had a real and a cooked set?" Ben suggested.

"Then why can't we find the cooked set?" Reaper asked. "You keep those separate from the real set so that you can show the cooked ones to the tax people or whoever. If there's a crooked set, they should have been in the desk. We've even got a copy of their sales tax and liquor licenses from the desk. Bear, where's that big briefcase that you picked up?"

"The one from the bottom drawer of the filing cabinet?" Bear said. "It must still be out in the camper. I'll get it."

Bear headed out to get the errant case. While he was gone, they all continued their examination of the documents. In a few minutes, Bear came back into the house, lugging the heavy salesman's case with him. He had a very odd look on his face.

"I think these guys were running on a cash basis," Bear said. To the astonishment of everyone, he tossed a thick bundle of hundred dollar bills on the table. The paper strip wrapped around the bills was printed in bright red: $10,000.

"Jesus, Bear," Reaper said as he picked up the bundle. "Where in the hell did you get that? Hey! Be careful there!"

Bear spread out a towel over the carefully sorted papers on the kitchen table.

"It was with its friends," Bear said, and he dumped the contents of the case onto the towel. Bundles of hundred dollar bills cascaded out of the case—piling onto the towel and spilling onto the floor.

"I always wanted to do something like that," Bear looked up from the huge pile of cash with a big grin.

"Have I called you an asshole recently?" Reaper said.

As they went through the bundles and stacked them up, the men soon came up with 250 sets of $10,000 each.

"So that's what two and a half million dollars looks like," Max said.

"Funny," said Bear, "I always thought it looked bigger on TV."

"What the hell would someone have this much cash on hand for?" Reaper said. "And why in the hell would they try to burn it rather than let it be captured?"

"Maybe Arzee wanted it as mad money for his vacation," Bear said.

"Vacation?" came up from Ben at the table.

"Yeah," said Bear. "He had this brochure for a hunting lodge in his desk."

He picked up the document and handed it to Ben.

"Northern Lake Michigan?" said Ben. "Wait a minute, I saw something else like that."

Going through the regular business papers stack from the filing cabinet, Ben pulled out a faxed receipt on shiny thermal paper.

"Here it is," Ben said as he handed the fax to Reaper. "It's a receipt for a load of diesel fuel and groceries going to someplace called South Wolverine Island."

"I know that place," Deckert said. "It was in the papers a few years back. Some article about the whole damned island being sold to a private party. The environmental and native Indian groups raised a big stink about it."

"That anywhere near Leland?" Reaper asked.

"North of there, yeah," Deckert said. "Why?"

"Because that's where this receipt came from," Reaper said. "It was sent from a fax machine at the Leland Yacht Harbor, and it's dated only three days ago."

"This is a lot of food and fuel," Deckert said as he looked at the papers. "Enough for a large group of people."

"Enough for a big hunting lodge," said Bear.

"Not just that," Deckert said. "There's nothing in the way of fresh foods on this list. This is all canned and frozen stuff. Not what you'd expect a hunting lodge to feed paying customers."

"Arzee started to say something about my family being 'up' somewhere right before the explosion," Reaper said.

"Up North is what everyone down here calls that part of Michigan," said Bear. "It sounds good enough to me. I think we may have found them, Ted, or at least a real good place to start."

Reaper was excited by what they had found, and he agreed with Bear's assessment. As they went through more of the papers with an eye for anything regarding that part of Michigan, they came up with some more clues. Fuel receipts for stops on I-75, the main drag heading up north in Michigan. Restaurant receipts, even motel receipts. And most of them were dated within the last month.

Going back to his computer, Deckert looked for everything he could find about South Wolverine Island and the lodge there. All information stopped as of the year before. The stated reason had been for renovation of the facilities by the new owners. More searching through databases failed to come up with any listings of the permits needed for such renovations. Even the public hearings required by law weren't listed as ever having happened.

Satellite images were available on-line regarding the island. It lay twenty-five miles north of Leland, the closest port on the mainland. It was part of a pair of islands, the smaller, North Wolverine Island only being about five miles northeast of the much larger South Wolverine Island. Both islands boasted heavily wooded areas, large game populations, and airstrips big enough to handle small planes.

"Okay, we need a boat and some additional gear," Reaper said.

"Don't have a boat," Deckert said, "powered chairs don't swim for shit."

"Let me call a friend," Bear said as he left the room.

They spent the rest of the day and into the evening learning everything they could about South Wolverine Island and what might be happening there. When the other men finally went to sleep that night, Reaper remained awake until Bear reminded him that not getting any sleep wouldn't do Reaper any good. Finally, the big man agreed and went to get some rest himself.

———

At the lodge on South Wolverine Island, Paxtun had a bad situation he needed to discuss with Ishmael. Even as remote as the island was, the news of a major fire at the Factory in Detroit, and the incredible traffic jam it caused, had made the local broadcast media.

In addition to the loss of the building and the club, Paxtun had lost something he would have a very hard time replacing; a man he could trust. While he had trusted Arzee, his second in command, only because he could firmly control him, he still counted it a loss. The material and personal losses, the bulk of the liquid funds to finance Ishmael's operations in North America, the hawala bankroll, had gone up in smoke.

The terrorist leader's reaction was anything but what Paxtun had expected. Ishmael considered the loss of funds little more than *in'shallah*—Allah's will. Paxtun found his fatalism shocking.

"You feel that this very inconvenient fire resulted from some direct action by the authorities?" Ishmael said as he sat pensively in Paxtun's inner office. He accepted the will of Allah, but would listen to others' suspicions.

"I don't see how it could be," Paxtun said from where he sat behind his desk. "The Detroit police and federal agencies just don't work like that in this country, no matter what some conspiracy theorists might say. There is no profit in it for them, nothing for them to gain. Even if they were going after the drugs, and we never had any intelligence indicating any kind of active investigation, our police agencies are interested in confiscation and evidence, not destruction."

"You may be correct in this matter," Ishmael said. "Even if you are not, little can be done immediately. The blow to my further operations by the loss of the funds is not insignificant. We have been having difficulty moving finances around the world's banking system since your new president has seen fit to try and become something other than the adulterer, coward, and fornicating paper tiger that your last leader was. The best thing that I can do in reaction to the situation is move up my operational timetable."

"What," said Paxtun, "for Shaitan's Blessing?"

"Yes," Ishmael said. "I had originally planned for our most ambitious operation to be launched next week. That is the three-day holiday your corrupt people hold to celebrate their criminal military forces."

"You mean Memorial Day," Paxtun volunteered.

"A proper name," Ishmael said ominously. "It certainly will be a memorable day this year."

"Why this weekend?" said Paxtun. "There aren't that many major celebrations within range that would make a good target, a target with a great many people concentrated in a small area. Those gatherings that have large crowds of people usually do so because of celebrities or some of our leadership being there. This year, anything like that would be under very heavy security."

"But what also happens at that time," Ishmael said, "is that a large number of people and their boats are in this area all at once for the first time during the year. It is the beginning of the tourist season."

"Unofficially, yes," Paxtun said. "But the cold weather this year may put off a lot of the usual people from coming up here this early in the season."

"It doesn't matter," Ishmael said, "I shall not wait any longer. My people are here and we shall strike."

"Strike at what?" Paxtun asked. "Tourists? And aren't you limited for weapons?"

"Since no one will now leave this island or communicate with the rest of the world until after the action is underway and it is too late to interfere," Ishmael said magnanimously, "I will explain it to you."

Paxtun reasoned that Ishmael desperately wanted to brag about what he had planned to someone who didn't know the details. Despite all of Ishmael's talk about martyrdom and sacrifice, when it finally came down to it, he wanted someone to know about his personal dedication and sacrifice. Bragging was a weakness of megalomaniacs, and Paxtun was sure Ishmael was one. Besides, it wouldn't be any fun to be a martyr if no one knew you had been one.

"Our experts," Ishmael went on, "have been carefully examining the new security arrangements that have been put in place in this country since the Prince so successfully struck a blow at the heart of the Great Satan in 2001. The destruction of the World Trade Center and the damage to the heart of the Great Satan's war machine are things true believers look to with pride. And they shall be given even more to be proud of by my actions.

"The loss of Iraq to the Great Satan's invaders eliminated one source of weapons that could have struck a telling blow against this land's decadent population of unbelievers. A nuclear bomb would have been the greatest of tools, but Saddam was not able to deliver one before that country's holy Muslim soil was defiled by infidels. Even the diseases and poisons he had promised us had not been completed, though the materials were on hand.

"We searched out and located a potent weapon right here on the soil of the Great Satan itself. It is one the unbelievers created themselves in their foolish arrogance. And they barely recognize its existence."

"A weapon of mass destruction?" said Paxtun. "Here, in the United States? How? The nuclear storage sites always have tight security. Since the 9/11 attacks, that security has been beefed up a lot. Those sites are some of the most secure locations in the country. And there just aren't any stores of chemical or biological weapons that could even be approached."

"Allah, all blessings be upon Him, provides for the dedicated true believers," Ishmael said. "Not more than thirty miles from our location is the source for the mighty sword Allah has seen fit to put into my hands."

"Thirty miles!" Paxtun gulped. "But there's nothing within thirty miles, or even forty or fifty miles of here for that matter. Even the old Big Rock nuclear power plant is gone. They tore it down some time back."

"It is not quite gone," said Ishmael. "There are still some very useful materials on the site."

"What, reactor fuel rods?" Paxtun said. "Those are in a high-security bunker that's alarmed and guarded."

"The weapons and skills my men have can deal with the guards," Ishmael said. "They would not be expecting a boat full of fishermen to open fire on them as we will. It would have been better to have more firepower, but the shipment we received from our brother holy warriors will be enough, *in'shallah.*"

"But you can't move the fuel rods," Paxtun said. "They're in massive armored containers. The containers are designed to be too big to move without some special handling gear and that isn't kept on-site. The rods are too radioactive for anyone to remove from the containers without some very sophisticated equipment. If you even had some, what would you make with them, a dirty bomb? Spray radiation all over a target?"

"The fuel rods are as you say," Ishmael said. "They are highly radioactive and difficult to handle. The raid to obtain them would alert the authorities, and searching for such material can be done from aircraft and satellites. It would take too much time and be technically very difficult to grind the fuel rods into the fine powder needed for a radioactive bomb. And the faithful who did such work would die before they could complete the weapon. No, a radioactive dirty bomb would not be practical for us right now.

"But fuel rods are hardly the only useful materials on the site. When they disassembled the reactor, the sodium metal that they used as a coolant in that old model was also removed and stored for later disposal. That very radioactive sodium has been stored in fifty kilogram lots, each lot is in its own four-hundred-pound steel container. Those containers can be moved, given the strength of the faithful I have with me. And there is the special equipment that I had you install on the large fishing boat you acquired for us."

"What could you do with such a material?" Paxtun said as he sat stunned at his desk. "You can't make a bomb out of it. And it can't be made into an explosive."

"There are many more ways to apply such a poison than from a bomb," Ishmael said. "Just as you said, sodium metal is reactive, very reactive. It explodes violently on contact with water, and makes lye, in this case, radioactive caustic lye. All that has to be done is punch a hole in the steel containers and allow the water that is so abundant all around us, to react with the metal. My technician says that creating the holes will be easy when we use the shaped charges he has fabricated. The charges he made with the explosives you supplied.

"The fuses for the shaped charges will detonate when dropped in the water after a very short delay. A salt crystal is the only thing that will be keeping the detonator from initiating once the fuse is armed. The water will do all of the work for us."

"You're going to poison Lake Michigan with radioactive sodium?" Paxtun said incredulously.

"Perhaps not the whole lake," Ishmael said. "It will be enough to contaminate a great deal of the lake. The panic of this country's sheeplike people would be massive no matter where we dropped the containers. Imagine just how much greater that panic would be if we dropped the sodium overboard, say, on the fresh water intakes for the city of Chicago? The panic should be beautiful to watch. I have the GPS coordinates for those intakes programmed into the navigation equipment on both of my boats. And Chicago is well within the range of those boats given their additional fuel loads. We will poison Lake Michigan and, if Allah wills, Chicago itself.

"Even if our actions were discovered, it would be too late for the Great Satan's minions to do anything to stop us. My men are all dedicated mujahideen—they have waged the jihad, they are Islam's holy warriors. They would not balk at becoming martyrs. Becoming such guarantees their entrance into Paradise. I have confirmed it through my sources that the sodium is in place and we have what we need to seize it.

"There will be a major panic and destruction of a large part of the economies of a number of states and Canada. That would happen even if only a small part of the radioactive poison got into the water. The lakes would be destroyed. The water would be considered poison for years, if not decades. People are frightened by what they can't see or don't know. They could not see the poison, and they would be terrified of the radiation. Even a little bit of the sodium contamination would be enough to create a panic—and we shall have hundreds of kilos. An elegant plan, don't you think?"

Paxtun simply sat at his desk—too stunned to think of anything to say. The plan could work. Because of his involvement in something of such magnitude, he would be hunted forever and not be able to enjoy the wealth he had accumulated. He would have to disappear, and his mind was already considering how to do it as Ishmael continued to speak.

"Regarding practical matters," Ishmael said. "We

will launch the operation Sunday. My followers, my sons, will be forgiven by Allah, all blessings upon His name, if they continue their preparations for the operation over His Sabbath on Saturday."

Chapter Twenty-five

Dawn had been over hours earlier on Saturday morning, the day after the Factory raid. Friday afternoon had passed without the cell phone ringing to demand more weapons. It may have been that Bear had delivered the only extra Jackhammer in existence to Arzee's people the day before. But now Reaper and his men were running on borrowed time. Whoever had Reaper's family had to eventually learn about the fire at the Factory. Then they would probably decide to get rid of any excess baggage and Reaper would be too late to save his wife and child.

Reaper had been up since long before the sun had risen. He was studying all of the intelligence they had collected. Deckert had gone out and bought some Great Lakes navigation charts detailing the waters off Leland and North and South Wolverine Islands. The charts indicated extremely deep waters off the islands for the most part—except for some shallow reefs to the south of the main island.

The rest of the papers had been dealt with. The documents in Arabic had been collected and secured in boxes. Reaper knew that whatever those documents contained, their anonymous delivery to certain authorities would get the information they contained into the proper hands. He made certain that nothing on those documents, or the boxes that held them, could identify Reaper or any members of his team.

The men with him in the house that day were people that he felt closer to than blood kin. They were his brothers in arms who had offered all they had when he needed it. That meant a great deal to him and he swore to keep them as safe as he knew how. Part of this commitment came from the fact that Reaper knew he would have to ask them for their help once more. His family wasn't safe yet.

Reaper directed that the cash they had recovered from the factory be packed back into the salesman's case for the time being. He intended that his partners would all get to share in the proceeds, but for the time being, they had decided the bag was nothing more than a war chest. It would be used to pay for what they needed to get Reaper's family back.

As Reaper went over the papers that remained spread out on the kitchen table, counter, and just about every available surface in the room, he heard a heavy knock at the front door. The "Open" sign for the shop hadn't been lit in several days, and it was far too early for a weekend customer anyway. The police wouldn't have knocked like that and waited, and the men they hunted wouldn't have knocked at all.

Going to the front door, Reaper could see a

shadow through the optical peephole in the center of the door. Since no light illuminated the interior of the house, Reaper knew that his looking out the peep wouldn't make a shadow that someone else could see from the other side. That kind of shadow could show a gunman that a target was poised on the other side of the door. The huge man standing on the porch made Reaper very glad he had looked, and more than a little surprised at what he saw. He had to move quickly to unlock and open the door before many more of the heavy-handed knocks took it off its hinges.

"Enzo!" Reaper said as he pulled open the door. "God damn, it's good to see you."

The big man on the porch resembled a reincarnation of some pirate from centuries past. The huge muscular frame, square face framed off by a thatch of dark red hair, and a beard the same color, fit perfectly with the small gold earring in the man's left ear. The booming voice that sounded out of that barrel-chested individual also fit the pirate image.

"Reaper, you grim-looking bastard, good to see you, too," Enzo Caronti almost bellowed. "Now let me in before some woodland critter drags me off into this wilderness you live in."

"If it did, it would be too bad for the critter," Reaper said as he stood to the side and let his old friend and Teammate in. "How the hell did you know to show up? No, don't tell me—Bear called you, didn't he?"

"Well if I hadn't, it's not like you would have," Bear said with a big grin plastered on his face as he came down the stairs.

"Well, ho, ho, ho, yourself, Bearski," Enzo said as

the two men clasped in a strong hug. Stepping back, Enzo held open the door for Bear and Reaper to look out.

"It's time for Santa to bring all the bad little boys their presents," Enzo said as he indicated with his chin where the two SEALs should look. "I brought my sleigh."

In the driveway was a shining black Chevrolet Silverado Suburban with silver trim and dark-tinted windows. The big SUV was covered with road dust but still loomed impressively. What looked even more impressive to Reaper at the moment was what rode behind the Suburban.

Almost dwarfing the vehicle that towed it was a big, black boat on a multiaxle trailer. The boat looked a bit like an enlarged version of the inflatable vessels the two SEALs had long been used to, but its up-curved bow and other lines indicated it had a hard hull. Standing near the center of the craft they saw a glass-paneled "phone booth" coxswain's station. Surrounding the station was a canvas cover that secured the inner hull of the boat. At the stern of the vessel hung two large, powerful Evenrude Mercury 250-horsepower outboard motors. The black-painted covers on top of the outboards looked as if they could encase an average-size car engine.

"There you go," Enzo said. "Bear told me to bring a boat up from the Creek, and this is one of the newest available."

"This is from the base at Little Creek?" Reaper said.

"Not from the Navy, if that's what you mean," Enzo said. "This is the USIA Swift Attack Vessel II.

It's a low-profile attack vessel. Since I left the Special Boat Teams, I've set up my own marine security outfit. We're using these boats at my company for tactical waterborne training. This is the twenty-four footer, the biggest I could get on short notice that had a trailer available for it."

"She looks great," Bear said. "What's it like?"

"The design is based on the inflatable boats we used at the Teams," Enzo explained. "But the hull's made of welded aluminum for strength and durability. The boat's stable as all hell in almost any sea state and the aluminum tubes are individually sealed so sinking it is a real job. With those twin Mercs on the back, it'll hit fifty to fifty-four knots, so she's fast and agile as hell too. These boats practically dance across the water.

"Rangewise, the motors will draw a gallon a mile wide open. There's a 180-gallon fuel tank so that should take us as far as you want to go. If we need any more range, we can always pick up a couple of extra fuel tanks at any boat chandlers."

"Two outboards," Reaper said.

"You know the rule," Enzo said. "Two is one, one is none. If an engine folds, we still have the other to move us along. That top will protect the coxswain, and there's also a Global Positioning System, marine radios, marine radar, and a fishfinder sonar rig. Everything is a stand-alone system and there's a triple battery rig for power. The cooler is a little small, though."

"Damn," said Bear. "A small cooler, you say?"

"Yeah, we'll have to stock up on beer twice," Enzo laughed. "Speaking of beer, aren't you going to offer a Teammate one? I've been on the road for fifteen hours getting here, and that included a stop off for some more gear."

"More gear?" asked Bear as the trio headed back into the house.

"Yeah," said Enzo, "your message said to bring some heavy hardware if I could put my hands on some in a hurry. I couldn't get much, but I think you may like one particular item."

When Enzo entered the house, he met Ben and Max. He and Max stared at each other until Enzo recognized the ex-marine as the sniper he and Reaper had pulled out of a hot spot in Kafji shortly before Desert Storm kicked into high gear. That immediately made the two men fast friends. Meeting Ben MacKenzie and Keith Deckert resulted in the automatic mutual respect given among fellow warriors.

Seeing all of the documents spread out everywhere told Enzo that the mission Bear had spoken about was a very real one. It didn't take much of Reaper's explanation of the situation to convince Enzo to put his hat in the ring. These were his Teammates and one of them needed him—that's all it took.

After a few minutes of discussion, everyone went out to Enzo's Suburban to bring in the gear he had brought. The man had filled the back of the SUV, and there were more containers, packages, boxes, and tubes in the SAV II, secured under the canvas tarp.

What they found in the back of the Suburban intrigued Bear the most. He had asked Enzo to bring a heavy weapon in case they had to take on a small boat—in the paperwork they had gone through they had found a receipt for a forty-one-foot commercial fishing boat and a twenty-nine-foot Fountain

"Fever" power boat. They knew the group that had these boats were well financed.

What Enzo had brought was big; it filled two Army duffel bags locked together with a chain. It extended from the back door of the Suburban almost to the front seat, requiring the smaller side passenger seat in the rear to be folded down to let the bags fit. The package was heavy. One man could carry it, but it had to have weighed more than a hundred pounds.

Once back inside the house with everything, it became Christmas exactly as Enzo had suggested it would. Only this Santa had brought a bunch of really nasty presents. Enzo apologized for not being able to bring a .50-caliber Browning machine gun as Bear had suggested. What he had brought proved to be pretty fair-sized.

The twin barracks bags held a massive World War II 20mm L/39 Finnish antitank rifle. All the men in the house had a lifetime interest in weapons, but this blaster was something unusual even for them.

Enzo explained that the semiautomatic rifle measured eighty-eight inches long and weighed 109 pounds empty. One of the larger boxes held an unusual short wooden ski-folding bipod mount that attached to the bottom of the impressive weapon. And it was definitely impressive.

The stainless-steel harmonic-style flash hider on the muzzle of the weapon had five holes along the sides of the long, flat, rectangular device, each hole larger than an average man's finger. Two large triangular steel boxes with flat bottoms accompanied the gear, the boxes were outfitted with shoulder straps to make carrying them easier. Inside each of the boxes lay two huge black-metal magazines. A magazine held only ten rounds of ammunition—but what ammunition!

Each cartridge weighed three-quarters of a pound and launched a projectile the size of an entire 12-gauge shotgun shell. The foot-long rounds were mostly loaded with black-painted pointed steel projectiles. One magazine had been loaded with rounds with yellow-painted projectiles that had flat-nosed aluminum fuses screwed into their tips. The men all knew high-explosive ammunition when they saw it.

"Where in the hell did you get this rifle?" Reaper asked, "Steal it from a dinosaur hunter?"

"Naw, I didn't steal it," Enzo responded in a hurt tone of voice. "There are these older, what you might call 'southern Miami expatriates' who had it left over from their days of shooting up some island or other down south. They gave it to me some while back in partial payment for a debt. When Bear mentioned an island, I thought of this and brought it along. There's a ground mount for it, that bipod over there, and there's a specially machined pedestal mount that's in the front of the SAV. It's kind of a classy old cannon, isn't it?"

"I like it," Bear said from down on the floor where he played with the big gun.

"That hand crank on the side pulls the bolt back with a gear arrangement," Enzo said. "The big thing on the pistol grip under the trigger is a bolt release, you squeeze that in and the bolt slams shut—don't leave your fingers there. It's semiautomatic—they made a fully automatic version for shooting at planes, but this isn't it. If you want it to autoload each shot, you have to hold the bolt release in."

"Is that it?" Bear asked.

"Isn't that enough?" Enzo replied.

"What's in the other containers?" Reaper asked.

"More stuff," Enzo said. "Bear didn't give me a lot of time to grab shit, so this is what I could get. I have ballistic dry suits since Lake Michigan is going to be real cold this time of year."

"What are ballistic dry suits?" Reaper asked.

"Yeah, they're new," Enzo said. "They have pockets front and back to take a slip-in waterproof panel of Point Blank's Legacy I premier level 2A soft body armor. Give you a hell of a lot more protection than the old suits, and they keep you warm.

"The other boxes have the leg-inflator tanks for the suits in case you want to blow them up for more buoyancy. Also some Military Exotherm II jumpsuits for keeping you warm under the dry suit. Fins, masks, weight belts, waterproof bags for weapons. And that barracks bag over there has two M72A3 LAW rockets."

"LAW rockets?" Reaper gaped at him.

"Yeah, well, I could only come up with two of them. I got you two M26A1 frag grenades, too."

"Only two fragmentation grenades?" Reaper said with an eyebrow raised. "Enzo, you must be slipping."

Enzo just shrugged his shoulders.

"What's in the long tubes we left back in the boat?" Ben asked from where he stood near the door.

"Fishing poles," Enzo said.

"Of course," said Ben.

"I've also got an M14 rifle with a folding stock I use on the boat," Enzo said. "There are ten twenty-round magazines for that. And this thing's kinda cool," he said reaching for another box. "I couldn't come up with an M60 or a .30-caliber machine gun fast enough, but this should do for your guys."

Pulling up the box and opening it, Enzo lifted up what looked like half of a very strange machine gun.

"What's that?" Deckert said, looking on.

"It's a new weapon just on the market," Enzo said. "Really it's not a whole weapon. It's called a Shrike. It's an upper receiver assembly that lets you turn an M16-style weapon into a belt-fed 5.56mm light machine gun. The Teams are just starting to look at it and there are damned near none available. I talked the owner of Ares Inc., the company that's making this, into letting me have it."

"That must have been some talk," Deckert said as Enzo handed him the part.

"Well, that was the stop I had to make on the way here," Enzo said. "Bear told me on the phone that you guys had an M4. This can mount on that easily."

"Yeah, we can come up with something like that," Deckert said. "You got any belted ammo?"

"Four hundred rounds in two assault packs," Enzo said. "They clip on to an adapter that's in the box. The adapter goes up in the magazine well. If the belt runs out, you can drop the adapter and immediately load up a regular magazine."

"Or a hundred-round Beta C-mag," Bear said with a grin.

"Sure," Enzo said. "But when are you going to use all of this firepower? Bear just said get up here as fast as I could."

"Well, Enzo, I hope your ass isn't flat yet," Reaper said, "because we're leaving as soon as we can all pack our gear in your suburban and the pickup truck. It's about a five-hour drive to where we're going and I want to get on the road as soon as we can."

"Can we stop somewhere to grab a bite to eat?" Enzo said. "I'm hungry enough to eat a bear."

"You stay the hell away from me," Bear said.

"Not a problem," laughed Reaper. "I know a pretty good place for chow, Tony's at Birch Run. They can probably even fill a guy your size."

Chapter Twenty-six

The vehicles were packed and on their way within an hour of Enzo's arrival. Deckert volunteered to man the phone lines at the farm and maintain a communications base in case a call came in regarding Reaper's family or the demand for guns. Ted knew that his friend wanted more than anything to go with them on the operation, but Keith had long ago come to grips with his disability, and he considered going out in an assault boat something he shouldn't do.

The stop at Birch Run north of Flint proved to be a funny one. Enzo found Tony's to be a home-style Italian restaurant that seemed as if it had time-warped from the 1950s. The triple eggs, toast, hash browns, and one-pound of bacon were almost too much of a good thing even for him. The break refreshed them and lightened the atmosphere in the vehicles.

The men traded off driving at rest stops along the way. Reaper didn't want to use much time, but they all had to be as fresh as they could when they arrived in Leland. Ben and Max swapped off driving in Max's pickup truck while Reaper, Bear, and Enzo went tooling along in the Suburban towing the boat. They looked like either a part of a football team out on a jaunt, or the most dangerous fishermen the Great Lakes had seen in a long time.

The Suburban took the lead when the short caravan turned to the west off I-75 and headed out toward Traverse City along M72. About a quarter-hour west of Kalkaska, Bear suddenly told Reaper to turn up a short road they were rapidly approaching.

Bear had been in the back of the Suburban for much of the trip, complaining about a miserable headache. The demand to turn off seemed unusual for him, but Reaper didn't feel like arguing. The spot turned out to be a scenic turnoff that went partway up a hill to where the road spread out into a wide parking area. Picnic tables and a place to stand and look out over the inland lakes had been added. The view made it worth the stop, even Reaper admitted to that.

"Damn, look at that," Bear said as the rest of the guys piled out of both vehicles.

The sun had slid lower in the sky and stretched out in front of their eyes were three magnificent lakes, the blue water of one going on past the horizon. Far to the west they could see the barest sliver of blue that was Lake Michigan.

"That short lake in front of us is Skegemog," Bear said. "To the left there is Elk Lake, and that really long one is Torch."

"How do you know so much about the lakes up here?" Ben asked.

"I used to ride my bike all around up here," Bear said with a faraway look in his eye. "I used to camp in the state forest up off of Dockery Road just west of here. This used to be a town called Barker Creek. Or at least it was near here."

"Nothing of a town here but that little fenced-in graveyard over there," Max said as he looked off to the west of where they were standing.

"Yeah," Bear said, "that would be a real nice place to rest for a while. Nice view and all."

"A while?" Max said. "That's a graveyard, Bear, you'd have to want to rest for a long while there. And that nice view of yours doesn't include the trees around here, does it? That one across the road way down there looks like the top got stepped on and squashed."

"Damn," said Bear, "you are a city boy. That's an eagle's nest. I heard they were back up here in numbers—never seen one though."

"You okay, Bear?" Reaper asked. "You don't usually talk like this."

"I'm fine," Bear said shaking his head. "I must be a little dingie from the trip."

Ben leaned close to Bear and looked him square in the eyes.

"No, really," Bear insisted, "I'm fine. Just wanted to take a look is all. We'd better get moving."

Reaper agreed and they got back into their vehicles. In spite of the rush, Reaper didn't begrudge Bear a few minutes in an area he seemed to know so well and cared about.

The little caravan hit the road again, heading farther out past Traverse City and on to Leland on the shores of Lake Michigan. Leland was a small town on the Leelanau Peninsula, a large finger of land bordered by Lake Michigan on the west and Grand Traverse Bay on the east. The town itself rested on a thin strip of land that lay between Lake Michigan and Lake Leelanau on the peninsula.

When the men finally reached the Leland harbor, right at the mouth of the Leland River, it was already after six-thirty in the evening. Several hours of daylight remained, enough for them to launch and get to South Wolverine. Enzo had said that the SAV II would do more than fifty knots, close to sixty miles an hour, fast enough to get them over the twenty-five miles to the island before sunset. The team wanted to keep a low profile and launching a big boat that late in the day would draw some unwanted attention—attention they received in spite of their efforts.

At the large public boat ramp area were a number of fishing boats, most of them tied up to the docks. It was an active fishing area and the Michigan Department of Natural Resources, the DNR, kept a close watch on sports activities at the ramp.

Wearing a green uniform and looking like a police officer, down to his SIG P-226 sidearm and handcuffs, was a DNR man, a Michigan game warden. He came up to Reaper and Bear as they got out to check the boat ramp.

"How you boys doing today?" the man said. His name tag read BERINSKI.

"Not bad officer. How's yourself?" Bear said.

"Well enough," Berinski said. "You going out kind of late, aren't you?"

"Not really," Bear said. "We planned on maybe doing some night fishing."

"Oh, fishing for what?" Berinski asked.

"Brown trout," Enzo said as he walked up to the three others. "The news down south said they were running off the peninsula and farther out in the lake. We thought we might get an early start before the crowds came up next weekend."

"That's a good idea," Berinski said, "if you don't mind the cold."

"We aren't bothered a lot by cold," Reaper said with a smile.

"Good, a lot better than some of the people who have been coming up here recently," Berinski said. "To look at how they acted, you'd think they were freezing. You've got all of your approved flotation devices, signaling and emergency gear, radios?"

"Not a problem on all counts," Enzo said. "You need to check anything out?"

"No, by the looks of you, I'd say I can take your word for it," Berinski said easily. "I see that's an out of state plate on the SUV. Got your fishing licenses?"

"Damn, I knew there was something I was supposed to stop for," Enzo complained loudly. "Weren't you supposed to get one for me?" he said as he looked at Reaper.

"Shit, I'm sorry," Reaper said, "I was asleep in the car. Do you know where we can pick some up, Officer?"

"Sure," Berinski said. "There's a sporting goods store just up the docks. They'll still be open this time of night. You can get what you need there."

"Is there a good motel nearby?" Reaper said. "It looks like it may be getting late and we might just strike out in the morning."

"Sure," Berinski said. "The closest one is the Anchor Motel, that's just a block up the street there," he said, pointing the direction.

"Thanks," Reaper said, "we'll get our act together now."

"Not a problem," Berinski said. "Good luck tomorrow."

Back in the Suburban, Bear leaned over the front seat and looked at Reaper.

"Well, that was fun," he said. "I can see about the licenses, the devil is in the details. But just what the hell was all that crap about a motel? We're not going out tonight?"

"No, we may have something else to do," Reaper said cryptically. "Do you still have those notes from the OP?"

"Somewhere here," Bear said. "You've been going through all of that stuff since we left the farm. What do you need?"

"Remember the van we saw come and go that night?" Reaper said. "I need to know the license number."

"YXLC-493," Bear said. "Why?"

Then Bear caught the stare coming his way from Enzo in the driver's seat.

"Hey, it's something I do, okay?" Bear said.

Astounded by this display of recall, Enzo shook his head.

"Take a look at the parking area left of where that officer was when we got here," Reaper said. "Does that van look familiar?"

"Damn," Bear said. "YXLC-493. There can't be two of them. We found them."

"I think so, too," Reaper said. "Now let's go get the

others and shop for some fishing licenses. I don't think that officer is going to be leaving for a while. It's a Saturday night and he's checking boats as they come in. I'll bet he's going to issue one or two tickets this evening. And I don't want him to see us loading up the boat. That cannon looks like anything but fishing gear—even in the bags. By the time he's gone, it will be too late to head out. The sun will be down and the sign says the ramp will be closed."

"Looks like we need that motel," said Enzo.

———

An hour before sunrise the next morning the two vehicles returned to the boat ramp. They arrived twenty minutes before the ramp officially opened to avoid any traffic from other boaters. Enzo put the boat in the water with ease, rolling the trailer down the ramp. Years of practice had eliminated his need for a ground guide to help him back up a trailer. As Reaper tied the boat up to the dock, Enzo drove the Suburban over to the parking area and left it.

All of the men hustled to hump their equipment and gear into the boat. The weapons had been packed up in USAI waterproof bags delivered by Enzo. No one was around in the early Sunday morning hours, but Bear still paused for a minute while he surveyed the parking lot. Then he pulled the Lahti 20mm cannon from the back of the SUV and hoisted it up to his shoulder. Trotting, he hurried the huge gun in its duffel bag case over to the boat.

Enzo emerged from the SUV already dressed in his ballistic dry suit. He busied himself prepping the boat and checking over everything while the rest of the guys stowed the gear on board. He didn't have time to suit up, so he had worn the gear he wanted from the motel under loose-fitting street clothes.

The Exotherm III insulating fleece jumpsuit that Enzo had on under the dry suit would have kept him warm in a winter wind. The ballistic dry suit prevented any water from getting to the jumpsuit. The armor panels of the dry suit made it feel that much more assuring.

Since he wore one of the ballistic dry suits on a regular basis, Enzo had modified his for his own comfort by cutting off the integral boots. The mottled green-black-and-brown camouflage pattern of the outer suit didn't extend to the boots. He preferred different footwear for his movements on the boat. On top of his head, he had squashed down a badly worn boonie hat, a veteran of many missions over the water.

The suit was warm, but it could quickly become very hot if you weren't in the cold water or blowing wind. To add to his comfort level, Enzo wore a neck ring that held the soft black rubber neck seal away from his throat. The ring kept the suit from being watertight at the neck, but it made Enzo's working on the boat a lot easier.

The rest of the men dressed in their suits while Enzo checked the boat and warmed up the engines. They all had the same ballistic dry suits as Enzo wore, but none of them expected to keep them on during the land operation on the island. So instead of the extremely comfortable Exotherm II jumpsuits they had available, Ben and Max both wore a standard woodland camouflage battle dress uniform (BDU) under their dry suits. Reaper and Bear had put on the same black shirts and Royal Robbins range pants they had worn during the Factory raid.

To put the suits on, over the uniforms and clothes, was a two-man job if you wanted to get dressed fast. The entry to the suit came through a long zipper across the shoulders. Once one had pulled the boots up onto his feet, the person stood and pulled up the rest of the pants portion of the suit. Arms went through the sleeves and the tight, soft black rubber seals at the wrists. Ducking one's head, the wearer pulled the neck part over his head and settled the neck seal in place. Then a partner was needed to pull the zipper across the back of the shoulders and seal up the suit. No one had arms flexible enough to pull the zipper by himself.

The suits crackled as they moved. The rustle of the waterproof material would be lessened when it got wet, but the new suits remained stiff. Yet they would keep each of the men protected from the thirty-nine-degree water of Lake Michigan. It had been a long, cold winter, and the spring had not been a warm one. Unprotected exposure to the water could kill a man almost instantly from the shock—and within half an hour from hypothermia if the shock hadn't gotten him.

The men placed all the gear on board and secured it. The boat's outboards were warmed up and running smoothly and everyone was now aboard. Ben had a particularly hard time gearing up because his suit was too big for him. Enzo said it was the smallest size he had in stock. When Ben accidentally dipped his hand into the lake water, he fully appreciated the suit, too large or not.

A gleam of sunrise came up over the land as the boat sped across the waves. Enzo reveled in his element, and he handled the small, agile craft with the steady hand of a master. All the waves only swelled a few feet high at the most, but Ben MacKenzie was not used to the pounding. He crawled into the crowded but protected cockpit area and tried not to look as miserable as he felt.

Reaper, Bear, and Max, all having spent a lot of time on the water while in the service, found the trip cold and wet but nothing new. As they skimmed over the water, they checked out their gear as much as they were able to. When they lost sight of the mainland, Enzo reached into the huge pocket on the outside of his dry suit and pulled out an Eagle tactical thigh holster. The rig held his favored 9mm SIG P-226 which he strapped to his leg with practiced fingers.

The marine radar screen in the cockpit showed open water ahead of the speeding small boat. With one eye on the screen, another on the water, and occasional glances at the GPS locator, Enzo knew the boat's position, where it was headed, and that no other craft moved on the water around them. They traveled swiftly across a steel-blue lake, the water spewing white as the wave tops broke in the wind. As the sun came up, so did the view of an island on the horizon.

A dark mound arose from the water, the darker covering of trees and brush became more distinct as they approached. Now Reaper stood behind Enzo, focusing on the island on the radar screen. He also checked for any signals that radar from the island might be painting them electronically, but was pleased that the screen remained clear of interference.

As they approached to within five miles of the island, Enzo cut back on the power and the SAV II settled in the water a bit. At Reaper's questioning glance, Enzo pointed to the fish finder. The simple sonar showed that the lake bottom rose rapidly ahead. From more than a hundred feet down, it quickly came to thirty, twenty, ten feet. Off to the right a buoy marked the top of the rocky reef only a few feet under the surface.

They were unknown waters to everyone on the boat, and Enzo wanted to play the situation as safely as he could. Only danger awaited them on that chunk of land in front of the boat. With the sunrise, the colors of the trees and brush could be made out against the tan and browns of the sand and earth. Reaper pointed and Enzo nodded as he swung the boat to the west.

They would land on the western shore of the island, close to the southern tip. Deckert's research had shown that the only major structures on the island were the mansion that made up the hunting lodge and a scattering of smaller support buildings at the airstrip and boat dock. On the southern point of the island stood an old lighthouse, which had been abandoned and dark for years. They would put in on the shore just to the north of that lighthouse, above the sandbar that separated it from the main body of the island.

A tree-covered rise above the sand concealed a small valley with a stream or a ravine that cut through its center from west to east. That rise would be where the men could look down on the lodge facilities only a few hundred meters away. Everything should be visible to them in the one panoramic view. From the base of the ridge to the eastern shore of the island, all the aerial and satellite images had shown a gentle grass-covered slope. The time had come to see if that intelligence was true.

Chapter Twenty-seven

With the arrival of the boat at the island, Reaper and Bear once again slipped into a comfortable, familiar mode of operating. They had performed the actions they would be doing countless times before during training and real-world operations, two combat-experienced SEALs about to slip onto an enemy-held beach as a pair of swimmer-scouts. Before the rest of the team could land, the swimmer-scouts would check the shoreline for unfriendlies, select the specific beach landing site, and provide security for the landing.

Reaper and Bear prepared to enter the water. They kept the weapons and equipment to a bare minimum: Their dry suits for protection, a nine-pound lead weight belt, a set of 3XL Turtle fins over the suit's boots, and a black U.S. Divers Maui model face mask made up the bulk of the two SEALs' swimming gear.

With a look to his partner, Reaper gave a ready signal and saw it returned. Then the two men slipped silently over the side of the boat and into the dark waters. The frigid water closed over their heads with barely a splash as they sank out of sight.

The USIA ballistic dry suits now proved their value. The hands of both men were red from the compression of the soft rubber wrist seals that kept out the water. But their hands still had their feeling and flexibility. Now those hands told them exactly how cold the water all around them was as they went numb within a minute of leaving the boat.

Discomfort in the water means little to a SEAL; it can't mean much because they spend more than half of their operational lives in the water all over the world and Reaper and Bear were no different in this respect. They quickly sorted out their locations in relation to each other and the island ahead. Bubbles gushed out of the two and one-half-inch-diameter round black plastic valve on their upper left arms. The pressure of the water pushed at the suits, squeezing out the excess air. If they had lost too much buoyancy, a quick squirt of air from the gas bottle in a pocket on their upper left thigh would reinflate the suit.

The arms and legs of the dry suits clamped around their limbs as the water squeezed down. The armor panels on their chest and backs kept the suits stiff across the chest and back and they barely felt the effects of the water there. Slowly and carefully returning to the surface, the two swimmer-scouts headed toward the beach.

The strong legs of Reaper and Bear pushed the black Turtle power-fins toward the beach, the big neoprene blades of the flippers driving the SEALs effortlessly through the water. SEALs regularly swam for miles, and ran for even more miles, in order to build up their leg strength for just such an operation. The driving force of the fins allowed the two SEALs to keep their hands free to move them over the lake bottom as they approached the softly pounding surf on the beach.

Reaper and Bear crawled up to the edge of the surf zone and lay there as the cold waves swirled around them. Raising his AKMS-47, the same weapon that Bear had picked up at the Factory, Reaper prepared it for action.

During the years Reaper had been in the Teams, the SEALs had not found another weapon that worked as well in the surf zone as an AK-47. The sand, mud, and water just didn't jam up the rugged Russian design. It wasn't as accurate, long-ranged, or comfortable to shoot as one of the weapons from the M16 family, but it always worked. And it was the weapon of choice for scout-swimmers passing through the surf zone. But Reaper and Bear only had one of the rugged Soviet designs. As the primary point man, Reaper carried their AK.

Over his shoulder, Reaper wore a yellow canvas pouch holding four thirty-round magazines for the AK. From somewhere in the boxes and from the shelves of their shop, Deckert had come up with the Iraqi ammo pouch and magazines along with fresh ammo for the weapon itself. The experienced gunsmith had gone over every inch of the weapon, making sure that even its rugged design didn't have any flaws. Reaper now held a weapon as dependable as anything mechanical ever could be.

The only thing Reaper had done to prepare his weapon for the swim in was to stretch a latex condom over the muzzle. The thin rubber could have been fired through if necessary without any damage to Reaper or the weapon. And the latex helped keep the water from entering the AK's barrel.

Now Reaper stripped the latex condom from the muzzle of the AK, as he pulled the bolt back partway. While he prepped his weapon, Reaper also kept watch along the beach and the tree line just beyond. Even though the condom would have kept the bore of the weapon relatively clear of water, cracking open the breech would release the seal of the cartridge in the chamber insuring that any water in the barrel drained away.

For his weapon, Bear didn't have to worry about water exposure. He was carrying Reaper's preferred MP5K-PDW. With the Gemtech Raptor suppressor secured on the barrel, the compact submachine gun had been secured in a special small waterproof weapons container Enzo had brought. The MP5K-PDW fit snugly in the bag. The flexible weapon container even had an inflator tube that allowed air to be blown into the bag to make it buoyant. The feature of the bag that Bear liked best was the built-in glove. The glove allowed the shooter to fire his weapon if necessary without taking it from the bag, the reason Bear had carried it out in front of him during the insertion.

After waiting a few minutes in the surf zone to be sure they hadn't been spotted, or that anyone else might be around, Reaper and Bear quickly moved inland to conduct a recon of the area. The aerial views of the island they had all studied had shown a small valley along the side of the ridge line where Reaper wanted to establish their observation post.

What the views hadn't shown was a wide inlet of water extending into the tree line along the floor of that valley. This would be their beach landing site and would be a safe place to cache their gear and secure the boat.

Going back to the shore, Reaper pulled a flashlight from a pocket of his ammunition pouch. The operators had devised a system to ensure that the operation hadn't been compromised on insertion. The man on shore would use a series of flashes to signal the men in the boat. The returned countersign had to add up to seven flashes. Any other result would mean that the men had to break off contact. Holding out his flashlight, Reaper squeezed off four slow flashes.

Three flashes returned from the boat. As Reaper watched, the SAV II emerged from the mist that had come up from the water. As it approached the shore, Reaper could see Ben and Max on either side of the bow, their weapons at the ready. Following his arm signals, Enzo spotted the opening in the beach that led into the valley. Slowly guiding the boat along, Enzo entered the crevasse with just one outboard engaged, cutting off the other motor in case he ran aground in the unknown waters and lost his propeller. The water in the gorge ran deep enough that he managed to scrape by and come in under the cover of the trees.

Not a word had been spoken since they left the boat. Every member of the team had studied the maps and photos of the island. The routes they would take had been committed to memory. The whole operation had been originally planned to take place under the cover of darkness. Circumstances now denied them that option.

The men would only have to patrol about four hundred meters to reach the top of the ridge line at the point Reaper had selected. While travelling only a short distance, their patrol needed to go through an unknown area with the possibility of discovery a very real one. They would stay off any paths they might find along the route and proceed as silently as ghosts through the woods and brush.

Returning to the water, Ben and Max helped Enzo turn the boat around so that its bow pointed toward open water only fifty meters away, preparing the group for a fast extraction. Then all except Enzo stripped off their ballistic dry suits. He would stay and secure the boat, their only sure means of extraction from the island.

If the men got separated or forced apart by heavy combat, the emergency rally point was at the tree line overlooking the old lighthouse. If everything went completely to hell, Enzo would call in the Coast Guard and the men would have to trust that they could hold off any forces until help arrived. The Motorola Talkabout radios they each had in their uniform pockets had a two-mile range. These would have to do as a final backup in case the boat's radio became unavailable.

It might be a loose plan, but that also made it flexible. Though they preferred stacking the deck in their favor at every opportunity, all of the men had long operated right out on the edge. One took chances only when he had to and prepared for as many contingencies as possible, and saved his luck for when he really needed it by training constantly.

Taking the lead as the point man in the patrol, Reaper moved out with his favored MP5K-PDW back in his hands. Now that he was on dry land, the suppressed MP5K-PDW would be the best choice in case he had to fire a shot. So Reaper had taken the MP5K from Bear and given the AK and ammo pouch to Ben.

Reaper's Chalker sling again spanned his chest and shoulders. Too bad that he would never be able to tell the retired command master chief just how well the sling had worked for him. Somehow, Reaper figured that this operation wouldn't be a story that got a lot of public release.

The gear Reaper had strapped on was almost a mirror of what he had carried at the Factory only the day before. That thought gave him pause. Had it only been a day?

This time, Reaper had loaded the Serbu Super-Shorty shotgun in the holster on his thigh with Winchester 00 buckshot. Every person on the island could be considered an armed enemy except for the hostages—Reaper's family. There would be little need for less lethal ammunition. Also, the nasty little shotgun would be useful for blasting locks or hinges if they had to open secured doors. In case he encountered a larger group of hostiles, Reaper had one of Enzo's M26A1 fragmentation grenades in the flash-crash pocket of his ammunition pouch. The deadly little green ovoid would spray out hundreds of steel fragments when detonated—enough to wreck anyone's day.

Immediately behind Reaper in the patrol came Max, who filled the position of automatic weapons man. He carried the Shrike belt-fed conversion unit mounted on the receiver of the M4. Slung across his back was the TTR-700 sniper rifle in its compact case. Max could place a single round exactly where he wanted with the bolt-action rifle. But he could also practically write his name with an automatic weapon when he wanted to—Bear had been right in nicknaming the young man "War."

Coming next in the patrol line was Bear. The stout SEAL now had the Jackhammer shotgun he liked so much hanging from a sling. Across his shoulders, Bear held the massive 20mm Lahti rifle. Ahead of them lay a long downhill, potential field of fire they would have to cross before they reached the lodge. Bear had accepted the responsibility of dragging the big gun along in order to give them the best base of fire they could have to cover that crossing.

The brochure for the lodge had pictures that showed the castlelike walls to be made of light brown stone. The 20mm cannon could make large, precise holes through that stone. The weight of the gun had become Bear's burden. The bipod and heavy ammunition magazines had been spread out among the rest of the patrol.

Bringing up rear security came Ben, armed with the AKMS-47. He watched their backs, "covering their six," in militaryspeak. While he made sure that no one came up from behind them, Ben also tried to wipe out the marks of the patrol's passage as much as he could. He walked backward much of the time, scanning behind them as well as to either side.

Reaper led the patrol along the sides of the ridge to the north of the valley. The group climbed higher as they continued to move generally eastward. Coming up to a saddle, a depression in the middle of the ridge, Reaper silently called a halt by raising his clenched fist. As the men settled down into a diamond formation, their weapons pointing outward into the brush, Bear breathed heavily, even his great stamina sapped by carrying the huge 20mm weapon.

Getting down low on his hands and knees, Reaper crawled forward to approach the edge of the saddle. As the ground started to open up and fall away to the east, he dropped down even flatter. Finally, he slithered on his belly. Reaper pulled up to a huge fallen tree and slowly peered over it, his head partly blocked and hidden by a big branch forking out from the fallen trunk.

The lodge was standing only a few hundred meters away. It stood in the open surrounded only by flower gardens. Though the gardens hadn't been kept up, they seemed almost out of place in what Reaper perceived as a hostile environment.

No one moved down at the lodge. The huge mansion had the appearance of an old castle with its rock walls and crenelated roof line. Bear had the right idea in struggling up here with the big Lahti.

A further hundred meters along the ridge, as it slanted down to the east, the tree line came to within a hundred meters of the lodge. That would be the most secure approach Reaper and Bear could take to reach the big house and penetrate inside. Withdrawing from the log, Reaper spoke into his radio headset.

"Come up, stay low," he said.

Going back up to peer down at the lodge, Reaper maintained a watch as the balance of his small patrol moved up to where he lay. Max came up and placed his Shrike down after looking over the fallen tree. Snuggling down next to the log, Max pulled up his case, opened it, and pulled out the parts to his sniper rifle. His skilled fingers almost assembled the rifle solely by touch as Max leaned his head against the log and looked over at Reaper.

As the sniper prepared his hardware, Bear crawled up, pulling the Lahti along by its barrel. Placing the big antitank rifle alongside the log, Bear then pulled up the rest of the components—taking a magazine box from Max as he handed it over. Finally, Ben came up and lay next to Max, lifting up the Shrike from where it lay.

Max and Ben would provide cover fire as needed. Ben could handle his gun well enough to allow Max to concentrate on precision shooting to cut down opposing numbers. When he saw everything was in hand and his two men set up and in position, Reaper signaled for Bear to come with him. The red-faced, shorter SEAL looked up and gave an okay signal by circling his thumb and forefinger. Bear was a little short of breath, but anyone would have been after dragging that big gun through the woods.

——

"Did you hear that?" Hadeed said in a loud whisper.

"Hear what?" Joseph replied. "I didn't hear anything. You've been jumpy about everything ever since you got here. You hear shit that no one else does."

"Hey, I didn't join up with this mob to wander in the woods," Hadeed said. "I grew up in Dearborn, not the forest, just like you did. Arzee told me that I would have to drive the van, and I've been driving that thing up and down from here to Detroit for weeks now. It's not like you or I are one of those Afghan chosen ones."

"Yeah, well now you've been told to walk the property line," Joseph said as he hitched the sling of the AK-47 rifle on his shoulder up to a more comfortable position. Turning to his partner in misery, he continued. "Or do you want to tell one of the chosen brethren that you are too good to watch trees? You do that and Paxtun will let them eat you when they get back from the other island."

"I don't give a shit about those better-than-us sand-soldiers. All they do is think they're better than we are and run around on the other island firing their guns. Put them in the street and I'll do just fine keeping up with them," Hadeed said. "It's only these damned woods. There are critters all over around here—and none of them are people. It's cold and windy, there's nothing to guard against but some trees and birds—I'm going back inside."

As the street tough turned, his eyes grew large as a shadow from the trees suddenly stood up in front of him. He saw no face on the black apparition, only a pair of piercing eyes that looked out from a blank, black-painted face. The AK-47 in his hands went unremembered as Hadeed never even noticed the slight cough and flash on the muzzle of the weapon in the spirit's hands.

Joseph had even less time to react to Reaper's appearance. As he turned, Bear simply said "War," into his radio's headset. A solid "thunk" rang out a moment later as a subsonic 220-grain 7.62mm EBR Thumper put the other thug's lights out.

Though he would never know it, the initial kills of the island assault had been the two men who had actually kidnapped Reaper's family. He and Bear then ran to the lodge not quite a football field away. They had been watching to see if any other guards appeared. The lodge remained silent as they approached. The two SEALs knew they were exposed and at risk during the rush across the open field—but the eyes and muzzles of their teammates up on the ridge covered them.

With a swift dart across the terrace at the south end of the main building, Reaper and Bear immediately went through the big doors in front of them. If they had been spotted from inside the house, the faster they could get to cover the better.

No one responded to their rapid entry.

The two SEALs didn't know they had entered the old music room, only that they didn't find any threats immediately visible. Instead of their normal shout of "clear," the two partners remained silent as they moved through the richly paneled room. Dark woods and paintings looked down on the two black-clad and heavily armed SEALs as they penetrated deeper into the lodge.

They passed through what had been the billiard room, the muzzles of their weapons sweeping across the stone fireplace and wall like lethal extensions of their arms. The living room was next, and another sweep turned up nothing. Only after they moved into the next hallway did they find a target—an unexpected one.

Hassan Akrit had been a kitchen helper at the Factory. Arzee had given him a bonus to come to the island and cook for a large group of men. The cook didn't know what Paxtun did with the extra food tray he had Hassan bring him twice a day. He only knew that the boss ate in his office upstairs. And Paxtun didn't look like someone who ate double meals, yet that's the amount of food he packed away. Sometime after being served, the second tray always came back, brought to the kitchen for Hassan to clean.

The young man froze in place as a tall, black-clothed ninja suddenly jumped out in front of him, waving a big, black gun under his nose. The trays he had stacked on top of one another shook in his hands, but they didn't fall—which boded well for him, Hassan reasoned, because the noise might have caused that awful gun to make some horrible noise itself.

"Where are they?" the tall ninja growled.

Hassan stared blankly, uncomprehending. The shorter ninja went past with an even bigger gun and did something behind Hassan. The terrified young cook did not even think to turn and see what the other was doing, but remained hypnotized by the black spot in the center of the weapon he was staring at.

"Don't you understand English?" the tall ninja snarled in a low voice. "Where are they!"

Being poked at with the big gun finally broke Hassan's concentration on the hole in the muzzle.

"Who they?" he said, totally confused. "They what?"

"Where are the hostages?" Tall ninja said.

"Hostages? What hostages?" Hassan asked in a quavering voice. "All of the others left in the boats this morning. Only the boss and four of the guys are around. There are no hostages."

Once Hassan's vocal logjam had been broken, the SEALs found it hard to shut him up.

"Enough," the tall ninja said. "Six tangos on site," he said, apparently to no one. "Six tangos. No hotels as yet."

"Who are you talking to?" Hassan asked.

Now that his initial shock seemed to have fled, the cook became positively talkative. Maybe he could tell Reaper something useful besides who else was on the island.

"Where's the boss you mentioned?" Reaper said.

"Upstairs in his office waiting for breakfast," Hassan said lightheadedly, the shock beginning to make him sway. "At the head of the stairs, to the left, last door on the right . . ." He was anxious to please the deadly strangers. Then Bear tapped the panicking man in the back of his head and the world went black. The cook had just enough time to hope this wasn't a permanent change.

Reaper barely managed to catch the young man as he wilted and sank to the floor. Grabbing the trays, Reaper noticed that there was a hell of a lot of food for one person. This boss would be the next person he would talk to.

"Bear, take him," Reaper said as he placed the trays on the floor. They hadn't made any real noise yet and it would be worthwhile to keep it that way.

"Secure him," Reaper ordered seconds later as he looked up the huge stairway.

Bear pulled the unconscious cook to the side and stuffed him into a small cloak room under the stairs. Before leaving his unconscious acquaintance, Bear secured his hands and feet with nylon tie-ties brought for the purpose. The very strong nylon ties were intended to hold bundles of heavy cables and wires together. They would have to be cut to get them off the cook's arms and legs. The white apron the cook had been wearing was made into a quick gag and the door to the big closet shut tight.

Reaper already had a foot on the first step, set to head up the stairs. Bear hustled over to catch up with him and they both went up to the landing in three short flights. The upstairs of the lodge was huge—and there were still at least four people around based on what the cook had said. But the boss was supposed to be down the hall on the left. So they would clear that room first.

Stacking up outside the last door on the right, Reaper gave Bear the squeeze signal since this time he would go first through the door. Reaper reached over and checked the knob, and saw that the door was unlocked. Instead of barging in, he decided to try another tack to see if they couldn't maintain the advantage of surprise. He squeezed Bear's shoulder again and raised one finger. Bear looked up and nodded—then Reaper knocked on the door.

"It's about goddamned time," a strangely familiar voice said inside. "Get in here with my breakfast."

Now the two SEALs flashed into the room, Reaper breaking high and right, Bear low and left. It was hard to say who had the greater surprise; the man standing inside the room, or the two SEALs as they recognized Cary Paxtun.

In spite of his astonishment, Paxtun was quick as

he jerked back and slammed the door to his private office. Bear covered the rest of the room and the door they had come in through while Reaper darted to the door Paxtun had slammed and forced it open.

Paxtun was behind a big desk, scrabbling through a drawer. He froze with his hand in the drawer as Reaper pointed the suppressed submachine gun at him.

"Both hands on the desk, now," Reaper said.

Paxtun wasn't about to argue with those eyes peering at him through the sights of a weapon. He slowly sat down with both of his hands on the desk in plain sight. He sweated heavily and could feel his heart beating its way out of his chest. It was the look in those eyes. All he wanted to do right then was to just keep his heart beating.

"Where are they, you son of a bitch?" Reaper asked slowly and distinctly.

"Who?" Paxtun tried to bluff as a cold chill came over him. "Where are who? Who are you, anyway?"

Reaper reached up with his left hand and pulled back the black balaclava he had over his head. As his features came into view, Paxtun blanched as recognition flooded his face. Then he started to panic.

"Where are who? There's no one here. I don't know what you're talking about," Paxtun's tongue started to trip up as the words poured from him. Then Reaper glanced over to his right.

A wooden box lay open on a set of drawers, a box that looked very familiar. And what looked even more familiar was the shining bright broadsword that lay inside of it. Reaper walked over to the case, never taking his eyes off Paxtun. Reaper switched hands on his weapon and reached down to grasp the hilt of the big sword.

"My family, now," the Grim Reaper said to Paxtun. "Give them to me and I'll let you live."

Paxtun collapsed. To the SEAL it seemed like watching a wax dummy melt in the sun.

"They're in the basement," Paxtun said in a cold whisper. "A storeroom under the south wing. They're fine, nothing has happened to them. No one has harmed them at all."

For a moment, rage swept through Reaper like a white-hot flame. He looked at Paxtun and his hand clenched on the grip of the sword.

"Why?" Reaper said through gritted teeth. "Why me? Why the fuck did you screw with me and my family?"

Paxtun looked up with a blank, hopeless look on his face. He was lost and knew it.

"You were just available," Paxtun said in a neutral voice. "It wasn't anything special. We needed something you could supply. Besides, you had fucked me over once. It was a chance for payback. That's all, just payback."

Paxtun dropped his face into his hands. His shoulders shook and his knees bent slightly. From the sound of it the former spook was having trouble breathing.

"So, it was all just something personal," Reaper said. "Well, payback's a bitch, or didn't you know that?"

Reaper looked at the suddenly broken man who had caused him so much grief. He didn't even seem worth wasting a bullet on. Reaper looked down at the sword in his hand and sighed. Then he turned his back and looked at the glass-fronted case on the wall over the chest of drawers.

Paxtun wasn't completely done yet. Seeing Reaper's back turned, he slipped his hand back into the drawer. His fingers finally closed over the cool plastic grips of the SIG 228 pistol he kept there. There would be more men between him and safety, but he could kill Reaper and still get away.

"Now that I know where my family is, I'll let the cops deal with you," Reaper said. "Now it's your turn to face a court."

"I don't think so," Paxtun said as he started to lift the pistol.

From his position in the other room, Bear glanced in to where Reaper was standing. He could see Paxtun slip his hand into the drawer. Before Bear shouted a warning or aimed his weapon, he saw Reaper's hand lift the sword. Then he saw his Teammate's eyes looking intently at the wall in front of him. The whole of Paxtun's movements had been clear to Reaper in the reflection in the glass of the case. As Paxtun stood, Reaper spoke.

"I thought you might see it that way," he said as he spun around with the sword extended out from his right hand. The reverse grip swung the razor-sharp blade out, and it barely slowed as it sliced through Paxtun's neck. The head fell from the shoulders of the body as blood fountained out and sprayed the wall nearby. Like a child's abandoned ball, Paxtun's head rolled across the floor and bumped up against the wall, his unseeing eyes staring in shock.

Chapter Twenty-eight

"Downstairs now," Reaper said as he left the room where Paxtun's body lay cooling. Reaper had stopped and picked up the leather scabbard that had been in the top of the case.

Nodding at the bloody sword in Reaper's hand, Bear said, "Better wipe that off or it'll rust."

Reaper stood and looked at his friend for a moment, then bent down and wiped the blade off on what looked to be a priceless Persian rug. Then he slipped it into its scabbard and stuck it diagonally down across his back, underneath his Chalker sling. It had been made for his son and he would give it to the boy personally.

"Better?" Reaper said.

"Oh, much," Bear agreed almost smiling, and led the way out the door.

As the two SEALs reached the head of the stairs, below them Paxtun's remaining two men, Kerah and Pali finally came in for some breakfast. The two men had been on guard at the front of the lodge, covered from Ben or Max's view from the hillside.

As they saw the two black-clad SEALs appearing on the stairs, Pali bellowed a strangled cry and pulled up his AK-47, squeezing off a long burst. The 7.62mm steel-jacketed slugs did nothing more than tear up a lot of expensive paneling as Reaper dropped backward out of sight.

Bear pulled up his Jackhammer and fired off a burst as Pali tried to swing his AK-47 around. The thunder of the Jackhammer roared out as Pali jerked and danced from the impact of the buckshot. It was something barely recognizable as human that dropped its AK-47 and slid down the far wall.

Now the problem was that Kerah controlled the downstairs landing. And Reaper wanted down those steps and into the basement. Having seen what happened to Pali, Kerah had pulled back under the stairs and was firing wildy in all directions.

With no desire to expose either himself or Bear to fire, Reaper reached into his pouch and pulled up an M26A1 fragmentation grenade. Holding the grenade up so that Bear could see it, Reaper pulled the pin. He popped off the safety spoon, and counted a long "one" before tossing the grenade over the landing they crouched upon. As the deadly green bomb bounced on the floor, Reaper and Bear scuttled back off the landing.

Kerah had few choices of where to go and no time to decide. The concussive blast of the 156 grams of Composition B explosive inside the grenade, boosted by eight grams of tetryl pellets, shattered the sheet metal body and broke up the notched square steel-wire fragmentation coil. The tiny steel fragments flew out at thousands of feet per second, shredding anything they hit, wood, plaster, cloth, or human flesh.

As they rolled to their feet, Bear and Reaper darted down the stairs, following the rolling thunder of the explosion. It was most definitely no longer a silent operation. Neither of the two men could hear very well right then, but that seemed of little concern.

At the bottom of the stairs, a quick shotgun blast from Bear made certain that the horrible mess inside the front door didn't suffer, or cause the SEALs any more trouble. The gruesome pile against the wall obviously didn't need a finishing shot. Moving quickly down the hall, Bear led the way to the stairs he had seen while Reaper had been questioning Hassan.

Both SEALs quickly moved down the stairs into the basement of the lodge. The basement consisted of an area as big as the rest of the building, with a lot of storage rooms.

"Mary, Ricky," Reaper bellowed, "Mary, Ricky!"

"Here," Reaper heard a muffled voice. "We're in here."

"Keep talking," Reaper shouted as he followed the sound to a padlocked door. While Bear kept cover on the stairs and passages they had just crossed through, Reaper reached behind his back and swept the padlock and hasp from the door with one stroke of the sword, then yanked the door open. Inside the bleak room he saw two mattresses, a bucket, and a blanket that had been pinned up to give anyone using the bucket a fraction of privacy.

And standing at the far corner of the room he saw his wife Mary and their son Ricky.

Mary ran into her husband's arms, ignoring the blood and stink of powder smoke on him. Ricky wrapped himself around his father's leg, hugging him as if he were a dream that had suddenly come true. If the boy let go, the dream might disappear.

Then Ricky noticed the blood on his father's leg.

"Daddy, you're hurt," he said in sudden fear.

"It's all right, I'm fine," Reaper said to his son.

"Ted . . ." Mary started to say.

"It's not mine," Reaper said quietly. "Come on, we have to go."

"But . . . Ted," Mary said, suddenly afraid to leave her prison, "those men."

"They aren't going to bother anyone ever again," Reaper said.

Mary shrank back for a moment from the man she had married years before. She knew what Ted had done while in the military. He had been a SEAL and she knew that he had been a good one. Yet the tone in his voice and the look of him remained alien to her. Swallowing her fear, she followed Reaper out the door.

"Think you can carry this for me, Ricky?" Reaper said as he handed his son the big broadsword.

The feel of the large weapon reassured the boy. It contained the power of his father, something he needed right then. For Reaper, he felt it gave the boy something to do that would distract him from the escape they had to make.

With Bear leading the way, the four ran through the passages and back up the stairs. As they passed through the hallway, and headed back to the music room and the doors there, Bear suddenly stopped and dove back toward Reaper and his family.

"Down!" he bellowed as a shattering burst of AK-47 fire roared out. The bullets slammed into the house from outside, moving across the room toward Reaper. One of the steel-jacketed Russian slugs smashed into the receiver of Reaper's MP5K, almost tearing the weapon out of his hands. Only the shackle of his Chalker sling kept the weapon from hitting the floor.

Reaper could see his assailant. One lone figure crouched on the porch at the front of the house, trying to reload the smoking AK-47 in his hands. Without conscious thought, Reaper reached down with his right hand and pulled the Serbu Super-Shorty shotgun from the thigh holster—his thumb pushing free the safety strap.

The SEAL grabbed the folding operating lever with his left hand, pulling the shotgun up and into line with the man on the porch. A single shot boomed from the weapon's short barrel, tearing into the man and knocking him back. Reaper then pulled back and down on the folding handle on the operating slide, rotating it away from the gun. As it locked into place, he pumped the gun's action, ejecting the spent case and putting a fresh round into the chamber. Another rolling boom sounded out as he made certain that the man who crawled on the porch couldn't get to his weapon—empty or not.

But the four escapees didn't emerge unscathed from the attack. Bear lay on the ground, not moaning, but struggling to push himself up, his legs refusing to support him.

"Bear, are you hit?" Reaper asked.

"No, but I think I'm screwed," Bear said in a weak voice.

They were interrupted by a call coming in over their radio headsets.

"Death, Pestilence, this is War," Max said over the radio, "you had better get out of there fast."

"We have the hotels," Reaper said, "repeat, we have the hotels, but Pestilence is down. Do you have tangos?"

"Two boatloads of them," Max said, abandoning procedure for expediency. "Get up here now. Do you need assistance?"

"Negative," Bear said as he struggled to a sitting position. "Okay, Boss," he said through gritted teeth. "You have what you came for. Now let's get out of here."

Giving an arm up to his partner, Reaper helped Bear to his feet. The man's legs were barely able to support him, and he struggled to make a step. Finally, Reaper picked Bear up and slung him across his back.

"Let's go, Mary, Ricky," Reaper said. Taking two rounds from the three on the outside of the holster, he reloaded the Super-Shorty with his free hand as he went along. With one hand still hanging on to his partner, the SEAL walked with the shotgun held out in front of him like a big pistol.

Once they got outside, Reaper could see across to the east and what had been bothering Max. Two boats headed in toward the island, one long one and a short, broad one. They looked like the sports boat and fishing boat that they had found the receipts for. The sudden zip . . . zip . . . above their heads told

Reaper that someone was shooting at them from the boats.

With Reaper in the lead and Bear across his back, Mary and Ricky followed him to the cover of the trees. They ran, stumbled, and ran some more to get back to the ridge where Ben and Max lay. Reaper hit the ground next to Ben, then rolled Bear to the ground.

"He's hurt," Reaper said quickly. "His legs don't work and he can't walk."

While Ben turned to his patient, Reaper moved to where Max lay with his rifle up to his shoulder.

"Who's out there?" Reaper asked.

"I have no idea," Max said as he looked through the Leupold scope on his rifle. "But there's a bunch of them in two boats, and they're waving weapons over their heads."

"Coast Guard?" Reaper said.

"Not unless the Coasties have taken to carrying AKs," Max said. "Those curved magazines are kind of distinctive. And they have a bunch of them."

"Time to go, Boss," Bear said from where he leaned against a log.

"Fine, get up." Reaper turned to Ben. "What can you do for him?"

"Nothing," Ben said quietly.

"Nothing he can do," Bear said with a ghost of his old grin across his face. "The cancer's finally winning."

"Cancer?" Reaper said. "What the hell are you talking about, Bear?"

"What they call a high-grade brain stem glioma," Bear said simply, "I don't have time to explain it and you don't have time to listen, but it's inoperable. It's why I've been so weak. Not that old yet, guess I never will be. Ask Ben when you get back on the boat."

Reaper looked at Ben who sadly nodded.

"You knew?" Reaper said.

"Don't blame him," Bear said. "He couldn't tell you. I met up with him back when he drove an ambulance for the VA hospital where I got my treatments. He couldn't tell you, I wouldn't let him."

Just looking into the pain showing in Ben's eyes told Reaper that he had heard the truth.

"So get the hell out of here," Bear said. "My arms still work and I have a machine gun, bullets, and a really big rifle. I carried it, I get to shoot it. I'll give those suckers out there in the boats something to work with while you get everyone away."

"No," the word seemed to tear from Reaper's chest. "We all came, we all go home."

Bear pulled an orange plastic pill bottle from his shirt pocket.

"These are painkillers," Bear said, "really powerful ones. You know those headaches I've been having? Well, these are the only things that have been able to make that hurt go away, and then only for a while. You think I can keep living like this? My legs don't seem to think so. It's check-out time for me, Ted. There's nothing anyone can do to change that. My only choice left is when and how. Let me do this."

Almost in a panic, Reaper looked to Ben for help. All the smaller man could do was look back at him.

"No," Reaper snarled through clenched teeth. "I carried you out here, I can carry you to the boat. No one gets left behind—ever!"

"Fuck you," Bear said. "One stays or we all stay. Think your boy would like that? Ted," Bear said in a quiet voice, "let me do this, please. It's a pretty good way to go."

Reaper looked to his son, and then to his wife. Tears streamed down both of their silent faces as they watched the man who had come to get them, pull them out of hell, struggle with a fight he didn't know how to win, or accept.

"Company's just about here," Max said from where he watched the approach of the terrorists. "It's time to go."

Reaper looked at his son, who took a tighter grip on his father's sword. Then he looked down at his friend, his Teammate, his brother.

"Are you sure, mate?" Reaper said softly.

"Yes," Bear said with a lopsided smile. "Now go."

Without another word, Reaper turned away. He signaled to the others, who melted into the tree line as more bullets started snapping around them.

Max came over and moved the Shrike closer to Bear.

"Have fun, you crazy squid," Max said.

"Go puke in the lake you cross-eyed Jarhead," Bear said with a wide smile now on his face.

Max turned and went into the woods.

———

It had taken an argument, but now Reaper quickly got the heck out of Dodge with his family. His family's safety depended on Bear to buy them the time they needed to get clear.

Lying by his weapons, Bear looked around for a

second. It really hadn't turned out a bad day at all, the sun shone brightly now and only a few clouds floated in the sky. It was not a bad day at all.

Bear pulled the Shrike up and quickly checked out the belt. There were two feed boxes and one was clipped to the weapon with the belt fed into the feed way. As he snugged himself down into the prone position, Bear felt something sticking into his chest from inside his left shirt pocket. Realizing what it was, Bear paused for a moment and then reached into his pocket. It was his bottle of OxyContin, the pain killers that he had been taking for weeks now. He had put them back where he could reach them easily without thinking about it after showing them to Reaper.

Bear held the bottle in his hand for a moment, looking at the orange plastic container with all of its warning labels. Slowly, he closed his hand in a crushing grip, first cracking and finally collapsing the bottle. He threw the smashed plastic and pills from him, knowing that he wouldn't be having any of his headaches any more. Yup, he thought as he snugged the light machine gun into his shoulder, it was going to be a good day.

The fishing boat had pulled up to the dock and a bunch of shouting men charged toward the house and the hillside beyond. Bear let them exit the boat. Then he opened fire.

Normally, a machine gun is fired in short, controlled bursts. But Bear had no interest in keeping to regulation fire right then. He hadn't anywhere to go, and had plenty of ammunition. The time had come to burn some up. The belt zipped from the ammunition box, feeding the voracious appetite of the machine gun as Bear watched his bullets rip gouts of dirt and grass from the lawn. A lot of those bullets also tore into terrorists. When the first ammunition box emptied, Bear pulled it from the weapon and tossed it away. Quickly reloading with another box, he laid the Shrike back down on his targets.

The long bursts of 5.56mm fired from the Shrike up on the hill ripped across the walls of the mansion. The thick limestone rock that faced the walls of the structure chipped a bit as they easily resisted the onslaught. Windows, doorways, and other openings proved another matter. The high-speed, steel-cored bullets whizzed through the open doorways and tore through the house, ripped and smashed furniture as cushions, dishes, books, and artwork burst and exploded off the shelves and walls.

Three of the terrorists took the weapons they had brought from the boat and ran up to the second floor of the mansion. Quickly diving through several of the rear bedroom's windows, the terrorists made it to the roof above the rear porch without being hit from the machine gun on the point of the ridge only a few hundred meters away. Shooting at that range would be nothing for the men of the Sons of Ishmael; they had trained to fire accurately at much longer ranges.

Bear knew that he would see some real trouble from the roof if he didn't do something about it. He fired the last of his belt through the Shrike in one long burst of fire, raking the lower floors and making sure that anyone who was there would be keeping their heads down for a while. Then he rolled over to the big Lahti antitank rifle. The limestone walls of that big castle might keep the bullets from the Shrike from penetrating into the house, but the builders had never envisioned a rifle this big when they were putting that place up. And the terrorists who took cover behind those upper walls probably thought themselves safe for the moment.

Crawling up to the weapon, Bear picked up the butt end of the big cannon and loaded it. Bright shiny brass shone through each of the three holes in the back of the magazine, indicating that the box was fully loaded. That meant that ten of the foot-long 20mm shells sat in the mag, ready to be fired. Each hardened-steel projectile had been designed to penetrate more than half an inch of armor plate at five hundred meters. They wouldn't have a lot of trouble with the rock walls of the mansion.

Snugging the curved, padded shoulder rest into place, Bear grabbed the silver knob of the rack-and-pinion cocking mechanism on the right side of the gun, right above the pistol grip. Pushing in on the knob unlocked the mechanism. One and a half rotations of the knob pulled the massive bolt back against its springs until it locked in place in the fully rearward position.

A squeeze on the switch on the pistol grip, underneath the trigger guard, released the bolt and it surged forward, stripping a round from the magazine and ramming it into place in the breech of the barrel. Just the sound of the big bolt slamming forward startled Bear a little bit and he jerked his head up. Dirt and wood chips flew from the log he lay behind as a powerful rifle slug slammed right next to where Bear's head had been a moment before.

Somebody in the house had a good idea of where Bear was, but the SEAL had managed to catch a glimpse of the muzzle flash of the rifle that shot at him from behind cover on the roof of the mansion. With the big weapon pulled in hard against his shoulder, Bear tracked the cannon across the house and settled in on the roof area where he had seen the shot come from. He started to squeeze the trigger.

The thundering concussion of the big antitank weapon smashed into Bear's face and the muzzle blast kicked up dirt and leaves in front of his position. Whoever had fired at him absolutely knew where the SEAL hid now. There was no use saving it, he wouldn't be moving this massive gun from his present position. So Bear gritted his teeth, and kept pulling the trigger and the Finnish war machine he controlled started to pump out over 2,200 grain (148 gram) slugs, pushing them through its fifty-one-inch barrel until they left the muzzle at more that 2,600 feet per second (800 meters per second).

———

Kedar had been a sniper during the jihad against the Soviet invaders of Afghanistan. Many troopers fell to his marksmanship with the long SVD Dragunov rifle. His first shot had been rushed and aimed at nothing more than movement up on the ridge. He had missed but the machine gun fire had stopped for the moment and he had the patience of all who had fought the infidels in Afghanistan.

All Kedar had to do was get a single glimpse of whoever fired at them from the woods and he knew that he could bring him down easily. Distances on the island were nothing to someone who had shot across the crags and valleys of Afghanistan. Hidden as he was behind one of the rock crenelations decorating this decadent infidel house, he knew it was only a matter of time before his prey fell to him. Then there came a brilliant flash up on the hillside.

Before the sound of the shot even reached the house, the first of the huge, hardened-steel projectiles fired from the 20mm rifle smashed its way through twelve inches of limestone. The round had been intended to kill the smaller and lighter tanks of World War II and the soft limestone of Ohio was no match for its power. Shards and chips exploded from the inner face of the rock, spraying the terrorists crouching on the roof with the razor-edged fragments. In spite of passing through several layers of rock, the shotgun-shell-sized projectile still had more than enough energy to kill.

Before Kedar could think "Allah is great" and long before he could react to seeing the dust and debris kicked up by the muzzle blast on the crest of the ridge, he fell dead. The Finnish-made tank killer entered his left shoulder, at the base of his neck. The thundering bullet bisected the terrorist's body completely—exiting at his upper right thigh after making a hash of almost every one of his internal organs.

Bear's second and third rounds struck little more than limestone as they smashed through what proved nothing more than a decorative parapet. The mansion may have looked like a castle, but it couldn't stand up to a siege with modern weapons— not even those sixty years old.

The blue-painted steel projectiles and whizzing rock fragments caused three of the terrorists— Mibsam, Dumah, and Adbeel—on the roof to duck down and cover their heads. They had all been under fire in the mountains of Afghanistan, and 7.62mm steel-cored slugs from Soviet PKM machine guns had tossed rock splinters at them before. Even the finger-sized 12.7mm slugs from the powerful DShK "Dashaka" machine guns on the Soviet tanks had smashed up rocks and caused injuries from the chips and shards. But nowhere had they faced bullets that passed right through the rock, causing the stone itself to explode.

Some of the projectiles from the 20mm cannon may not have struck anything more than stone, but the stone itself did more than a little damage. Adbeel had faced Soviet fire in Afghanistan, military weapons in the Sudan, and Serbian steel in Bosnia. In his combat experience, he had never felt pain such as that coursing through his body at that moment. Screaming, he looked at the shattered remnants of his right hand, and the red-stained six-inch splinter of stone that stuck through it, severing the median nerve as it eliminated any future use of the now paralyzed lump of bleeding flesh.

Adbeel's suffering was short-lived, as was the terrorist, when Bear's 20mm cannon finished the job.

As Adbeel screamed and reacted to his wound, his left hand lifted the PG-7 rocket grenade it held. He had prepared the missile for Mibsam's launcher; his fellow warrior was kneeling right next to him. The blast of the powerful RPG-7v launcher was capable of killing a main battle tank, it would have made short work of a simple machine-gun position. But before the round had been loaded, it had been pushed into the path of Bear's fourth shot.

The 20mm projectile smashed through the fluted-metal cone that made up the nose of the RPG-7 rocket warhead. The 380-gram (over half a pound) loading of A-IX-1 high explosive in the shaped-charge RPG-7 warhead did not react to being violated by the 20mm steel slug passing through it. The smaller, but much more sensitive, base detonating element of the fuse was not so forgiving. When the 20mm slug smashed into the 21.8 grams of PETN that made up the detonating booster, it reacted and the fuse element initiated the detonation of the 95 percent RDX explosive filler of the warhead. The resulting blast also detonated the other two RPG-7 rocket rounds that were in a pouch lying on the rooftop. All three high-explosive warheads went up in a sympathetic detonation.

The multiple explosions turned the area behind the parapets into a maelstrom of thundering concussions, flying steel splinters, and ripping shards of rock. The blasts cleared the parapets of functioning terrorists. The body of Miasma, the most experienced RPG gunner of the Sons of Ishmael, flew from the roof, over the crenelations, and down to the flagstones below. Even in death, Miasmaa held on to the weapon he had used so much in life. The loaded RPG-7v launcher lay across the terrorist's body and it sprawled across the stones like an ugly, abandoned puppet.

———

The size and ferocity of the explosion surprised Bear as he lay next to the Lahti antitank rifle. The SEAL didn't know what he had hit, only that the results were spectacular. The orange-white ball of flame from the exploding Soviet munitions put on a good show in addition to the bad guys on the other side of the wall.

Five more rounds from the big antitank rifle fired across the parapets, the big slugs smashing stone, wood, and anything else that got in their way with equal contempt. Even a man as big as Bear got slammed around by the recoil of the Lahti as it rocked back against the springs in its bipod mount. If it hadn't been for the efficiency of the multiholed harmonica muzzle break mounted to the barrel of the gun, the recoil would have been uncontrollable. As it was, the recoil, though fierce, seemed not as bad as the thundering concussion of each shot as it fired.

It took a lot of powder to push that big slug down the long barrel of the Lahti. And that much powder also made a really big bang. His ears now rang painfully, so Bear could no longer hear anything around him, but he could still see quite well.

From the far side of the house, initially out of his sight, the remaining terrorists made a break for the boats that they had left only short minutes before. The docks lay almost four hundred meters away from the house, but the remaining terrorists made a good attempt at imitating Olympic sprinters. They had no idea of the nature of the big gun that had started to tear through the house around them, but they did know they wanted no part of it. Besides, the bulk of their remaining weapons and ammunition remained aboard the two boats.

As the terrorists ran, Bear yanked the now-empty magazine from the top of the Lahti. By his count, there was still a round in the chamber. But he would need something with a little more power, though maybe not as much penetration, as the armor-piercing rounds had given him. One magazine had a broad red stripe around its body. That bright red tape identified the only magazine out of the four they brought that held high-explosive (HE) rounds.

Pulling the big magazine over to him, Bear struggled to lift the heavy ammunition device up and into the Lahti. The massive muscles of his strong body started to fail him at last, his shoulder being badly bruised from the 20mm's recoil not helping any. But he still had the energy and determination to lift the HE magazine up and snap it down and back into place.

Bear knew that his end had finally come. He didn't fear it—death was not only something he had worked with during his SEAL career, but something that he had learned to live with over the past six months. Everybody died, no one got off the planet alive, at least not permanently. But he still had this job to do. His Teammates, his friends, his brothers, all depended on him. It was not in his makeup to let them down and it somehow made his dying have more meaning.

For a few seconds the world seemed to darken, the raging tumor announcing itself in a new way.

The terrorists split up into two groups, the larger band of four men piled aboard the broad-hulled fishing boat and fired up its still-warm engine. The smaller group of three men, including the retreating leader, Ishmael himself, clambered aboard the Fountain Fever speedboat. The big, twin 320-horsepower Mercury engines of the speedboat rumbled and then roared as they started and quickly came up to full throttle. The big, heavy diesel of the fishing boat made much less noise as black smoke belched out of its exhaust stacks.

The speedboat pulled away and accelerated swiftly as Bear finally brought the big 20mm gun into play against the vessels. He slid the rear sight adjustment forward to account for the range he had to use to get to the boats. The speedboat moved too fast for Bear to expect to get a clean shot into it. The fishing boat was another matter.

Steeling himself against the recoil and punishing noise of the shots, Bear opened fire on the fishing boat. From the muzzle of the cannon, 20mm high-explosive shells, intended to destroy light-skinned vehicles or rip apart World War II fighter planes, slashed into the boat hull, passed through the fiber-glass and exploded on the other side.

Tearing open the fuel tanks of the fishing boat, the HE rounds soon had even the hard-to-burn diesel fuel merrily ablaze. As the small vessel started to list to one side and founder, survivors of Bear's high-explosive fusillade tried to jump over-board. When the flames and explosions of the 20mm shells reached the ammunition and explosive stores aboard the terrorist boat only a few seconds later, the thunderous blast left little more than a hole in the water, which immediately closed over the heads of the terrorists' bodies to form a watery grave.

———

The youngest, but most enthusiastic and driven member of the Sons of Ishmael, had chosen to re-main behind and fight the infidel to cover the withdrawal of his brothers and their leader. Hadad's youth limited his experience, yet his fanaticism burned with a white-hot heat, and he fully believed in the cause of Ishmael and his followers. He wasn't only courageous, he had made himself completely unafraid of death. Dying in battle against the infidels simply insured his arrival in Paradise that much sooner.

The booms of the infidel's monster weapon up on the hillside still sounded out, but the deadly shells had stopped crashing through the building. Hadad lifted his head up as he crawled across the floor and looked through the open door out across the porch and to the woods beyond. The flash and spray of materials kicked up by the muzzle blast of the infidel marked his position clearly. He was sure that the AK-47 in his hands would do little to the emplacement.

On the path a short way past the porch walls the body of Mibsam lay sprawled where it had landed after being thrown from the roof. Hadad could plainly see that his brother was dead. No one could survive having his head so flat from hitting the rock walkway. But lying across Mibsam's body was his favored RPG-7v—and the round loaded into the launcher had survived the explosion on the roof. Allah was great and He would see to it that the weapon remained intact and functional, the young terrorist believed with surety. Why else would Allah, all blessing be upon Him, leave such a tool in his path?

Darting forward, Hadad grabbed the RPG-7v and continued to move away from the house. He took cover behind one of the many decorative flower bushes in the huge garden that spread along the rear of the mansion. The fanatic looked over his weapon. Allah be praised! The weapon looked unbroken and functional.

Pulling the pin from the nose of the grenade, Hadad stripped away the safety cap, completing the final preparation of the round for firing. Lifting the almost-twenty-pound launcher and rocket grenade to his shoulder, Hadad pushed the safety button behind the trigger in from the right, taking the firing mechanism off safe. As he brought the weapon to his shoulder, he thumbed back the hammer on the rear of the trigger group.

Knowing he would have only one real chance to make his shot, the terrorist offered a short prayer to Allah, all blessings be upon Him, and then he stood up. Swinging the nose-heavy weapon around to the left, Hadad stuck his right eye firmly to the rubber cup on the back of the 2.5-power PGO-7 prismatic telescopic sight. Setting the two-hundred-meter stadia lines on the top of the grid of the sight reticule on the hillside where the muzzle flashes came from, he pulled the trigger on the firing mechanism.

The huge blast of the propelling charge roared out the back of the launcher, canceling the recoil of the projectile ejected out of the muzzle. Four thin metal fins unfolded from the PG-7 rocket as it flew forward, the sustainer rocket motor firing up with a roar ten meters in front of the launcher. Hadad felt only a puff of warm air from the igniting of the sustainer motor. But the initial blast of launching had deafened him, and shattered several windows in the house behind him.

Unfortunately for Hadad the big antitank rocket

whooshed forward and impacted ten feet below and to the left of Bear's position. The blast of the explosion rocked the big SEAL as he lay behind the Lahti. Steel shards from the rocket's warhead and splinters from the log cover sprayed across his left side. Bleeding badly from a number of wounds, Bear was slammed against the Lahti from the force of the explosion and slumped down onto his weapon.

A warm sensation spread along Bear's left side as he tried to clear the spinning in his head. He knew that there was something very important that he had to do, something that couldn't wait. But he just didn't have the energy to act on it. Then he remembered his Teammates. The same force of will that pushed him through Basic Underwater Demolition/SEAL training, that kept him from quitting during that awful cold and strained exhaustion, that will pushed at him now.

He lifted his head and tried to wipe away whatever had run into his eyes. To his shock Bear's left arm wouldn't obey him anymore. Letting go of the pistol grip, Bear wiped away enough of the blood that had sprayed across his face to see again. Blinking at his blurred vision, Bear could see through what looked like a tunnel. At the end of that tunnel somebody stood and waved something over his head. Bear didn't know the identity of the person, but he knew he had to do something to him.

Blood gushed from his wounds, the worst being at the left side of his neck. Bear didn't know what had happened to him. And if he did, he wouldn't have cared. As the tunnel vision got worse, Bear tried to swing the big cannon around and force the muzzle down and in line with the target. Blurred vision focused on the front sight blade as something in the back of Bear's mind kept saying. "Shoot him in the ass."

The sights of the Lahti remained set for a much longer range than Bear would shoot at now. Only his subconscious mind maintained function well enough to tell him to aim low on his target.

As he started to feel warm all over and the buzzing lessened in his ears, Bear pulled the trigger of the big cannon for the last time. He never even felt the recoil slam him back, or his head fall to the ground. He just lay there and let the warmth and softness finally sweep over him. Satisfied that he had done his job, that his mission was over, he gave up the fight. His last conscious thought was a pleasant one—that it had been a really good day.

The young terrorist didn't have any real thoughts after firing the RPG-7v. As his youthful exuberance caused him to jump up in joy at hitting the infidel's weapon, he waved his arms, yelled, and never thought of the consequences. Turning back to the house, he started to walk back past the body of his brother. He stopped and looked down at the man and realized that he had been better than Mibsam. He could be better than any of them. What they hadn't been able to do, he had done. Yes, him. Hadad. He was the best of them all.

Hadad never felt the big 20mm slug smash into his upper back. As the high-explosive-filled steel projectile crushed into the young terrorist's spine, the old Nazi German-made nose fuse initiated and detonated the filler. The PETN blast went off inside the chest of the terrorist—literally blowing him apart as the shock wave of the explosive combined with the kinetic energy of the projectile.

The combined energies of Bear's last shot blew Hadad's chest open and shattered his torso—it tore him apart as if he had been drawn and quartered by four charging stallions. It was a suitably barbaric end for a barbarian.

Chapter Twenty-nine

Once the decision to move had been made, the team moved fast. Slipping quickly down the side of the small valley, Reaper, his family, and the rest of his men made their way back to the boat much faster than they had left it. With no need for silence, and very little for concealment, speed was what mattered most. As they approached the boat, a voice sounded from within the trees.

"Four," Enzo said.

"Shit," Reaper cursed, having forgotten the countersign for just a moment, "three, I mean three."

Stepping from the brush where he had concealed himself, Enzo held his M14 at high port as he looked at the group.

"Where's Bear?" he asked.

"He had something to do," Reaper said gruffly. Just then, they heard the first burst of machine-gun fire from the far side of the ridge.

"Sounds like he's doing it, too," the SEAL said as he glanced back at the hillside.

The look in everyone's eyes told Enzo that this wouldn't be the best time to ask what had happened. The bursts of fire in the distance were long ones. Whoever was shooting didn't care a whole lot about what they were doing to his gun's barrel. Enzo noticed that along with Bear, the Lahti and the Shrike weren't in sight either. Bear's Jackhammer shotgun was slung across Reaper's back, but that was the only sign of the other SEAL.

The thoughts took only an instant as Enzo started moving and within seconds they had the boat in the water and he was pulling Mary and Ricky on board. Then he moved into the coxswain's position to operate the boat. The rest of the men moved through the water, pushing the SAV II back out into the lake. The little bay's water was cold, but not nearly as bad as that out in the deeper lake. With the weight of the rest of the men off the boat it made the SAV II ride a little higher in the water and helped insure that the props didn't drag on the bottom as Enzo fired up the outboards.

In the background came the thundering booms of the 20mm rifle. After a few rounds had sounded out from the big gun, a much louder blast reached them as something exploded. Reaper was climbing aboard as the roar thundered out. He almost turned and headed back to shore when nothing but silence followed the explosion. Then the thunder of the 20mm opened up again and Reaper knew his friend still played in the game. He climbed aboard the boat and joined his family.

With everyone on board who was coming, Enzo pushed the throttles wide open. The agile boat leaped like a racehorse leaving the starting gates as the outboards roared, the boat dancing across the waves as it picked up speed. Now was not the time for niceties, Enzo thought. They had the precious cargo on board and they had better get a move on.

Another large explosion boomed out from the island, the sound mostly drowned out by the roar of the outboards as the distance between the boat and the island increased. They did not slow down to see what had exploded. One of their own had just given his all so that they had a chance to get away—they were not going to squander that sacrifice.

Off the eastern coast of the island, Ishmael did more than think about the attack; he screamed and cursed about it. Even Bear would have been impressed by the terrorist's command of invective as he swore in Arabic and five other languages. His mission, Shaitan's Blessing, had been destroyed before it was even launched. He cared little for the men he had lost, but the glory he would have reaped and the blow to the Americans was impossible now.

They had been training out on their range at the smaller island, the same place where they practiced with their boats, and had come back to heavy fire—fire that came from near their own headquarters! It had been less than twenty-four hours before they would have launched the greatest operation of Ishmael's career, his life's crowning glory, and it was a shambles! What had happened? How had he brought down this retribution on himself and his men?

As he took a breath and assessed the situation, Ishmael told Naphish at the helm to immediately head south and get them to the mainland as quickly as possible. Maybe whoever had raided the island, probably one of those accursed special operations groups of the American police or military, had missed the transportation that waited in the parking lot back at the harbor. If not, they still had enough arms and ammunition on board the speedboat to come close to wiping out that lakeshore city.

As the 29 Fever sports boat passed the southern-most point of the island, Jetur shouted and pointed. Off to the southwest, skimming across the low waves not more than a few miles ahead, was some black watercraft. It had to be the boat that had been involved with the raid on the island. No helicopters or planes had been heard approaching and no parachutes had been seen dropping in. The only way the raiders could have come in was by boat.

If the people on this boat off in the distance had nothing to do with the shattering of Ishmael's plans, then that was too bad for them. The letting of their blood would help slake his thirst for vengeance for the destroyed Sons of Ishmael.

———

Aboard the SAV II, a signal started beeping from the console of the marine radar. Looking at the panel and then studying the water to starboard, Enzo saw the approaching sports boat.

"We've got company!" Enzo shouted to Reaper.

Staring out to where Enzo was pointing, Reaper saw the long, pointed shape of the 29 Fever sports boat. It moved fast and headed in their direction. It looked like one of the boats from the island.

"Can you outrun them?" Reaper asked.

"Not if that's the boat you had listed back at the farm," Enzo said. "That craft can put on a third more speed than we can. And with the seas having gone down since this morning, we can't outmaneuver them here in the open."

As the sports boat gradually drew closer, Enzo performed a dazzling display of seamanship as he put the SAV II through her paces. No matter how he twisted or turned, the other boat followed his every move. All he accomplished was to give the other boat some time to come a little closer. Finally, Enzo decided on a desperate trick.

"What are you doing?" Reaper said as the boat turned hard to the east and remained on that heading.

"I'm heading for the Wolverine Shoals," Enzo shouted. "Maybe we can sucker these guys in a little too close. The lake's gone down over the last couple of years and the charts don't show the real water over those rocks. We only draw about a foot of water, but that long bastard needs three feet under her keel. With any luck, we can gut them on the rocks."

The idea sounded like something from an old pirate movie, and Enzo was as close to a pirate as they had right now. He had thought it a desperate action, and it was. As the 29 Fever drew closer to the SAV II, the crew aboard it started shooting at the smaller boat.

Behind his beard, Enzo gritted his teeth as he headed for the buoys marking the shoals. Two buoys were anchored on the shallow shoals. Much deeper water lay between them. Enzo wanted to tease the bigger, faster boat around the buoys, draw them in as he made a pass through safe water. Cutting across the shoal would put the bigger boat in real danger.

As he swept through the channel, Enzo wished the buoys indicating the underwater threat weren't so obvious. It became plain to him that whoever drove the sports boat knew just where the dangerous waters were, and would not be suckered in by his risky stunt.

Bullets snapped by overhead as Ishmael and his men fired their AKM-47s wildly at the SAV II. Pointed steel slugs cracked past, and bounced off the water all around the smaller boat. Inside the tiny booth, Mary and Ricky crouched down at Enzo's feet. The rest of the men had covered them with the ballistic dry suits so that the armor panels gave them some small degree of protection. With the AKs puncturing the air around the SAV II, the inevitable finally happened.

An AK slug fired by Jetur skipped off the water, went between the two laboring outboards, and passed through the frame of the seat supporting Enzo. The pointed spitzer slug smacked the big man square in the back, missing his spine by less than an inch. Enzo grunted and staggered, but stayed upright at his station.

The armor panel in the back of his ballistic dry suit had never been intended to stop such a round. But the bounce off the water had taken much of the energy from the 123-grain bullet. The resistance of the armor panel slowed the steel-jacketed projectile and almost stopped it. Enzo wouldn't die from that round, but he would have an incredibly sore back for a while with a spectacular bruise.

Moving quickly up to the big man when he heard him get hit, Ben MacKenzie quickly checked his wound as best he could. When Ben saw that the slug stuck out from the armor in Enzo's suit, he knew the big man was not in any danger from that wound.

Max then opened fire at the sports boat with Enzo's M14. The powerful rifle had the range to hit the other craft, but the bouncing and swerving on the SAV II made any kind of accuracy nearly impossible. The best Max hoped for was to keep the other crew's heads down and reduce their fire. But his shooting had no apparent effect on the 29 Fever.

When Reaper caught a nod from Ben that Enzo was all right, he realized that they had about reached the end of their run. They were being outrun, were outgunned and his family had to be protected. A very dangerous plan formed in his mind. When they had heeled over as Enzo made a turn across the shoal, he could see the rocks speed past no more than a foot or two beneath the surface. That formed the seed of an idea in Reaper's mind. There would be a danger to the SAV II, which would be nothing compared to what the risk would be to him. But Reaper had never been one to consider the risks when the need was great.

"Enzo," Reaper said, "I want you to cut back and make another turn near that buoy. I want you to cut across the shallows back there and then turn her hard to starboard."

"But that will put us even closer to that boat, and they aren't suckering in," Enzo said.

"They might if they think they could grab someone who had fallen overboard," Reaper replied.

"Overboard?" Enzo said. "Who in the hell would go overboard while . . ."

As he asked the question, Enzo looked over at Reaper and saw the M72A3 LAW antitank rocket he had in his hand. His eyes lit up as Reaper's plan became clear to him.

"You got it, Chief," Enzo said as he leaned the boat hard over in a tight turn back along the way they had come.

The M72A3 LAW was a light antitank weapon contained in a green Fiberglas tube. The tube was sealed at both ends and only had to have the covers removed and the tube pulled open to be ready to fire. The 66mm high-explosive rocket in the tube burned all of its propellant while still inside the launcher, making a horrendous boom of a launch signature. But that launch put out a high-explosive warhead that held 304 grams, over half a pound, of the 60-40 HMX/TNT explosive known as Octal. The rocket packed a wallop. The shaped-charge warhead could put a hole in a foot of armor plate once the rocket had traveled past its arming point nine meters from the point of launch.

The buoy flashed past and Enzo put the wheel over hard. Pushing off with his strong legs, Reaper sprang away and catapulted from the side of the boat. He landed and skipped out across the water like a flat, flung rock. Mary screamed and Ricky cried out as they both saw Reaper ejected from the boat as if shot from a cannon. Ishmael also saw the "accident," and he indeed relished the idea of a prisoner. They had been firing back so these were the heathens responsible for his failure. This one could tell him how the Americans had known of Shaitan's Blessing, and he would relish taking a long time finding this out.

Directing Naphish to turn toward where the man had fallen in, Ishmael searched the waters to find a body, but he saw nothing. He hoped the American was just wounded. Having studied the charts of the area carefully as part of his preparations for Shaitan's Blessing, Naphish was careful not to approach the shallows too closely.

———

The almost freezing water crushed into Reaper with much more impact than his slam across the waves had done. He could hold his breath for several minutes if necessary, and this was the most necessary time for that in his life. Yet he found it hard not to gasp as the frigid waters closed over his head.

The weight of the gear he had on helped pull him down. Only a couple of feet of water washed over the rocky floor of the lake. He stayed down and swam away from where he had hit to try to give him a better shot at the sports boat. He held the M72A3 LAW cradled protectively in his arms, but the sealed rocket couldn't take a long submersion. Reaper listened to the sound of the sport boat's engines as it drew closer to where he held fast. The noise of the engines slowed and almost stopped. Reaper crouched and braced his legs against the bottom.

———

As Ishmael watched astounded, the water burst upward as a figure suddenly rose not fifty meters from where they floated. Even as he overcame his surprise and brought his AKM up to fire, the terrorist leader could see the figure struggle with something in his arms, tossing a line away and pulling something apart in his hands. Suddenly, Ishmael understood that was preparing to fire a weapon.

As Ishmael opened his mouth to scream an order at Naphish, the tube on the figure's shoulder exploded with noise, smoke, and flame. The rocket streaked across the waves only a few feet above the water as it passed the nine-meter point where the M412 fuze fully armed. The rocket smashed into the Fiberglas hull of the boat and detonated. The explosive jet formed by the shaped-charge warhead tore through the hull and ruptured the fuel tank. The fury of the rocket's explosion became magnified by the gasoline spray, the boat consumed by a billowing cloud of flame.

EPILOGUE

It was a long four days later that Reaper once again traveled down into Detroit from the farm. Mary hadn't been able to handle what had happened to her and Ricky, and Reaper couldn't blame her. She had decided to move away and take up her maiden name again. That seemed a polite way of telling Reaper that the divorce would go through—and he wouldn't fight it. He had become a danger to Mary and his son, and that wasn't something he could accept.

The divorce might not matter much after the meeting he was headed for. The summons was an official one and he rode his bike to the Federal Building in downtown Detroit. At least they hadn't sent a car full of federal marshals for him.

Moving through downtown on his Harley, Reaper passed the ruins of what had once been a six-story factory and successful nightclub. Construction equipment already worked to clear the mess. The SEAL couldn't see the young black man who had gotten his first real job working with the construction people. A meeting with the devil a week before had changed at least one person's life for the better.

Arriving at the Federal Building, Reaper had a hard time finding a parking space anywhere close to the structure, and an even harder time waited for him as he tried to enter the building. The intense security check included a detailed pass with a magnetometer after going through the normal metal detector. Identification was carefully checked and matched up against the appointments list.

The nation had gone to Orange Alert status only a few days earlier. The heightened state of alert against a terrorist attack was caused by a credible threat to the country. Reaper wondered if he might not have met someone more closely involved with that terrorist threat. If he had, they weren't much of a threat anymore.

The office he finally arrived at had the nondescript look of bureaucracy. The only thing missing was the one-way mirror in the wall. Then the spartan room would have looked just like a police interrogation office—which Reaper suspected it most likely was.

He had no choice in the matter He had fought as part of the system for too long to now fight against it. He hadn't even brought a lawyer to the meeting, over the protests of the rest of the guys at the farm. They had pointed out that they could afford the best defense available for Reaper. But he hadn't wanted to take advantage of the money they had.

Not that Reaper had a fatalistic streak, he simply accepted what he had done. And he would take the blame for everything that had happened on his own shoulders. None of the men who had helped him would even come into the equation. And he wouldn't cost them any more than what they already had given to save his family.

So Reaper sat in one of the available steel-framed, gray upholstered chairs. He placed his hands on the brown-plastic top of the steel-framed table that dominated the center of the room. When a person finally came through the door, Reaper's eyes went wide with the shock of recognition, his reflexes bringing him immediately to his feet.

"At least you still know how to show respect," said Admiral Alan Straker gruffly. "Although you exhibit little for the law. Now, sit down, Reaper, I'm retired now."

Sitting again, Reaper looked over at the man who had once tried to save his career. The admiral, Reaper would always think of him as that, wore a spotless blue suit, snowy white shirt, and a black tie. On his lapel was an American flag pin, and below it a miniature gold SEAL Trident. At least Reaper would be taken down by one of his own.

As Straker sat at the table, he began shuffling through some papers in a file he had brought with him. Long moments stretched out as he read the reports—moments that seemed an eternity for Reaper. Finally, the admiral closed the file and pushed it away.

"It appears that someone thought to ship the feds a box full of illegally obtained intelligence documents," Straker said. "I'm with the Office of Homeland Security now and those documents quickly ended up in my hands. Whoever came up with them knew their value and where to send them so they could do the most good.

"Just to be plain with you, Reaper, you and your partners have broken enough federal, state, and local laws to be put away for roughly forever. Even the Fish and Game people want a piece of your ass. And, pardon the image, but that ass is squarely in my hands right now, Chief.

"You fought your own undeclared war against terrorism, Reaper. I know what drove you to it. It seems that when a Coast Guard team investigated the explosions they found a cook, someone named Hassan Akrit, had survived what I've been informed had to be a serious firestorm on an island resort up in Lake Michigan. He mentioned someone in black, and evidence we found there suggested that there had been two prisoners held against their will—a female and young male. That this evidence resided in the same house as a headless corpse, the corpse of an officer you have had a serious history with, will go unmentioned.

"Chief, the United States is at war now, a declared war against international terrorism. That war has to follow precise rules, and it has to follow international law. And some of those laws prevent certain actions from being officially taken.

"Reaper, I have a choice for you. You can pick what's outside that door or what I'm going to put on the table right here. And what's outside the door are federal marshals waiting to see if I hand them a prisoner."

"And what's on the table?" asked Reaper.

"Not quite a free pass," Straker said, "but as close to one as you're ever going to see. I'll make all of the legal problems go away—but the only way that can happen is if you admit that you've been working for my office as a special consultant over the last several weeks. And that offer extends to those four who are waiting for you out at that farm north of here. Yes, we know about them. And you will remain as my special consultant for an undetermined length of time, receiving support and assignments as my office issues them . . . and only as we do."

Reaper just looked at the man who was one of the leaders he had followed for years. He had been willing to do so then, and he would be willing to do so again. But he had some questions that had to be addressed first.

"All I can do is speak for me, Admiral," Reaper said, "and I will agree to work for you as you see fit. But I have two conditions first—and they aren't really negotiable."

"Conditions!" Straker exploded. "I offer you a part of your life back and you want to list conditions? Exactly what are they?"

———

It was only a few days later when Ted Reaper, Keith Deckert, Max Warrick, Ben MacKenzie, and now Enzo Caronti found themselves back in northern Michigan. This time, they had come to pay their final respects to a fallen comrade. They found it fitting that it was Memorial Day, a holiday when America pays homage to its fallen heroes, because it was a hero who the men came to bury that day. Though had someone called him that while he was alive, he probably would have punched that guy's lights out. There are no heroes in the Teams, only operators.

"How the hell did he get this place opened on a holiday?" Max said as they looked at the closed grave.

"He's an admiral," Enzo said. "They can do things we mere mortals can't. Besides, he said he really liked this place."

"I'm just glad they got his body back for us," Ben said.

"Amen to that," said Deckert. Looking around he added, "It is a nice place, though."

Reaper just looked at the ground where they had placed his Teammate. Bear was in his casket in his motorcycle leathers. A Cuban cigar, its aluminum tube never having been opened, resided in his jacket pocket. On the front of that pocket, polished and gleaming now for all eternity, was the gold Trident of Naval Special Warfare. It had been the last Trident that Reaper had worn while on active duty. He wanted his Teammate to have it.

A glass rested in the casket as well, a twin to the glasses in the hands of the men around the grave. The premium Canadian Club whiskey in the coffin remained in a bottle, the bottle that had already filled the glasses that the men now drained to their friend.

As Reaper stood, smoking a really good Cuban cigar, the sound of a screeching cry in the sky caused him to look up.

Max pulled his own cigar from his mouth as he said in astonishment, "Son of a bitch, is that an eagle?"

Soaring overhead was a bald eagle. It had come back with its mate to the nest that they built up every year. The nest would grow larger, and the eagles would be flying over the area for a long time to come.

"Oh, that's way too corny," Enzo said with a big smile. "Bear would have loved this. Think he set it up?"

"I wouldn't put it past him," Reaper laughed as he watched the magnificent bird fly overhead.

Presents

What can you expect in Harlequin Presents?

Passionate relationships

Revenge and redemption

Emotional intensity

Seduction

Escapist, glamorous settings from around the world

New stories every month

The most handsome and successful heroes

Scores of internationally bestselling writers

Find all this in our November books—on sale now!

Harlequin Presents®

UNCUT

Even more passion for your reading pleasure!

Escape into a world of intense passion and scorching romance! You'll find the drama, the emotion, the international settings and happy endings that you've always loved in Harlequin Presents® novels. But we've turned up the thermostat just a little, so that the relationships really sizzle. Careful, they're almost too hot to handle!

Look for some of your favorite bestselling authors in the UNCUT miniseries!

Sarah Morgan

Million-Dollar Love-Child

uNcut

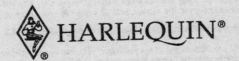

HARLEQUIN®

TORONTO • NEW YORK • LONDON
AMSTERDAM • PARIS • SYDNEY • HAMBURG
STOCKHOLM • ATHENS • TOKYO • MILAN • MADRID
PRAGUE • WARSAW • BUDAPEST • AUCKLAND

ISBN-13: 978-0-373-12582-1
ISBN-10:   0-373-12582-8

MILLION-DOLLAR LOVE-CHILD

First North American Publication 2006.

Copyright © 2006 by Sarah Morgan.

This edition published by arrangement with Harlequin Books S.A.

® and TM are trademarks of the publisher. Trademarks indicated with ® are registered in the United States Patent and Trademark Office, the Canadian Trade Marks Office and in other countries.

www.eHarlequin.com

Printed in U.S.A.

All about the author...
Sarah Morgan

SARAH MORGAN was born in Wiltshire and started writing at the age of eight when she produced an autobiography of her hamster.

At the age of eighteen she traveled to London to train as a nurse in one of London's top teaching hospitals, and she describes what happened in those years as extremely happy and definitely censored! She worked in a number of areas in the hospital after she qualified.

Over time her writing interests had moved on from hamsters to men, and she started creating romance fiction. Her first completed manuscript, written after the birth of her first child, was rejected by Harlequin, but the comments were encouraging, so she tried again; on the third attempt her manuscript *Worth the Risk* was accepted unchanged. She describes receiving the acceptance letter as one of the best moments of her life, after meeting her husband and having her two children.

Sarah still works part-time in a health-related industry and spends the rest of the time with her family trying to squeeze in writing whenever she can. She is an enthusiastic skier and walker, and loves outdoor life.

**To Kim Young, for being a great friend
and a fantastic editor.
Thank you.**

CHAPTER ONE

SHE'D never known fear like it.

Breathing so rapidly that she felt light-headed, Kimberley stood in the imposing glass-walled boardroom on the executive floor of Santoro Investments, staring down at the throbbing, vibrant streets of Rio de Janeiro.

The waiting was torture.

Everything rested on the outcome of this visit—*everything*—and the knowledge made her legs weaken and her insides knot with vicious tension.

It was ironic, she thought helplessly, that the only person who could help her now was the one man she'd sworn never to see again.

Forcing herself to breathe steadily, she closed her eyes for a moment and tried to modify her expectations. He'd probably refuse to see her.

People didn't just arrive unannounced and gain access to a man like Luc Santoro.

She was only sitting here now because his personal assistant had taken pity on her. Stammering out her request to see him, Kimberley had been so pale and anxious that the older woman had become quite concerned and had insisted that she should sit and wait in the privacy of the air-conditioned boardroom. Having brought her a large glass of water, the assistant had given her a smile and assured her that Mr Santoro really wasn't as dangerous as his reputation suggested.

But Kimberley knew differently. Luc Santoro wasn't just dangerous, he was lethal and she knew that it was going to take more than water to make her face the man on the other side of that door.

What was she going to say?

How was she going to tell him?

Where was she going to start?

She couldn't appeal to his sense of decency or his conscience because he possessed neither. Helping others wasn't high on his agenda. He *used* people and, more especially, he used women. She knew that better than anyone. Pain ripped through her as she remembered just how badly he'd treated her. He was a ruthless, self-seeking billionaire with only one focus in his life. The pursuit of pleasure.

And for a short, blissful time, she'd been his pleasure.

Her heart felt like a heavy weight in her chest. Looking back on it now, she couldn't believe how naïve she'd been. *How trusting.* As an idealistic, romantic eighteen-year-old, she'd been willing and eager to share every single part of herself with him. She'd held nothing back because she'd seen no reason to hold anything back. He'd been the one. Her everything. *And she'd been his nothing.*

She curled her fingers into her palms and reminded herself that the objective of today was not to rehash the past. She was going to have to put aside the memory of the pain, the panic and the bone-deep humiliation she'd suffered as a result of his cruel and careless rejection.

None of that mattered now.

There was only one thing that mattered to her, *only one person*, and for the sake of that person she was going to bite her tongue, smile, beg or do whatever it took to ingratiate herself with Luc Santoro—because there was no way she was leaving Brazil without the money she needed.

It was a matter of life and death.

She paced the length of the room, trying to formulate some sort of plan in her mind, trying to work out a reasonable way to ask for five million dollars from a man who had absolutely no feelings for her.

How was she going to tackle the subject?

How was she going to tell him that she was in serious trouble?

And how could she make him care?

She felt a shaft of pure panic and then the door opened and he strolled into the room unannounced, the sun glinting on his glossy black hair, his face hard, handsome and unsmiling.

And Kimberley realised that she was in even more trouble than she'd previously thought.

She looked like a baby deer caught in an ambush.

Without revealing any of his thoughts, Luc surveyed the slender, impossibly beautiful redhead who stood shivering and pale on the far side of his boardroom.

She looked so frightened that he almost found it possible to feel sorry for her. Except that he knew too much about her.

And if he were in her position, he'd be shaking, too.

She had one hell of a nerve, coming here!

Seven years.

He hadn't seen Kimberley Townsend for seven years and *still* she had the ability to seriously disturb his day.

Endless legs, silken hair, soft mouth and a wide, trusting smile—

For a time she'd truly had him fooled with that loving, giving, generous act that she'd perfected. Accustomed to being with women who were as sophisticated and calculating as himself, he'd been charmed and captivated by Kimberley's innocence, openness and her almost childlike honesty.

It was the first and only occasion in his adult life when he'd made a serious error of judgement.

She was a greedy little gold-digger.

He knew that now. And she knew that he knew.

So what could possibly have possessed her to throw herself in his path again?

She was either very brave or very, *very* stupid. He strolled towards her, watching her flinch and tremble and decided that she didn't look particularly brave.

Which just left stupid.

Or desperate?

Kimberley stood with her back to the wall and wondered how she could have forgotten the impact that Luciano Santoro had on women. *How could she ever have thought she could hold a man like him?*

Time had somehow dimmed the memory and the reality was enough to stun her into a temporary silence.

She was tall but he was taller. His shoulders were broad, his physique lithe and athletic and his dark, dangerous looks alone were enough to make a woman forget her own name. The truth was that, even among a race renowned for handsome men, Luc stood out from the crowd.

She stared at him with almost agonizing awareness as he strolled towards her, her eyes sliding over the glossy blue-black hair, the high cheekbones, those thick, thick lashes that shielded brooding, night-dark eyes and down to the darkened jaw of a man who seemed to embody everything it meant to be masculine. He was dressed formally in standard business attire but even the tailored perfection of his dark suit couldn't entirely disguise a nature that bordered on the very edges of civilised. Although he moved in a conventional world, Luc could never be described as 'safe' and it was that subtle hint of danger that added to his almost overwhelming appeal.

His attraction to the opposite sex was as powerful as it was predictable and she'd proved herself to be as susceptible as the rest when it came to his particular brand of lethal charm.

Feeling her heart pound against her chest, she wondered whether she'd been mad to come here.

She didn't move in his league and she never had. They played by a completely different set of rules.

And then she reminded herself firmly that she wasn't here for herself. Given the choice she never would have come near Luc again. But he was her only hope.

'Luciano.'

His eyes mocked her in that lazy, almost bored way that she used to find both aggravating and seductive. 'Very formal. You used to call me Luc.'

He spoke with a cultured male drawl that held just a hint of the dark and dangerous. The staggeringly successful international businessman mingled with the raw, rough boy from the streets.

There was enough of the hard and the tough and the ruthless in him to make her shiver. Of course he was tough and ruthless, she reasoned, trying to control the exaggerated response of her trembling body. Rumour had it that he'd dragged himself from the streets of Rio before building one of the biggest multinational businesses in the world.

'That's in the past.' And she didn't want to remember the past. Didn't want to remember the times she'd cried out his name as he'd shown her yet another way to paradise.

He raised an eyebrow and from the look in his dark eyes she knew that he was experiencing the same memories. The temperature in the room rose by several degrees and the air began to crackle and hum. 'And is that what this meeting is

about? The past? You want closure? You have come to beg
forgiveness and repay the money you stole?'

It was typical of him that the first thing he mentioned was
the money.

For a moment her courage faltered.

'I know it was wrong to use your credit cards—' she licked
her lips '—but I had a good reason—' She broke off and the
carefully prepared speech that she'd rehearsed and rehearsed
in her head dissolved into nothing and suddenly she couldn't
think how on earth she was going to say what needed to be
said.

Now, she urged herself frantically, *tell him now!*

But somehow the right words just wouldn't come.

'You *did* give me the cards—'

'One of the perks of being with me,' Luc said silkily, 'but
when you spent the money, you were no longer with me. I have
to congratulate you. I thought that no woman had the ability
to surprise me—' he paced around her, his voice a soft, lethal
drawl '—and yet you did just that. During our relationship you
spent nothing. You showed no interest in my money. At the
time I thought you were unique amongst your sex. I found your
lack of interest in material things particularly endearing.' His
tone hardened. 'Now I see that you were in fact just clever. Very
clever. You held back on your spending but once you realised
that the relationship was over, you showed your true colours.'

Kimberley's mouth fell open in genuine amazement. What
on earth was he implying? It was *definitely* time to tell him
the truth. 'I can explain where the money went—' She braced
herself for the ultimate confession but he gave a dismissive
shrug that indicated nothing short of total indifference.

'If there is one occupation more boring than watching a
woman shop, it's hearing about it after the event.' Luc's tone
was bored. 'I have absolutely no interest in the finer details
of feminine indulgence.'

'Is that what you think it was?' Kimberley stared at him, aghast. 'You think I spent your money in some sort of childish female tantrum?'

'So you cheered yourself up with some new shoes and handbags.' He gave a sardonic smile. 'It is typically female behaviour. I can assure you I'm no stranger to the perceived benefits of retail therapy.'

Kimberley gasped. 'You are unbelievably insensitive!' Her voice rang with passion, anger and pain and her carefully planned speech flew out of her brain. He thought she'd been *shopping?* 'Shopping was the last thing on my mind! This was *not* retail therapy.' Her whole body trembled with indignation. 'This was *survival*. I needed the money to survive because I gave up everything to be with you. *Everything*. I gave up my job, my flat—*I moved in with you*. It was what you demanded.'

His gaze was cool. 'I don't recall a significant degree of protest on your part.'

She tilted her head back and struggled with her emotions. 'I was in love with you, Luc.' Her voice cracked and she paused for just long enough to regain control. 'I was *so* in love with you that being together was the only thing in my life that made sense. I couldn't see further than what we shared. I certainly couldn't imagine a time when we wouldn't be together.'

'Women do have a tendency to hear wedding bells when they're around me,' he observed dryly. 'In fact I would say, the larger the wallet, the louder the bells.'

'I'm not talking about marriage. I didn't *care* about marriage. I just cared about *you*.'

A muscle flickered in his lean jaw and his eyes hardened. 'Obviously you were planning for the long term.'

It took her a moment to understand the implication of his words. 'You're suggesting it was an act?' She gave a tiny laugh of disbelief and lifted a hand to her throat. Beneath the tips of her fingers she felt her pulse beating rapidly. 'You think I was pretending?'

'You were very convincing,' Luc conceded after a moment's reflection, 'but then the stakes were high, were they not? The prospect of landing a billionaire is often sufficient to produce the most commendable acting skills in a woman.'

Kimberley stared at him.

How could she ever have been foolish enough to give her love to this man? Was her judgement really that bad?

Tears clogged her throat. 'I don't consider you a prize, Luc,' she choked. 'In fact I consider you to be the biggest mistake of my life.'

'Of course you do.' He spread lean bronzed hands and gave a sympathetic smile, but his eyes were hard as flint. 'I can understand that you'd be kicking yourself for letting me slip through your fingers. All I can say is, better luck with the next guy.'

She stared into his cold, handsome face and suddenly she just wanted to sob and sob. 'You deserve to be alone in life, Luc,' she said flatly, battling not to let the emotion show on her face, 'and every woman with a grain of sense is going to let you slip right through her fingers. Given the chance, I'd drop you head first on to a tiled floor from a great height.'

He smiled an arrogant, all-male smile that reflected his unshakeable self-confidence. 'We both know you couldn't get enough of me.'

She gasped, utterly humiliated by the picture he painted. 'That was before I knew what an unfeeling, cold-hearted bastard you were!' She broke off in horror, *appalled* by her rudeness and uncharacteristic loss of control. What had come over her? 'I—I'm sorry, that was unforgivable—'

'Don't apologise for showing your true colours.' Far from being offended, he looked mildly amused. 'Believe it or not,

I prefer honesty in a woman. It saves all sorts of misunderstanding.'

She lifted a hand to her forehead in an attempt to relieve the ache between her temples.

It had been so hard for her to come here. So hard to brace herself to tell him the things that he needed to know. And so far none of it had gone as planned.

She had things that had to be said and she just didn't know how to say them. Instead of talking about the present, they were back in the past and that was the one place she didn't want to be. Unless she could use the past to remind him of what they'd once shared—

'You cared, Luc,' she said softly, her hands dropping to her sides in a helpless gesture. 'I *know* you cared. I felt it.'

She appealed to the man that she'd once believed him to be.

'I was very turned on by the fact I was your first lover,' he agreed in a smooth tone. 'In fact I was totally knocked out by the novelty of the experience. Naturally I was keen for you to enjoy it too. You were very shy and it was in both our interests for you to be relaxed. I did what needed to be done and said what needed to be said.'

Her cheeks flamed with embarrassment. In other words he was so experienced with women that he knew exactly which buttons to press. In her case he'd sensed that she needed closeness and affection. *It hadn't meant anything to him.*

'So you're saying it was all an act?' The pain inside her blossomed. 'Being loving and gentle was just another of your many seduction methods?'

He shrugged as if he could see no problem with that. 'I didn't hear you complaining.'

She closed her eyes. How could she have been so gullible? Yes, she'd been a virgin but that was no excuse for bald stupidity. Sixteen years of living with a man like her father should have taught her everything she needed to know about men. He'd moved from one woman to another, never making a commitment, never giving anything. Just using. Using and discarding. Her mother had walked out just after Kimberley's fourth birthday and from that moment on she had a series of 'Aunties', women who came into her father's life and then left with a volley of shouts and jealous accusations. Kimberley had promised herself that she was never, *ever* going to let a man treat her the way her father treated women. She was going to find one man and she was going to love him.

And then she'd met Luc and for a short, crazy period of time she'd thought he was that man. She'd ignored his reputation with women, ignored any similarities to her father, ignored her promise to herself.

She'd broken all her own rules.

And she'd paid the price.

'What did I ever do to make you treat me so cruelly?' Suddenly she needed to understand. Wanted to know what had gone wrong—how she could have made such an enormous mistake. 'Why did you need other women?'

'I've never been a one woman kind of guy,' he admitted without a trace of apology or regret, 'and you're all pretty much the same, as you went on to prove with your truly awesome spending spree.'

She flinched. This would be a perfect time to confess. To tell him exactly *why* she'd needed the money so badly. She took a deep breath and braced herself for the truth. 'I spent your money because I needed it for something very important,' she said hesitantly, 'and before I tell you exactly what, I want you to know that I *did* try and talk to you at the time but you wouldn't see me, and—'

'Is this conversation going anywhere?' He glanced at his watch in a gesture of supreme boredom. 'I've already told you that your spending habits don't interest me. And if you'd needed funds then maybe you should have tapped your other lover for the cash.'

She gasped. 'I didn't *have* other lovers. You *know* I didn't.'

There'd only ever been him. Just him.

'I don't know anything of the kind.' His eyes hardened. 'On two occasions I returned home to be told that you were "out".'

'Because I was tired of lying in our bed waiting for you to come home from some other woman's arms!' She exploded with exasperation, determined to defend herself. 'Yes, I went out! And you just couldn't stand that, could you? And why not? Because you *always* have to be the one in control.'

'It wasn't about control.' His gaze simmered, dark with all the volatility of his exotic heritage. 'You didn't need to leave. You were *mine*.'

And he thought that wasn't about control?

'You make me sound like a possession!' Her voice rang with pain and frustration. She was *trying* to say what needed to be said but each time she tried to talk about the present they seemed to end up back in the past. 'You treat every woman like a possession! To be used and discarded when you're had enough! That's why our relationship never would have worked. You're ruthless, self-seeking and totally without morals or thought for other people. You expected me to lie there and wait for you to finish partying and come home!'

'Instead of which, you decided to expand your sexual horizons,' he said coldly and she resisted the temptation to leap at him and claw at his handsome face.

How could such an intelligent, successful man be so dense about women? He couldn't see past the end of his nose.

'You went out, so I went out.' Wisps of hair floated across her face and she brushed them away with an impatient hand. 'What was I supposed to do when you weren't there?'

'You were supposed to get some rest,' he delivered in silky tones, 'and wait for me to come home.'

Neanderthal man. She was expected to wait in the cave for the hunter to return.

Exasperated beyond belief, she resisted the temptation to walk out and slam the door. 'This is the twenty-first century, Luc! Women vote. They run companies. They decide their own social lives.'

'And they cheat on their partners.' He gave a sardonic lift of his brows. 'Progress, indeed.'

'I did *not* cheat!' She stared at him in outrage, wondering how such an intelligent man could be so dense when it came to relationships. *She'd loved him so much.* 'You were the one photographed in a restaurant with another woman. Clearly I wasn't enough for you.' She gave a casual shrug and tried to keep the pain out of her voice. 'Naturally I assumed that if you were out seeing other people then I could do the same. But I did not cheat!'

'I don't want the details.'

They were closing in on each other. A step here, a slight movement there.

'Well, perhaps you should, instead of jumping to conclusions,' she suggested shakily, 'and if a sin was committed then it was yours, Luc. I was eighteen years old and yet you seduced me without even a flicker of conscience. And then you moved on without a flicker of conscience. Tell me—did you give it any thought? Before you took my virginity and wrecked my life, *did you give it any thought?'*

His dark gaze swept over her with naked incredulity. 'You have been back in my life for five minutes and already you are snapping and snarling and hurling accusations. You were only too willing to be seduced, my flame-haired temptress, but if you've forgotten that fact then I'm happy to jog your memory.' Without warning he closed lean brown fingers around her wrist and jerked her hard against him. The connection was immediate and powerful.

'That first night, in the back of my car, when you wrapped that amazing body of yours around mine—' his voice was a low, dangerous purr and the warmth of his breath teased her mouth '—was that not an invitation?'

The air around them crackled and sparked with tension.

She tugged at her wrist but he held her easily and she remembered just how much she'd loved that about him. His strength. His vibrant, undiluted masculinity. In fact she'd positively relished the differences between them. His dark male power to her feminine softness. *Her good to his very, very bad.*

He was *so* strong and she'd always felt incredibly safe when she was with him. At the beginning that had been part of the attraction. Particularly that first night, as he'd just reminded her. 'I'd been attacked. I was frightened—'

And he'd rescued her. Using street fighting skills that didn't go with the sleek dinner jacket he'd been wearing, he'd taken on six men and had extracted her with apparently very little damage to himself. As a tactic designed to impress a woman, it had proved a winner.

'So you wanted comfort.' His grip on her wrist tightened. 'So when you slid on to my lap and begged me to kiss you, was that not an invitation? Or was that comfort too?'

Hot colour of mortification flooded her smooth cheeks. 'I don't know what happened to me that night—'

She'd taken one look at him and suddenly believed in fairy tales. Knights. Dragons. Maidens in distress. *He was the one.* Or so she'd thought—

'You discovered your true self,' he said roughly. 'That's what happened. So don't accuse me of seducing you when we both know that I only took what you freely offered. You were hot for me and you stayed hot—'

'I was innocent—'

His breath warmed her mouth and he gave a slow, sexy smile that made her heart thud hard against her chest. 'You were desperate.'

He was going to kiss her.

She recognised the signs, saw the darkening of his eyes and the lowering of those thick, thick lashes as his heated gaze swept her flushed face.

The tension throbbed and pulsed between them and then suddenly he released her with a soft curse and took a step backwards.

'So why are you here?' His tone was suddenly icy cold, and there was anger in the glint of his dark eyes. 'You wish to reminisce? You are hoping for a repeat performance, perhaps? If so, you should probably know that women only get one chance in my bed and you blew it.'

A repeat performance?

Erotic memories flashed through her brain and she took a step backwards, as if to escape from them. 'Let's get this straight.' Despite all her best efforts, her voice shook slightly. *'Nothing* would induce me to climb back into your bed, Luc. Nothing. That was one life experience I have no intention of repeating. Ever. I'm not that stupid.'

He stilled and a look of masculine speculation flickered across his handsome face. 'Is that a fact?'

Too late she realised that a man like Luc would probably consider that a challenge. And he was a man who loved a challenge.

She looked at him helplessly, wondering how on earth the conversation had developed into this. For some reason they were right back where they'd left off seven years before and it wasn't what she'd planned.

She'd intended to be cool and businesslike and to avoid anything remotely personal. Instead of which, their verbal exchange had so far been entirely personal.

And still she hadn't told him what she needed to tell him. Still she hadn't said what needed to be said.

He prowled around her slowly and a slightly mocking smile touched his firm mouth. 'Still so much passion, Kimberley, and still trying to hold it in check and pretend it doesn't exist. That it isn't a part of you and yet how could your nature be anything else?' He brushed a hand over her hair with a mocking smile. 'Never get involved with a woman who has hair the colour of dragon's breath.'

Kimberley lifted her chin and her green eyes flashed. 'And never get involved with a man who has an ego the size of Brazil.'

He laughed. 'Ours was never the most tranquil of relationships, was it *meu amorzinho?*'

Meu amorzinho. He'd always called her that and she'd loved hearing him speak in his native language. It had seemed so much more exotic than the English translation, 'my little love'.

His unexpected laughter released some of the throbbing tension in the room and she felt the colour flood into her face as she remembered, too late, that she'd promised herself she wasn't going to fight with him. She couldn't afford to fight with him. 'We both need to forget the past.' Determined not to let him unsettle her, she took a deep breath and tried to find the tranquillity that usually came naturally to her. 'Both of us have moved on. I'm not the same person any more.'

'You're exactly the same person, Kimberley.' He strolled around her, like a jungle animal assessing its prey. 'Inside, people never really change. It's just the packaging that's different. The way they present themselves to the world.'

Before she could guess his intention, he lifted a lean bronze hand and in a deft, skilful movement removed the clip from her hair.

She gasped a protest and clutched at the fiery mass that tumbled over her shoulders. 'What do you think you're doing?'

'Altering the packaging. Reminding you who you really are under the costume you're wearing.' His burning gaze slid lazily down her body. 'You come in here, suitably dressed to teach a class of schoolchildren or sort books in a library, that hot red hair all twisted away and tamed. On the outside you are all buttoned up and locked away, yet we both know what sort of person you are on the inside.' His dark eyes fixed on hers and his voice was rich and seductive. 'Passionate. Wild.'

His tongue rolled over the words, his accent more pronounced than usual, and she felt her stomach flip over and her knees weaken.

'You're wrong! That's not who I am! You have no idea who I am.' Despite her promise to herself that she'd remain cool, she couldn't hold back the emotion. 'Did you really think I'd be the same pathetic little girl you seduced all those years ago? Do you really think I haven't changed?'

Despite her heated denials, she felt a flash of sexual awareness that appalled her and she squashed it down with grim determination.

She wasn't going to let him do this to her again. She wasn't going to feel anything.

She'd come here to tell him something she should have told him seven years ago, not to resurrect feelings that she'd taken years to bury.

'You weren't pathetic and neither,' he said softly, touching a curl of fiery red hair, 'did I seduce you, determined though you seem to be to believe that. Our passion was as mutual as it was hot, *meu amorzinho*. You were with me all the way.' He said the words 'all the way' with a smooth, erotic emphasis that started a slow burn deep within her pelvis. 'The only difference between us was that you were ashamed of how you felt. I assumed that maturity would allow you to embrace your passionate nature instead of rejecting it.'

To her horror she felt her body start to melt and her breathing grow shallow and she shrank away from him, desperate to stop the reaction.

How?

How, after all these years and all the thinking time she'd had, could she still react to this man?

Did she never learn?

And then she remembered that she *had* learned. The hard way. And it didn't matter how her body responded to this man, this time her brain was in charge. She was older and more experienced and well able to ignore the insidious curl of sexual desire deep in her pelvis.

'This isn't what I came here for.' She lifted a hand to her hair and smoothed it away from her face. 'What happened between you and me isn't important.'

'So you keep saying. So what *is* important enough to bring you all the way back to Rio de Janeiro when you left and swore never to return, I wonder? Our golden beaches? Our dramatic mountains?' His rich accent rolled over the words. 'The addictive beat of the samba? I recall that evening that we danced on my terrace...'

He flicked memories in front of her like a slide show and she looked away for a moment, forcing herself to focus on something bland and inanimate, trying to dilute the disturbing images in her head. The chair drew the full force of her gaze while she composed herself and plucked up the courage to say what she had to say.

'I want us to stop talking about the past.' She paused for a moment and felt her knees turn to liquid. It was now. It had to be now. 'I'm here because—' Her voice cracked and she licked dry lips and tried again. 'I'm trying to tell you—w-we had a son together, Luc, and he's now six years old.' Her heart pounded and her body trembled. 'He's six years old and his life is in danger. I'm here because I need your help. I've no one else to turn to.'

CHAPTER TWO

How could silence seem so loud?

Was he ever going to speak?

Relief that she'd finally told him mingled with apprehension. What was he going to say? How was he going to react to the sudden discovery that he was a father?

'Well, that's inventive.' His tone was flat and he sprawled in the nearest chair, his eyes veiled as he watched her, always the one in control, always the one calling the shots. 'You certainly know how to keep a guy on his toes. I never know what you're going to come up with next.'

Kimberley blinked, totally taken aback.

He didn't believe her?

She'd prepared herself for anger and recrimination. She'd braced herself to be on the receiving end of his hot Brazilian temper. She'd been prepared to explain why she hadn't told him seven years before. But it hadn't once crossed her mind that he might not believe her.

'You seriously think I'd joke about something like that?'

He gave a casual shrug. 'I admit it's in pretty poor taste, but some women will stoop to just about anything to get a man to fork out. And I presume that's what you want? More money?'

It was exactly what she wanted but not for any of the reasons he seemed to be implying.

Her mouth opened and shut and she swallowed hard, totally out of her depth. She hadn't even entertained the possibility that he wouldn't believe her and she honestly didn't know what to say next. She'd geared herself up for this moment and it wasn't going according to her script.

'*Why* wouldn't you believe me?'

'Possibly because women don't suddenly turn up after seven years of silence and announce that they're pregnant.'

'I didn't say I was p-pregnant,' she stammered, appalled and frustrated that he refused to take her seriously. 'I told you he's *six*. He was born precisely forty weeks after we had— after you—' She broke off, blushing furiously, and his gaze dropped to her mouth, lingered and then lifted again.

'After I had my wicked way with you? You're so repressed you can't even bring yourself to say the word "sex".' His dark eyes mocked her gently and she bit her lip, wishing she was more sophisticated—better equipped to deal with this sort of situation. Verbal sparring wasn't her forte and yet she was dealing with a master.

He'd wronged her and yet suddenly she felt as though she should be apologising. 'You're probably wondering why I didn't tell you this before—'

'The thought had crossed my mind.'

'You threw me out, Luc,' she reminded him in a shaky voice, 'and you refused to see me or take my calls. You treated me *abominably*.'

'Relationships end every day of the week,' he drawled in a tone of total indifference. 'Stop being so dramatic.'

'*I was pregnant!*' She rose to her feet, shaking with emotion, goaded into action by his total lack of remorse. 'I decided that you ought to know about your child. I tried to tell you so many times but you cut me out of your life. *And you hurt me.* You hurt me so badly that I decided that no child of mine was going to have you as a father. And *that's* why didn't tell you.' She broke off, waiting for an angry reaction on his part, waiting for him to storm and rant that she hadn't told him sooner.

Instead he raised an eyebrow expectantly. 'Seven years and this is the best you can come up with?'

She stared at him blankly, unable to comprehend his callous indifference. 'Do you think I made that decision lightly? *Have you any idea what making a decision like that does to a person?* I felt screwed up with guilt, Luc! I was depriving my son of a father and I knew that one day I'd have to answer to him for that.' She broke off and dragged a shuddering breath into her starving lungs. 'I have felt guilty every single day for the last seven years. *Every single day.*'

'Yes, well, that's another woman thing—guilt,' Luc said helpfully, 'and I suppose that all this *guilt* suddenly overwhelmed you and that's why you've suddenly decided to share your joyous news with me?'

She shook her head. 'I can't *believe* you're behaving like this. Do you *know* how hard it was for me to come here today? *Have you any idea?*' He was even more unfeeling than she'd believed possible. How could she feel guilt? She should be *proud* that she'd protected her son from this man. But the time for protection had passed and, unfortunately for everyone, she now needed his help. She couldn't afford the luxury of cutting him out of her life. 'What do I have to do to prove that I'm telling the truth?'

Luc turned his head and glanced towards the door expectantly. 'Produce him.' He lifted broad shoulders in a careless shrug. 'That should do the trick.'

She looked at him in disbelief. 'You seriously think I'd drag a six-year-old all the way to Brazil to meet a man who doesn't even know he's a father? This is a huge thing, Luc. We need to discuss how we're going to handle it. How we're going to tell him. It needs to be a joint decision.'

There was a sardonic gleam in his dark eyes. 'Well, that's going to be a problem, isn't it? I don't do joint decisions. Never have, never will. I'm unilateral all the way, *meu amorzinho*. But in this case it really doesn't matter because we both know that this so called "son" of yours, oh, sorry—' he corrected himself with an apologetic smile and a lift of his hand '—I should say son of *"ours"*, shouldn't I?—is a figment of your greedy, money-grabbing imagination. So it would be impossible for you to produce him. Unless you hired someone to play the part. Have you?'

Kimberley gaped at him.

He was an utter bastard!

How could she have forgotten just how cold and unfeeling he was? What a low opinion of women he had? How could she have thought, even for a moment, that she'd made a mistake in not persisting in her attempts to tell him that she was expecting his child? At the time she'd decided that she could never expose a child of hers to a man like him and, listening to him now, she knew that it had *definitely* been the right decision.

People had criticised her behind her back, she knew that, but they were people who came from safe, loving homes— homes where the father came home at night and cared about what happened to his family.

Luc wasn't like that. Luc didn't care about anything or anyone except himself.

He was *just* like her father and she knew only too well what it was like to grow up with a parent like that. She'd been right to protect her child from him and if it hadn't been for her current crisis she would have continued to keep Luc out of his life.

But fate had intervened and she'd decided that she had no choice but to tell him. He *had* to help her. He *had* to take some responsibility, however distasteful he found the prospect of parenthood.

But at the moment he didn't even believe that his son existed—

He seemed to think that their child was some sort of figment of her greedy imagination.

She sank on to the nearest chair, bemused and sickened by his less than flattering assessment of her. 'Why do you have such a low opinion of me?'

'Well, let's see—' he gave a patient smile, as if he was dealing with someone very, *very* stupid '—it could have something to do with the volume of money you spent after we broke up. Or the fact that you're now stooping to depths previously unheard of in order to sue me for maintenance. *Not* the actions of someone destined for sainthood, wouldn't you agree?'

She stared at him blankly. Her mind didn't work along the same lines as his and she was struggling to keep up. 'I'm not suing you for maintenance.'

He gave an impatient frown. 'You want me to pay money for the child.'

She licked her lips. 'Yes, but not to *me* and it's nothing to do with maintenance. I can support our son. I took the money from you because I was pregnant, alone and very scared and I couldn't think how I could possibly bring a child into the world when I didn't even have somewhere to live. I used your money to buy a small flat. If I hadn't done that I would have had to find a job and put the baby into a nursery, and I wanted to care for him myself. And I bought a few essentials.' She gave a tiny frown, momentarily distracted. 'I had no idea how many things a baby needed. I bought a cot and a push-chair, bedding, nappies. I didn't use any of the money on myself. I *know* that technically it was stealing, but I didn't know what else to do so I told myself it was maintenance. If I'd chased you through the courts you would have had to pay a lot more to support Rio.'

One dark eyebrow swooped upwards. *'Rio?'*

She blushed. 'I chose to name him after the city where he was conceived.'

'How quaint.' Luc's tone was a deep, dark drawl loaded with undertones of menace. 'So if I've already paid for the pushchair and the nappies, what else is there? He needs a new school coat, perhaps? His feet have grown and his shoes no longer fit?'

He still didn't believe her.

'Last week I received a kidnap threat.' Her voice shook as she said the words. Perhaps the truth would shake him out of his infuriating cool. 'Someone out there knows about our son. They know you're a father. And they're threatening Rio's life.'

There was a long silence while he watched her, his dark eyes fixed on her pale face.

They were sitting too close to each other. *Much too close.*

Her knee brushed against his and she felt the insidious warmth of awareness spread through her body. Against her will, her eyes slid to the silken dark hairs visible on his wrist and then rested on his strong fingers. *Those long, clever fingers—*

Her body flooded with heat as she remembered how those fingers had introduced her to intimacies that she'd never before imagined and she shifted slightly in her chair. His eyes detected the movement. Instantly his gaze trapped hers and the temperature in the room rose still further.

'Show me the letter.'

Did she imagine the sudden rough tone to his voice? Relieved that she could finally meet one of his demands, she delved into her bag and dragged out the offending letter, dropping it on the table next to him as if it might bite her.

He extended a hand and lifted the letter, no visible sense of urgency apparent in his movements. He flipped it open and read it, his handsome face inscrutable.

'Interesting.' He dropped the letter back on the table. 'So I'm expected to shell out five million dollars and then everyone lives happily ever after? Have I got that right?'

She stared at him, stunned, more than a little taken aback that he didn't seem more concerned for the welfare of his son. Still, at least now he'd seen the evidence, he'd know she was telling the truth.

'Do you think paying is the wrong approach? You think we should go to the police?' She looked at him anxiously and rubbed her fingers across her forehead, trying to ease the pain that pulsed behind her temples. She'd gone over and over it in her head so many times, trying to do the right thing. 'I have thought about it, obviously, but you can see from the letter what he threatened to do if I spoke to the police. I know everyone always says you shouldn't pay blackmailers, but that's very easy to say when it isn't your child in danger and—' her voice cracked '—and I can't play games with his life, Luc. He's everything I have.'

She looked at the strong, hard lines of Luc's face and suddenly wanted him to step in and save her the way he'd saved her that first night they'd met. He was hard and ruthless and he had powerful connections and she knew instinctively that he would be able to handle this situation if he chose to. He could make it go away.

'I think involving the police would *not* be a good idea,' he assured her, rising to his feet in a lithe, athletic movement and pacing across the office to the window. 'Police in any country don't generally appreciate having their time wasted.'

Her eyes widened. 'But why would this waste their time?'

He shot her an impatient look. 'Because we both know that this is all part of your elaborate plan to extract more money from me. I suppose I should just be grateful it took you seven years to work your way through the last lot.' His voice was harsh and contemptuous. 'It was a master stroke suggesting we contact the police because it does add credibility to the situation, but we both know that would have proved somewhat embarrassing if they'd agreed to be involved.'

She stared at him in stunned silence. 'You still think I'm making this whole situation up, don't you?'

'Look at it from my point of view,' he advised silkily. 'You turn up after seven years, demanding money to help a child I know nothing about and whose existence you cannot prove. If he's my child, why didn't you tell me you were pregnant seven years ago?'

'I've already explained!' She ran a hand over the back of her neck to relieve the tension. 'Over and over again I rang and came to your office and you refused to see me. You wouldn't even *talk* to me.'

He'd cut her dead and she'd thought she'd die from the pain. She'd missed him *so* much.

'Our relationship was over and talking about it after the event isn't my forte.' Luc gave a careless shrug. 'Talking is something else that's more of a woman thing than a man thing. A bit like guilt, I suppose.'

'Well, just because you're totally lacking in communication skills, don't blame me now for the fact you weren't told about your child!' Her emotions rumbled like a volcano on the point of eruption. 'I *tried* to tell you, but your listening skills need serious attention.'

His eyes hardened. 'It's a funny thing, but I always find that I become slightly hard of hearing when people are begging me for money.'

She stared at him helplessly. 'He's your *son*—'

He held out a hand. 'So show me a photograph.'

'Sorry?'

'If he exists, then at least show me a photograph.'

She felt as though she was on the witness stand being questioned by a particularly nasty prosecutor. 'I—I don't have one with me. I was in a panic and I didn't think to bring one.' *But she should have.* Should have known Luc would ask to at least see a picture of his child. 'I wasn't expecting to have to prove his existence, so no, I don't have a photograph.'

One dark eyebrow swooped upwards and his hand fell to his side. 'What a loving mother you must be.' His tone was dangerously soft. 'You don't even carry a photograph of your own child.'

She exploded with exasperation. 'I don't *need* to carry a photograph of him because I'm with him virtually every minute of every day and have been since he was born! I used your money to buy a little flat so that I could stay at home and look after him. And now he's older I work from home so that I don't miss a single minute of being with him. I don't need photographs! I have the real thing!'

He inclined his head and a ghost of a smile touched his firm mouth. 'Good answer.'

She shook her head slowly, helpless to know what to do to convince him. 'You think I'm making all this up just to get money for myself?'

'Frankly?' The smile vanished. 'I think you're a greedy, money-grabbing bitch who wants five million dollars and is prepared to go to most distasteful lengths to achieve that goal.' His eyes scanned her face. 'And you can abandon the wounded look—it's less convincing once you've already ripped a guy off big time.'

Her mouth fell open and her body chilled with shock. '*Why* would you think that about me?'

'Because I already know you're greedy,' he said helpfully, checking his watch. 'And now you'll have to excuse me because I have a Japanese delegation waiting in another meeting room who are equally eager to drain my bank account. If they're even half as inventive as you've been then I'm in for an interesting afternoon.'

She stared at him in horrified disbelief.

Was that it?

Was he really going to walk out on her?

She knew instinctively that if he left the room now, she wouldn't see him again. Gaining access to Luciano Santoro was an honour extended only to a privileged few and she sensed that she was on borrowed time.

'No!' She stood up quickly and her voice rang with panic. Her feelings didn't matter any more. Nothing mattered except the safety of her son. 'You can't just send me away! I'm telling the truth and I'll prove it if I have to. I can get Rio on the phone, I can arrange for you to talk to the school, I'll do anything, *absolutely anything,* but you have to give me the money. I'm *begging* you, Luc. *Please* lend me the money. I'll pay you back somehow, but if you don't give it to me I don't know what else to do. I don't know where else to turn—'

She broke off, her slim shoulders drooped as the fight drained out of her, and she slumped into a chair.

He wasn't going to help her. The responsibility of being a single parent had always felt enormous, but never more so than now, when her child's safety was threatened.

She wanted to lean on someone. She wanted to share the burden.

Luc stilled and his dark eyes narrowed. 'For five million dollars you'd do *absolutely anything*?'

There was something in his tone that made her uneasy but she didn't hesitate. 'I'm a mother and what mother wouldn't agree to anything if it meant keeping her child safe?'

'Well, that's a very interesting offer.' His eyes scanned her face thoughtfully. 'I'll think about it.'

She bit her lip and clasped her hands in her lap. 'I need an answer quickly.'

'This is Brazil, *meu amorzinho,*' he reminded gently,

stretching lean muscular legs out in front of him, 'and you of all people should know that we don't do anything quickly.'

She caught her breath, trapped by the burning heat in his eyes and the tense, pulsing atmosphere in the room. All at once she was transported back to long, lazy afternoons making love on his bed, in the swimming pool—afternoons that had stretched into evenings that had stretched into mornings.

She swallowed as she remembered the slow, throbbing, intense heat of those days.

No, Brazilians certainly didn't rush anything.

'The deadline is tomorrow night.'

His eyes gleamed. 'So many shoes, so little time. You think I will just give you the money and let you go? Is that what you think?'

She swallowed, hypnotised by the look in his eyes. 'Luc—'

'Let's look at the facts, shall we?' Lean bronzed fingers beat a slow, menacing rhythm on the glass table. 'You clearly hold me responsible for seducing you seven years ago. You come into my office ignoring the past as though it is a vile disease that you could catch again if you stay close to me for long enough.' His gaze swept over her. 'Everything about you is buttoned up. You are wearing your clothes like armour, protecting yourself and the truth is—' he leaned towards her, his dark eyes mocking '—you are afraid of those things I made you feel, are you not? You are afraid of your own response to me. That is why you deny your feelings. It is so much easier to pretend that they don't exist.'

The breath she'd been about to take lodged in her throat. 'I don't feel anything—'

He gave a lethal smile. 'You forget, *minha docura*, that I was once intimately acquainted with every delicious inch of you. I know the signs. I recognise that flush on your cheeks, I recognise the way your eyes glaze and your lips part just before you beg me to kiss you.'

Completely unsettled by his words, Kimberley rose to her feet so quickly she almost knocked the chair over. 'You're insufferably arrogant!'

Her heart was pounding heavily and everything about her whole body suddenly felt warm and tingly.

'I'm honest,' he drawled, swivelling in his seat so that he could survey her from under slightly lowered lids, 'which is more than you have ever been, I suspect. It is so much easier to blame me, is it not, than to accept responsibility yourself? Why is it that you find sex so shameful, I wonder?'

She couldn't catch her breath properly. 'Because sex should be part of a loving relationship,' she blurted out before she could stop herself and he gave a smile that was totally male.

'If you believe that then clearly maturity has added nothing to your ability to face facts.'

Tears pricked her eyes. '*Why* are you so cynical?'

He shrugged. 'I am realistic and, like most men, I don't need the pretence of love to justify enjoying good sex.'

How had she ever allowed herself to become involved with this man?

They were just *so* different. 'I—I hate you—'

'You don't hate me—' his relaxed pose was in complete contrast to her rising tension '—but I know you *think* you do, which makes this whole situation more intriguing by the minute. You would so much rather be anywhere else but here. Which makes your greed all the more deplorable. You must want money very badly to risk walking into the dragon's den.'

'I've told you why I need the money and this situation has nothing to do with *us*—we've both moved on.' Her fingers curled into her palms. 'I know you're not still interested in me, any more than I'm still interested in you.'

'Is that a fact?' His voice was a deep, dark drawl and he lounged in his seat with careless ease, contemplating her with lazy amusement. 'And what if you're wrong? What if I *am* still interested in you?'

Her mouth dried. 'You're being ridiculous.'

'A word of advice—' His voice was suddenly soft and his eyes glittered, dark and dangerous. 'When you're trying to relieve someone of an indecent sum of money, don't accuse them of being ridiculous.'

She swallowed. How could she ever have thought she was a match for this man? She was a different person around him. Her brain didn't move and her tongue didn't form the right words.

She should never have come, she thought helplessly. 'If you won't lend me the money then there's no more to be said.'

She'd failed.

Panic threatened to choke her and she curled her fingers into her palms and walked towards the door.

'Walk out of that door and you won't be allowed back in,' he informed her in silky tones. 'Come back and sit down.'

Would he be ordering her to sit down if he had no intention of lending her the money?

Hope mingled with caution and she turned, her hand on the door handle and her heart in her mouth.

'I said, sit down.' His strong face was expressionless and, with barely any hesitation, she did as he ordered and then immediately hated herself for being that predictable. For doing exactly what he said.

Wasn't that what her whole life had been like for that one month they'd spent together? He'd commanded and she'd obeyed, too much in love and in lust to even think of resisting. Completely overwhelmed by him in every way. And here she was, seven years on, in his company for less than an hour and still obeying his every command.

Well, it wasn't going to happen that way again.

She wasn't that person any more, and being in the same room as him didn't make her that person.

Her expression was defiant as she looked at him. 'It's a simple question, Luc. Yes or no. It doesn't matter whether I sit or stand and it doesn't matter whether I leave the room. All the information you need is in that letter in front of you.'

The letter he clearly thought was a fake.

She watched in despair as he gave a casual shrug and pushed it away from him in a gesture of total indifference. 'I have no interest in the letter or in your stories about phantom pregnancies. What *does* interest me, *meu amorzinho*, is the fact that you came to me.'

She froze. 'I already told you, I—'

'I heard—' he interrupted her gently, 'you came to me to tell me you would do *absolutely anything* for five million dollars and now I simply have to decide exactly what form *absolutely anything* is going to take. When I've worked it out, you'll be the first to know.'

CHAPTER THREE

BACK in her hotel room, Kimberley dragged off the jacket of her suit and dropped on to the bed, fighting off tears of frustration and anxiety.

She'd blown it. She'd totally blown it.

She'd planned to be calm and rational, to tell him the facts and explain the reasons for having kept Rio's birth a secret from him for so long. But from the moment he'd walked into the room her plans had flown out of the window.

She'd been catapulted back into the past.

And she had less than twenty-four hours before the deadline came and went. Less than twenty-four hours in which to persuade a man with no morals or human decency to deposit five million dollars into the blackmailer's bank account.

The blackmailer he didn't even believe existed.

She took several deep breaths, struggling to hold herself together emotionally. It had been the hardest thing in the world to leave her child at this point in time, when all her instincts as a mother told her to keep him close. But she had known that to bring him on this trip would have been to expose him to even greater danger. And she'd hoped that she would only be in Rio de Janeiro for two days at the most. And after that—

She closed her eyes briefly and took a deep breath. She

hadn't dared think further than this meeting. Hadn't dared think what would happen if Luc refused to lend her the money.

Even now, with the letter still lurking in her handbag, she couldn't quite believe that this was happening. Couldn't believe that someone, somewhere, had discovered the truth about her child's parentage. She'd been so careful *and yet somehow they knew.*

And she'd left her son with the only person in the world that she trusted. The man who was a father figure to him.

As if by telepathy the phone in her bag rang and she answered it swiftly.

'Is he all right?'

Jason's voice came back, reassuringly familiar. 'He's fine. Stop fussing.' They'd agreed not to discuss any details on the phone. 'How are you? Any luck your end?'

Kimberley felt the panic rise again. 'Not yet.' She couldn't bring herself to tell Jason that Luc didn't believe her. Part of her was still hoping for a miracle.

'But Luc agreed to see you this time? You met with him?'

Kimberley's fingers tightened on the phone. 'Oh, yes.' And her whole body was still humming and tingling as a result of that encounter. 'But he won't give me an answer. He's playing games.'

'Did he fall on bended knee and beg your forgiveness for treating you so shoddily?'

Kimberley tipped her head back and struggled with tears as she recalled every detail of their explosive meeting. 'Not exactly—'

'I don't suppose "sorry" is in his vocabulary.' Jason gave a short laugh that was distinctly lacking in humour. 'Hang in there. If he doesn't come banging on your door in the next hour then he isn't the man I think he is.'

Banging on her door? Why would he do that?

Kimberley gave a sigh. She knew only too well that Luc
Santoro didn't go round banging on women's doors. Usually
they fell at his feet and he just scooped them out of his path
and dropped them in his bed until he'd had enough of them.

'I wish I had your confidence. What if he refuses?'

'He won't refuse. Have courage.' Jason's voice was firm.
'But I still think we should talk to the police.'

'No!' She sat bolt upright on the bed and swept her tangled hair out of her eyes. *Not* the police. You saw the note.
You *know* what that man threatened to do—'

'All right. But if you change your mind—'

'I won't change my mind.' She wouldn't do anything that
would jeopardize the safety of her child. 'All I want is to deposit the money in his account as he instructed. I don't want to
do anything that might upset him or give him reason to hurt
Rio.'

Limp with the heat and exhaustion, Kimberley snapped the
phone shut and lay back on the bed and closed her eyes. For
a moment she questioned her decision to stay in this small
hotel with no air-conditioning in a slightly dubious part of Rio
de Janeiro. At the time it had seemed the right thing to do because she didn't want to squander money, but now, with the
perspiration prickling her skin and her head throbbing, she
wished she'd chosen somewhere else. She was hot, she was
miserable and she hadn't eaten or slept since the letter had
arrived two days previously.

Instead she'd spent the time pacing the floor of her London
flat, planning strategy with Jason. It had been hard to act as
if nothing was wrong in front of her little boy. Even harder
to board a plane to Rio de Janeiro without him, because apart
from the time he spent at school or playing with friends, they
were hardly ever apart.

She'd stayed at home when he was little and, with the help
of Jason, a top fashion photographer who she'd met when she

was modelling, she'd started working from home, selling her own designs of jewellery. She'd managed to fit her working hours around caring for her new baby and she'd worked hard to push all thoughts and memories of Luc Santoro out of her system.

And she'd dealt with the enormous guilt by telling herself that there were some men who just weren't cut out to be fathers and Luc was definitely one of them. He was a man like her father—a man who shifted his attention from one woman to the next without any thought of commitment—and she vowed that no child of hers was ever going to experience the utter misery and chronic insecurity that she'd suffered as a child.

Finding the heat suddenly intolerable, Kimberley sprang to her feet and stripped off the rest of her clothes before padding barefoot into the tiny bathroom in an attempt to seek relief from the unrelenting humidity.

The shower could barely be described as such, but it was sufficient to cool her heated flesh and she washed and dried herself and then slid into clean underwear and collapsed back on to the bed, wishing that the ceiling fan worked.

'Presumably this is all part of your plan to gain the sympathy vote, staying in a hotel with no air-conditioning in a part of town that even the police avoid.' His deep, dark drawl came from the doorway and she gave a gasp of shock and sprang off the bed.

She hadn't even heard the door open.

'You can't just walk in here!' She made a grab for her robe and dragged it around herself, self-conscious and just horrified that he'd caught her in such a vulnerable state. Her hair was hanging in dark, damp coils down her back and she wasn't wearing any make-up. She felt completely unprepared for a confrontation with a man like him. 'You should have knocked!'

'You should have locked the door.' He strolled into the room and closed the door firmly behind him, turning the key with a smooth, deliberate movement. 'In this part of town, you can't be too careful.'

Hands shaking, she tied the robe at the waist, still glaring at him. 'What are you doing here?'

'I was under the impression that you wanted an urgent answer to your request for funds.' He strolled across the cramped, airless room and stared out of the smeared window into the grimy, litter infested street below. His broad shoulders all but obliterated the light in the room and she couldn't see his face. 'If your finances are in this bad a state, perhaps you ought to be asking me for more than five million.'

She didn't answer. She couldn't. She could hardly breathe, trapped in this tiny, airless room with Luc Santoro, who dominated every inch of available space with his powerful body. He was still wearing the sleek business suit and the jacket moulded to his shoulders, hinting at masculine strength and power. His glossy hair brushed the collar of his white silk shirt, just on the edges of what would be considered respectable in the cut-throat world of corporate finance. His hard jaw betrayed the tell-tale signs of dark stubble and at that precise moment, even dressed in the suit, he looked more bandit than businessman.

He was wickedly, dangerously attractive and with a rush of horror she felt her nipples harden and push against the soft fabric of her robe.

Mortified by her own reaction, she wrapped her arms around her waist and tried to remind herself that none of that mattered. It didn't matter how her body reacted to this man. This time around, her brain was running the show and all that mattered was her child.

Would he agree to the loan? Would he have come in person if he was going to refuse to help her? Surely he would have sent a minion—one of the thousands of people who worked into the night to ensure that the Santoro empire kept multiplying.

'I've already told you that the money isn't for me.' Nervous and self-conscious, she blurted the words out before she could stop herself. 'I don't know what else to do to convince you.'

He turned to face her, his voice soft. 'To be honest, I'm not particularly interested in your reasons for wanting the money. What does interest me is what you intend to give me in return for my—' he lingered over the word thoughtfully '—let's call it an *investment*, shall we?'

There was something in his eyes that made her suddenly wary and nerves flickered in her stomach, her feminine senses suddenly on full alert. 'I don't understand—'

'No?' He moved away from the window. 'Then allow me to give you a basic lesson in business.' His voice was smooth and he watched her with the unflinching gaze of a hunter studying its prey for weakness. 'A business deal is an exchange of favours. No more. No less. I have something you want. You have something I want.'

Feeling as though she was missing something important, her heart beat faster and she licked dry lips with the tip of her tongue. 'I have nothing that you can possibly want. So I assume you're saying no.'

He lifted a hand and trailed a lean, strong finger down her cheek. 'I'm saying that I'm willing to negotiate.' His finger lingered at the corner of her mouth and his smile was disconcerting. 'I will give you money but I want something in return.'

Not his son.

Dear God, please don't let him ask for his son.

Trying to ignore the sudden flip of her stomach, she stared at him helplessly, hardly daring to breathe. 'What?' What else did she have to offer that could possibly be of interest to him? Her flat in London was ridiculously modest by his standards and she had few other assets. 'What is it you want?'

Not Rio. Please, not Rio—

His hand slid into her hair and his eyes didn't shift from hers. 'You.' He said the word with simple clarity. 'I want you, *minha docura*. Back in my bed. Naked. Until I give you permission to get dressed and leave.'

There was a stunned silence. A stunned silence while parts of her body heated to melting point under the raw sexuality she saw in his dark gaze.

She couldn't believe she'd heard him correctly.

He wanted *her?*

Relief that he hadn't mentioned Rio mingled with a shivering, helpless excitement that she didn't understand.

Somehow she managed to speak, but her voice was a disbelieving croak. 'You *can't* be serious.'

'I never joke about sex.'

'But why?' The blood pounded in her ears and she felt alarmingly dizzy. She wished he'd move away from her. *He was too close.* 'Why would you want me in your bed? We've been there, done that—'

His eyes burned into hers. 'And I want to do it again.' He gave a lazy, predatory smile. 'And again. *And again—*'

The air jammed in her lungs. 'You can have any woman you want—'

'Good,' he said silkily, withdrawing his hand from her hair slowly, as if he were reluctant to let her go. 'Then that's settled.'

He stood with his legs planted firmly apart, in full control mode, completely confident that he could manipulate any situation to his advantage.

'Hold on.' She wished desperately that she hadn't taken off the crisp business suit. It was hard to maintain an icy distance dressed in a virtually transparent robe, especially when the conversation was about sex. 'Are you saying that you'll give me the money if I agree to—' she broke off, having difficulty getting her tongue around the words '—sleep with you?'

'Not sleep, no.' His mouth curved into a slow smile that mocked her hesitation. 'I can assure you that there will be very little sleeping involved.'

Her mouth dried and she hugged the robe more closely around herself, as if to protect herself from the feelings that shot through her body. 'It's a ridiculous suggestion.'

Winged dark brows came together in a sharp frown. 'What's ridiculous about it? I'm merely renewing a relationship.'

'A relationship?' Her voice rose. 'We did *not* have a *relationship*, Luc, we had *sex!*' Relentless, mindless, incredible sex that had neutralized her ability to think straight.

Someone in the next room thumped on the wall and Kimberley closed her eyes in embarrassment.

Luc didn't even register the interruption, his handsome face as inscrutable as ever. 'Sex. Relationships.' He shrugged broad shoulders. 'It's all the same thing.'

Her eyes flew wide and she stared at him in appalled dismay. 'No! It is not the same thing, Luc!' She was so outraged she could hardly breathe and she barely remembered to lower her voice. 'It is not the same thing at all! Not that I'd expect a man with your Neanderthal, macho tendencies to understand that.'

He clearly hadn't changed a bit!

Luc shrugged, supremely indifferent to her opinion. 'Women want different things from men, it's an acknowledged fact. I don't need fluffy romantic to make me feel OK about good sex, but if fluffy romantic makes you feel better then that's your choice.'

Her jaw dropped. He just didn't have a clue. 'I can't believe you'd think I'd even *consider* such a proposition. What sort of woman do you think I am?'

'One who needs five million dollars and is willing to do *"absolutely anything"* to get it.' He was brutal in his assessment of the situation. 'I have something you want. You have something I want. This is a business deal at its most basic.'

It was typical of Luc that he viewed sex as just another commodity, she thought helplessly. Typical that he thought he could just buy whatever he wanted. 'What you're suggesting is immoral.'

'It's honest. But you're not that great at being honest about your feelings, are you?' His gaze locked on hers with burning intent. 'Tell me that you haven't lain in your bed at night unable to sleep because you're thinking about me. Tell me that your body doesn't burn for my touch. *Tell me that you're not remembering what it was like between us.*'

Her breathing grew shallow. She didn't want to remember something she'd spent seven years learning to forget.

Kimberley licked dry lips and her stomach dropped. 'You're prepared to pay to go to bed with a woman, Luc?' She struggled to keep her tone light, not to betray just how much he'd unsettled her. 'You must have lost your touch.'

'You think so?' He smiled. 'There is nothing wrong with my touch, *meu amorzinho*, as you will discover the moment you say yes. And, as for paying—' he gave a dismissive shrug '—I can be a very generous lover when I want to be. The money is nothing. Call it a gift. Only this time I will pay you for your services up front to save you the bother of taking the money afterwards.'

Her desperate need for the money warred with her own powerful sense of self-preservation. It had taken her years to recover from the fallout of their relationship. Years to rebuild her life. How could she even contemplate putting herself back in that position?

She knew from bitter experience that he was incapable of connecting with a woman on any level other than the physical. He was incapable of showing or even *feeling* emotion. *He'd break her heart again if she was foolish enough to let him.*

Except that this time she wasn't an idealistic teenager, she reminded herself. Her expectations were realistic. This time round she knew the man she was dealing with. Understood his shortcomings. Understood that he wasn't capable of a relationship.

And, most of all, this time she would have more sense than to fall in love with him.

She almost laughed at her own thoughts. She was weighing up the facts as if she had a decision to make but the truth was there was no decision to make. What choice did she have?

Given the circumstances, how could she say no?

The only thing that mattered was her son.

So what were Luc's reasons? Why would he want her back when he'd been so determined to end their relationship all those years before?

'Why do you want this when our relationship was over years ago?' She just couldn't bring herself to refer to it as sex, even though that was what it had been. 'I just don't understand.'

'Don't you?' His gaze dropped to her mouth and his dark eyes heated with molten sexuality. 'We have unfinished business, *meu amorzinho*, as you well know.'

Her heart thudded hard against her chest. 'I need time to think about it.' *Time to talk herself into doing something that left her almost breathless with panic.*

'You can have ten seconds,' he offered in a smooth tone, glancing around the basic, threadbare room with an expression of appalled distaste. 'And then we're leaving.'

'Ten seconds?' How she wished she'd booked a room with air-conditioning. It was too hot to think properly and she *needed* to think. Just in case there was an alternative—'That's ridiculous! You can't expect me to make a decision that quickly!'

'And yet it was you who said that you needed the money immediately,' he reminded her, thick dark lashes shielding his expression, 'you who told me there was no time to linger over this decision. The blackmailer is waiting, is he not?'

His tone dripped sarcasm and she stared at him helplessly, looking for a hint of softness, a chink in that solid armour plating which might suggest that for him this arrangement was about something deeper than just animal hunger.

But there was nothing soft about Luciano Santoro and no break in the armour. He was hard, ruthless and he took what he wanted.

And it seemed that he wanted her.

'Why?' The words fell from her lips like a plea. 'Why do you want me back? You yourself said that women don't get a second chance with you. It doesn't make sense.'

'It will make perfect sense when you're naked and underneath me,' he assured her in the confident tone of a man who knew a negotiation was all but over. 'Your thinking time is up, *meu amorzinho*. Yes or no?'

She looked at him with loathing, wondering how he could be so cold and detached. Was he capable of feeling *anything*? All her instincts were warning her to say no and run a mile. But then she thought of her son— 'You leave me no choice.'

'How typical of you to pretend that this isn't what you want. Again I'm cast in the role of big bad wolf.' His smile was faintly mocking and he lifted a hand and gently drew his thumb over her lower lip. 'You can always refuse.'

She stared at him, hypnotised by the heat in his eyes.

How? How could she say no, knowing what that would mean for her child?

And yet how could she say yes, knowing what it would mean for her?

'Unfortunately I cannot refuse.' Her voice didn't sound like her own. There was a cold, bitter edge to it that she didn't recognise. 'Unlike you, my commitment to our child is absolute. And to keep him safe I need the money in my account by to-night.'

'My, we are desperate.'

She lifted her chin. 'I'll climb back into your bed, Luc, if that's what it takes, but you'd better be warned. I'm not the same innocent girl you seduced seven years ago. I'm a very different person now. Be sure you know what you're getting. You may not be able to handle me.'

Having agreed to his terms, a tiny part of her refused to let him have it all his own way. Where in their contract did it say that she had to be nice to him?

She didn't feel nice. She didn't feel nice at all.

She was boiling inside and *angry*.

His eyes gleamed dark and his voice lowered to a sexy purr. 'I can handle you with both hands tied behind my back.'

She lifted her chin and her eyes flashed in blatant challenge. 'You can force me into your bed, Luc, but you can't make me enjoy the experience.'

'You think not?'

He moved remarkably quickly for such a powerfully built man, his mouth coming down on hers with a fierce, driving compulsion which shocked and thrilled in equal measure.

It was savage and basic and he stole, plundered and seduced with the warm promise of his mouth and the hot slide of his tongue until her head swirled and her senses exploded.

He kissed with a sexual expertise that made the pleasure roar in her head and she kissed him back, greedy, starved and desperate for more.

And he gave her more. Gave her exactly what he knew she needed.

With a grunt of masculine satisfaction he kissed her deeper, harder, his hands sliding down her back and anchoring her hard against the proud thrust of his arousal. Her starved body melted and hungered for the virile male feel of him and she pressed closer still, her movements feminine and instinctive.

She shivered with wicked excitement and then gave a soft gasp of protest as he dragged his mouth away from hers, leaving her shaking and gasping. She felt the roughness of male stubble graze the soft skin of her cheek and then he released her so suddenly that she almost fell.

'As I said,' he drawled softly, spreading his hands like a magician who had just performed an incredible trick for the benefit of a rapt audience, 'I can handle you with both hands tied behind my back if necessary. No problem.'

Dazed and still fighting the explosion of sensual fireworks that his touch had released, she struggled to bring herself back to the present. Her insides were spinning and her brain was foggy.

If she'd needed proof that she was still vulnerable to Luc Santoro's particular brand of macho sex appeal, then she had it now and she found the knowledge that he could still make her forget everything, just by kissing her, deeply humiliating.

'Thank you for reminding me that I really, *really* hate you.'

'I think I've just proved that you don't.' He gave a shrug that suggested that her feelings were a matter of complete indifference to him. 'And stop pretending that this deal is going to be a hardship to you when we both know you're going to be sobbing and begging the moment I get you back in my bed.'

Goaded past the point of self-control, she lifted a hand and slapped him hard across his lean bronzed cheek—so hard that her palm stung. Shocked and mortified, her hand fell to her side and she stepped back with a gasp of horror.

Never before in her life had she struck anyone or anything, but the image he'd painted of the person she'd been in his bed had been so agonisingly embarrassing that she'd been unable

to control herself, and her cheeks flamed at the less than subtle reminder of how eager she'd once been for his caresses.
Instantly she vowed that, no matter what happened, *no matter what he did to her,* the next time he touched her she
wouldn't respond. She wasn't going to give him the satisfaction. *Whatever it took,* she was going to just lie there.

'You're so wrong about me. I *do* hate you—' Her passionate declaration fell from her lips like a sob. 'I truly hate you
for turning me into a person that I don't even recognise.'

'That's because you've conveniently forgotten the person
you really are.' He touched long fingers to the livid red streak
that had appeared high on his cheek, his expression thoughtful. 'I look forward to reminding you. Over and over again,
meu amorzinho.'

She stared at him, her chest rising and falling as she struggled to contain the emotion that boiled inside her. 'You're
about to discover the woman I really am, Luc, and I just hope
it doesn't come as a shock because there's no refund.' She
lifted a hand to her throat, struggling to calm herself. 'How
long do you expect this charade to last?'

'Until I've finished with you.'

She felt a shaft of maternal panic. 'I have to get home to
my son.'

'I don't want to hear any more about this "son",' Luc
growled, 'and, just for the record, next time you decide to pin
a paternity suit on a guy, don't wait seven years to do it.'

If she'd had a gun she would have shot him for his total
insensitivity. Instead she stared at him, angry and frustrated,
wondering what she had to do to convince him of Rio's existence. But then she realised that she really didn't *need* him
to believe her. All she needed was the money, and it seemed
he was willing to give her that.

Providing she agreed to resume their relationship.

She closed her eyes and allowed herself one last frantic attempt to find an alternative, but there wasn't one. And she knew there wasn't one because he had always been her last resort. If there'd been any other conceivable way of raising the money, then she would have found it, but who else could give her five million dollars as easily as blinking?

Her son would be fine without her for a short time, she assured herself firmly, trying to ignore the maternal anxiety that twisted inside her. Jason was like a father to him. Jason would make sure that no harm came to her child. As for her—*she couldn't escape the feeling that she was now in more danger than her child.*

She opened her eyes. 'Two weeks. I can stay no more than two weeks.' She needed to put a time frame on it. Needed to know when she was going home. 'And I didn't pack for a long stay so I'll need to buy something to wear.'

She was proud of her flat, practical tone but he merely smiled in that maddening fashion that never failed to raise her pulse rate. 'Dress by all means, because I have no desire to share your more private attractions with the rest of Brazil, but you don't need to buy anything to wear. For what I have in mind,' he purred softly, 'you're not going to need clothes.'

Her eyes widened. 'But—'

'My car is parked outside and drawing attention even as we speak,' he said smoothly, 'so, unless we wish to begin the second chapter of our relationship the way we began the first, with a brawl on the streets, I suggest we make a move.'

He was no stranger to violence, she knew that from the way he'd handled himself the first night they'd met. And he was no stranger to the darker, rougher side of Rio de Janeiro. But the rumours that he had taken himself from the poverty of the *favelas*, the famed slums of Rio, to billionaire status, had never been confirmed, because Luc Santoro flatly refused to talk about his personal life.

He would talk about the money markets and business in

general, but questions of a more personal nature were skilfully deflected. Luc Santoro remained something of an enigma, which simply served to increase his fascination for the media. *And for women.*

Grabbing her clothes, Kimberley took refuge in the bathroom and dressed quickly. She twisted her hair back on top of her head, buttoned the jacket of her suit and gave her reflection a grim smile. This was a business deal. Nothing more. She was not going to scream or beg. And, most of all, she was *not* going to fall in love.

She almost laughed at the thought.

That was the one aspect of this deal of which she could be entirely confident. There was absolutely *no* risk of her falling in love with him. This time she'd be walking away from the relationship with both her heart and her head in perfect working order.

Drawing confidence from that fact, she opened the bathroom door, picked up her bag and walked towards the door. 'Shall we go?'

Luc cast a disparaging look at the lift and took the stairs. 'If we risk climbing into that thing we may find ourselves stuck for the foreseeable future. Why did you pick this hotel when Rio de Janeiro has so much better to offer?'

Because she'd been saving money.

'It has charm,' she said blithely and his eyes gleamed with appreciative humour.

'If this is the standard that is required to win your approval then I'm not going to have to work very hard to impress you.'

Momentarily transfixed by his smile, her heart gave a tiny flip and then she remembered that Luc used charm like a weapon when it suited him.

'Nothing you do could ever impress me, Luc.'

She'd never been particularly interested in material things.

For her, the true attraction had been the man himself. Luc
Santoro approached life with a cool confidence in his own
ability to win in every situation. To him, obstacles existed to
be smashed down and the greater the problem then the bigger the challenge. And he was a man who loved a challenge.
His belief in himself was nothing short of monumental and
that, combined with his indecent wealth and staggering dose
of sex appeal, made him a prime target for every single
woman on the planet.

And he'd chosen her.

There were mornings she'd woken up in his enormous
bed, limp and exhausted after a night of relentless sensual exploration, and feasted her eyes on his bronzed male perfection, unable to believe that he was really her man and that this
was actually *her life*.

But it hadn't been her life for anywhere near long enough
and yet how could anything so perfect ever be anything but
ephemeral?

Real life wasn't like that, she reminded herself gloomily
as they arrived in the foyer of the hotel. Sixteen years of living with her father had taught her that.

Luc gestured towards the long silver limousine that was
parked at the front of the hotel. A driver stood by the open
door while a bodyguard stood eyeing the streets around them.

Kimberley frowned. Because Luc was so obviously capable of looking after himself physically, it hadn't really occurred to her that he was a target for crime, but of course he
must be, and she gave a little shiver, once more reminded of
the letter that lay in her bag.

'Let's go.' His hand was planted firmly in her back but she
tried to stop, still reluctant to relinquish her independence.

'I need to settle my bill.'

'You mean they charge to stay in this place?' There was a
glimmer of humour in his dark eyes as he urged her into the

mousine without allowing her time to pause. 'My staff will deal with it. We need to get out of here before the press arrive, unless you wish to find yourself plastered all over tomorrow's newspapers as an object of speculation for half the world. I have a feeling that *"Woman sold to highest bidder"* would make a very appealing headline for the tabloid press.'

She ignored his sarcasm and frowned slightly. She'd forgotten that Luc Santoro was always an object of press attention and so was any woman seen with him. As one of the richest, most eligible bachelors in the world, it was inevitable that he attracted more than his fair share of media interest and attention.

Out on the street in the sun several flash bulbs went off in her face and Kimberley froze, dazzled and taken by surprise.

'Get into the car,' Luc ordered harshly, just as his bodyguard leaped forward to deal with the photographers.

CHAPTER FOUR

KIMBERLEY slid into the luxurious interior of the vehicle, grateful for the darkened windows that afforded a degree of privacy for those inside.

'How did they know you were here?' She stared at the group of photographers, watching as Luc's bodyguard ushered them out of the way.

'The press follow me everywhere and they also follow anyone who is linked to me in any way,' Luc reminded her in a grim tone, his lean, handsome face taut as he leaned forward and issued a string of instructions to his driver, who promptly accelerated away, leaving the photographers scrambling for their own transport.

'Perhaps if you didn't drive around in a car that shrieks "look at me" you might escape their attention,' she muttered, knowing even as she said the words that it would be virtually impossible for Luc Santoro to be incognito. Everything about him was high profile. He headed up a hugely successful global business and was no stranger to controversy. Added to that, his continued status as a rich playboy meant that he was a constant source of fascination for the world's media. Every woman he was seen with provided days of speculation in the newspapers. *Was this the one? Had a woman finally tamed the Brazilian bad boy?*

It had been the same when she had been with him. They hadn't even been out in public, she recalled bitterly, and yet still the press had managed to snap photos of her climbing into his car. And it had been the media that had alerted her to the fact that he'd left her bed to spend an evening with another woman. *And the media who'd printed pictures of her on the day he'd had her driven to the airport, her expression traumatised, her eyes huge and bruised from too much crying.*

Luc lounged back in his seat, indifferent to what was happening outside the confines of his car. 'I hardly need to remind you that you were the one who chose to book into a hotel in one of the seedier parts of Rio. At least the car is air-conditioned so we can indulge in conversation without risking heatstroke.'

'You were born here. You don't feel the heat.'

He reached across the back of the seat and twisted a coil of her hair around lean bronzed fingers, his eyes trapping hers. 'Whereas you, *minha docura,*' he breathed softly, 'with your blazing hair and your snowy white skin, were designed to be kept indoors in a man's bed, well away from the heat of the sun.'

Her heart thudded against her chest and she felt a vicious stab of sexual awareness deep inside her. 'I prefer the more traditional approach of a hat and sunscreen. And your attitude to women is positively Neolithic.'

The truth was, the heat that could do her the most damage, *the heat that she feared most,* didn't come from the sun.

She felt the gentle pressure on her scalp as he twisted the hair around his fingers and felt her stomach tumble. For a moment she just gazed at him helplessly, captivated by the burning masculine appraisal she saw in his eyes.

It had always begun like this—with his hands in her hair. He'd used her hair as a tool in his seduction. How many times had he murmured that it was the sexiest part of her? How many times had he raked his fingers through the thick copper waves and then wound the strands round his hands to hold her head still for his kiss? Her hair had become an erotic, sensual part of their lovemaking.

Hypnotised by the memories and by the look in his eyes, Kimberley felt a curl of heat low in her pelvis. Her breath jammed in her throat and for a brief, crazy moment her body swayed towards his, lured by the look in his partly veiled eyes and the almost irresistible draw of his hard mouth.

She remembered only too well what that mouth could do to her. *How it felt to be kissed by him.*

And then she also remembered what a cold-hearted, unfeeling man he was and she lifted a hand, removing her hair from his toying fingers with a determined jerk.

'*Don't* touch me—'

'I'm paying you for the privilege of doing just that,' he reminded her in soft tones, 'but I'm prepared to wait until there are no camera lenses around.'

She waited for him to slide back across the seat but he didn't move, his powerful shoulders only inches from hers.

'It's strange that you're so flushed,' he observed in a soft purr, his eyes raking her face. 'Why is that, I wonder?'

She tried to move further away from him but she was trapped against the door of the car with nowhere to go. 'As you yourself pointed out, I'm not great in the heat,' she stammered hoarsely and he gave a knowing smile.

'The car is air-conditioned and we both know perfectly well that it isn't the heat that's bothering you. You want me, *meu amorzinho*, every bit as much as I want you and eventually you're going to stop playing games and admit it.'

Her heart lurched. 'You have an exaggerated opinion of your own attractions,' she said witheringly and he gave a laugh of genuine amusement and slid back across the seat, finally giving her the space she'd thought she craved.

Alarmingly, it didn't seem to make any difference to the growing ache deep in her pelvis. Trapped within the confines of his car, she was still agonizingly aware of his lean, muscular body, sprawled with careless ease in the leather seat.

His phone rang and he gave a frown of irritation as he answered it in his native tongue, switching to rapid, fluent Italian once he identified the caller.

Kimberley watched helplessly, trying not to be impressed by the apparent ease with which he communicated in yet another language, wondering what it was about this man that affected her so deeply. She'd met plenty of handsome men in her time and plenty of clever, successful men. But none of them had once threatened her equilibrium in the way that Luc Santoro did. What was it that made him different? What was it that made her respond to him even though she knew he was so bad for her?

They were *completely* unsuited. They didn't want the same things out of life.

Luc didn't do relationships. Luc just did sex. And the really appalling thing was that he didn't believe there was a difference.

Not for the first time, she wondered what had happened in his life to bring him to that conclusion, but she knew better than to ask. Luc didn't talk about his past. In fact, in the short time they'd spent together, they'd barely talked at all. All their communication had been physical. As a result, she knew next to nothing about him.

He ended the call, snapped the phone shut and she cast a speculative look in his direction.

'Just how many languages do you speak?'

'My business is global, so enough to ensure that everything runs smoothly and I don't get fleeced.' As usual he gave nothing away and she rolled her eyes in exasperation.

'Your conversation skills are so limited that I don't suppose you need a very extensive vocabulary,' she muttered sarcastically. 'You just need to be able to boss people around. You're definitely fluent in He-man.'

He dropped the phone back into his pocket with a laugh. 'It was interesting,' he observed smoothly, 'that you were in my bed for almost a month and only at the end did I see that glorious temper. The signs were always there, of course, only your passion was otherwise directed.'

Kimberley felt a stab of pain as he dropped in yet another reminder of just how uninhibited she'd been during the month they'd spent together. The truth was she'd been so deliriously, ecstatically in love with him that she hadn't seen any reason to hold back. Hadn't realised what sort of man Luc Santoro really was. *Hadn't understood how totally different they were.*

'I hadn't been to bed with a man before,' she said tonelessly. 'It was the novelty factor.' It was a feeble attempt to defend herself and it drew nothing but a mocking gaze from her tormentor.

'The novelty factor?'

Breathing was suddenly a challenge. 'Of course. I was young and I discovered sex for the first time. What did you expect? It would have been the same with anybody.'

'You think so?' His eyes gleamed dark and dangerous as he leaned towards her, his gaze disturbingly intense. 'We barely touched the surface of sensuality,' he drawled huskily, 'but now I think you're ready to be moved on to the next level, *meu amorzinho.*'

Her mouth dried, her heart thudded hard against her chest and suddenly everything around her seemed to be happening in slow motion. She felt a flicker of alarm, mixed with a tinge of an intense excitement that horrified her. 'What do you mean, the next level?'

'Seven years ago you were a virgin. I was your first sexual experience, so naturally I was very careful with you.' His firm mouth curved into a smile of masculine anticipation. 'Now, as you keep reminding me, things are different. The girl is grown up. It's time to discover the woman. This time there will be no holding back.'

Holding back?

Recalling the fierce intensity of their lovemaking, Kimberley wondered exactly what he'd been holding back. She remembered how they'd hungered for each other. She remembered the burning desperation as they slaked their need time and time again. She remembered the heat and the explosive passion. But she didn't remember anything that could have been described as holding back.

Her stomach clenched.

So what exactly did he have in mind this time?

She tore her gaze away from his, horrified by the sexual awareness sizzling through her body. She wanted so badly to feel nothing, to be indifferent, and yet she felt *everything* and the knowledge just appalled her.

She'd spent the last seven years concentrating on making a good life for her child and never once during that time had she experienced even the smallest inclination to become involved with another man.

Her experience with Luc had put her off men completely. It had taken her so long to piece herself back together that she'd assumed she was no longer capable of experiencing such depth of feeling. The discovery that she *was* shocked and horrified her.

It was just physical, she told herself firmly, nothing more than that.

She'd denied herself for so long that it was hardly surprising that her body had reawakened. And so what? She gave a mental shrug. As he rightly said, she was a woman now. She wasn't a naïve girl. She knew that Luc wasn't capable of love and she no longer expected it. They could have sex and then she could walk away back to her old life.

'The question is, can you cope with the woman, Luc?' She threw him a cool, challenging look. 'As you rightly said, the girl has grown up. And, like I said, be careful you don't find yourself with more than you can handle.'

'We've already established that I can handle you.' His dark eyes narrowed. 'And the mere fact that you've agreed to this shows that you are as eager as me to renew our relationship.'

'We didn't have a relationship,' she said flatly. 'We had sex, and I agreed to this because you left me no choice.'

'We always have choices.' For a brief second his expression was bleak and then the moment passed and his eyes held their customary mocking expression. 'It's just that some of them are more difficult than others. That's life.'

She stared at him with mounting frustration. He really thought she was willing to go to bed with him just to satisfy an indecent lust for retail therapy? Did he really have such a low opinion of her?

For a wild moment she was tempted to try one more time to convince him about the existence of his child, but she knew there was no point. 'You're paying me to sleep with you,' she reminded him coldly, 'not to indulge in conversation. That's going to cost you extra.'

Far from being annoyed, he laughed. 'I believe my bank balance will remain unthreatened. You still don't know men very well, *meu amorzinho*. Talking is something that women want, not men. I have no intention of paying you to talk. To be honest, I couldn't care less if you don't speak at all for the next two weeks.'

His gaze shimmered with molten sexuality and suddenly the luxurious interior of the car seemed hotly oppressive. She shifted in her seat, trying desperately to ignore the wicked curl of her stomach.

'Where are we going, anyway?'

He threw her a predatory smile. 'My lair.'

The smooth intimacy of his tone was more than a little disturbing and she felt her breath catch. 'Which one?'

'To my office and from there we'll fly to the island.'

Her fingers curled into her palms. His island. West of Rio was the beautiful Emerald coast, littered with islands, some of them owned by the rich and privileged.

'You mean you're prepared to abandon work?'

'Some things are worthy of my full attention.'

The fact that he was planning to sequester her somewhere secluded increased her tension.

As an impressionable eighteen-year-old, she'd fallen in love with the stunning scenery of this part of Brazil, the forests and the mountains and most of all the beaches. And she'd been overwhelmed by the sheer indulgence of staying on Luc's private island, with all the accompanying luxury and privacy.

During the time they'd spent there, she'd been cocooned in a romantic haze, so sexually sated and madly in love with Luc and the exotic beauty of her surroundings that she couldn't imagine ever wanting to live anywhere else. All her memories of him were tied up with that one special place and she had no desire to return there.

It was just too raw.

'You have other homes,' she croaked. 'Can't we stay somewhere else?'

Somewhere that wouldn't remind her of the past—*of the humiliating completeness of her surrender.* Somewhere that wasn't brimming with memories.

She knew he had an apartment in New York and homes in Paris and Geneva. In fact, one of the reasons she'd chosen to settle in London was because it was the one place where Luc didn't have a home so she was unlikely to bump into him.

His eyes gleamed with masculine amusement. 'For what I have in mind, I require privacy and the island is perfect for that. And anyway—' he gave a careless shrug '—I'm still close enough to the office to be able to fly back if necessary.'

'Business. Business. Business.' She stared at him in exasperation, her nerves jumping and her senses humming. 'Is that all you ever think of?'

'No.' His reply was a sensual purr. 'I also think about sex. Like now, for instance.' He leaned his head back against the seat, his expression inscrutable. 'I'm cursing the need for me to return to the office to sign some papers when all I want to do is fly straight to the island and strip you naked.'

His words should have shocked her, but instead a wicked thrill flashed through her and her tummy muscles tightened. Suddenly she was aware of every masculine inch of him and just hated herself for feeling excitement when what she wanted to feel was indifference. 'You have a totally one track mind, do you know that?'

She told herself that it didn't matter what she felt as long as she didn't reveal those feelings to him. Last time she'd offered every single part of herself and he'd rejected her. This time she would give nothing except her body.

'If by "one track mind" you mean that I know what I want and I make sure that I get it, then yes—' he gave a lethal smile '—I have a one track mind. And as soon as these papers are signed, my mind is going to be on you, *meu amorzinho,* and you're going to discover just how fixed on one track my mind can be.'

His gaze slid down her body in a leisurely scrutiny and she struggled and fought against the wicked excitement that burned low in her pelvis.

He was the sexiest man she'd ever encountered, Kimberley thought helplessly, dragging her eyes away from his shimmering dark eyes and staring out of the car window in quiet desperation. She didn't want to notice anything about him, but instead she found herself noticing *everything*.

Determined not to sink under his seductive spell a second time, she tried to talk some sense into herself.

Sexy wasn't enough.

She reminded herself that this man was a control freak who was incapable of feeling or expressing normal human emotions.

She reminded herself that he'd taken her heart and chopped it into a million tiny pieces.

She reminded herself that she'd spent years building a new life after their scorching, intense, but all too brief relationship had ended.

Suddenly aware that the car had stopped, she realised that she'd barely even noticed the journey. All her attention had been focused on Luc.

A perfectly normal reaction, she tried to assure herself as she unfastened her seat belt. She hadn't seen him for years and he was the father of her child. They shared plenty of history. It was understandable that she'd find him impossible to ignore.

His driver held the door for her and she stepped out. For a wild moment she was tempted to turn and run along the sun-baked pavement and lose herself in the streets of Rio, but her bag was on her shoulder and in her bag was the letter.

The letter that had changed her life.

She wasn't in a position to run anywhere.

She needed five million dollars and the only man who could give her that was Luc Santoro.

And perhaps he read her mind because he paused for a moment on the pavement, watching her with those amazingly sexy dark eyes. Then he placed a hand firmly in the small of her back and walked her into the building.

'Loitering on pavements is not an occupation to be commended,' he observed dryly, striding towards the express lift without looking left or right, very much the king of his domain.

He urged her inside, hit a button and the doors slid together, closing out the outside world. A tense, intimate silence folded around them. Suddenly she was breathlessly, helplessly aware that she was alone in this confined space with the one man capable of turning her perfectly ordered life upside down.

Struggling to control the tiny tremors that shook her body, Kimberley stared at the floor but she felt the attraction pulsing between them like the pull of a magnet.

With a quiet desperation she risked a glance at him, expecting to find him watching the passage of the lift upwards. Instead their eyes locked and the last of her sanity fizzled out, torched by the sexual awareness that flared between them.

His handsome features grim and set, he gave a harsh curse and powered her back against the wall of the lift, his mouth hard and hungry as he kissed her with unrelenting passion.

Driven to fever pitch by the tension that had been mounting between them since she'd walked back into his office less than twenty-four hours earlier, she kissed him back, their tongues blending, her desperation more than matching his.

Her arms slid round his neck and her fingers jammed into his dark hair as he took her mouth with erotic expertise, exploring and seducing until her body was humming with unrelieved sexual need and her mind was numb. Every rational thought slid from her brain and she ceased to be a thinking, intelligent woman. Instead she responded with almost animal desperation, her head swimming with a wild hunger that was outside her control.

His eyes still burning into hers, he released a throaty groan of masculine appreciation and, without lifting his mouth, he yanked her skirt upwards and his hands slid down to her bottom. He hauled her hard against him and she gave a gasp of shock as she felt the unmistakable thrust of his erection against her.

The last of her resistance fell away to be replaced by a driving need so basic and powerful that she was completely controlled by its force. Her body throbbed and ached and cried out for satisfaction while her heart raced madly in a flight of excitement.

She forgot all her resolutions. Forgot all the promises she'd made to herself.

Instead she yanked at his shirt and slid her hands underneath, needing to touch, *to feel*, just desperate to get closer to him. Her seeking fingers found warm flesh, male body hair and hard muscle and she moaned her pleasure against his mouth as her starved senses leapt into overdrive and her body awakened.

She'd denied herself for so long that there was no hope of denying herself now. Not when what she needed so badly was standing right in front of her.

She felt every male inch of him pumped up and hard against her, and then his hands tore aside her panties and he lifted her, crashing her back against the wall with a thud as he took the weight of her body, his fingers digging hard into her thighs.

The lift gave a muted 'ping' but he merely reached out and thumped a button with an impatient hand, his eyes never leaving her eyes, his mouth never lifting from her mouth.

Helpless with excitement, Kimberley curled her legs around him, driven by an urgency that she didn't understand, her body throbbing with almost agonising excitement.

'Luc, please—' She sobbed his name into his mouth and moved her hips in a desperate plea for satisfaction and he gave a low grunt and cupped her with his hand.

Immediately Kimberley exploded into a climax so intense that she could hardly breathe. And still he kissed her, trapping her wild cries and sobs with his mouth as he slid his fingers deep inside her, his touch so shockingly intimate and amazingly skilled that the agonizing spasms just went on and on. She trembled and gasped, trapped on a sexual plateau until finally her body subsided.

Only then did he lift his mouth from hers, his breathing harsh and ragged as he scanned her flushed cheeks.

Gradually her own breathing slowed and her vision cleared and she became aware of exactly what she'd just done. *What she'd let him do to her.* In a public place.

'*Meu Deus*—' As if realising the same thing, he lowered her to the floor, streaks of colour highlighting his stunning bone structure as he lowered her to the floor. 'I don't know myself when I'm with you.'

His breathing was far from steady and his dark hair was roughened where her fingers had tugged and pulled. Still without uttering a word, he gently freed himself from the twisting, clinging coils of her fiery hair.

Tangled and wild from his hands and her own frantic movements, it tumbled in total disarray over her shoulders, half obscuring her vision.

Which was just as well, she reflected miserably as she ducked her head and tried frantically to straighten her clothing, because she couldn't bring herself to look at him and her hair provided a convenient curtain.

Deeply shocked by her own behaviour, she wanted to slink into a dark hole and never re-emerge.

She'd done it again.

For the past seven years she'd had absolutely no trouble resisting men. And it hadn't been for a lack of invitations. In fact she'd been so uninterested in the opposite sex that she'd assumed that her relationship with Luc had killed something inside her. And she'd been hugely relieved by that knowledge. It meant that her one all-consuming experience of love had rendered her immune to another attack of a similar nature. It meant that she was never again at risk of experiencing that out of control burning desire for a man, which had left her broken-hearted and soaked with humiliation.

How wrong could she have been?

Five seconds in an enclosed space with Luc was all it had taken for her to revert to her old self. She responded to him in the most basic animal fashion and no amount of logic or reason seemed to quell the burning need she had for him. The searing attraction between them was more powerful than common sense and lessons learned. So powerful that it outweighed all other considerations.

Like the fact that they were in a public lift.

Suddenly aware of their surroundings and the risk they'd just taken, various scenarios flashed across her brain and she lifted her head and stared at him in horror. 'Someone could have called the lift—'

For a long pulsing moment he didn't speak and she had a vague feeling that he was as stunned as she was, but then he stepped away from her and gave a casual shrug.

'Then they would have had a shock,' he drawled, adjusting his own clothing with a characteristic lack of concern for the opinion of others.

'You may be into public displays, but I'm not.'

In response he stroked a leisurely finger down her burning cheek. 'As usual you appear to be blaming me, but face it, *meu amorzinho*, you were as hot for it as I was. You didn't know where you were or what you were doing.' As if to prove his point, he stooped to retrieve something from the floor. 'These are yours, I believe.'

Kimberley stared down at the torn panties he'd given her and wanted to sink to the bottom of the lift shaft. Before she had a chance to comment, he stretched out a hand, hit a button on a panel on the wall and the lift doors opened.

Furious with him for not giving her more time to compose herself and still shrinking with mortification,

Kimberley was forced to stuff the remains of her underwear into her handbag. She stared after him with growing frustration and anger as he strolled out into his suite of offices without a backward glance in her direction, and for a wild moment she was tempted to take the lift back down to the ground floor and make a run for it. How could he seem so indifferent? He was totally relaxed and in control, as if indulging in mind-blowing sex in a lift was an everyday occurrence for him.

And perhaps it was, she reflected miserably as she reminded herself of the reason she was here and forced herself to follow him, her heels tapping on the polished marble floor. Women threw themselves at Luc Santoro wherever he went. She was sure there were endless numbers of females only too eager to indulge in a spot of elevator-sex with a drop dead gorgeous billionaire, given the opportunity.

Spotting a door marked 'Ladies', Kimberley took the opportunity to slip inside and do what she could to rectify her appearance.

When she emerged she saw that Luc was talking to the same personal assistant who had brought her the water and shown her such kindness.

She possessed the same exotic dark looks as her boss, but she was about twenty years older than Kimberley would have expected. Somehow she'd assumed that his personal assistant would be young and provocative.

The woman ended a phone call and gave her boss a wry smile. 'Well, you've stirred them all up as usual.'

'Is everything arranged?'

'You just need to check these figures, sign these because the fifth floor lot almost passed out with horror when I told them that you were planning to be out of the office—' she pushed some papers in his direction '—and everything else I can cope with. I'll speak to Milan about rescheduling that

presentation and Phil will be over from New York next
Wednesday as you requested. All sorted.'

'The helicopter?'

'Your pilot is waiting for you both.'

Horribly self-conscious and uncomfortably sure that, despite her attempts to freshen up her make-up, the evidence of
their passionate encounter must be somehow visible,
Kimberley hovered in the background, wondering how Luc
could make the shift from hot lover to cool-headed businessman with such casual ease.

There was no trace of the hungry, passionate, out of control man who'd driven her to vertiginous heights of sexual
pleasure only moments earlier.

Instead he seemed icy cold and more than a little remote
and detached, his mind well and truly back on business as he
scanned the papers and held his hand out for a pen.

Sex and business—the only two things that interested him
in life.

Clearly their steamy encounter in the lift hadn't affected
him in the same way it had affected her, Kimberley thought,
and the knowledge depressed her more than she cared to
admit. Even in the bedroom their relationship was one-sided.
He turned her into a shivering, sobbing wreck, willing to do
anything for his touch, while he was perfectly capable of
walking away from their steamy encounters with equa-
nimity.

*She had a horrid lowering feeling that she could have
been anyone.*

Glancing at his lean, handsome profile, she decided that
there was nothing to suggest that he'd shared anything but polite conversation with the woman who had been his companion in the lift. In total contrast, her own body was still
throbbing from the intimacies they'd shared. Her heart was
pounding and her lips were sore and swollen from his touch

and she was sure that it must be completely obvious to any-one who cared to look at her that their trip in the lift hadn't involved a single moment of conversation.

Having handed Luc another file, the older woman looked across and gave her a slightly harassed apologetic smile. *'Como vai você?* How are you? I'm Maria. Sorry to hold you up but we weren't expecting him to be out of the office next week. He just needs to take a look at these figures for me, then you can go off and spoil yourselves.'

Spoil themselves?

Kimberley looked at her in consternation, not sure how to respond. Just how much did his PA know about their deal? She made it sound as though they were going to take a holi-day. And Luc's proposed absence was clearly causing no end of problems for everyone. She glanced back at him but he had his eyes on the screen, scanning the figures.

He made a few comments, signed the rest of the papers and then glanced at his watch in an impatient gesture. Restless en-ergy pulsed from his powerful frame and he closed lean, strong fingers around her wrist and hauled her against his side in a proprietary gesture.

'Enough. Let's go.' Like a man on a mission, he virtually dragged her across the floor and through the glass doors that led directly to the roof of the building and the helicopter pad.

His pilot and another man who Kimberley assumed to be another bodyguard immediately snapped to attention as Luc strode towards them, a look of purposeful intent in his shim-mering dark gaze.

'There's no need to drag me,' she muttered, stumbling to keep up with him and he flashed her a smile that was noth-ing short of predatory.

'I'm in a hurry. It's either this or we go straight back in that lift. Take your pick.'

She shot him a look of naked exasperation. 'Your behaviour is well and truly locked in the Stone Age, do you know that? Have you ever even heard of the feminist movement and equal opportunities?'

'You will certainly have equal opportunity to experience pleasure once you're in my bed,' he assured her in silky tones, nodding to the pilot as he urged her into the helicopter with an almost indecent degree of haste.

Left with no choice, she slid into the nearest seat and shot him a look of helpless disbelief. 'You're unbelievable. Do any women actually agree to work for you?'

'Of course.' He loosened his tie and gave a tiny frown, clearly thinking it an odd question. 'You just met Maria.'

'Yes, she wasn't at all what I expected.' Kimberley's fingers tightened on her bag. She was horribly conscious of his proximity and the quivering, aching response of her own body, which seemed to be totally outside her control. No matter what she thought or what she wanted, it seemed she was destined to be fatally drawn to his raw male sex appeal.

Dangerous black eyes gleamed with amusement as he fastened his seat belt. 'And just what were you expecting?'

Kimberley looked away from him and focused on a point outside the window. 'I don't know. Someone younger? More glamorous. You're addicted to beautiful women.' *As she'd discovered to her cost.* For a short blissful time, she'd thought he was addicted to *her* and then she'd discovered just how short his attention span was. He'd cured his addiction to her all too easily.

'The secret of success in business is to be clear about the job description and then select the right person for the job,' he informed her in cool tones. 'The attributes I require in a PA are not the same as those I require in my bedroom. I never confuse the two roles and I never mix business with pleasure.'

This evidence of his ruthless self-discipline was in such stark contrast to her own dismal lack of control when she was around him that she felt her frustration slowly mounting. Was he really able to be that detached?

Recalling the way he'd strolled out of the lift and clicked his mind into business mode, she decided that he clearly was and the realisation wasn't flattering.

Evidently the effect she had on him was less than overwhelming.

She glanced across at him. 'So what would you do if you wanted a relationship with someone who worked for you?'

'Fire them and then sleep with them,' he replied without hesitation. 'But I don't understand why that would interest you. You're not working for me, so there's absolutely no barrier to our relationship.'

'Apart from the fact that we can't stand the sight of one another.'

'Cast your mind back to the lift,' he suggested silkily, dark lashes lowering as he studied her with blatantly sexual intent. 'And if that doesn't jog your memory, then try asking yourself why you're not currently wearing underwear.'

She gave a tiny gasp of shock and her heart skipped a beat. 'You didn't give me the opportunity to put them back on, they were in tatters,' she murmured, trying without any confidence of success to emulate the cool indifference that he constantly displayed.

'That's because I believe in economy of effort and I don't see the point in removing them twice.'

'Aren't you ever interested in anything other than sex?' she blurted out suddenly. 'Don't you want to know a single thing about me?'

'I know that you excite me more than any woman I've ever met,' he responded instantly, night-black eyes raking her tense, quivering body with raw masculine appreciation. 'What else would I want, or need, to know?'

She gazed at him helplessly, both fascinated and appalled by his total lack of emotional engagement. He was a man who operated alone. A man who appeared to need no one.

Luc didn't have a single vulnerable bone in his body.

Then she thought of Rio and she was stifled by a maternal love so powerful that it almost choked her.

In a sudden rush of panic, she fumbled for her seat belt and unclipped it. 'I can't do this, Luc, I'm sorry,' she stammered. 'You have to take me to the airport. I have to go home now. I need to be there for my son. I've never left him before, not for this long, and he's in danger—'

Luc lounged in his seat, watching her with interest. 'Drop the act, *meu amorzinho*,' he advised gently. 'The money is already paid. The deal is done.'

Her breathing quickened. 'But what if it isn't enough?' She bit her lip. 'Don't blackmailers often come back for more?'

Luc paused, his eyes glittering dark in his handsome face. 'I think it will take our "blackmailer" a little while to work her way through five million dollars, don't you?' His tone was mocking and she flushed with anger and frustration.

'You're making *such* a big mistake.'

'I don't make mistakes. I make decisions and they're always the right ones,' he said in a cool tone, 'and my decision on this is to pay you what you've asked for. It's done. Now you have to play your part and I don't want to hear any more mention of blackmailers or sweet, vulnerable children who need you at home.'

What could she do?

The helicopter was already in mid-flight and, if what Luc said was correct, then the money was already in the hands of the blackmailer.

Kimberley turned her head so that he couldn't see the tears in her eyes.

This was about *her,* not her son, she acknowledged helplessly. She'd always been hideously over-protective. From the moment Rio was born, her love for him had been absolute and unconditional. She'd tried hard not to smother him but she found it incredibly hard. She just loved him *so* much and she couldn't bear the thought that anything might make him unhappy, even for a moment.

But Rio would be fine, she told herself firmly. He adored Jason and Jason adored him back and would never let anything happen to him.

It was she who was going to suffer by not being close to her child.

Two weeks. She straightened her narrow shoulders and forced herself to get a grip on her emotions. Just two weeks and then her life would be back to normal again.

No blackmailer and no Luc.

Would it really be that hard? What was he asking for? Sex without love?

Well, she could do that.

She was just going to lie there, she vowed fiercely to herself. She wasn't going to sob and she wasn't going to beg.

And when eventually she bored him and he decided to let her go, she was going to walk away without a backward glance, as emotionally detached as he was.

CHAPTER FIVE

THE helicopter had barely settled on dry land before Luc was out of his seat. If he was aware of the mystified glances exchanged between his bodyguards and his pilot then he gave no sign, his darkly handsome face a mask of cool indifference as he strode the short distance to the villa with Kimberley clamped firmly by his side.

For a man who prided himself on his rigid self-discipline and self-control, he was suffering from no small degree of discomfort and irritation because at that precise moment he'd never felt *less* in control. Only once before in his life could he remember acting in such a wild and impulsive manner and that was seven years before when Kimberley had first entered his life.

The knowledge did nothing to soothe his volatile and uncertain mood.

He was frustrated, exasperated and more than a little disturbed by his own behaviour, and he didn't need to read the body language of his clearly stunned staff to confirm that his behaviour was totally out of character.

It wasn't just the incident in the lift, he mused grimly as he walked with single-minded purpose through the grounds of the villa, indifferent to the visual temptation presented by the lush gardens. His fingers were still clamped around her slender wrist as he headed directly for the master suite, skirting round the tempting blue of the pool, which sparkled and shimmered in the sunlight.

No. It definitely wasn't about the lift. What did that prove, apart from the fact that he was a normal red-blooded guy with a healthy appetite for an attractive woman and an ability to make the most of the moment?

He could even have dismissed the more seedy aspects of seducing a woman in a public place if the experience had left him clear-headed and sated and with his sanity fully restored. But that wasn't the case. Like an alcoholic who had allowed himself the dark indulgence of just one drink, that one taste of the forbidden had left him with a throbbing, nagging need for still more and he had an uncomfortable feeling that even a gawking crowd wouldn't be enough to tempt him to exercise restraint should the situation arise again.

And that was what he found uncomfortable about the whole situation in which he now found himself.

He never lost control. In fact he prided himself on his ability to remain cool when others around him were reaching boiling point. He prided himself on his ability to maintain a rational approach to decision making when others around him became emotional. It was his ability to think, unencumbered by the emotional baggage that seemed to trouble some people, which was a major contributor to his current success.

And, although women played an important part in his life, never *ever* had a woman compromised his business decisions.

Until now.

From the moment Kimberley had re-entered his life, all that mattered to him was getting her back in his bed and keeping her there until his body was sufficiently sated for him to be able to think clearly again.

His behaviour since Kimberley had walked back into his

life had been so completely out of character that he was not in the least surprised that his bodyguards and pilot were looking at him strangely. Even Maria, who knew more about him than most, had been openly shocked by his sudden request that she completely rearrange his diary in order to accommodate his need to be absent from the office for the foreseeable future. In fact he was entirely sure that a large proportion of his staff would be huddled together at this very moment discussing the question of their boss's personality transformation.

And he was asking himself the very same question.

Given the delicate stage of the business deal he was currently negotiating, it was nothing short of reckless to cancel meetings and leave the office at a time when his presence was mandatory.

But that was exactly what he'd done and he was ready to ignore the consequences.

He was ready to ignore everything except the building sexual tension that nagged at his body. Their torrid encounter in the lift had succeeded in heating his blood to intolerable levels and, if it hadn't been for the fact that halting the lift for any longer would have attracted the attentions of a maintenance team with embarrassing consequences, he would have satisfied his baser urges and taken her there and then, against the mirrored wall of his express lift.

The knowledge would have disturbed him more had he not been grimly aware that there had never been a woman who had succeeded in holding his attention longer than a few weeks. Given that knowledge, he was entirely confident that, with the right degree of dedication to the task in hand, he could easily work Kimberley out of his system.

She really was pushing her luck, he mused, trying to slap him with a paternity suit seven years after their relationship had ended. Did she think he was entirely stupid? Still, her greed had thrown her back into his path and for that he was grateful. He'd been given the chance to get her out of his system once and for all.

This time he was going to take the relationship to its inevitable conclusion.

Despite the number of corporate headaches bearing down on him from all sides, he'd decided to dedicate the next few weeks of his life to becoming bored by Kimberley. He owed it to his sanity and his ability to concentrate. And all he required to fulfil that task was privacy and an extremely large double bed, both of which were very much available in his villa. It was the one place in the world where he was guaranteed not to be disturbed. The one place where the press and the public were unable to gain any sort of access.

The one place where he could be truly alone to concentrate on Kimberley.

And, if the episode in the lift was anything to go by, they really, *really* needed to be alone.

Hot, sticky and thoroughly overheated by factors far more complex than a tropical climate, Kimberley glanced longingly at the cool water of the pool, but Luc didn't alter his pace as he strode towards the bedroom suite that she remembered all too well.

Her pulse rate increased and her mouth dried.

During the time they'd spent on the island she'd hardly left that room and going back there now simply intensified the shame she already felt at the uninhibited way she'd responded to him all those years ago.

She wanted to dig her heels in and resist but the tight grip of his strong fingers on her wrist and the grim, set expression on his face were warning enough that any argument on her part was futile.

And anyway, she reasoned helplessly, how could she argue?

She'd agreed to this.

For the sum of five million dollars and to protect her child, she'd agreed to it and she just wanted to get the next two weeks over with as quickly as possible and get home.

She wanted to be with her son. She missed him dreadfully.

And she was afraid. Desperately afraid that she might turn back into the helpless, needy woman Luc had seduced all those years before.

When she'd met him she'd been a hard working, successful model. She'd never missed a shoot or been late for an appointment in her life. Then she'd met Luc and all that had changed.

One hot glance from those dark eyes and she'd been dazzled, unable to see anything except *him.* She'd abandoned her job, forgotten her responsibilities and ceased to care about anything except Luc.

She'd been so drunk on her love for him that she'd failed to see that, for him, their relationship was all about sex. Even when he'd left her in bed to date other women, she hadn't truly accepted that their relationship had no future. Only when she'd discovered that she was pregnant, only when she'd turned to him for help and been rejected, had she finally accepted that it was over.

And now here she was, about to walk back into Luc Santoro's bedroom again. *About to risk everything.*

Last time he'd hurt her so badly with his cruel indifference that it had taken years for her to piece her life back together again, but she'd done it and she was proud of the woman she'd become. Proud of her son and the small business she'd built. Proud of her life. And she'd been very careful to preserve and protect that life.

But this wasn't like the last time, she reminded herself firmly. The last time she'd been young, naïve and hopelessly in love with the man she'd wanted Luc to be. Now she was a very different person and, no matter how powerful the sexual attraction, she wasn't going to lose sight of the man he really was. She had no intention of making that mistake a second time in her life.

She knew now that Luc didn't have an emotional bone in his perfectly put together body and he was never going to change.

She lifted her chin. He'd proved to her time and time again that he was capable of enjoying sex without emotion, so why shouldn't she be able to do the same thing? In many ways he was the perfect man for the task, she thought, sneaking a sideways glance at his hard, handsome profile. Whatever criticisms could be levelled at him in the emotional stakes, his bedroom technique was surely unsurpassed.

Remembering the wild, mindless encounter in the lift, her breathing hitched in her throat and a sudden flare of delicious, forbidden excitement scorched her body.

She would approach the next two weeks with the same emotional detachment that he did, she vowed silently, ignoring the bump of her heart as he all but dragged her into the bedroom that opened directly on to the pool area.

In front of her was a huge bed, *the* huge bed that she remembered well. She should do, she thought wryly, because she had barely left it for the entire time they'd spent at the villa.

Covered with sheets of the finest Egyptian cotton, it faced both the pool and the sea, but Kimberley recalled with a lowering degree of clarity that on the previous occasion she'd lain in that very bed and been totally unaware of the view. When she had been with Luc, for her the outside world had ceased to exist.

Well, not any more.

This time she was going to enjoy the pool and the sea along with any other hidden delights that his private island had to offer.

She'd enjoy the sex for the two weeks, just as she'd agreed, but this time everything else would be different. She'd enjoy his incredible body in the most superficial way possible. She wasn't going to fall in love and she wasn't going to pretend that Luc might fall in love with *her*.

That way she'd be sure of being able to walk away with her heart completely intact.

If he could do it, so could she, and just to prove that fact she turned to him with a cool smile on her face.

'Well—' She waved a hand towards the bed in an almost dismissive gesture. 'We seem to have everything we need, so shall we make a start?'

Wasn't that what it was all about? Practicality versus romance.

She just needed to learn to play by different rules. *His rules.*

His dark eyes sharpened on her face. 'Sarcasm doesn't suit you. It isn't part of your personality and it isn't part of who you are.'

'You have no idea who I am, Luc, and we both know that it isn't my personality that interests you.' She kept her tone casual as she strolled towards the bed and dropped her bag on the cover. 'And you're the one who keeps reminding me that you didn't pay five million dollars to indulge in conversation.'

She saw the flicker of incredulity cross his handsome face and suddenly felt like smiling.

He'd expected her to stammer and protest. He'd been prepared to control and dominate in his usual fashion. But this time she wasn't going to allow it. This time, she was the one with the upper hand. Instead of fighting against the tide she was swimming with it.

She'd surprised him and it felt *good*.

With a sense of power and confidence that she couldn't ever remember feeling before in his company, she casually undid the buttons of her shirt and strolled towards the luxurious bathroom. 'I'll just take a shower and I'll meet you in the bed in five minutes.'

She was doing brilliantly, she told herself gleefully as she stripped her clothes off and stepped under the power shower. Even though this situation wasn't of her choice, there was no reason why she had to allow Luc to call all the shots.

The spray was the perfect temperature and she closed her eyes and gave a soft moan of pleasure as the cool water drenched her heated flesh.

For a moment she just stood there, humming softly to herself, revelling in the feel of the water on her skin and the knowledge that, for once, she was the one in control.

Her feeling of smug satisfaction lasted all of eight seconds.

'I never knew you had such a good singing voice,' came a dark male drawl from directly next to her and with a soft gasp of shock she opened her eyes and brushed the water away from her face to clear her vision.

Luc stood only inches away from her, gloriously naked and unashamedly aroused, his body as close to male physical perfection as it was possible to get.

'I must congratulate you.' The water clung to his thick, dark lashes and he watched her with a slumberous expression in his wicked dark eyes. 'A shower together was the perfect idea, *meu amorzinho*. I more than approve.'

Her new-found confidence vanished in an instant.

He wasn't supposed to approve. He was supposed to be feeling deflated and frustrated and slightly at a loss by the fact she'd taken control.

Instead he looked like a man who was well and truly in command of the situation.

Remembering her promise to herself not to play the part of the shrinking maiden, she resisted the temptation to flatten herself against the wall of the shower.

'You didn't need to join me,' she said in a cool voice, averting her eyes from the tantalising vision of curling black hair shadowing a bronzed, muscular chest. She didn't dare look lower. Her one brief glimpse when she'd opened her eyes had been more than enough to remind her of his undeniable masculinity. 'We have a contract and I intend to honour it. You don't need to worry about me escaping.'

'Do I look worried?' His eyes gleamed dark with amusement and he lifted a hand and smoothed her damp hair away from her face. 'Why would I worry when I know you can't say no to me?'

She gritted her teeth and tried to ignore the tiny spasms of excitement that licked through her body. 'You need a private island to accommodate your ego.'

He gave a soft laugh and reached out to pull her closer in a gesture that was pure caveman. 'I love the fact that you pretend you can resist me. It's going to make your final surrender all the more satisfying. You present me with a challenge and I *love* a challenge.'

She stared at him helplessly, appalled by his arrogance and yet fascinated by his undiluted masculinity. 'What you're saying is that you just can't take no for an answer.'

'Perhaps my English isn't always perfect.'

'Your English is f-fluent,' she stammered, heat piercing through her pelvis as the roughness of his thighs brushed against her bare legs. 'It's just that you always have to get your own way in everything.'

'And what's wrong with that?' He gave a casual shrug and curved an arm around her narrow waist, bringing her hard against him. 'Especially when we both want the same thing.'

Her heart was thumping so hard that she could hardly breathe and as she felt him reach for the soap and slide his hands down her bare back she couldn't hold back the moan.

'You have an amazing body,' he said hoarsely, turning her round and sliding his strong hands down her spine.

Her eyes closed and she forced herself to think about something else. But the only thing in her mind was Luc and when she felt his hands move to her hair she gave a shudder of approbation.

He lathered her hair, his fingers delivering a slow, sensual massage to her scalp, and she closed her eyes, unable to resist the amazingly skilful pressure of his fingers. It had always been like this, she thought helplessly as she sank into his caress. He knew exactly how to touch her. Exactly how to melt resistance. *Exactly how to drive her wild.*

He washed the rest of her body, lingering in some parts just long enough to make her squirm and then moving on to concentrate his attentions elsewhere.

He carried on until her entire body was quivering with anticipation. *Until she was desperate to explore him the way he was exploring her.* Unable to wait a moment longer, Kimberley reached out and slid a hand over his chest and then lower still, following the track of dark hair that led downwards.

But he caught her wrists in his hands and drew her arms round his neck, refusing her the satisfaction of touching him.

Need and frustration pounding in her veins, she tried to free her arms but he held her firm, a glimmer of mockery in his dark eyes as he lowered his mouth to hers.

But he refused to kiss her properly.

Still in teasing mode, he licked at the corners of her mouth, played with her lower lip and kissed his way down her neck until she was gasping and writhing against him, but still he wouldn't give her what she craved.

Her whole body throbbed and ached with an intensity that approached pain, but there was nothing she could do to relieve the mounting frustration. Only he could do that and he was careful to give her just enough to build the excitement while withholding the ultimate satisfaction that she craved.

He teased her and seduced her until every nerve in her body was throbbing and humming, until she was unable to think about anything except the man in front of her. Her mind ceased to function and she was driven entirely by her senses to the point where she wasn't even aware that he'd switched off the shower until she felt herself wrapped in a soft towel and lifted into his arms.

Somewhere in the back of her mind something nagged at her. Something about him being the one in control once more. But she couldn't hold on to the thought long enough to examine it, let alone act on it, so she lay still in his arms, drugged and dizzy from his slow, expert seduction.

He laid her on the bed, removed the towel with a gentle but determined tug and then came down on top of her, a gleam of masculine purpose in his dark eyes.

Almost breathless with desperation, she ran her hands down the sleek muscle of his back and shifted her body under his in an attempt to gain access to the male power of him. He slid away from her in a smooth movement and she gave a sob of frustration, her hips writhing against the sheets.

'You touch me—why can't I touch you?'

'Not yet—' He anchored her wrists in his hands and held them above her head and then finally he lowered his head to hers.

His mouth took hers in a kiss so hot and sexual that the room spun around her and she thought she might actually lose consciousness.

His tongue explored every inch of her mouth with erotic expertise and she was so drugged by his skilful touch that she didn't realise that he'd tied her wrists until she tried to slide her arms round his neck and discovered that she couldn't.

Her hands were firmly secured to the head of the bed.

He gave a low laugh of masculine satisfaction and slid down her body. 'Now I have you *exactly* where I want you, *meu amorzinho.*'

A flicker of alarm penetrated the sensual fog that had paralysed her brain and she tried to tug at her wrists but he chose that precise moment to flick his tongue over her nipple and she gave a gasp as sharp needles of sensation pierced her body.

She writhed and shifted on the bed, trying desperately to rediscover her powers of speech and demand that he let her go, when he sucked her into his mouth and proceeded to subject her to the skill of his tongue.

It was maddeningly good and she felt the burning ache in her pelvis increase to almost intolerable levels but he was in no hurry, his seduction slow and leisurely as he skilfully caressed first one breast and then the other.

She squirmed and gasped and tugged at her bound wrists and just when she thought she couldn't stand it any longer he slid down her body.

Barely able to form the words, she gave a moan of protest, horribly embarrassed. 'Untie me, Luc, please—'

He lifted his dark head, 'Not yet. You still have too many inhibitions. You think too much. I want to show you what your body can feel when the freedom of choice is removed. You are quite safe, *meu amorzinho*. All that is going to happen is that I intend to torture you with pleasure and you will be totally unable to resist.'

Horror and disbelief mingled with a sense of wicked anticipation as he slid further down the bed and closed his strong hands round her trembling thighs.

Realising his intention, she tried desperately to keep her legs together, but he gave a low laugh and ignored her feeble resistance, opening her to his hungry gaze with the gentle pressure of his hands.

She'd never felt so exposed before, so vulnerable, and her face burned hot under his probing, masculine gaze. Her whole body tensed as she felt his fingers slide through the fiery curls at the apex of her thighs and then he was parting her and she felt the damp flick of his tongue exploring her intimately.

She gave a gasp of shock and tried to free herself but her hands were securely tied and she had no way of protecting herself from his determined seduction. And soon the very thought of protecting herself vanished from her brain because what he was doing to her body felt so impossibly, exquisitely good she thought there was a very strong chance that she might pass out.

When he slid his fingers deep inside her, Kimberley shot into a climax so intense that she cried out sharply in almost agonised disbelief. The sensation went on and on, his fingers and his mouth witness to the sensual havoc he was creating within her body.

It was so wild that she lost touch with reality, lost touch with everything, controlled entirely by erotic sensation caused by one man.

Finally the spasms eased and he slid up her body in a smooth movement and ran his fingers through her damp, tangled hair.

Limp and dazed, she stared up at him blankly, slowly registering the triumphant expression in those night-black eyes as they raked her flushed cheeks.

Without shifting his gaze from hers, he reached up and freed her in one simple movement, trailing the scarlet silk ribbon that had held her captive to his sexual whims over one hardened nipple.

'*Now* you can touch me,' he informed her in silky tones and she wished she had the energy or the inclination to smack the smug smile from his indecently handsome face. He was all too aware of his own abilities to drive a woman to the edge of sanity, but unfortunately she was suffering such an overload of excitement that she could think of nothing but her own need for him.

She reached for him urgently, closing her slender fingers over the impressive throb of his erection with a moan of feminine approval.

With a grunt deep in his throat, he slid an arm under her hips, positioned her to his satisfaction and thrust deeply into her shivering, quivering body and it felt so shockingly good to have him inside her again that she gave a sob of relief. Wrapping her legs around him, she moved her hips instinctively and he muttered something against her mouth before driving into her hard and setting a rhythm that was pagan and primitive and out of control.

She raked her nails down his back and he dug his fingers into her thighs, bringing his mouth down hard on hers, connecting them in every way possible until the inevitable sensual explosion engulfed her, suspending thought and time.

Kimberley felt her mind go blank, felt her body come apart as fierce excitement gripped her. For a moment, everything was suspended and exaggerated and she struggled to breathe as her body convulsed around the plunging, primal force of his. Dimly she registered a masculine groan and knew that her climax had driven him to the same peak. She felt the liquid force of his own release, felt him thrust hard as he powered into her, felt the rasp of male chest hair against her sensitised breasts as his body moved against hers. The spasms went on and on and she clung to him, overpowered by sensation, riding the storm, waiting for the world around her to settle.

And eventually it did. Her senses cleared and calm was restored. She opened her eyes and saw a bronzed male shoulder, became aware of the slick heat of his body against hers, the harshness of his breathing against her cheek and the weight of him pressing down on her.

And then he rolled on to his back, taking her with him. Her hair tumbled and slid across his chest and he gave a satisfied groan and brushed it gently away from her face so that he could kiss her mouth.

'That was amazing.' His tone was slightly roughened and Kimberley shifted her head slightly so that she could look at him, her eyes trapped by his slumberous dark gaze. 'You are so wild in my bed. And, just in case you're tempted to pretend that you didn't enjoy it, then I ought to warn you that you'd be wasting your time,' he drawled lazily, smothering a yawn. 'You were completely mad for me and I still have the wounds on my back to prove it.'

His less than subtle reminder of just how uninhibited she'd been horrified her and she pulled away from him, suddenly realising that, despite her best intentions, he'd taken all the control right back. And, judging from the satisfied macho smile on his sickeningly handsome face, he knew it.

Ignoring the fact that her limbs felt weak and her body ached and throbbed, she sprang out of bed. It was the only way she could fight the impulse to snuggle against him. And their relationship wasn't about affection.

'Well, I thought that five million dollars required an above average performance on my part.' Her casual tone drew a quick frown from him but she turned and strolled into the bathroom with what she hoped was a convincing degree of indifference.

Inside the palatial bathroom she bolted the door and then slid in a boneless heap on to the marbled floor and covered her face with her hands.

She remembered his words as he'd untied her with a whimper of horror.

'Now you can touch me.'

Even in the middle of lovemaking, he'd still been the one in control and she'd been so desperate for him that she hadn't even noticed. In fact she'd ceased to care about anything else except satisfying the maddening, almost intolerable ache in her body. He'd orchestrated every second of her seduction, without once allowing her the same privileged, unlimited access to his body. And, although he'd clearly enjoyed their encounter, at no point in the proceedings had he appeared to lose control or been consumed by the same degree of sexual abandon.

She remembered how pleased she'd been with herself earlier when she'd taken control back for a few moments. And she remembered the surprise in his eyes. But it hadn't lasted. From the moment he'd stepped into the shower with her, he'd been in full command mode. The truth was that in the bedroom he would always be in charge. And his skills in that department were such that he could turn her into a mindless squirming mass within seconds and she just hated herself for being unable to resist him.

Dragging herself over to the mirror, she gazed at her reflection, seeing flushed cheeks and a soft, bruised mouth.

What had happened to her?

In the last seven years she'd raised a child and built a successful business from scratch. She considered herself to be competent and independent. She was proud of the woman she'd become.

And yet in Luc Santoro's bed that woman vanished and in her place was the same clingy, needy, desperate girl that she'd been at eighteen.

Two weeks, she reminded herself grimly as she splashed her face with cold water and tidied her hair. She just had to get through two weeks and then she could return home to her child and put Luc Santoro back in the past where he well and truly belonged.

CHAPTER SIX

STRETCHED out in the shade by the exquisite pool almost two weeks later, Kimberley decided drowsily that she'd undergone a complete personality change. Far from being an independent thinking woman, she now felt more like a sex slave, ready and willing to obey the commands of her master.

Luc only had to cast a burning glance in her direction and she fell into his arms with an enthusiasm as predictable as it was humiliating.

Underneath the sensual addiction that fuelled her every move she was secretly *appalled* at herself and she didn't know which was worse—the knowledge that she'd reverted to her old self the moment he'd brought his extremely talented mouth down on hers, or the fact that she was actually enjoying herself and she was far too honest a person to pretend otherwise. How could she when she couldn't take her eyes off him? *Couldn't stop wondering when he was going to reach for her next?*

If it hadn't been for the fact that she was missing Rio horribly, she would have been completely and totally happy.

Even though Luc had assured her that the money had immediately been transferred into the right account, as per her instructions, and that her surreptitious calls to Jason had assured her that everything seemed fine at home, she couldn't stop worrying.

It made no difference that she'd sneaked off at least once a day, and sometimes twice, to phone her son and chat about what was happening in his life. It made no difference that he'd sounded happy and buoyant and didn't seem to be missing her at all.

She missed him.

Desperately.

And she wanted to go home.

Which just left her to finish her part of the deal with Luc. And so far he'd certainly been getting his money's worth. They'd barely left the bed.

Maybe it was being back in this villa, she thought helplessly as she glanced across the pool to the lush gardens that led down to the beach. It had such powerful associations with the first time they'd met that it was impossible for her to remember how much she'd changed since those days.

She'd regressed to the girl she'd been at eighteen.

'You are dreaming again.' Luc lifted himself out of the swimming pool in a lithe, powerful movement and ran a hand over his eyes to clear the water from his face. He reached for a towel and flashed her a predatory smile. 'There is no need to dream when you have the real thing. If you wish to return to the bedroom, *meu amorzinho*, then you only have to say the word.'

His arrogant assumption that her dreams had all been about him should have made her slap his face or at least deliver an acid comment about the size of his ego. But she was prevented from speaking because it was true. Her dreams *were* all about him.

And that was the most annoying thing of all, she mused as she stretched out a hand and reached for her drink. Apart from being with her child, there was no place in the world she'd rather be than in Luc's bed and she just hated herself for feeling like that. It might have been different if the relationship had been equal, but it wasn't.

He was *always* the one in control. He decided when they ate, when they slept, when they made love, even *how* they made love. Any attempt on her part to take the lead was always brushed aside.

It wasn't that Luc didn't enjoy the sex, because he clearly did, but she was humiliatingly aware that he never lost control in the way that she did. He orchestrated every move in the bedroom.

He strolled over to her, the towel looped over his broad shoulders, water clinging to the hairs on his chest and the hard muscles of his thighs. He had a body designed to scramble a woman's brain and she felt her stomach clench. No wonder she couldn't resist him. What woman could? He was as near to masculine perfection as it was possible to get.

'You've been out here for almost an hour.' He dropped the towel, a frown in his eyes as he studied her semi-naked body. 'Go back inside before you burn.'

She opened her mouth to point out that he was being controlling again, when she realised that it would give her the perfect opportunity to call home again.

She could have been open about phoning her son but, given that Luc hadn't mentioned the subject since they'd arrived on the island, it seemed more sensible to let the matter drop.

Suddenly she missed Rio so acutely that the pain was almost physical.

She needed to hear his voice.

Trying to look suitably casual, she swung her legs over the edge of the sunbed and stood up. 'You're right, I'm burning,' she stammered quickly, reaching for her bag and sliding her feet into her sandals. 'I'll go inside for a while and lie down. I'm feeling a little tired.'

It was true. Unlike Luc, who seemed possessed of almost supernatural energy levels and stamina, she found it hard to go through an entire night with virtually no sleep without then dropping off to sleep at various intervals throughout the day.

Ignoring the hot slide of his gaze over her body, she hurried into the bedroom, reaching into her bag for her mobile phone.

With a quick glance over her shoulder, she checked that Luc was still safely on the terrace by the pool and then dialled the number.

Rio answered. 'Mum?' He sounded breathless with excitement and older than his six years. 'You have to buy me a fish!'

She closed her eyes and felt relief flood through her. He sounded so normal. *And so like his father.* Life with Rio was one long round of commands and orders.

'What sort of fish?'

'Like the one we've just got at school; it's *really* cool.'

Kimberley smiled. To her six-year-old son, everything was cool.

They talked for a few more minutes and then she cut the connection reluctantly, feeling as though she was tearing her own heart out.

But as she dropped the phone back into her bag she saw the letter and remembered the reason she was doing this. *She was keeping her baby safe.*

Something glinted underneath the envelope and she gave a slight frown and delved into the bag again, this time removing a set of handcuffs. She gave a disbelieving laugh and then remembered that her son had borrowed a policeman's outfit from one of his friends and had been dressing up on the day before she'd flown out to Brazil. He must have dropped the cuffs into her bag. How they hadn't been detected by the airport authorities, she had no idea.

She fingered the handcuffs thoughtfully and a wickedly naughty idea suddenly shot through her brain.

Did she dare?

Before she could lose her nerve, she quickly looped them round the bed head and covered them with a pillow.

'I've decided that I'm risking sunstroke by staying outside and that I'm also in serious need of a rest.' Luc's sardonic masculine drawl came from the doorway and she gave a start and quickly jumped off the bed, her heart thumping, convinced that the guilt must be written all over her face.

Had he noticed what she'd just done?

Her eyes clashed with his and her stomach dropped in instinctive feminine response to the masculine intent she read in his eyes. He hadn't noticed. He was too busy looking at her legs and other parts of her openly displayed by the almost non-existent bikini that had been part of her newly acquired wardrobe.

'The sun doesn't bother you and you never get tired,' she reminded him, watching him stroll towards her in a pair of swimming trunks that did nothing to conceal his rampant arousal. 'And anyway, we only got up an hour ago.'

Her mouth dried and wicked excitement curled deep in her pelvis as she stared at him helplessly.

He was unbelievably good-looking and it was no wonder he affected her so strongly.

'An hour is a long time,' he said silkily, reaching for her and dragging her to her feet. 'Especially when you are wearing that particular bikini.'

His eyes dropped to her mouth and suddenly breathing seemed difficult. 'You chose the bikini.' It had been one of a selection of clothing that had been waiting for her at the villa. 'I didn't bring any clothes, remember?'

He gave a predatory smile. 'And so far, *minha docura*, you haven't needed any.'

'When it comes to sex, you're insatiable,' she said breathlessly. 'Do you know that?'

'When it comes to *you*, I'm insatiable,' he informed her and then frowned slightly as if the thought made him uncomfortable.

'Why are you frowning?'

'I'm not.' The frown on his brow lifted as he clearly dismissed the thought with his customary single-minded determination.

She felt his hand slide down her back and gave a shiver of response. Her reaction to him was so predictable, she thought helplessly. He only had to touch her and she surrendered.

Except that this time—

He slid his hand into her hair and tugged gently, exposing the smooth skin of her neck for his touch. She gasped as she felt the burning heat of his mouth and then she was tumbled back on to the bed with Luc on top of her, his seductive gaze veiled by thick, dark lashes.

'I can't get enough of you,' he raked hoarsely as he quickly stripped her of her bikini and then fastened his mouth on hers again.

He rolled on to his back, taking her with him, and she dragged her mouth away from his. She couldn't think straight when he was kissing her. Couldn't concentrate. *And she needed to concentrate because she had a plan.*

For once she was determined to take control. She was determined to torture him the way he always tortured her.

Payback time.

Knowing that she had to act quickly, she drew his hands above his head, moving the pillow to reveal the handcuffs she'd already looped round the bed. Heart thumping, she snapped the cuffs on his wrists before he had time to realize her intentions.

He stilled and a look of stunned incredulity illuminated his dark gaze. '*What* do you think you are doing?'

She held her breath, watching as the muscles of his shoulders bunched as he jerked his wrists in an attempt to free himself. *Would the handcuffs hold?*

Deciding that she needed to use more than one method of

holding him captive, she bent her head and teased the corners of his mouth with her tongue. 'You said you could handle me with both hands tied behind your back,' she reminded him in a husky voice, 'so I thought I'd give it a try. Both of your hands are well and truly behind your back, or above your head if you want to be precise. I'm all yours, Luc.' Her tongue slid between his lips in a teasing, erotic gesture and she saw his eyes darken. She lifted her head and licked her lips slowly, savouring the taste of his mouth. 'Or perhaps you're all mine. Let's find out, shall we?'

She saw the shock flicker across his handsome face and for the first time in her life had the pleasure of seeing Luc Santoro out of his depth. She saw him struggling to shake off the raw desire so that he could think clearly and almost smiled. *How many times had she tried to do the very same thing in his bed and failed?*

'No woman has ever done this to you before, have they?' She slid her body over his, soft woman over hard man, felt the power of his erection brush against her abdomen and immediately moved away. *She wasn't ready to touch him there yet.* 'You're about to discover what it's like to be ruled by the senses and to be totally at the mercy of another person.'

His dark eyes were fierce. '*Meu Deus*, Kimberley. Let me go, now!'

With agonising slowness she dragged a slender finger through the hairs on his chest, her mouth curving into a smile as he shuddered.

'You're not in a position to give orders,' she pointed out in a husky voice, 'so you might just as well relax and go with the flow. Who knows, you might find that you enjoy having someone else in the command position for a while.'

His aggressive jaw hardened. 'Kimberley—' his tone was hoarse and he jerked at his hands again '—I demand that you let me go.'

'Order—' she bent her head and trailed her tongue along the hard ridge of his jaw '—demand—' her tongue snaked upwards towards his ear '—they're not the words I want to hear,' she informed him huskily, enjoying herself more and more. 'By the time I've finished with you, you're going to scream and beg, Luc. In exactly the same way that you make me scream and beg.'

'That's *different*—'

'How is it different?' She lowered her mouth again and trailed hot kisses over his bronzed muscular shoulder. *She just adored his body.* 'Because you're a man and I'm a woman?' Her teeth nipped his shoulder and she heard the hiss of his breath as he fought for control. 'You told me that you believed in equal opportunities, Luc. Let's find out whether you were telling the truth, shall we? I've just turned the tables on you.'

For the first time in their relationship she had the chance to admire his body the way he insisted on admiring hers. *She could take her time.* And she had every intention of doing just that.

Registering his stunned and slightly dazed expression with a sexy, satisfied smile, she slid her hands down his body and removed his swimming trunks in a smooth movement, sliding them down his legs and exposing him fully to her gaze.

He was hard and proud and totally ready for all the dark, sensual exploits she had in mind.

For a moment she just stared and he swore fluently in his own language and shifted his lean hips on the bed.

'Release me, now! This is *not* funny—'

'It isn't supposed to be funny.' The atmosphere in the room crackled and throbbed as the tension mounted. *He was magnificent,* she thought to herself. Hot, aroused and more of a man than he had a right to be. And she wanted him badly.

But she was going to make herself wait.

And, more to the point, she was going to make *him* wait.

With a low laugh of triumph and a heated glance that was pure seductress, she slid her fingers down his body until her hand lingered teasingly on his taut abdomen, just short of the straining shaft of his manhood.

'Release me!' He swore softly and pulled hard at the handcuffs but they held firm and Kimberley lifted her head and smiled a womanly smile, her confidence and power increasing by the minute.

'No way.' Her hand slid to the top of his thigh. 'For once I've got you exactly where I want you and you're going to stay there until I've finished with you.'

'You can't do this—'

'I *am* doing it. It's time you learned that you can't always be the one in control. I'm going to show you what it feels like to be tortured by sensual pleasure.'

He gave a soft curse and jerked at the handcuffs again but still they held fast and Kimberley bent her head, her glorious fiery hair trailing over his body as she used her tongue to trace the line of hair that ran below his navel. Her touch was slow and teasing and she saw the muscles of his abdomen tense viciously. He wanted her to touch him, badly, but she was determined not to. Not yet. She wasn't ready. And neither was he.

She had never been given unrestricted access to his body before and suddenly she needed to touch and taste all of him. To know him in every way possible.

Dimly she heard the harshness of his breathing, but she was too caught up in the sensual feast she'd made for herself to be distracted. She licked and nibbled and tasted him everywhere except his throbbing, pulsing masculinity.

Once, her fingers brushed against him fleetingly and she heard his guttural groan and felt him jerk his body towards her but she pulled back and slid up his body, raking her fingers through his chest hair and using her tongue to tease his nipples.

His breathing was harsh in her ears and she saw the muscles in his shoulders bunch as he pulled at the restraints, but he failed to free himself and cursed again, his eyes burning dark in his handsome face.

He muttered something in his own language and she lifted her head and gave him a mocking smile.

'If you expect me to understand what you're saying, you're going to have to speak English.' Her voice was smoky and softened by desire. 'What is it you want, Luc?'

For a moment he just stared at her, obviously unable to form the words, his eyes glazed and fevered. Then he licked his tongue over his lips. 'I want you to touch me,' he muttered hoarsely. 'Touch me now.'

There was no mistaking just how much he wanted her and she felt a flash of womanly triumph. 'Not yet. I'm not ready, and neither are you.'

He closed his eyes and beads of sweat appeared on his brow. 'Kimberley, please—'

A feeling of power spread through her veins and she gave a slow womanly smile. 'When I'm ready, I'll touch you,' she told him in a husky, smoky voice. 'All you have to do is lie there.' She shifted up the bed and teased the corner of his mouth with her tongue. Instantly he moved his mouth to capture hers but she was too quick for him, moving just out of reach and smiling as he swore fluently.

'This isn't a joke, Kimberley!'

'I know that. I never joke about sex.' She saw from the flash in his eyes that he recognised the words that he'd spoken to her. 'Just relax, Luc. It may have escaped your notice, but this time *I'm* the one in control. I've got you exactly where I want you and you're not going anywhere until I've finished with you.'

He swore under his breath but she saw him harden still further and gave a low laugh of satisfaction. He wanted her every bit as much as she wanted him and the knowledge thrilled her. Suddenly aware of her own power, she raked a nail down his chest and ran her tongue over her lips.

'I'm going to make you sob and beg, Luc,' she said softly, leaning forward and tracing the line of his rough jaw with her tongue. 'I'm going to make you so desperate that you can't even remember who you are or what you're doing here.'

She slid a hand slowly down his taut body and rested her palm just millimetres away from his straining manhood.

His hard jaw clenched and his eyes glittered dangerously. 'I will make you suffer for this.'

'You're the one who's suffering, Luc.'

But the truth was that she was suffering too. Her body ached and throbbed with a need that she hadn't experienced before. She was supposed to be the one doing the seducing but having his perfect masculine physique stretched out for her enjoyment was a temptation too great to resist.

She proceeded to lick her way down his body, exploring him everywhere except that one place that was straining to be touched. Her long hair fell forward, sliding over his naked, straining body like a sensual cloak.

'Kimberley—' His hoarse plea made her lift her head and she gazed at him, her mouth damp and her eyes shimmering with need.

'Not yet—' Desire curled low in her pelvis but she held it in check, determined to delay his satisfaction the way he always delayed hers. 'You haven't begged.'

'*Meu Deus*—' he cursed softly and closed his eyes, thick dark lashes brushing his bronzed skin as he struggled against his body's natural desire for satisfaction.

Her gaze slid down his body and her mouth dried. He was rock-hard and so aroused that she felt her mouth dry in anticipation. Why hadn't she thought of doing this before? she wondered.

For the first time she felt strong and powerful.

For the first time she felt like his equal.

For the first time she was able to torment him the way he always took pleasure in tormenting her.

She waited until every muscle was straining in his powerful body, until she couldn't wait any longer.

'Kimberley—' His voice shook and his lean hips thrust upwards. 'I'm begging—'

And then she touched him.

With the hot slide of her mouth, she took him and tasted, his harsh moans of pleasure fuelling her own sense of power and need. She explored every part of him with her fingers, with her tongue until she could no longer bear the ache deep in her body.

Only then did she lift her head and slide on top of him. She positioned herself over him, her hair trailing over his chest, her eyes fixed on his face as she allowed only the tip of his manhood to touch her intimately. With a soft curse he strained upwards trying to fill her, trying to take her breast in his mouth, but she held herself slightly away from him and leaned forward to kiss him.

'I'm still the one in control, Luc,' she whispered against his lips, but she knew that, strictly speaking, it wasn't true. She wanted him every bit as desperately as he wanted her.

But still she was going to make him wait.

She made him wait until the beads of sweat gathered on his brow, until he could no longer see straight, *until she wanted him so badly that she couldn't hold herself back a moment longer.*

And then finally she took him. Deep inside her so that she could feel the hard throb of his erection with every pulse of her body, so that she forgot that they were supposed to be separate, man and woman. Instead they were one.

And when the inevitable explosion came it was so blisteringly intense that for a moment she was afraid of what she'd unleashed. It was a beast that couldn't be tamed. A beast that savaged both of them. A beast that had to be allowed to run riot until finally it burned itself out.

Which it finally did. In a riot of soft cries, harsh groans, gasps and sobs and slippery flesh, the beast finally left them.

Struggling to breathe, Kimberley slid sideways, her arm over his chest, her leg over his leg.

Eventually her senses settled and she dared to lift her head.

He lay with his eyes closed, dense dark lashes brushing his perfect bone structure, his arms still locked above his head.

Suddenly, in the aftermath of such intimacy, she felt ridiculously shy and self-conscious. 'Luc?'

He didn't respond and she gave a frown and reached up and undid the handcuffs.

Instantly strong arms came around her and he rolled her on to her back, his eyes burning into hers. 'I can't believe you just did that—'

She felt the power and strength of his body pressing into her and gave a soft gasp. 'Are you angry with me?'

'Angry?' He groaned and brushed his mouth over hers in a lingering kiss. 'How could I be angry with you for giving me the best sex of my life? And anyway I don't have the energy to be angry. I don't have the energy for anything.'

She smiled, feeling clever and beautiful and every inch a woman. 'It was good, wasn't it?'

He rolled on to his back, taking her with him. 'It was amazing,' he said huskily, stroking her tangled hair away from her flushed cheeks with a gentle hand. '*Where* did you get those handcuffs?'

She tensed. That was a question she hadn't anticipated and she didn't want to spoil the moment by mentioning Rio. 'Someone I know was playing a joke on me,' she muttered vaguely, hoping that he wouldn't delve further.

Fortunately he didn't. Instead he hauled her closer still, snuggling her against him.

She felt a flicker of surprise. Luc tolerated a cuddle after sex but she could never recall him initiating that kind of contact before.

Luc did sex. He didn't do the emotional stuff.

He kissed the top of her head. 'I can't believe you just did that. And I can't believe I just let you.'

She gave a low laugh, more than a little pleased with herself. 'You didn't have any choice. For the first time in your life, you weren't the one in control. I was.'

To her surprise, he laughed. 'You're right, you are a different woman now,' he said in husky tones as he slid a hand over her heated flesh with undisguised masculine appreciation. 'You never would have had the courage to do what you just did seven years ago. In fact, you were pretty shocked by me.'

'You were my first lover,' she reminded him. 'I hadn't done any of those things before and you were totally controlling.'

'Necessary,' he assured her arrogantly, 'because you were too tied up with your inhibitions to let go. You were only able to do so when you could convince yourself that I was the one who seduced you. It was all my fault, isn't that right, *meu amorzinho*?'

There was laughter in his voice and she lifted her head and gave him a reproachful look. 'I was a virgin.'

He gave a macho, self-satisfied smile. 'I *know* that. And being the only man who had ever slept with you gave me an incredible high. Now, go to sleep.' He tightened his grip. 'You need to get some rest and recover your energy.'

Having delivered that command, he closed his eyes and promptly fell asleep himself, his arms locked firmly around her.

And it felt so good that Kimberley hardly dared move in case he woke up and changed his mind about the cuddle.

Being held by him made her feel safe and secure. *And it felt totally right.*

Which was ridiculous, she told herself, because there was nothing right about a relationship based on nothing more than sex.

Slowly, the happiness drained out of her as realisation dawned.

For her it was so much more than sex, and it always had been. She'd dismissed what she'd felt for him at eighteen as childish infatuation. Who wouldn't have been dazzled by a man as sophisticated as Luc? But the truth was that she'd loved Luc almost from the first moment she'd set eyes on him and time had done nothing to dilute her feelings. What she'd felt as a girl was no different to what she felt now, as a woman. Love was the reason she was so vulnerable to Luc. Love was the reason she hadn't looked at another man in the last seven years. It didn't matter that he was controlling and that he revealed nothing of himself. *It didn't matter that he was totally the wrong man.*

It didn't even matter that he didn't love her.

She still loved him.

She closed her eyes tightly, refusing to allow her bleak thoughts to spoil the moment. It would be over soon enough because they were almost at the end of their two weeks.

Luc woke several hours later to find the sun setting and Kimberley gone.

He felt a flicker of something that he didn't recognise. *Disappointment,* he decided immediately, rejecting the opportunity to examine his emotions in more detail.

The most explosive sex of his entire life had left him feeling refreshed and invigorated and more than ready to appreciate the woman who had been part of the experience.

Was it surprising that he felt disappointed that she wasn't still lying in his arms?

He sprang out of bed, noted the abandoned handcuffs with an appreciative male smile, and reached for a pair of casual trousers.

He found her by the pool, her expression pale and strained, her mobile phone in her hand.

The tension in her slender frame stopped him dead. 'Is something wrong?'

After what they'd shared, he'd expected to find her relaxed and smiling, recovering her energy levels in the sun, ready for the next bout of lovemaking. Instead she gave a start and shot him a guilty look before stuffing the phone back in her bag. 'Nothing's wrong.'

More unfamiliar emotions boiled up inside him. 'Who were you calling?'

She dipped her head, her long fiery hair concealing her expression from him. 'Just a friend.'

A friend?

Luc felt the sharp claws of jealousy dig into his flesh. What sex was the 'friend'? Had she been talking to another man? What was her life like when she was at home? Did she date? *Had she tied another man to the bed and rendered him unable to think?*

He realised with no small degree of discomfort that, although he'd spent weeks in bed with this woman, he knew next to nothing about her, and suddenly he was driven by a burning desire to discover *everything*.

'We're dining on the terrace tonight,' he said firmly as she glanced up at him, clearly as startled by hearing this unusual announcement as he had felt making it. 'And we're going to talk.'

She blinked and her lips parted. Those perfectly shaped lips that had driven him wild only hours earlier.

Resolutely Luc pushed the thought away. He wasn't going to think about that now. The same instincts that had made him an unbeatable force in business were currently telling him that something wasn't right about this situation. And he intended to make it right. He had a sudden burning need to see her smiling again. The reason *why* he should suddenly feel the urge to make a woman happy outside the bedroom didn't occur to him as he searched his brain for an answer.

Obviously she wasn't short of sex, so the problem couldn't possibly lie there. Just to confirm that fact, his mind ran speedily through the time they'd spent together and he concluded with a warm feeling of masculine satisfaction that she *definitely* couldn't be feeling unappreciated in that department.

Which meant that the problem must lie elsewhere.

Romance.

With a sudden burst of clarity, he identified the reason for her long face.

Perhaps the last two weeks had been a little too bedroom focused, he conceded. Wasn't it true that women needed different things to men? Apparently whole books had been written on the subject. For some inexplicable reason women needed to *talk* and certainly during the past two weeks he and Kimberley hadn't indulged much in the way of conversation. Acknowledgment of that fact would normally have left him nothing short of indifferent, but for some reason that he didn't entirely understand he suddenly felt a driving need to give her everything she wanted. *He wanted to make Kimberley happy.* And if conversation was what it took, then he was willing to make that sacrifice.

Convinced that he'd found the solution to the white, pinched look on her face, he waved a hand towards the bedroom with the smug look of a man who knew he had all the answers when it came to women.

'There are clothes in the wardrobe,' he informed her silkily. 'Choose something and meet me out here when you're dressed.'

She stared at him blankly, as if he'd just delivered a command that was nothing short of incomprehensible.

'What's the point of getting dressed when you're just going to strip me naked again?' she asked him and there was a hint of wariness in her tone that triggered his male early warning system.

Telling himself that he could exercise restraint when there was a higher purpose, he gave a smile. 'Because tonight I'm more interested in your mind than your body. We're going to *talk, meu amorzinho,* and I'm going to find out everything there is to know about you.'

That soft mouth, *the same mouth that had taken him to paradise and back,* curved into a wry smile. 'And what about you, Luc? Are you going to talk too? Or am I going to be the one doing all the giving? Perhaps I want to know everything there is to know about you too.'

Luc gave a brief frown but recovered himself in time. If she wanted him to talk too, then he could do that. True, it wasn't his favourite pastime, but he dealt with inquisitive journalists on a daily basis and was used to talking about a wide range of subjects. He was more than confident that he could maintain conversation over dinner with an attractive woman if the incentive was great enough.

'I look forward to telling you everything you want to know,' he said diplomatically, urging her back towards the villa with the palm of his hand. 'Change and I'll ask the staff to serve dinner by the pool.'

She walked away from him with the fluid, graceful movement of a dancer. Luc's eyes automatically slid down her slender back and he struggled briefly against a powerful impulse to forget this whole 'romantic' approach and indulge the caveman that was threatening to burst out from inside him.

Remembering the desolate expression on her face, he reminded himself that a small investment could often yield surprising results and that might well be the case with Kimberley.

He was entirely confident that exercising physical restraint for a short time would pay dividends in the bedroom.

All he needed to make his investment complete were pretty flowers, good wine and plenty of delicious food and the smile would soon be back on her face.

Easy, he thought to himself as he strode purposefully towards the kitchen to brief his chef and his housekeeper. Handling women was no different from any other business negotiation. It was just a question of identifying their weakness, and then moving in for the kill.

Before the evening was out, she'd be smiling again.

And he could satisfy the caveman inside him.

CHAPTER SEVEN

'So why did you give up modelling?'

Luc lounged across from her, his face bronzed and lethally handsome in the flickering candlelight. The setting couldn't have been more romantic. The pool was illuminated by what seemed like hundreds of tiny lights, the evening was warm and the air was filled with the heady scent of exotic flowers. It was a setting fit for seduction and yet he'd already seduced her. More times than she cared to count.

So why the exotic arrangement of flowers on the table?

Why the tablecloth and the sparkling crystal?

And why was he dressed in a pair of tailored trousers and an exquisite silk shirt when he'd barely bothered to get dressed for the past two weeks?

If it hadn't been Luc sitting across from her, she would have thought that the setting had been designed for romance.

But Luc didn't do romantic. Luc did white-hot sex. Luc did blistering, uncontrollable passion. Luc did control and domination. He most certainly, *definitely* didn't do romantic.

So why was he doing it now?

And why the sudden desire to acquaint himself with her every thought and feeling? Ever since she'd emerged on to the terrace he'd been openly solicitous about every aspect of her comfort and asked her endless questions about herself until she felt like a candidate in an interview. Especially because it was impossible to relax in case she gave the wrong answers and revealed too much.

Kimberley concentrated on her food, wondering what had sparked Luc's sudden uncharacteristic desire for conversation. Had he guessed that she was hiding something? Had he overheard her on the phone?

'Modelling gave me up,' she said dryly, 'when I chose not to turn up for any of the swimwear shots on the beach because I was in your bed. It was a lucrative account for the agency and I lost it for them. They took me off their books and made sure I wasn't given work again.'

Luc's eyes hardened. 'Give me the name of the agency.'

She blinked. 'Why?' Amusement lit her eyes. 'Are you going to close them down?'

He didn't smile. 'Maybe.'

'There's no need. I was glad to give up modelling. The life-style never suited me. You know I was never comfortable with the partying, the drugs—any of that.'

'I know you were incredibly naïve and innocent when I met you,' he drawled softly, leaning across to top up her glass. 'Why else would you have been walking along the beach in Rio de Janeiro at midnight in a non-existent dress with your hair dazzling like an Olympic torch? I couldn't believe my eyes. You were like some sort of virgin sacrifice, left out for the lions to consume.'

She gave a wry smile, acknowledging how stupid she'd been. 'The other girls persuaded me to go to a party but I hated every moment. I just wanted to get back to my hotel and there were no taxis,' she said simply, remembering that evening with a small shudder. If Luc hadn't come along when he had—

'It had been a long time since I'd been required to test my skills against a flick-knife,' Luc observed lightly, his eyes rest-

ing on her face in an intense male scrutiny that she found more
than a little disturbing.

'You were impressive,' she conceded, wondering if the
moment when he'd taken on a gang of six thugs, all with
knives, had been when she'd fallen in love with him.

But even dressed in a shockingly expensive designer suit
Luc Santoro looked like a man who could handle himself.
And she'd be less than honest if she didn't admit that his
spontaneous demonstration of physical skill and courage had
been one of the elements that had initially drawn her to him.
When in her life, before that moment, had anyone ever defended her? Never, and the novelty of meeting a man prepared to risk his life to extract a female from a situation that
had been entirely of her own making had proved more than
a little intoxicating.

In the single second it had taken him to identify the leader
of the gang, he'd moved with such speed and skill that
Kimberley had wondered for a moment whether her rescuer
might not be more dangerous than her attackers.

*Where exactly had he learned those street-fighting tactics
that he'd used to extricate her from danger that night?*

Kimberley fingered her glass and glanced across at him,
remembering the gossip that she'd heard about his past.
Nothing specific. Just speculation.

Her eyes hovered on his blue-shadowed jaw and the hard
male perfection of his bone structure. No one with a grain of
common sense would mess with Luc Santoro.

'Where did you learn to fight?' She asked the question before she could stop herself and she saw his hand still en route
to his glass.

'*Não entendo*. I don't understand.' He frowned at her.
'What do you mean, "fight"?'

She swallowed. 'The night you rescued me, you took on
six men. How did you learn to do that? *Where* did you learn?'

He picked up his glass. 'I'm a man. Fighting is instinctive.'

'I don't believe that.' Something made her push the point. 'You were outnumbered six to one and you anticipated all their tricks. As if you'd been trained in the same school of fighting.'

There was the briefest pause. 'The school of fighting I attended is called life,' he said dryly. 'I learned a great deal and I learned it early on.'

'What was it about your life that made it necessary for you to learn those skills? I've never learned them. If I had, perhaps I wouldn't have got myself into trouble that night,' she admitted. 'I wasn't very streetwise. To be honest, there wasn't any need to be where I was brought up.'

He gave a short laugh and drank deeply. 'You once told me that your home was a leafy English village where everyone knew everyone. Very middle class. Perhaps it's hardly surprising that you didn't find yourself learning self-defence.'

Maybe that was why he fascinated her. He was a man of contradictions. On the one hand he had great wealth and sophistication and he moved in the highest, most glittering social circles. But that veneer of sophistication didn't entirely hide the dark, dangerous, almost primitive side of his nature that she'd sensed from the very first moment they'd met. There was nothing tame or safe about Luc Santoro.

Which was one of the reasons he was so irresistible to women.

'I take it your upbringing wasn't middle class,' she ventured. 'Were you born in Rio de Janeiro?'

'Yes.' His smile was slightly mocking. 'I'm a genuine *Carioca.*'

She knew that was the name given to someone born or living in Rio de Janeiro.

'So how did you make it from *Carioca* to billionaire tycoon?' she asked lightly and he delivered her a smile that both charmed and seduced.

'Motivation and hard work.' He leaned forward, his eyes fixed on her face. 'If you want something badly enough, *meu amorzinho*, you can have it. It's just a question of careful planning and letting nothing stand in your way.'

His cold, ruthless approach to life, so different from her own, made her shiver. 'Just because you want something you can't just go out there and take it!'

His gaze didn't shift from hers. 'Why not?'

'Because you have to consider other people.'

A slightly mocking smile touched his beautifully shaped mouth. 'That's a typically female approach.' The smile faded. 'I, on the other hand, believe that trusting people is a hobby for fools. You decide what you want in life and then you go for it. You build something up until no one can take it away from you.'

There was such passion and volatility in the sudden flash of his dark eyes that Kimberley found that she was holding her breath. For one brief tantalising moment she felt she'd been given a glimpse of the real Luc—the man underneath that cool, emotionless exterior.

Sensing the sudden turbulence in his mood, she reached across the table in an instinctive gesture of comfort. 'Is that what happened?' Her voice was soft. 'Did someone take something away from you?'

He removed his hand from hers and leaned back in his chair, dark eyes veiled. 'Why do women always search for the dramatic? Everyone's character is formed by events in their lives.' He gave a dismissive shrug. 'I'm no different.'

'But you shut everyone out,' she said passionately and he gave a cool smile.

'I'm a man, *meu amorzinho*, and like most men I hunt alone. And I don't allow another male to poach on my territory. The friend you were speaking to earlier—' the warmth of his tone dropped several degrees '—was it a man?'

His slick change of subject took her by surprise and she answered without thinking. 'Yes.'

She saw his eyes glint dangerously and his lean, strong fingers tighten on his glass. Suddenly the atmosphere changed from comfortable to menacing.

His mouth was set in a grim line and his body held a certain stillness that raised the tension several notches. 'And have you been together long?'

'It isn't like that—'

'Evidently not,' he delivered with ruthless bite, 'if he allows his woman to spend two weeks in another man's bed. Or doesn't he know?'

She bit her lip. 'He's just a friend—'

'How good a friend?'

'The very best!' Loyalty to Jason made her tell the truth. 'He's stood by me through everything.'

'I'm sure he's done far more than stand.' The sardonic lift of his dark brow stung her more than his sarcasm.

She dropped her fork with a clatter. 'Not everyone is like you, Luc! Some people have proper relationships.' She rose to her feet, so angry and upset that she almost knocked the chair over. 'Relationships that aren't all about sex and nothing else. But you're so emotionally stunted you couldn't possibly understand that.'

'*Meu Deus*, what is this about?' He rose to his feet too, six-foot-four of powerful, angry male. Tension throbbed and pulsed between them. 'I am *not* emotionally stunted.'

She lifted her hands in a gesture of exasperation. 'Then *tell* me something about yourself! Anything.'

'Why? What does the sharing of past history bring to a relationship?' His eyes burned dark with temper. 'Does it change things between us if I tell you that I was born in the *favelas*, the slums of Rio, so poor that food was a luxury? Does it change things between us if I tell you that my father and mother worked like animals to take themselves and me away from that place? *Does it help you to know that they succeeded, only to lose everything and be forced back into the lifestyle they'd fought so hard to leave behind?*' He paced round the table and dragged her hard against him, his face grim and set as he raked her shocked face with night-black eyes. 'Tell me, *meu amorzinho*, now that you know the truth of where I came from, now that you know that I have emotions, has our relationship improved?'

Somehow she found her voice. 'That's the first time you've ever told me anything about yourself.'

'Then savour the moment,' he advised silkily, raking lean bronzed fingers through her silky hair in an unmistakably possessive gesture, 'because mindless chatter about past events doesn't rank as my favourite pastime.'

Had she been in any doubt, one breathless glance into his dark eyes enlightened her as to exactly what constituted his favourite pastime.

'I thought tonight was about conversation and getting to know each other.'

'You now know more about me than almost any other person on the planet,' he delivered in husky tones, tugging at her hair gently and fastening his mouth on the smooth pale skin of her neck. 'Let's leave it at that.'

His tongue flickered and teased and she felt her stomach shift and her eyes drifted closed. 'Luc—'

'A man can only stand so much talking in one night,' he groaned against her skin, sliding his hand down her back and bringing her hard against him. 'It's time to revert to body language.'

With that he scooped her up and carried her through to the bedroom.

She stared up at him in a state of helpless excitement, part of her simmering with exasperation that his ability to sustain a conversation about himself had been so short-lived and part of her as desperate for him as he clearly was for her.

They'd made progress, she thought, as he stripped off his shirt and dropped it on the floor with indecent haste and a careless disregard for its future appearance. Small progress, perhaps, but still, it was progress.

They'd dressed. They'd shared a meal. They'd talked—sort of.

And that was her last coherent thought as he stripped her naked with ruthless precision and brought his mouth down on hers.

Kimberley waited for all the usual feelings to swamp her but this time something was different. He was different. More gentle. More caring?

The thought popped into her head and she pushed it away ruthlessly. No! She wasn't going to do that again—make the mistake of believing that Luc was interested in anything other than her body. She'd done that once before and allowing herself to dream about something that could never happen had almost broken her heart.

But it *was* different.

Instead of dominating or being dominated, they *shared* and when they finally descended from an explosive climax he held her firmly against him, refusing to let her go.

As the delicious spasms died and they both lay spent and exhausted, he still refused to let her go, curving her into his body and locking his arms tightly around her as if he was afraid she might leave.

Which was ridiculous, she told herself sleepily, because they both knew that she was leaving and they both knew he wouldn't care.

The two weeks was almost up.

But she was too sleepy to make sense of any of it and eventually she stopped wondering and asking herself questions and drifted off to sleep in the warm, safe circle of his arms.

The day before she was due to fly home, Kimberley awoke late and found the bed empty.

Her heart gave a thud of disappointment and then she noticed that the French doors on to the terrace were open and she heard the rhythmic splashing of someone swimming in the pool.

She lay there and smiled.

Obviously Luc had decided on an early swim. Or maybe not that early, she thought ruefully as she cast a glance at her watch.

Now would be a good time to phone home for the final time, to check on the arrangements for the following day.

She scraped her tangled hair out of her eyes, flinched slightly as her bruised aching body reminded her of how they'd spent most of the night, and reached for her phone.

Jason answered and they talked for a bit and then she spoke to Rio, a soft smile touching her mouth as she listened to his excited chatter.

She couldn't wait to see him.

'I miss you, baby.'

'Are you coming home soon, Mummy?' Suddenly he sounded very young. 'I miss you.'

Tears clogged her throat. 'I'll be home tomorrow. And I miss you too.'

She heard a noise behind her and, with a horrified premonition, she turned round to see Luc standing there. A towel was looped carelessly around his waist, his breathtakingly gorgeous bronzed body was glistening with water and his expression black as thunder.

She said a hasty goodbye to Rio, cut the connection and turned to face the music.

'So your "*friend*" is missing you.' His tone was icy cold

as he padded towards her, all simmering anger and lethal menace. 'Next time you can tell the "*friend*" that he's poaching on my time.'

She couldn't understand why he was so angry.

'Our two weeks are up tomorrow, Luc,' she reminded him, trying to keep her tone reasonable, 'and I was making arrangements.'

He stopped dead and stared at her blankly, as if she'd told him something that he didn't already know. Something flitted across his handsome face. Surprise? Regret?

'It was just a phone call—' If she hadn't known better she would have said that he was jealous, but how could he be jealous of a phone call?

For a moment her heart skittered slightly and then she remembered that in order to be jealous you had to care, and Luc didn't care about anything except sex. He enjoyed the physical side of their relationship but nothing more.

'This is ridiculous,' she said, trying to keep her voice steady. 'You were the one who negotiated the terms. You agreed to two weeks, Luc, and those two weeks are up today.'

'I didn't agree to two weeks. You really can't wait to get home to him, can you?'

She gaped at him in disbelief. 'Why are you behaving like this? It doesn't make sense. Especially as we don't even have a proper relationship.'

His breath hissed through his teeth. 'We *do* have a relationship. What do you think the last two weeks have been all about?'

'Sex,' she replied in a flat tone. 'The last two weeks have been all about sex.'

The anger faded and he eyed her warily, like a man who knew he was on extremely rocky ground. '*Not* just about sex. Last night we talked.'

'*I* talked,' she pointed out wryly. '*You* questioned me.'

His hard jaw clenched. 'I told you about my past.'

'You yelled and shouted and lost your temper,' she reminded him in a calm voice, 'and then reluctantly disclosed a tiny morsel of your experiences in childhood! Prisoners under torture have revealed more!'

'Well, I'm not *used* to talking about myself,' he exclaimed defensively, pacing across the floor and throwing her a simmering black look. 'But if that's what you want, we'll have dinner on the terrace again tonight and we'll talk again.'

She stared at him, stunned into silence by his uncharacteristic offer to do something that was so completely against his nature.

Why would he bother?

'I have to go home, Luc,' she said quietly and he stopped pacing and simply glared at her.

'*Why?*'

'Because I have a child,' she said flatly, 'a child who I love and miss and need to be near. We've carefully avoided mentioning it for the past two weeks but the fact that we haven't mentioned it doesn't change the facts. My *life* is in London and tomorrow I'm going home.'

A muscle flickered in his lean jaw. 'You have a *lover* in London.'

Was he ignoring the issue of Rio once again?

She rose to her feet, totally bemused. 'Why are you acting in this jealous, possessive fashion when we both knew that this was just for two weeks?'

'I'm *not* jealous,' he refuted her accusation in proud tones, the disdainful look he cast in her direction telling her exactly what he thought of the mere suggestion that he might suffer from such a base emotion. 'But I don't share. Ever. I told you that once before.'

Kimberley closed her eyes briefly and decided that if she

lived to be a hundred and read every book written on the subject, she'd never understand men.

'My flight leaves tomorrow afternoon,' she reminded him steadily and his eyes narrowed.

'Cancel that flight,' he advised silkily, 'or I will cancel it for you.'

She'd done it again, she thought helplessly as she dragged her eyes away from his magnificent body. Given herself to him, heart, body and soul. And now she was going to have to find a way to recover.

How could she ever have thought she'd be able to walk away from him and feel nothing?

They had clinics for coming off drugs and drinks, she reflected with almost hysterical amusement. What she needed was a clinic for breaking her addiction to Luciano Santoro. Otherwise she was going to live the rest of her life craving a man she couldn't have.

Jealous?

Luc powered through the swimming pool yet again in an attempt to drive out the uncomfortable and unfamiliar thoughts and feelings that crowded his brain. The fact that he'd spent an unusual amount of time in the pool in pursuit of calm that continued to elude him hadn't escaped him.

If he was totally honest, then he didn't exactly know what was happening to him at the moment. Certainly he'd never felt the same burning need to keep a woman by his side as he did with Kimberley.

But was that really so surprising? he reasoned. She was *incredible* in bed. What normal sane man would want to let her go? It had nothing to do with jealousy and everything to do with sanity, he decided as he executed a perfect turn and swam down the pool again.

The fact that the agreed two weeks hadn't been enough to

get her out of his system troubled him slightly, but he was entirely sure that a week or two more would be sufficient to convince him of the merits of moving on to another willing female, this time someone less motivated to discover everything about him.

He'd simply work out a way of persuading Kimberley to extend their deal, he decided, confident that the problem was now all but solved.

With his usual limitless energy, he sprang out of the pool and reached for a towel.

The fact that she appeared to be determined to fly home the following day didn't trouble him in the slightest. He would simply talk her out of it. How hard could that be for a man who negotiated million dollar deals before breakfast on virtually a daily basis? He dealt with hard-nosed businessmen all the time. One extremely willing woman would be a piece of cake, even if she did have red hair, an extremely uncertain temper and what could almost be termed as a conversation disorder.

He had one more night.

He'd start by proving to her that he could talk as much as the next man when the situation called for it. Then he'd take her to bed.

By the end of the night he was entirely confident that she would be the one calling the airline to cancel her flight.

The following morning Kimberley checked her flight ticket and her passport and tucked them carefully back into her handbag. A small piece of hand luggage lay open on the bed. She'd found the case in her dressing room and, since it was clearly for her use and the clothes had been purchased specifically for her, she'd decided that she might as well take her favourites. Probably none of Luc's other girlfriends ever wore the same outfit twice, she thought wryly as she slipped the silk dress off the hanger and placed it carefully in the case, trying not to think too hard about what leaving would mean.

The previous evening they'd dined on the terrace again, and this time Luc had made what could only be described as a heroic effort to talk about himself. In fact he hadn't stopped talking and if she hadn't been so touched she would have laughed.

It was such an obvious struggle for him to discuss anything remotely personal but he'd tried extremely hard, sharing with her all manner of snippets about his childhood and the way his office worked.

The question of *why* he was trying so hard slid into her mind, but she dismissed it because the answer was so obvious. He wanted her to stay because he wanted more sex and for some reason he'd worked out that the way to change her mind about leaving was to start talking.

But of course her mind hadn't been changed, even by what had followed. Before last night she'd thought that she'd already experienced the very best in sex. But Luc had been relentless in his determination to drive her to the very pinnacle of ecstasy, proving once again that he was a skilled and sophisticated lover.

And she couldn't imagine living without him.

She was *desperate* to go home and be with her son, but she wanted to be with Luc too.

At that moment he walked out from the bathroom, his dark jaw freshly shaved, his hair still damp from the shower. Despite his almost total absence of sleep, he looked refreshed and invigorated and sexier than any man had a right to be.

Her eyes feasted on him, knowing that it would probably be the last time.

If she didn't have her son to think of, would she have stayed?

No, because she wasn't going to get her heart broken a second time in her life, she told herself firmly as she dropped a bikini into the case.

His gaze fastened on the case and he gave a sharp frown. 'Why are you packing?'

'Because I'm going home,' she reminded him, slightly bemused by his question. He knew she was going home that afternoon. 'I'm presuming your pilot will take me to the airport.'

'He certainly will not.' The Rolex on his bronzed wrist glinted as he reached out to remove the bag from her hand in a decisive movement. 'Because you're not going home. I thought we both agreed that.'

Kimberley racked her brain and tried to recall having said anything that might have given him that impression. 'We didn't agree that.'

He stepped closer to her and slid a possessive hand into her hair. 'Did we or did we not,' he enquired in silky tones, 'spend the entire night making love?'

Her face heated at the memory and the breath caught in her throat. 'Yes, but—'

His dark head lowered towards hers, an arrogant smile on his sexy mouth. 'And was it, or was it not, the most mind-blowing experience of your life?'

The flames flickered higher and higher inside her. 'It was amazing,' she agreed huskily, 'but I still have to go.'

The arrogant smile faded and blank incomprehension flickered across his handsome face. 'Why?'

'Because I have to go home.'

His brow cleared. 'Easily solved. Your home is now here. With me.'

She stared at him in amazement and a flicker of crazy hope came to life inside her. 'You want me to live with you?' She was so stunned that her voice cracked and he gave a smile loaded with an abundance of male self-confidence.

'Of course. The sex between us is simply amazing. I'd have to be out of my mind to let you go. So you stay. As my mistress. Until we decide that we've had enough of each other.'

The hope disintegrated into a million tiny pieces, blown away by his total lack of sensitivity, and she stared at him in disbelief.

'Your *mistress?* Are we suddenly living in the Middle Ages?'

'Mistress, girlfriend—' He gave a casual lift of his broad shoulders to indicate that he considered the terms both interchangeable and irrelevant. 'Choose whatever title you like.'

'How about "mug" or "idiot"?' Kimberley suggested helpfully, her temper starting to boil, 'because that's what I'd be if I accepted an invitation like that from a man like you.'

How could she have allowed herself to think for one single solitary minute that he might care for her just a little bit?

Luc wasn't capable of caring for anyone.

He raked long fingers through his dark hair, his expression showing that he was holding on to his patience with visible effort. 'I don't think you understood,' he said stiffly. 'I'm suggesting that you move in with me on a permanent basis, at least for the foreseeable future—'

'That's semi-permanent, Luc, and I understood you perfectly. Sex on tap, until I bore you.' Kimberley reached for the nightdress she'd worn before he'd stripped it from her quivering, pliant body. 'Very convenient for you—very precarious for me. So no thanks. These days I have more self-respect than to accept an offer like that.' She stuffed the nightdress in the case, as angry with herself as she was with him.

How could she have been so stupid as to fall for this man again?

How could she have been that shallow?

'*No thanks?*' Night-black eyes raked her flushed cheeks

with a lethal mixture of naked incredulity and stunned amazement. 'Do you realise that I have never made that offer to a woman before in my entire life? I will need to start visiting the office occasionally but believe me, *meu amorzinho*, we will be spending plenty of time together.' His voice dropped to a sexy drawl as he clearly dismissed her refusal as a misunderstanding. 'From now on I'll be extremely motivated to finish my working day early.'

Clearly he thought that was sufficient inducement for her to empty the contents of the case back into the drawers.

'You're unbelievable, do you know that?' She stared at him with a mixture of amazement and exasperation, wondering whether a sharp blow to the head would be of any help in bringing him to his senses. 'It is *not* a compliment to know that someone wants you just for sex!'

He frowned. 'If you're pretending the sex isn't amazing between us then you're deluding yourself again and I thought we'd moved past that point.'

'There's nothing wrong with the sex. The sex is great. The sex is amazing.' She spoke in staccato tones as she turned back to the bed and continued to stuff and push things into the tiny bag. 'But there are other things that are just as important as sex and there's *everything* wrong with those.'

'What do you mean, other things? What other things?' There was a hint of genuine confusion in his handsome features, as if he couldn't for one minute imagine there being anything more important than sex. And for him there probably wasn't, she conceded helplessly, flipping the lid of the case shut.

She scraped her hair back from her face and lifted her chin, her eyes challenging as she met his scorching dark gaze. 'Sharing a life, for one thing. Everyday activities. But you wouldn't understand about that because you're well and truly stuck in the Stone Age. For you, a woman's place is flat on her back, preferably stark naked, isn't that right, Luc?' She dropped the bag and spread her hands in a gesture of pure exasperation. 'Do you realise that you've never actually taken me out, Luc? Never. I mean, what exactly was the point of buying me a whole wardrobe full of flashy clothes when I have no need to dress up?'

'Because I like stripping them off you and because I can't see you naked without wanting to be inside you,' he admitted with characteristic frankness and she gave a gurgle of exasperation and fought the temptation to stamp her foot.

'Sex again! Do you realise that once again we haven't actually left this island?'

His dark brows came together in a sharp frown. 'There was no reason to leave. Everything we need is here.'

'Of course it is.' Her voice shook. 'Because all you need when a relationship is based on nothing but sex is a very large bed and maybe not even that if there happens to be a comfortable lift handy.'

His dark eyes narrowed warily. 'You're becoming very emotional—'

'Dead right I'm emotional.' She flung her head back and her hair trailed like tongues of fire down her back. 'I'm a woman and I like being emotional. Believe it or not, I *like* being able to feel things because feeling is what makes us human. You should try it some time; you might find it liberating.'

A muscle flickered in his lean cheek and he gritted his teeth, hanging on to his temper with visible difficulty. 'I can't talk to you when you're like this.'

'You can't talk to me whatever I'm like, Luc.' She dragged the case off the bed and dropped it on the floor. 'You *try* and talk to me but it's such an effort, such an act, that I feel exhausted for you. And you always treat me like a journalist. Giving me sound bites. Things that you're happy for me to hear. Things that sound good. I never get near to the real you.'

'You have been naked underneath the real me for the best part of two weeks,' he reminded her silkily. 'How much nearer could you get?'

Suddenly the fight drained out of her.

He just didn't get it. And he never would. And the sooner she gave up trying to make him understand, the better it would be for both of them.

They were so different it was laughable.

'And those two weeks are now finished,' she reminded him flatly, picking the case up and taking it to the bedroom door. 'You don't know the meaning of the word compromise. There's a flight leaving for London this afternoon. I'd be grateful if you'd ask your pilot to fly me to the airport so that I can catch it. I'm going home to my child. The child you still don't believe exists.'

He stared at her in stunned silence, his expression that of a man trying to comprehend the incomprehensible. Then he muttered something in his own language and turned on his heel, striding out of the room without a backward glance.

Exhausted and drained, Kimberley stared after him, her heart a solid lump of misery in her chest. What had she expected? That he'd argue with her? That he'd make her stay?

That he'd suddenly have a personality transplant and they'd live happily ever after?

She gave herself a mental shake and decided that she was losing her mind.

The two weeks were over and Luc was never, ever going to change. And neither was she. The truth was that the physical attraction between them was so breathtakingly powerful that it blinded her to the truth.

He wasn't what she wanted in a relationship and that was the end of it.

She was never going to share anything other than passion with Luc, and it wasn't enough for her.

She'd done what was needed. Her son was safe. It was time to get on with her life.

Time to go home.

CHAPTER EIGHT

LUNCHTIME came and went with no sign of Luc and Kimberley glanced at her watch with increasing anxiety, afraid that she was going to miss her flight. By mid-afternoon she was sure of it. There was no sign of the helicopter and no sign of Luc.

Short of swimming or flagging down a passing boat, there was no other way off the island.

Feeling hot and tired and furious with Luc for blatantly sabotaging her plans, she was on the point of picking up the phone and seeing whether she could arrange a helicopter taxi to take her to the airport when she finally heard the distinctive sound of a helicopter approaching.

She breathed a sigh of relief. There was no way she'd make it to the airport in time to catch her flight to London, but at least she'd be at the airport ready to take the first available flight the following day.

Keen to leave the island as soon as possible, Kimberley picked up her bag and walked quickly through the lush gardens towards the helicopter pad, wondering whether Luc was even going to bother to say goodbye.

The late afternoon sun was almost unbearably hot and she exchanged a few polite words with the pilot before climbing into the helicopter, eager to protect herself from the heat.

Moments later Luc came striding towards her and he looked so staggeringly handsome that she caught her breath. The casual trousers, swimming trunks, bare torso were gone to be replaced by a designer suit that outlined the male perfection of his body.

There was more to a relationship than the physical, she reminded herself firmly, gritting her teeth and glancing in the opposite direction in an attempt to break the sensual spell his presence cast over her.

He exchanged a few words with one of the bodyguards who was hovering and then joined her in the helicopter, seating himself beside her.

Surely he wasn't coming with her?

She looked at him in surprise, trying not to notice the way his immaculate grey suit showed off the impressive width of his shoulders. He looked every inch the sophisticated, successful tycoon, cool and more than a little remote.

'What are you doing?'

'Exploring the meaning of the word compromise,' he informed her in silky tones, fastening his seat belt in a determined gesture. 'Showing you that I can be as flexible as the next guy when the need arises. If you won't stay here, then I'll come with you.'

She gaped at him.

Luc? Flexible?

He was about as flexible as a steel rod. But, on the other hand, he was sitting next to her, she conceded, feeling slightly weakened by that realisation.

'You're seriously coming with me?' Delight and excitement mingled with sudden panic. Was he coming to see his son? Was he seeking the proof he'd demanded? Or was there another reason? 'Do you have business interests in London?'

'I have business everywhere,' he informed her in a lazy drawl, 'and London is no exception, although perhaps it's only in the last few hours that I developed this burning need to give that particular area of my business my personal attention.'

He leaned forward and issued some instructions to his pilot before relaxing back in his seat.

'Well, I hate to tell you this but we won't be going anywhere today because we've missed the flight,' she informed him and he threw her an amused look.

'The flight leaves when I give orders for it to leave. Not before. We most certainly won't miss it.'

'It takes off in—' she glanced at her watch and pulled a face '—ten minutes, to be precise. And even you can't command a commercial airline.'

'But we're not flying by commercial airline,' he informed her in lazy, almost bored tones as he stretched his long legs out in front of him. 'My private jet is already refuelled and waiting for our arrival.'

His private jet? She blinked at him. 'You have your own plane?'

'Of course.' A dark eyebrow swooped upwards and the amusement in his eyes deepened. 'I have offices all over the world which require my presence on an all too frequent basis. How else did you think I travelled? Flying carpet?'

She blushed and gritted her teeth, feeling ridiculously naïve. 'I've never thought about it at all,' she admitted, 'but I suppose if I had I would have naturally assumed you caught a flight like other people.'

His smile widened. 'But I'm *not* like other people—' he leaned forward, his dark gaze burning into hers '—and two weeks naked in my bed should have convinced you of that fact.'

Vivid, erotic images burst into her brain and she struggled with a ridiculous impulse to slide her arms round his neck.

He was an addiction, she reminded herself firmly, *and no one cured an addiction by continuing to enjoy the addictive substance.*

'Luc—' she cleared her throat and wished he wasn't quite so close to her '—we agreed two weeks and the two weeks is finished.'

'And the next two weeks are just beginning,' he told her helpfully and she looked at him in exasperation.

'Do you know the meaning of the word no?'

He gave a careless shrug of his broad shoulders. 'I'm not that great with "no" or "maybe",' he admitted without a trace of apology, 'but I'm working on "compromise" and "conversation" so who knows?'

She didn't know whether to laugh or hit him. And, no matter how much the rational part of her brain told her that having Luc in London would complicate her life in the extreme, another part lifted and floated with sheer excitement that he'd changed his plans for her. That he was coming to London to be with *her*.

In desperation she tried to stifle that part of herself but failed dismally and spent the entire helicopter flight in a dreamy haze, trying not to read too much into his actions, *trying to drag herself back down from the clouds*. He was still Luc, she reminded herself firmly, and he was never going to change.

At the airport they transferred on to his private jet and Kimberley found it hard to appear cool and indifferent as she was greeted on to the aircraft like royalty.

Once inside, she eyed the luxurious seating area in amazement. 'It's bigger than the average house. And more comfortable, come to that.'

'I do a lot of travelling, so comfort is essential.' He urged her forward into the body of the plane. 'There's a bathroom, a meeting room, a small cinema and an extremely large bedroom.' The sudden gleam in his eyes warned her that they'd be making use of the latter and hot colour touched her cheeks as she gazed around her in amazement.

'Just how rich are you?'

'Shockingly, indecently, *extravagantly* rich,' he assured her calmly, amusement lighting his dark eyes as he registered her ill-disguised awe at this visual demonstration of his wealth, 'which is presumably why you came to me for the five million dollars you needed to pay for your—er—*expenses*.' He waved a hand at the sofa. 'Sit down. We missed lunch and I'm starving and there's an extremely good bottle of Cristal waiting for our attention.'

She sank into the soft embrace of a creamy leather sofa and wondered what it was like to have so much money that you never, ever had to worry again.

They were served by a team of staff who discreetly tended to their every need and then vanished into a different part of the plane, leaving them alone.

'I didn't know you had an office in London.' She sipped her champagne and tucked into spicy chicken served with a delicious side salad.

'I have offices in most of the major cities of the world,' he observed in dry tones, the amusement back in his dark eyes. 'And I didn't know that you had such a burning interest in the detail of my business.'

'That's because we never talk,' she reminded him and he gave her a mocking smile.

'You wish to spend our evenings discussing fourth quarter sales figures?'

She sipped her champagne and realised that she was only just appreciating the true size of his business empire. The truth was that when she was with him she never saw further than the man himself and she'd somehow managed to remain oblivious to the power he yielded. 'And what will you be doing while you're in London?'

One dark eyebrow lifted in abject mockery. 'If you have to ask me that question then I obviously haven't made the objective of my visit clear enough,' he drawled and she felt her heart skitter in her chest.

She shouldn't be flattered. She really shouldn't. *But she was.*

'You're seriously travelling to London to be with me?' She just couldn't contain the little jump in her pulse rate.

'You thought I required a change of scenery?'

Remembering the beauty of his island, she gave a smile. 'Hardly. I just can't quite believe that you changed your plans to be with me.'

Hope flared inside her.

Maybe she'd got him wrong.

Would he cross an ocean just for physical satisfaction? Or was there something more to their relationship, after all?

'The sex between us is truly amazing, *meu amorzinho*,' he replied, 'and in any relationship there must be compromise. You taught me that.'

Hope fizzled out. 'So what you're saying is that you're willing to change countries in order to carry on having sex with me.'

So much for believing that he actually wanted to spend time with her.

'If you're about to pick a fight then I ought to warn you that there is sufficient turbulence outside the plane without causing more on the inside.' He stretched long legs out in front of him, infuriatingly relaxed in the face of her growing tension. 'As you yourself pointed out, I have never before changed my plans for a woman. It's a compliment.'

She bit her lip and refrained from lecturing him on the true definition of the word compliment. It was true that she didn't want to pick a fight. What was the point? He was never going to change and the sooner she accepted that, the happier she'd be.

'Well, we won't be able to spend much time together. I have a business that needs my attention,' she said flatly. And a son. *A son who Luc still didn't believe existed.* 'Unlike you, I don't have a massive staff willing to do the work in my absence. Having been away for two weeks, I have lots of catching up to do.'

'My hotel suite comes complete with my own staff and full office facilities, which you are welcome to use,' he offered smoothly and she felt herself tense.

'I don't need office space,' she said quickly. 'I've been away for two weeks, Luc. There are people I need to see.'

There was a sardonic gleam in his dark eyes as he studied her. 'But presumably your evenings and nights will be available.'

She should say no. She should tell him that their relationship was over. 'Possibly.' She put down her fork, leaving her food untouched. Being with Luc unsettled her stomach so much that she couldn't face food. 'I'll meet you for dinner.'

Once Rio was tucked up in bed and asleep.

What was wrong with that? she asked herself weakly. She was already crazily in love with Luc. What did she have to lose by spending more time with him?

They landed in the early morning in time to get stuck in the commuter traffic that crawled its way into London on a daily basis during the week and Luc had plenty of opportunity to contemplate the distinct possibility that he'd suffered a personality change.

Never in his life before had he suffered an impulse to adjust his plans for a woman, least of all follow one halfway across the world. The fact that he was now in London, a city that hadn't featured as part of his immediate plans, left him suffering from no small degree of discomfort.

And if he needed any confirmation of the fact that he

was acting out of character, then he simply had to look at Kimberley's face.

It was hard to say who was more shocked, he mused with wry amusement as he cast a sideways look at the woman who had wrought this miraculous change in him. She was clearly wondering what on earth was going on and he could hardly blame her. He was still telling himself that it was just about great sex and certainly the night they'd spent on his plane had given him plenty of evidence to support that assumption. The fact that he'd never gone to similar lengths for any woman before was something he preferred not to dwell on.

'I haven't even asked you where you live.'

The way she looked at him reminded him of a small vulnerable animal trapped in the headlights of an oncoming car. 'I bought a small flat with your money,' she reminded him calmly. 'If you just drop me at your office I'll make my own way home and meet you at your hotel later.'

Luc watched her intently. *Was she planning to meet her lover?*

'Fine.' He agreed to her terms, taking the way she immediately relaxed as confirmation of his suspicions.

She'd assured him that she didn't have a man in her life, but the evidence appeared to suggest otherwise, he thought grimly.

It started to rain heavily as they approached the London office of Santoro Investments, which was situated in Canary Wharf along with many of the other leading merchant banks.

'My driver will take you home,' he informed her smoothly, leaning across to give her a lingering kiss on the mouth. 'I'll order dinner for eight.'

After which he intended to drive all thoughts of other men clean out of her mind.

His relationship with women was the one area of his life

where he'd never before encountered competition but he was
entirely confident that he was more than up to the task.

Having issued a set of instructions to his driver in his native language, Luc stepped out of the car and contemplated
the degree of havoc he was about to cause in an office unprepared for his imminent arrival.

Flanked by members of his security team, who had been
in the car behind, he strode towards the building, trying to recall exactly how he'd intended to justify his unexpected visit
to his London office to his amazed staff.

Kimberley spent the day catching up on some urgent business issues, talking to Jason and watching the clock, anxious for the moment when she could pick her son up from
school.

When his little figure finally appeared at the school gates
she was struck by his powerful resemblance to his father. He
had the same night-black hair and the same dark eyes. Perhaps
it was because she'd just spent two weeks with Luc that the
similarity was so marked, she thought as she swept him into
her arms and cuddled him close. *She'd missed him so much.*

They chatted non-stop all the way home to the tiny flat she
shared with Jason and carried on chatting while she made tea.

Kimberley had just cleared Rio's plate when the doorbell
rang.

'I'll get it.' Jason stood up and gave her a smile. 'You two
still have a lot to talk about.'

He strolled out of the room to answer the door but was back
only moments later, this time without the smile.

'Who was—?' Kimberley broke off as she caught sight of
the tall, powerfully built figure standing beside him. Her heart
dropped like a stone.

'Luc.' She stood up quickly, her chair scraping on the tiled
floor of the kitchen, her knees shaking and the breath sud-

denly trapped in her lungs. *What was he doing here?* 'I was going to come to you at eight.'

'I finished in the office early and decided to surprise you.' There was an edge to his voice that alerted her to danger and she lifted a hand to her throat.

'But you didn't know my address—'

He gave a cool smile. 'You were careful to keep it a secret. I wanted to know why.' His eyes slid to Jason and then he noticed the child. A slight frown touched his dark brows and then his expression shifted swiftly from cool to shattered.

'Meu Deus, it can't be—' His voice was hoarse and his handsome face was suddenly alarmingly pale under his tan. He looked totally shell-shocked.

Kimberley suddenly found she couldn't move. She made a nervous gesture with her hand. 'I *did* tell you—'

His gaze fixed on her, his dark eyes fierce and hot and loaded with accusation. 'But you *knew* I didn't believe you—'

She stared at him helplessly. 'We should go outside to talk about this—'

For a long moment he didn't respond. Appeared to have lost his ability to speak. Then, finally, he found his voice.

'Why?' He didn't shift his gaze from the child. 'If this is really how it appears, then *why* am I discovering this now? *After seven years!'*

Kimberley held her breath, trapped by the anger and emotional tension that throbbed in his powerful frame. She was on the verge of sweeping Rio into her arms, afraid that he'd pick up the same vibes as her, afraid that he'd be upset. But, far from being upset, he was staring at his father in blatant fascination.

'You look like me.'

Luc inhaled sharply and his proud head jerked backwards as if he'd been slapped. 'Yes.'

Kimberley closed her eyes and asked herself why her child couldn't have been born with red hair. As it was, the resemblance between father and son was so striking that there could be absolutely no doubt about the boy's parentage.

She felt Luc's tension build. Felt his anger, his uncertainty, *his agony*, and guilt sliced through her like the blade of the sharpest knife.

For the first time since she'd known him, all his emotions were clearly etched on every plane of his handsome face for all to read, and the vision of such a private man revealing himself so completely deepened her guilt still further.

She held her breath, not knowing how to rescue the situation, just praying that he wouldn't say anything that would upset their child.

He didn't.

Instead he hunkered down so that his eyes were on the same level as the boy's. 'I'm Luc.'

Her son's eyes fixed on his father for the first time in his life. 'You look cross. Are you cross?'

'*Not* cross,' Luc assured him, his voice decidedly unsteady and his smile a little shaky. 'I just wasn't expecting to meet you, that's all.'

'I'm Rio.'

Luc closed his eyes briefly and the breath hissed through his teeth. 'It isn't a very common name.'

'I'm named after a very special city,' Rio confided happily, sliding off his chair and walking over to a wall of the kitchen which was covered in his paintings, photos and cards. 'This is it.' He tugged a card from the wall and handed it to Luc with a smile. 'That's where I get my name. That's the mountain Corcovado with the statue *Cristo Redento*—' he pronounced it perfectly '—doesn't it look great? I'm going to go there one day. Mum's promised. But it's a long way away and we don't have enough money yet. We're saving up.'

There was a long painful silence as Luc stared down at the postcard in his hand and then he lifted his gaze and looked straight at Kimberley, raw accusation shimmering in his dark eyes.

She stood totally still, unable to move, paralysed by the terrifying anger she sensed building inside him. But this was like no anger she'd ever encountered before. This wasn't a raw red anger, quick to ignite into flames of vicious temper. This was a blue cold anger, a simmering menace that threatened a far more lethal outcome.

Her courage shifted and, for no immediate reason that she could identify, she felt afraid. 'Luc—'

'Not now and not in front of the child,' he growled before dragging a deep breath into his lungs and turning his attention back to Rio.

Kimberley watched in a state of breathless tension, marvelling at the change in him, at how much he softened his attitude when he looked at their son. The anger seemed to drain away to be replaced by a gentle fascination. 'It's a lovely picture. A great city.' His voice was soft and he smoothed a bronzed hand over Rio's dark curls in a surprisingly tender gesture. 'Those paintings on the wall—did you do them?'

'I'm going to be an artist,' Rio confided, slipping his hand into Luc's and dragging him towards the wall where the paintings were proudly displayed. 'That's my favourite.' He pointed to one in particular and Luc nodded.

'I can see why. It's very good.' His expression was serious as he studied every childish brushstroke with enormous interest.

Kimberley felt her heart twist with guilt.

She'd made the wrong decision.

She'd robbed him of the right to know his son. And her son of the right to know his father. Suddenly she could hardly breathe. But what else could she have done? she reasoned.

She'd *tried* to tell him. She'd wanted, *needed*, his support right at the beginning. But he'd made it clear that the relationship was over. And she'd seen a man like her father.

'You can have it if you like,' Rio offered generously and there was a long silence while Luc continued to stare at the painting. Then he swallowed hard and cleared his throat.

'Thanks.' He glanced down at his son and the roughness of his tone betrayed his emotion. 'I'd like that.'

He carefully removed the painting from the wall and held it as if it were priceless. Then he crouched down again and started to talk to his son. He asked questions, he listened, he responded and all the time Kimberley watched, transfixed by what she was seeing.

How could he be so good with children?

He had absolutely no experience with children. He should have been at a loss and yet here he was, totally comfortable, talking to a six-year-old boy about football, painting and any other subject that Rio chose to bring up.

Eventually he glanced at his Rolex and brought the conversation to a reluctant halt. 'Unfortunately, I have to go now.'

Rio frowned. 'Will I see you again?'

'Oh, yes.' Luc's voice was still gentle but his broad shoulders were rigid with simmering tension. 'You'll definitely see me again. Very soon.'

Kimberley's heart kicked hard against her chest as she was forced to face the inevitable. 'Luc—'

Finally he looked at her, his gaze hard and uncompromising. 'Eight o'clock.' His tone was icy cold. 'I'll send my driver for you. We'll talk then. I think you might find it's a skill I've finally mastered.'

CHAPTER NINE

KIMBERLEY paused outside the door to Luc's suite and took a moment to compose herself.

Was he still as angry as he'd been when he'd left the house?

She took a deep breath and felt dread seep through her like a heavy substance, weighing her down. Whichever way you looked at it, this wasn't going to be an easy meeting.

And she didn't feel at all prepared. For the past seven years she'd convinced herself that even if she *had* managed to get close enough to Luc to tell him about her pregnancy then he would have completely rejected the prospect of fatherhood. This was a man who couldn't sustain a relationship for longer than a month, whose lifestyle was so far removed from that of a family man that it was laughable. There had been nothing about him to suggest that hearing the word 'pregnancy' would have stimulated a reaction other than panic and after he'd flatly refused to see her she'd managed to convince herself that it was all for the best.

But today, seeing him interacting with his son, she'd asked herself the same question she'd been asking herself for the past seven years. *Had she done the wrong thing by not persisting in her attempts to contact Luc and tell him the truth?*

Certainly Luc had appeared far from horrified by the realisation that he actually did have a son. Shocked, yes. Angry with her, yes. But horrified? No. In fact, his reaction had been so far from what she'd predicted all those years ago that it merely confirmed, yet again, how little she knew him. *He'd surprised her.*

And now he was expecting an explanation.

She was shown into the enormous living room of the suite by one of the security guards, who immediately melted into the background, leaving her alone with Luc. He was standing with his back to the window, facing into the room.

Waiting for her.

He watched her in silence, his handsome face cold and unsmiling, his long legs planted firmly apart in an attitude of pure male aggression.

The silence dragged on and on and in the end she was the one to break it, unable to bear the rising tension a moment longer.

She curled her fingers into her palms. 'Luc—'

'I don't even want to talk about this until we have resolved the issue of the blackmailer. Evidently someone really is threatening my child. I want that letter and I want it now.' He held out his hand and she delved in her handbag and produced it.

'There are absolutely no clues as to who sent it, he—'

'It isn't your job to look for clues.' Luc spoke into his mobile phone and moments later a man who Kimberley recognised as his head of security walked into the room.

He spoke briefly to Luc, took the letter and then walked out of the room, pausing only to give a reassuring smile to Kimberley, who stared after him in surprise.

'Doesn't he want to ask me anything?'

Luc gave a cool smile. 'I don't micromanage my staff. I appoint people based on their skills to do the job and then I leave the job up to them. Ronaldo is the best there is. If he feels the need to question you then doubtless he'll do so. In the meantime I have arranged for Rio to have twenty-four hour security both inside and outside the home.'

She gaped at him and her stomach curled with fear. 'You think he's still in danger?'

'He's my son,' Luc pointed out coldly, 'and that alone is enough to put him in danger. He'll be under guard here until I can arrange to take him back to Brazil.'

The room spun. 'You're *not* taking my child to Brazil! I know you're angry about all this, but—'

'*Our child*, Kimberley. We are talking about *our* child and angry doesn't even *begin* to describe what I am feeling at this precise moment,' he informed her in dangerously soft tones, every muscle in his powerful body pumped up and tense as he struggled for control. 'I am waiting for an explanation and I don't even know why, because frankly there *is* no explanation sufficient to justify your failure to inform me that I have been a father for the past six years.'

'I told you two weeks ago—'

'Because you needed my help! If it hadn't been for the blackmail letter the chances are I *never* would have found out, isn't that right?' He paced the floor of the hotel suite, his anger and volatility barely contained. 'I can't believe you would have kept my son from me!' His eyes flashed bitter condemnation and she stiffened defensively, his total lack of self-recrimination firing her own anger.

The fact that he hadn't even considered his own behaviour in the whole situation filled her with outrage.

He was laying the blame squarely on her and yet she knew that had he agreed to see her when she'd tried to contact him she would have told him immediately.

'I don't have to justify anything, Luc.' Her voice shook but she carried on anyway, determined not to let him bully her. 'You treated me abominably.'

'And this was my punishment?' He stared at her in derision. 'Because I ended our relationship, you decided that I'd forfeited the right to know about my child?'

'No.' Her own temper exploded in the face of his accusing look. 'But you're supposed to take responsibility for your actions. You were eager enough to sleep with me but considerably less eager to find out whether I was pregnant, weren't you, Luc?'

The faintest flicker of a frown touched those strong dark brows. 'I did *not* ignore the possibility,' he gritted, 'but I used protection. There was no reason for you to become pregnant.'

'And that's it? Your responsibility ends there? Well, I'm sorry to be the one to point out that you're not infallible,' she said bitterly, 'and your so-called "protection" didn't work. I discovered I was pregnant the day after I left your house.'

'You were still in Rio de Janeiro when you discovered your pregnancy?' His gaze changed from startled to scornful and he swept a hand through the air in a gesture of disgust. 'Then it would have taken *nothing* for you to come and find me and tell me.'

His condemnation was the final straw. 'You have a selective memory. It's so easy for you to stand there now and say that, but at the time you wouldn't let me come *near* you!' Her body trembled with outrage and her hair tumbled over her shoulders, emphasising the pallor of her face. 'You'd had enough of me, Luc. Remember? You went out partying, just to prove that you were bored with me. And when I did the same you lost your temper. We hardly parted on good terms.'

His gaze was ice-cold. 'This wasn't about us. It was about a child. You had a responsibility to tell me.'

'*How?*' She almost choked on the word. 'How was I supposed to tell you? Do you realise how *impossible* it is to get near to you unless you give permission? It's easier to see royalty than get an audience with you!'

He frowned. 'You're being ridiculous—'

'*Not* ridiculous, Luc.' She smoothed her hair away from her face and forced herself to calm down. 'You are totally inaccessible to the public and you should know that because you made yourself that way.'

'But you were not the public.' His gaze raked her face with raw anger. 'We had a relationship.'

'But once that relationship was over I had no better access to you than anyone else. I couldn't get through the walls of bodyguards and frosty-faced receptionists to exchange a single word with you.'

'You obviously didn't try hard enough.'

The injustice of the suggestion stung like acid in an open wound. 'Cast your mind back, Luc.' She wrapped her arms around her waist to stop the shivering. It was a warm June evening but suddenly she felt cold. 'Twice I rang asking to see you and twice you refused to take my call. You thought I'd left Brazil and then suddenly, two weeks after our relationship had ended, I made a final attempt to tell you I was pregnant. This time I turned up in your office asking to see you. I thought that if I came myself then it would be harder to send me away. Your response was to arrange for your driver to take me to the airport, just to make sure that this time there could be no doubt that I'd left the country. It was what you wanted, Luc, so it was what I did.'

He stiffened but had the grace to look uncomfortable. 'I assumed you wanted to talk about our relationship.'

'No. I wanted to tell you I was *pregnant*. But you wouldn't listen. So I went home and did everything by myself. You thought I was a gold-digger—' Shaking with anger and the sheer injustice of it all, she dug a hand into her bag and pulled out a sheaf of papers. 'Here are the receipts, Luc. Everything I spent is itemised there, down to the last box of nappies, and there isn't a single pair of shoes on the list. Just for the record, I *hated* having to use your money and I only did it for Rio.'

She stuffed the papers into his hand and had the satisfaction of seeing him speechless.

He stared at the papers for a moment, his handsome face unusually pale. 'I did *not* know you were pregnant.'

'You didn't give me a chance to tell you! You'd already made up your mind that our relationship was over.' She felt tears clog her throat. 'And it *was* over. Maybe it's a good thing I didn't manage to tell you the truth. What would have happened? You'd never stayed with a woman for more than a month, Luc.'

He threw the papers on to the nearest sofa and paced the length of the suite until he ran out of room. Then he turned to face her, his eyes glittering dark and fierce. 'I would *not* have abandoned a child—'

'But the child would have come with a mother,' she reminded him flatly. 'Complicated, isn't it? Would you have abandoned your playboy lifestyle to give your son a home?'

He jabbed long fingers through his sleek dark hair, clearly driven to the edges of his patience. 'I do not know what I would have done—but finding out this way, it is very difficult—'

Goaded past the point of noticing that his usually fluent English was less than perfect, she turned on him. '*You're* finding it difficult? Try discovering you're pregnant at the age of eighteen when you're unemployed and on your own in a foreign city. I was totally alone, scared, jobless and homeless. *That's* difficult, Luc!'

His broad shoulders tensed. 'You must have had family who could help you—'

'Well, I didn't exactly meet their parental expectations.' She tried to hide the hurt because the truth was that she still couldn't quite believe that her parents had both turned away her pleas for help. She couldn't imagine any situation where she would refuse to help her son. 'They didn't approve of my modelling career but they approved even less of my career as your mistress and the fact that I'd abandoned *everything* to be with you.'

From the moment she'd laid eyes on him she'd been dazzled. Everything else in her life had become inconsequential. *Nothing* had mattered except Luc.

His eyes meshed with hers and she could see that he too was remembering the sensual madness of the time they'd spent together.

Disapproval emanated from every inch of his powerful frame. 'They should have supported you—'

'Perhaps. But you don't always get what you deserve in life and people don't always behave the way they should.' She shot him a meaningful look and had the satisfaction of seeing two spots of colour appear high on his cheekbones. 'The only support I had were your two credit cards, so don't talk to me about difficult, Luc, because I've been there and done that. And don't keep telling me that I did the wrong thing. I tried to tell you. Yes, I failed, but some of the responsibility for that failure lies with you, so don't give me that self-righteous, I'm-so-perfect look! Maybe you should rethink the way you run your life. Ex-girlfriends who think they might be pregnant should be given priority when your staff are handing out appointments to see you.' She picked up her bag and walked towards the door, suddenly feeling a desperate need for fresh air and space. The past was closing in on her and she had to get away.

His voice stopped her. 'You're *not* walking out of here.'

'Watch me!' She turned to look at him, her hair tumbling past her shoulders, her gaze challenging him to stop her if he dared. 'This conversation is clearly going nowhere and I'm tired.'

'Then we will continue the conversation sitting down.' He gestured towards the nearest sofa. 'We have much to discuss still.'

'But we're not discussing,' she pointed out tightly, 'we're arguing, and I've had enough for one night. I've had enough of your accusations and your total inability to see the situation from anyone's point of view but your own. So I'm going home. And when you've calmed down enough to think properly, then maybe we'll talk.'

His hard jaw clenched. 'I have arranged dinner.'

'I'd rather starve than eat dinner with you.' Driven by hurt and frustration, she yanked the door open, ignoring the startled gaze of the bodyguard stationed outside the door. 'And if you've got an appetite at this particular moment in time, then you're even more insensitive than I thought.'

After a sleepless night spent reliving every moment of their conversation, Kimberley was drinking strong coffee at the kitchen table when the doorbell rang.

It was Luc and judging from the shadows under his eyes and the growth of stubble on his hard jaw, his night hadn't been any better than hers.

But he still managed to look devastating, she thought helplessly, running her eyes over his broad shoulders.

His eyes were wary, as if he wasn't sure what reaction to expect. 'Can I come in?'

'What for?' She lifted her chin. 'More recriminations, Luc? More blame?'

A muscle flickered in his hard jaw. 'No recriminations or blame. But you have to admit that we do have things to talk about.'

'I'm not sure that we do.'

His eyes flashed, dark and angry. '*Meu Deus*, I am doing my best here but you won't even meet me halfway!'

'It isn't you or I that matter in this, Luc! It's Rio. I won't have him upset. And I don't trust your temper.'

'There is nothing wrong with my temper!' Luc inhaled deeply and dragged long fingers through his hair, visibly struggling for control. 'I admit that I was angry last night but I'm over that now and I would never upset Rio. Did he look upset yesterday, when he met me?' His voice was a masculine growl. 'Did he?'

She forced herself to stand her ground. 'No. But he didn't know who you were. It isn't just about your temper, Luc, although you definitely need to work on that. You're about to upset his life and I won't let you do it.'

Luc's jaw clenched. 'I have no intention of upsetting anyone.'

'No?' Her tone was cold. 'The way you didn't upset me last night?'

A muscle flickered in his jaw. 'I may have been slightly unfair to you—' he conceded finally and she fought a powerful temptation to slap his handsome face.

'Slightly?'

He shrugged broad shoulders and looked distinctly uncomfortable. 'All right, very possibly more than slightly—' his accent was more pronounced than usual '—but that is all in the past now and we have to talk about the future.'

'That's it?' Kimberley gave an incredulous laugh. 'That's your idea of an apology? Push it into the past and forget about it? How very convenient.'

He swore under his breath. 'It is true that there are many things I regret about what has happened but the past is history and the most important thing is that we concentrate on the future.'

'That's it?' Kimberley shook her head in weary disbelief. 'You need to add "apology" to your list of things you're going to work on, along with "no", "compromise" and "conversation".'

'*Meu Deus, what* do you expect me to do?' He displayed all the explosive volatility of a man well and truly wedged in a tight corner. 'I can't change what happened but I *can* make it right now. But we need to talk.'

'We said everything that needed to be said last night,' Kimberley said stiffly and he gave a driven sigh.

'We were both in a state of shock last night and we have both had time to do some thinking,' he muttered, glancing over his shoulder to where his car and driver waited. 'This is all new territory for me and I certainly don't want to explore it in public. Are you going to let me come in or are we going to provide headlines for tomorrow's newspapers?'

What was the point of refusing? She'd known when she'd walked away from him the night before that she was only postponing the inevitable.

She opened the door a little wider and he strode past her and made straight for her kitchen.

'This is a nice room—' His eyes drifted to the French windows that opened on to the tiny garden. 'It has a nice atmosphere. You chose well.'

Given that her entire flat would have fitted into one room of the villa, she took his words as a sign that he was at least attempting to be conciliatory.

'Thanks.'

He tilted his head and scanned the four corners of the room. 'Its value must have increased considerably since you purchased it.'

She stared at him with undisguised incredulity. 'Do you only ever think about money and return on investment?'

'No, sometimes I think about sex and now I also have a child to think about.' His eyes were cool as he glanced around him. 'Has Jason lived with you from the start? It was Jason you were talking to on the phone?'

'Yes.' She made a pot of coffee. 'He was the only friend I had.'

'It's good that I'm aware that Jason's sexual preferences don't run to beautiful female models,' Luc drawled and something in his tone made her glance at him warily.

'Why's that?'

'Because it saves me having to knock his teeth down his

throat,' he said pleasantly, the gleam in his dark eyes making her catch her breath.

'You and I were no longer an item, Luc,' she pointed out, pouring them both a coffee and taking the mugs to the table, 'so jealousy on your part is nothing short of ridiculous. I could have been with any number of men quite legitimately.'

The atmosphere in the room instantly darkened.

'And were you?' His voice was a threatening male growl and she gave an impatient sigh.

'No, Luc, I wasn't. I had a baby, I was struggling to build a business and I was always exhausted. The last thing I needed was the additional mental strain of a man. And, frankly, my experience with you was enough to put me off men for life.'

'Not exactly for life,' he said softly, lifting his mug to his lips and sipping his coffee. 'I seem to recall you displaying no small degree of enthusiasm over the past two weeks. Not exactly the reaction of a woman who has gone off men.'

Her eyes met his and she swallowed hard. 'That's different.'

'*Not* different.' He looked at her thoughtfully, his gaze curiously intent. 'Perhaps what you're saying, *meu amorzinho*, is that you failed to find another man who made you feel the way I did. Perhaps what you're saying is that being with me put you off other men for life because none of them matched up.'

Her jaw dropped at his arrogance even while a tiny voice in her head told her that he was absolutely right. No man had ever come close to making her feel what she felt for Luc and she doubted that any man ever would. 'Your ego is amazing—'

'I'm merely telling the truth.' He was cool, confident and totally back in control. It was as if that split second moment of regret and apology had never happened. 'It is time to be totally honest with each other. It's essential if our marriage is to work.'

If she'd been holding her coffee she would have dropped it. 'Our marriage?' She almost choked on the word. 'What marriage?'

'It's the obvious way forward.' He gave a dismissive shrug as if marriage had frequently featured in his plans in the past. 'We share a child. It makes sense for us to share the other aspects of our lives as well.'

She gaped at him and struggled to find her voice. 'We share nothing.'

He gave a smug male smile. 'I think the last two weeks have proved that isn't true.'

'You're talking about sex again, Luc!' Kimberley rose to her feet, resisting the temptation to scream with frustration. She couldn't believe what she was hearing. 'You cannot possibly base a marriage on what we have!'

His smile faded. 'We have a son,' he said coldly, 'and that's more than enough of a basis for a marriage.'

She flopped back down on to her chair. 'You're delusional,' she said flatly and he stared at her with naked incredulity.

'Is that any way to respond to a proposal of marriage?'

'Possibly not, but you didn't make a proposal of marriage,' she said bitterly, standing up again and pacing round her tiny kitchen in an attempt to work off some of her anger and frustration. 'You marched in here and announced that we're getting married because we have a child.'

Jaw clenched, he stood up too. 'I have never proposed to a woman before—'

'Then trust me, you need more practice.' She lifted an eyebrow in his direction. 'Perhaps by the fourth or fifth attempt you might get it right.'

He reached out and grabbed her, his lean strong fingers gripping her arms as he forced her to look at him. 'Stop pacing and listen to me. I mean that you should be flattered. Do you know how many women have wanted to hear me say those words?'

'What words exactly?' She stared at him in helpless frustration. '"*We share a child. It makes sense for us to share the other aspects of our lives as well*"? That certainly wasn't in any of the fairy tales I read as a child.'

'*Stop* making a joke—'

'Do I look as though I'm laughing?' She tried to wriggle away from him but he held her firmly. 'Believe me, Luc, I've never been as far away from laughing. You've just insulted me beyond belief.'

'*Meu Deus*, how have I insulted you?' He stared down at her with ill-concealed exasperation. 'I am asking you to marry me.'

She tilted her head to one side, significantly unimpressed. 'And why would I want to do that? Because it's an honour bestowed on so few?'

'Because it is the best thing for our child,' he growled with a dangerous flash of his dark eyes. 'And because it's what women always want from men.'

And the stupid thing was it was exactly what she wanted. *But not like this.*

'You think so?' Her tone dripped sarcasm. 'Well, not this woman, Luc. I can't think of anything worse than tying myself to you.'

'You are not thinking straight.'

'I'm thinking perfectly straight. Marriage to you would be a nightmare. I'd never be able to go out because you're so hideously possessive, we wouldn't have any sort of social life because your idea of an evening with me is to be naked in bed. You probably wouldn't allow me to get dressed!'

He inhaled sharply, his face unusually pale under his tan. 'You're becoming very emotional.'

'Too right I'm emotional! "*We share a child. It makes sense for us to share the other aspects of our lives as well.*" What about the things that matter, Luc, like love and affection? I grew up with a man like you. My father felt the need to go to bed with every woman who smiled at him! Our house was filled with "aunties" and, believe me, there is absolutely no way I'd inflict a similar childhood on a child of mine.'

'That is *not* the way I would behave.' His hand sliced through the air in a gesture of outrage. 'It's true that there is no love between us but marriage can be successful based on other things.'

'Like what? Sex?' She threw him a derisory look. 'For a marriage to work a couple at least have to be able to spend time in each other's company, preferably dressed. That's the bare minimum, Luc, especially when there's a child involved.'

Luc studied her thoughtfully. 'So if we spend time together, then you'll say yes? Those are your terms?'

Terms?

'You make it sound like another of your business negotiations.'

He gave a slight shrug. 'And in a way it is. We each have something that the other wants.'

'You have nothing that I want.'

He leaned back in his chair, his eyes holding hers. 'You want Rio to grow up not knowing his father?'

She bit her lip and shifted slightly. 'No, but—'

'So if we can find a way of sharing an existence amicably then it would be what you would want for him?'

'Well, yes, but—'

'Name your terms.'

She stared at him in stupefied silence. *Name your terms?* Was he that desperate to get his hands on Rio?

'It isn't that simple. I—'

'It is exactly that simple.' As usual he was arrogantly confident of his ability to manoeuvre the situation to his advantage. 'Tell me what it is you want and I will give it to you.'

Love. She wanted him to love her.

She bit back a hysterical laugh, imagining Luc's reaction

if she were to deliver that as her ultimatum. He thought that he could deliver anything she asked, but of course he couldn't. And she would be asking the impossible.

'So I tell you what I want, you say yes and then we get married.'

'That's right.' He gave a confident smile, evidently relieved that she'd finally understood.

'And then you revert to your old ways.'

He frowned. 'I want this marriage to work—'

'But you've never exactly excelled at commitment before, have you, Luc? What's your longest relationship up until now? A month? Two months?'

'There has never been a child involved before—'

'Maybe not, but two months to a lifetime is still rather a stretch,' she muttered, 'and I think it might tax your staying power.'

'I will do whatever it takes to make it work.'

'Really?' She looked at him curiously. 'You'll do whatever it takes?'

'Whatever it takes.'

What did she have to lose?

'All right, this is what it's going to take.' She folded her arms and tilted her head to one side. 'For the next month all our meetings will take place fully clothed. You're going to take me out and you're going to take Rio out. We're going to behave like a family, Luc. And every evening you're going to have me home by ten o'clock. No overnight stays and no sex. And no sex with anyone else, either. If I see one incriminating photograph of you in the press, the deal is off.'

The air throbbed with sudden tension. 'No sex?'

It was hard not to laugh at his tone of utter disbelief.

'No sex. I'm sure you'll be able to hold yourself back for the greater good of proving that being a good father to your child is what really matters to you. And it will give us a chance to find out whether we can stand being together when there is no sex involved. If we can—' she shrugged her slender shoulders '—then I'll marry you.'

She smiled placidly, safe in the knowledge that he was about to leap to his feet and reject her terms as totally unreasonable.

He was a red-blooded highly sexed male in his prime. He was *never* going to agree to her terms.

And that was fine by her. She didn't want to marry Luc. He didn't love her and he never would, and spending every day with him, knowing that he was only with her because of their child, would be torment.

'All right.'

She was so busy smiling to herself that at first she thought she'd misheard him. 'Sorry?'

'I said all right.' He rose to his feet and walked towards her, a slightly dangerous glint in his dark, sexy eyes. 'I accept your terms.'

She looked at him dubiously. 'All of them?'

'All of them.'

'You do?' She stared at him in confusion and a slight smile touched his hard mouth.

'I do. And pretty soon I'll be saying those words in a marriage ceremony, *meu amorzinho*, because you are going to enjoy spending time with me, and so is Rio.'

Kimberley gaped at him. Did anything dent his confidence?

He'd never manage it, she told herself firmly.

Deprived of sex and forced to communicate on a daily basis would soon put an end to his desire for marriage, she thought wryly, and then perhaps her life could return to normal. Obviously Luc would need access to his son, but that could be easily arranged.

'Fine,' she said airily. 'It's a deal.'

* * *

Luc strode away from the house, wondering at exactly what point he'd lost his sanity.

He'd just agreed to a month without sex with a woman who made him think about nothing but sex.

What sort of normal healthy guy would agree to terms like that?

Had he gone totally and utterly mad?

For a man who'd made a point of avoiding commitment at all costs, he was more than a little disturbed by how far he was prepared to go to persuade Kimberley to marry him.

And she *would* marry him, of course, because he would meet all her terms.

How hard could it be? Conversation? Easy—he was getting better at it by the day. Family trips out—easy. No sex—not so easy, he conceded ruefully, ignoring the waiting car and striding purposefully in the opposite direction. But perhaps if she was fully clothed the whole time they were together and he took lots of cold showers, he might just be able to manage it.

Which meant that the deal was as good as done.

One month, that was all it was, he reminded himself as he crossed the road without noticing the cars.

And then he could be a proper father to his son.

Because that was what this marriage was all about.

What other possible reason could there be?

CHAPTER TEN

ONE month later Kimberley sat in the pretty, airy sitting room of her flat, wondering what had happened to her life.

The room was filled with the scent of yet more fresh flowers, which had arrived from Luc that morning, and around her neck lay a beautiful necklace, which he'd given her only the night before as they'd shared another intimate dinner on her patio.

If she'd thought he wasn't capable of sustaining a relationship outside the bedroom then she'd been proved more than wrong.

She stared down at her sketch-book, which lay in front of her, open and untouched. She'd promised herself that today she was going to do some rough designs of a necklace for a very wealthy French client, but so far she hadn't as much as glanced at the page in front of her. She was too distracted.

She couldn't stop thinking about Luc.

It was ironic, she mused as she gazed out of the window without so much as a glance at the sketch-pad in front of her, that the first time she and Luc had spent time together fully clothed and without a double bed in sight had been on a visit to London Zoo with their son.

And the ridiculous thing was that *they'd felt like a family.*
It didn't matter how many times she reminded herself that

he didn't love her and that this amazing, romantic month was all about him trying to manipulate her into marrying him so that he could have full access to his son, she still couldn't stop feeling ridiculously happy.

The almost agonizing anxiety she'd felt over the kidnap threat had finally vanished, partly because she'd heard nothing more from the man and partly because Luc's security team were now part of her everyday life.

But the real reason for her happiness was that she just adored being with Luc. And today she was missing him. That morning he'd been forced to fly to Paris for an urgent business meeting and already she was watching the clock, anticipating the time when his flight would land.

She'd been fast discovering that as well as being amazing in bed, Luc was also incredibly entertaining company when he wanted to be and she was enjoying seeing a completely different side of him.

From the moment he had announced his intention of marrying her, his entire focus had been on her and Rio. He'd contacted lawyers, changed his will, signed countless documents and presented her with countless documents to sign, all designed to ensure that Rio was well provided for. And he'd spent endless hours with his son, waiting at the school gates to collect him at the end of the school day and then taking him on trips, giving him treats and just *talking*.

With the insensitivity of youth, Rio was always asking him questions and Luc had started to relax and respond, gradually becoming more open about himself and his past. And that willingness to reveal intimate details about himself had extended into the evenings, when Rio was safely tucked up in his bed. London was experiencing a heatwave and Luc and Kimberley had fallen into a habit of eating dinner in the tiny walled garden that led from her kitchen and the intimacy of their surroundings had somehow stimulated conversations of a deeply personal nature.

In the past few days alone she'd learned that both his parents had died when he was thirteen and that he'd been given a home by Maria, the woman who was now his personal assistant. And in return he'd given her a job. And she'd been with him for over twenty years.

Maybe Luc *was* capable of commitment, Kimberley mused as she picked up her pencil and attempted to translate the design in her head into a drawing that would provide the basis of her first discussion with her client. After all, he was obviously committed to Maria. And he was showing all the signs of being equally committed to his son.

Committed enough to make an effort in his relationship with her.

She was far too realistic to pretend, even for one unguarded minute, that all this effort on his part was driven by anything other than a desire to secure unlimited access to their child.

With her agreement, he'd revealed his identity to Rio immediately and if she'd harboured any doubts about the sense of marrying a man who clearly didn't love her, then they had dissolved once she'd seen the undiluted excitement and delight on her child's face when he'd finally realised that this vibrant, energetic, exotic man was his father.

How could she deprive her child of the chance to grow up in a normal family? Particularly as Luc himself was so clearly determined to be the very best father possible.

And he'd met every one of her terms. All too easily, it would seem.

Was she the only one who was sexually frustrated? she wondered ruefully.

Evidently the answer was yes. Luc hadn't made one single move in her direction in the past month. He kissed her on both cheeks when they met and when they parted and that was the limit of their physical contact. Very formal. Very restrained.

The desperate need to touch him and be touched by him was driving her mad.

And they were getting on well, she conceded as her pencil danced over the page, creating a stunning individual design. She enjoyed the time they spent together. Enjoyed spending time with him, even though she knew he was doing it with a distinct purpose in mind.

All right, so their relationship wasn't perfect, but what relationship was? She'd learned at eighteen that fairy tale endings didn't happen in real life and at least she was with Luc and Rio had a father. The fact that Luc didn't love her had almost ceased to matter.

As long as she was careful not to reveal the strength of her feelings, careful to do nothing which might frighten him off, what could go wrong?

Kimberley glanced at the clock again. She'd arranged to pick Rio up from school half an hour early so that they could go and meet Luc at the airport. Wasn't that what families did?

The phone rang and, expecting Luc's call, she lifted the receiver and tucked it under her ear, leaving her hands free to gather up her sketches.

But it wasn't Luc and her face turned pale as she immediately recognised the voice.

'So—this time you've really hit the jackpot.'

The papers slid from her nerveless fingers and her knees shook so much she sank on to the nearest chair. It was that or slide to the ground.

Anxiety and panic slammed through her with the force of an express train. 'What do you want?'

'If you have to ask that then you're a lot stupider than you look.'

'W-we already paid you.' Her confidence fell away and her fingers clenched on the phone. 'A fortune. You promised that would be it—'

'Well, let's just say that circumstances have changed. You're a wealthy lady. This time I want ten million.'

She closed her eyes briefly. 'That's ridiculous.'

'You've snagged the attentions of a billionaire.'

'It isn't my money. I can't—'

'Bad decision.' The voice was harsh. 'Goodbye.'

'Wait!' She stood up, panic and anguish in her tone. 'Don't hang up!'

'Are you going to be reasonable?'

What choice did she have? Her eyes filled and her voice was little more than a whisper. 'Yes. I—I'll do anything—'

There was a cold laugh from the other end of the phone. 'Now you're being sensible. And because I'm in a generous mood I'll give you twenty-four hours to get the money. Then I'll contact you again. And if you tell the police or Santoro, then the deal is off.'

Twenty-four hours?

How was she going to get the money in twenty-four hours? *It wasn't long enough.* She couldn't possibly—

'I won't tell Luc, I promise I won't tell Luc, but—' She broke off as she realised that the connection was dead.

'So what exactly are you not going to tell me?' An icy voice came from the doorway and the phone fell from her fingers with a clatter to join the papers on the floor.

She stared at Luc in horror, wondering just how much he'd heard. 'You're early—'

'Clearly ploughing through obstacles in order to spend more time with my family wasn't a sensible move,' he said flatly, walking into the room and pushing the door shut behind him, hostility and condemnation pulsing from every inch of his powerful frame. 'I have spent the last month jumping through hoops to be the sort of man you want me to be. You accuse me of not being able to communicate and yet time and time again the person with the secrets in this relationship is *you*.'

She could hardly breathe, but her panic was all for Rio. 'I don't have secrets—' She couldn't handle this now. She just needed to be left on her own to think and plan and yet how could she do either when her mind was full of anxiety for her child?

Luc planted himself in front of her, his powerful frame a wall of tension. 'So what is it that you've promised not to tell me and who were you making that promise to?'

For a moment she stared at him, sickened by the icy remoteness she saw in his eyes and the disdainful slant of his beautiful mouth. She wanted to defend herself but how could she when the blackmailer had insisted she didn't tell Luc? What if she told him and something happened to Rio?

She tried to comfort herself with the knowledge that Luc had security staff watching Rio, but she still couldn't relax.

'I can't talk about this now.' She needed to talk to Jason. She needed to go to the school. She needed to pick up her child. Urgently. In a complete fluster, she dropped to her knees to gather up the papers she'd scattered but her hands were shaking so badly she immediately dropped them again. Tears pricked her eyes and she blinked them back. 'Can we go back to Brazil this afternoon?' she blurted out impulsively, tilting her head to look at him. 'All three of us? Please?'

Luc lifted stunned dark eyes from the mess on the floor and stared at her with unconcealed amazement. 'The school term isn't ended yet. You said you wanted to wait until the summer holidays. Those were your terms. Remember?'

'I kn-know what I said,' she stammered, gathering up the sketches she'd dropped and then promptly dropping them again. Her hands were shaking so much she couldn't hold anything. 'I've changed my mind. I want us to go now. As soon as we can.'

If she took Rio out of school, then they could go to the island and he'd be safe there, she reasoned desperately. He'd be surrounded by water and Luc's security team. In a place like that they'd be able to protect him, *keep him safe*.

Luc studied her with a visible lack of comprehension. 'Suddenly you want to fly to Brazil. Why?'

She started picking up papers again, her brain paralysed by terror. 'Why must you always ask so many questions?'

'Perhaps because you're not giving me anything that looks even remotely like an answer,' he ground out, reaching for her and hauling her against him. '*Stop* picking up papers and dropping them again, *stop* avoiding my gaze and stand still for just one minute so that we can *talk*.'

'I can't. Not now.' Not ever. She didn't dare think what might happen to Rio if she told Luc the truth. 'And anyway, there's nothing to say.' Her voice was barely audible and he took such a long time to react that for a moment she wondered whether he'd even heard her.

Then he released her so suddenly that she almost fell. 'Fine.' His tone was ice-cold. 'Clearly I was the one who was crazy to even think we could have a relationship. Go and do whatever it is you have to do that I mustn't find out about. I'm going to the office. I'll be back later to pick Rio up and take him for tea. And then my lawyer will contact you to discuss arrangements for the future. Finally I agree with you. Marriage is not on the agenda. I can't marry a woman whose behaviour I'm not even *close* to understanding.'

She wanted to hurl herself into the safety of his arms.

She wanted to tell him *everything* and let him sort it out the way he'd sorted everything out. But she didn't dare.

So instead she stood there, watching through a haze of tears as he strode out of the room like a man with no intention of ever coming back.

Kimberley wanted to break down and just sob and sob until her heart was empty of emotion and her body was dry, but she knew she couldn't allow herself that luxury. She had to get to her son. *Before anyone else did.*

She made it just as far as the door when the phone rang again.

This time it was the school and they were ringing to say that Rio had gone missing.

Luc strode towards his car, struggling to contain the fierce rage of jealousy that threatened to consume his usually cold and rational approach to life. The guilt on Kimberley's face when she'd dropped the phone had ignited feelings inside him that he had never before experienced. For a wild, primitive moment he'd been tempted to throw her over his shoulder, carry her to his nearest property and lock all the doors so that she could have no contact with the outside world.

No contact with other men.

Because he was completely and utterly sure that it was a man who was causing her to be so secretive.

Hadn't she already told him on several occasions that there was no reason why she shouldn't have another man in her life?

And hadn't he spent the last month trying to prove to her that she didn't *need* another man in her life?

Was that why she'd put that ridiculous ban on sex? Because she was spending her nights with another man?

He uttered a soft curse and wondered why he should be suddenly experiencing a depth of insecurity hitherto completely alien to him.

He'd left Paris earlier than planned, overwhelmed by a sudden inexplicable need to be with Kimberley, only to find her white-faced and clearly horrified to see him. His dreams of an ecstatic romantic reunion had dissolved on the spot. The rare diamond that he'd chosen with such care and hidden securely in his pocket until such time as he deemed it appropriate to present it to his future wife, had remained in his pocket, a cruel reminder of how life with Kimberley never turned out the way he expected.

In fact *nothing* had gone the way he'd planned.

For a man used to nothing short of adulation from the female sex, Kimberley's less than flattering reaction to his arrival had come as a severe shock. But over the past month he'd been convinced on several occasions that she was actually enjoying their time together.

Which simply went to prove that a desperate man was a deluded man, he thought grimly as he strode towards his car.

How had he expected her to react to his early arrival?

So surprised by his unexpected appearance that she'd drop her guard, throw herself into his arms and declare her love?

That she'd show him the same unquestioning devotion she'd offered him at the age of eighteen?

Hardly. As she kept reminding him, she wasn't that person any more. Instead of warmth and affection, she displayed nothing but cool reserve and nothing in her body language suggested that she was missing the physical side of their relationship.

Was that because her affection was given elsewhere?

He ground his teeth at the very thought and wondered what it was that she was hiding from him. Whatever it was had been enough to drain the colour from her cheeks and put a look of raw terror into her green eyes.

As the first punch of jealousy receded and his brain once more clicked into action he frowned, recalling her extreme pallor and the papers scattered over the floor.

He stopped dead, oblivious to the curious glances of his security staff and his chauffeur, who was poised to take him to his next appointment. *The papers had already been on the floor before he'd entered the room.*

With the same single-minded focus and ruthless attention to detail that characterised all his business dealings, Luc applied his mind to every moment of their meeting, searching for clues and answers.

She had been pale from the moment he'd walked into the

room, he reminded himself. He hadn't caused the pallor. The papers had already been on the floor. His unexpected arrival hadn't caused her to drop them.

The only thing she'd dropped when she'd seen him had been the phone.

He frowned as he mentally ran through the exact sequence of events.

Like a woman who was desperate, she'd begged him to take them back to Brazil, even though she'd been the one to insist that Rio needed stability and should finish his term at school before they considered travelling.

Why would she want to go back to Brazil if she had another man in her life?

Something didn't feel right.

Like so many men before him, he cursed fluently and wished that women didn't have to be so extremely complicated and perverse in their behaviour.

At that moment his mobile phone rang and he answered the call immediately, all his senses on full alert when he saw that it was Kimberley's number displayed on the screen.

She whispered three words. 'I need you.'

Where was Luc and when would he come?

Kimberley was huddled on the floor, shaking so badly that she couldn't speak.

Her worst nightmare had come true.

'Calm down and tell me again what the school said—' Jason held a glass of brandy to her lips but she pushed it away, her eyes wild with fear. For a moment she thought she might be swallowed up by panic and then she heard the firm, determined tread of Luc's footsteps on the wooden floor and almost wept again with relief because she needed him badly, even though she knew she wasn't supposed to need him.

He strode into the room, his expression grim as his dark

eyes swept the room. He took in Jason holding the glass and then registered her tear-stained face with a soft curse.

In two strides he was by her side. 'From the beginning,' he commanded in rough tones as he lifted her easily and sat in the nearest chair with her on his lap, 'and this time you're going to leave nothing out.'

For a brief moment Kimberley rested a hand against his chest, feeling the solid strength of hard male muscle under her fingers, allowing herself the luxury of comfort. And then she remembered that she didn't have time for comfort.

'I have to go—' She went to slide off his lap but his arms tightened around her waist, preventing her from moving.

'You're going nowhere.'

'You don't understand—' Almost whimpering with fear, she pushed at his arms, trying to free herself. 'He's been taken.'

Luc stilled. '*Who* has been taken?'

'Rio.' Her eyes were frantic. 'He was supposed to give me twenty-four hours to get the money but the school just phoned and he's disappeared.'

'You are making absolutely no sense.' Luc narrowed his eyes as he tried to decipher her garbled statement. Then he inhaled sharply, his expression suddenly grim. 'The blackmailer has contacted you again? Is that what you're saying?'

Kimberley turned to Jason for support, not knowing what to do or say.

'You want my opinion?' Her friend gave a helpless shrug. 'You need to tell him everything. He might be able to help. We both know that Luc's a nasty bastard when he's crossed.'

'Thanks.' Luc cast an ironic glance at the other man, who gave an apologetic shrug.

'Take it as a compliment. You have assets that we need at the moment.'

'They made me promise not to tell you. What if they find out?' Kimberley was shivering with fear but Luc was totally calm, his handsome face an icy mask as he reached for his phone. Without providing them with any explanation, he made three calls in rapid succession, his tone cold and unemotional as he issued what she assumed to be a string of instructions in his own language. Then he slipped the phone back into his pocket and gave her a gentle shake.

'You should have told me. Do you know nothing about me? Do you think I would allow anyone to take our child?' His tone was rough and his fingers tightened on her arms and she looked at him blankly, too afraid to think straight.

'I suppose not—' Suddenly there was a glimmer of light in the darkness. She'd forgotten how strong Luc was, even though she'd seen the evidence of that strength on several occasions. Even now he was strong. Unlike her, he was showing no sign of panic. Instead he was cold and rational and very much in control.

Jason dumped the glass down on the table. 'How can a child of six go missing from a school?'

Despite the warmth and safety of Luc's arms, Kimberley couldn't stop shivering. 'Because someone took him.'

'Calm yourself, *meu amorzinho*,' Luc urged roughly. 'No one has taken him. It isn't possible. My team have not left his side since I discovered his existence.'

His phone rang suddenly and he answered it immediately, his expression revealing nothing as he listened and responded. He ended the call with a determined stab of one bronzed finger. 'As I thought—all is well. Rio is safe. One of my security team picked him up two minutes ago, just to be on the safe side. You can relax, *minha docura*.'

'They've found him?' Kimberley's voice was a strangled whisper and Luc gave a soft curse and stroked her tangled hair away from her blotched face.

'He had crossed the road to the sweet shop,' he said gruffly, 'apparently to buy me a present to take to the airport. He had much to say to my driver about your plans to surprise me.'

Kimberley blushed. 'We were going to meet you, but you were early—'

His dark eyes were unusually penetrating. 'A mistake I will remember not to make again,' he said softly, pushing her gently off his lap but maintaining a firm grip on her hand as they stood up. 'My team are taking Rio straight back to my hotel. He'll be safe there. I'll take you to him, but first you need to wash your face and practise your smile. We don't want him to know that anything is wrong.'

'But what about the man? He's still out there and he gave me twenty-four hours—'

'It is not your problem,' Luc informed her with the cool confidence of a man totally comfortable in the command position. 'He slipped up when he called you here. We now have his identity and his whereabouts. He'll be dealt with.'

For once she was more than willing to let him take control of the situation.

Something in the grim set of his mouth made her feel almost sorry for the blackmailer but then she reminded herself that the man had threatened her child and deserved to be on the receiving end of Luc's wrath.

She splashed her face in the bathroom and when she came out there were two security staff waiting to escort her to the hotel.

Luc had gone.

CHAPTER ELEVEN

KIMBERLEY spent the rest of the afternoon and evening playing with Rio in the safety of the hotel suite. Despite the comforting presence of Luc's security staff, she didn't let him out of her sight, all too aware that the threat to his safety still remained.

And as the hours passed and there was still no sign of Luc, she suddenly discovered that her anxiety wasn't only confined to the safety of her child.

What if something had happened to Luc?

Finally, long after Rio had been tucked up in bed asleep, Luc walked into the suite and she dropped on to the nearest sofa, worn out with worrying and almost weak with relief.

'Thank goodness—I was *so* worried and no one would tell me where you were.'

'Why were you worried?' His shirt was undone at the collar and he strolled towards her, as cool and unconcerned as ever. 'You have Rio safe with you.'

'I know, but I thought something might have happened to *you*,' she confessed and then almost bit her tongue off as she realised what she'd revealed.

He didn't want her love or affection.

He just wanted their son. And suddenly she knew that she couldn't marry him, no matter how much she wanted to. It wouldn't be fair on Luc. Eventually he would find someone he could love and she didn't want to stand in the way of his happiness.

They'd have to come to some other arrangement.

He stopped in front of her and dragged her gently to her feet.

'I think it's time you learned to trust me, *meu amorzinho*,' he urged, sliding a hand under her chin and forcing her to look at him. 'You accuse me of being controlling, yet there are times when it is good to allow another to take charge and this was one of them. You have proved time and time again that you are capable of running your own life, but I think when it comes to dealing with blackmailers you can safely leave the work to others. You need to learn to delegate.'

His eyes hardened and she caught her breath, hardly daring to ask the question. 'Did you find him?'

His hand dropped to his side and he gave a smile that wasn't altogether pleasant. 'Of course. The problem is solved.'

'Thank you,' she breathed, almost weak with relief. She suddenly discovered that she didn't even want to know what had happened. She was just glad that it was over. 'Thank you so much.'

Luc released her abruptly and raked long fingers through his sleek, dark hair as he paced away from her. 'Before you bestow your gratitude in my direction I should probably tell you that the whole situation was my fault.' His voice was harsh as he turned back to her. 'He made your life a misery because of me, *minha docura*. I am entirely to blame for your recent trauma so you might want to hold on to your thanks.'

She frowned. 'I don't understand—'

'He was an employee of mine. One of my drivers.' Luc's hands dropped to his sides and he walked towards the window, his expression grim and set, his tone flat. 'I fired him.

He was dishonest and I won't tolerate dishonesty in my employees. That was seven years ago.'

Kimberley stared at him. 'I was with you seven years ago.'

'That's right.'

She looked at him blankly, still not understanding. 'But what does that have to do with me?'

He let out a driven sigh. 'He wanted to make money the easy way. You presented him with the opportunity to do that.'

'But *how*? How did he even know about Rio?'

Luc loosened more buttons of his shirt. 'He was my driver. I suspect he overheard something which he then used to his advantage.'

'But I never—' Kimberley broke off and Luc gave a wry smile.

'You never?' he prompted her gently and she lifted a hand to her mouth.

'Oh, God—the very last time I tried to see you, I came to the office and you arranged for a car to take me away. I was terribly upset—I called Jason to ask him if I could stay with him—'

'And naturally you told him why,' Luc finished for her with a dismissive shrug of his broad shoulders. 'I think you have your answer.'

'Then it's *all* my fault,' she whispered in horror and Luc frowned sharply.

'Not true. If it is anyone's fault it is mine, for sending you away that day without even giving you the courtesy of a hearing. And on the other occasions.' He hesitated, his bronzed face unusually pale as he surveyed her stricken expression. 'I am very much to blame for everything that has happened to you and for that I am truly sorry. My only defence is that you were so very different from every other woman I've ever met.'

She gaped at him, so startled and taken aback by the previously unimaginable vision of Luc Santoro *apologising* that she wasn't aware that he'd even taken her hands until he pulled her against him.

'But the thing that makes me most sorry is that I didn't believe you when you said you were being blackmailed. I'm truly sorry that you've had so much worry to cope with alone,' he said roughly, his dark eyes raking her pale face. 'That day you came to my office and asked me for five million dollars; I should have believed you, but I've never been able to think clearly around you. The truth is that I wanted to believe that you were a cold-hearted little gold-digger.'

'But *why?* Why would you want to think a thing like that about someone?' She stared at him in amazement and he spread his hands, as if the answer should be obvious.

'Seven years ago it was the only way I could keep myself from following you and bringing you back. But I should have known better. You were never interested in possessions. It wasn't until recently that I realised that you truly had no idea just how wealthy I am—'

She bit her lip, more than a little embarrassed that she'd been so naïve. 'To be honest, I'd never really given it any thought.'

She'd never been interested in Luc the businessman. *Only Luc the man.*

'Unlike every other woman I've ever been with, all of whom thought about little else,' he informed her, a hard edge to his voice. 'In contrast, the only thing you've ever asked me for is conversation. You're not interested in material things, so I should have known that when you told me about Rio you were telling the truth. I should have listened to you but unfortunately my temper is as hot as my libido.'

She blushed. 'I can understand that you were still angry with me,' she conceded hastily, more than willing to forgive him. 'I did spend a great deal of your money. Which was probably wrong of me, but I was very upset and scared about the future and I badly wanted to be able to stay at home and look after our baby.'

'You spent next to nothing compared to your predecessors,' he informed her in a dry tone and she blinked in astonishment.

'I bought a *flat*.'

'Which has turned out to be an excellent investment,' he pointed out with some amusement. 'I have had girlfriends who have spent a similar amount expanding the contents of their wardrobes. It appears that the flat has more than trebled in value since you first bought it.'

It was typical of Luc to have already discovered that fact, she thought dryly. 'But if you truly thought I was a gold-digger, why did you want me back in your bed? I never understood that. You'd so obviously had enough of me when we parted seven years ago.'

He grimaced. 'I wish that was the case, but sadly the complete opposite was true.'

She stilled. 'But you drove me away.'

'That's right.'

'You'd *definitely* had enough of me—'

'I doubt I would ever have enough of you, *meu amorzinho*. And that was the very reason I had to make you leave.'

She felt thoroughly confused. All these years she'd made certain assumptions and it seemed now that she'd been wrong. 'You knew I'd leave?'

'Of course—' His smile was self-mocking. 'You were very possessive. I knew that if I was photographed with another woman that would be the end for you. And us.'

'I can't believe you did that.' She struggled to find her voice. 'I was *so* hurt.'

He flinched as though she'd hit him. 'I know and for that I am truly sorry. If it makes it any better, it was all staged. I let the photographer do his stuff and then spent the rest of the evening getting blind drunk. I never touched another woman when we were together.'

She lifted a hand and rubbed the frown between her eyes. 'You hated the fact I was so affectionate, hated the fact that I loved you—because you didn't feel the same way about me.'

He gave a short laugh that was totally lacking in humour. 'You're wrong. I felt *exactly* the same way about you and those feelings scared me.'

Luc, *scared*?

There was a long painful silence while she stared at him. 'You felt the same way I did?'

'That's right.'

Her heart thudded against her chest. 'I *loved* you.'

He tensed slightly. 'I know.'

She licked her lips. 'You accused me of acting—'

'Some men will say anything rather than accept that he's been well and truly hooked by a woman.' Luc ran a hand over the back of his neck, visibly discomfited by the admission. 'I guess I'm one of those men. I didn't know how to handle the situation. For the first time in my life I found myself seriously out of my depth.'

She stared at him. 'You're saying you felt the same way about me?'

'Why do you think I refused to see you on those three occasions? I've always considered myself to be a self-disciplined man but that went out of the window when I met you. I didn't trust myself to turn you away. I was relieved when you spent all that money because it meant that I was finally able to bracket you with all the other women I'd ever been with. It made it easier to push you away.'

'I don't understand.' Her voice was little more than a whisper as she tried to comprehend what he was telling her. 'If you loved me, why did you want to push me away?'

He inhaled sharply. 'Because I didn't want to be in love. I've spent my life avoiding emotional entanglements and I succeeded very well until you came along. I was always careful to pick the same type of woman. Cold, hard and with an eye set firmly on my money. I suppose, in a way, it was a guarantee. I knew there was no chance that I'd ever fall in love with a woman like that so I was perfectly safe. But I made a mistake with you. A big mistake.'

'What's wrong with being in love if it's mutual?' She stared at him in confusion. 'I *adored* you.'

There was a long silence and she saw a shadow cross his hard, handsome face.

He paced over to the window, keeping his back to her as if speaking was suddenly extraordinarily difficult. 'My father loved my mother so much and when she died his entire life fell apart. I watched it happen. I saw a strong man shrivel to nothing and become weak. He no longer wanted to live and he lost interest in everything, including me.' Luc's voice was flat. 'I was thirteen years old and it certainly wasn't a good advertisement for the benefits of love. My father ceased to function. His business folded. We lost our home. And finally he died.'

Kimberley stilled, appalled and saddened. And her heart ached for how he must have suffered as a boy, losing both his parents at such a young, impressionable age. She looked at the stiff set of his broad shoulders and wanted to go to him. *Wanted to hug him tight.* But she sensed that he didn't want her comfort. 'How did he die?'

Luc didn't turn, his eyes still fixed on a point outside the window. 'To be honest, I think he just didn't care enough to live. He gave up.'

She stared at his back helplessly, for the first time feeling as though she'd been given some insight into what made him the person he was. 'And you vowed that was never going to happen to you—'

'And it never did.' He turned, his dark eyes fixed on hers with shimmering intensity. 'Never even came close until I met you. And what I felt for you frightened me so much I refused to acknowledge it, even to myself.'

She swallowed. 'I wish I'd known about your childhood. I wish you'd *talked* to me—'

'I didn't want to talk. I just wanted to run a mile. I'd vowed that it was never going to happen to me. *That I would never make myself that vulnerable.* My father went from being a man with energy and drive to little more than a shell. We lost everything virtually overnight. Maria gave me a home. She was like a mother to me.'

And she guessed that he'd repaid that debt many times over.

'I still think you should have told me.'

He gave a wry smile. 'I didn't tell anyone anything, *meu amorzinho*. That's how I kept myself safe.'

She curled her fingers into her palms. 'So when I turned up at your office six weeks ago—'

'I couldn't resist the temptation to see you one more time and, having seen you, I couldn't resist the temptation to get you into my bed one more time,' he confessed with brutal frankness. 'I convinced myself that two weeks would be enough to cure me. Then I convinced myself that just a little longer would do the trick. I'm not good at being without you, *meu amorzinho*.'

She gazed at him, unable to suppress the bubble of happiness inside her. 'I never even guessed you felt that way.'

'I followed you to England,' he pointed out dryly, 'which should have told you something.'

'I thought it was just sex—'

'*Not* just sex,' he assured her, 'and the last month should have proved that. But if you still don't believe me you can talk to my board of directors, who are currently wondering if I'm ever going to work again. I have been absent from the office for so long they're all becoming extremely jittery.'

She chewed her lip, hardly daring to ask the question that needed to be asked. 'And what about now—' her voice cracked '—are you cured, Luc?'

Luc fixed her with his dark, possessive gaze. 'You really have to ask me that?' His accent was strangely thick, as if he couldn't quite get his tongue around the words that needed to be said. 'In the past month I have thought only of you and what you need in a relationship. I have talked until my throat is sore and told you *everything* about myself. I have expressed thoughts that I didn't even know I was thinking. But, most of all, I have ignored the fact that you only have to walk into a room and I want to strip you naked. You have stayed fully clothed for an entire month and I haven't so much as kissed you on the lips. I have done for you what I've never done for any woman before. And yet *still* you ask me if I love you?'

Suddenly Kimberley just wanted to smile and smile. 'I thought you just wanted to marry me because of Rio—'

'I want to marry you because I love you and because I can't live without you,' he confessed with a groan, pulling her against him. 'And if I was a decent sort of guy I'd be saying that I love you too much to marry you unless you love me. But, as you've pointed out so many times in the past, I'm ruthless and entirely self-seeking and don't understand the word no, so I'm going to keep on at you until you say yes.'

He sounded so much like his usual self that she laughed. 'Controlling again, Luc?' Her eyes twinkled suggestively. 'The handcuffs are still in my bag. Perhaps I should use them again. It isn't good for you to have everything your own way.'

'If it's any consolation, I am suffering badly for the way I treated you,' he confessed in a raw tone. 'It tortures me to think of how alone and afraid you were and that I was the cause of it. I don't know how you managed—'

'Well, your credit cards certainly helped,' she muttered and he gave an agonized groan.

'And you even kept the receipts for everything you bought. Do you know how that made me feel? To know that you felt the need to itemise everything?'

'I'm used to watching what I spend,' she said simply and then gave a rueful smile. 'And, I suppose, deep down I felt guilty spending your money. But you'd called all the shots and it was a way of taking some of the control back.'

His own eyes gleamed dark in response. 'Once we're safely married you can take control any time you like,' he assured her huskily, sliding his hands into her hair and tilting her face to his. 'But, in the meantime, I need you to put me out of my misery. I never dreamt that asking a woman to marry me could be so traumatic. No wonder I've avoided commitment for so long.'

'I didn't know you were asking—I thought you were telling.'

'I'm *trying* to ask; it's just that asking is all very new to me,' he confessed in a smooth tone that suggested that he had absolutely no intention of changing his ways in the near future.

'Like compromise and conversation,' she teased and he gave a tortured groan.

'*Don't* tease me—just give me an answer.' His dark head lowered and his mouth brushed against hers. 'Are you going to say yes or do you have still more challenges and tests for me to pass before you'll agree to tie yourself to me for ever?'

For ever.

How could two words sound so good?

'I think you've more than passed the test,' she whispered as she slid her arms round his neck. 'And the answer is yes.'

'And do you think, if I really concentrate on compromise and conversation, that you might manage to love me back one day, the way you used to love me?'

'I already do,' she said softly, standing on tiptoe and kissing him again. 'You were absolutely right when you said that no other man had ever matched up to what we shared. I've never found anyone who made me feel the way you do.'

'Seriously?' He looked stunned, as if he couldn't quite allow himself to believe what she was saying. 'You still love me?'

'I've never stopped loving you. Although I'm worried about what such a confession will do to your already massively over-inflated ego.'

He gave a delighted laugh and pulled her hard against him. 'So if I put a ring on your finger straight away, can we drop the "no sex" routine because, frankly, abstinence is something else that I don't excel at.'

'Me neither,' she confessed breathlessly, her cheeks heating at the hard, male feel of him against her, 'and there's no need to wait for a ring.'

'You're going to wear the ring,' he told her in his usual tone of authority, reaching into his jacket pocket and removing a velvet box. 'The ring says "hands off, she's mine" to any other man who happens to glance in your direction. I want you well and truly labelled so that there can be no mistake.'

'Not possessive at all then, Luc,' she teased and then gasped as he flipped open the box and the stunning diamond winked and sparkled at her. 'Oh, it's *beautiful*—'

'It's worth a small fortune, not that you care about things like that,' he added hastily. 'I bought it in Paris when I decided that I absolutely wasn't going to take no for an answer.' He slid it on to her finger and then pulled her back into his arms.

'And if I *had* said no?'

He stroked her hair away from her face. 'I don't understand no,' he reminded her in husky tones as he bent his head to claim her mouth again. 'I had a *very* limited education.'

She felt her head swim and her legs turn to liquid and forced herself to pull away briefly before she completely lost the ability to communicate. 'In that case I'd better say yes—' the look in his eyes made her breathless '—but you have to promise not to be too controlling or I might be forced to handcuff you to the bed again so that I can have my own way.'

His eyes gleamed. 'In that case, *meu amorzinho*,' he murmured huskily, 'it's only fair to warn you that I'm planning on being controlling any moment now.'

Her heart missed a beat and she ran her tongue over her lower lip. 'So perhaps we ought to move this conversation through to the bedroom.'

Luc gave a low, sexy laugh and scooped her into his arms. 'I'm finding the whole concept of conversation increasingly more appealing with practice.'

And he walked through to the bedroom and kicked the door closed behind them.

HARLEQUIN Presents

Legally wed, but he's never said… "I love you."

They're

Wedlocked!

Where marriages are made in haste… and love comes later….

This December,

Emily Vaillon was driven to leave her husband a year ago. She couldn't stay with a man who didn't love her—especially when she was pregnant. Now Luc is back, demanding to see his son….

THE FRENCHMAN'S CAPTIVE BRIDE

by Chantelle Shaw

#2594 On sale December.

Look out for more *Wedlocked!* marriage stories coming in Harlequin Presents:

THE FORCED BRIDE by Sara Craven
#2597 Coming in January!

www.eHarlequin.com

HPWED1206